WOLF CHILDREN

AME & YUKI

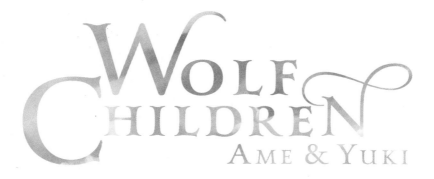

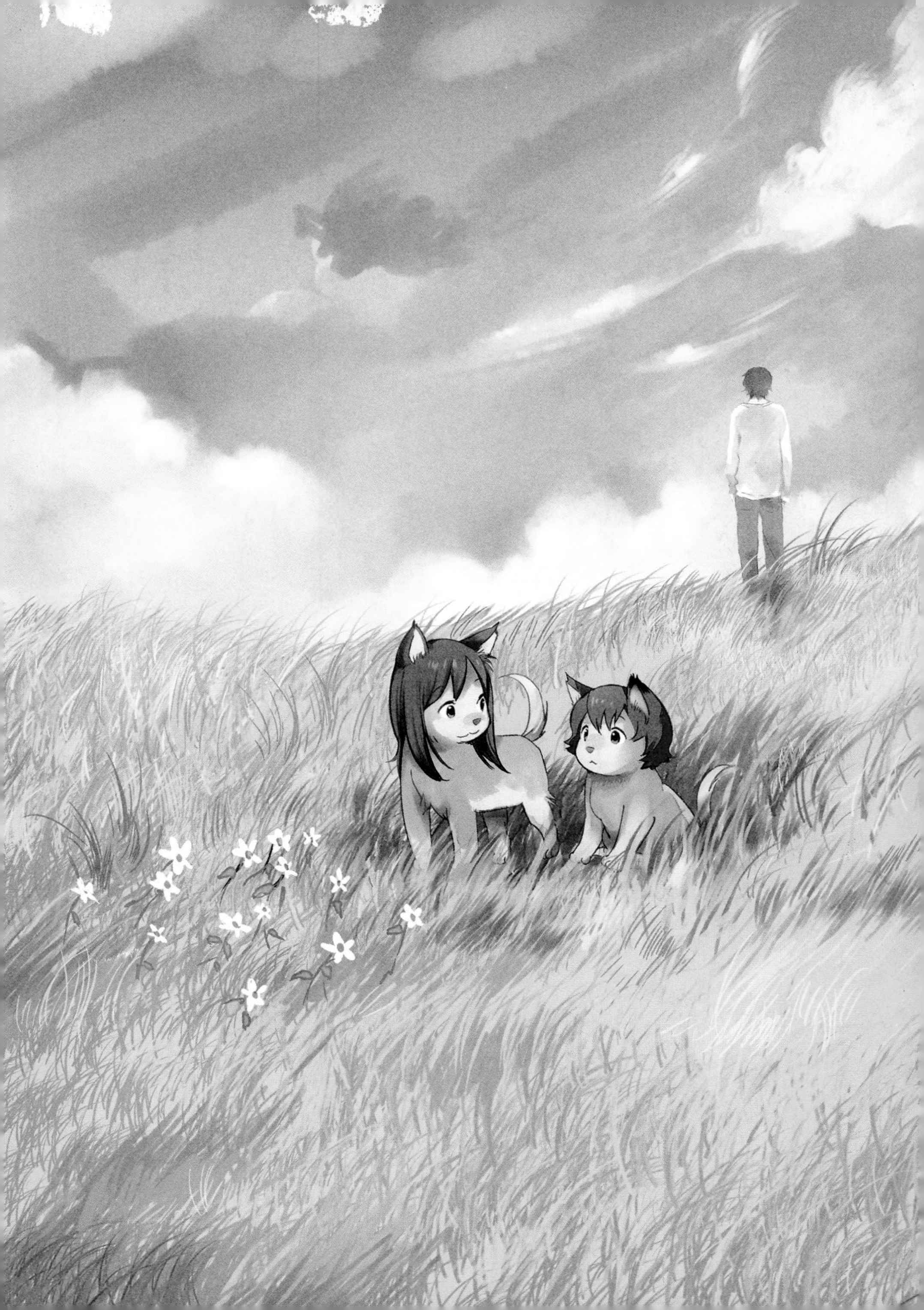

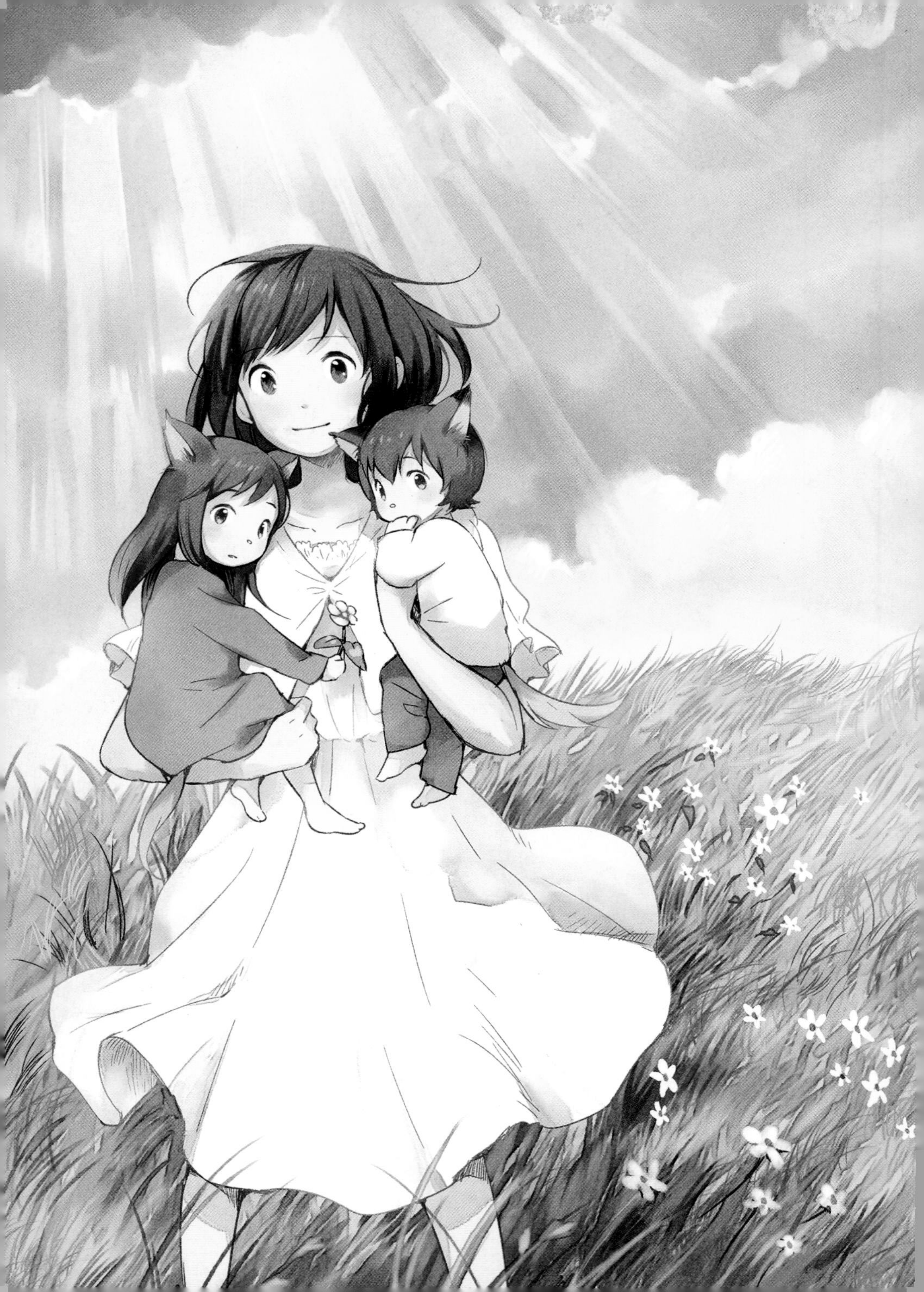

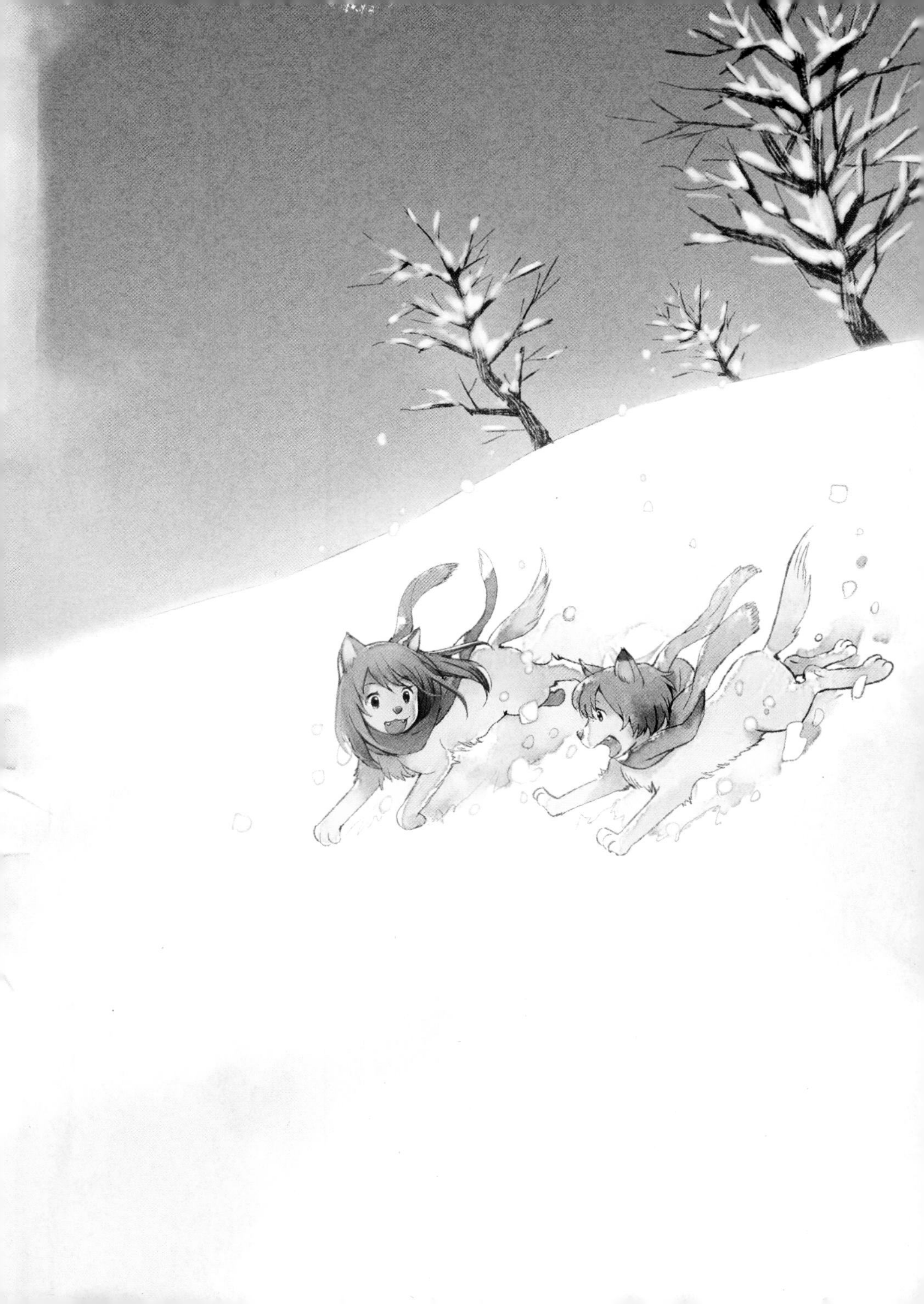

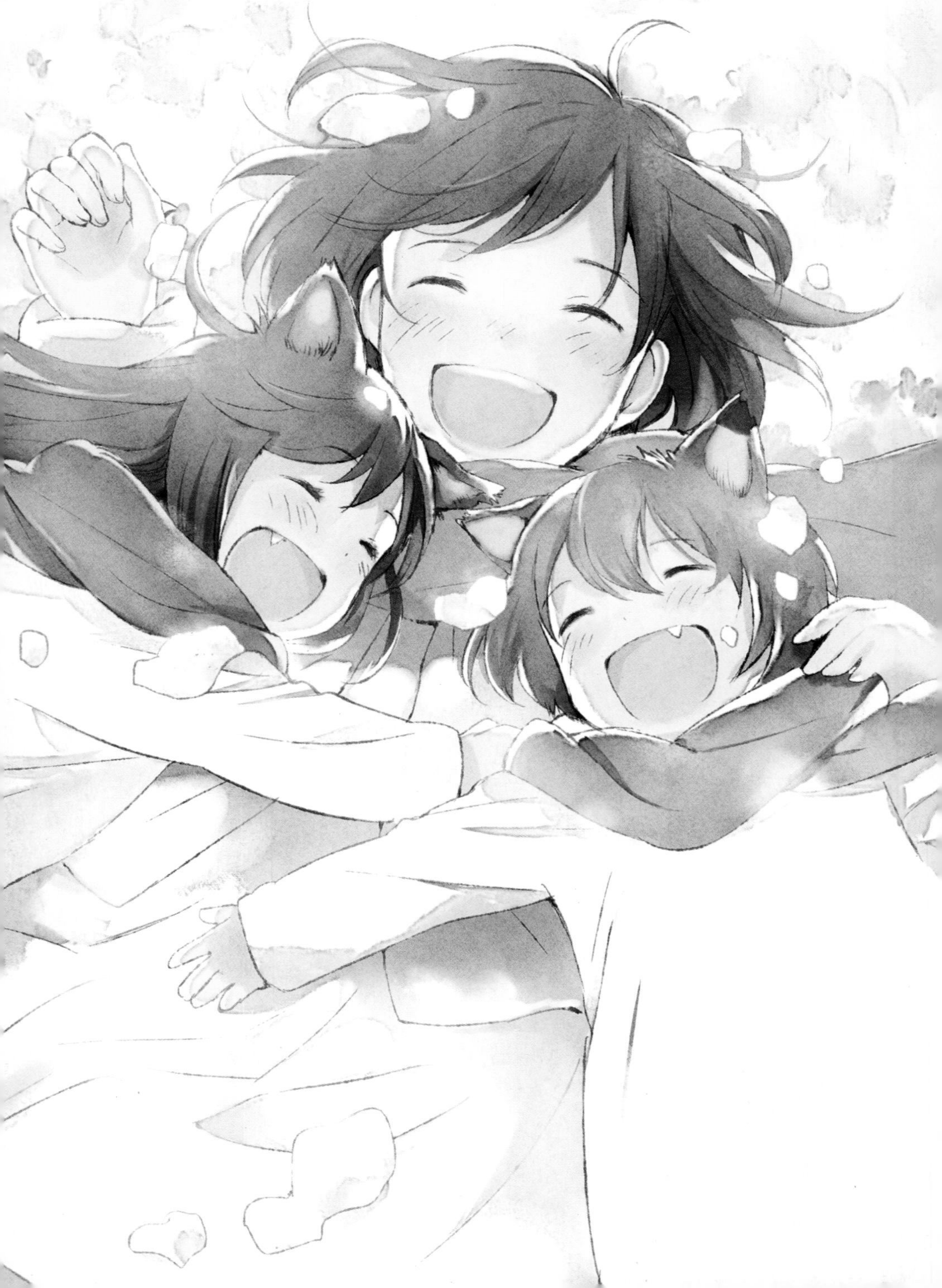

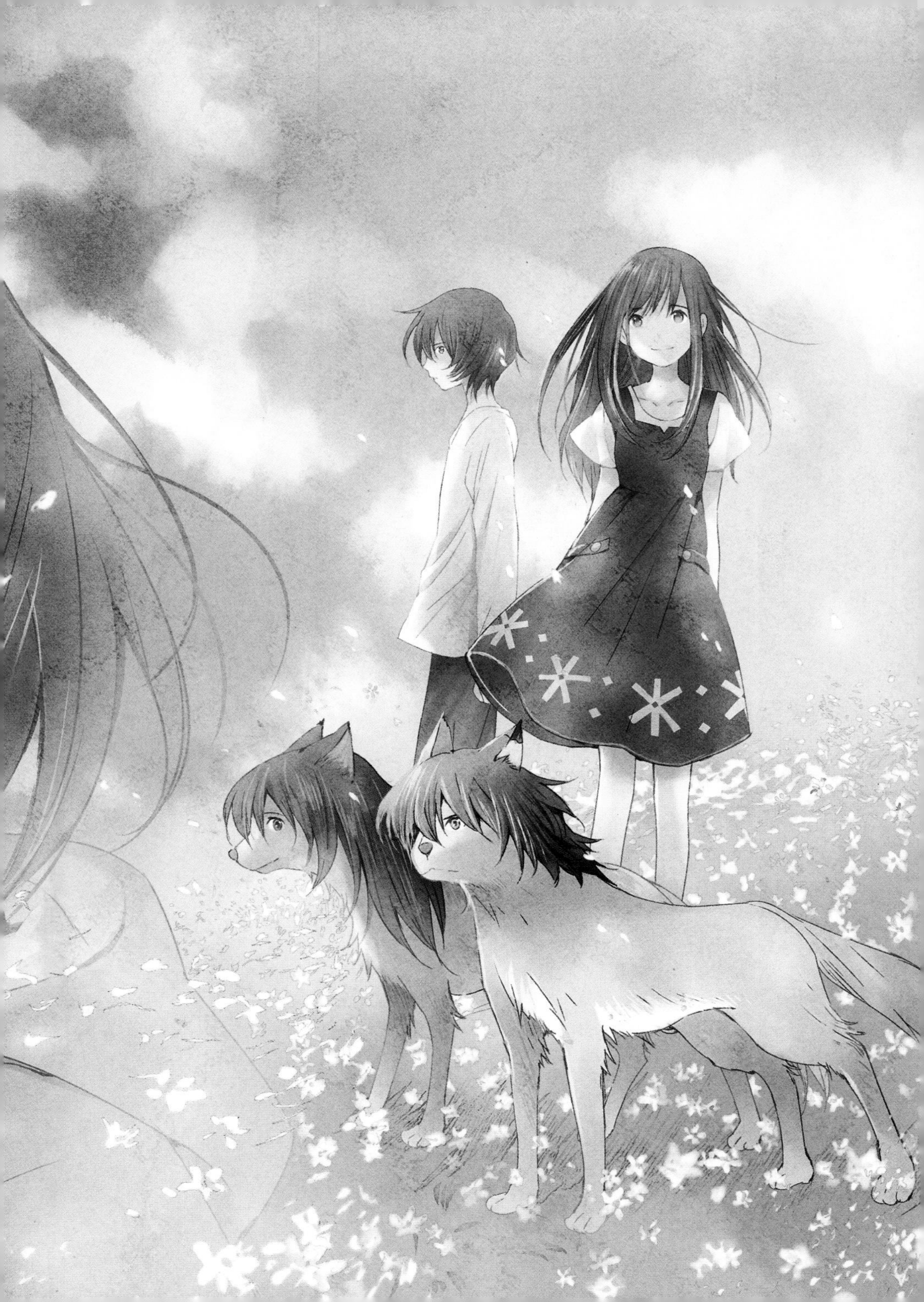

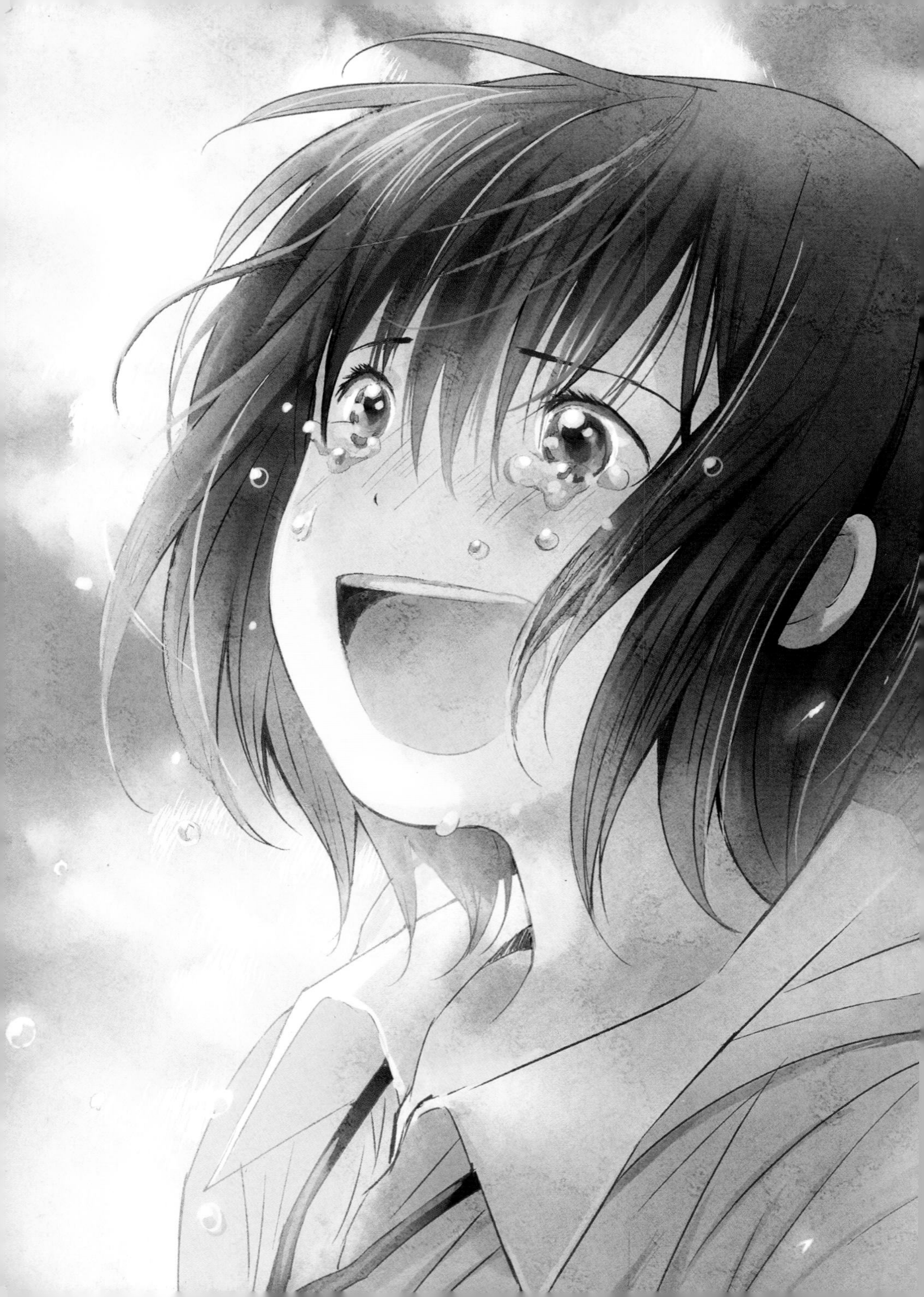

Contents

Chapter 1 Encounter

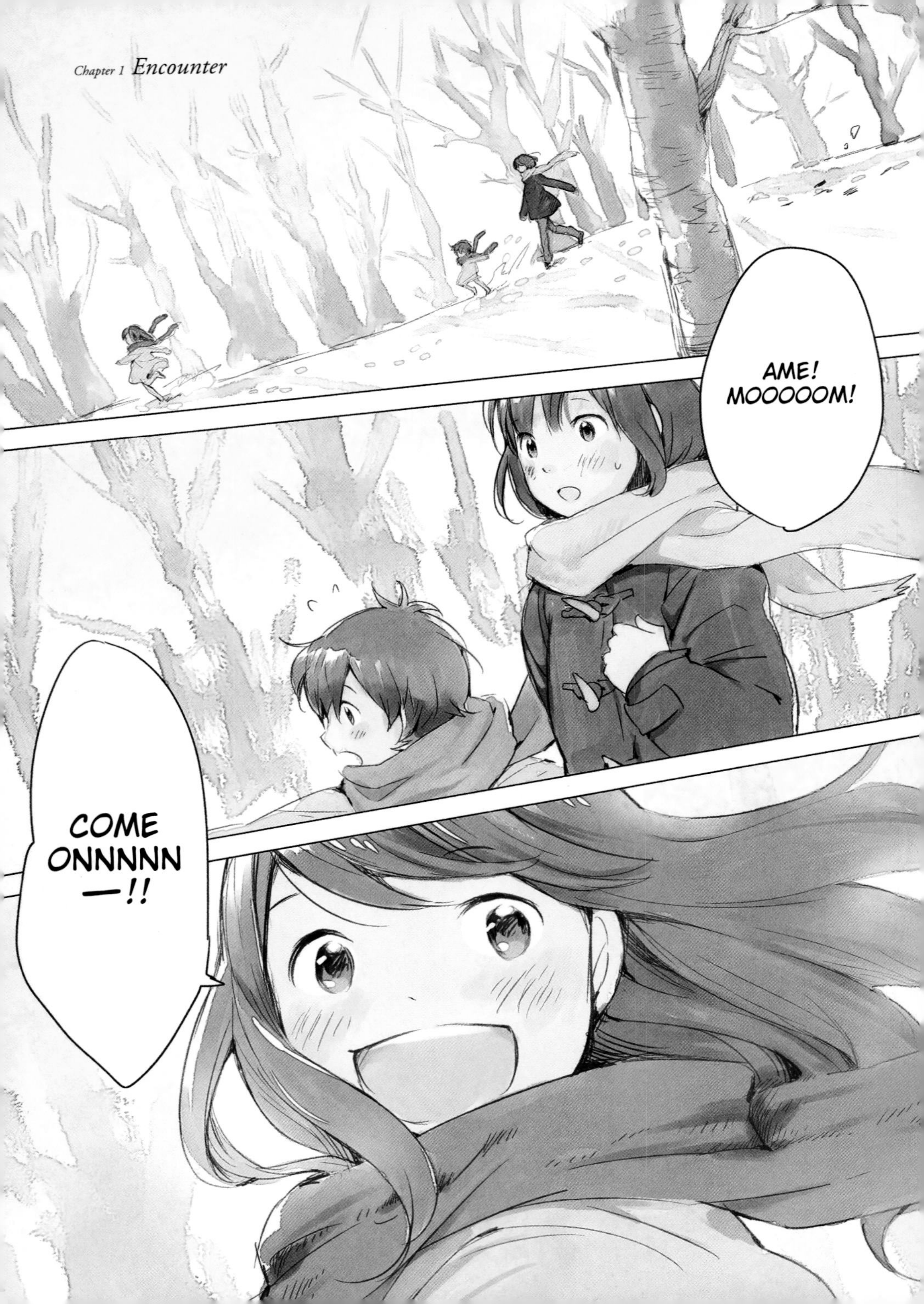
AME! MOOOOOM!
COME ONNNNN—!!

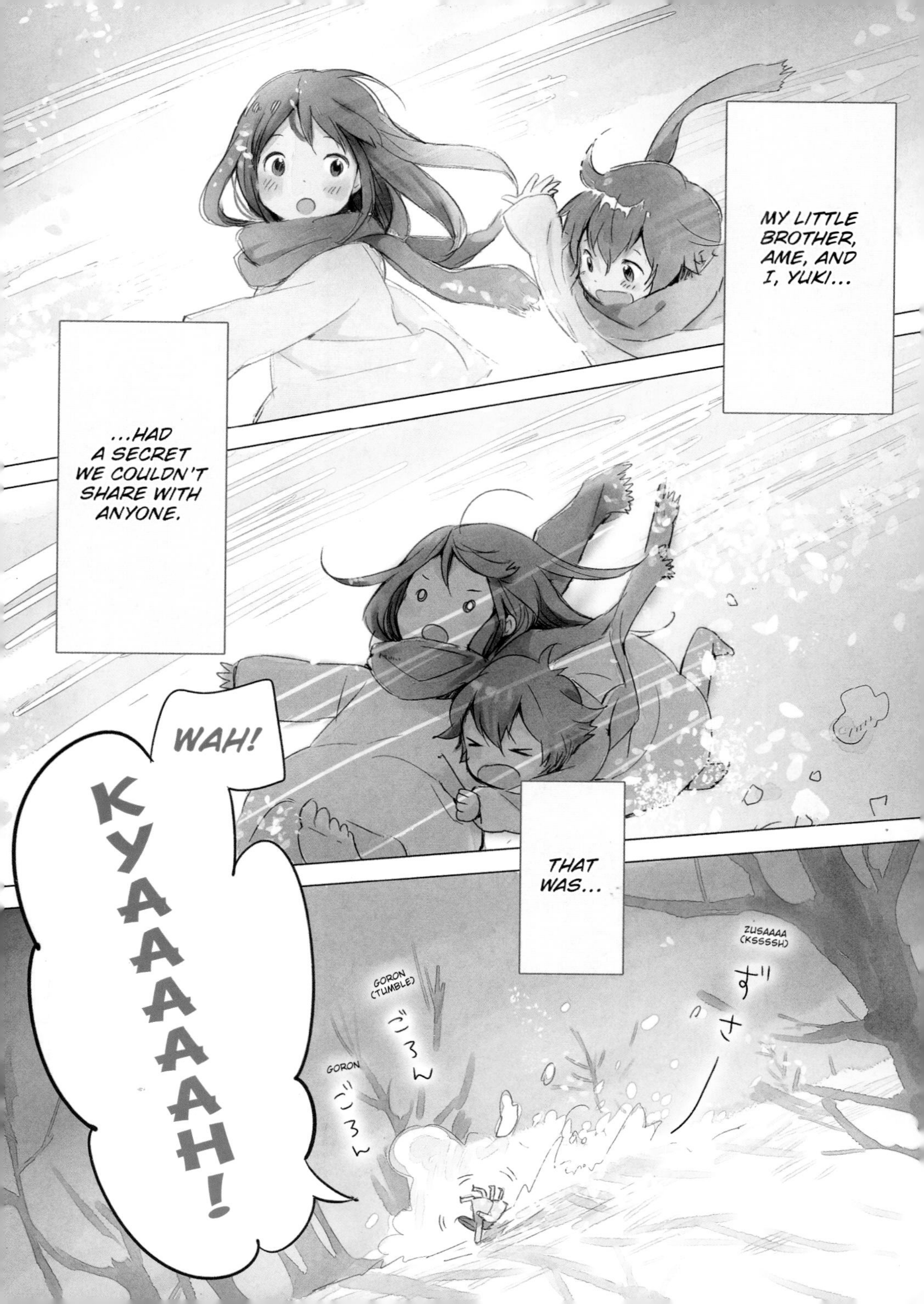
MY LITTLE BROTHER, AME, AND I, YUKI...
...HAD A SECRET WE COULDN'T SHARE WITH ANYONE.
WAH!
THAT WAS...
ZUSAAAA (KSSSSH)
ずさー
GORON (TUMBLE)
ごろん
GORON
ごろん
KYAAAAH!

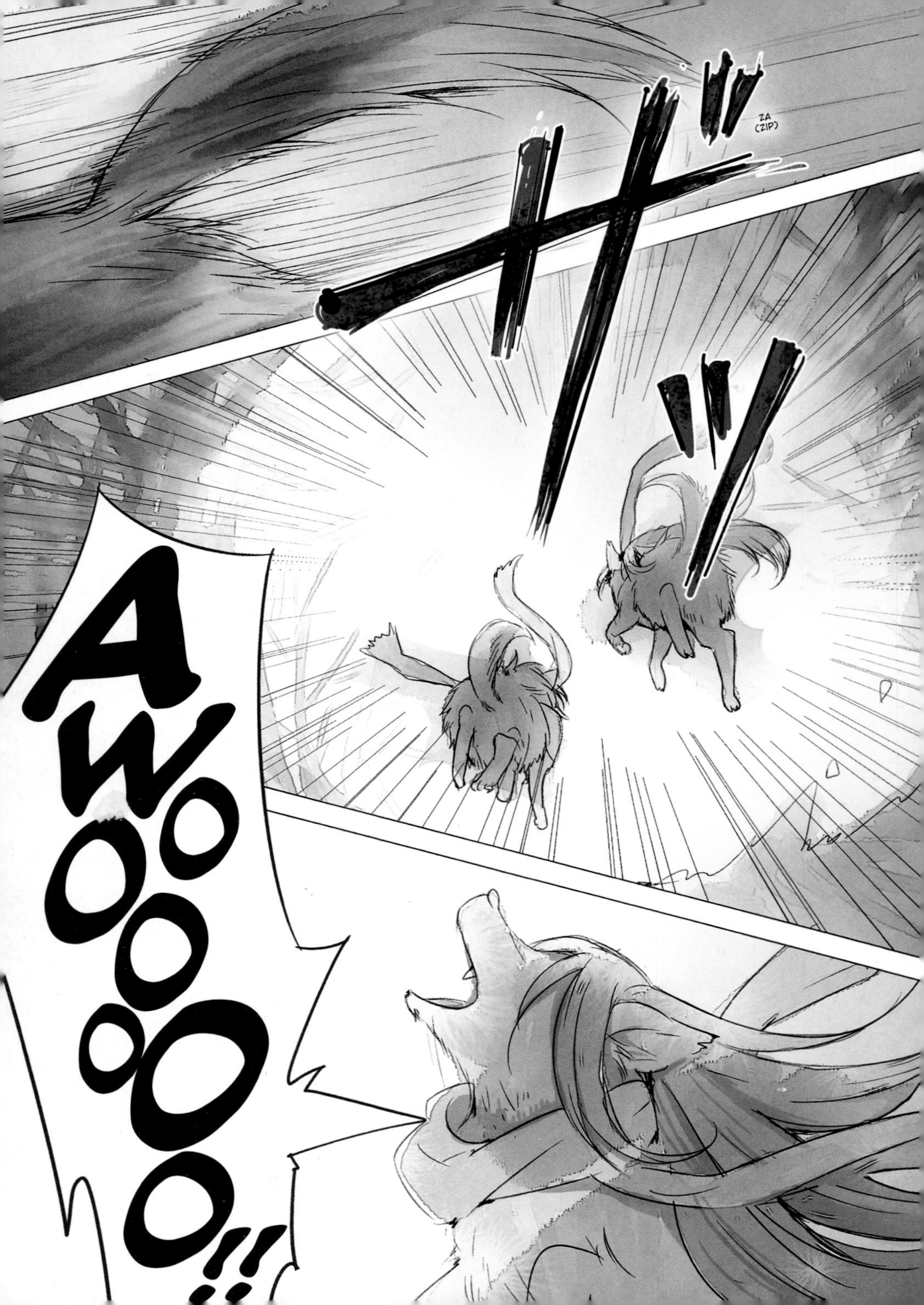
ZA
(ZIP)
AWOOOOOOO!!

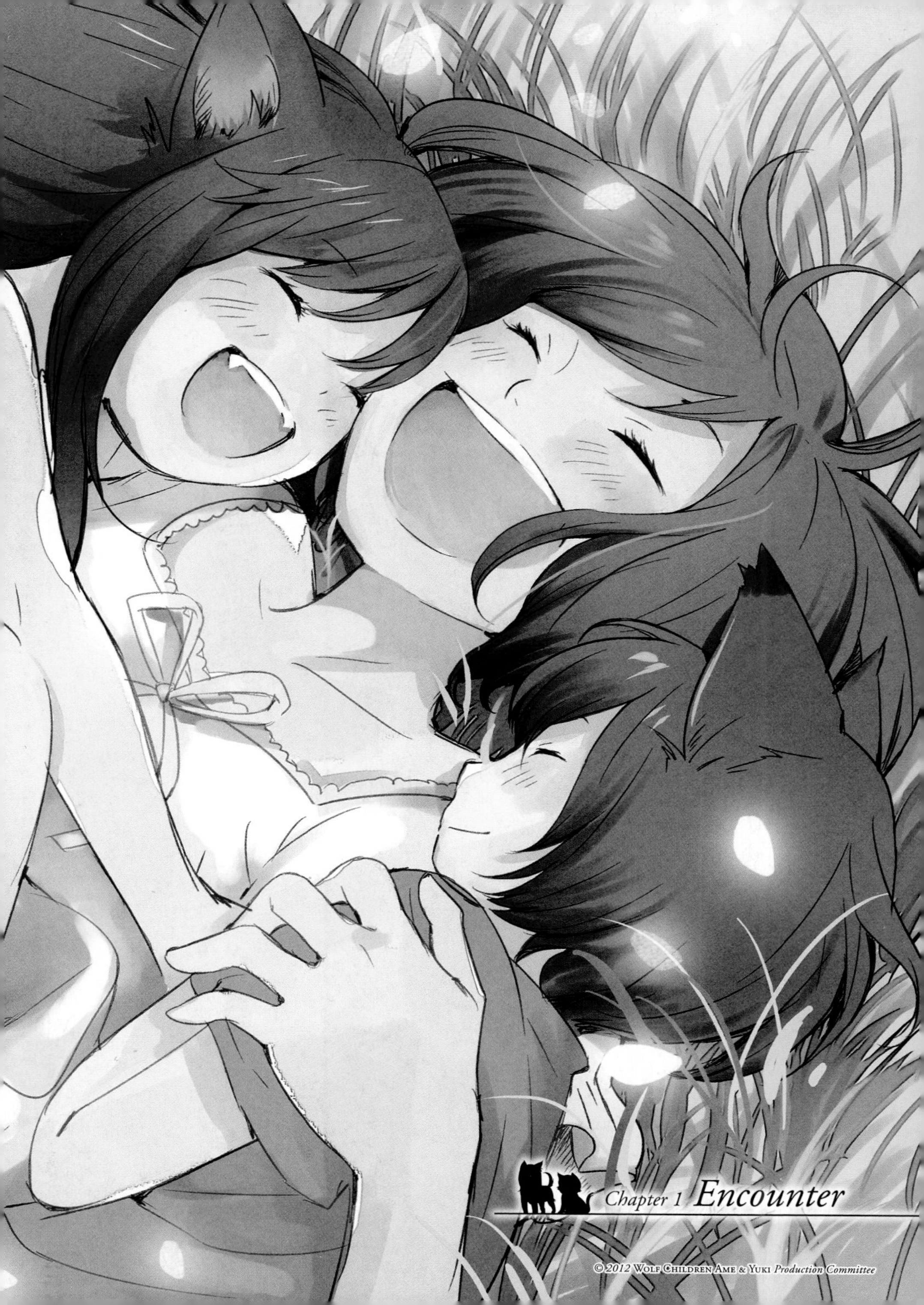

Chapter 1 Encounter

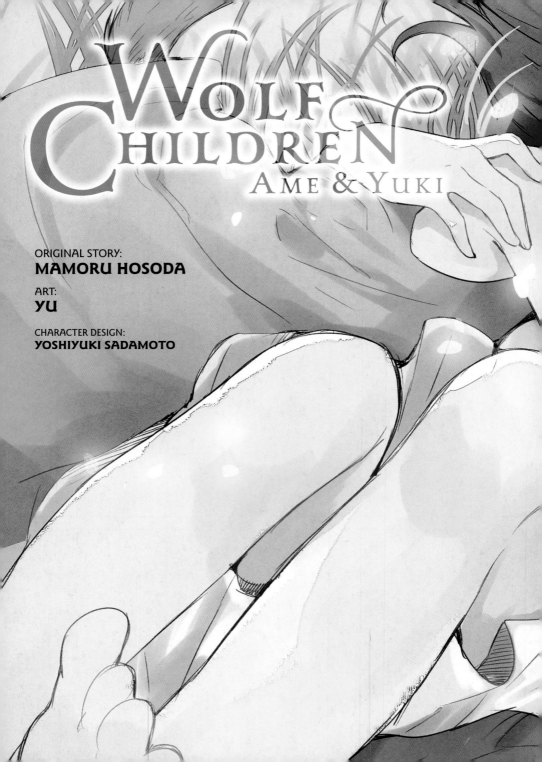

WOLF CHILDREN
AME & YUKI

ORIGINAL STORY:
MAMORU HOSODA

ART:
YU

CHARACTER DESIGN:
YOSHIYUKI SADAMOTO

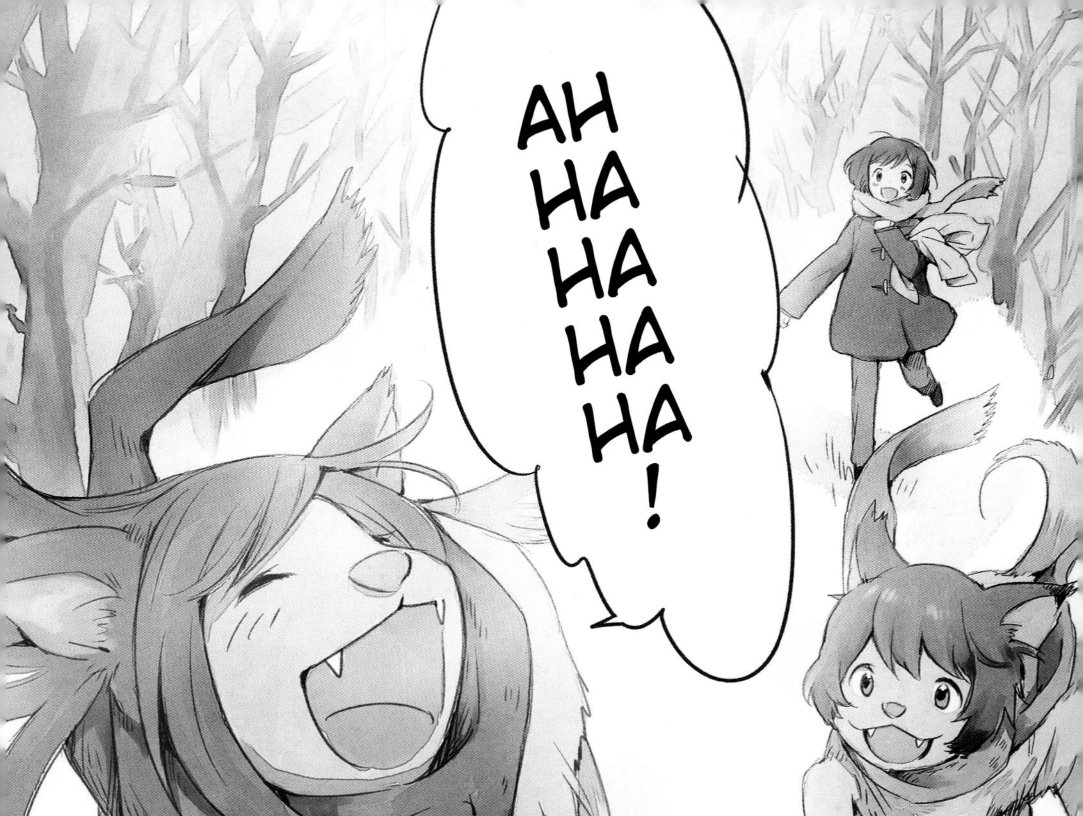
AH HA HA HA HA!

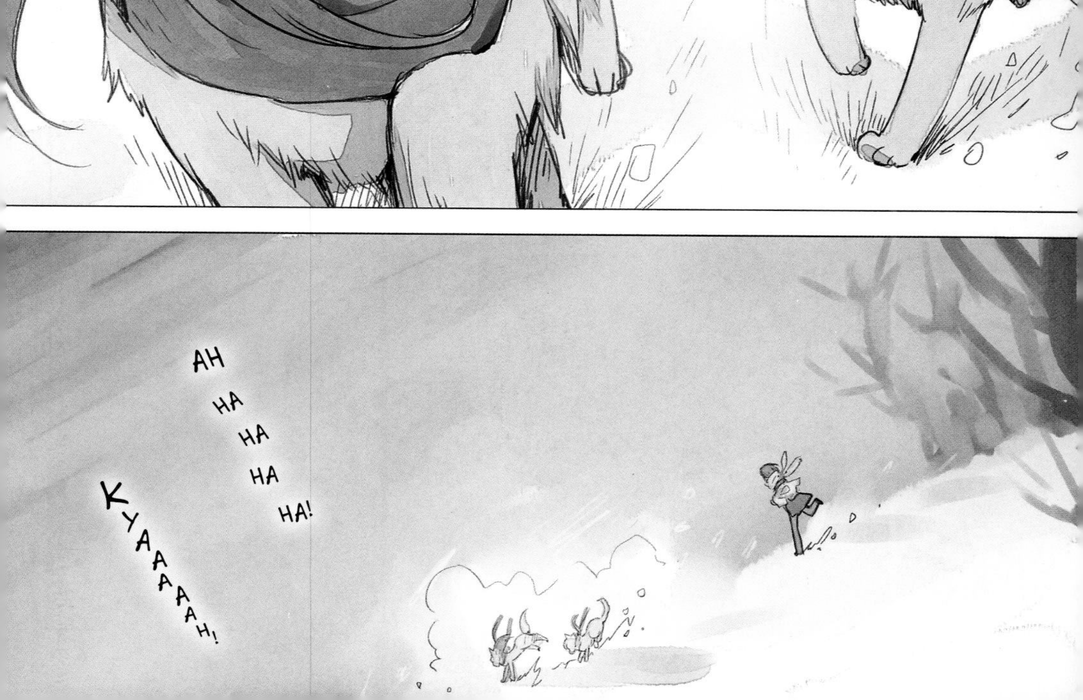
AH HA HA HA HA!
KYAAAAAAH!

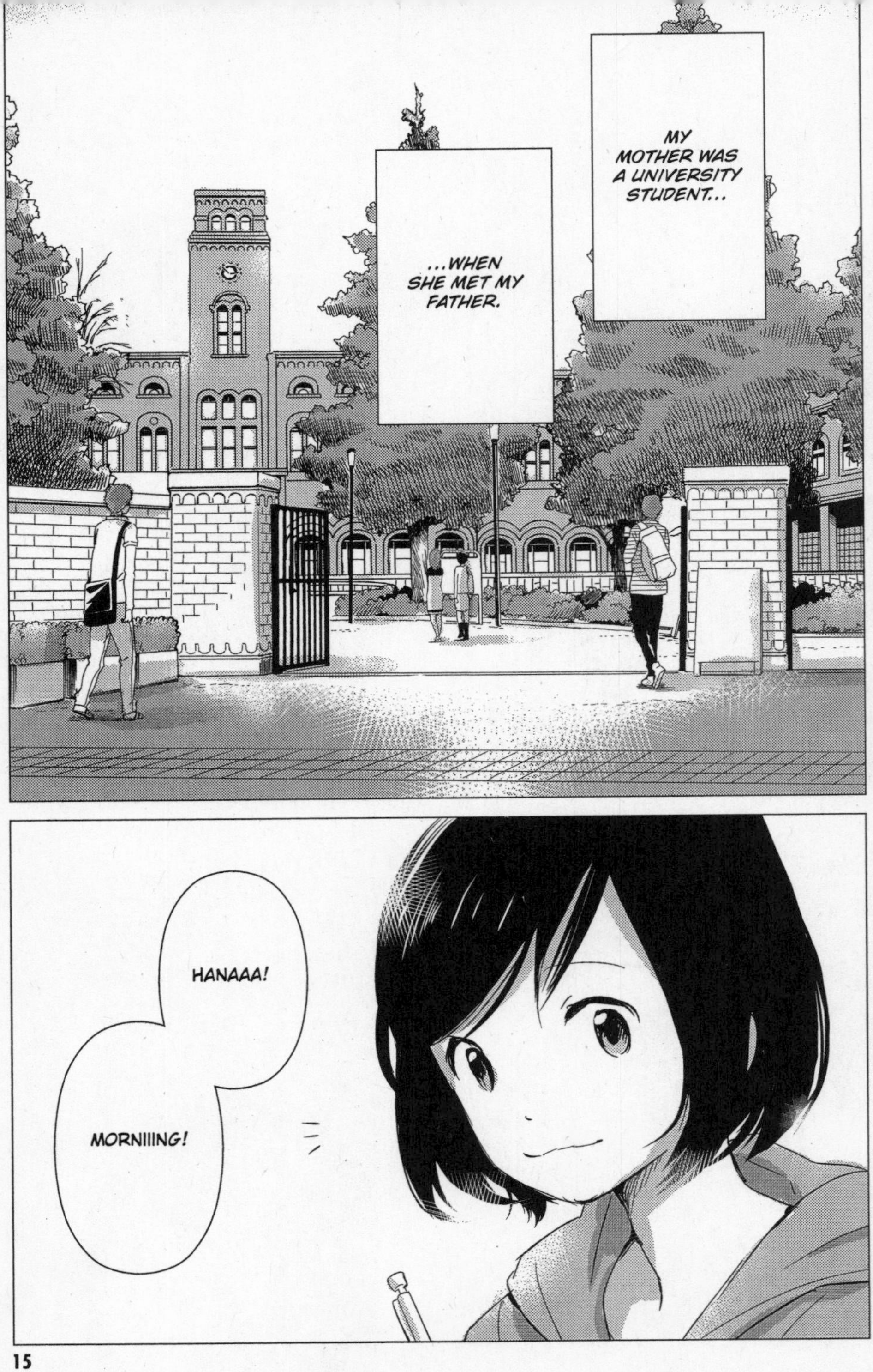
MY MOTHER WAS A UNIVERSITY STUDENT...
...WHEN SHE MET MY FATHER.
HANAAA!
MORNIIING!

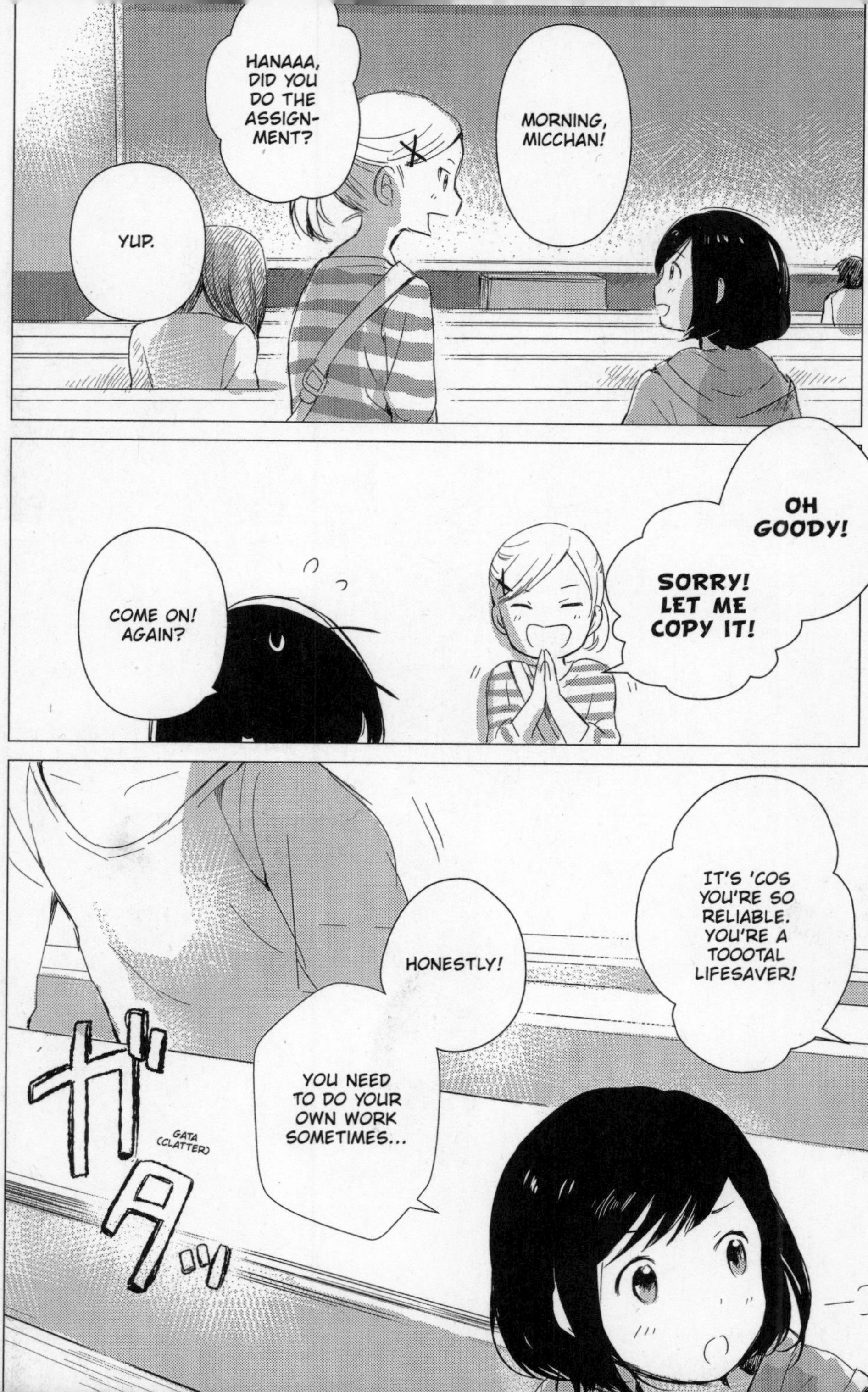
MORNING, MICCHAN!
HANAAA, DID YOU DO THE ASSIGN- MENT?
YUP.
OH GOODY!
SORRY! LET ME COPY IT!
COME ON! AGAIN?
IT'S 'COS YOU'RE SO RELIABLE. YOU'RE A TOOOTAL LIFESAVER!
HONESTLY!
YOU NEED TO DO YOUR OWN WORK SOMETIMES...
ガタッ
GATA (CLATTER)

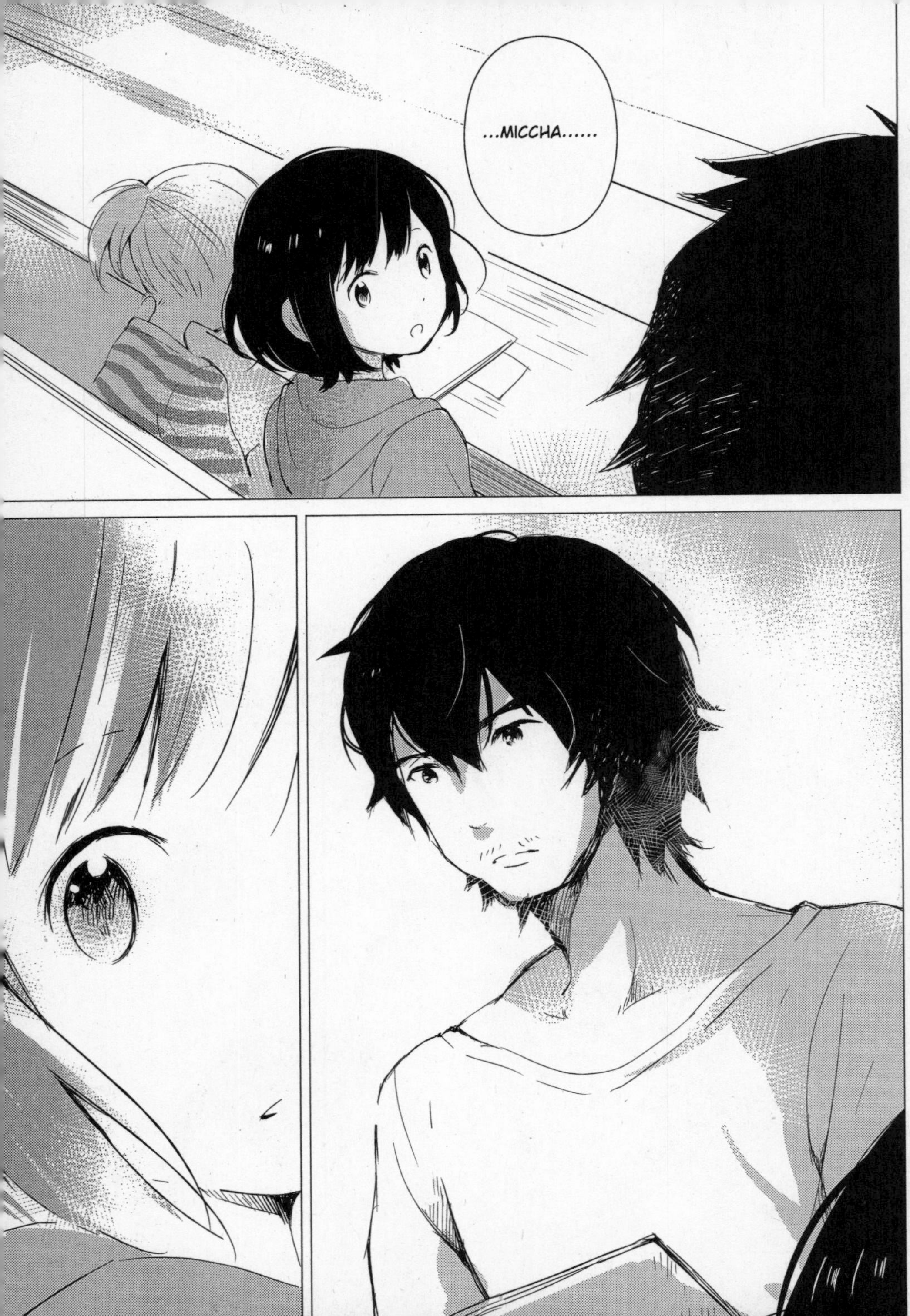
...MICCHA......

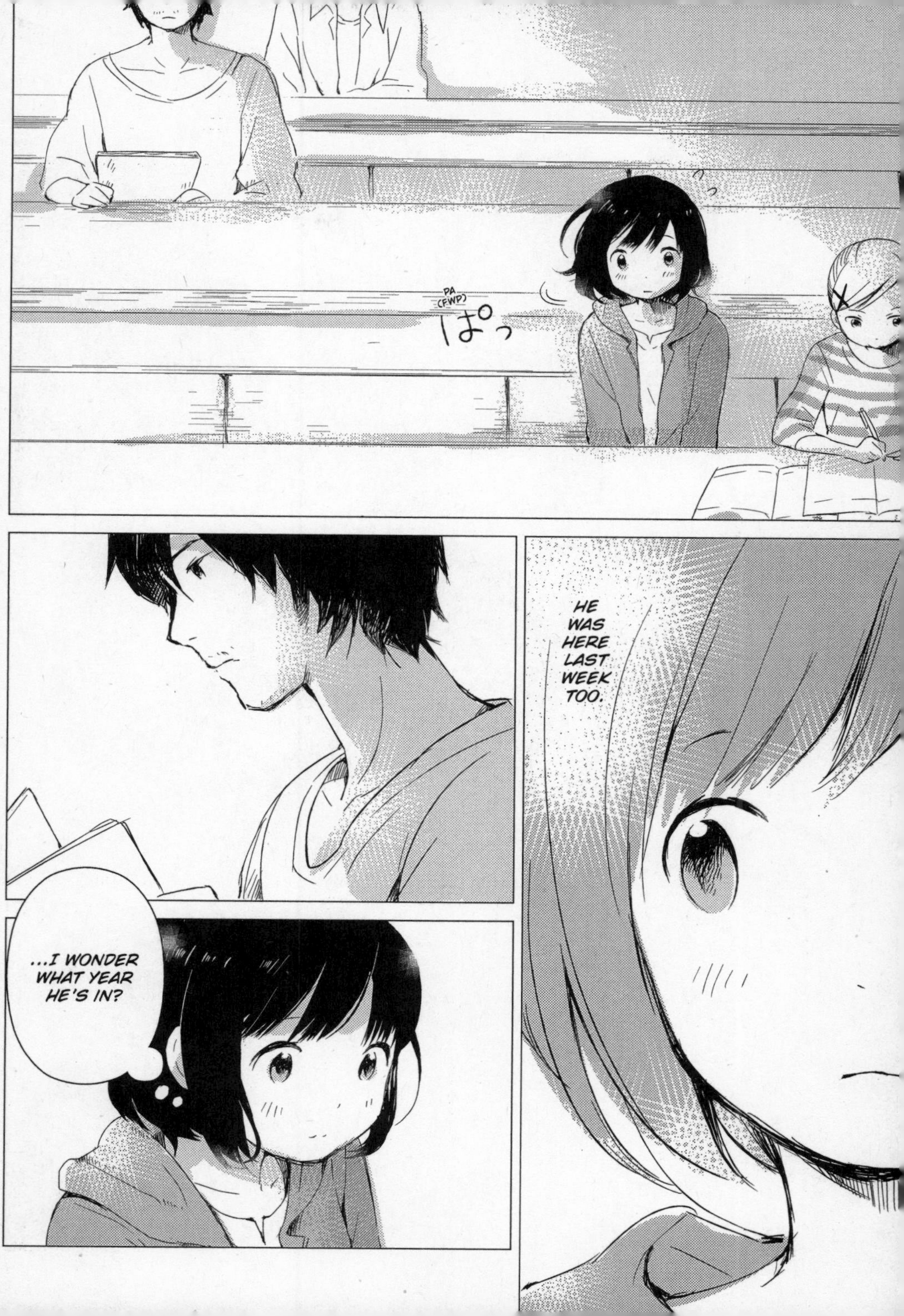
PA (FWP)
ぱっ
HE WAS HERE LAST WEEK TOO.
...I WONDER WHAT YEAR HE'S IN?

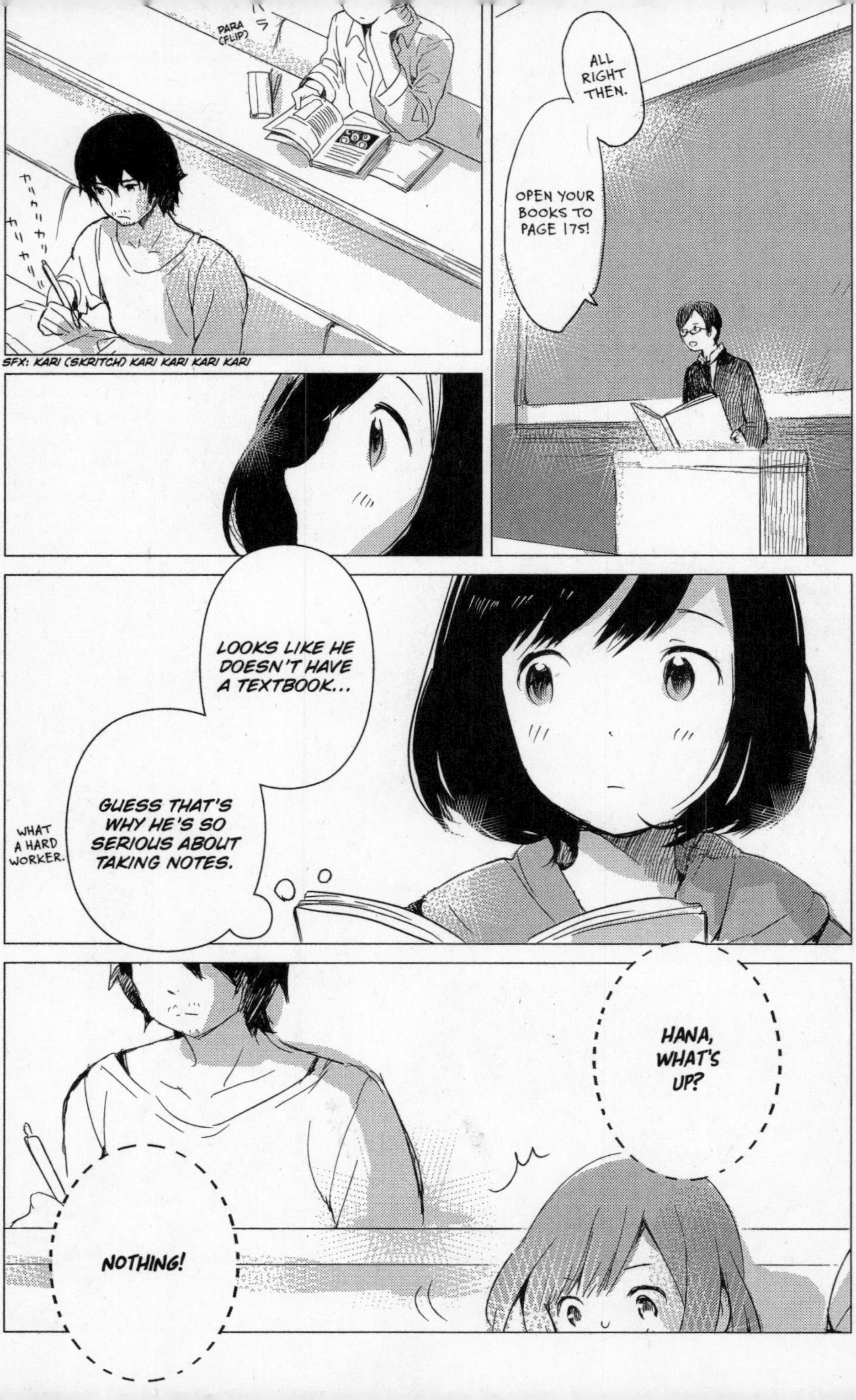
ALL RIGHT THEN.
OPEN YOUR BOOKS TO PAGE 175!
PARA (FLIP)
SFX: KARI (SKRITCH) KARI KARI KARI KARI
LOOKS LIKE HE DOESN'T HAVE A TEXTBOOK...
GUESS THAT'S WHY HE'S SO SERIOUS ABOUT TAKING NOTES.
WHAT A HARD WORKER.
HANA, WHAT'S UP?
NOTHING!

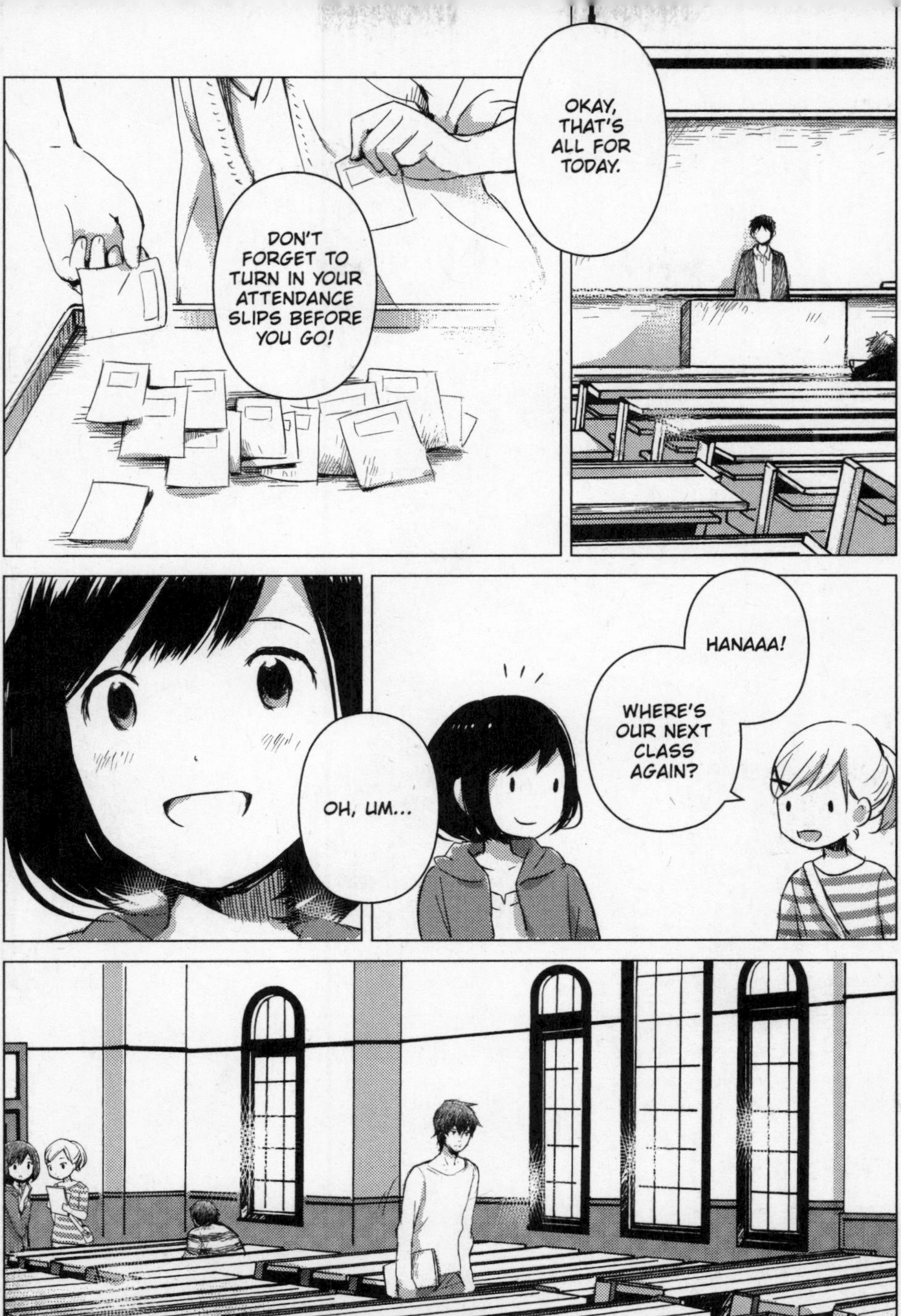
OKAY, THAT'S ALL FOR TODAY.
DON'T FORGET TO TURN IN YOUR ATTENDANCE SLIPS BEFORE YOU GO!
HANAAA!
WHERE'S OUR NEXT CLASS AGAIN?
OH, UM...

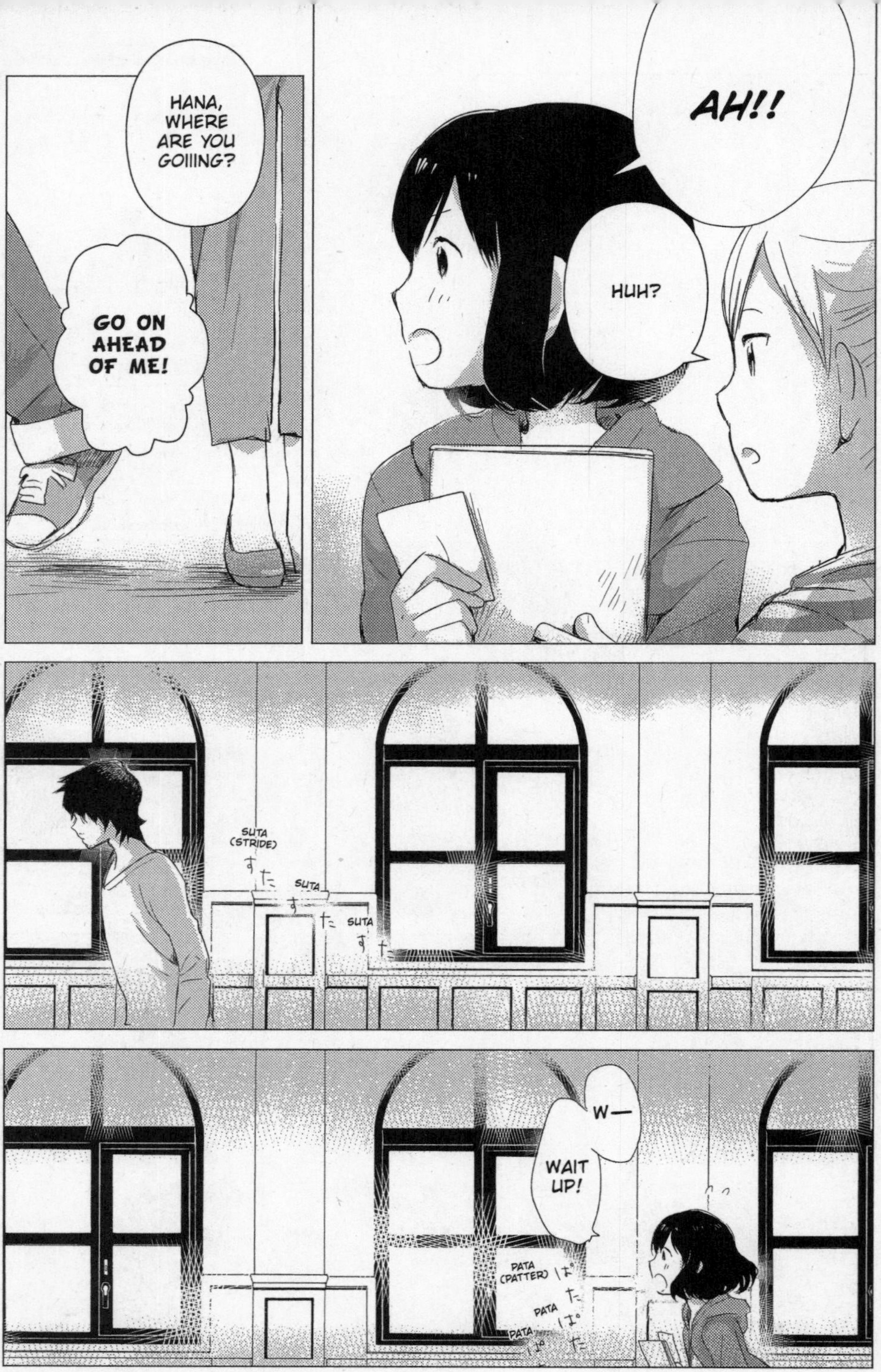
AH!!
HUH?
HANA, WHERE ARE YOU GOIIING?
GO ON AHEAD OF ME!
SUTA (STRIDE) すた
SUTA すた
SUTA すた
W—
WAIT UP!
PATA (PATTER) ぱた
PATA ぱた
PATA ぱた

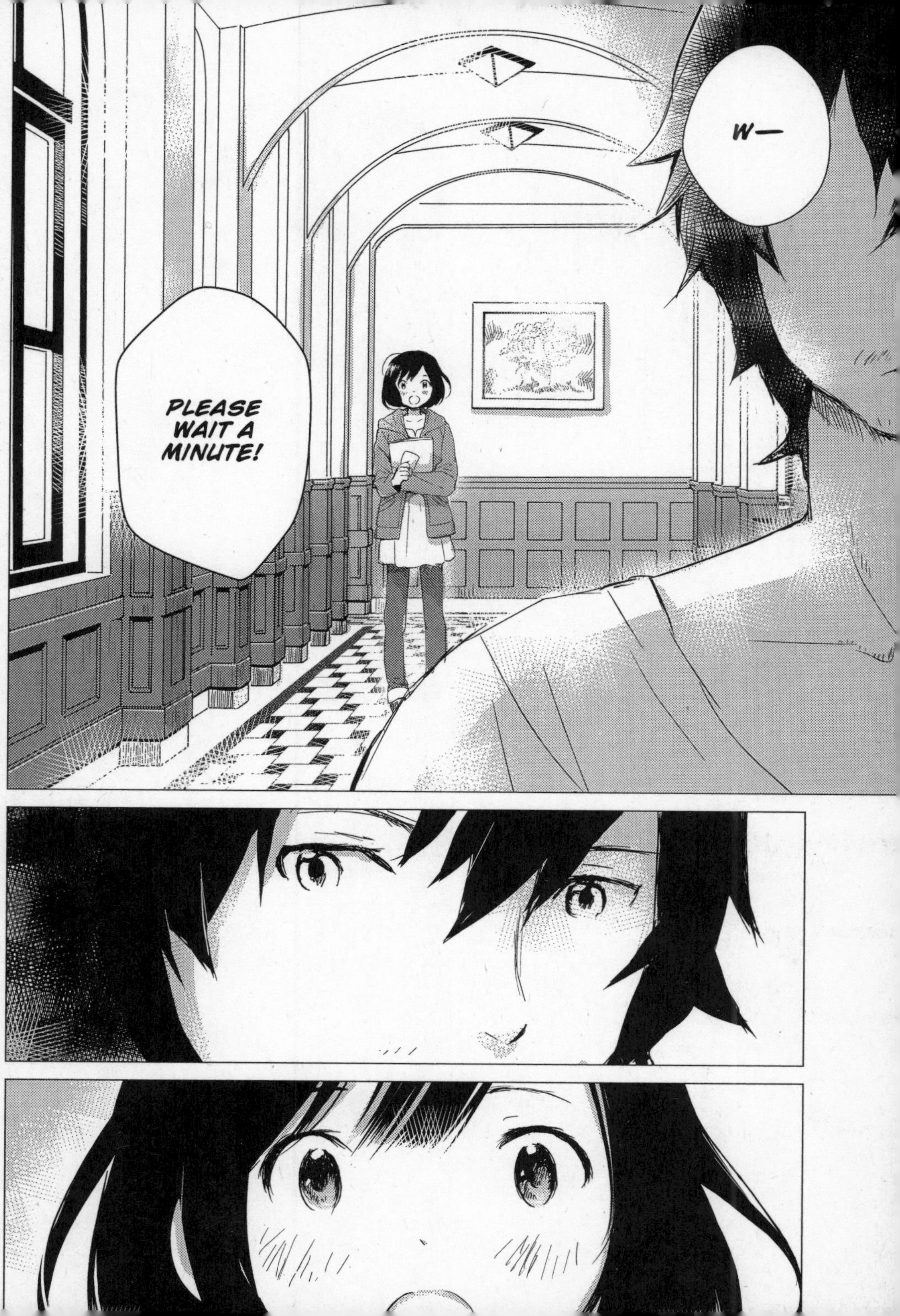
W—
PLEASE WAIT A MINUTE!

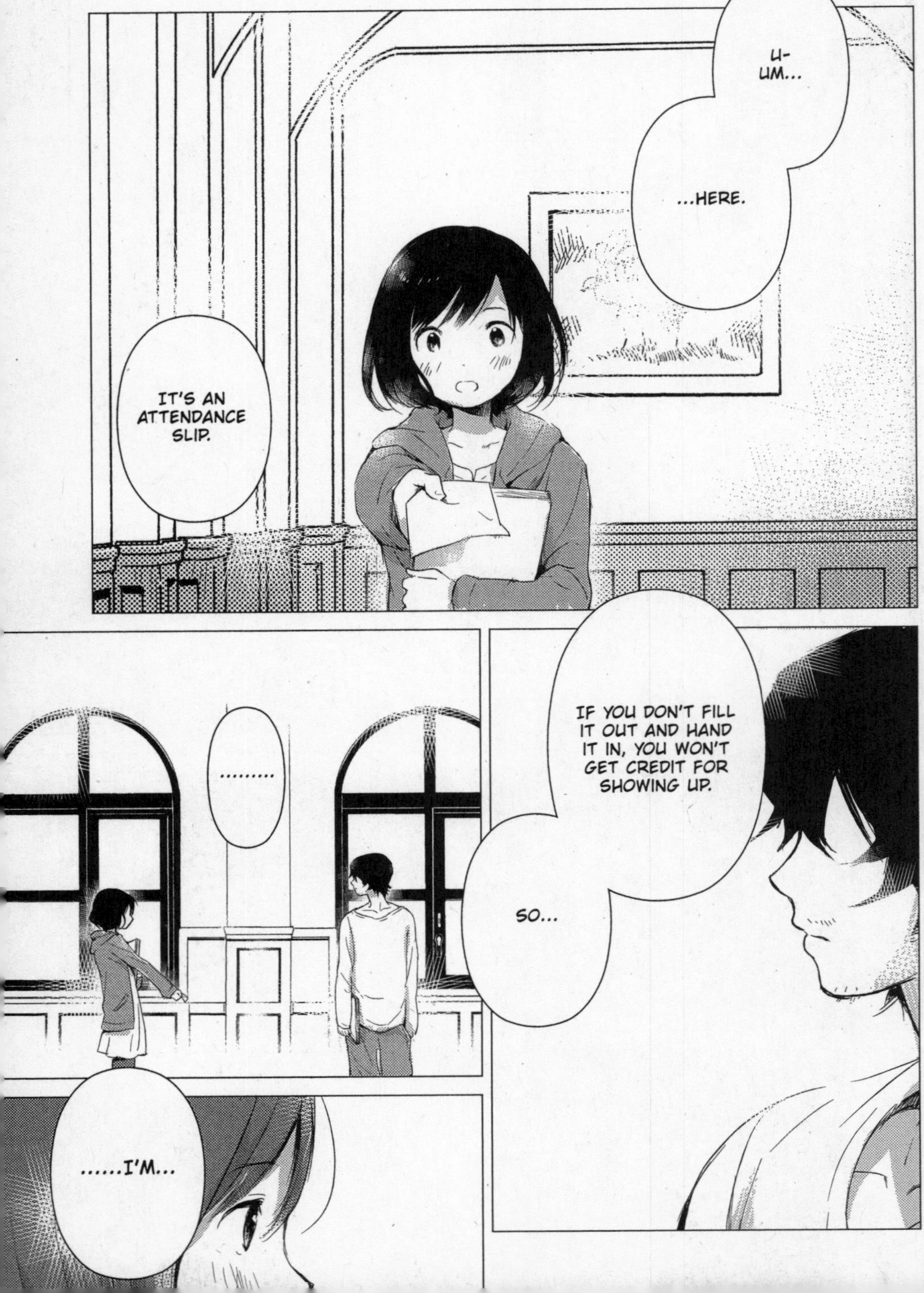
U-UM...
...HERE.
IT'S AN ATTENDANCE SLIP.
IF YOU DON'T FILL IT OUT AND HAND IT IN, YOU WON'T GET CREDIT FOR SHOWING UP.
SO...
....
......I'M...

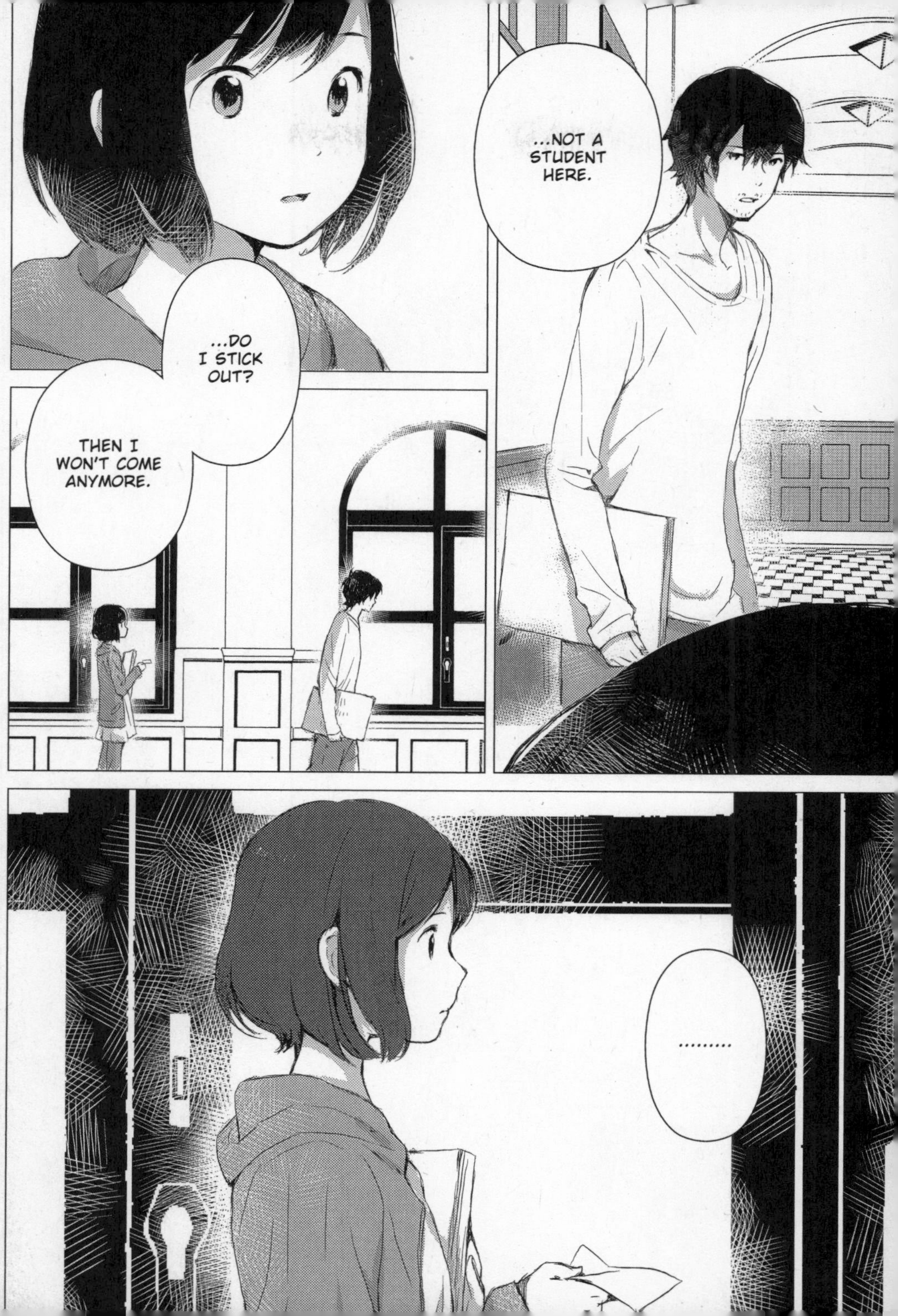
...NOT A STUDENT HERE.
...DO I STICK OUT?
THEN I WON'T COME ANYMORE.
....

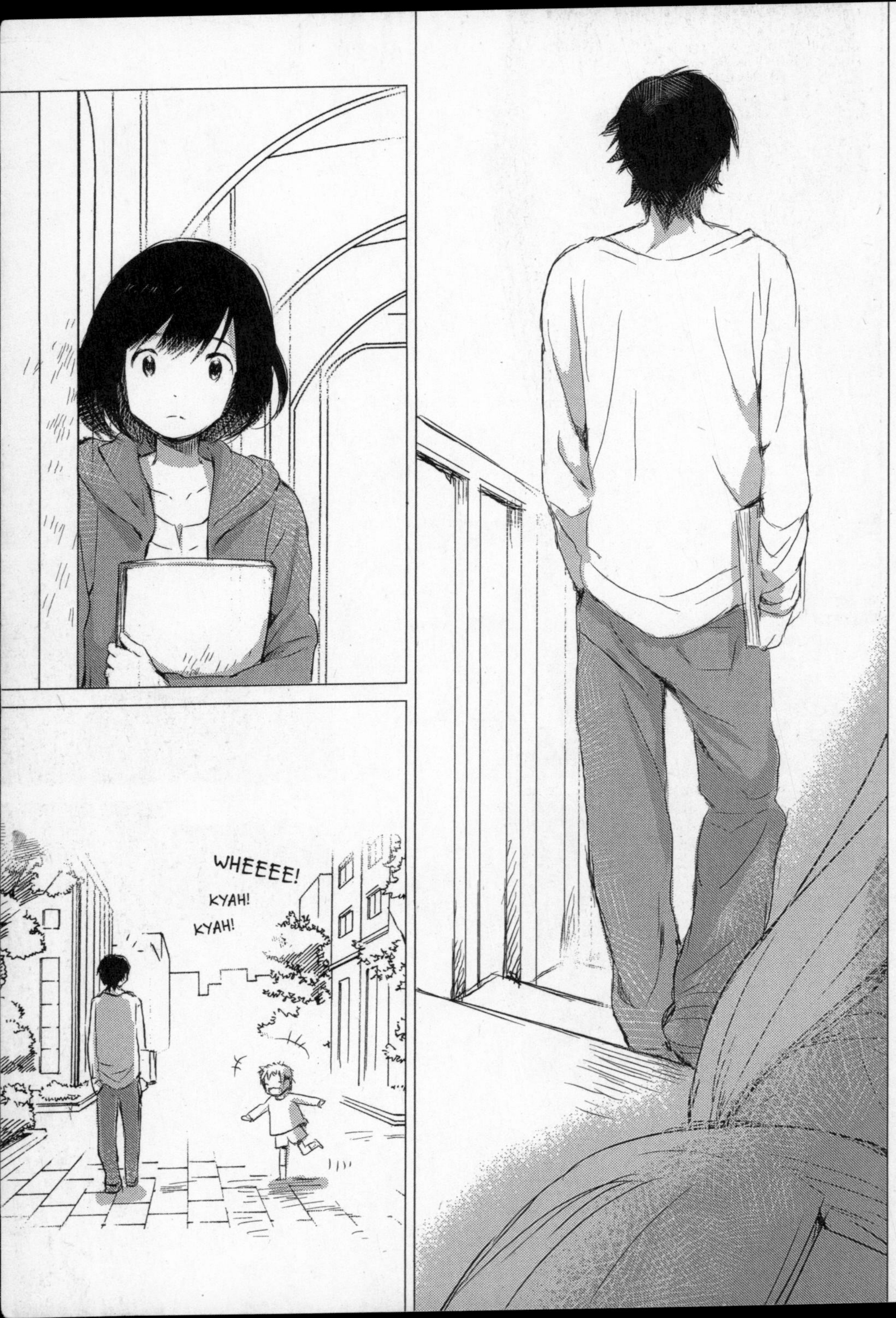
WHEEEE!
KYAH!
KYAH!

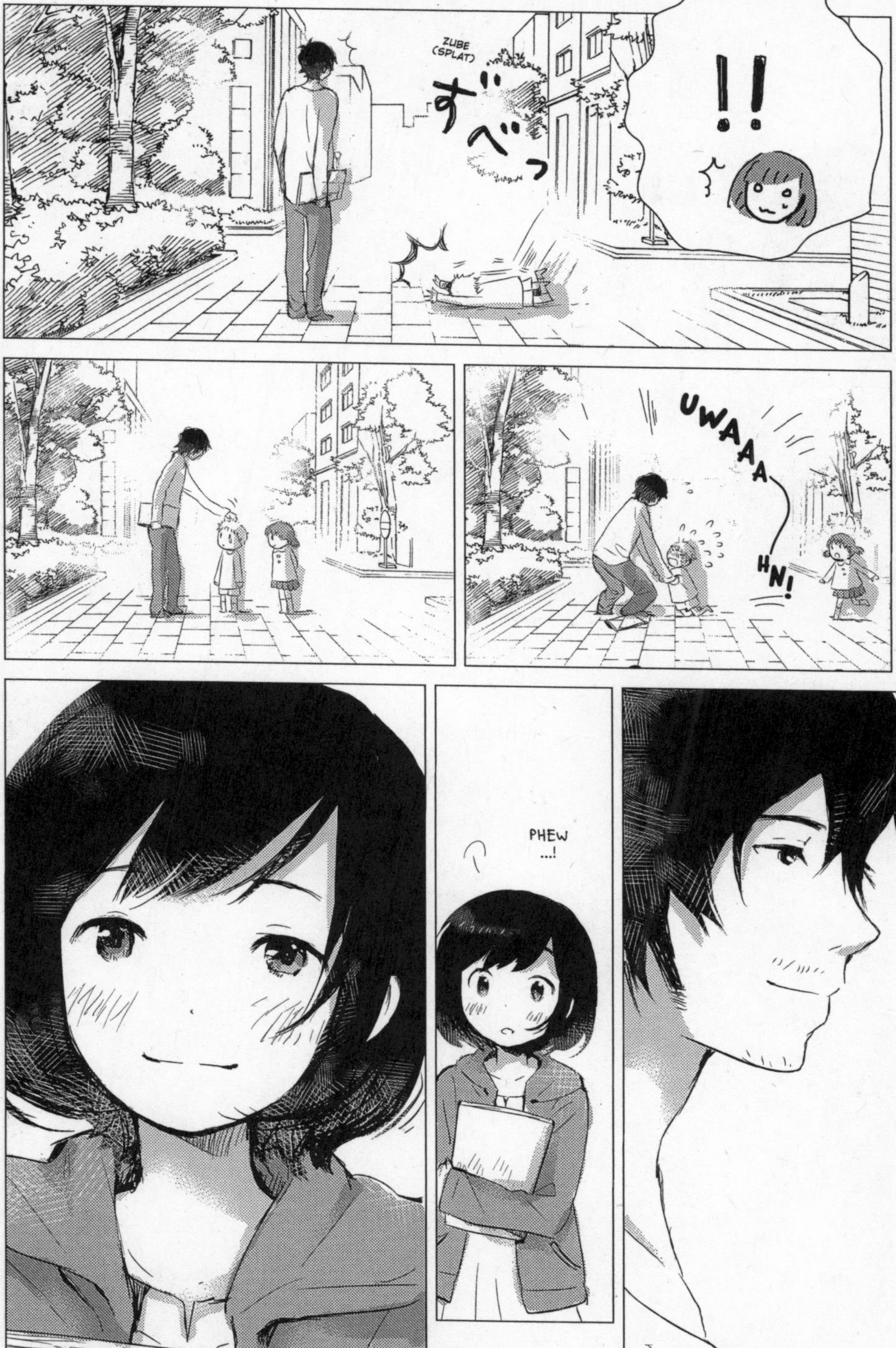
!!
ZUBE (SPLAT)
ずべっ
UWAAAAHN!
PHEW ...!

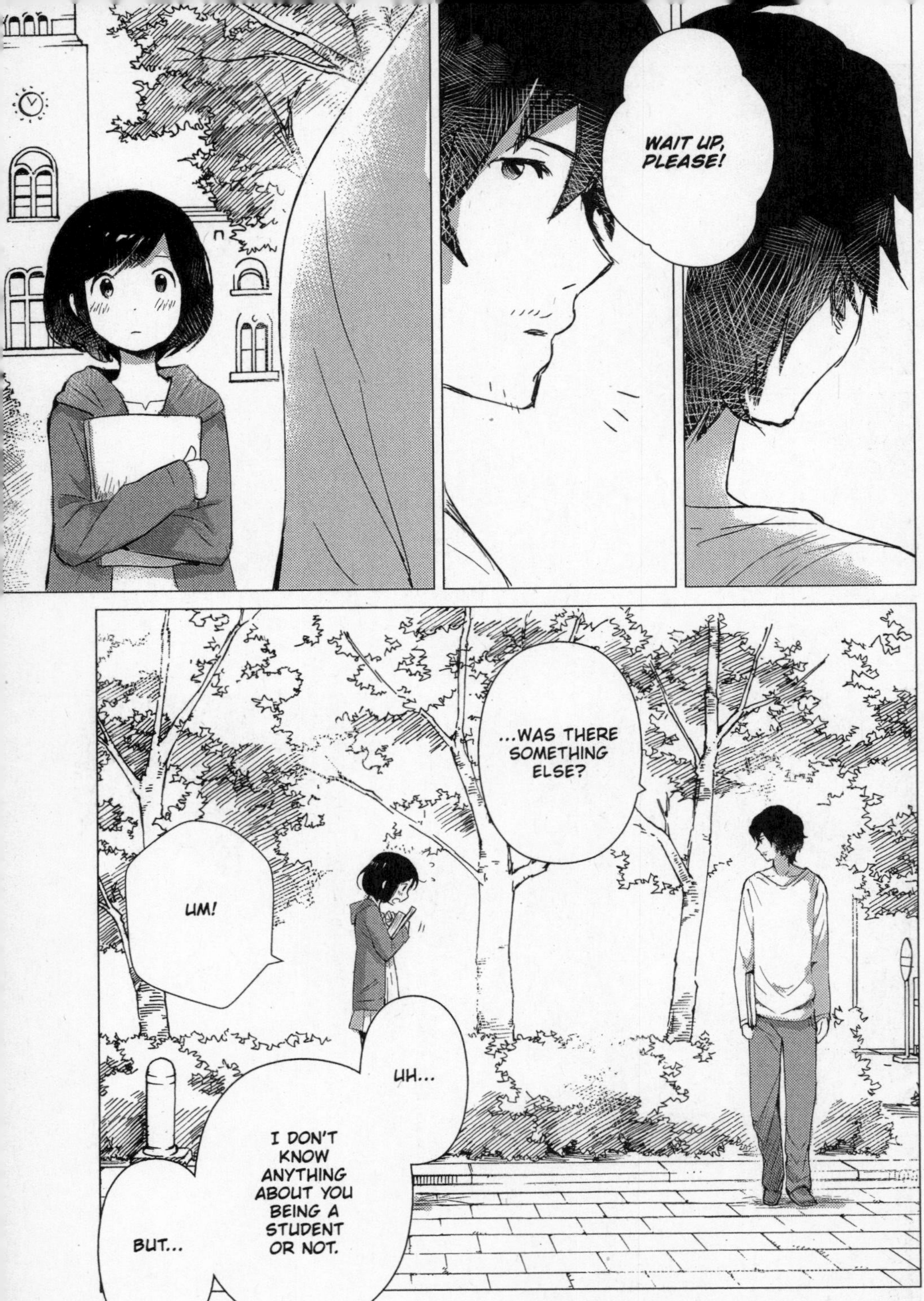
WAIT UP, PLEASE!
...WAS THERE SOMETHING ELSE?
UM!
UH...
I DON'T KNOW ANYTHING ABOUT YOU BEING A STUDENT OR NOT.
BUT...

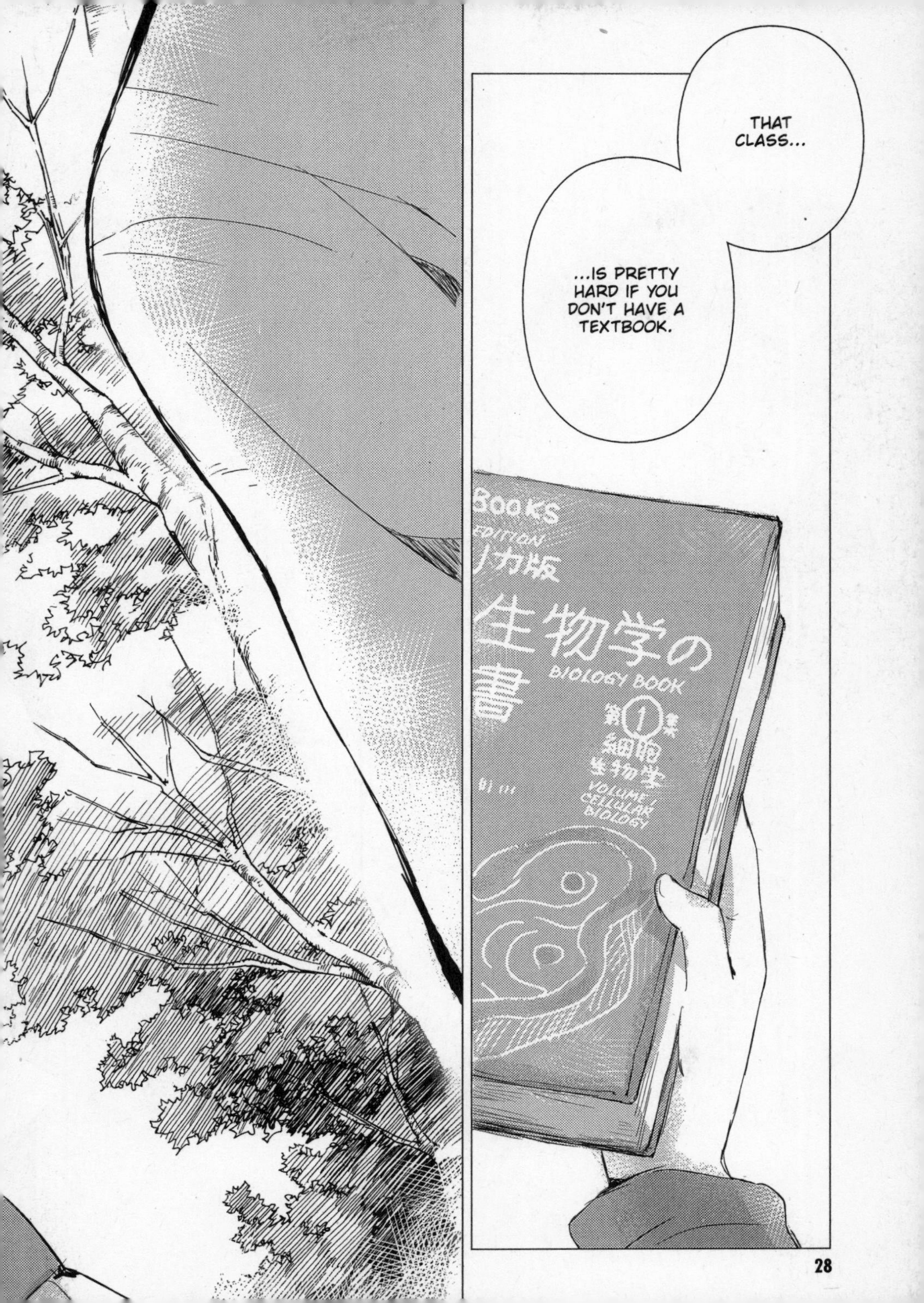
THAT CLASS...
...IS PRETTY HARD IF YOU DON'T HAVE A TEXTBOOK.
BOOKS
EDITION
生物学の
BIOLOGY BOOK
VOLUME 1 CELLULAR BIOLOGY

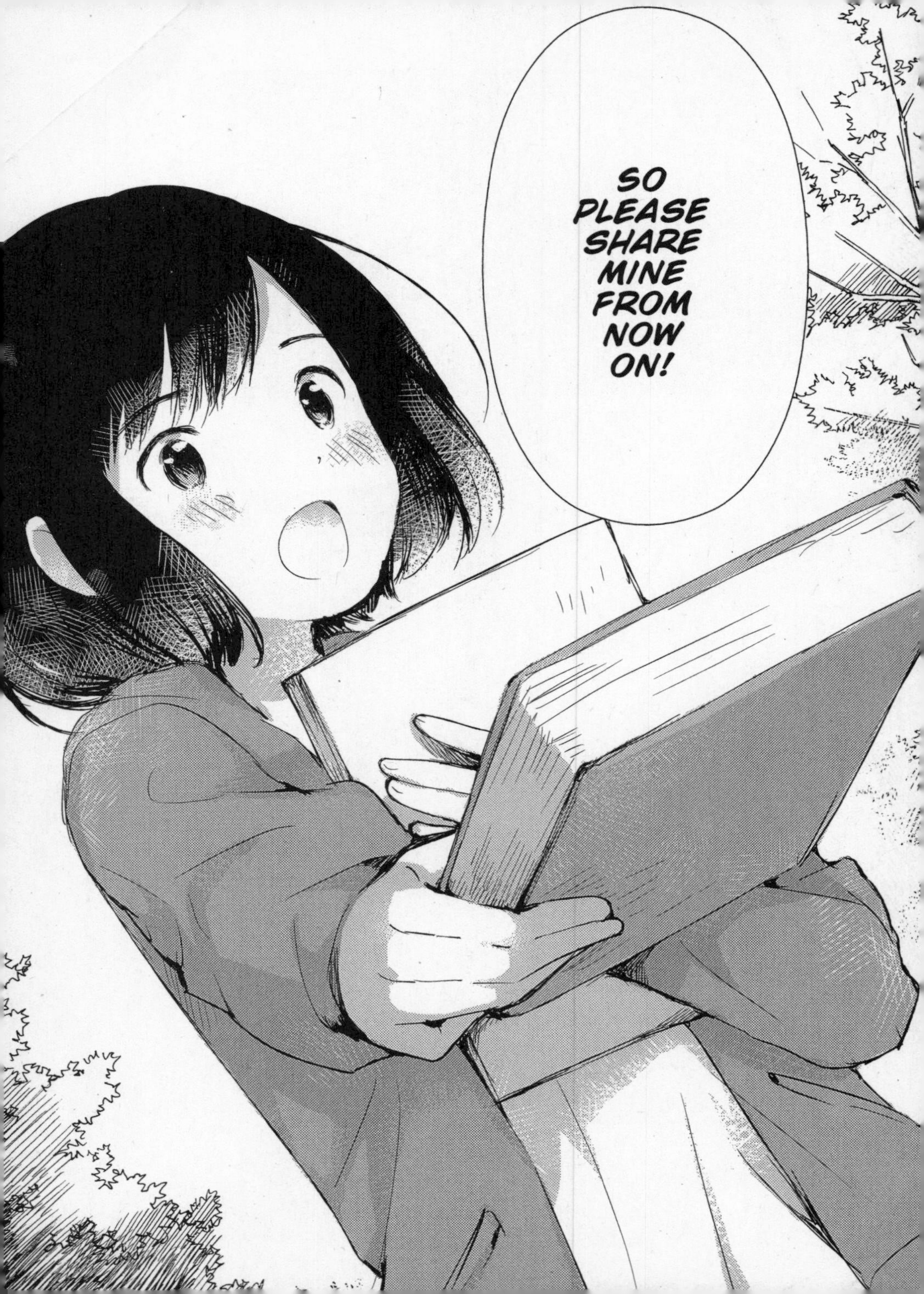
SO PLEASE SHARE MINE FROM NOW ON!

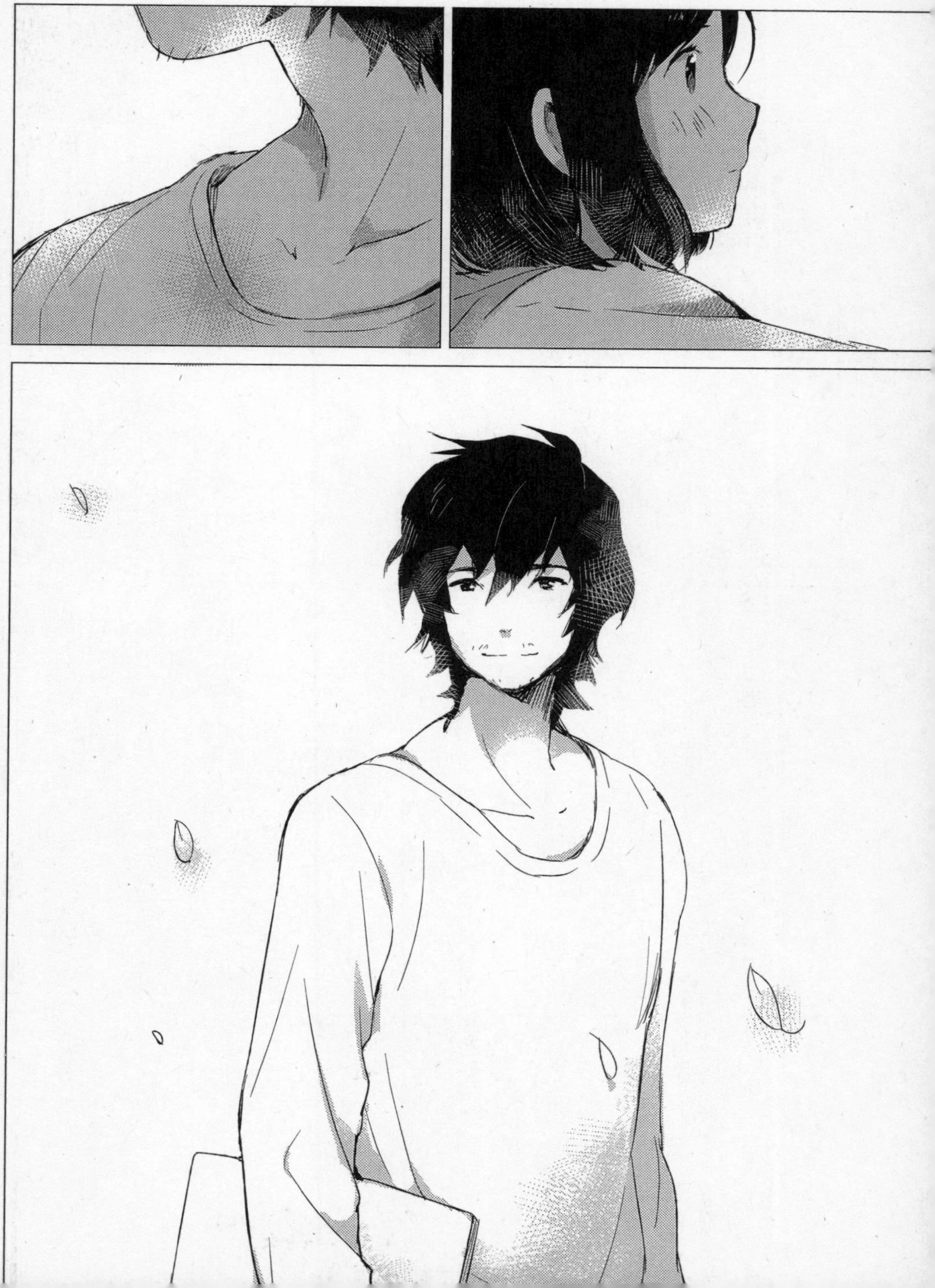

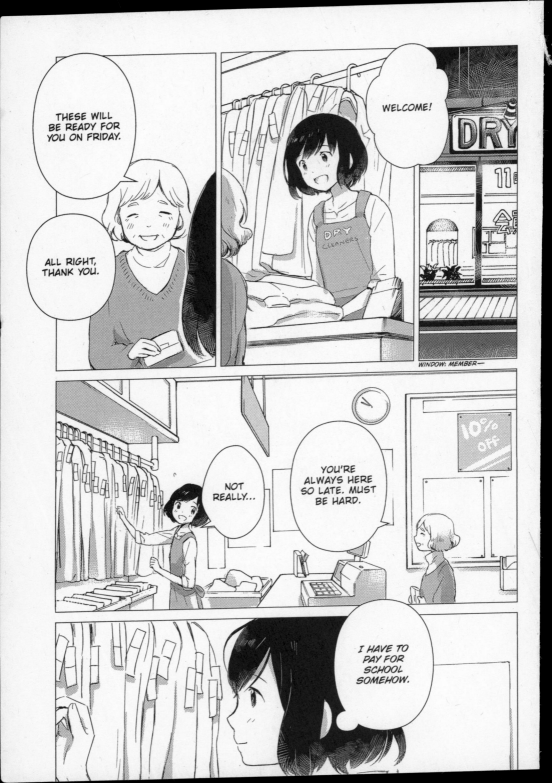

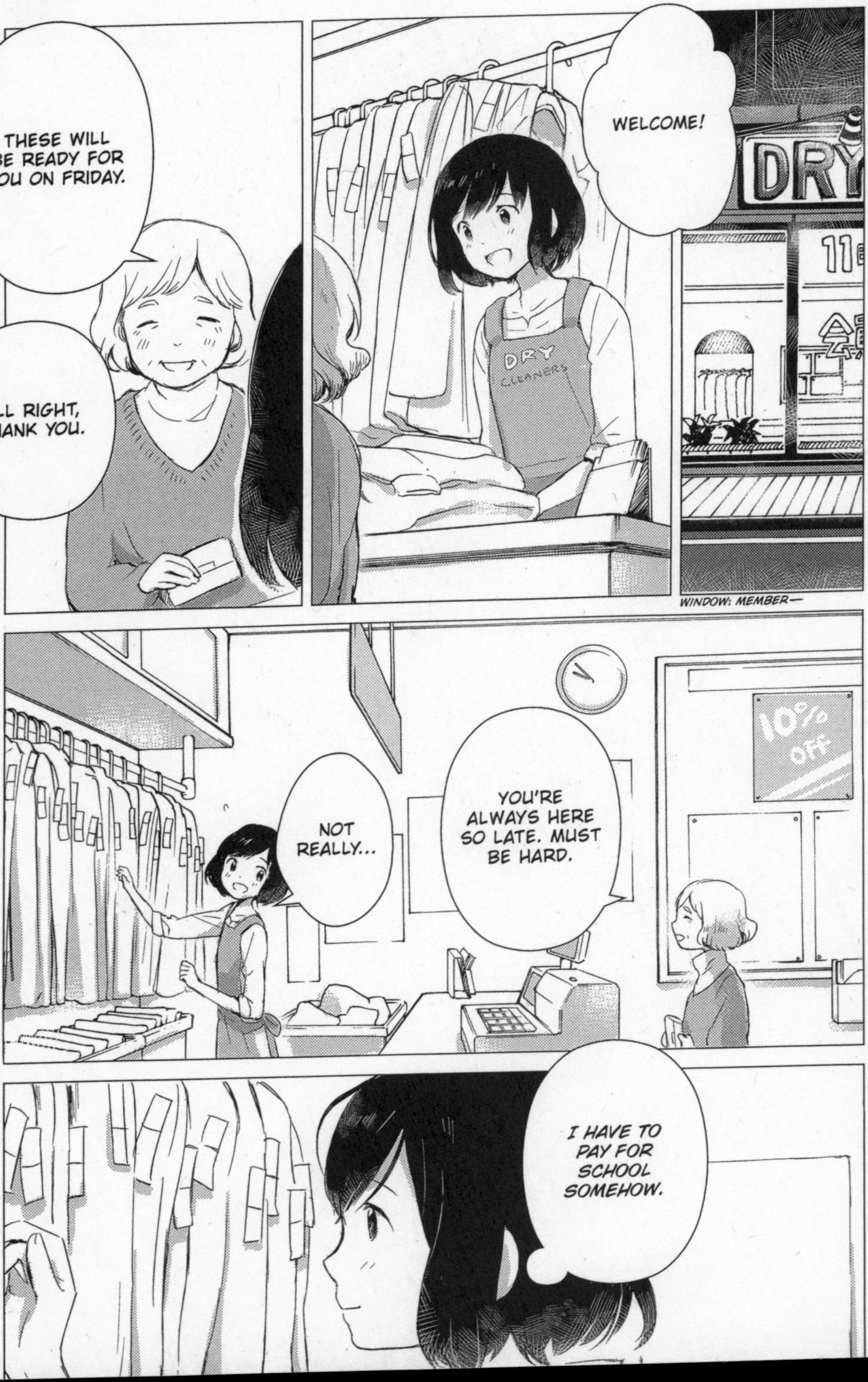
WELCOME!
DRY
DRY CLEANERS
WINDOW: MEMBER—
THESE WILL BE READY FOR YOU ON FRIDAY.
ALL RIGHT, THANK YOU.
10% OFF
YOU'RE ALWAYS HERE SO LATE. MUST BE HARD.
NOT REALLY...
I HAVE TO PAY FOR SCHOOL SOMEHOW.

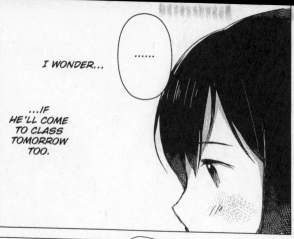

I WONDER...

...IF HE'LL COME TO CLASS TOMORROW TOO.

......

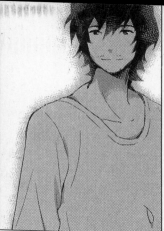

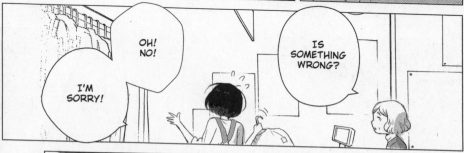

OH! NO!

I'M SORRY!

IS SOMETHING WRONG?

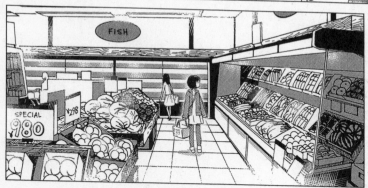

FISH

SPECIAL ¥780

¥298

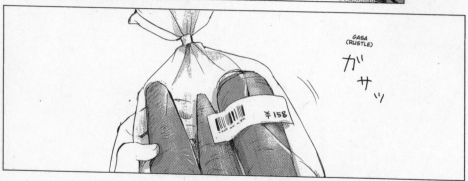

GASA (RUSTLE)

がサッ

¥158

32

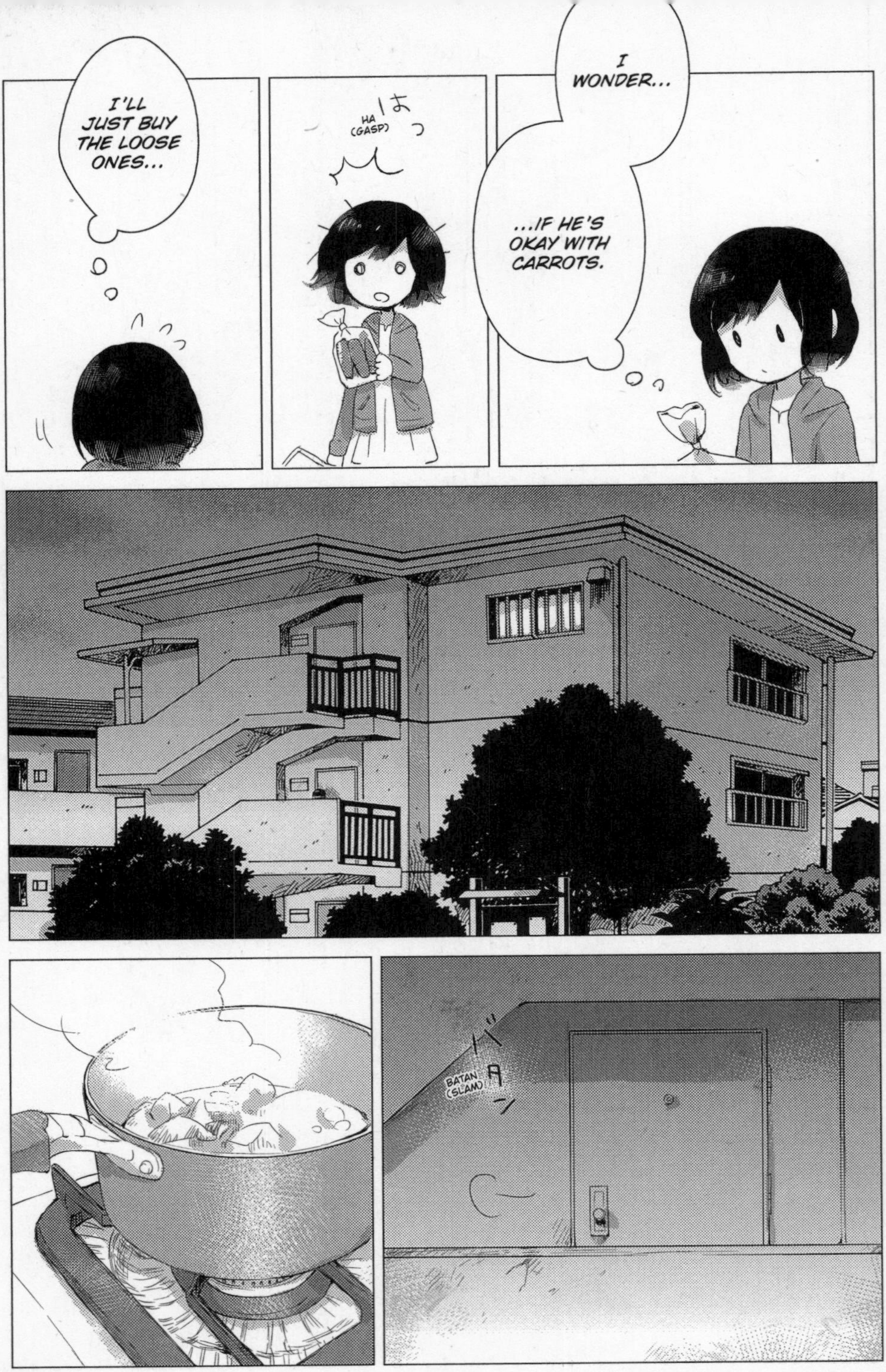
I WONDER...
...IF HE'S OKAY WITH CARROTS.
はっ
HA (GASP)
I'LL JUST BUY THE LOOSE ONES...
BATAN (SLAM)

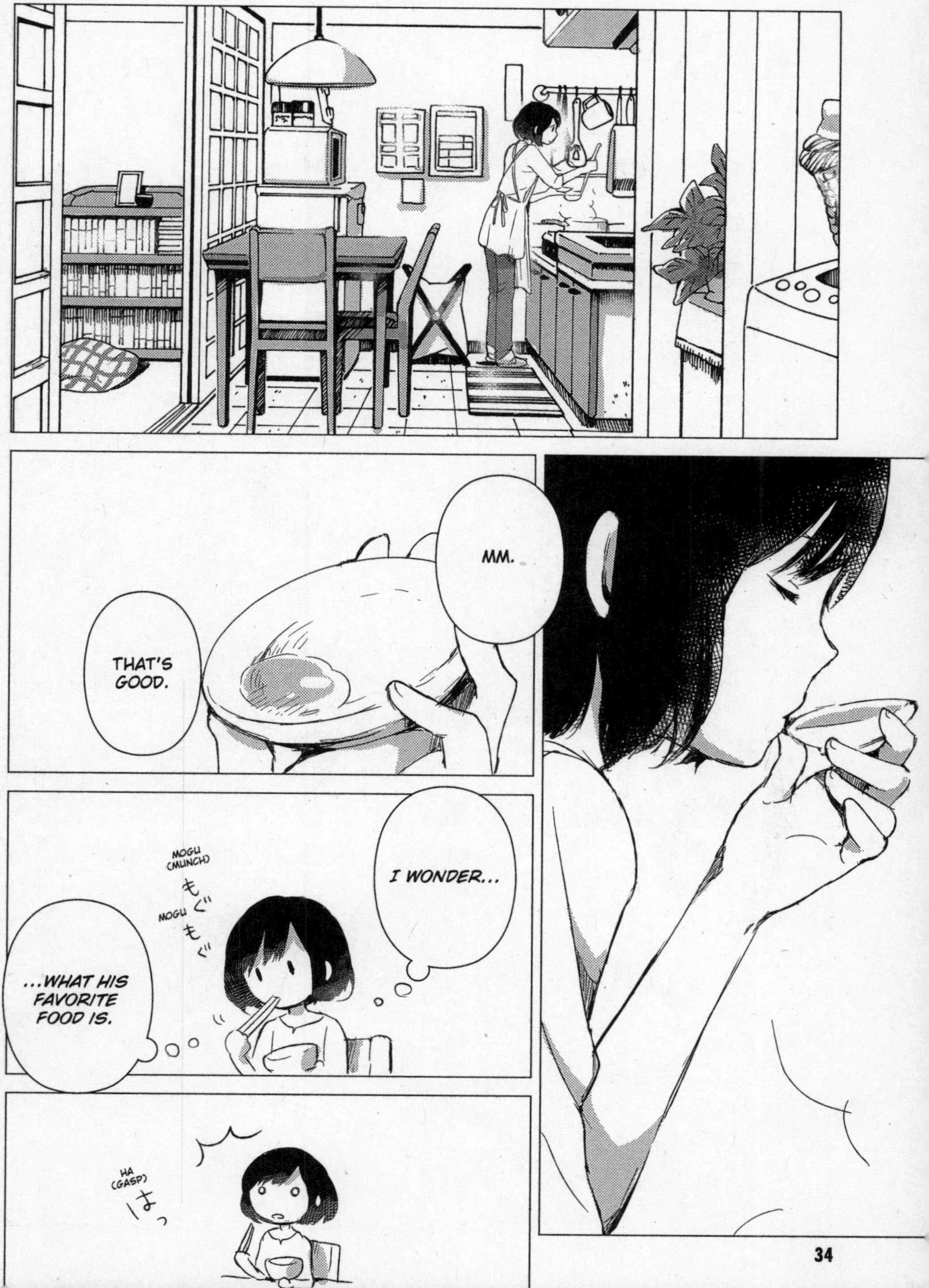
MM.
THAT'S GOOD.
I WONDER...
MOGU (MUNCH) もぐ
MOGU もぐ
...WHAT HIS FAVORITE FOOD IS.
HA (GASP) はっ

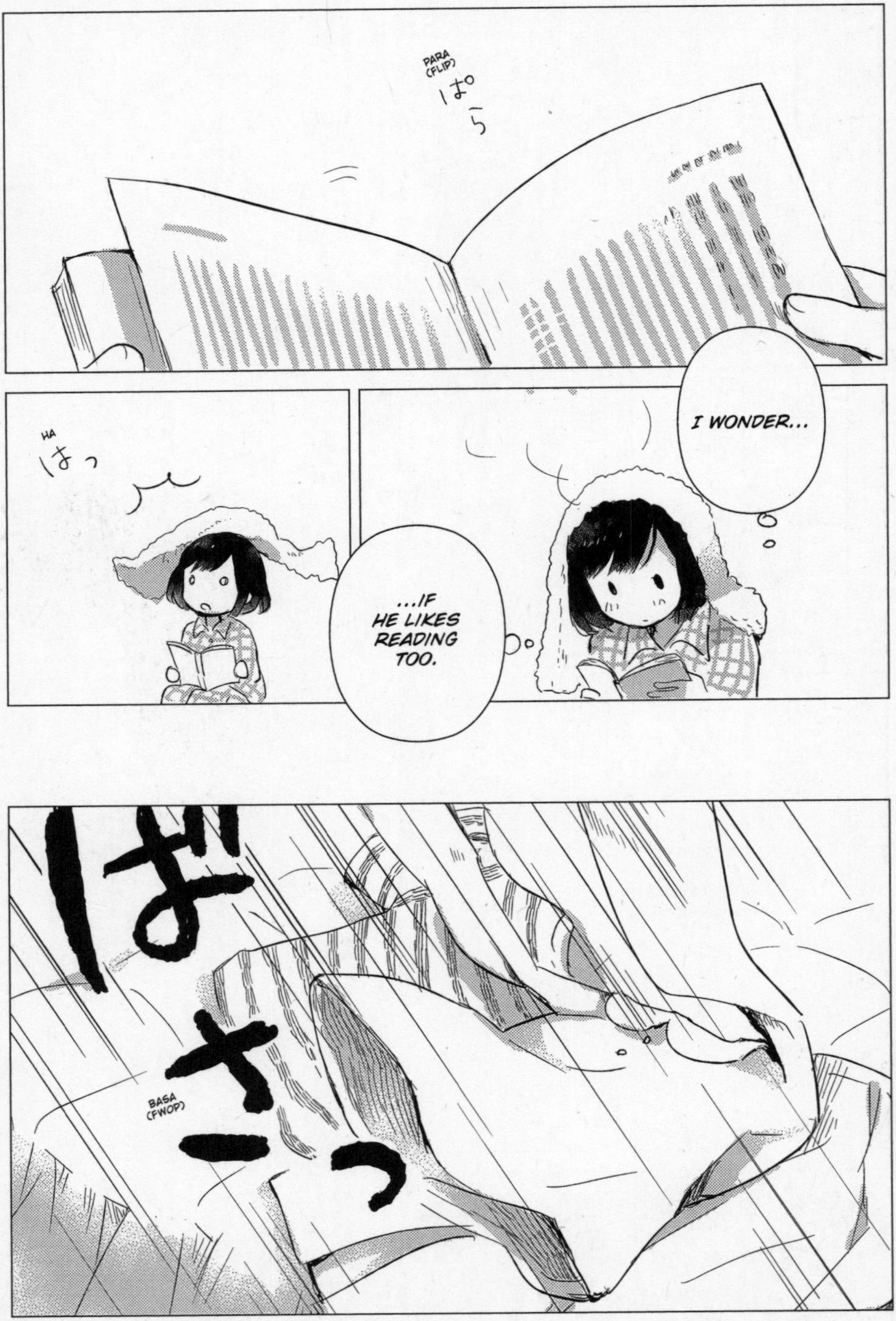
PARA (FLIP)
ぱら
I WONDER...
...IF HE LIKES READING TOO.
HA
はっ
BASA (FWOP)
ばさっ

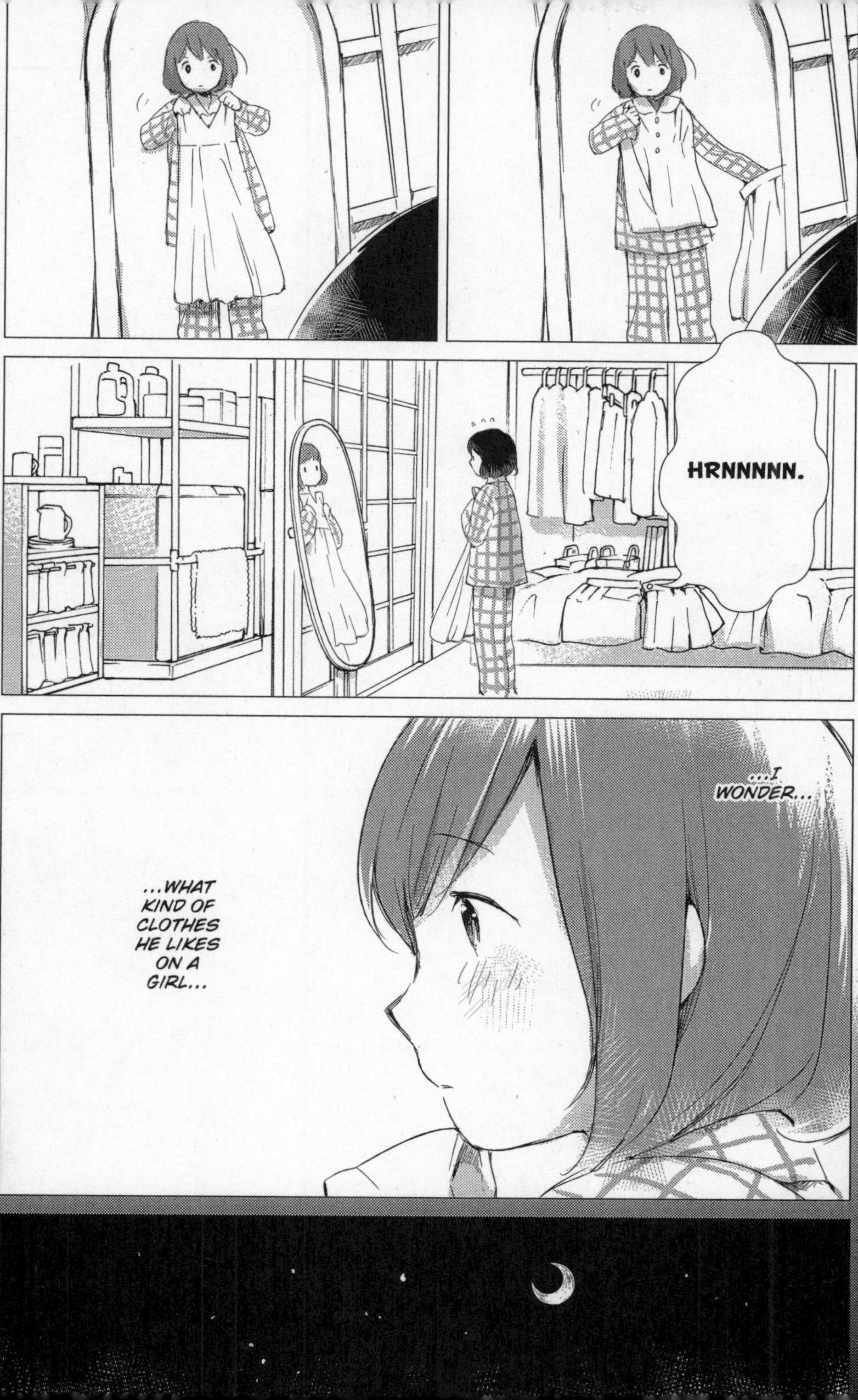
HRNNNNN.
...I WONDER...
...WHAT KIND OF CLOTHES HE LIKES ON A GIRL...

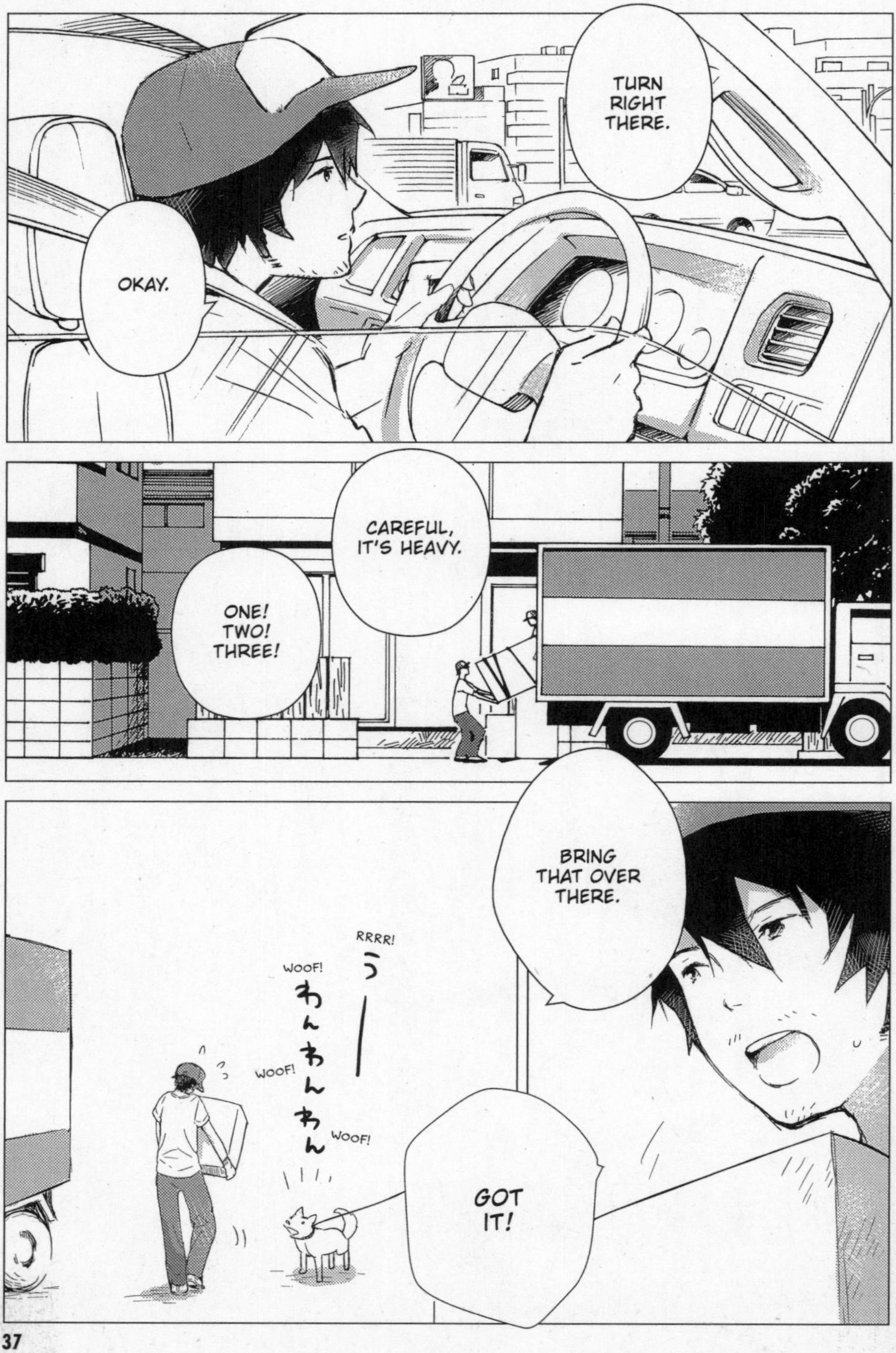
TURN RIGHT THERE.
OKAY.
CAREFUL, IT'S HEAVY.
ONE! TWO! THREE!
BRING THAT OVER THERE.
GOT IT!
RRRR!
うー
WOOF!
わんわんわん
WOOF!
WOOF!

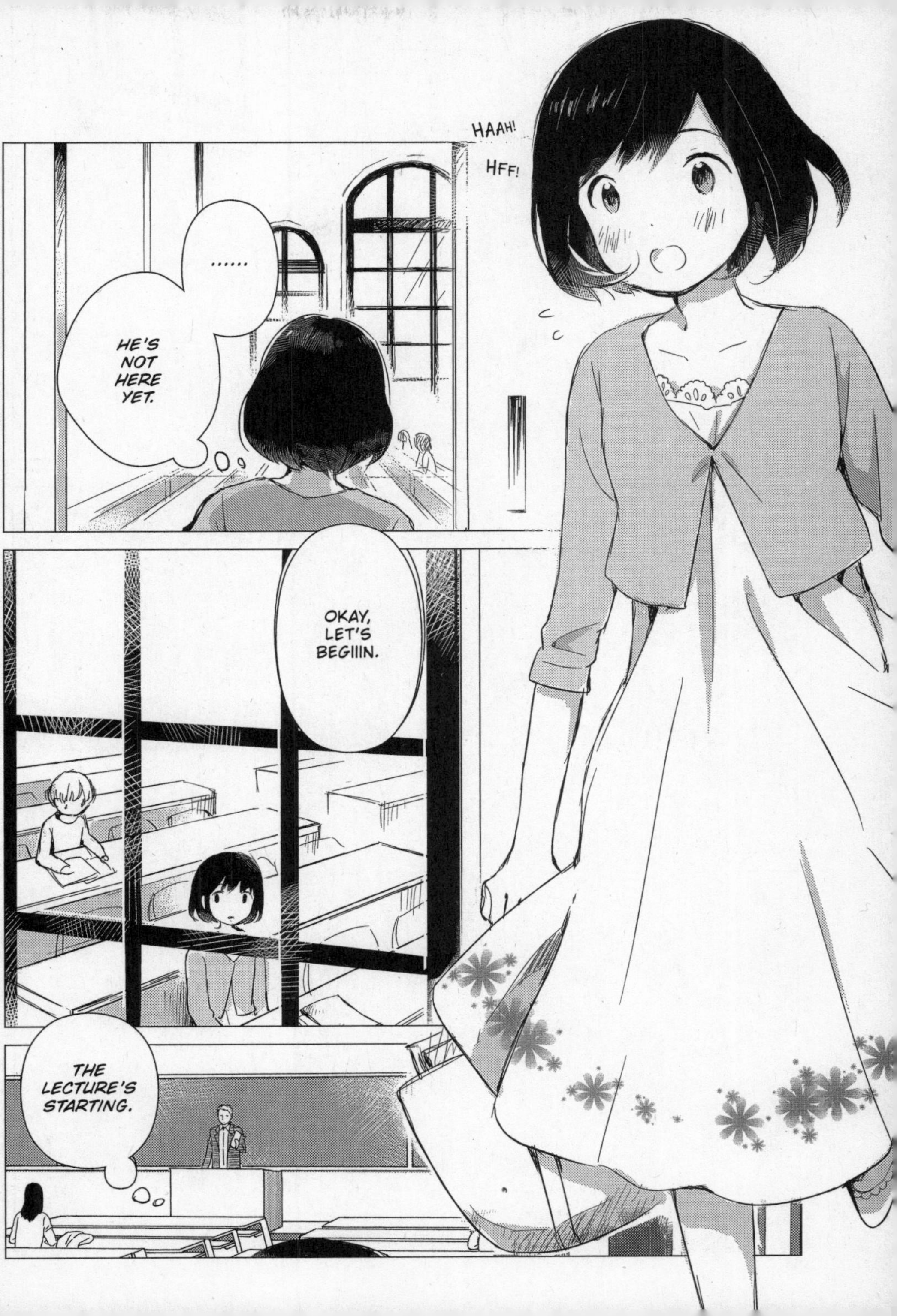
HAAH!
HFF!
......
HE'S NOT HERE YET.
OKAY, LET'S BEGIIIN.
THE LECTURE'S STARTING.

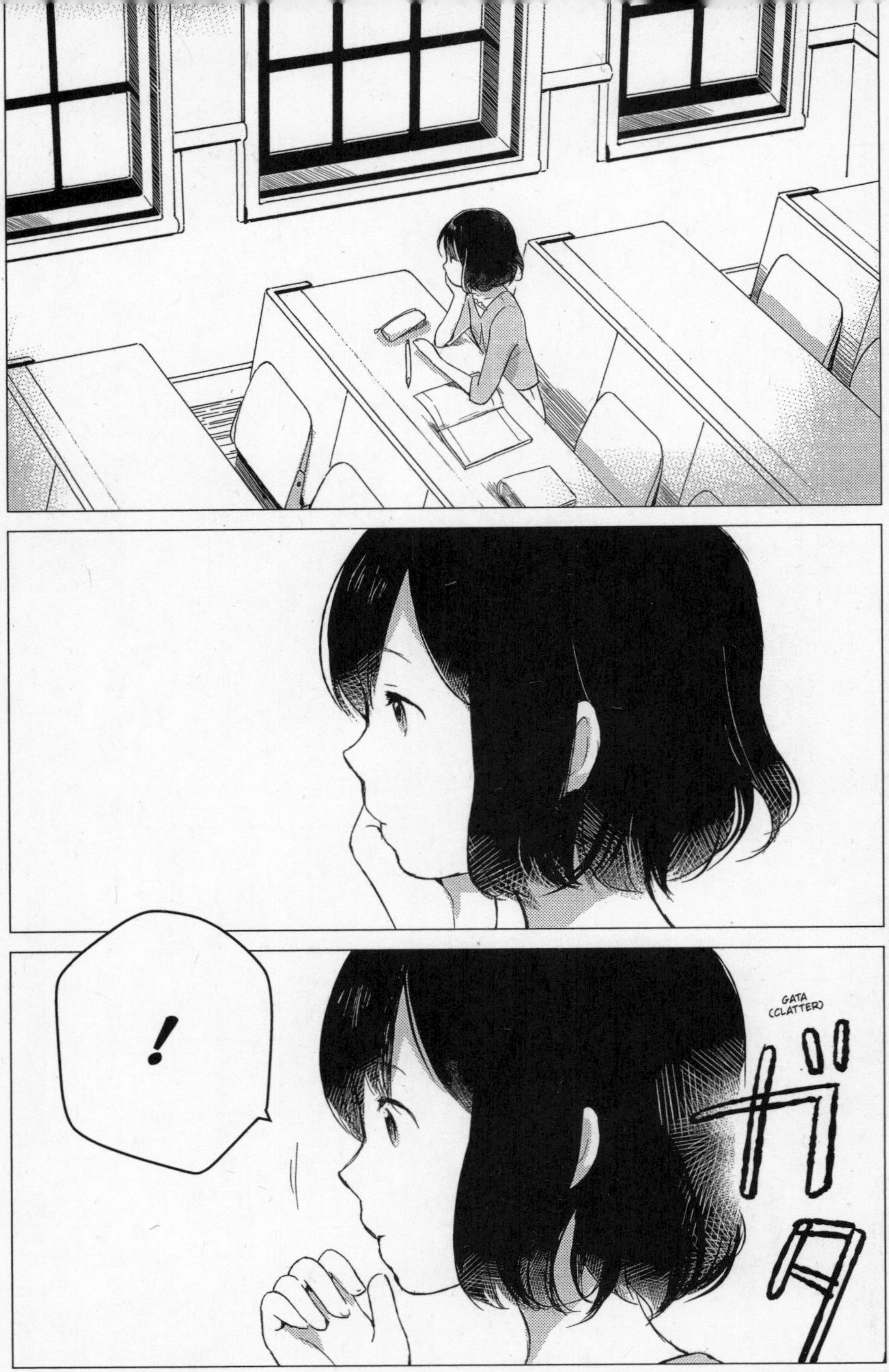
!
GATA (CLATTER)

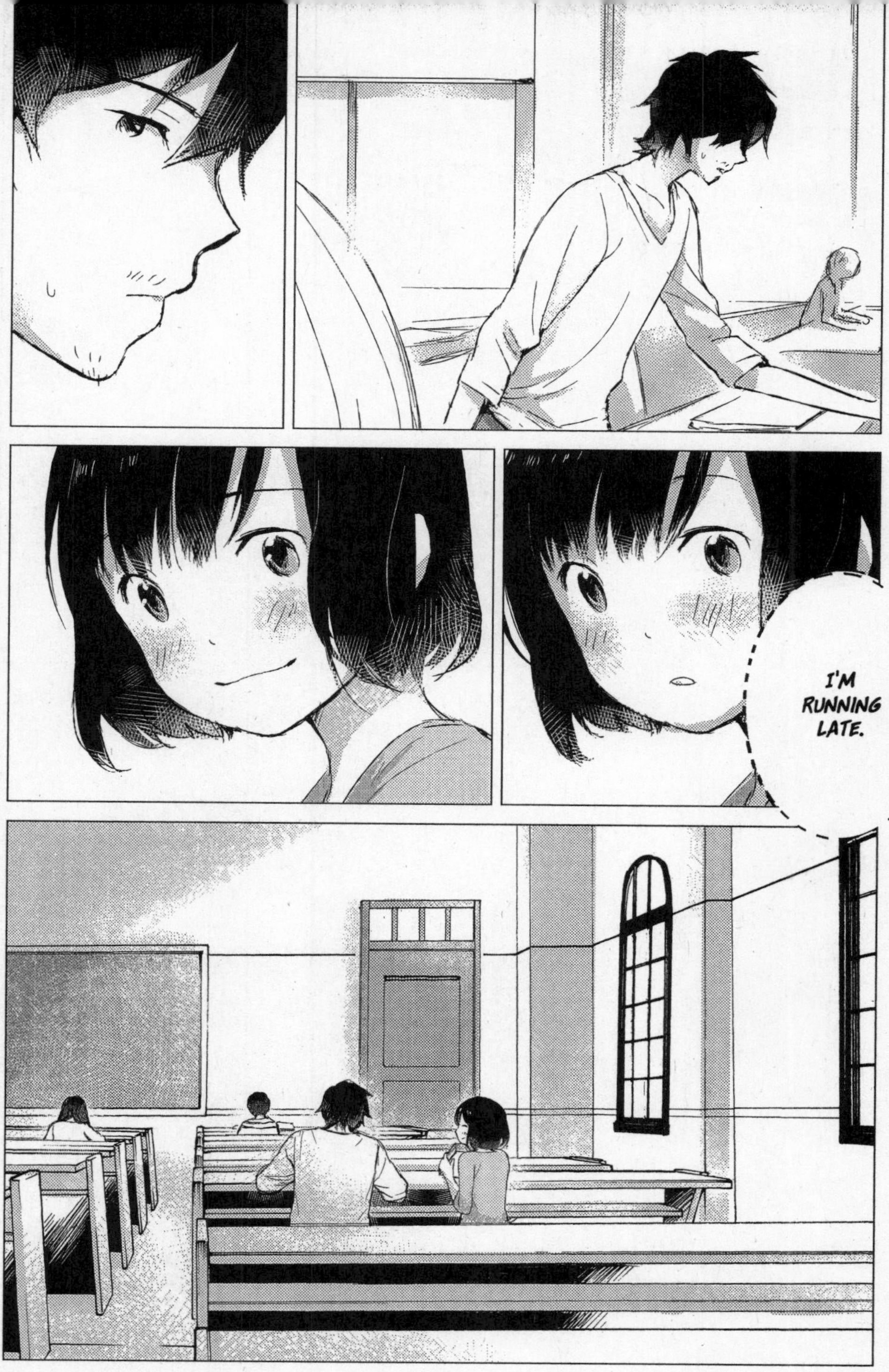
I'M RUNNING LATE.

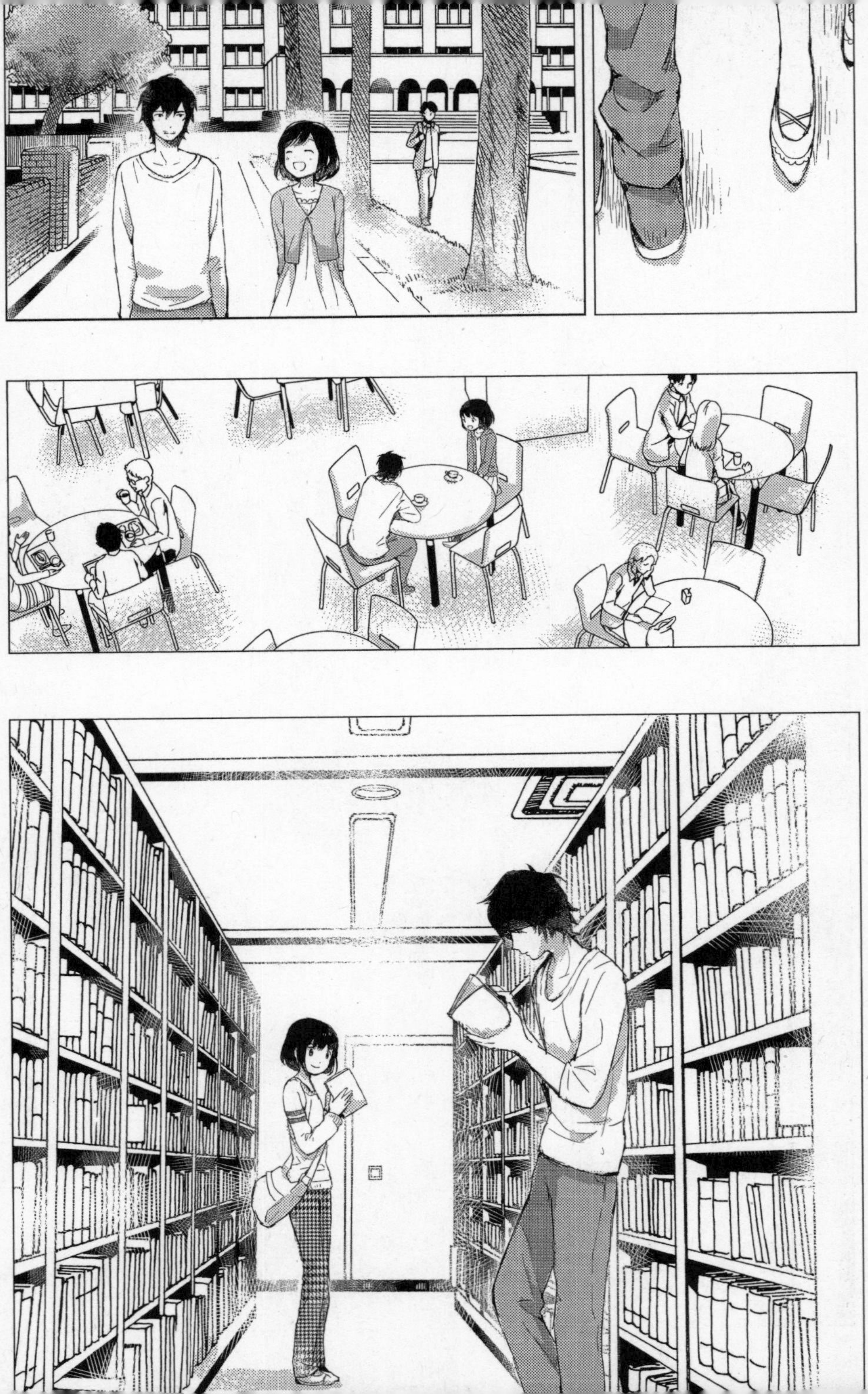

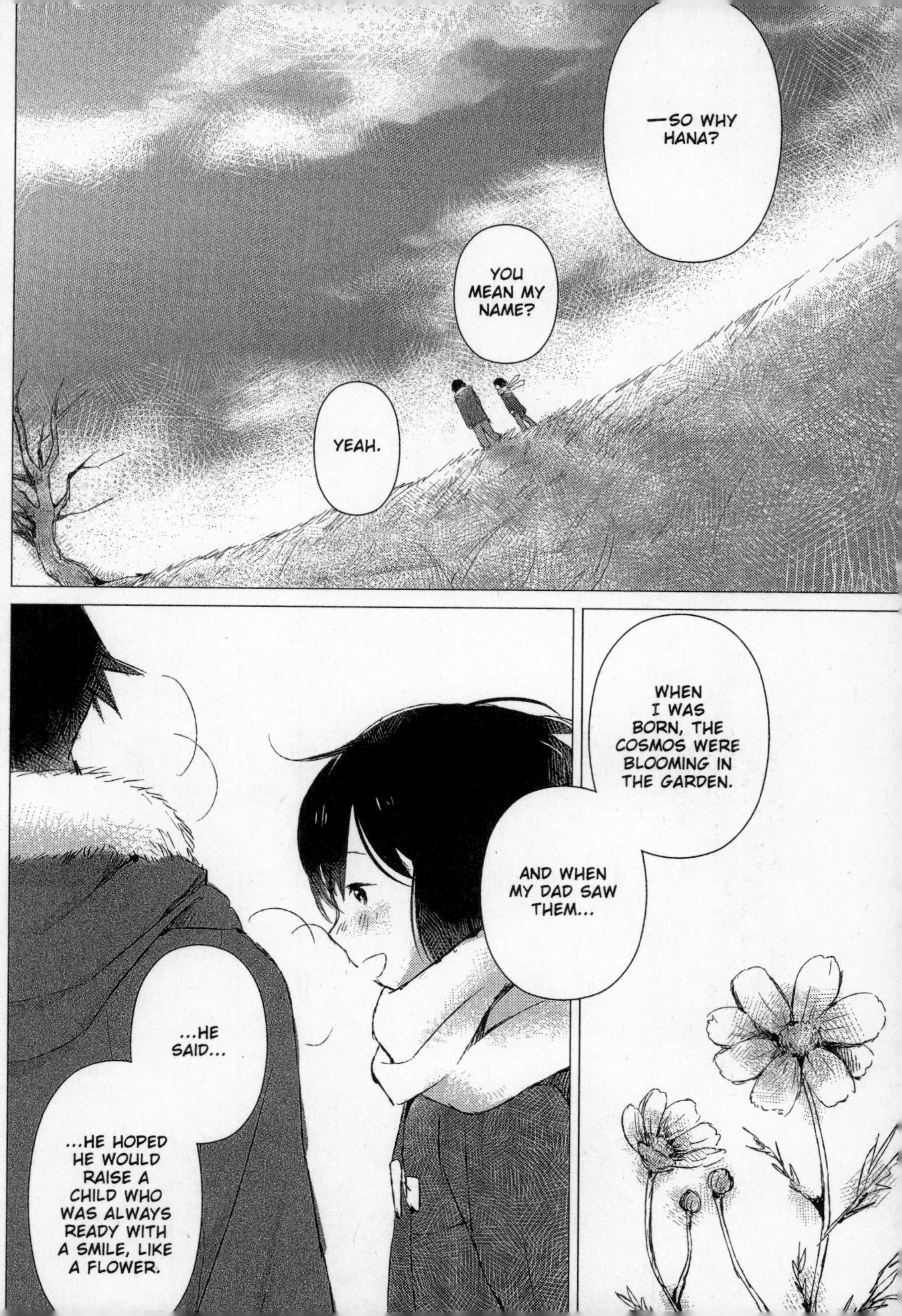
—SO WHY HANA?
YOU MEAN MY NAME?
YEAH.
WHEN I WAS BORN, THE COSMOS WERE BLOOMING IN THE GARDEN.
AND WHEN MY DAD SAW THEM...
...HE SAID...
...HE HOPED HE WOULD RAISE A CHILD WHO WAS ALWAYS READY WITH A SMILE, LIKE A FLOWER.

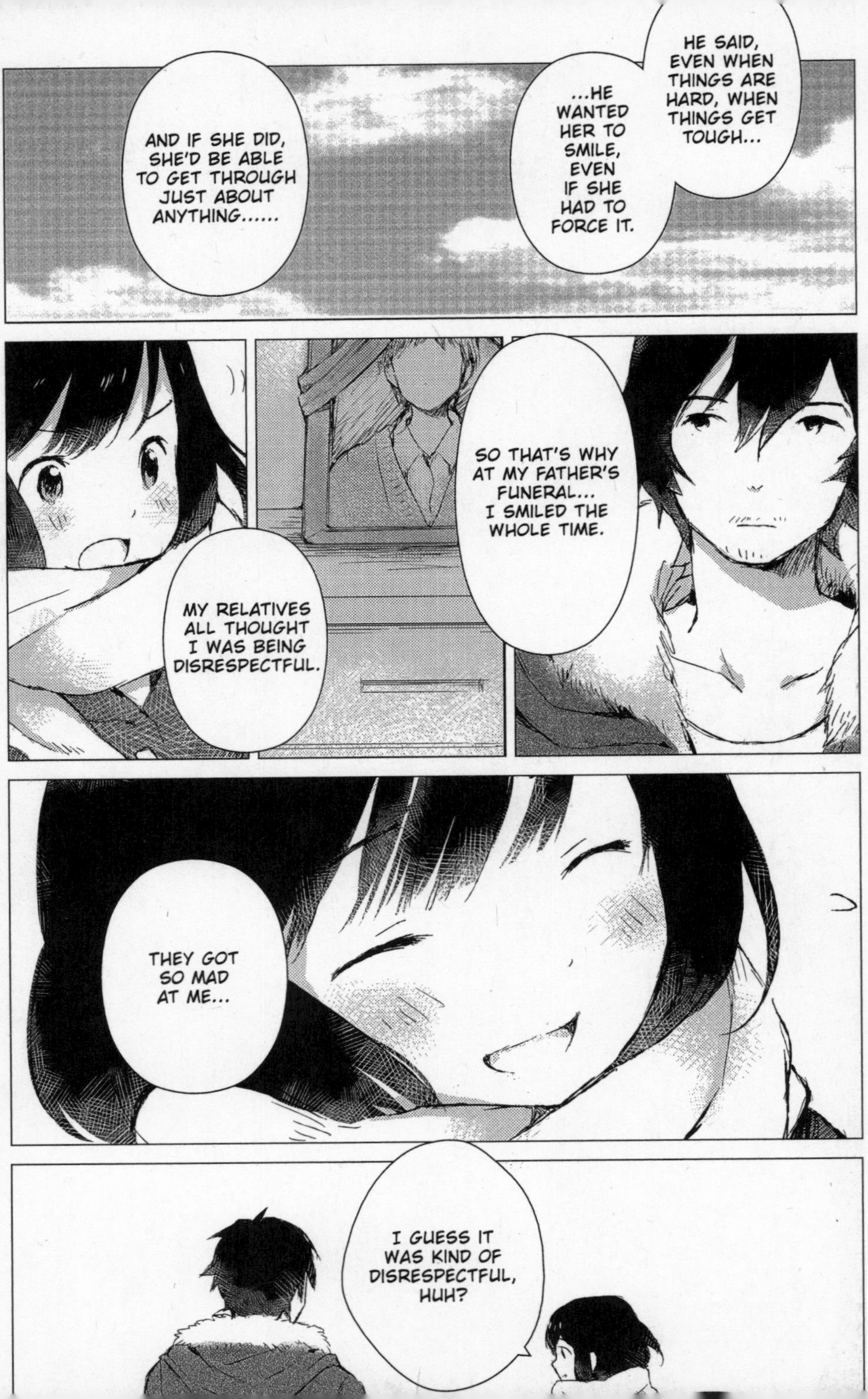
HE SAID, EVEN WHEN THINGS ARE HARD, WHEN THINGS GET TOUGH...
...HE WANTED HER TO SMILE, EVEN IF SHE HAD TO FORCE IT.
AND IF SHE DID, SHE'D BE ABLE TO GET THROUGH JUST ABOUT ANYTHING......
SO THAT'S WHY AT MY FATHER'S FUNERAL... I SMILED THE WHOLE TIME.
MY RELATIVES ALL THOUGHT I WAS BEING DISRESPECTFUL.
THEY GOT SO MAD AT ME...
I GUESS IT WAS KIND OF DISRESPECTFUL, HUH?

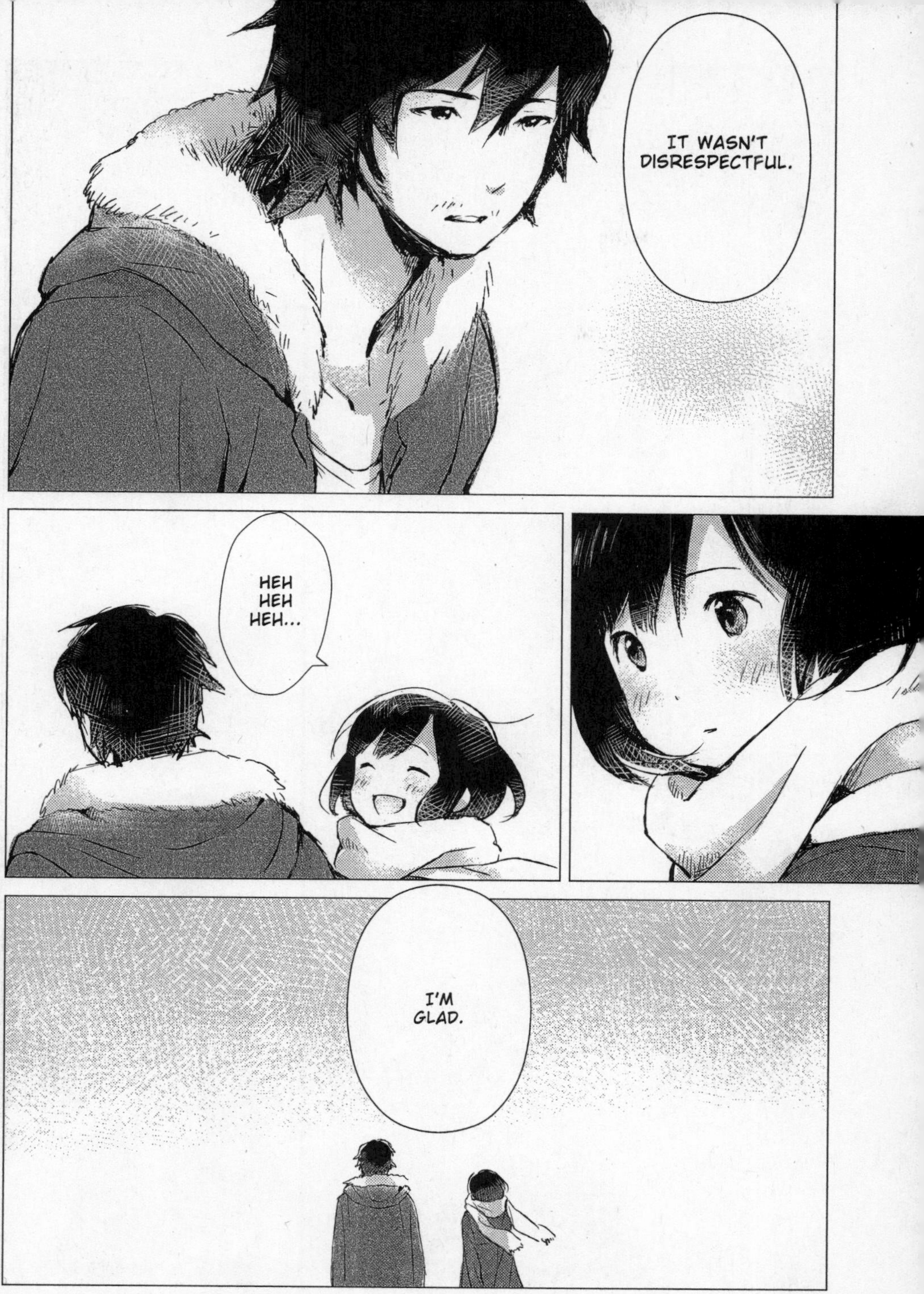
IT WASN'T DISRESPECTFUL.
HEH HEH HEH...
I'M GLAD.

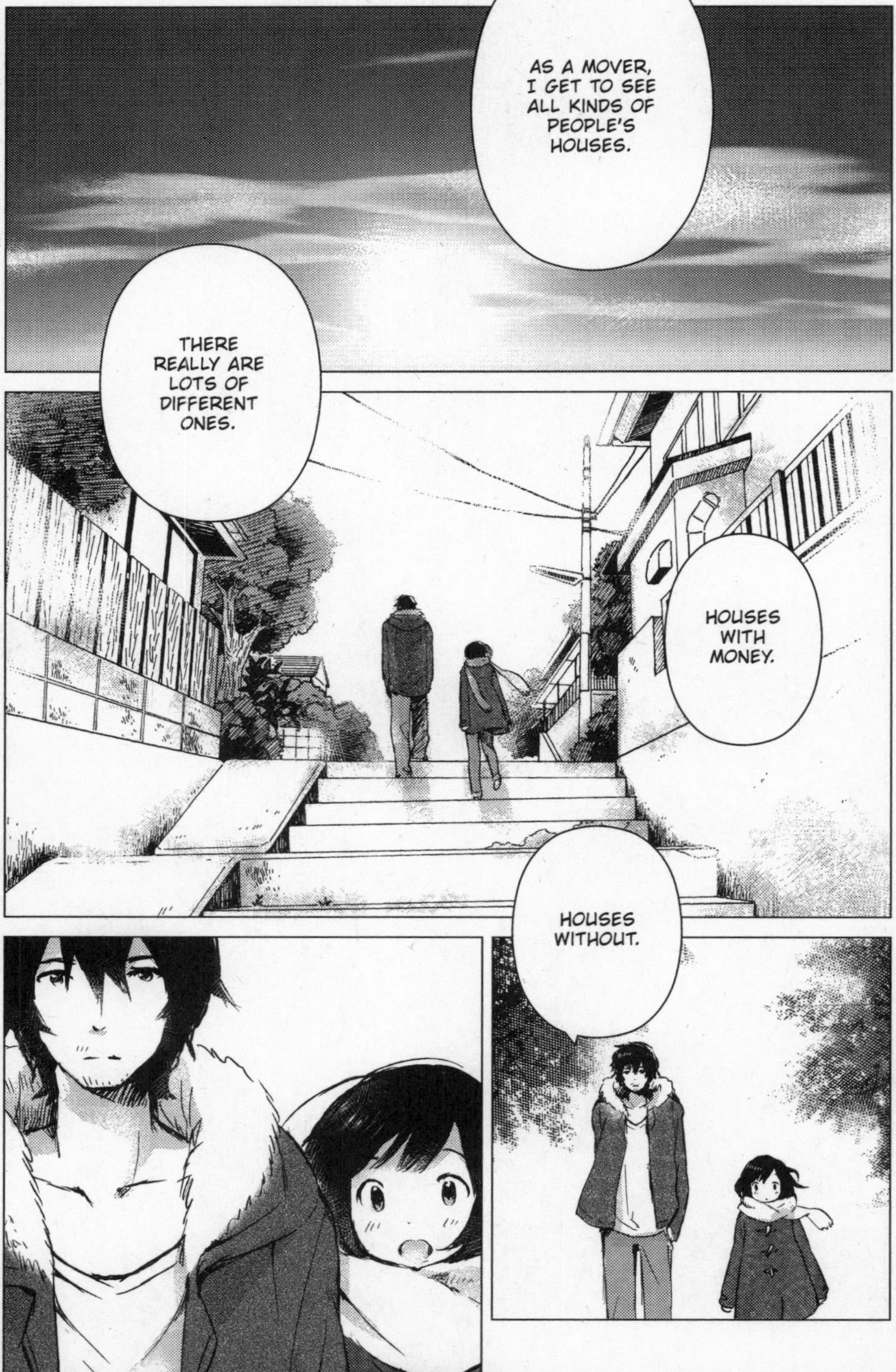
AS A MOVER, I GET TO SEE ALL KINDS OF PEOPLE'S HOUSES.
THERE REALLY ARE LOTS OF DIFFERENT ONES.
HOUSES WITH MONEY.
HOUSES WITHOUT.

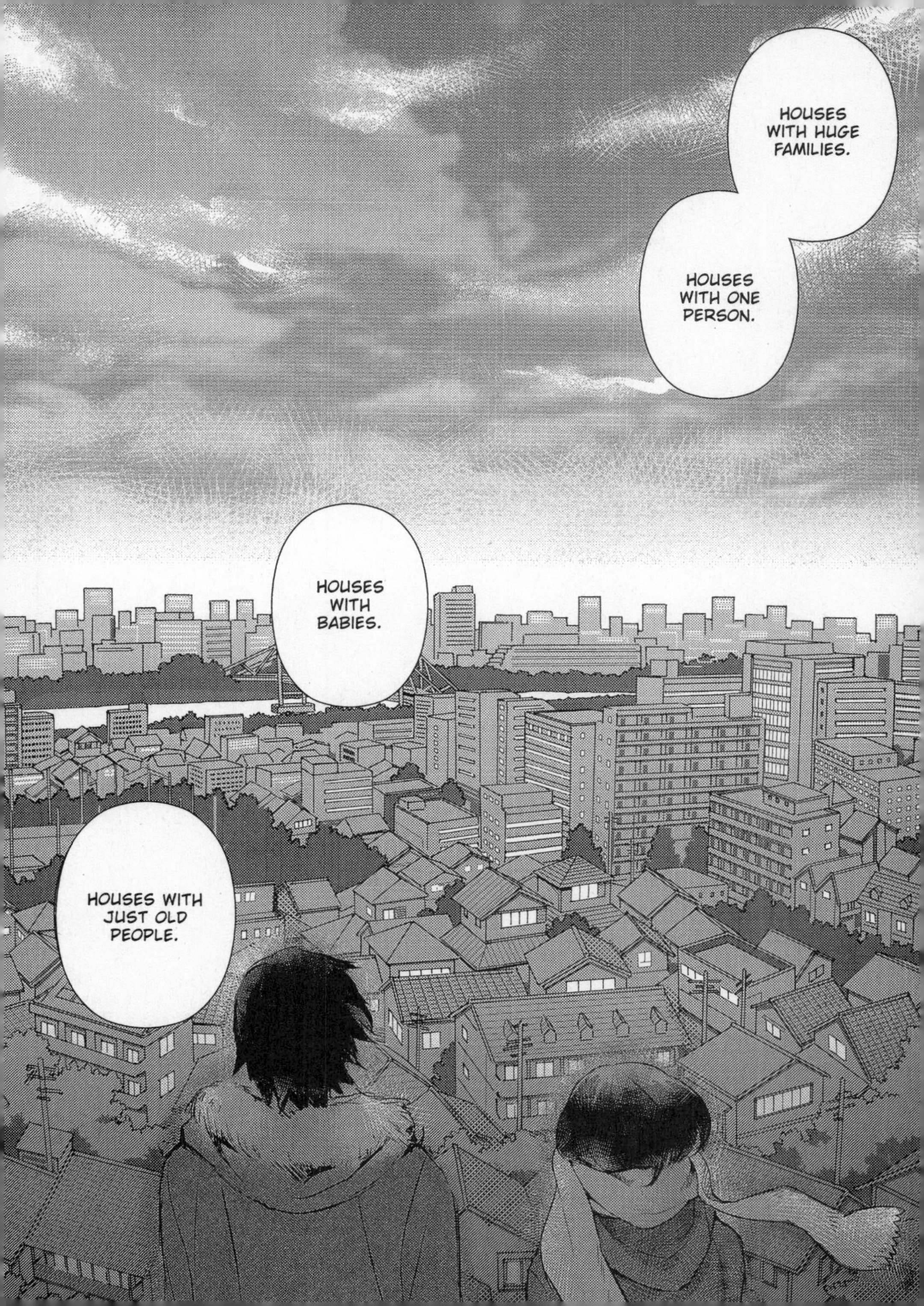
HOUSES WITH HUGE FAMILIES.
HOUSES WITH ONE PERSON.
HOUSES WITH BABIES.
HOUSES WITH JUST OLD PEOPLE.

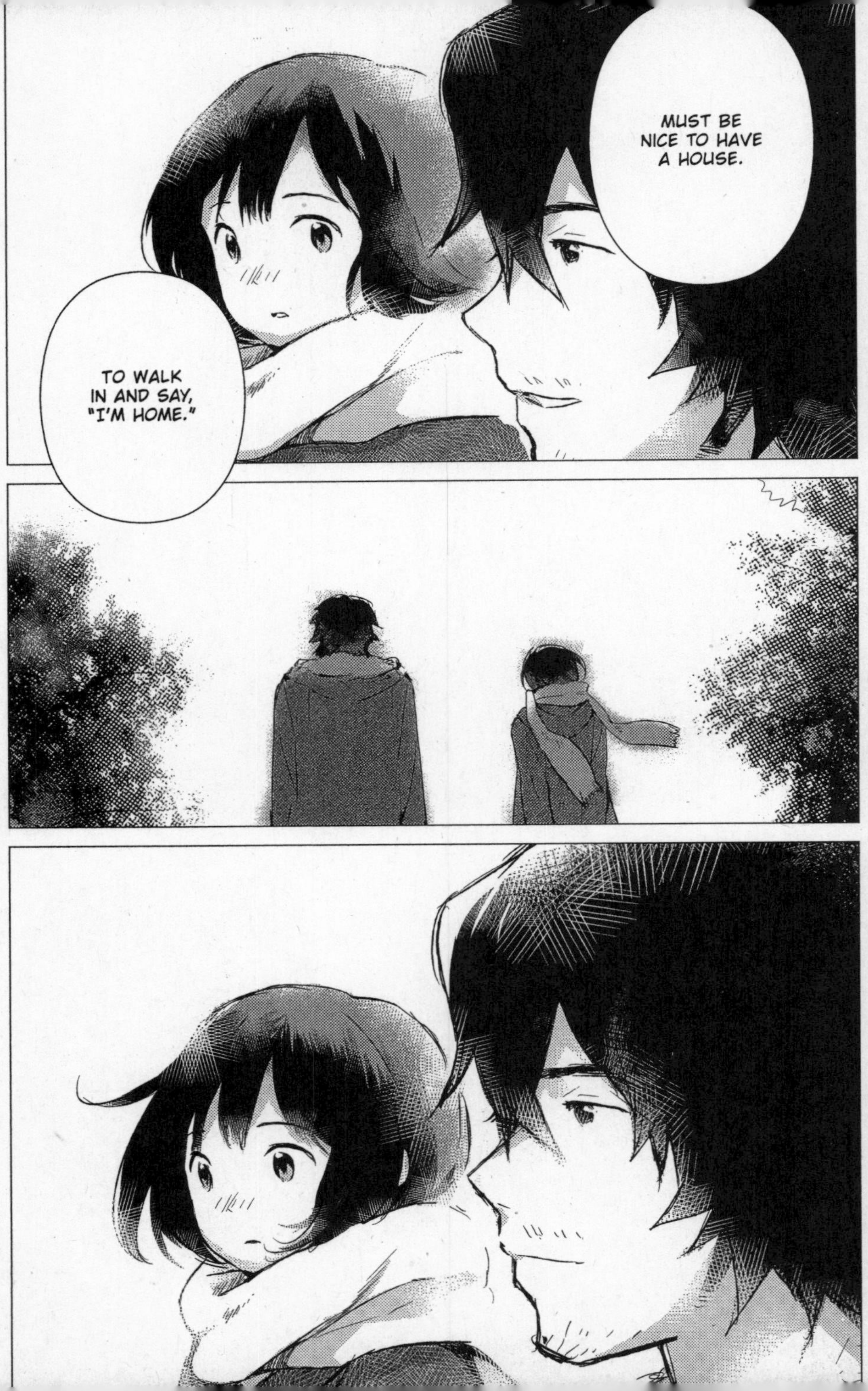
MUST BE NICE TO HAVE A HOUSE.
TO WALK IN AND SAY, "I'M HOME."

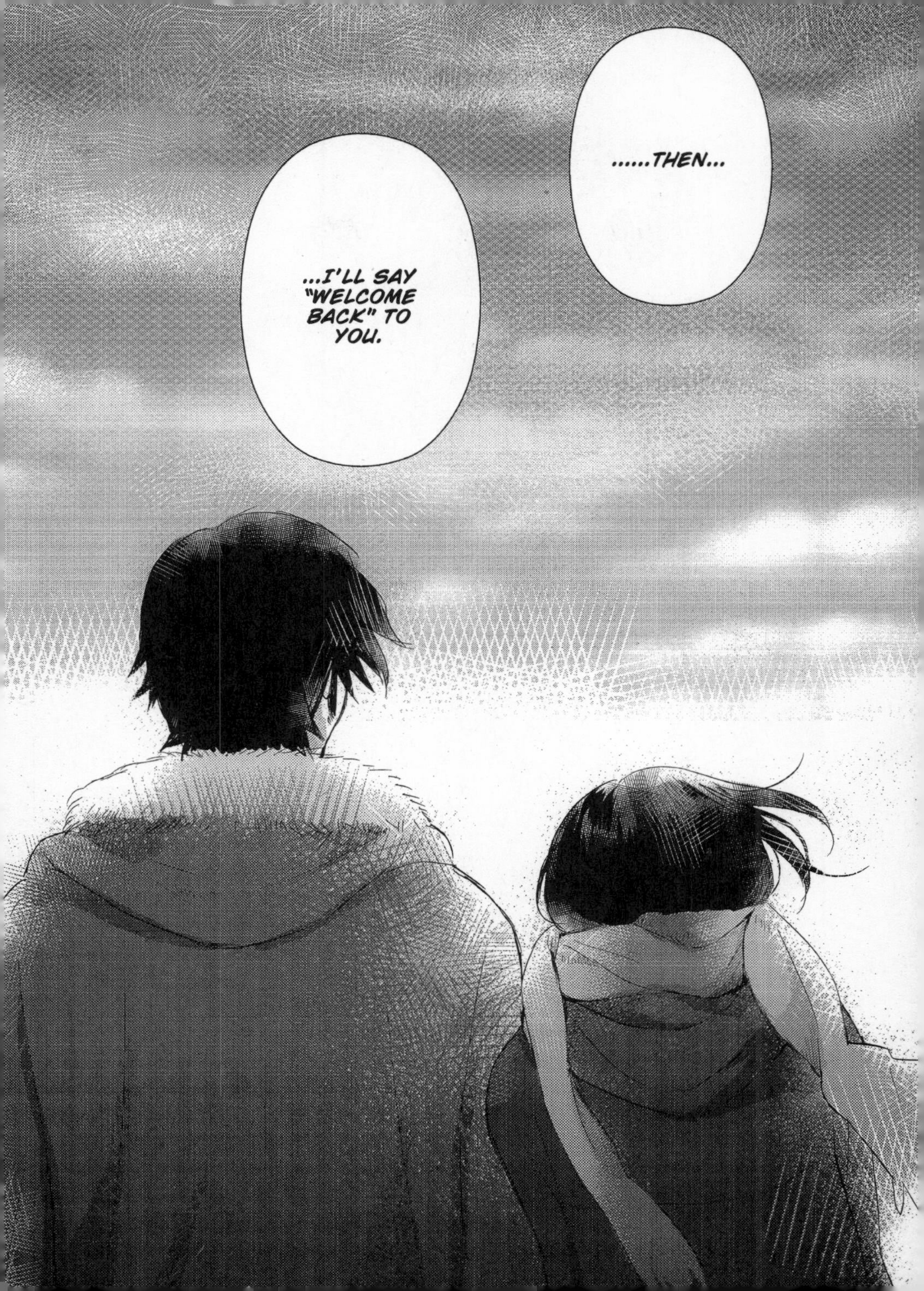
......THEN...
...I'LL SAY "WELCOME BACK" TO YOU.

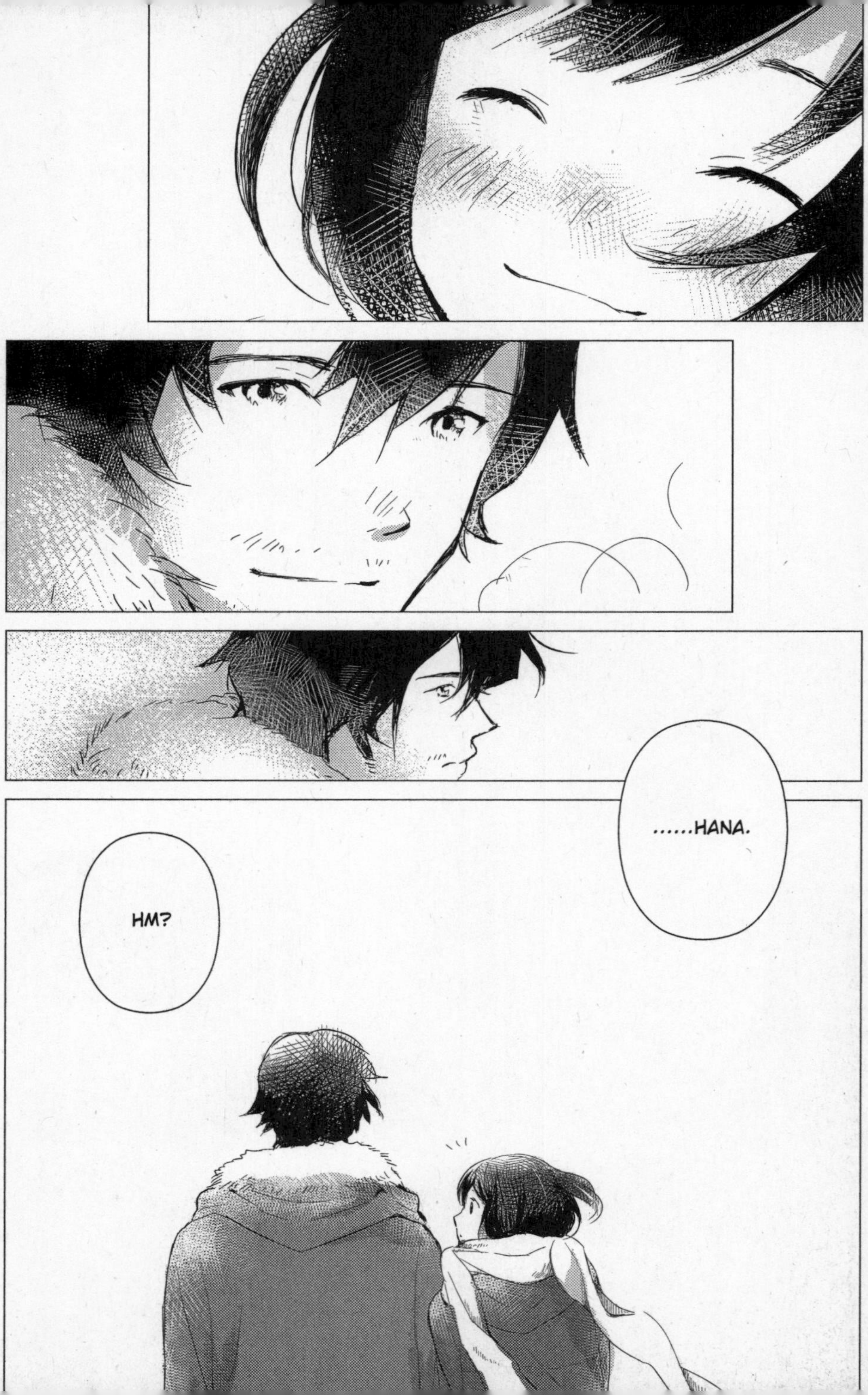
......HANA.
HM?

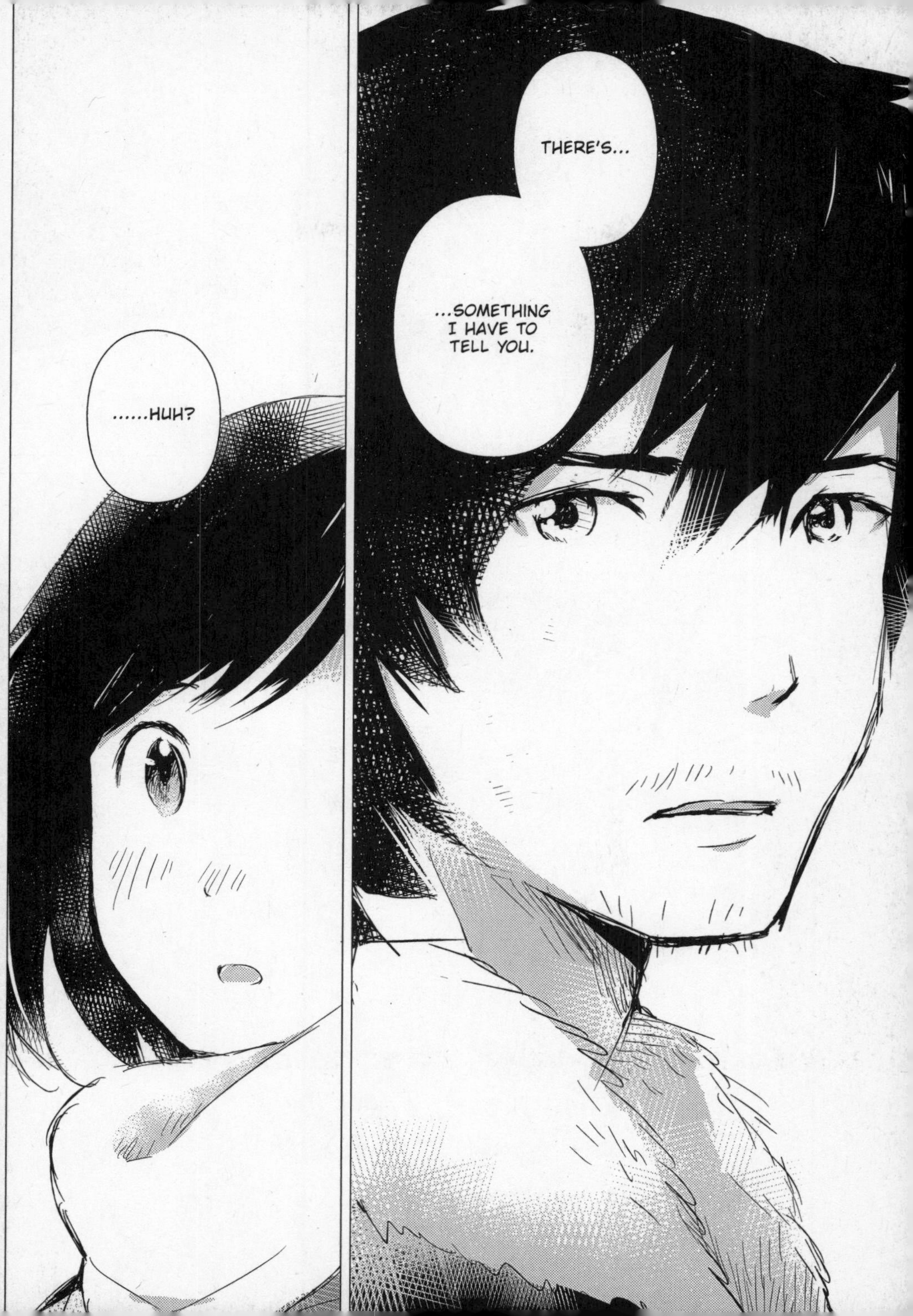
THERE'S...
...SOMETHING I HAVE TO TELL YOU.
......HUH?

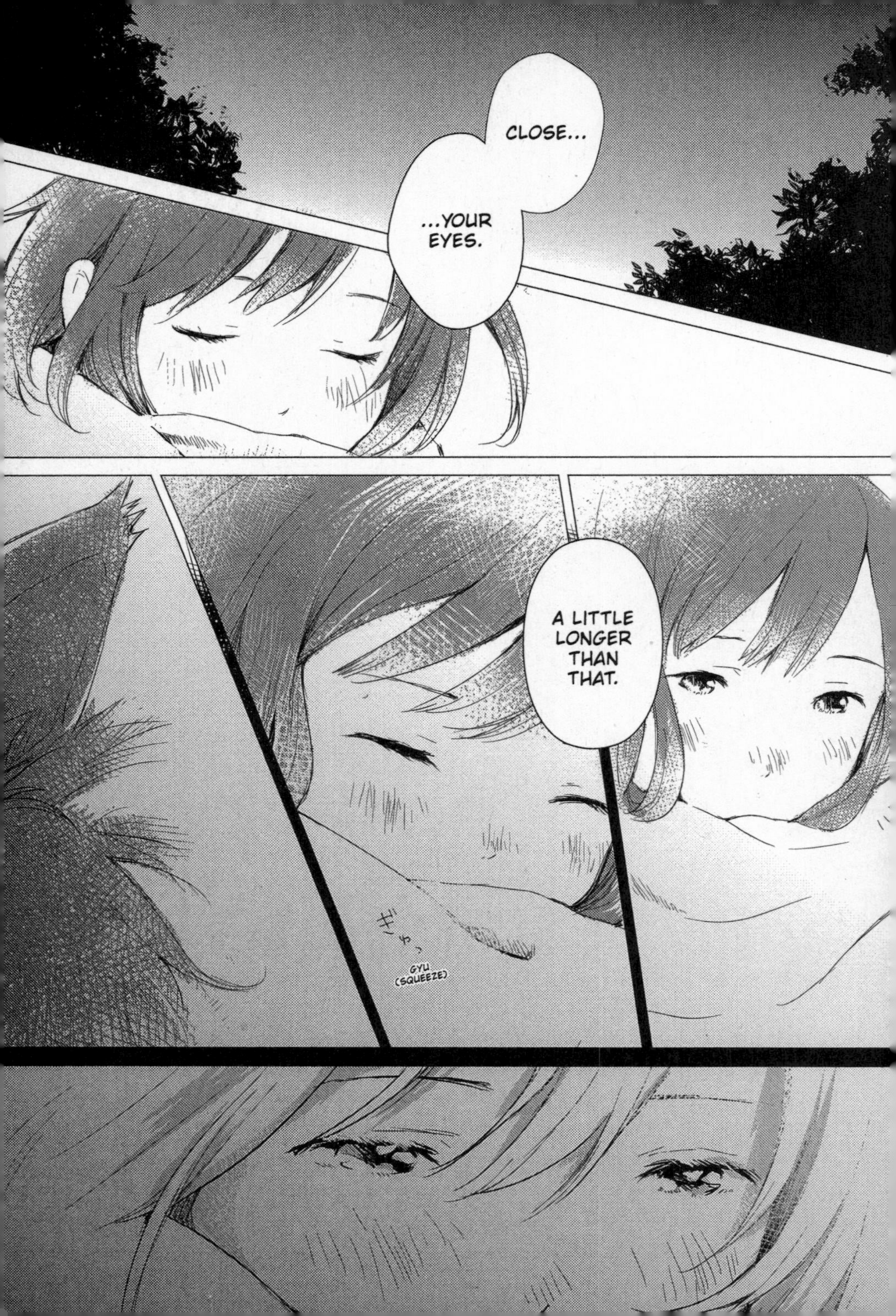
CLOSE...
...YOUR EYES.
A LITTLE LONGER THAN THAT.
ぎゅっ
GYU (SQUEEZE)

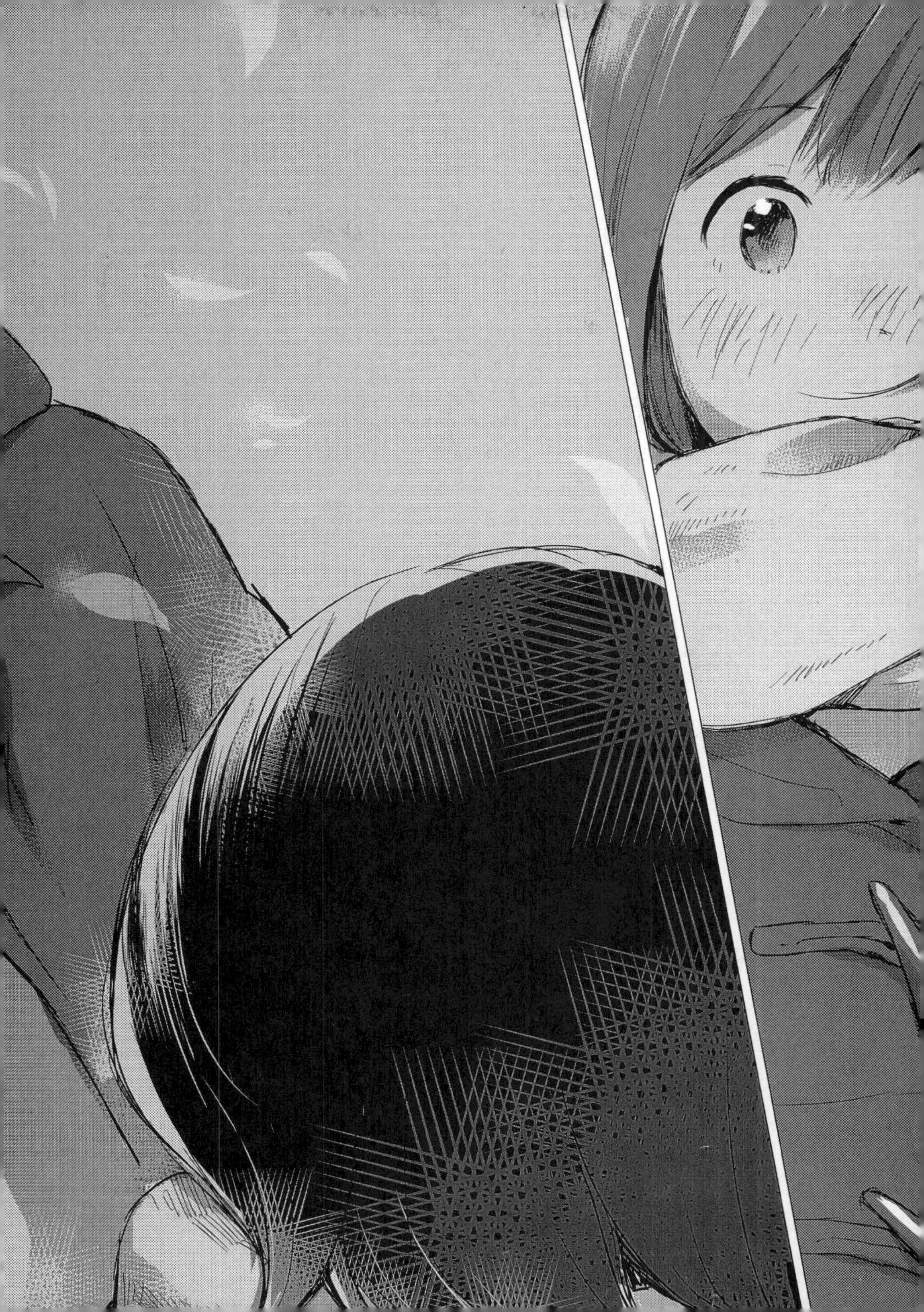

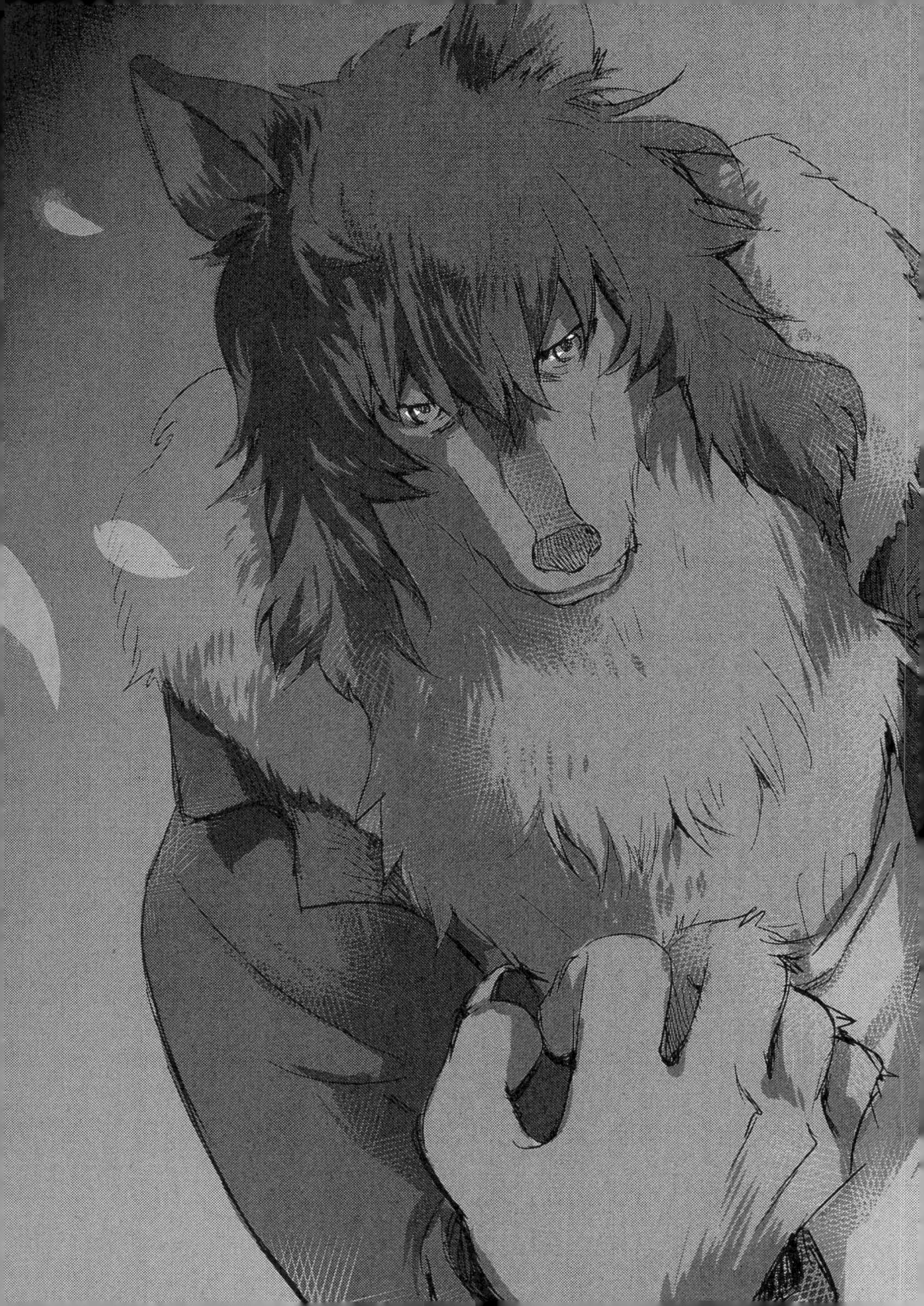

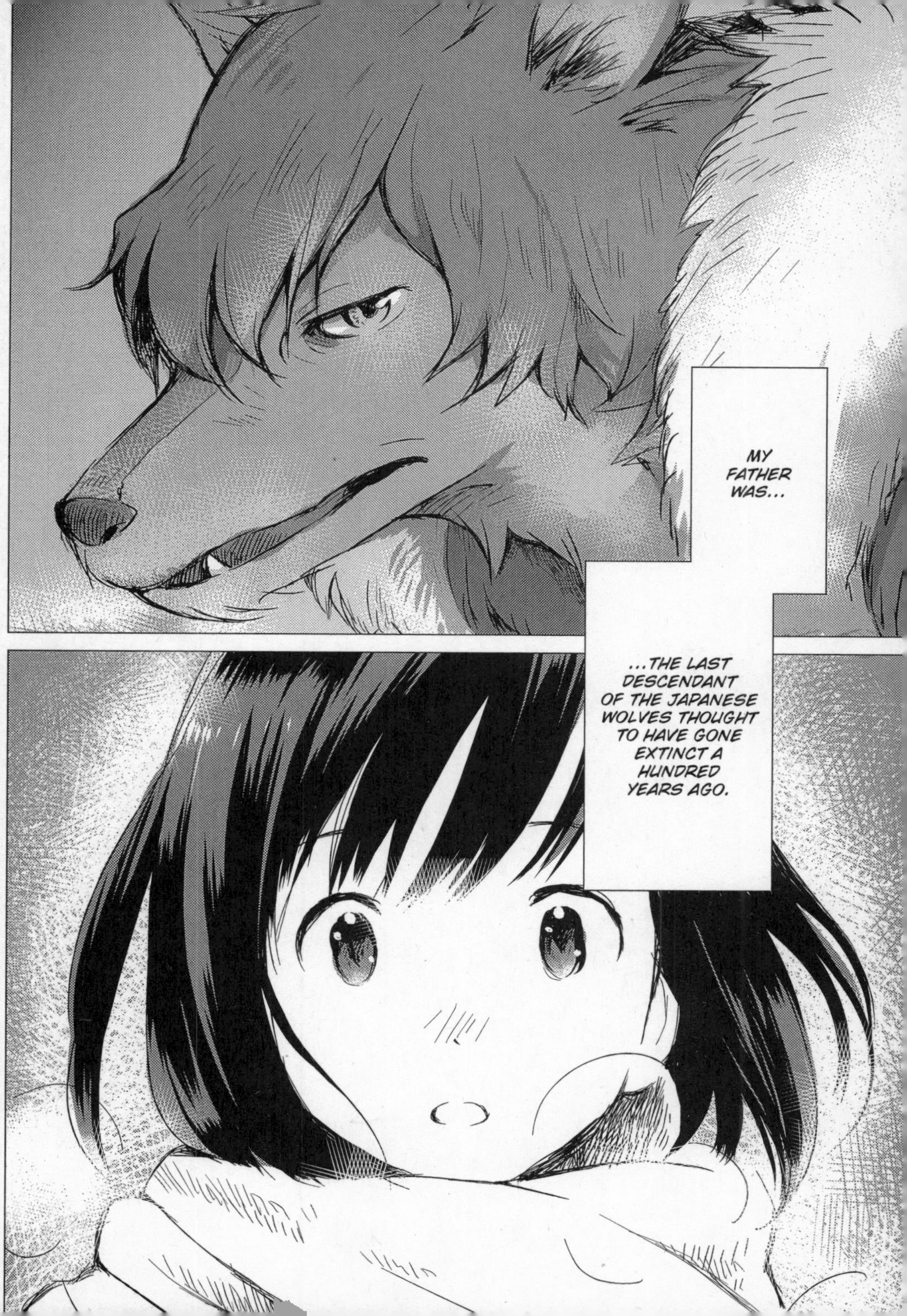
MY FATHER WAS...
...THE LAST DESCENDANT OF THE JAPANESE WOLVES THOUGHT TO HAVE GONE EXTINCT A HUNDRED YEARS AGO.

WOLF CHILDREN
AME & YUKI

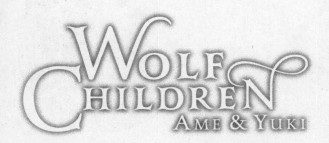

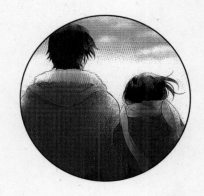

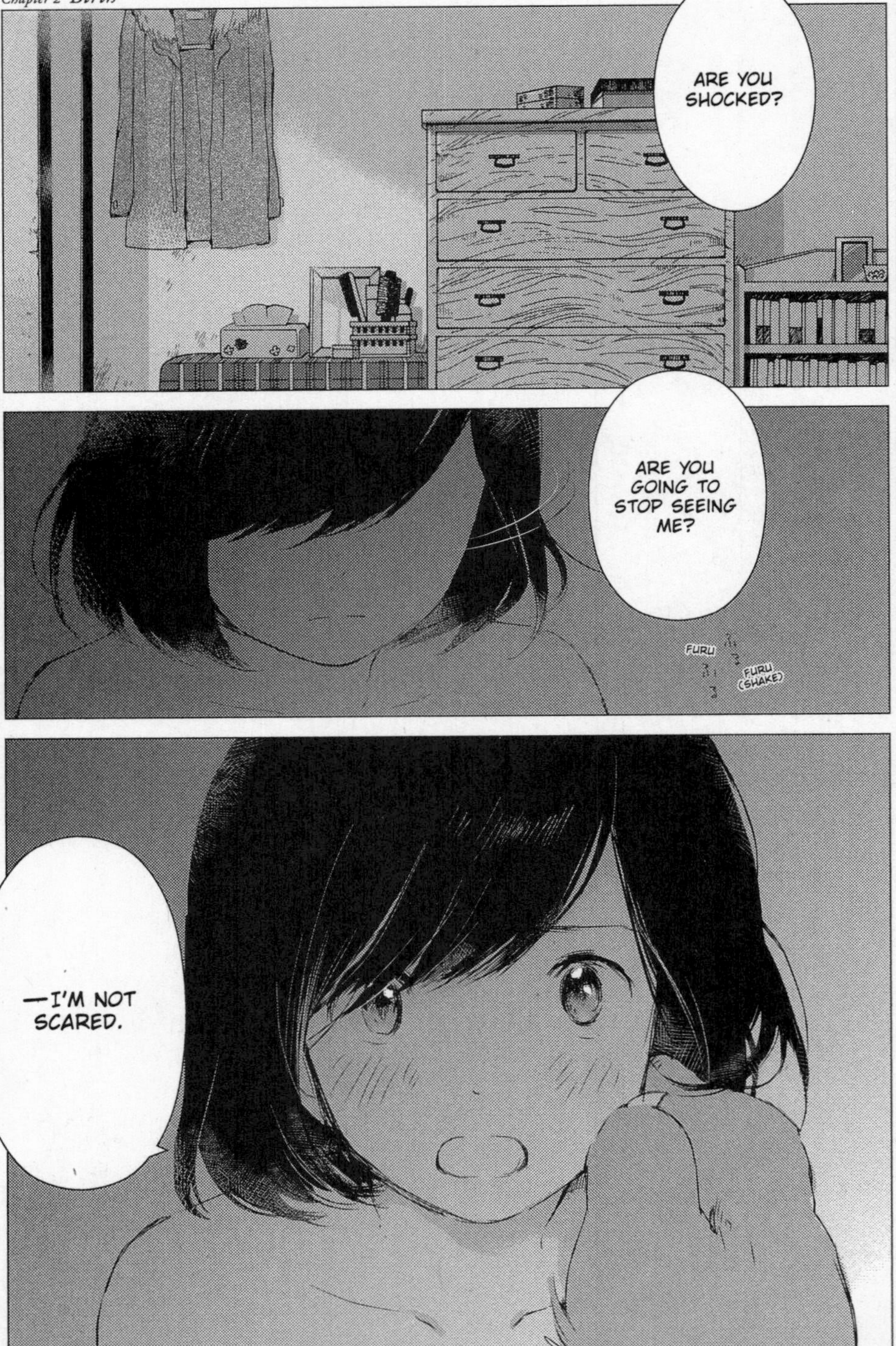
ARE YOU SHOCKED?
ARE YOU GOING TO STOP SEEING ME?
FURU
FURU (SHAKE)
—I'M NOT SCARED.

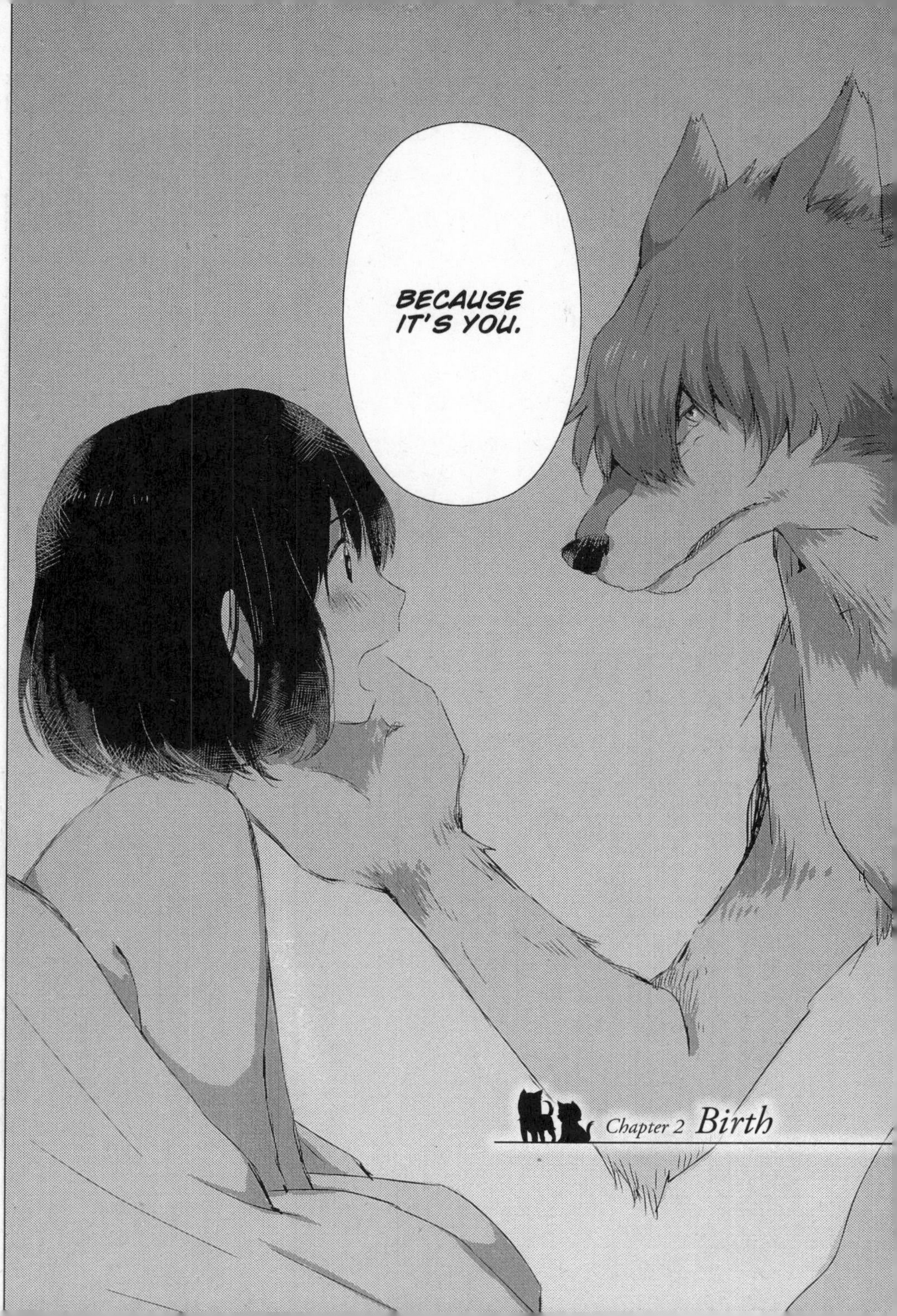
BECAUSE IT'S YOU.

Chapter 2 Birth

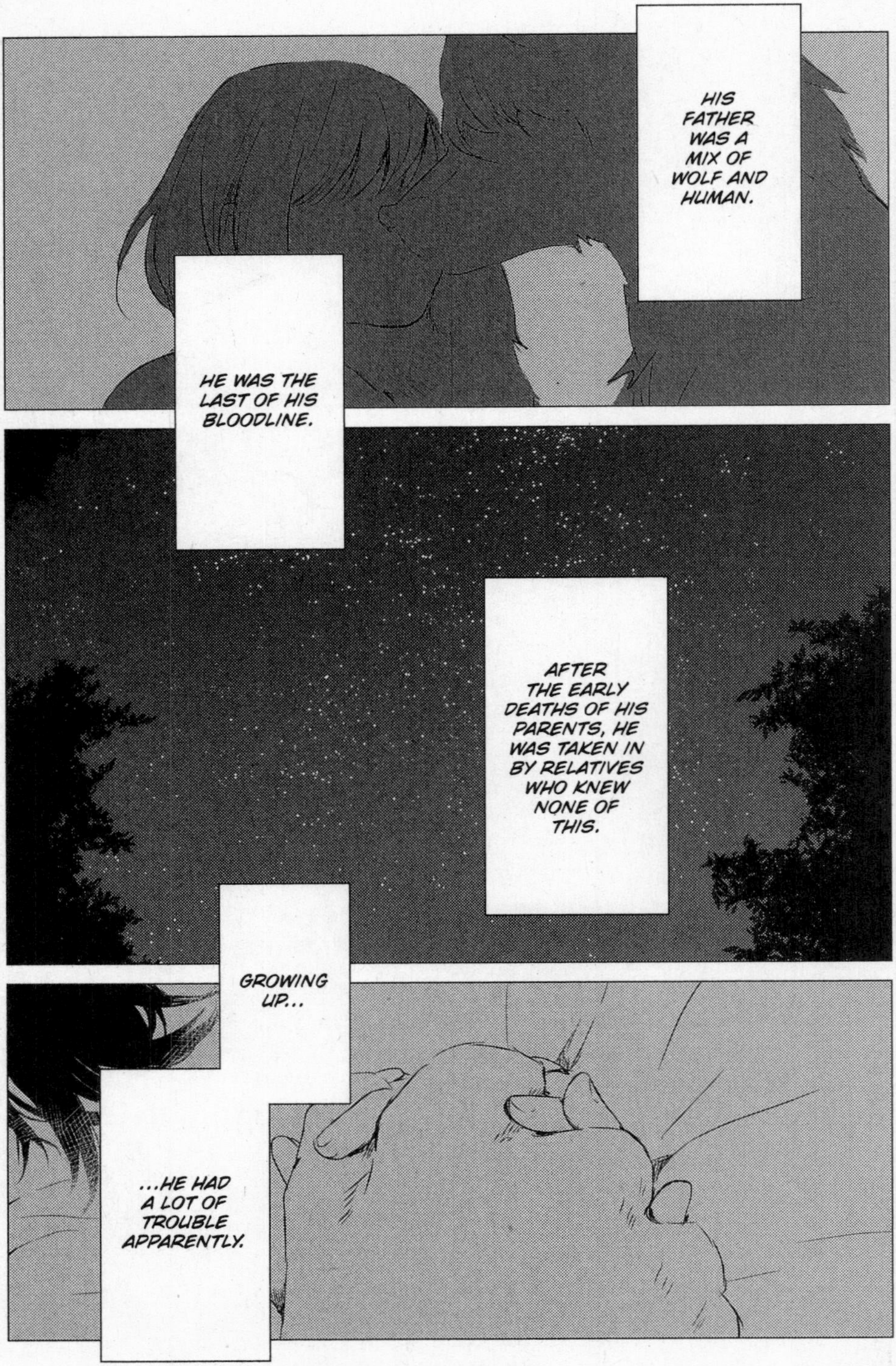
HIS FATHER WAS A MIX OF WOLF AND HUMAN.
HE WAS THE LAST OF HIS BLOODLINE.
AFTER THE EARLY DEATHS OF HIS PARENTS, HE WAS TAKEN IN BY RELATIVES WHO KNEW NONE OF THIS.
GROWING UP...
...HE HAD A LOT OF TROUBLE APPARENTLY.

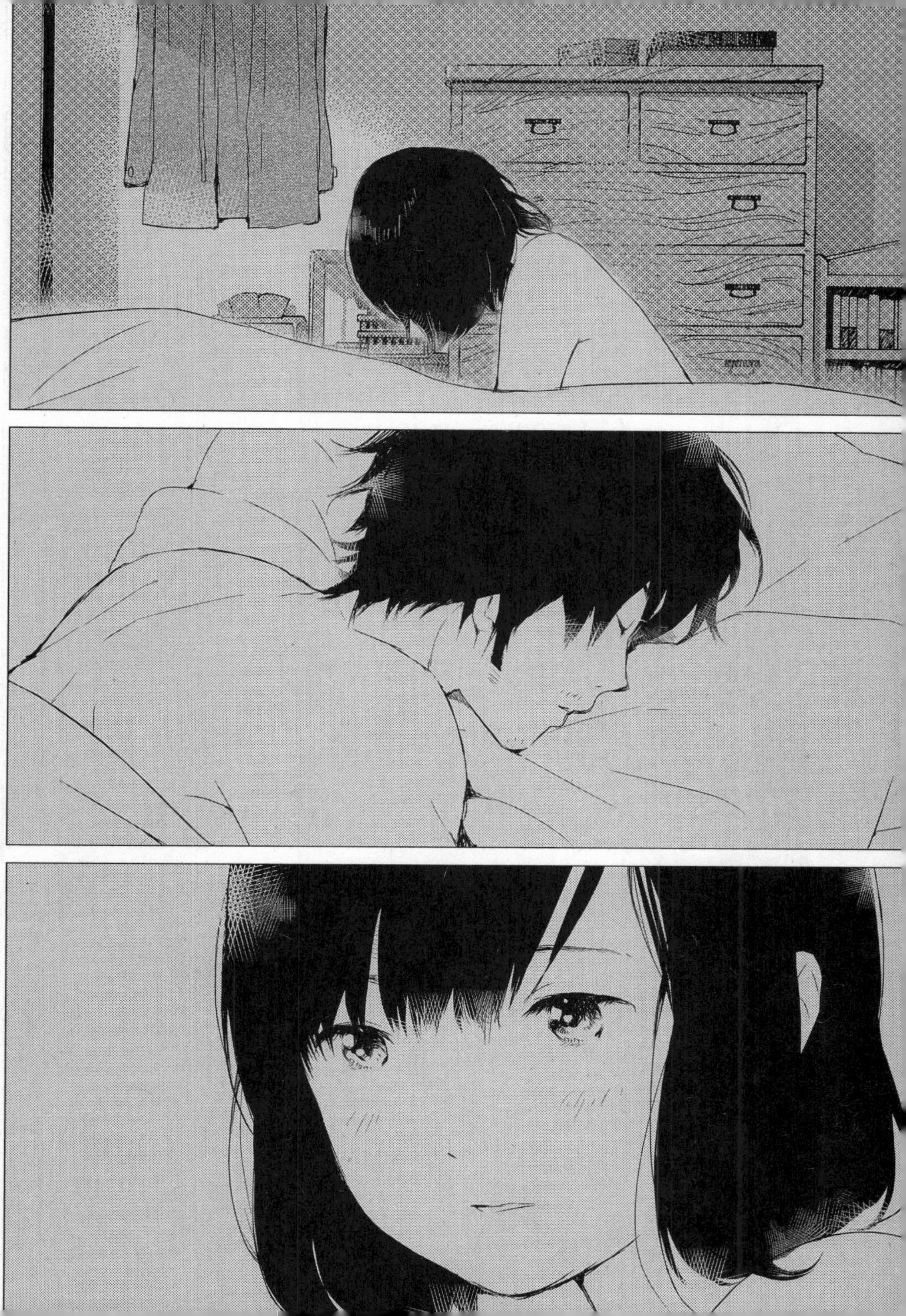

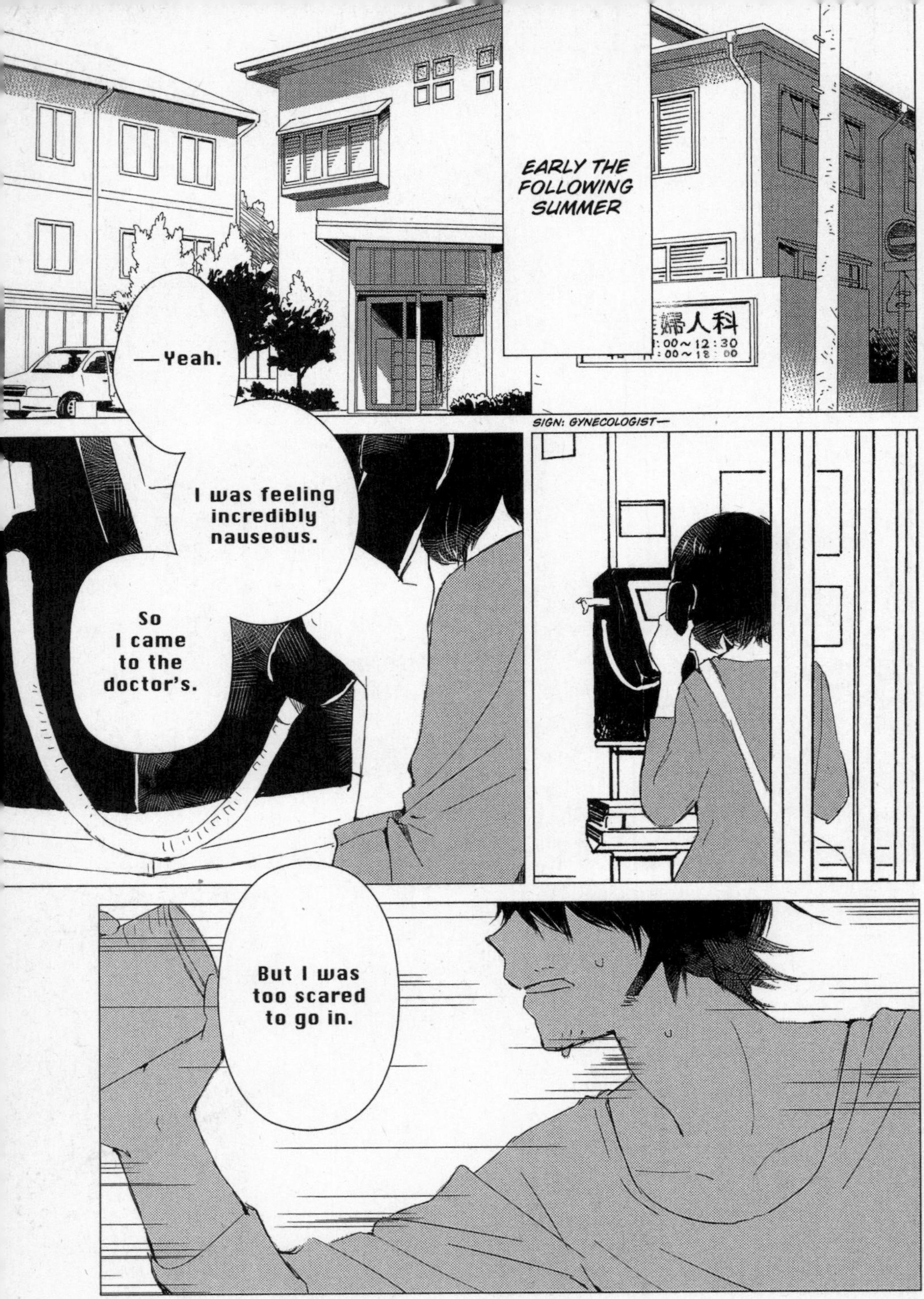
EARLY THE FOLLOWING SUMMER
婦人科
SIGN: GYNECOLOGIST—
—Yeah.
I was feeling incredibly nauseous.
So I came to the doctor's.
But I was too scared to go in.

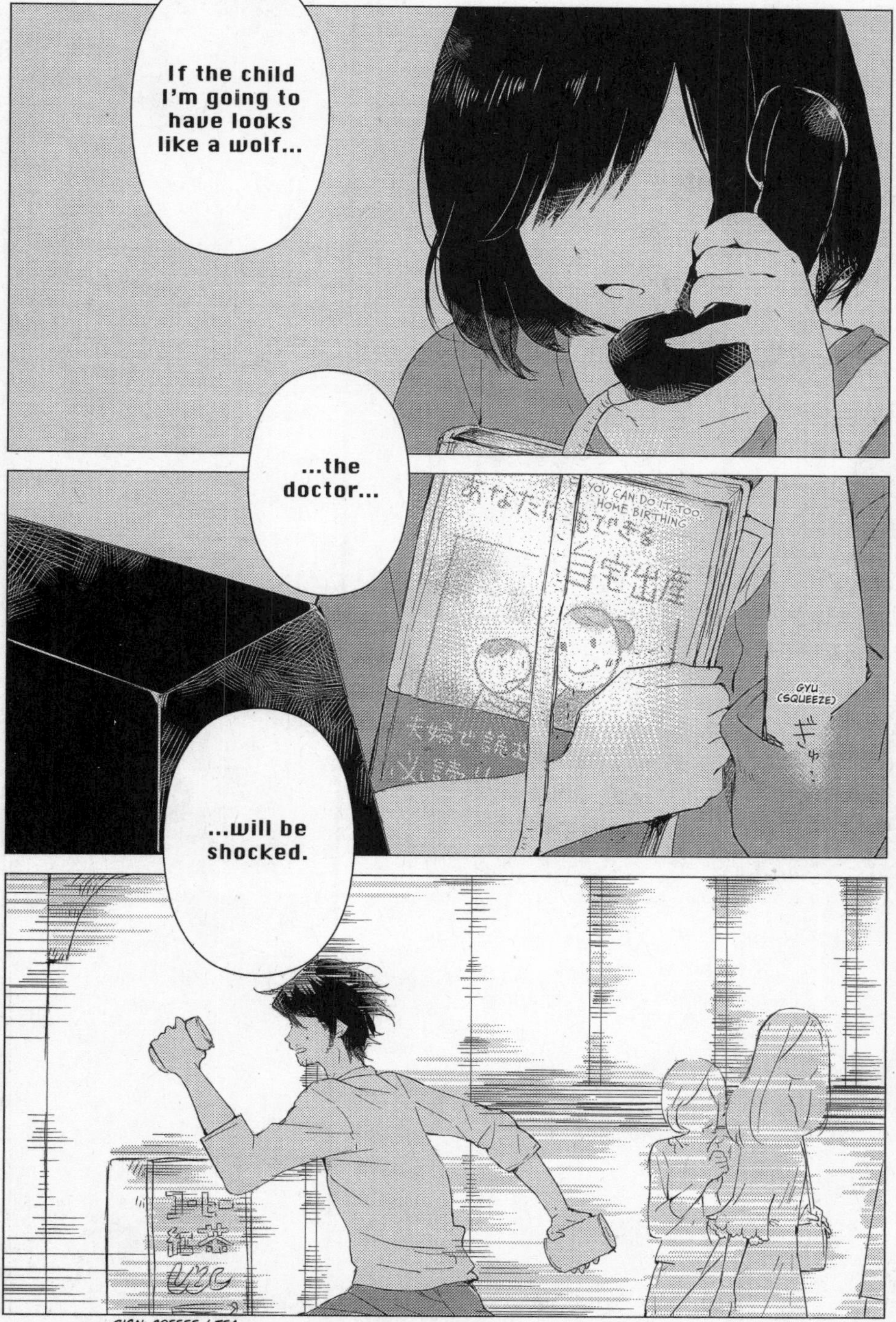
If the child I'm going to have looks like a wolf...
...the doctor...
YOU CAN DO IT TOO, HOME BIRTHING
自宅出産
GYU (SQUEEZE)
ぎゅ
...will be shocked.

SIGN: COFFEE / TEA

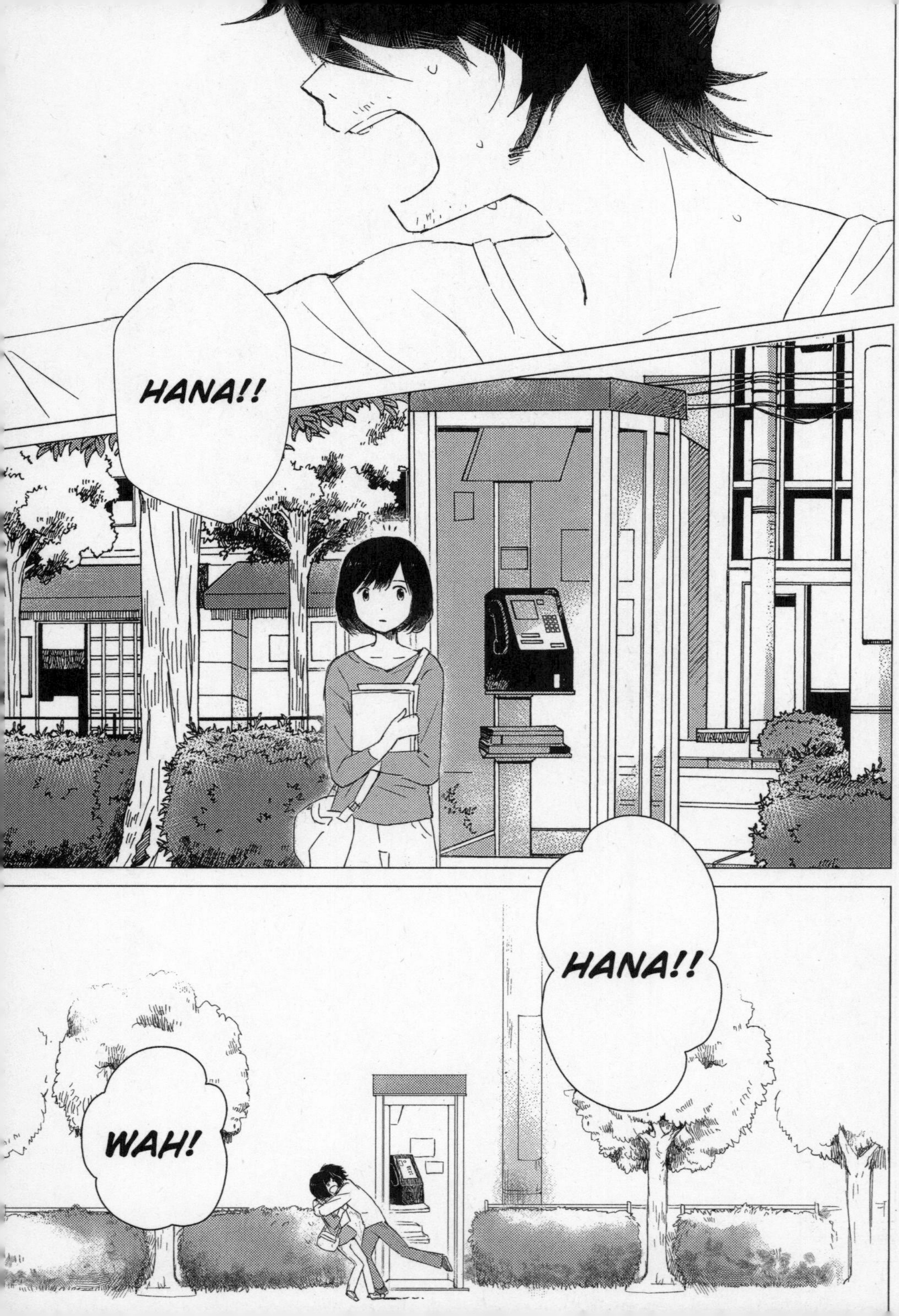
HANA!!
HANA!!
WAH!

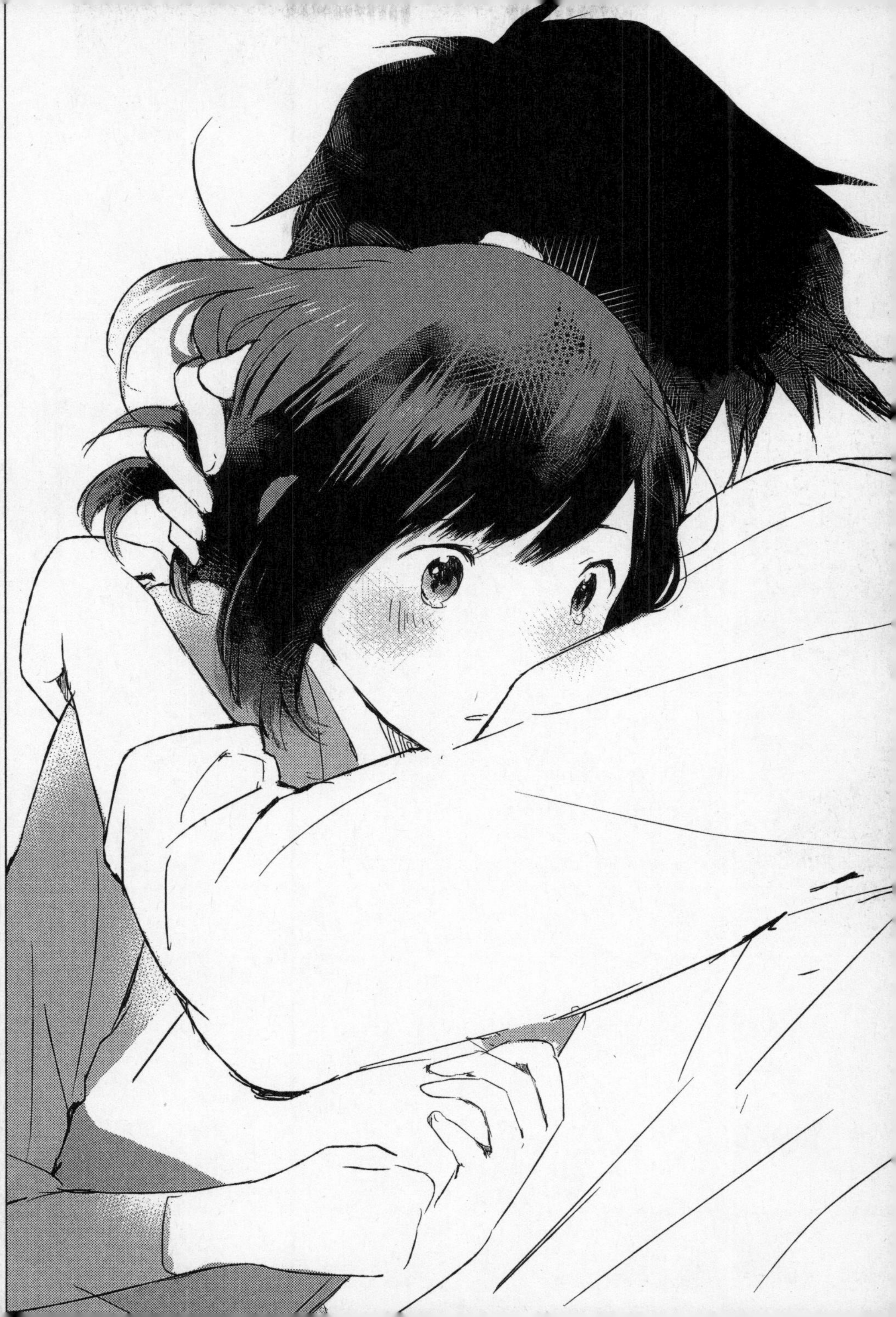

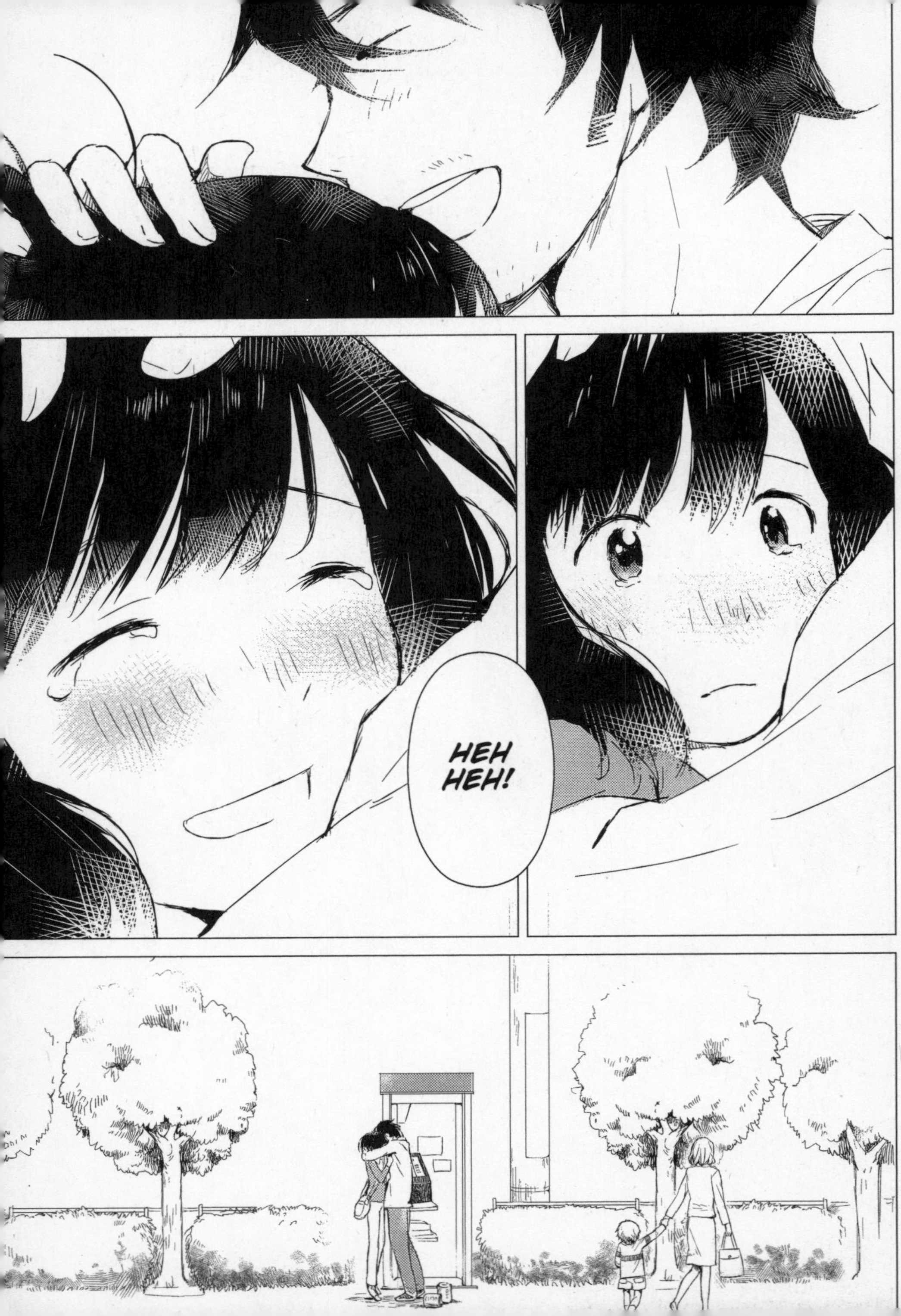
HEH HEH!

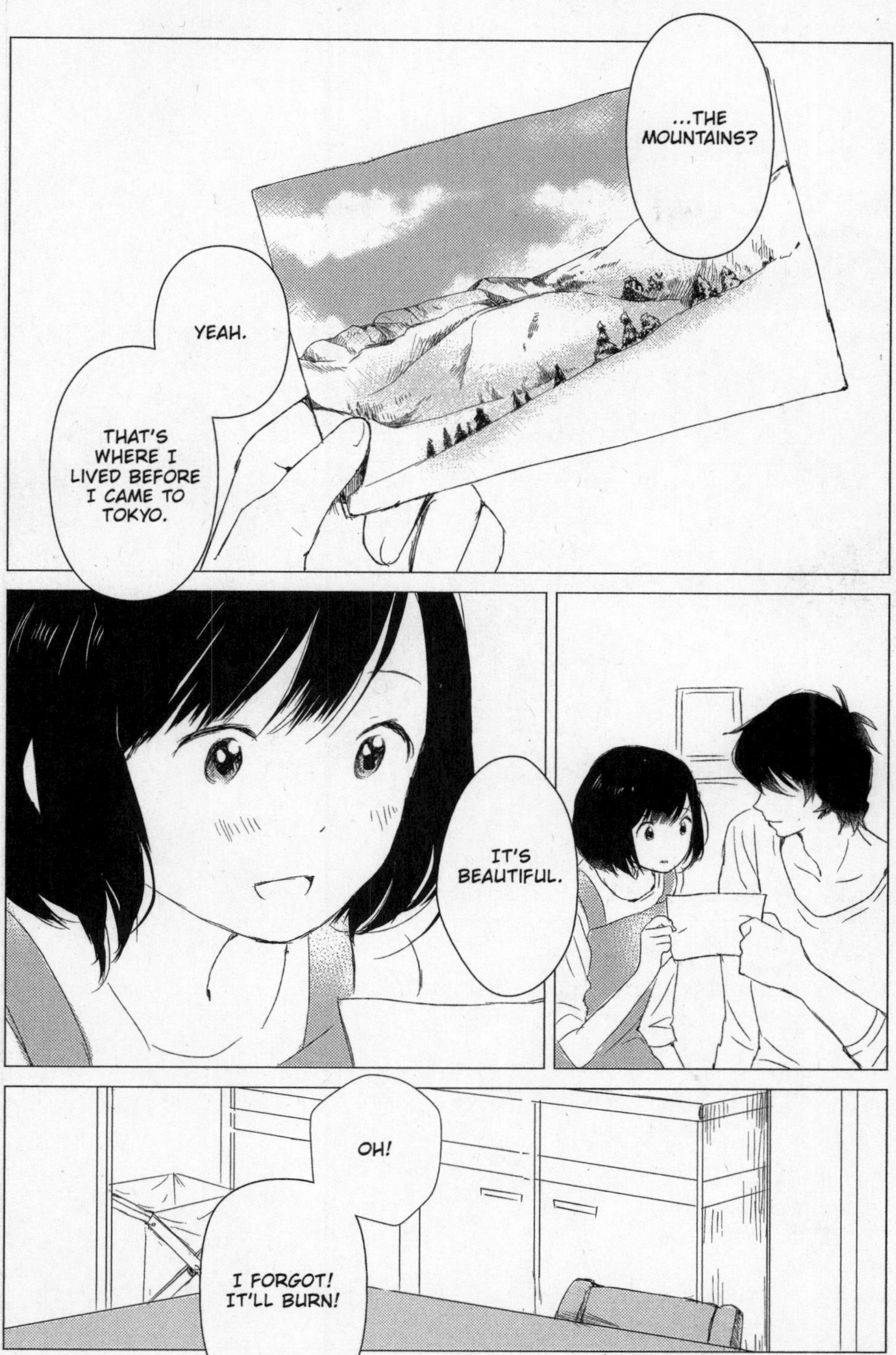
...THE MOUNTAINS?
YEAH.
THAT'S WHERE I LIVED BEFORE I CAME TO TOKYO.
IT'S BEAUTIFUL.
OH!
I FORGOT! IT'LL BURN!

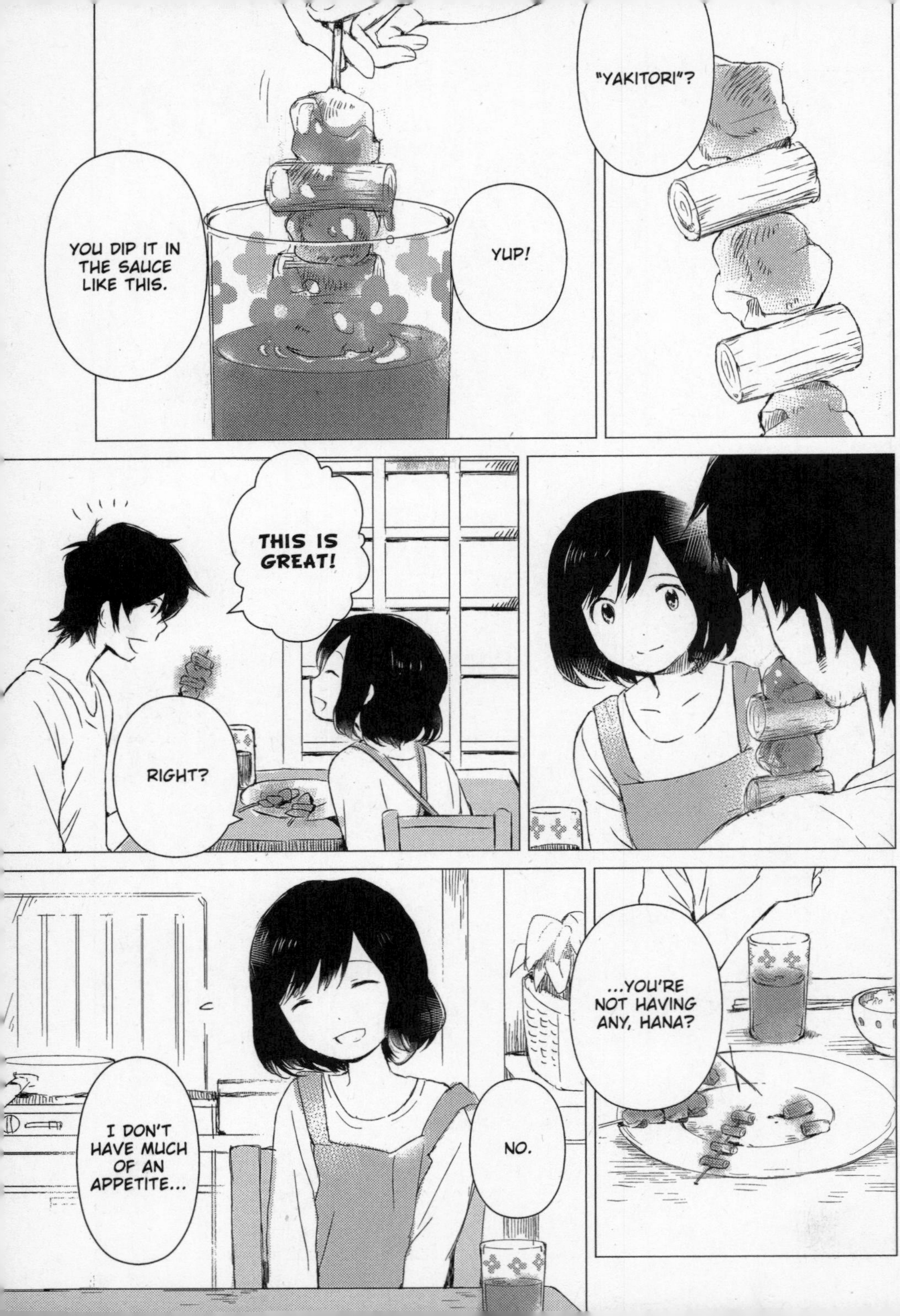
"YAKITORI"?
YUP!
YOU DIP IT IN THE SAUCE LIKE THIS.
THIS IS GREAT!
RIGHT?
...YOU'RE NOT HAVING ANY, HANA?
NO.
I DON'T HAVE MUCH OF AN APPETITE...

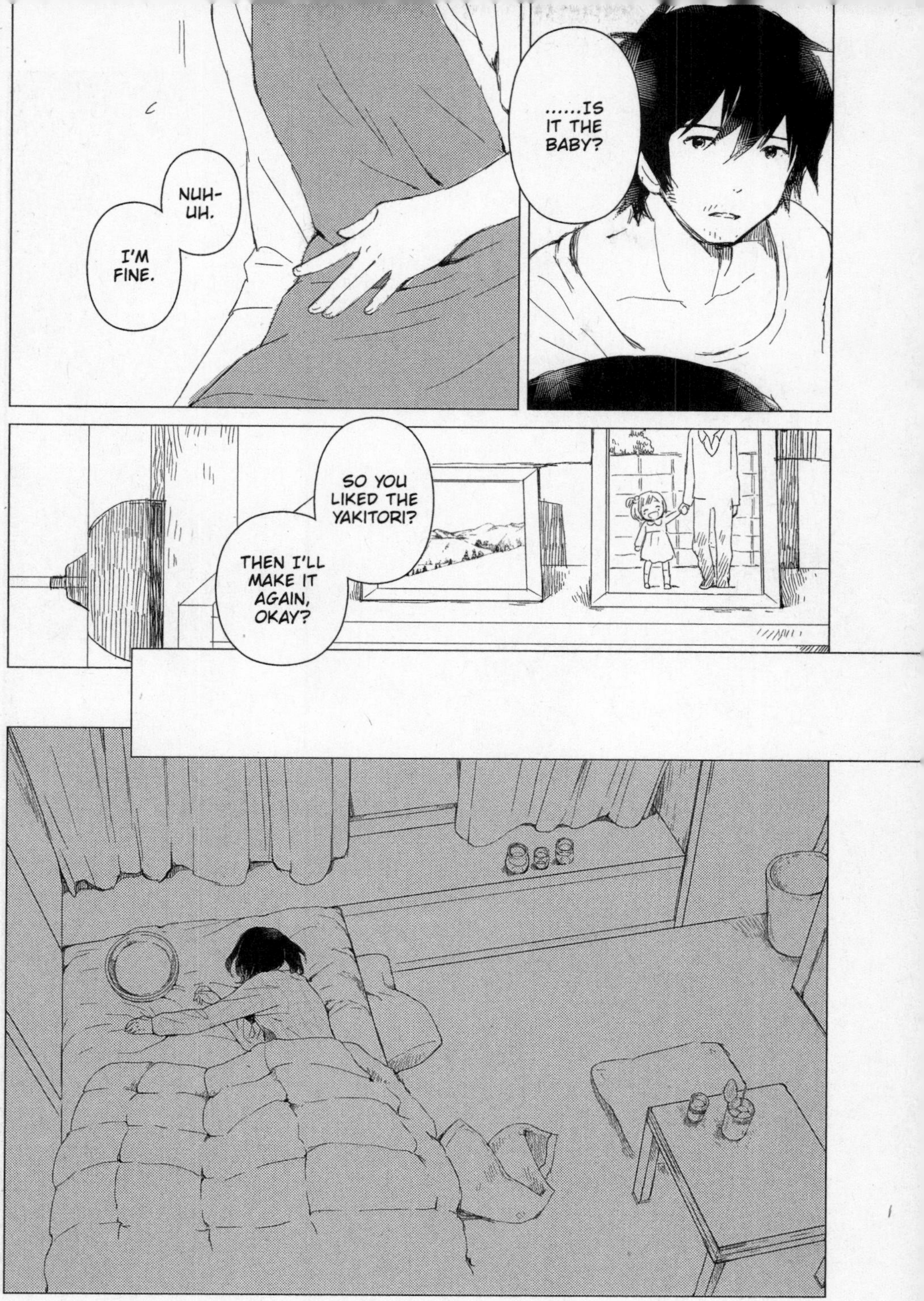
......IS IT THE BABY?
NUH-UH.
I'M FINE.
SO YOU LIKED THE YAKITORI?
THEN I'LL MAKE IT AGAIN, OKAY?

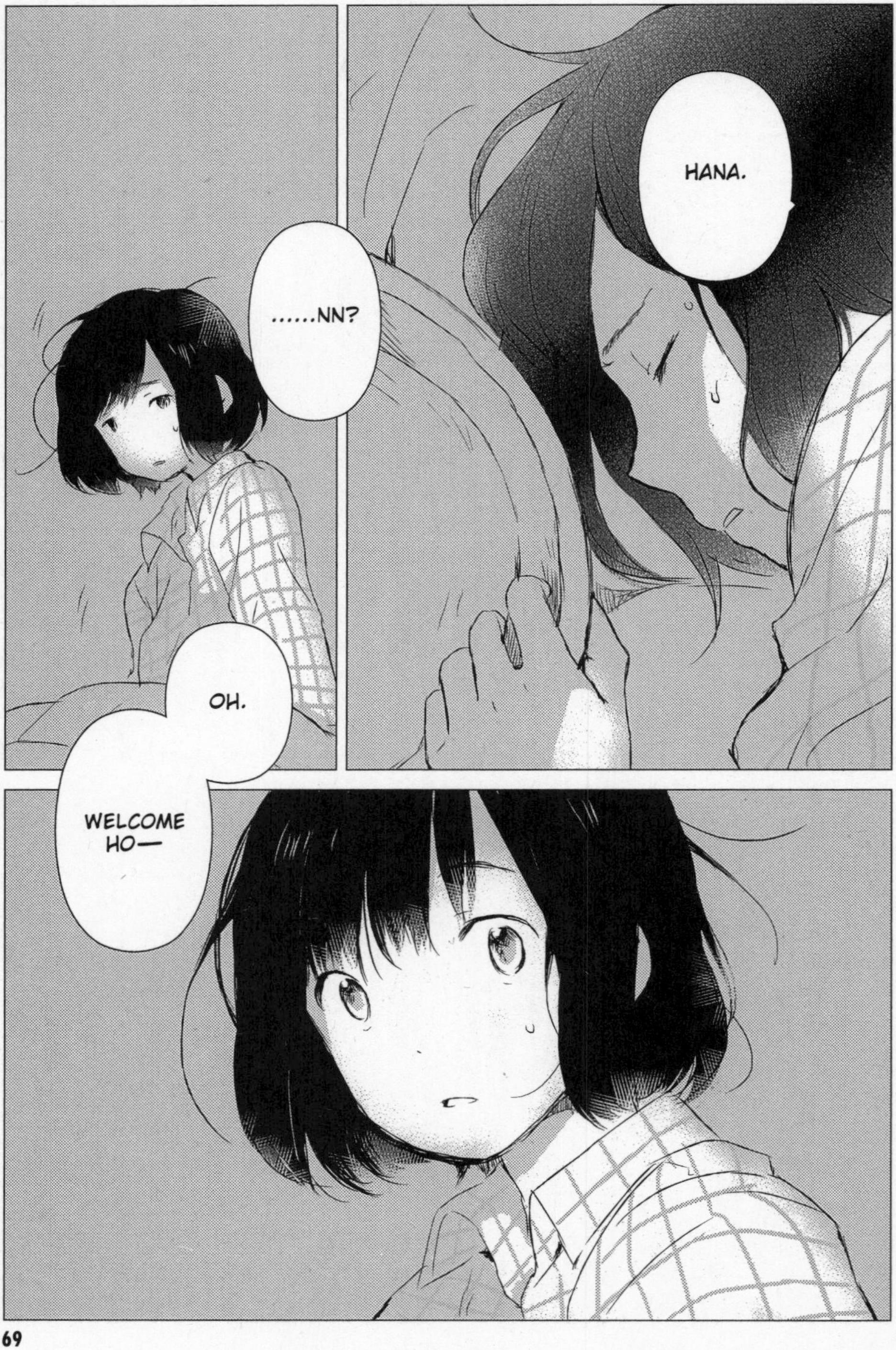
HANA.
......NN?
OH.
WELCOME HO—

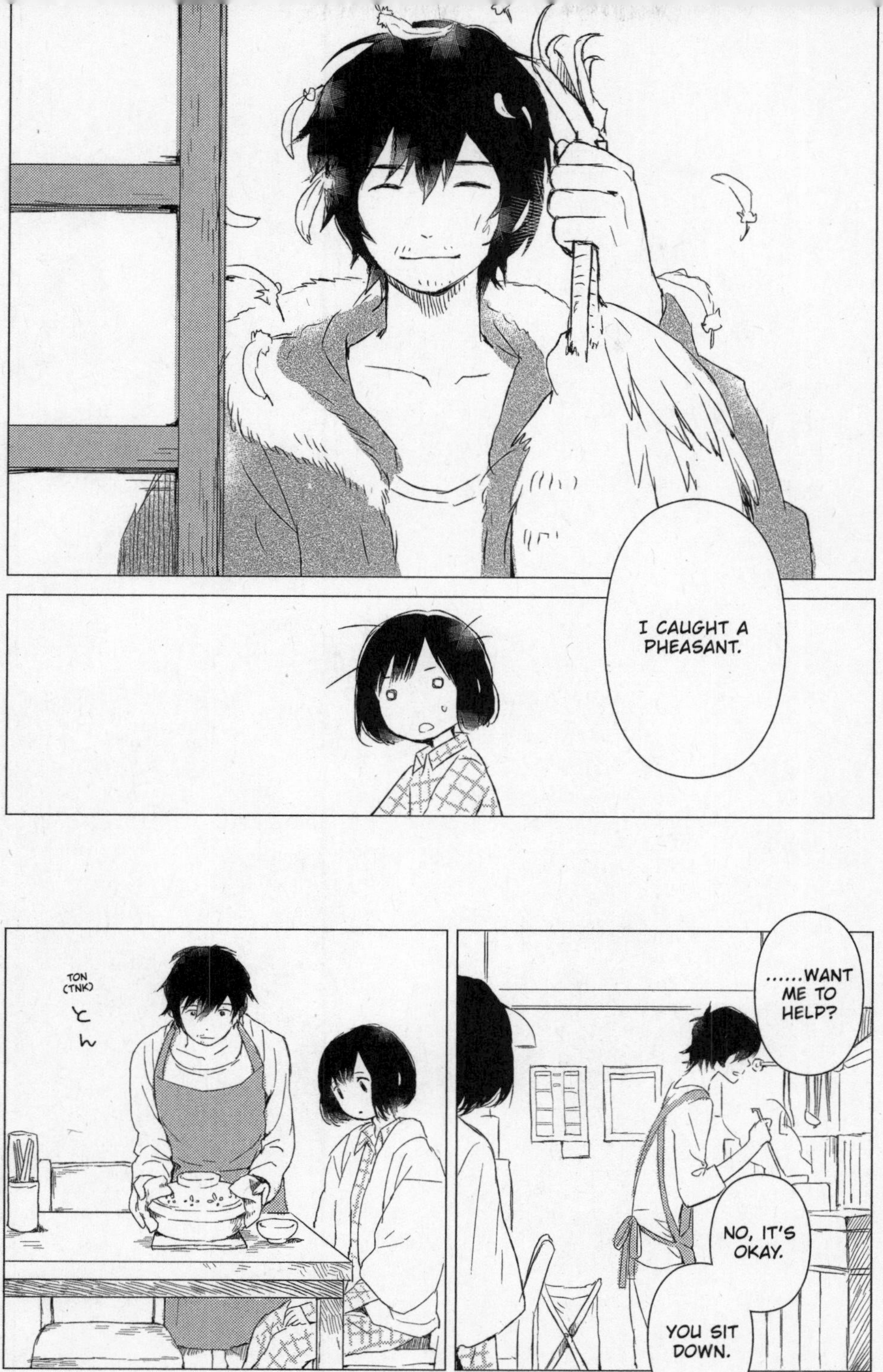
I CAUGHT A PHEASANT.
......WANT ME TO HELP?
NO, IT'S OKAY.
YOU SIT DOWN.
TON (TNK)
とん

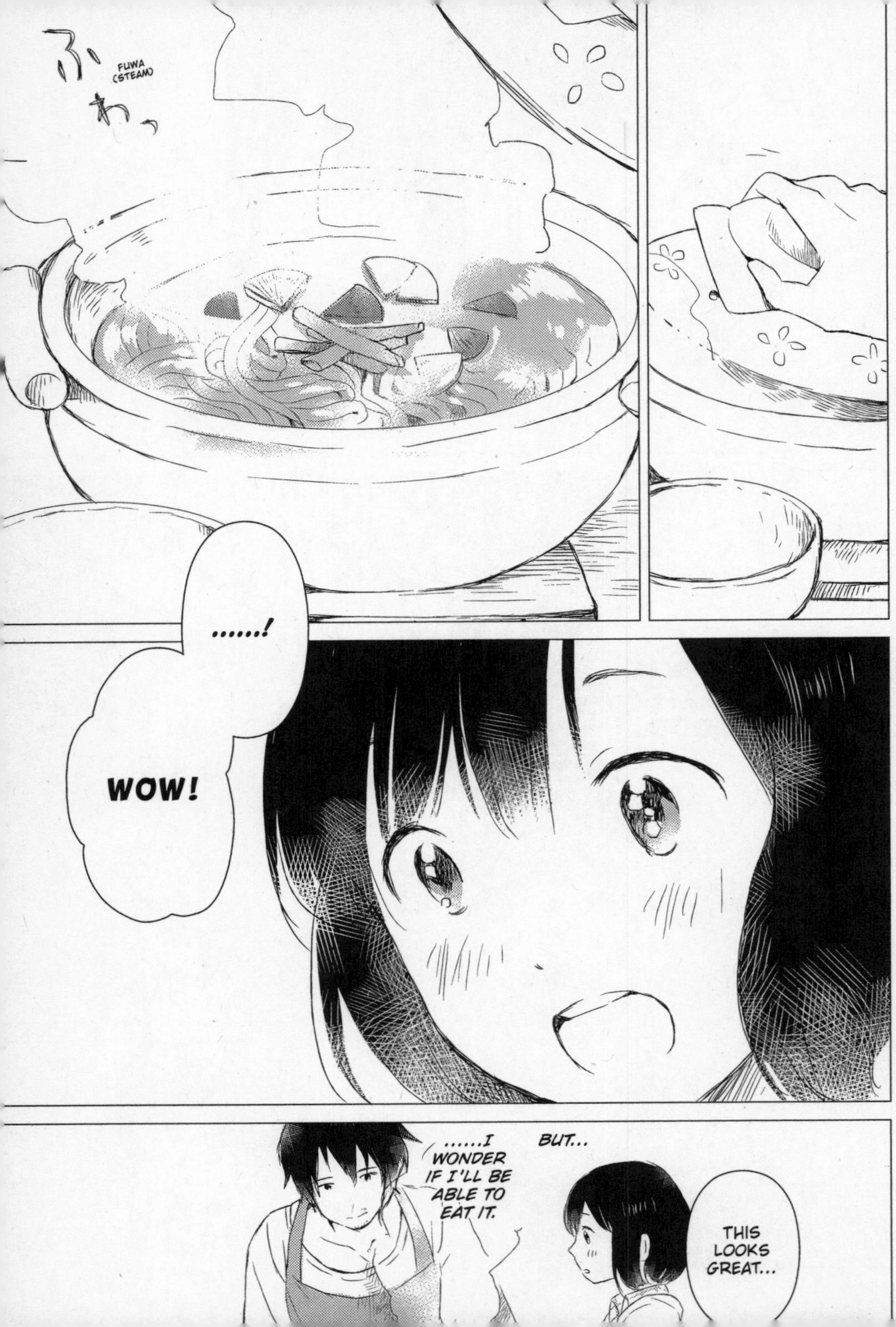
ふわっ
FUWA (STEAM)
......!
WOW!
THIS LOOKS GREAT...
BUT...
......I WONDER IF I'LL BE ABLE TO EAT IT.

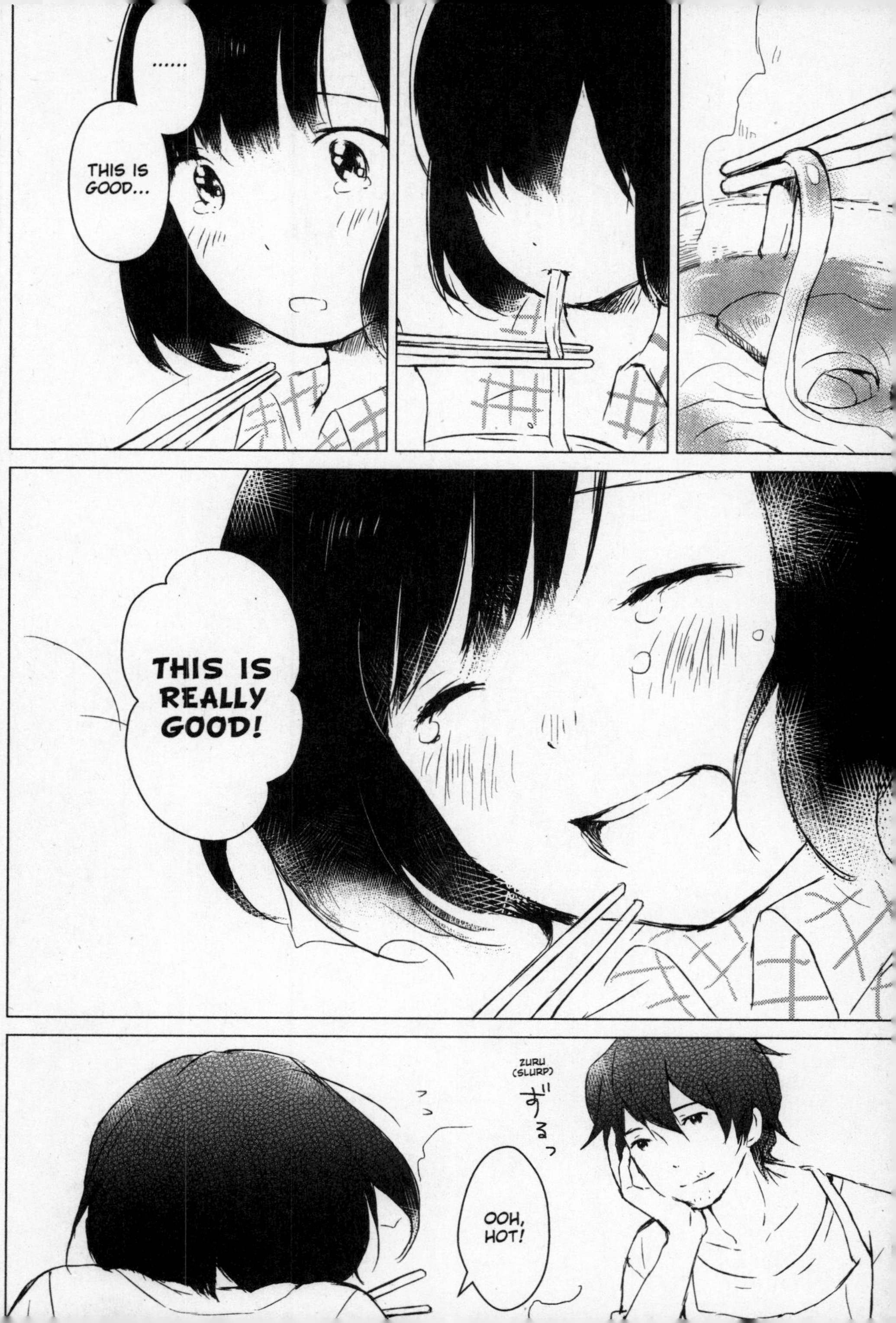
......
THIS IS GOOD...
THIS IS REALLY GOOD!
ZURU (SLURP)
ずるっ
OOH, HOT!

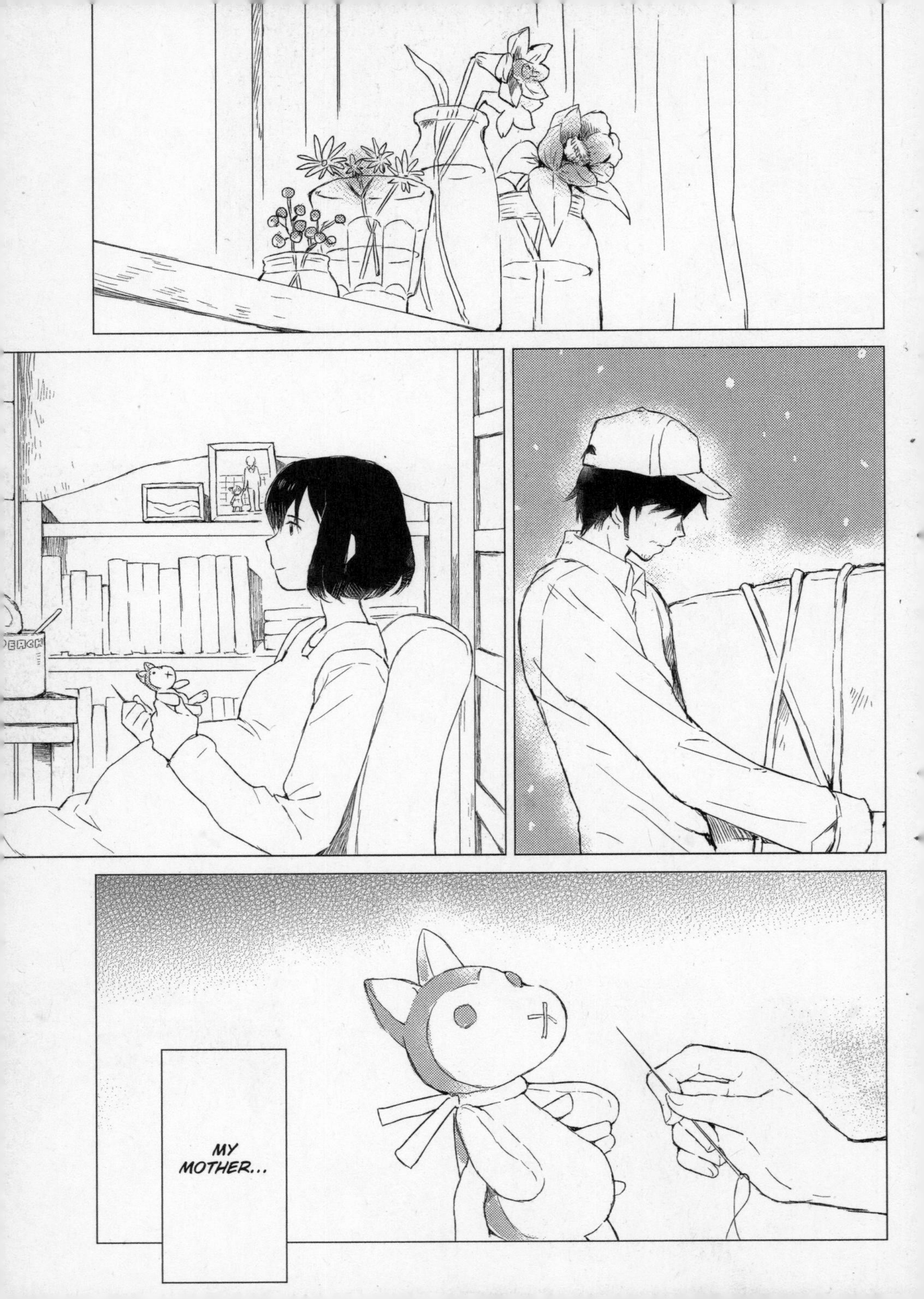
PEACH
MY MOTHER...

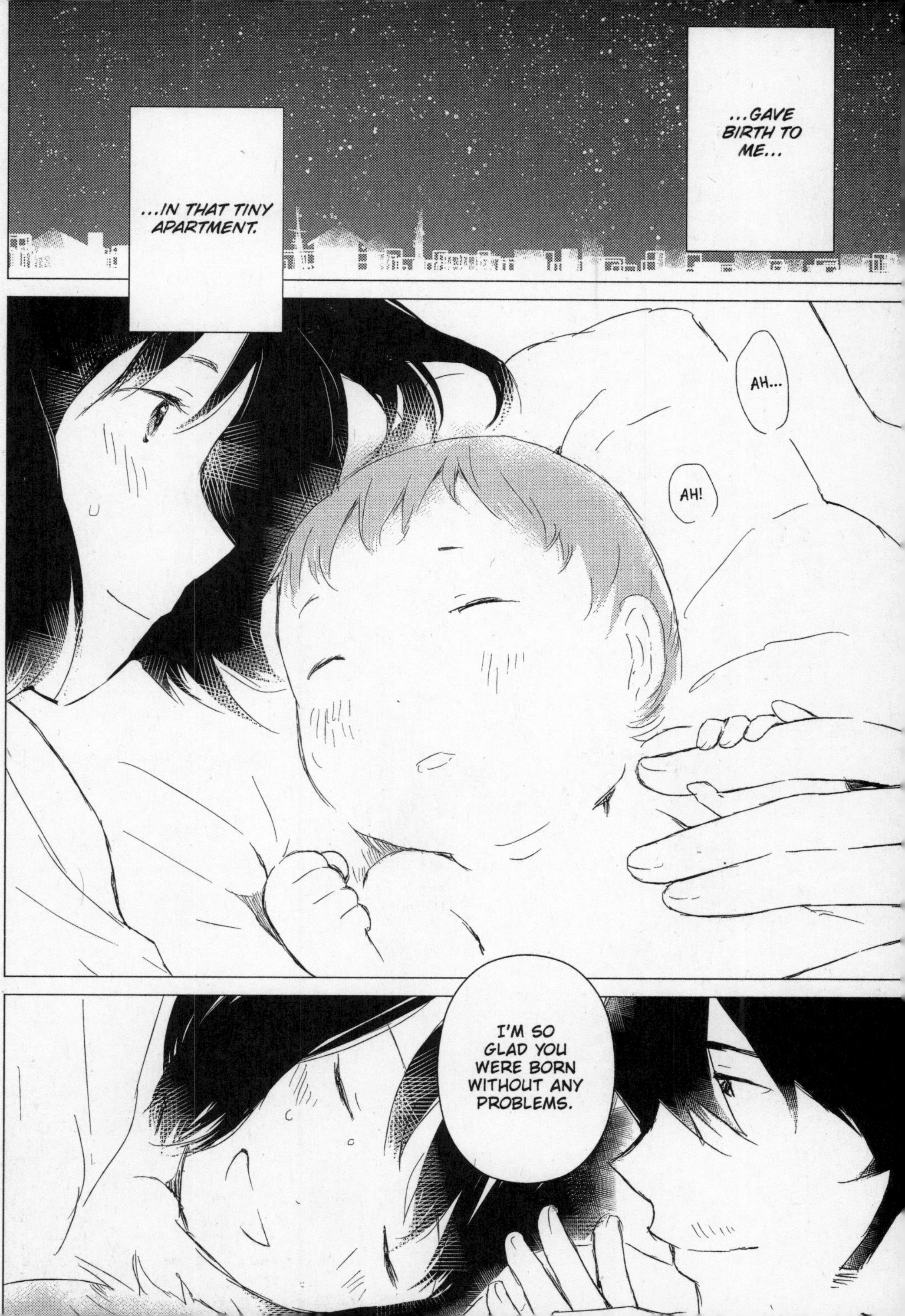
...GAVE BIRTH TO ME...
...IN THAT TINY APARTMENT.
AH...
AH!
I'M SO GLAD YOU WERE BORN WITHOUT ANY PROBLEMS.

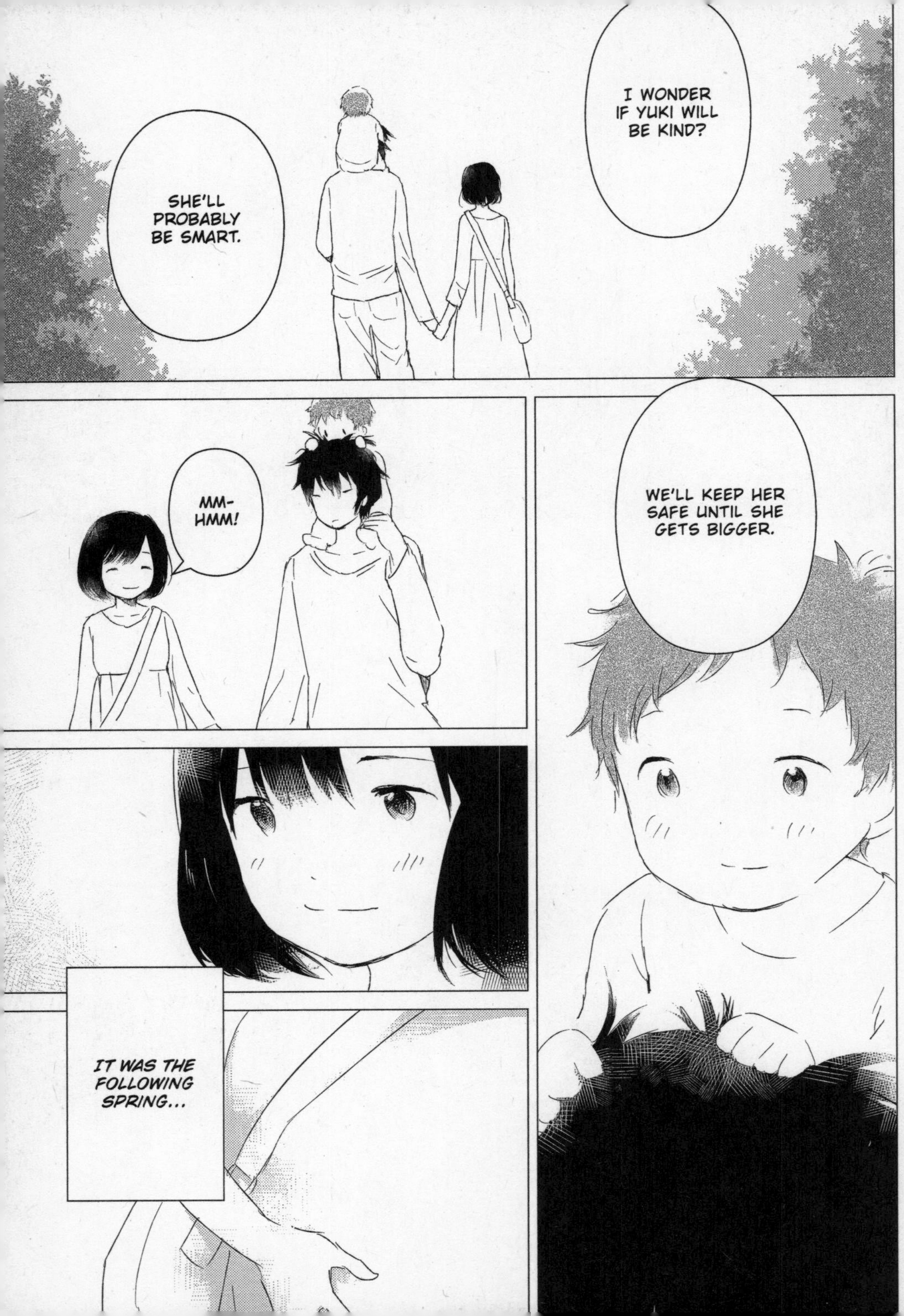
I WONDER IF YUKI WILL BE KIND?
SHE'LL PROBABLY BE SMART.
WE'LL KEEP HER SAFE UNTIL SHE GETS BIGGER.
MM-HMM!
IT WAS THE FOLLOWING SPRING...

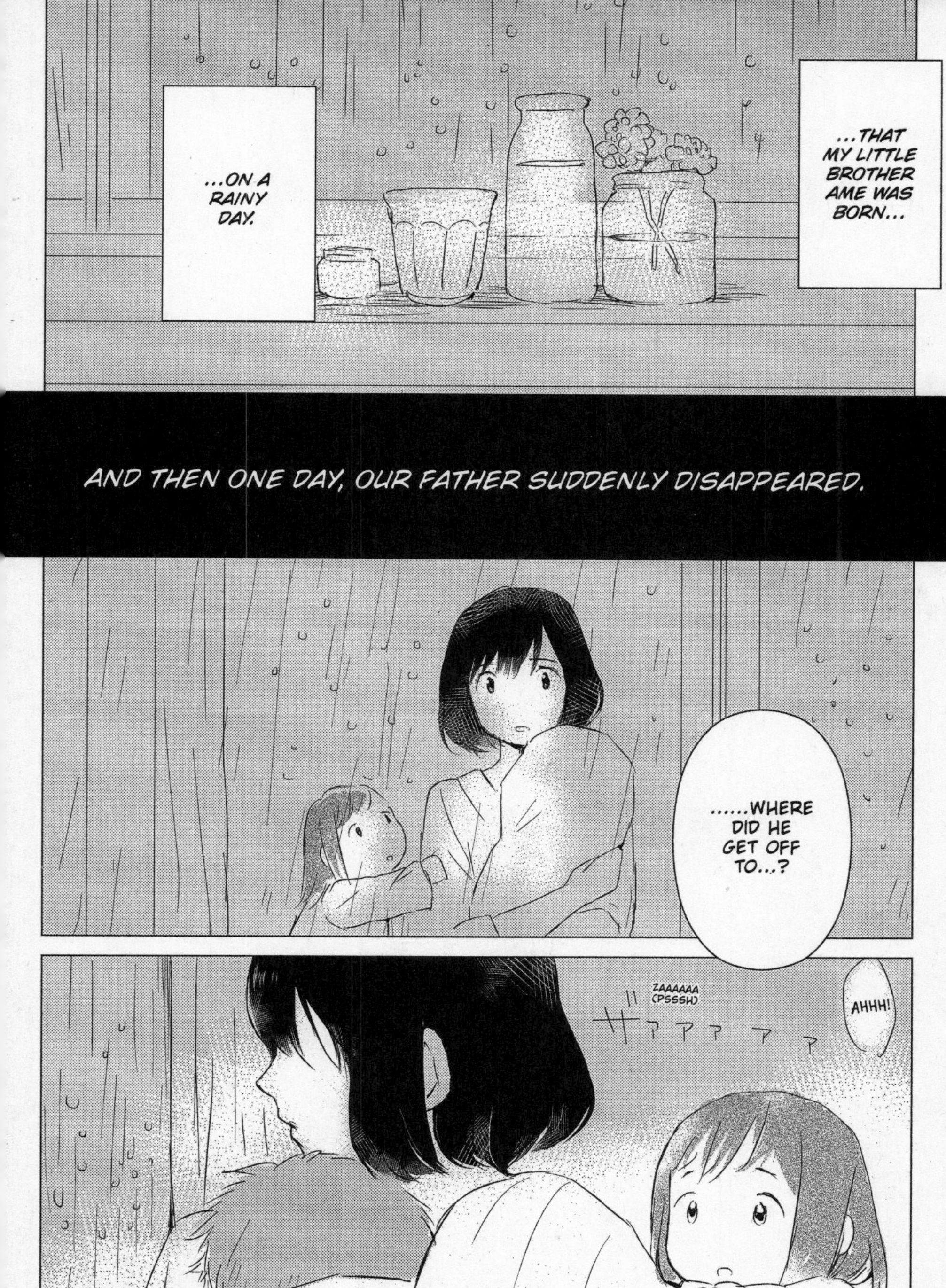
...THAT MY LITTLE BROTHER AME WAS BORN...
...ON A RAINY DAY.
AND THEN ONE DAY, OUR FATHER SUDDENLY DISAPPEARED.
......WHERE DID HE GET OFF TO...?
AHHH!
ZAAAAAA (PSSSH)

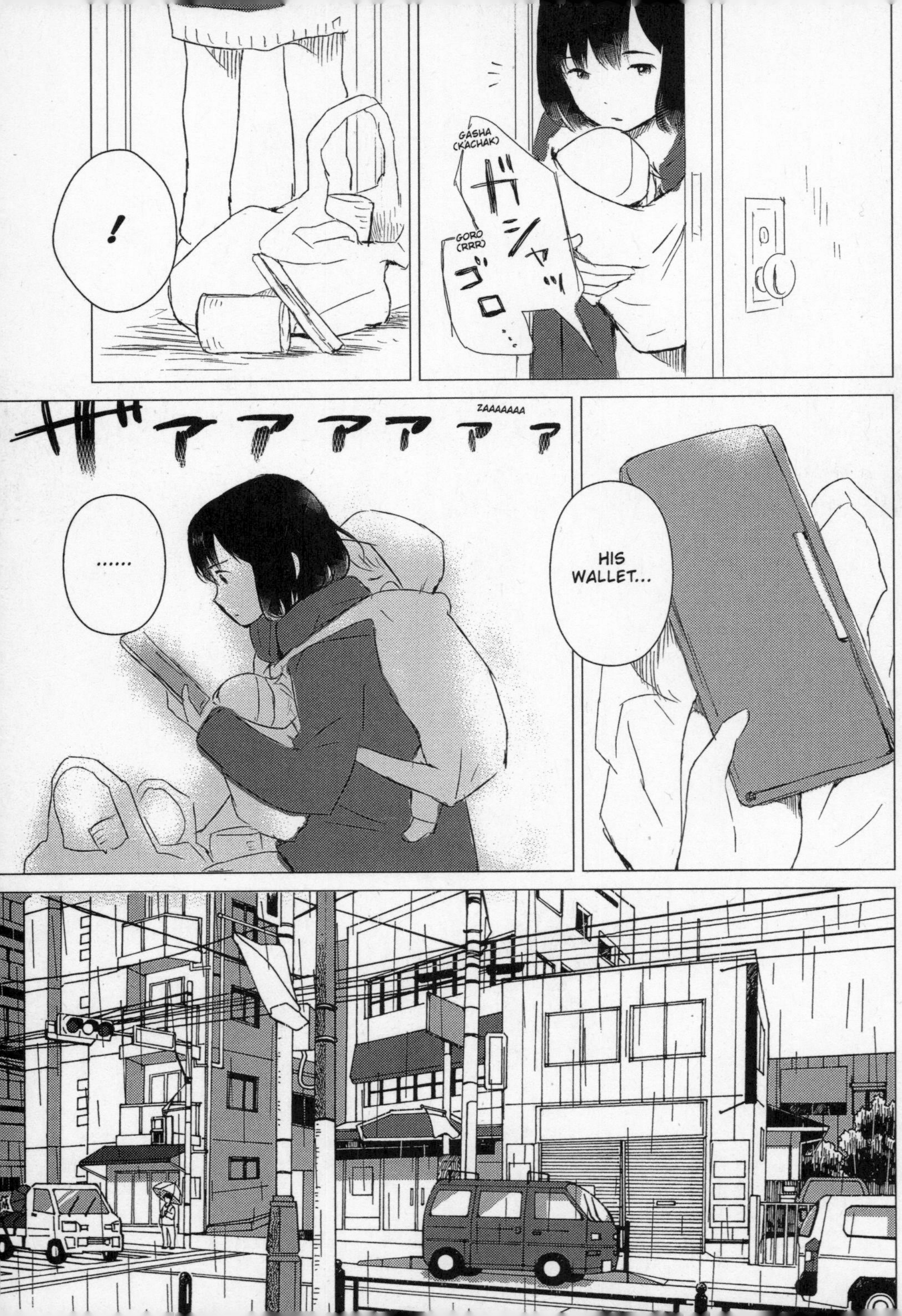

GASHA (KACHAK)
ガシャッ
GORO (RRR)
ゴロ…
!
HIS WALLET...
ZAAAAAAA
ザァァァァァァ
......

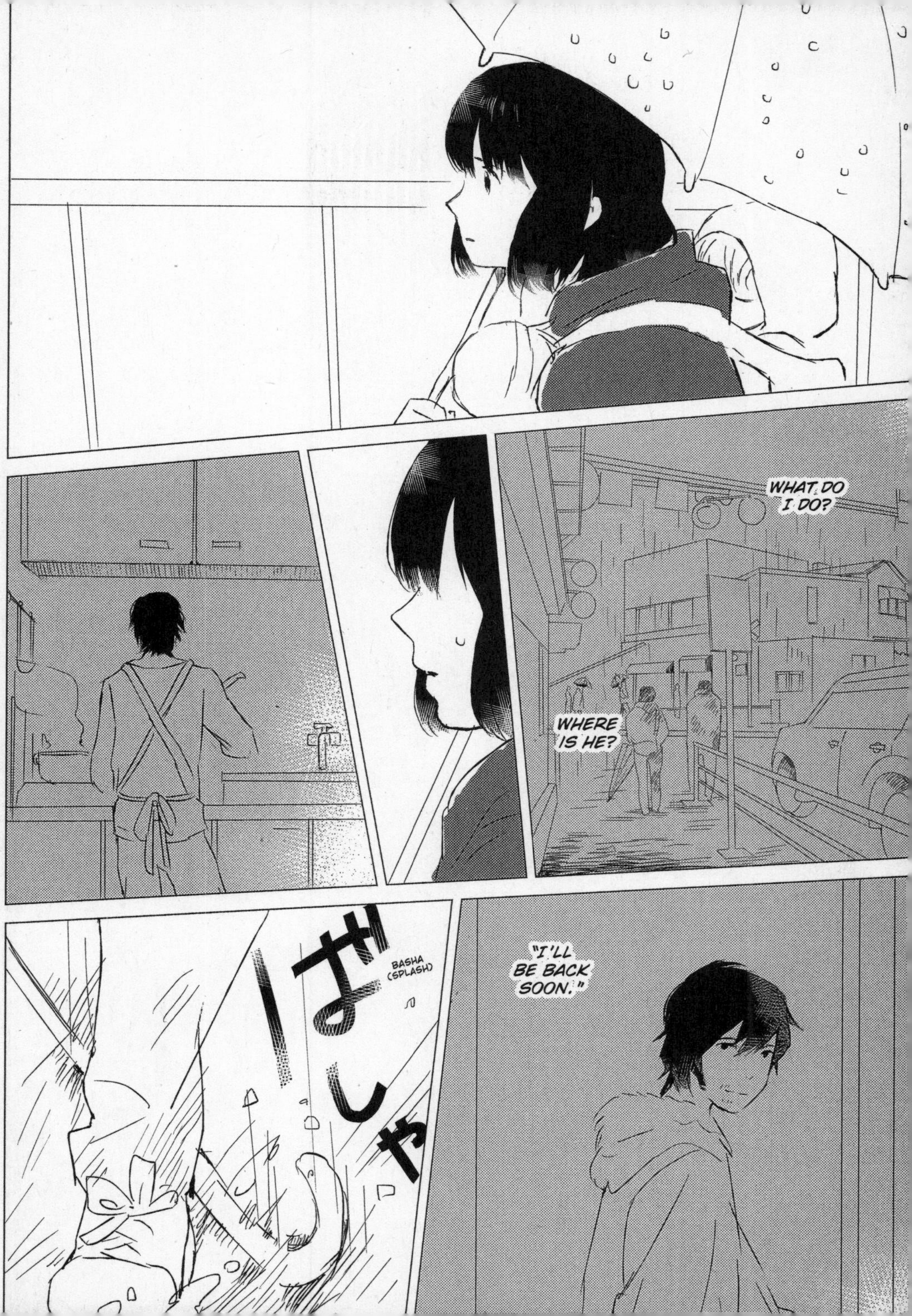
WHAT DO I DO?
WHERE IS HE?
"I'LL BE BACK SOON."
ばしゃ
BASHA (SPLASH)

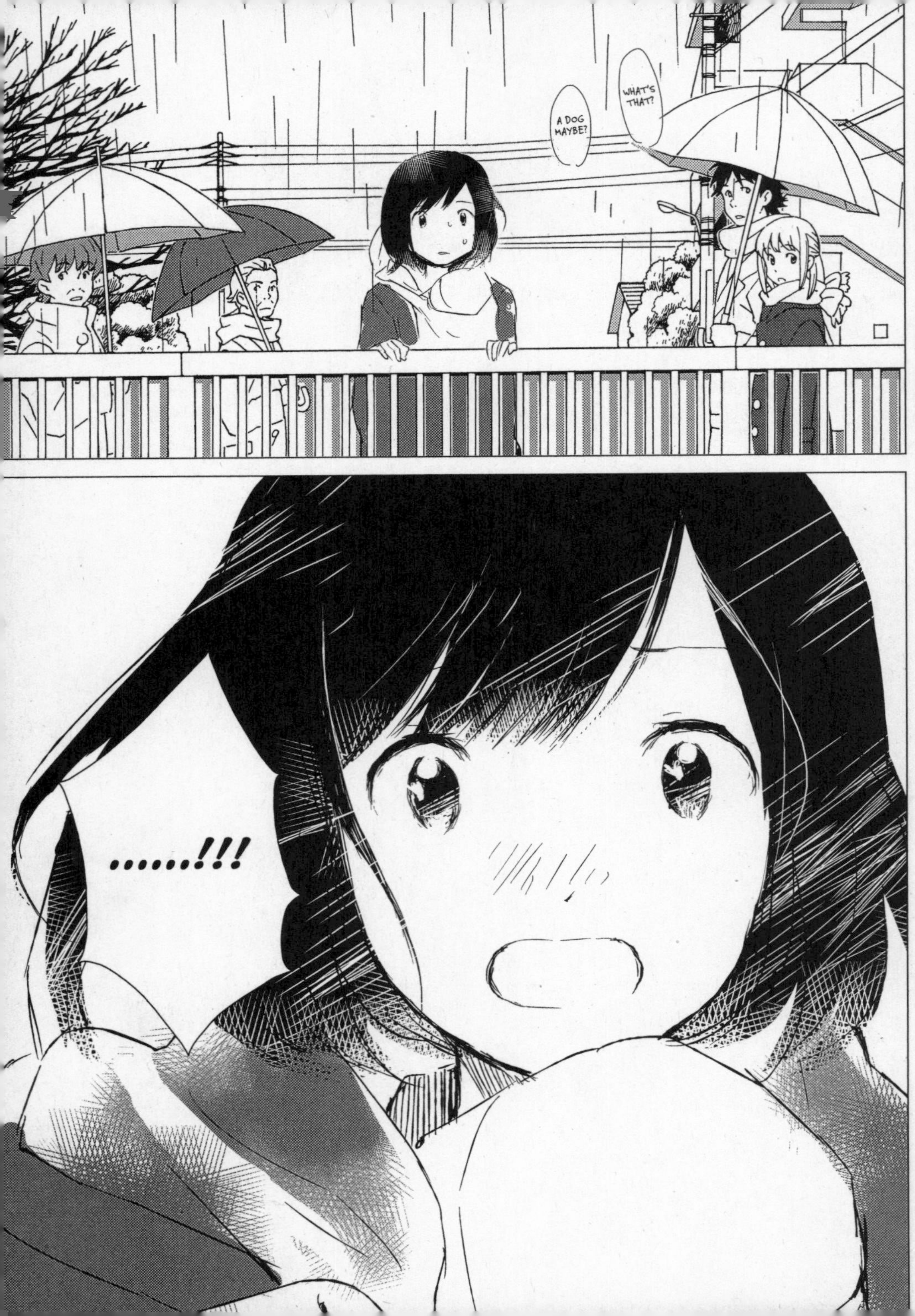
WHAT'S THAT?
A DOG MAYBE?
......!!!

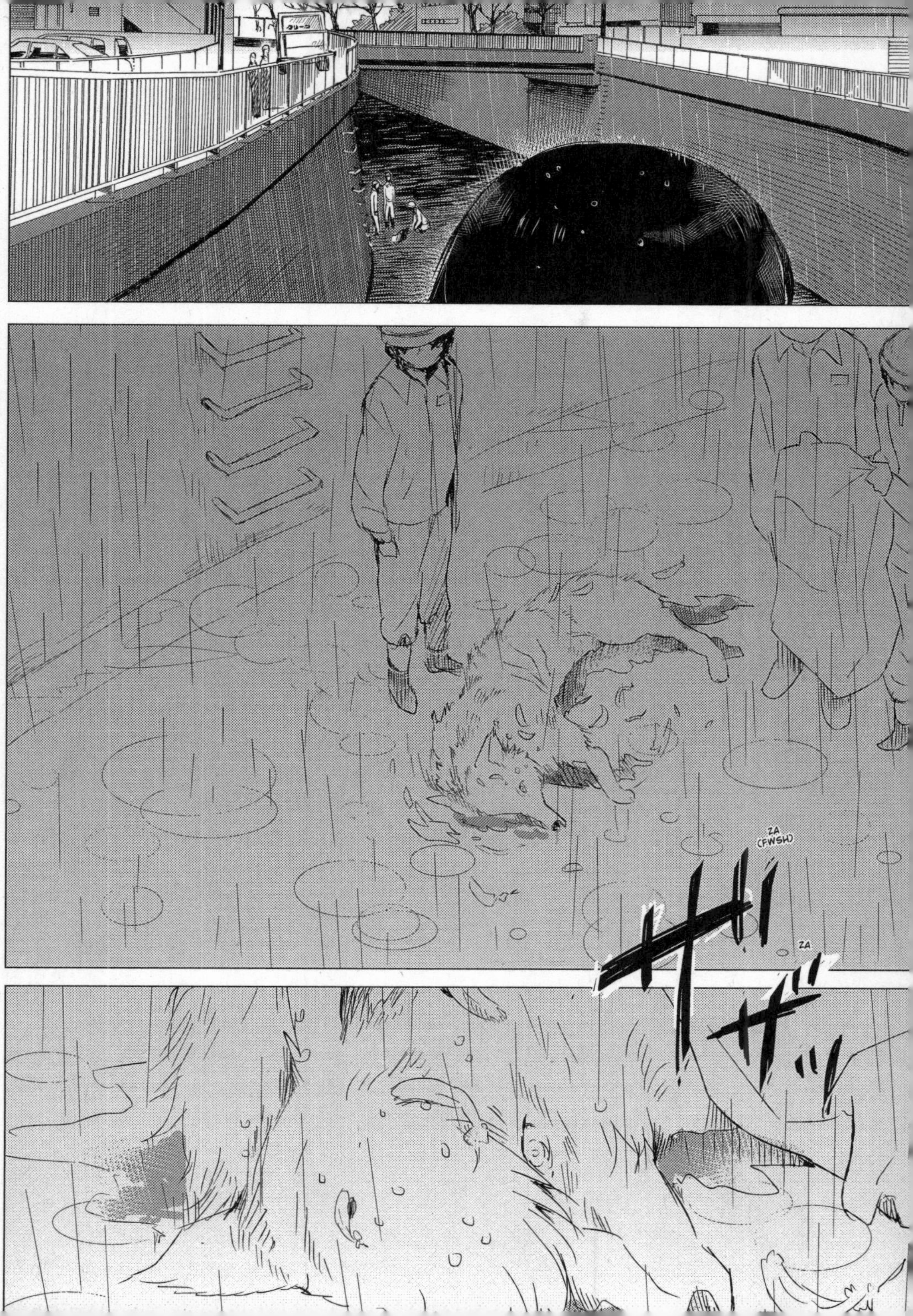
ZA (FWSH)
ZA

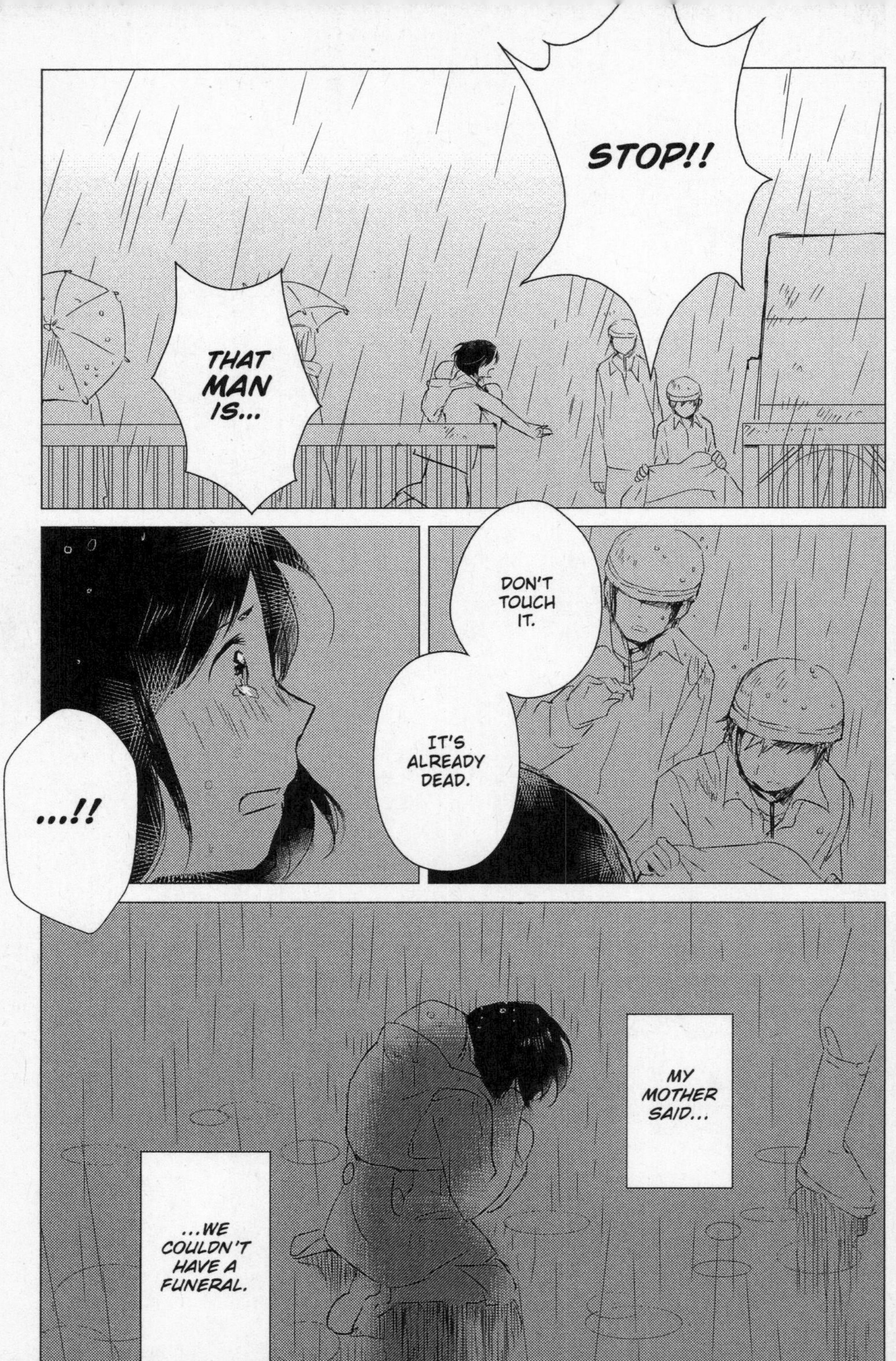
STOP!!
THAT MAN IS...
DON'T TOUCH IT.
IT'S ALREADY DEAD.
...!!
MY MOTHER SAID...
...WE COULDN'T HAVE A FUNERAL.

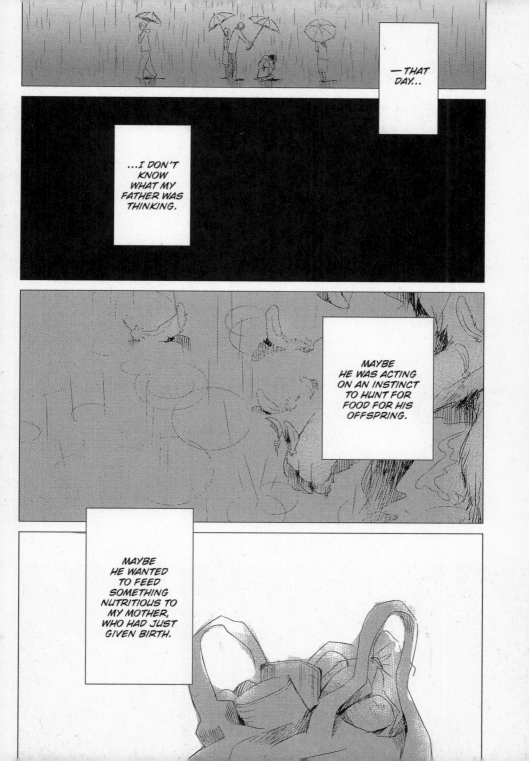

—THAT DAY...

...I DON'T KNOW WHAT MY FATHER WAS THINKING.

MAYBE HE WAS ACTING ON AN INSTINCT TO HUNT FOR FOOD FOR HIS OFFSPRING.

MAYBE HE WANTED TO FEED SOMETHING NUTRITIOUS TO MY MOTHER, WHO HAD JUST GIVEN BIRTH.

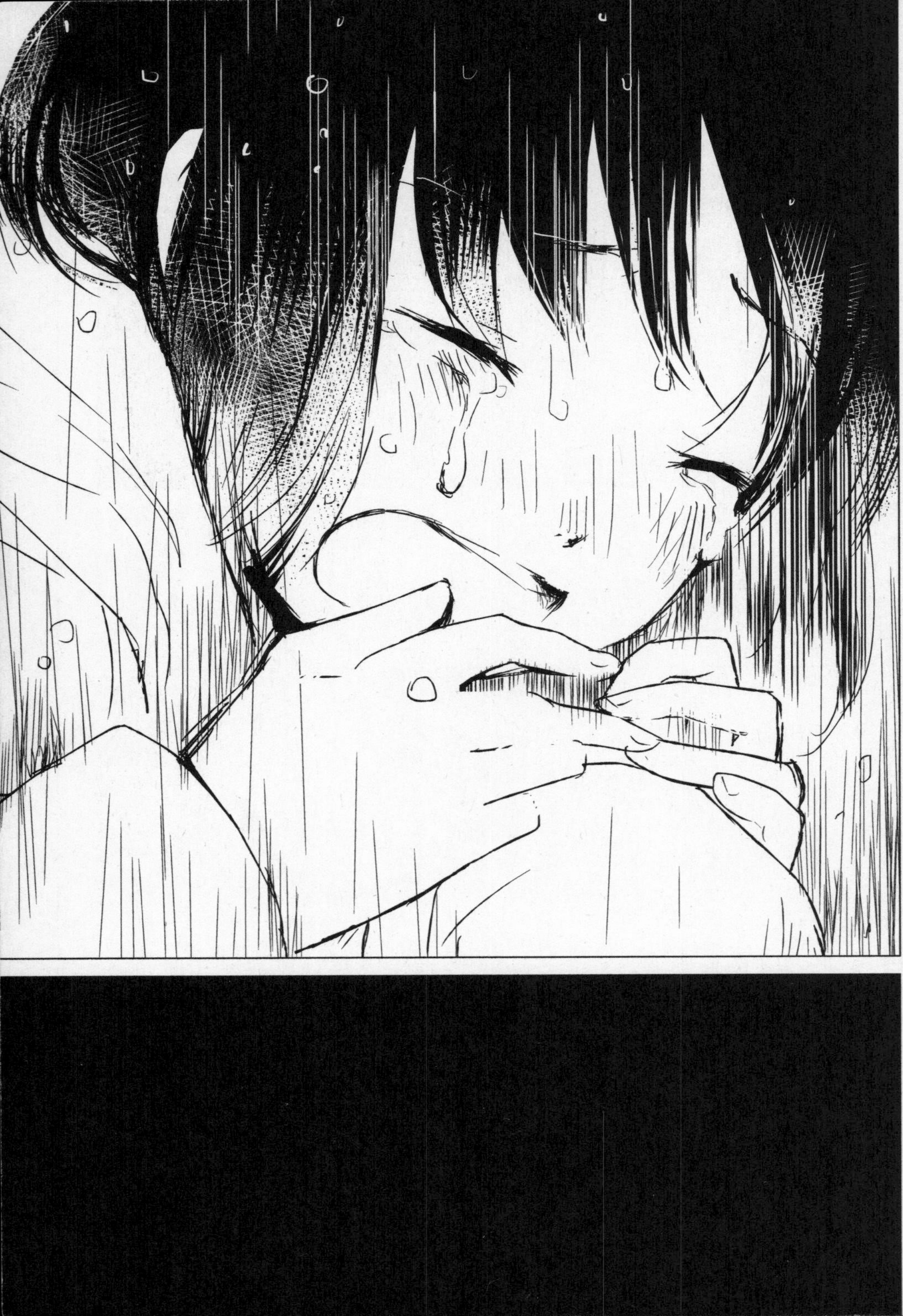

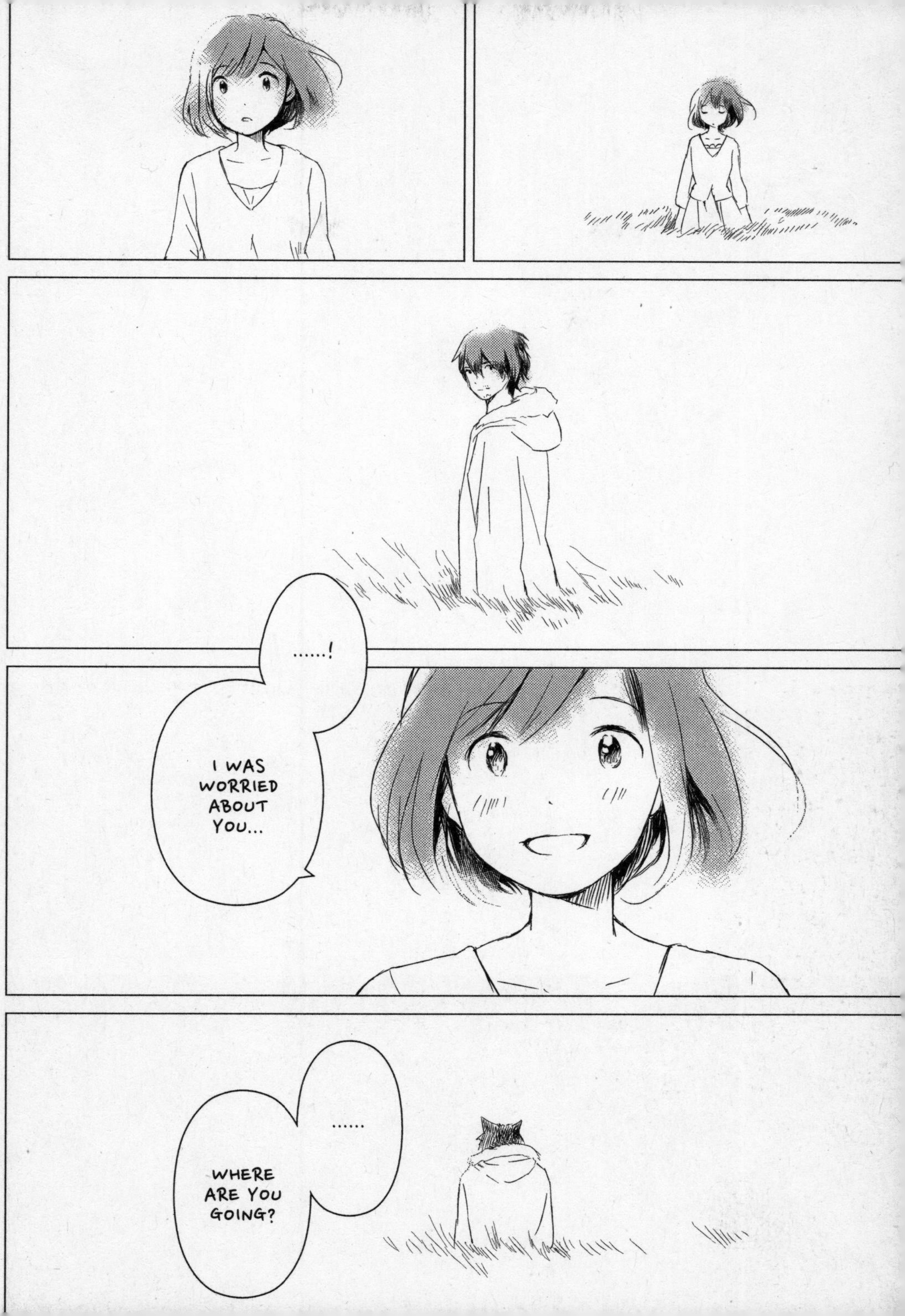
......!
I WAS WORRIED ABOUT YOU...
......
WHERE ARE YOU GOING?

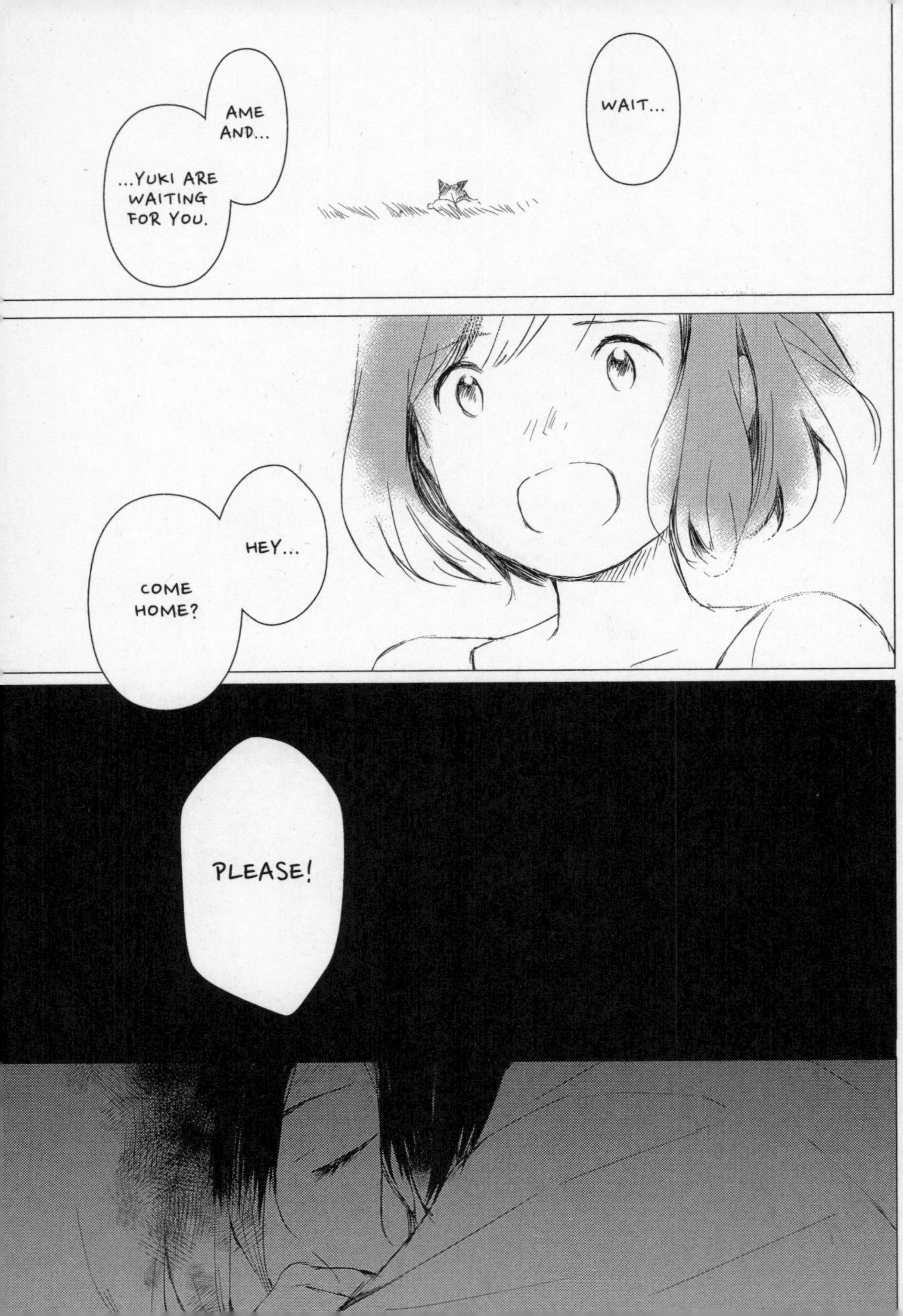
WAIT...
AME AND...
...YUKI ARE WAITING FOR YOU.
HEY...
COME HOME?
PLEASE!

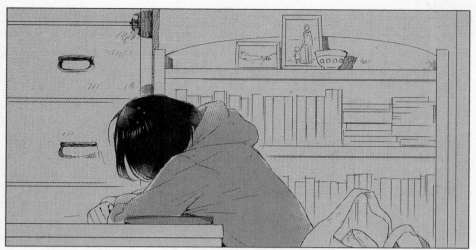

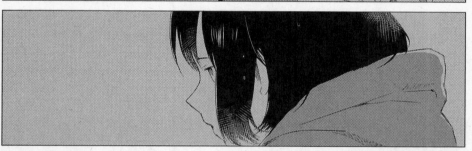

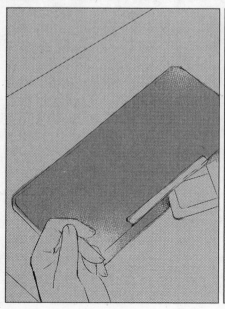

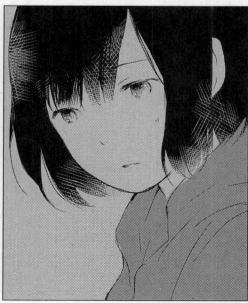

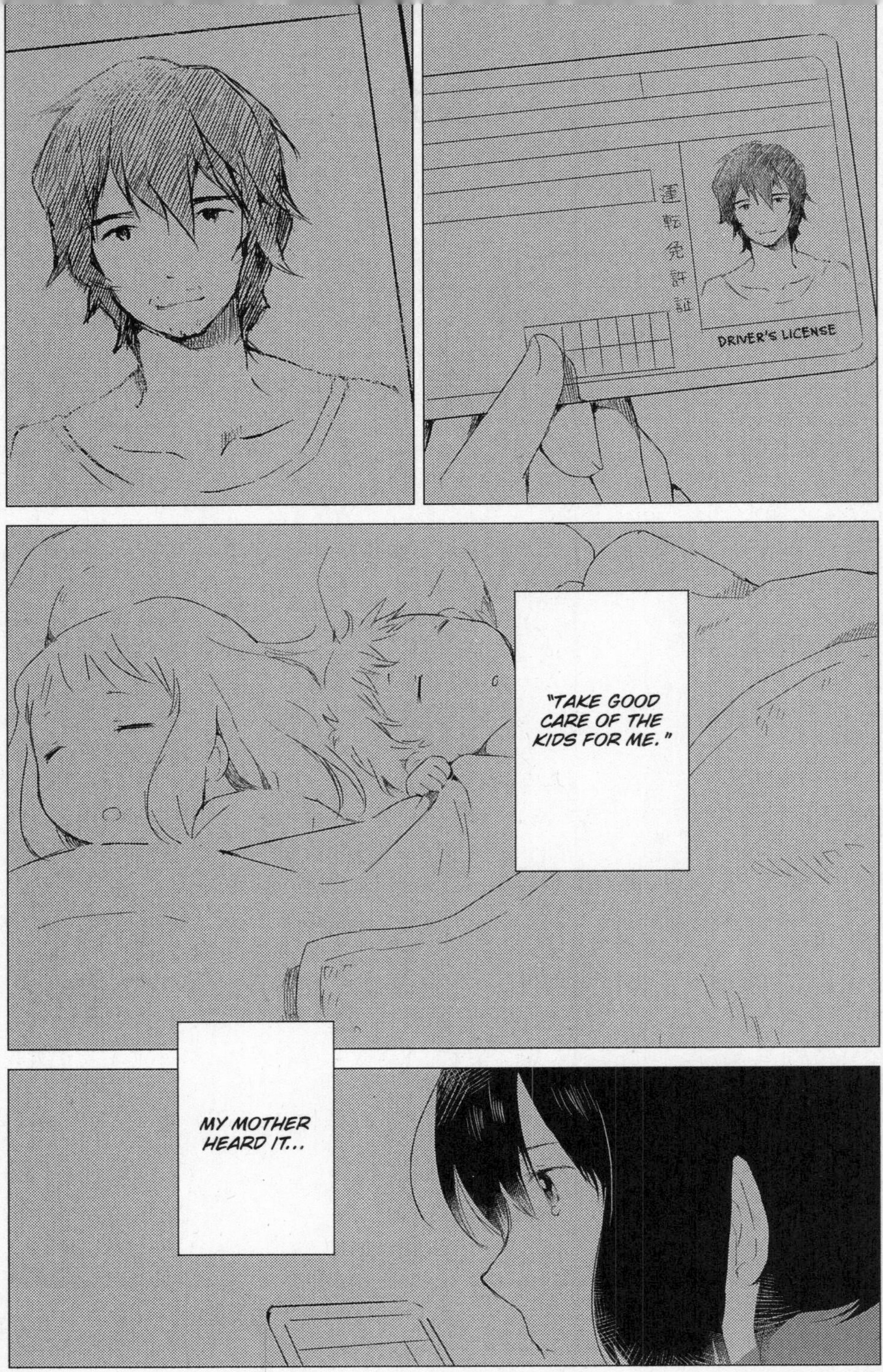
運転免許証
DRIVER'S LICENSE
"TAKE GOOD CARE OF THE KIDS FOR ME."
MY MOTHER HEARD IT...

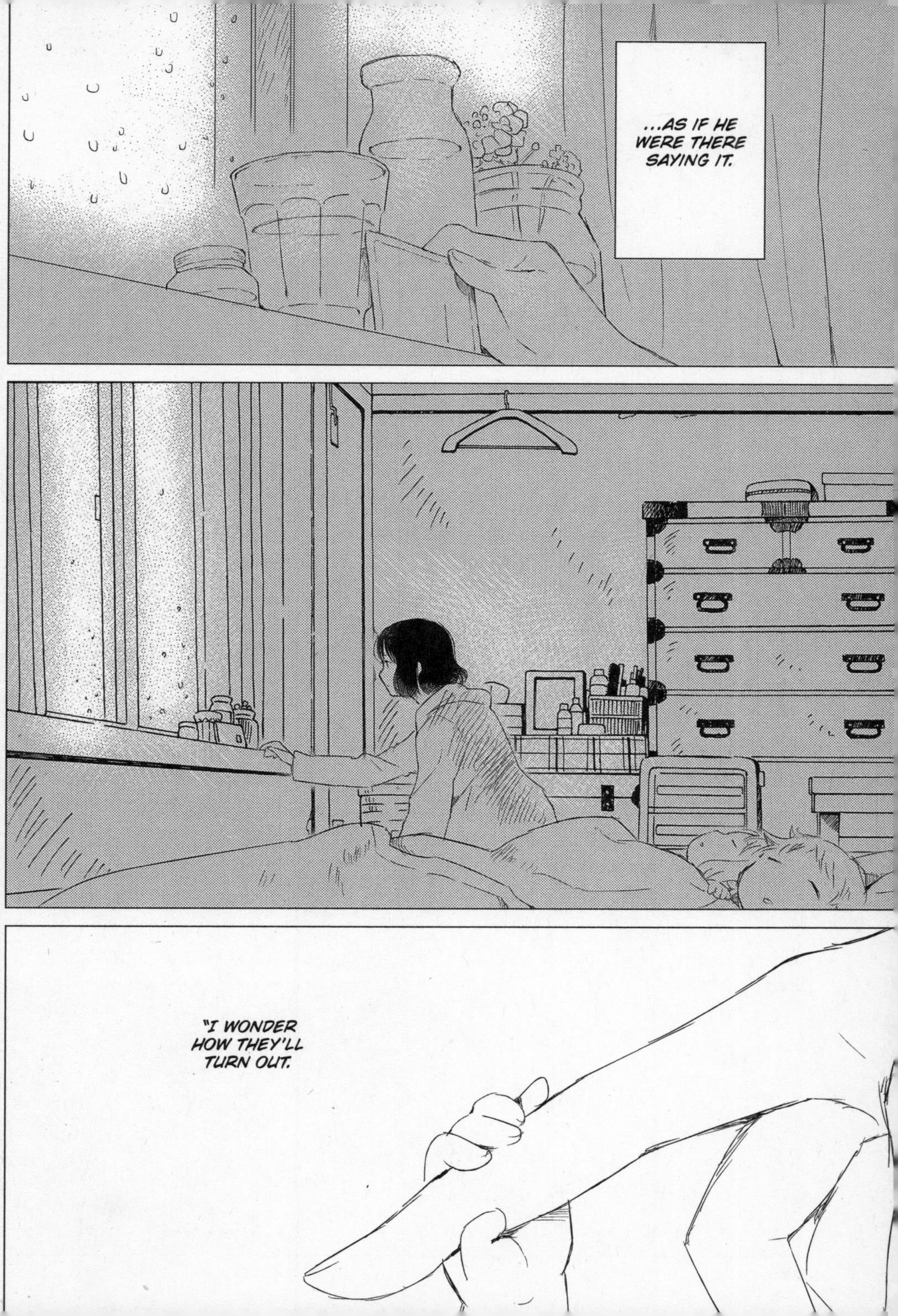
...AS IF HE WERE THERE SAYING IT.
"I WONDER HOW THEY'LL TURN OUT.

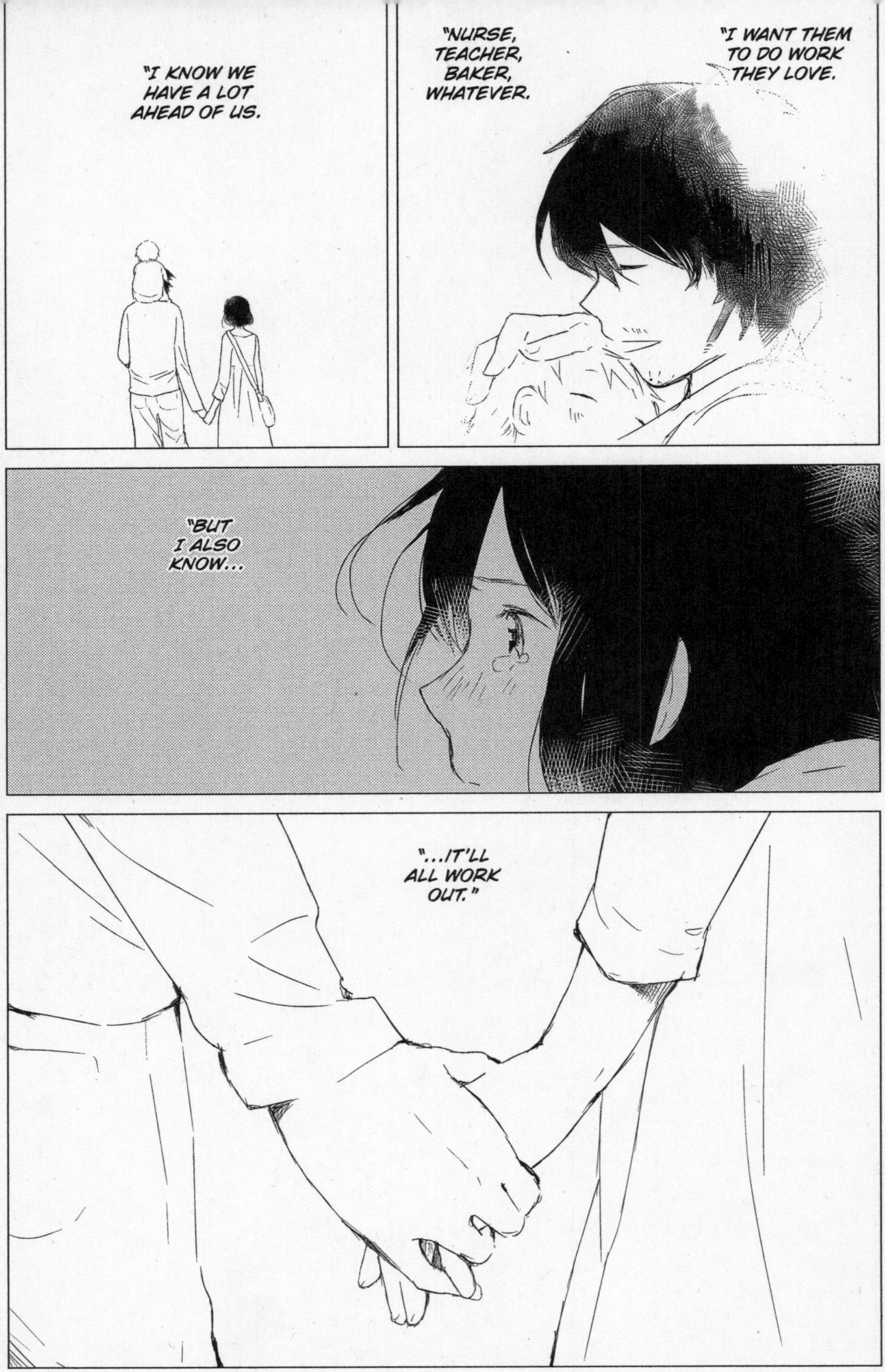
"I WANT THEM TO DO WORK THEY LOVE.
"NURSE, TEACHER, BAKER, WHATEVER.
"I KNOW WE HAVE A LOT AHEAD OF US.
"BUT I ALSO KNOW...
"...IT'LL ALL WORK OUT."

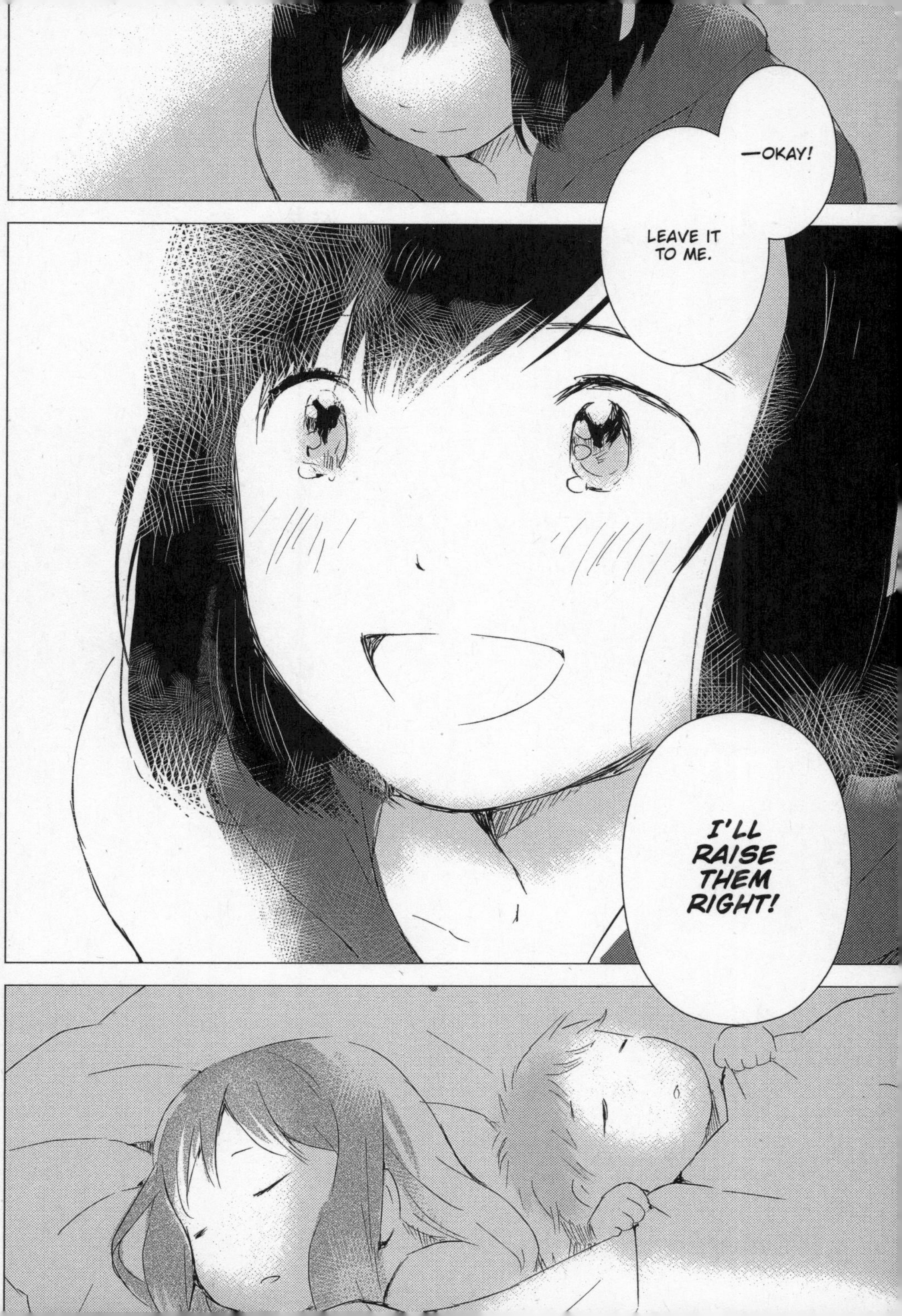
—OKAY!
LEAVE IT TO ME.
I'LL RAISE THEM RIGHT!

Wolf Children
Ame & Yuki

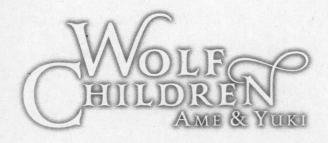

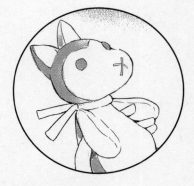

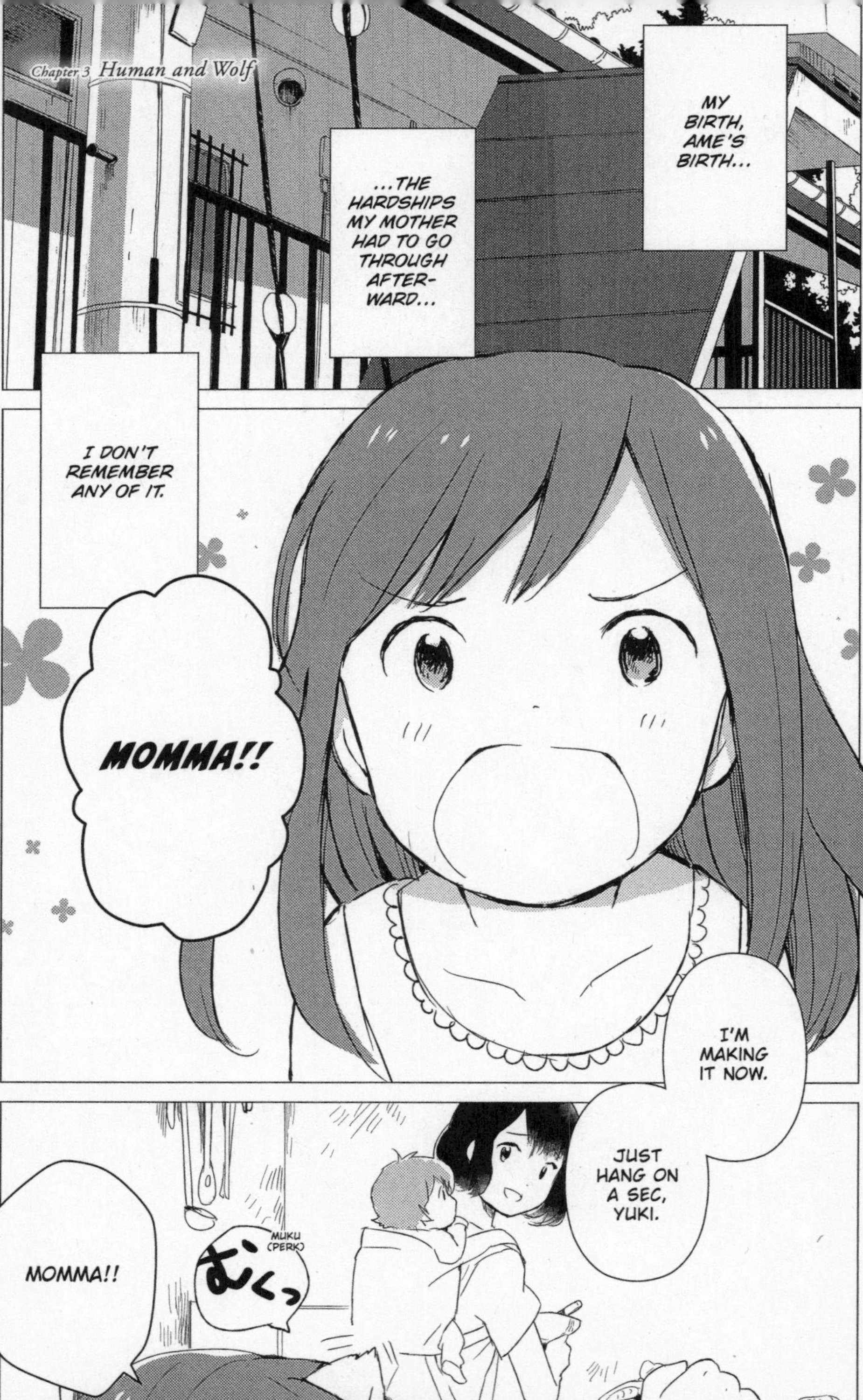
Chapter 3 Human and Wolf
MY BIRTH, AME'S BIRTH...
...THE HARDSHIPS MY MOTHER HAD TO GO THROUGH AFTER-WARD...
I DON'T REMEMBER ANY OF IT.
MOMMA!!
I'M MAKING IT NOW.
JUST HANG ON A SEC, YUKI.
MUKU (PERK)
むくっ
MOMMA!!

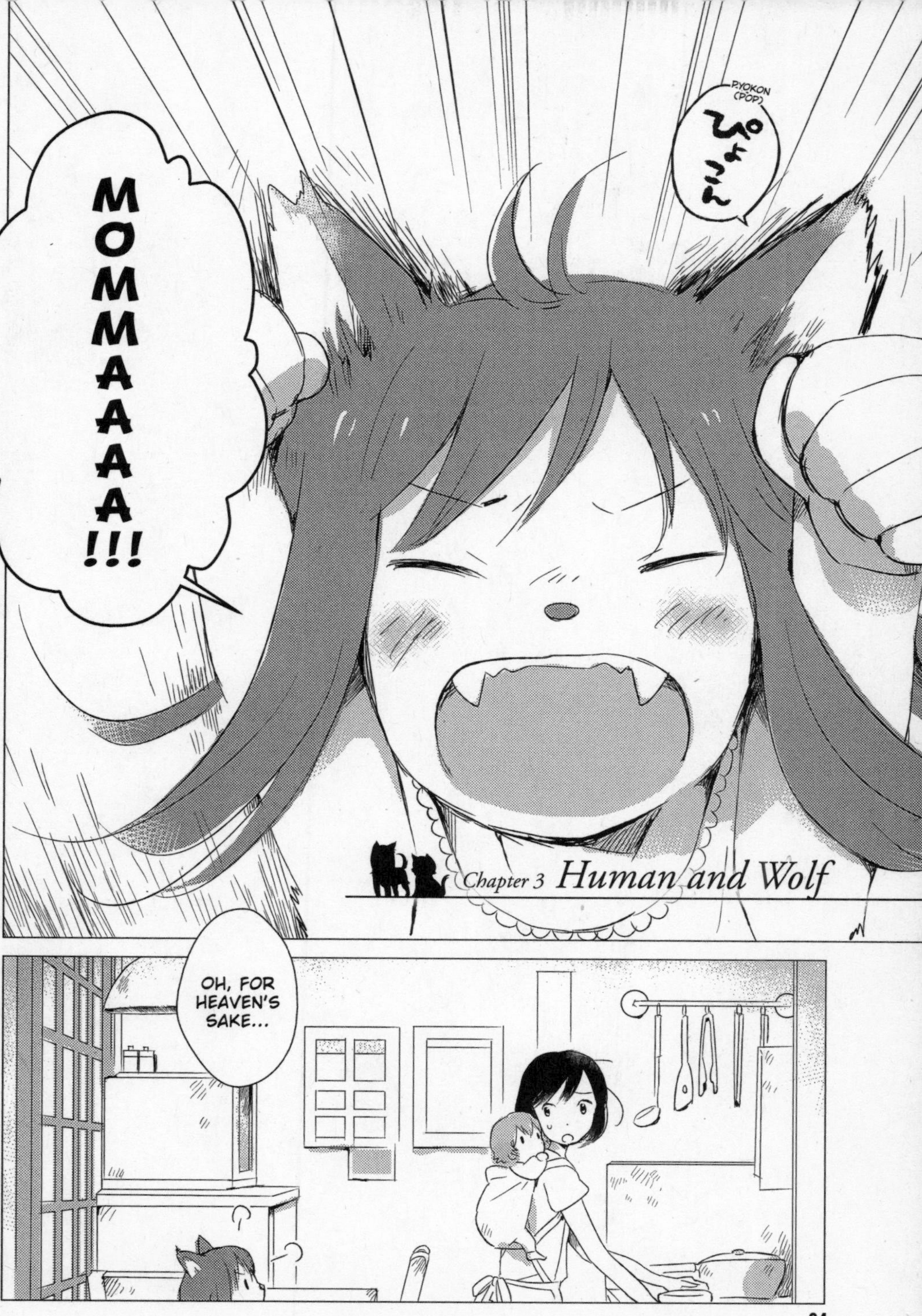
PYOKON (POP)
ぴょこん
MOMMAAAA!!!
Chapter 3 Human and Wolf
OH, FOR HEAVEN'S SAKE...

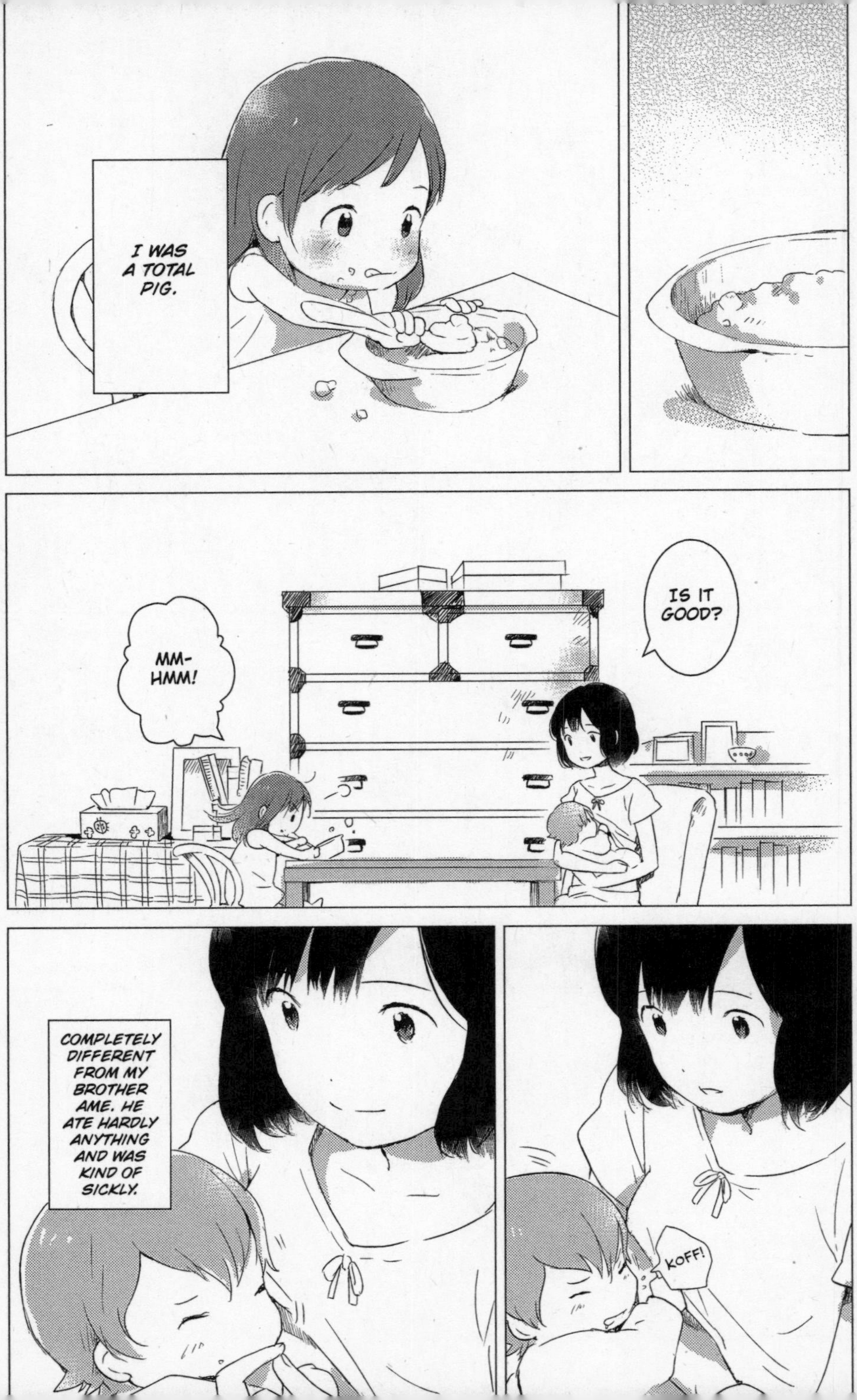
I WAS A TOTAL PIG.
IS IT GOOD?
MM-HMM!
KOFF!
COMPLETELY DIFFERENT FROM MY BROTHER AME. HE ATE HARDLY ANYTHING AND WAS KIND OF SICKLY.

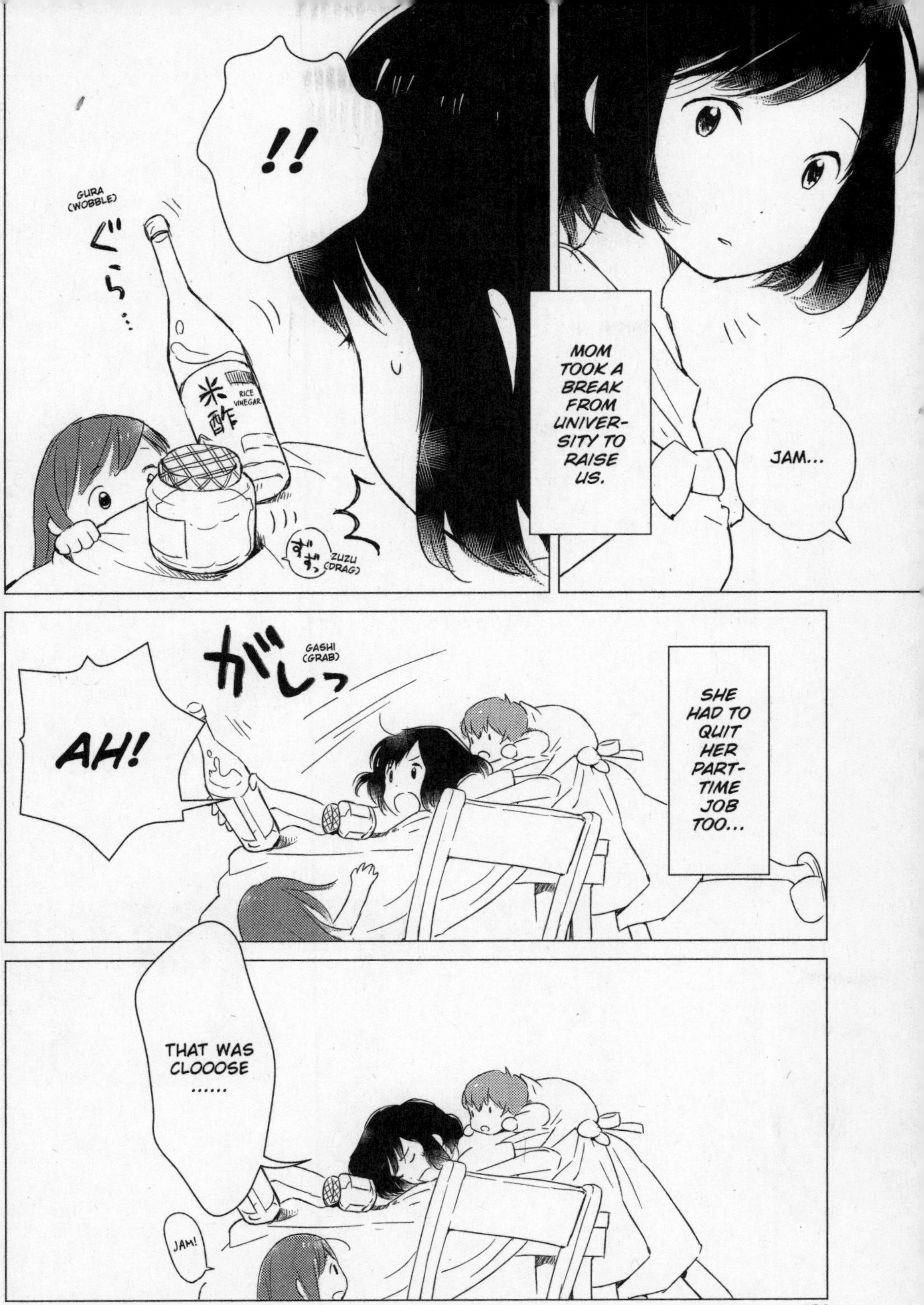

MOM TOOK A BREAK FROM UNIVERSITY TO RAISE US.
JAM...
!!
ぐら…
GURA (WOBBLE)
米酢
RICE VINEGAR
ずずっ
ZUZU (DRAG)
SHE HAD TO QUIT HER PART-TIME JOB TOO...
がしっ
GASHI (GRAB)
AH!
THAT WAS CLOOOSE ......
JAM!

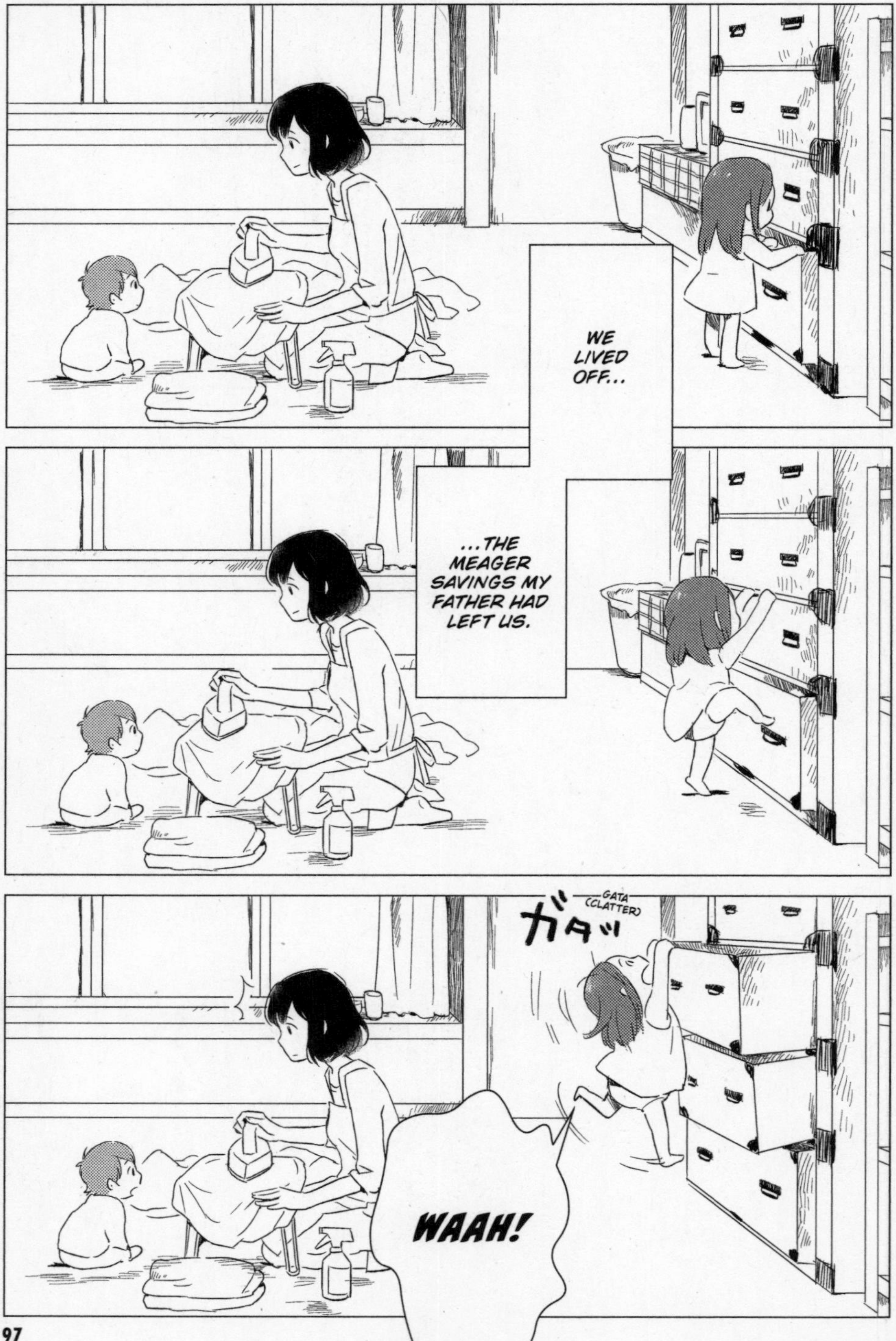
WE LIVED OFF...
...THE MEAGER SAVINGS MY FATHER HAD LEFT US.
ガタッ
GATA (CLATTER)
WAAH!

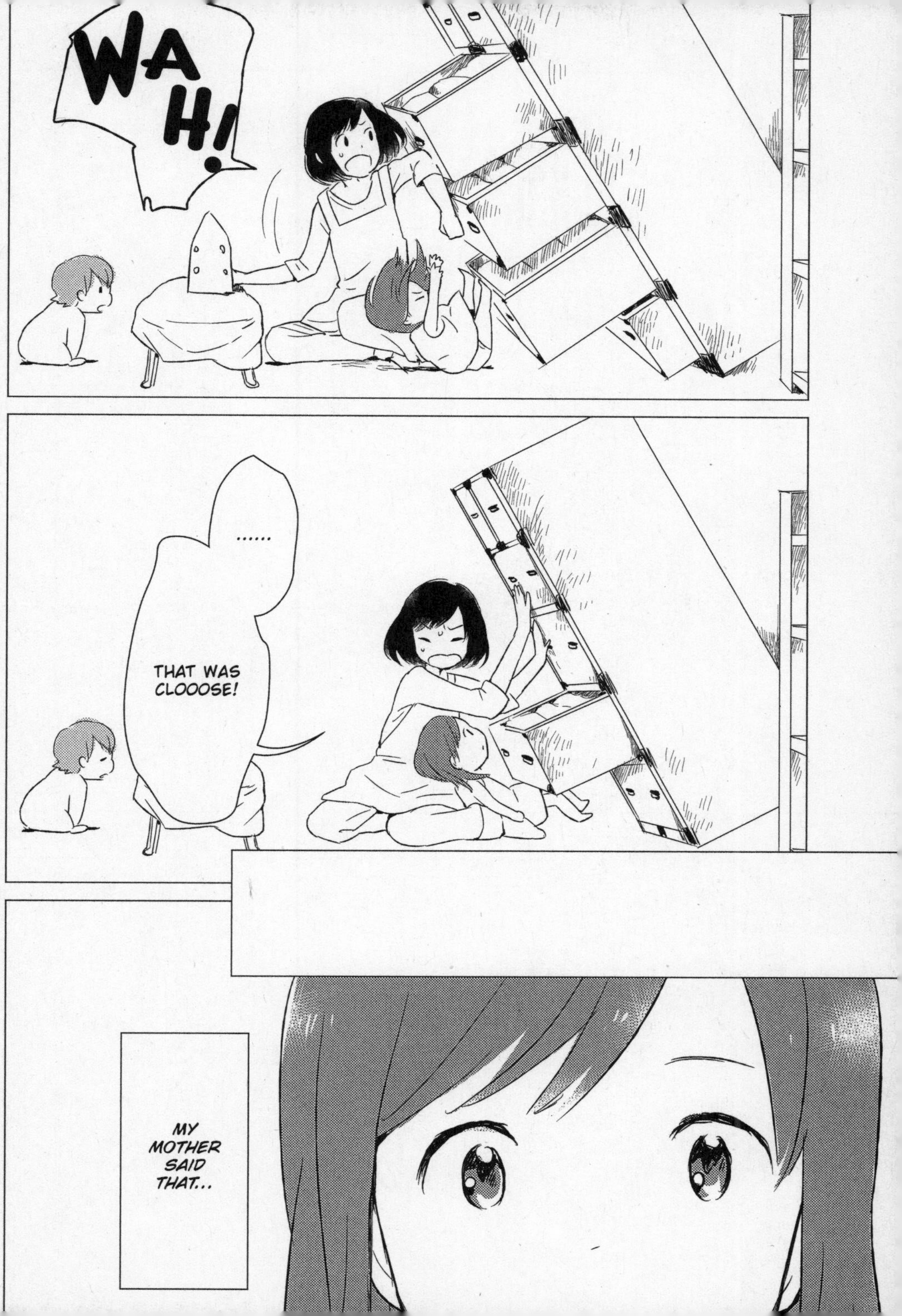
WAH!
......
THAT WAS CLOOOSE!
MY MOTHER SAID THAT...

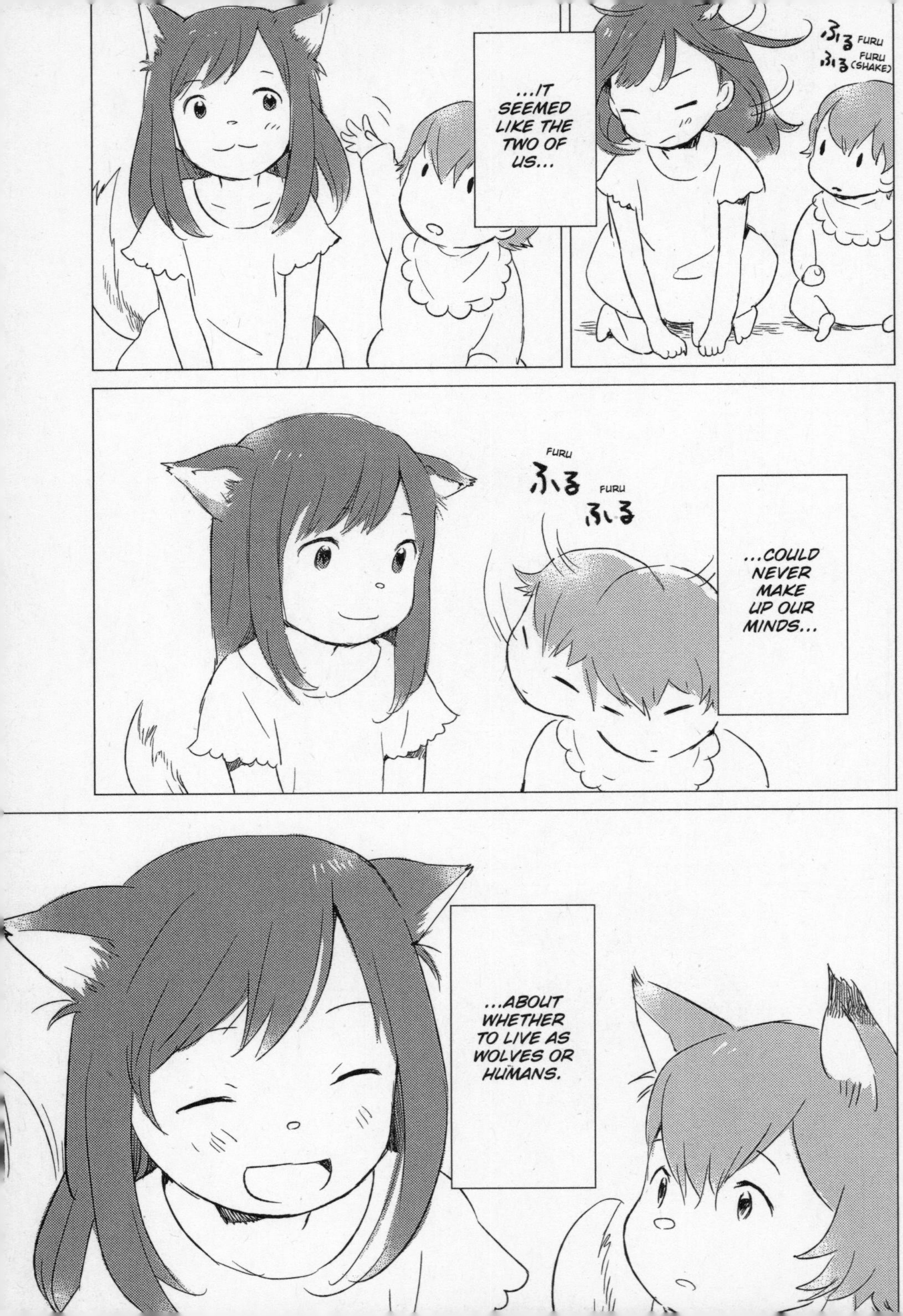
ふる FURU
ふる FURU (SHAKE)
...IT SEEMED LIKE THE TWO OF US...
FURU ふる
FURU ふる
...COULD NEVER MAKE UP OUR MINDS...
...ABOUT WHETHER TO LIVE AS WOLVES OR HUMANS.

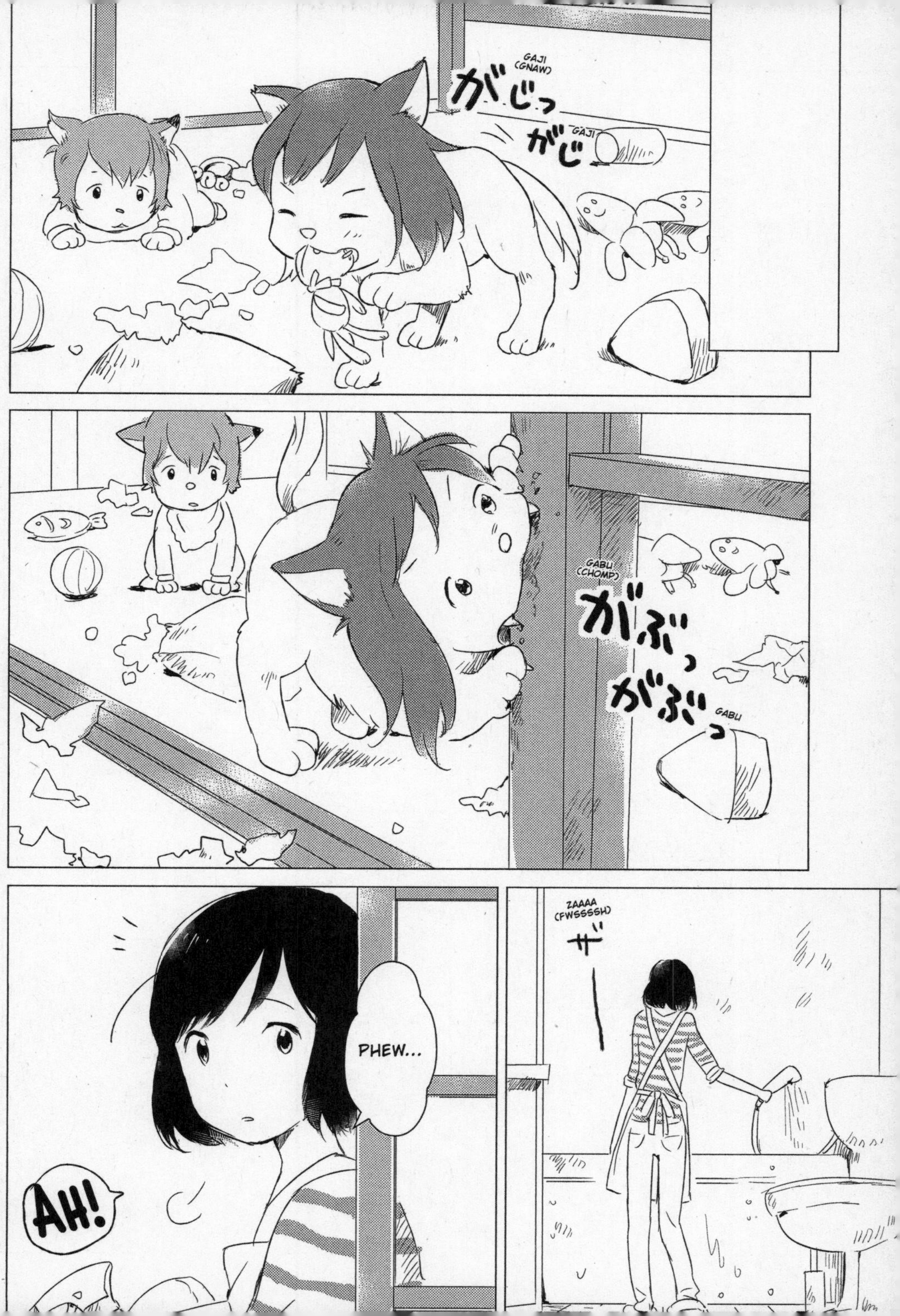

がじっ
GAJI (GNAW)
がじ
GAJI
がぶっ
GABU (CHOMP)
がぶっ
GABU
ザー
ZAAAA (FWSSSSH)
PHEW...
AH!

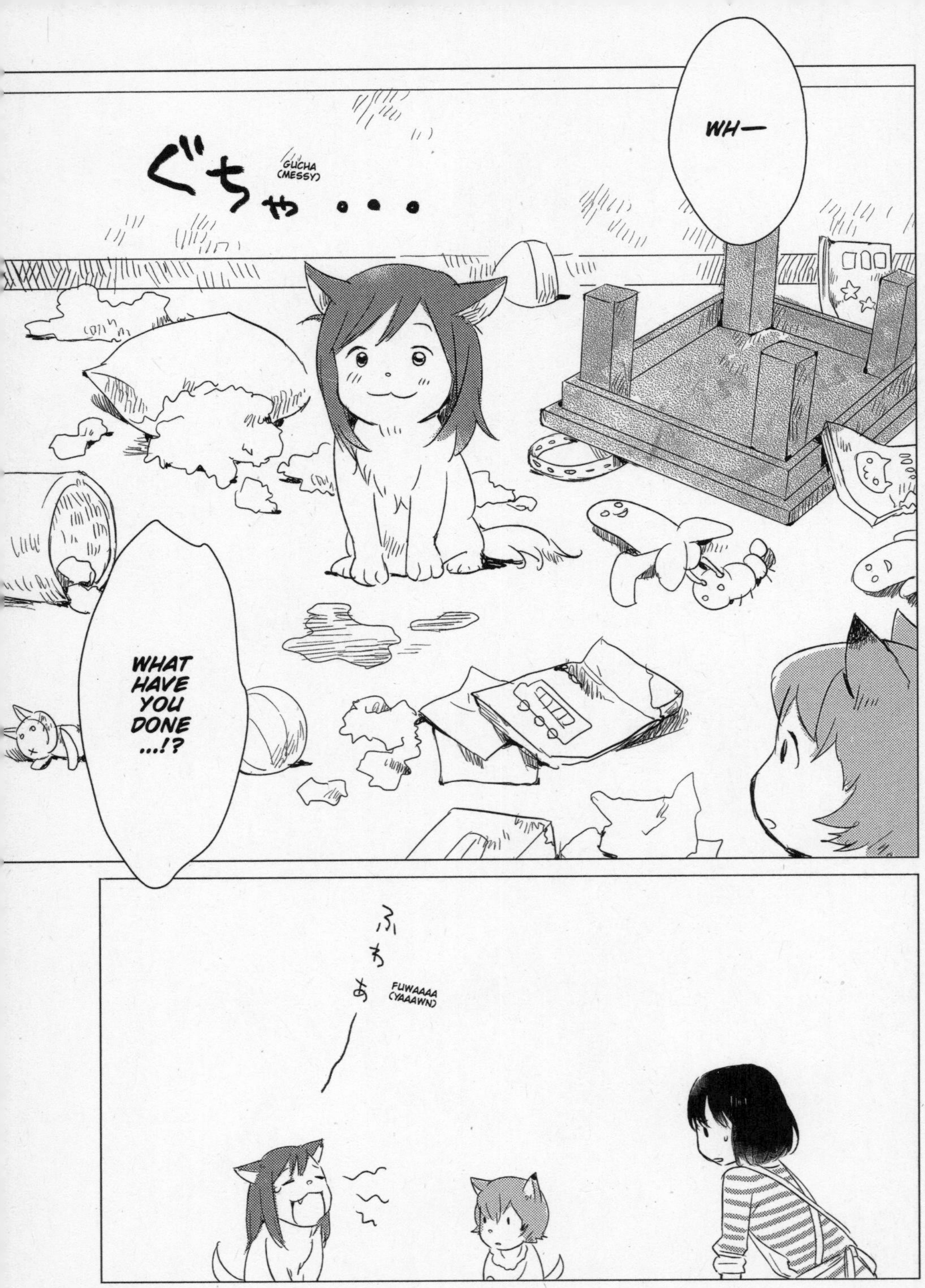
WH—
ぐちゃ・・・
GUCHA (MESSY)
WHAT HAVE YOU DONE ...!?
ふわあ
FUWAAAA (YAAAWN)

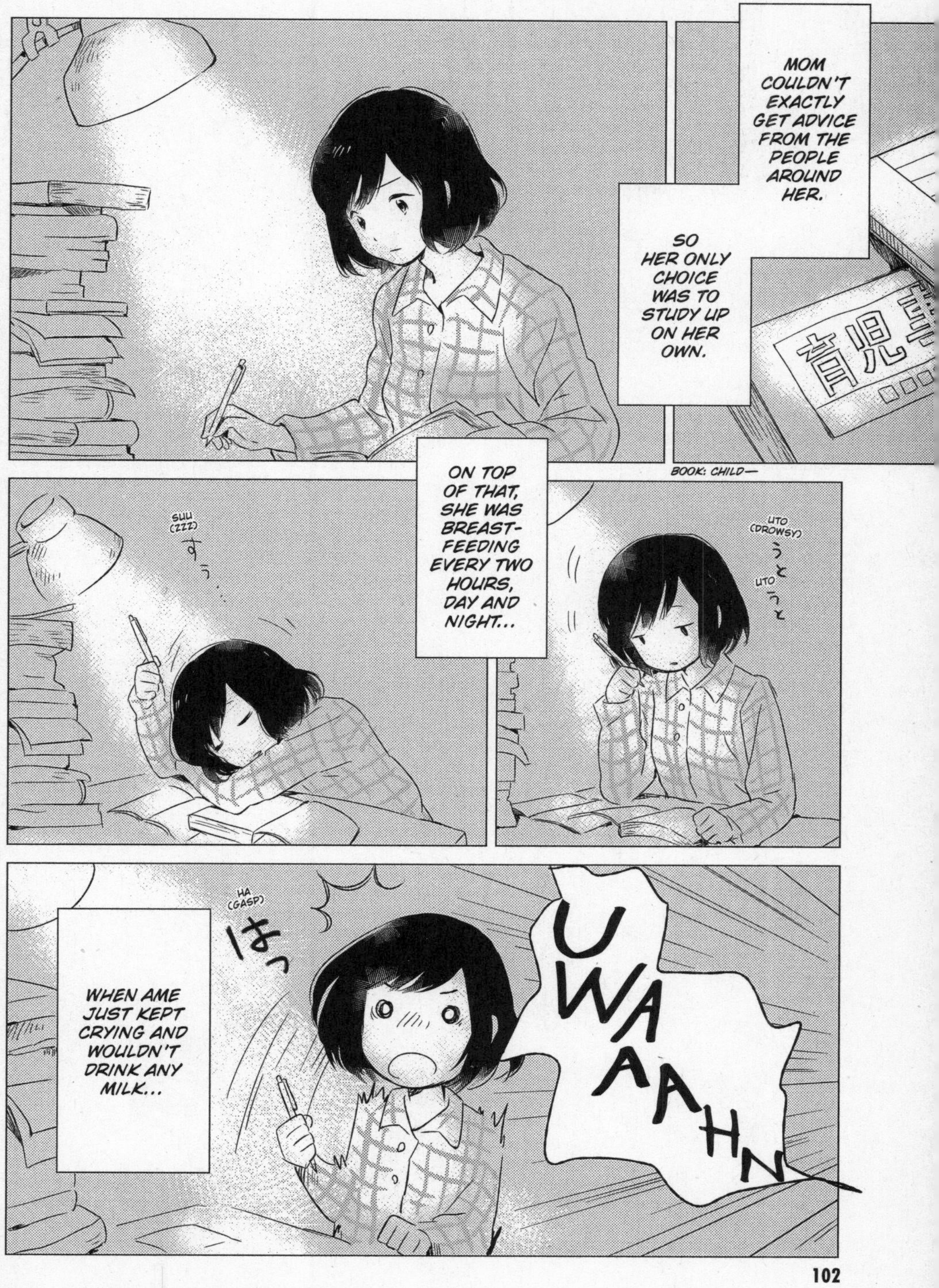
MOM COULDN'T EXACTLY GET ADVICE FROM THE PEOPLE AROUND HER.
SO HER ONLY CHOICE WAS TO STUDY UP ON HER OWN.
育児事
BOOK: CHILD—
ON TOP OF THAT, SHE WAS BREAST-FEEDING EVERY TWO HOURS, DAY AND NIGHT...
UTO (DROWSY)
うと
UTO
うと
SUU (ZZZ)
すぅ…
UWAAAHN
HA (GASP)
はっ
WHEN AME JUST KEPT CRYING AND WOULDN'T DRINK ANY MILK...

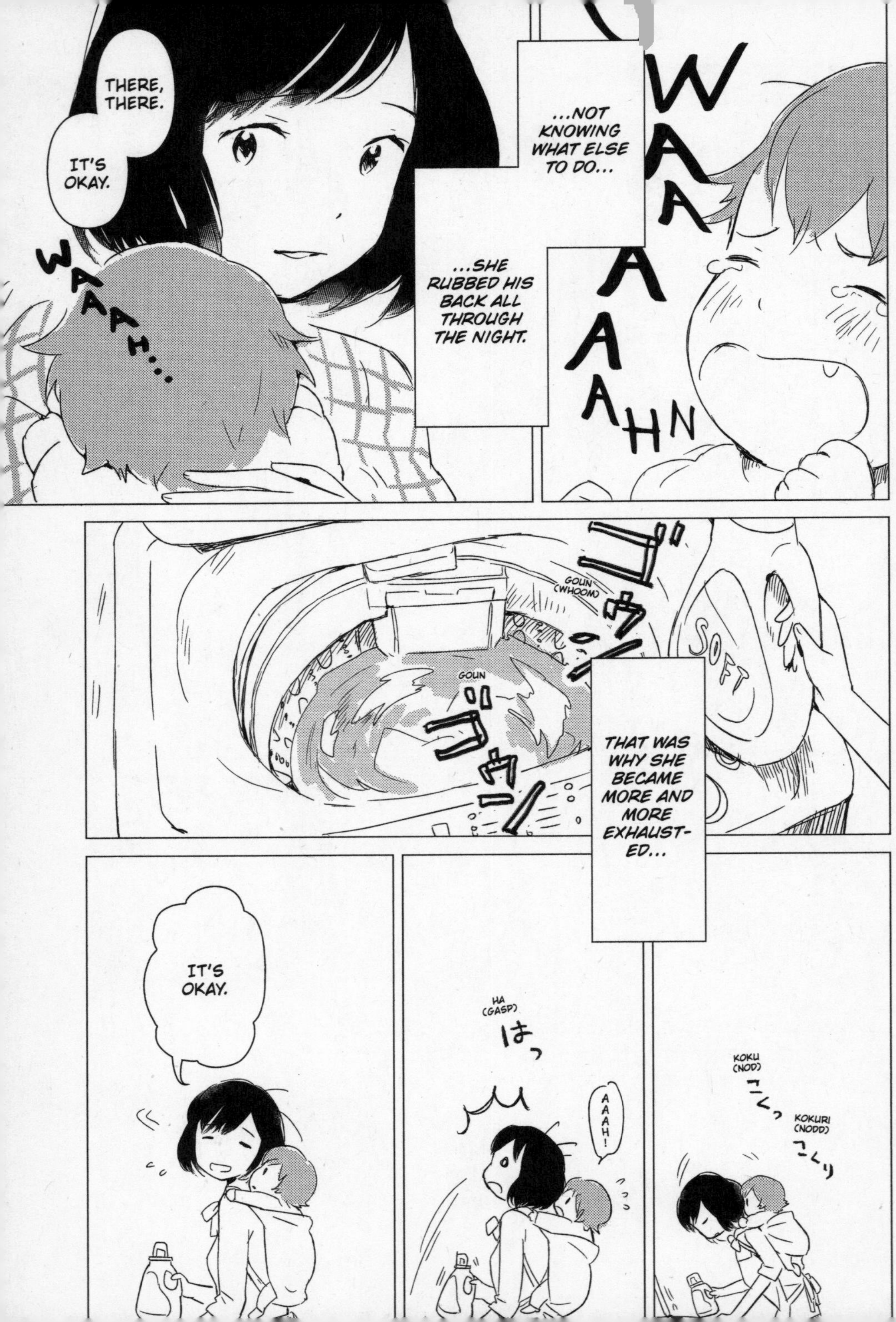
WAAAAAHN
...NOT KNOWING WHAT ELSE TO DO...
...SHE RUBBED HIS BACK ALL THROUGH THE NIGHT.
THERE, THERE.
IT'S OKAY.
WAAPH...
ゴゥン
GOUN (WHOOM)
ゴゥン
GOUN
THAT WAS WHY SHE BECAME MORE AND MORE EXHAUSTED...
KOKU (NOD)
こくっ
KOKURI (NODD)
こくり
HA (GASP)
はっ
AAAH!
IT'S OKAY.

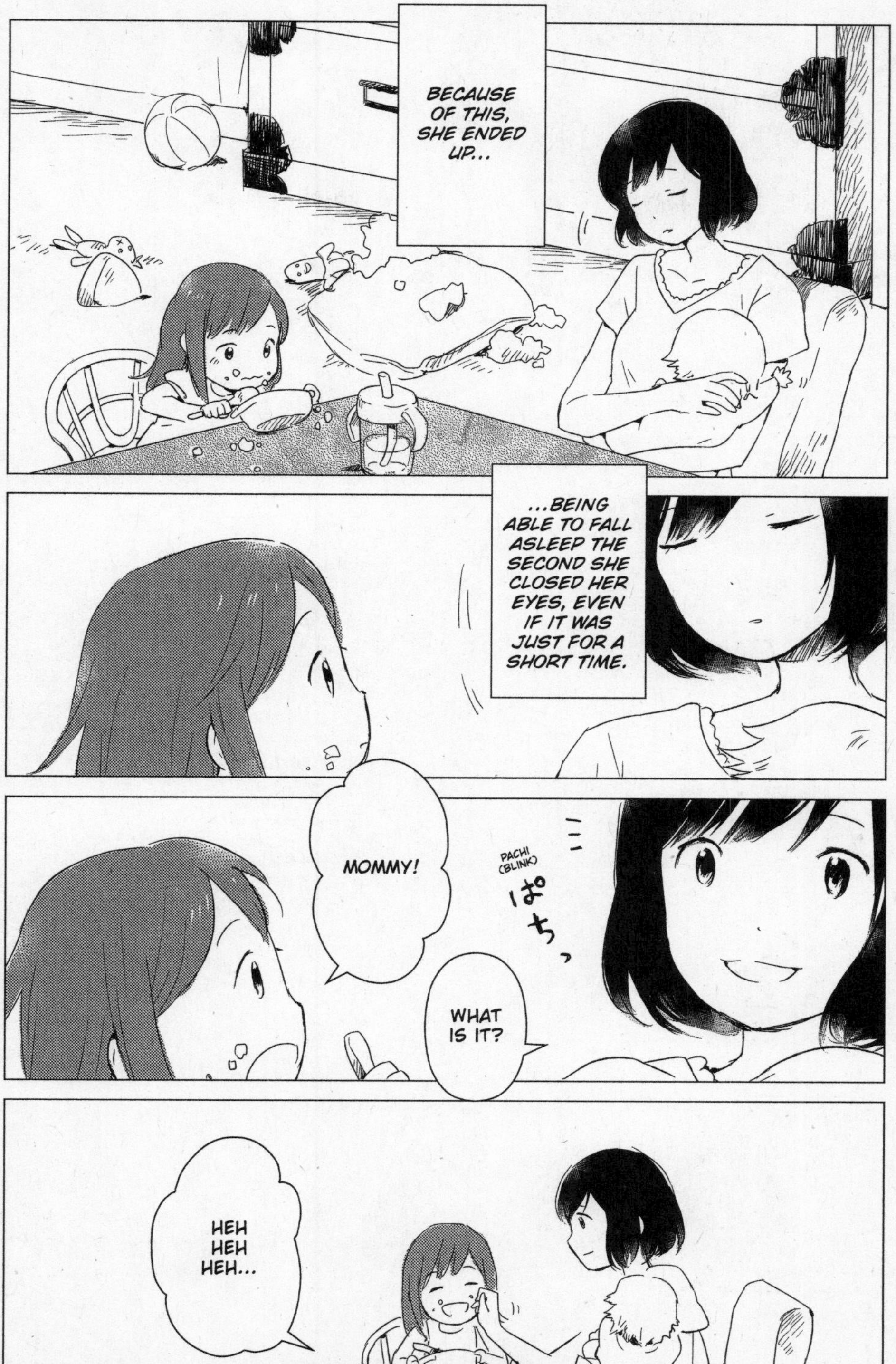
BECAUSE OF THIS, SHE ENDED UP...
...BEING ABLE TO FALL ASLEEP THE SECOND SHE CLOSED HER EYES, EVEN IF IT WAS JUST FOR A SHORT TIME.
PACHI (BLINK)
ぱちっ
MOMMY!
WHAT IS IT?
HEH HEH HEH...

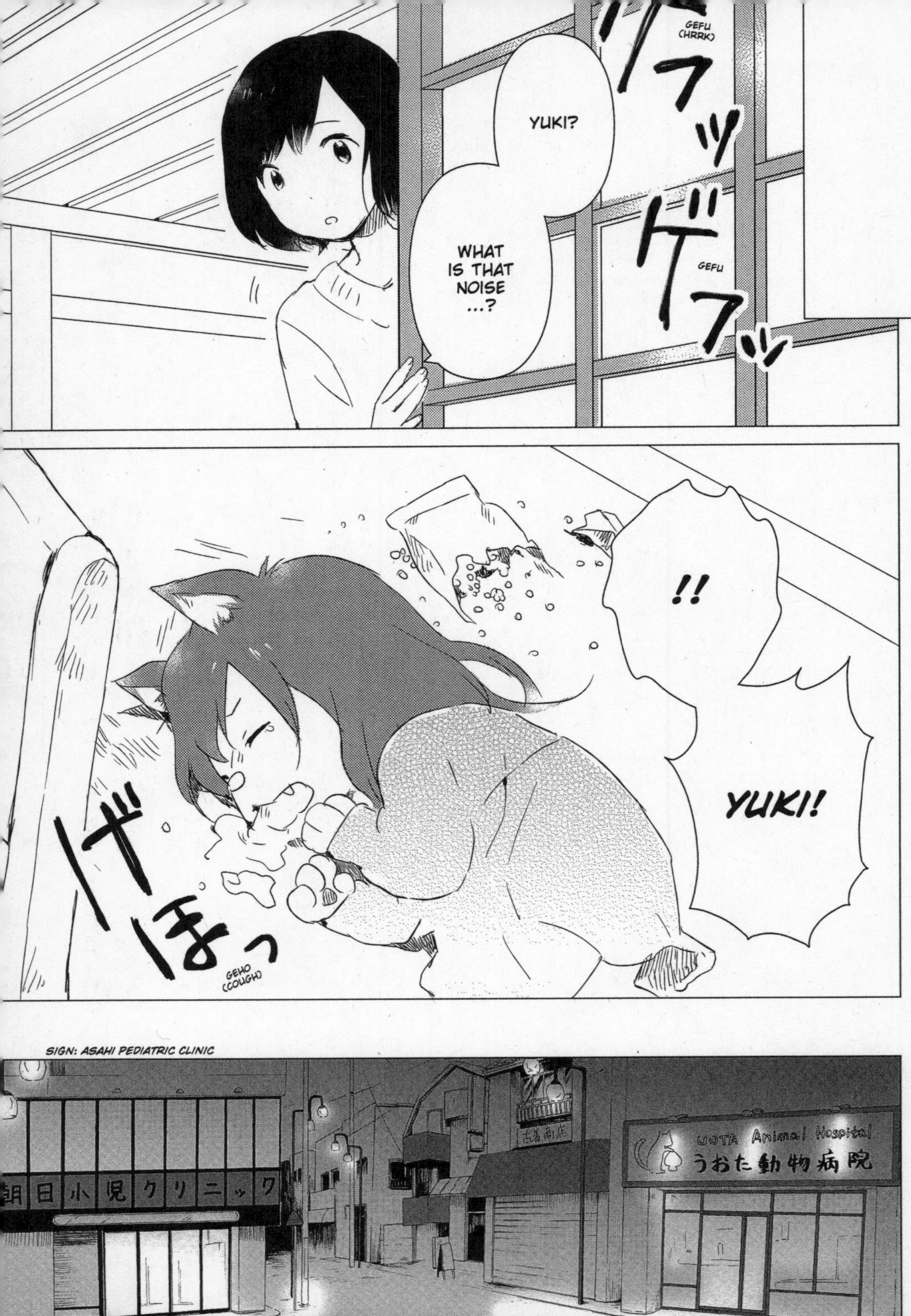
ゲフッ
GEFU (HRRK)
ゲフッ
GEFU
YUKI?
WHAT IS THAT NOISE ...?
!!
YUKI!
げほっ
GEHO (COUGH)
SIGN: ASAHI PEDIATRIC CLINIC
UOTA Animal Hospital
うおた動物病院
古着商店
朝日小児クリニック

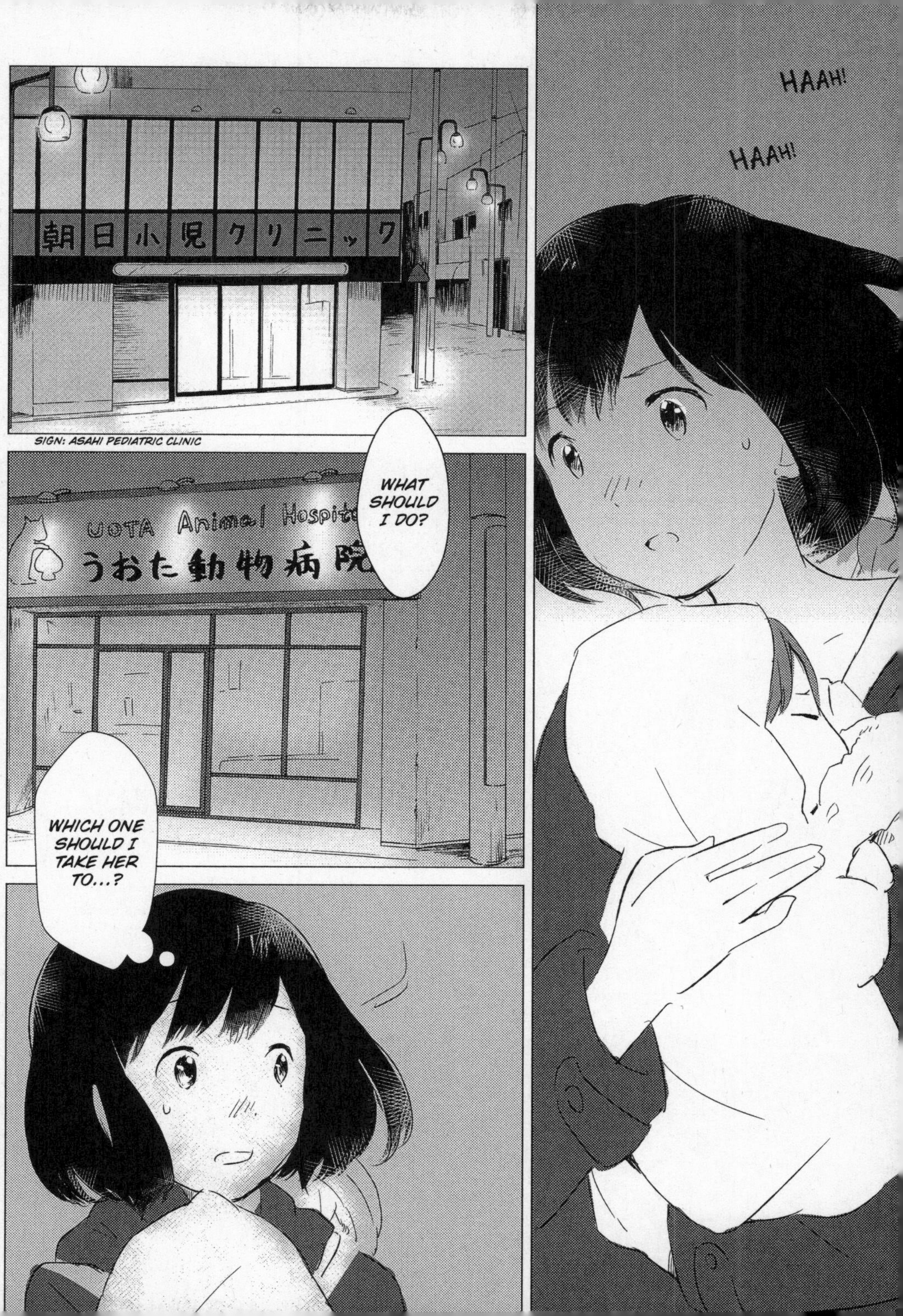
HAAH!
HAAH!
朝日小児クリニック
SIGN: ASAHI PEDIATRIC CLINIC
UOTA Animal Hospit
うおた動物病院
WHAT SHOULD I DO?
WHICH ONE SHOULD I TAKE HER TO...?

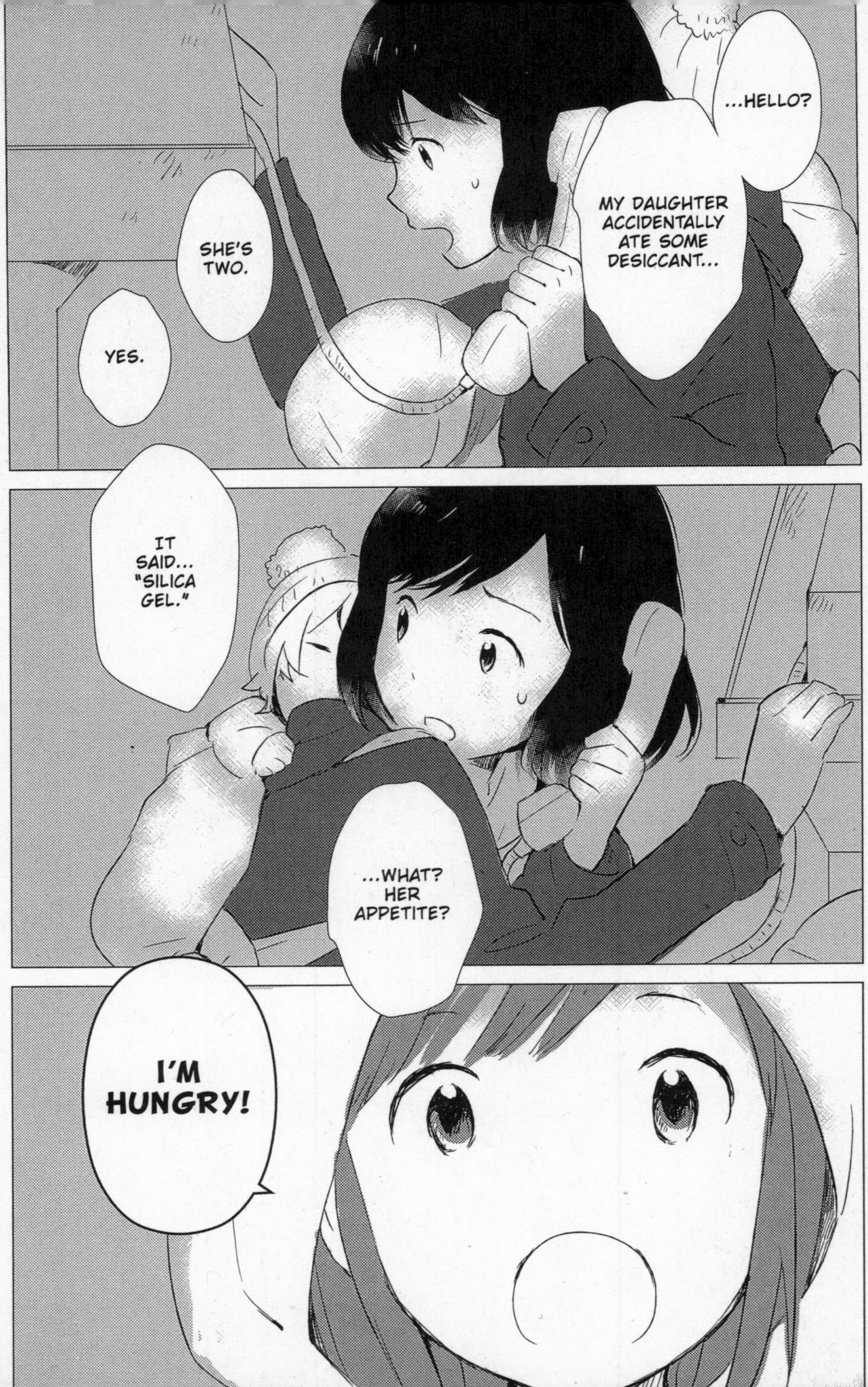
...HELLO?
MY DAUGHTER ACCIDENTALLY ATE SOME DESICCANT...
SHE'S TWO.
YES.
IT SAID... "SILICA GEL."
...WHAT? HER APPETITE?
I'M HUNGRY!

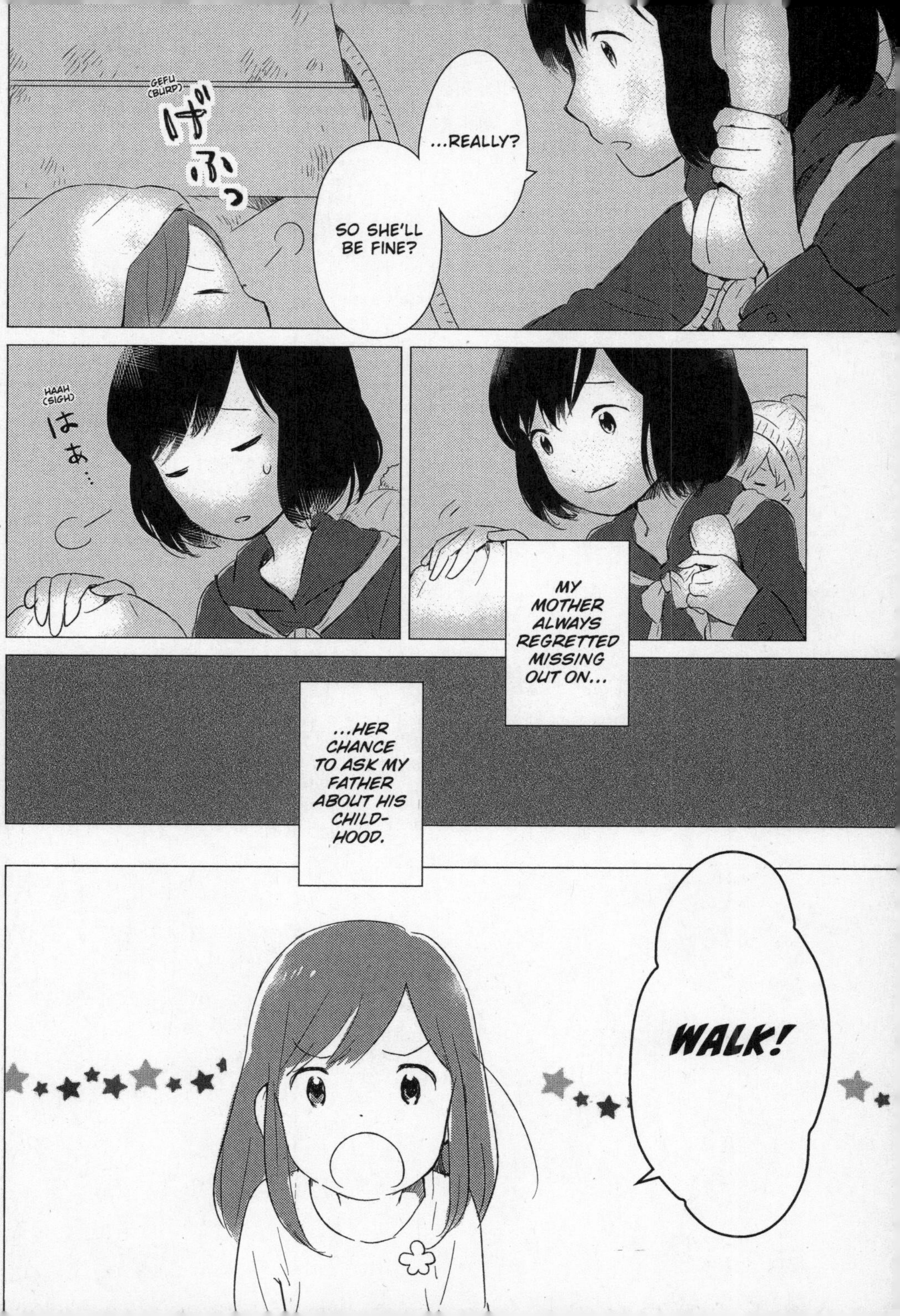
...REALLY?
SO SHE'LL BE FINE?
GEFU (BURP)
げふっ
MY MOTHER ALWAYS REGRETTED MISSING OUT ON...
HAAH (SIGH)
はぁ…
...HER CHANCE TO ASK MY FATHER ABOUT HIS CHILD-HOOD.
WALK!

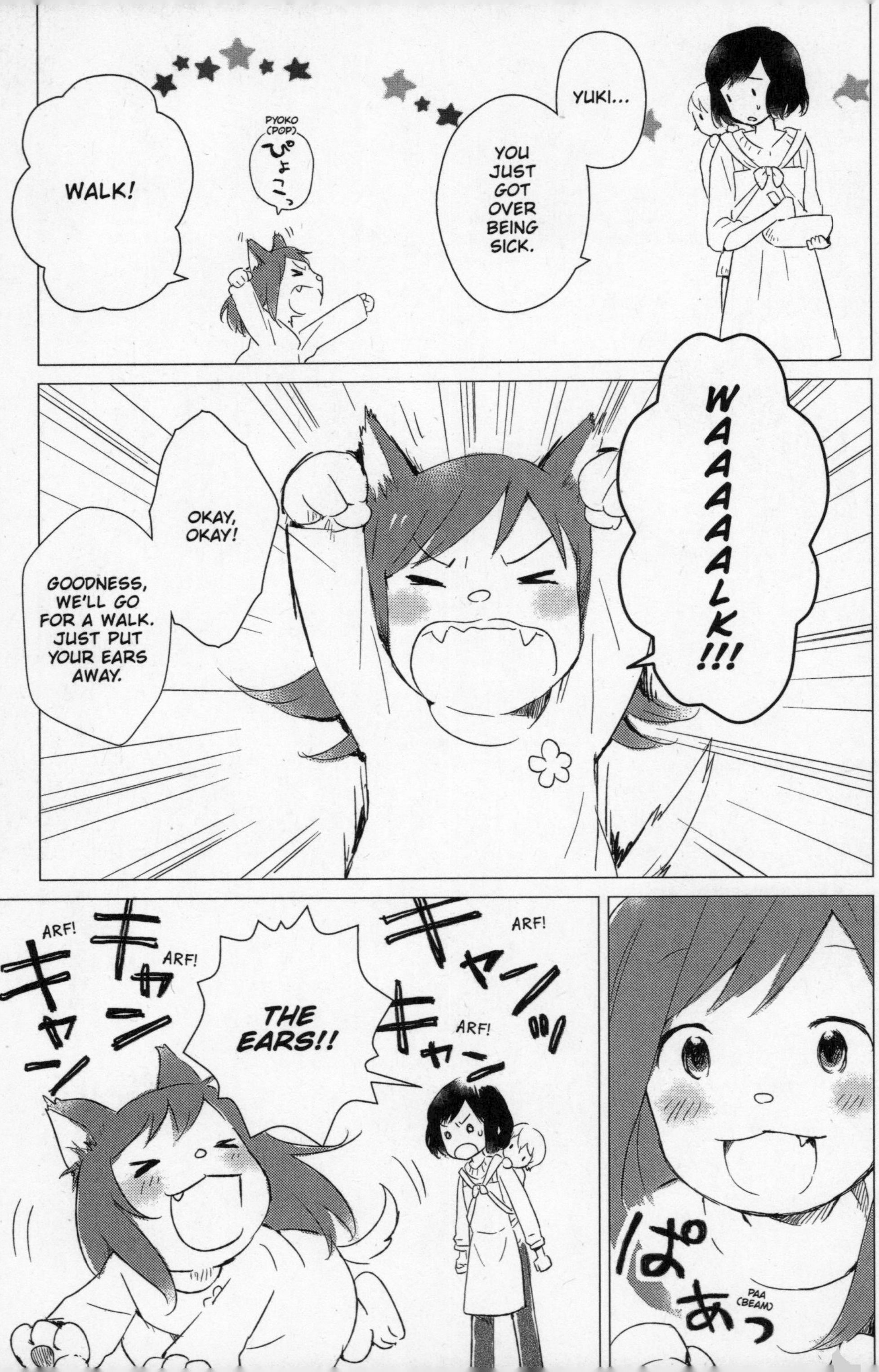
YUKI... YOU JUST GOT OVER BEING SICK.
PYOKO (POP)
ぴょこっ
WALK!
WAAAAALK!!!
OKAY, OKAY!
GOODNESS, WE'LL GO FOR A WALK. JUST PUT YOUR EARS AWAY.
ぱあっ
PAA (BEAM)
キャーン
ARF!
キャーン
ARF!
THE EARS!!
キャーン
ARF!
キャーン
ARF!

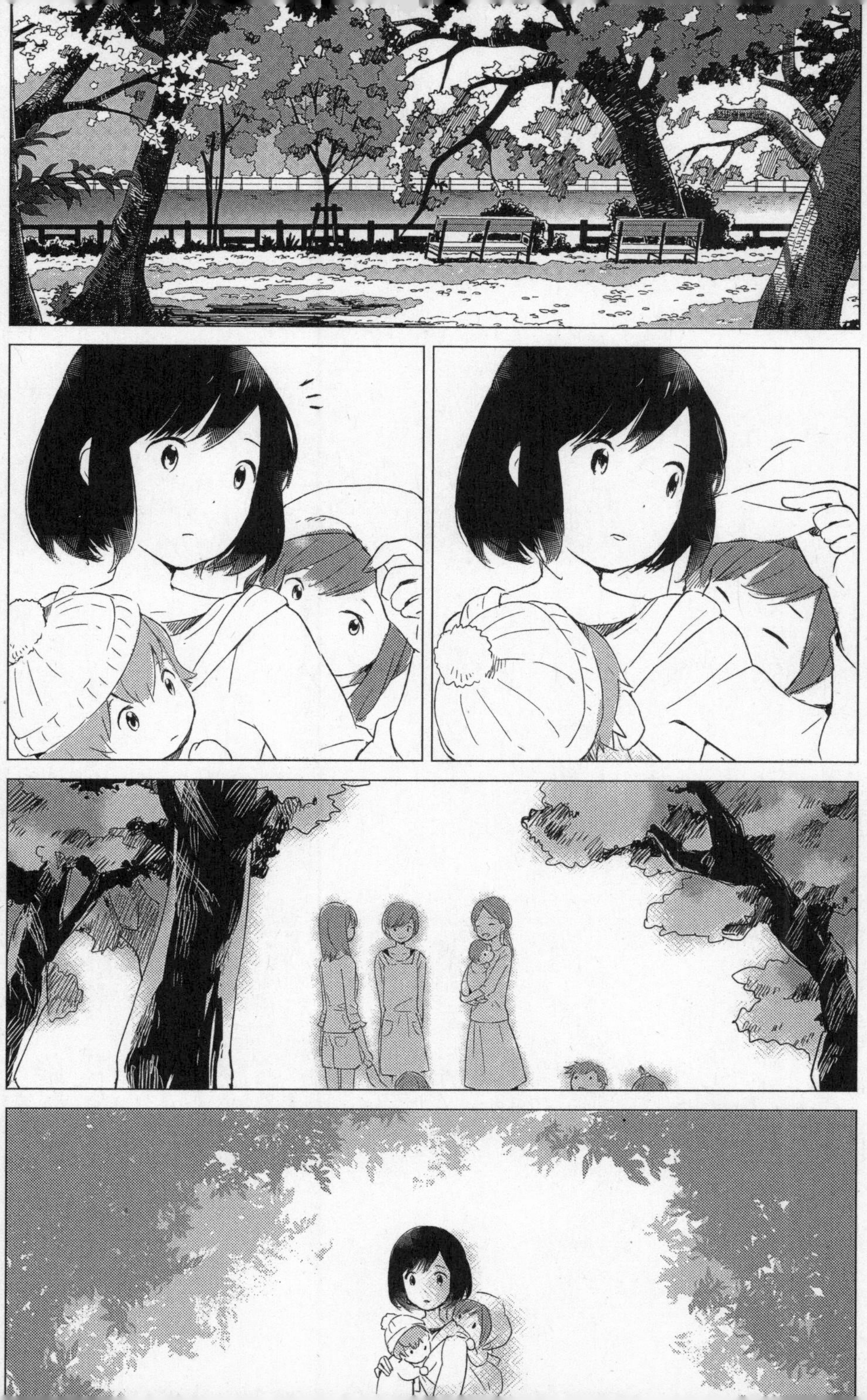

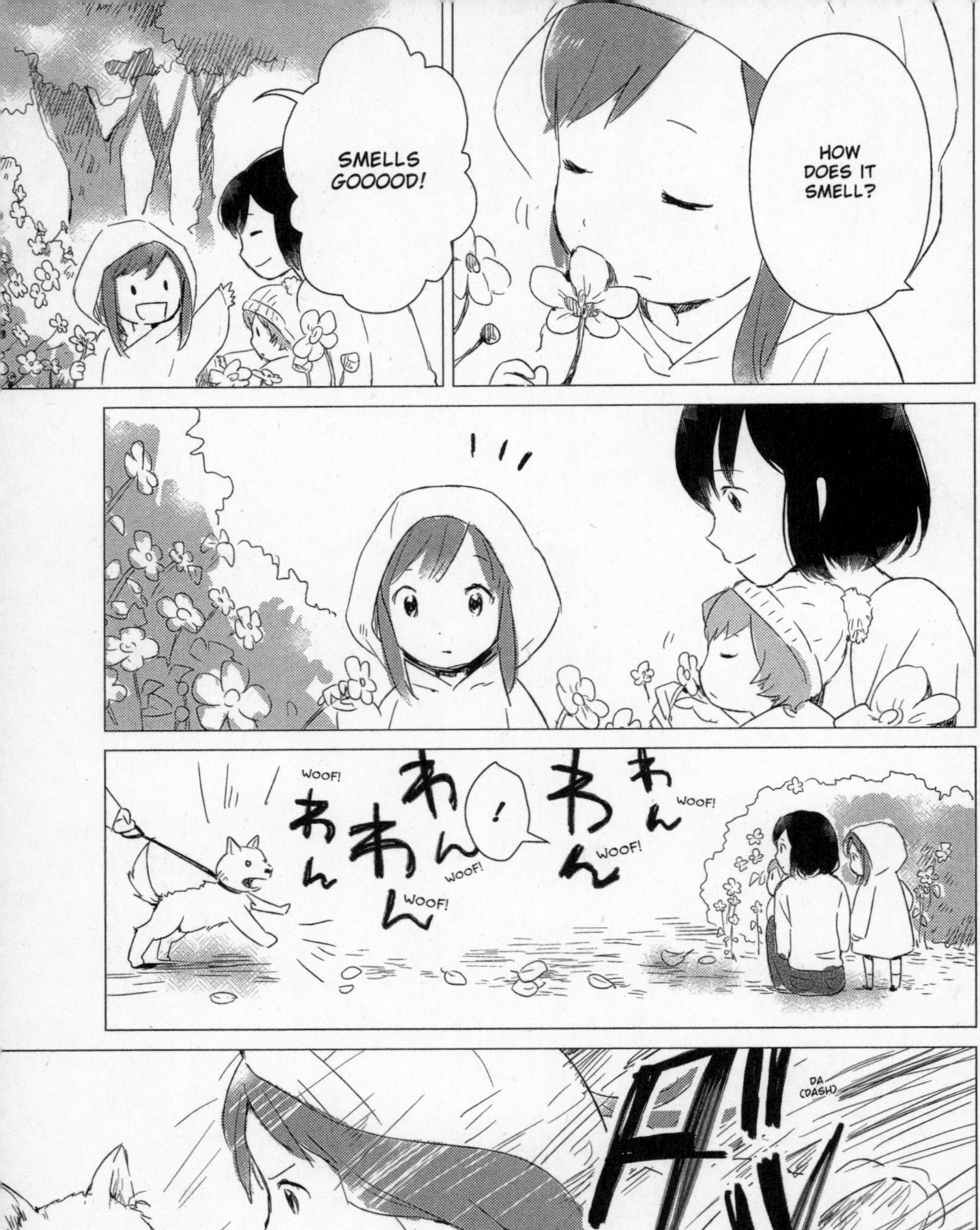
HOW DOES IT SMELL?
SMELLS GOOOOD!
わん
WOOF!
わん
WOOF!
!
わん
わん
WOOF!
わん
WOOF!
わん
WOOF!
ダッ
DA (DASH)

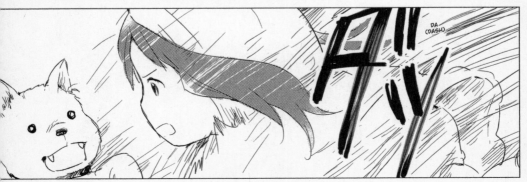

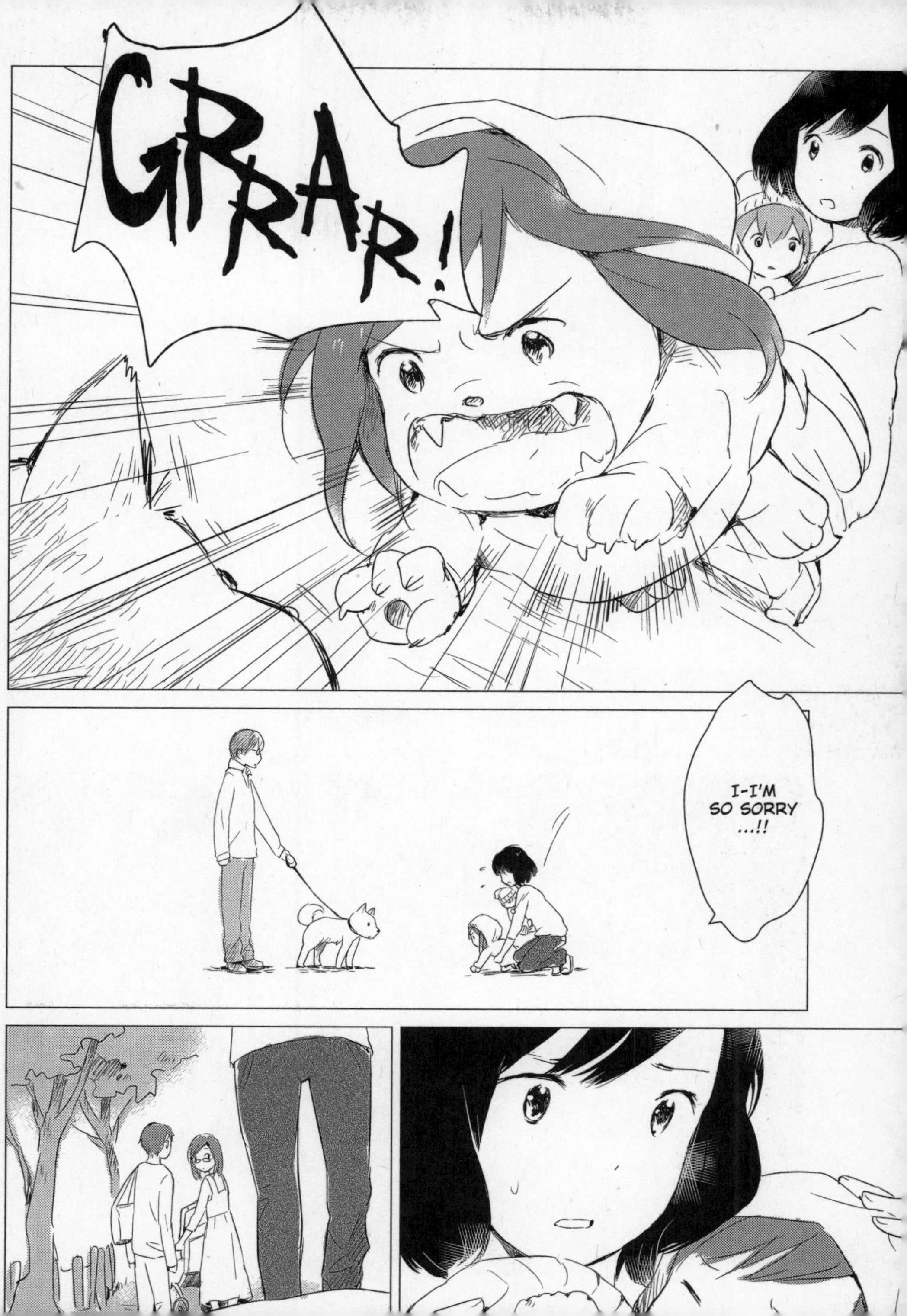
GRRAR!
I-I'M SO SORRY ...!!

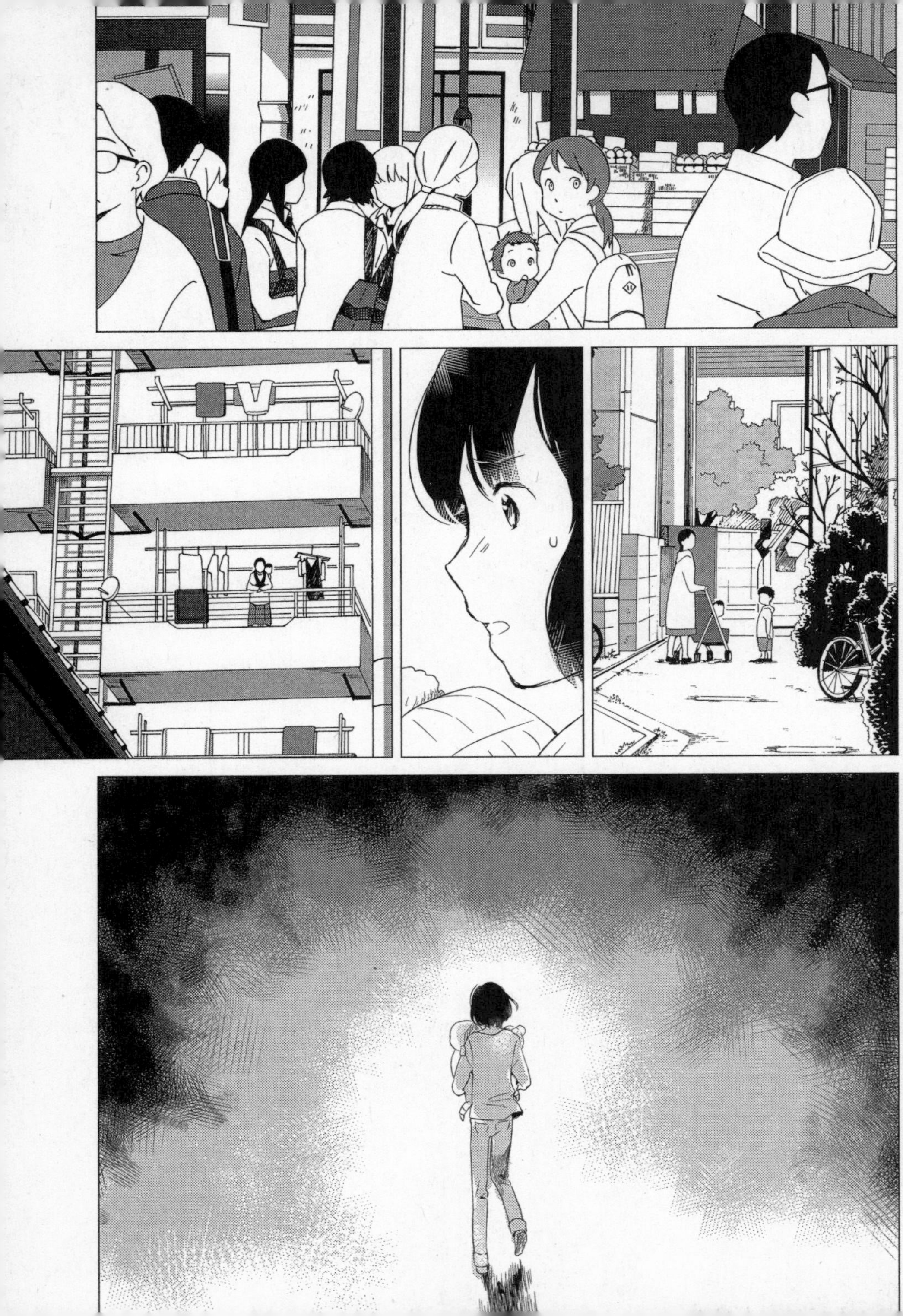

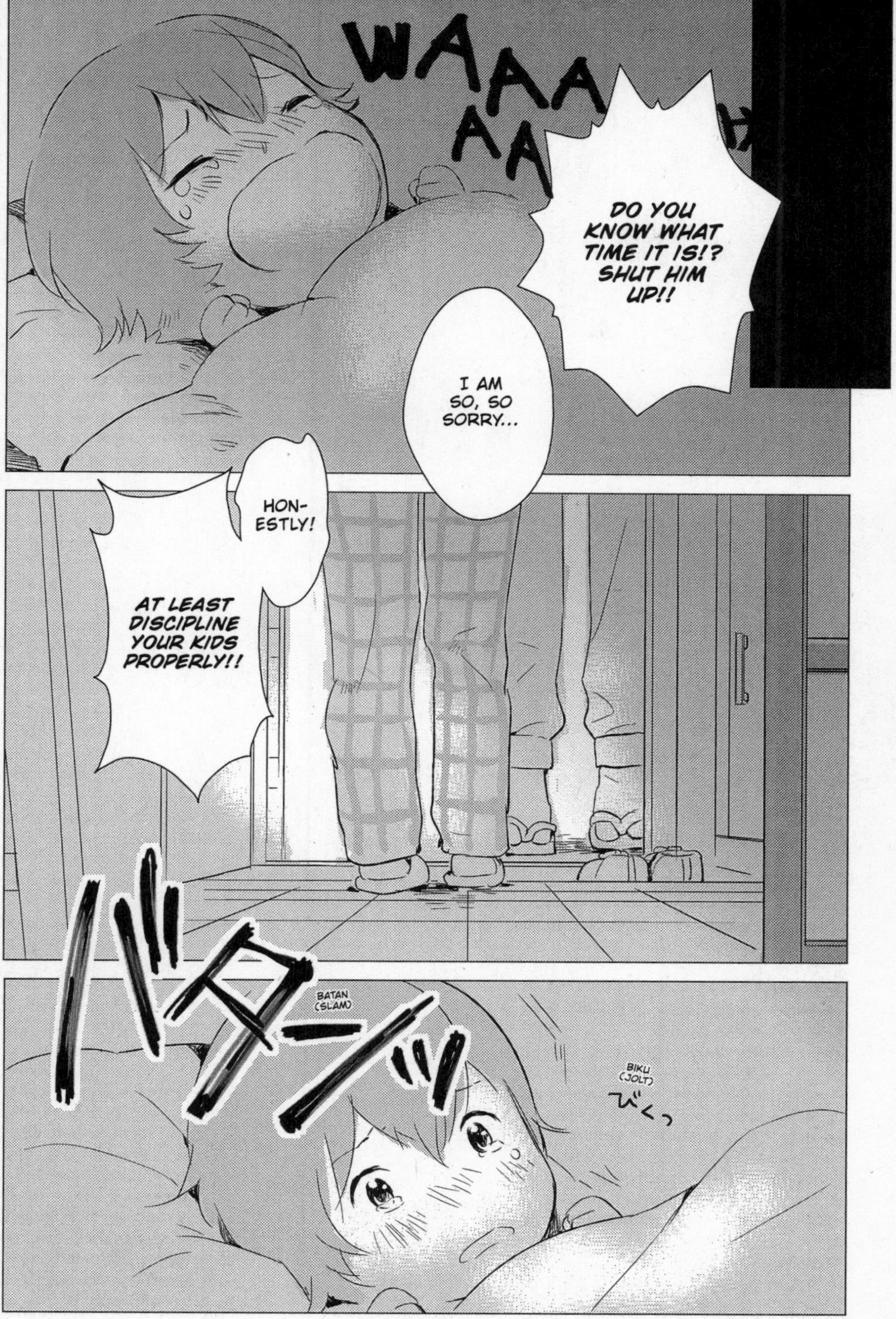
WAAAA
AAA
DO YOU KNOW WHAT TIME IT IS!? SHUT HIM UP!!
I AM SO, SO SORRY...
HON-ESTLY!
AT LEAST DISCIPLINE YOUR KIDS PROPERLY!!
バターンッ
BATAN (SLAM)
BIKU (JOLT)
びくっ

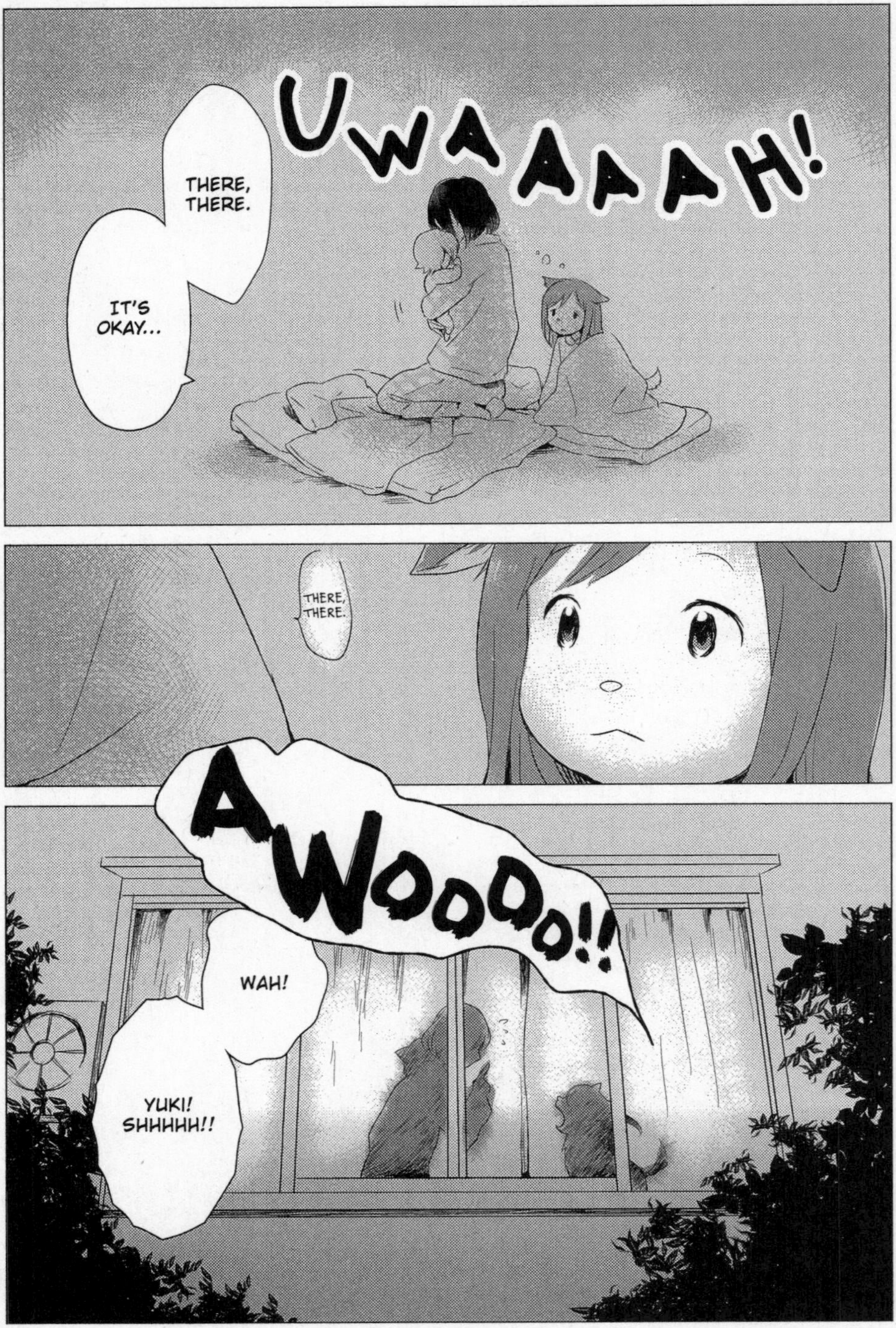
UWAAAAH!
THERE, THERE.
IT'S OKAY...
THERE, THERE.
AWOOOO!!
WAH!
YUKI! SHHHHH!!

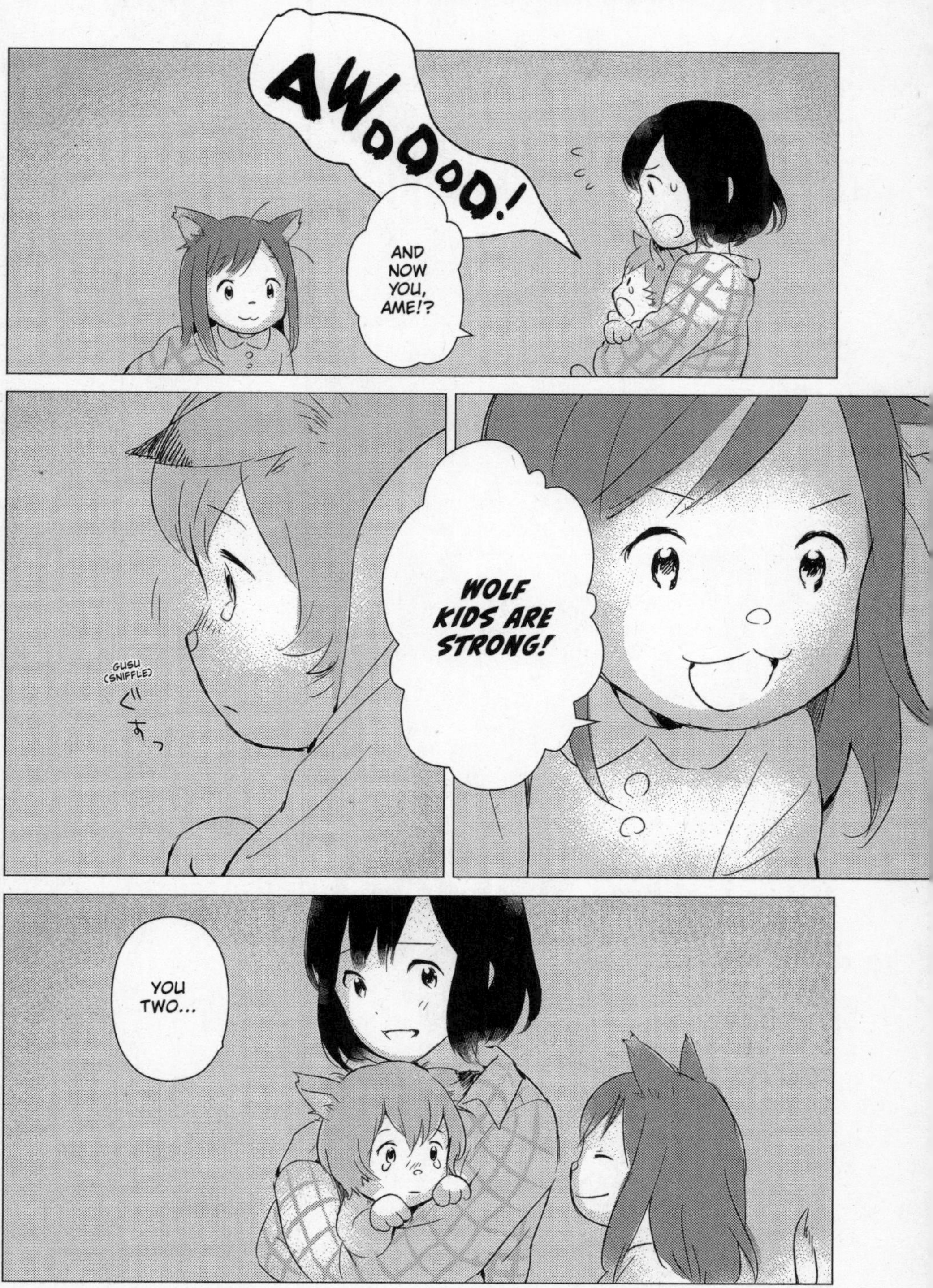
AWOOOOD!
AND NOW YOU, AME!?
WOLF KIDS ARE STRONG!
GUSU (SNIFFLE)
ぐすっ
YOU TWO...

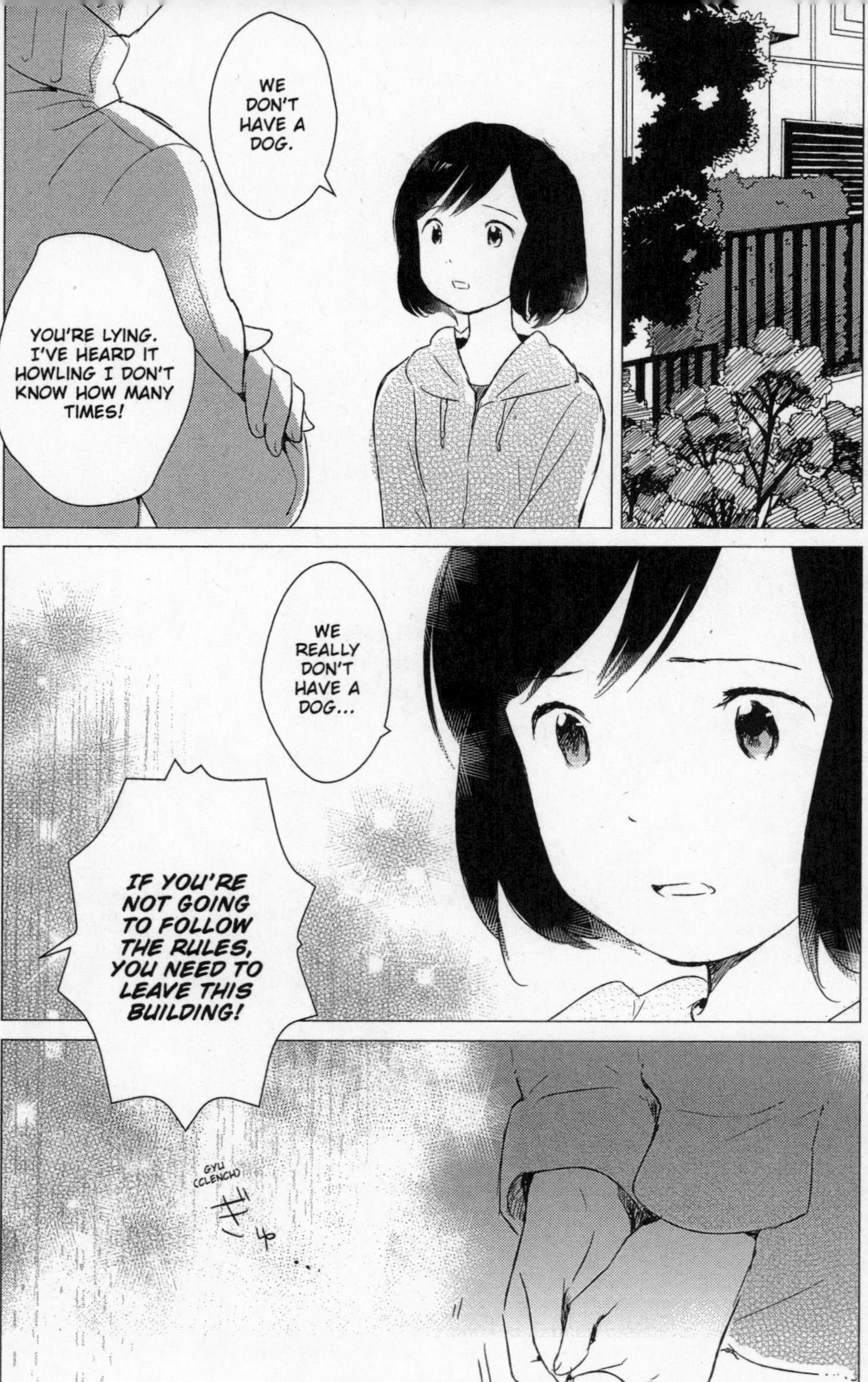
WE DON'T HAVE A DOG.
YOU'RE LYING. I'VE HEARD IT HOWLING I DON'T KNOW HOW MANY TIMES!
WE REALLY DON'T HAVE A DOG...
IF YOU'RE NOT GOING TO FOLLOW THE RULES, YOU NEED TO LEAVE THIS BUILDING!
GYU (CLENCH)

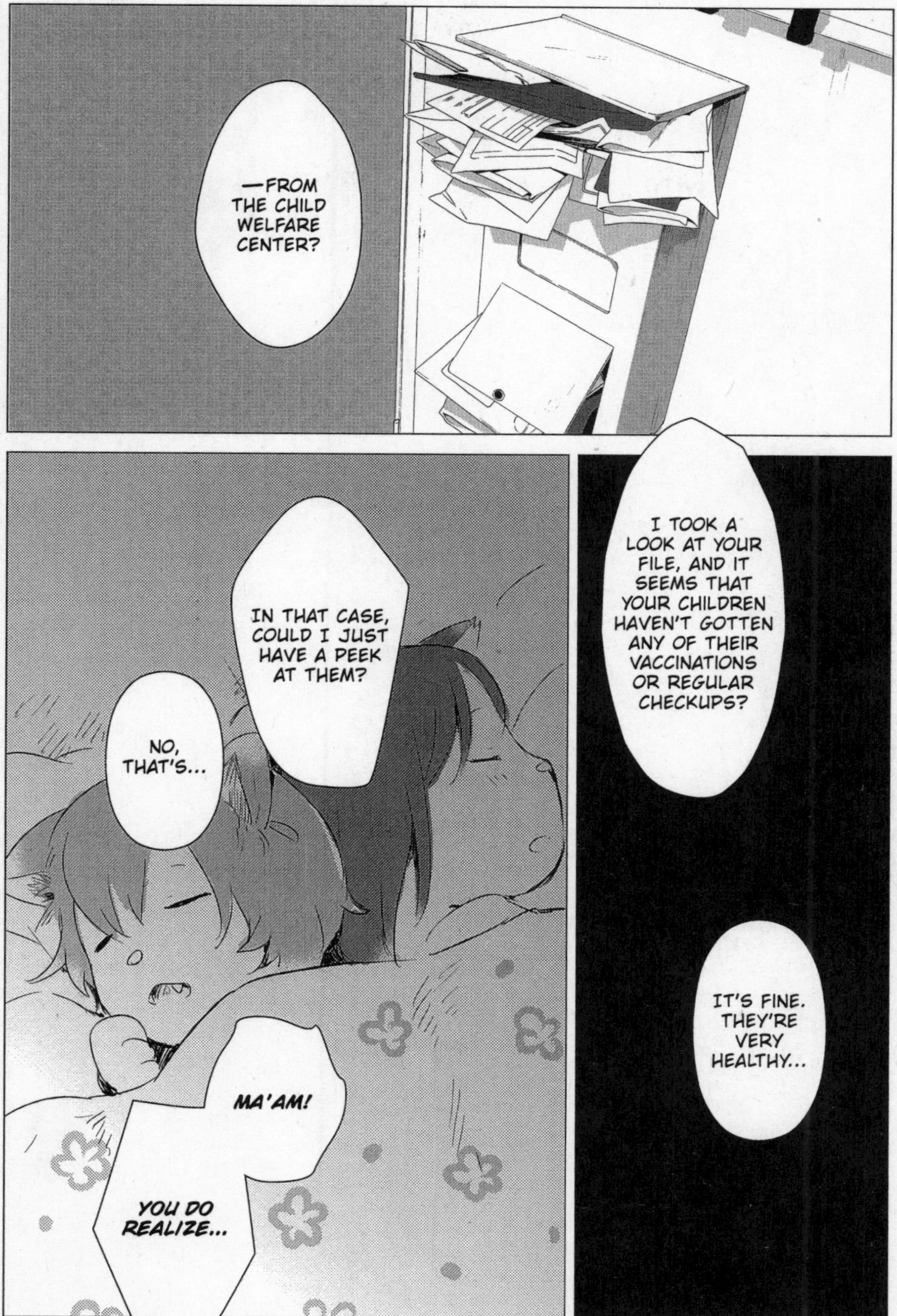
—FROM THE CHILD WELFARE CENTER?
I TOOK A LOOK AT YOUR FILE, AND IT SEEMS THAT YOUR CHILDREN HAVEN'T GOTTEN ANY OF THEIR VACCINATIONS OR REGULAR CHECKUPS?
IT'S FINE. THEY'RE VERY HEALTHY...
IN THAT CASE, COULD I JUST HAVE A PEEK AT THEM?
NO, THAT'S...
MA'AM!
YOU DO REALIZE...

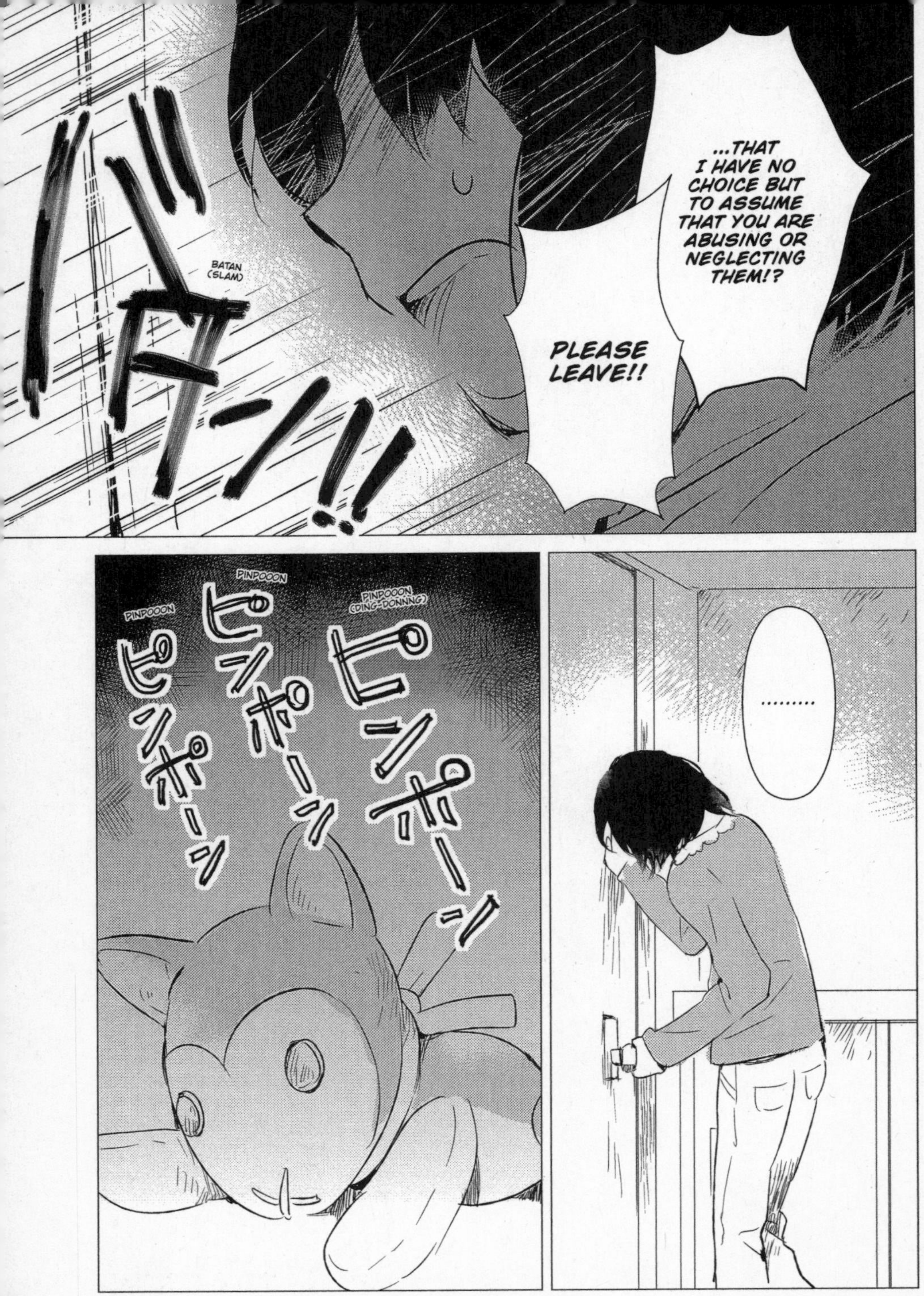
...THAT I HAVE NO CHOICE BUT TO ASSUME THAT YOU ARE ABUSING OR NEGLECTING THEM!?
PLEASE LEAVE!!
BATAN (SLAM)
バターン!!
....
PINPOOON (DING-DONNNG)
ピンポーン
PINPOOON
ピンポーン
PINPOOON
ピンポーン

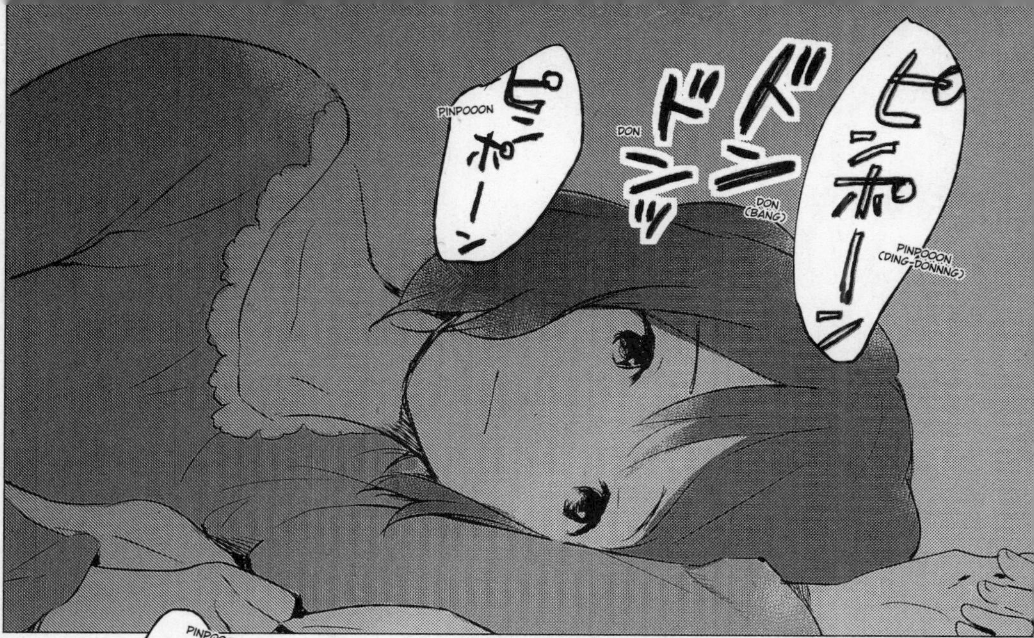
ピンポーン
PINPOOON
(DING-DONNNG)
ドンドンッ
DON
DON
(BANG)
ピンポーン
PINPOOON
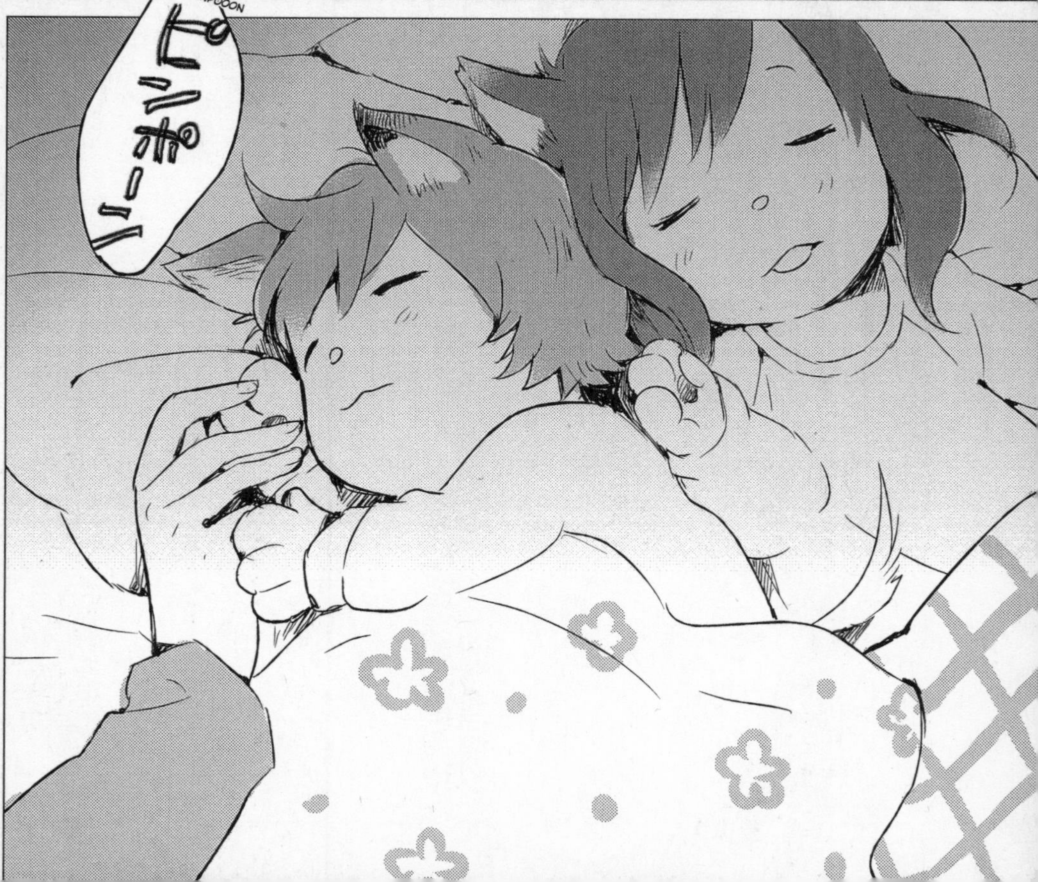
PINPOOON
ピンポーン

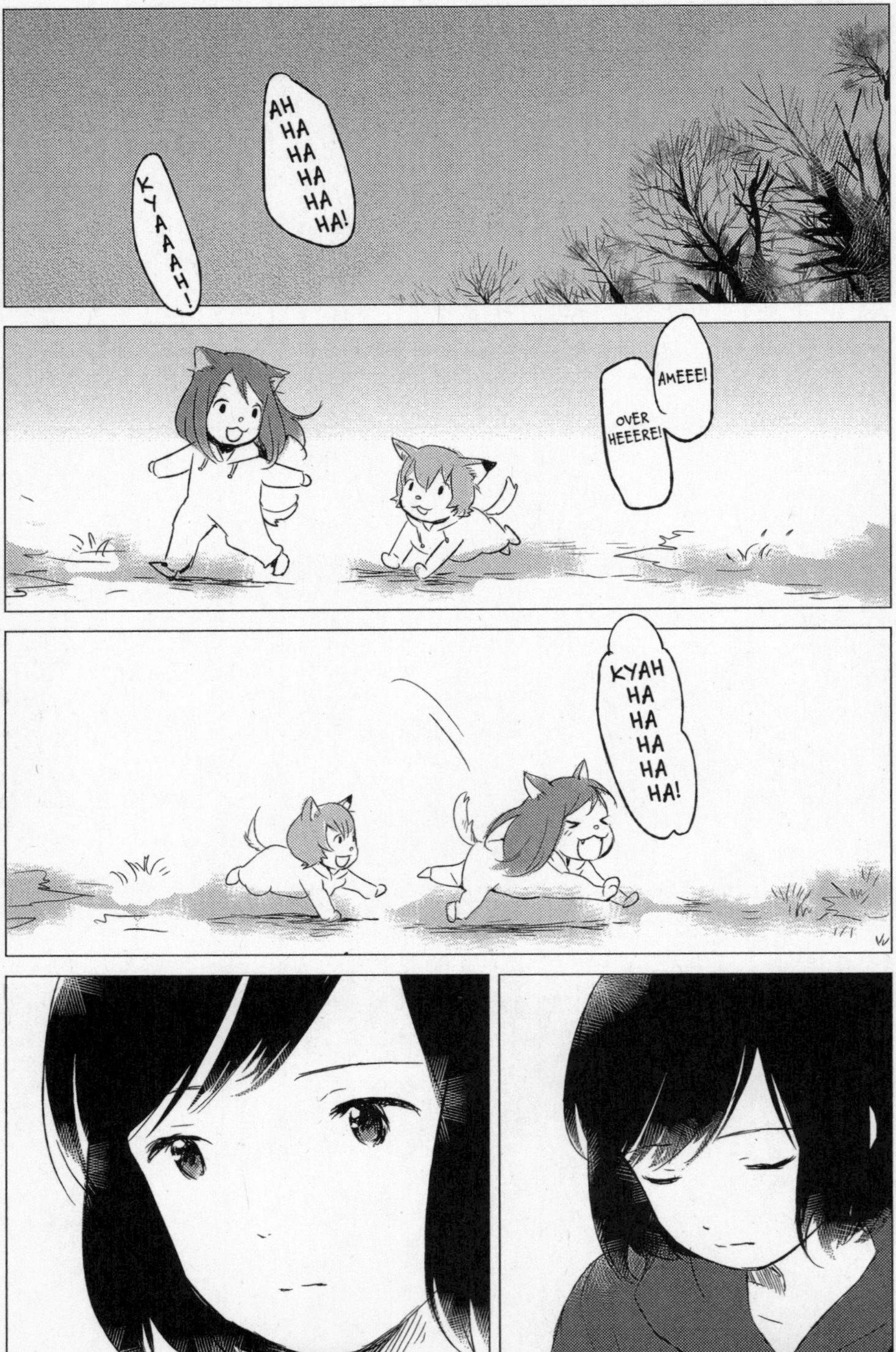
AH HA HA HA HA HA!
KYAAAAH!
AMEEE!
OVER HEEERE!
KYAH HA HA HA HA HA!

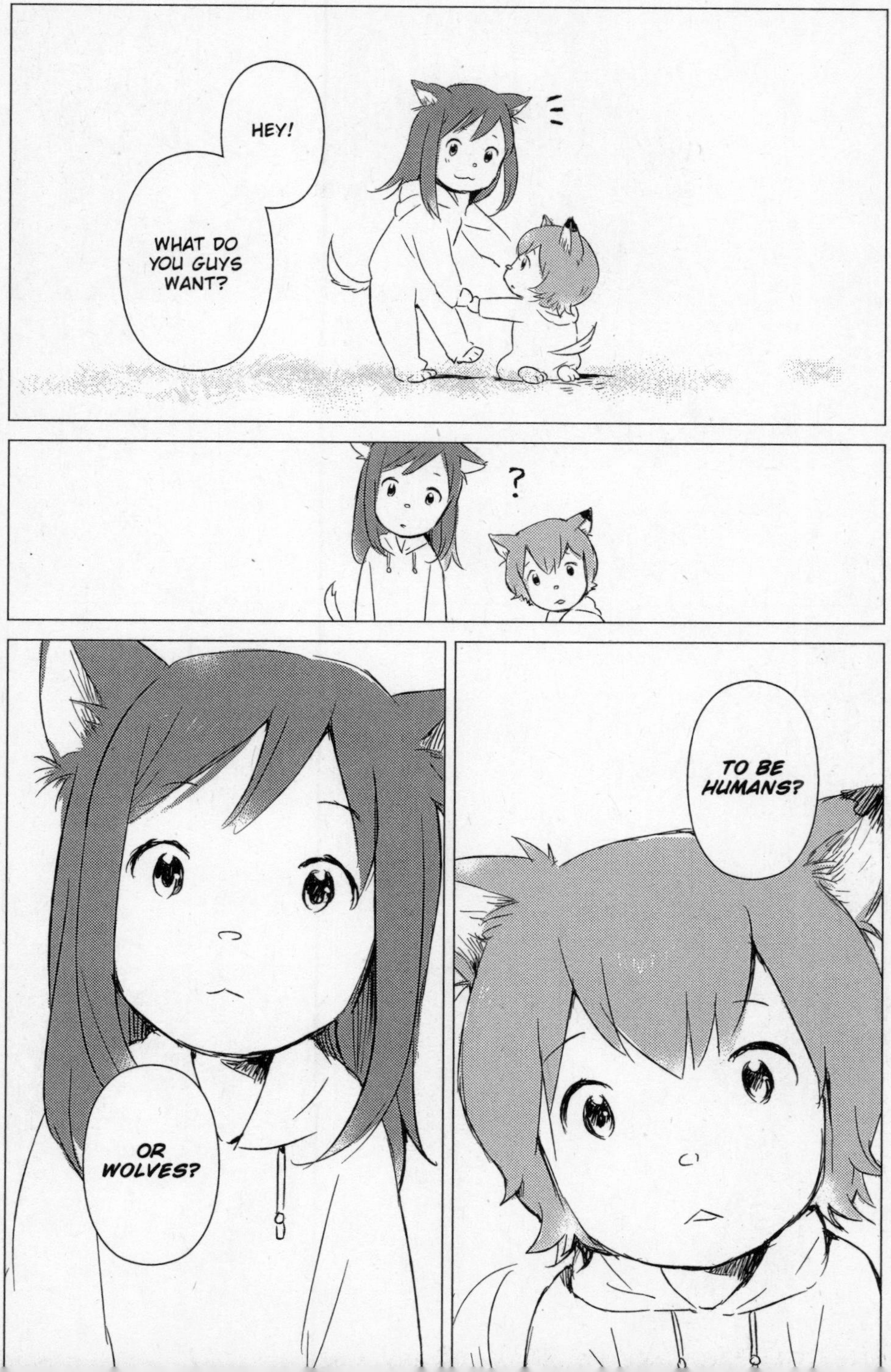
HEY!
WHAT DO YOU GUYS WANT?
?
TO BE HUMANS?
OR WOLVES?

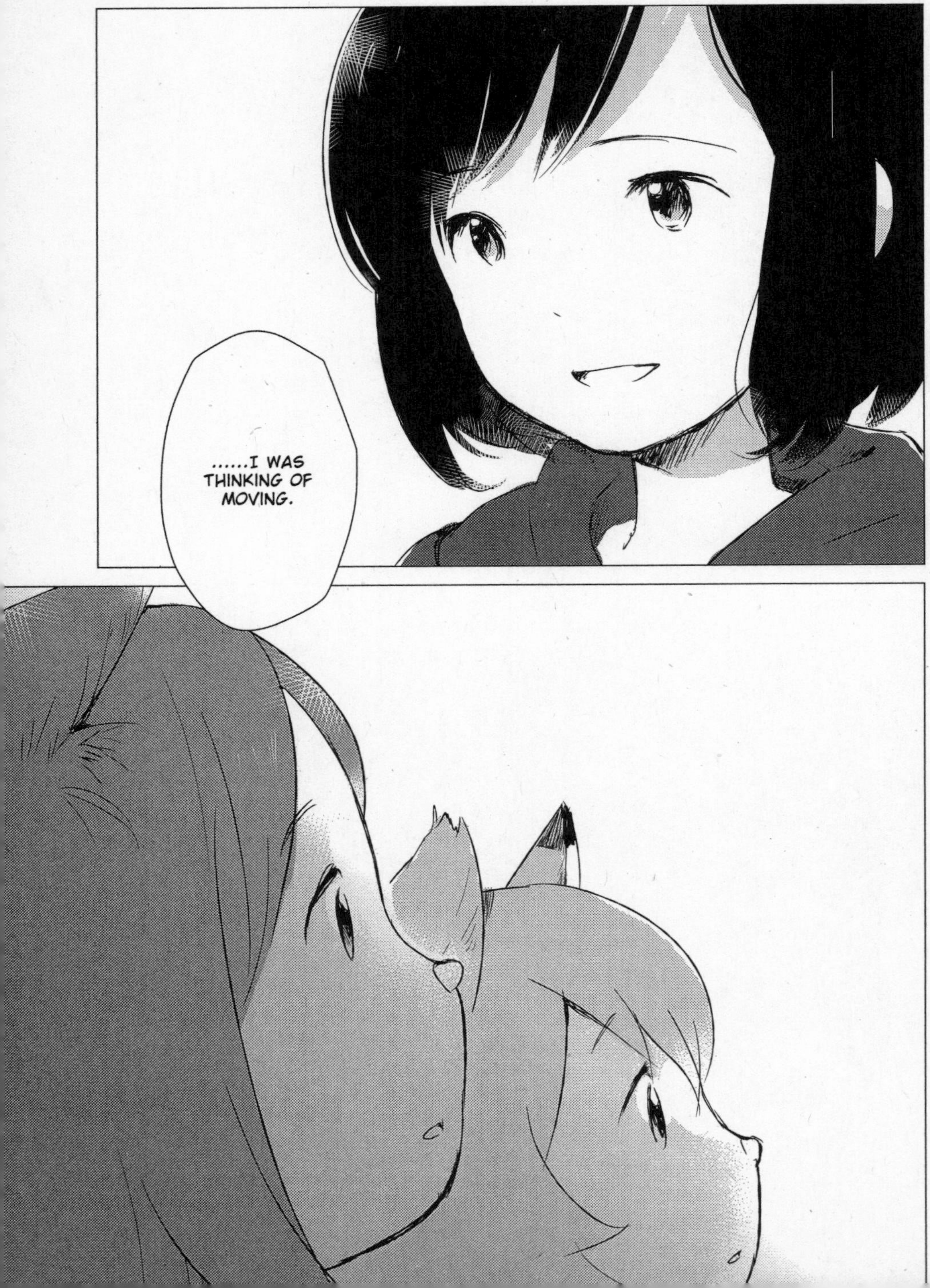
......I WAS THINKING OF MOVING.

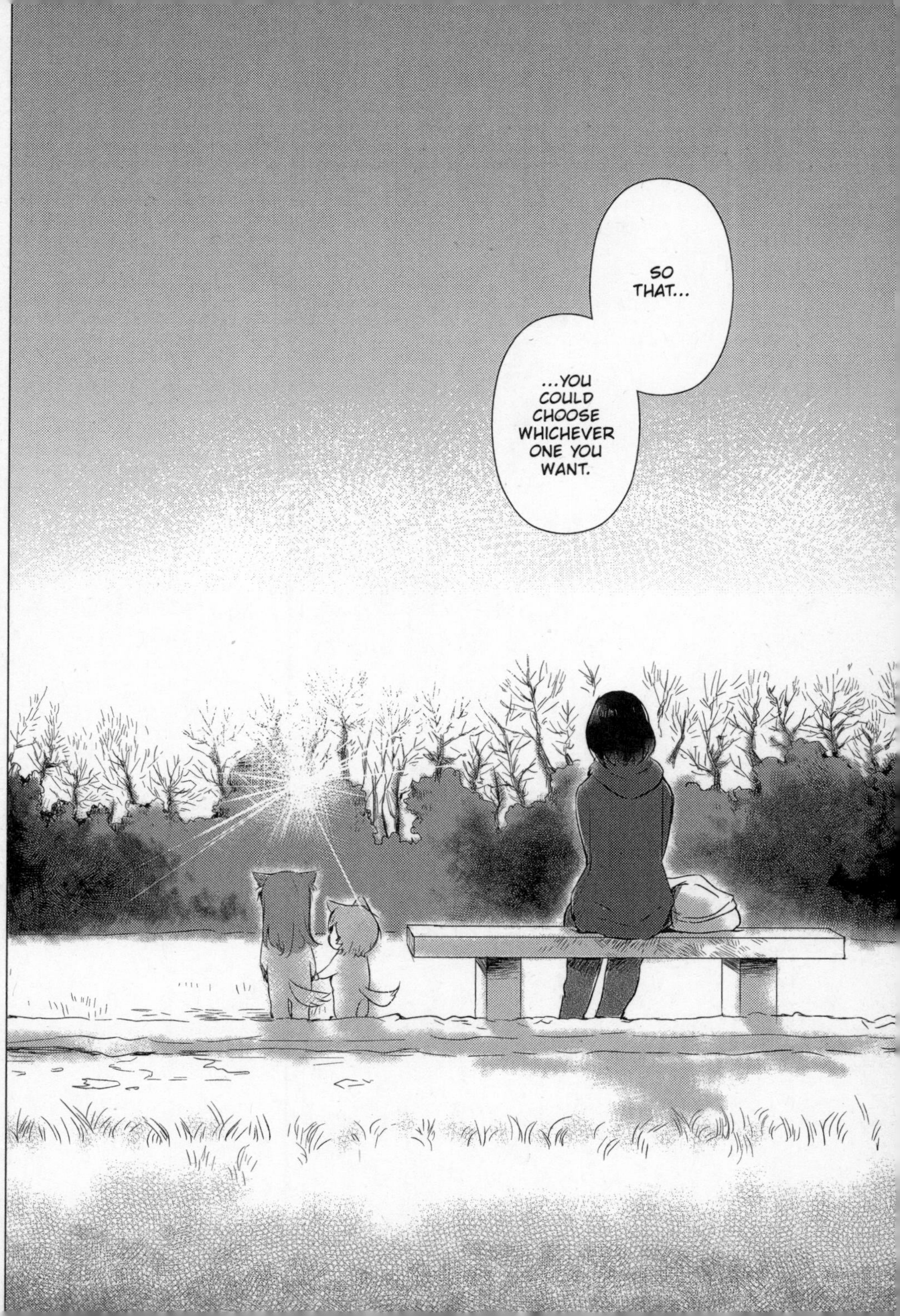
SO THAT...
...YOU COULD CHOOSE WHICHEVER ONE YOU WANT.

Wolf Children
Ame & Yuki

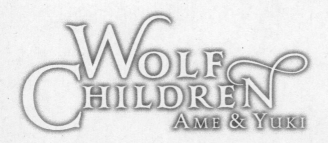

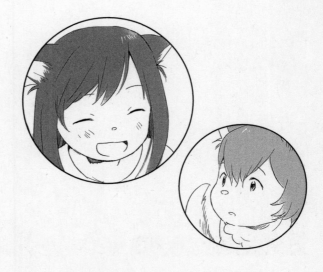

Chapter 4 The Middle of Nowhere

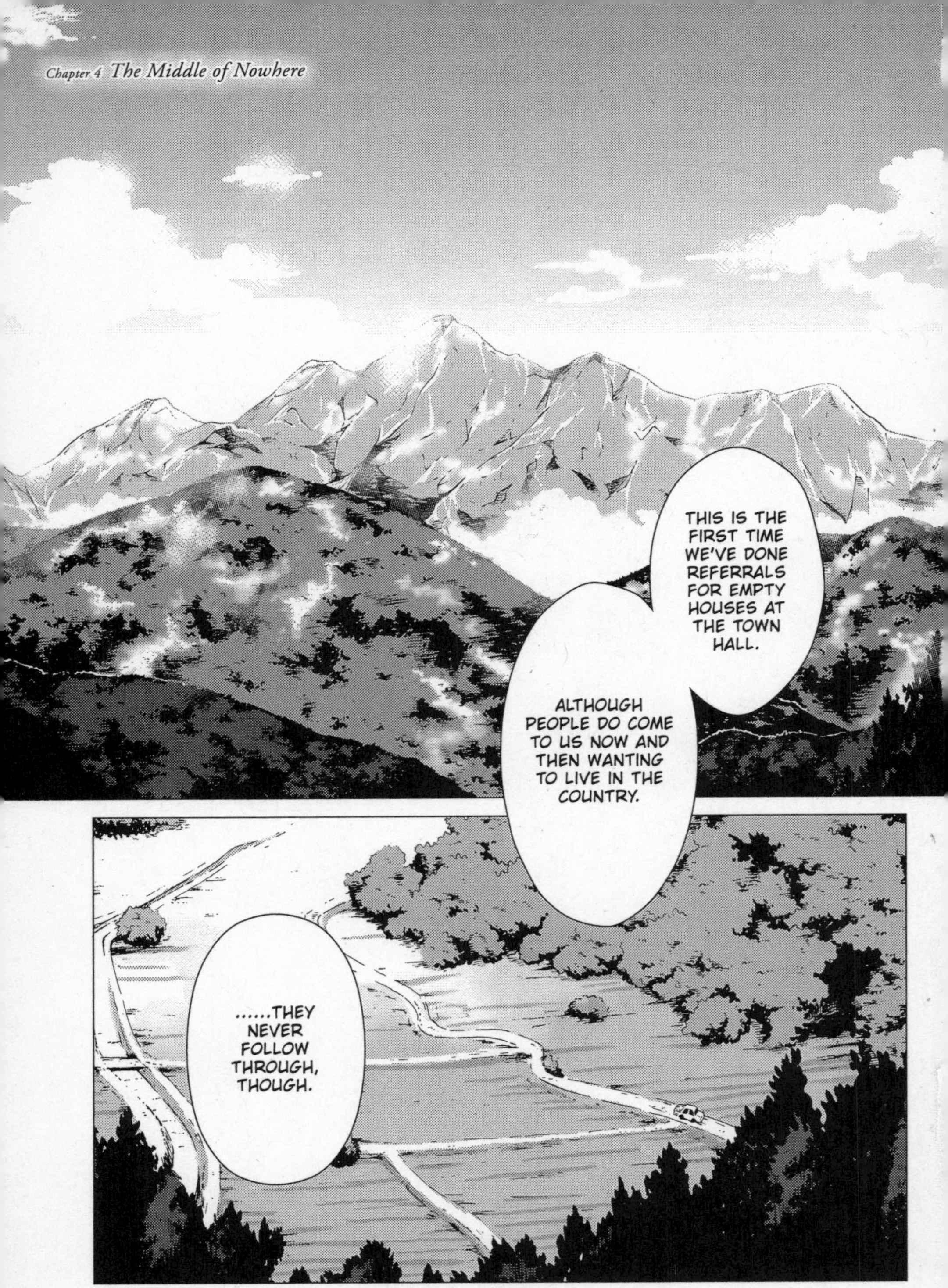
THIS IS THE FIRST TIME WE'VE DONE REFERRALS FOR EMPTY HOUSES AT THE TOWN HALL.
ALTHOUGH PEOPLE DO COME TO US NOW AND THEN WANTING TO LIVE IN THE COUNTRY.
......THEY NEVER FOLLOW THROUGH, THOUGH.

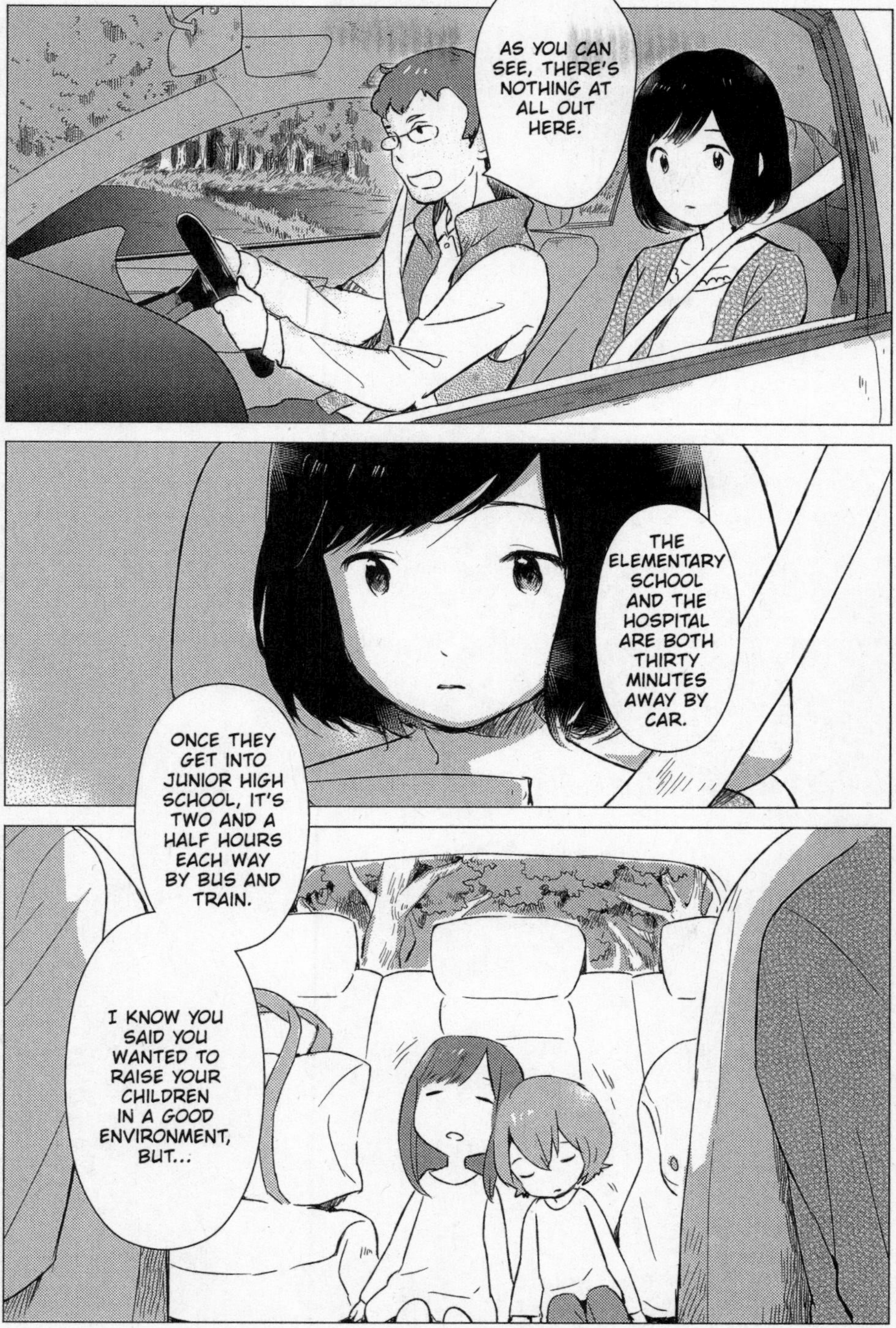
AS YOU CAN SEE, THERE'S NOTHING AT ALL OUT HERE.
THE ELEMENTARY SCHOOL AND THE HOSPITAL ARE BOTH THIRTY MINUTES AWAY BY CAR.
ONCE THEY GET INTO JUNIOR HIGH SCHOOL, IT'S TWO AND A HALF HOURS EACH WAY BY BUS AND TRAIN.
I KNOW YOU SAID YOU WANTED TO RAISE YOUR CHILDREN IN A GOOD ENVIRONMENT, BUT...

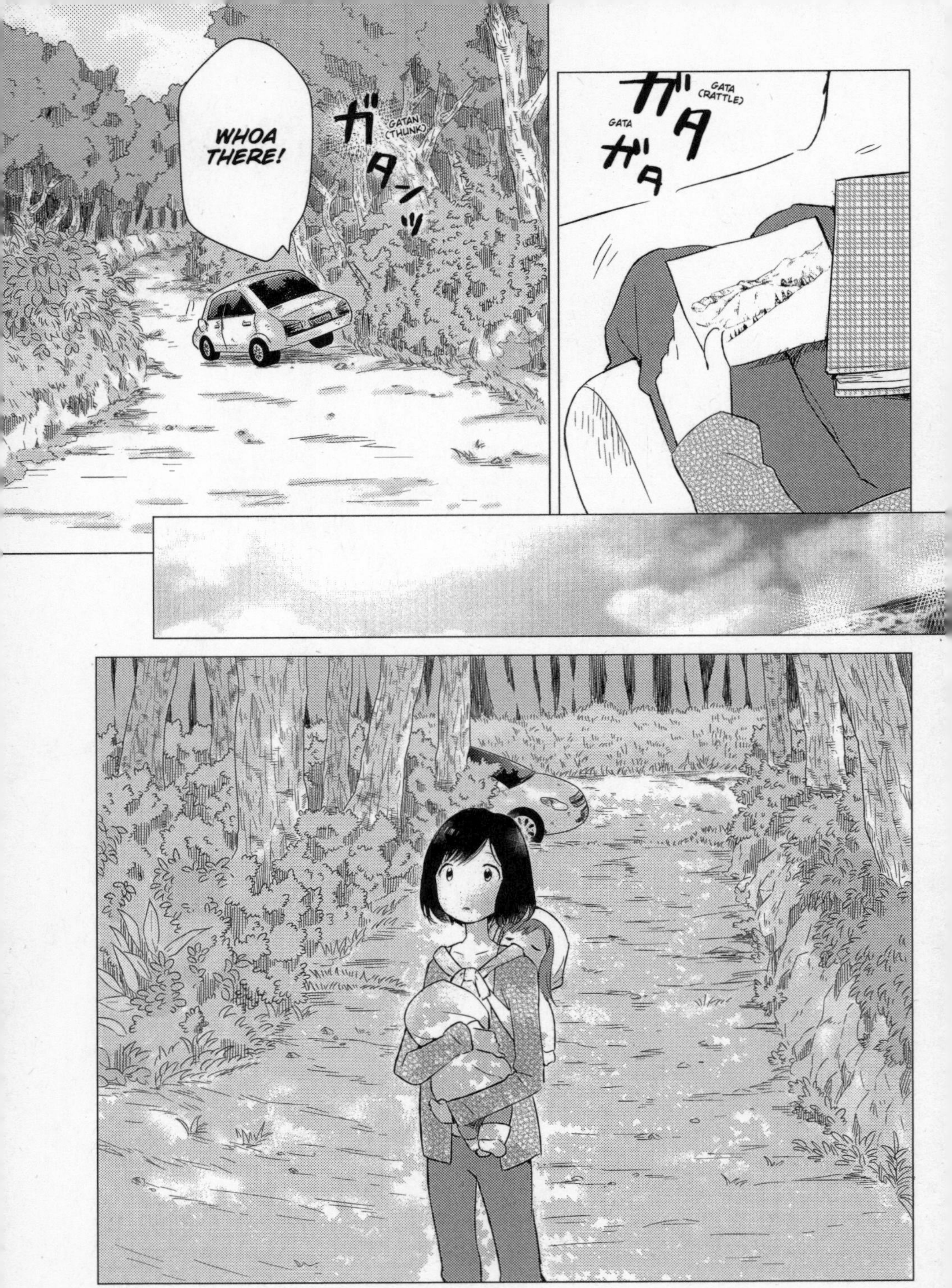
ガタ
GATA (RATTLE)
ガタ
GATA
WHOA THERE!
ガタンッ
GATAN (THUNK)

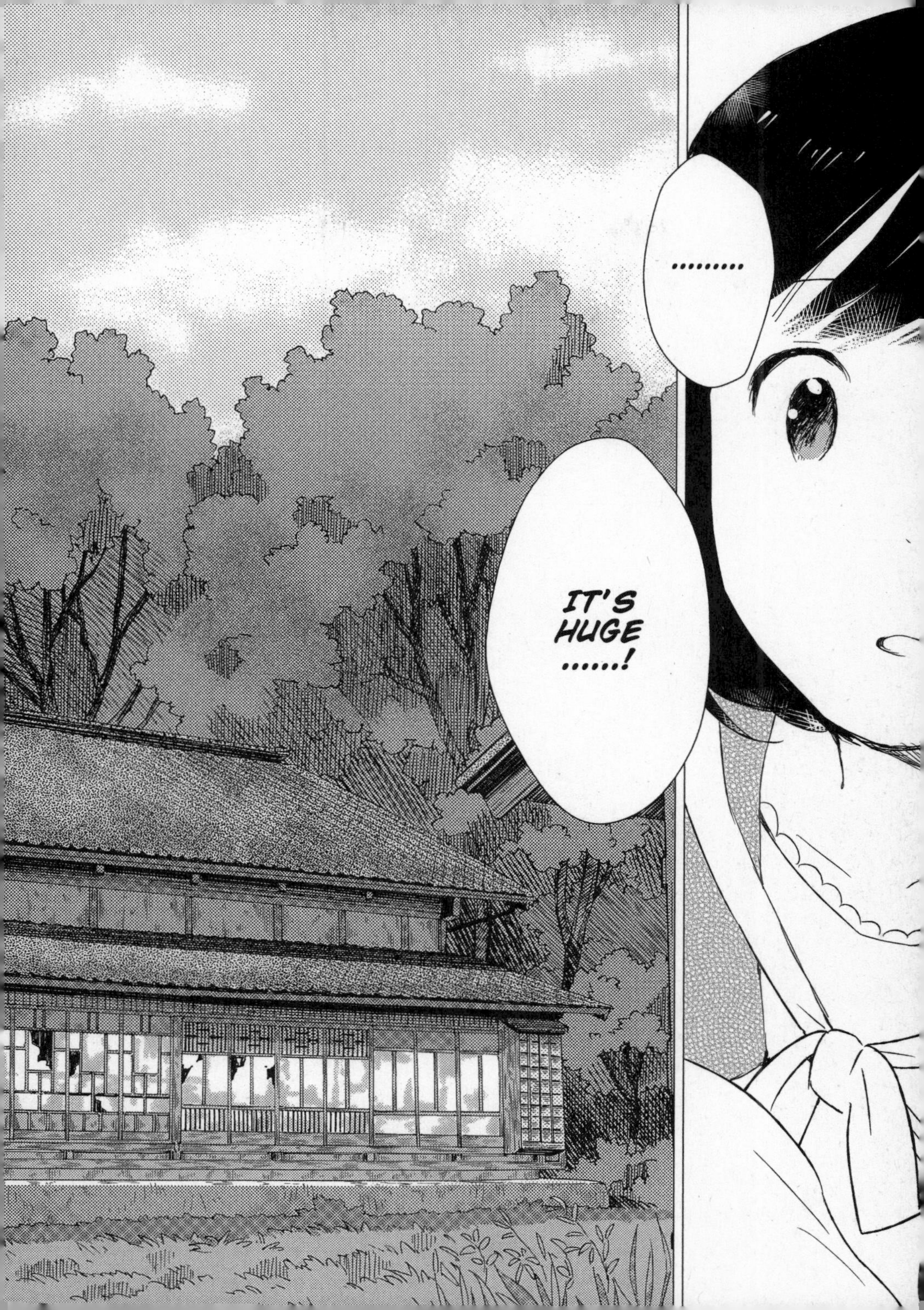
....
IT'S HUGE ......!

Chapter 4 The Middle of Nowhere

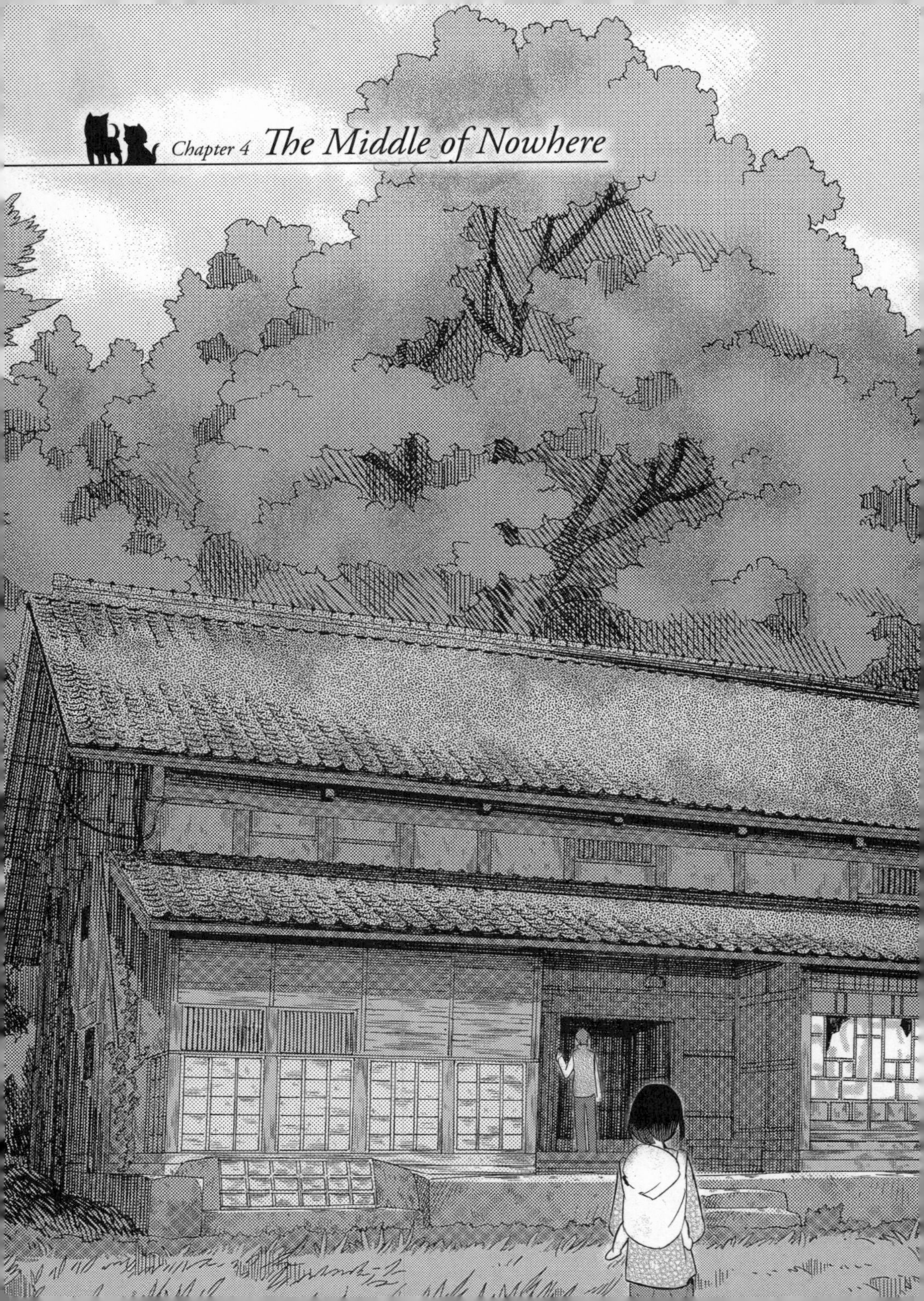

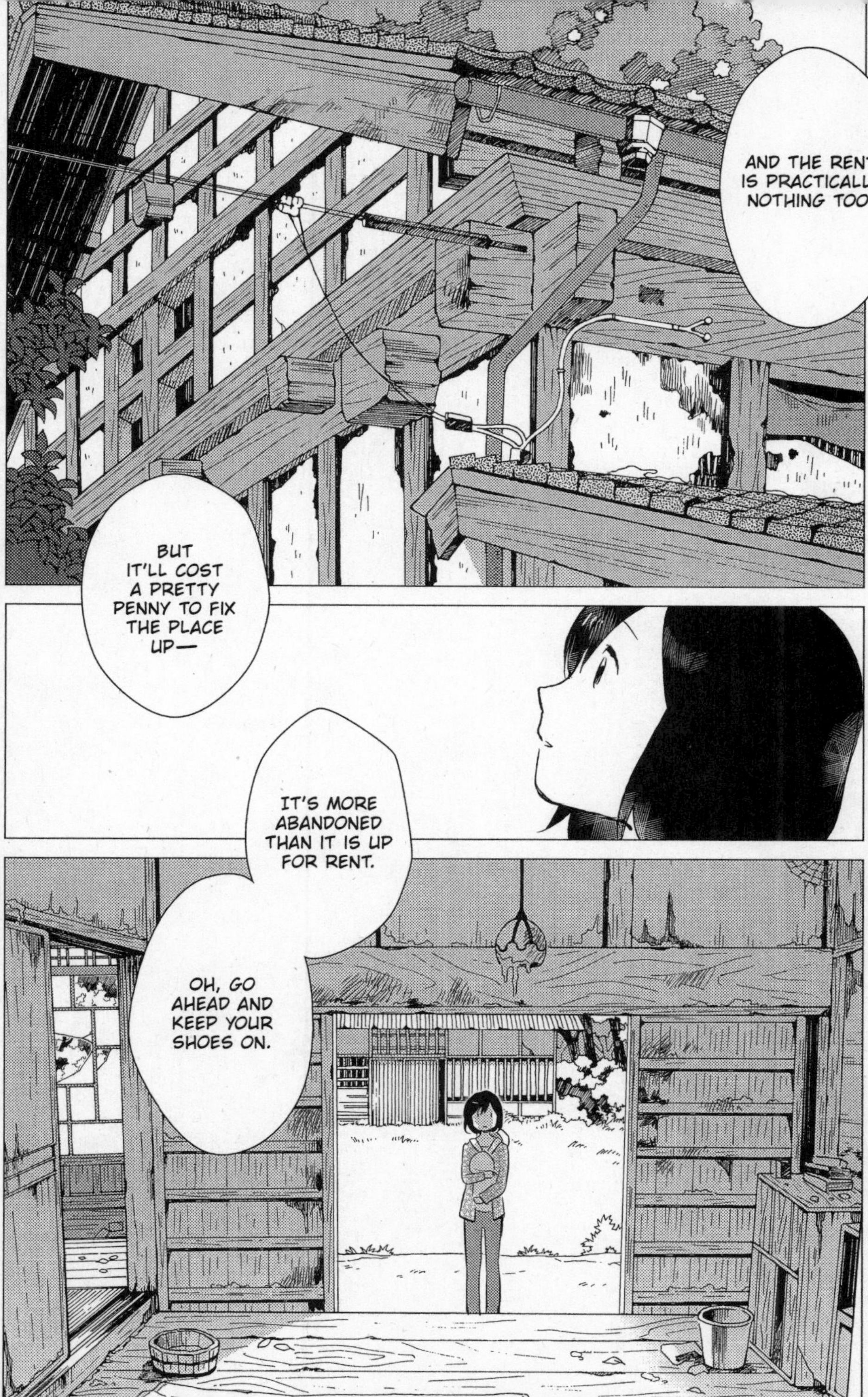
AND THE RENT IS PRACTICALLY NOTHING TOO.
BUT IT'LL COST A PRETTY PENNY TO FIX THE PLACE UP—
IT'S MORE ABANDONED THAN IT IS UP FOR RENT.
OH, GO AHEAD AND KEEP YOUR SHOES ON.

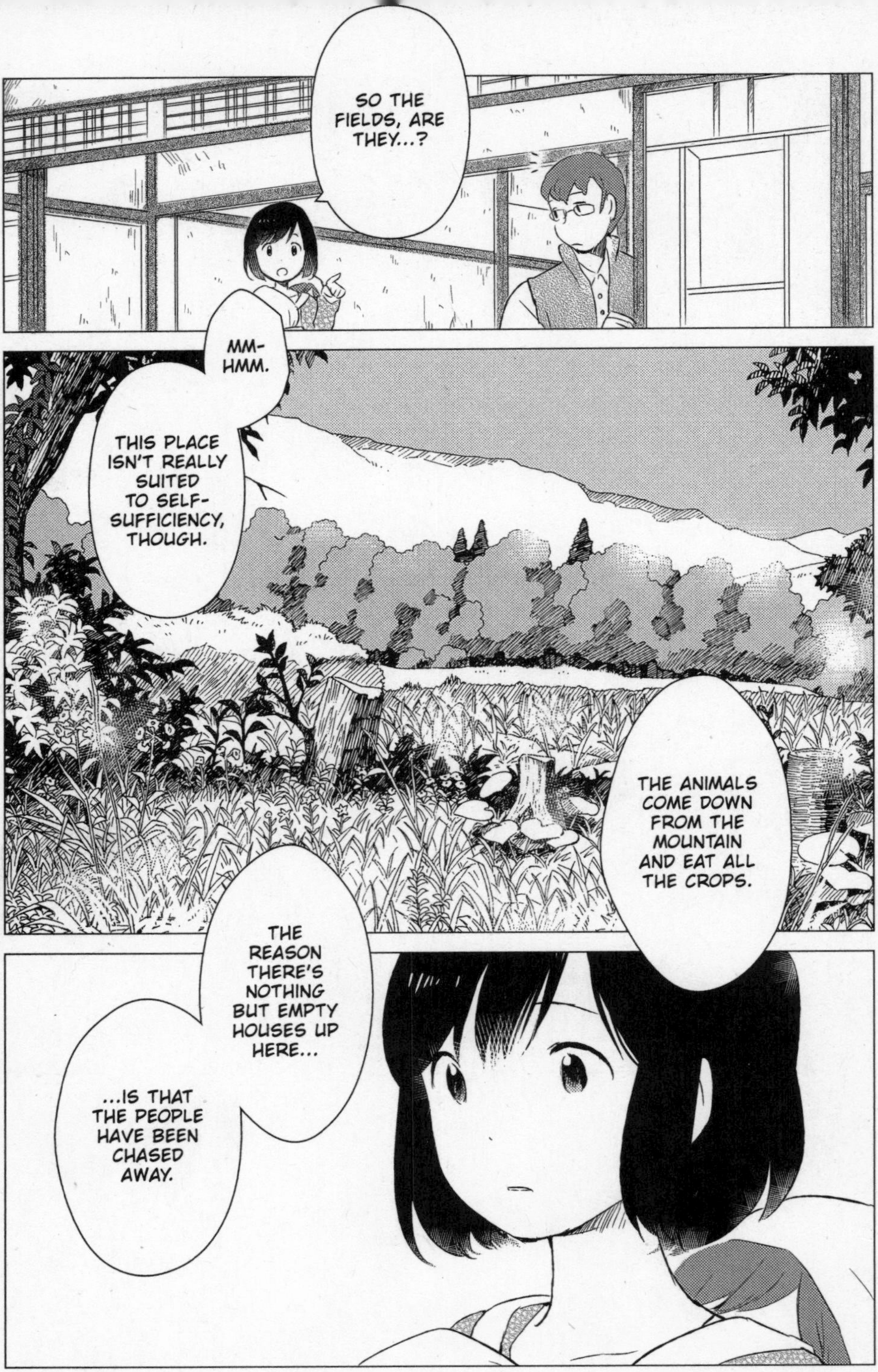
SO THE FIELDS, ARE THEY...?
MM-HMM.
THIS PLACE ISN'T REALLY SUITED TO SELF-SUFFICIENCY, THOUGH.
THE ANIMALS COME DOWN FROM THE MOUNTAIN AND EAT ALL THE CROPS.
THE REASON THERE'S NOTHING BUT EMPTY HOUSES UP HERE...
...IS THAT THE PEOPLE HAVE BEEN CHASED AWAY.

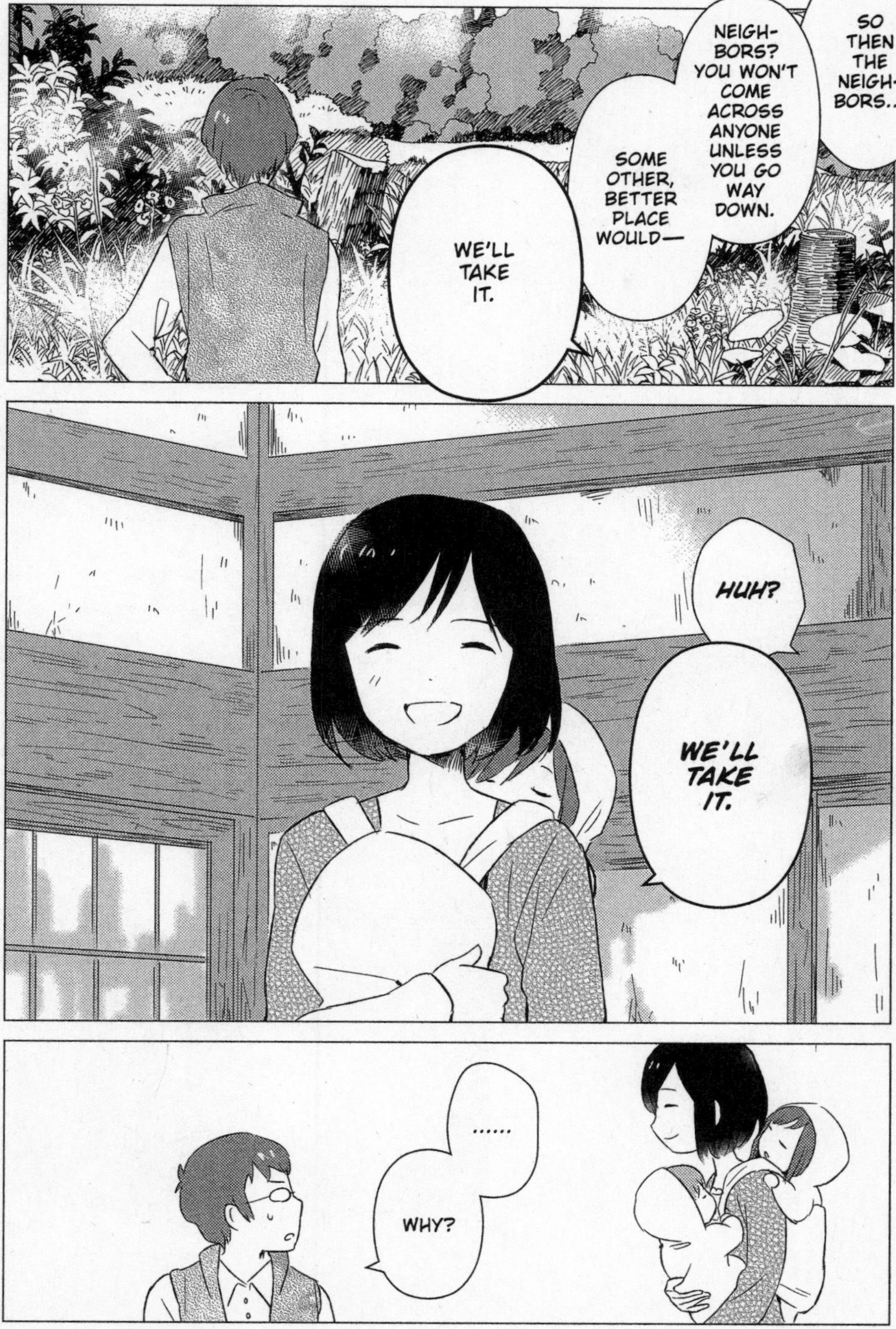
SO THEN THE NEIGH-BORS...
NEIGH-BORS? YOU WON'T COME ACROSS ANYONE UNLESS YOU GO WAY DOWN.
SOME OTHER, BETTER PLACE WOULD—
WE'LL TAKE IT.
HUH?
WE'LL TAKE IT.
......
WHY?

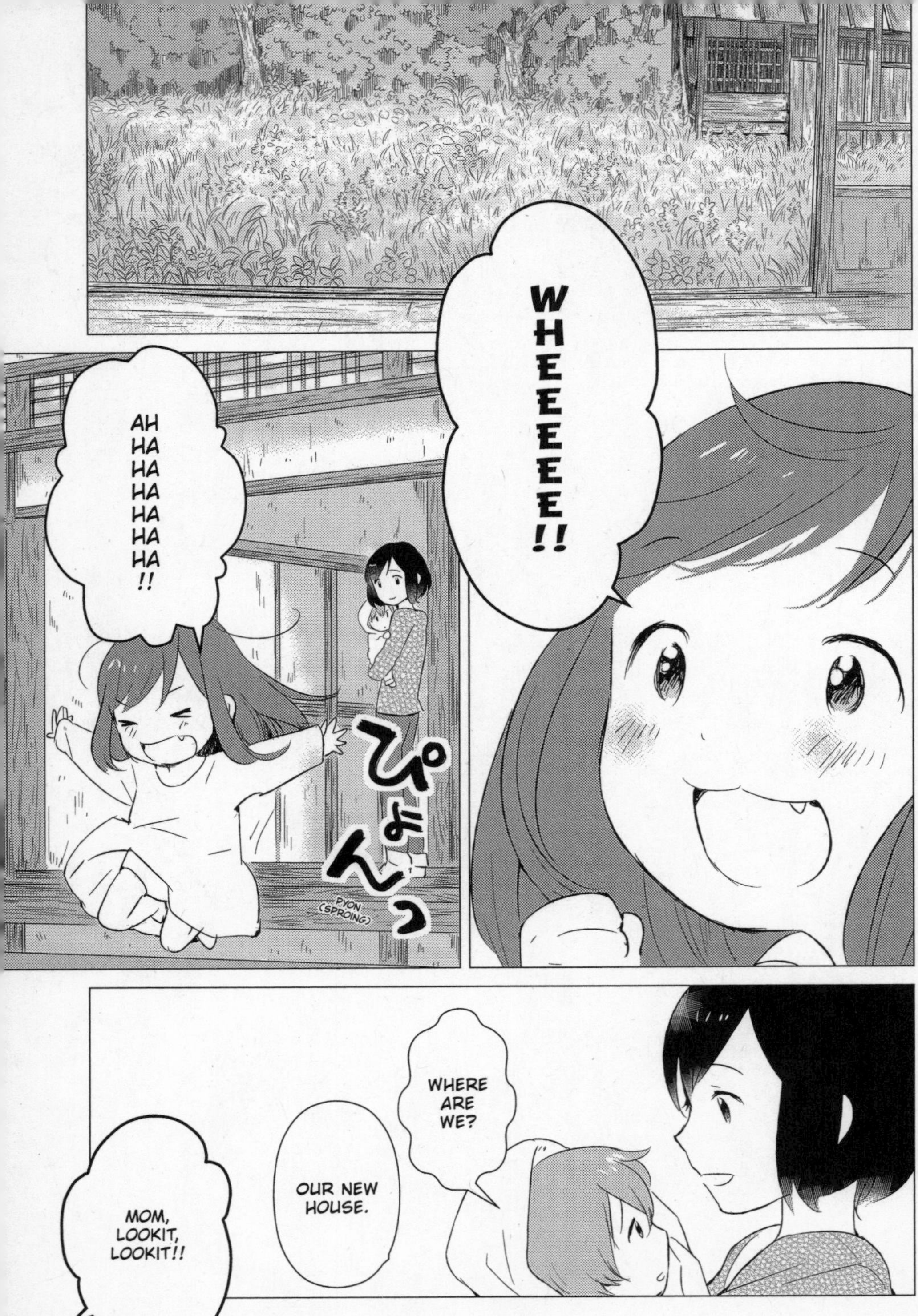
WHEEEEEE!!
AH HA HA HA HA HA HA!!
ぴょんっ
PYON (SPROING)
WHERE ARE WE?
OUR NEW HOUSE.
MOM, LOOKIT, LOOKIT!!

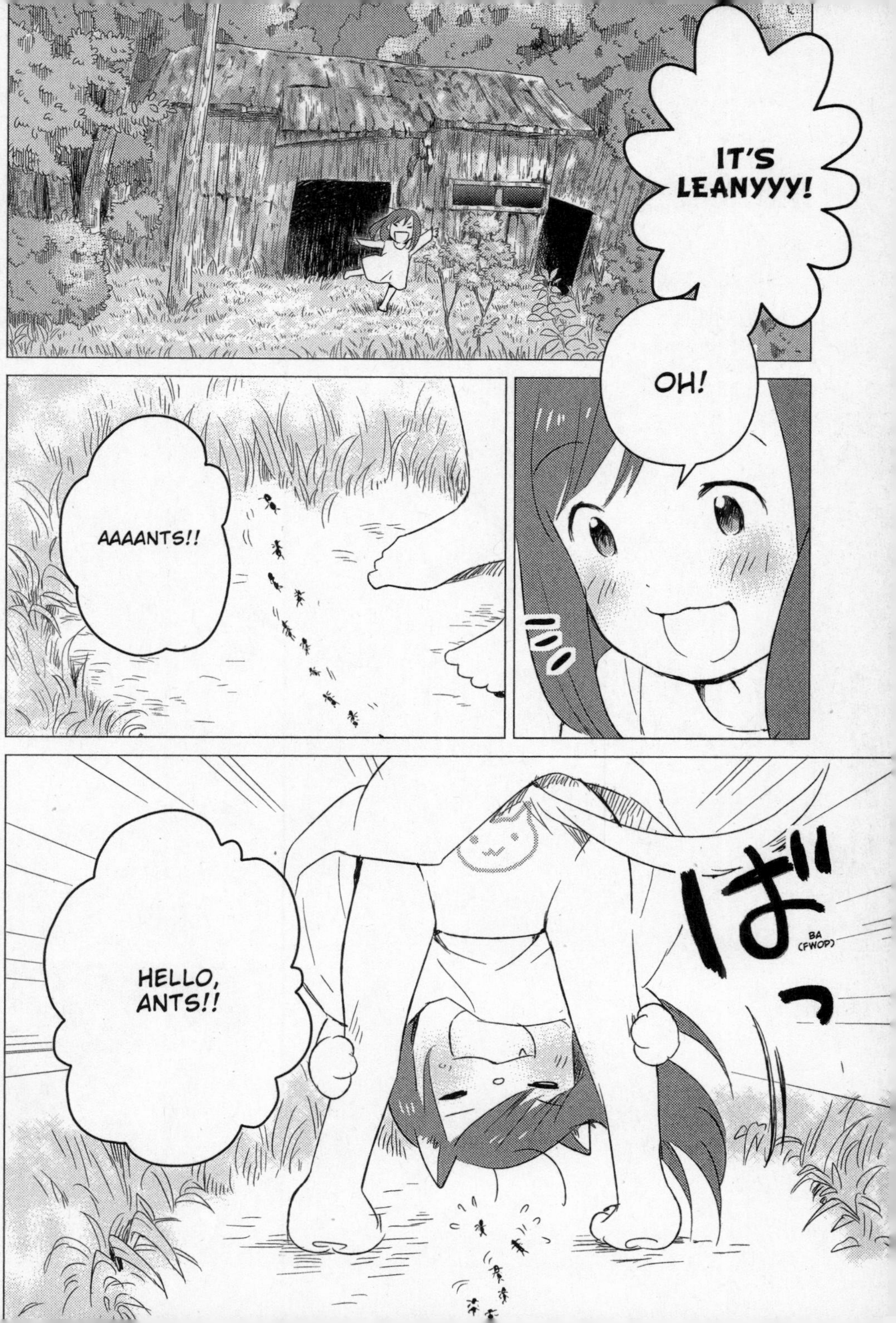
IT'S LEANYYY!
OH!
AAAANTS!!
ぱっ
BA (FWOP)
HELLO, ANTS!!

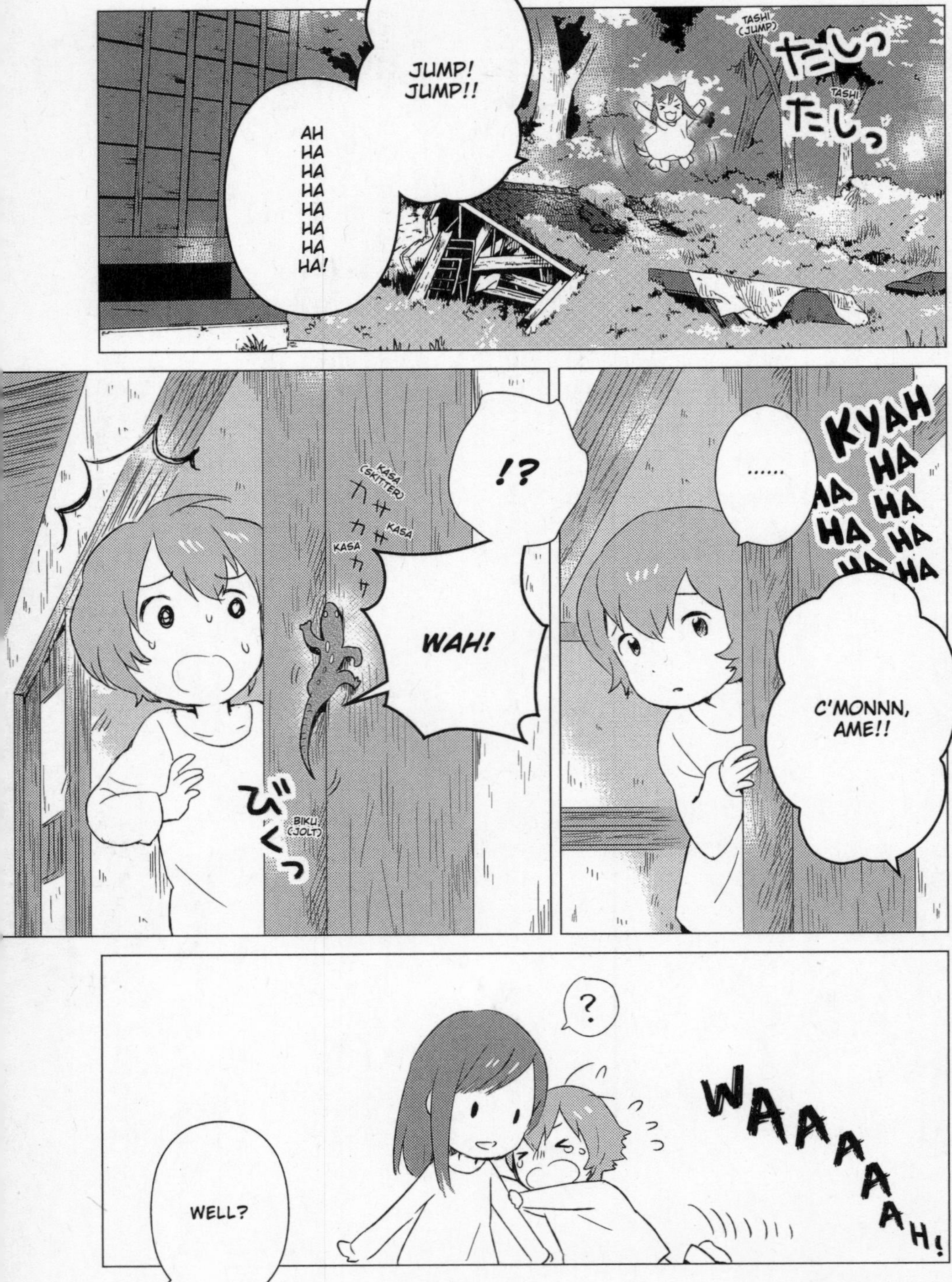
TASHI (JUMP)
たしっ
TASHI
たしっ
JUMP! JUMP!!
AH HA HA HA HA HA HA HA HA!
KYAH HA HA HA HA HA HA HA HA HA
......
C'MONNN, AME!!
!?
KASA (SKITTER)
カサ
KASA
カサ
KASA
カサ
WAH!
びくっ
BIKU (JOLT)
?
WAAAAAAAH!
WELL?

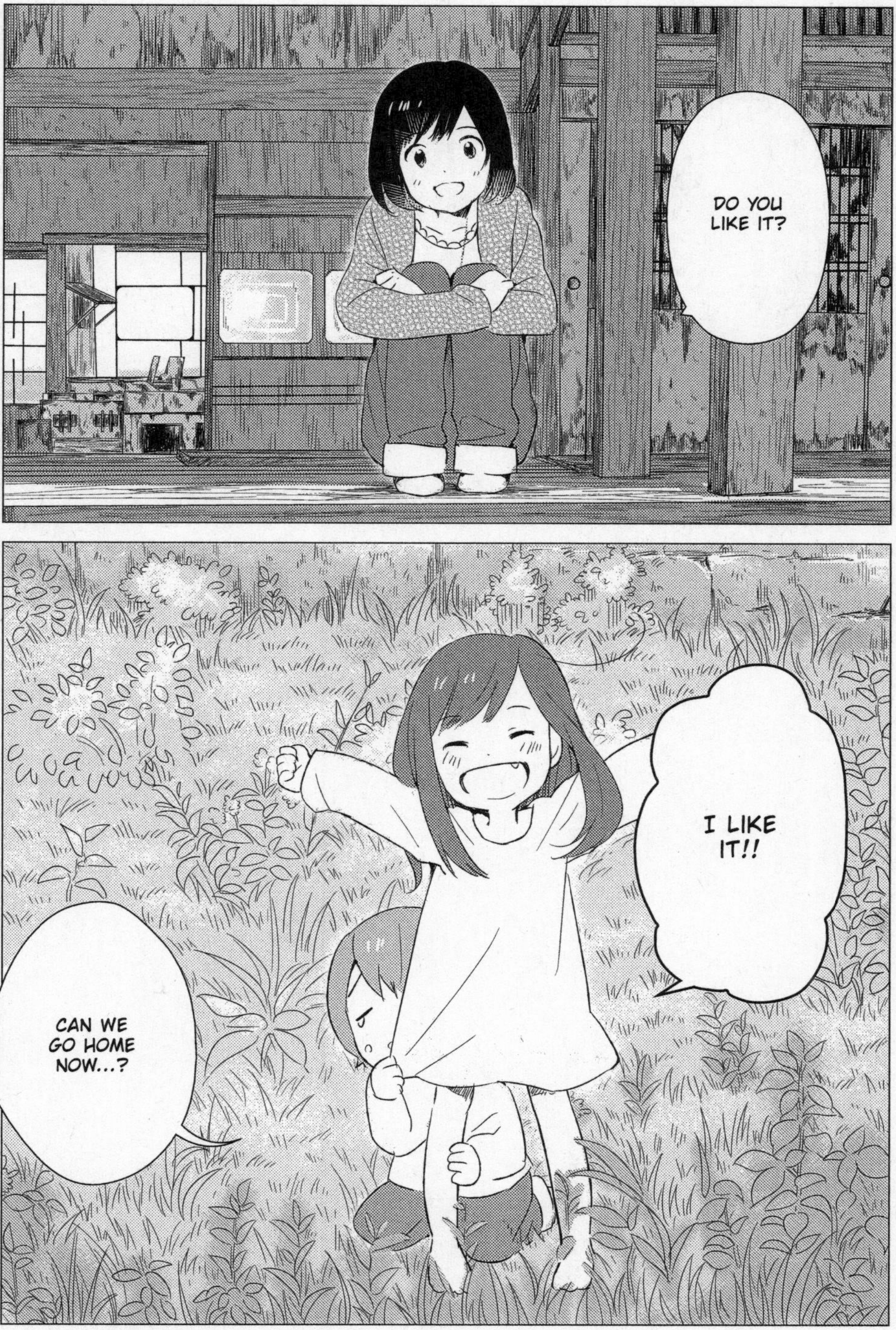
DO YOU LIKE IT?
I LIKE IT!!
CAN WE GO HOME NOW...?

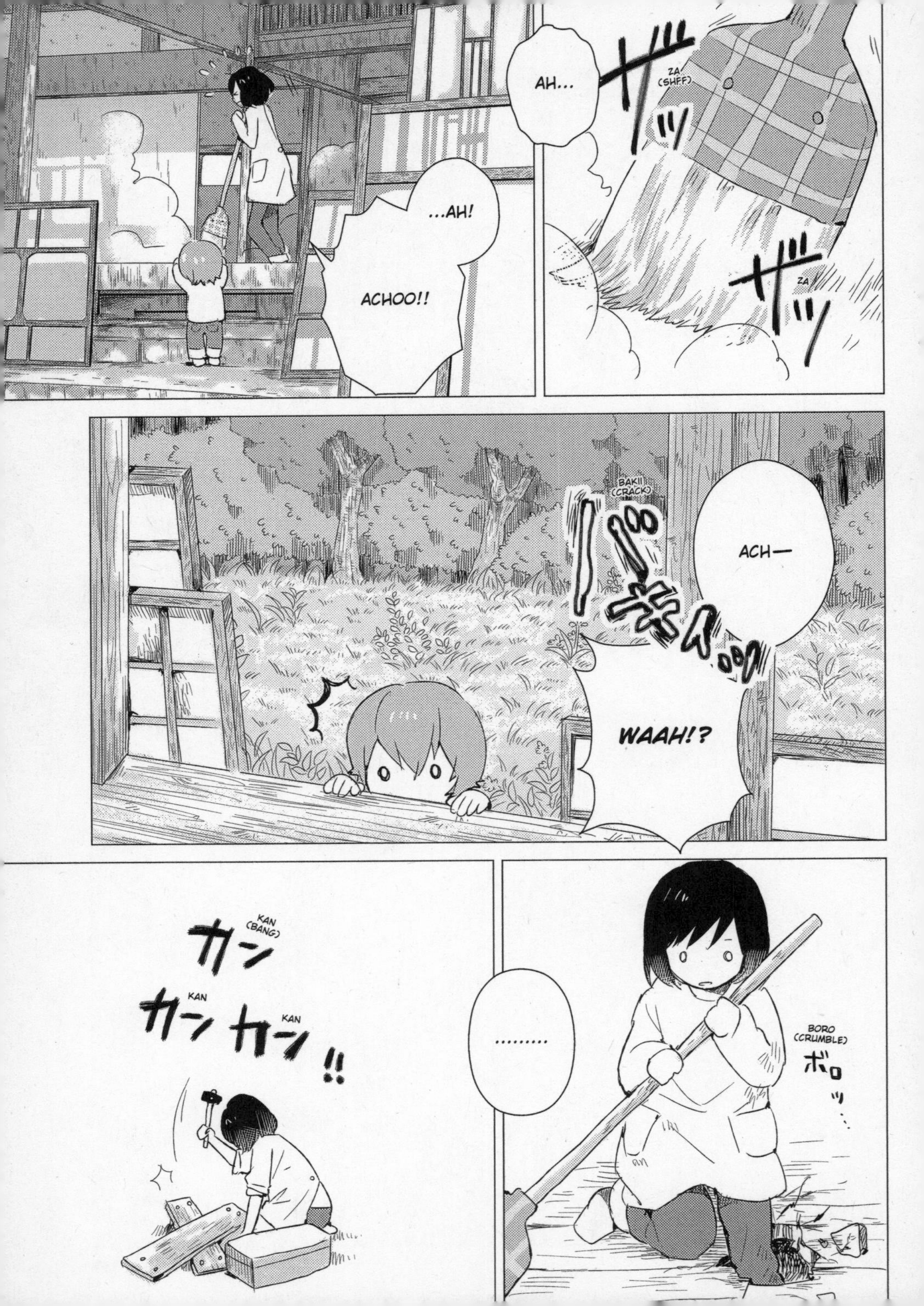
AH...
ZA (SHFF)
ザッ
ZA
ザッ
...AH!
ACHOO!!
BAKII (CRACK)
ACH—
WAAH!?
....
BORO (CRUMBLE)
ボロッ
KAN (BANG)
カン
KAN
カン
KAN
カン!!

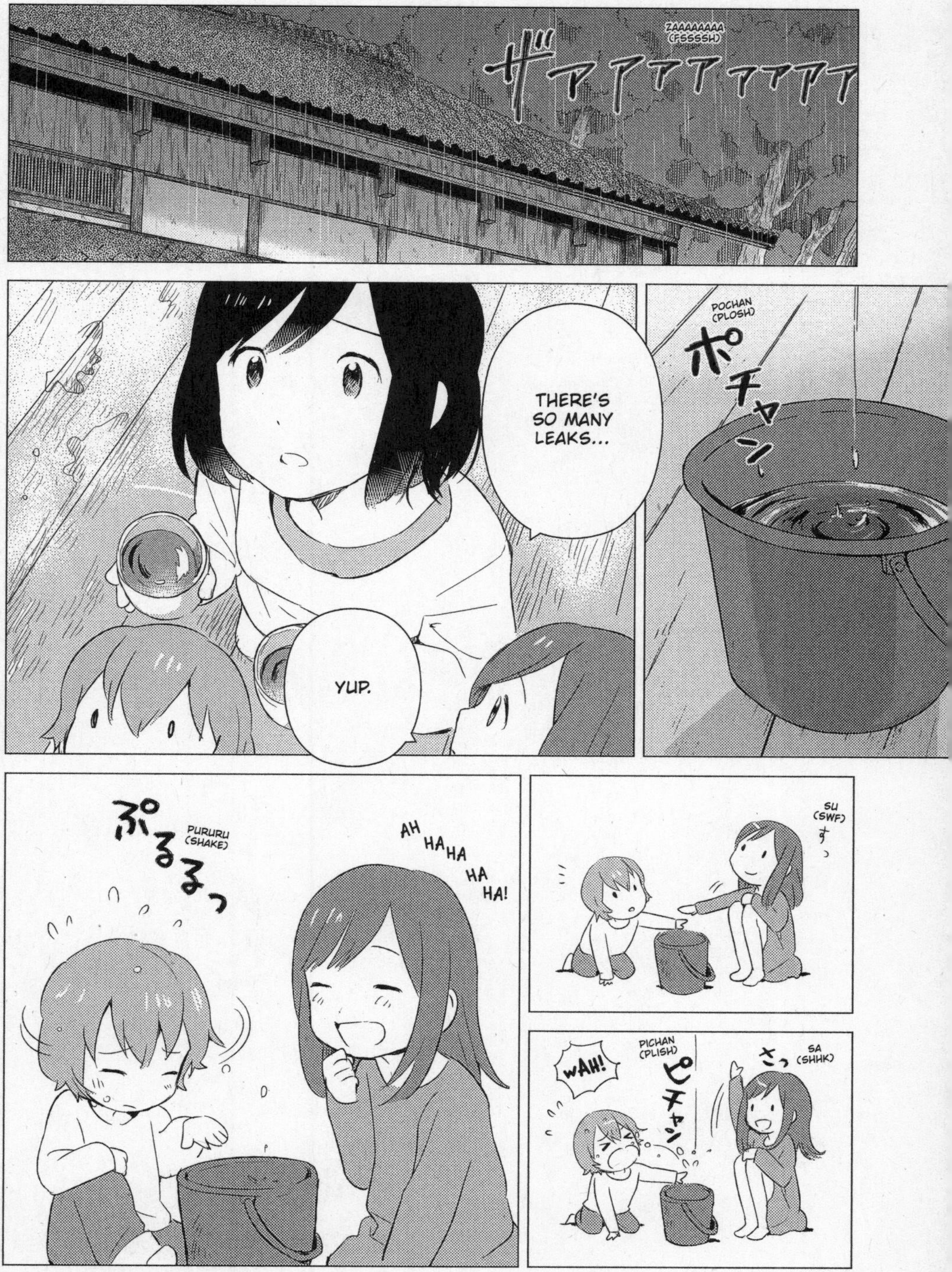
ZAAAAAAAA (FSSSSH)
ザアアアアアアア
POCHAN (PLOSH)
ポチャン
THERE'S SO MANY LEAKS...
YUP.
SU (SWF)
す
SA (SHHK)
さっ
PICHAN (PLISH)
ピチャン
WAH!
PURURU (SHAKE)
ぷるるっ
AH HAHA HA HA HA!

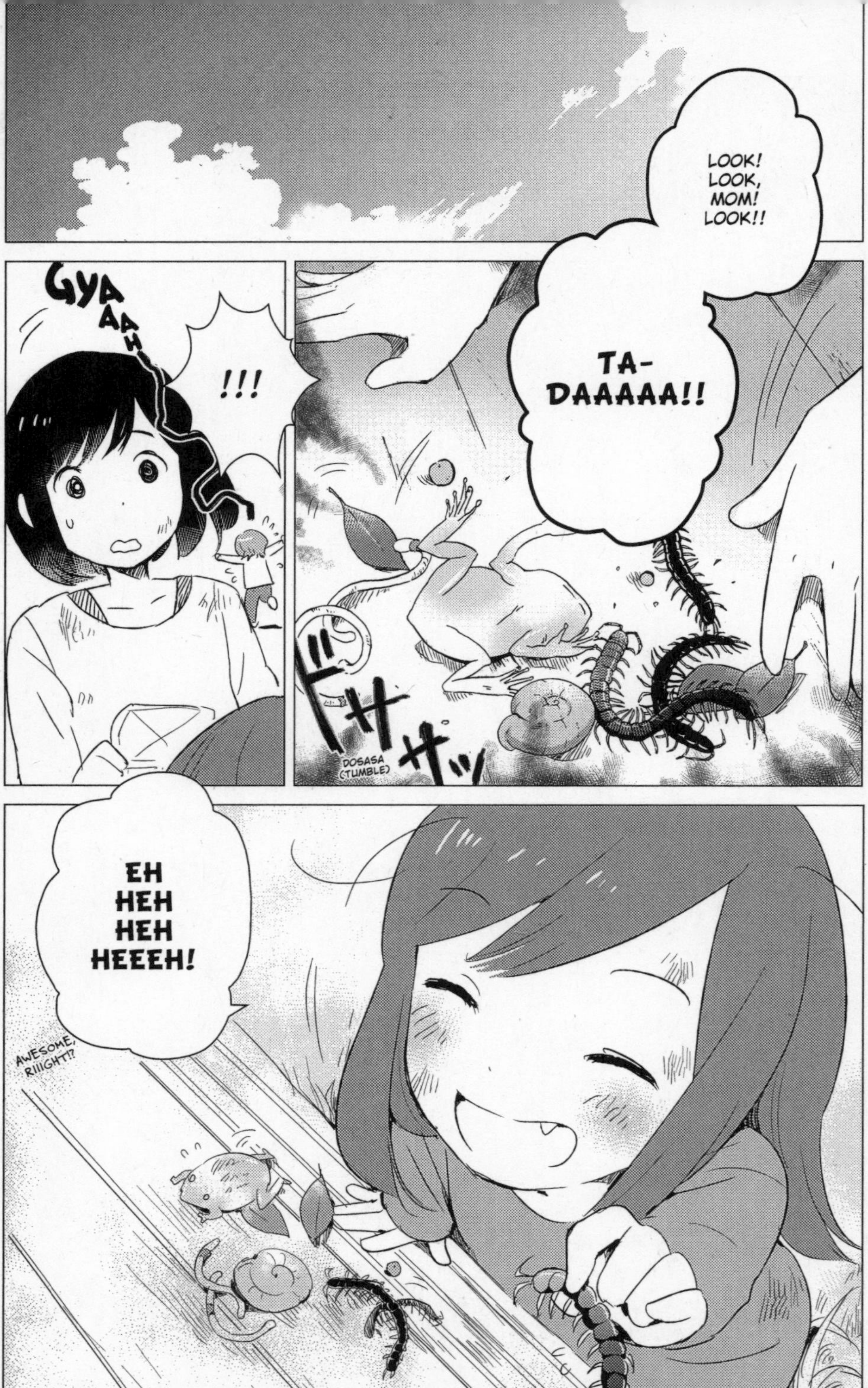
LOOK! LOOK, MOM! LOOK!!
TA-DAAAAA!!
DOSASA (TUMBLE)
GYAAAH
!!!
EH HEH HEH HEEEH!
AWESOME, RIIIGHT!?

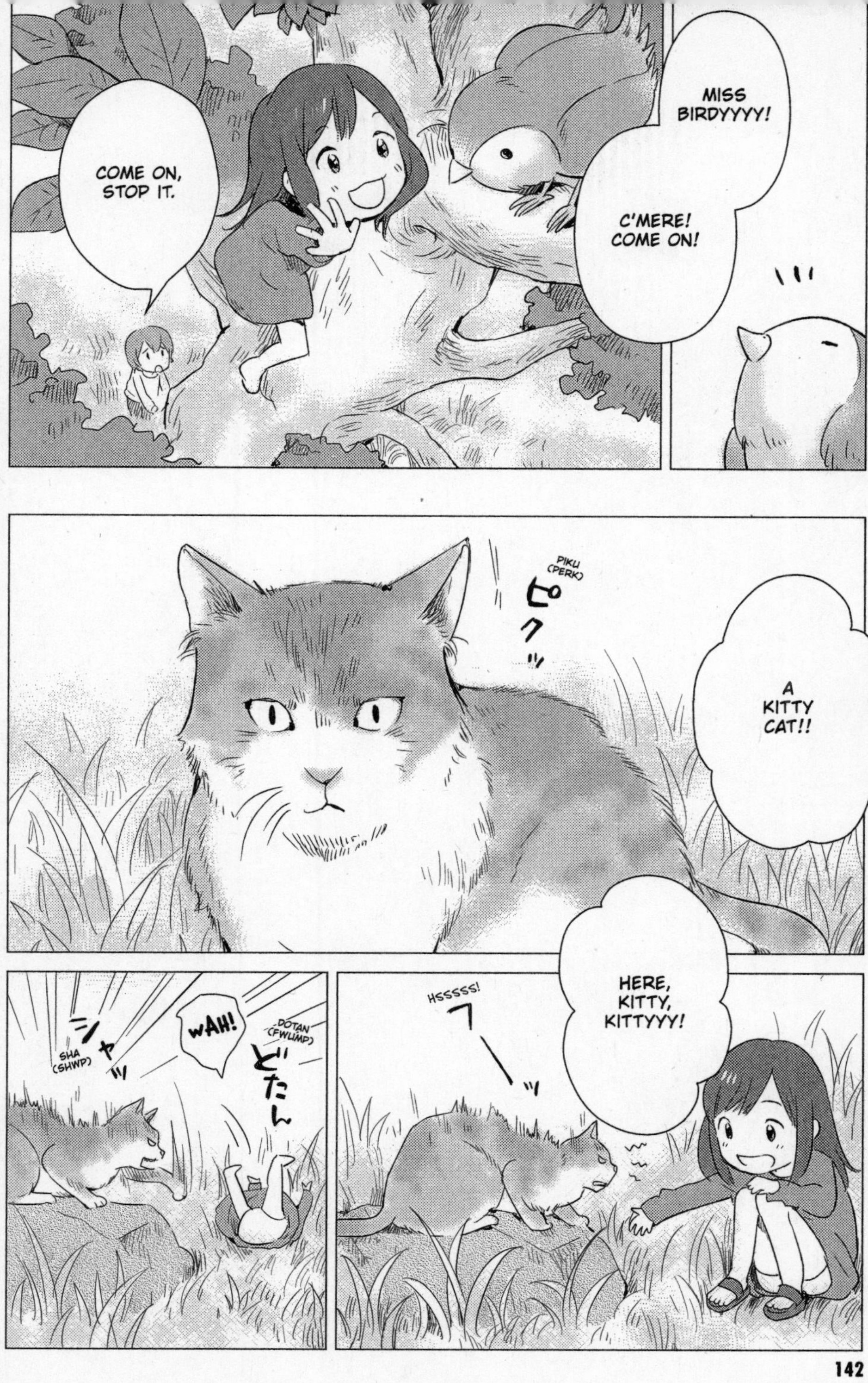
MISS BIRDYYYY!
C'MERE! COME ON!
COME ON, STOP IT.
PIKU (PERK)
ピクッ
A KITTY CAT!!
HERE, KITTY, KITTYYY!
HSSSSS!
ヘーッ
DOTAN (FWUMP)
どたん
WAH!
SHA (SHWP)
シャッ

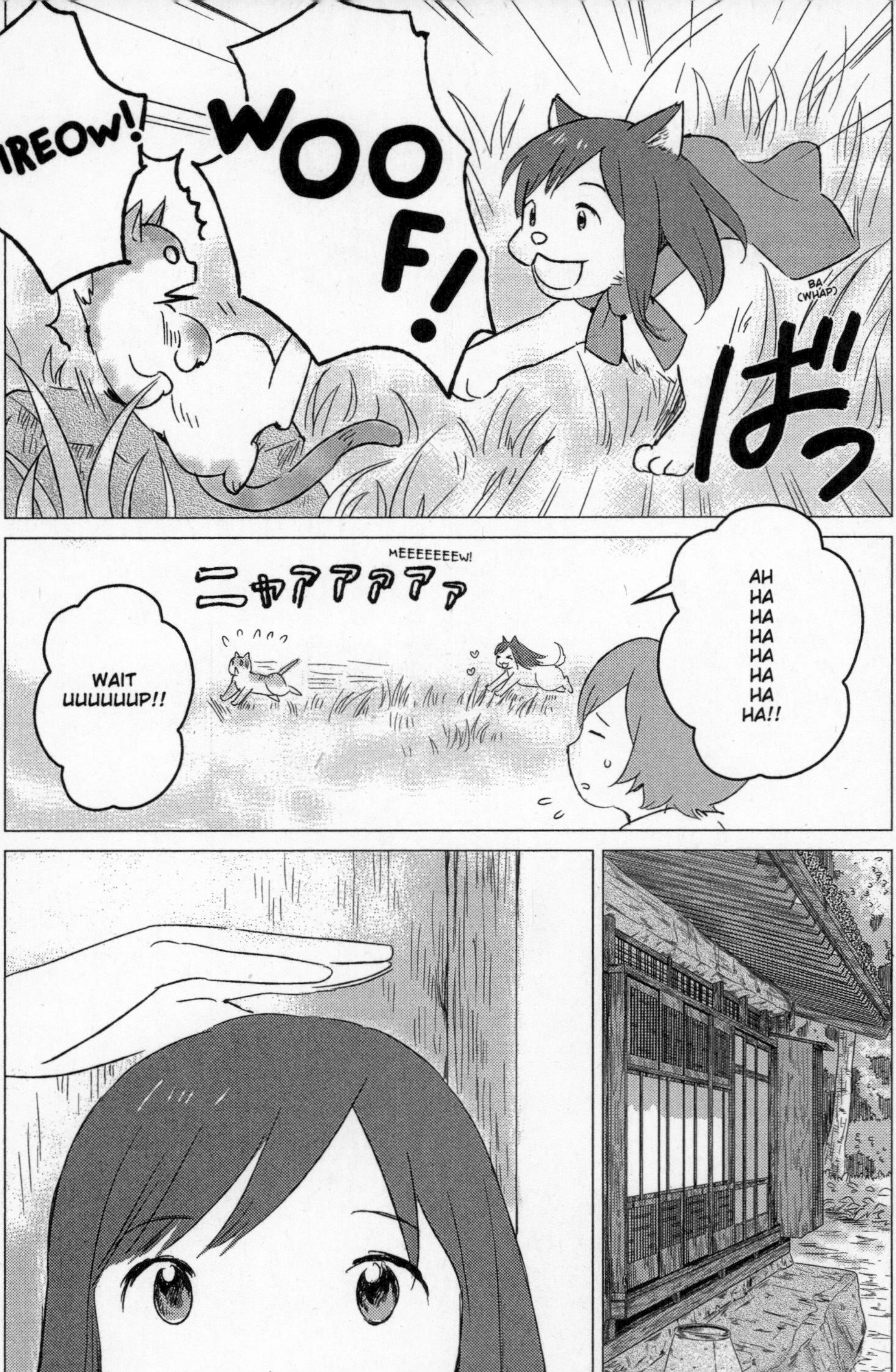
WOOF!
BA (WHAP)
ばっ
MREOW!
AH HA HA HA HA HA HA HA!!
MEEEEEEEW!
ニャアアアアァ
WAIT UUUUUUP!!

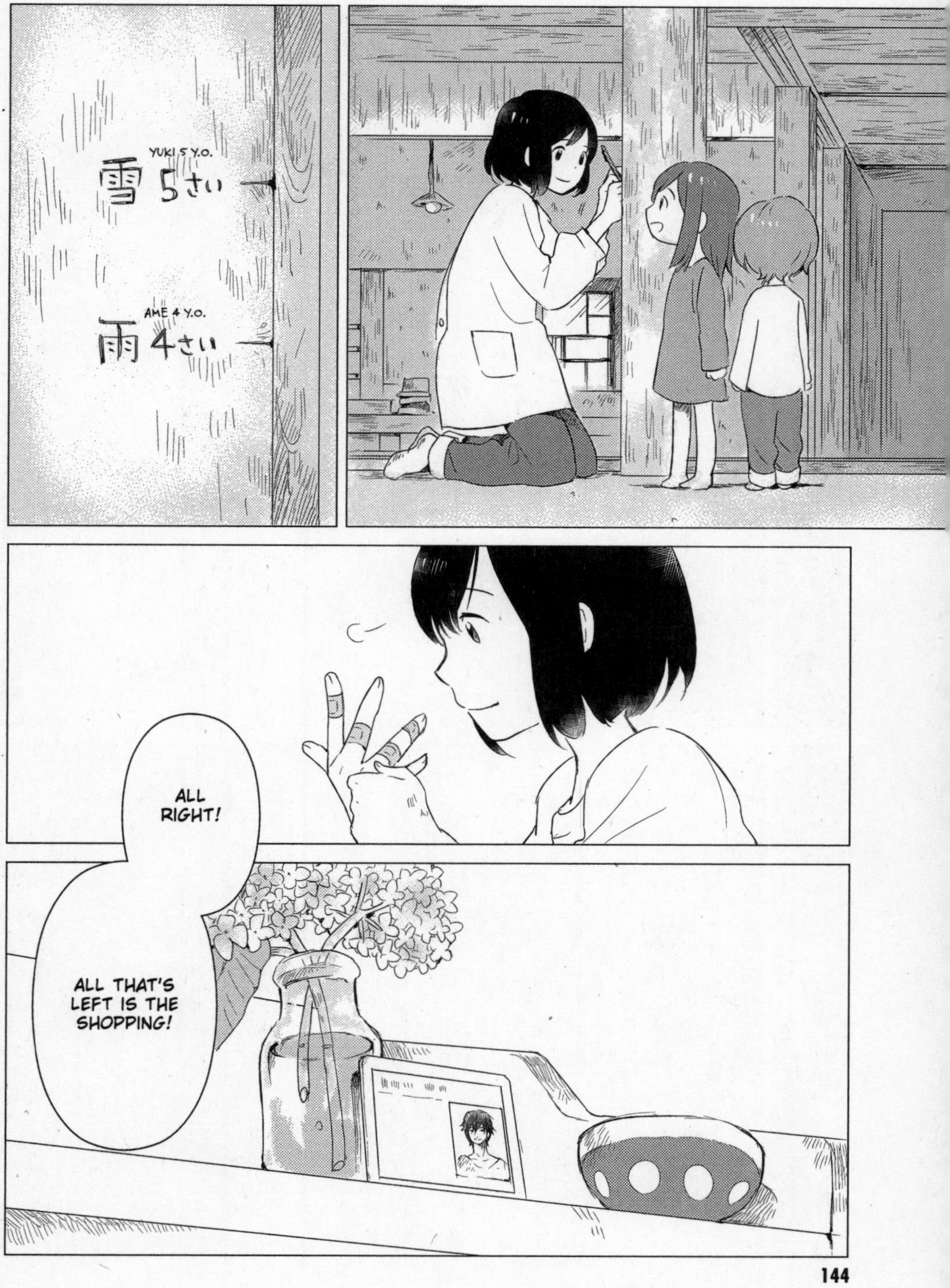
YUKI 5 Y.O.
雪 5さい
AME 4 Y.O.
雨 4さい
ALL RIGHT!
ALL THAT'S LEFT IS THE SHOPPING!

GATA (RATTLE)
ガタッ
GATA
ガタ
GATA
ガタ
WHEEEEEEEE!
AH HA HA HA HA!

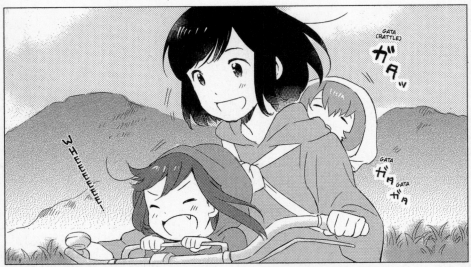

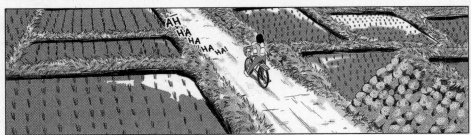

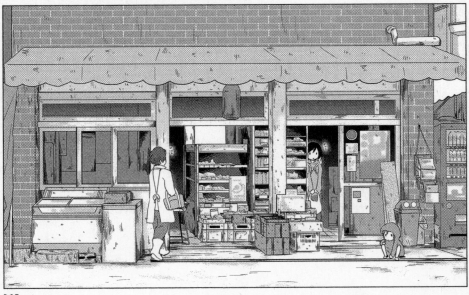

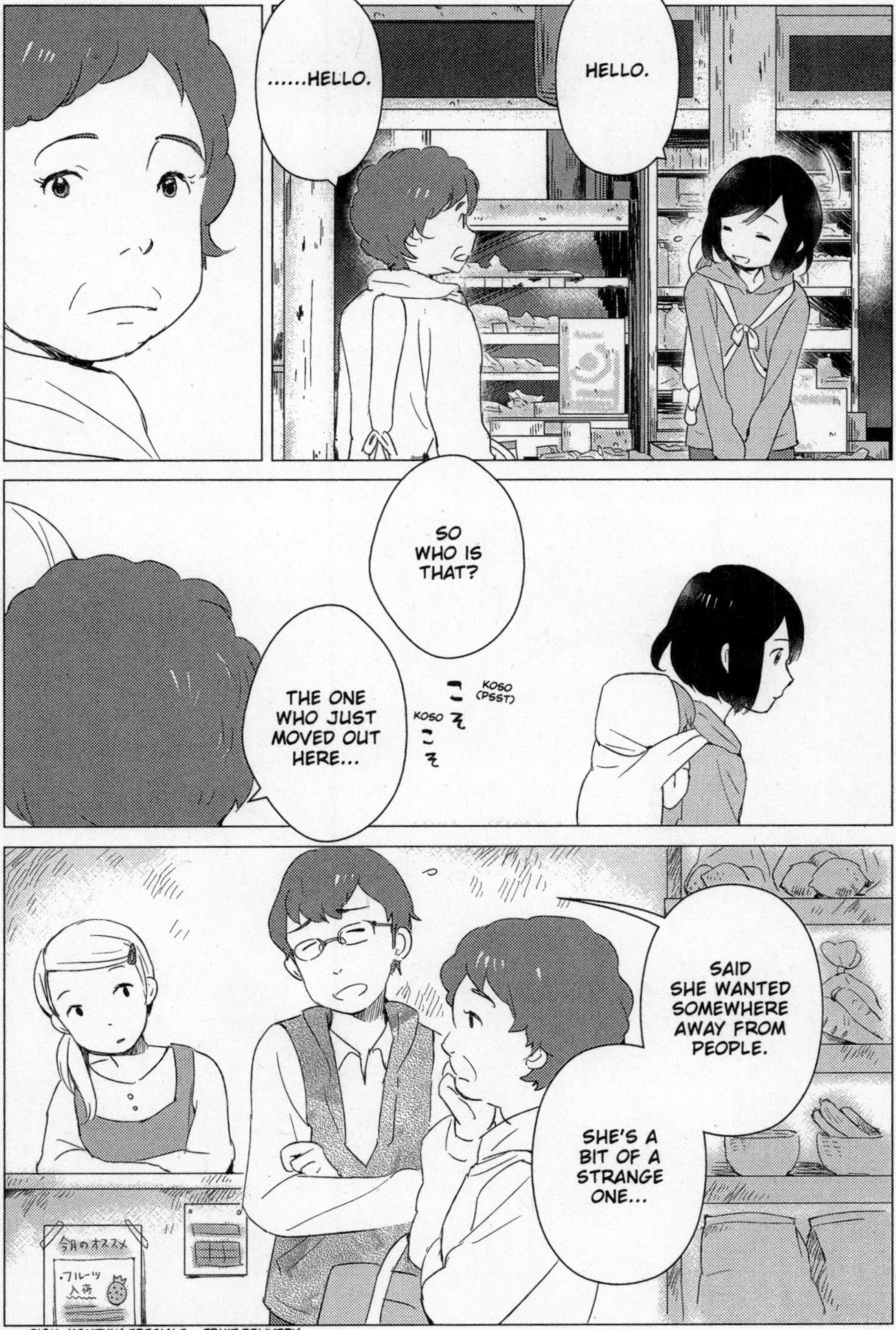
HELLO.
......HELLO.
SO WHO IS THAT?
こそ KOSO (PSST)
こそ KOSO
THE ONE WHO JUST MOVED OUT HERE...
SAID SHE WANTED SOMEWHERE AWAY FROM PEOPLE.
SHE'S A BIT OF A STRANGE ONE...
今月のオススメ
・フルーツ 入荷

SIGN: MONTHLY SPECIALS—FRUIT DELIVERY

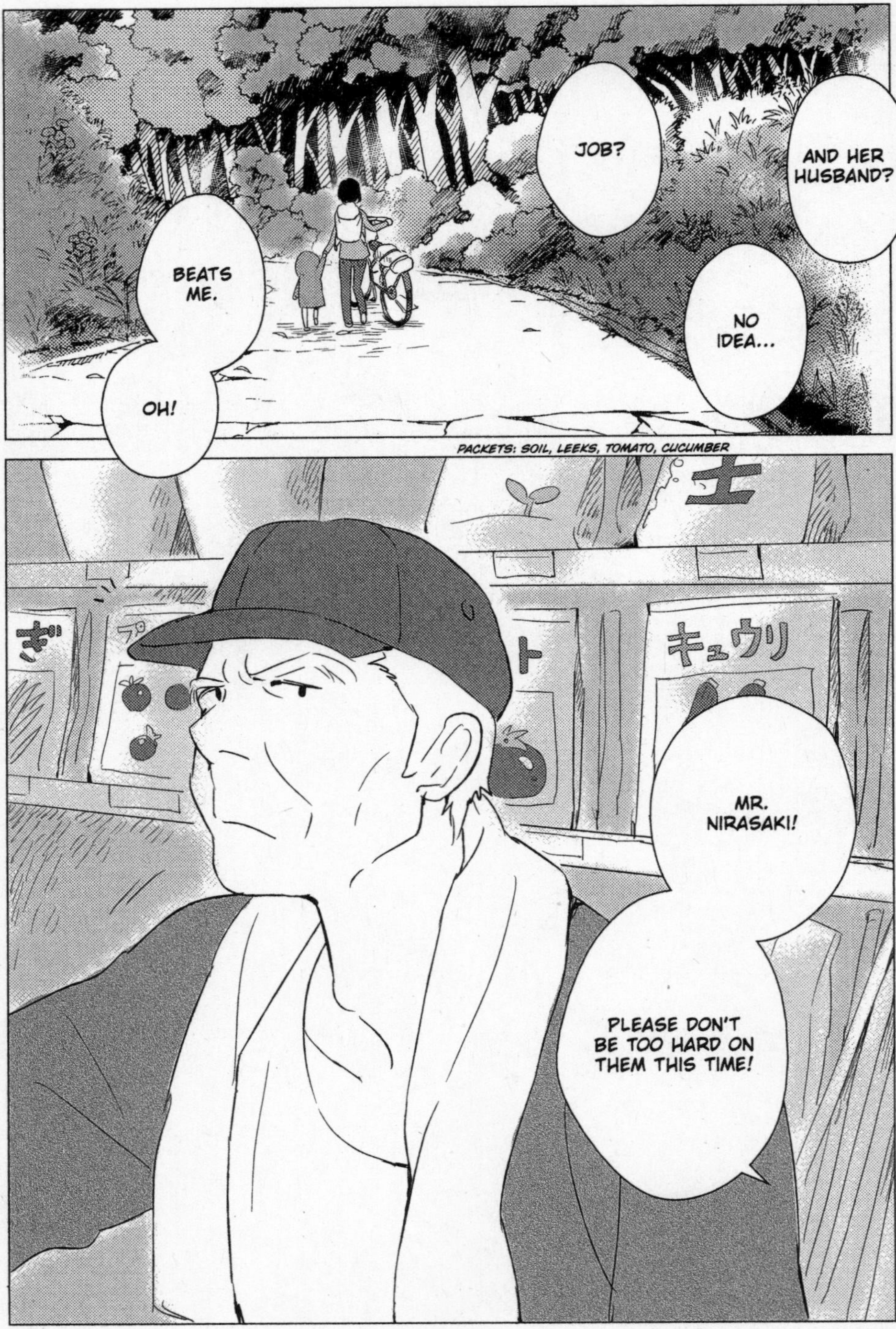
AND HER HUSBAND?
JOB?
NO IDEA...
BEATS ME.
OH!
PACKETS: SOIL, LEEKS, TOMATO, CUCUMBER
土
キュウリ
MR. NIRASAKI!
PLEASE DON'T BE TOO HARD ON THEM THIS TIME!

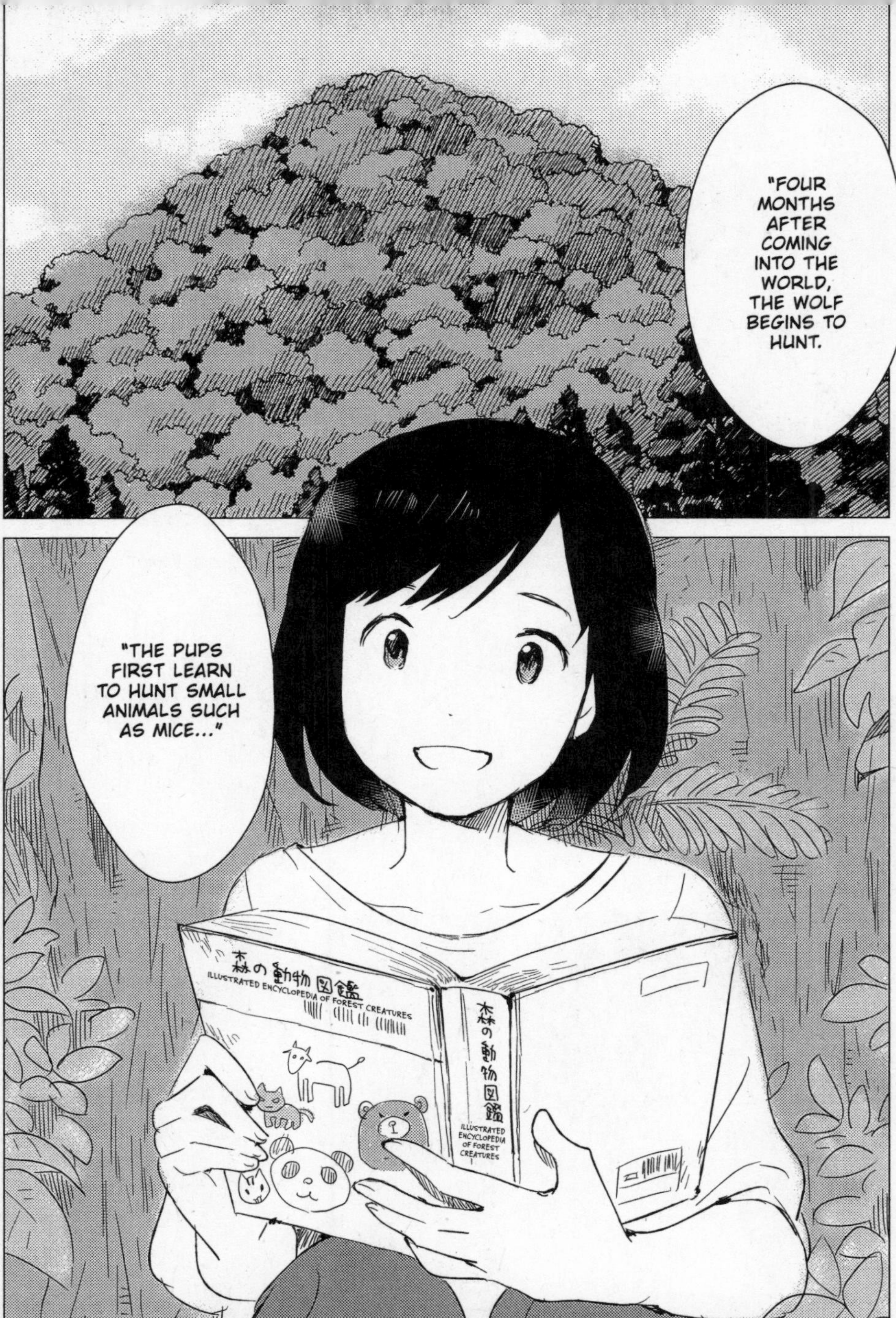
"FOUR MONTHS AFTER COMING INTO THE WORLD, THE WOLF BEGINS TO HUNT.
"THE PUPS FIRST LEARN TO HUNT SMALL ANIMALS SUCH AS MICE..."
森の動物図鑑
ILLUSTRATED ENCYCLOPEDIA OF FOREST CREATURES
森の動物図鑑
ILLUSTRATED ENCYCLOPEDIA OF FOREST CREATURES 1

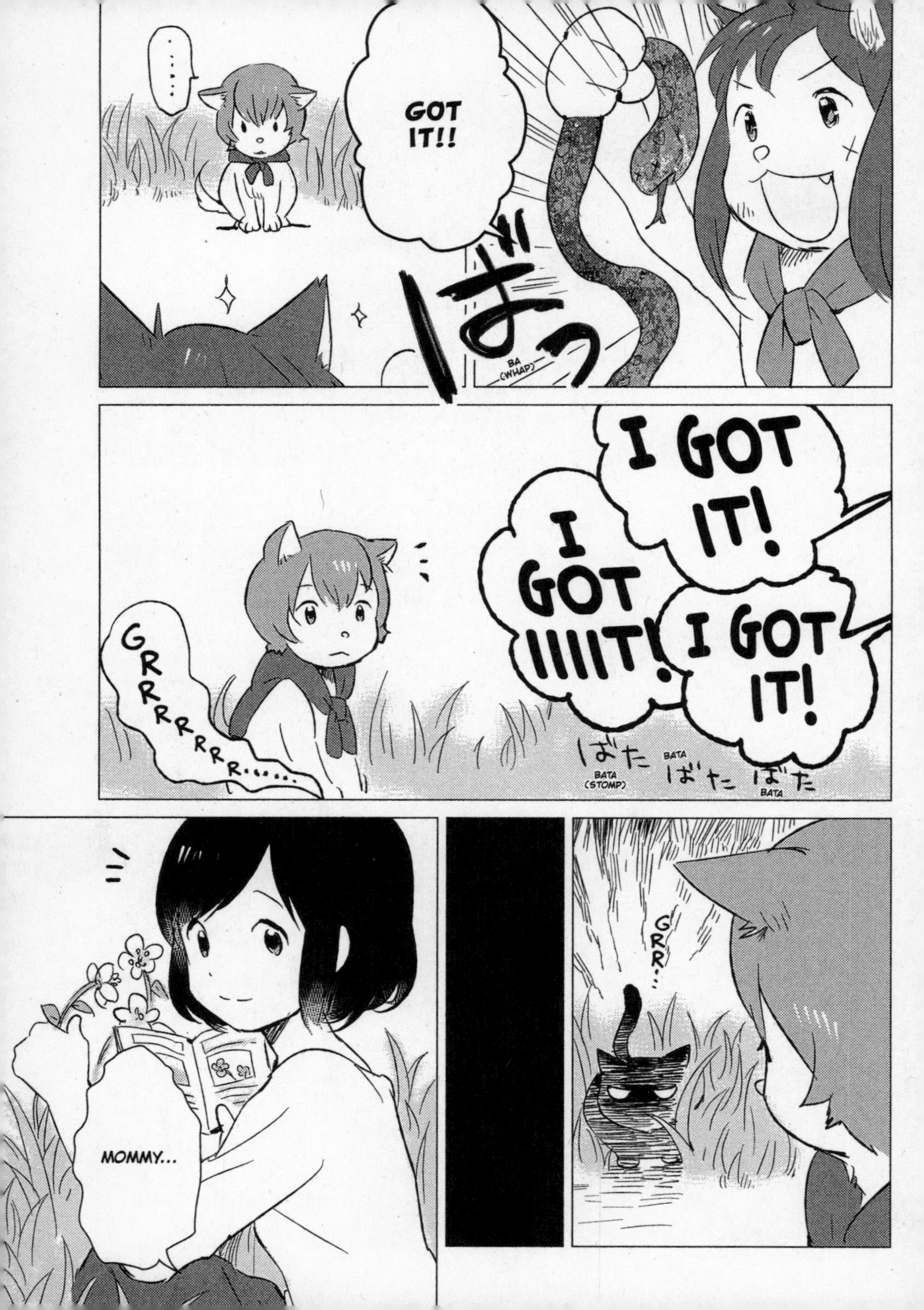
GOT IT!!
ばっ
BA (WHAP)
......
I GOT IT!
I GOT IT!
I GOT IIIIIT!
ばた
BATA (STOMP)
ばた
BATA
ばた
BATA
GRRRRRRR......
GRR...
MOMMY...

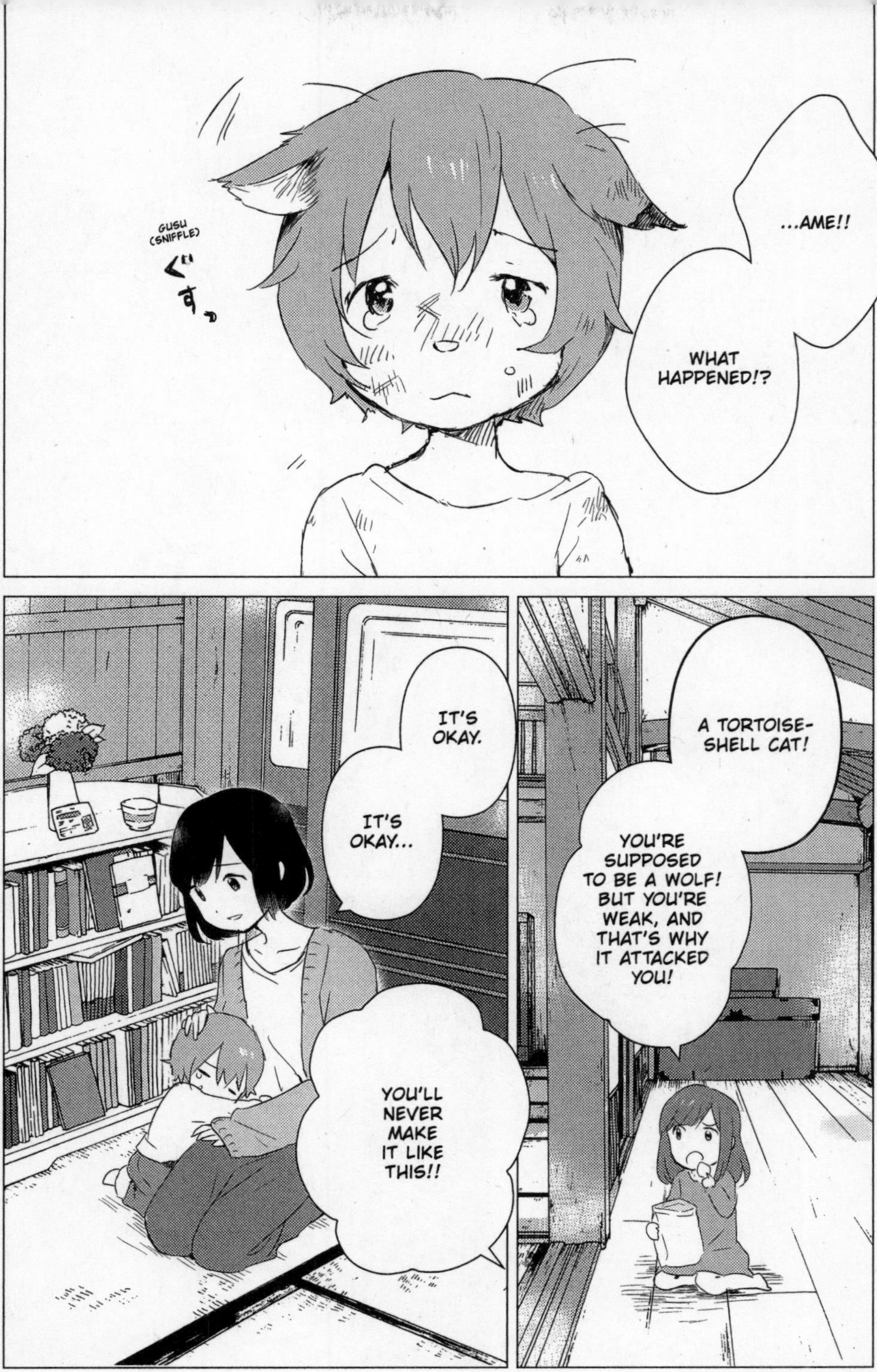
...AME!!
WHAT HAPPENED!?
GUSU (SNIFFLE)
ぐすっ
A TORTOISE-SHELL CAT!
YOU'RE SUPPOSED TO BE A WOLF! BUT YOU'RE WEAK, AND THAT'S WHY IT ATTACKED YOU!
IT'S OKAY.
IT'S OKAY...
YOU'LL NEVER MAKE IT LIKE THIS!!

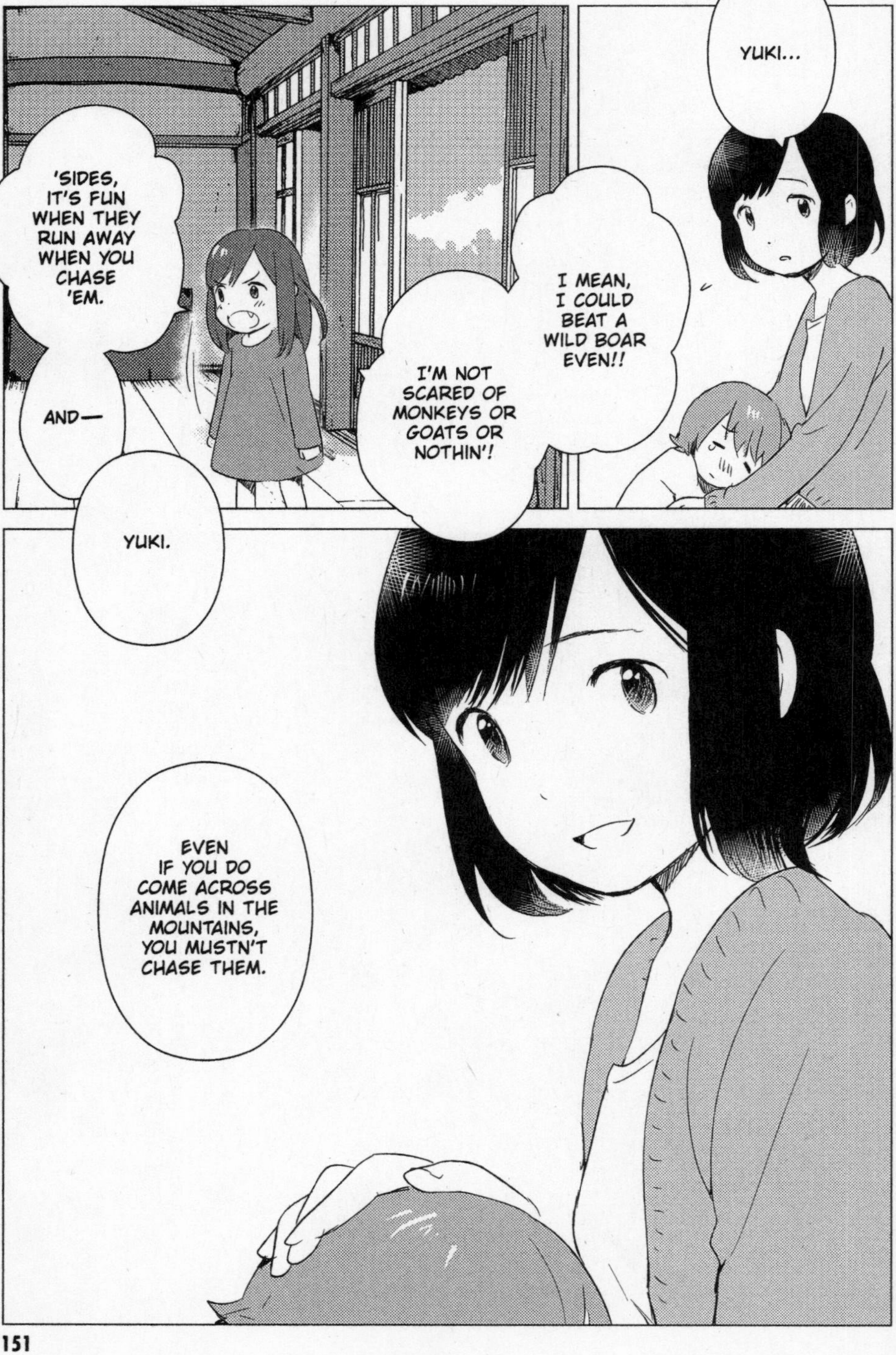
YUKI...
I MEAN, I COULD BEAT A WILD BOAR EVEN!!
I'M NOT SCARED OF MONKEYS OR GOATS OR NOTHIN'!
'SIDES, IT'S FUN WHEN THEY RUN AWAY WHEN YOU CHASE 'EM.
AND—
YUKI.
EVEN IF YOU DO COME ACROSS ANIMALS IN THE MOUNTAINS, YOU MUSTN'T CHASE THEM.

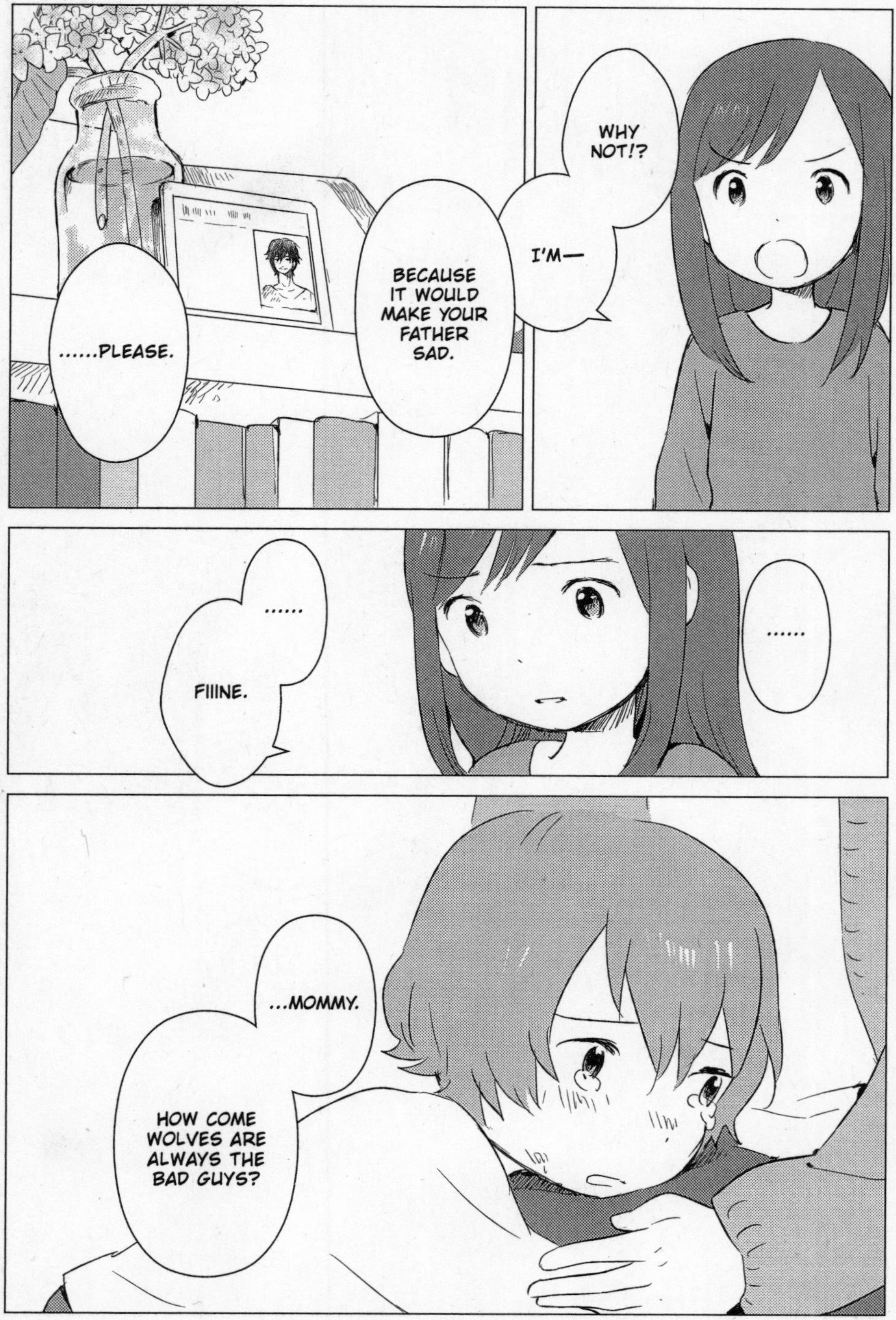
WHY NOT!?
I'M—
BECAUSE IT WOULD MAKE YOUR FATHER SAD.
......PLEASE.
......
......
FIIINE.
...MOMMY.
HOW COME WOLVES ARE ALWAYS THE BAD GUYS?

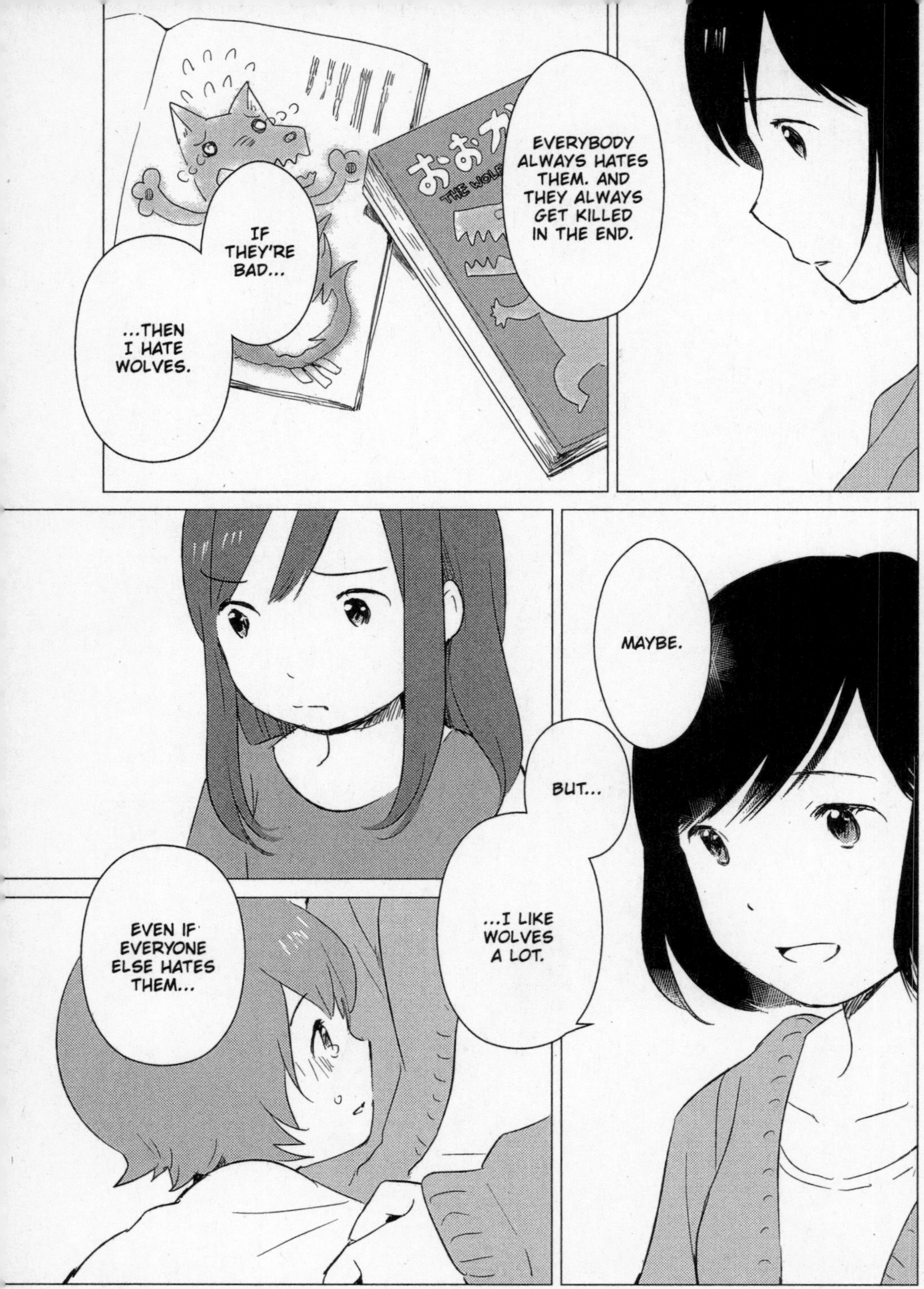
EVERYBODY ALWAYS HATES THEM. AND THEY ALWAYS GET KILLED IN THE END.
IF THEY'RE BAD...
...THEN I HATE WOLVES.
MAYBE.
BUT...
...I LIKE WOLVES A LOT.
EVEN IF EVERYONE ELSE HATES THEM...

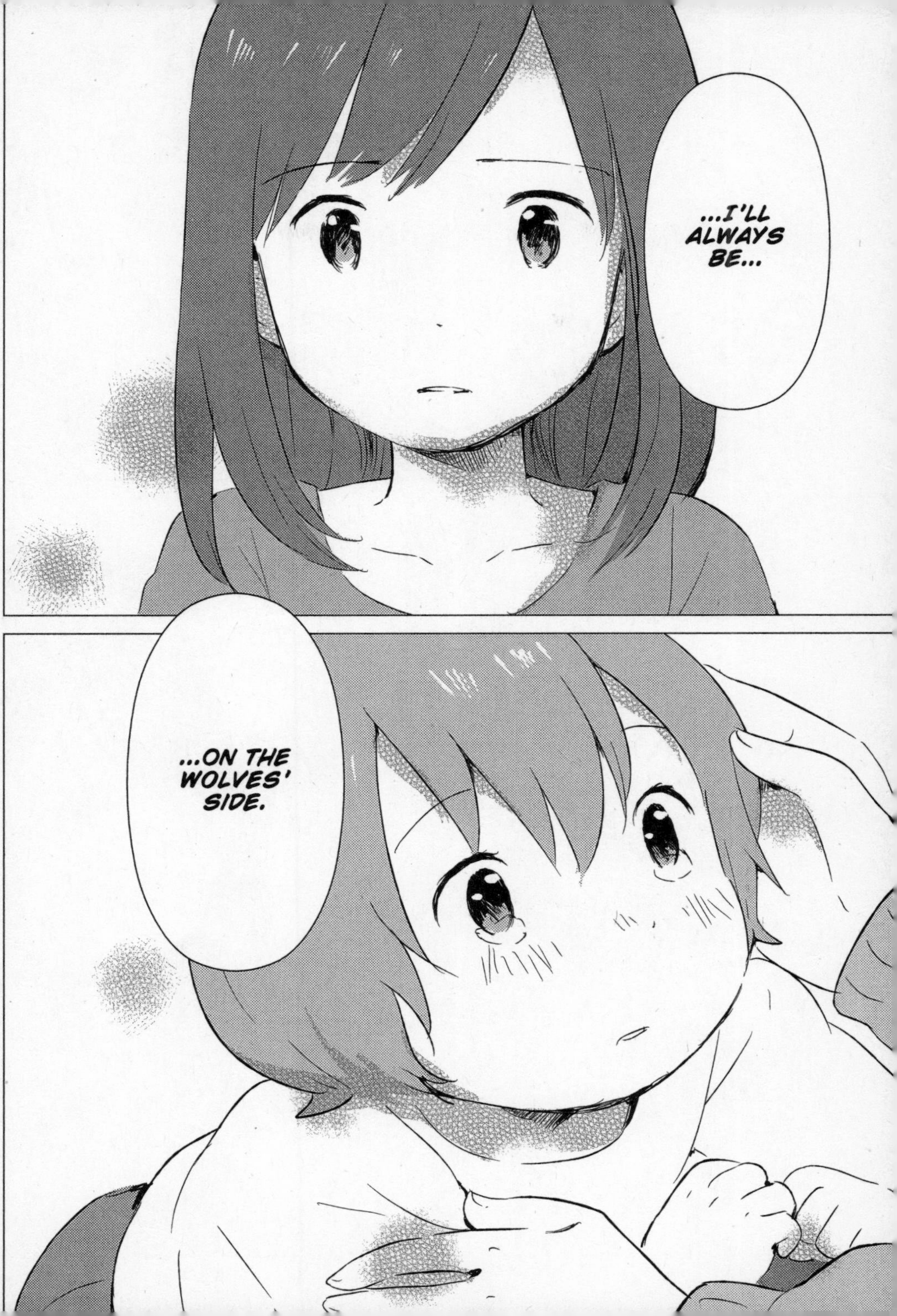
...I'LL ALWAYS BE...
...ON THE WOLVES' SIDE.

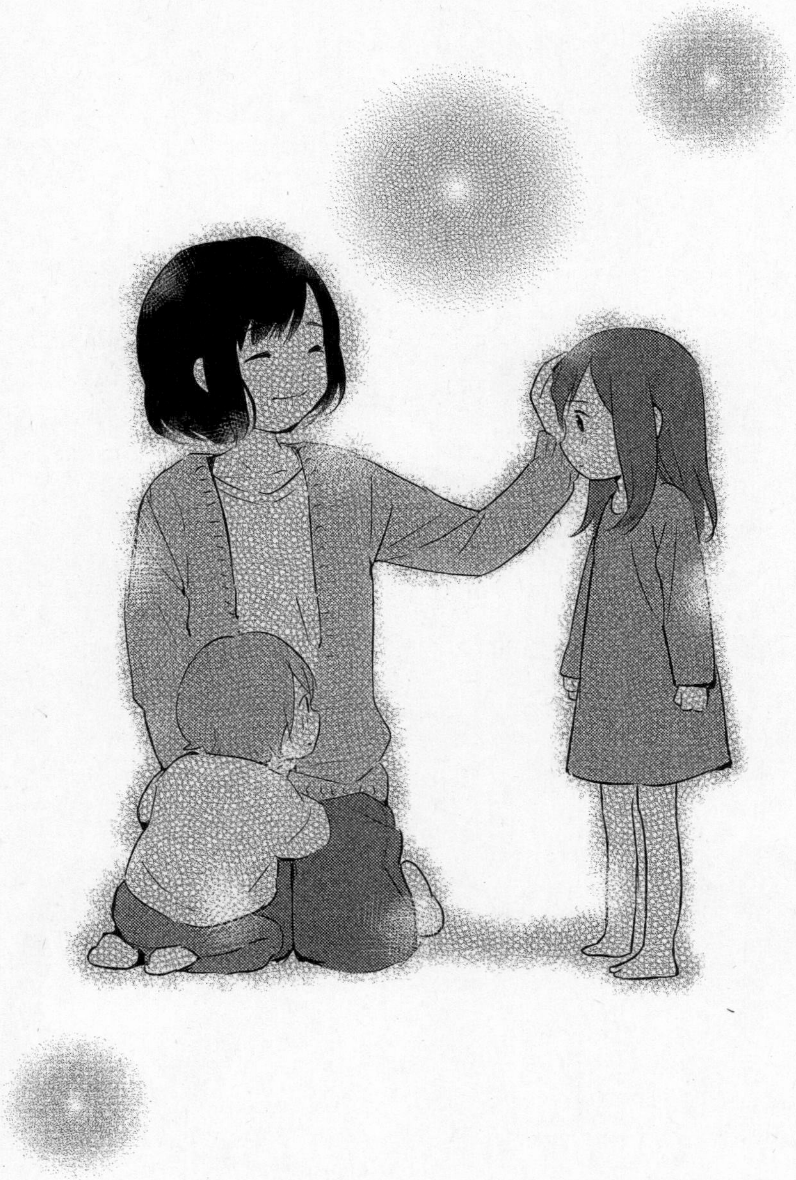

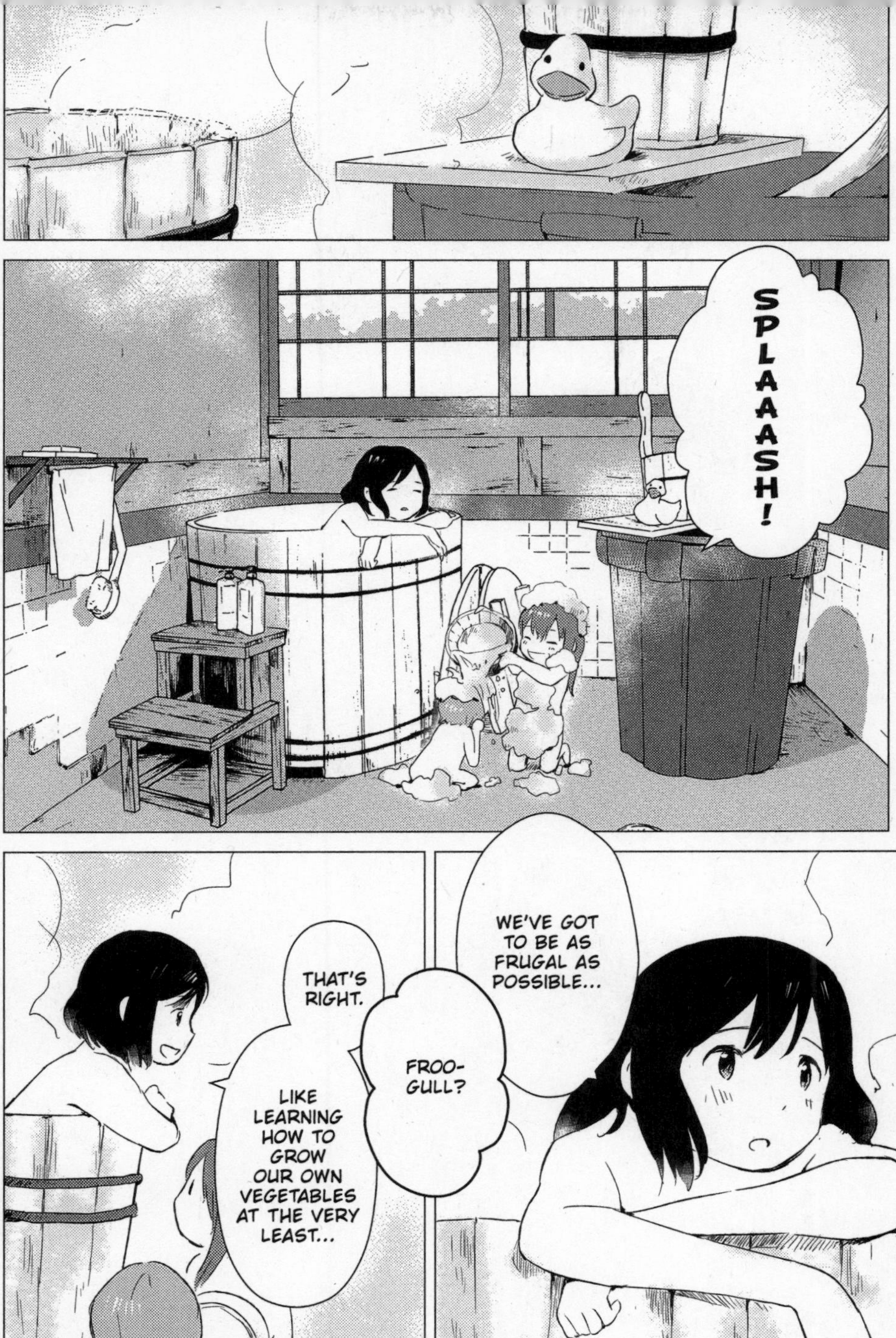
SPLAAASH!
WE'VE GOT TO BE AS FRUGAL AS POSSIBLE...
FROO-GULL?
THAT'S RIGHT.
LIKE LEARNING HOW TO GROW OUR OWN VEGETABLES AT THE VERY LEAST...

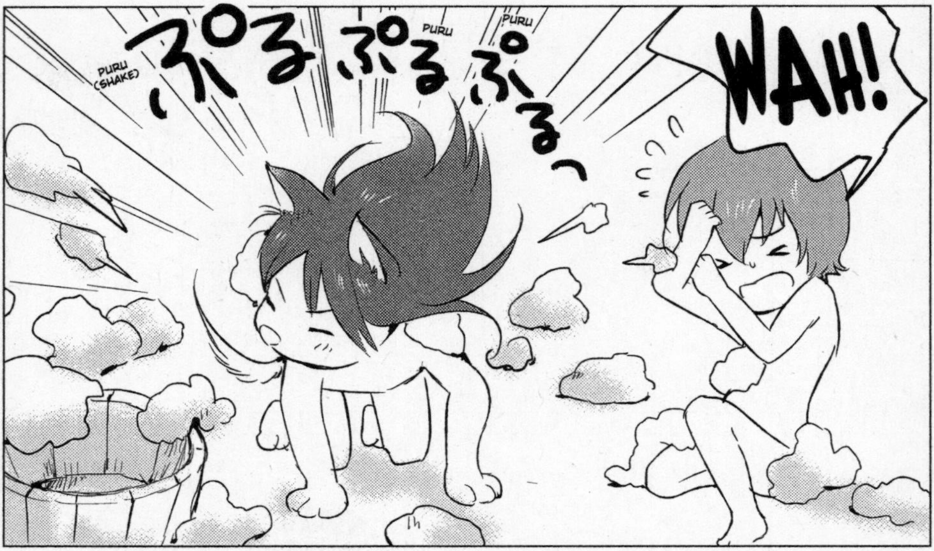
WAH!
ぷるぷるぷるっ
PURU (SHAKE)
PURU
PURU

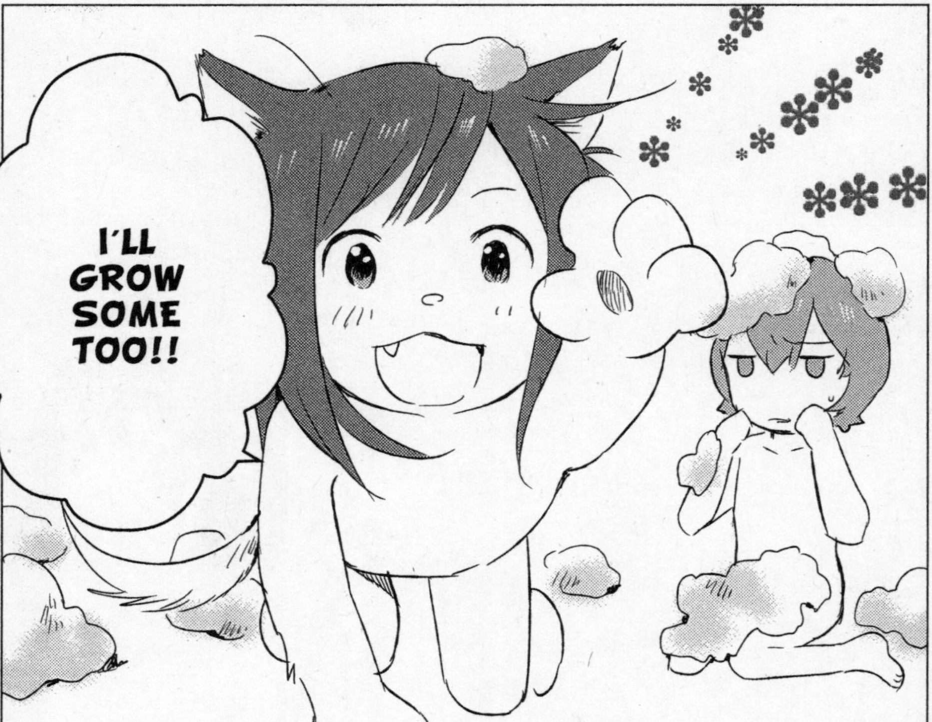
I'LL GROW SOME TOO!!

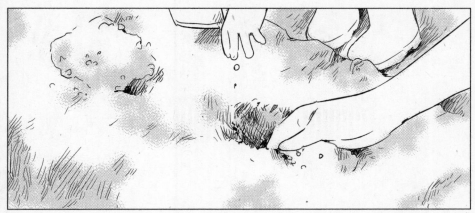

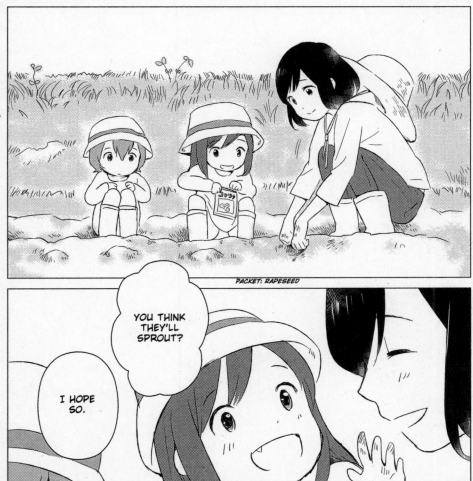

PACKET: RAPESEED

YOU THINK THEY'LL SPROUT?

I HOPE SO.

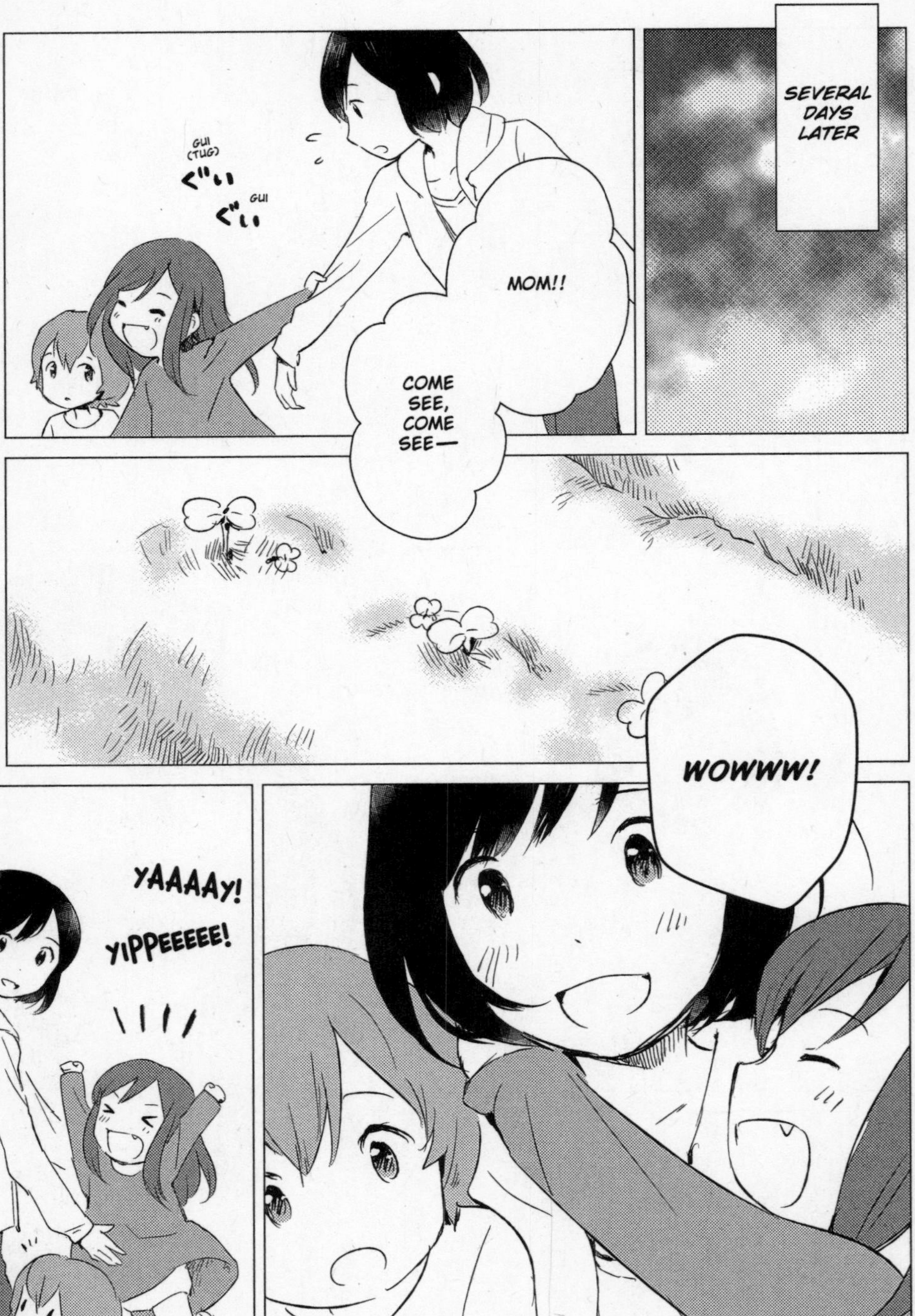
SEVERAL DAYS LATER
GUI (TUG)
ぐい
ぐい
GUI
MOM!!
COME SEE, COME SEE—
WOWWW!
YAAAAY!
YIPPEEEEE!

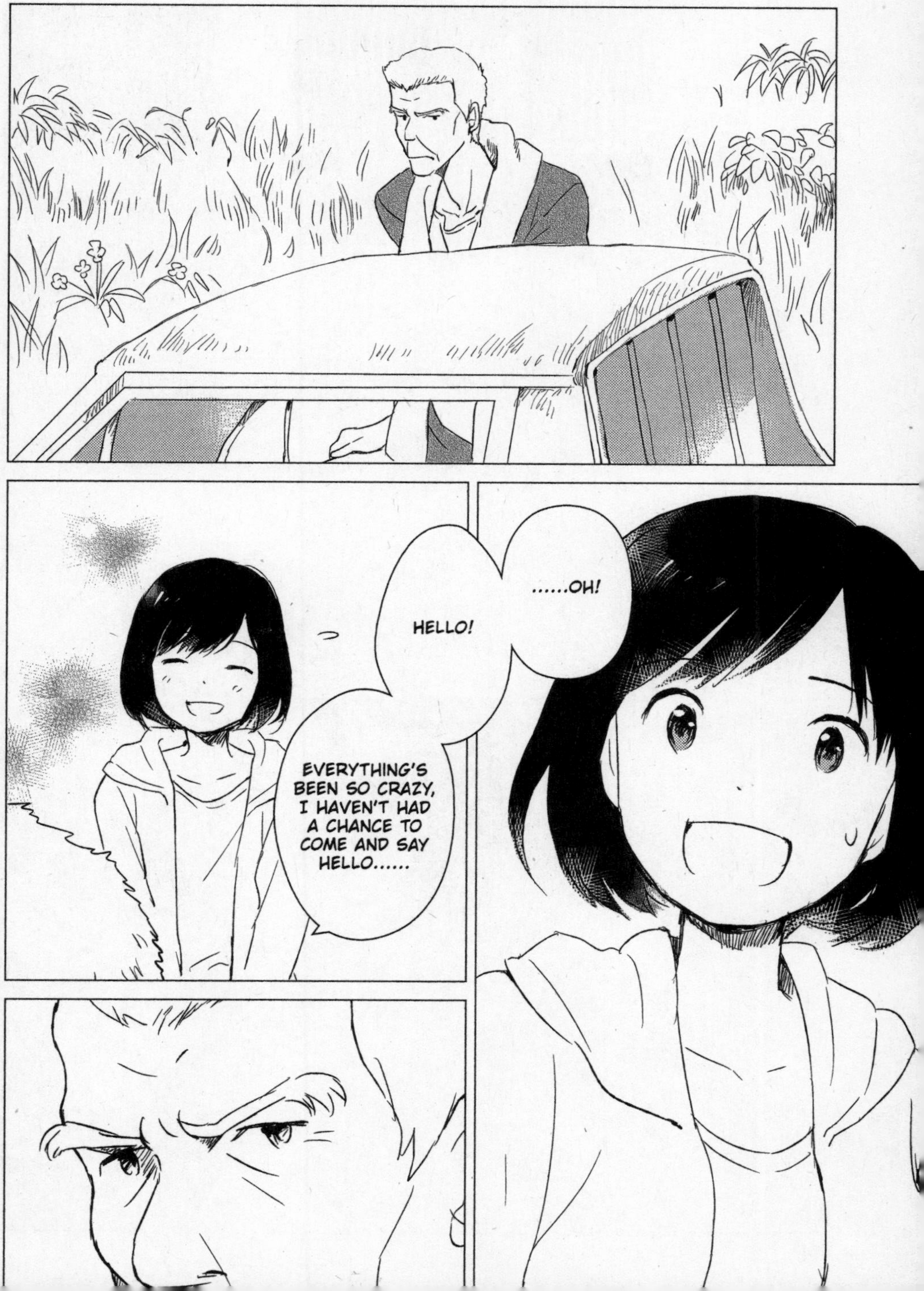
......OH!
HELLO!
EVERYTHING'S BEEN SO CRAZY, I HAVEN'T HAD A CHANCE TO COME AND SAY HELLO......

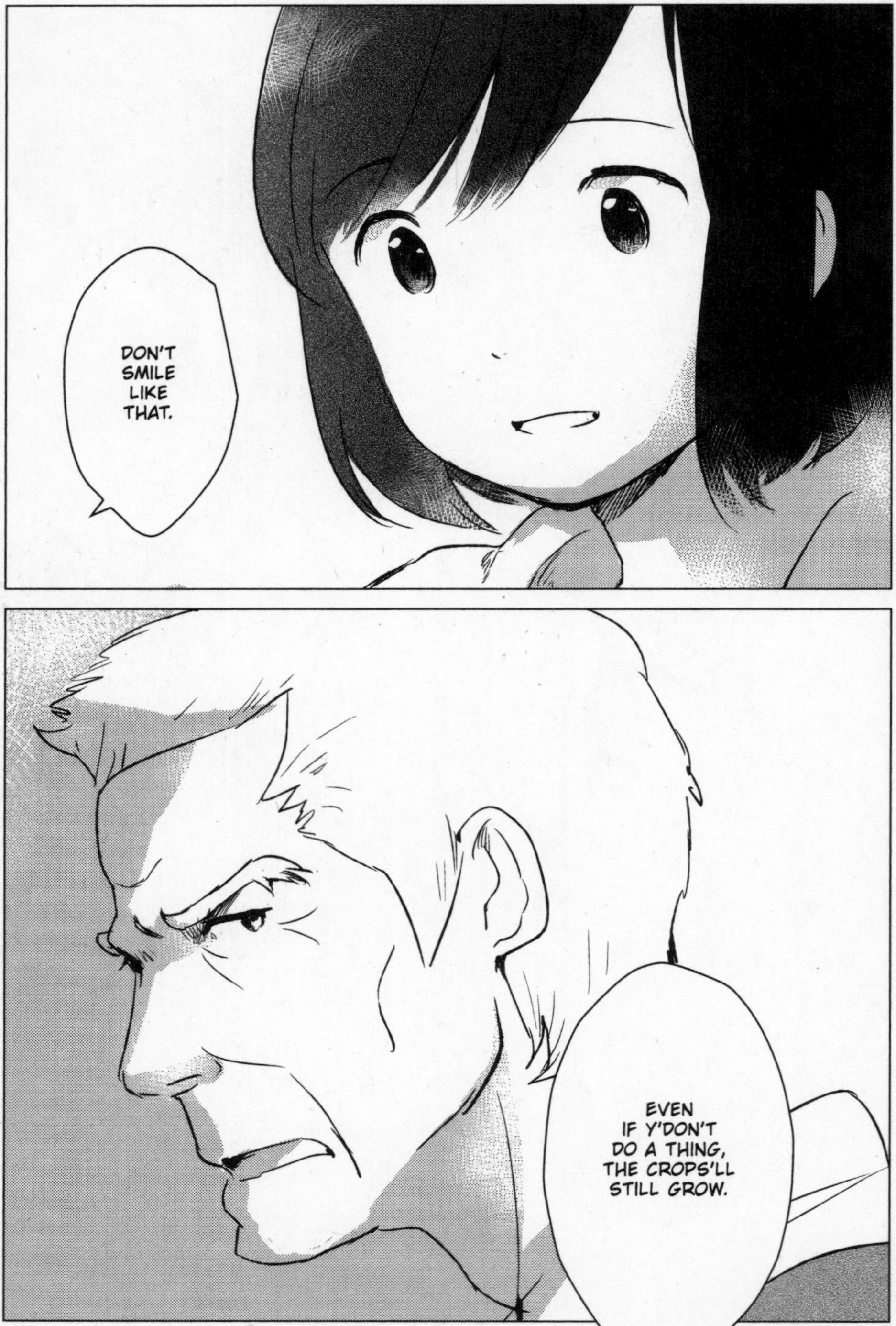
DON'T SMILE LIKE THAT.
EVEN IF Y'DON'T DO A THING, THE CROPS'LL STILL GROW.

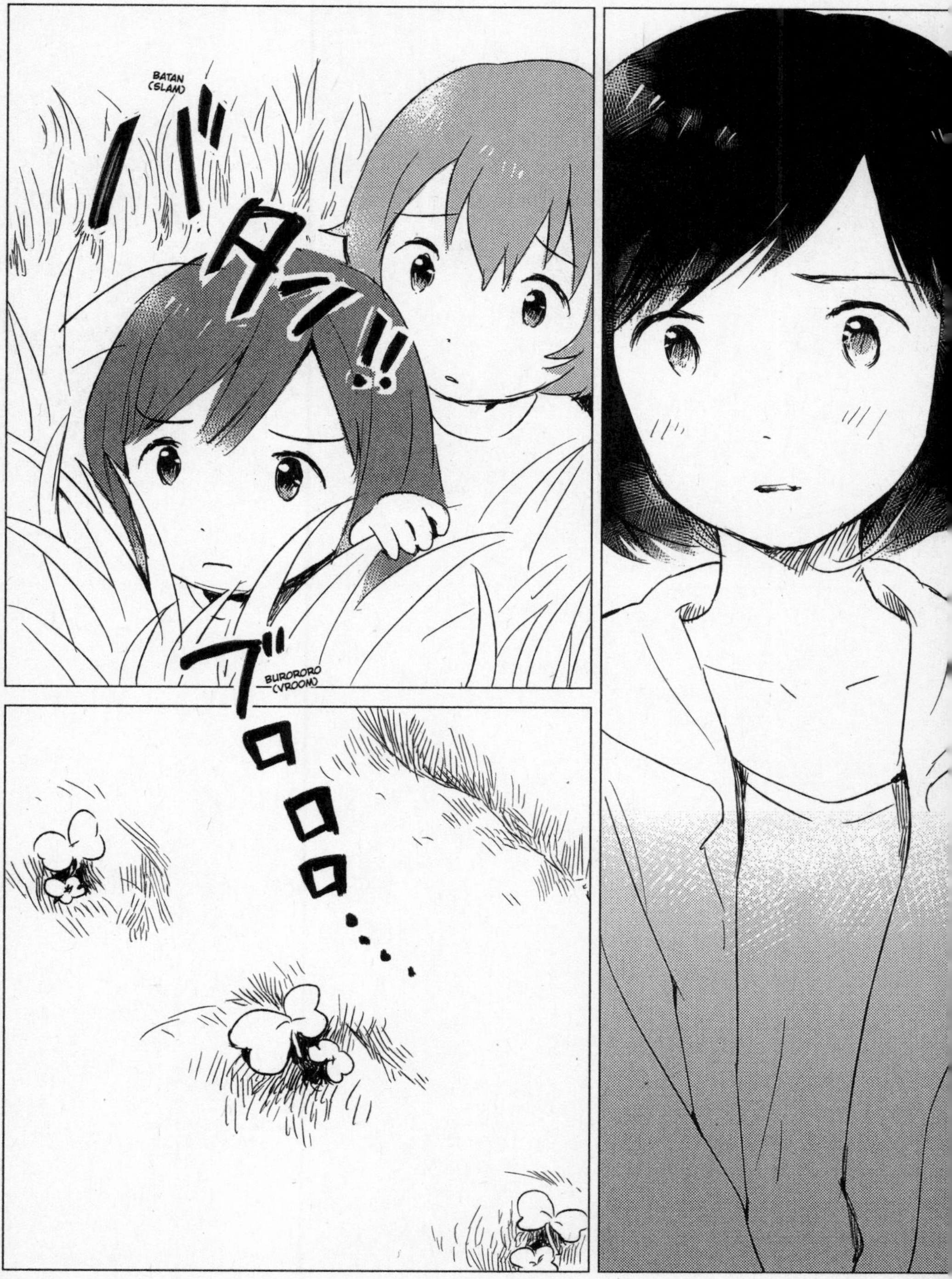
BATAN (SLAM)
バタン!!
BURORORO (VROOM)
ブロロロ…

WOLF CHILDREN
AME & YUKI

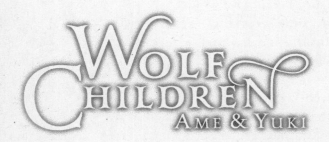

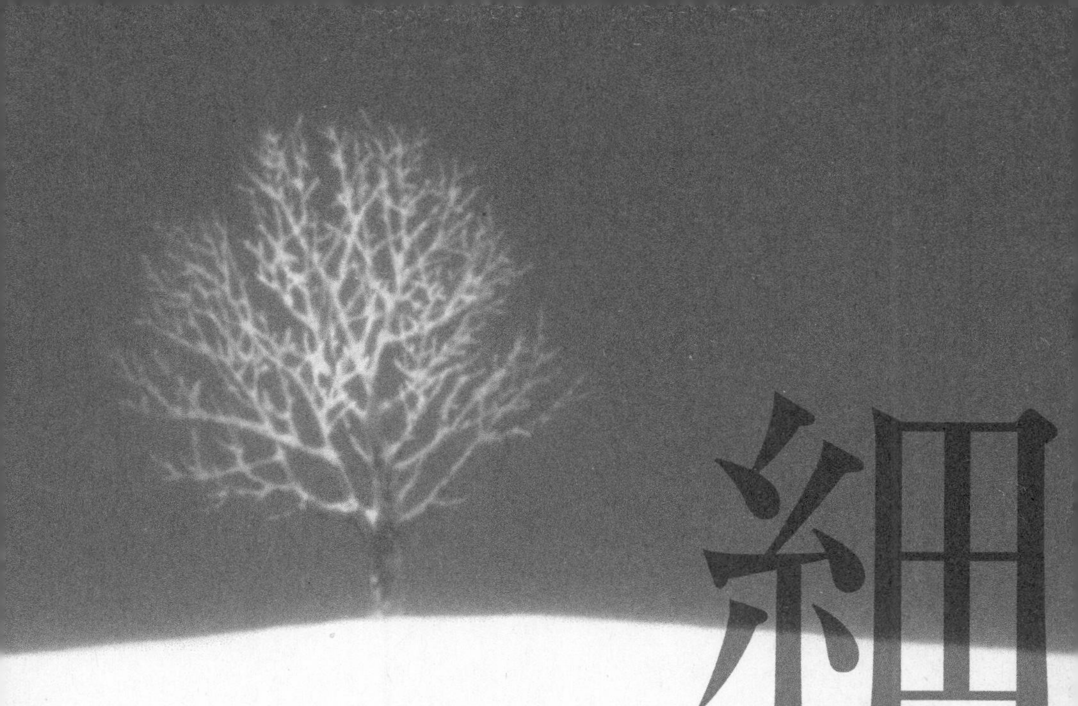

細田守

from
Mamoru Hosoda

Extraordinarily gentle, adorable, full of warmth——I believe this is the charm of Yu-san's illustrations. I felt the strong appeal of the characters themselves when I first saw her rough sketches of Hana, Yuki, and Ame, but now that they have been turned into a manga, there is an even greater richness of expression and even more warmth. And once again, I realize how fortunate I was to have come across the perfect manga artist for this fantastical work, *Wolf Children Ame & Yuki*.

This story is a thirteen-year journey, thirteen long years from the time Yuki and Ame are born until they are grown.

Adapting Wolf Children Ame & Yuki *into a Comic*

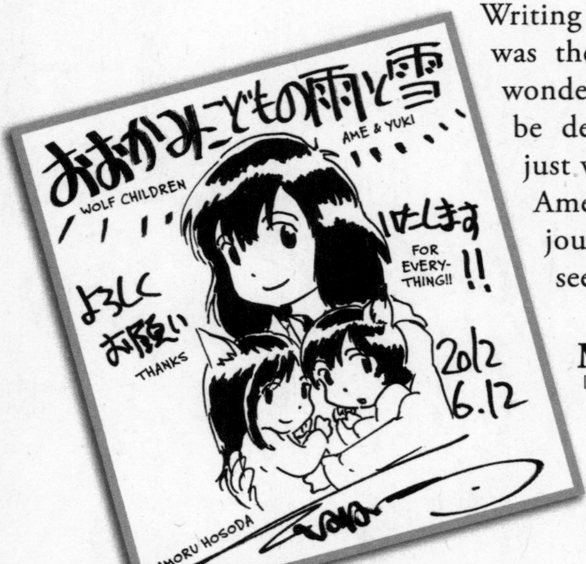

おおかみこどもの雨と雪
WOLF CHILDREN
AME & YUKI
よろしく
お願い
THANKS
いたします
FOR EVERYTHING!!
!!
2012
6.12
MAMORU HOSODA

Writing these events into a film was the first trial for me. Now I wonder how this flow of time will be depicted in the manga. And just what will Hana and Yuki and Ame look like at the end of their journey? I'm looking forward to seeing how it all plays out.

Mamoru Hosoda
[*Wolf Children Ame & Yuki* director, screenwriter, creator]

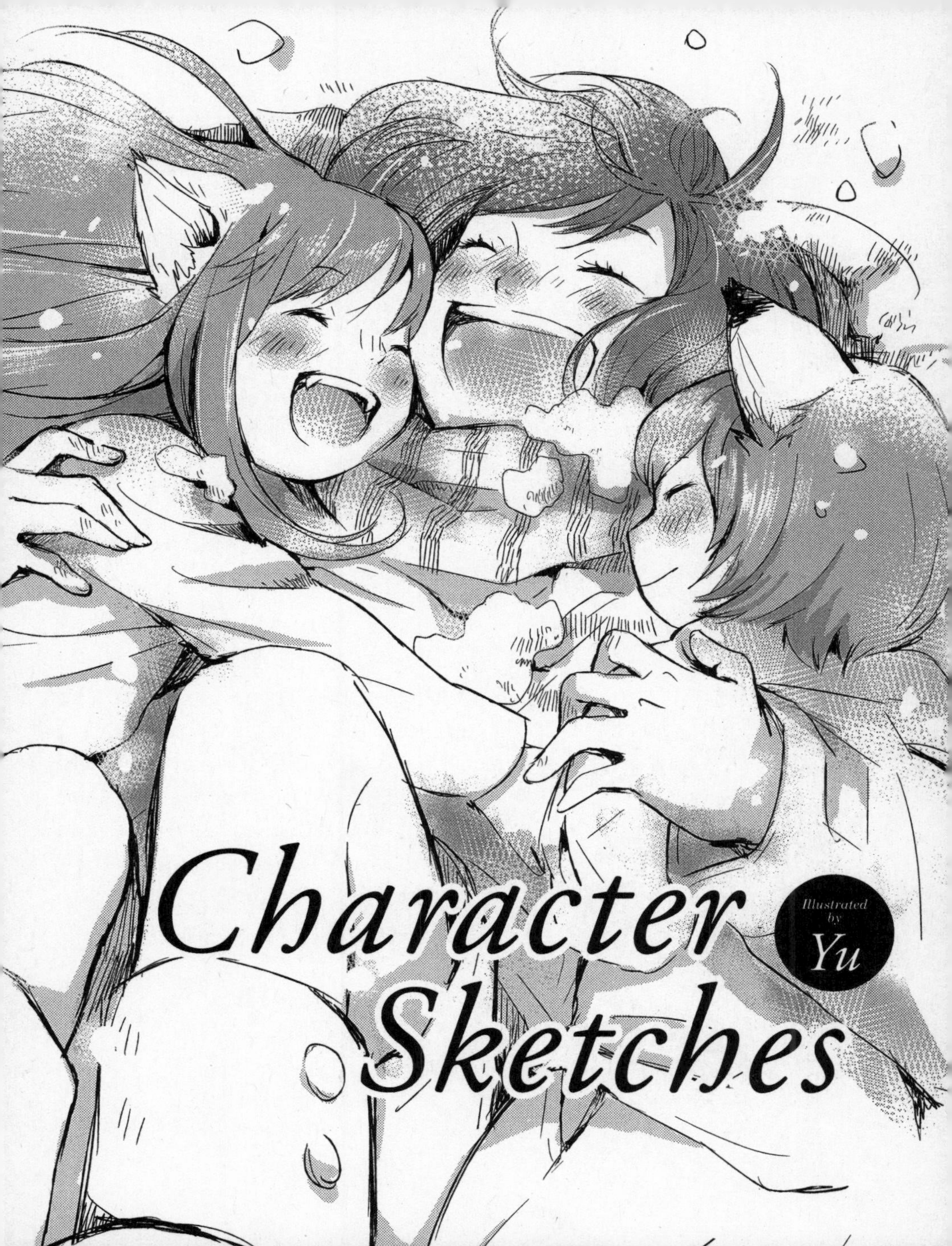
Character
Sketches
Illustrated by
Yu

Hana

A student at a university on the outskirts of Tokyo who falls in love with a wolfman. She takes on the challenge of child rearing for the first time in raising Yuki and Ame.

(Note: Hana's name is written with the kanji for "flower.")

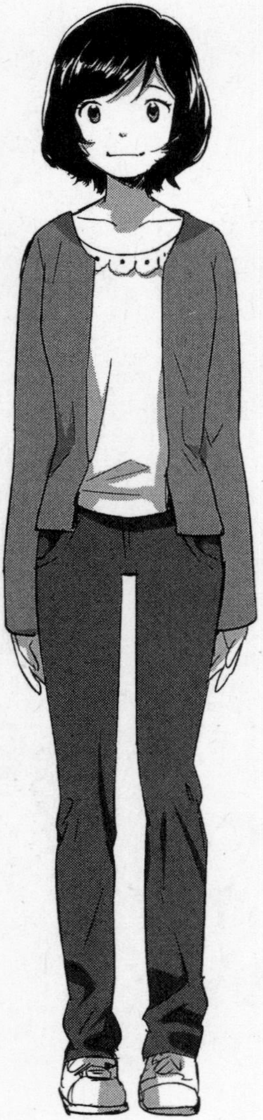

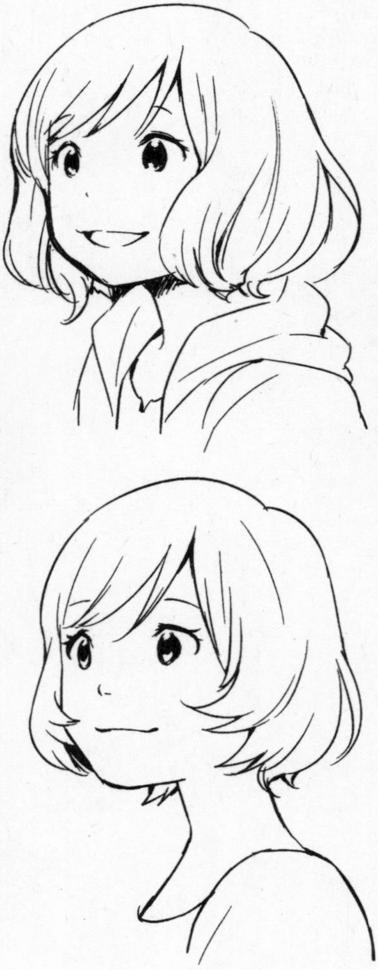

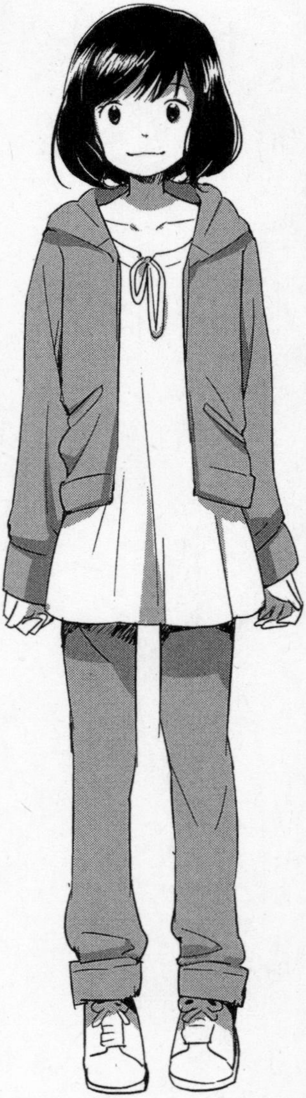

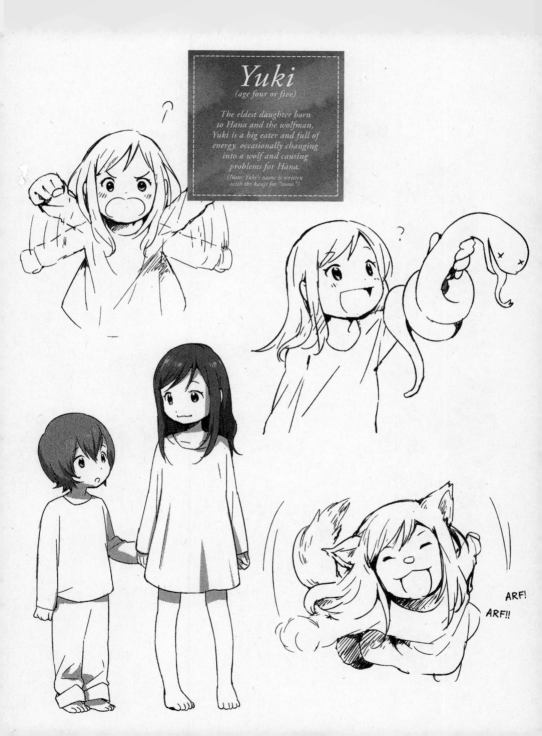

Yuki

(age four or five)

The eldest daughter born to Hana and the wolfman, Yuki is a big eater and full of energy, occasionally changing into a wolf and causing problems for Hana.

(Note: Yuki's name is written with the kanji for "snow.")

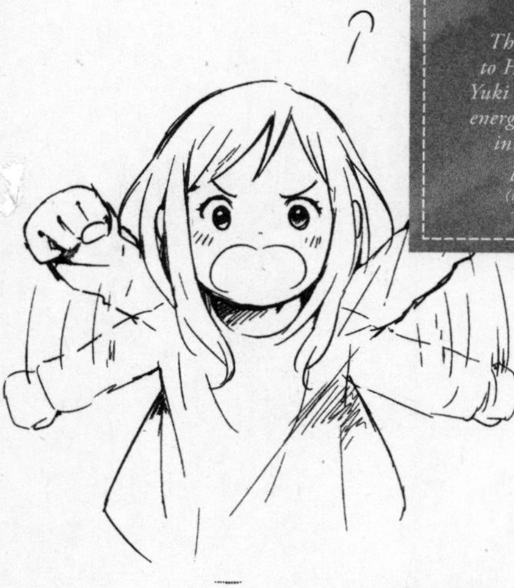

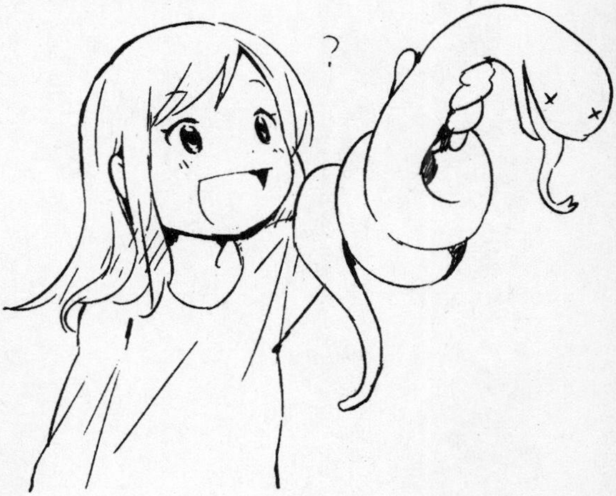

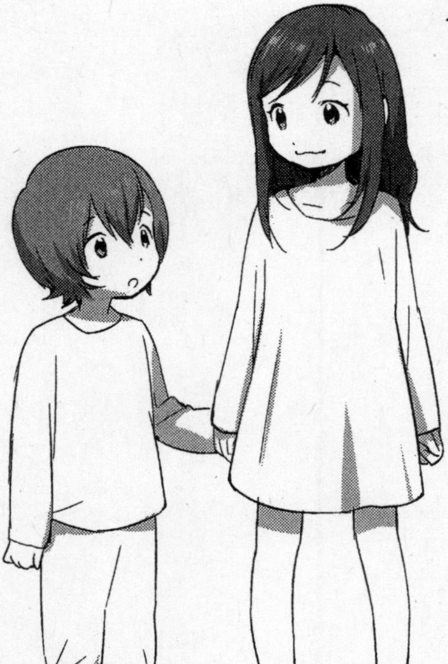

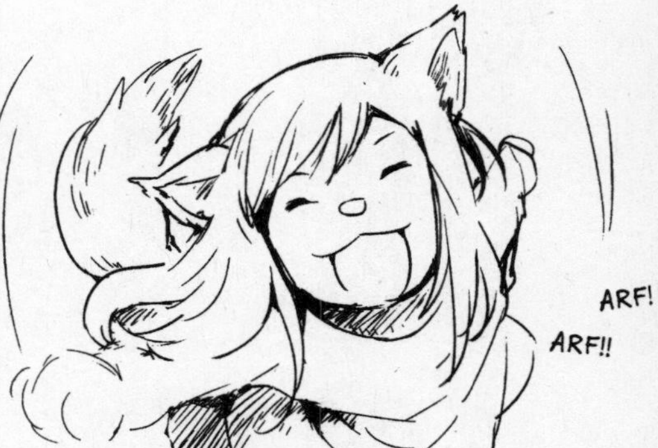
ARF!
ARF!!

Ame

(age four or five)

The eldest son, born a year after Yuki, he doesn't eat much compared to his big sister, and he can be a bit sickly. Personality-wise, he's a little withdrawn, contemplative, and quiet.

(Note: Ame's name is written with the kanji for "rain.")

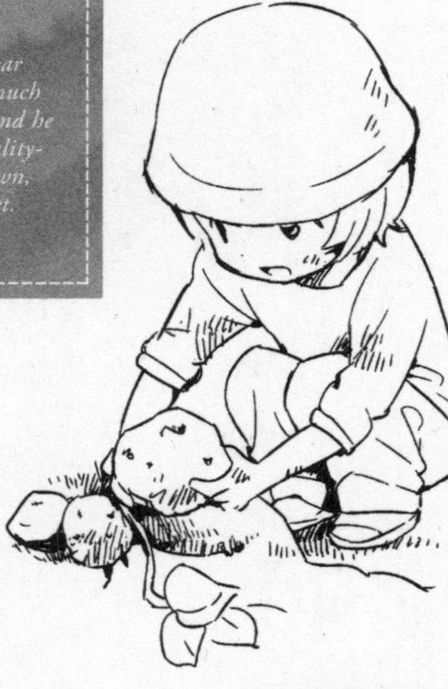

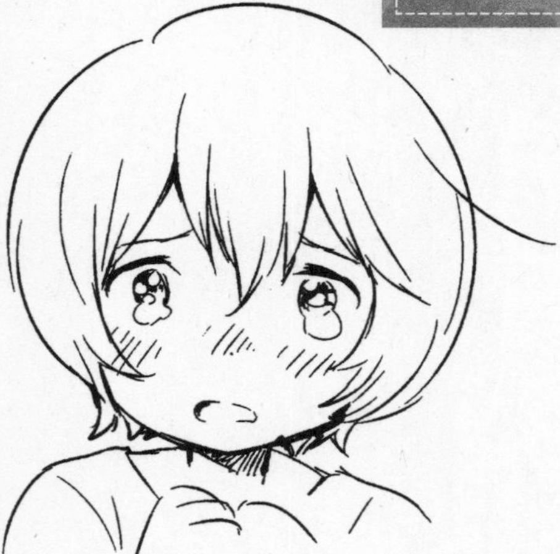

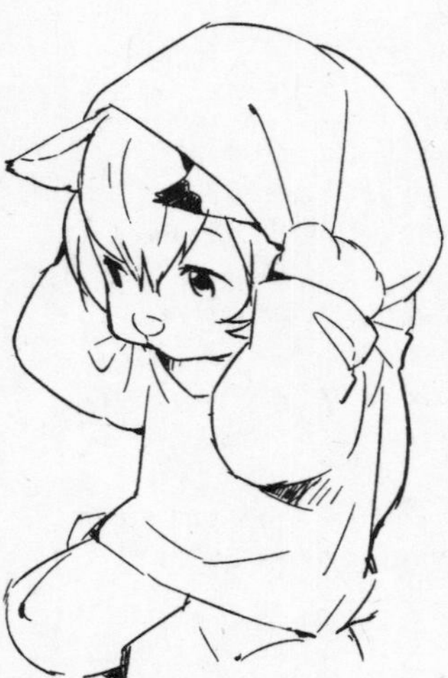

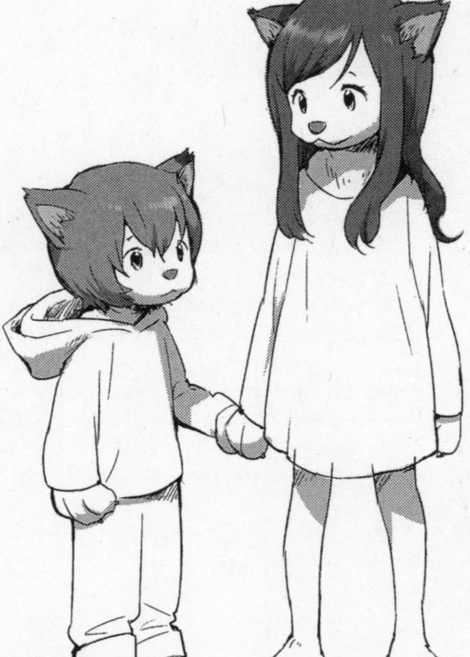

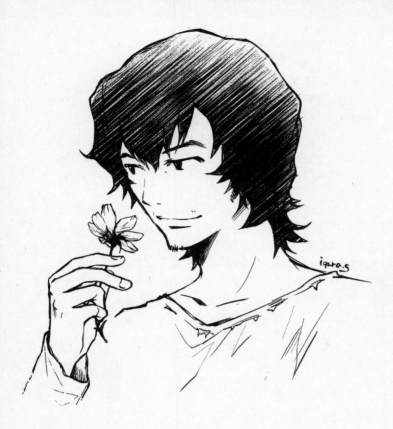

iqura.s

CONGRATULATIONS ON THE FIRST VOLUME OF THE COMIC ADAPTATION OF
WOLF CHILDREN AME & YUKI! I WAS FORTUNATE ENOUGH TO DRAW THE COMIC
ADAPTATION OF DIRECTOR HOSODA'S PREVIOUS WORK, SUMMER WARS, AND I'VE
BEEN VERY MUCH LOOKING FORWARD TO THIS EDITION OF WOLF CHILDREN AME & YUKI.

MAYBE IT'S BECAUSE HANA AND I ARE BOTH MOTHERS AND SHE'S DRAWN AS BEING
FROM THE SAME GENERATION AS ME, BUT THIS MAY BE THE FIRST WORK WHERE I HAVE
FELT SUCH EMPATHY FOR THE CHARACTERS. I CAN'T HELP BUT WANT TO CAREFULLY WATCH
OVER HANA'S FAMILY UNTIL THE END OF TIME IN THE HOPES THAT THEY KEEP ON SMILING.

I BELIEVE THAT YU-SENSEI'S GENTLE DRAWING STYLE GETS ACROSS THE EXACT WARMTH
OF THE ORIGINAL WORK. AS A READER, I'M EXCITED FOR THE NEXT VOLUME.

IQURA SUGIMOTO, JUNE 2012

Yu
Afterword

THANK YOU SO MUCH FOR PICKING UP WOLF CHILDREN AME + YUKI.

I PERSONALLY LOVE AND ADORE THE WORK OF MAMORU HOSODA-SAN, SO WHEN THE DECISION WAS MADE TO SERIALIZE THE COMIC VERSION, I WAS VERY HAPPY. IT WAS LIKE A DREAM. IT WAS THE FIRST COMIC I'D EVER HAD SERIALIZED, AND NOTHING WENT THE WAY I EXPECTED. I STRUGGLED WITH A LOT OF THINGS. BUT EVEN SO, I BELIEVE I WAS ABLE TO MAKE IT THIS FAR BECAUSE I HAD SO MANY PEOPLE SUPPORTING ME, INCLUDING YOU READERS. THANK YOU SO MUCH. I FEEL LIKE I STILL HAVE SO MUCH MORE TO LEARN, BUT I'M WORKING HARD SO THAT THE WONDER OF WOLF CHILDREN AME + YUKI COMES THROUGH IN THIS MANGA, EVEN IF IT'S JUST THE TINIEST BIT.

I HOPE YOU'LL KEEP READING!!

SPECIAL THANKS

MAMEKO-SAN
HABUKI-SAN
MIKI KAWARABAYASHI-SAN
MIKI KAMIYA-SAN
YUSUKE-SAN
EDITOR: NAKAZAWA-SAN

THANK YOU!

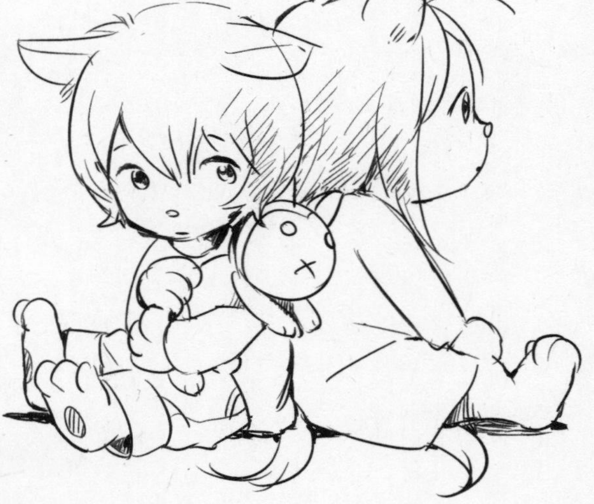

HERE'S TO HOPING WE MEET AGAIN!

優
YU

Words from the Artist

Volume 1

Nice to meet you. My name is Yu. This is my first serialization and also my first book. I still have a lot to learn, but I'm putting all of my heart into these illustrations. I hope you'll keep reading!

—Yu

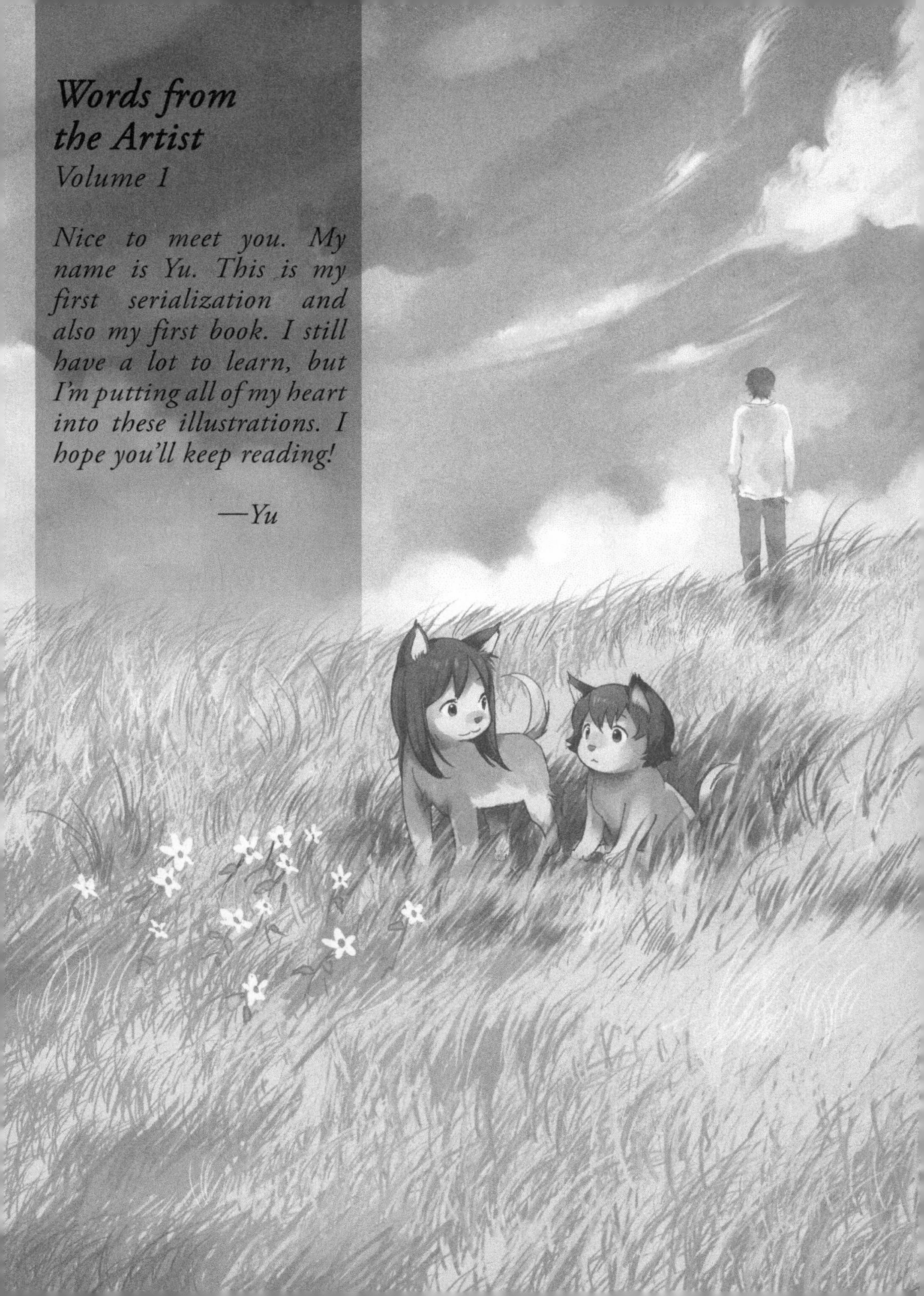

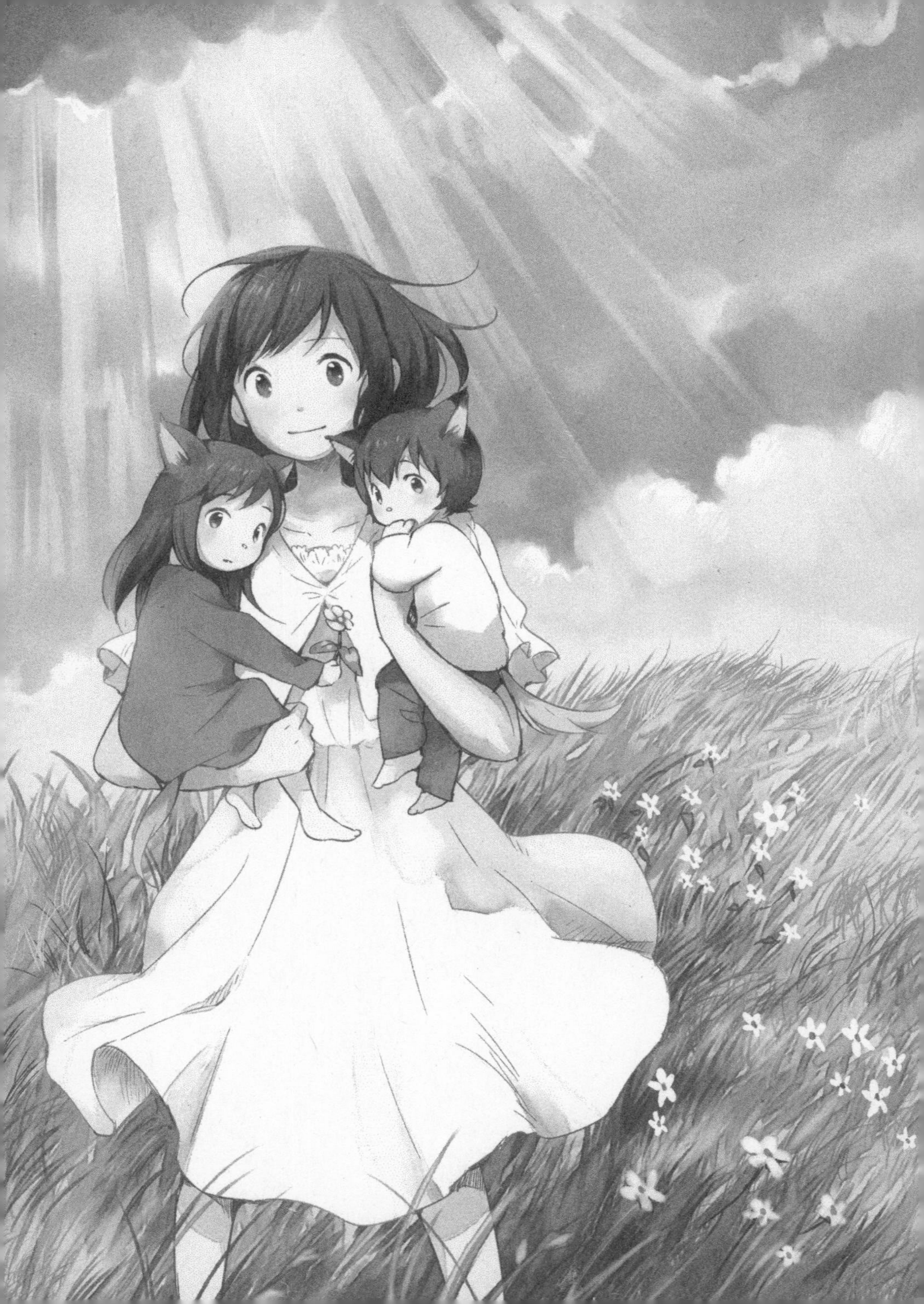

Wolf Children
Ame & Yuki

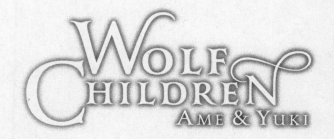

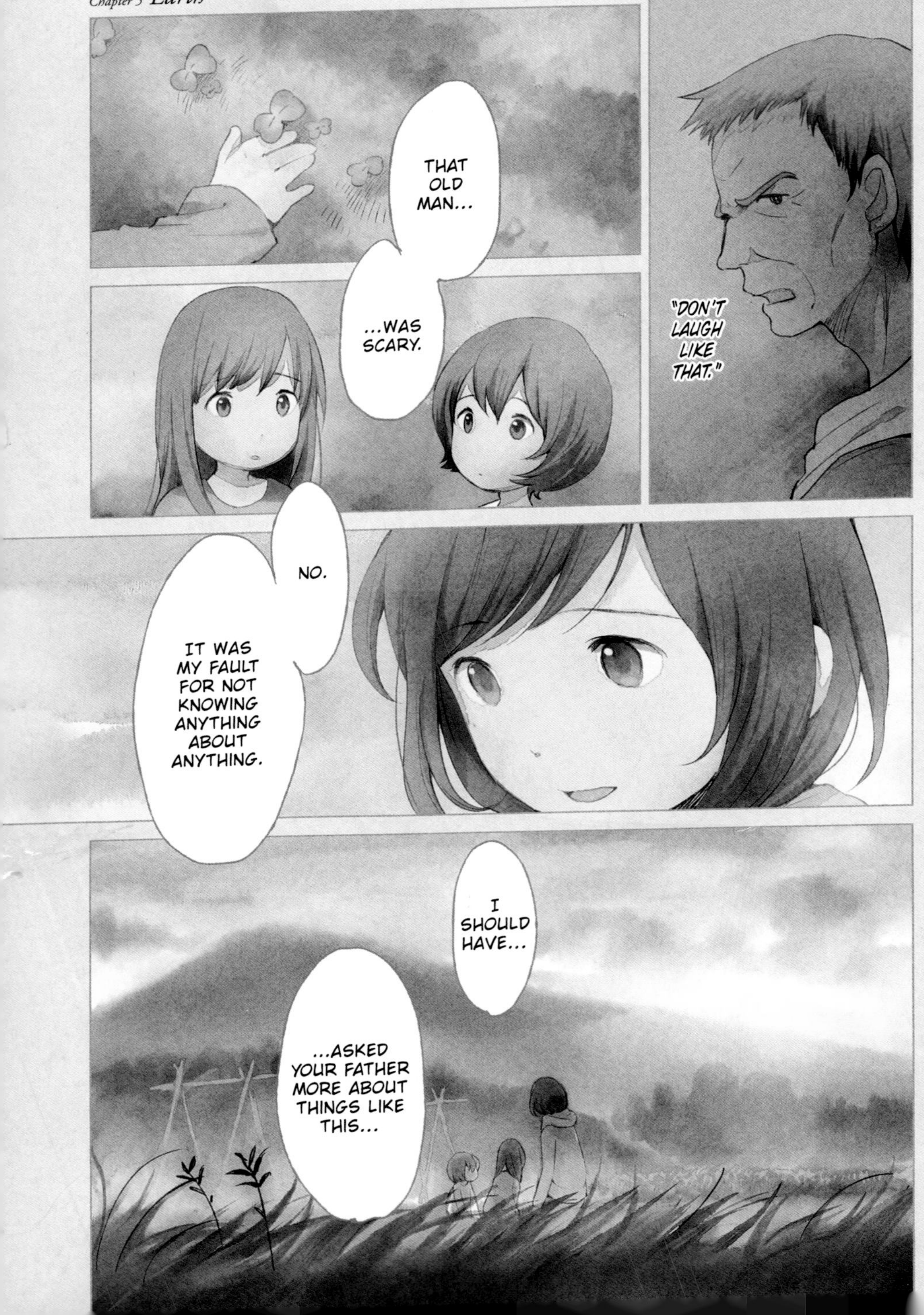
"DON'T LAUGH LIKE THAT."
THAT OLD MAN...
...WAS SCARY.
NO.
IT WAS MY FAULT FOR NOT KNOWING ANYTHING ABOUT ANYTHING.
I SHOULD HAVE...
...ASKED YOUR FATHER MORE ABOUT THINGS LIKE THIS...

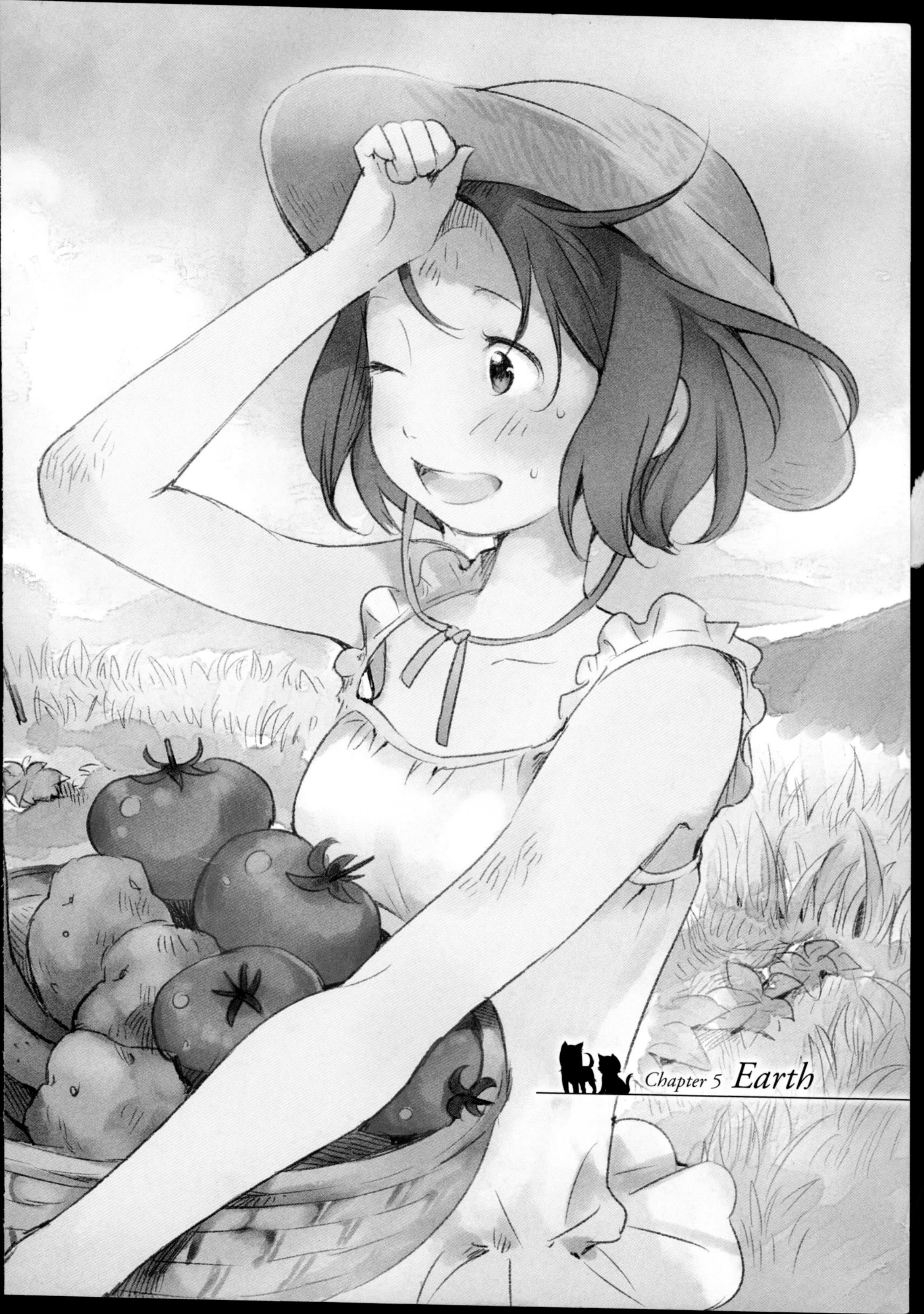

Chapter 5 Earth

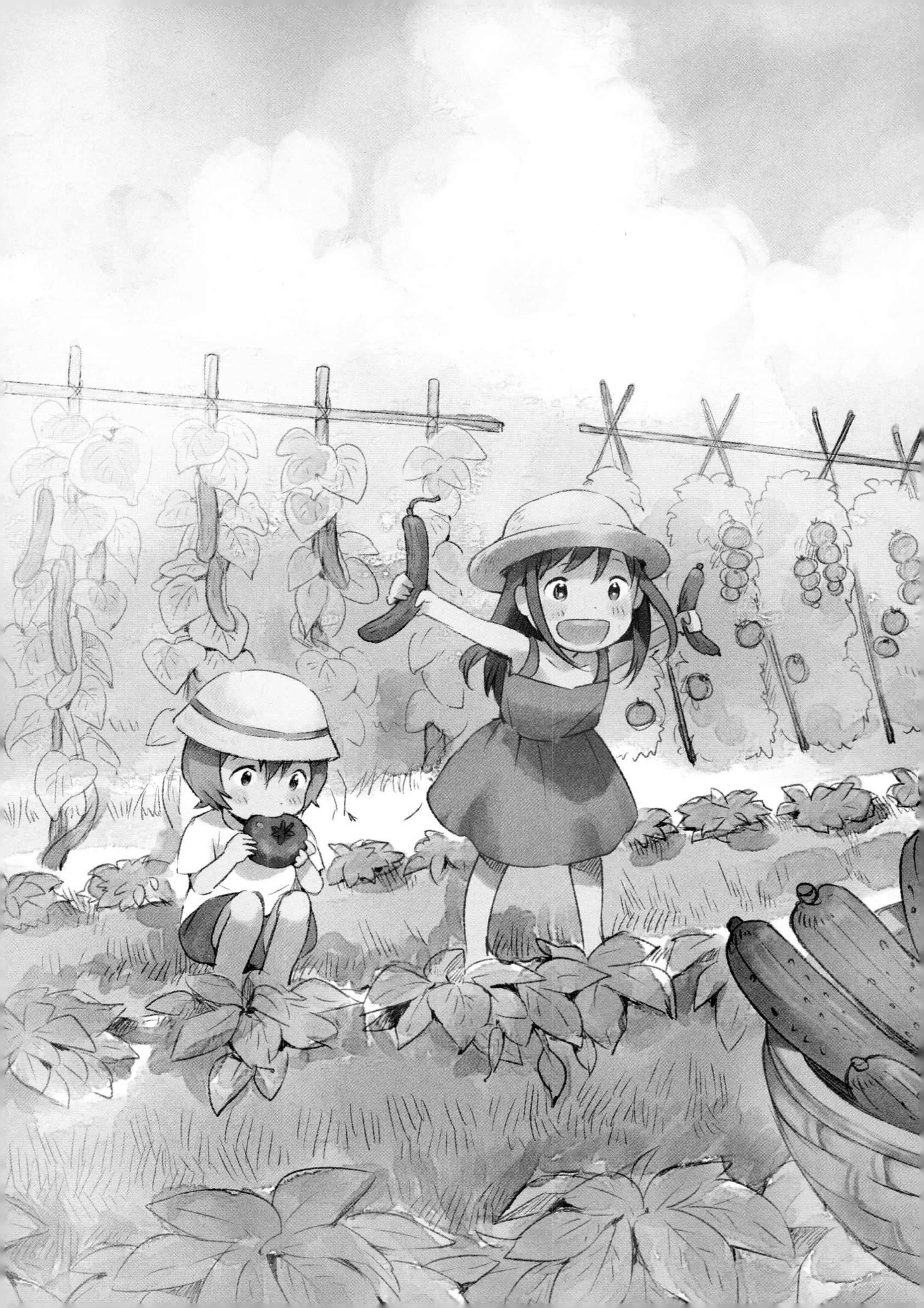

WOLF CHILDREN
AME & YUKI

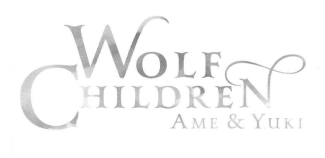

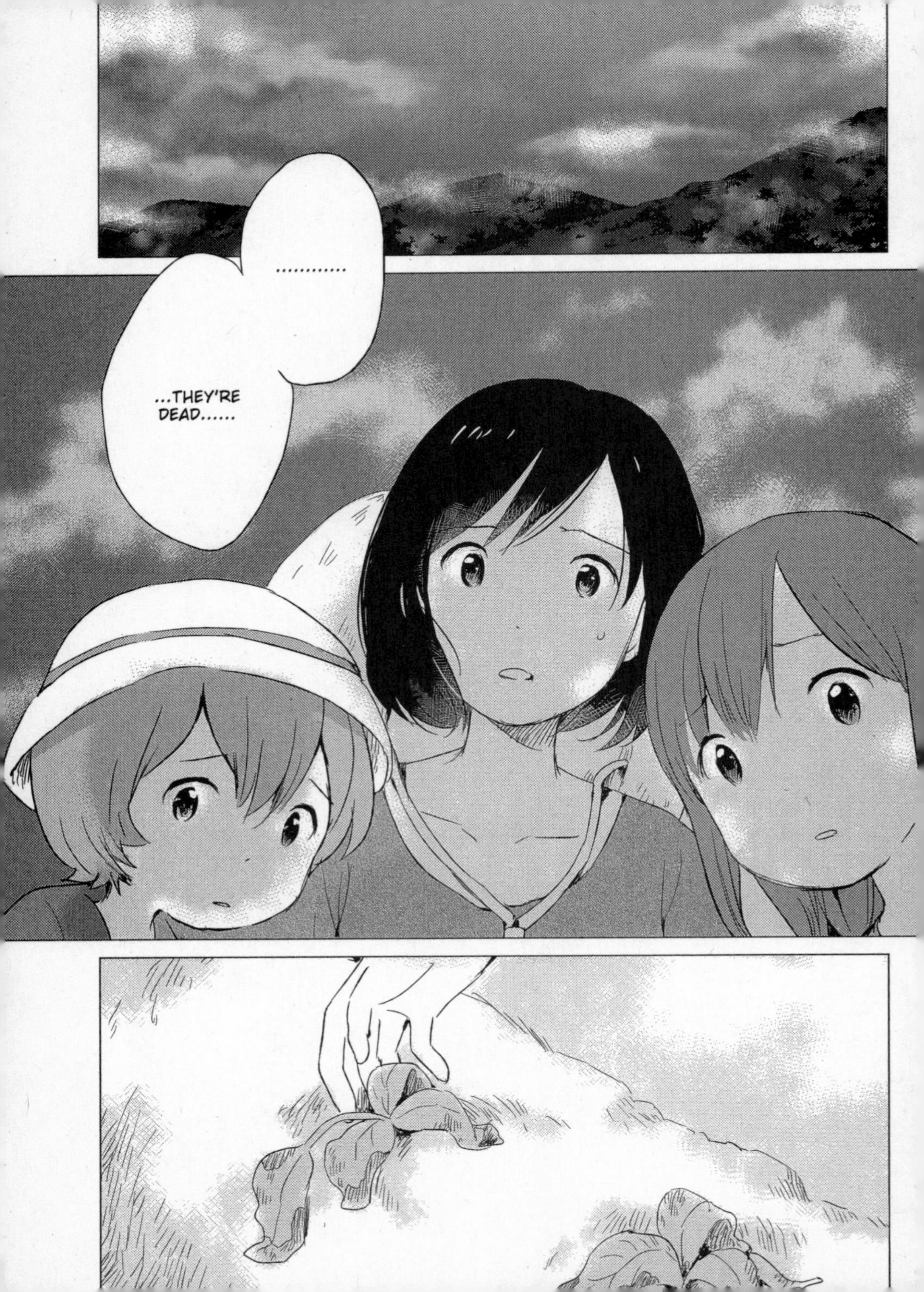
....
...THEY'RE DEAD......

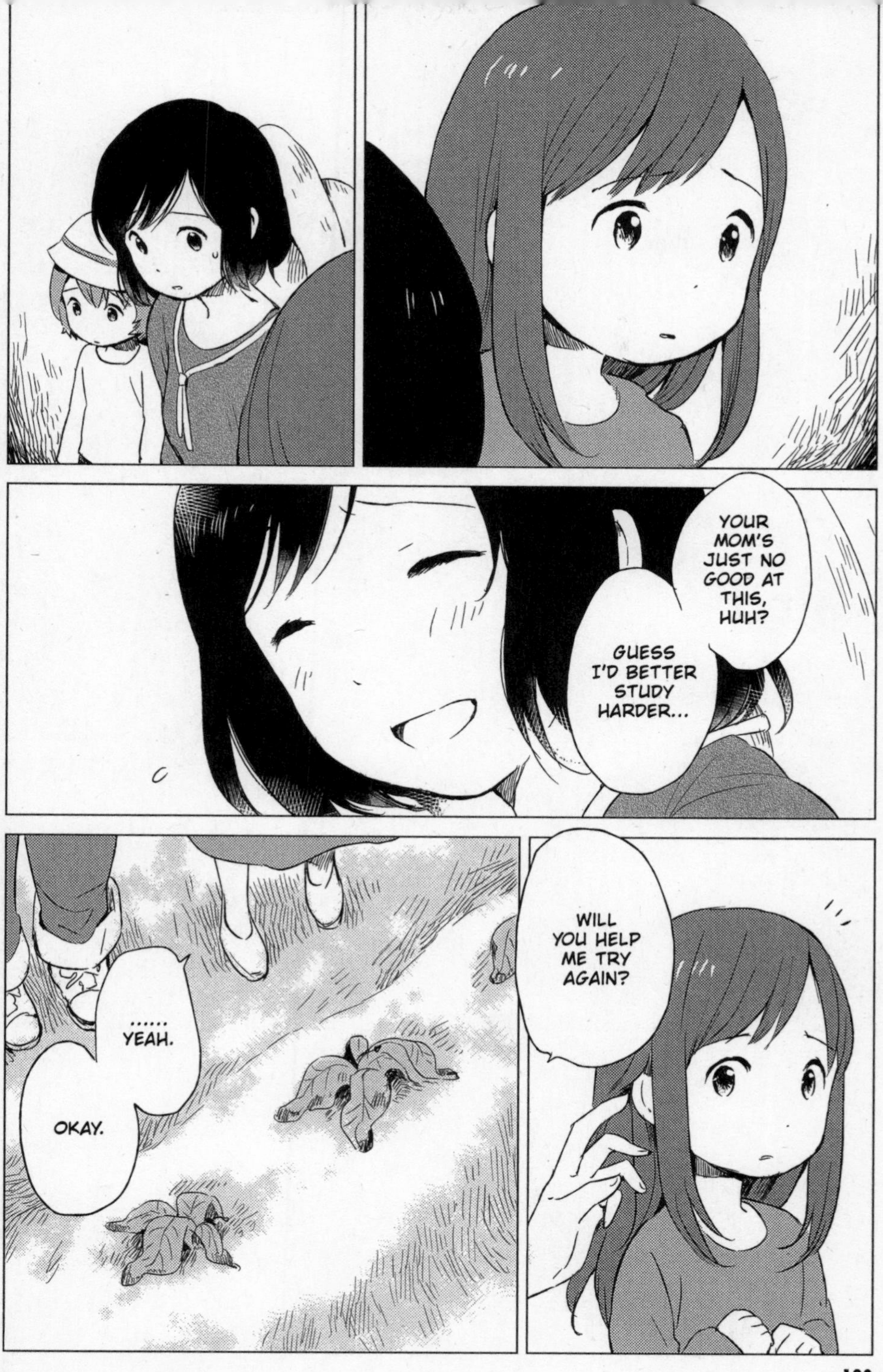
YOUR MOM'S JUST NO GOOD AT THIS, HUH?
GUESS I'D BETTER STUDY HARDER...
WILL YOU HELP ME TRY AGAIN?
...... YEAH.
OKAY.

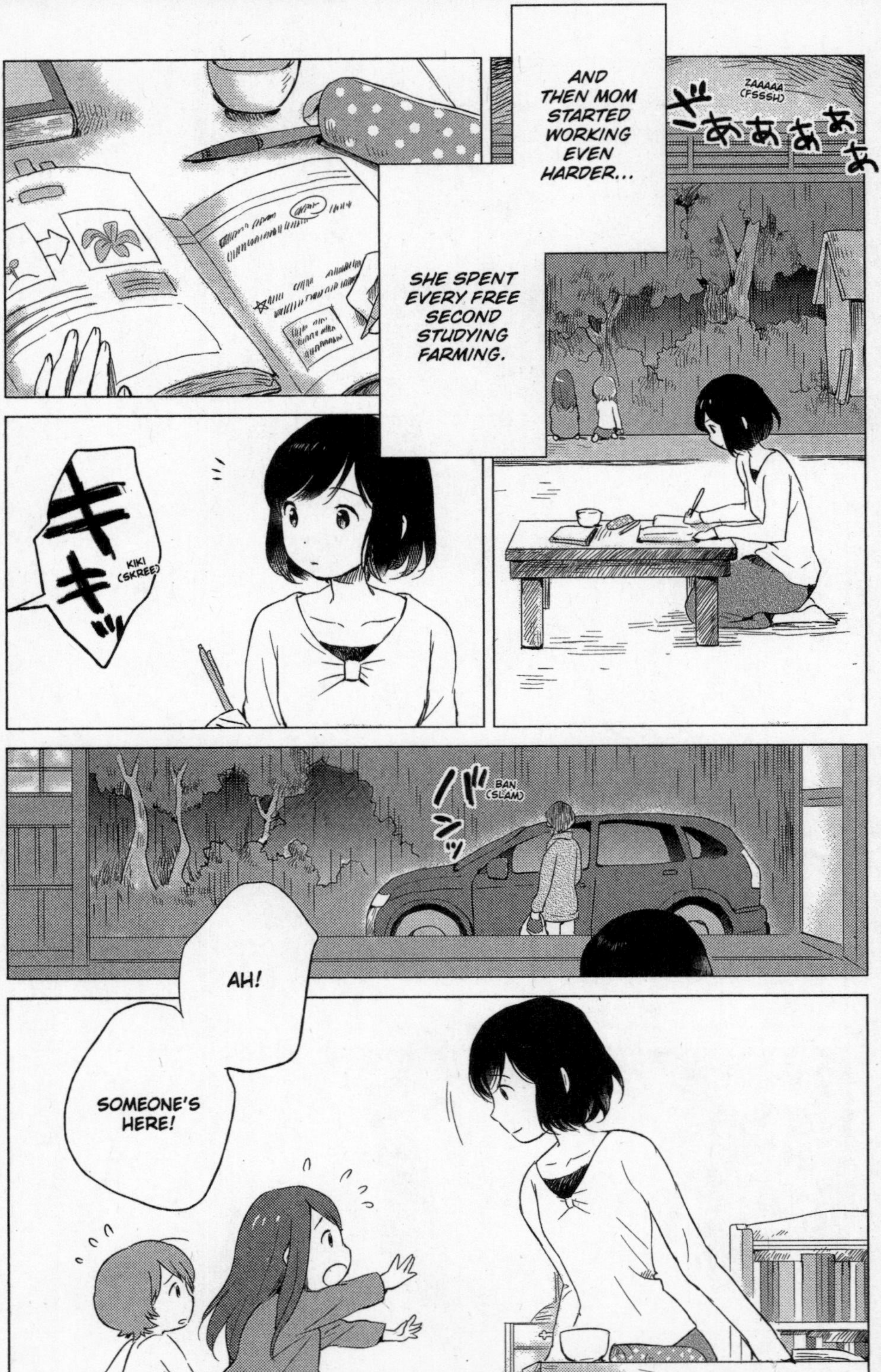
ざあああああ
ZAAAAA (FSSSH)
AND THEN MOM STARTED WORKING EVEN HARDER...
SHE SPENT EVERY FREE SECOND STUDYING FARMING.
キキッ
KIKI (SKREE)
バンッ
BAN (SLAM)
AH!
SOMEONE'S HERE!

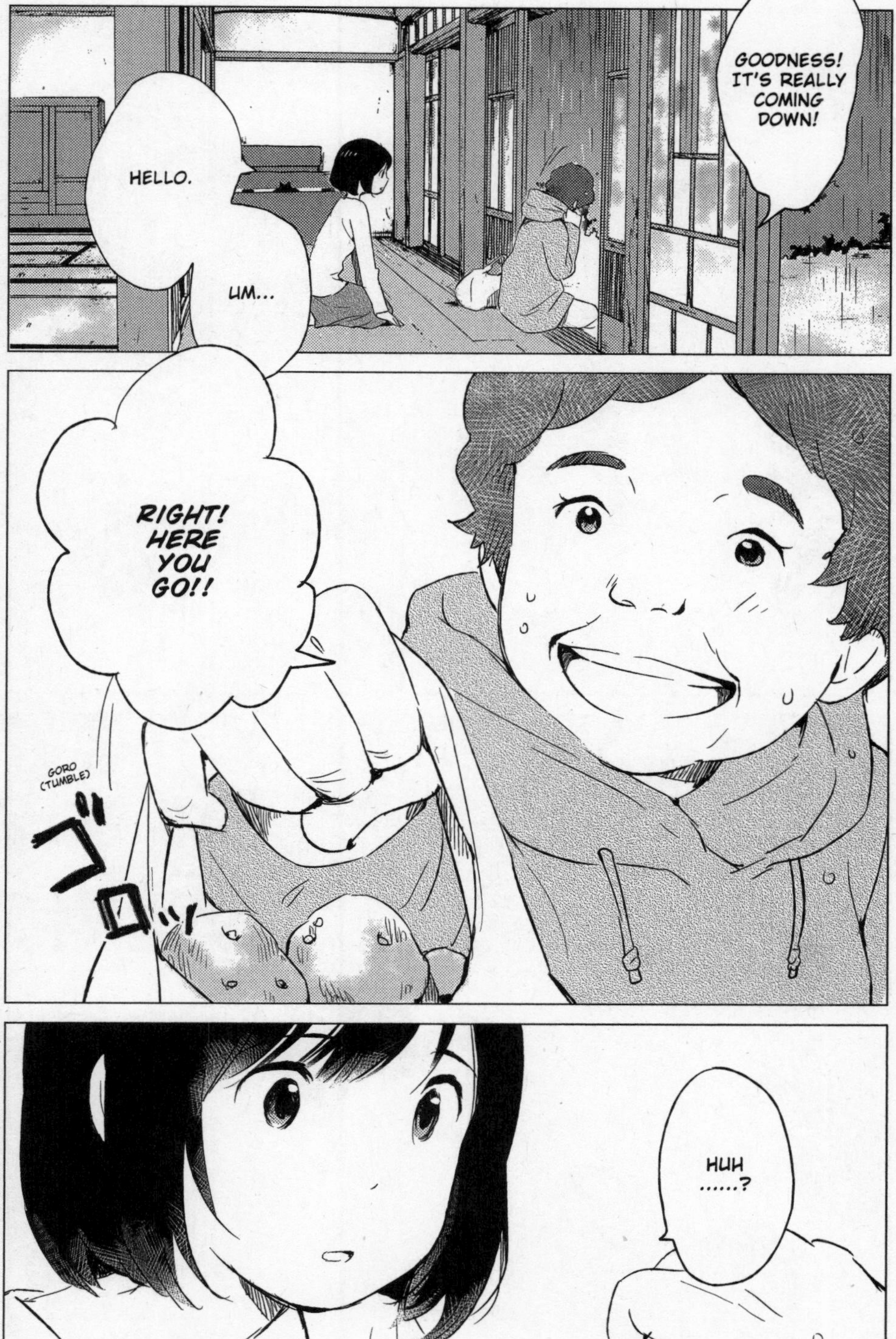
GOODNESS! IT'S REALLY COMING DOWN!
HELLO.
UM...
RIGHT! HERE YOU GO!!
GORO (TUMBLE)
ゴロッ
HUH ......?

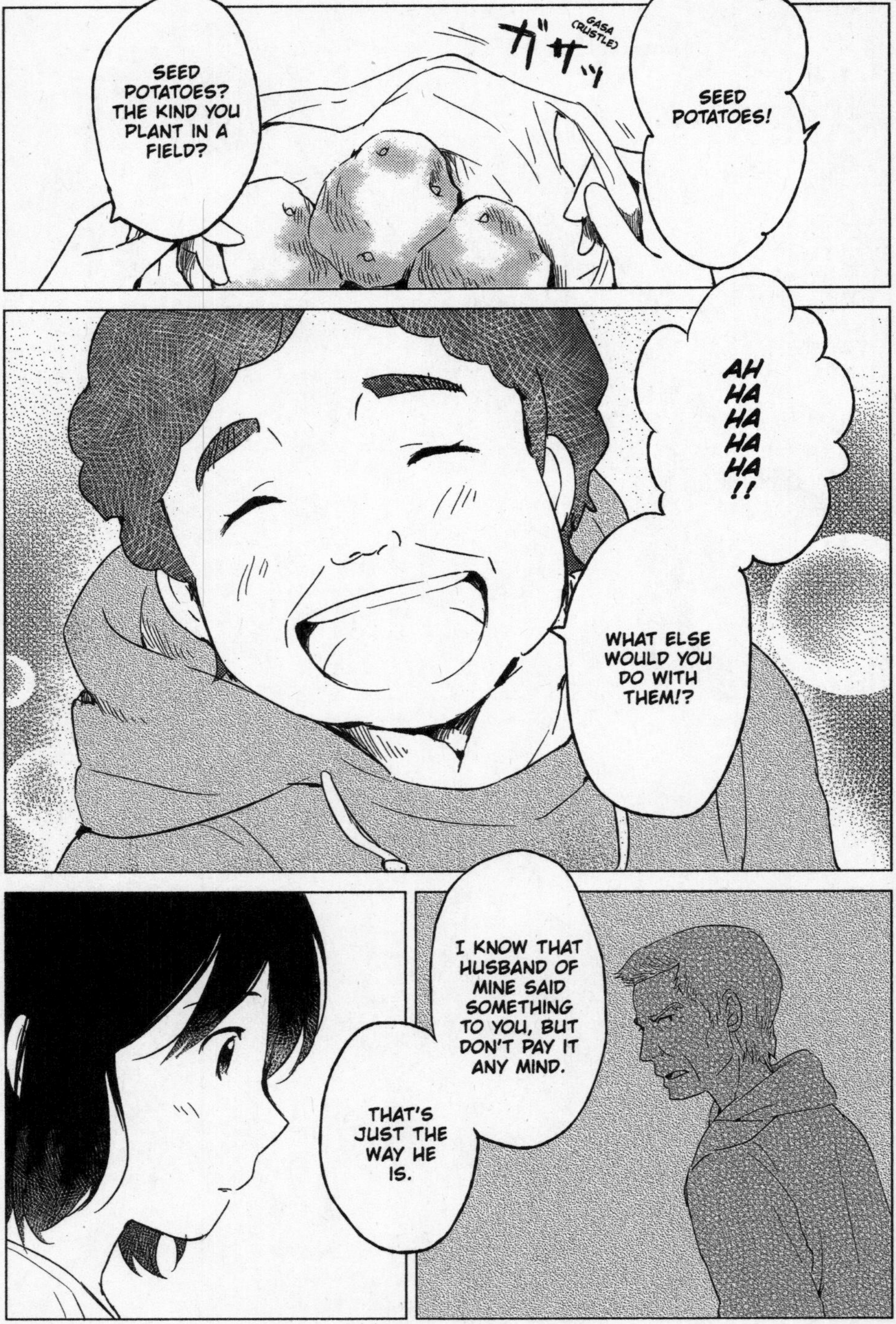
GASA (RUSTLE)
SEED POTATOES!
SEED POTATOES? THE KIND YOU PLANT IN A FIELD?
AH HA HA HA HA!!
WHAT ELSE WOULD YOU DO WITH THEM!?
I KNOW THAT HUSBAND OF MINE SAID SOMETHING TO YOU, BUT DON'T PAY IT ANY MIND.
THAT'S JUST THE WAY HE IS.

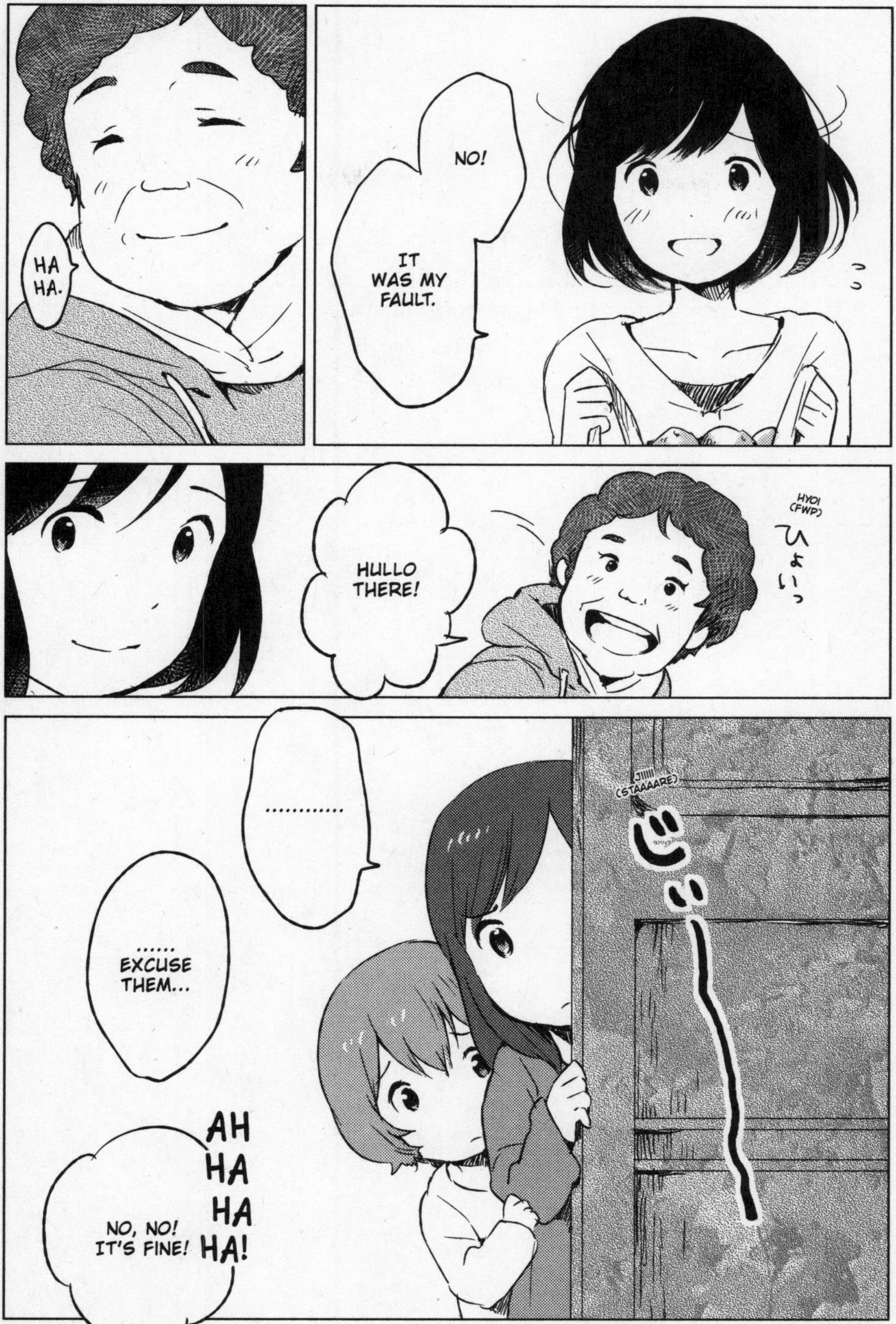
NO!
IT WAS MY FAULT.
HA HA.
HYOI (FWP)
ひょいっ
HULLO THERE!
JIIIII (STAAAARE)
じーー
....
......EXCUSE THEM...
AH HA HA HA!
NO, NO! IT'S FINE!

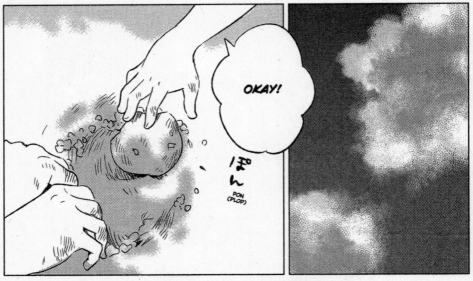

OKAY!

ぽん
PON
(PLOP)

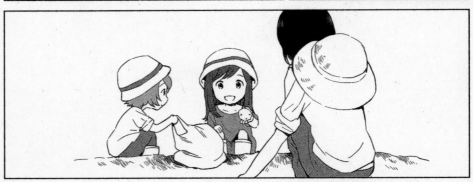

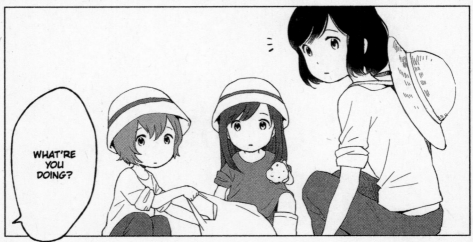

WHAT'RE YOU DOING?

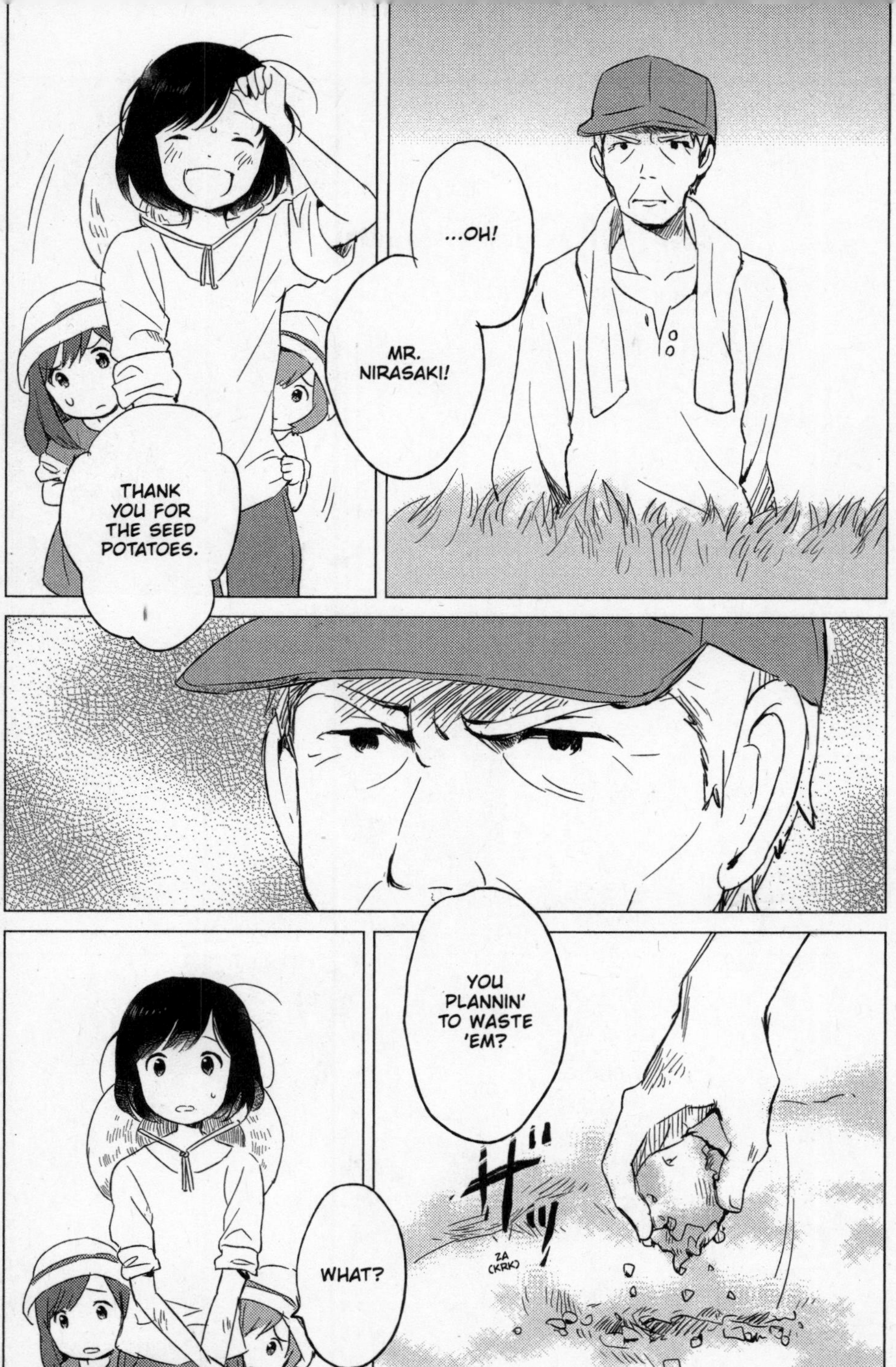
...OH!
MR. NIRASAKI!
THANK YOU FOR THE SEED POTATOES.
YOU PLANNIN' TO WASTE 'EM?
ZA (KRK)
WHAT?

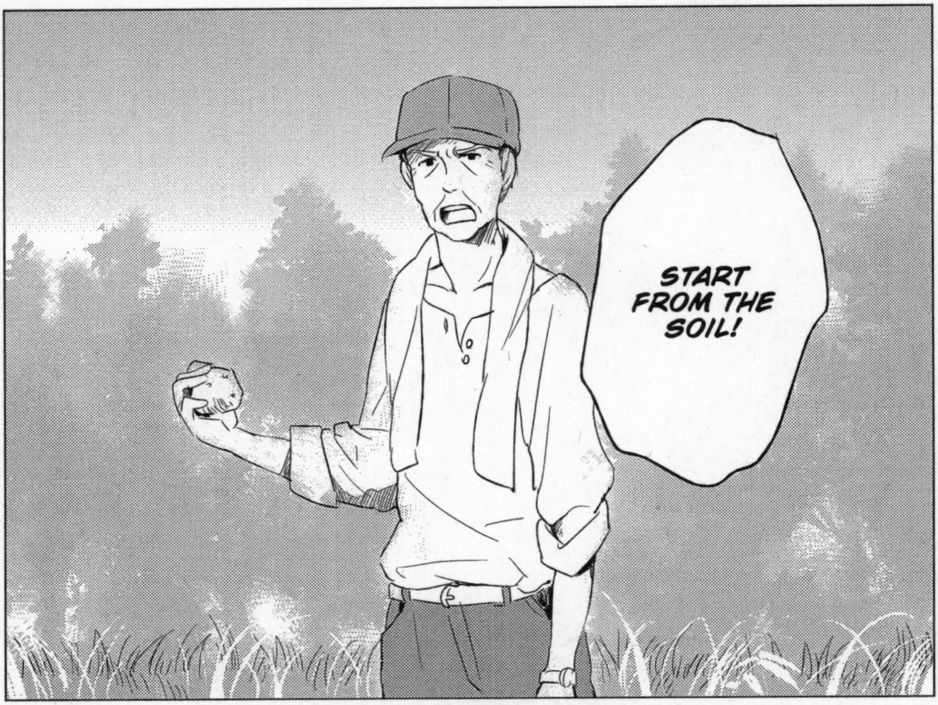
START FROM THE SOIL!

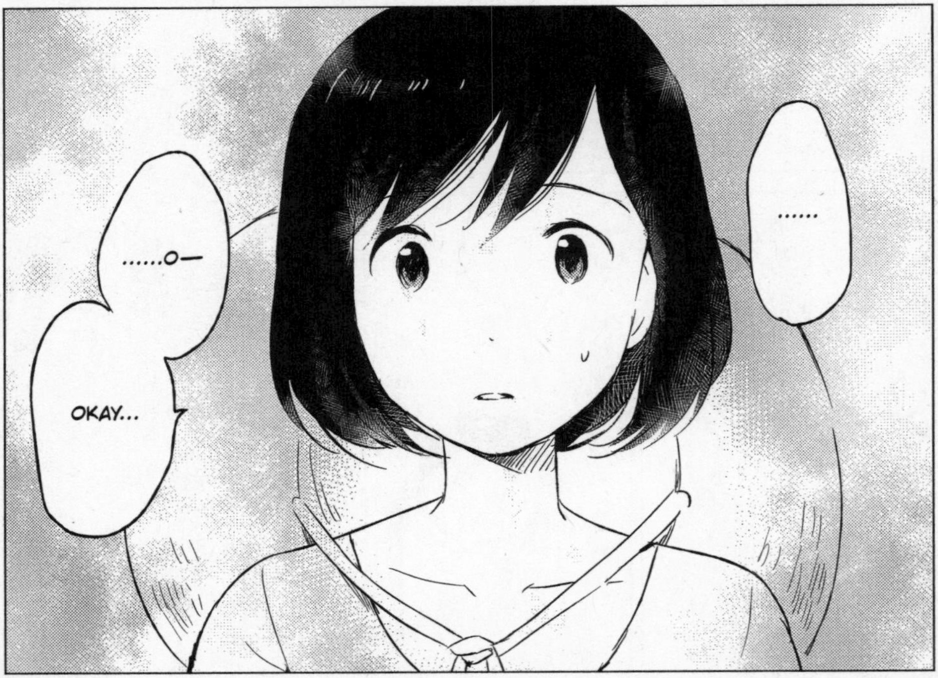
......
......O—
OKAY...

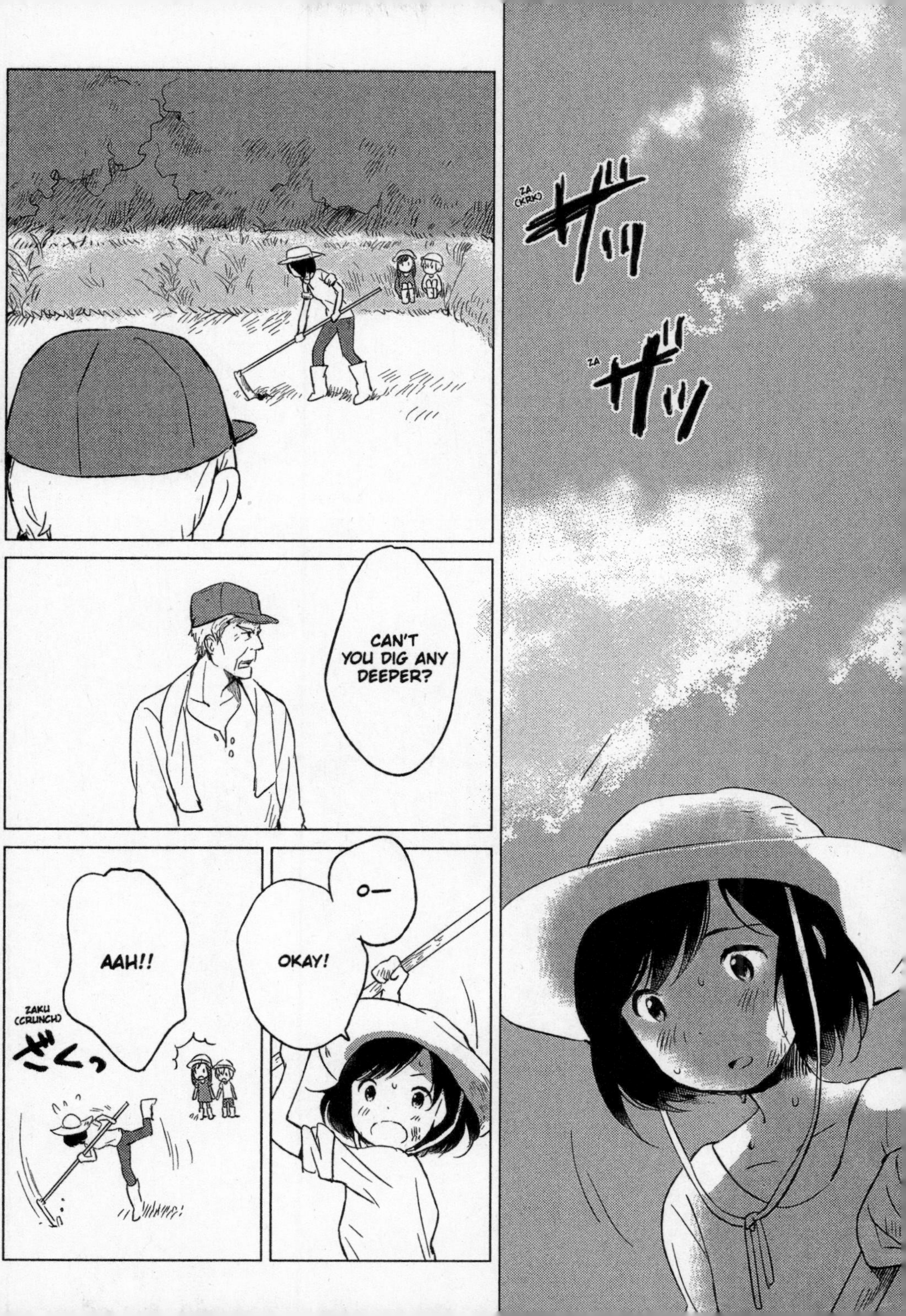
ZA (KRK)
ザリ
ZA
ザッ
CAN'T YOU DIG ANY DEEPER?
O—
OKAY!
AAH!!
ZAKU (CRUNCH)
ざくっ

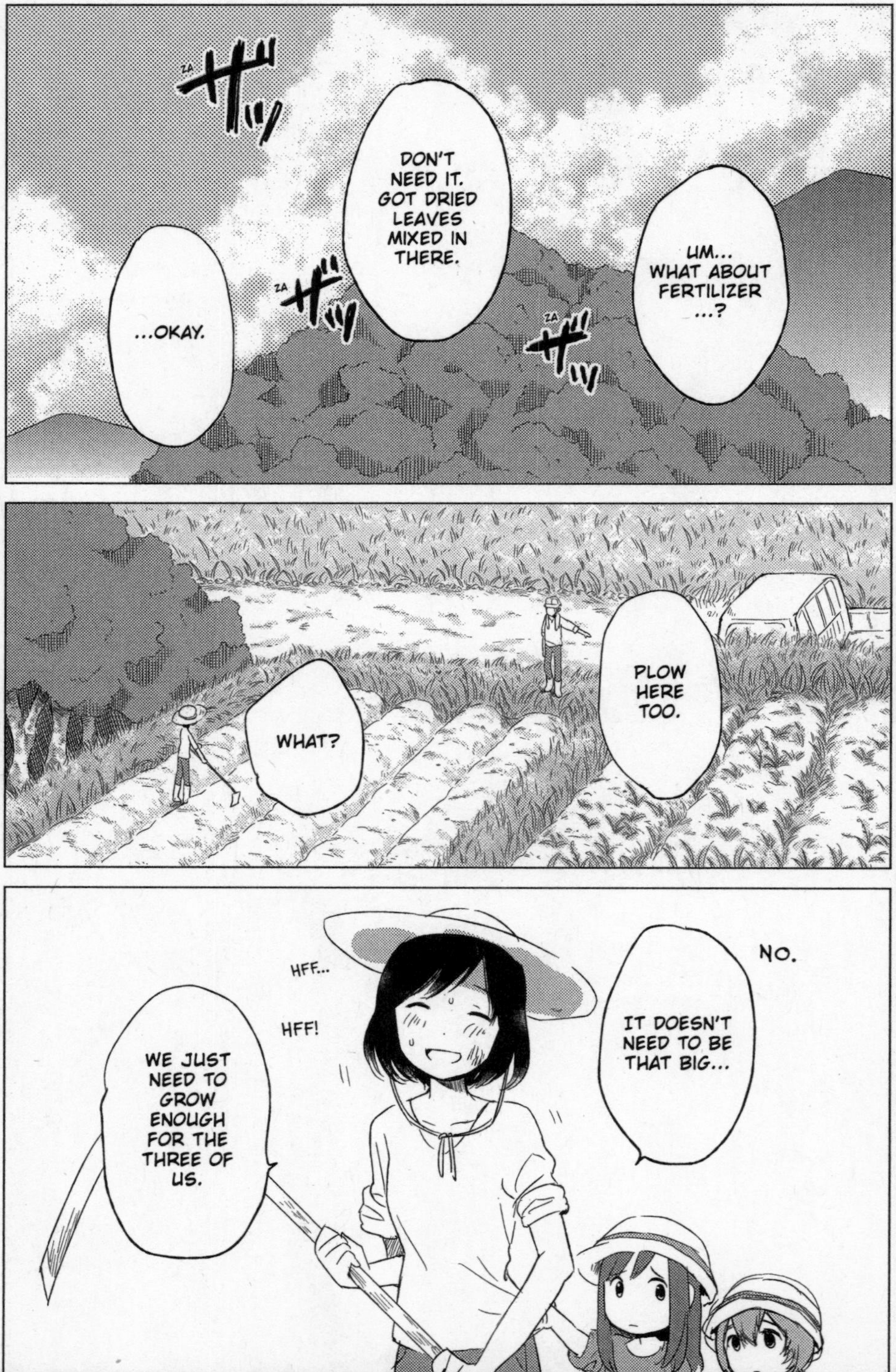
ZA
UM... WHAT ABOUT FERTILIZER ...?
DON'T NEED IT. GOT DRIED LEAVES MIXED IN THERE.
ZA
ZA
...OKAY.
PLOW HERE TOO.
WHAT?
NO.
IT DOESN'T NEED TO BE THAT BIG...
HFF...
HFF!
WE JUST NEED TO GROW ENOUGH FOR THE THREE OF US.

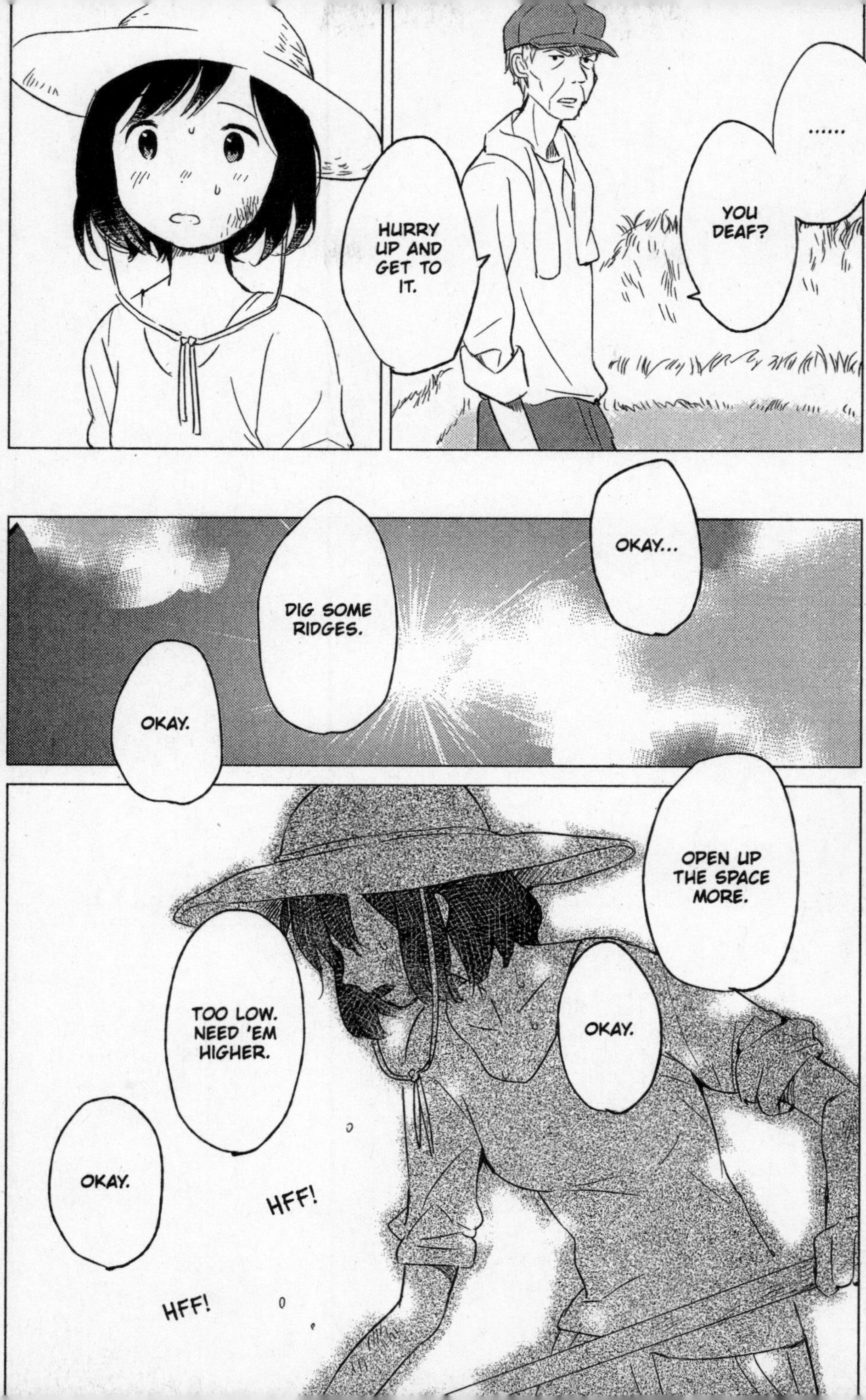
......
YOU DEAF?
HURRY UP AND GET TO IT.
OKAY...
DIG SOME RIDGES.
OKAY.
OPEN UP THE SPACE MORE.
OKAY.
TOO LOW. NEED 'EM HIGHER.
OKAY.
HFF!
HFF!

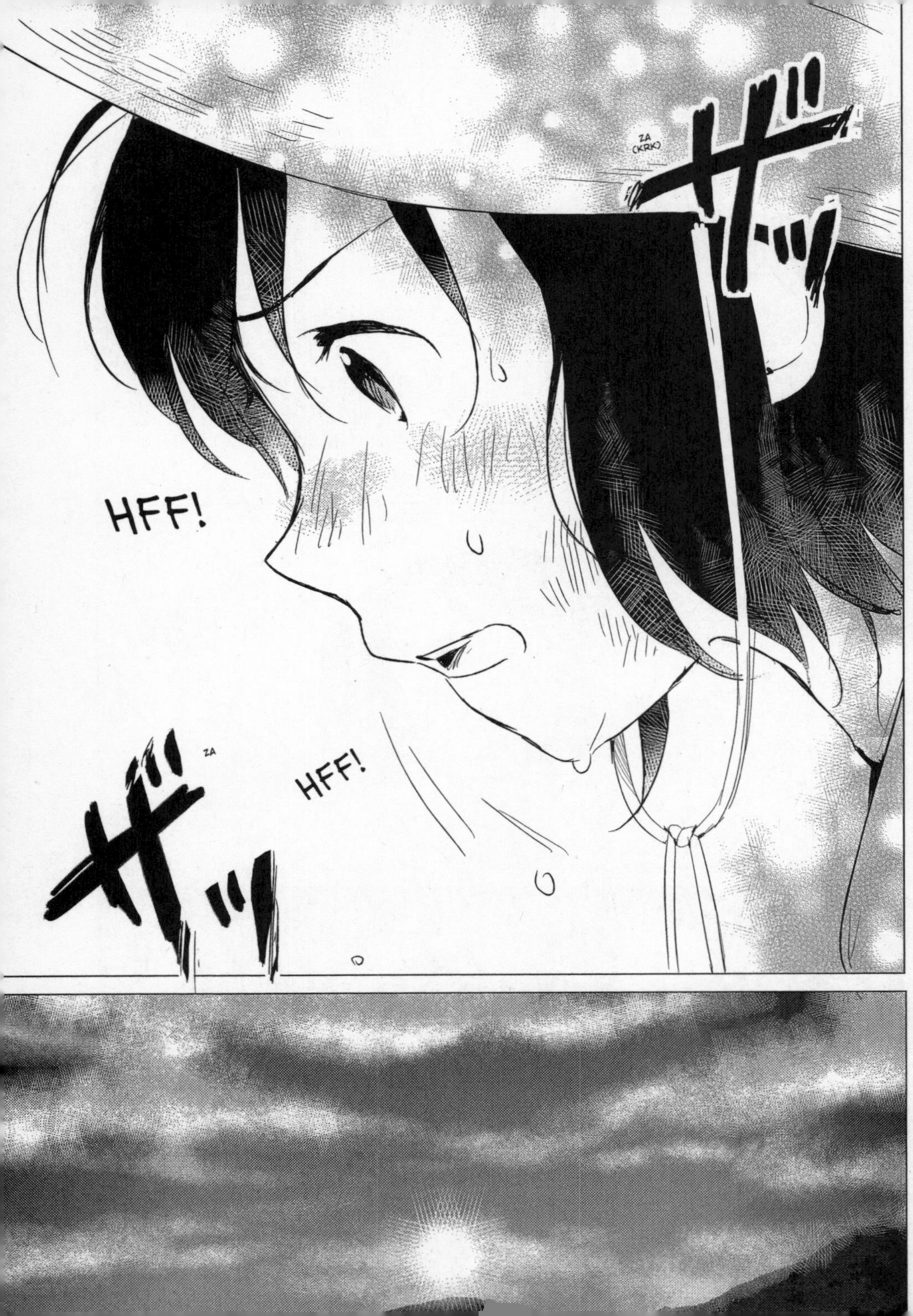
ザッ
ZA (KRK)
HFF!
HFF!
ザッ
ZA

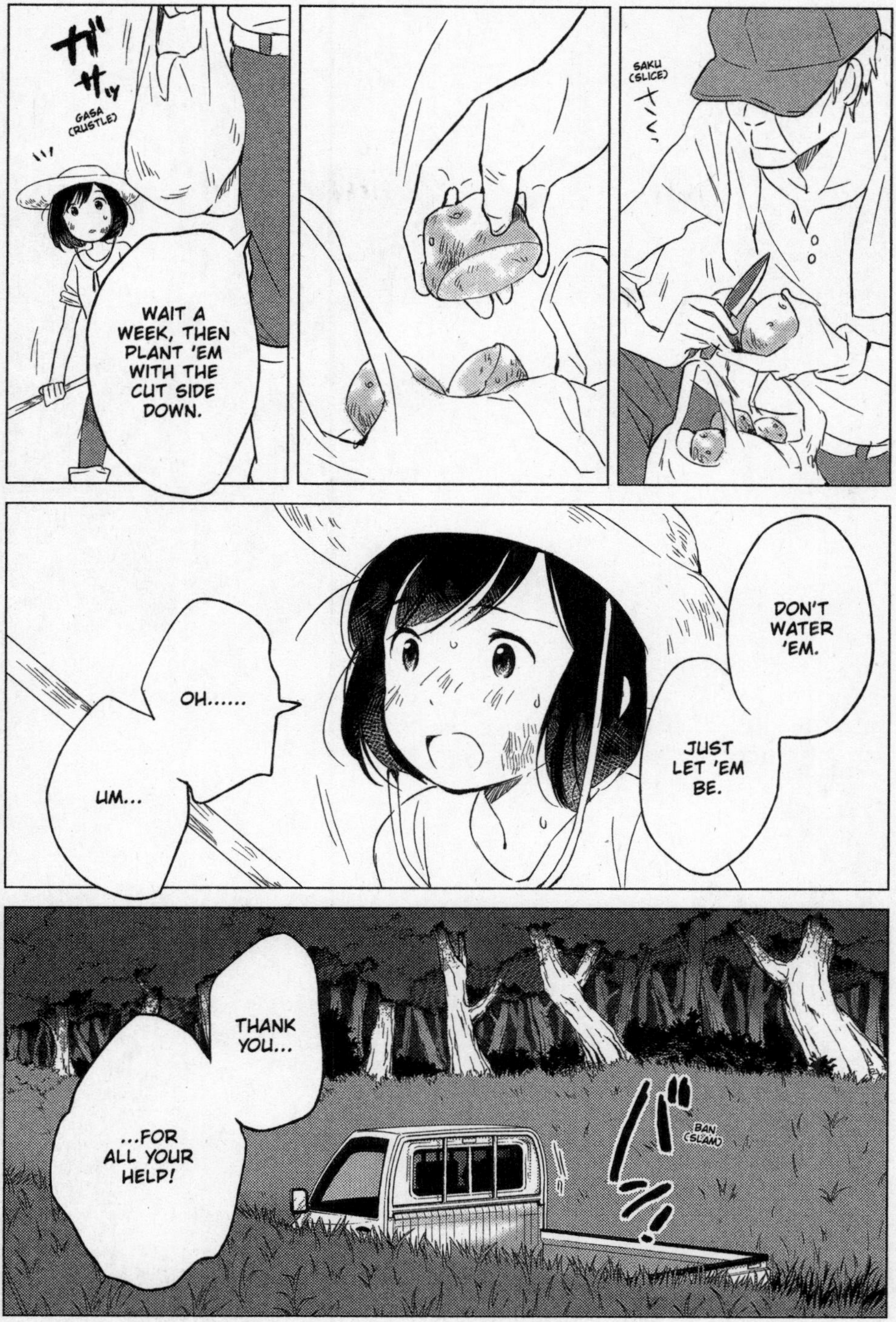
SAKU (SLICE)
GASA (RUSTLE)
WAIT A WEEK, THEN PLANT 'EM WITH THE CUT SIDE DOWN.
DON'T WATER 'EM.
JUST LET 'EM BE.
OH......
UM...
BAN (SLAM)
THANK YOU...
...FOR ALL YOUR HELP!

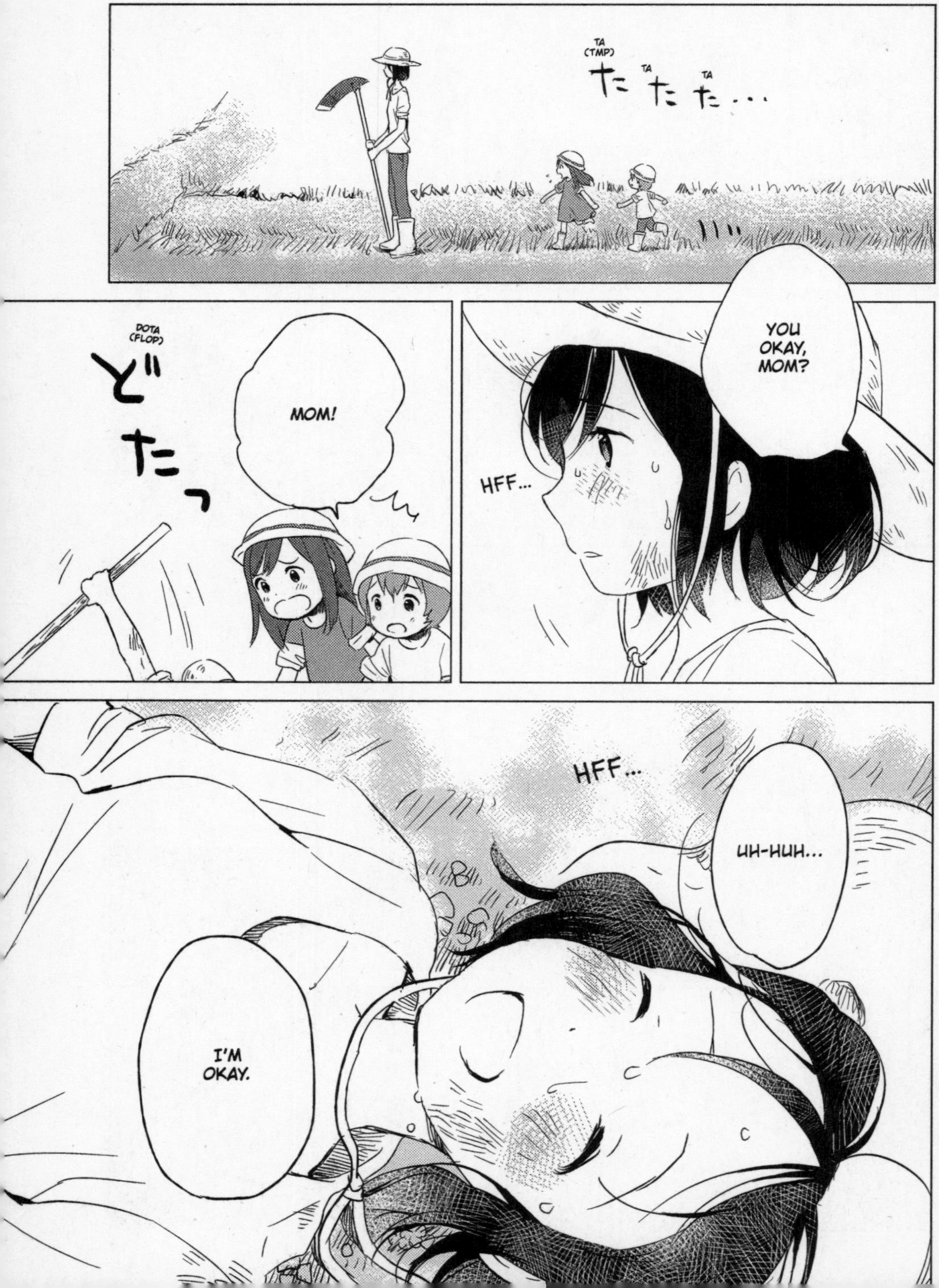
TA (TMP)
TA
TA
たたた…
YOU OKAY, MOM?
HFF...
DOTA (FLOP)
どたっ
MOM!
HFF...
UH-HUH...
I'M OKAY.

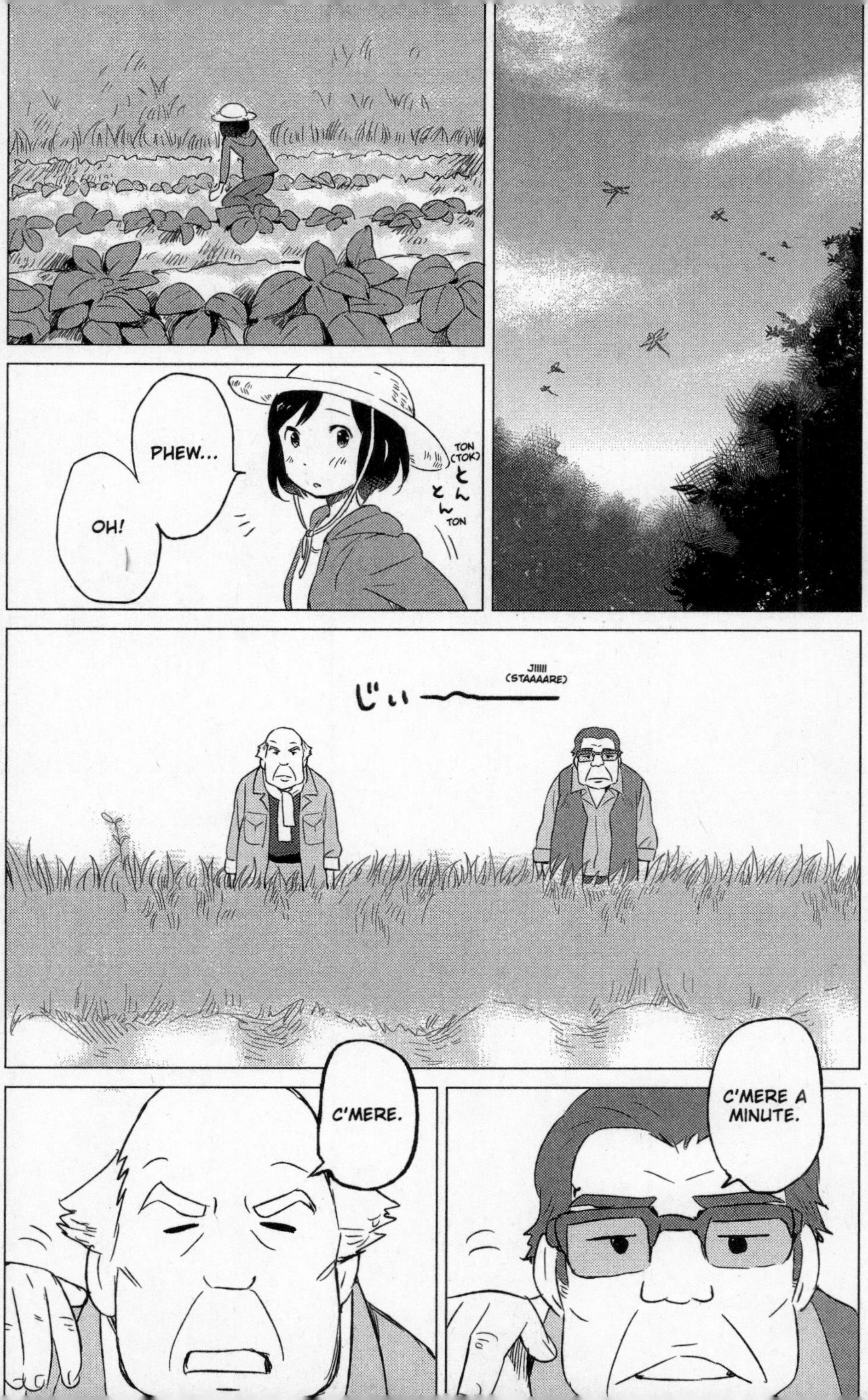
PHEW...
OH!
とん TON (TOK)
とん TON
じぃ〜〜〜
JIIIII (STAAAARE)
C'MERE A MINUTE.
C'MERE.

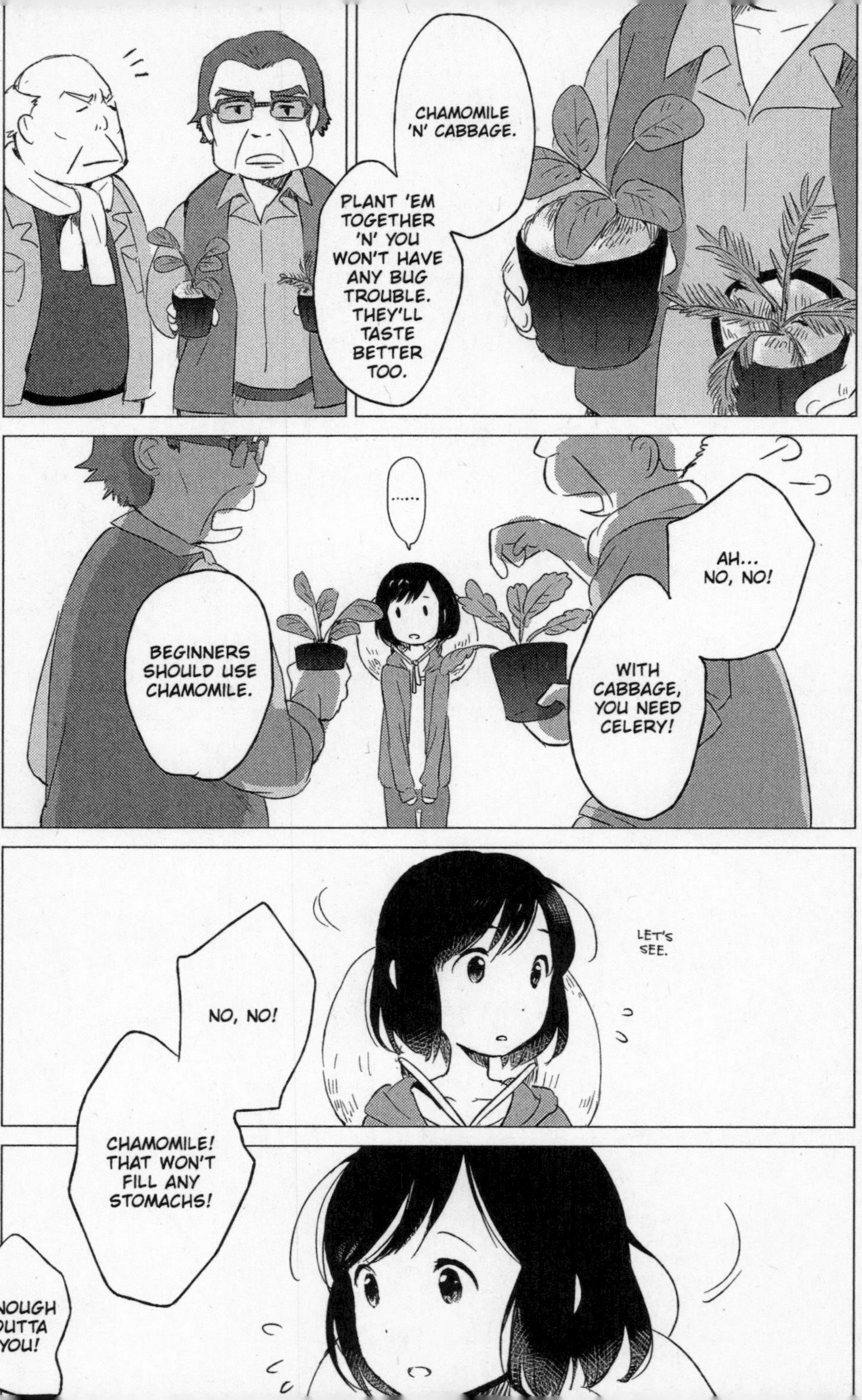
CHAMOMILE 'N' CABBAGE.
PLANT 'EM TOGETHER 'N' YOU WON'T HAVE ANY BUG TROUBLE. THEY'LL TASTE BETTER TOO.
……
AH... NO, NO!
WITH CABBAGE, YOU NEED CELERY!
BEGINNERS SHOULD USE CHAMOMILE.
LET'S SEE.
NO, NO!
CHAMOMILE! THAT WON'T FILL ANY STOMACHS!
ENOUGH OUTTA YOU!

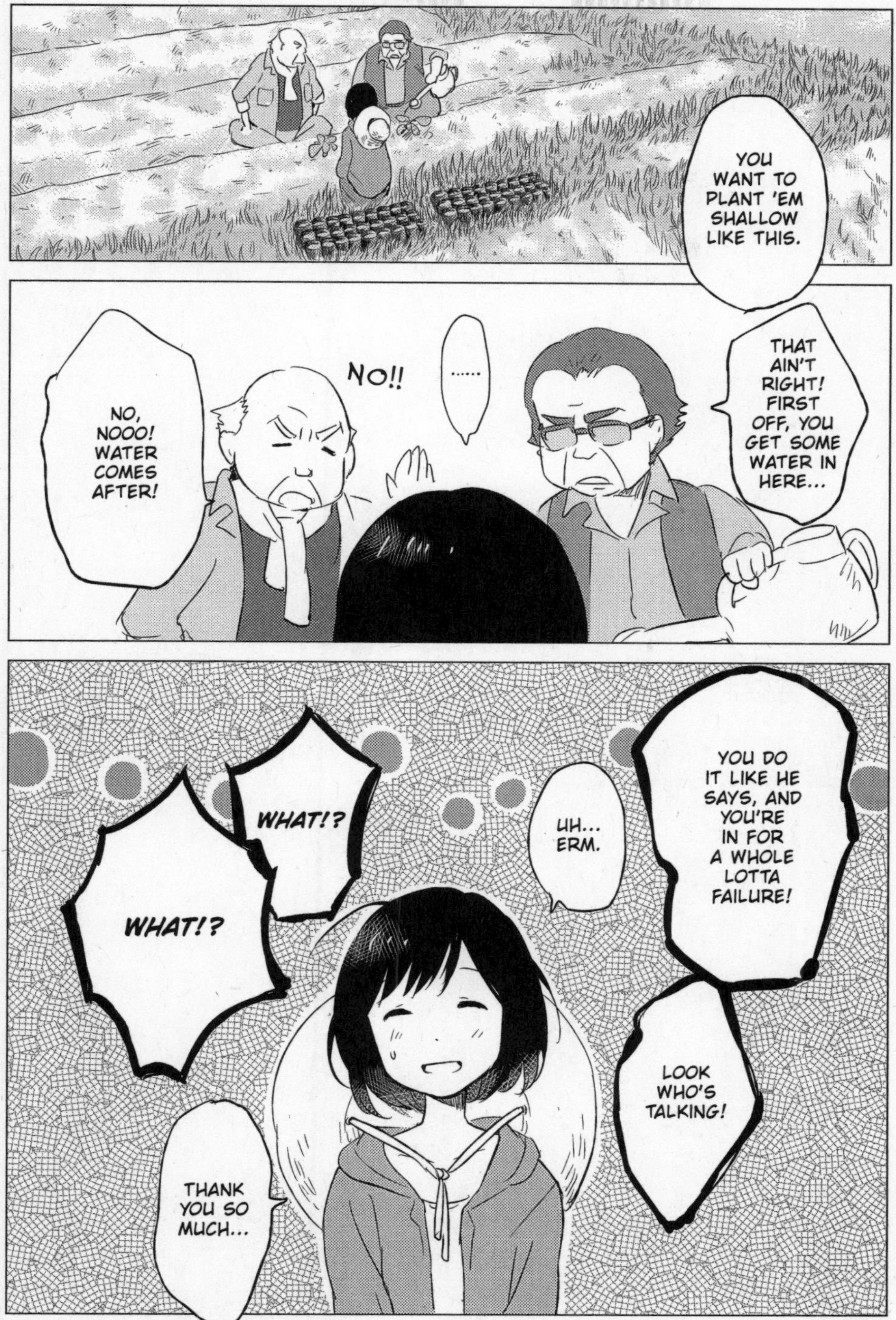
YOU WANT TO PLANT 'EM SHALLOW LIKE THIS.
THAT AIN'T RIGHT! FIRST OFF, YOU GET SOME WATER IN HERE...
......
NO!!
NO, NOOO! WATER COMES AFTER!
YOU DO IT LIKE HE SAYS, AND YOU'RE IN FOR A WHOLE LOTTA FAILURE!
UH... ERM.
WHAT!?
WHAT!?
LOOK WHO'S TALKING!
THANK YOU SO MUCH...

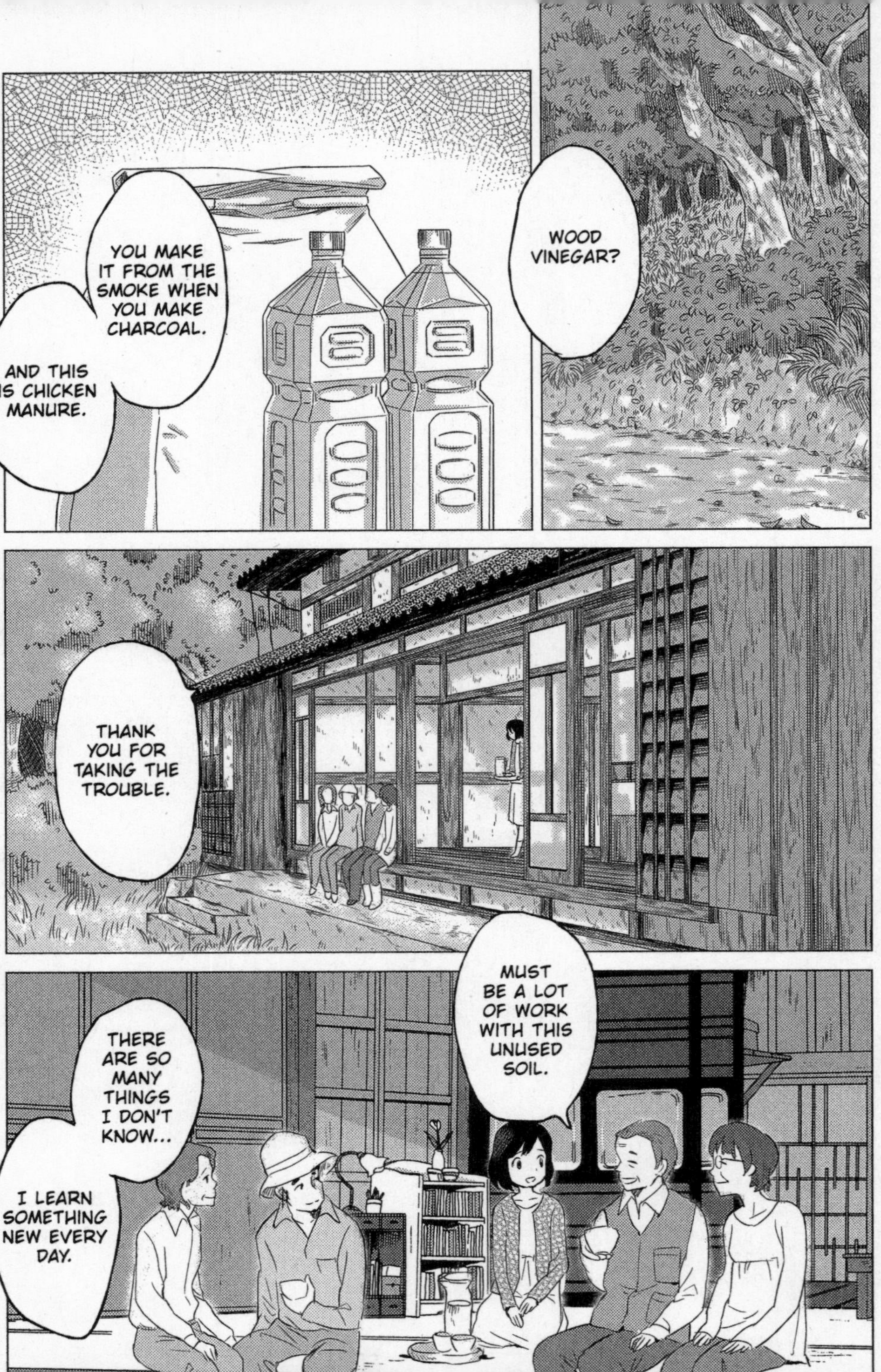
WOOD VINEGAR?
YOU MAKE IT FROM THE SMOKE WHEN YOU MAKE CHARCOAL.
AND THIS IS CHICKEN MANURE.
THANK YOU FOR TAKING THE TROUBLE.
MUST BE A LOT OF WORK WITH THIS UNUSED SOIL.
THERE ARE SO MANY THINGS I DON'T KNOW...
I LEARN SOMETHING NEW EVERY DAY.

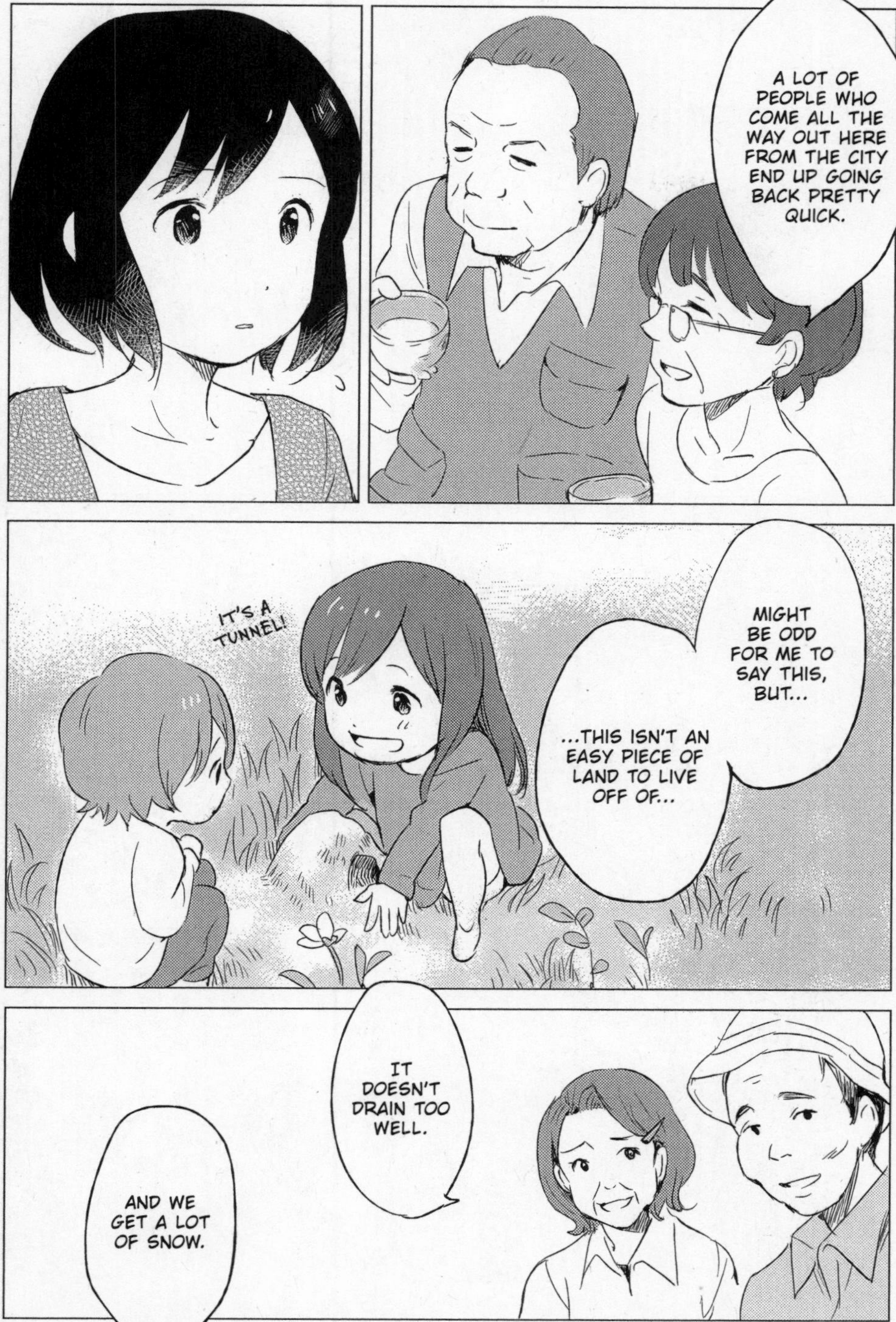
A LOT OF PEOPLE WHO COME ALL THE WAY OUT HERE FROM THE CITY END UP GOING BACK PRETTY QUICK.
MIGHT BE ODD FOR ME TO SAY THIS, BUT...
...THIS ISN'T AN EASY PIECE OF LAND TO LIVE OFF OF...
IT'S A TUNNEL!
IT DOESN'T DRAIN TOO WELL.
AND WE GET A LOT OF SNOW.

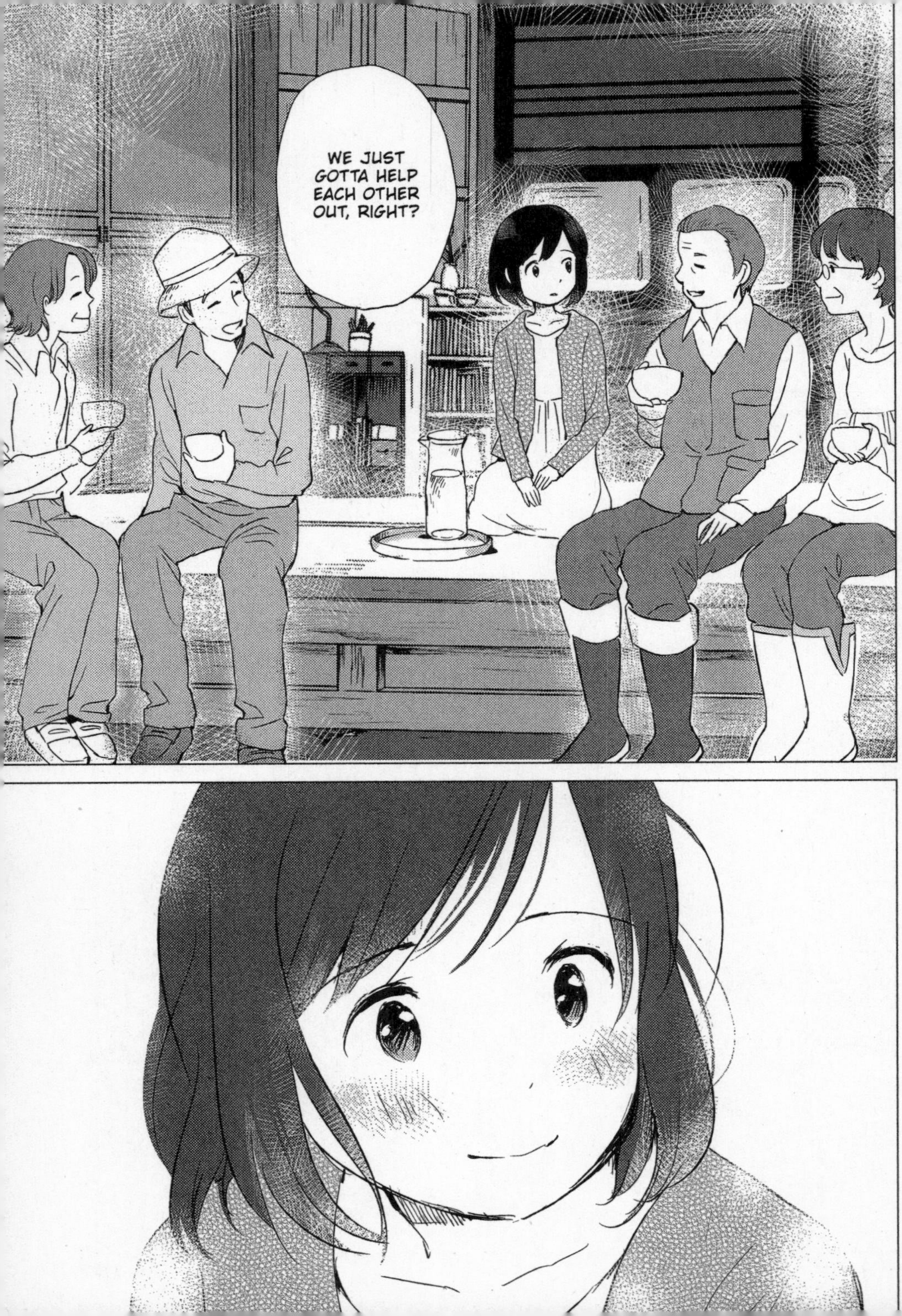
WE JUST GOTTA HELP EACH OTHER OUT, RIGHT?

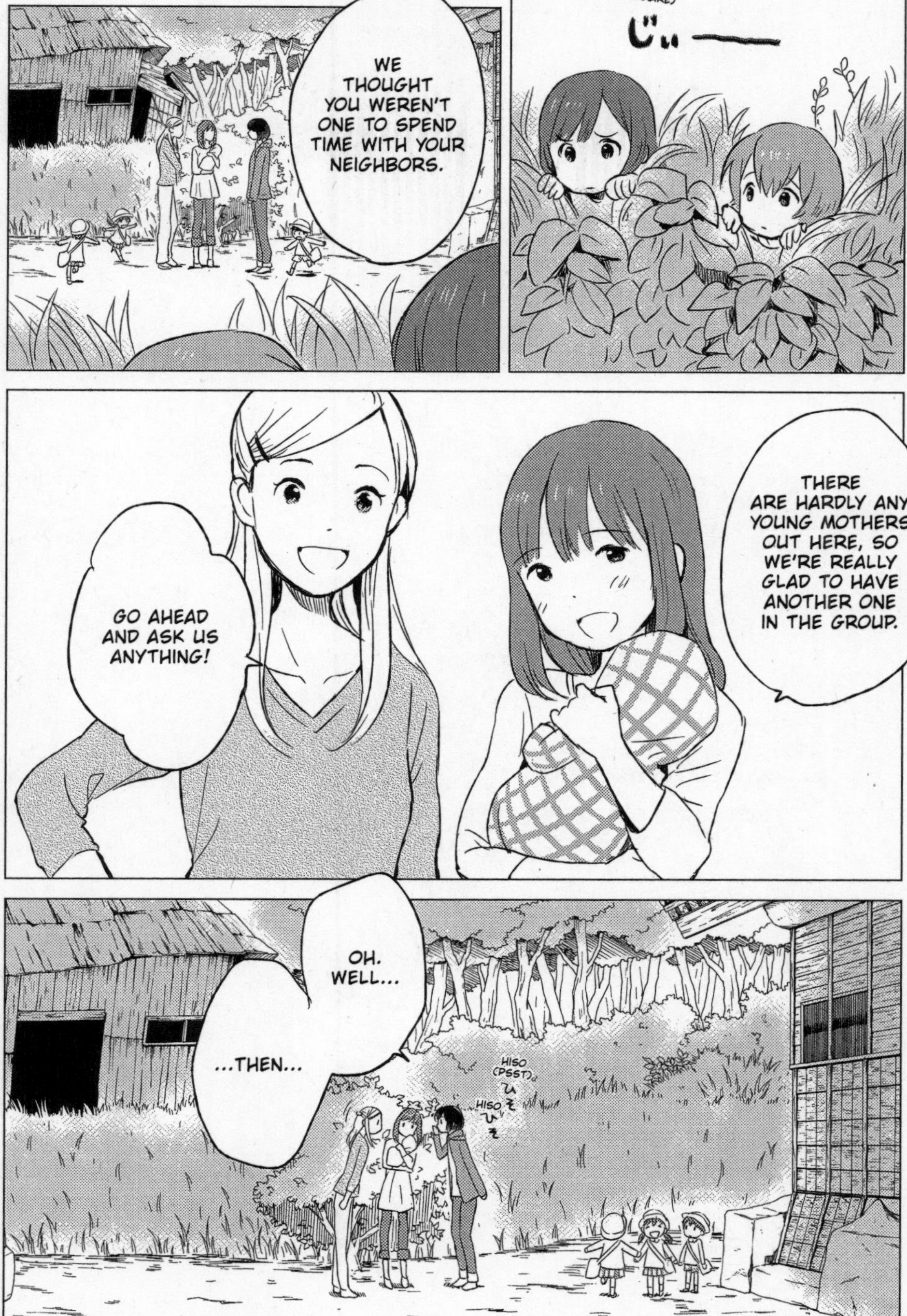
JIIIII
(STAAARE)
じぃーー
WE THOUGHT YOU WEREN'T ONE TO SPEND TIME WITH YOUR NEIGHBORS.
THERE ARE HARDLY ANY YOUNG MOTHERS OUT HERE, SO WE'RE REALLY GLAD TO HAVE ANOTHER ONE IN THE GROUP.
GO AHEAD AND ASK US ANYTHING!
OH. WELL...
...THEN...
HISO (PSST) ひそ
HISO ひそ

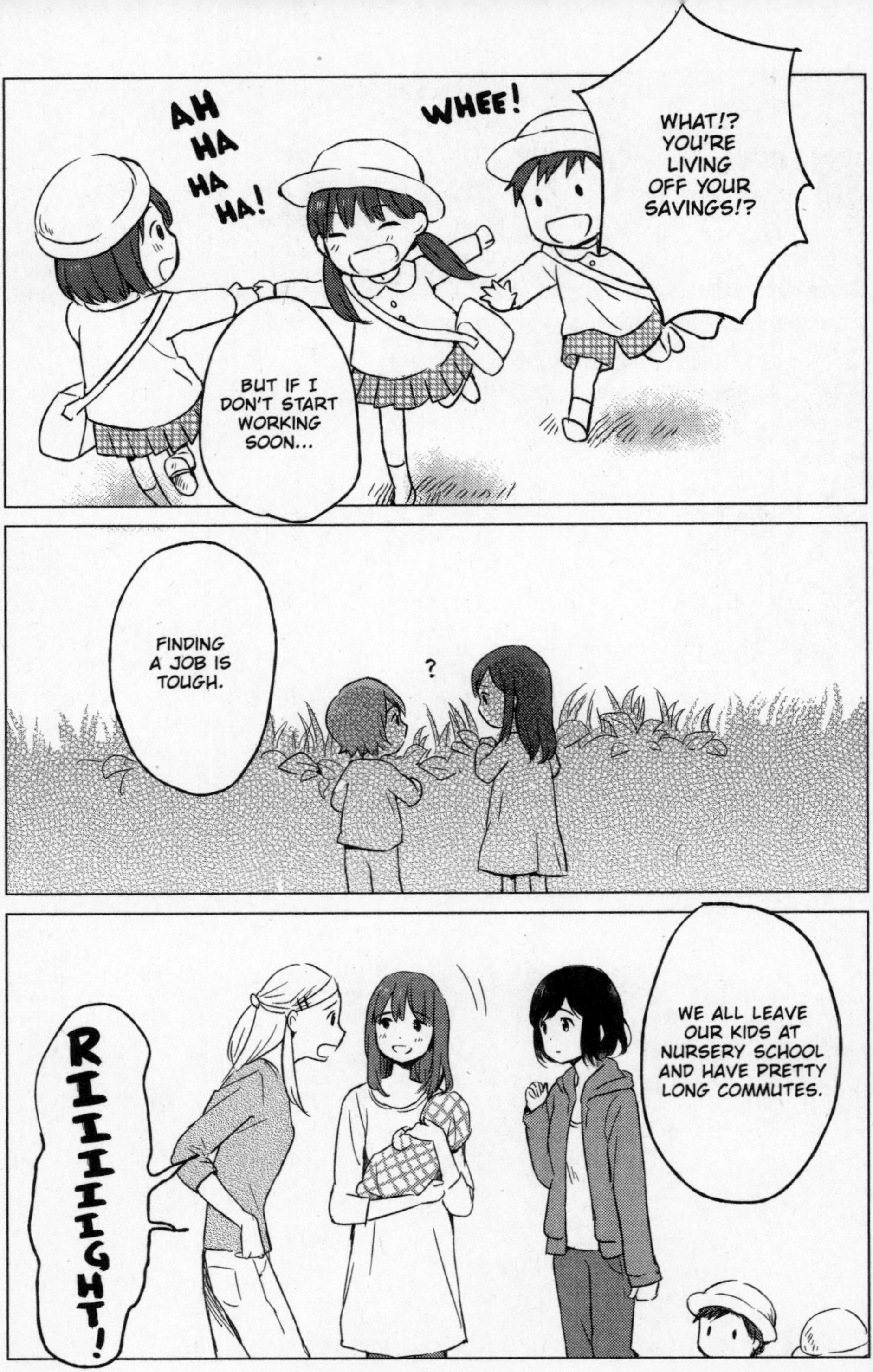
WHAT!? YOU'RE LIVING OFF YOUR SAVINGS!?
WHEE!
AH HA HA HA!
BUT IF I DON'T START WORKING SOON...
FINDING A JOB IS TOUGH.
?
WE ALL LEAVE OUR KIDS AT NURSERY SCHOOL AND HAVE PRETTY LONG COMMUTES.
RIIIIIGHT!

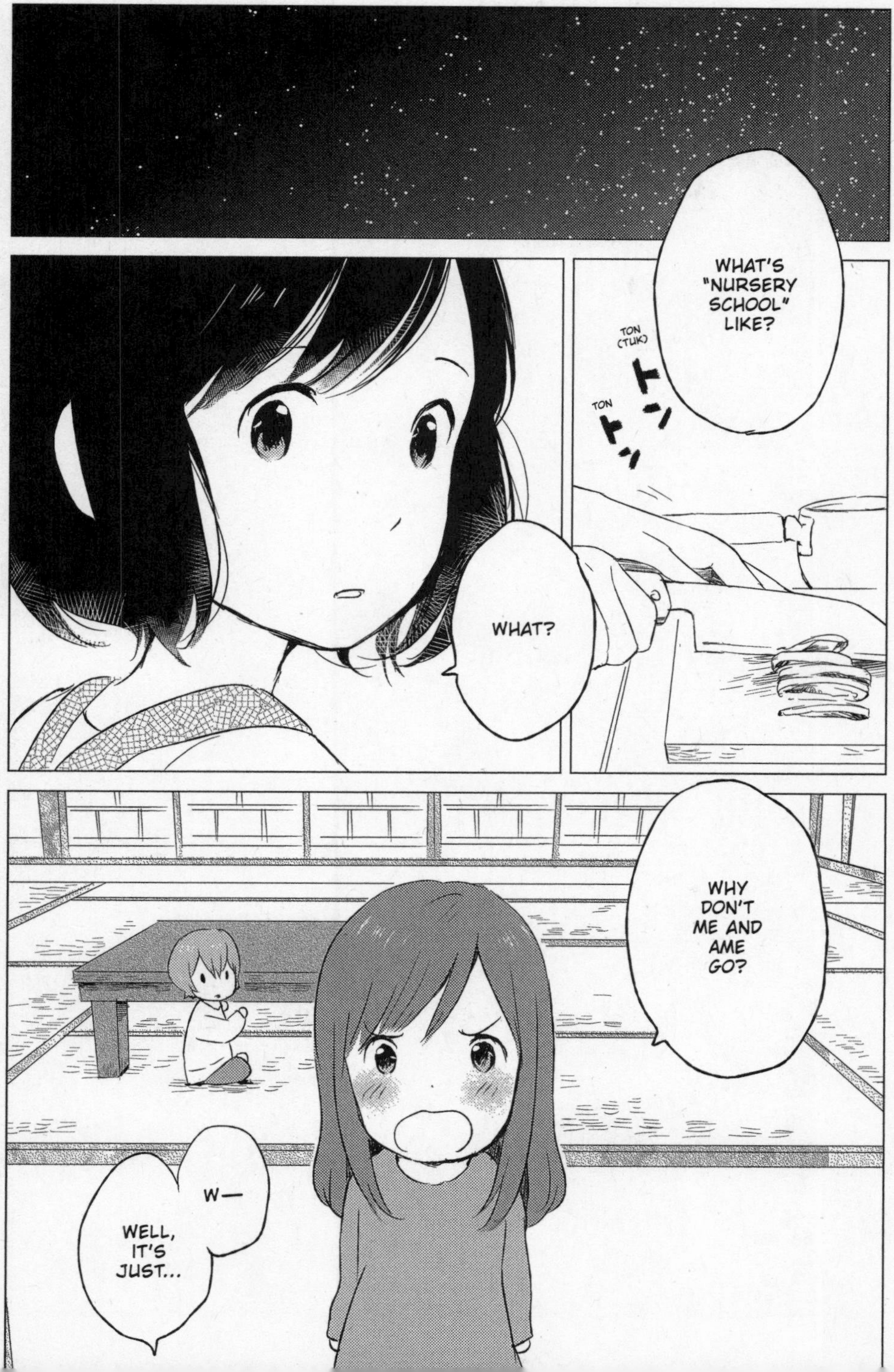
WHAT'S "NURSERY SCHOOL" LIKE?
TON (TUK)
TON
WHAT?
WHY DON'T ME AND AME GO?
W— WELL, IT'S JUST...

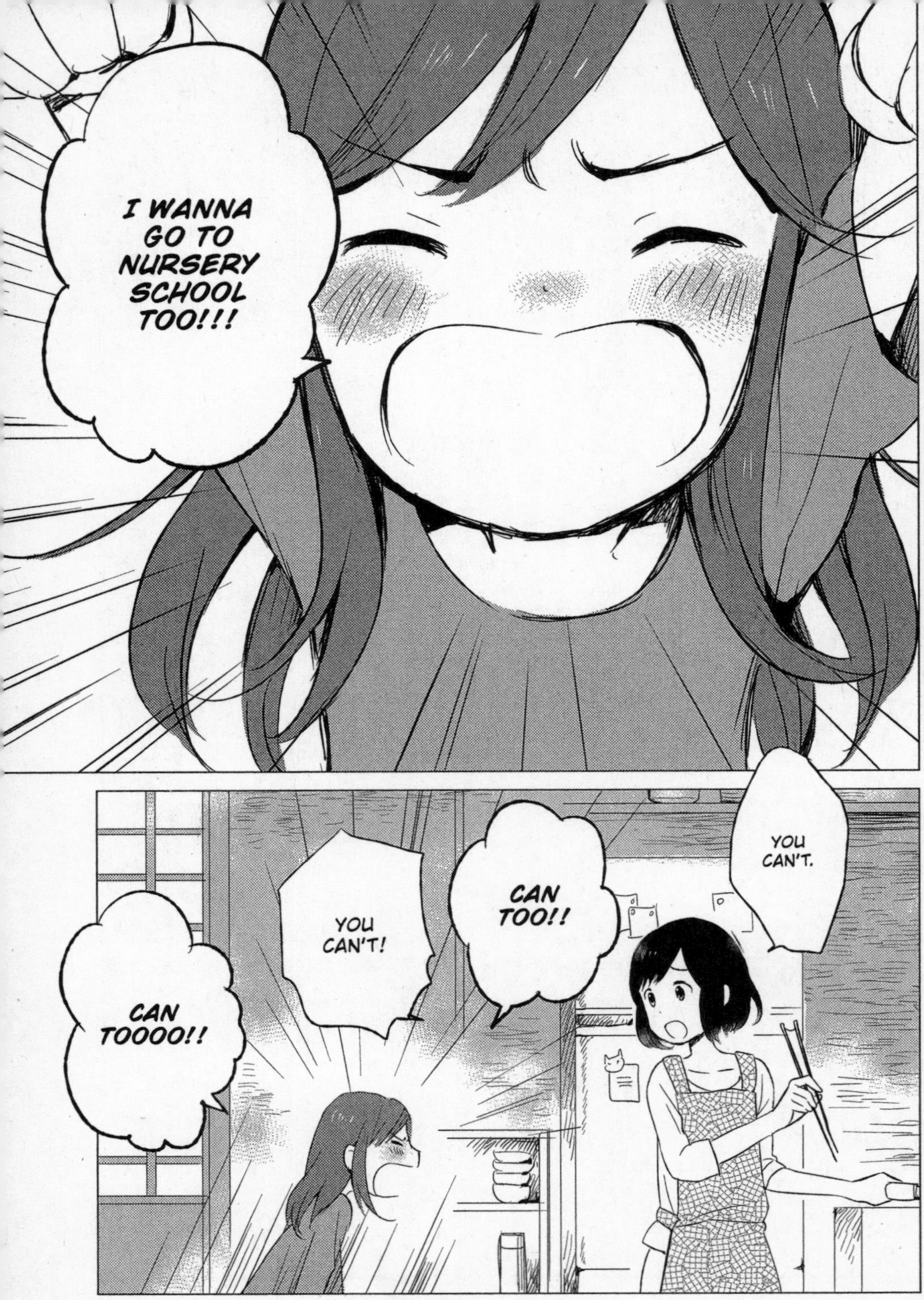
I WANNA GO TO NURSERY SCHOOL TOO!!!
YOU CAN'T.
CAN TOO!!
YOU CAN'T!
CAN TOOOO!!

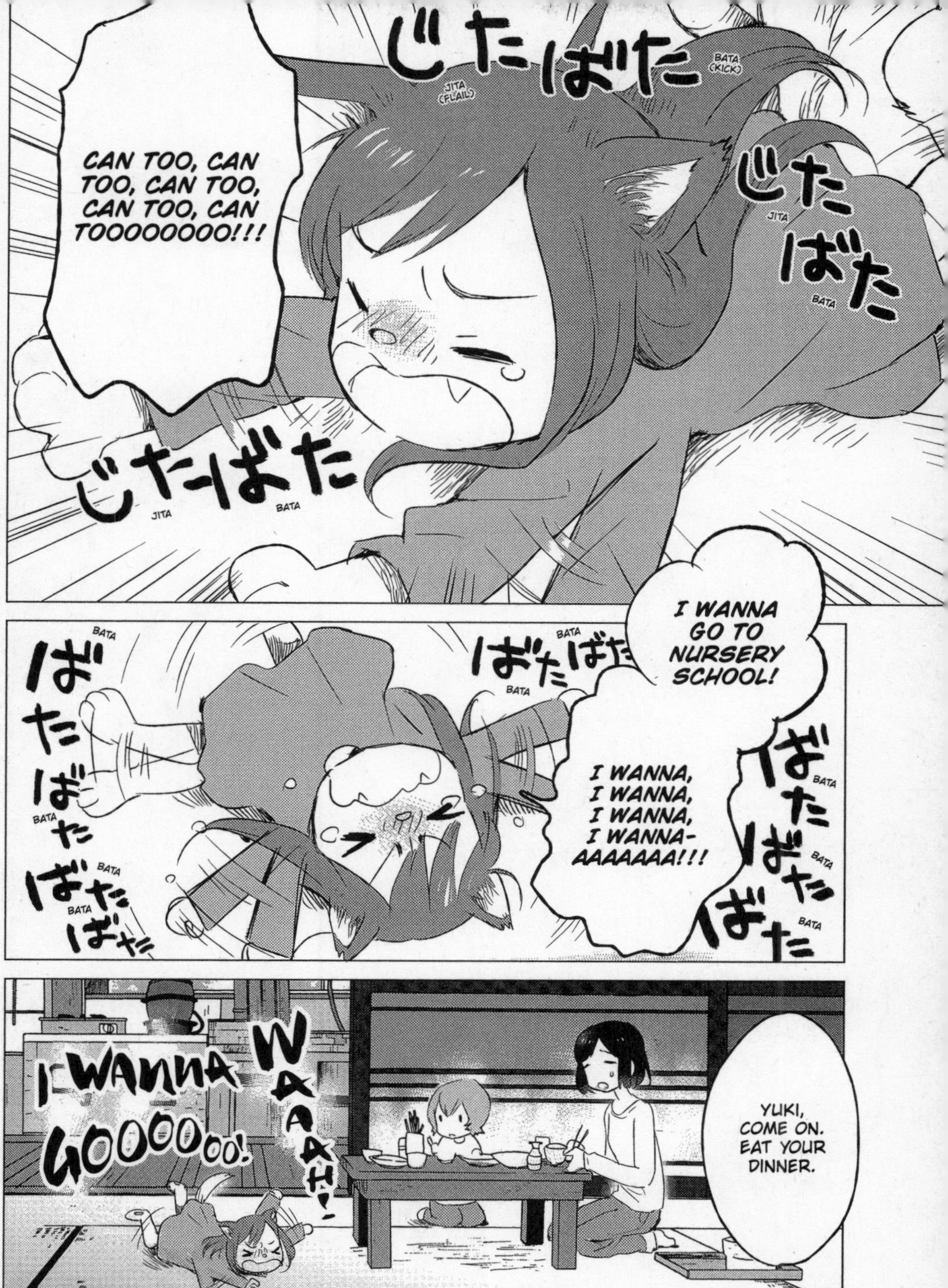
じたばた
BATA (KICK)
JITA (FLAIL)
じた ばた
JITA
BATA
CAN TOO, CAN TOO, CAN TOO, CAN TOO, CAN TOOOOOOOOO!!!
じたーばた
JITA
BATA
I WANNA GO TO NURSERY SCHOOL!
ばた ばた ばた
BATA
BATA
BATA
I WANNA, I WANNA, I WANNA, I WANNA-AAAAAAA!!!
ばたばた
BATA
BATA
ばた ばた ばた ばた
BATA
BATA
BATA
BATA
YUKI, COME ON. EAT YOUR DINNER.
WAAAH!
I WANNA GOOOOooo!

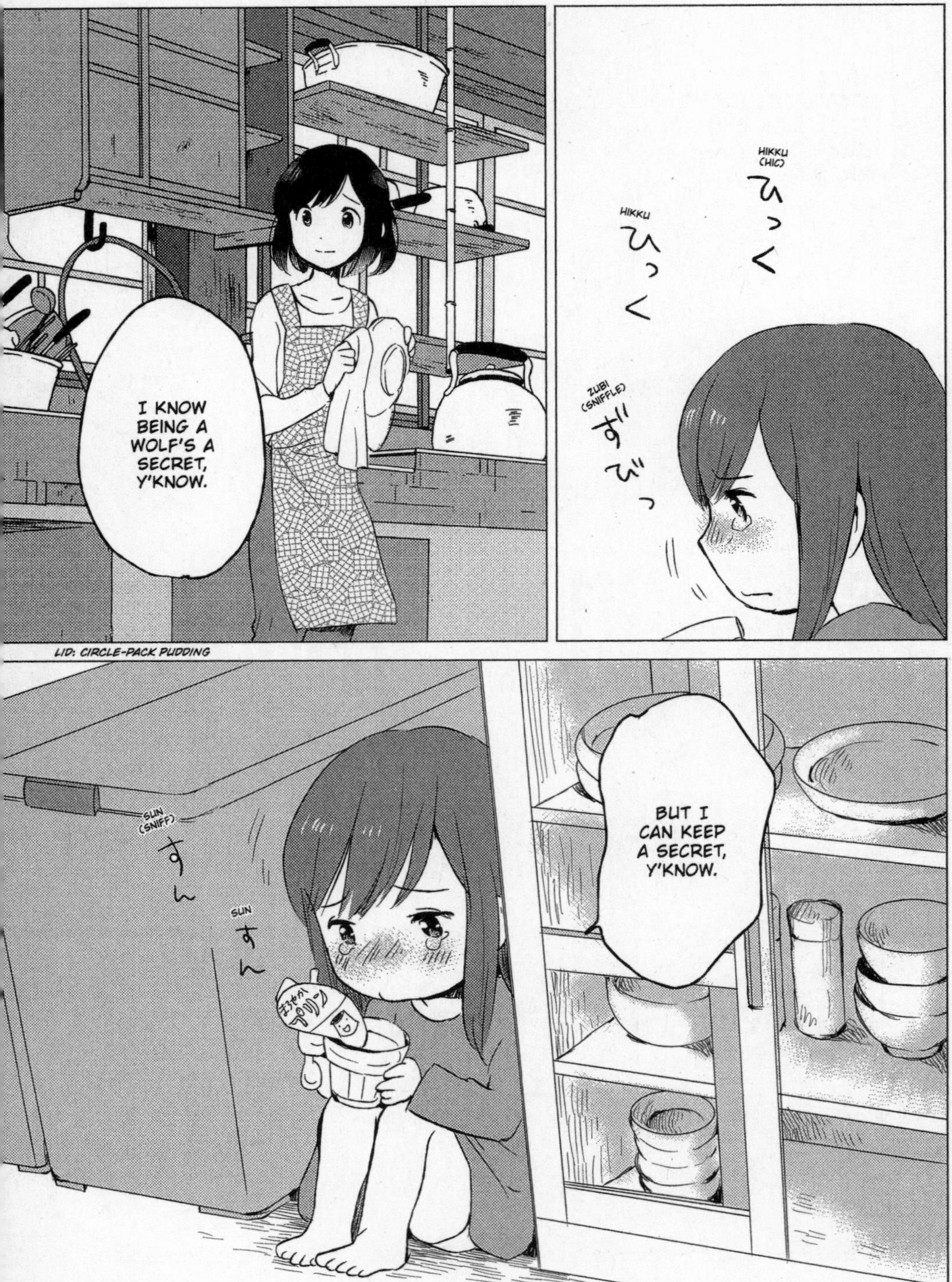
HIKKU (HIC)
ひっく
HIKKU
ひっく
ZUBI (SNIFFLE)
ずびっ
I KNOW BEING A WOLF'S A SECRET, Y'KNOW.
LID: CIRCLE-PACK PUDDING
BUT I CAN KEEP A SECRET, Y'KNOW.
SUN (SNIFF)
すん
SUN
すん

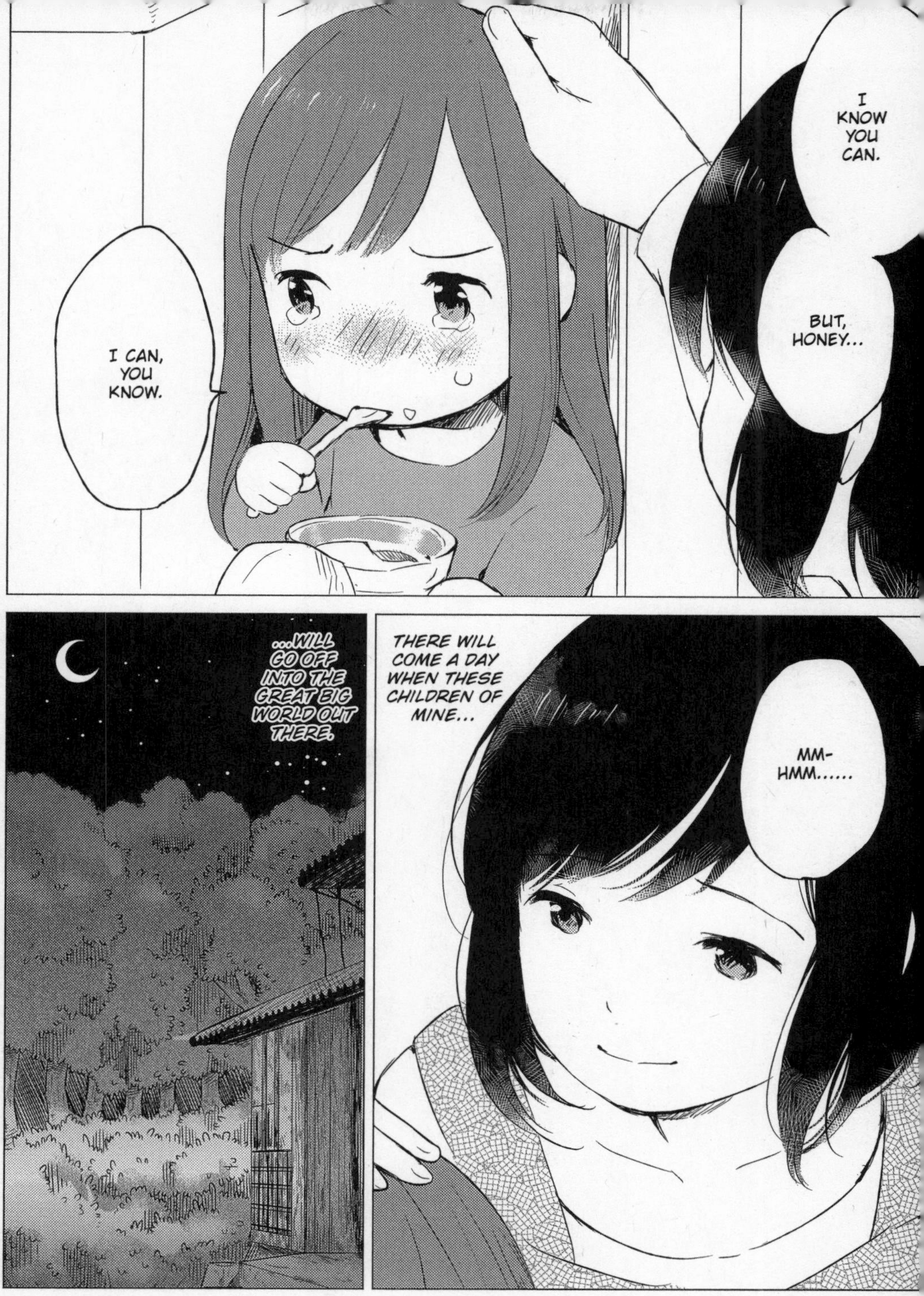
I KNOW YOU CAN.
BUT, HONEY...
I CAN, YOU KNOW.
MM-HMM......
THERE WILL COME A DAY WHEN THESE CHILDREN OF MINE...
...WILL GO OFF INTO THE GREAT BIG WORLD OUT THERE.

WOLF CHILDREN
AME & YUKI

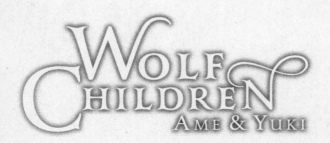

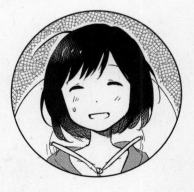

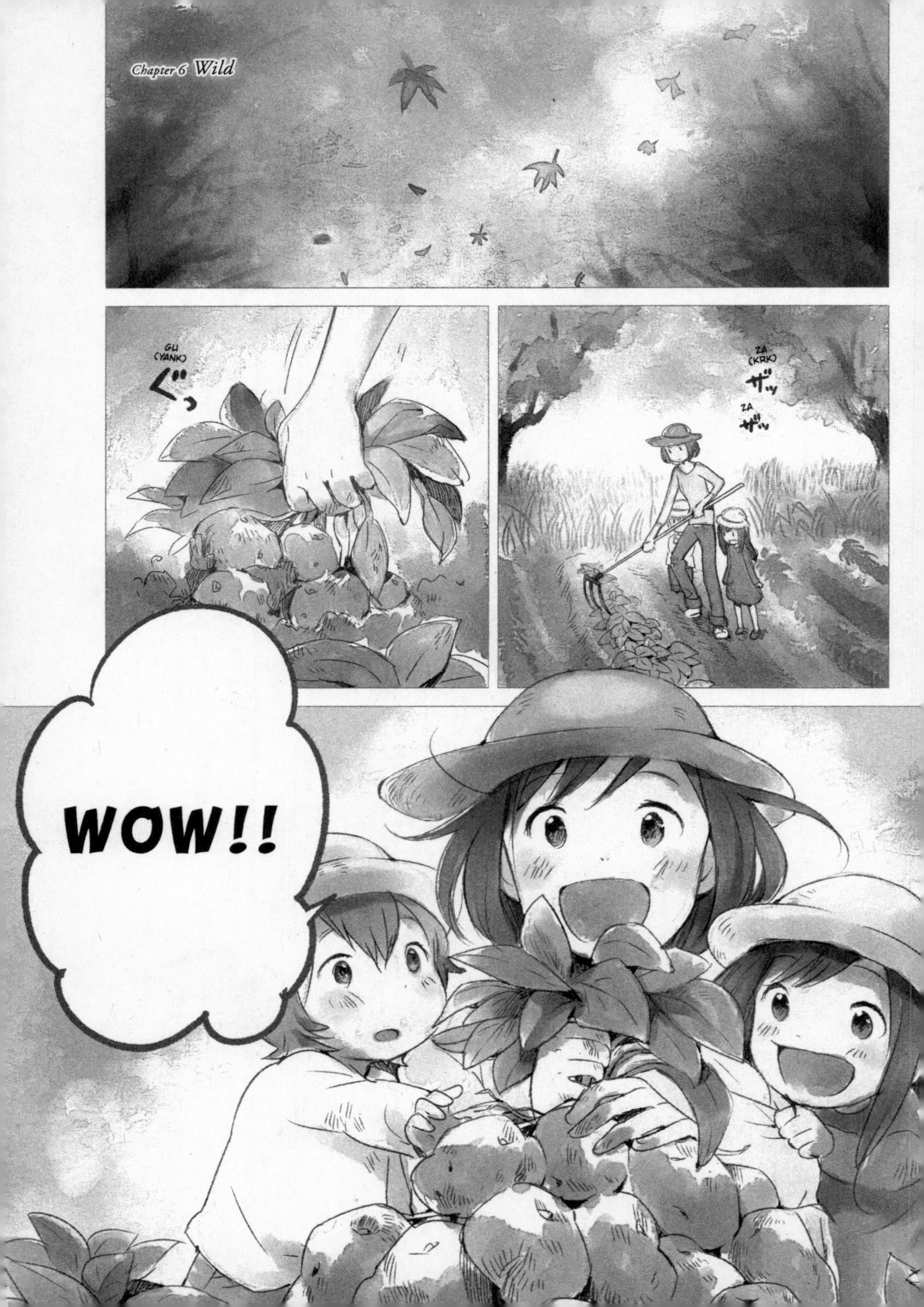
Chapter 6 Wild
ZA (KRK)
ザッ
ZA
ザッ
GU (YANK)
ぐっ
WOW!!

Chapter 6 Wild

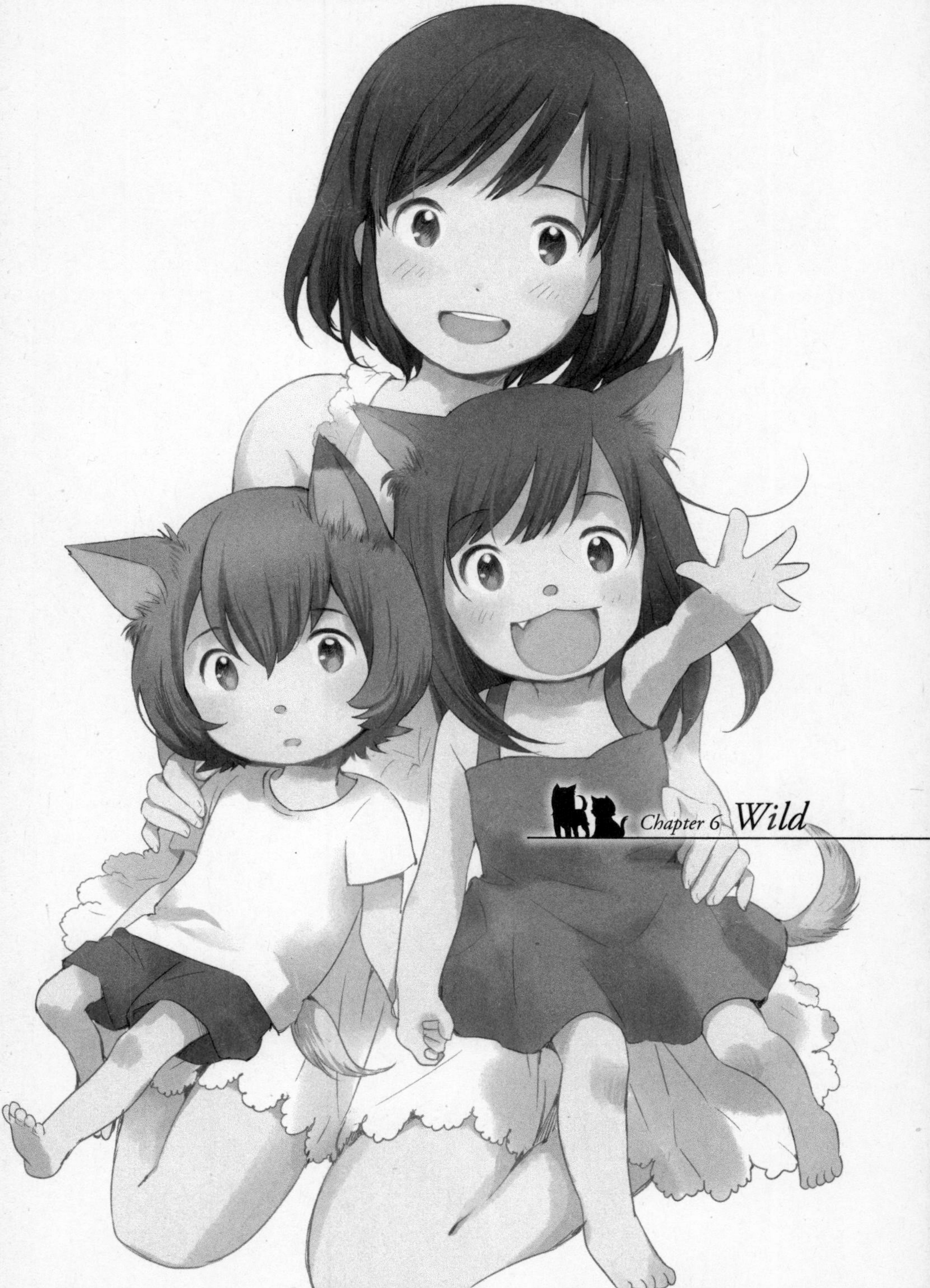

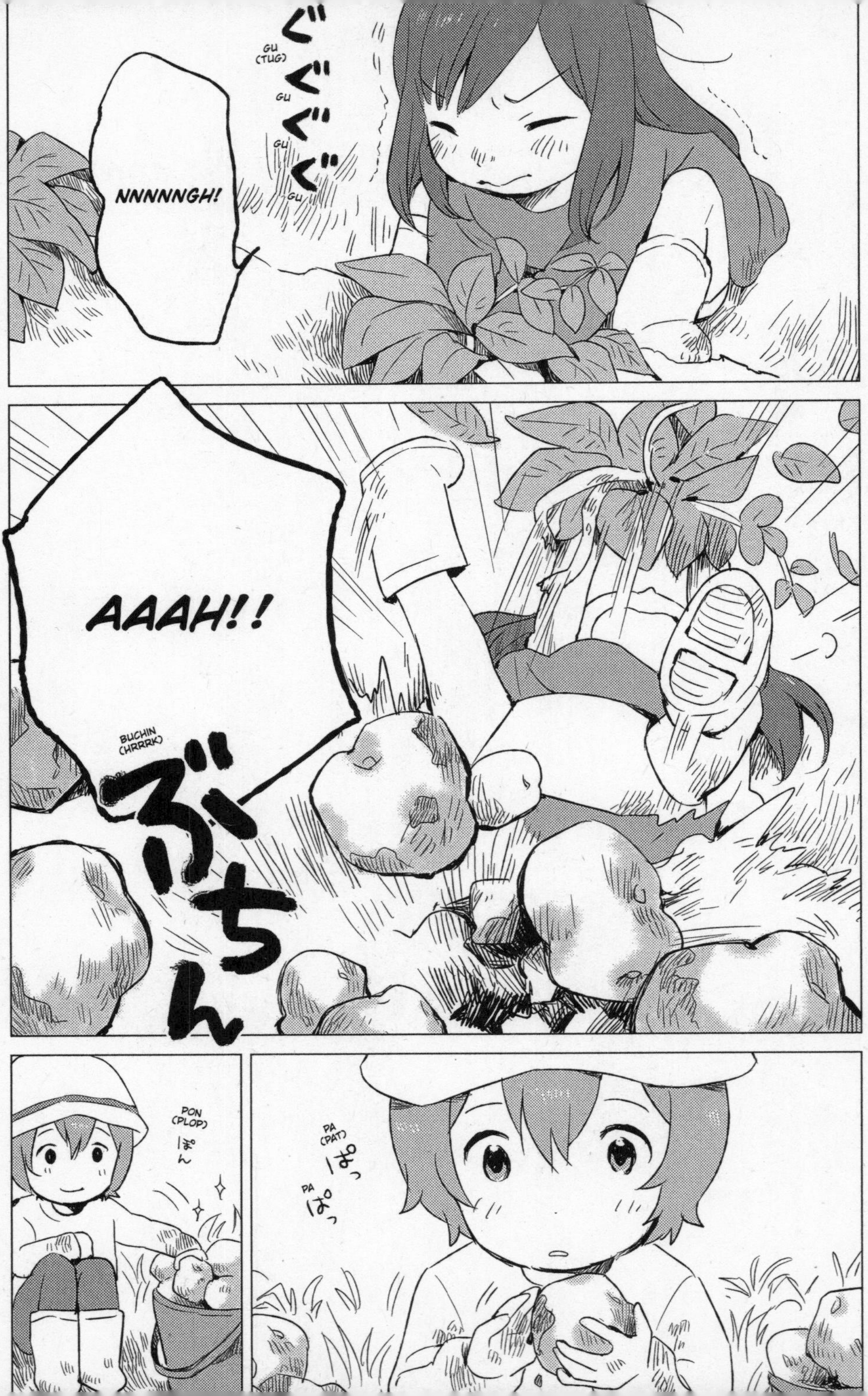

ぐ
GU (TUG)
ぐ
GU
ぐ
GU
ぐ
GU
NNNNNGH!
AAAH!!
ぶちん
BUCHIN (HRRRK)
ぱっ
PA (PAT)
ぱっ
PA
ぽん
PON (PLOP)

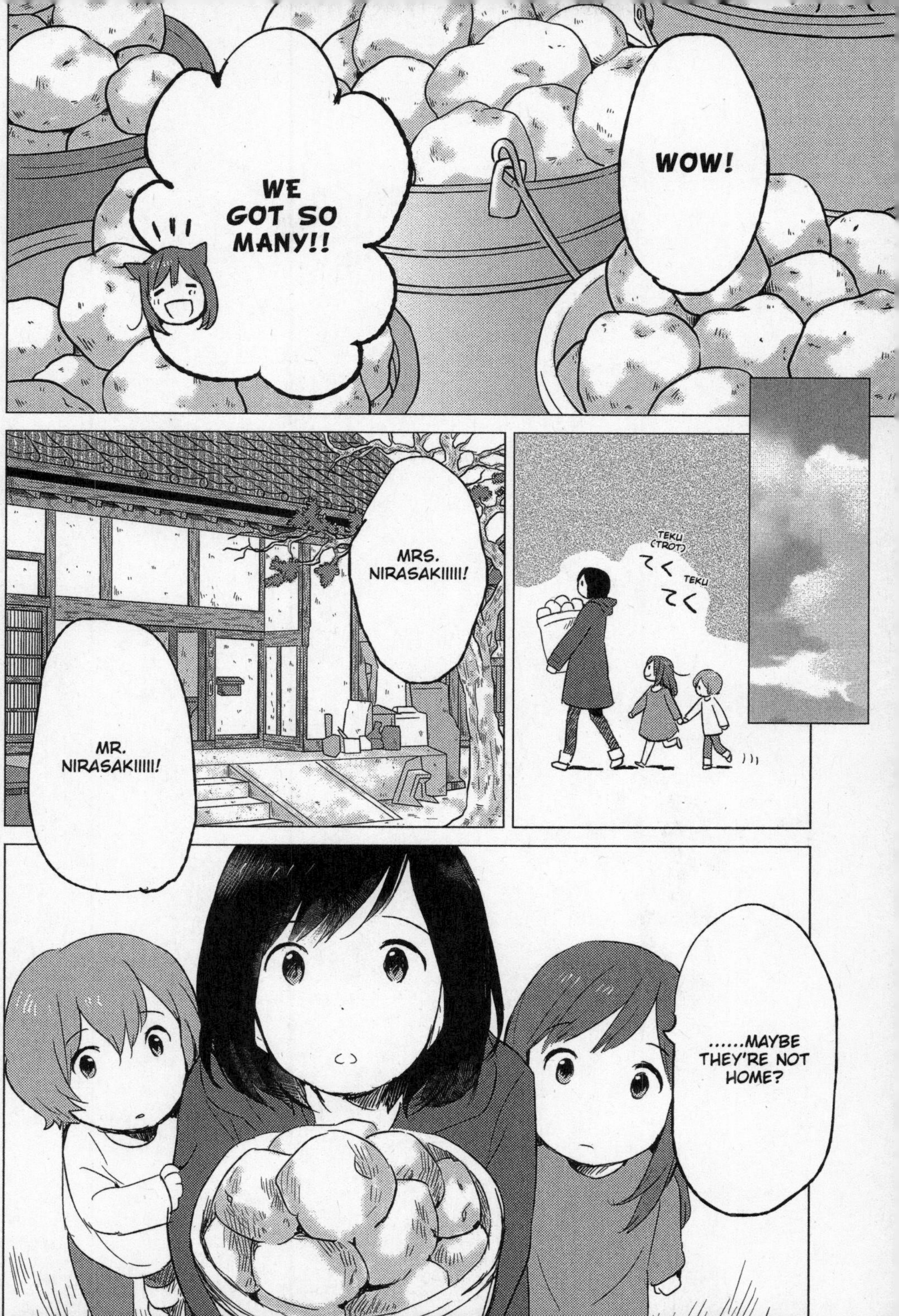
WOW!
WE GOT SO MANY!!
TEKU (TROT)
てく
TEKU
てく
MRS. NIRASAKIIIII!
MR. NIRASAKIIIII!
......MAYBE THEY'RE NOT HOME?

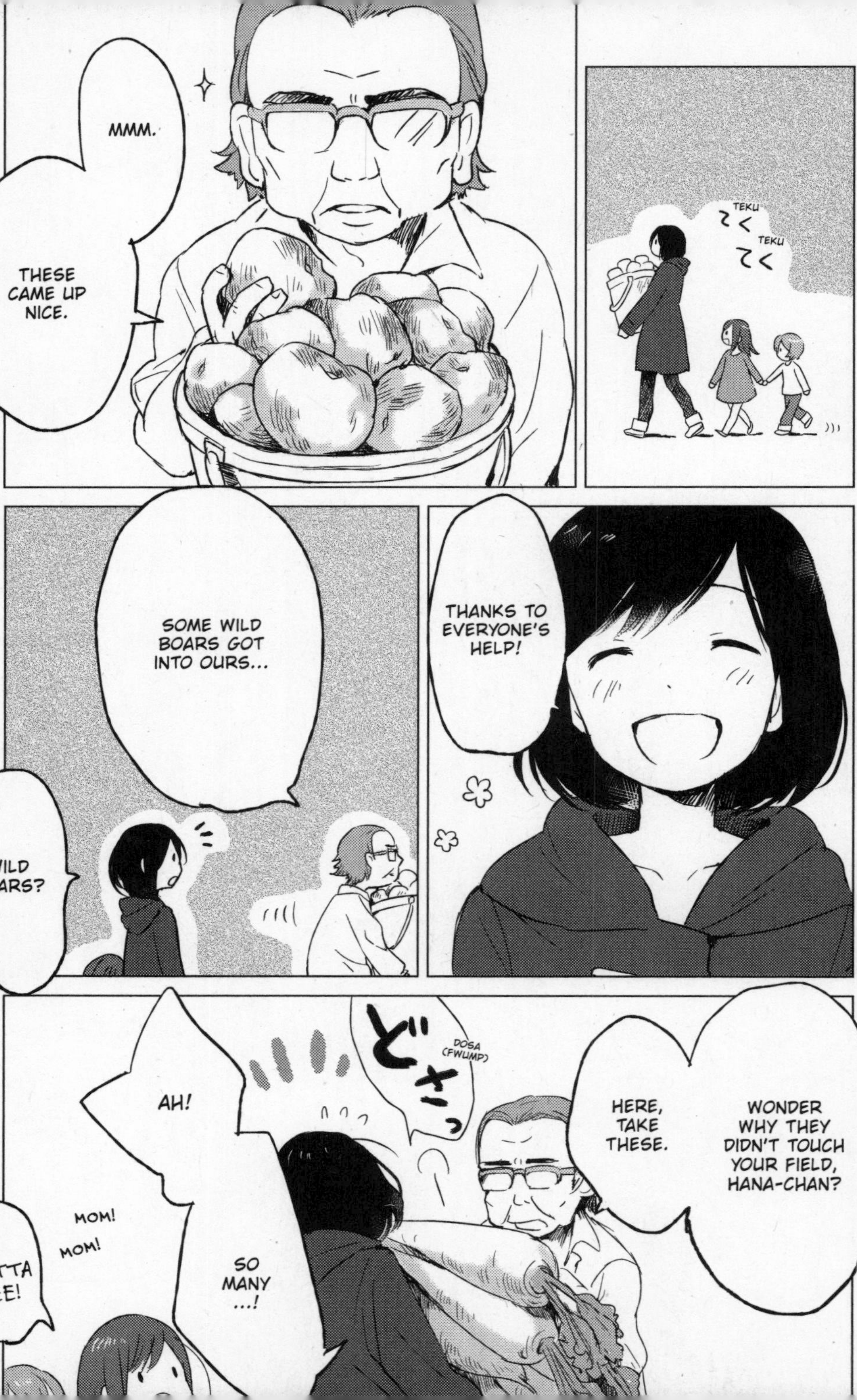
TEKU
てく
TEKU
てく
MMM.
THESE CAME UP NICE.
THANKS TO EVERYONE'S HELP!
SOME WILD BOARS GOT INTO OURS...
WILD BOARS?
WONDER WHY THEY DIDN'T TOUCH YOUR FIELD, HANA-CHAN?
HERE, TAKE THESE.
どさっ
DOSA (FWUMP)
AH!
SO MANY ...!
MOM!
MOM!
I GOTTA PEE!

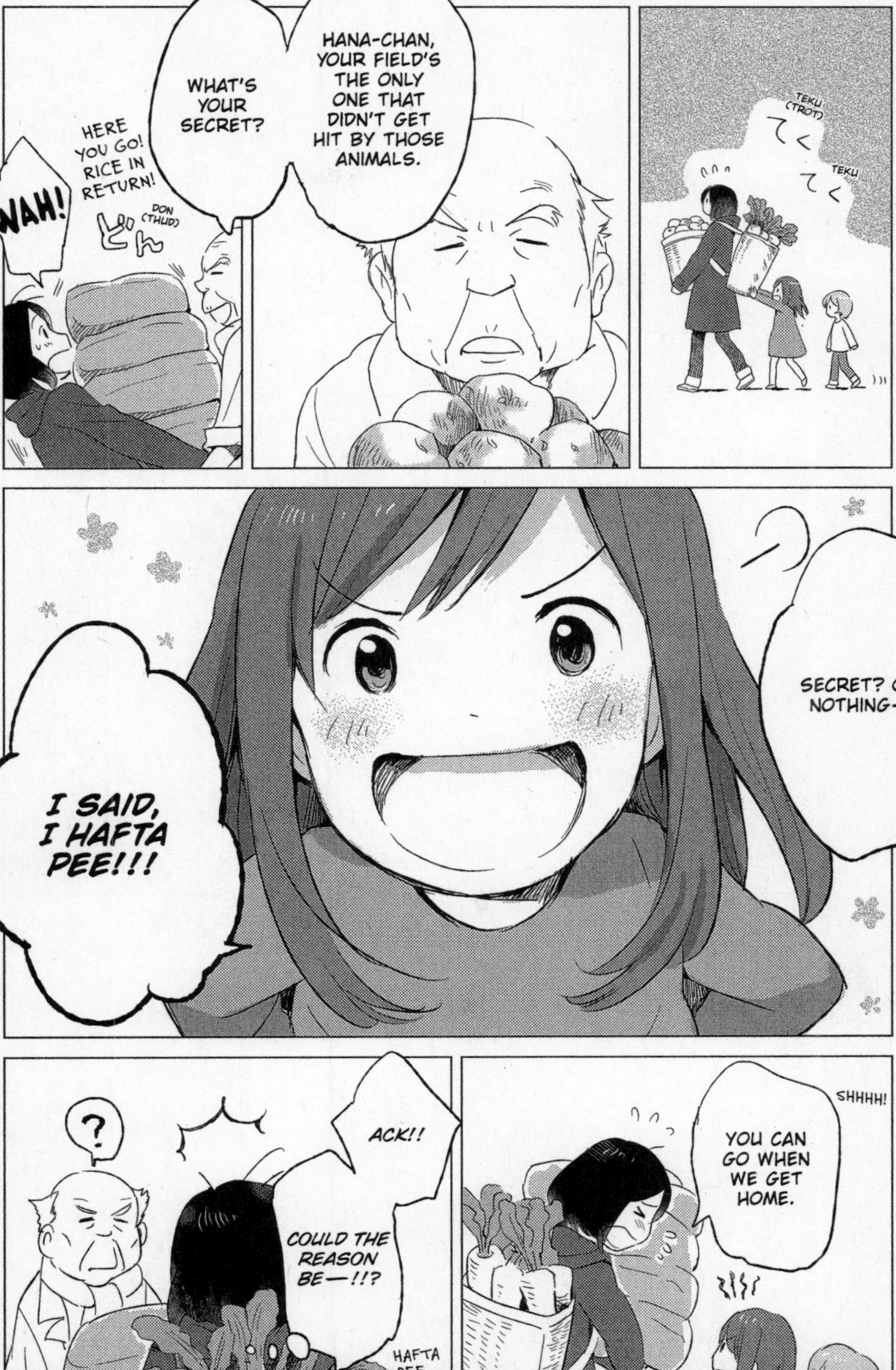
TEKU (TROT)
てく
TEKU
てく
HANA-CHAN, YOUR FIELD'S THE ONLY ONE THAT DIDN'T GET HIT BY THOSE ANIMALS.
WHAT'S YOUR SECRET?
HERE YOU GO! RICE IN RETURN!
DON (THUD)
どん
WAH!
SECRET? OH, NOTHING—
I SAID, I HAFTA PEE!!!
SHHHH!
YOU CAN GO WHEN WE GET HOME.
ACK!!
?
COULD THE REASON BE—!!?
HAFTA PEE...

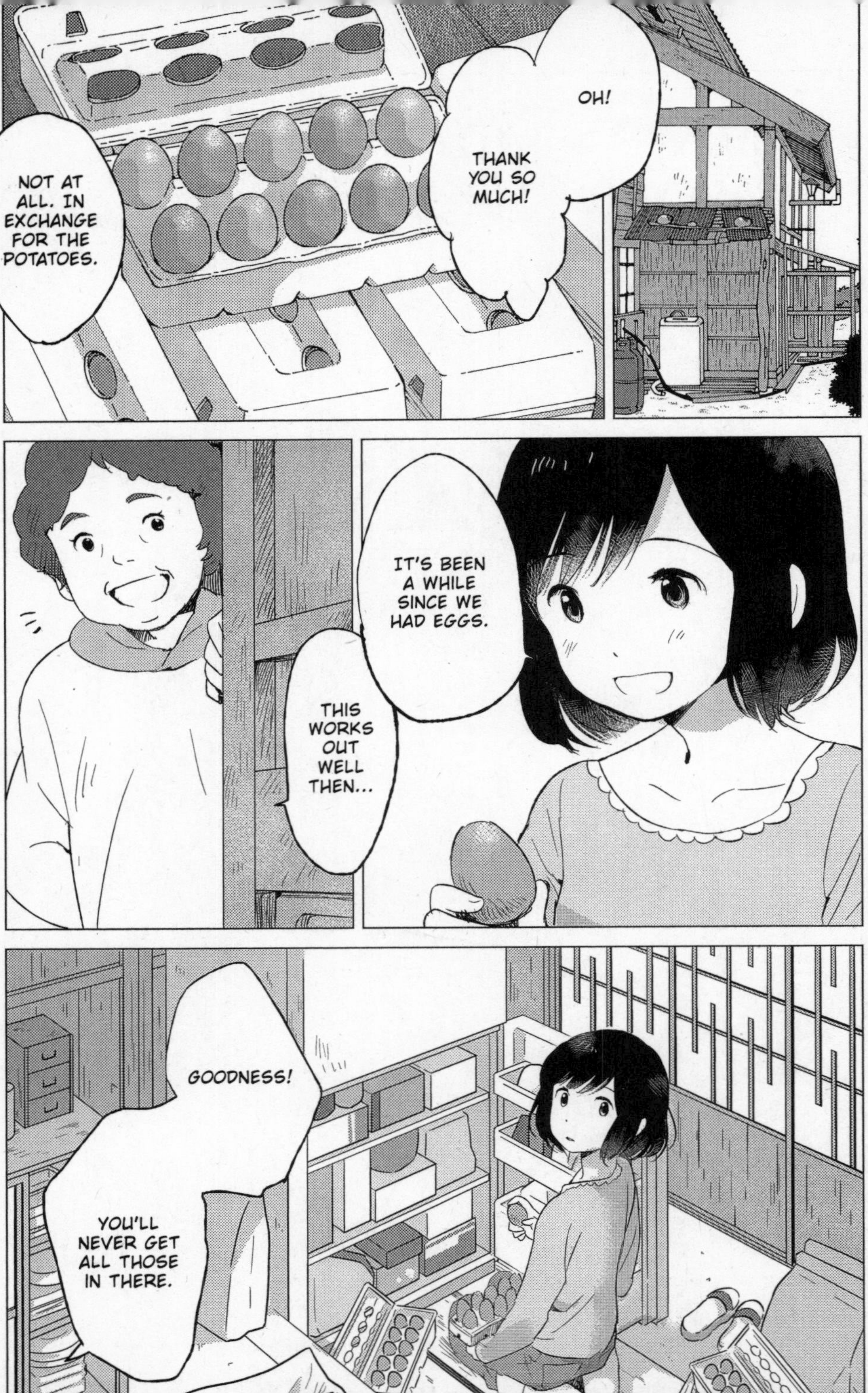
OH!
THANK YOU SO MUCH!
NOT AT ALL. IN EXCHANGE FOR THE POTATOES.
IT'S BEEN A WHILE SINCE WE HAD EGGS.
THIS WORKS OUT WELL THEN...
GOODNESS!
YOU'LL NEVER GET ALL THOSE IN THERE.

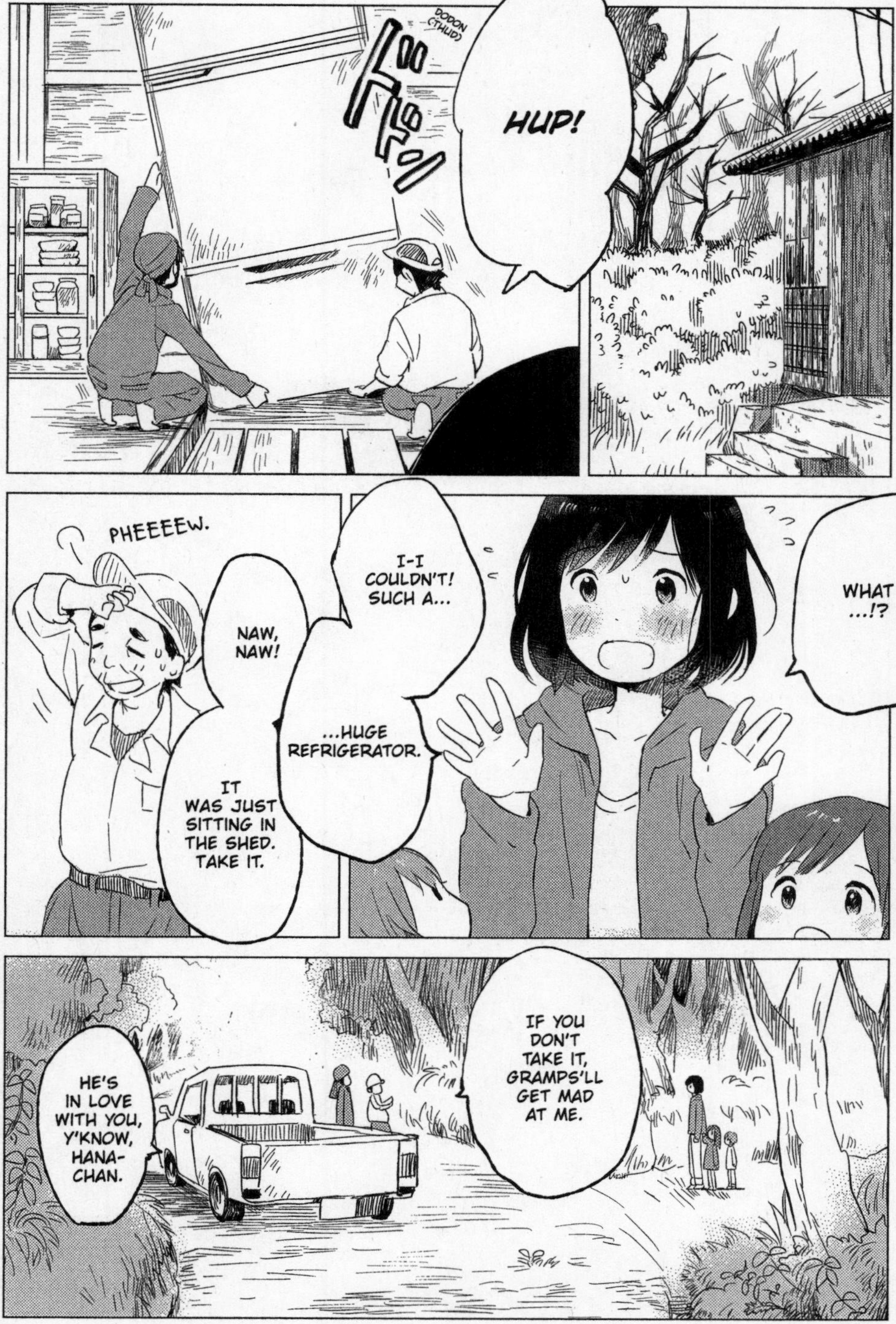
HUP!
DODON (THUD)
WHAT ...!?
I-I COULDN'T! SUCH A...
...HUGE REFRIGERATOR.
PHEEEEW.
NAW, NAW!
IT WAS JUST SITTING IN THE SHED. TAKE IT.
IF YOU DON'T TAKE IT, GRAMPS'LL GET MAD AT ME.
HE'S IN LOVE WITH YOU, Y'KNOW, HANA-CHAN.

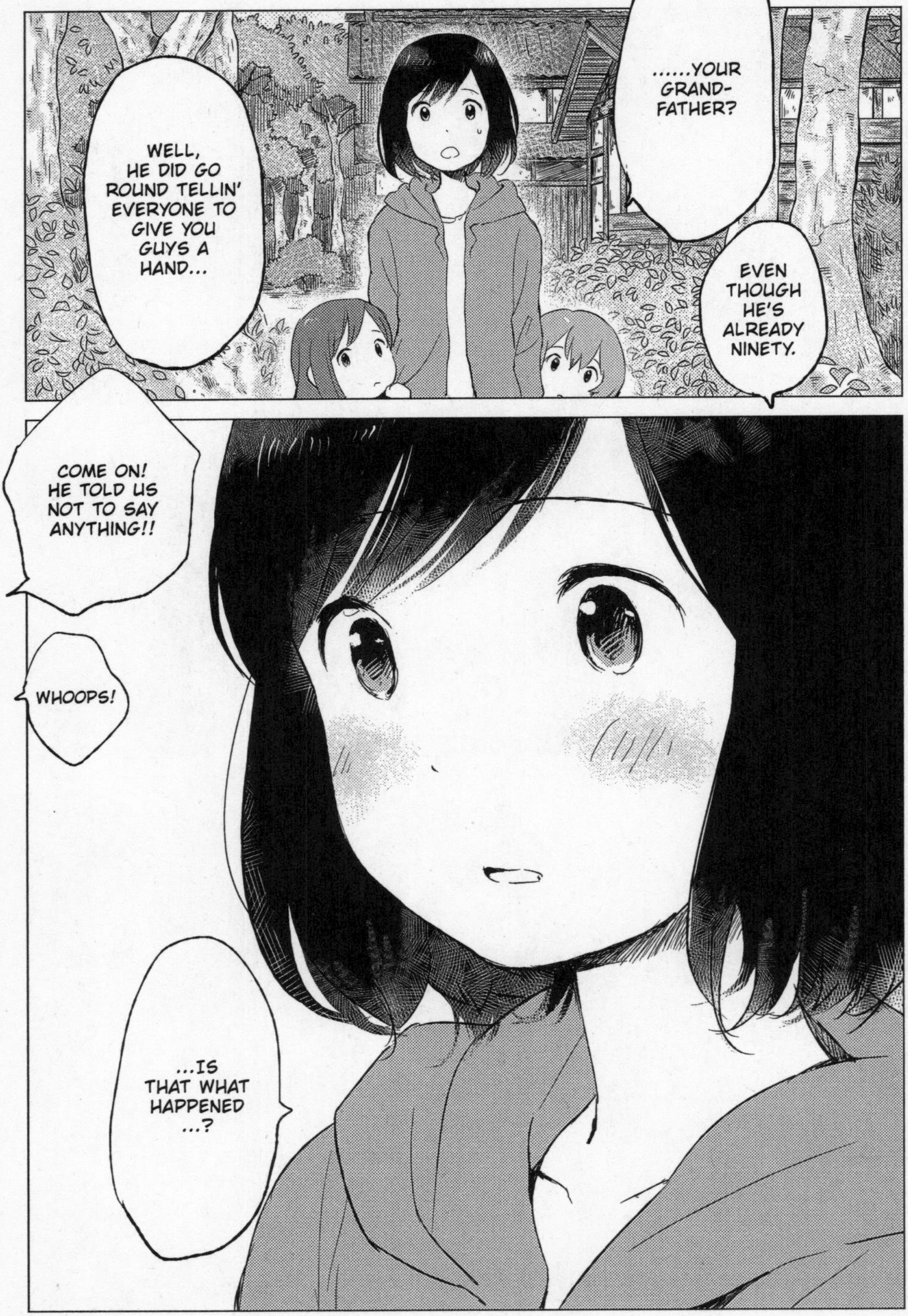
......YOUR GRAND-FATHER?
EVEN THOUGH HE'S ALREADY NINETY.
WELL, HE DID GO ROUND TELLIN' EVERYONE TO GIVE YOU GUYS A HAND...
COME ON! HE TOLD US NOT TO SAY ANYTHING!!
WHOOPS!
...IS THAT WHAT HAPPENED ...?

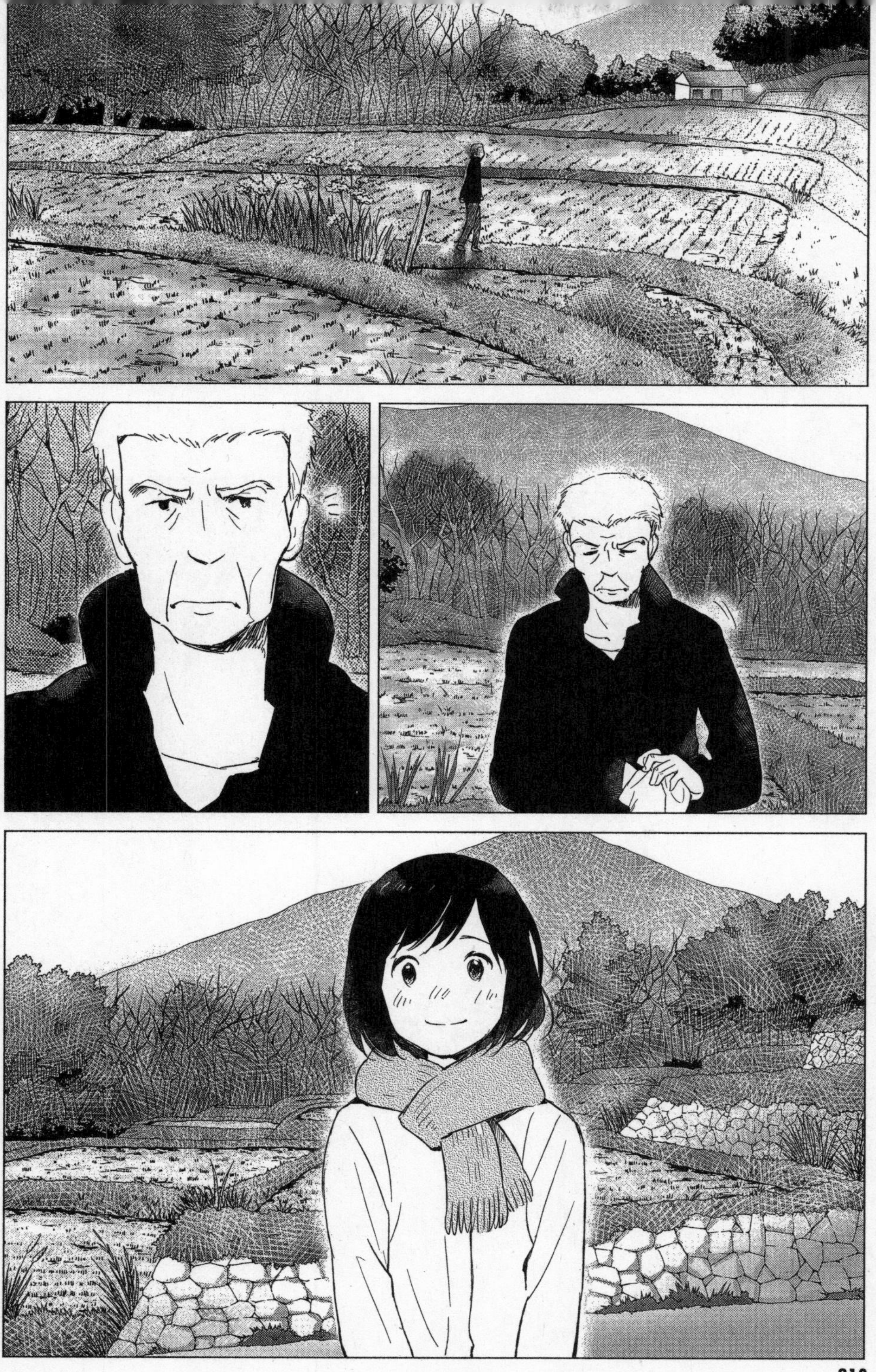

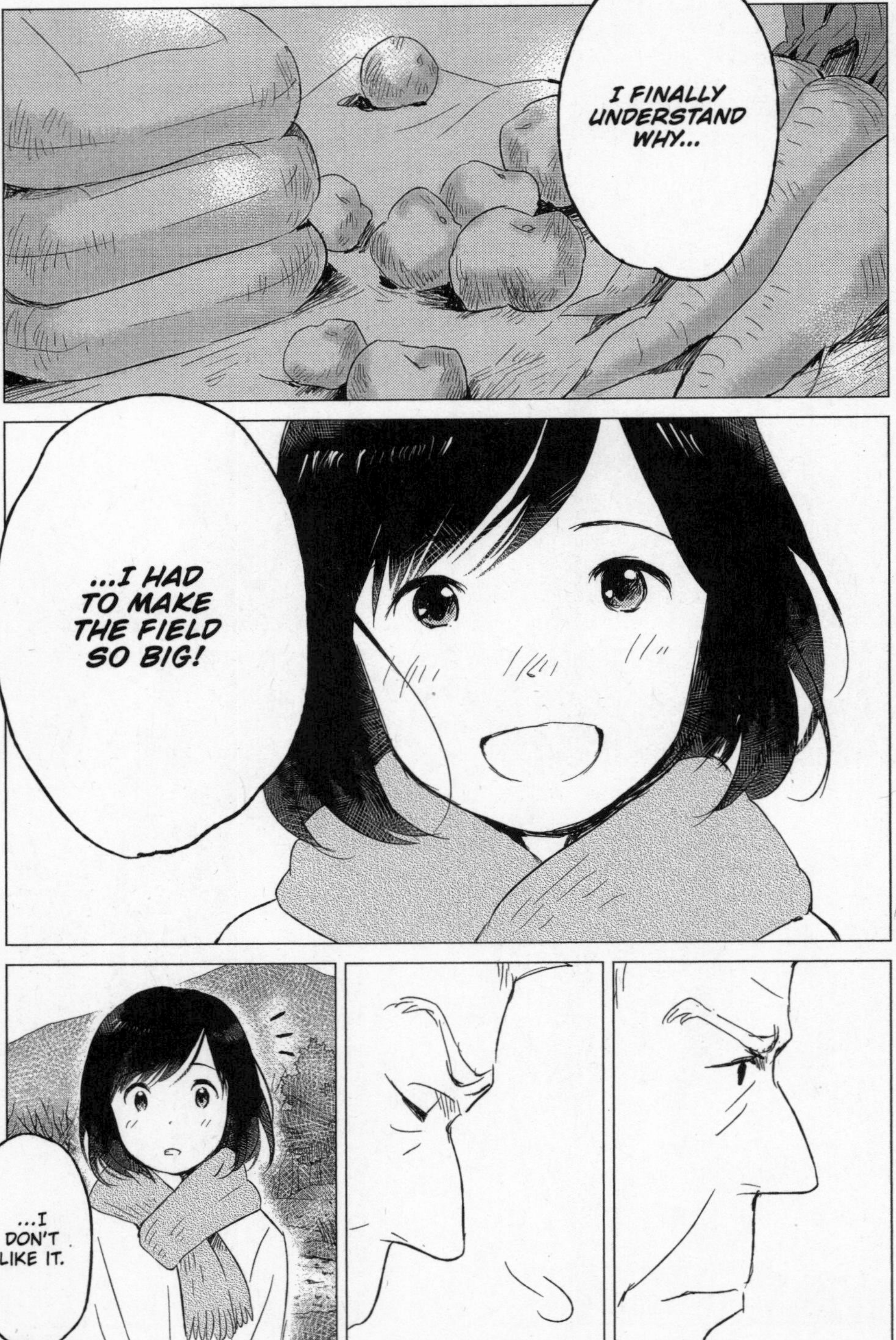
I FINALLY UNDERSTAND WHY...
...I HAD TO MAKE THE FIELD SO BIG!
...I DON'T LIKE IT.

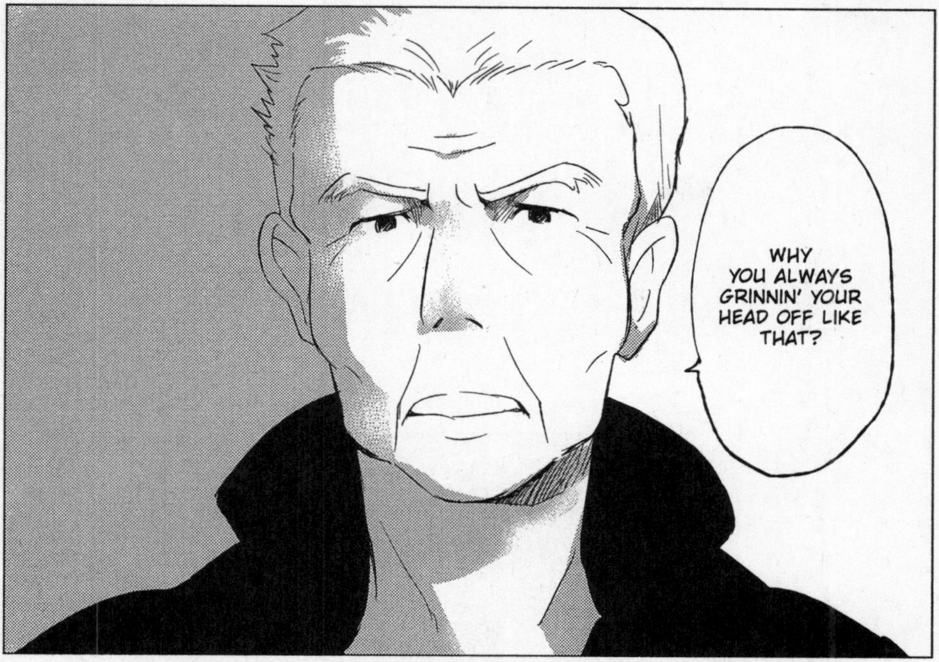
WHY YOU ALWAYS GRINNIN' YOUR HEAD OFF LIKE THAT?
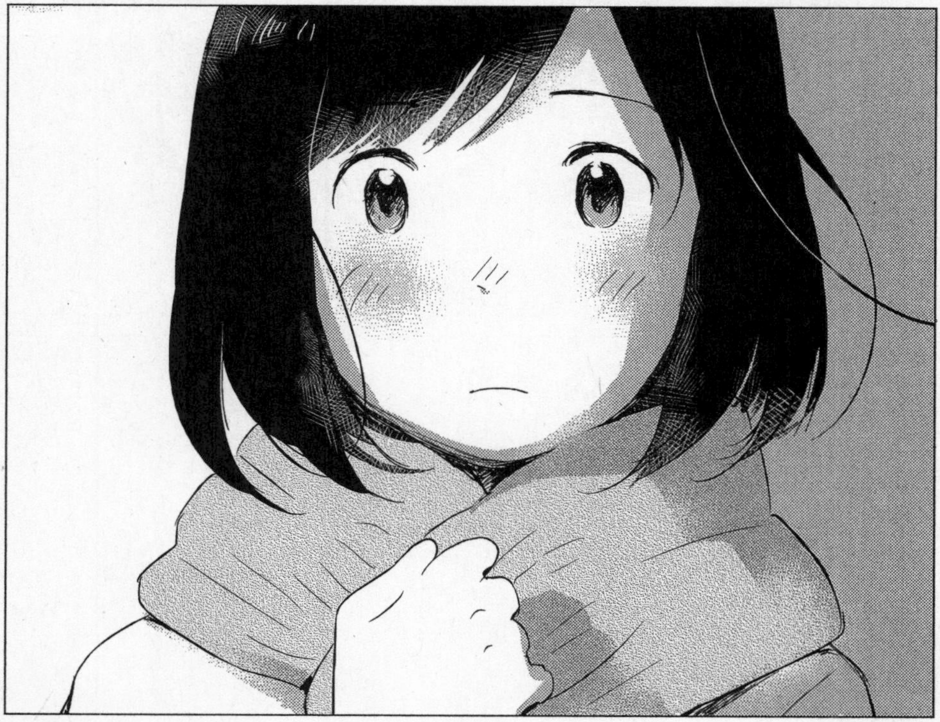

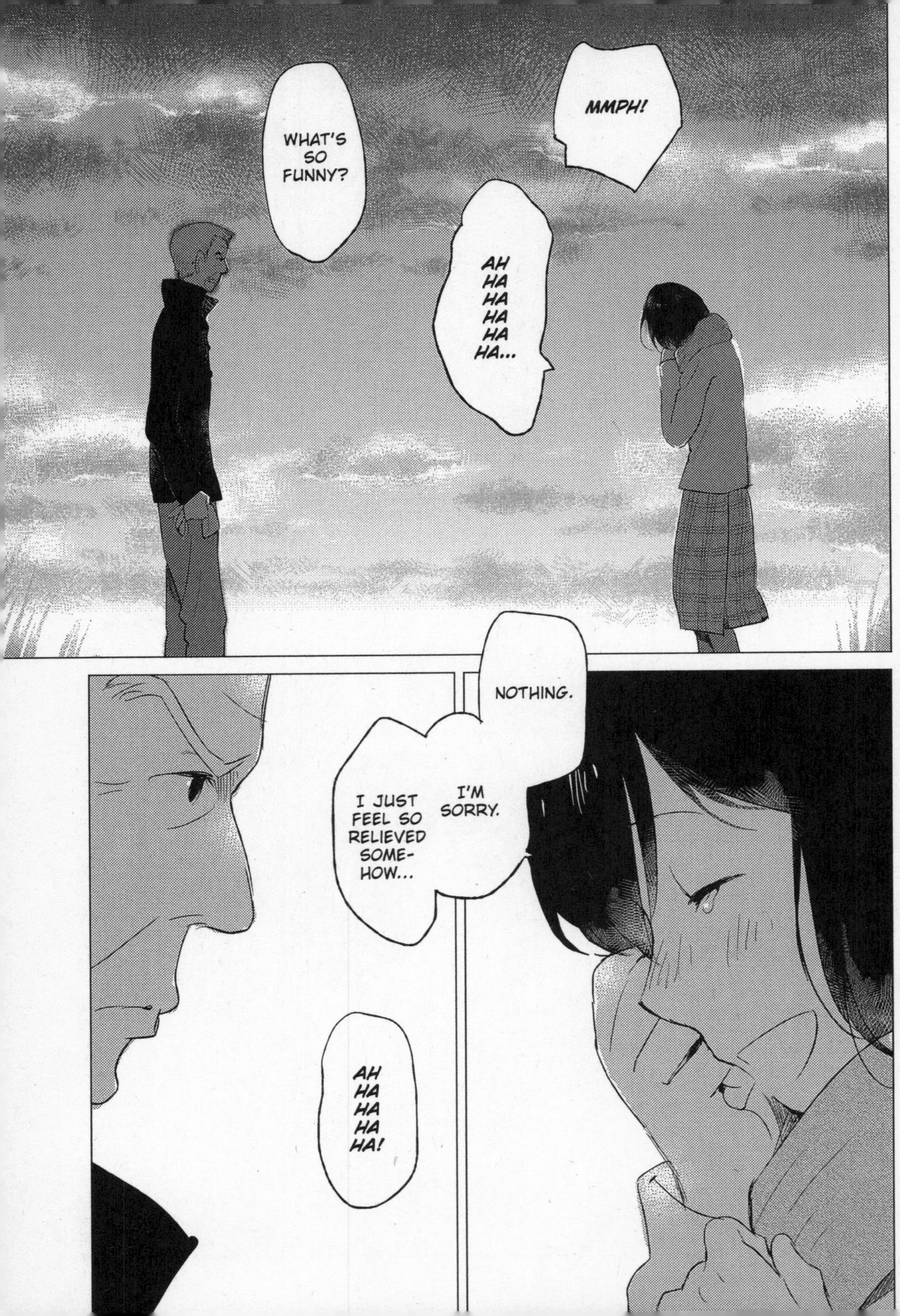
MMPH!
AH HA HA HA HA HA...
WHAT'S SO FUNNY?
NOTHING.
I'M SORRY.
I JUST FEEL SO RELIEVED SOME-HOW...
AH HA HA HA HA HA!

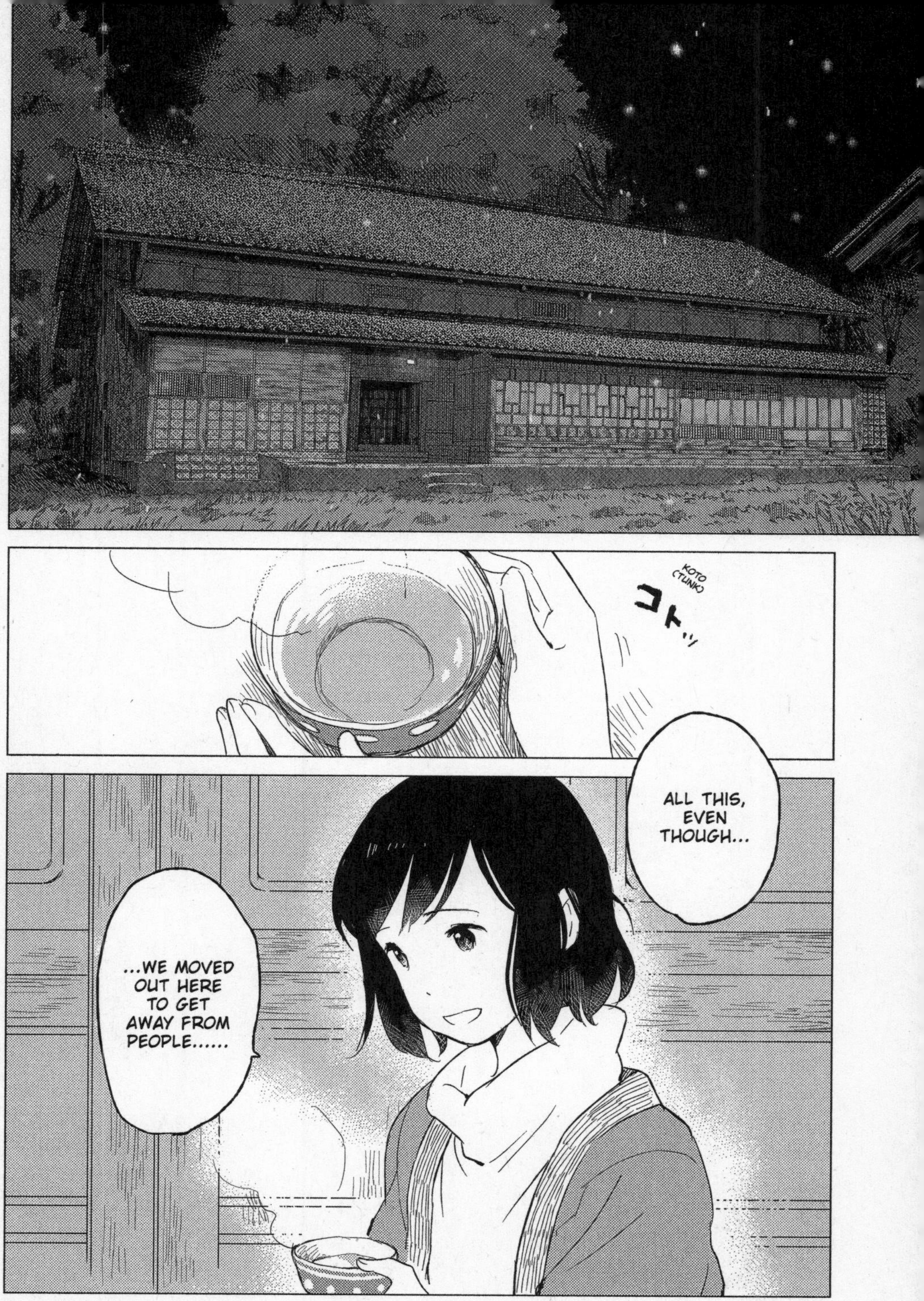
KOTO (TUNK)
コトッ
ALL THIS, EVEN THOUGH...
...WE MOVED OUT HERE TO GET AWAY FROM PEOPLE......

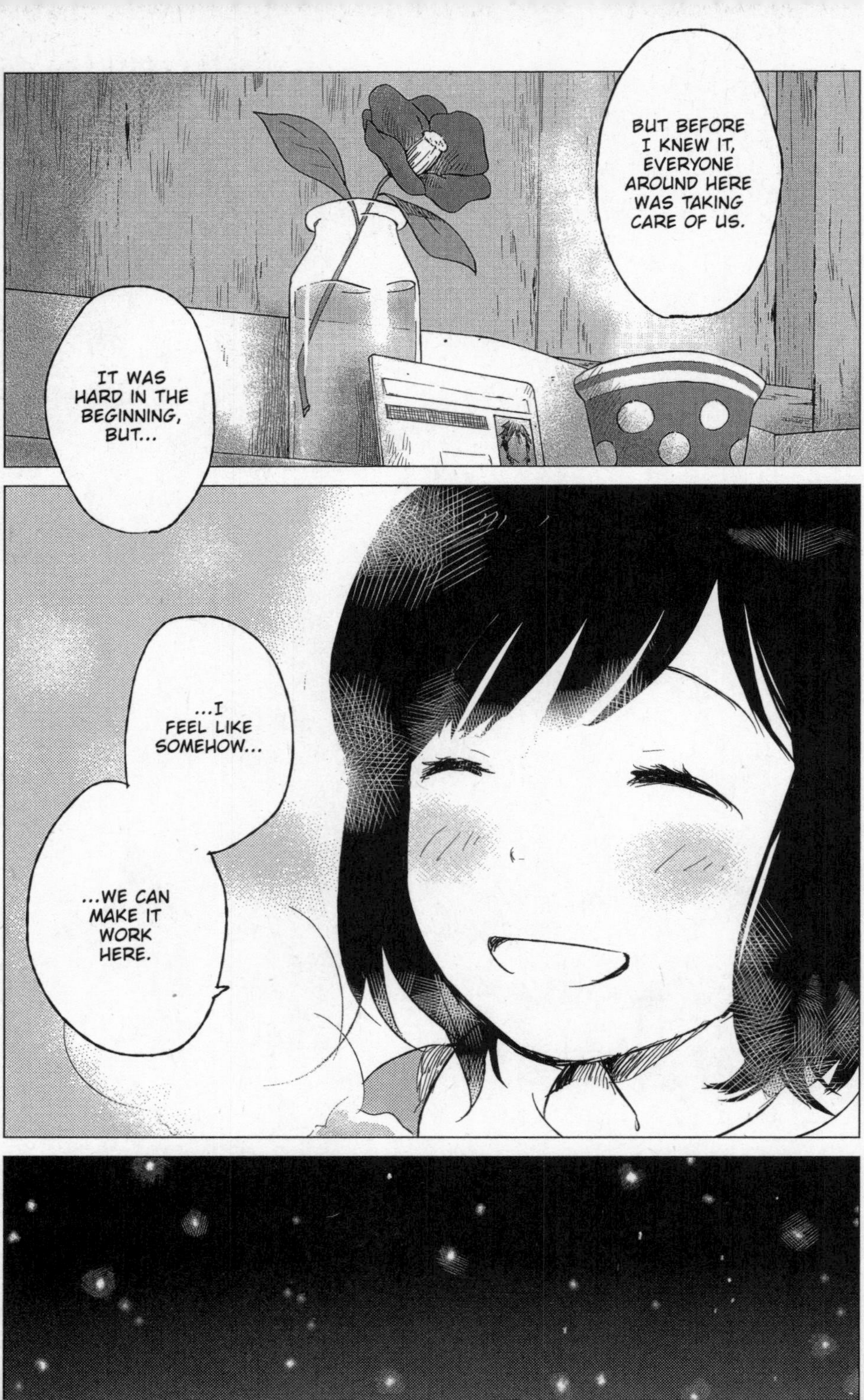
BUT BEFORE I KNEW IT, EVERYONE AROUND HERE WAS TAKING CARE OF US.
IT WAS HARD IN THE BEGINNING, BUT...
...I FEEL LIKE SOMEHOW...
...WE CAN MAKE IT WORK HERE.

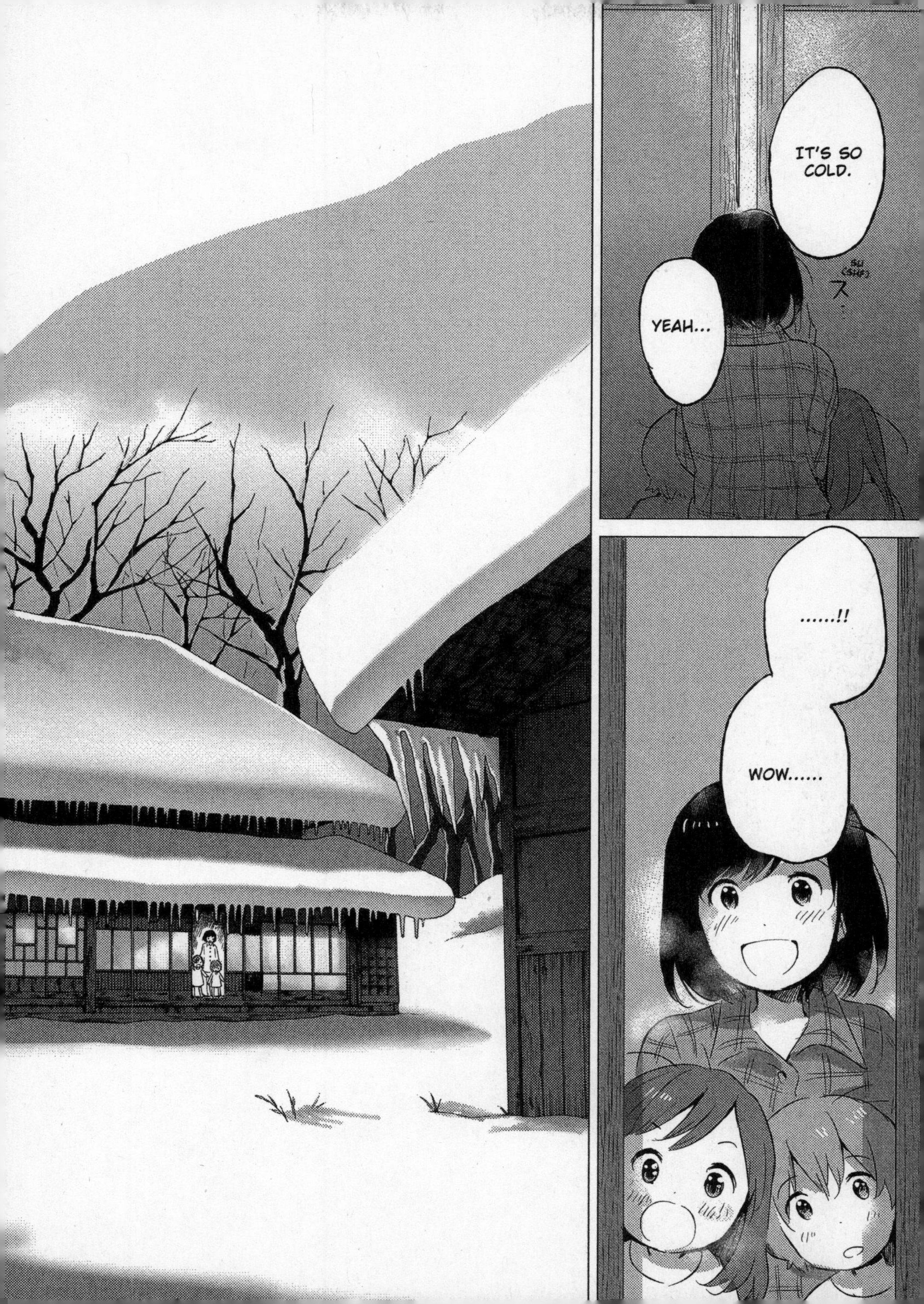
IT'S SO COLD.
YEAH...
SU (SHF)
ス
......!!
WOW......

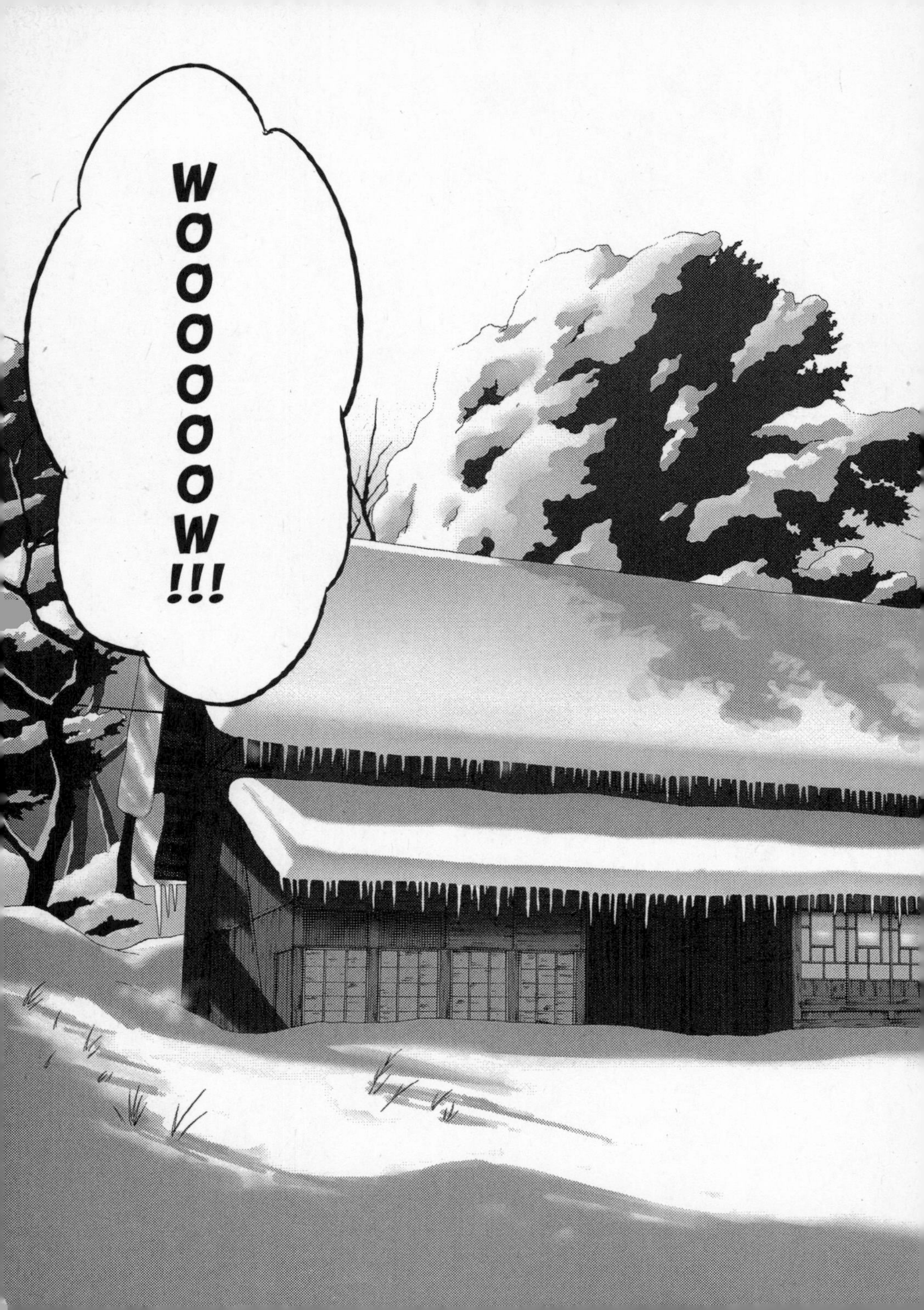
WOOOOOOW!!!

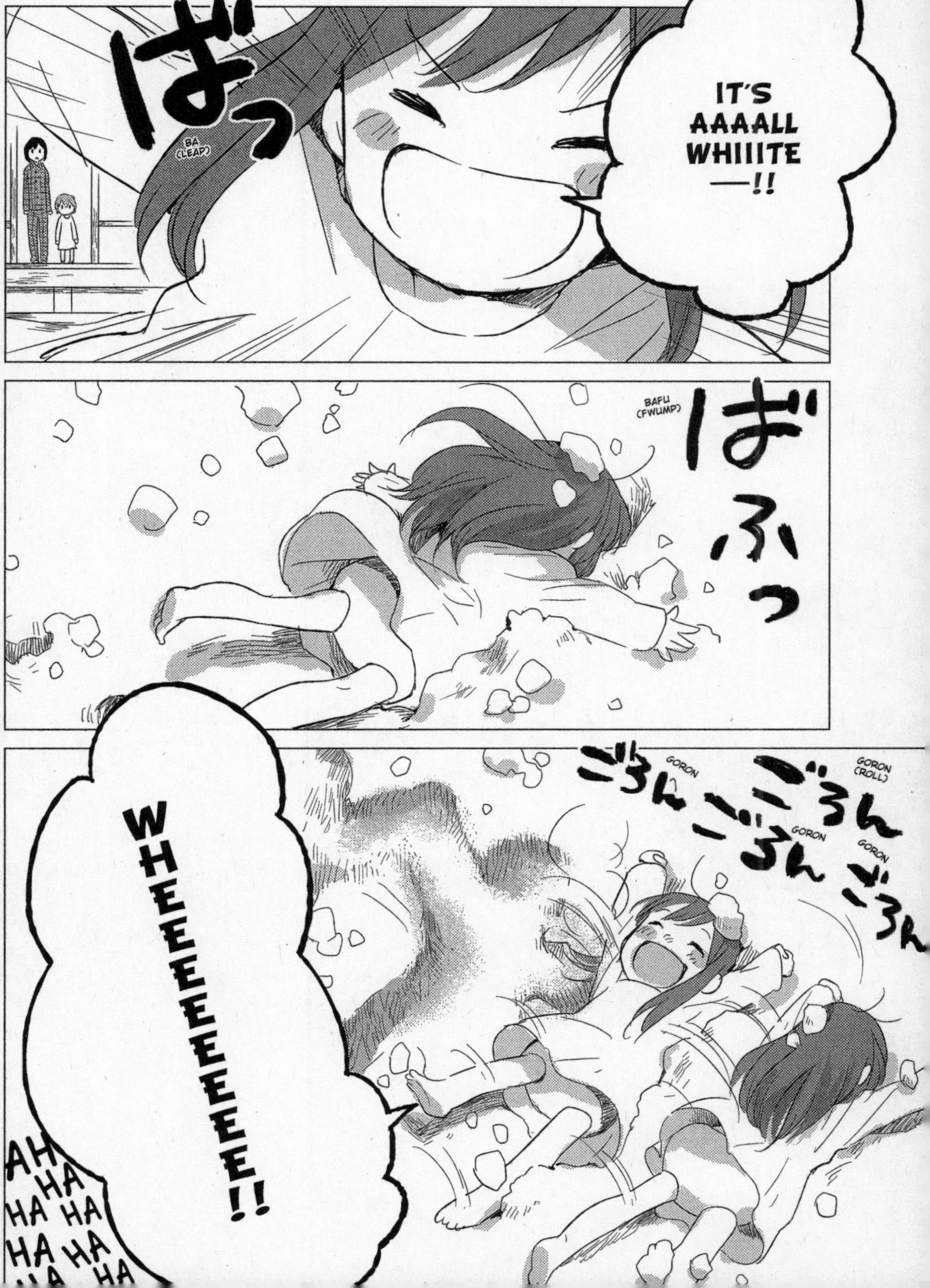
IT'S AAAALL WHIIITE—!!
ばっ
BA (LEAP)
ぼふっ
BAFU (FWUMP)
ごろん GORON (ROLL)
ごろん GORON
ごろん GORON
ごろん GORON
WHEEEEEEEEEEEE!!
AHAHAHAHAHAHAHAHAHA

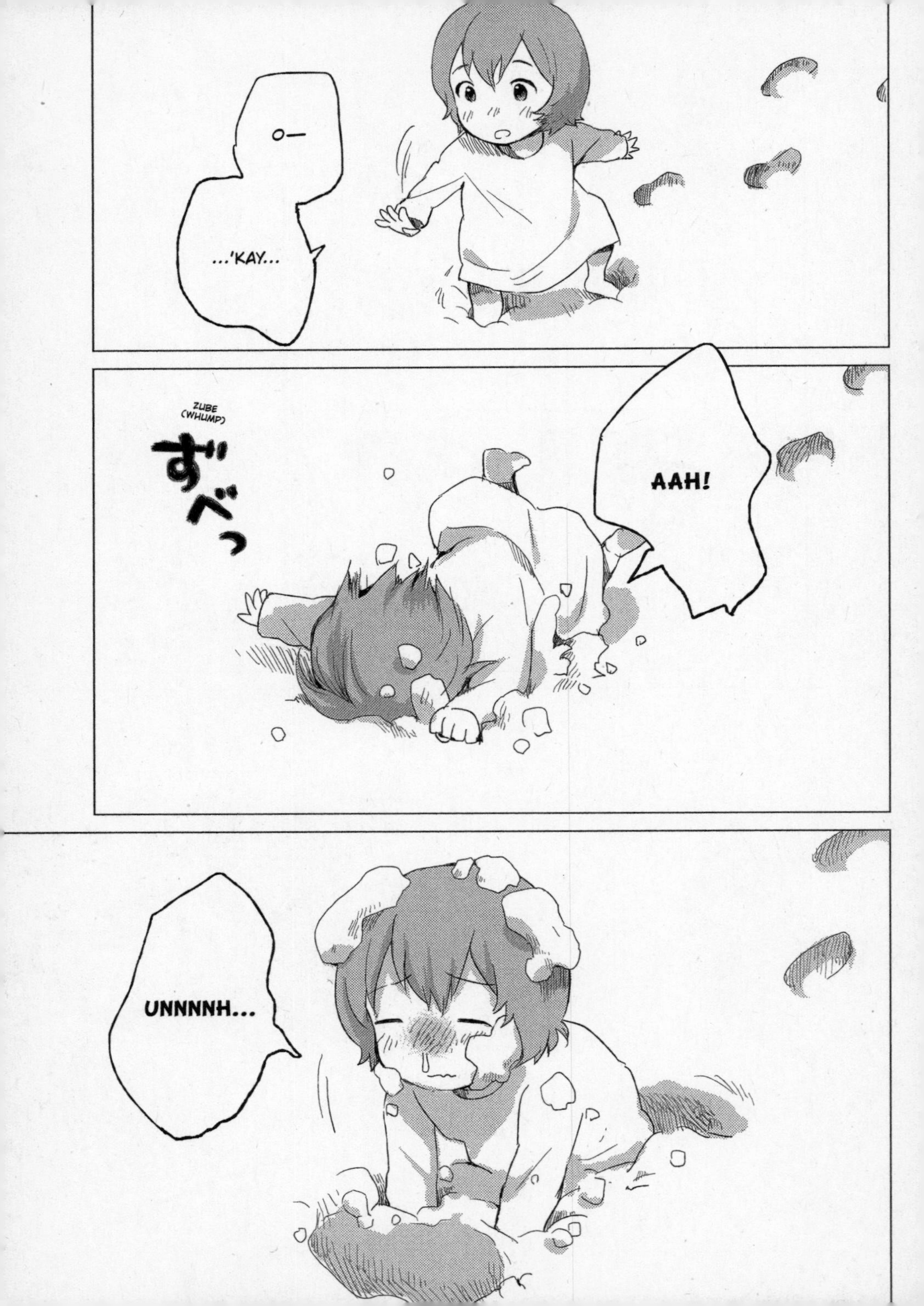

O–
...'KAY...
ZUBE (WHUMP)
ずべっ
AAH!
UNNNNH...

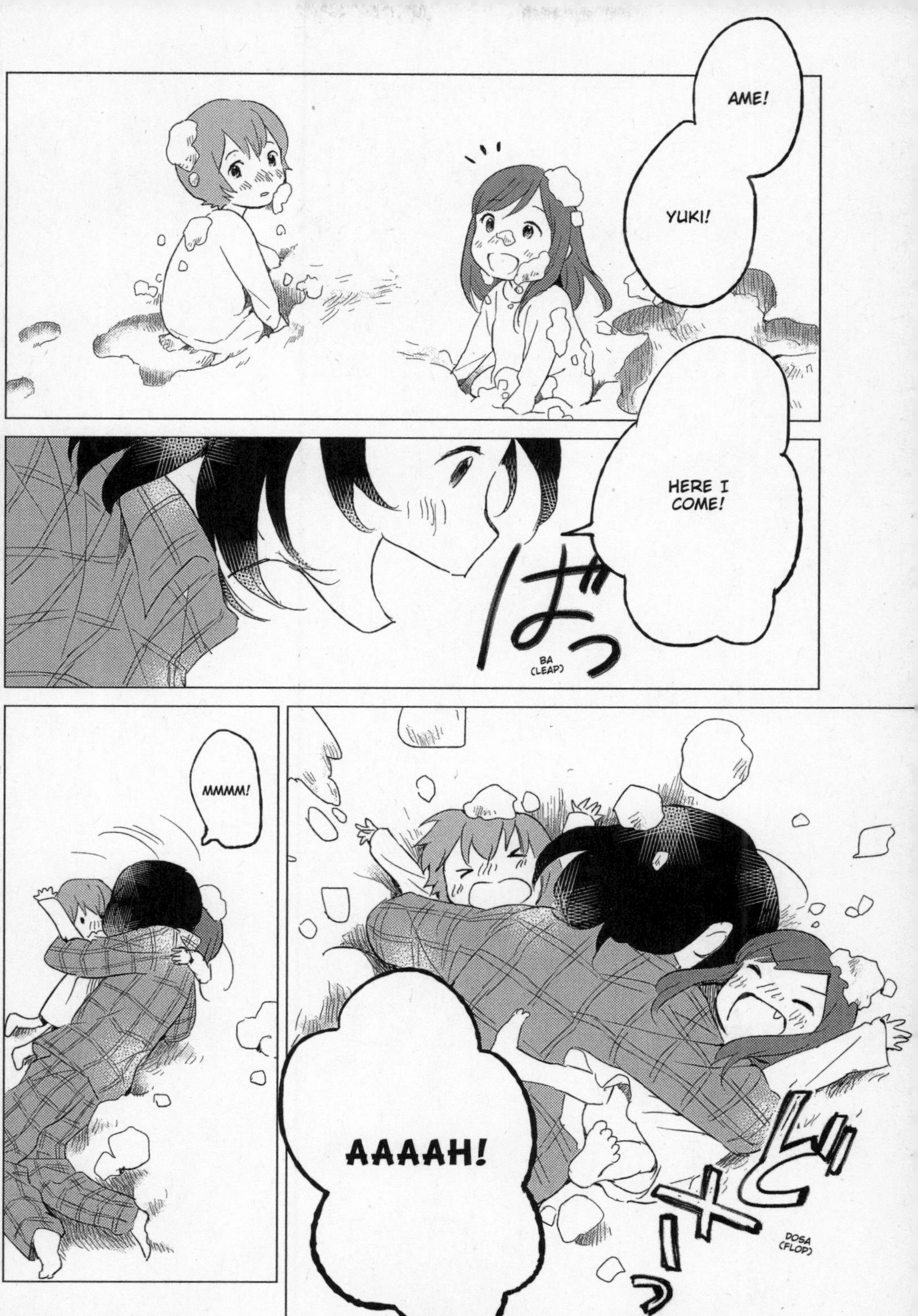
AME!
YUKI!
HERE I COME!
BA (LEAP)
AAAAH!
DOSA (FLOP)
MMMM!

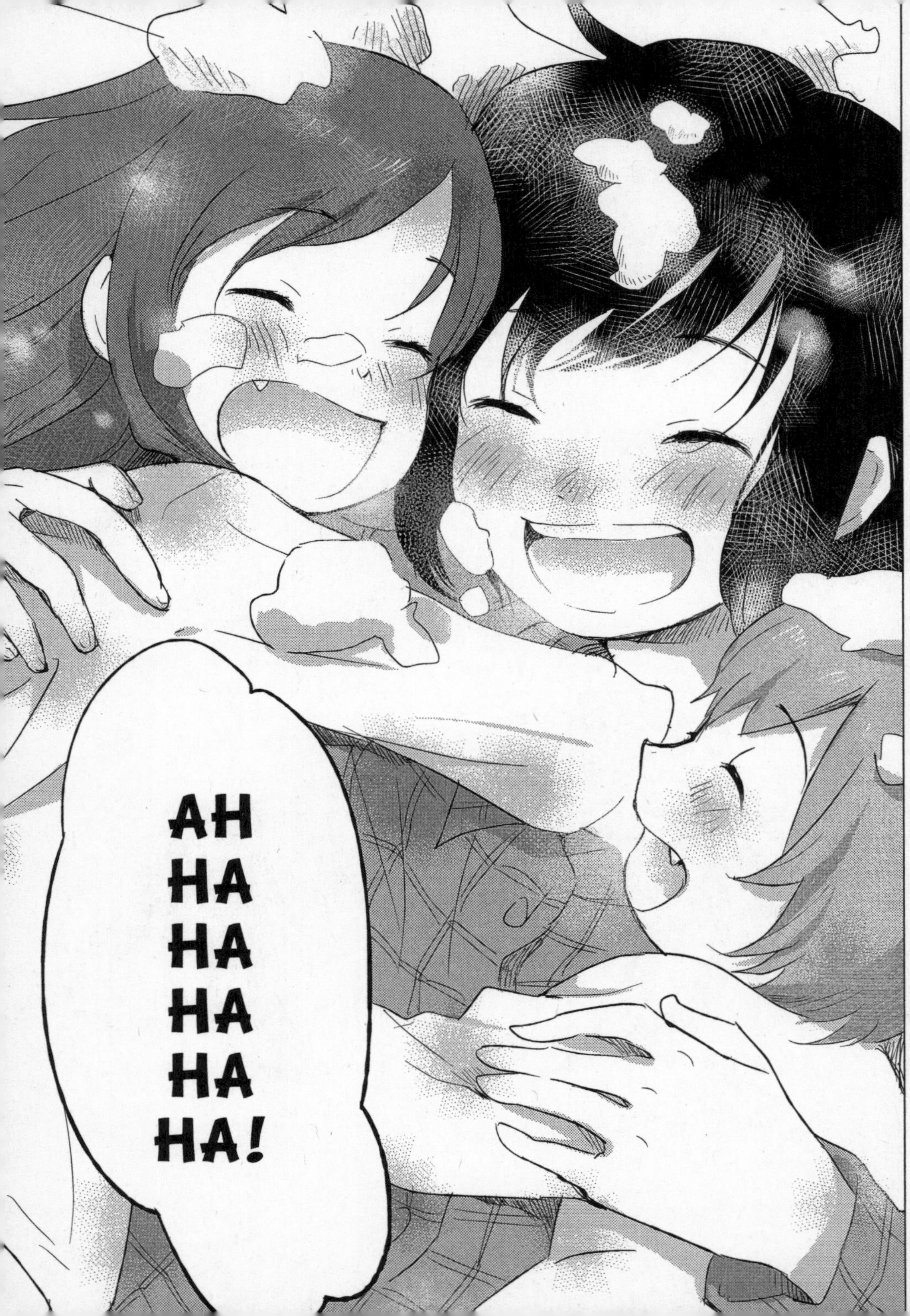
AH HA HA HA HA HA!

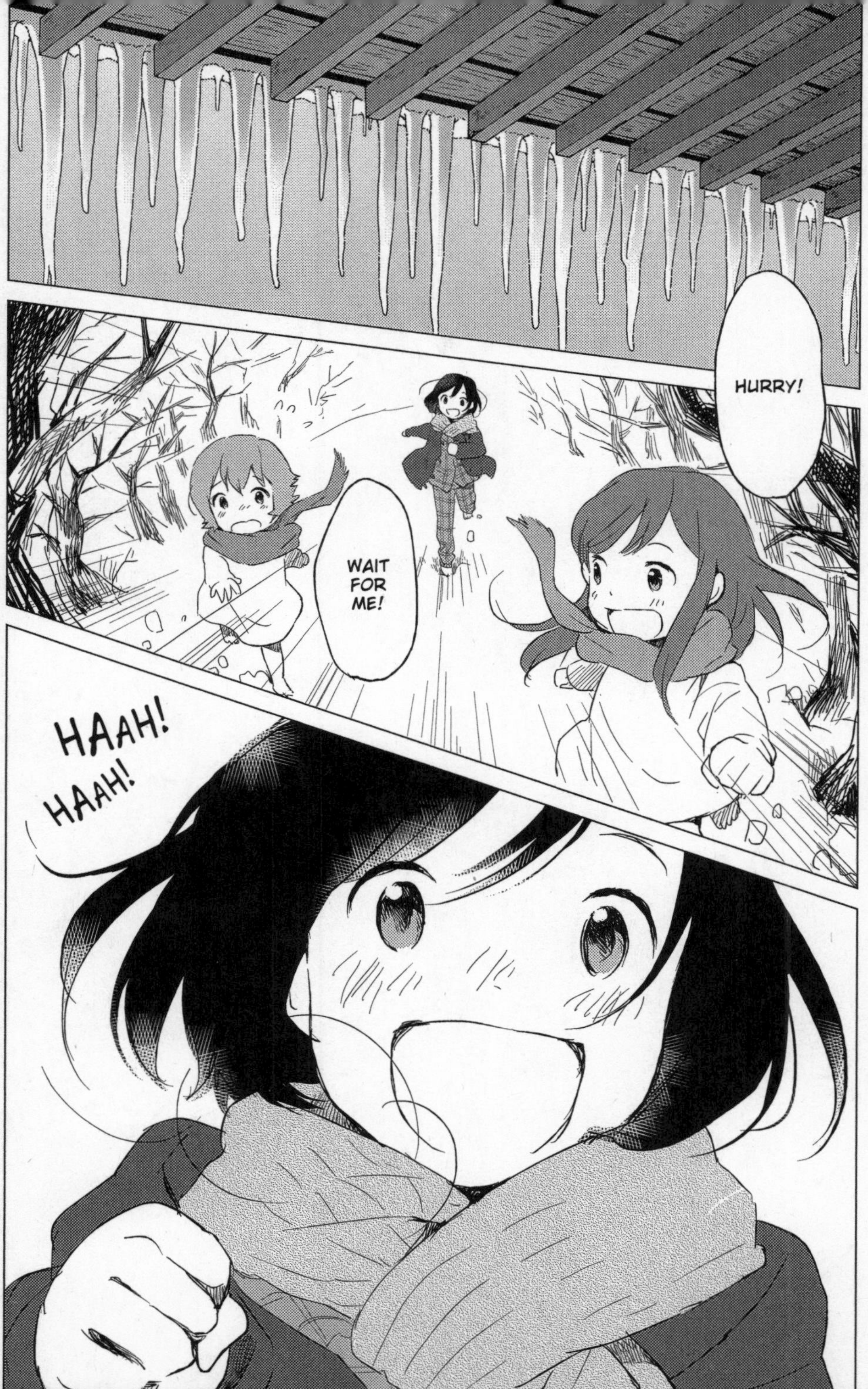
HURRY!
WAIT FOR ME!
HAAH! HAAH!

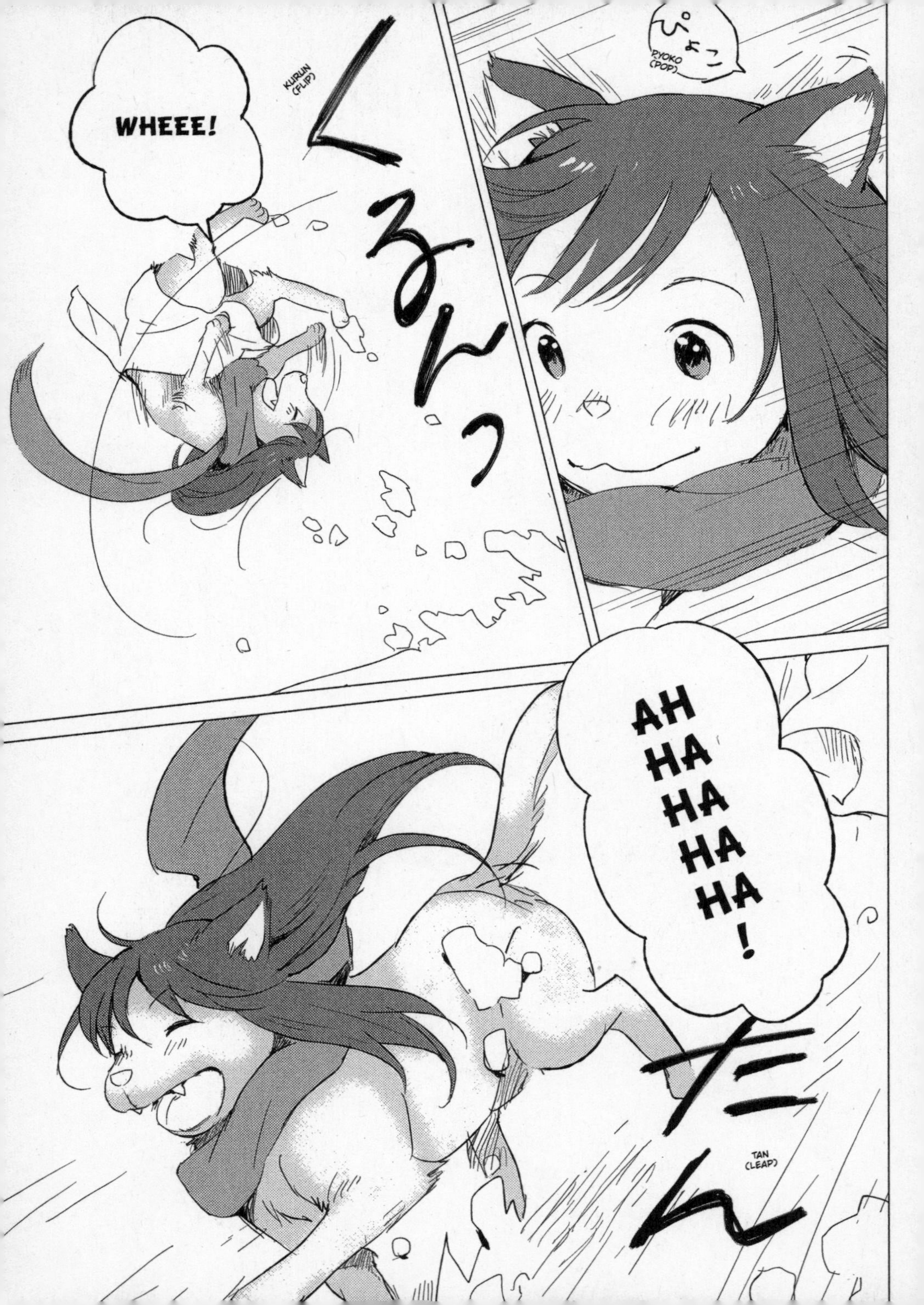
ぴょこっ
PYOKO (POP)
くるんっ
KURUN (FLIP)
WHEEE!
AH HA HA HA HA!
たーん
TAN (LEAP)

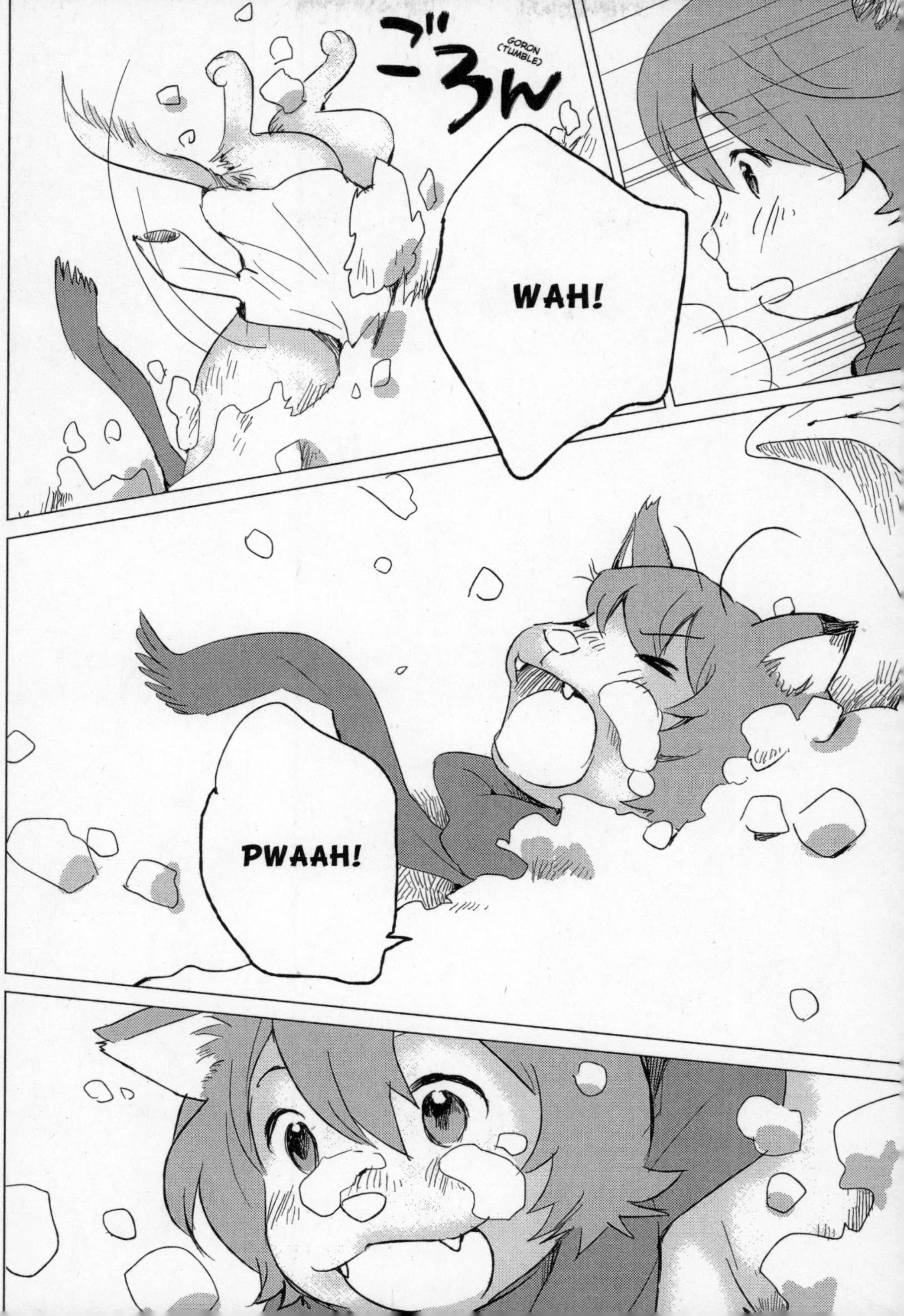
ごろん
GORON (TUMBLE)
WAH!
PWAAH!

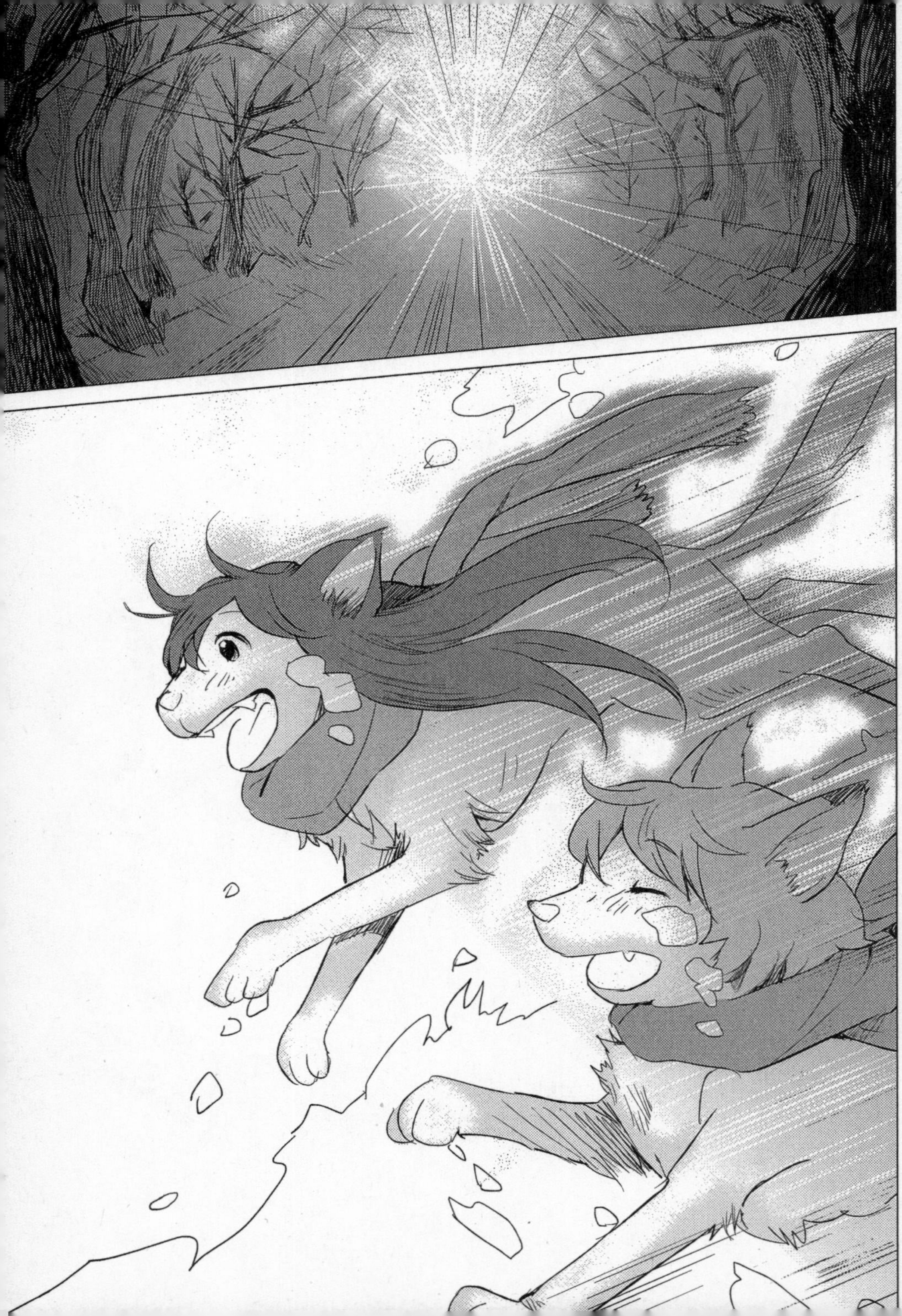

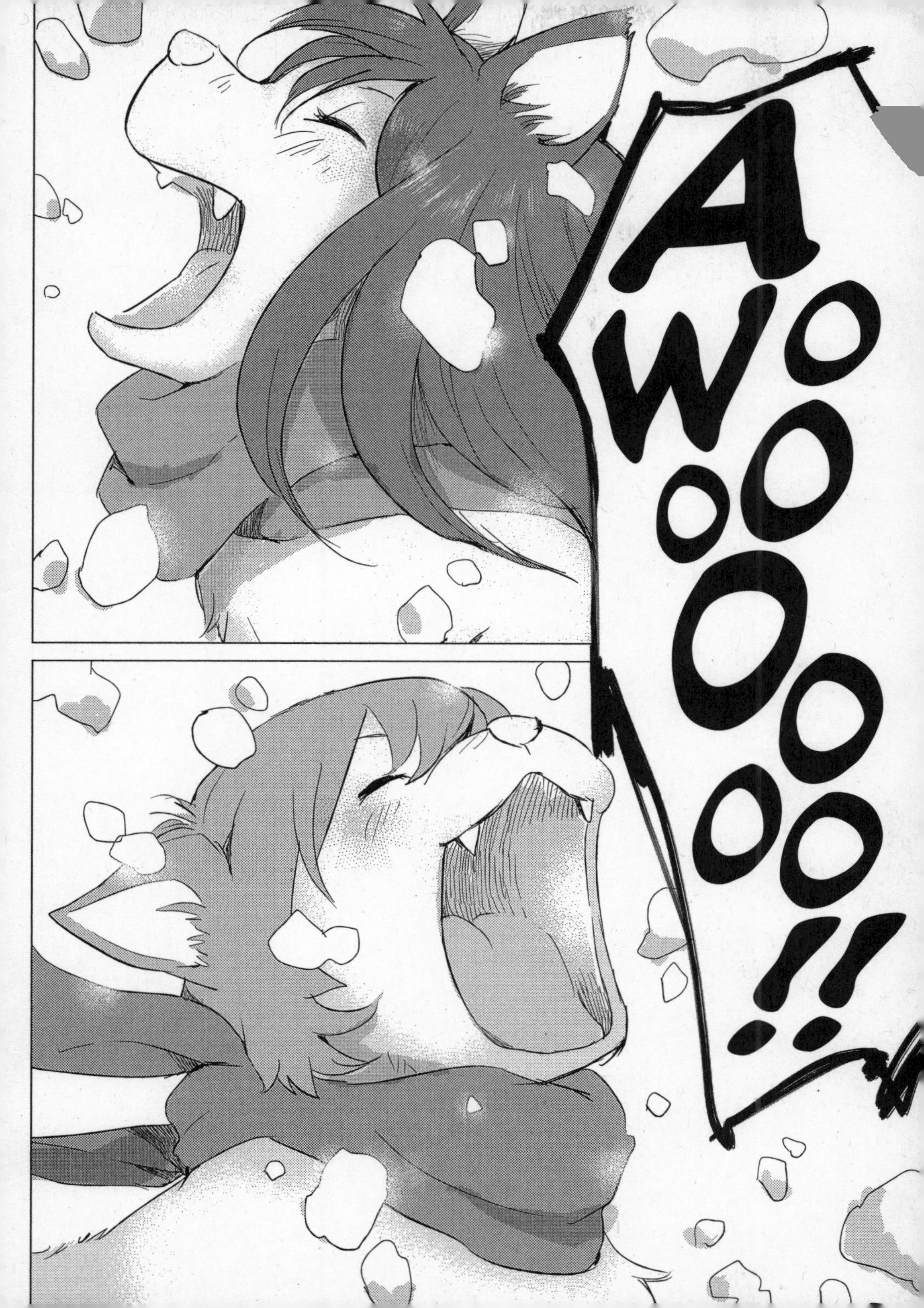
AWOOOOOOO!!

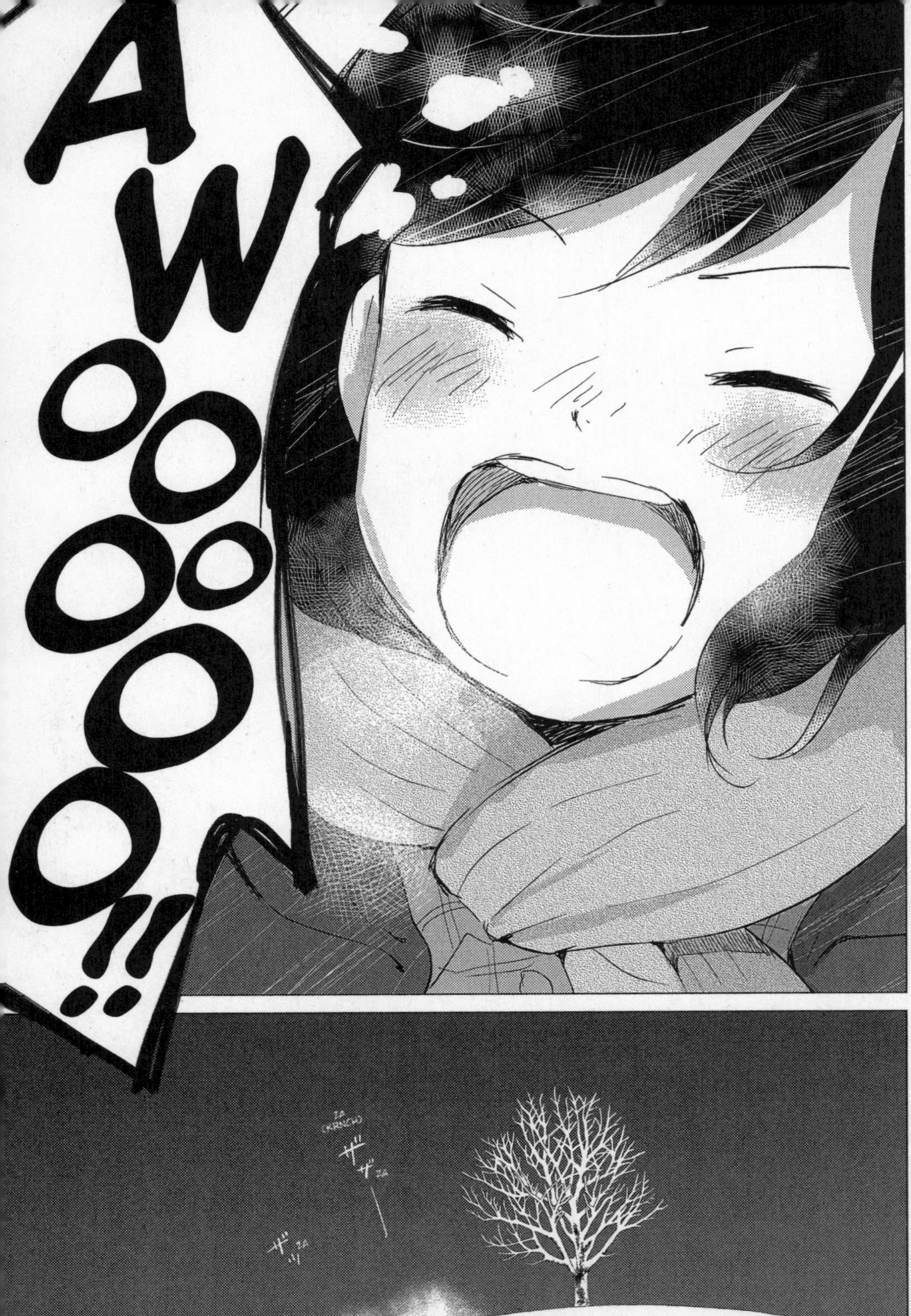
AWOOOOOOO!!
ZA (KRNCH)
ザ
ザ ZA
ザッ ZA

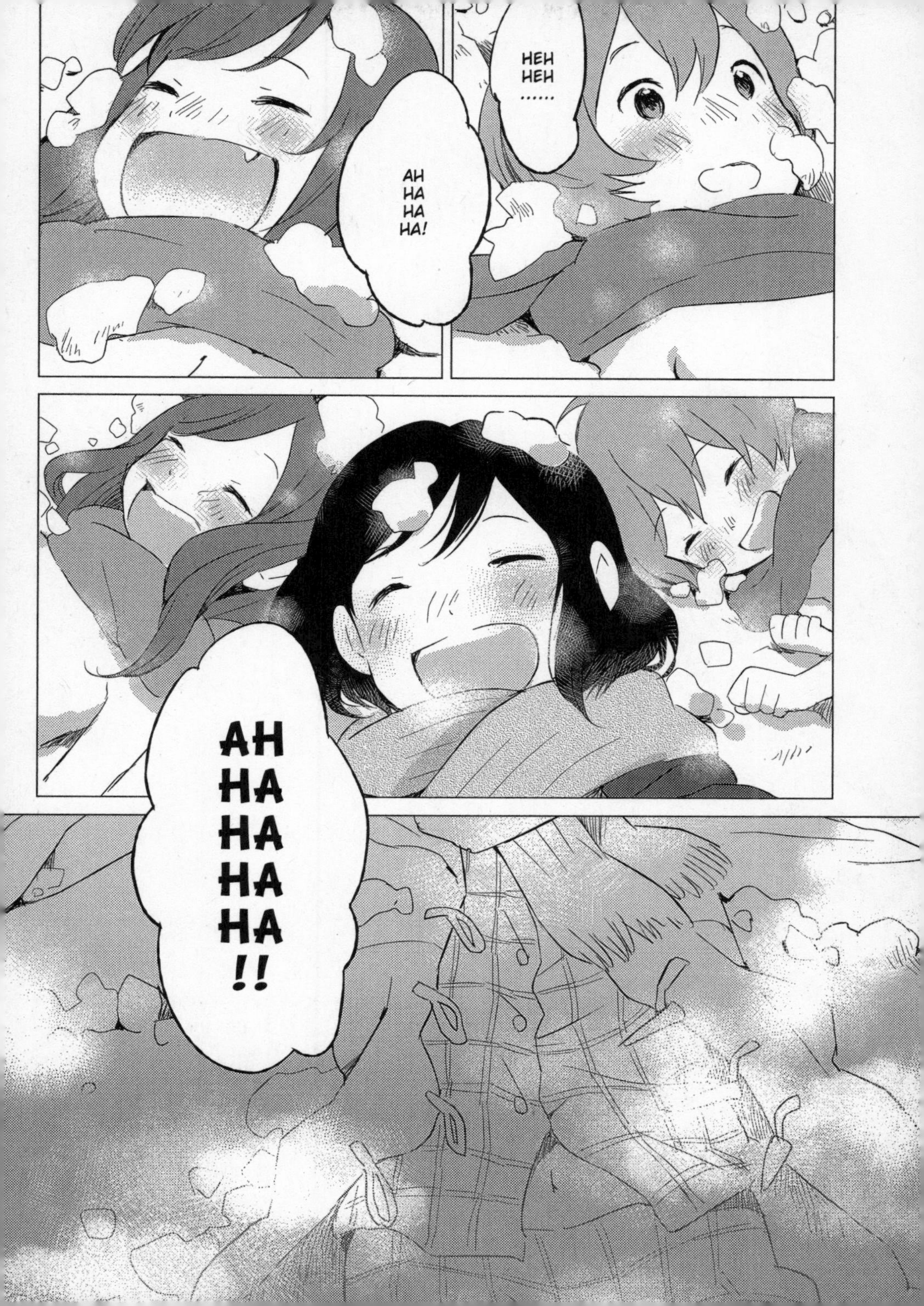
HEH HEH ......
AH HA HA HA!
AH HA HA HA HA!!

Wolf Children
Ame & Yuki

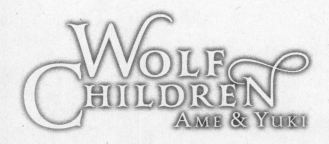

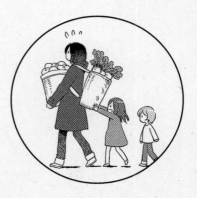

Chapter 7 Ame in Winter, Yuki in Spring

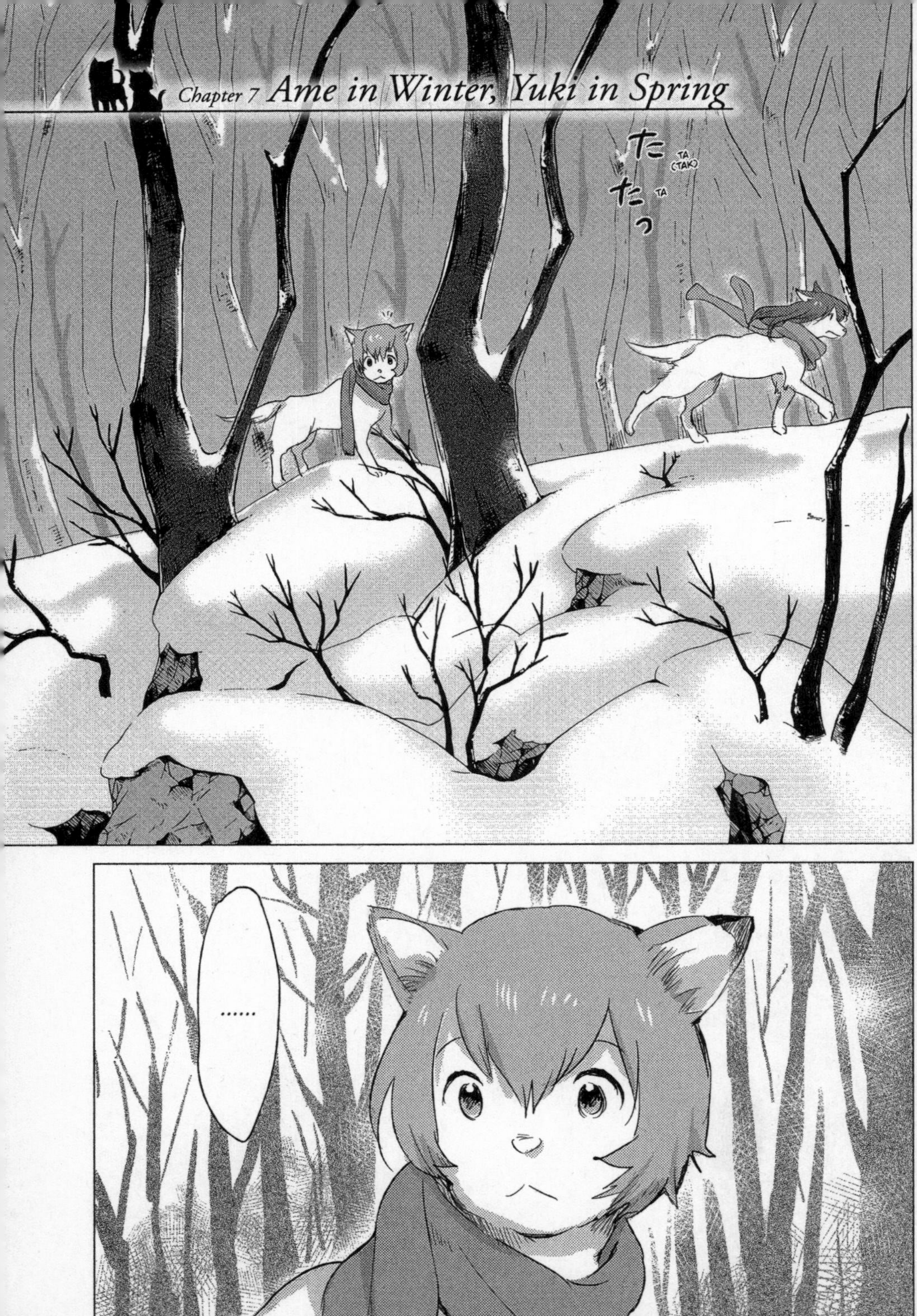
たたっ
TA (TAK) TA
......

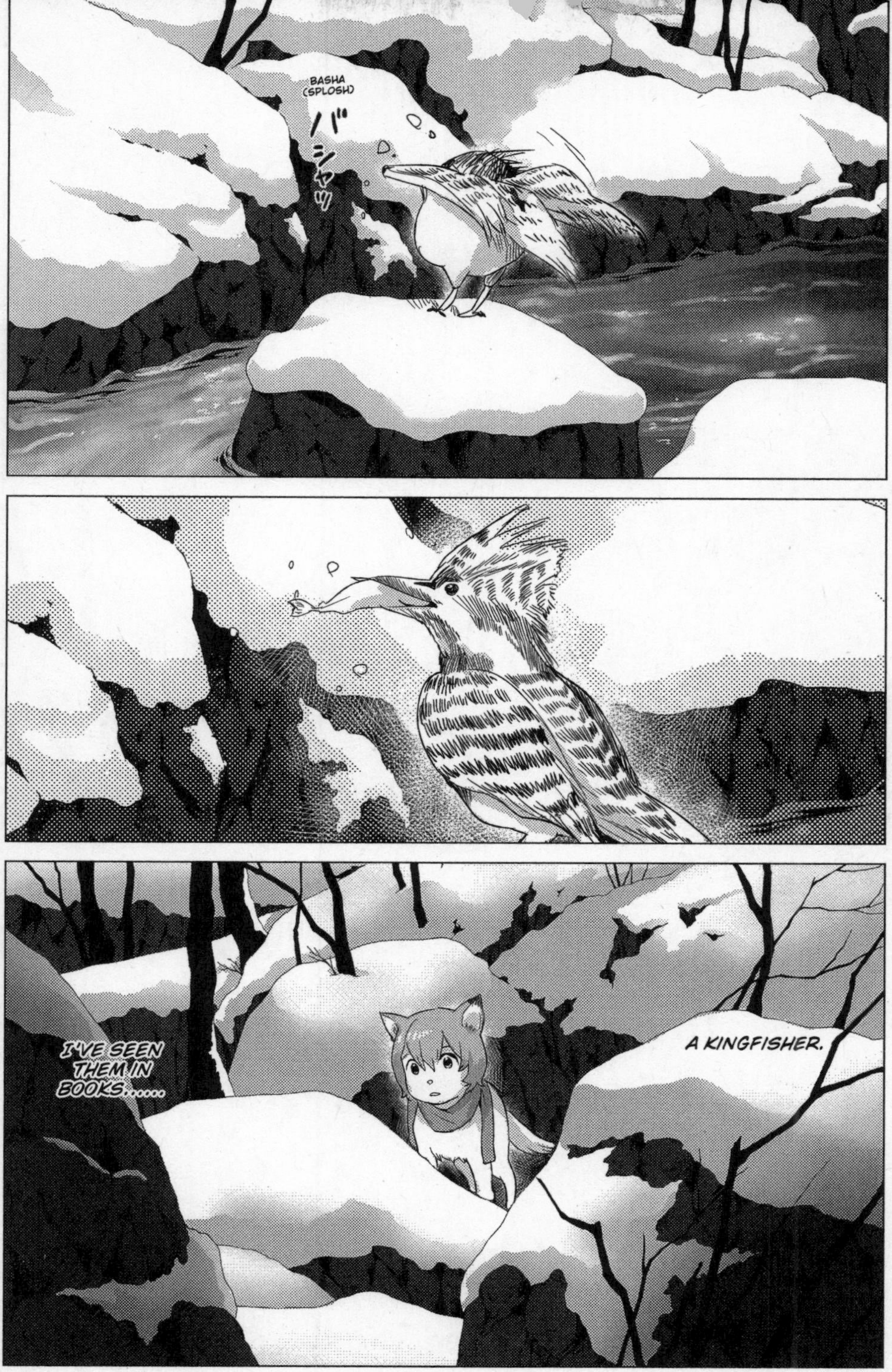
BASHA (SPLOSH)
バシャッ
A KINGFISHER.
I'VE SEEN THEM IN BOOKS......

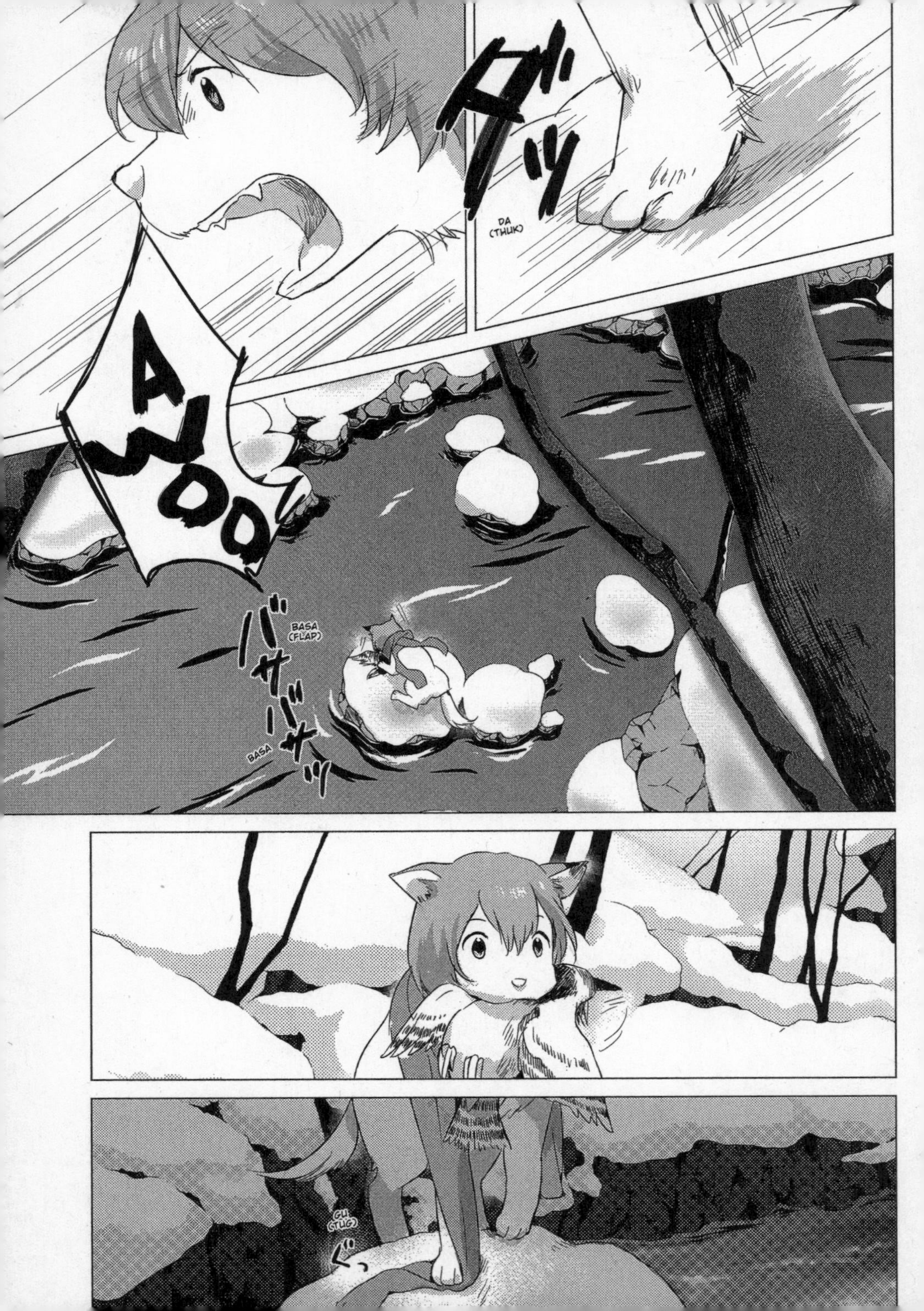
DA
(THUK)
AWOO
BASA
(FLAP)
BASA
GU
(TUG)

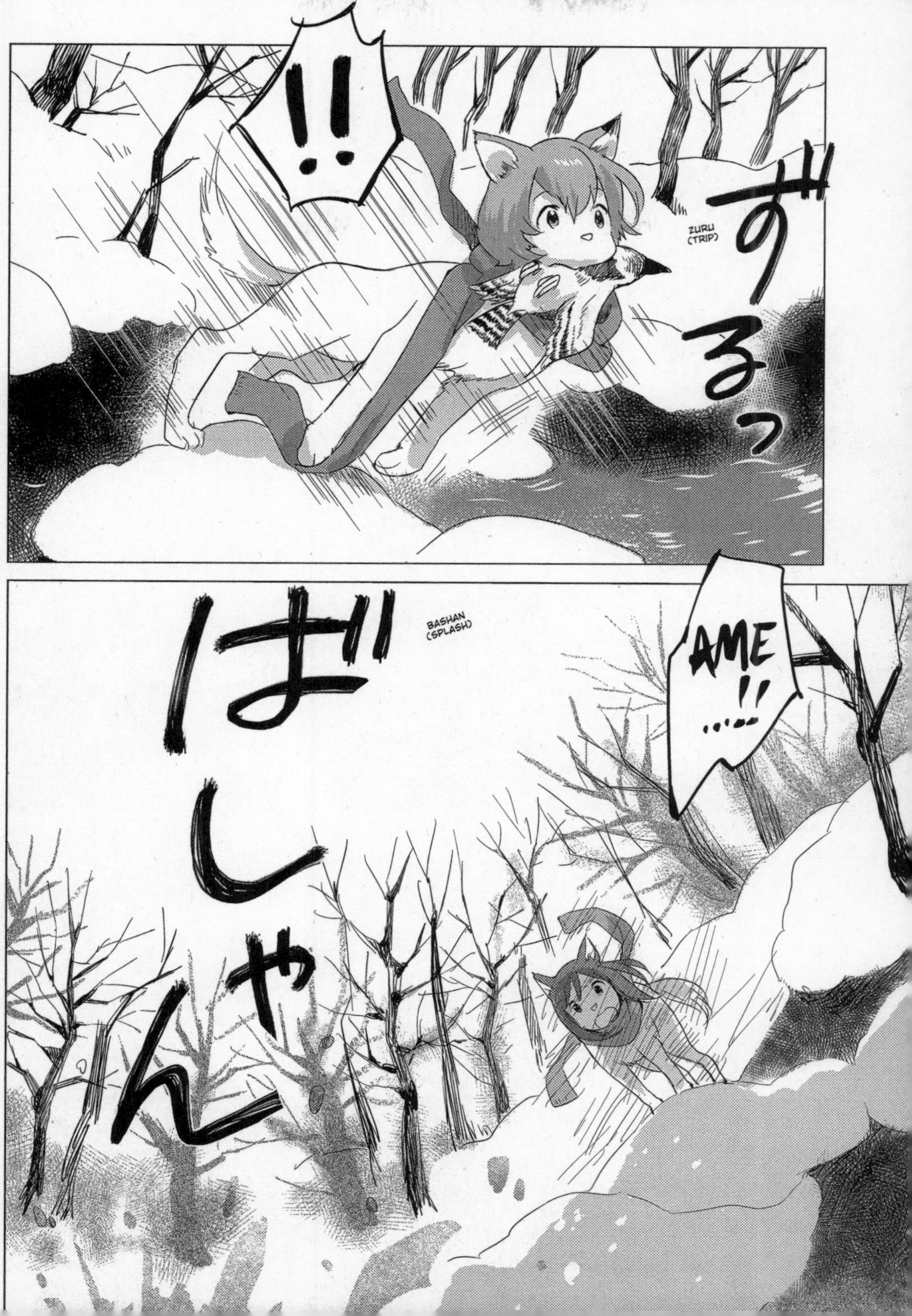
!!
ずるっ
ZURU (TRIP)
AME!! ......
ばしゃん
BASHAN (SPLASH)

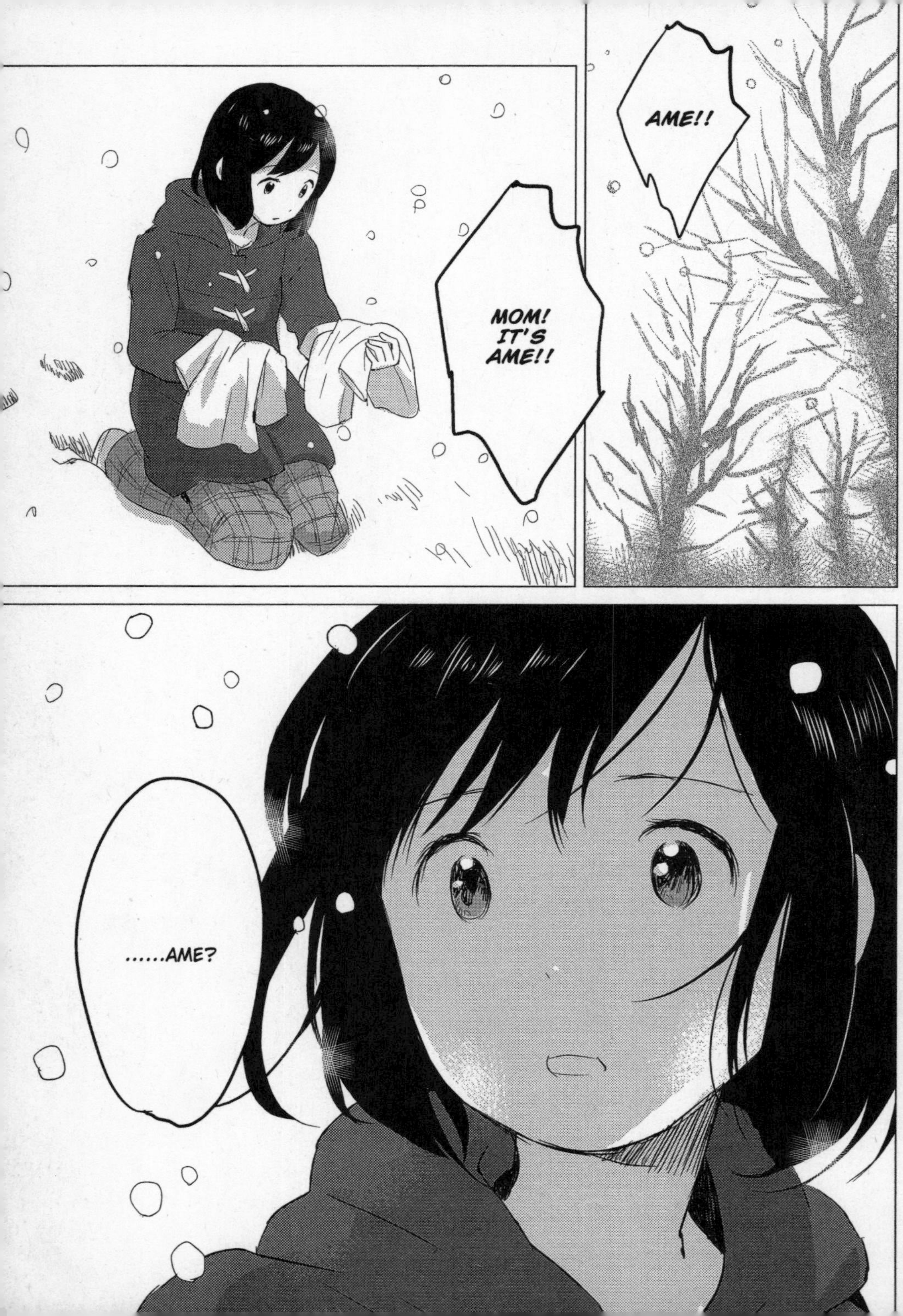
AME!!
MOM! IT'S AME!!
......AME?

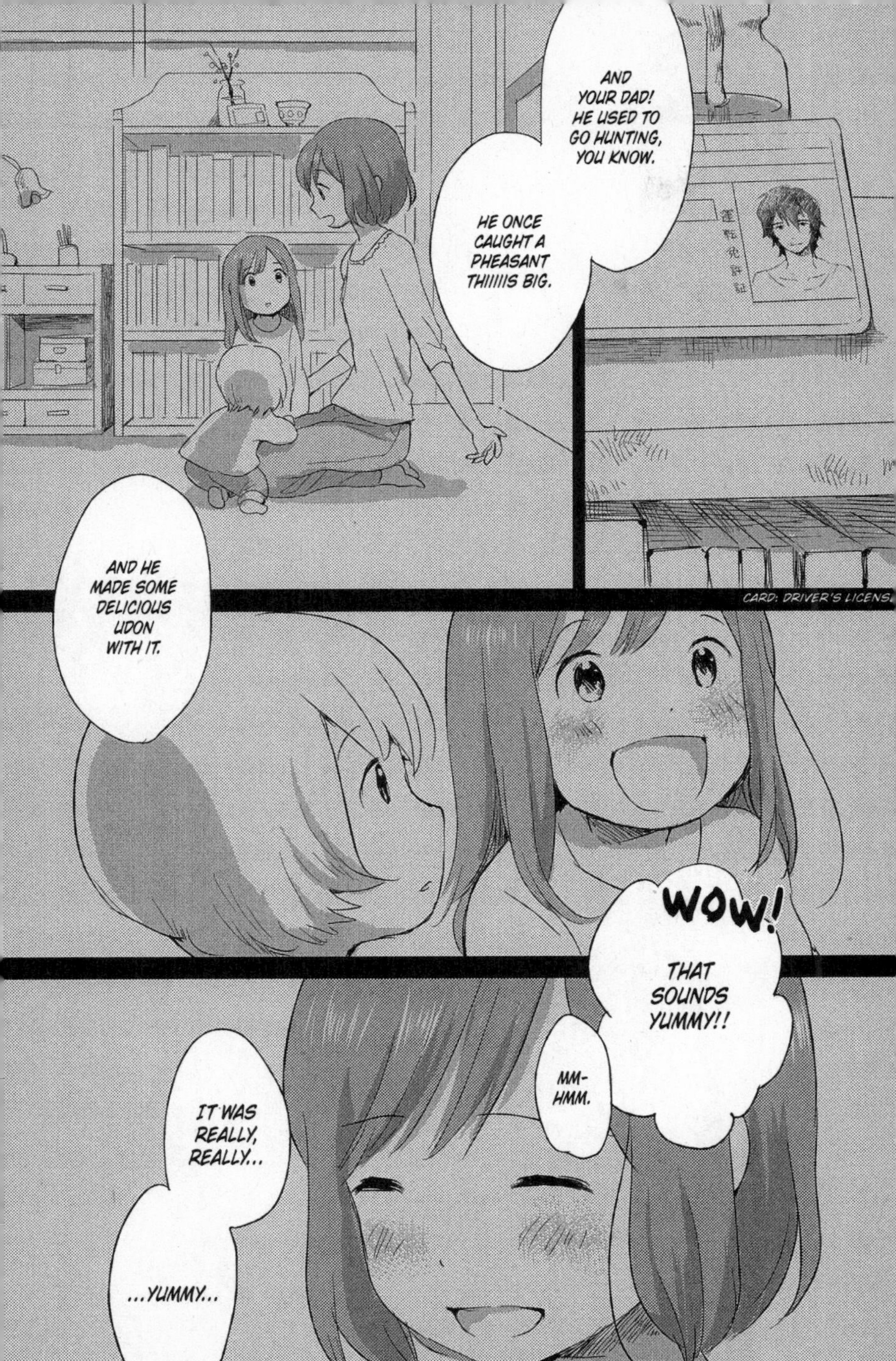
AND YOUR DAD! HE USED TO GO HUNTING, YOU KNOW.
HE ONCE CAUGHT A PHEASANT THIIIIIS BIG.
CARD: DRIVER'S LICENS
AND HE MADE SOME DELICIOUS UDON WITH IT.
WOW!
THAT SOUNDS YUMMY!!
MM-HMM.
IT WAS REALLY, REALLY...
...YUMMY...

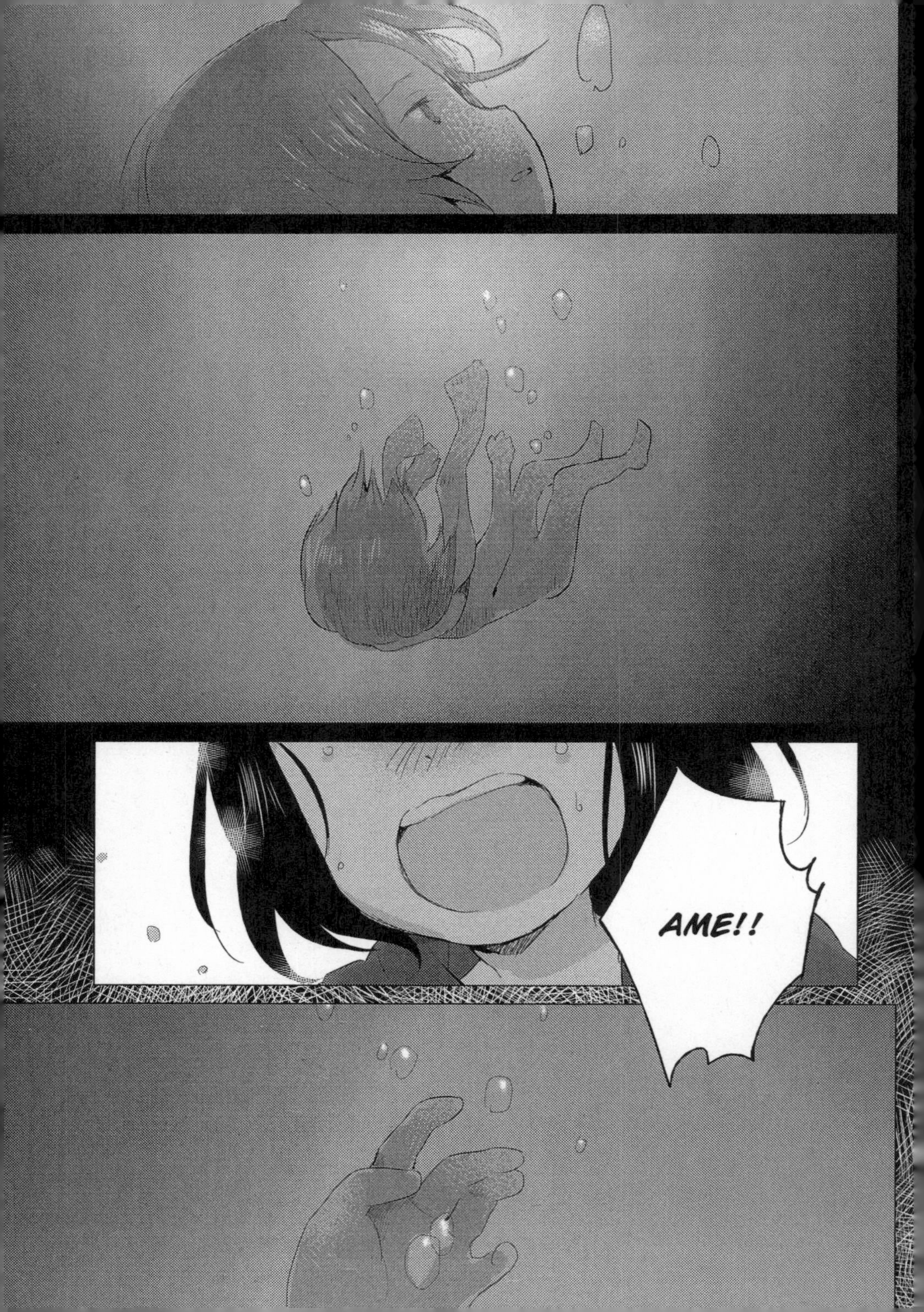
AME!!

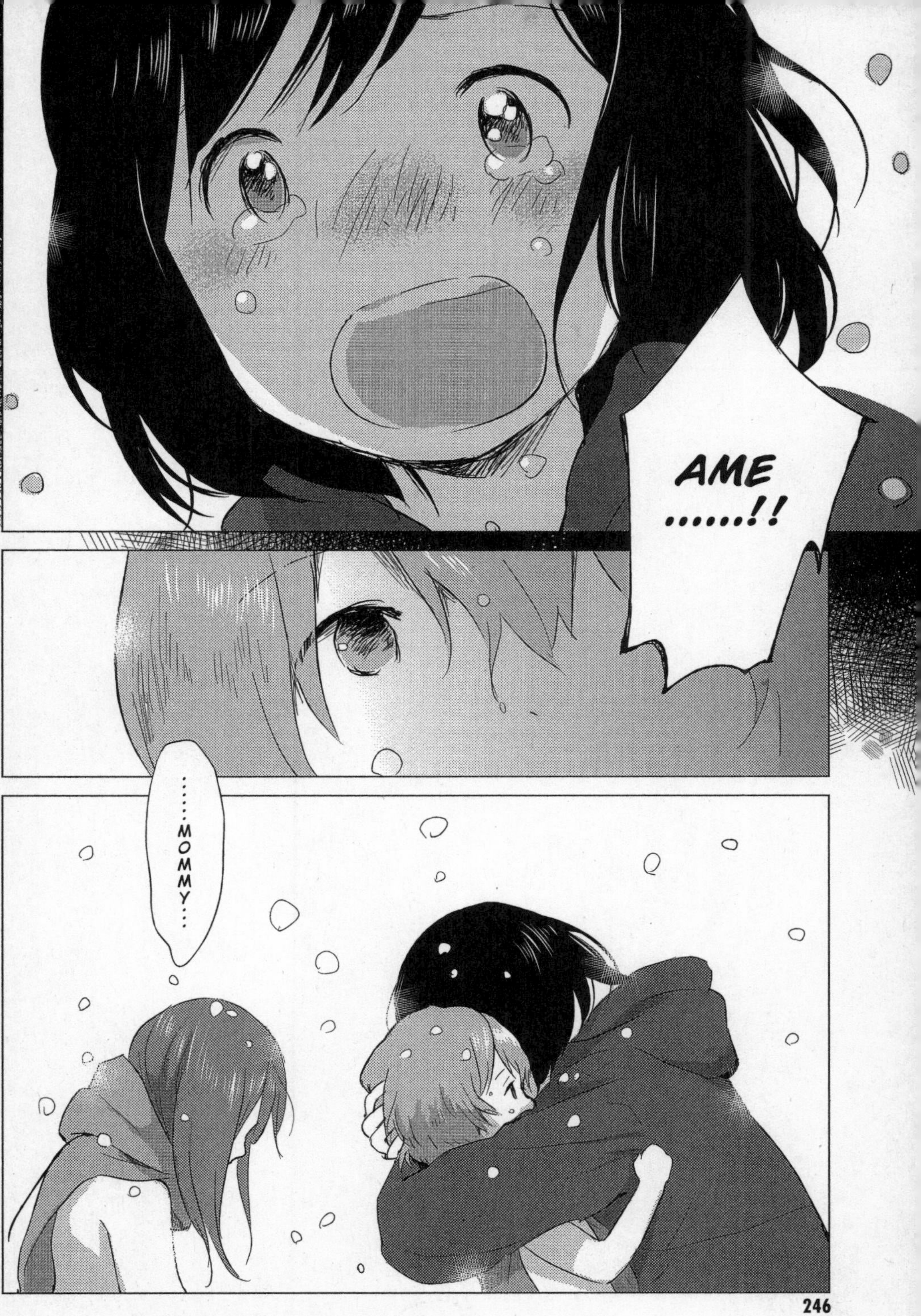
AME ......!!
......MOMMY...

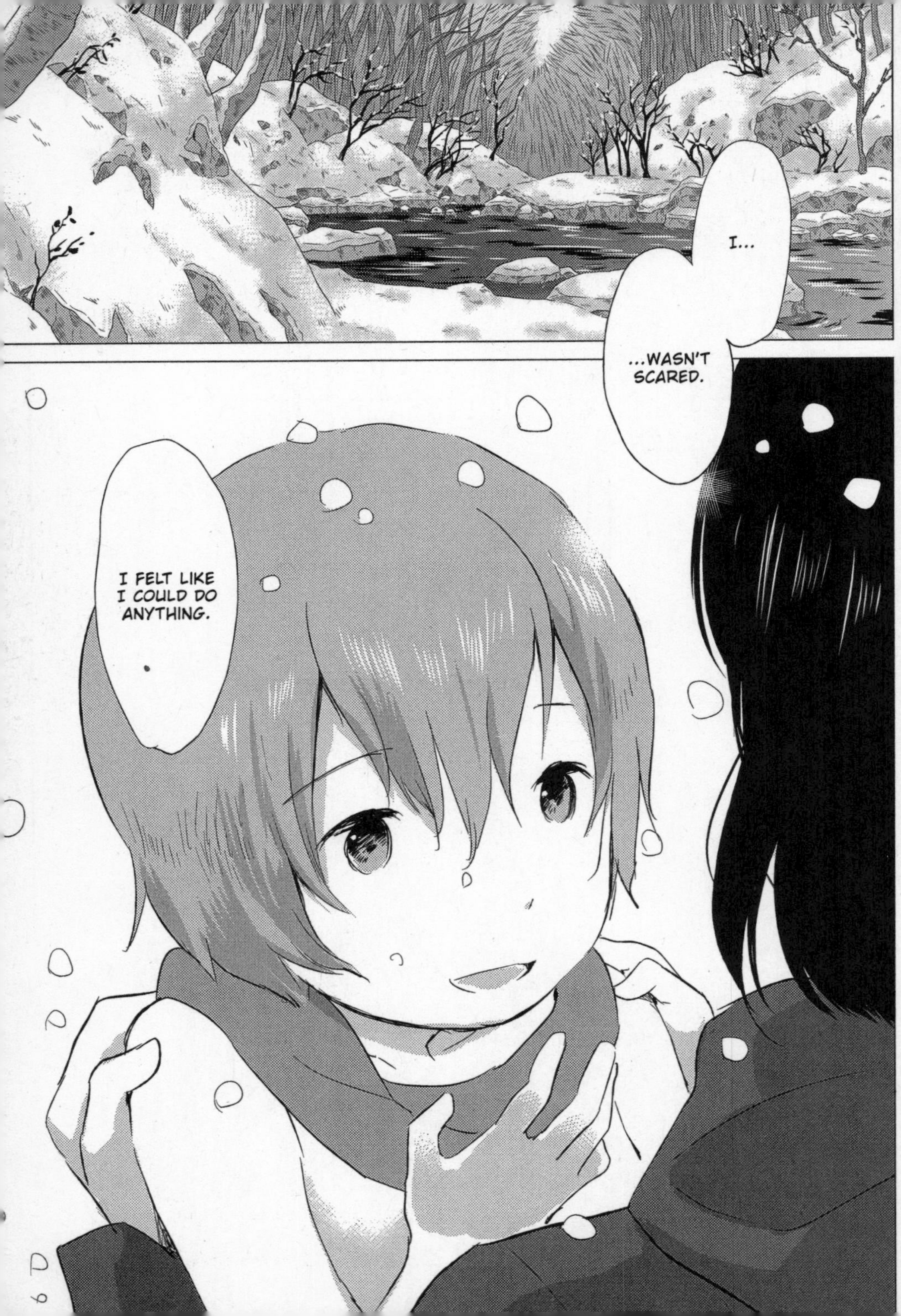
I...
...WASN'T SCARED.
I FELT LIKE I COULD DO ANYTHING.

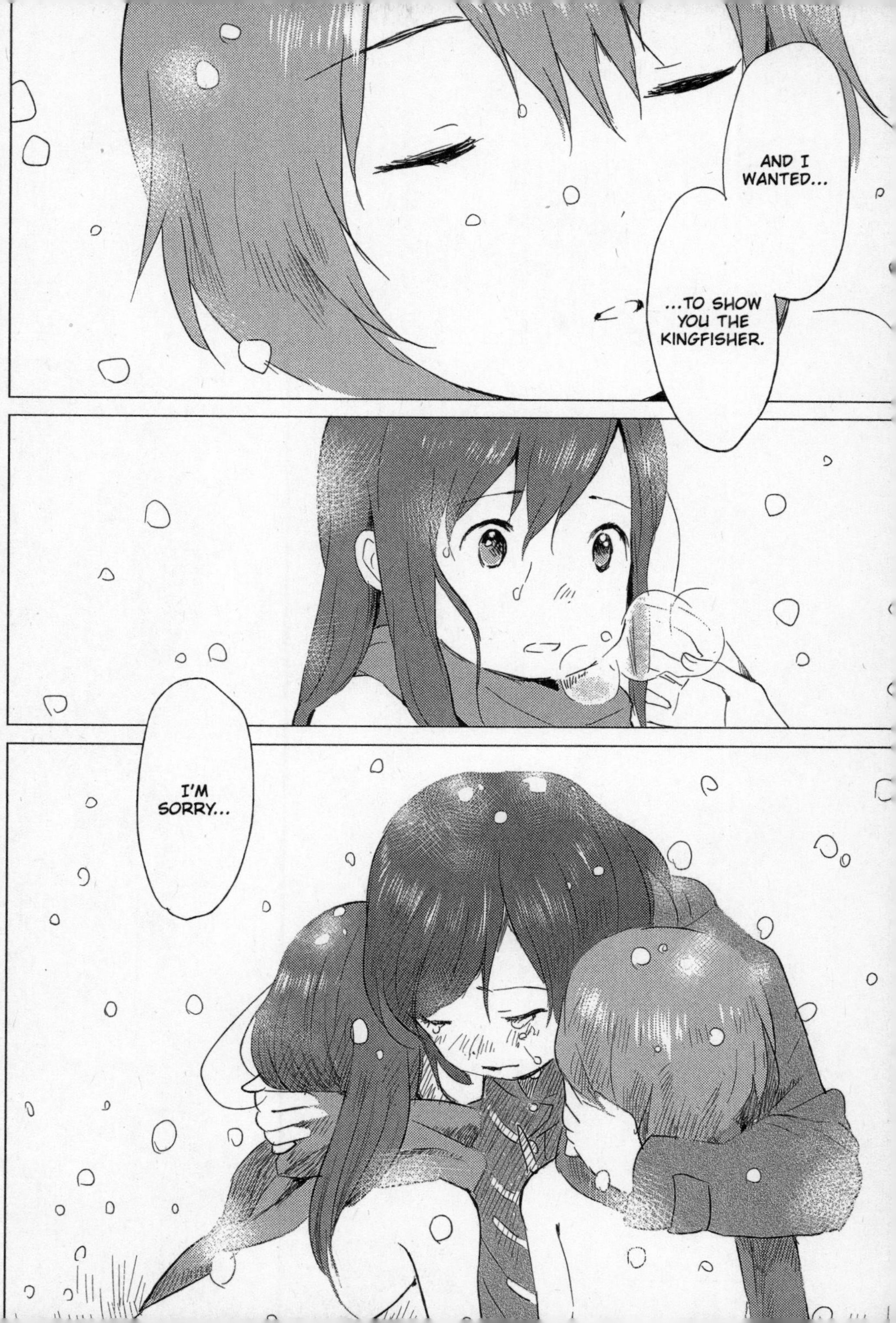
AND I WANTED...
...TO SHOW YOU THE KINGFISHER.
I'M SORRY...

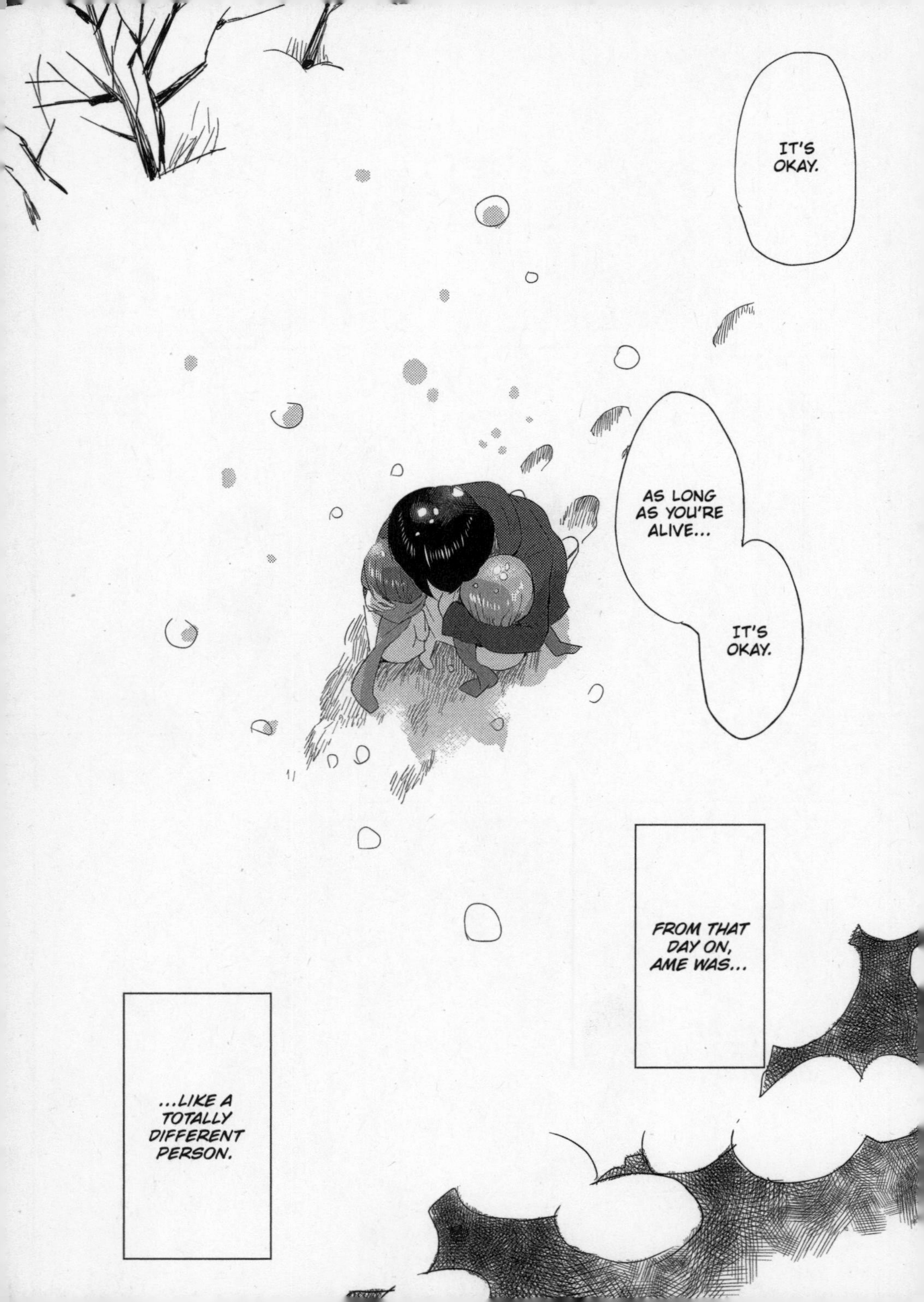
IT'S OKAY.
AS LONG AS YOU'RE ALIVE...
IT'S OKAY.
FROM THAT DAY ON, AME WAS...
...LIKE A TOTALLY DIFFERENT PERSON.

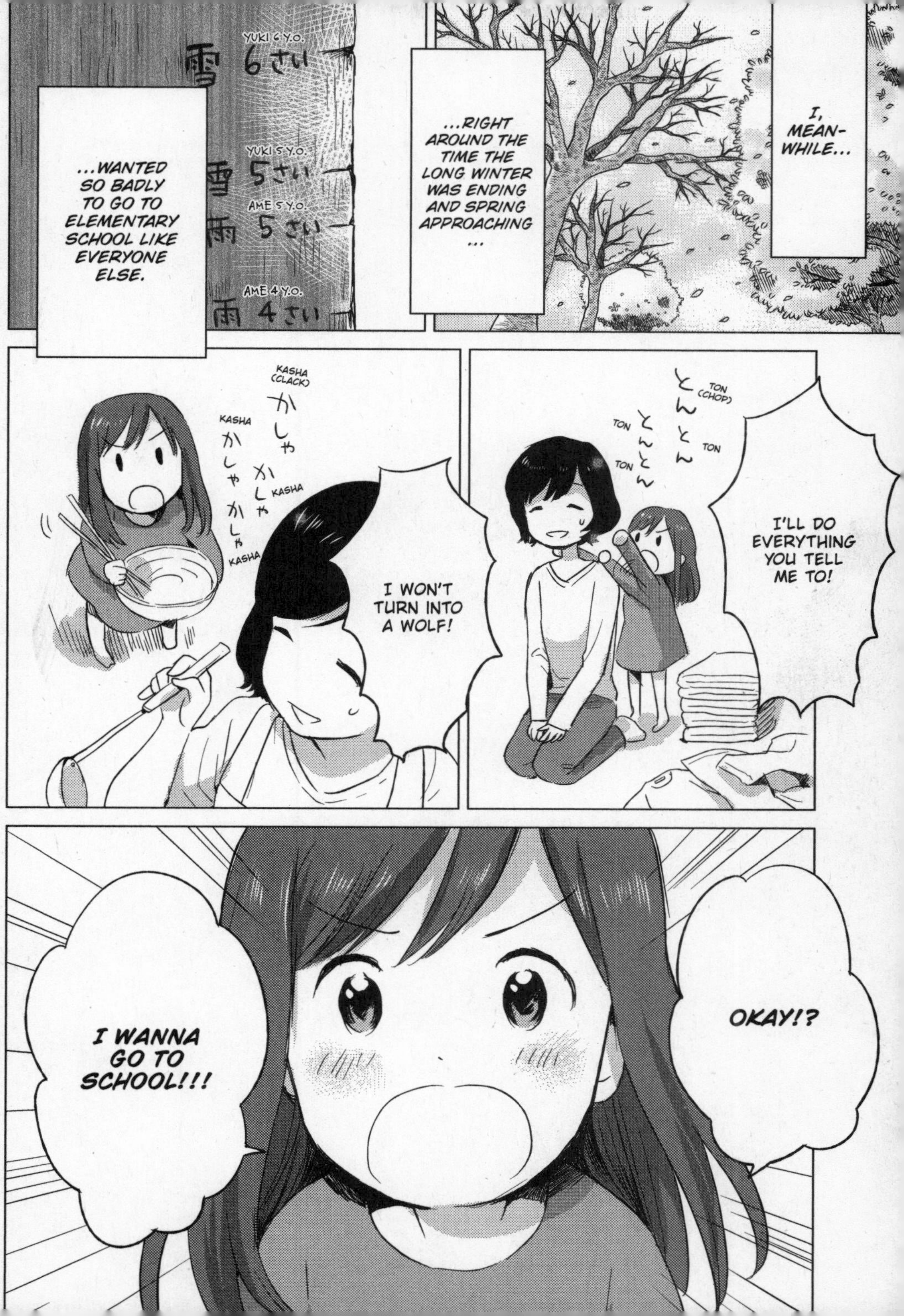
I, MEAN-WHILE...
...RIGHT AROUND THE TIME THE LONG WINTER WAS ENDING AND SPRING APPROACHING...
YUKI 6 Y.O.
雪 6さい
YUKI 5 Y.O.
雪 5さい
AME 5 Y.O.
雨 5さい
AME 4 Y.O.
雨 4さい
...WANTED SO BADLY TO GO TO ELEMENTARY SCHOOL LIKE EVERYONE ELSE.
とんとん TON (CHOP) TON
とんとん TON TON
I'LL DO EVERYTHING YOU TELL ME TO!
かしゃ KASHA (CLACK)
かしゃ KASHA
かしゃ KASHA
かしゃ KASHA
I WON'T TURN INTO A WOLF!
I WANNA GO TO SCHOOL!!!
OKAY!?

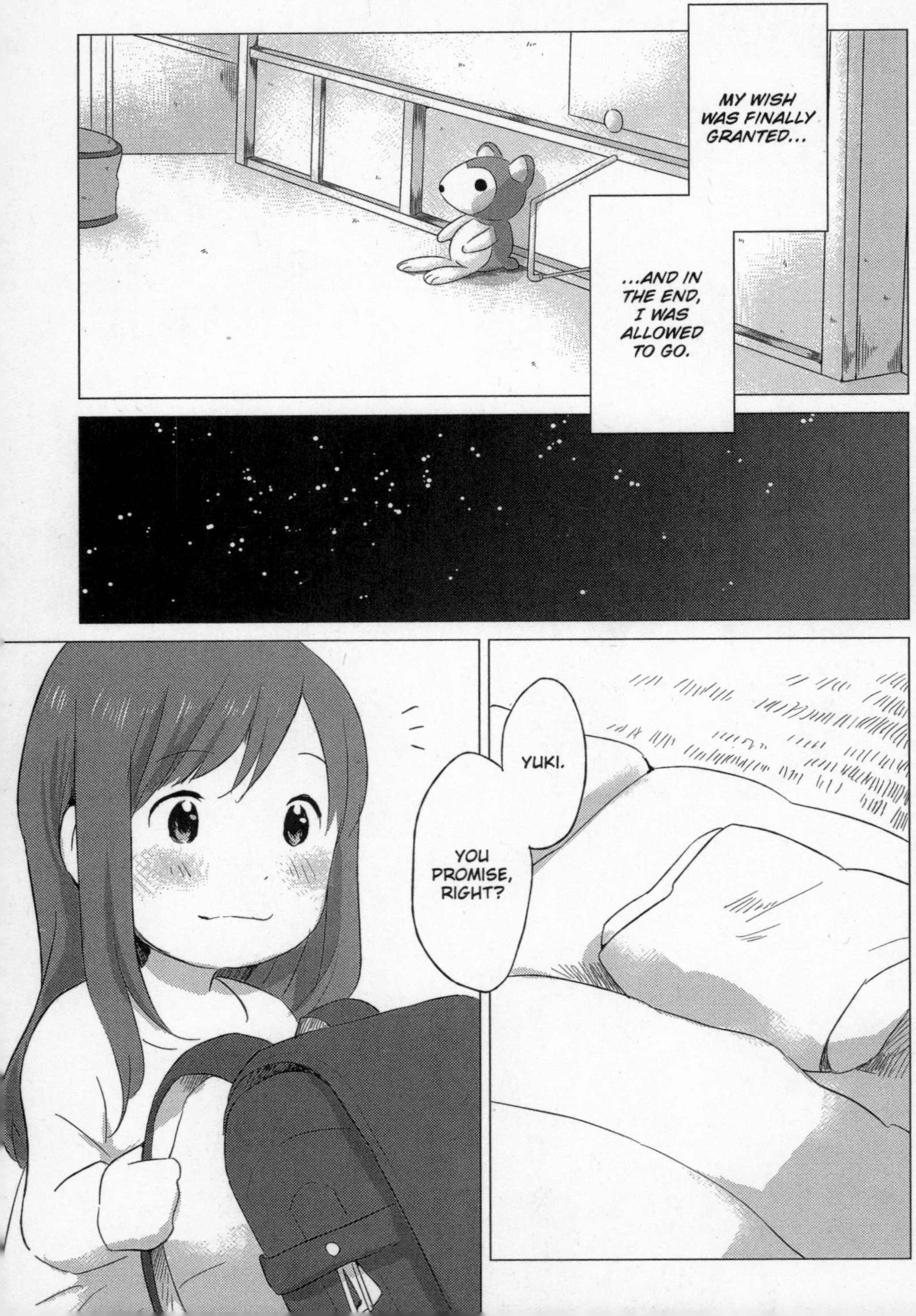
MY WISH WAS FINALLY GRANTED...
...AND IN THE END, I WAS ALLOWED TO GO.
YUKI.
YOU PROMISE, RIGHT?

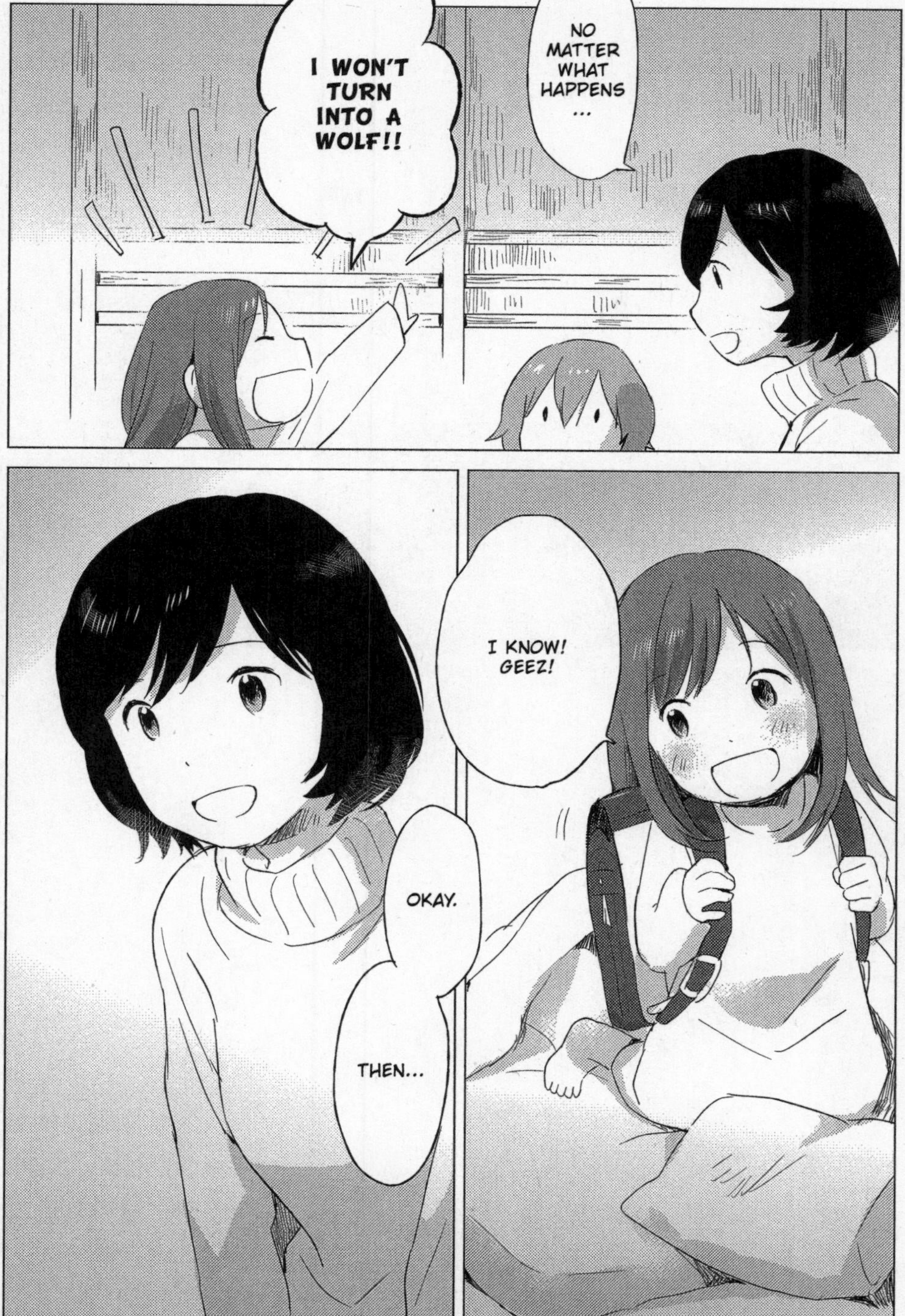
NO MATTER WHAT HAPPENS...
I WON'T TURN INTO A WOLF!!
I KNOW! GEEZ!
OKAY.
THEN...

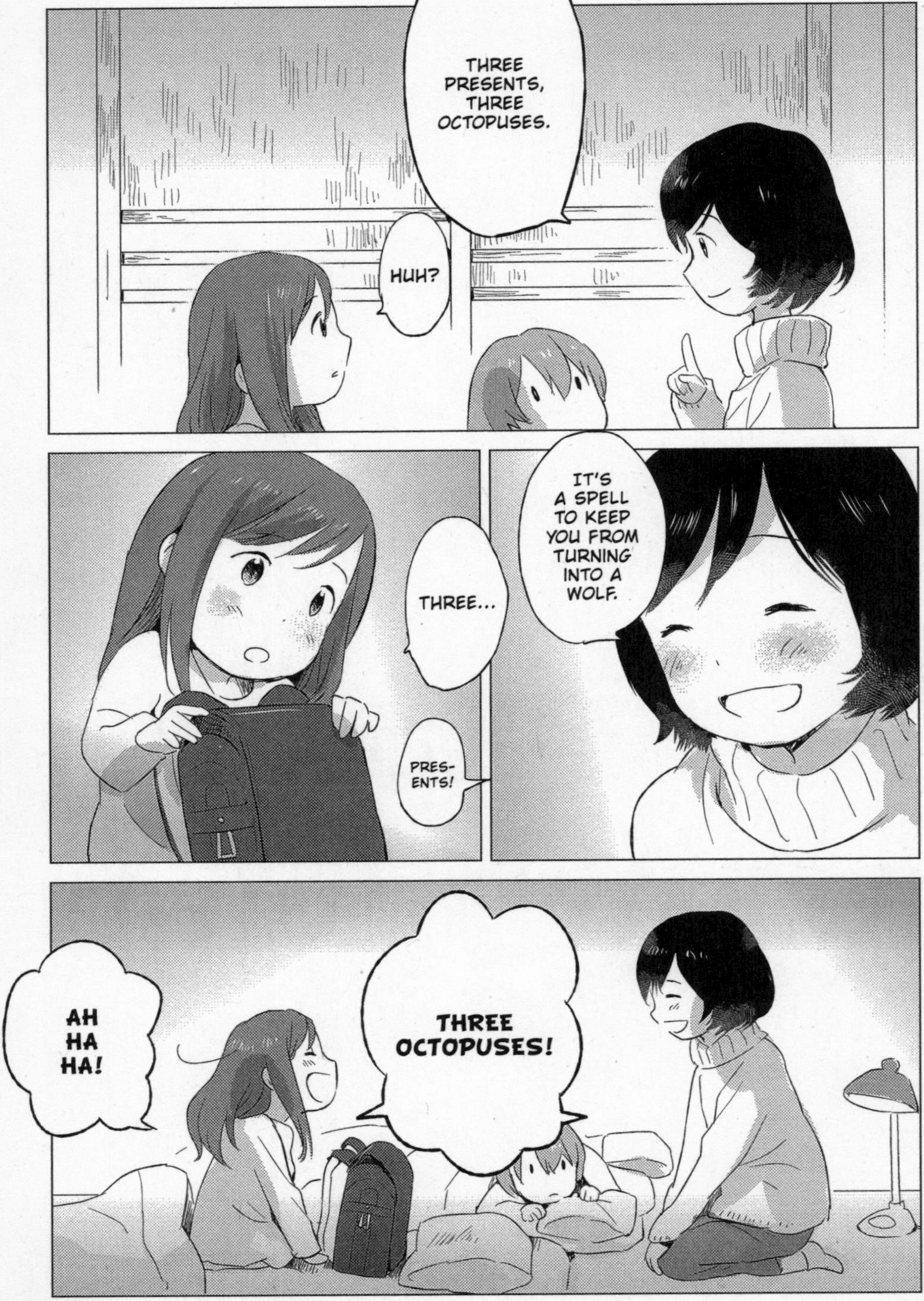
THREE PRESENTS, THREE OCTOPUSES.
HUH?
IT'S A SPELL TO KEEP YOU FROM TURNING INTO A WOLF.
THREE...
PRES-ENTS!
THREE OCTOPUSES!
AH HA HA!

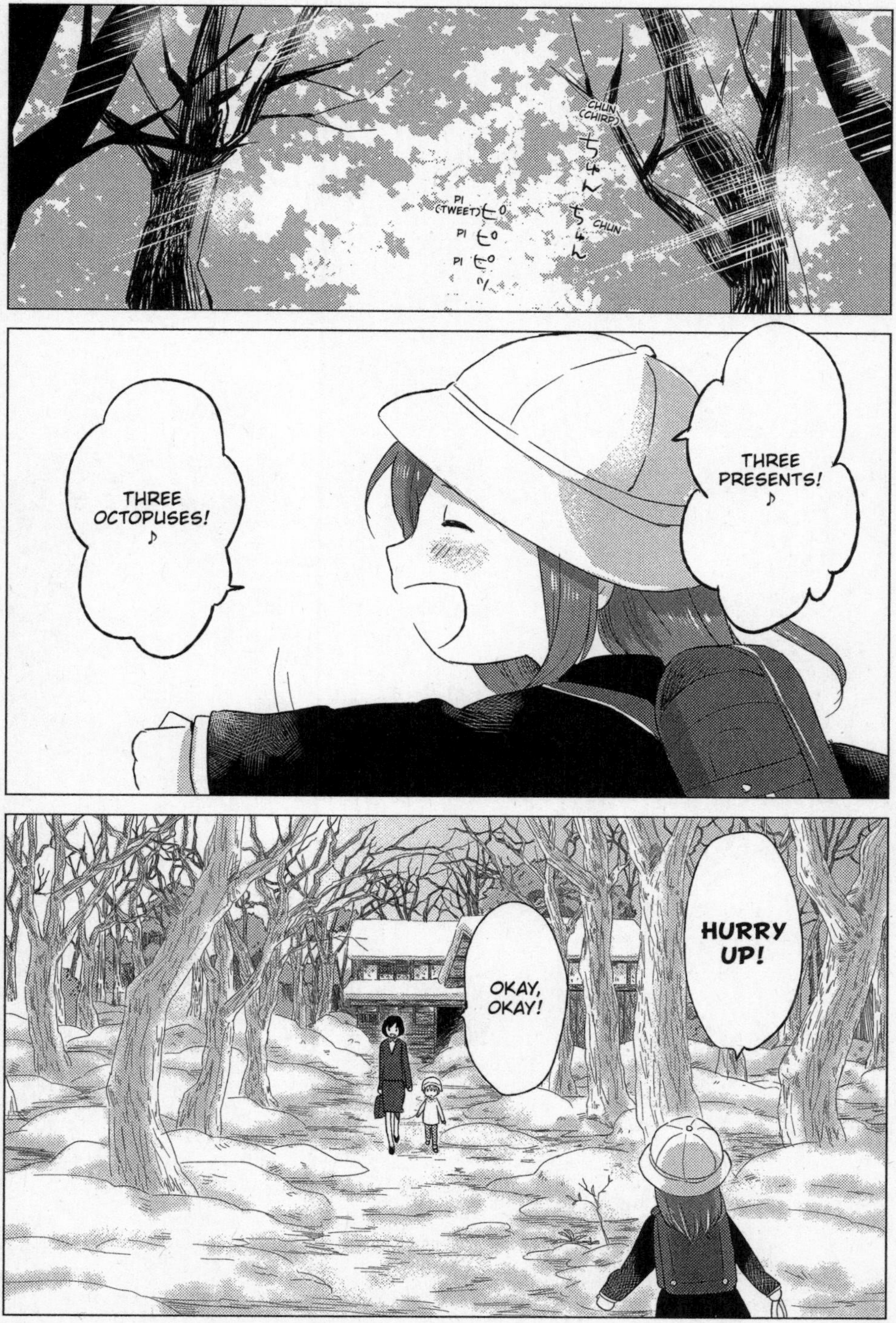
CHUN (CHIRP)
ちゅん ちゅん
CHUN
PI (TWEET)
PI
PI
THREE PRESENTS! ♪
THREE OCTOPUSES! ♪
HURRY UP!
OKAY, OKAY!

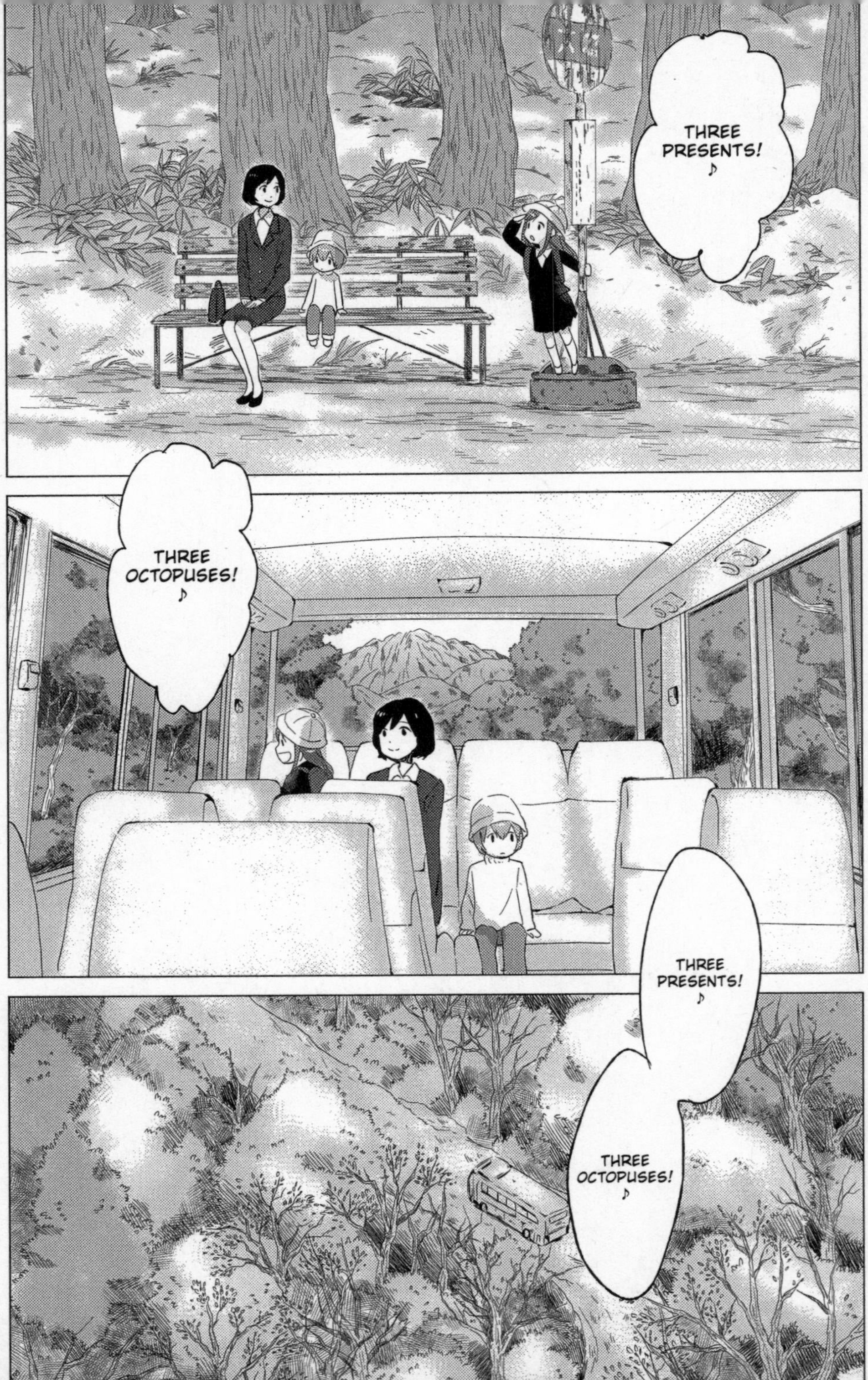
THREE PRESENTS! ♪
THREE OCTOPUSES! ♪
THREE PRESENTS! ♪
THREE OCTOPUSES! ♪

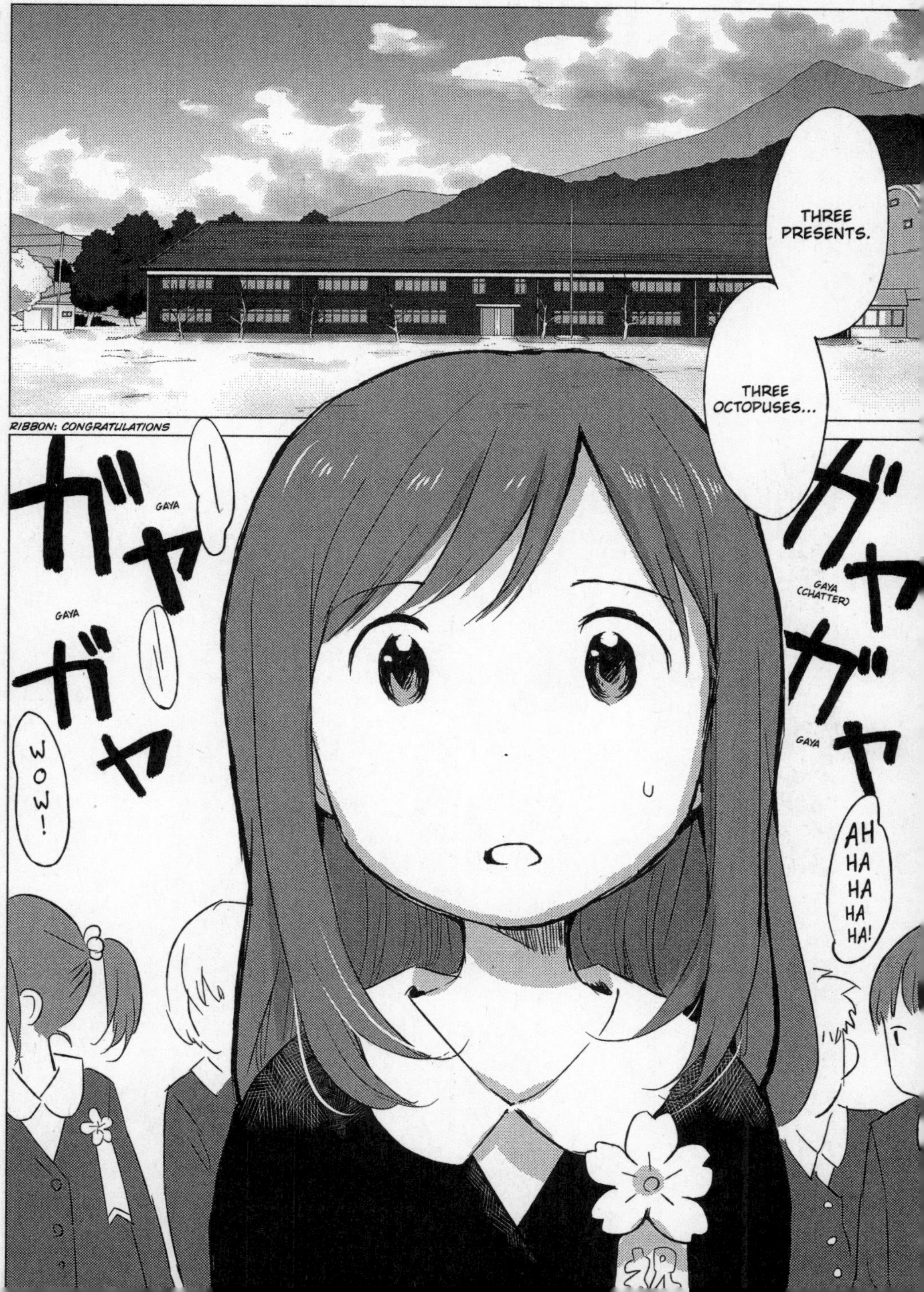
THREE PRESENTS.
THREE OCTOPUSES...
ガヤガヤ
GAYA (CHATTER)
GAYA
AH HA HA HA HA!
ガヤ
ガヤ
GAYA
GAYA
WOW!
RIBBON: CONGRATULATIONS

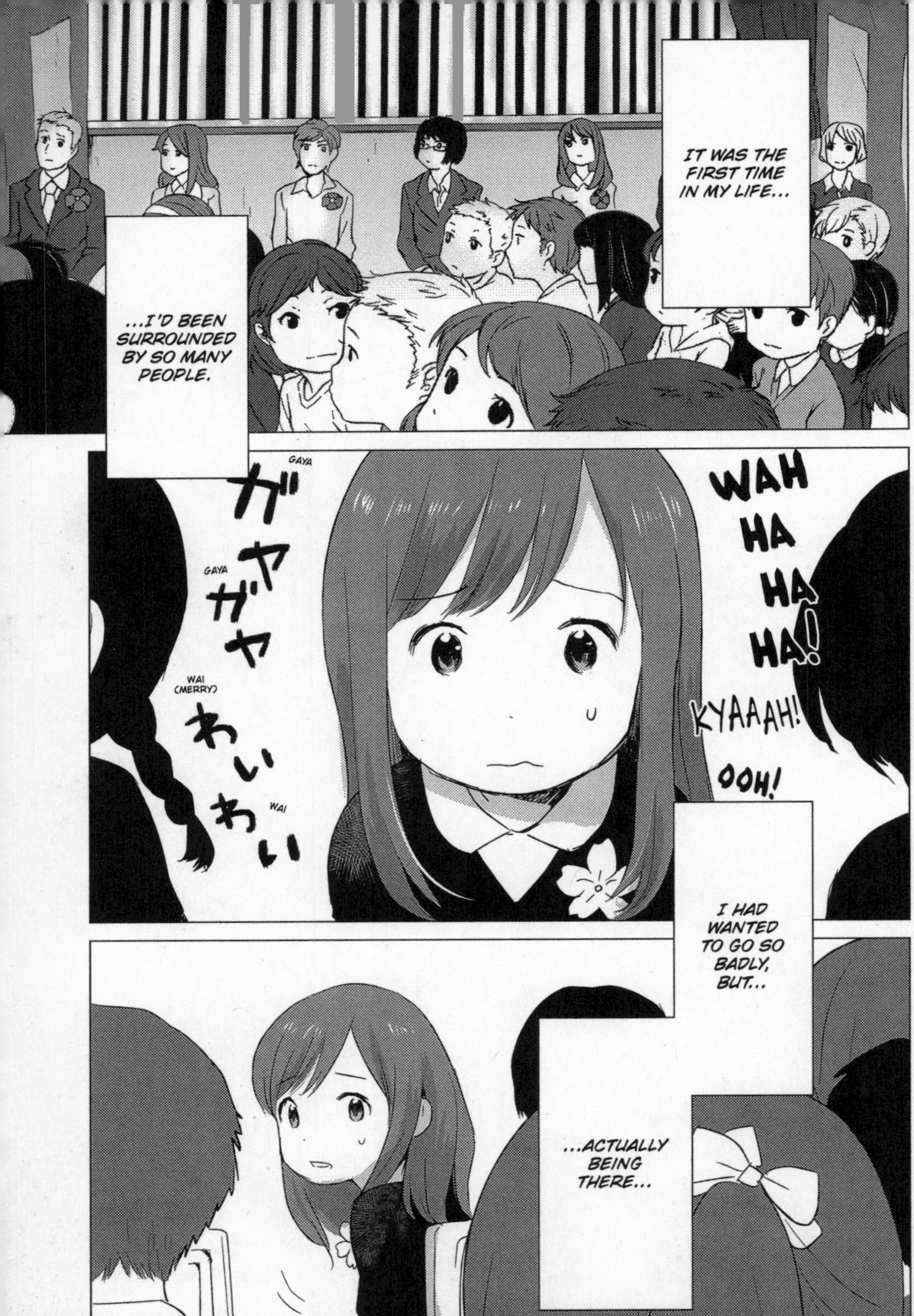
IT WAS THE FIRST TIME IN MY LIFE...
...I'D BEEN SURROUNDED BY SO MANY PEOPLE.
WAH HA HA HA!
KYAAAH!
OOH!
ガヤ
GAYA
ガヤ
GAYA
わい
WAI (MERRY)
わい
WAI
I HAD WANTED TO GO SO BADLY, BUT...
...ACTUALLY BEING THERE...

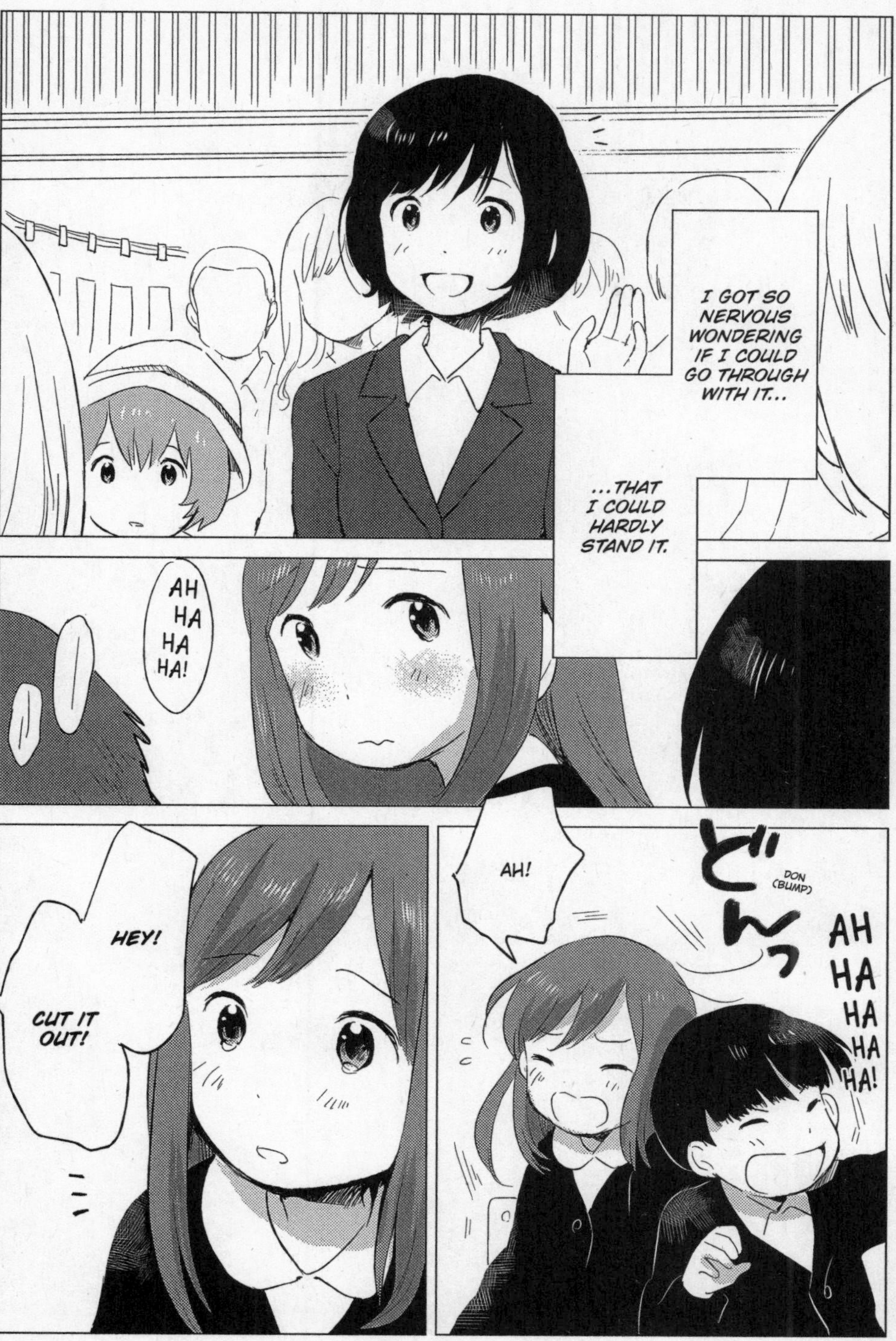
I GOT SO NERVOUS WONDERING IF I COULD GO THROUGH WITH IT...
...THAT I COULD HARDLY STAND IT.
AH HA HA HA HA!
AH!
どんっ
DON (BUMP)
AH HA HA HA HA HA!
HEY!
CUT IT OUT!

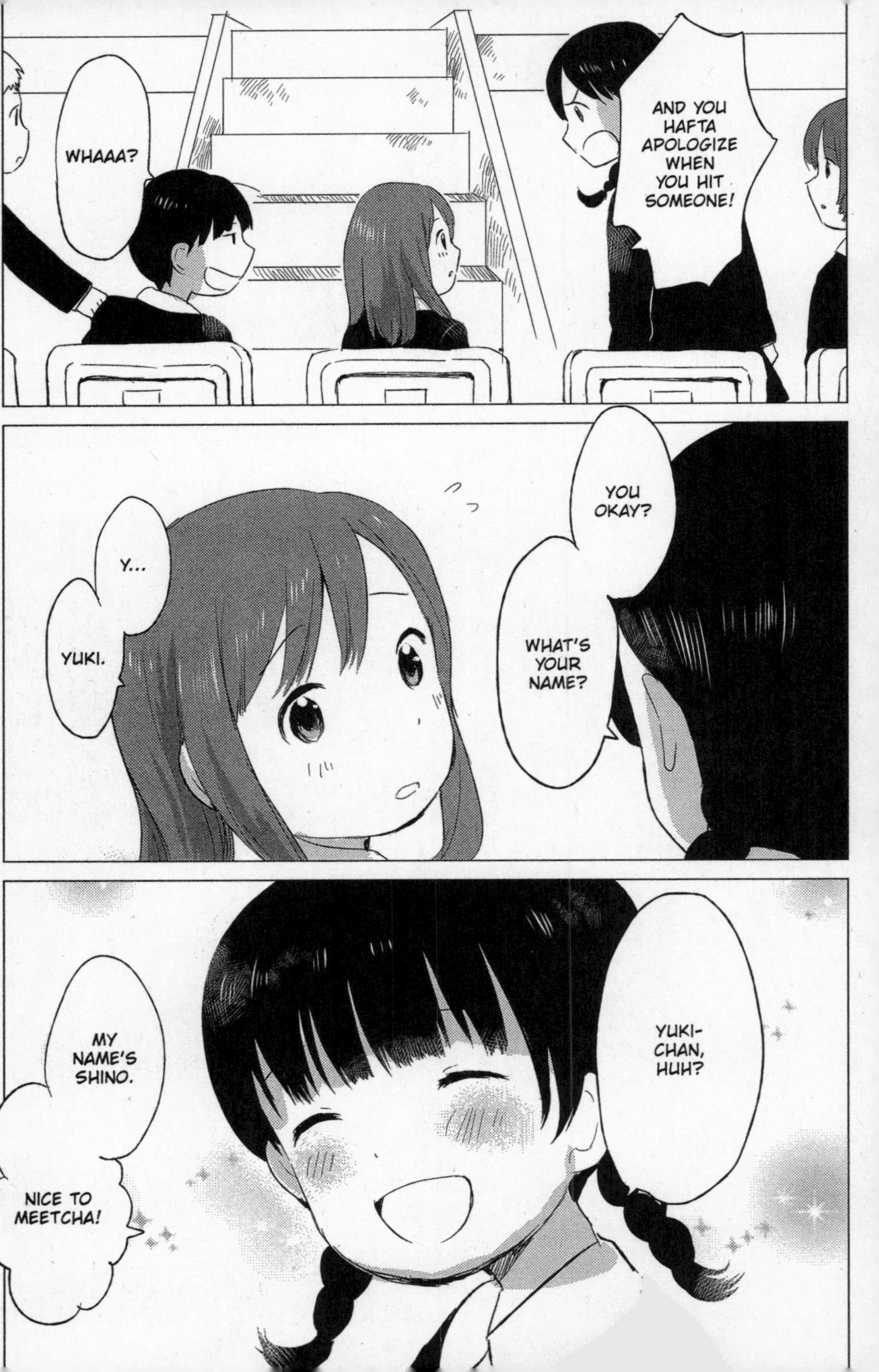
AND YOU HAFTA APOLOGIZE WHEN YOU HIT SOMEONE!
WHAAA?
YOU OKAY?
WHAT'S YOUR NAME?
Y...
YUKI.
YUKI-CHAN, HUH?
MY NAME'S SHINO.
NICE TO MEETCHA!

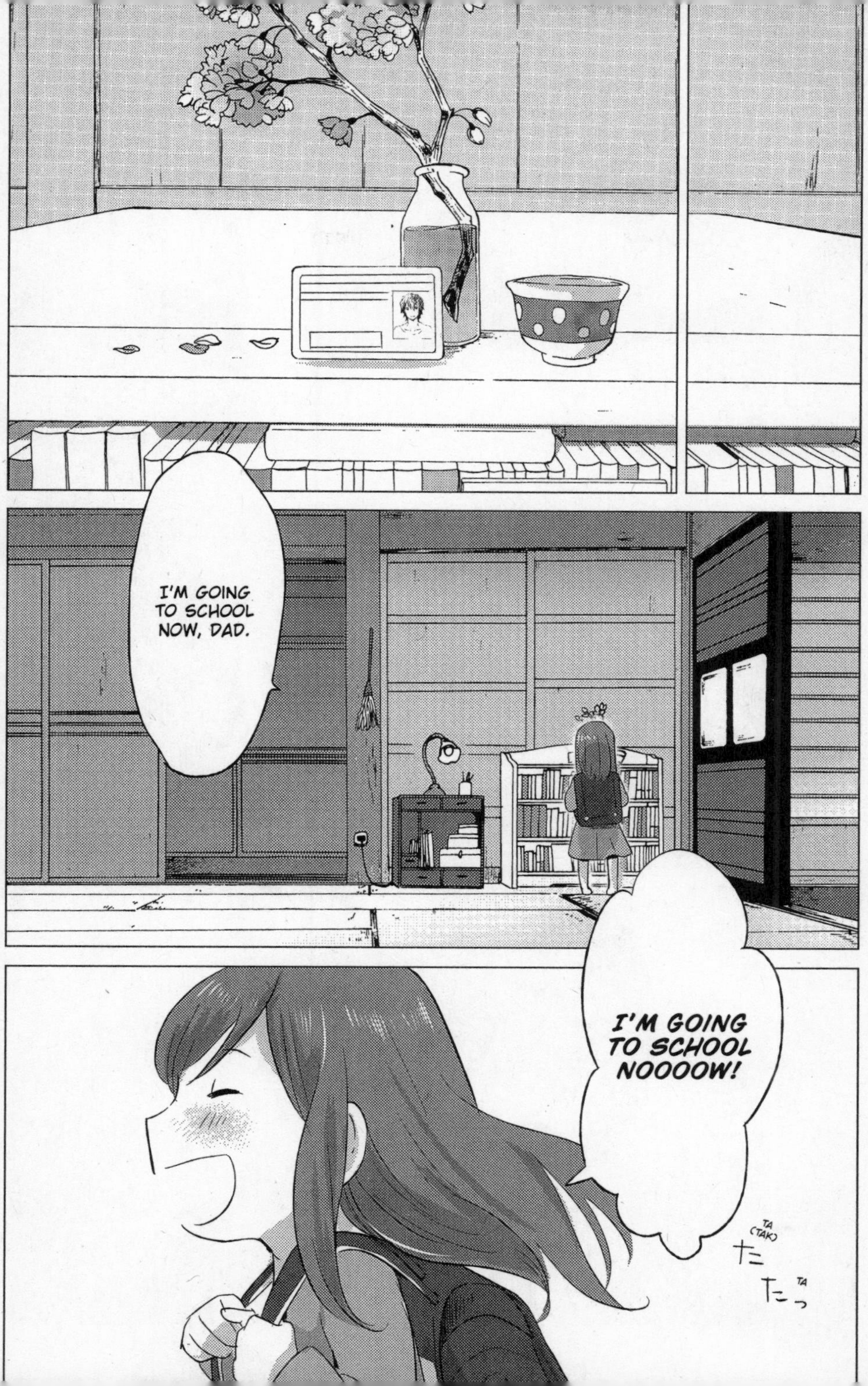
I'M GOING TO SCHOOL NOW, DAD.
I'M GOING TO SCHOOL NOOOOW!
たたっ
TA (TAK) TA

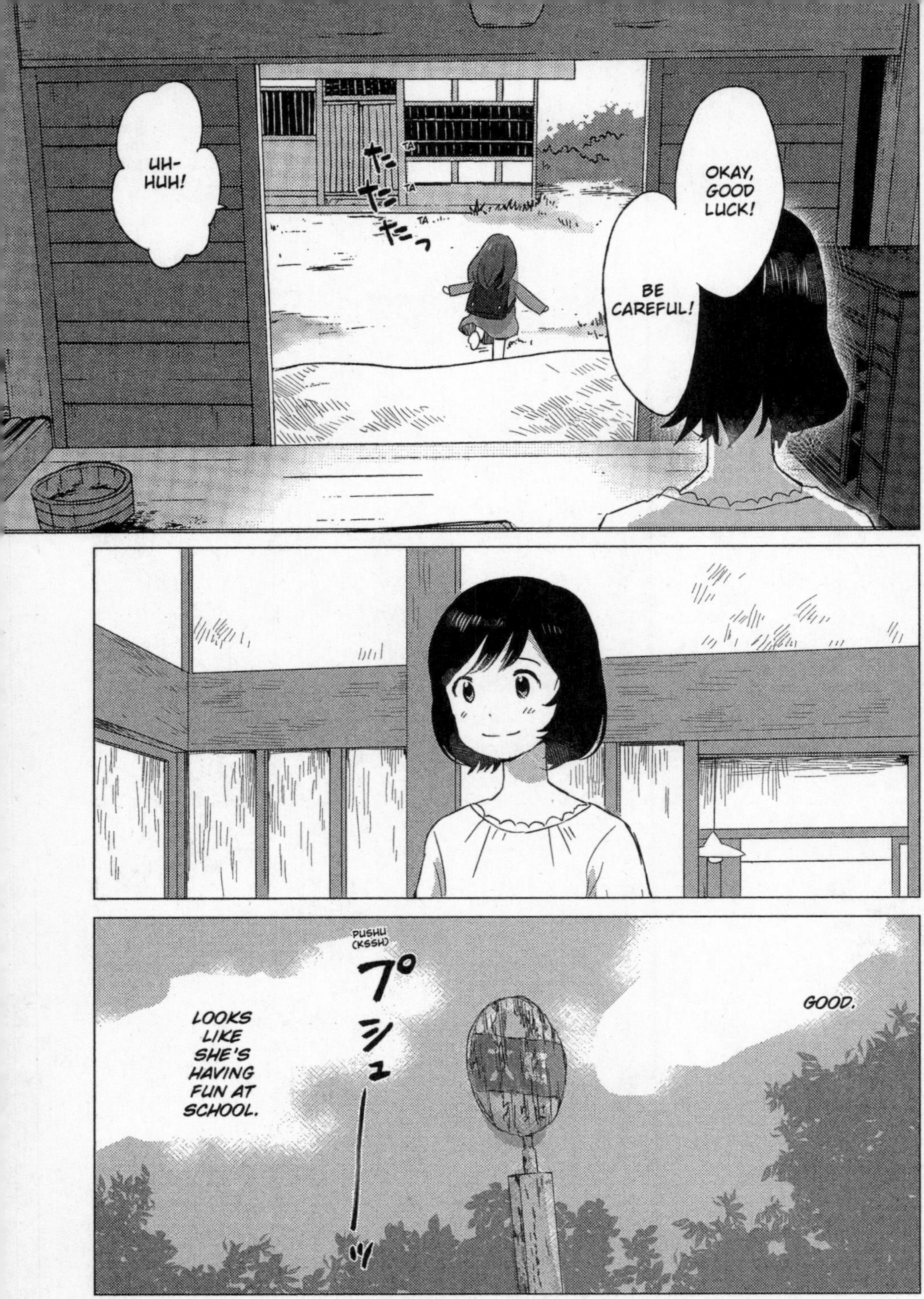
OKAY, GOOD LUCK!
BE CAREFUL!
TA
TA
TA
UH-HUH!
GOOD.
PUSHU (KSSH)
LOOKS LIKE SHE'S HAVING FUN AT SCHOOL.

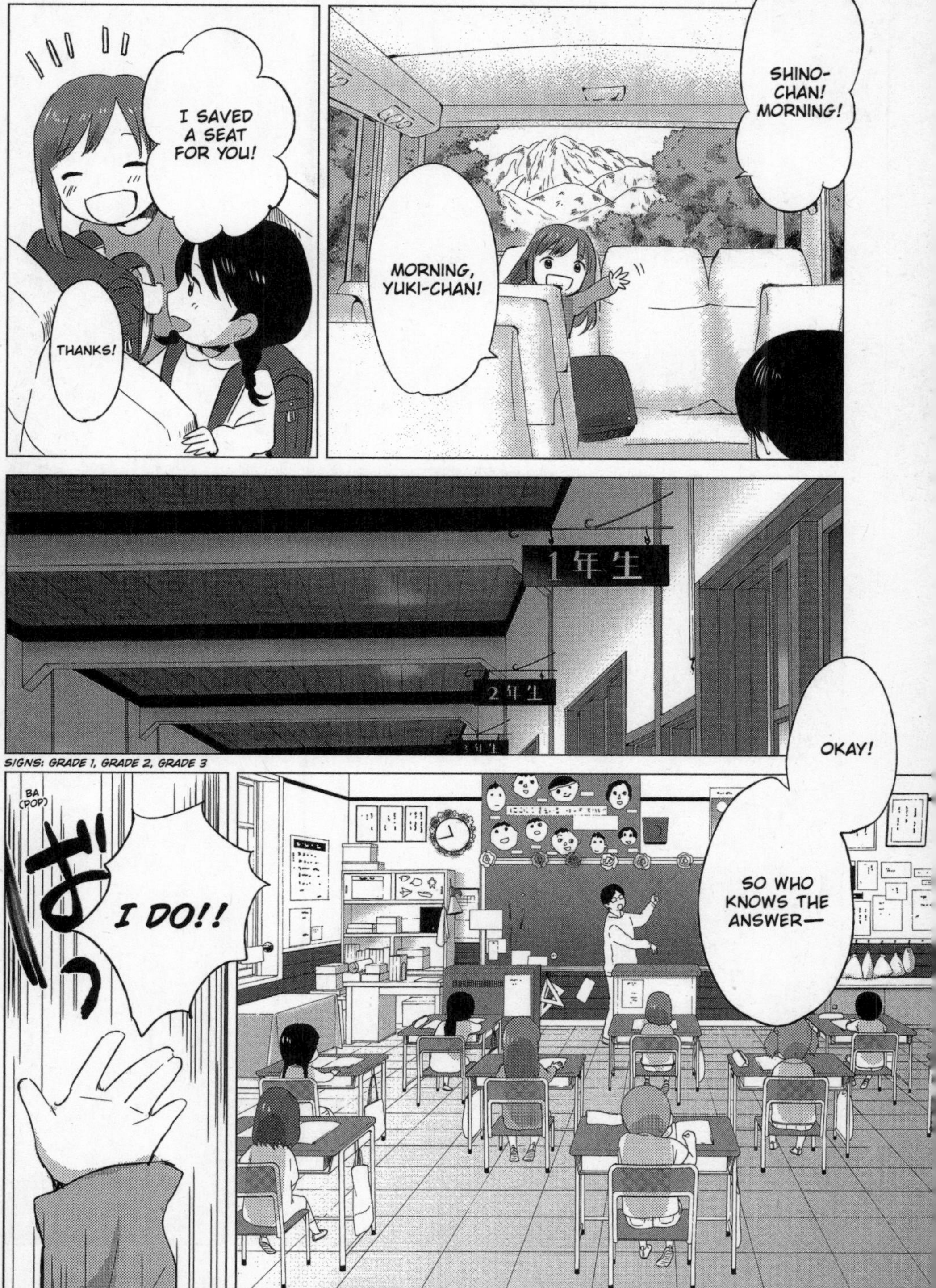
SHINO-CHAN! MORNING!
MORNING, YUKI-CHAN!
I SAVED A SEAT FOR YOU!
THANKS!
1年生
2年生
SIGNS: GRADE 1, GRADE 2, GRADE 3
OKAY!
SO WHO KNOWS THE ANSWER—
BA (POP)
I DO!!

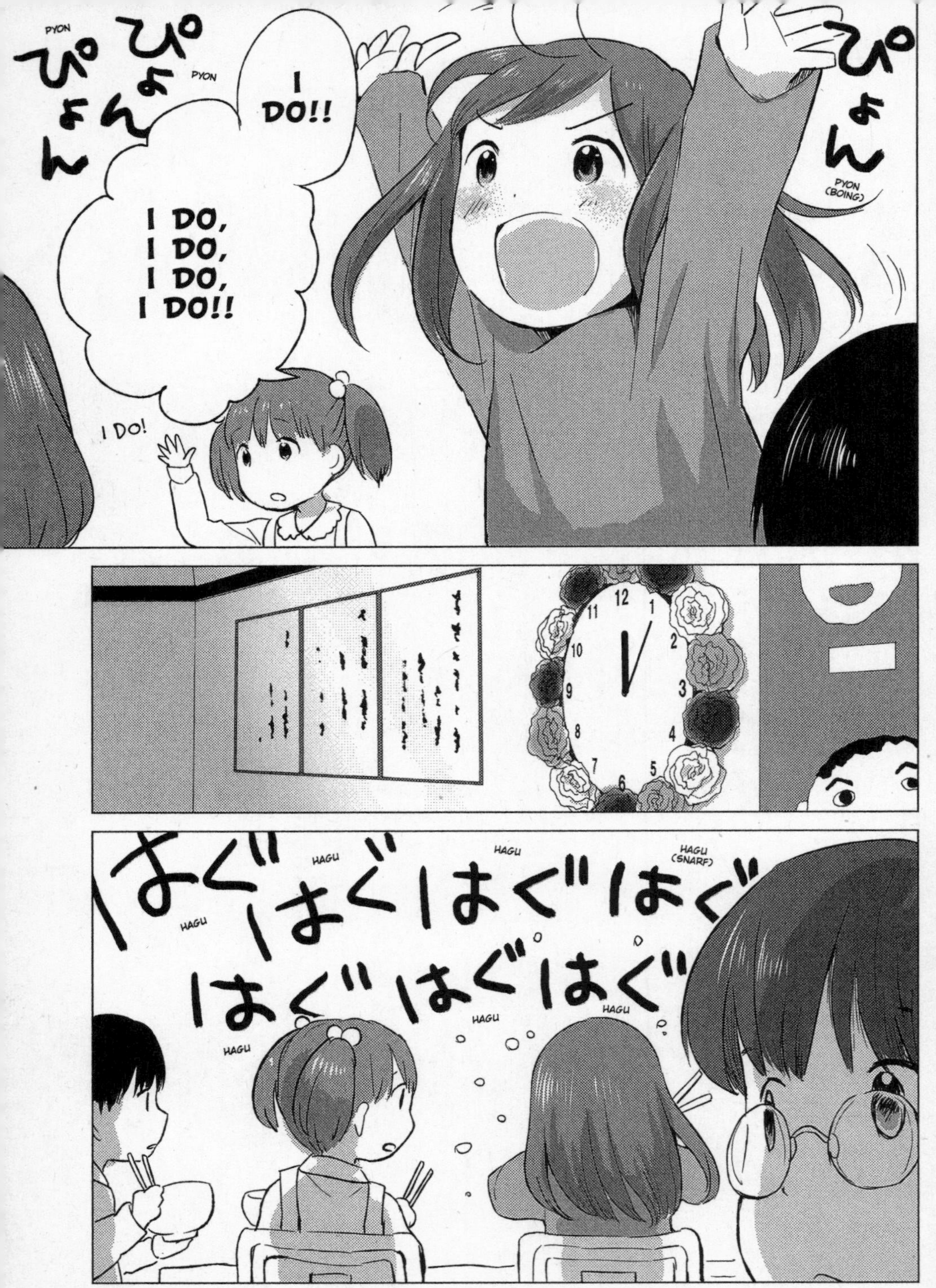
ぴょん
PYON (BOING)
I DO!!
ぴょん
PYON
ぴょん
PYON
I DO, I DO, I DO, I DO!!
I DO!
はぐはぐはぐはぐ
HAGU (SNARF)
HAGU
HAGU
HAGU
はぐはぐはぐ
HAGU
HAGU
HAGU

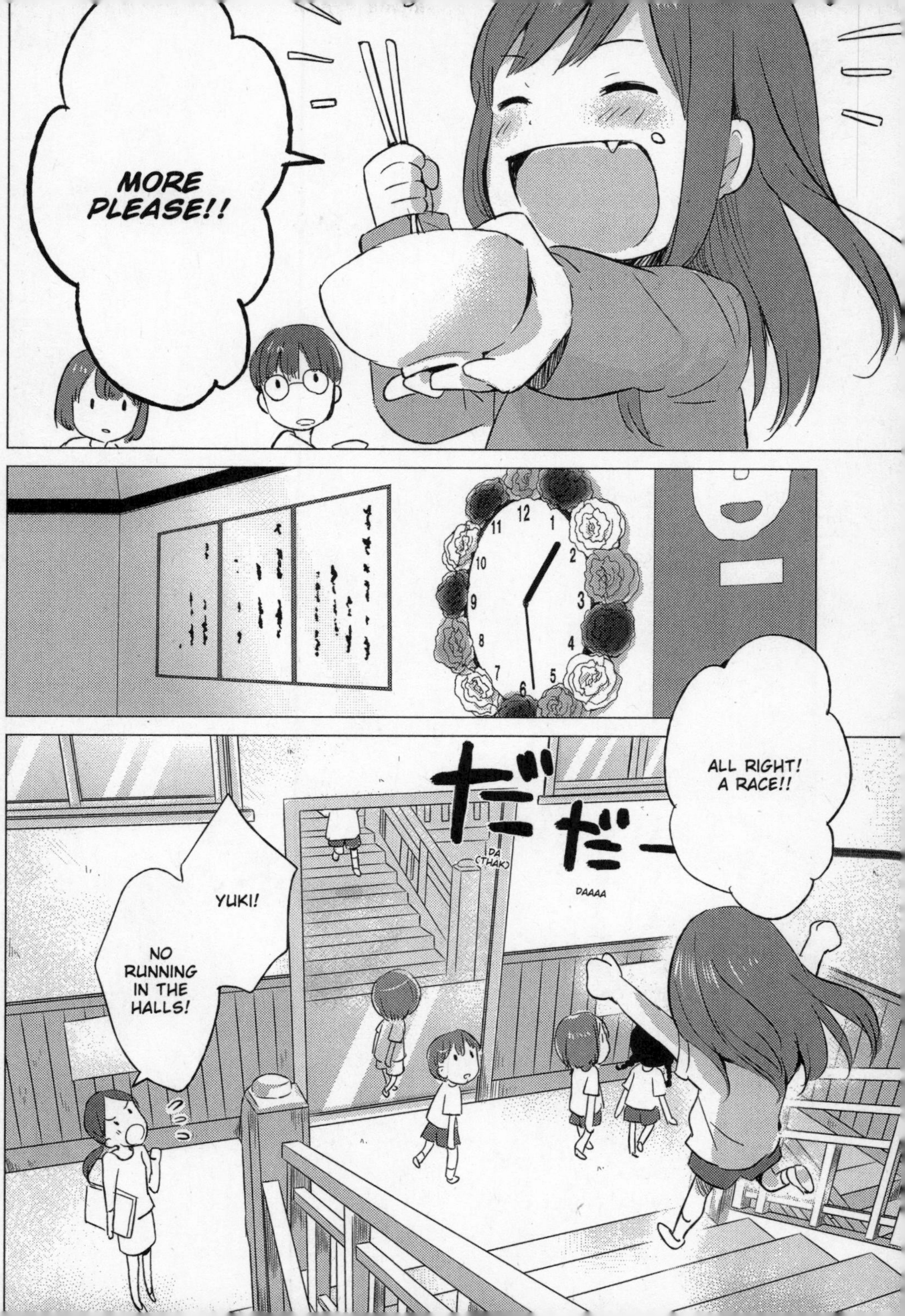
MORE PLEASE!!
ALL RIGHT! A RACE!!
だだー
DA (THAK)
DAAAA
YUKI!
NO RUNNING IN THE HALLS!

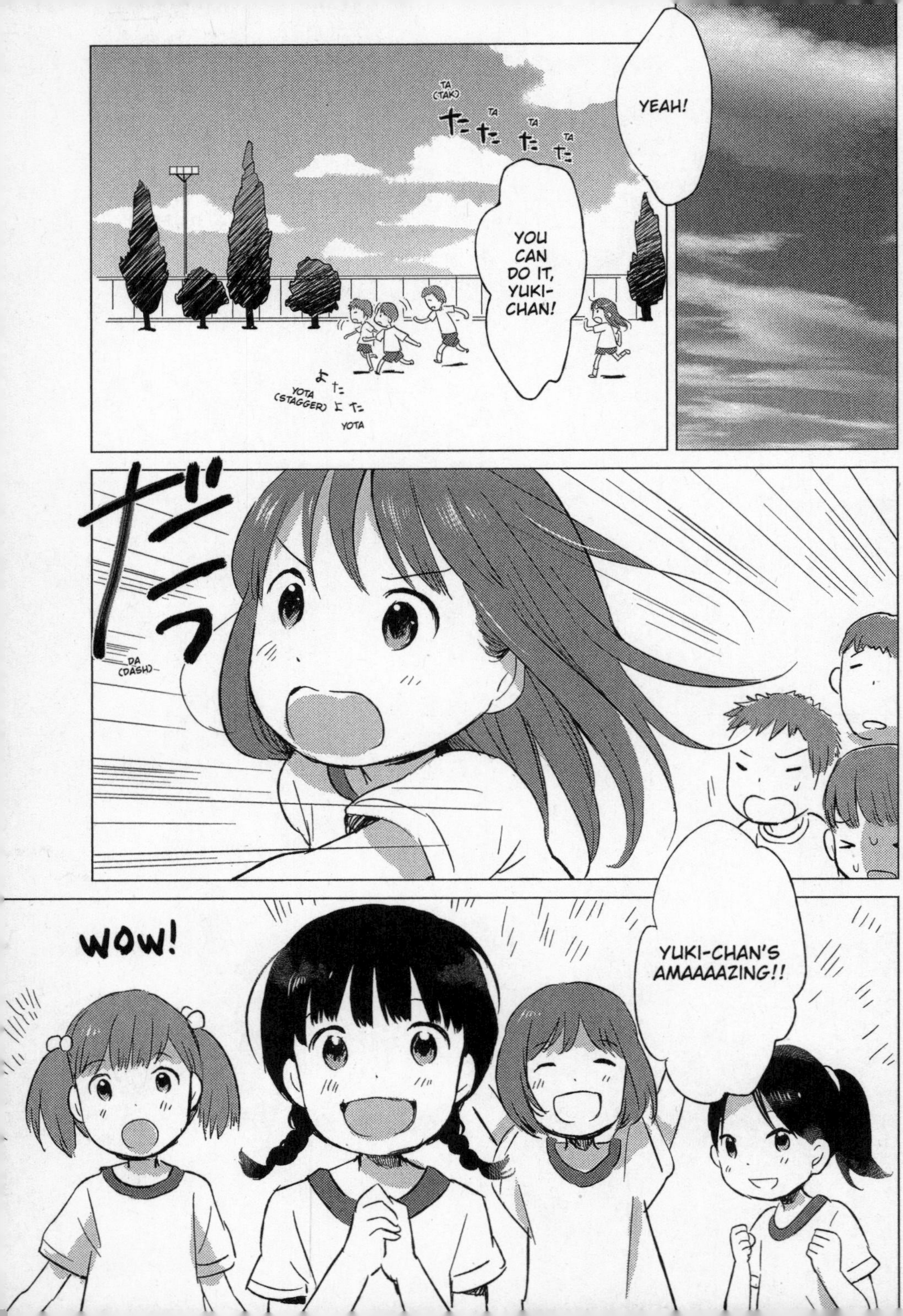
YEAH!
TA (TAK) TA TA TA
YOU CAN DO IT, YUKI-CHAN!
YOTA (STAGGER) YOTA
DA (DASH)
YUKI-CHAN'S AMAAAAZING!!
WOW!

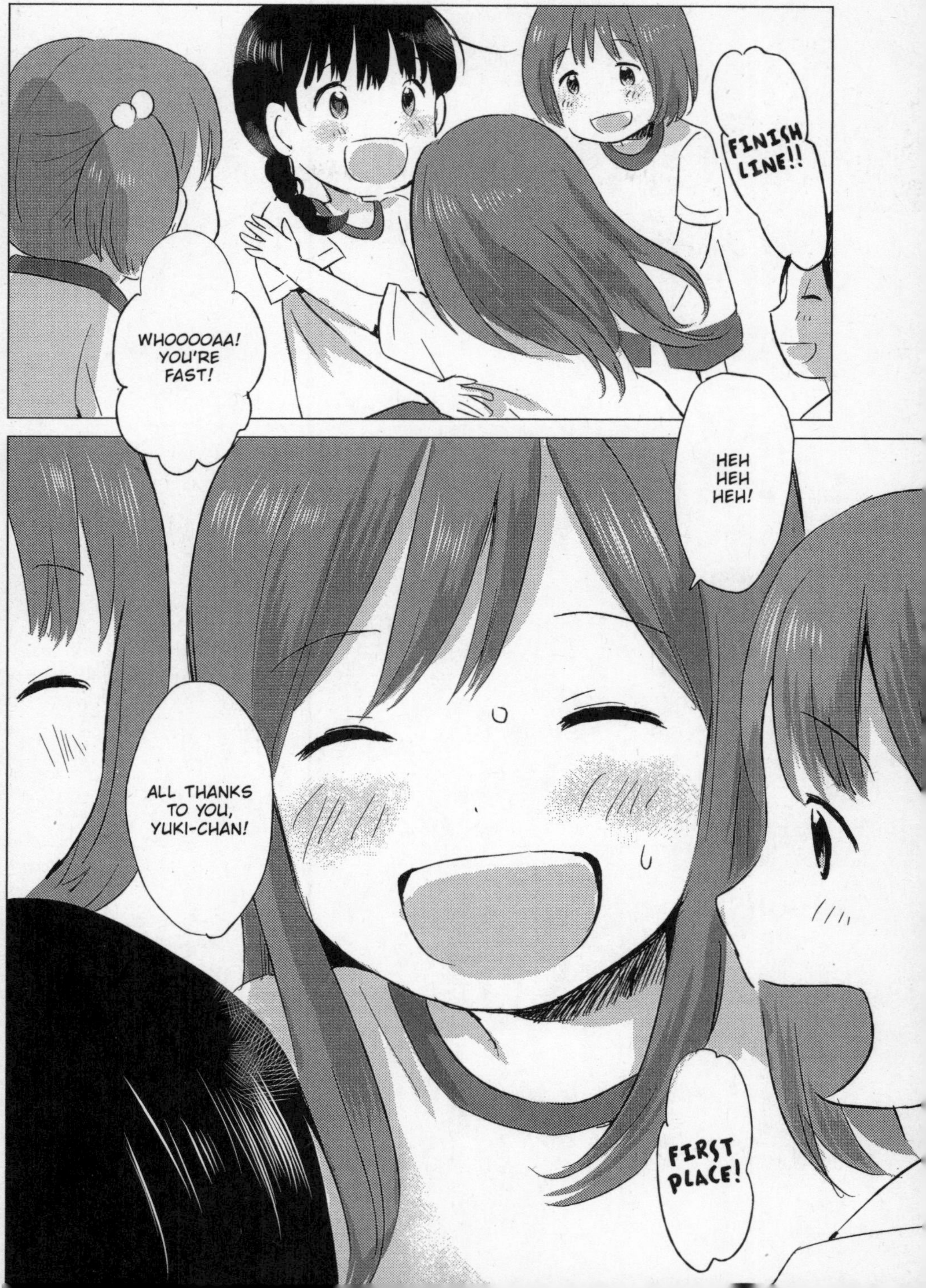
FINISH LINE!!
WHOOOOAA! YOU'RE FAST!
HEH HEH HEH!
ALL THANKS TO YOU, YUKI-CHAN!
FIRST PLACE!

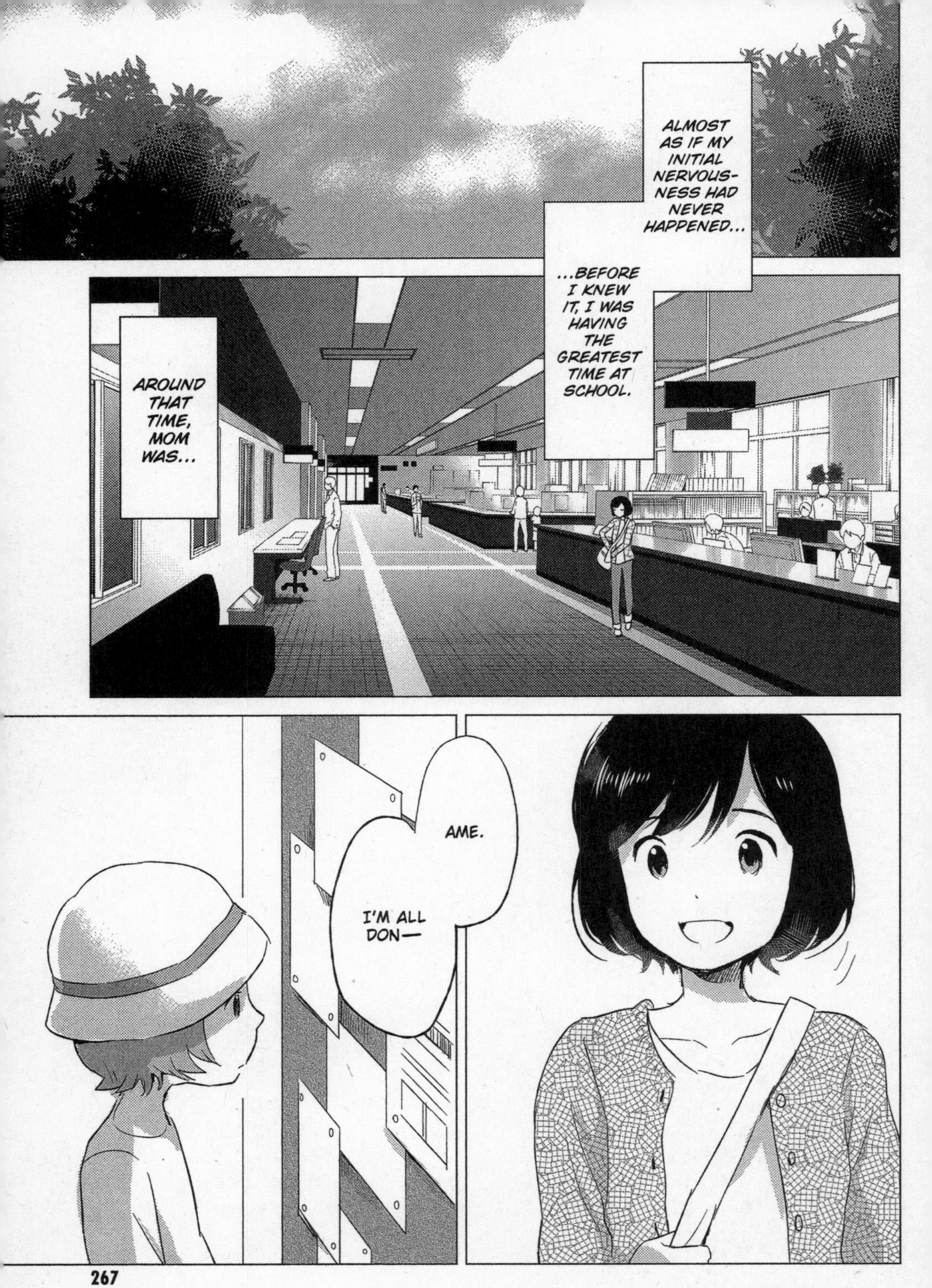
ALMOST AS IF MY INITIAL NERVOUSNESS HAD NEVER HAPPENED...
...BEFORE I KNEW IT, I WAS HAVING THE GREATEST TIME AT SCHOOL.
AROUND THAT TIME, MOM WAS...
AME.
I'M ALL DON—

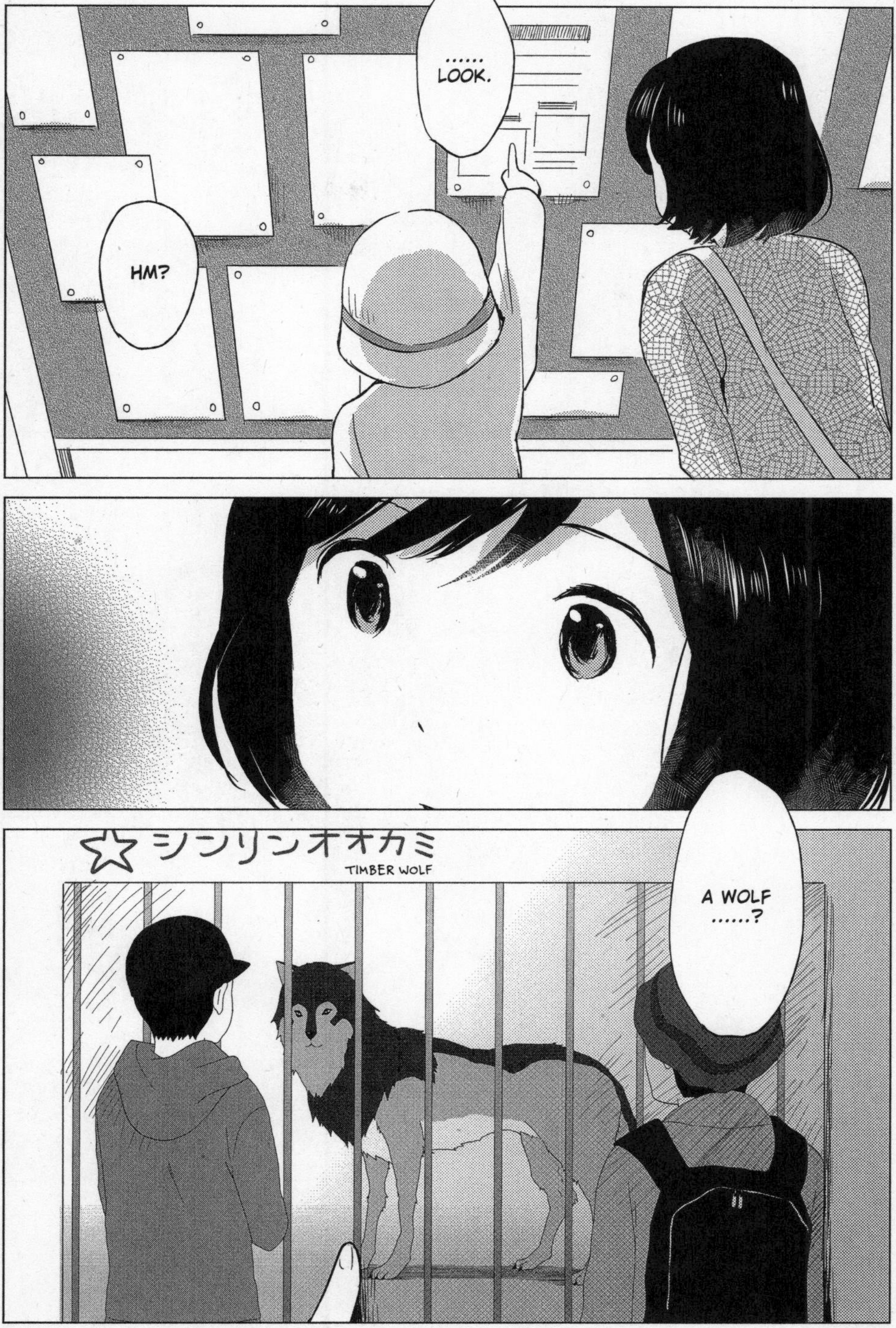

......
LOOK.
HM?
A WOLF
......?
☆ シンリンオオカミ
TIMBER WOLF

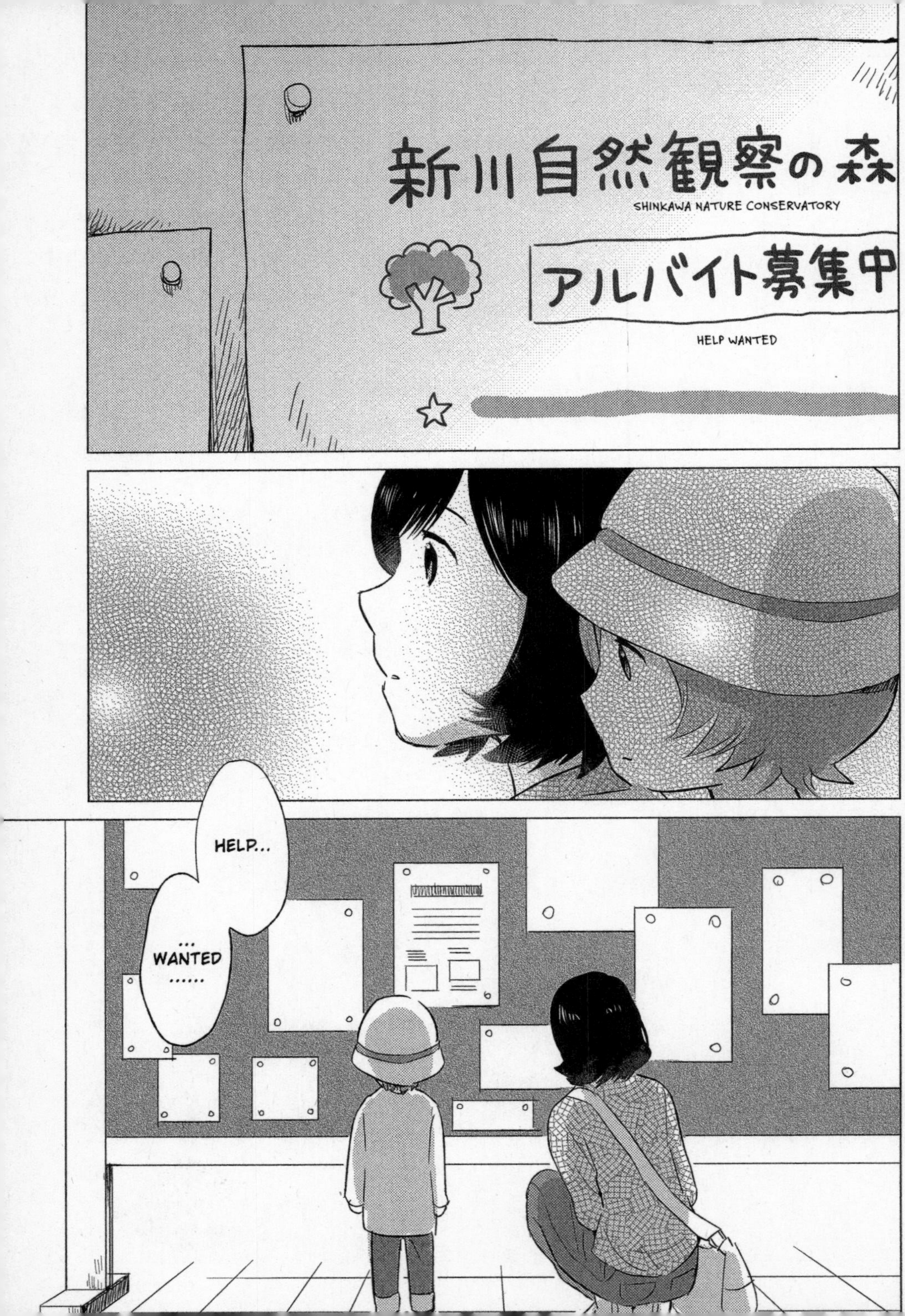
新川自然観察の森
SHINKAWA NATURE CONSERVATORY
アルバイト募集中
HELP WANTED
HELP...
...WANTED......

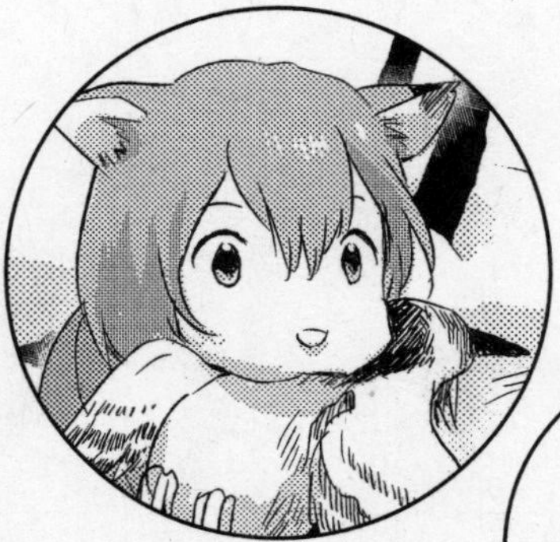
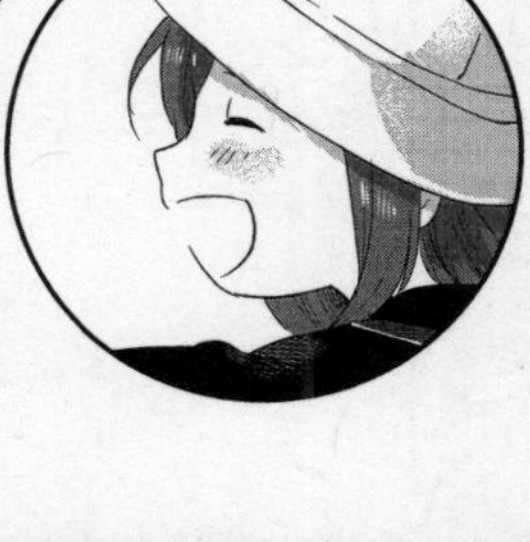

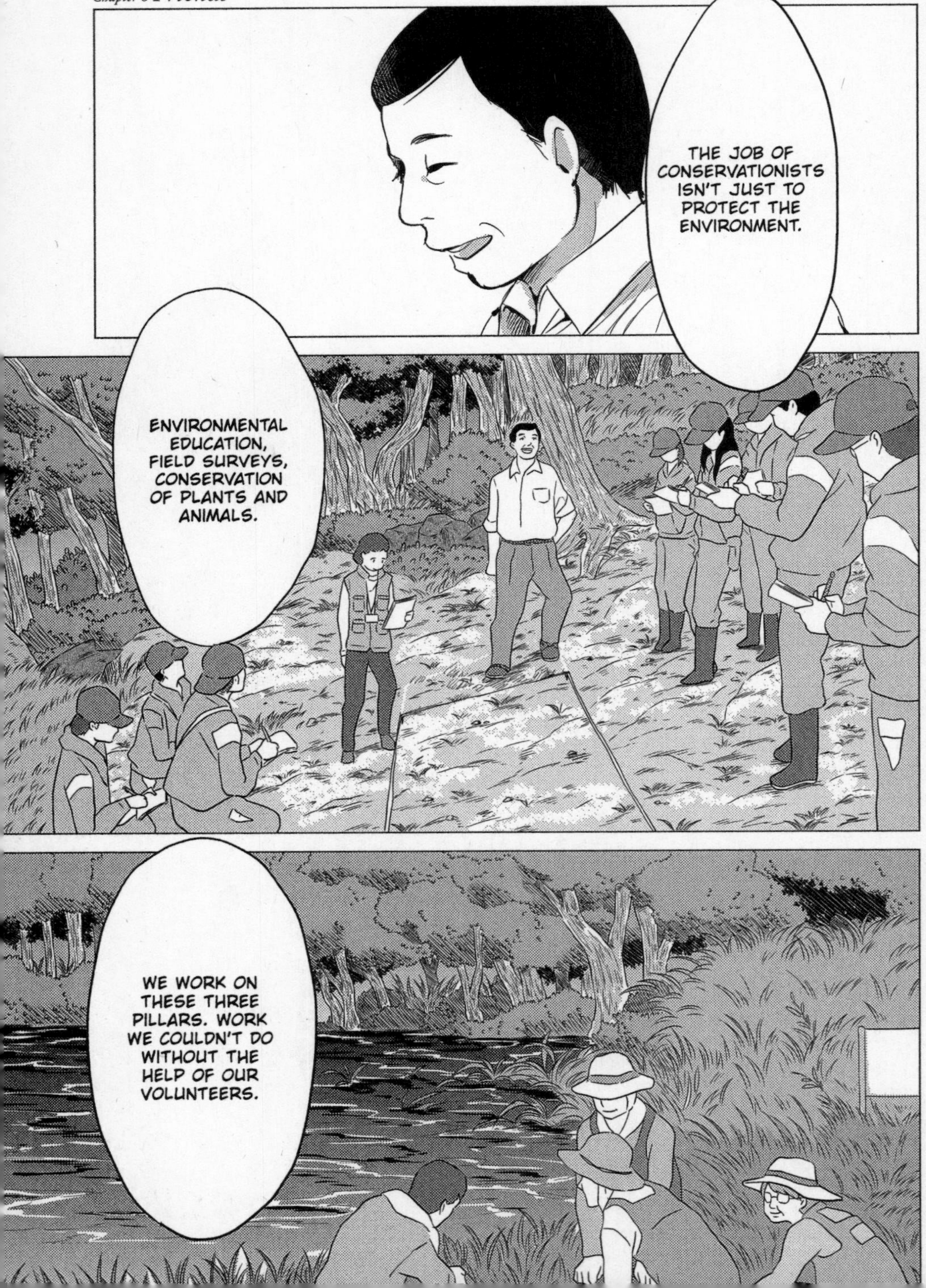
THE JOB OF CONSERVATIONISTS ISN'T JUST TO PROTECT THE ENVIRONMENT.
ENVIRONMENTAL EDUCATION, FIELD SURVEYS, CONSERVATION OF PLANTS AND ANIMALS.
WE WORK ON THESE THREE PILLARS. WORK WE COULDN'T DO WITHOUT THE HELP OF OUR VOLUNTEERS.

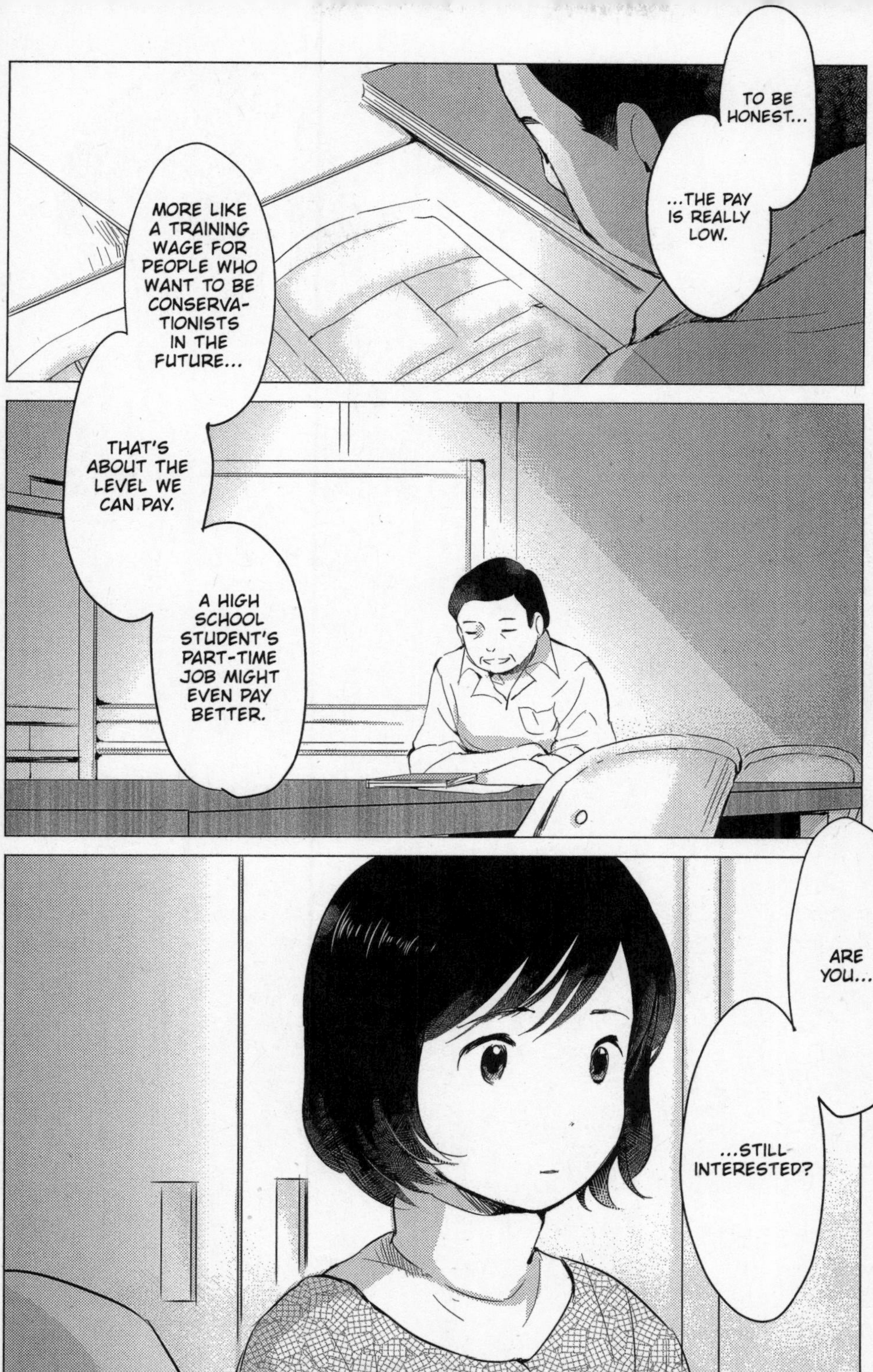
TO BE HONEST...
...THE PAY IS REALLY LOW.
MORE LIKE A TRAINING WAGE FOR PEOPLE WHO WANT TO BE CONSERVA-TIONISTS IN THE FUTURE...
THAT'S ABOUT THE LEVEL WE CAN PAY.
A HIGH SCHOOL STUDENT'S PART-TIME JOB MIGHT EVEN PAY BETTER.
ARE YOU...
...STILL INTERESTED?

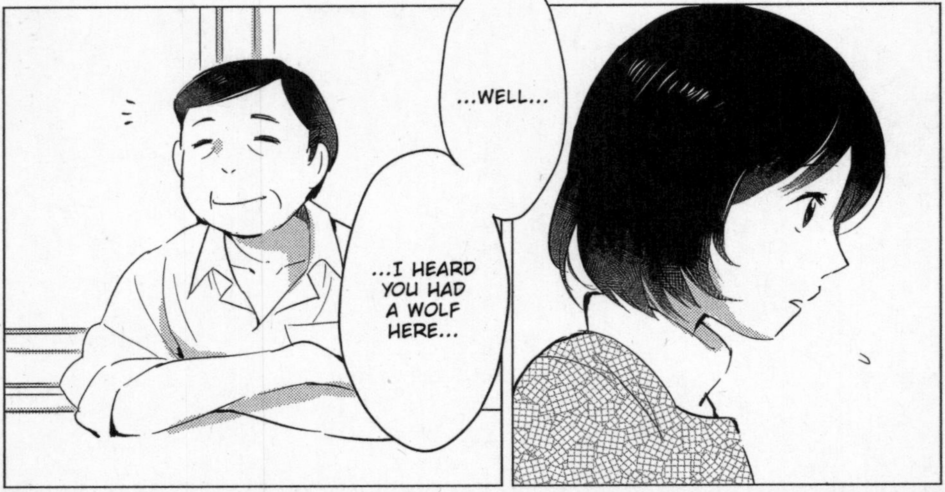
...WELL...
...I HEARD YOU HAD A WOLF HERE...

Chapter 8 Friends

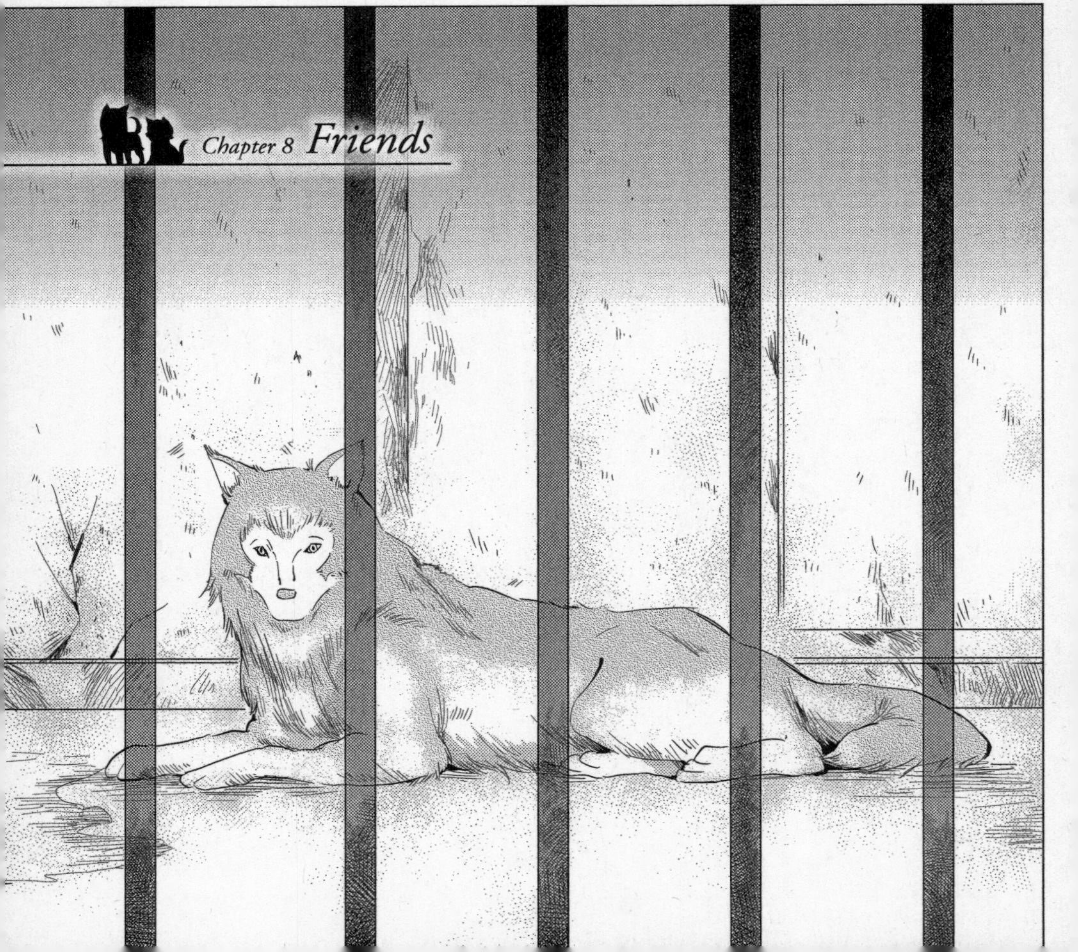

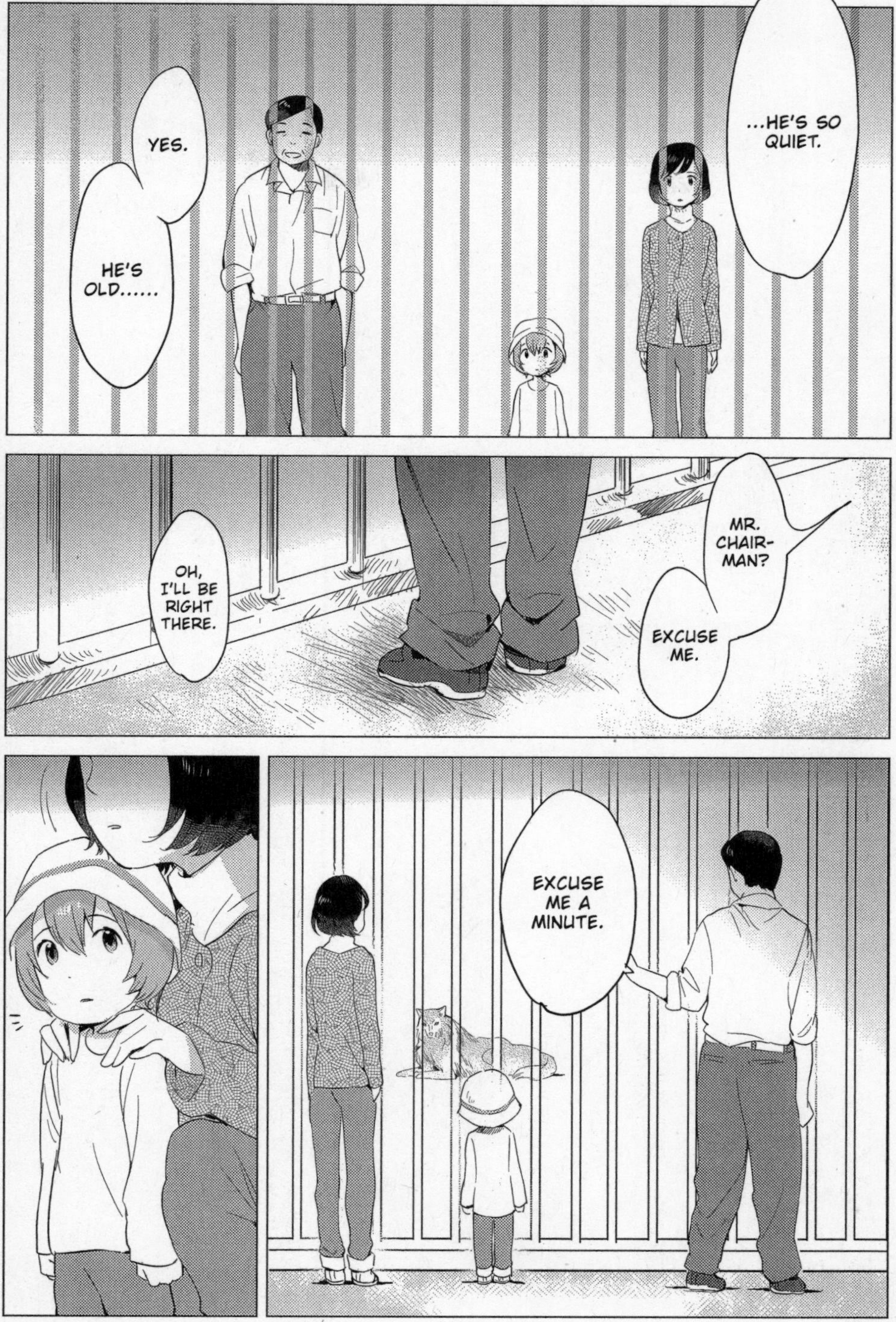
...HE'S SO QUIET.
YES.
HE'S OLD......
MR. CHAIR-MAN?
EXCUSE ME.
OH, I'LL BE RIGHT THERE.
EXCUSE ME A MINUTE.

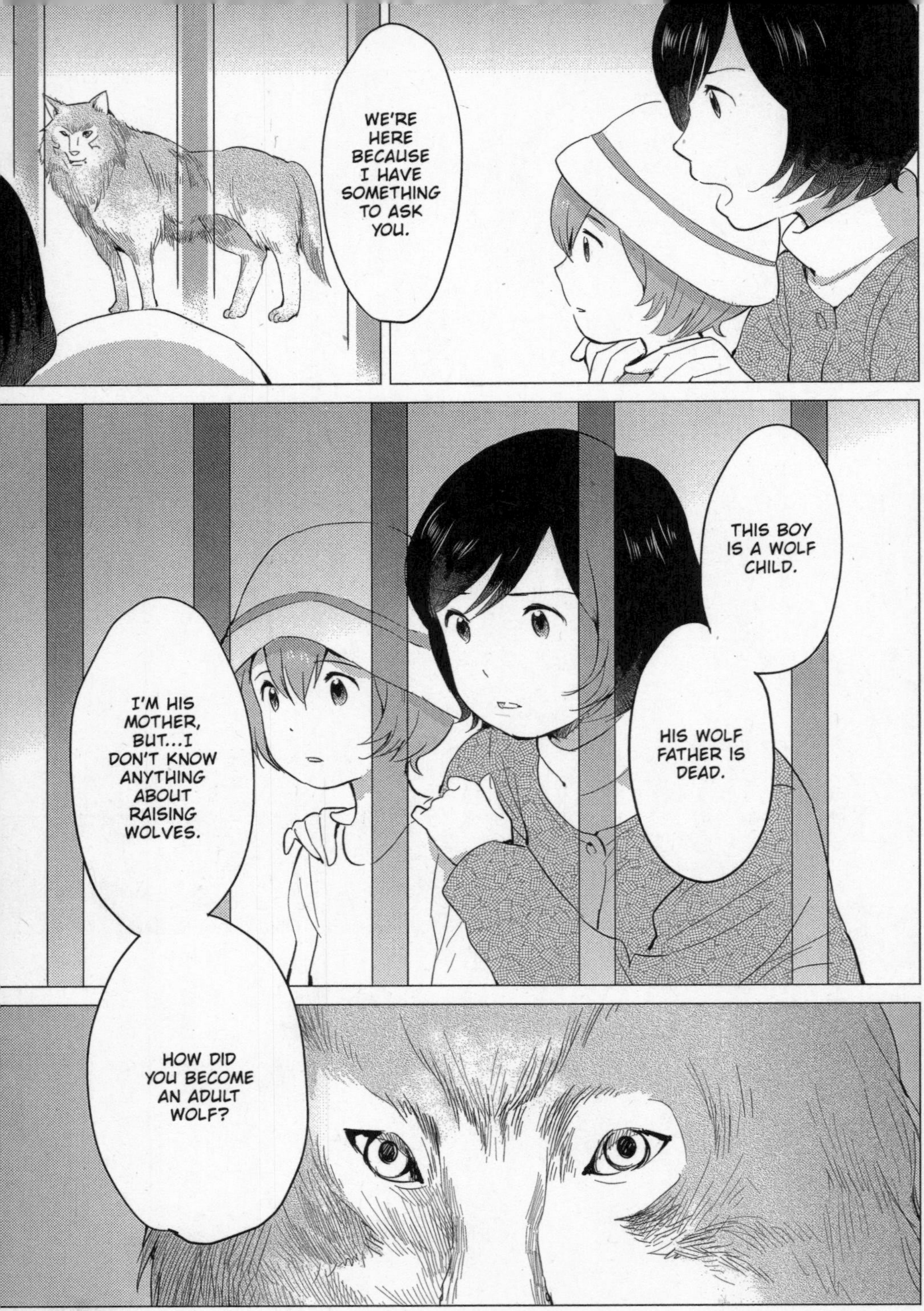
WE'RE HERE BECAUSE I HAVE SOMETHING TO ASK YOU.
THIS BOY IS A WOLF CHILD.
HIS WOLF FATHER IS DEAD.
I'M HIS MOTHER, BUT...I DON'T KNOW ANYTHING ABOUT RAISING WOLVES.
HOW DID YOU BECOME AN ADULT WOLF?

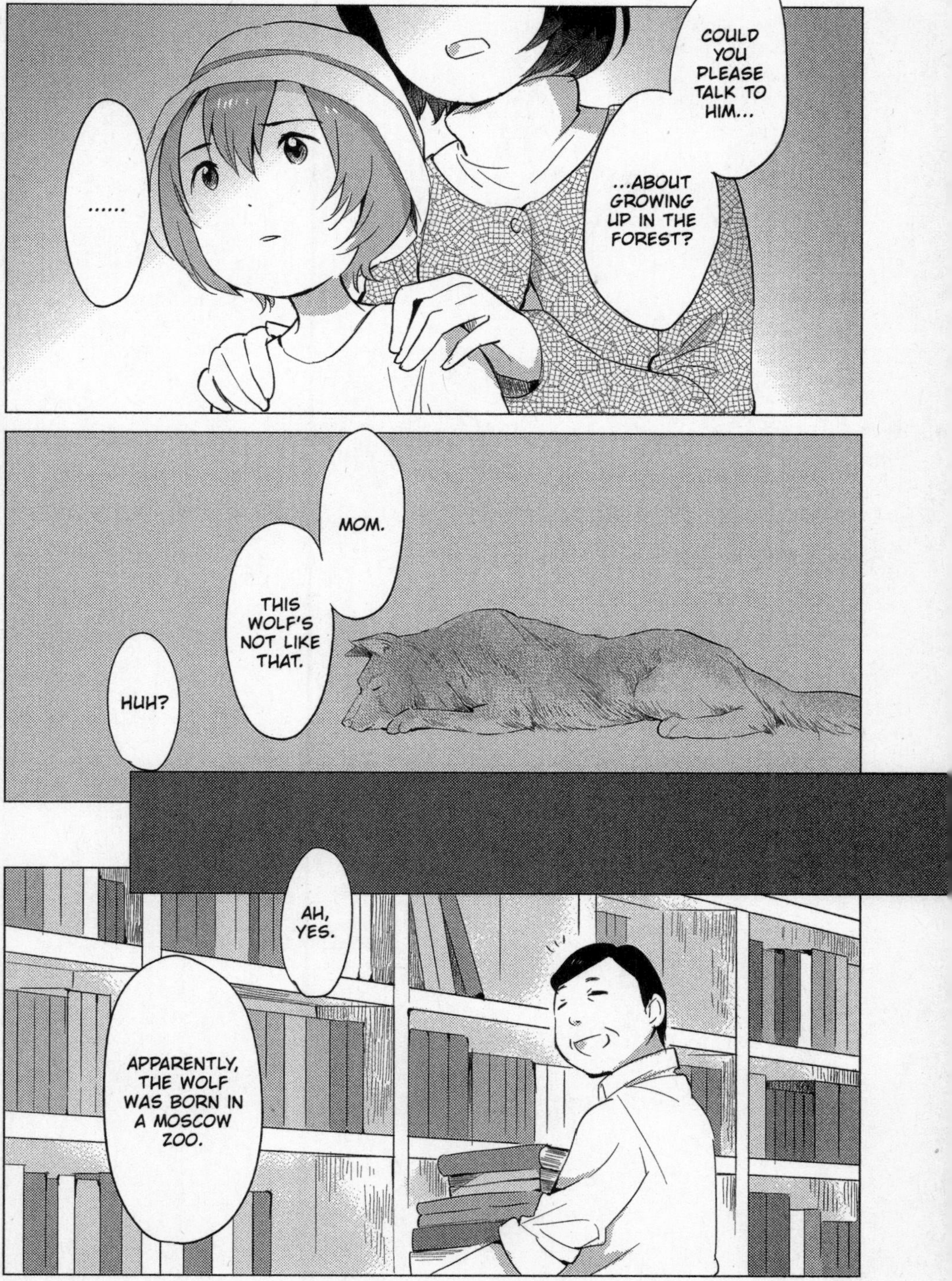
COULD YOU PLEASE TALK TO HIM...
...ABOUT GROWING UP IN THE FOREST?
......
MOM.
THIS WOLF'S NOT LIKE THAT.
HUH?
AH, YES.
APPARENTLY, THE WOLF WAS BORN IN A MOSCOW ZOO.

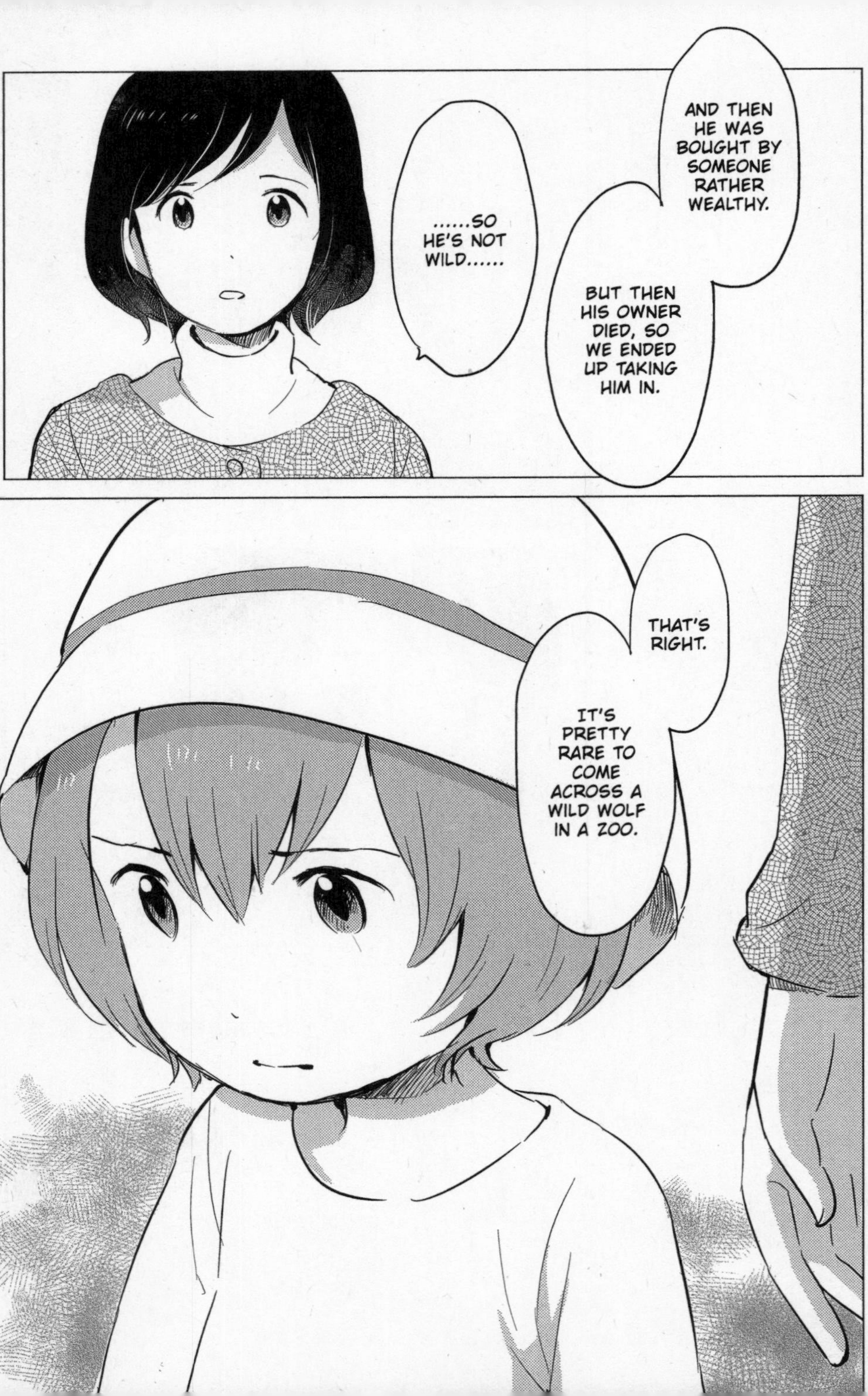
AND THEN HE WAS BOUGHT BY SOMEONE RATHER WEALTHY.
BUT THEN HIS OWNER DIED, SO WE ENDED UP TAKING HIM IN.
......SO HE'S NOT WILD......
THAT'S RIGHT.
IT'S PRETTY RARE TO COME ACROSS A WILD WOLF IN A ZOO.

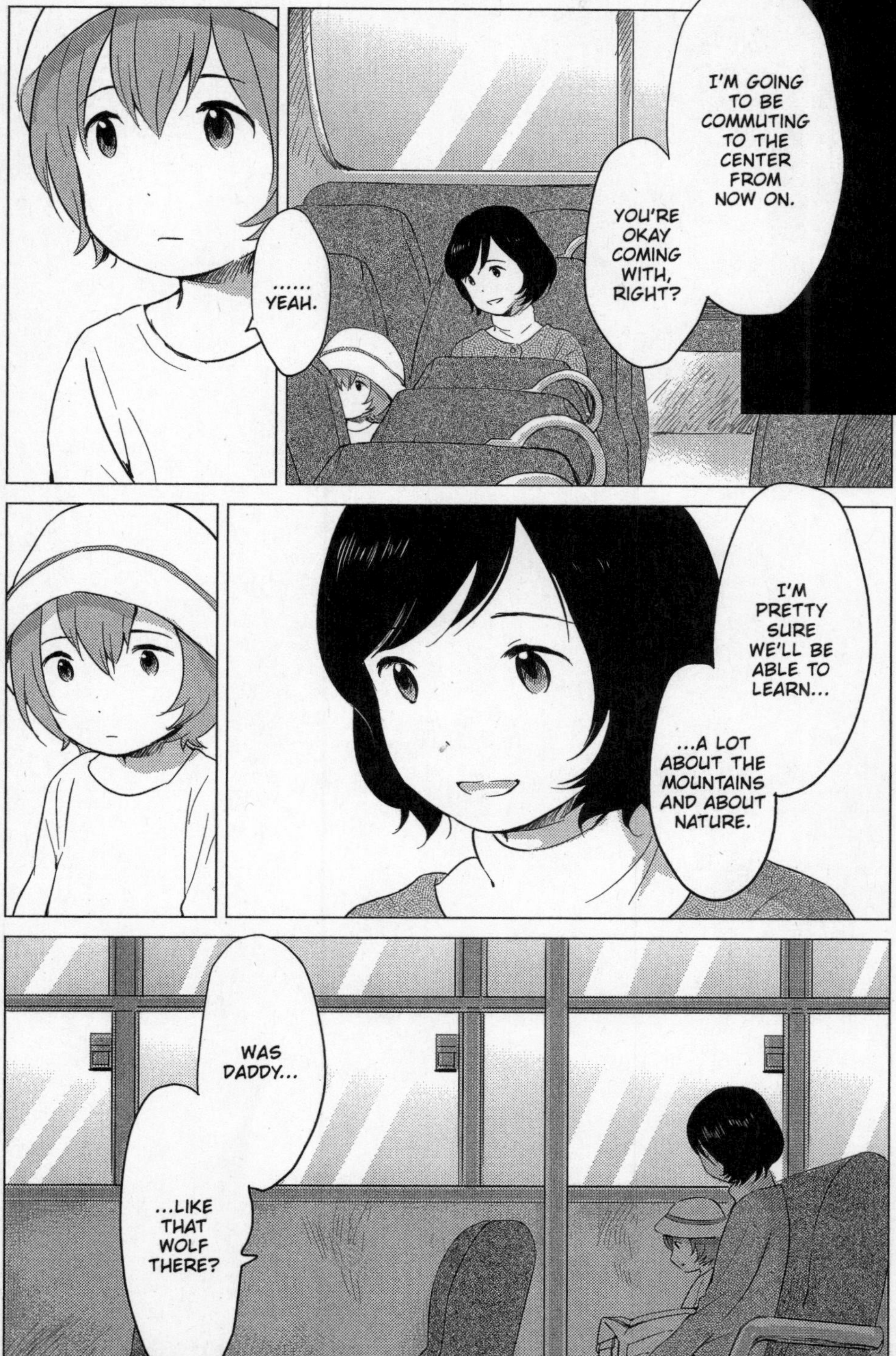
I'M GOING TO BE COMMUTING TO THE CENTER FROM NOW ON.
YOU'RE OKAY COMING WITH, RIGHT?
...... YEAH.
I'M PRETTY SURE WE'LL BE ABLE TO LEARN...
...A LOT ABOUT THE MOUNTAINS AND ABOUT NATURE.
WAS DADDY...
...LIKE THAT WOLF THERE?

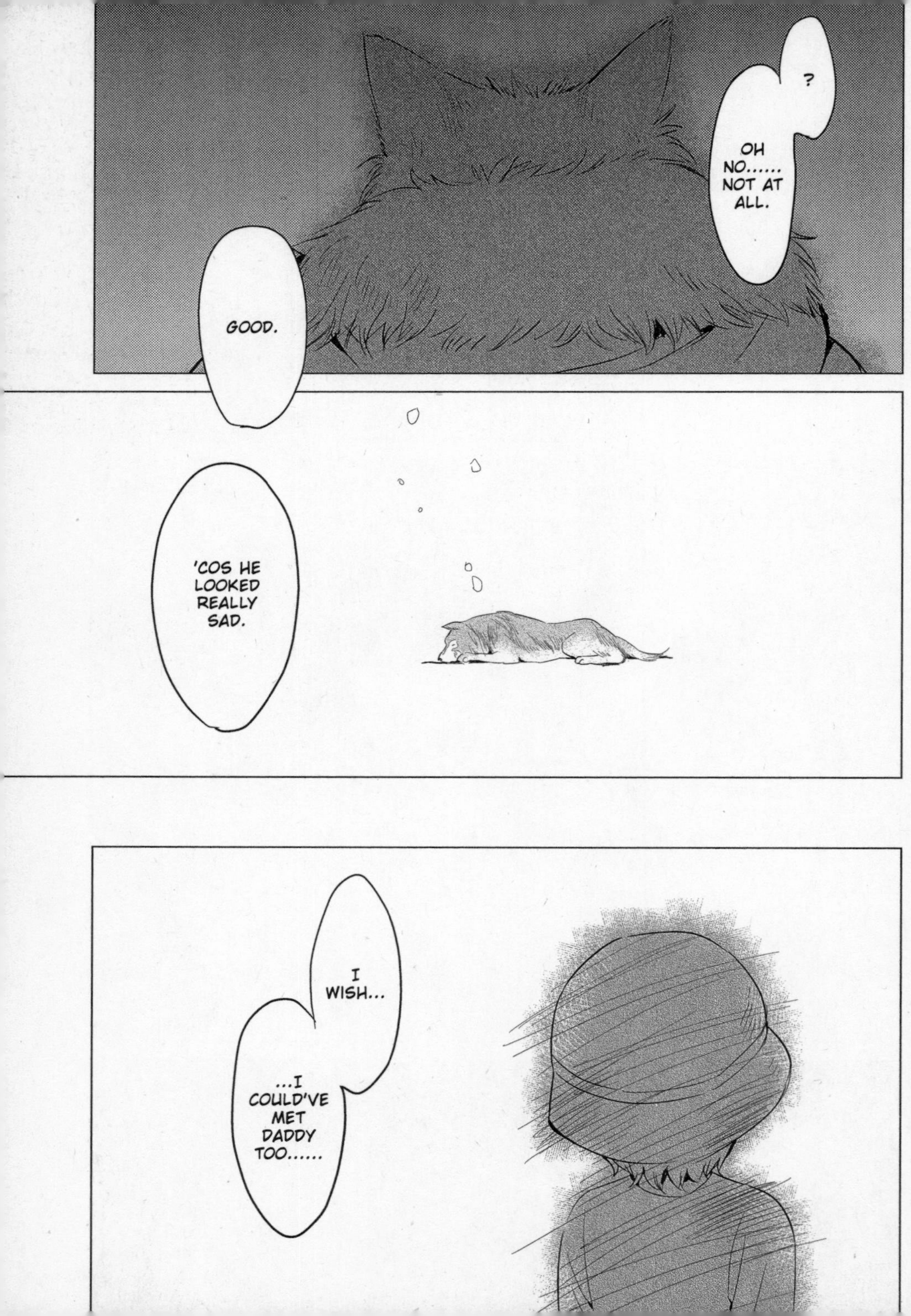
?
OH NO...... NOT AT ALL.
GOOD.
'COS HE LOOKED REALLY SAD.
I WISH...
...I COULD'VE MET DADDY TOO......

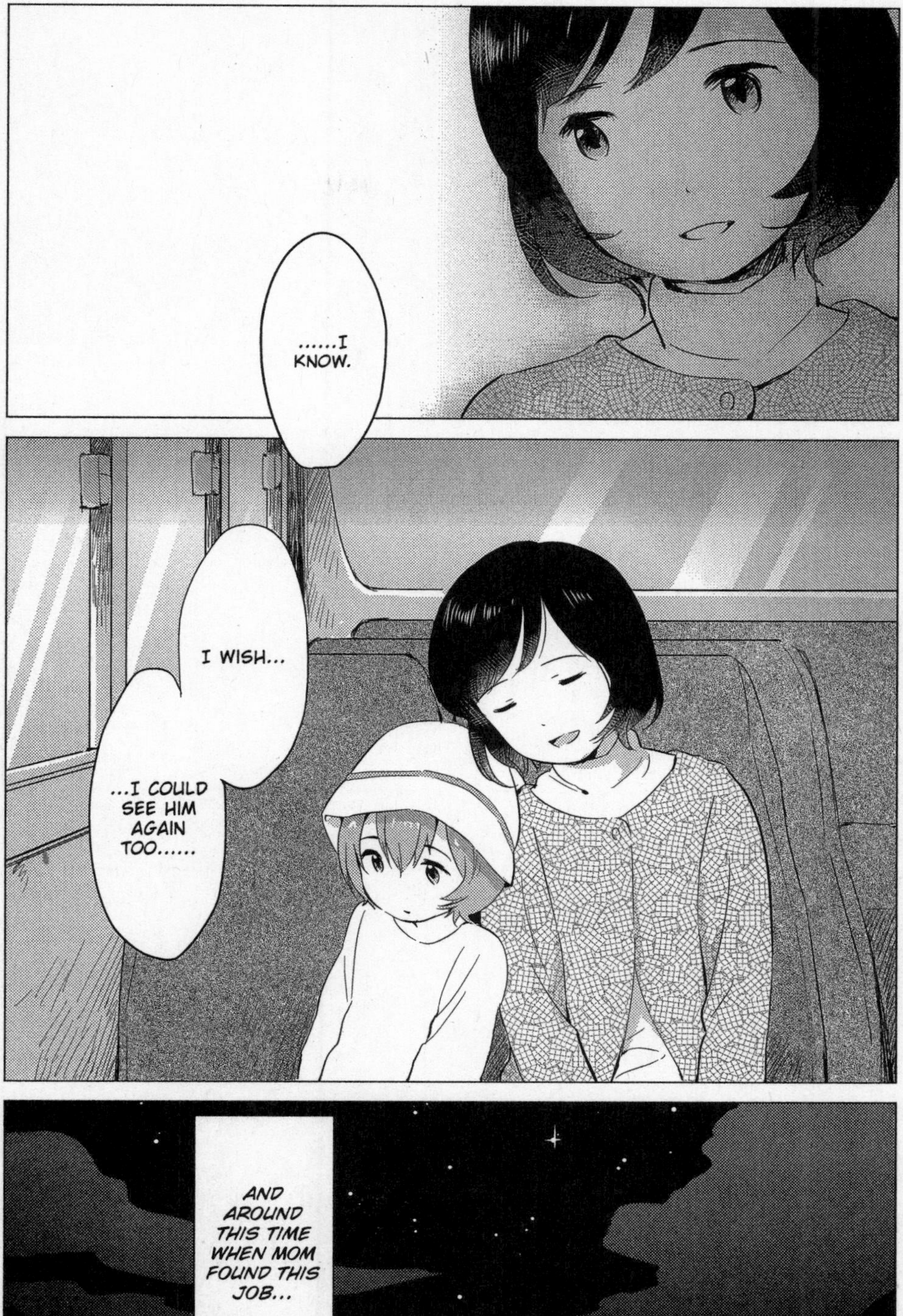
......I KNOW.
I WISH...
...I COULD SEE HIM AGAIN TOO......
AND AROUND THIS TIME WHEN MOM FOUND THIS JOB...

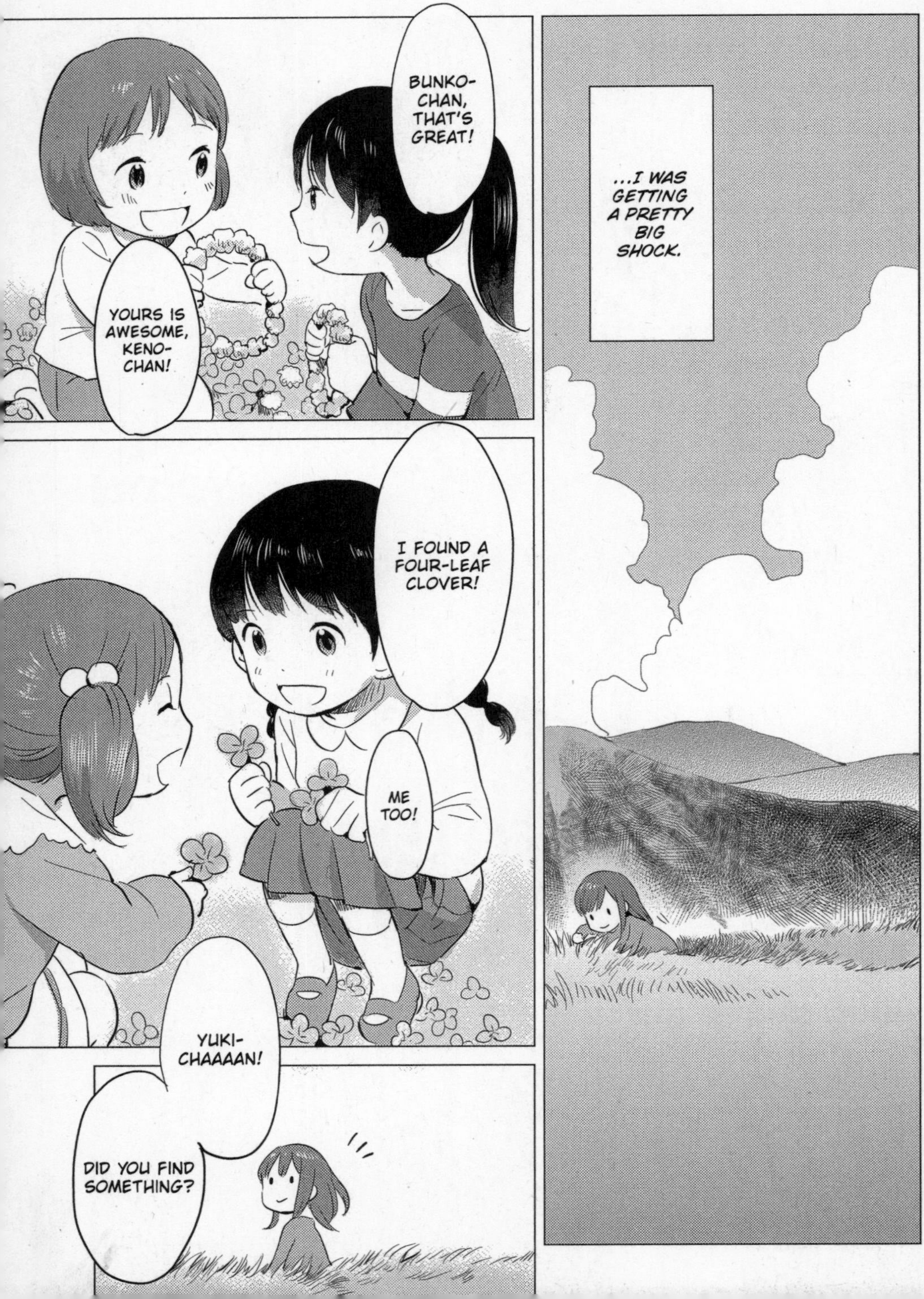
...I WAS GETTING A PRETTY BIG SHOCK.
BUNKO-CHAN, THAT'S GREAT!
YOURS IS AWESOME, KENO-CHAN!
I FOUND A FOUR-LEAF CLOVER!
ME TOO!
YUKI-CHAAAAN!
DID YOU FIND SOMETHING?

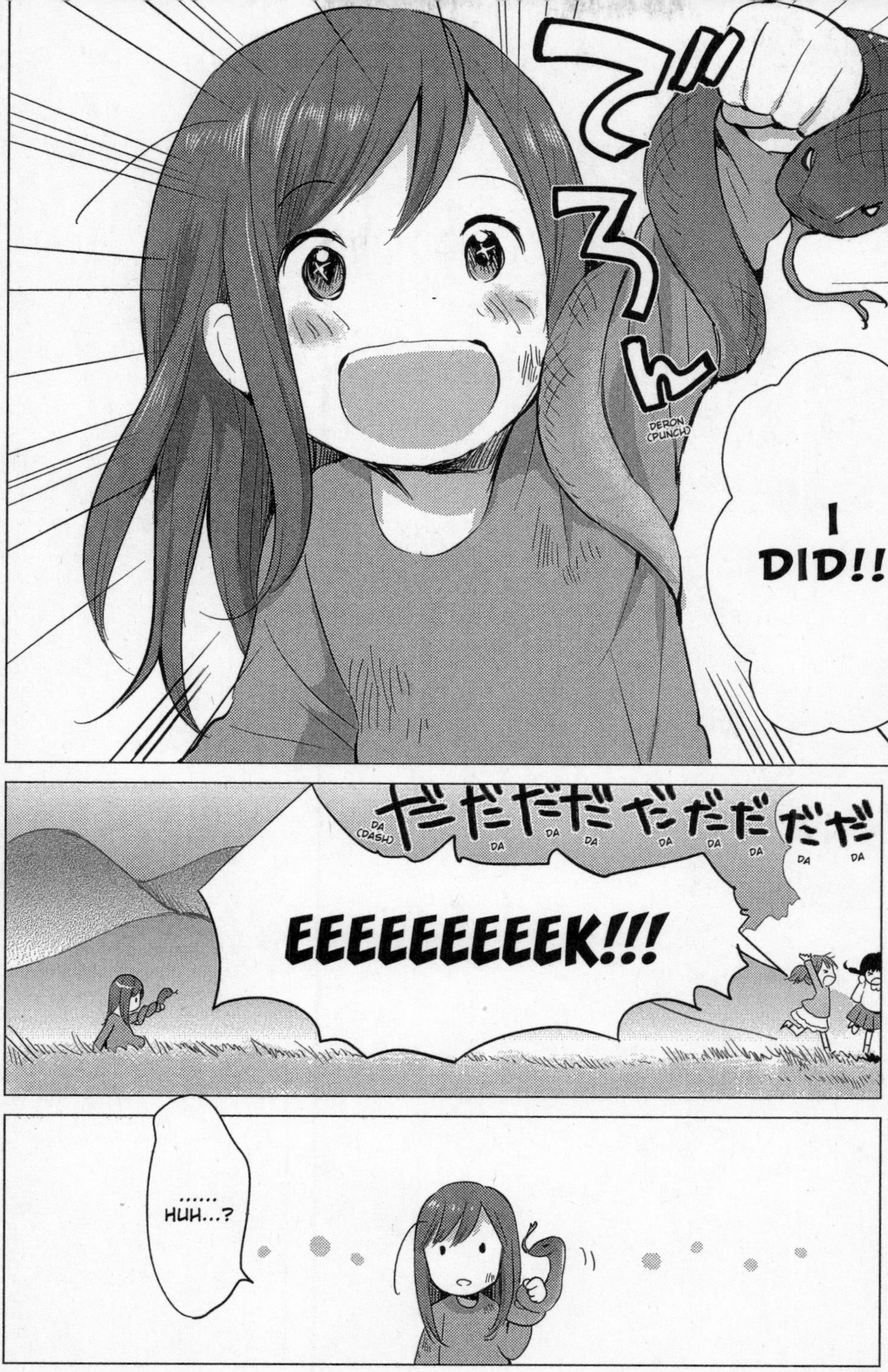
でろん
DERON (PUNCH)
I DID!!!
だだだだだだだだだ
DA (DASH) DA DA DA DA DA DA DA DA
EEEEEEEEEEK!!!
...... HUH...?

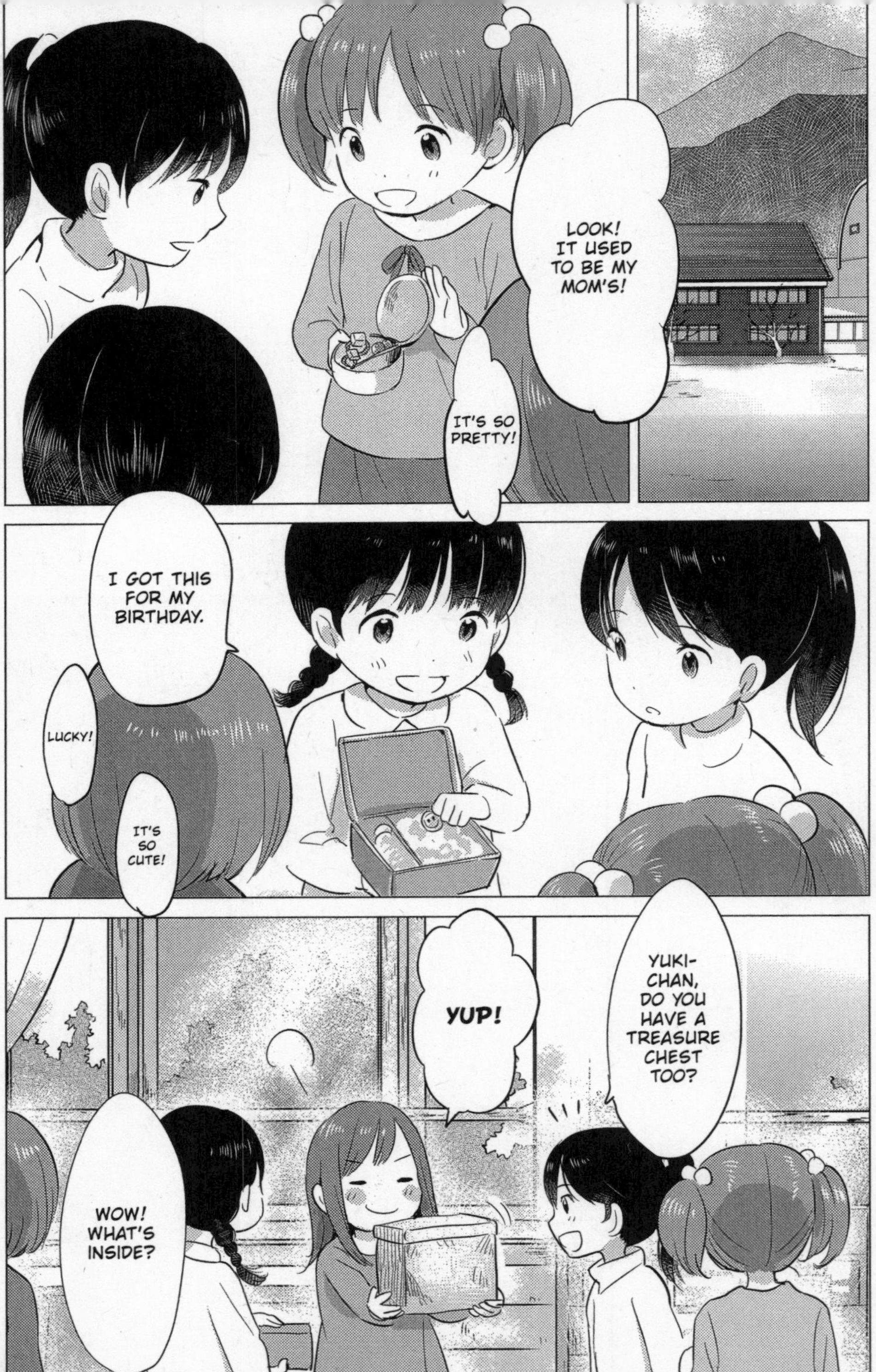
LOOK! IT USED TO BE MY MOM'S!
IT'S SO PRETTY!
I GOT THIS FOR MY BIRTHDAY.
LUCKY!
IT'S SO CUTE!
YUKI-CHAN, DO YOU HAVE A TREASURE CHEST TOO?
YUP!
WOW! WHAT'S INSIDE?

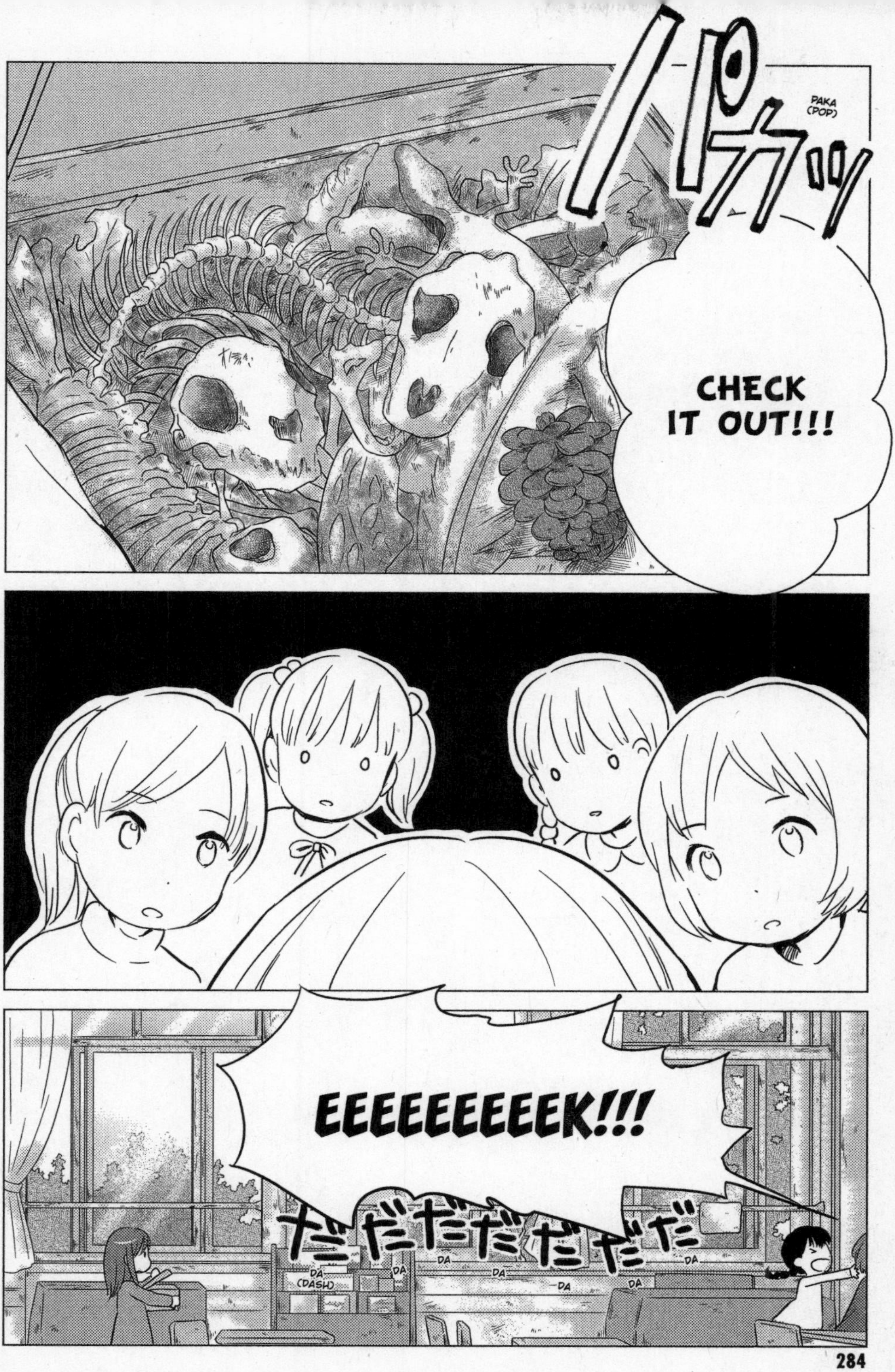

パカッ
PAKA (POP)
CHECK IT OUT!!!
EEEEEEEEEEK!!!
だだだだだだだ
DA
DA
DA
DA
DA
DA
DA (DASH)

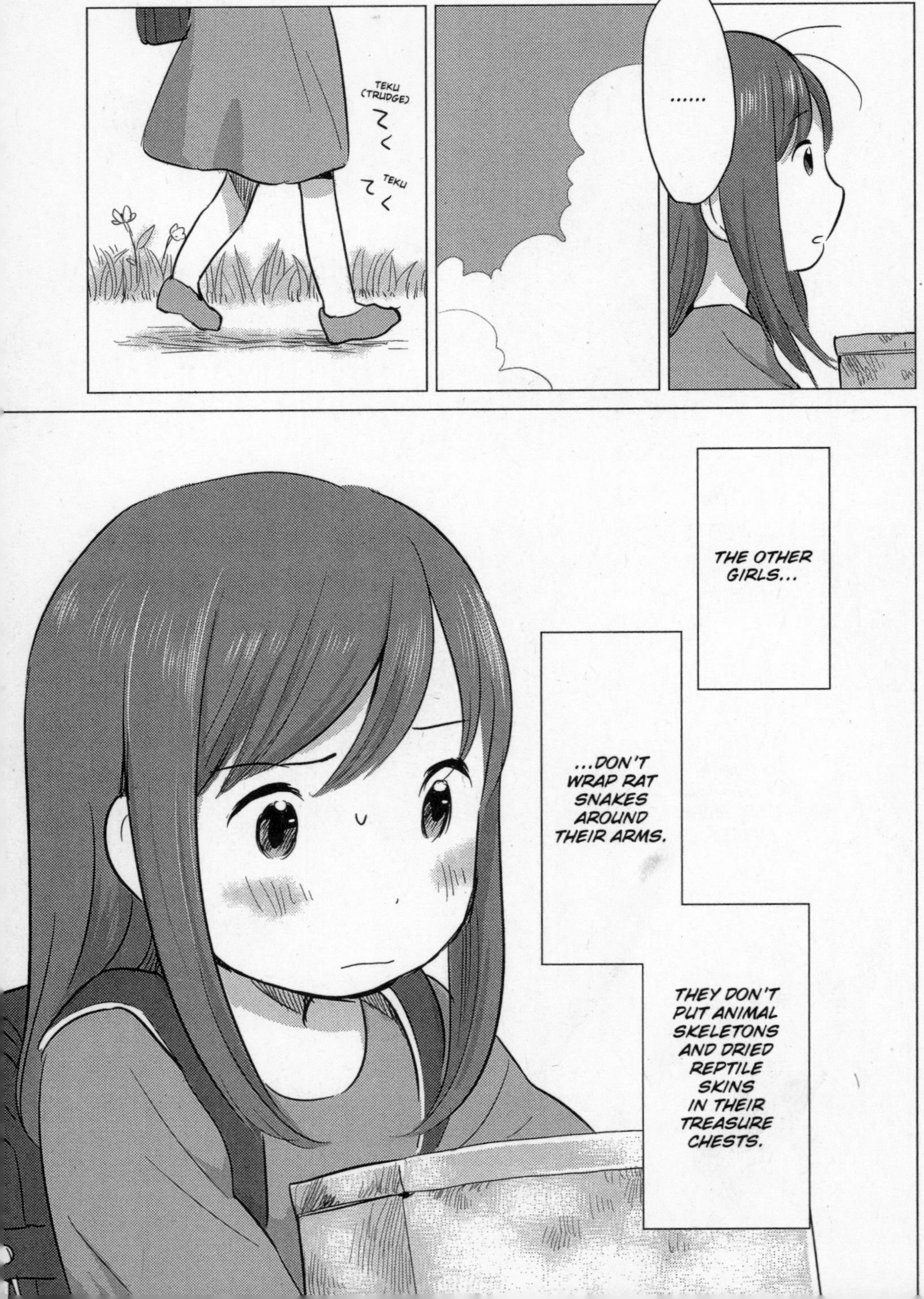
......
TEKU (TRUDGE)
てく
TEKU
てく
THE OTHER GIRLS...
...DON'T WRAP RAT SNAKES AROUND THEIR ARMS.
THEY DON'T PUT ANIMAL SKELETONS AND DRIED REPTILE SKINS IN THEIR TREASURE CHESTS.

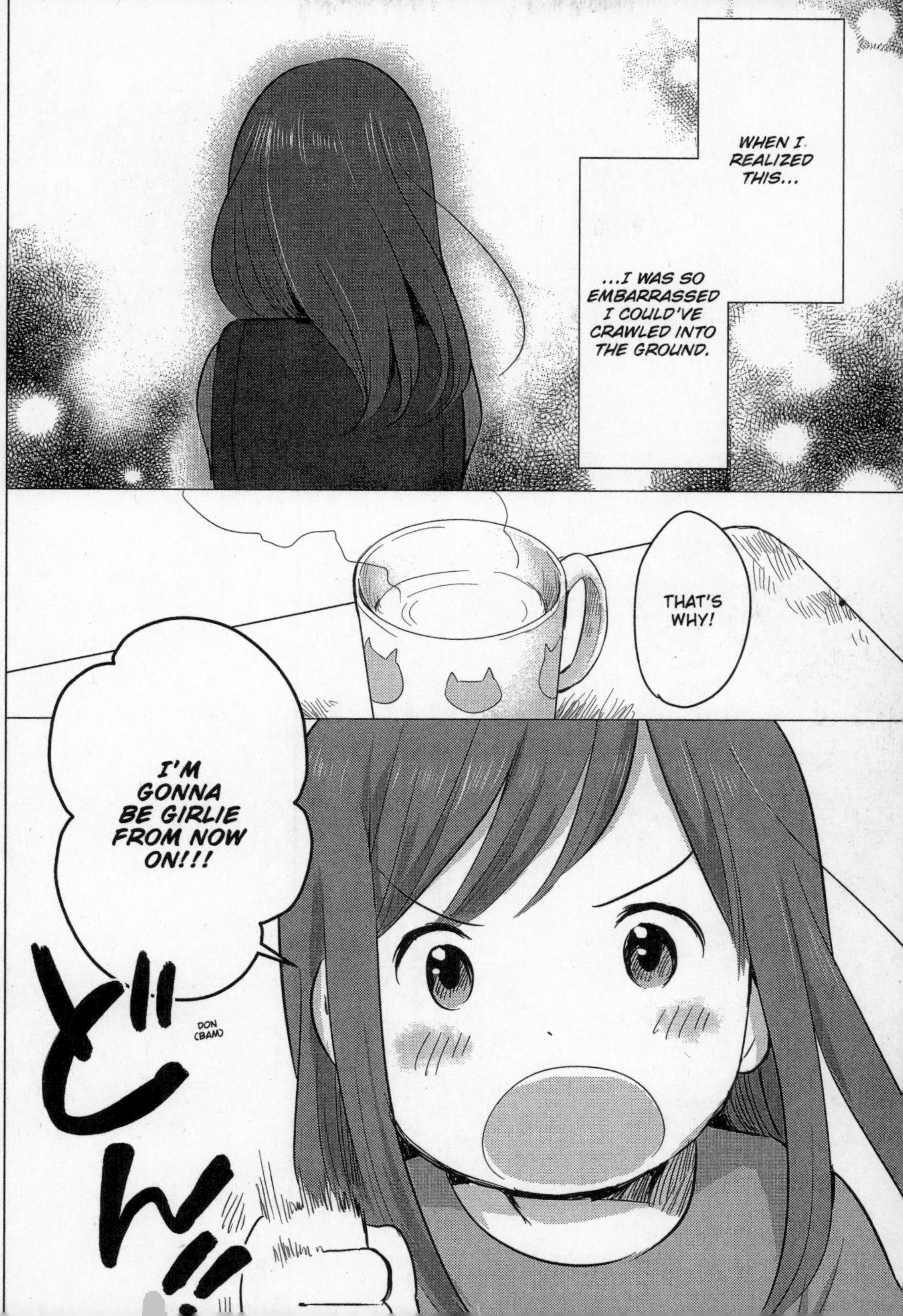

WHEN I REALIZED THIS...
...I WAS SO EMBARRASSED I COULD'VE CRAWLED INTO THE GROUND.
THAT'S WHY!
I'M GONNA BE GIRLIE FROM NOW ON!!!
どーん!!
DON (BAM)

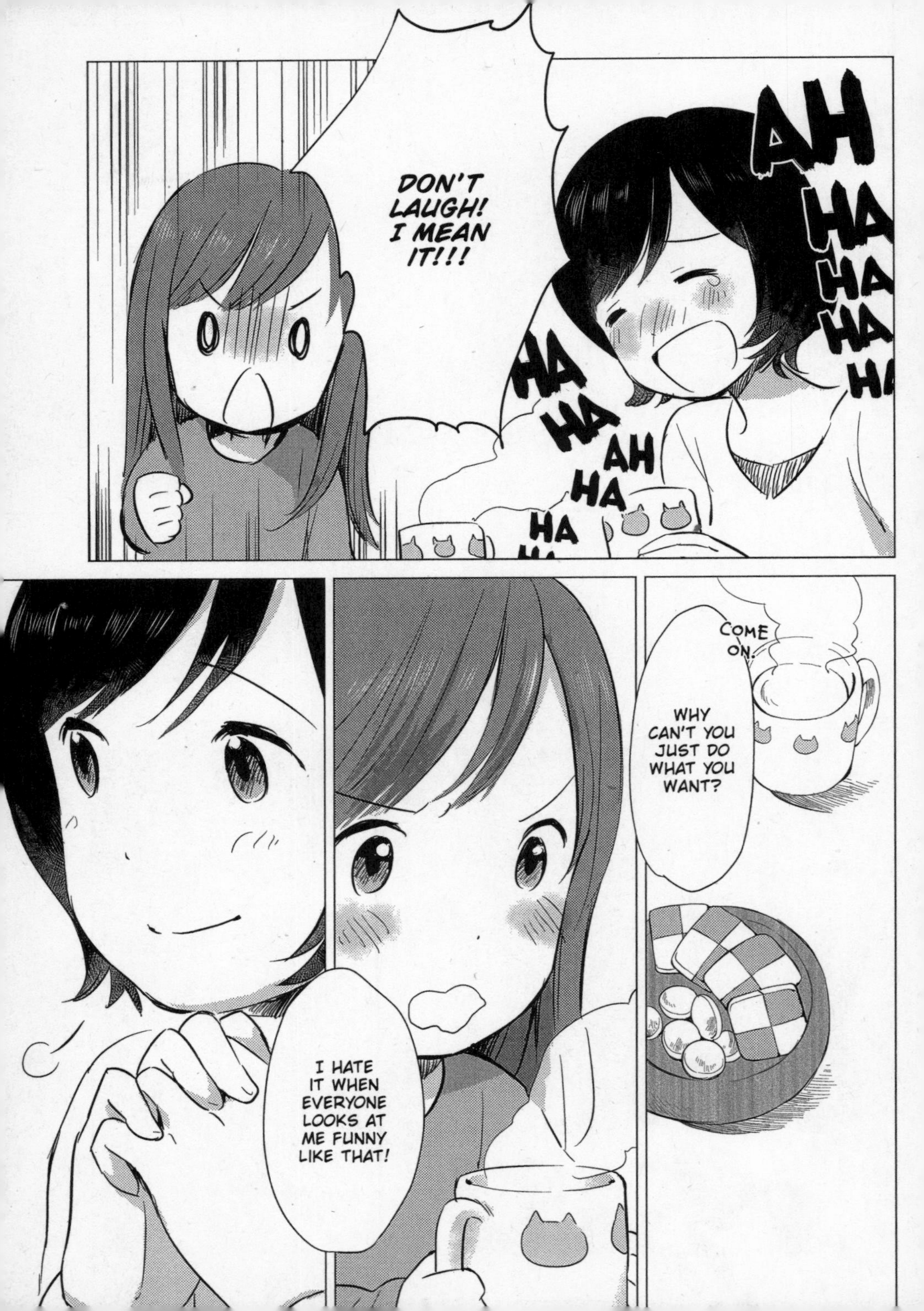
AH HA HA HA HA
DON'T LAUGH! I MEAN IT!!!
HA HA AH HA HA
COME ON.
WHY CAN'T YOU JUST DO WHAT YOU WANT?
I HATE IT WHEN EVERYONE LOOKS AT ME FUNNY LIKE THAT!

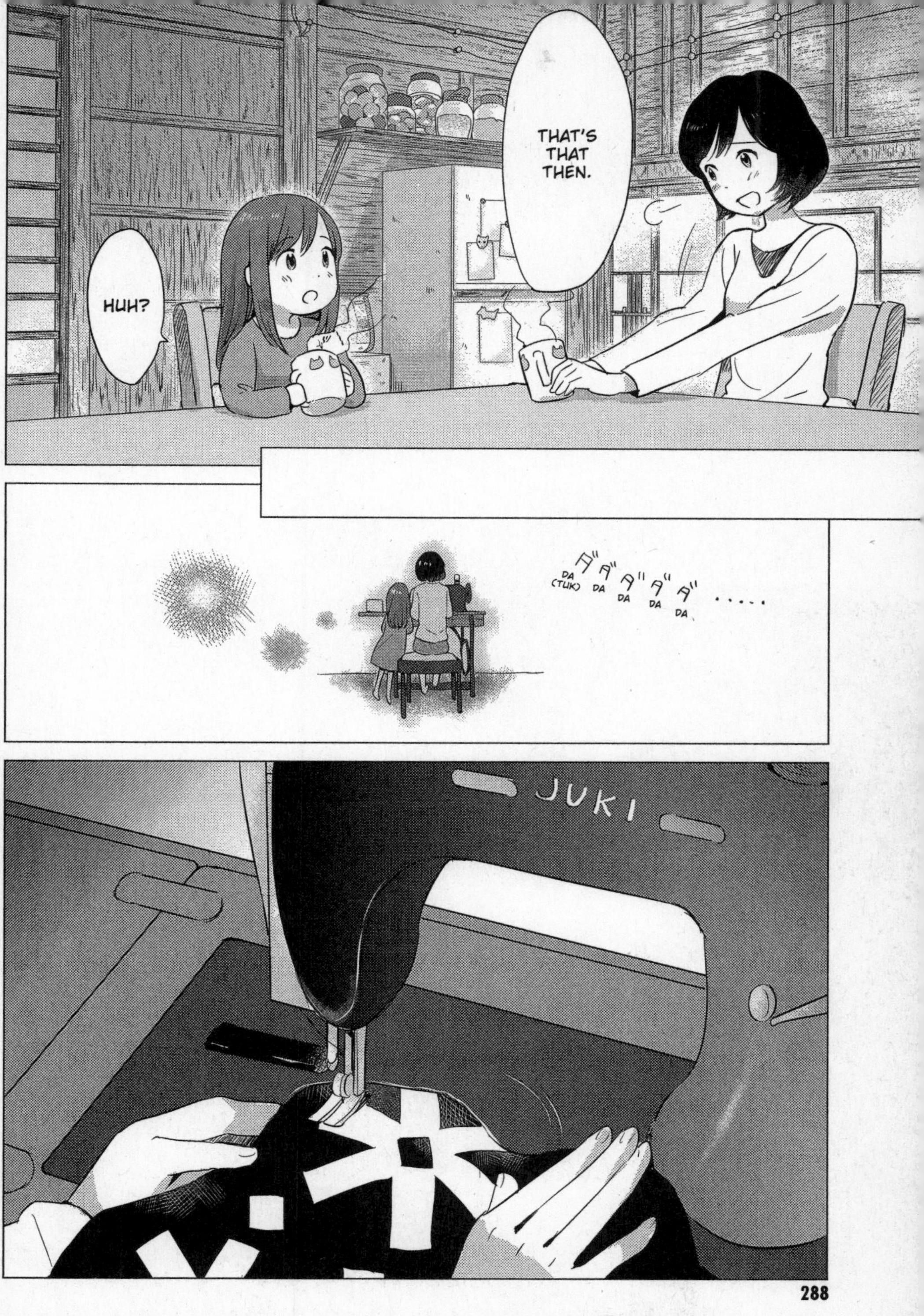
THAT'S THAT THEN.
HUH?
ダダダダダ.....
DA (TUK) DA DA DA DA
JUKI

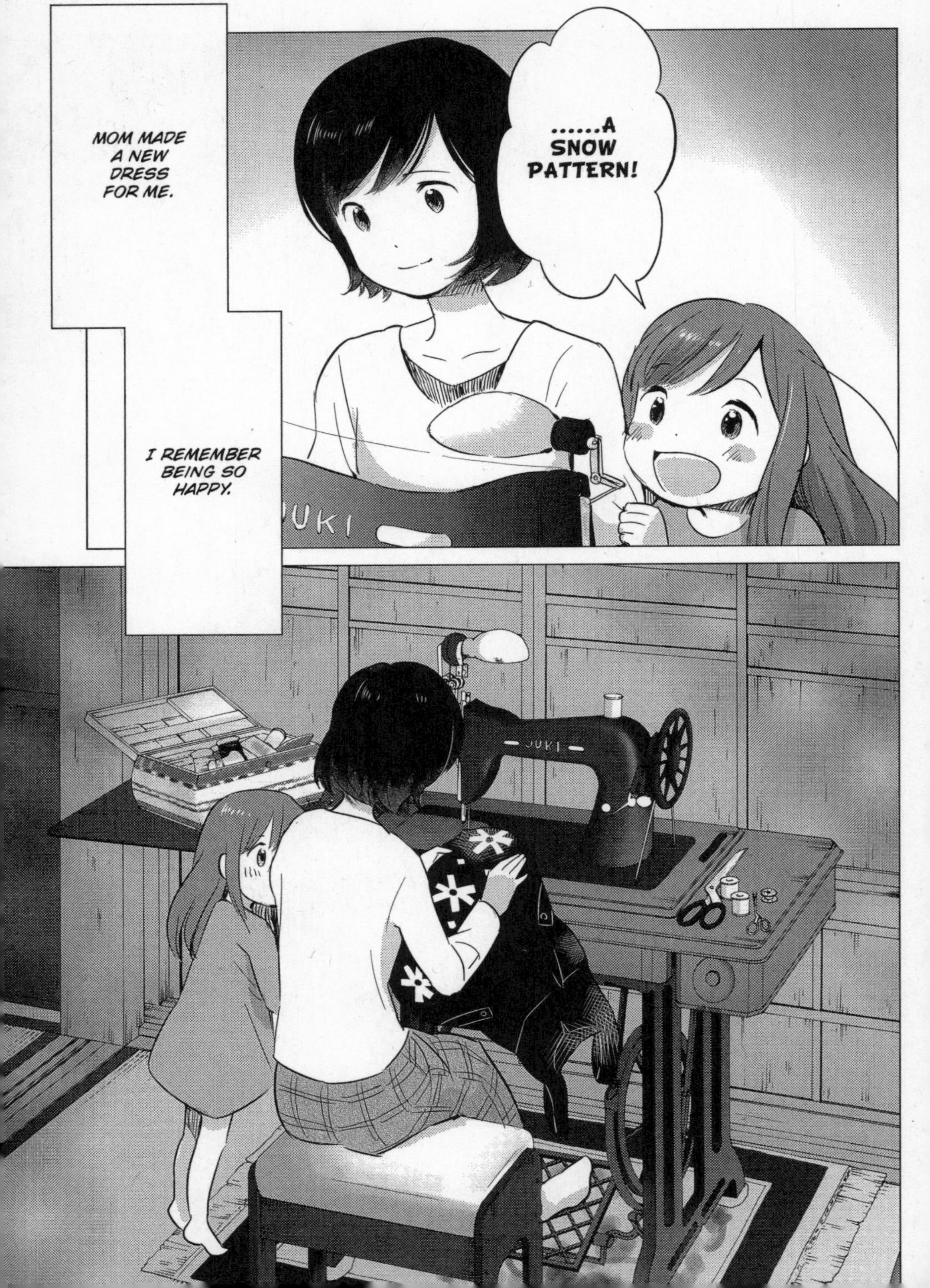
......A SNOW PATTERN!
MOM MADE A NEW DRESS FOR ME.
I REMEMBER BEING SO HAPPY.
JUKI
JUKI

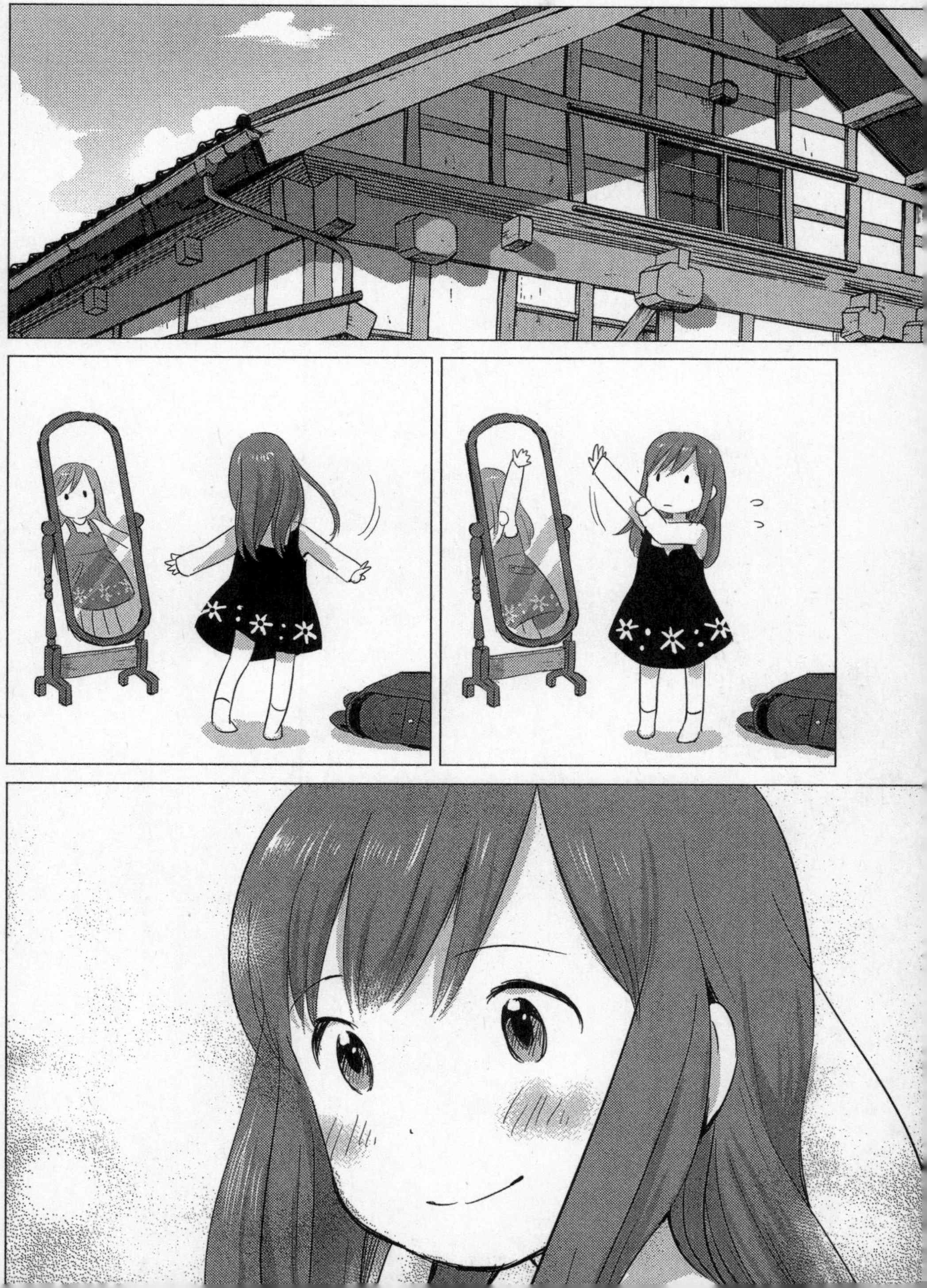

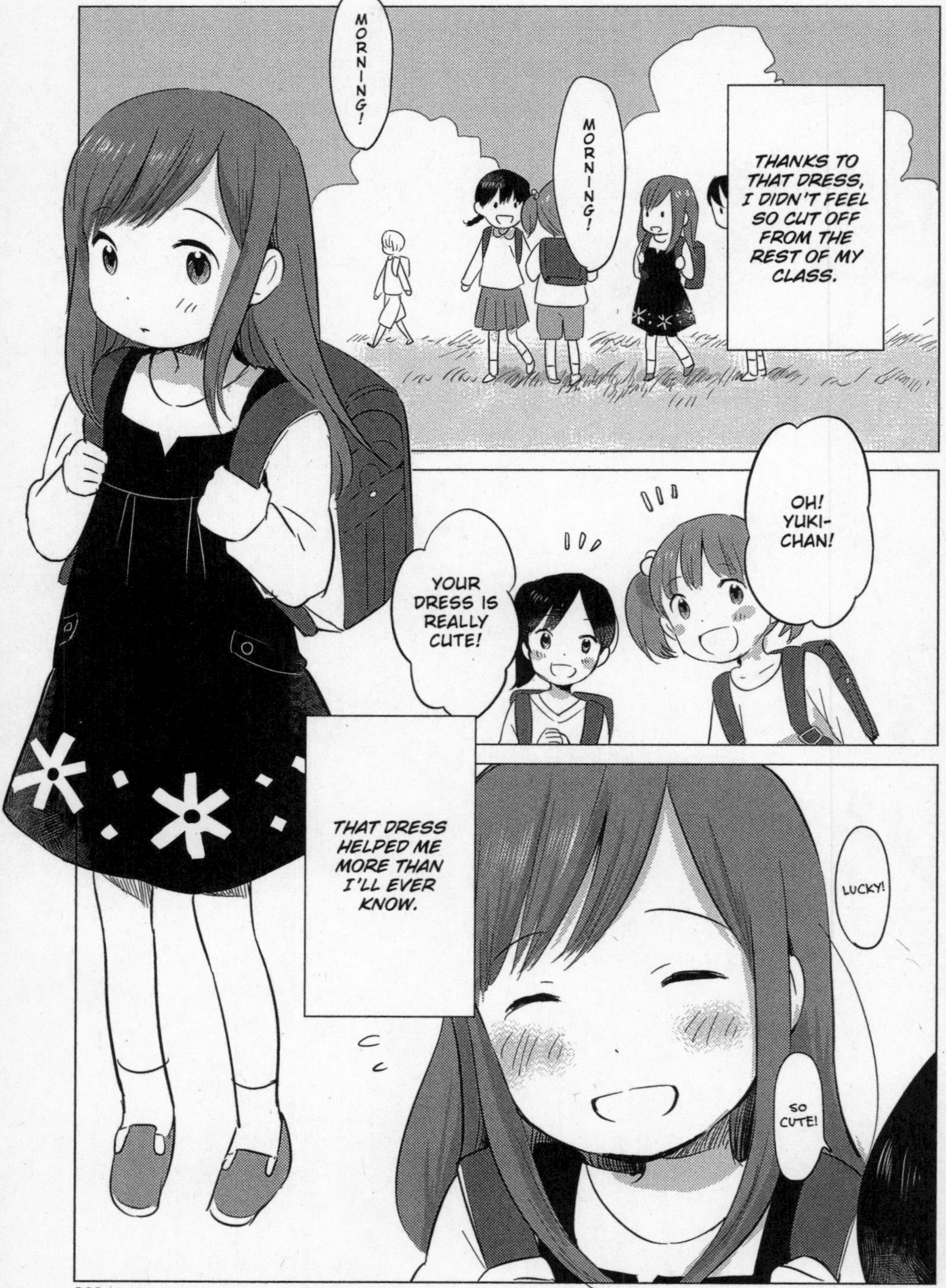
THANKS TO THAT DRESS, I DIDN'T FEEL SO CUT OFF FROM THE REST OF MY CLASS.
MORNING!
MORNING!
OH! YUKI-CHAN!
YOUR DRESS IS REALLY CUTE!
LUCKY!
SO CUTE!
THAT DRESS HELPED ME MORE THAN I'LL EVER KNOW.

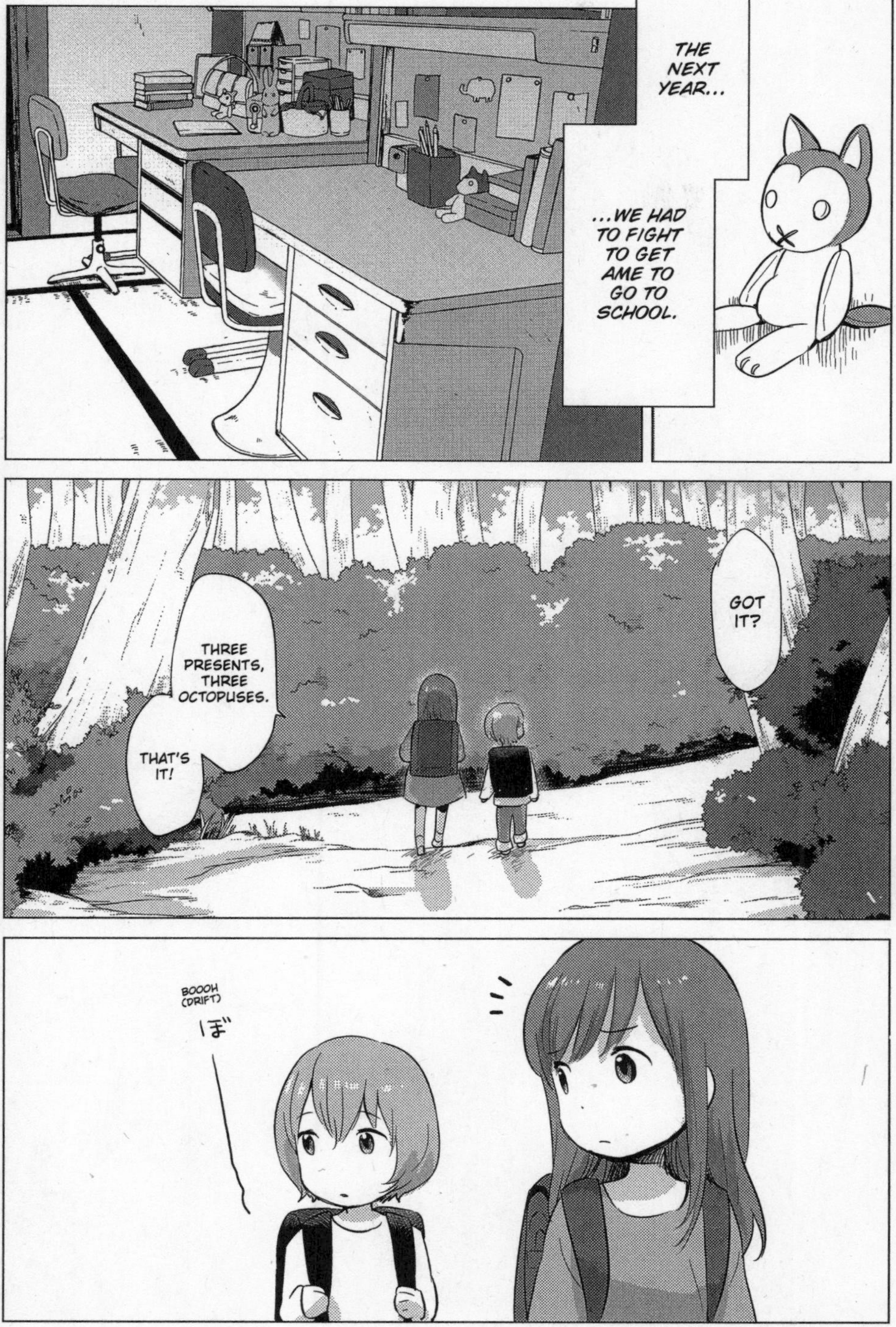
THE NEXT YEAR...
...WE HAD TO FIGHT TO GET AME TO GO TO SCHOOL.
GOT IT?
THREE PRESENTS, THREE OCTOPUSES.
THAT'S IT!
ぼ
BOOOH (DRIFT)

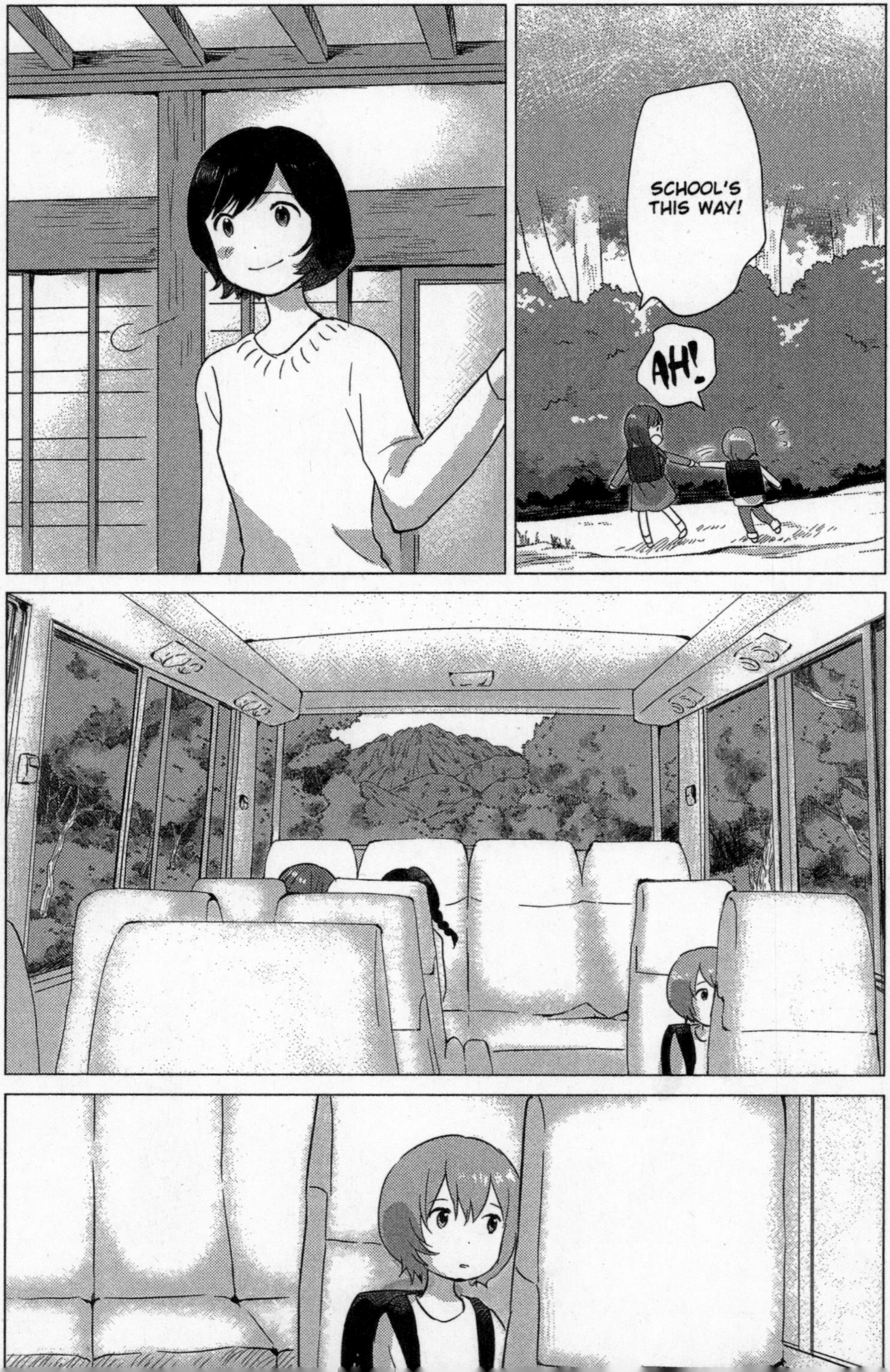
SCHOOL'S THIS WAY!
AH!

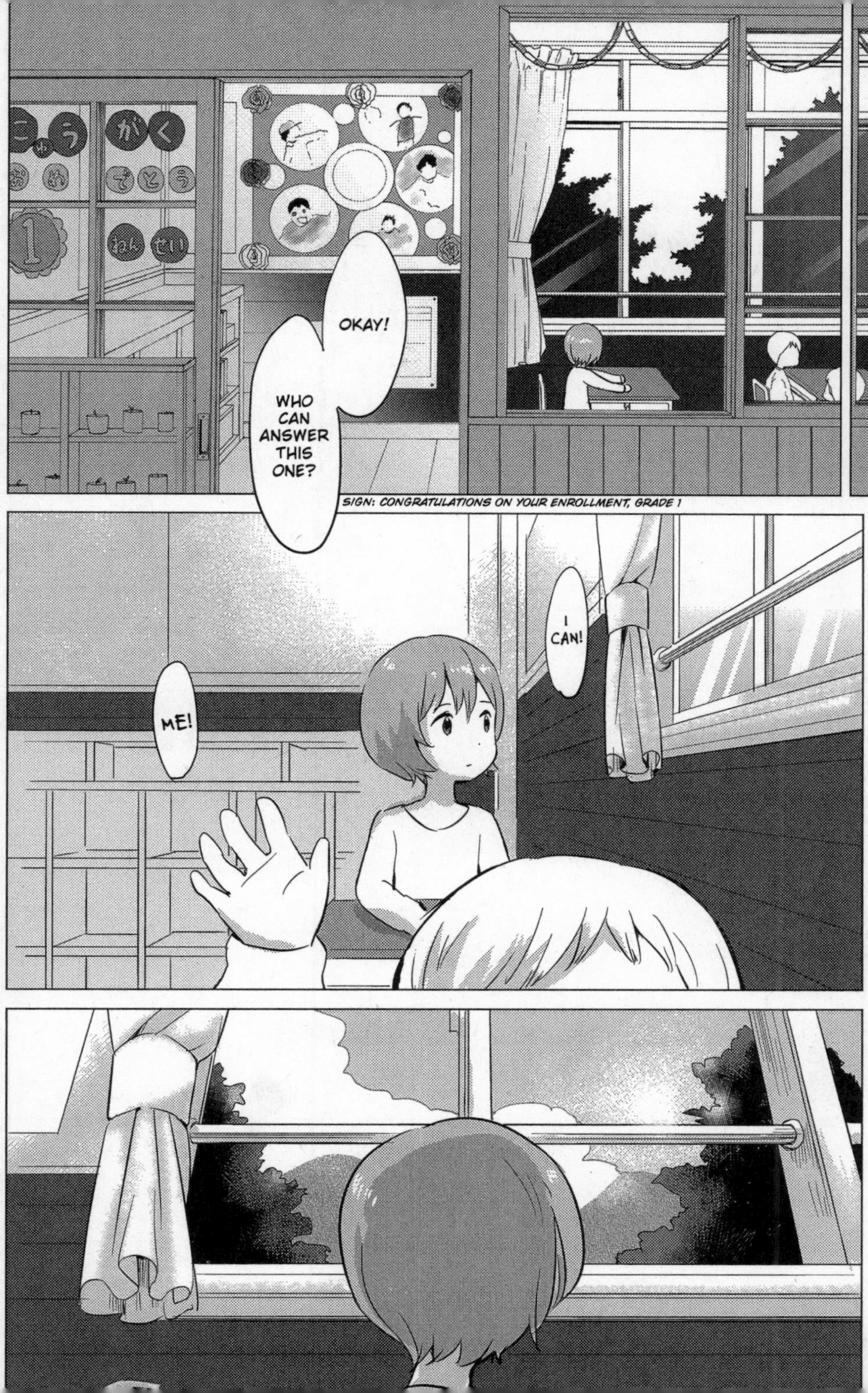
OKAY!
WHO CAN ANSWER THIS ONE?
SIGN: CONGRATULATIONS ON YOUR ENROLLMENT, GRADE 1
I CAN!
ME!

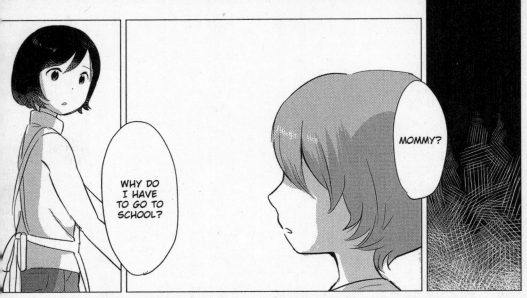

MOMMY?

WHY DO I HAVE TO GO TO SCHOOL?

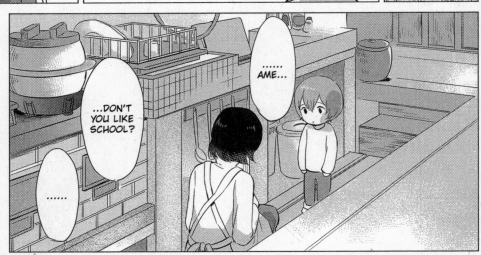

......AME...

...DON'T YOU LIKE SCHOOL?

......

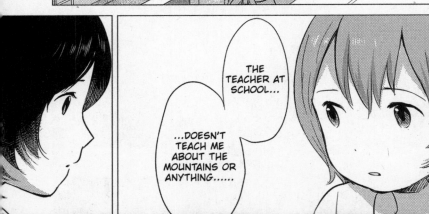

THE TEACHER AT SCHOOL...

...DOESN'T TEACH ME ABOUT THE MOUNTAINS OR ANYTHING......

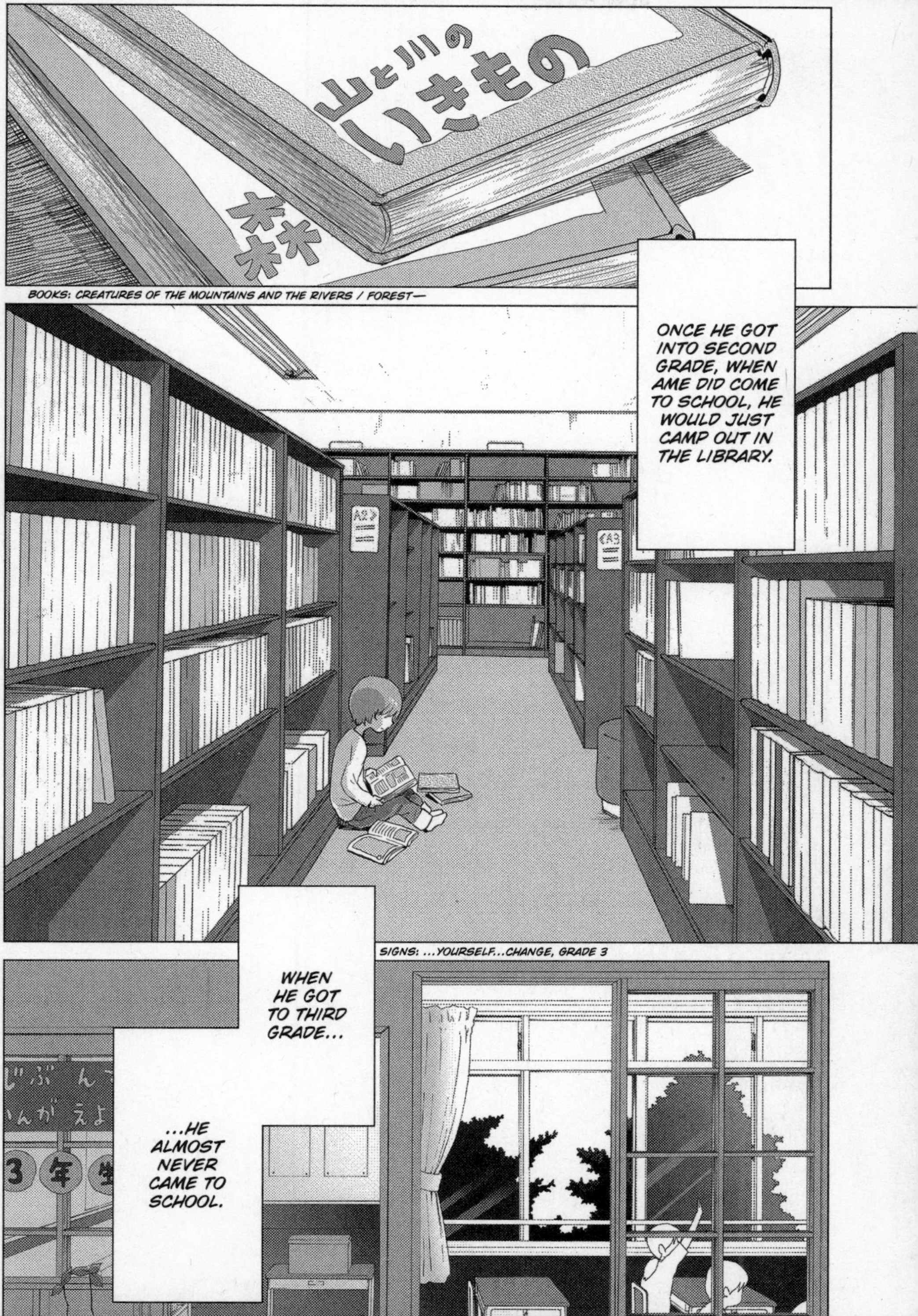
山と川の
いきもの
森
BOOKS: CREATURES OF THE MOUNTAINS AND THE RIVERS / FOREST—
ONCE HE GOT INTO SECOND GRADE, WHEN AME DID COME TO SCHOOL, HE WOULD JUST CAMP OUT IN THE LIBRARY.
SIGNS: ...YOURSELF...CHANGE, GRADE 3
WHEN HE GOT TO THIRD GRADE...
...HE ALMOST NEVER CAME TO SCHOOL.

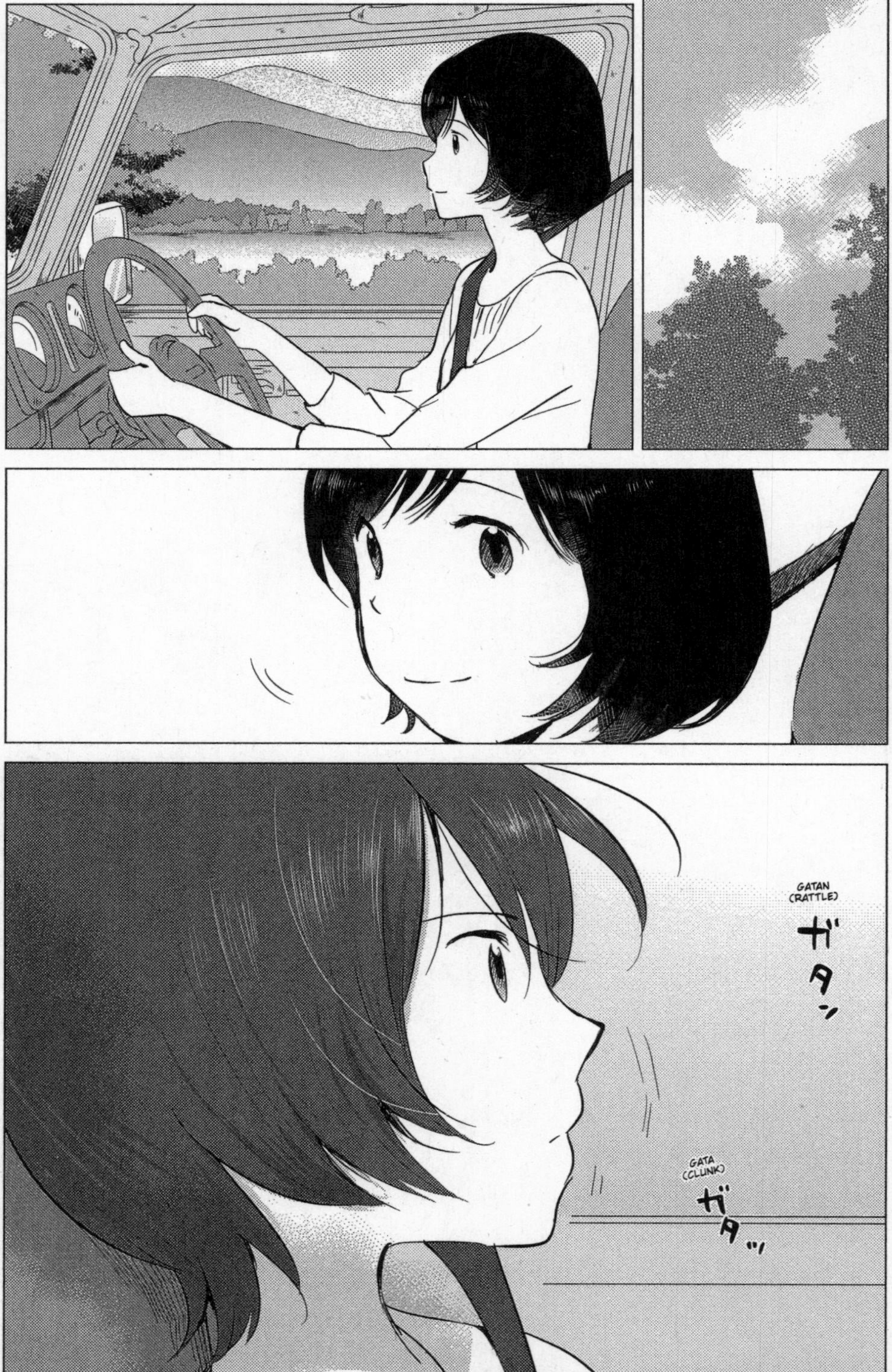
GATAN (RATTLE)
ガタン
GATA (CLUNK)
ガタッ

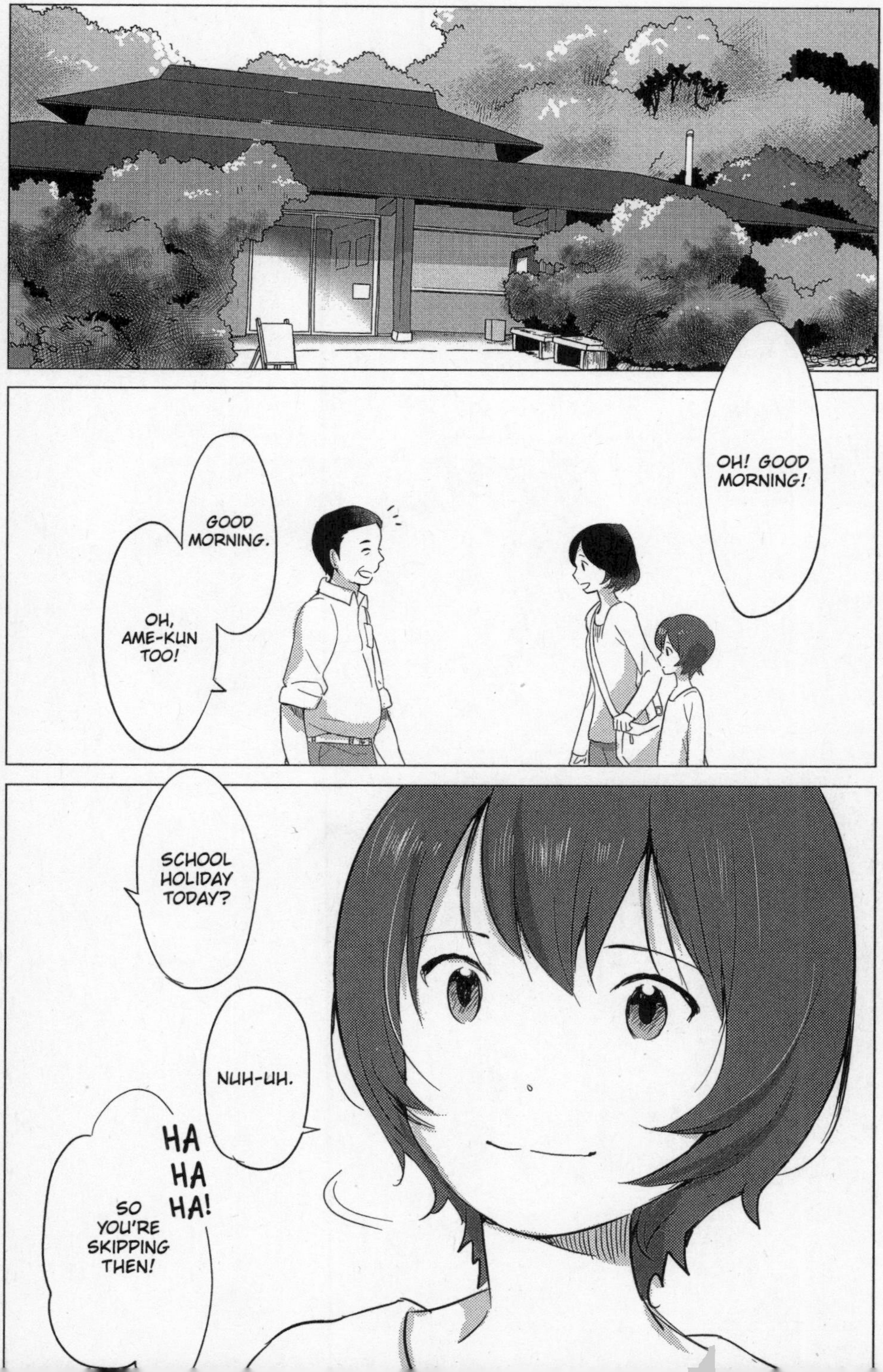
OH! GOOD MORNING!
GOOD MORNING.
OH, AME-KUN TOO!
SCHOOL HOLIDAY TODAY?
NUH-UH.
HA HA HA!
SO YOU'RE SKIPPING THEN!

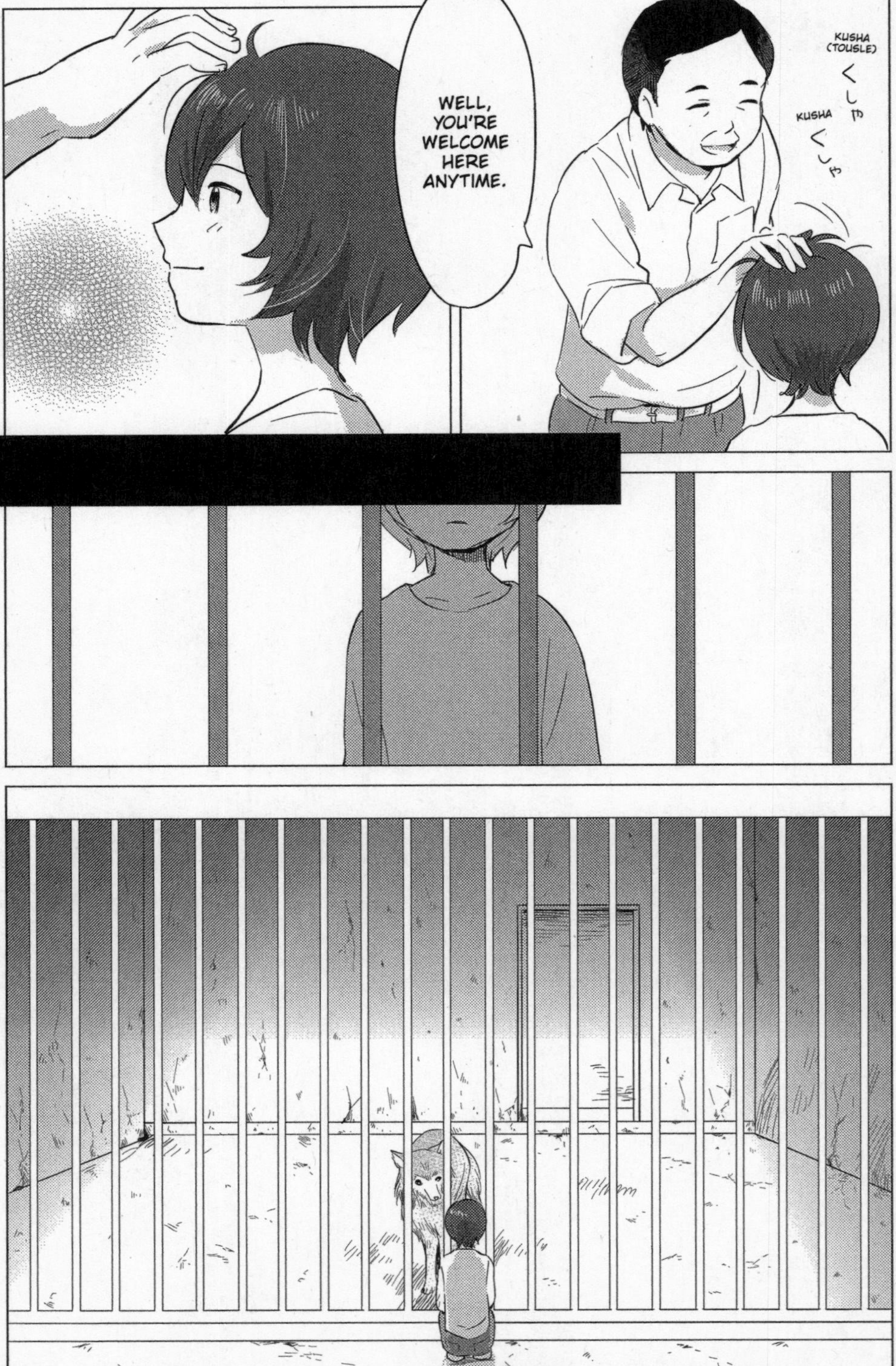
KUSHA (TOUSLE)
くしゃ
KUSHA
くしゃ
WELL, YOU'RE WELCOME HERE ANYTIME.

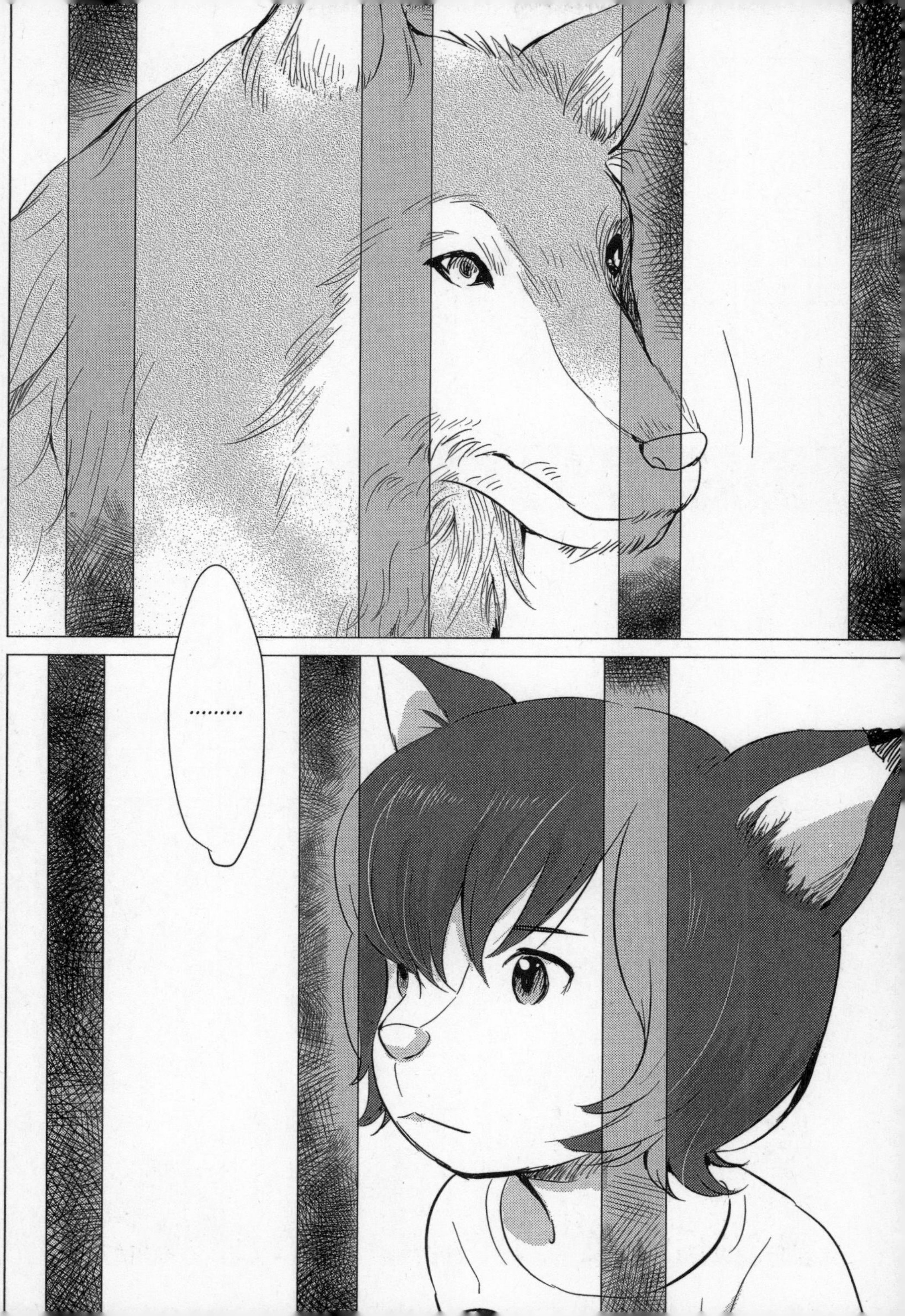
....

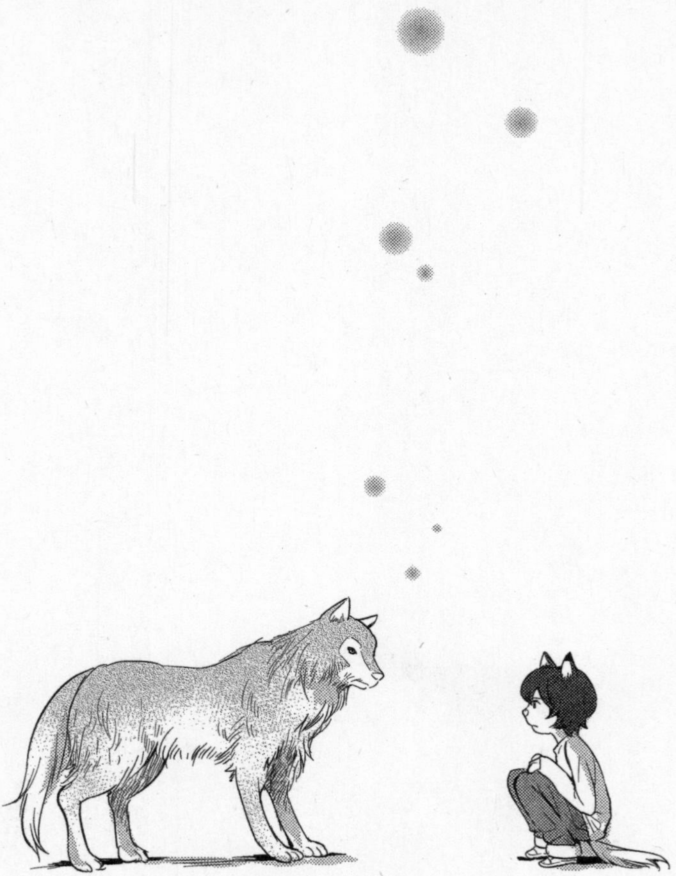

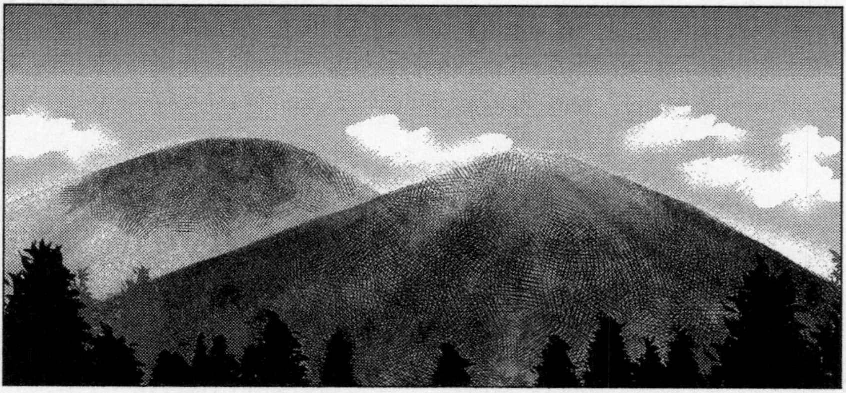

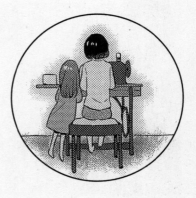

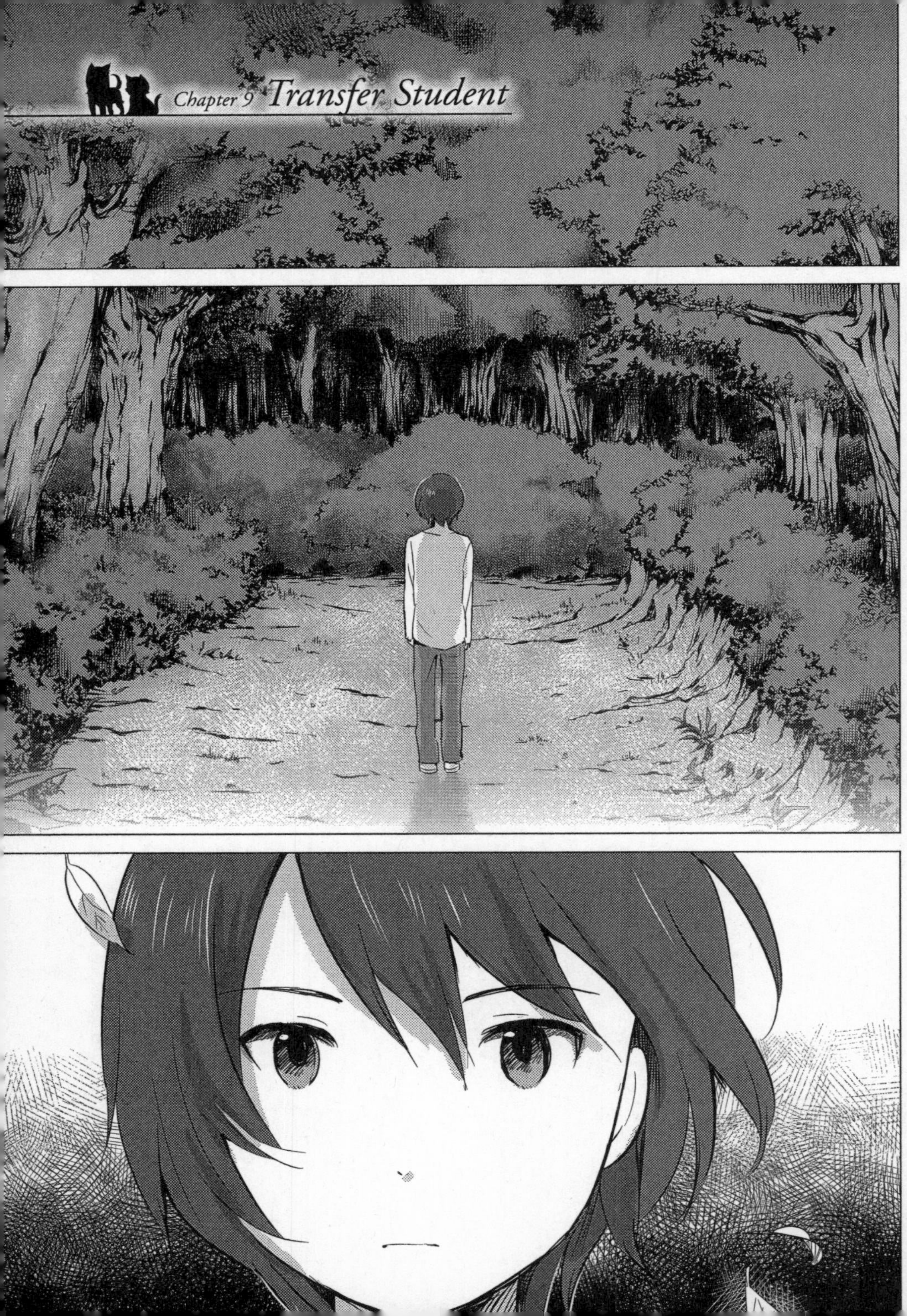
Chapter 9 Transfer Student

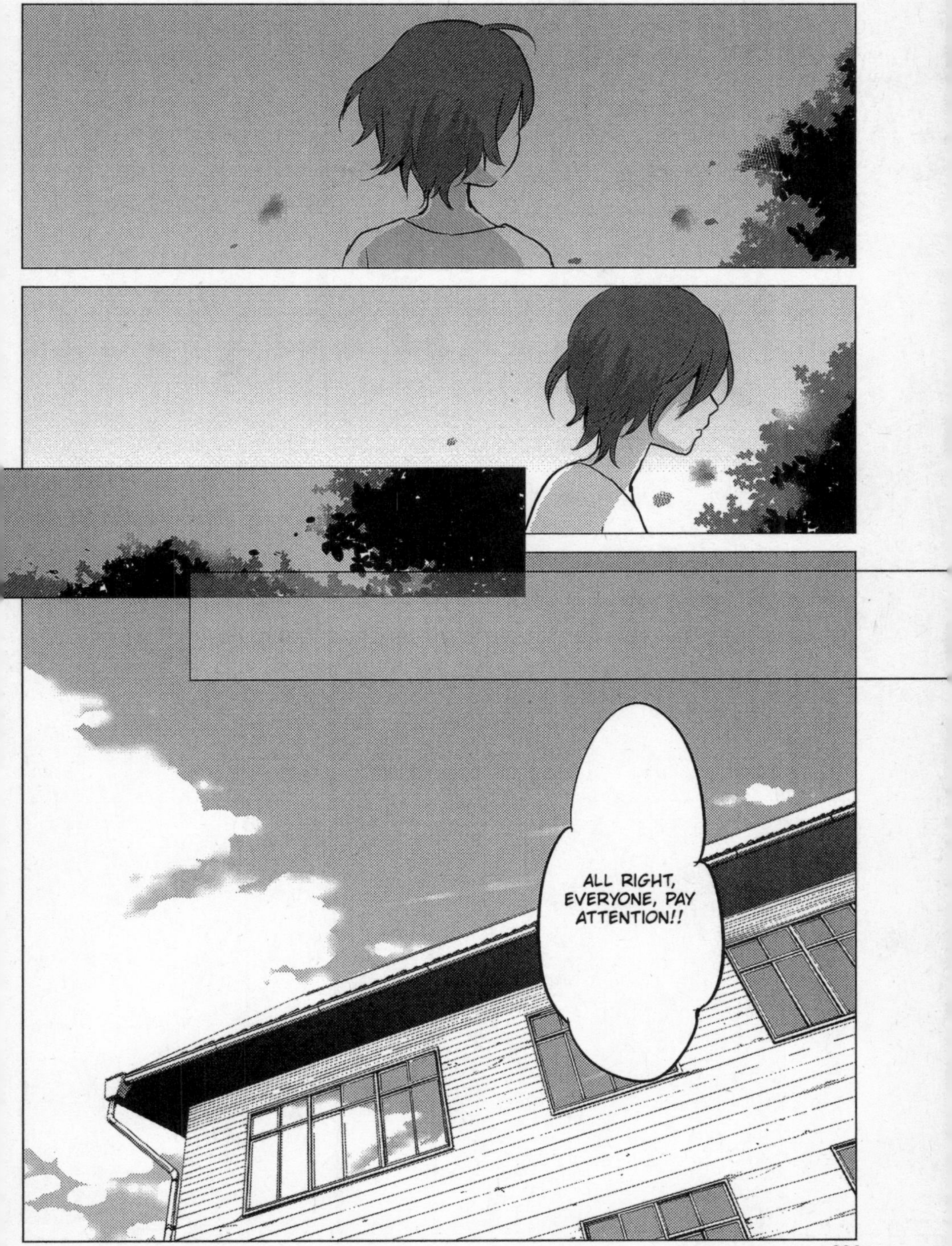
ALL RIGHT, EVERYONE, PAY ATTENTION!!

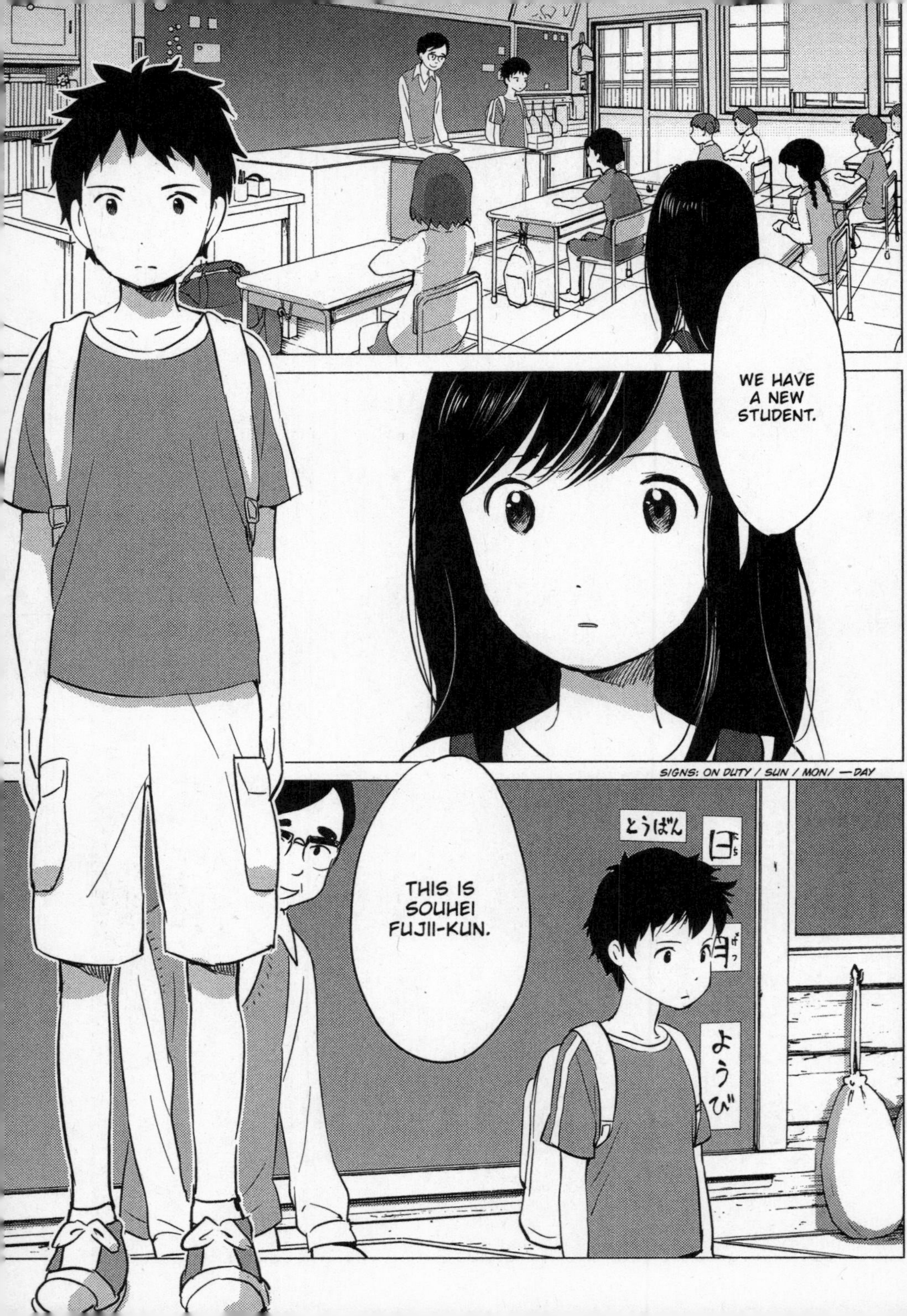
WE HAVE A NEW STUDENT.
SIGNS: ON DUTY / SUN / MON/ —DAY
THIS IS SOUHEI FUJII-KUN.
とうばん
日
月
ようび

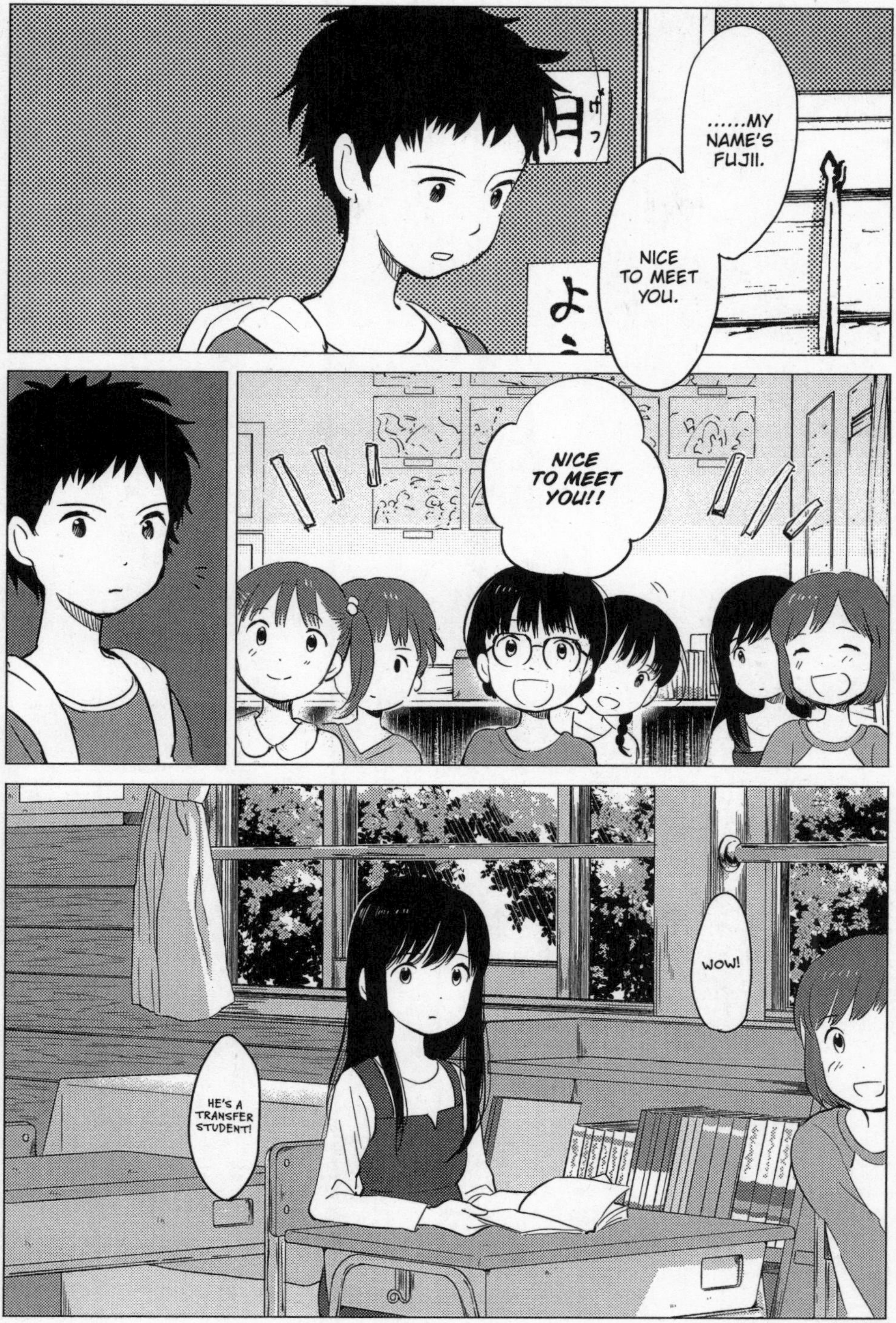
......MY NAME'S FUJII.
NICE TO MEET YOU.
NICE TO MEET YOU!!
WOW!
HE'S A TRANSFER STUDENT!

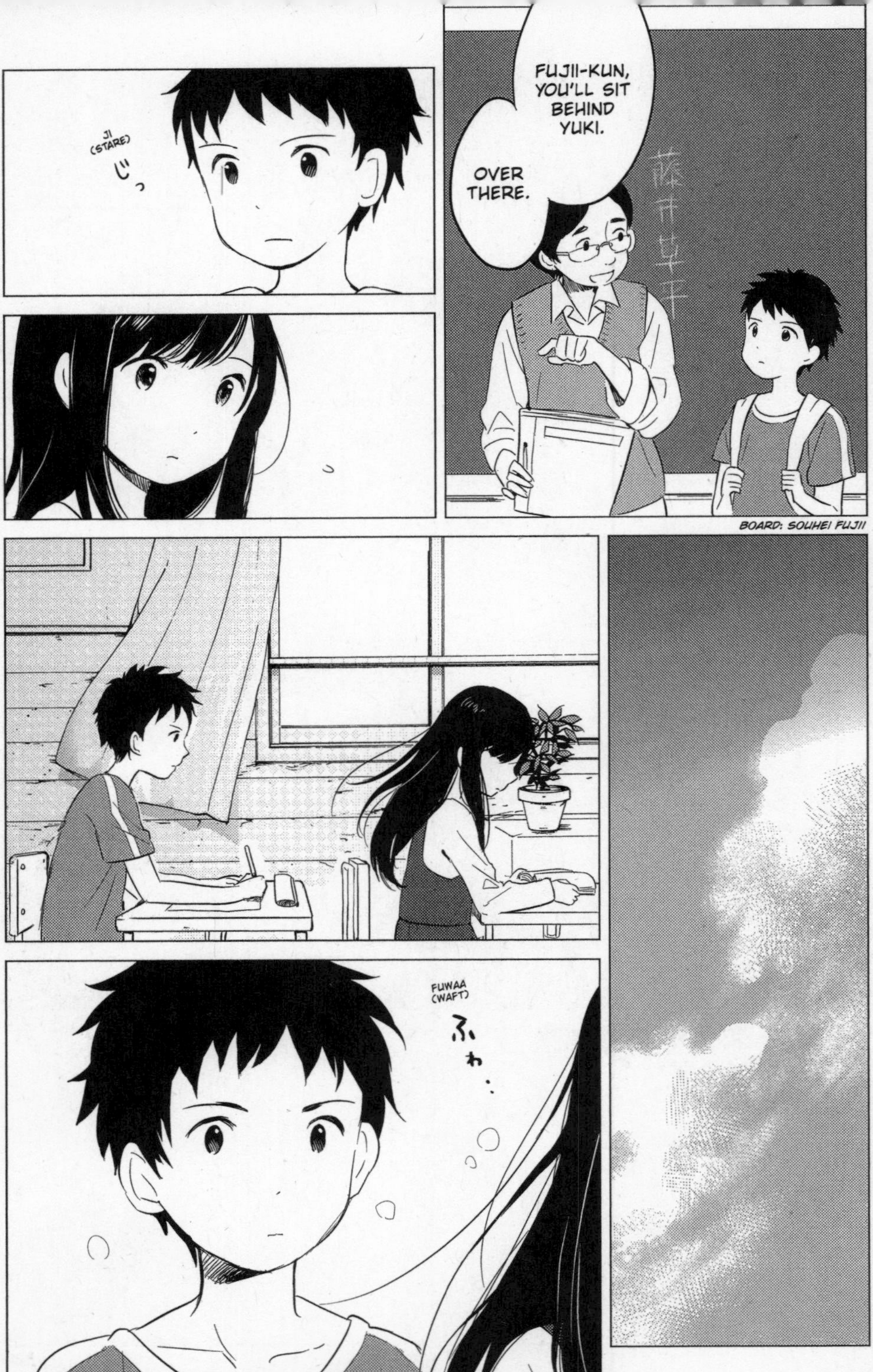
FUJII-KUN, YOU'LL SIT BEHIND YUKI.
OVER THERE.
BOARD: SOUHEI FUJII
JI (STARE)
じっ
FUWAA (WAFT)
ふわ‥

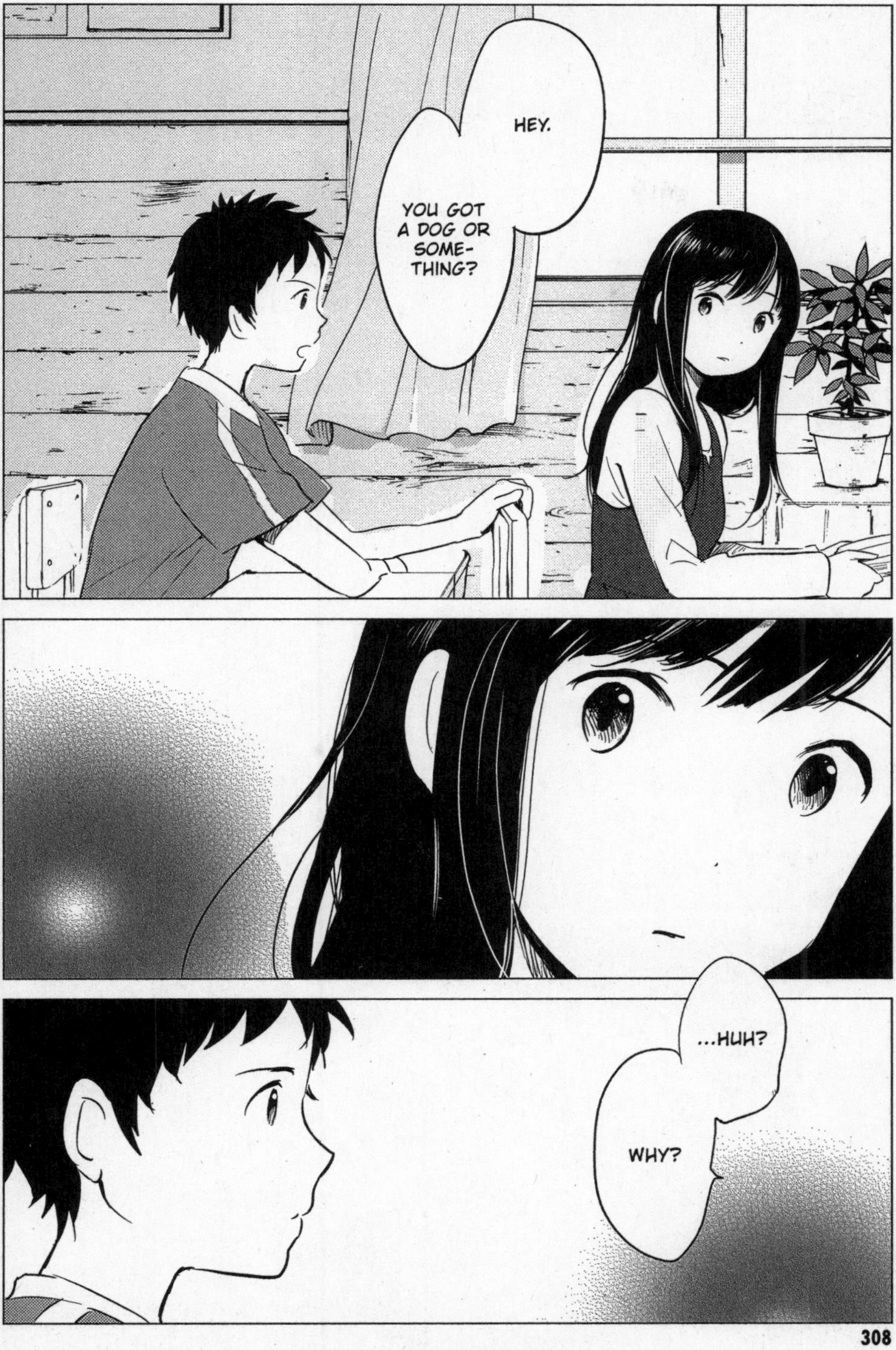
HEY.
YOU GOT A DOG OR SOME-THING?
...HUH?
WHY?

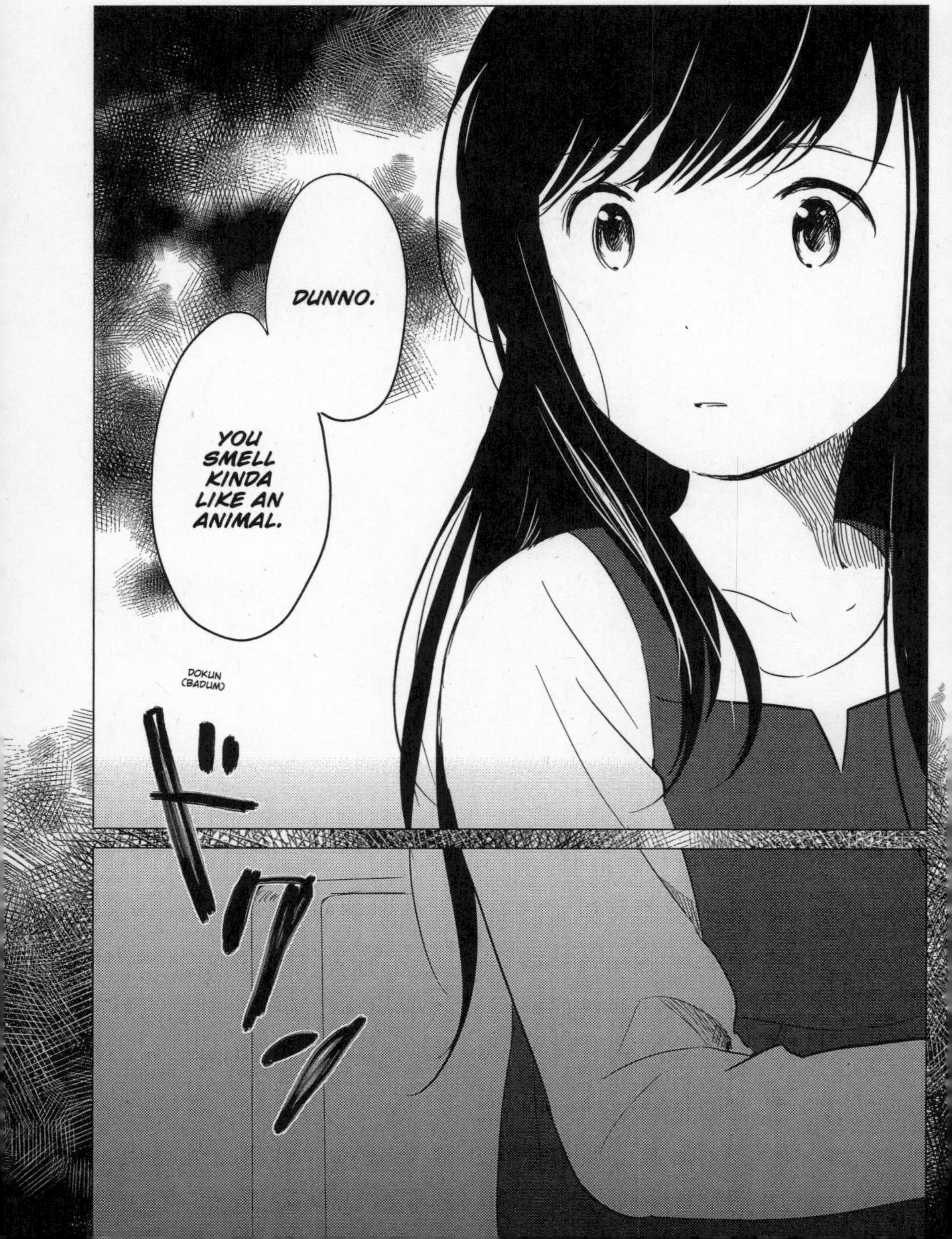
DUNNO.
YOU SMELL KINDA LIKE AN ANIMAL.
DOKUN (BADUM)
ドクン

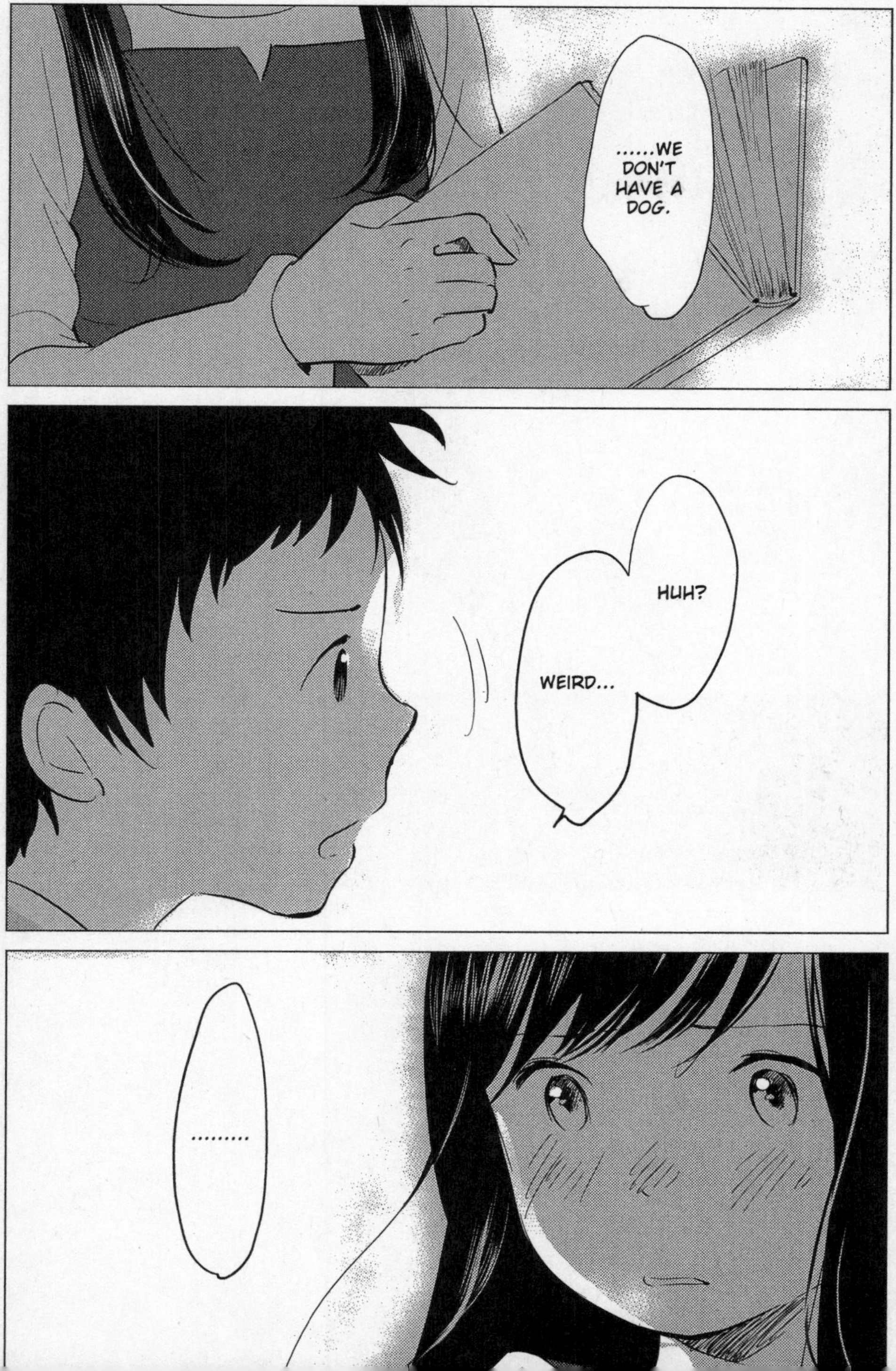
......WE DON'T HAVE A DOG.
HUH?
WEIRD...
....

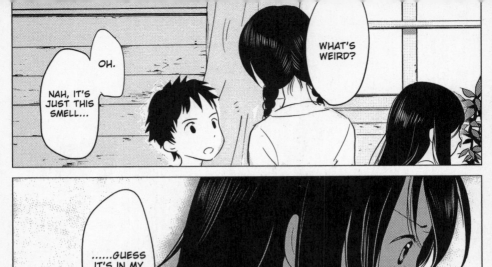

OH.

NAH, IT'S JUST THIS SMELL...

WHAT'S WEIRD?

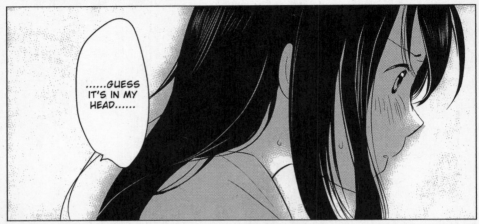

......GUESS IT'S IN MY HEAD......

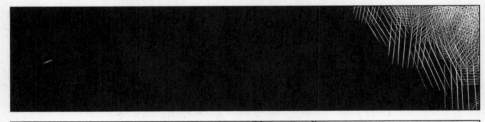

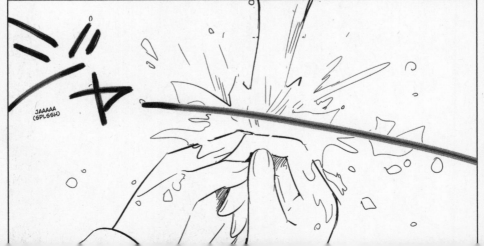

JAAAAA
(SPLSSH)

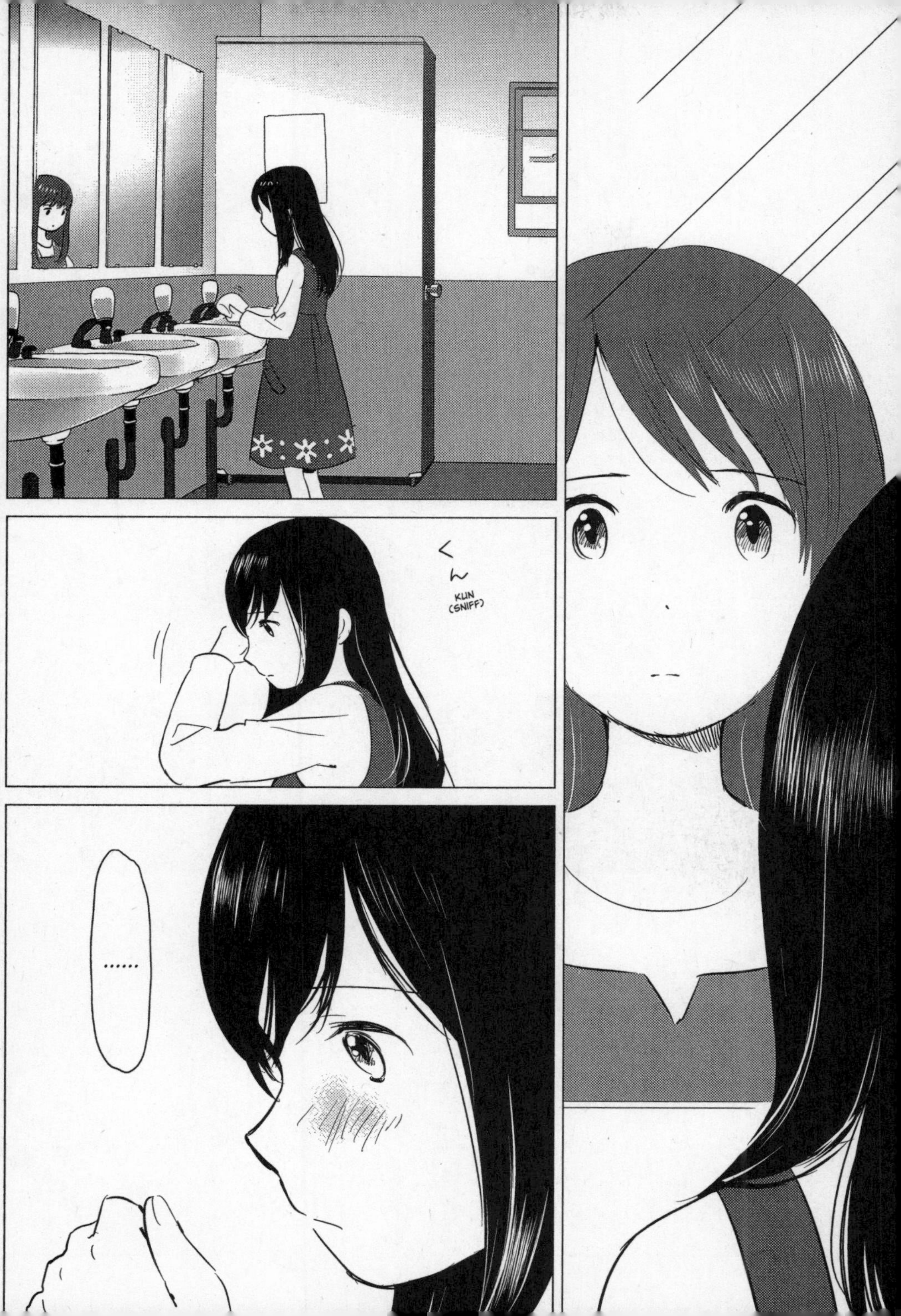
くん
KUN (SNIFF)
......

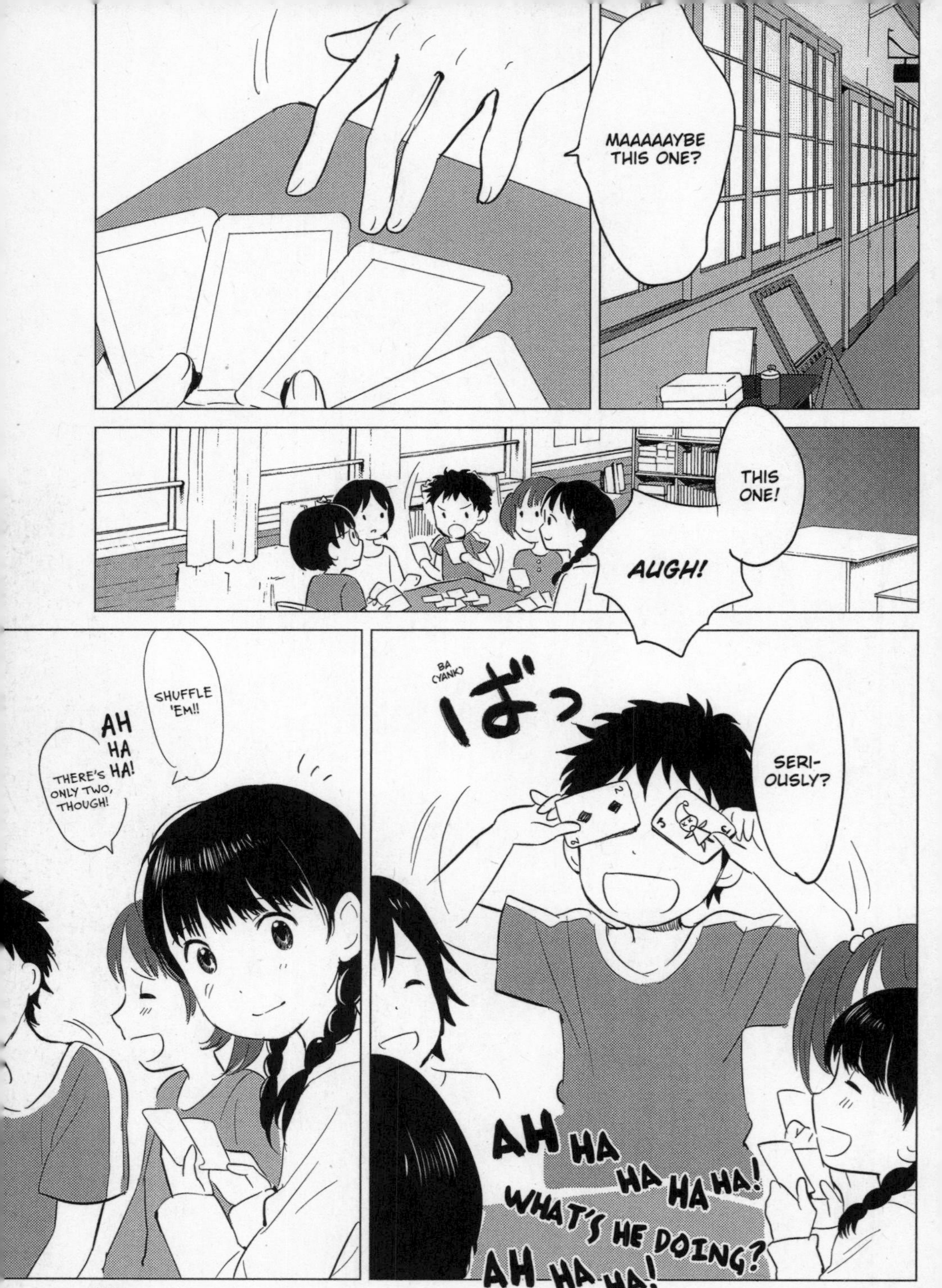
MAAAAAYBE THIS ONE?
THIS ONE!
AUGH!
BA (YANK)
ばっ
SERI-OUSLY?
AH HA HA HA HA! WHAT'S HE DOING? AH HA HA!
SHUFFLE 'EM!!
AH HA HA!
THERE'S ONLY TWO, THOUGH!

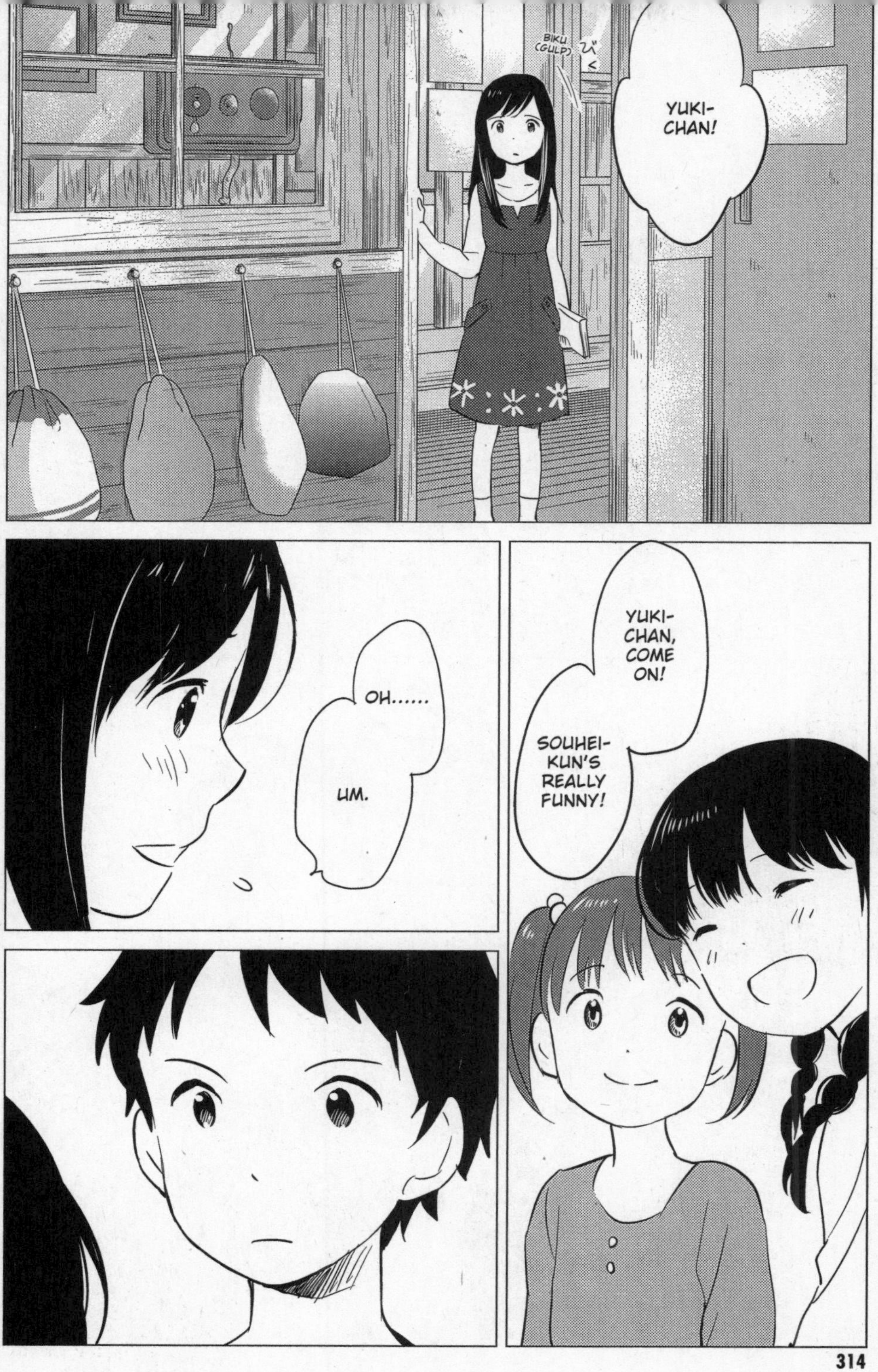
YUKI-CHAN!
BIKU (GULP) びく
YUKI-CHAN, COME ON!
SOUHEI-KUN'S REALLY FUNNY!
OH......
UM.

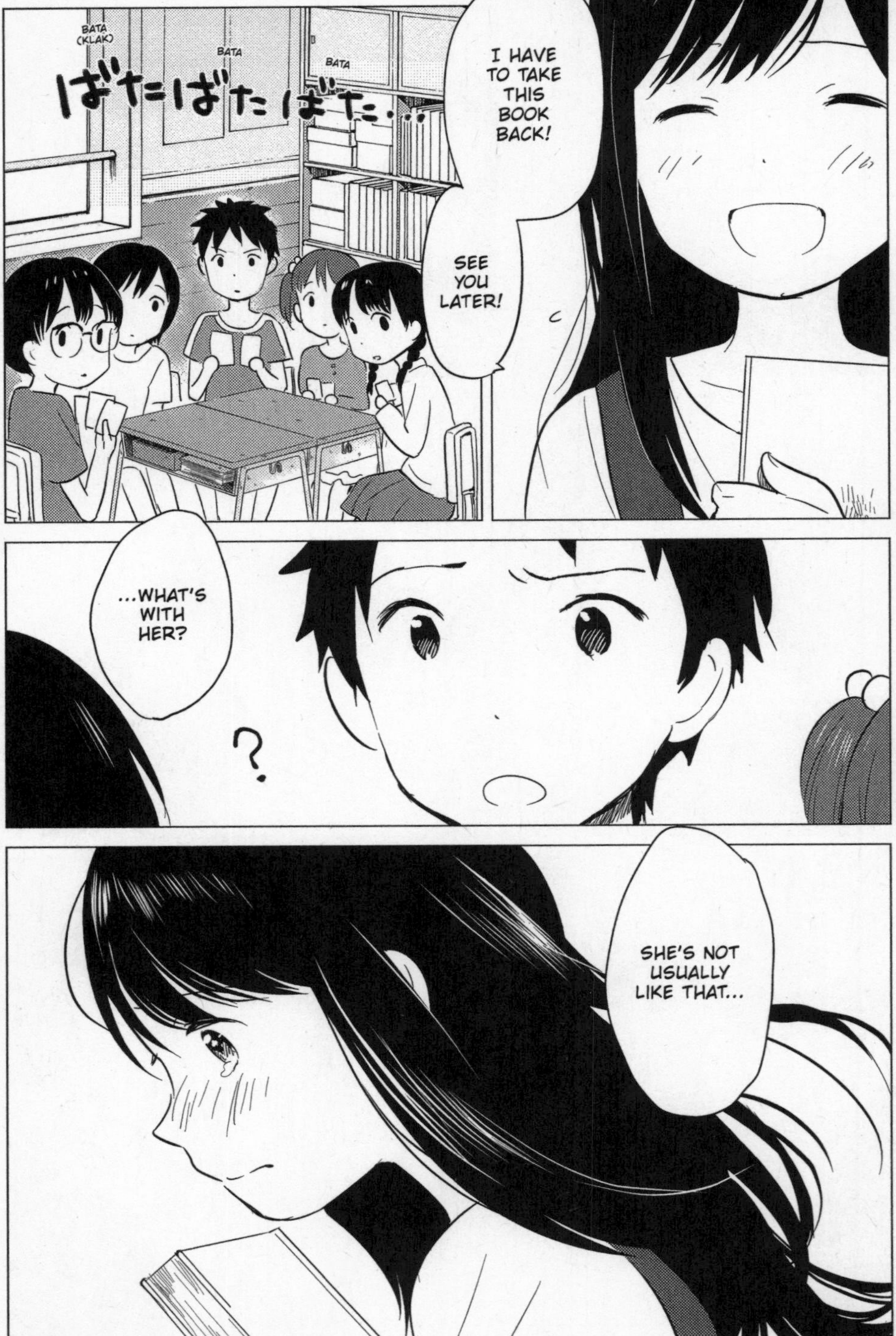
I HAVE TO TAKE THIS BOOK BACK!
SEE YOU LATER!
BATA (KLAK)
BATA
BATA
ばたばたばた…
...WHAT'S WITH HER?
?
SHE'S NOT USUALLY LIKE THAT...

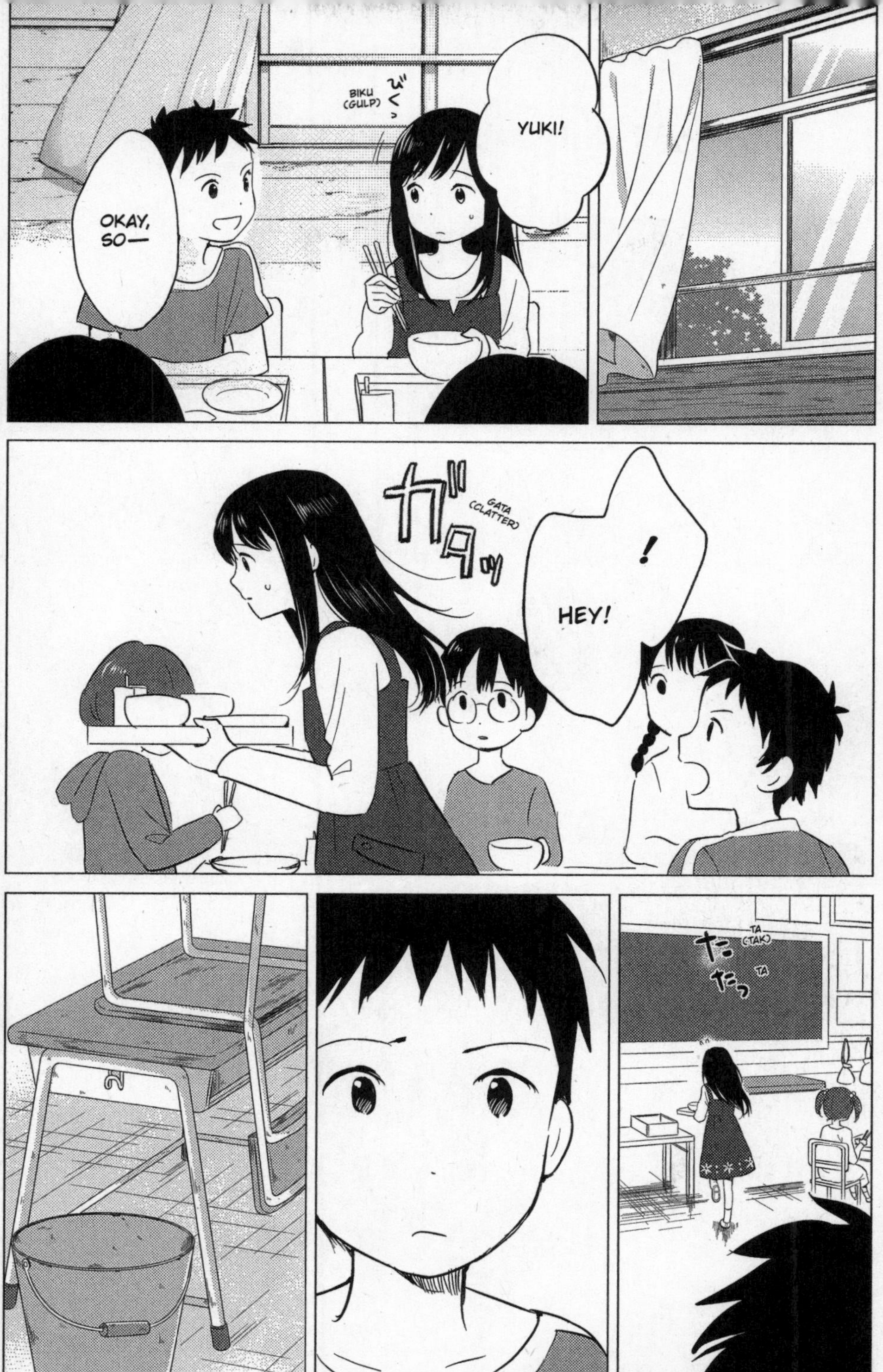

YUKI!
びくっ
BIKU (GULP)
OKAY, SO—
!
HEY!
ガタッ
GATA (CLATTER)
たっ たっ
TA (TAK) TA

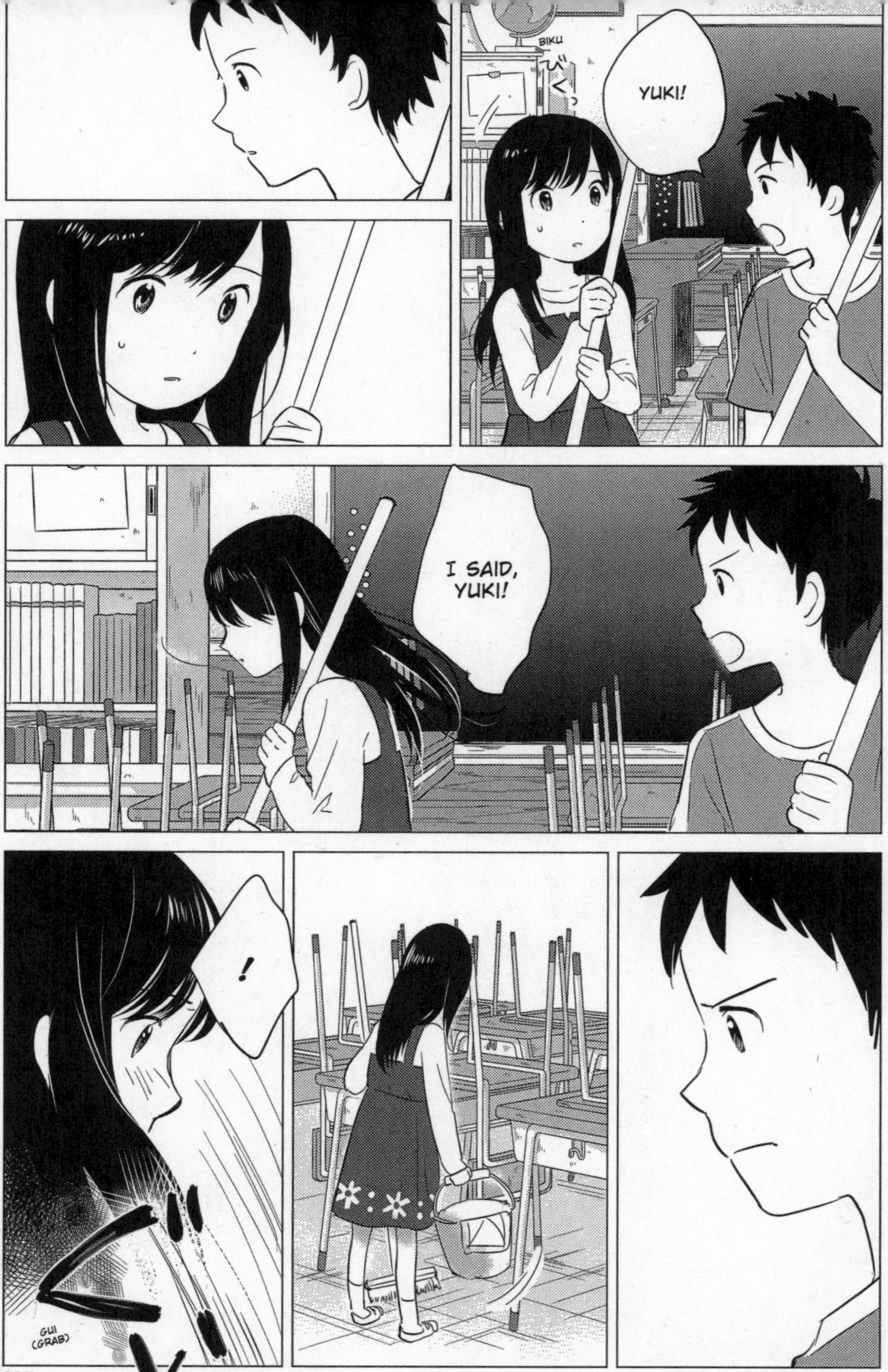
BIKU
YUKI!
I SAID, YUKI!
!
GUI (GRAB)

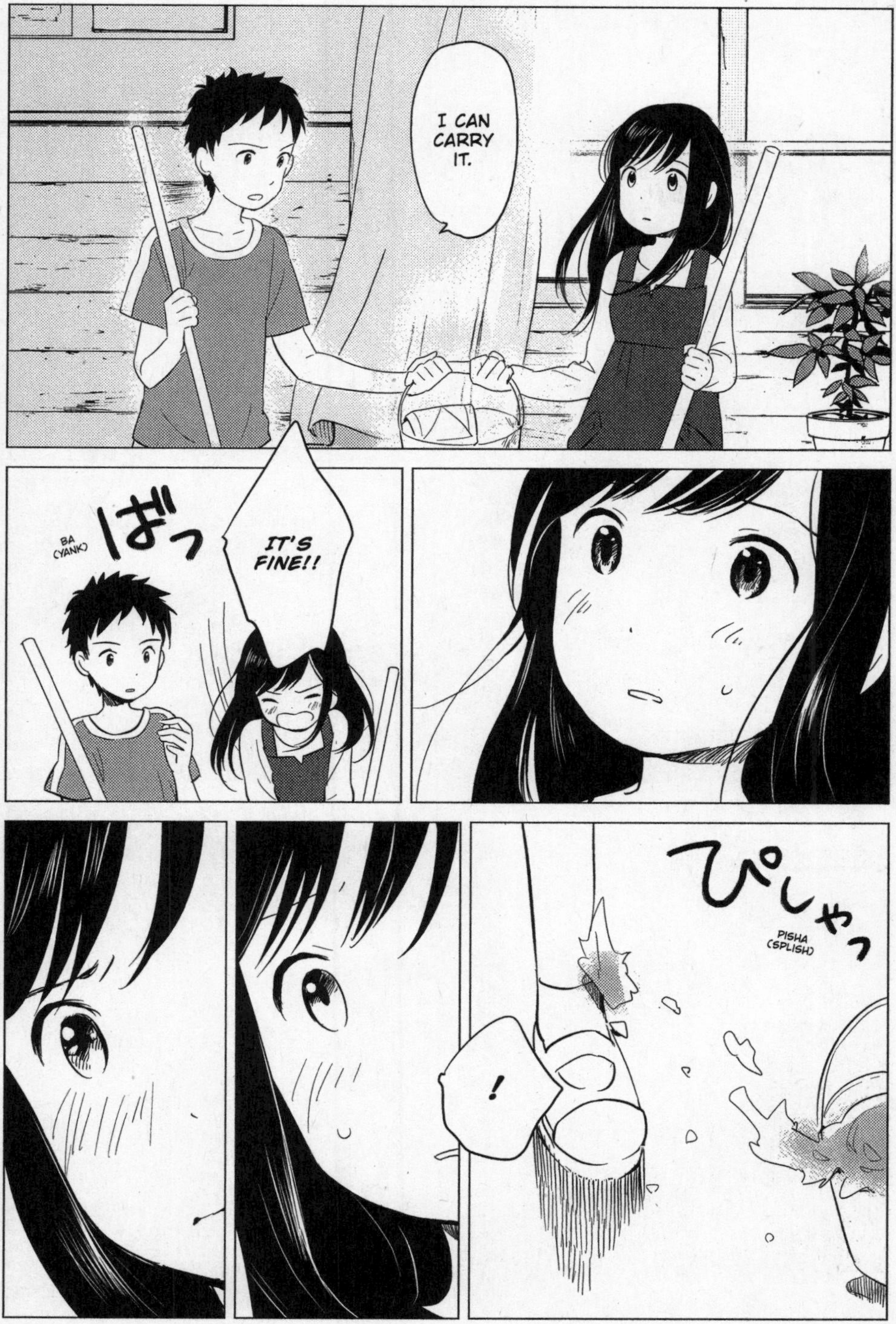
I CAN CARRY IT.
IT'S FINE!!
ばっ
BA (YANK)
ぴしゃっ
PISHA (SPLISH)
!

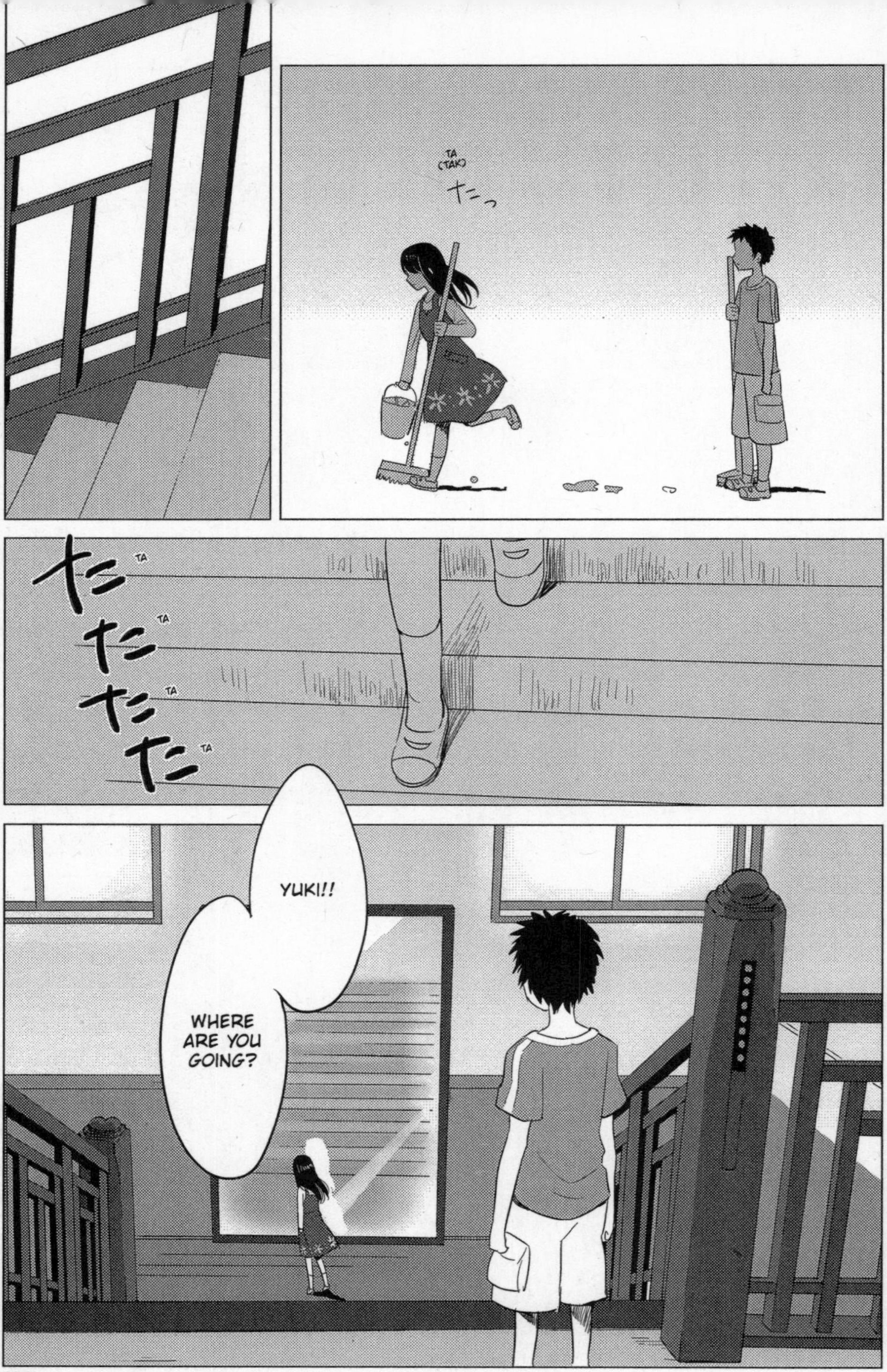

TA (TAK)
たっ
たたたた
TA TA TA TA
YUKI!!
WHERE ARE YOU GOING?

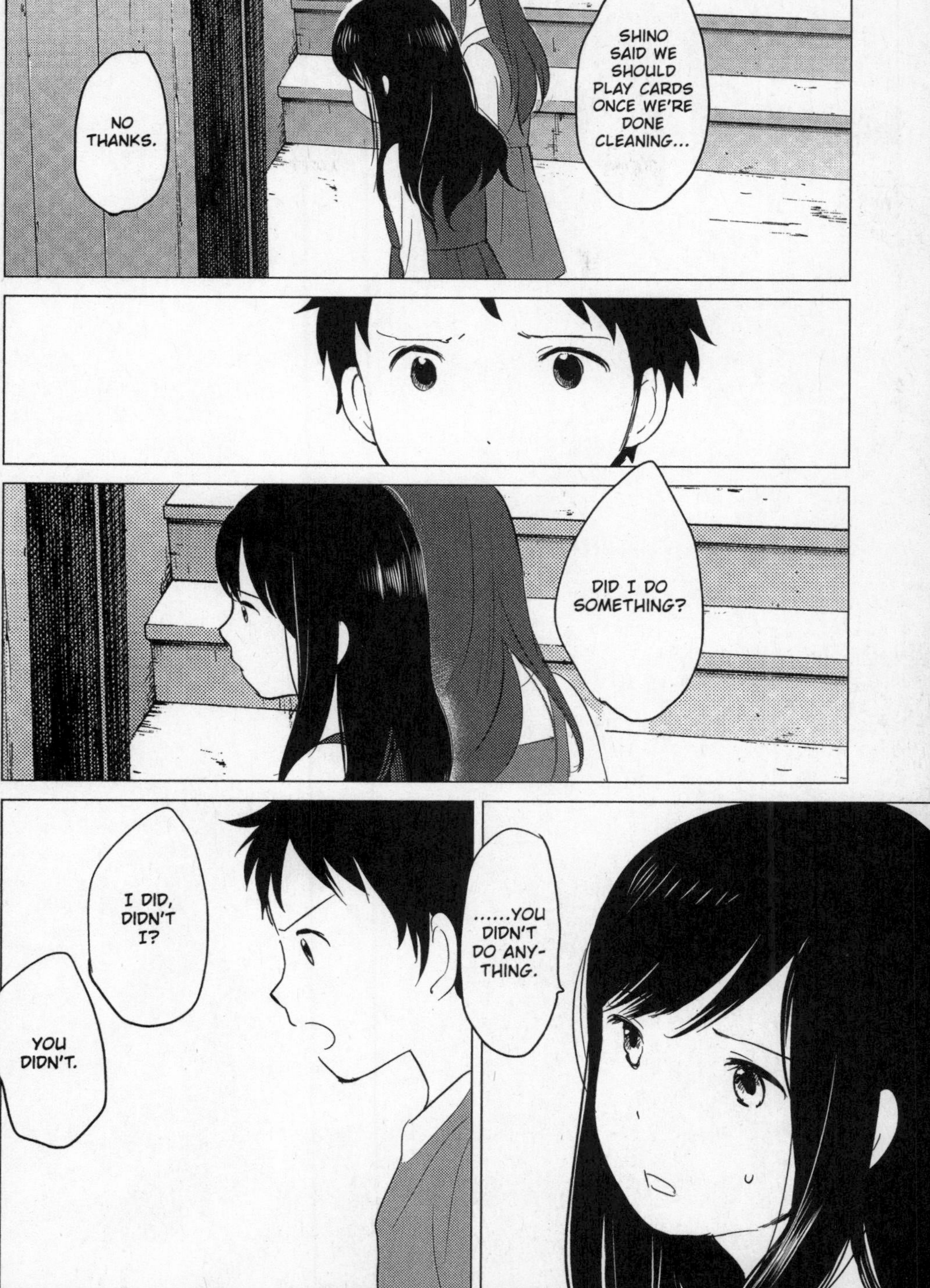

SHINO SAID WE SHOULD PLAY CARDS ONCE WE'RE DONE CLEANING...
NO THANKS.
DID I DO SOMETHING?
......YOU DIDN'T DO ANY-THING.
I DID, DIDN'T I?
YOU DIDN'T.

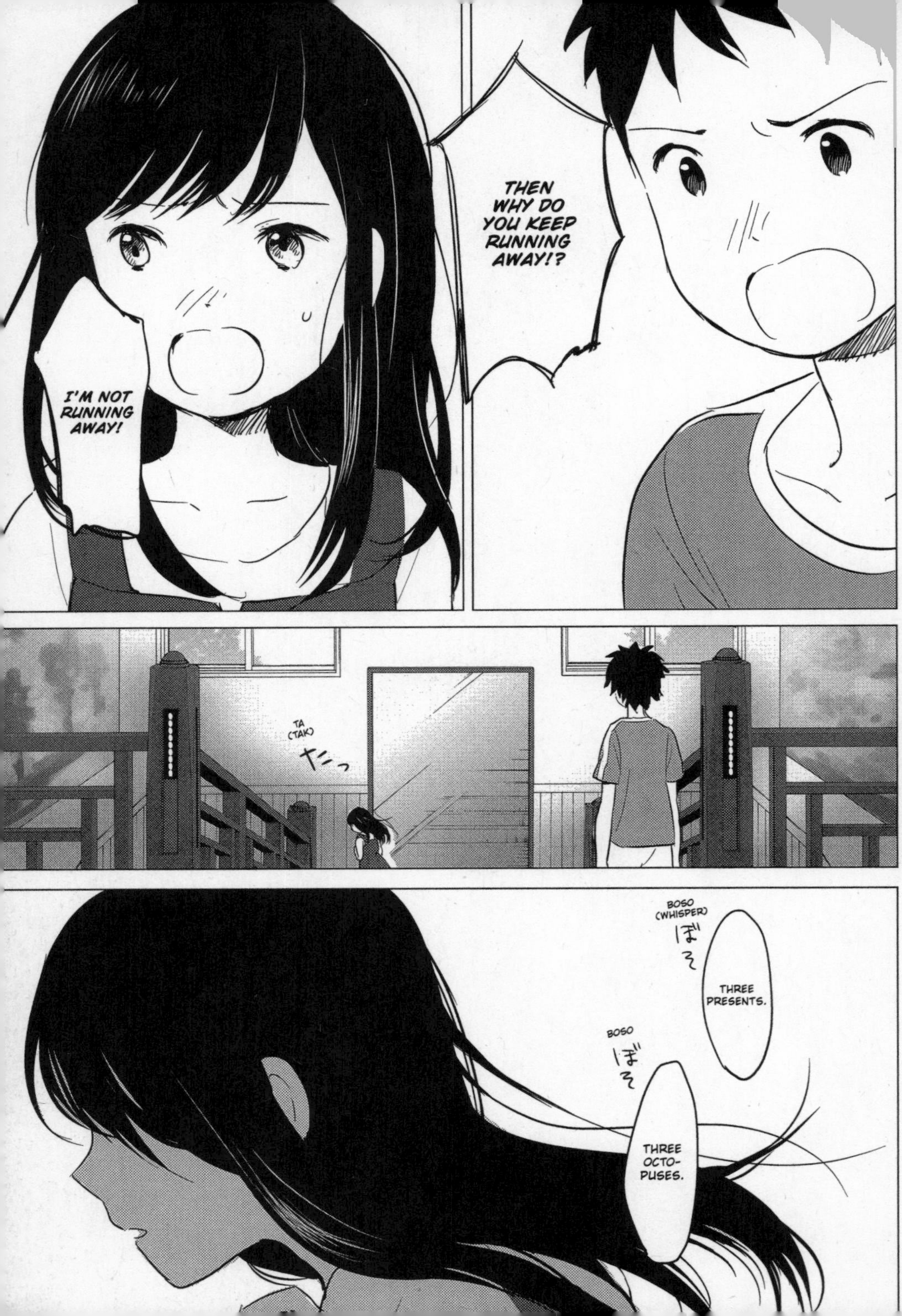
THEN WHY DO YOU KEEP RUNNING AWAY!?
I'M NOT RUNNING AWAY!
TA (TAK)
タッ
BOSO (WHISPER)
ぼそ
THREE PRESENTS.
BOSO
ぼそ
THREE OCTO-PUSES.

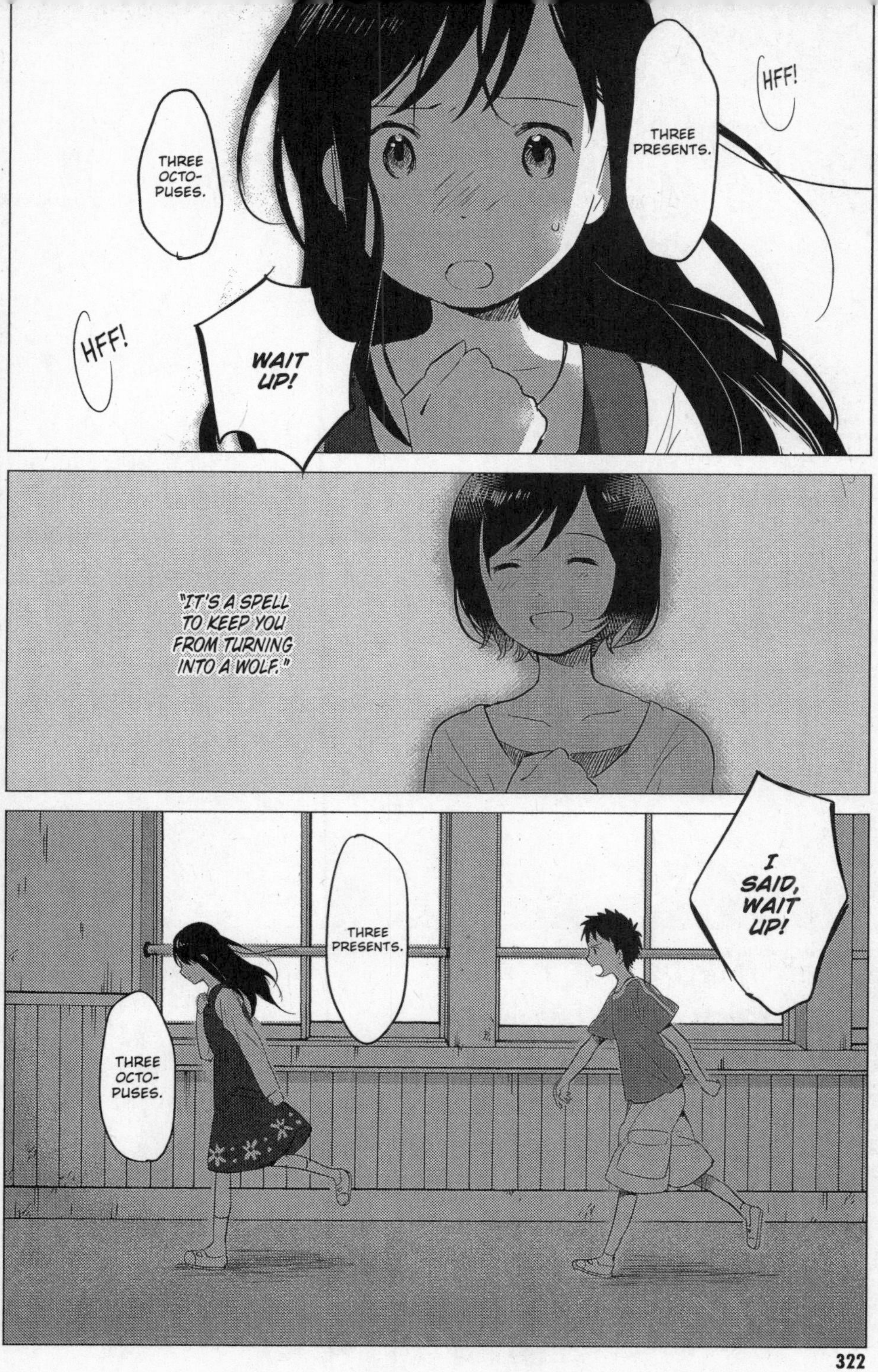
HFF!
THREE PRESENTS.
THREE OCTO-PUSES.
WAIT UP!
HFF!
"IT'S A SPELL TO KEEP YOU FROM TURNING INTO A WOLF."
I SAID, WAIT UP!
THREE PRESENTS.
THREE OCTO-PUSES.

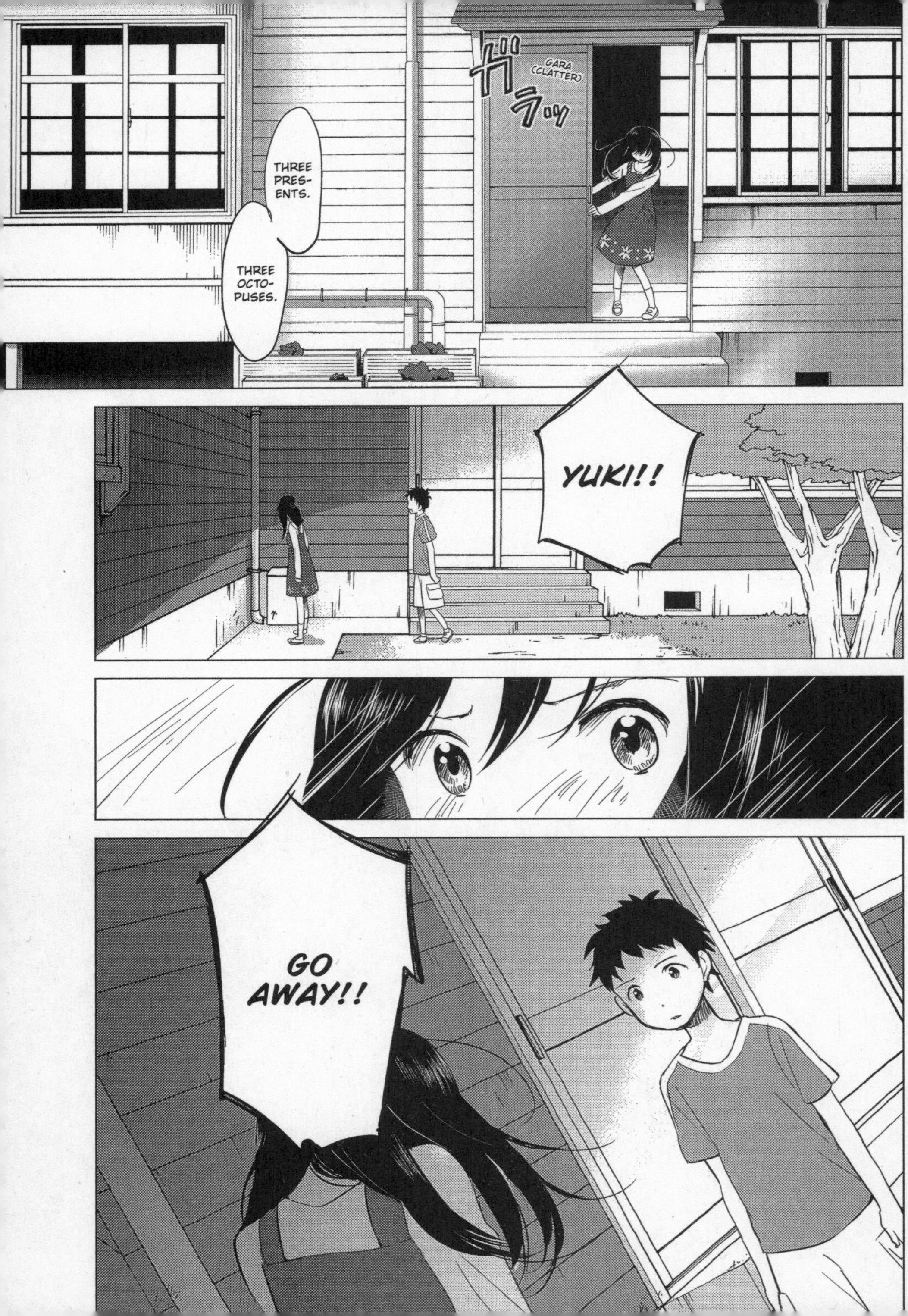
ガラッ
GARA (CLATTER)
THREE PRES-ENTS.
THREE OCTO-PUSES.
YUKI!!
GO AWAY!!

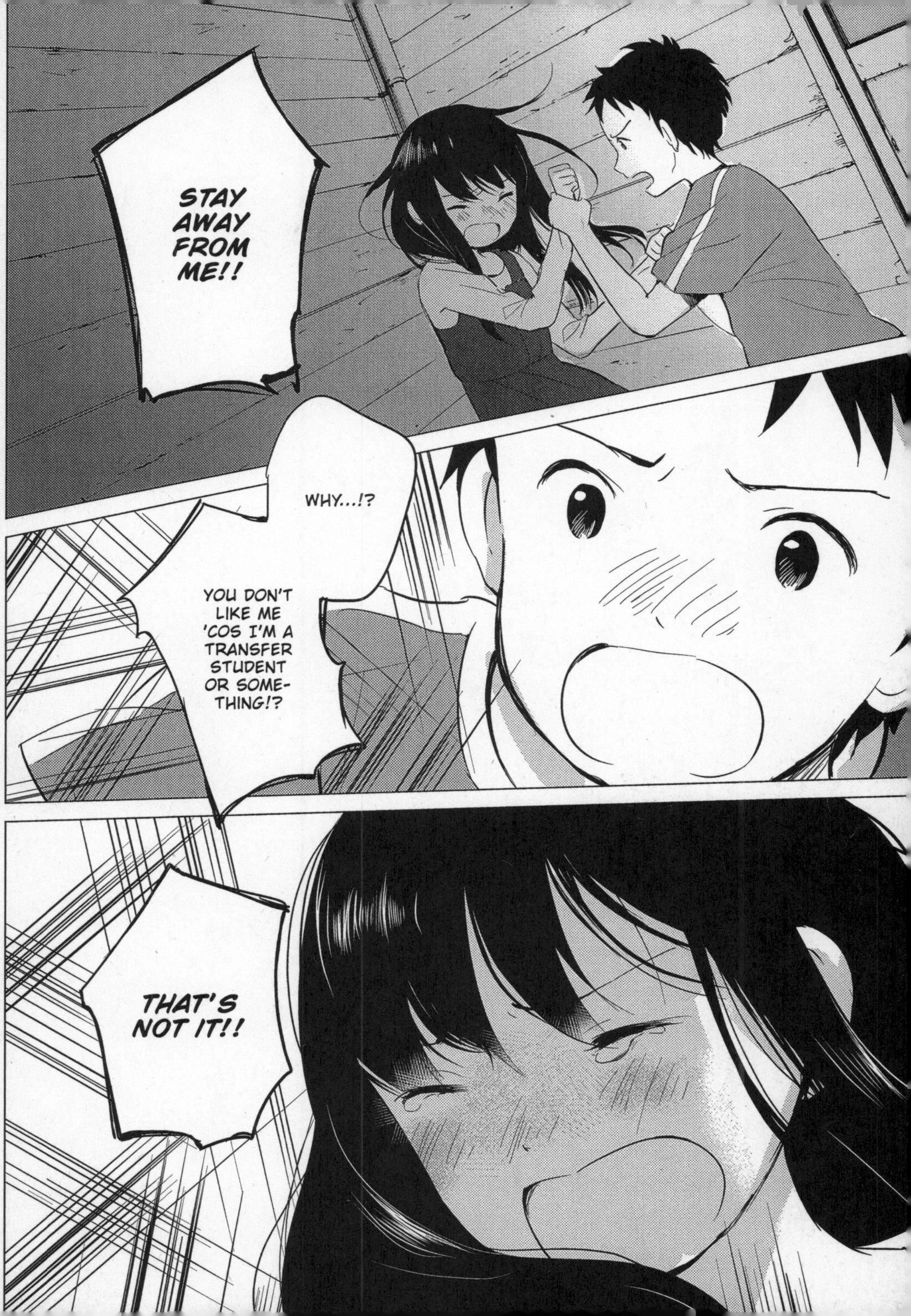
STAY AWAY FROM ME!!
WHY...!?
YOU DON'T LIKE ME 'COS I'M A TRANSFER STUDENT OR SOME-THING!?
THAT'S NOT IT!!

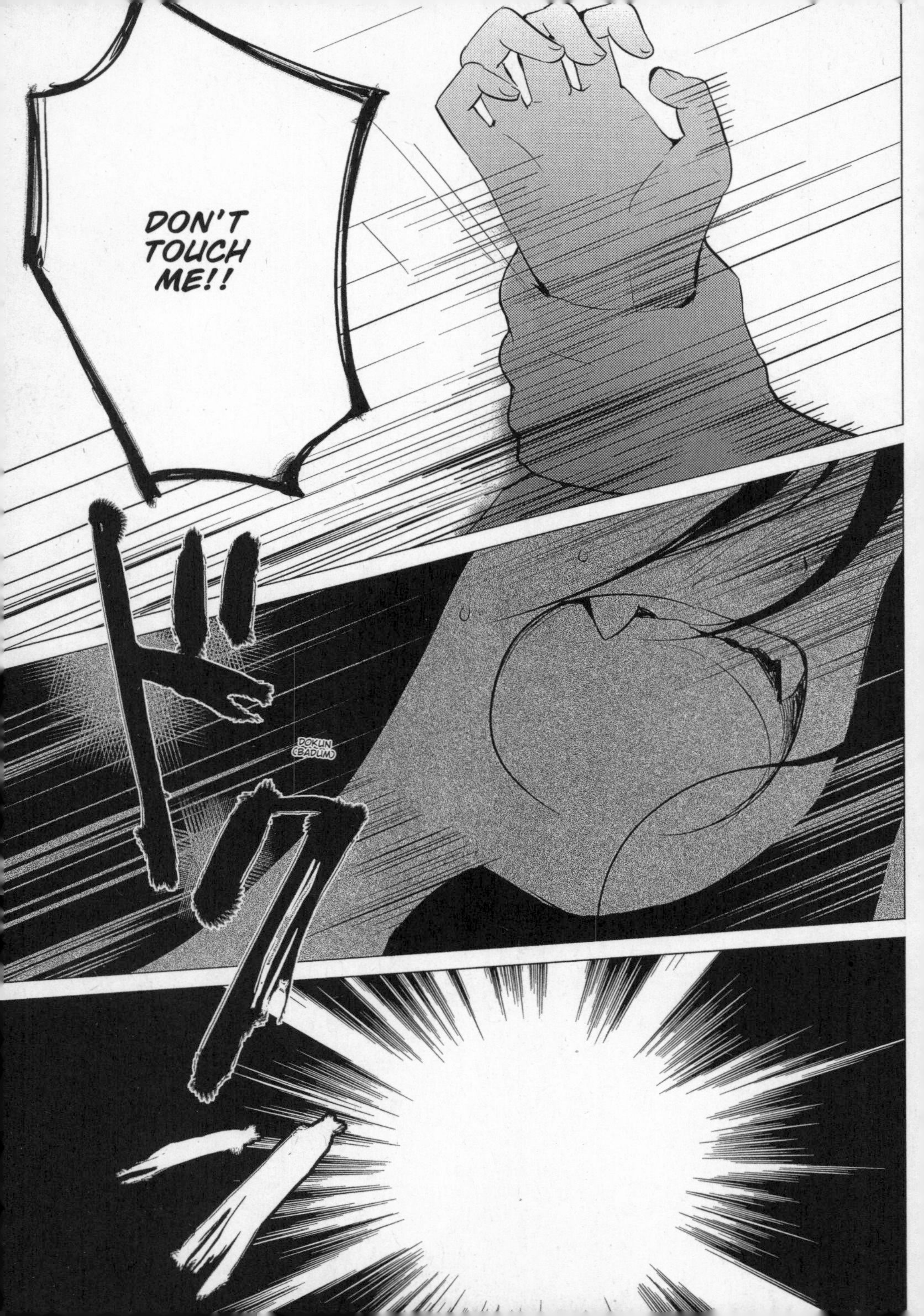
DON'T TOUCH ME!!
DOKUN (BADUM)

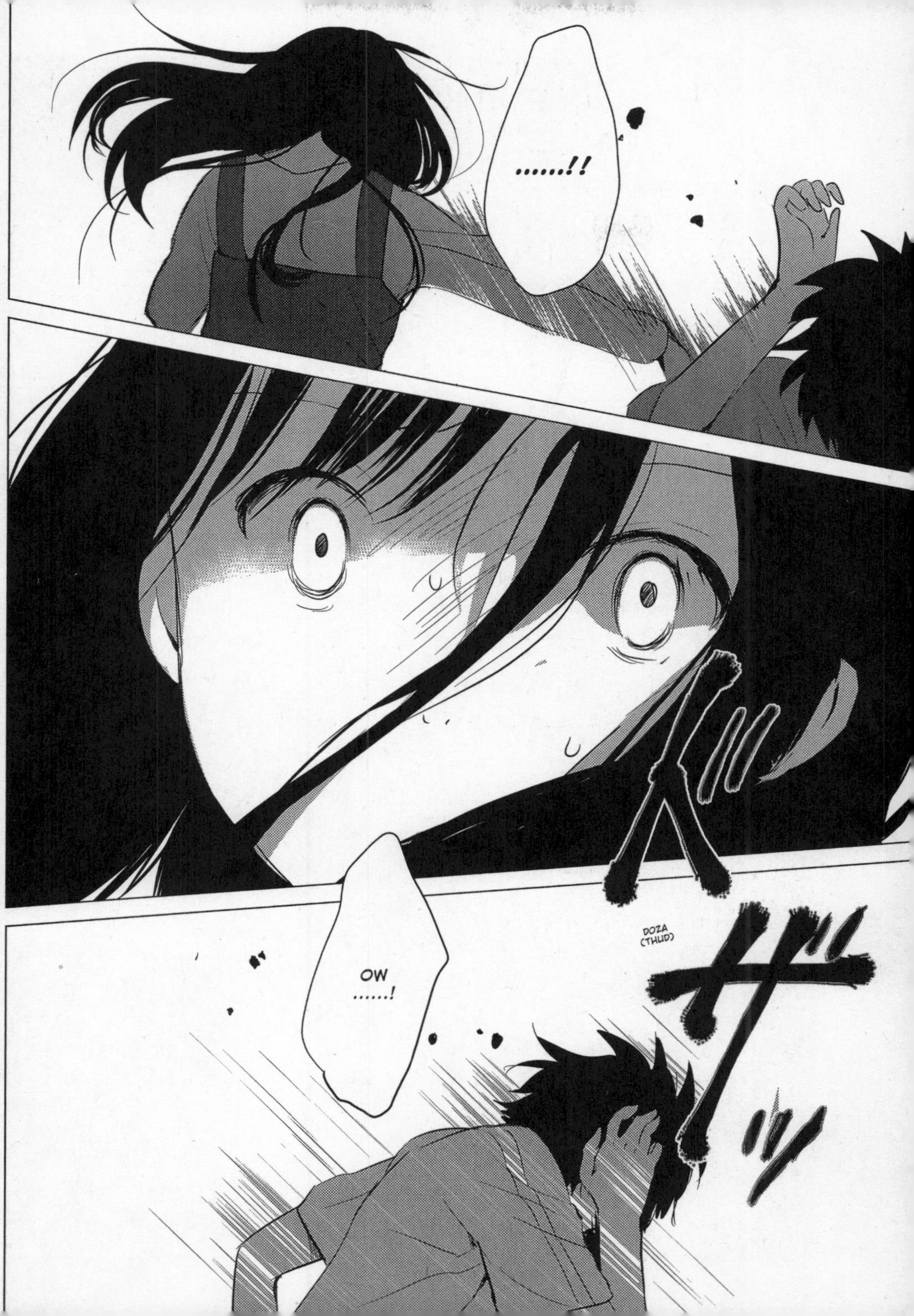
......!!
OW
......!
DOZA
(THUD)

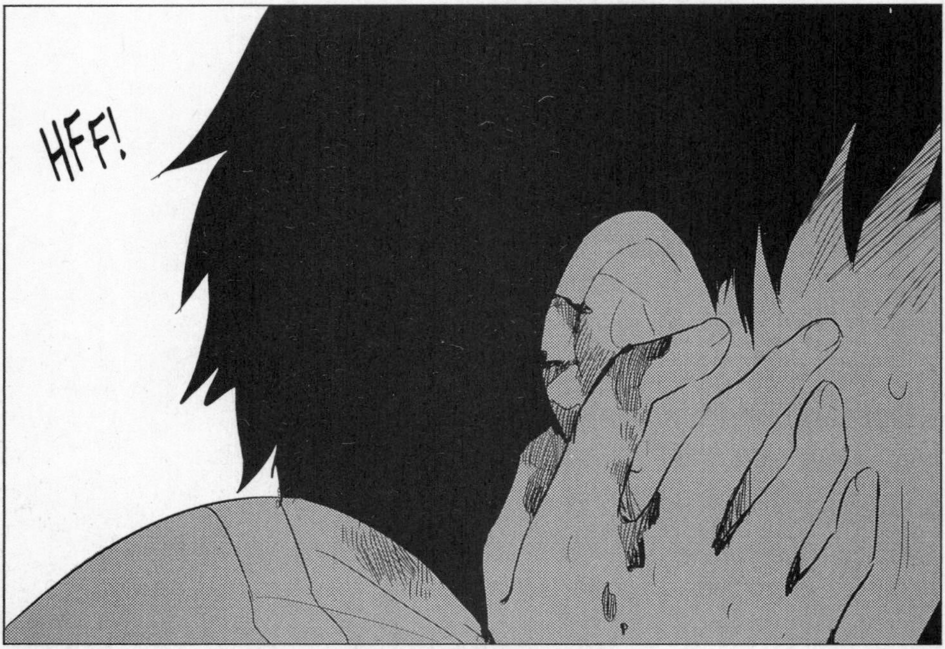
HFF!
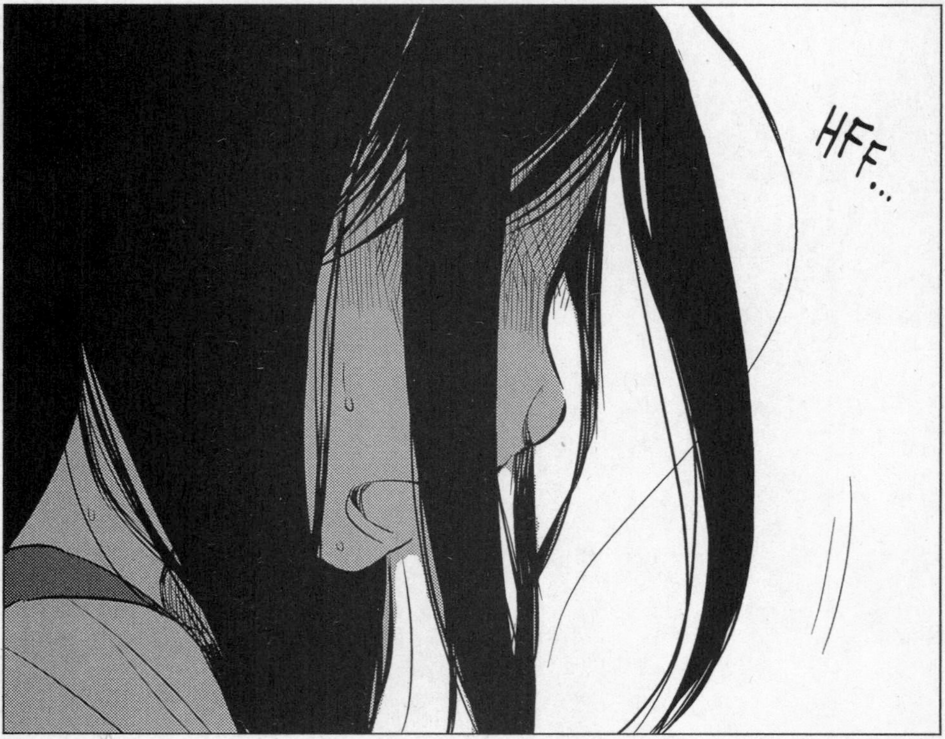
HFF...

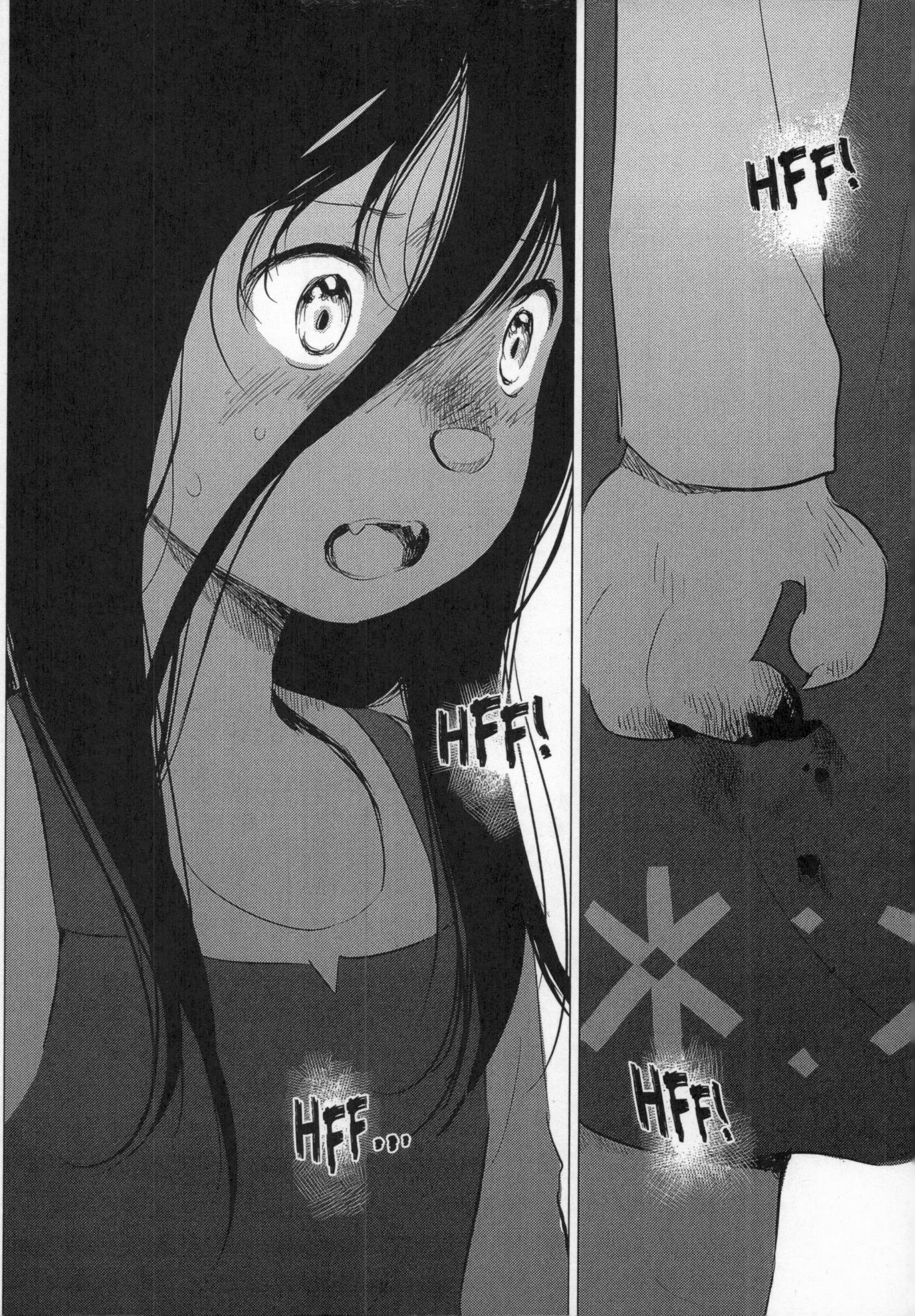
HFF!
HFF!
HFF!
HFF...

WOLF CHILDREN
AME & YUKI

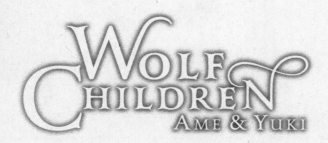

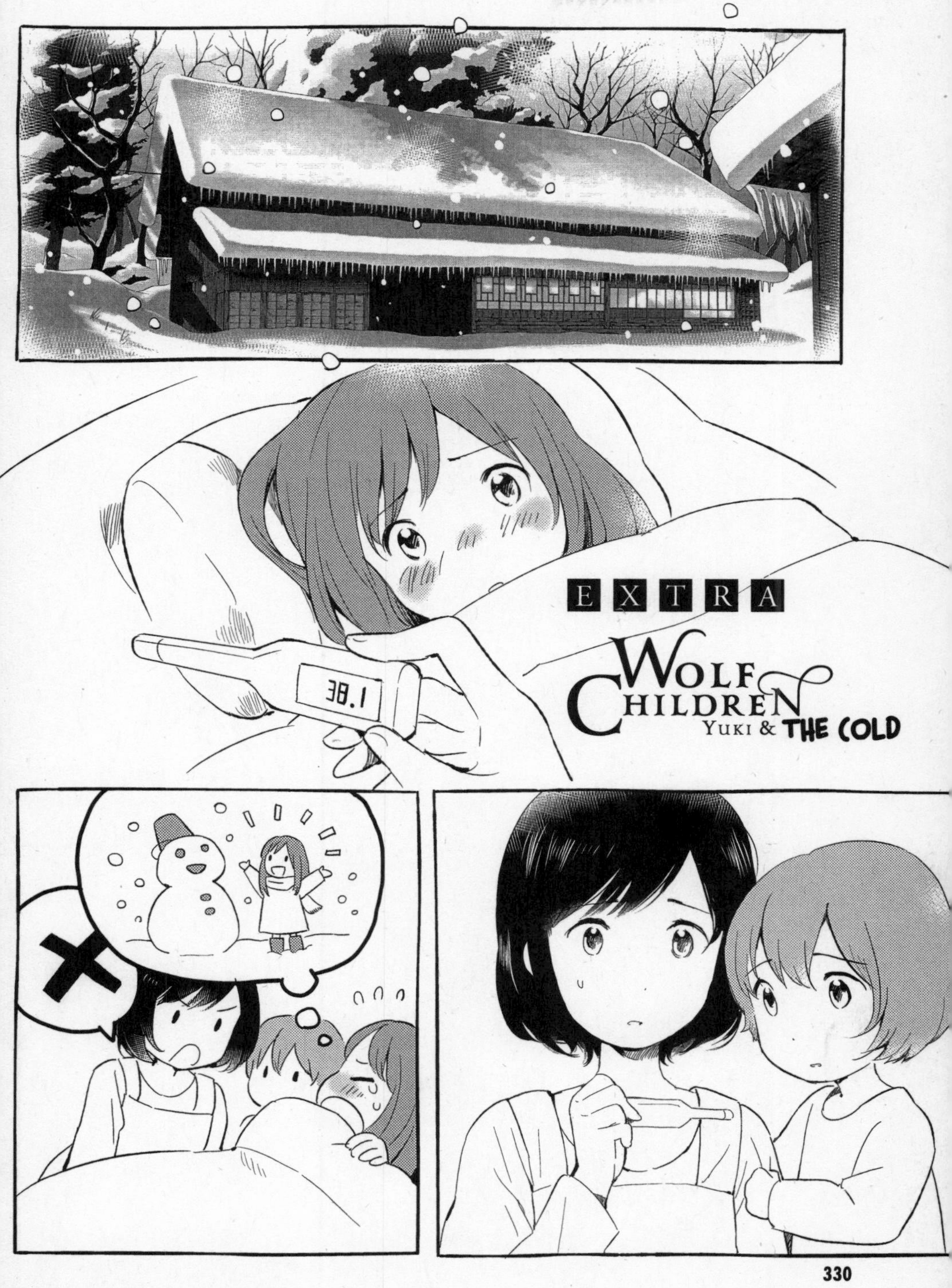
EXTRA
WOLF CHILDREN
YUKI & THE COLD
38.1

Check Out Receipt

Prince Albert - John M. Cuelenaere
(306) 763-8496
http://www.jmcpl.ca/

Monday, June 7, 2021 11:49:15 AM
05608

Item: 31234550017154
Title: A man and his cat. Volume 2
Material: Book
Due: 05/07/2021

Item: 33292013670777
Title: Wolf children Ame & Yuki
Material: Book
Due: 05/07/2021

Total items: 2

Thank you! If you would like to update your library notification to telephone, email or text message, please contact your local library.

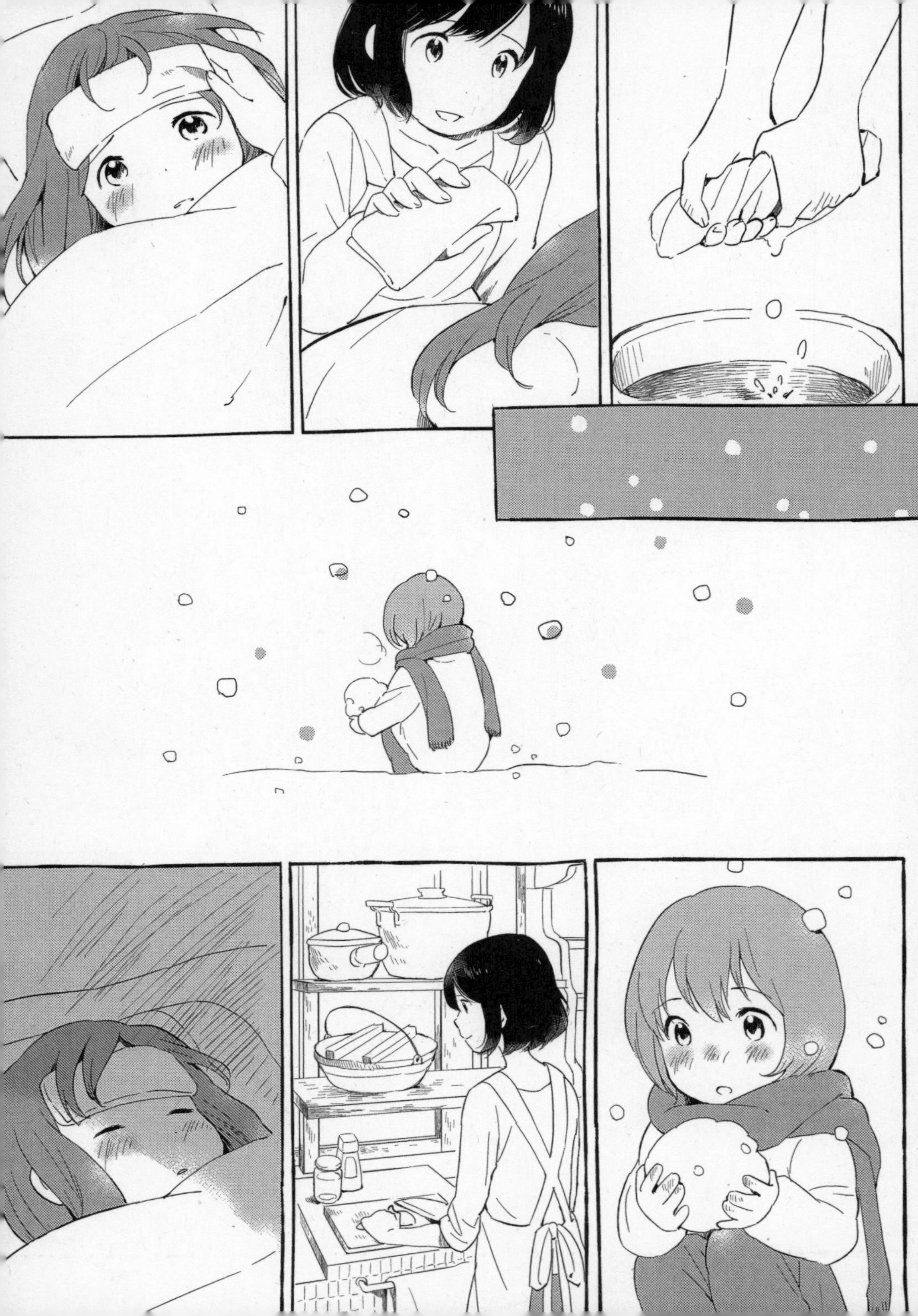

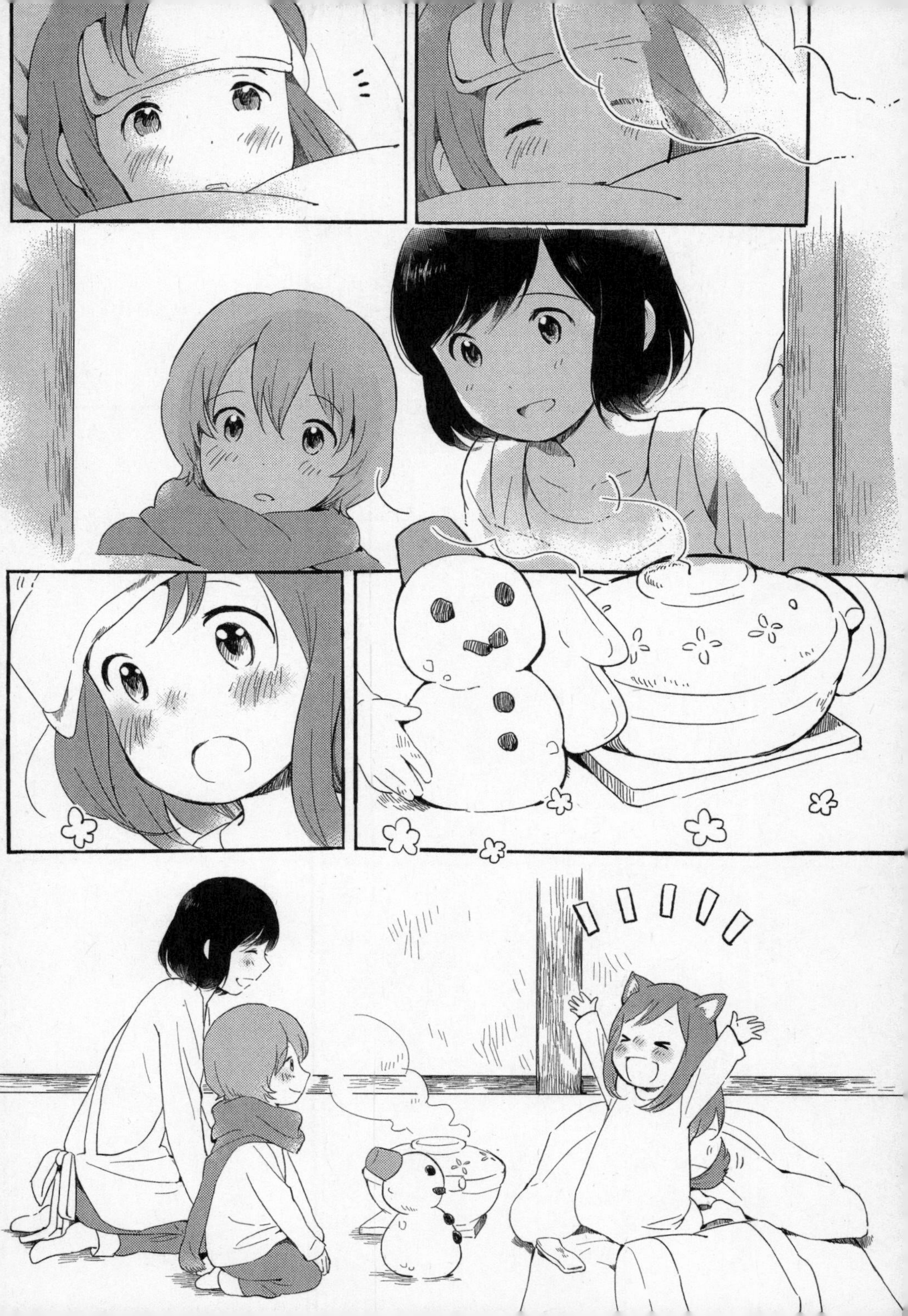

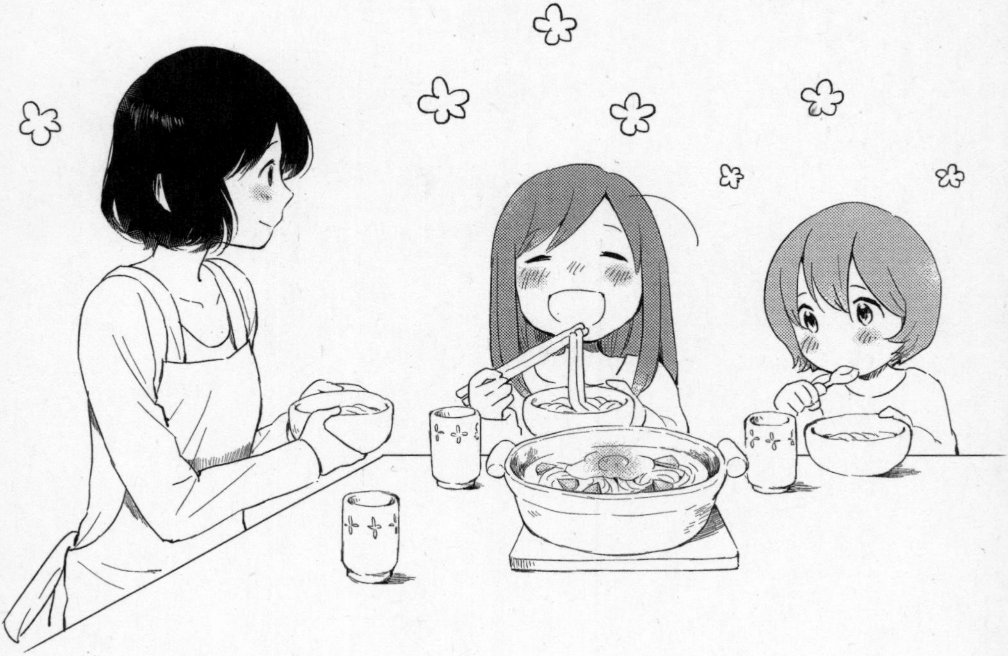

SPECIAL THANKS

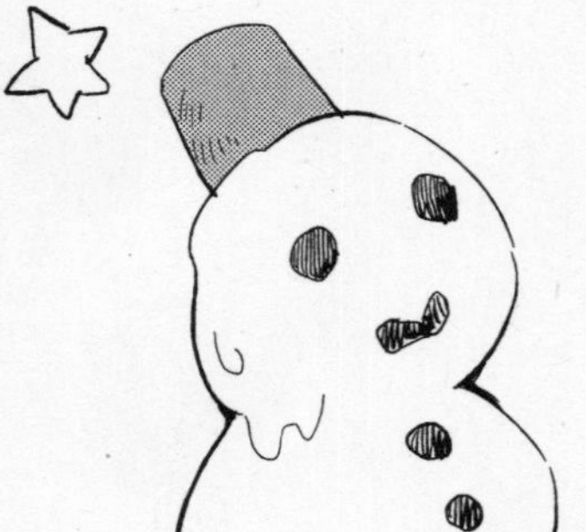

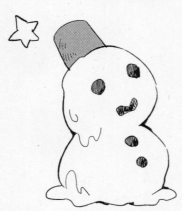

MIKI KAMIYA-SAN

MIKI KAWARABAYASHI-SAN

AYUKO SUZUKI-SAN

YUKINA SUZUKI-SAN

JURO SHIMIZU-SAN

EDITOR: NAKAZAWA-SAN

AND YOU.

THANK YOU SO MUCH. I HOPE WE MEET AGAIN IN VOLUME 3!

優

YU

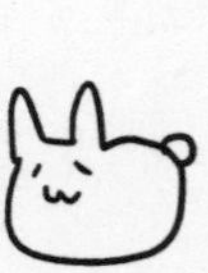

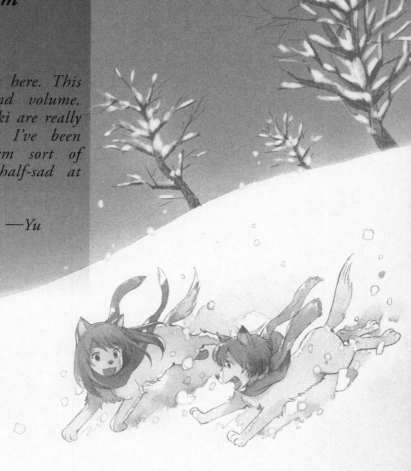

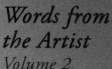

Words from the Artist
Volume 2

Hi there. Yu here. This is the second volume. Ame and Yuki are really growing up. I've been drawing them sort of half-happy, half-sad at this fact.

—Yu

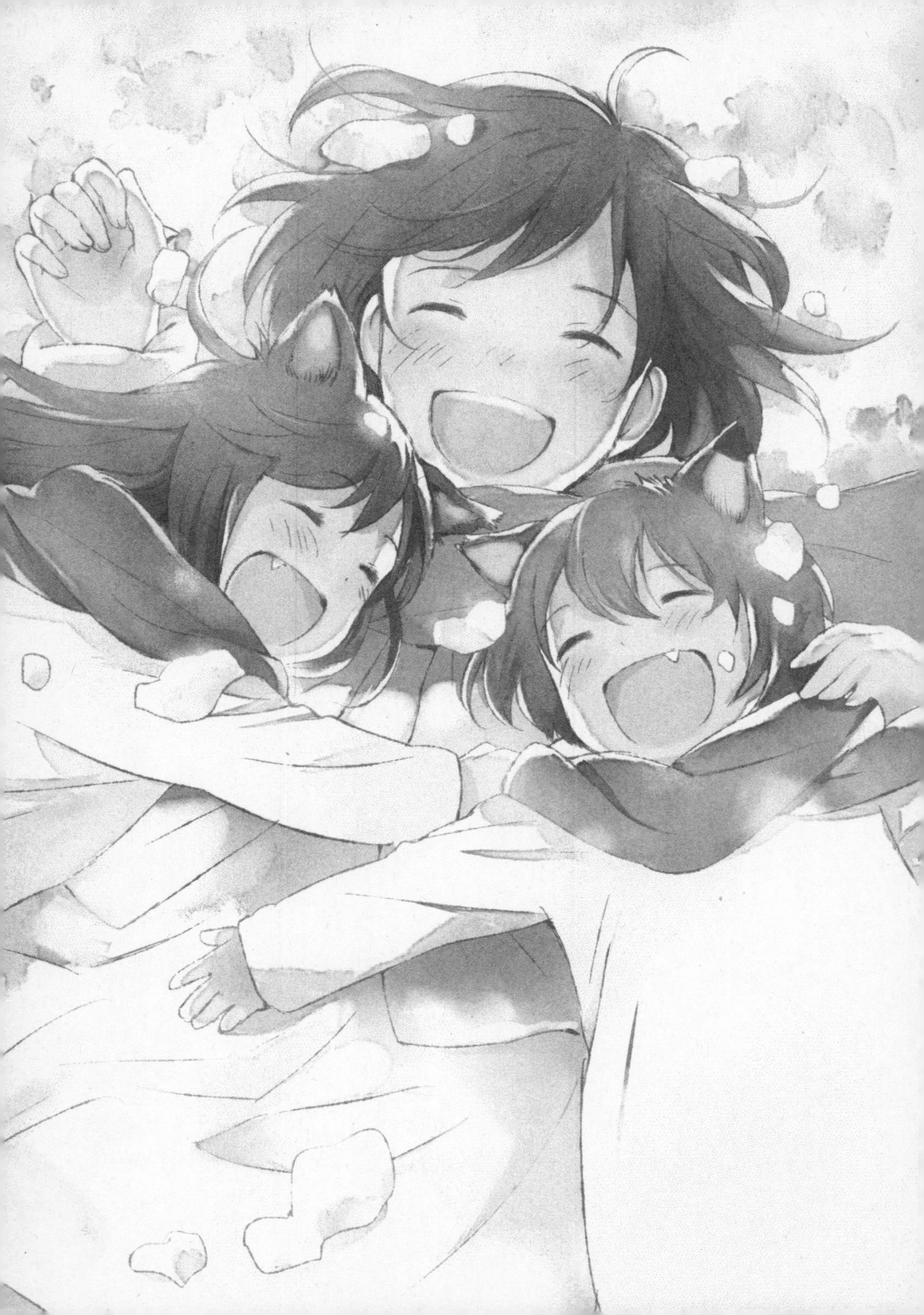

Words from the Artist

Volume 3

This is the final volume. Since this was my first serialization, I was often a little lost, and there were tons of difficult things and happy moments. I've been really content while doing this manga. I hope that Wolf Children Ame & Yuki *ends up being one of those works loved through the ages.*

—Yu

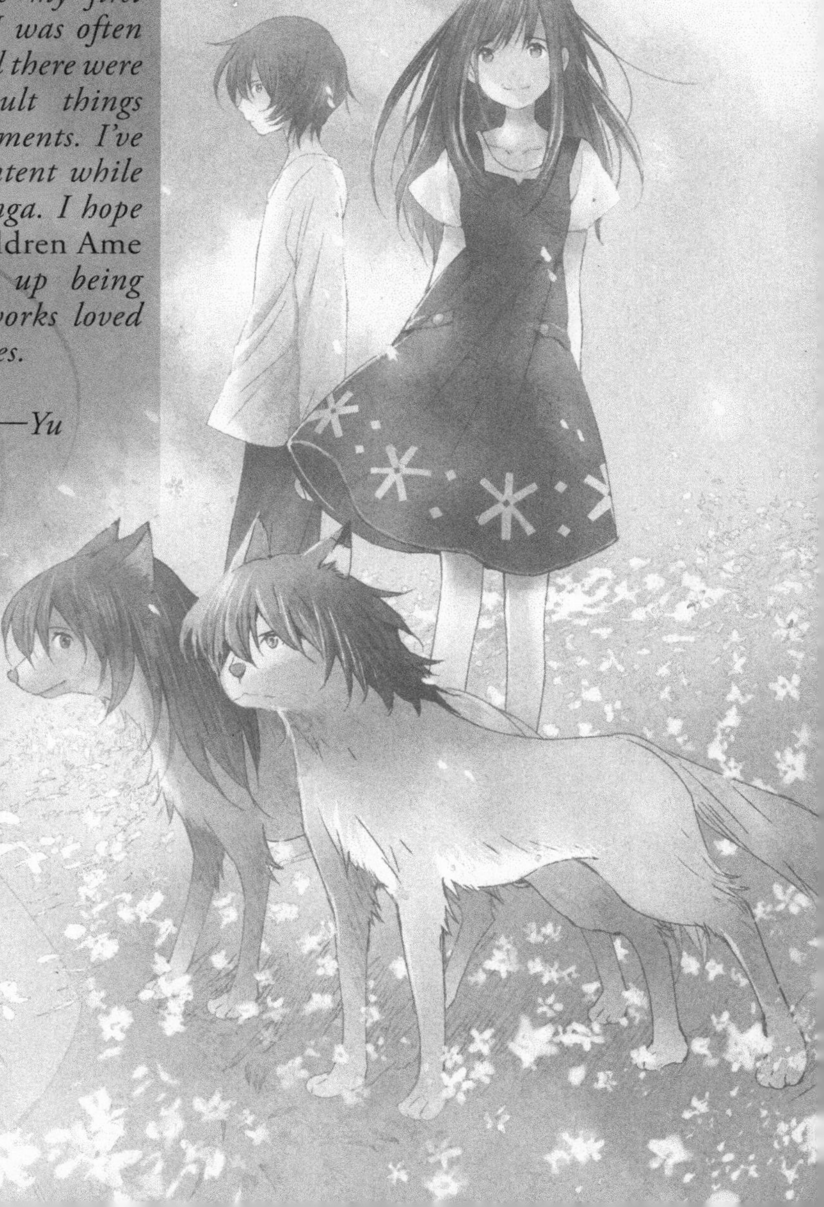

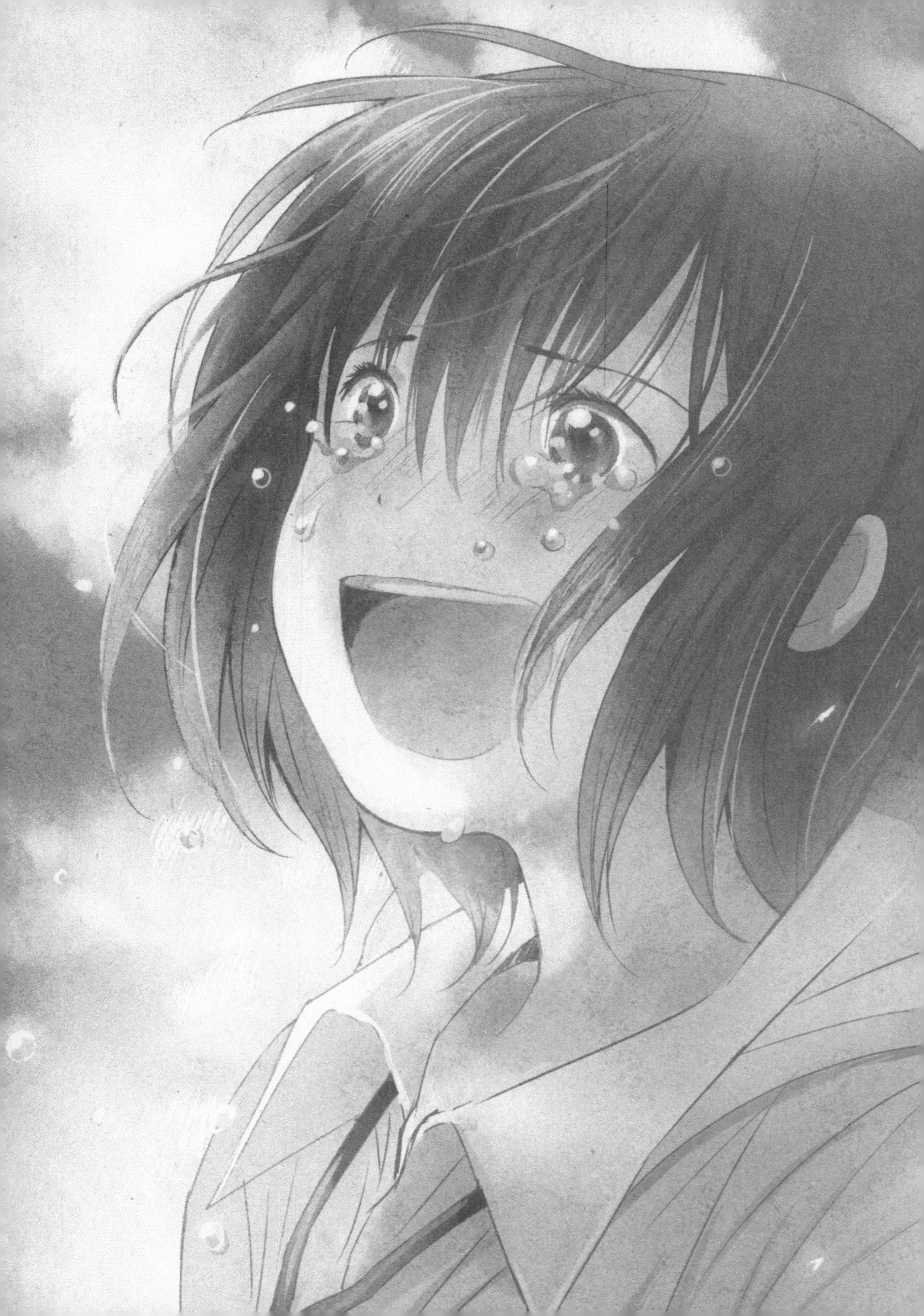

WOLF CHILDREN
AME & YUKI

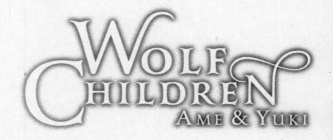

Chapter 10 Broken Promise

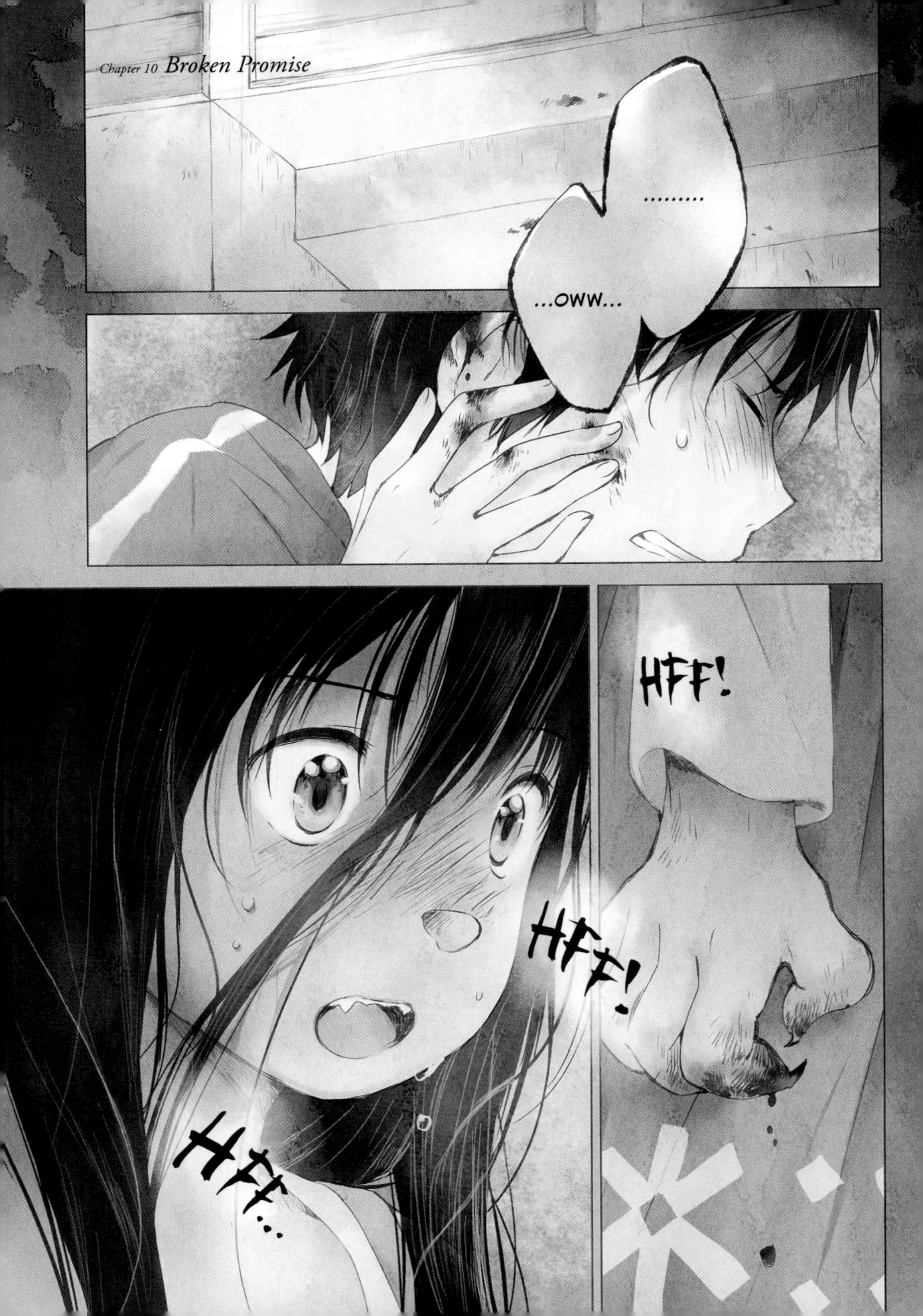
....
...OWW...
HFF!
HFF!
HFF...

Chapter 10 Broken Promise

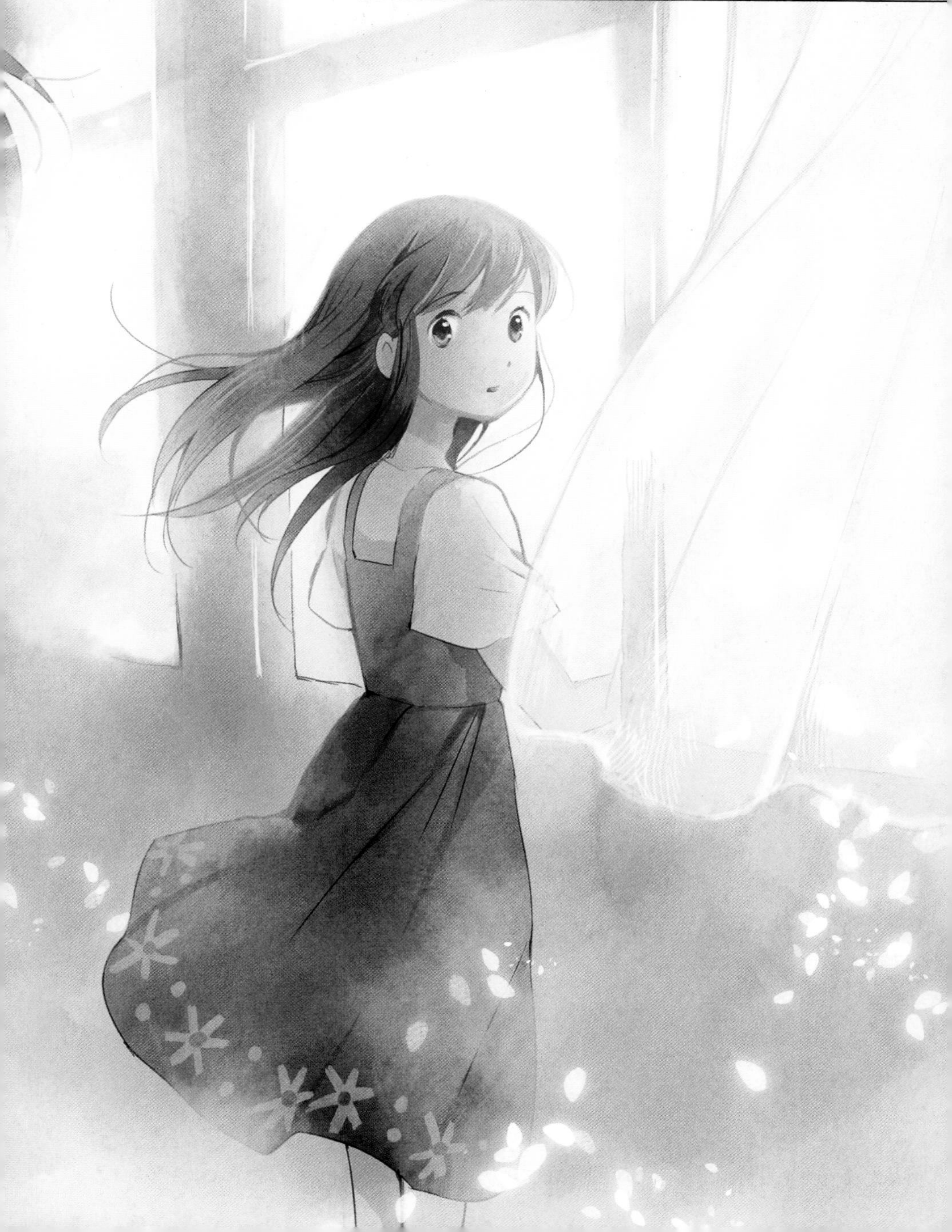

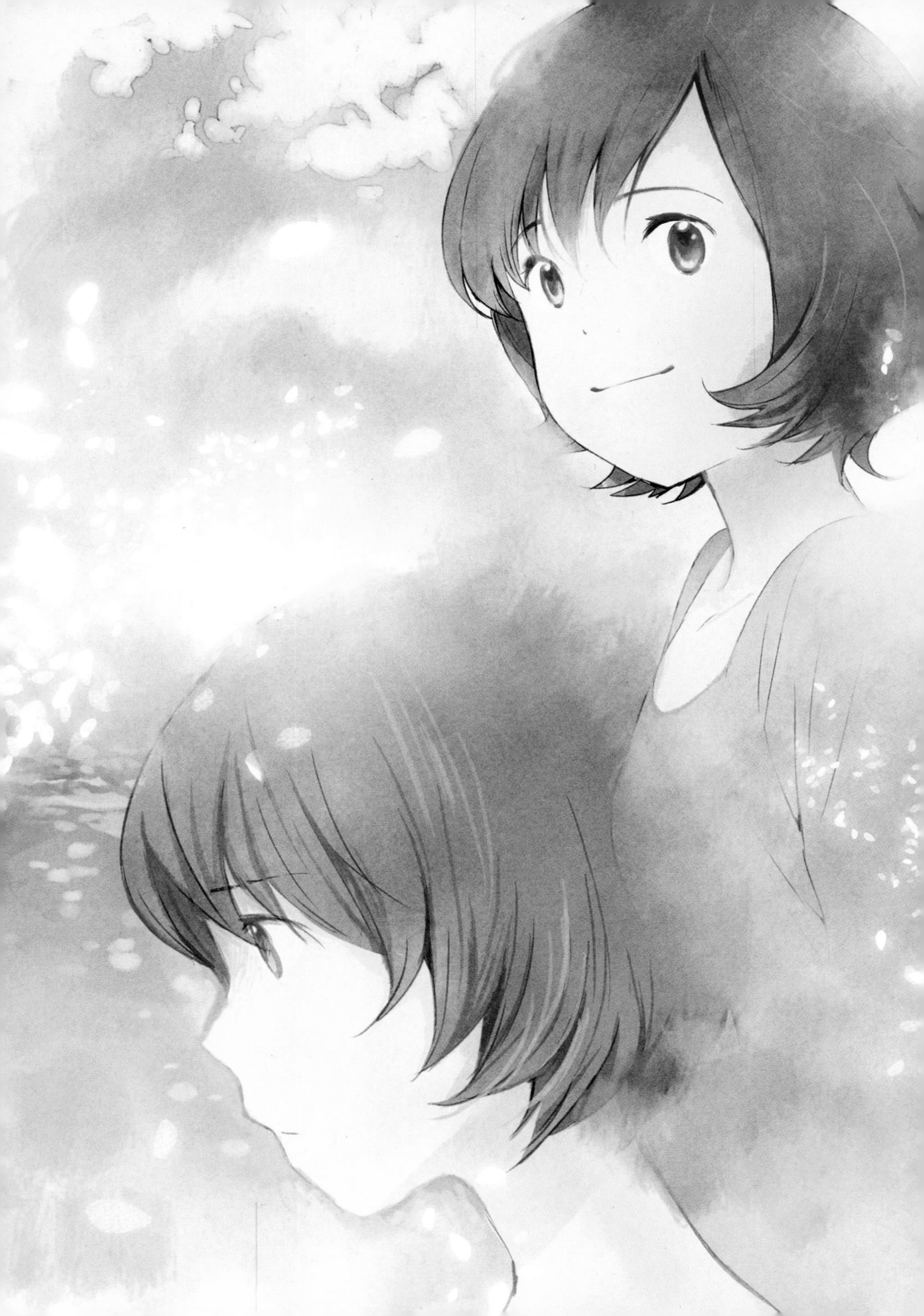

WOLF CHILDREN
AME & YUKI

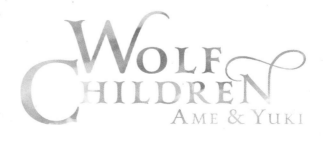

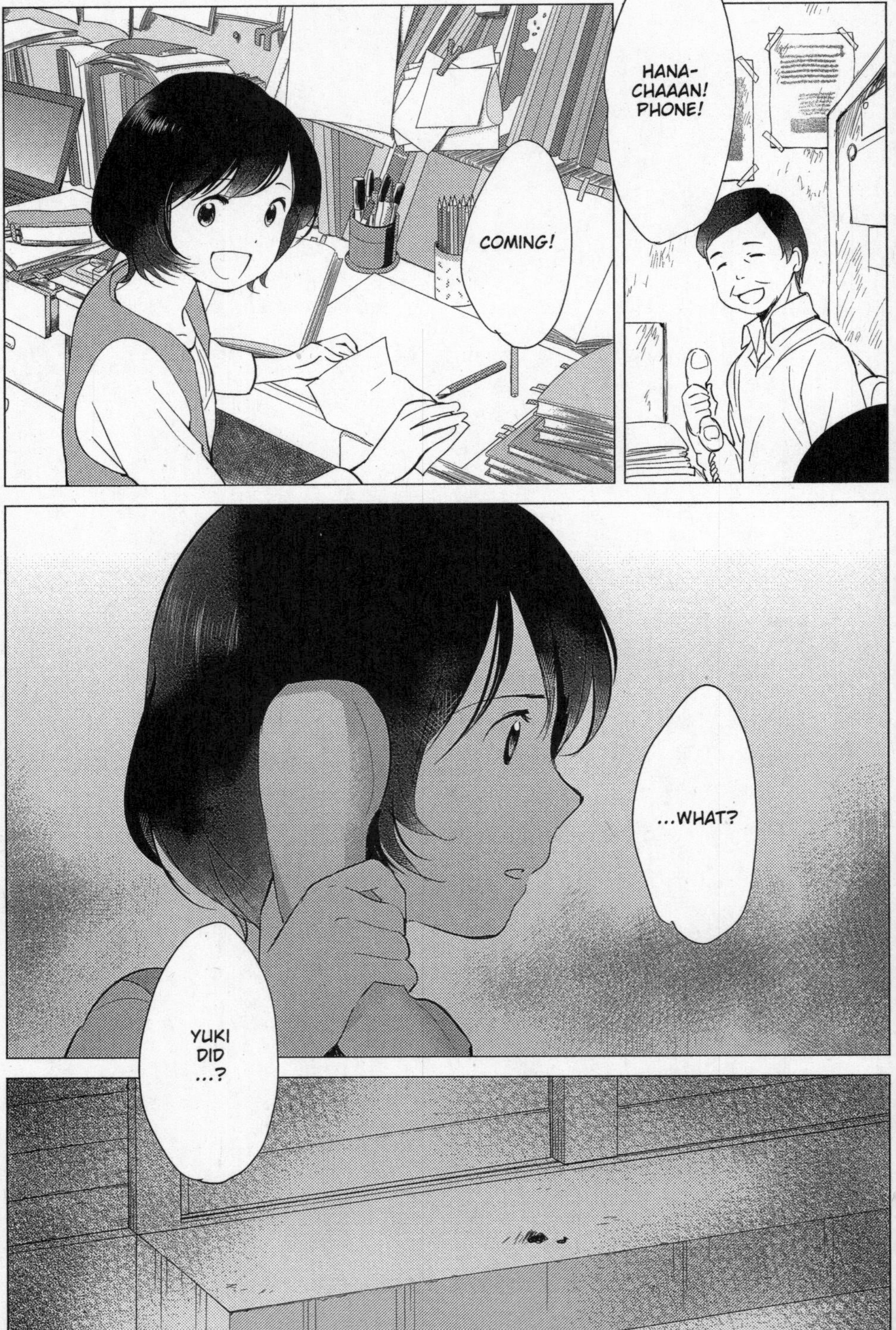
HANA-CHAAAN! PHONE!
COMING!
...WHAT?
YUKI DID ...?

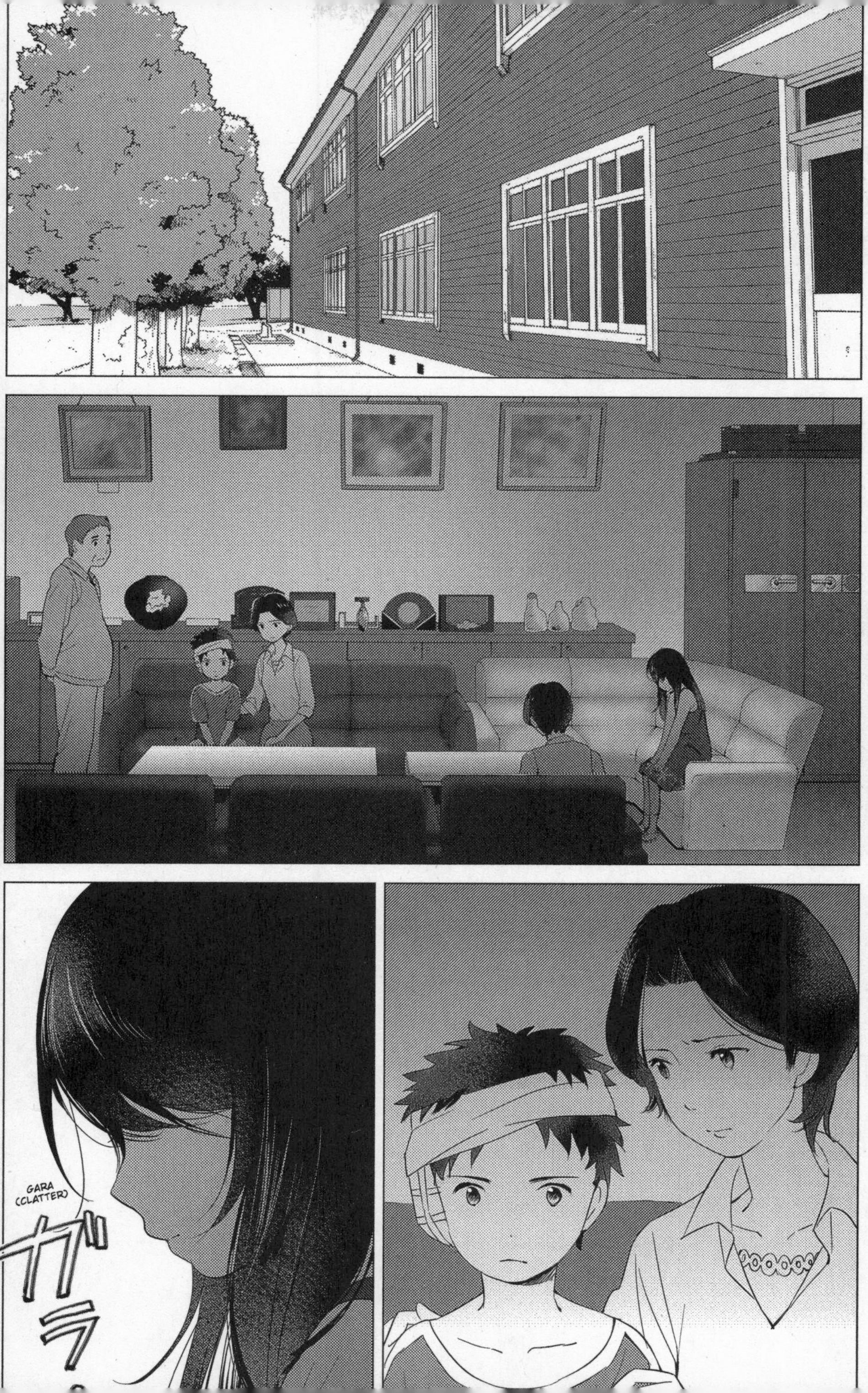
GARA (CLATTER)
ガラ

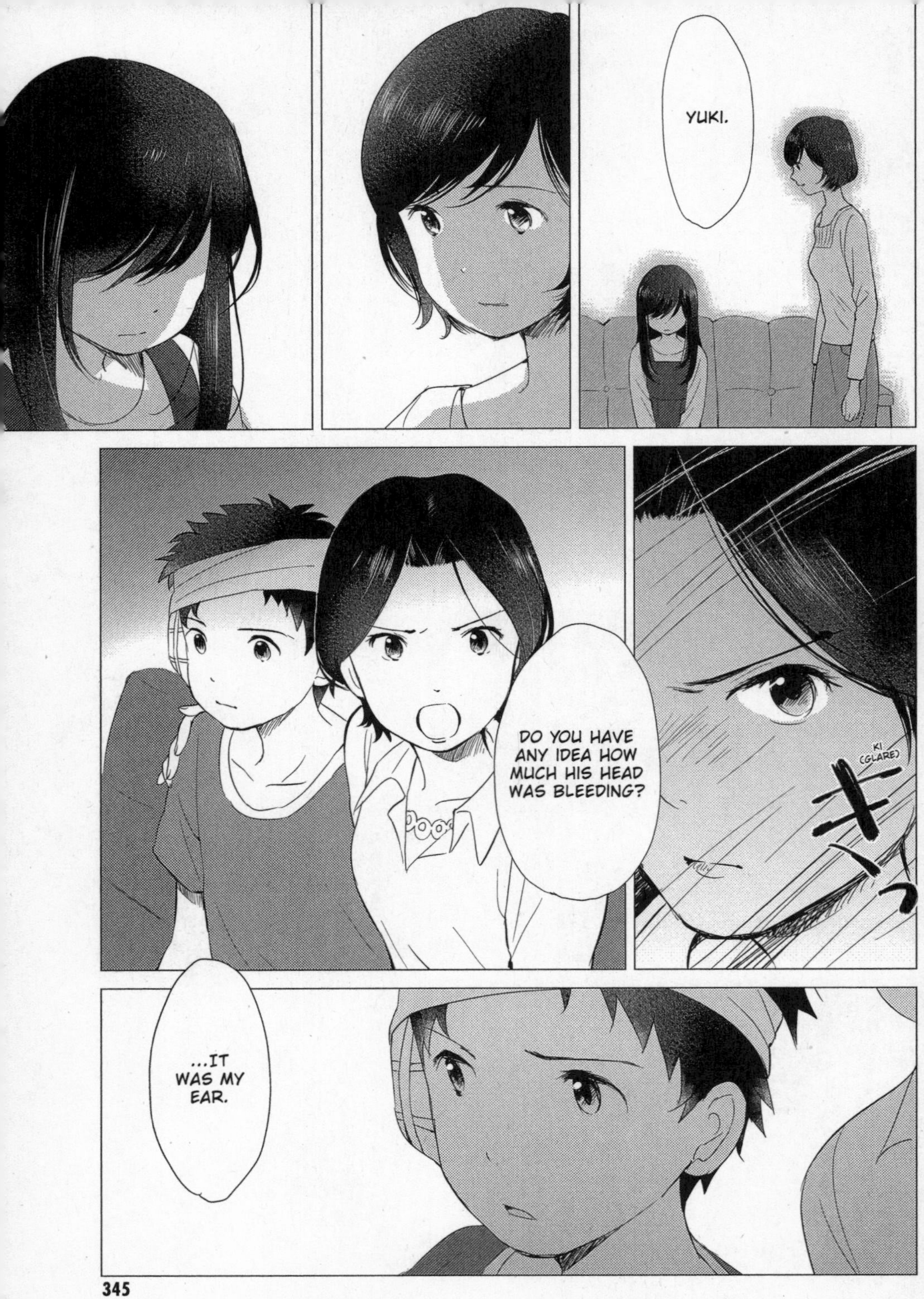
YUKI.
KI (GLARE)
DO YOU HAVE ANY IDEA HOW MUCH HIS HEAD WAS BLEEDING?
...IT WAS MY EAR.

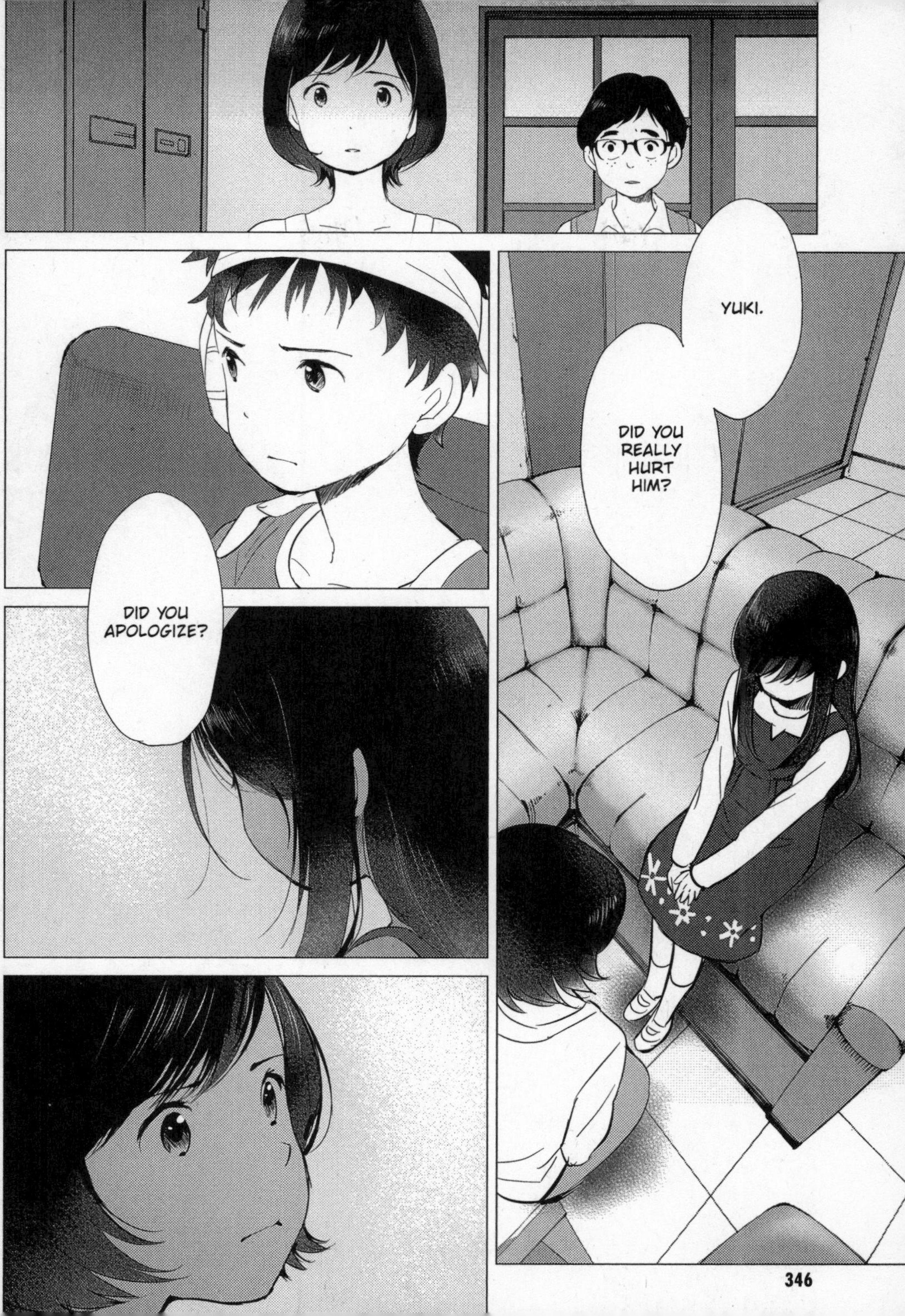
YUKI.
DID YOU REALLY HURT HIM?
DID YOU APOLOGIZE?

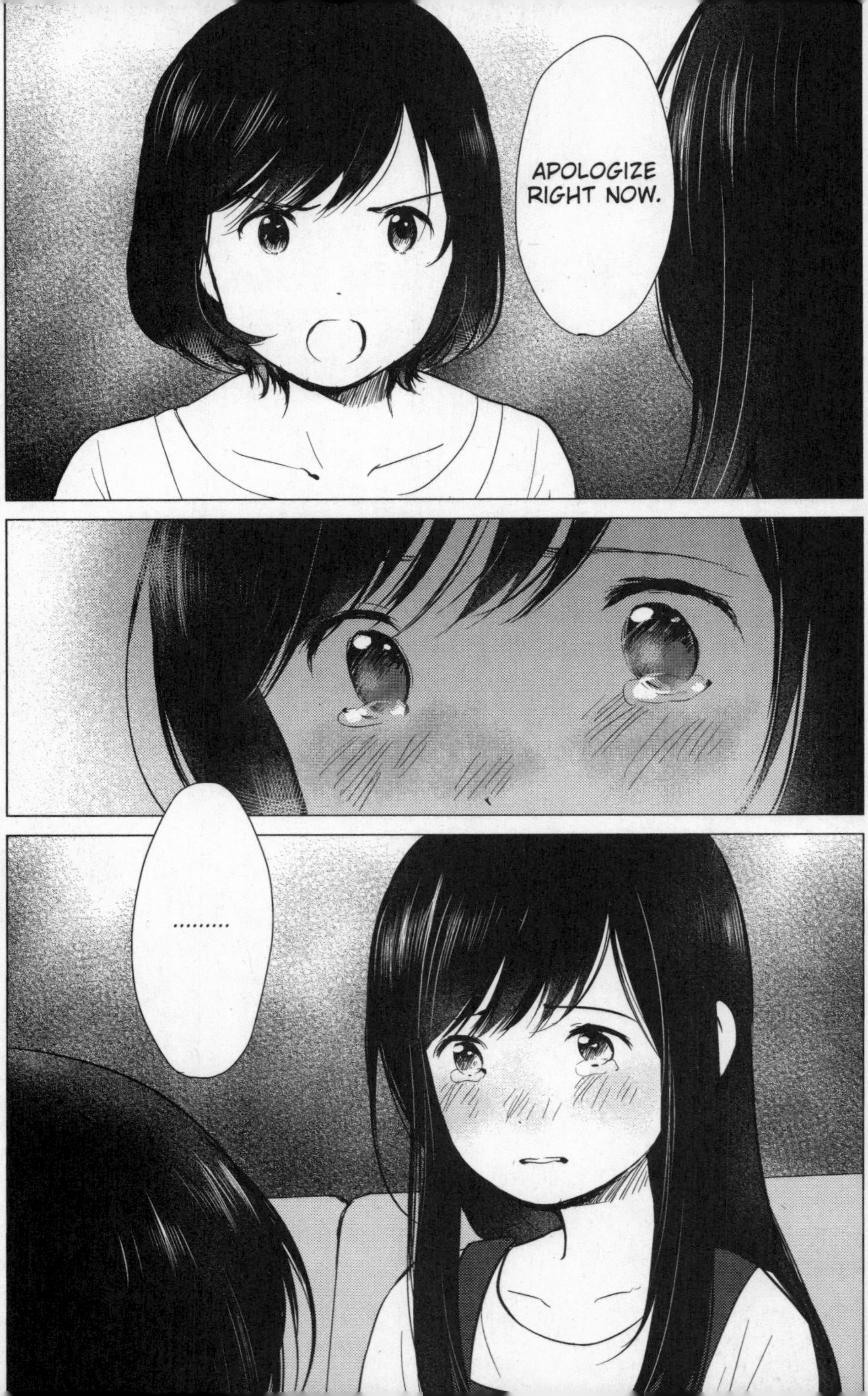
APOLOGIZE RIGHT NOW.
....

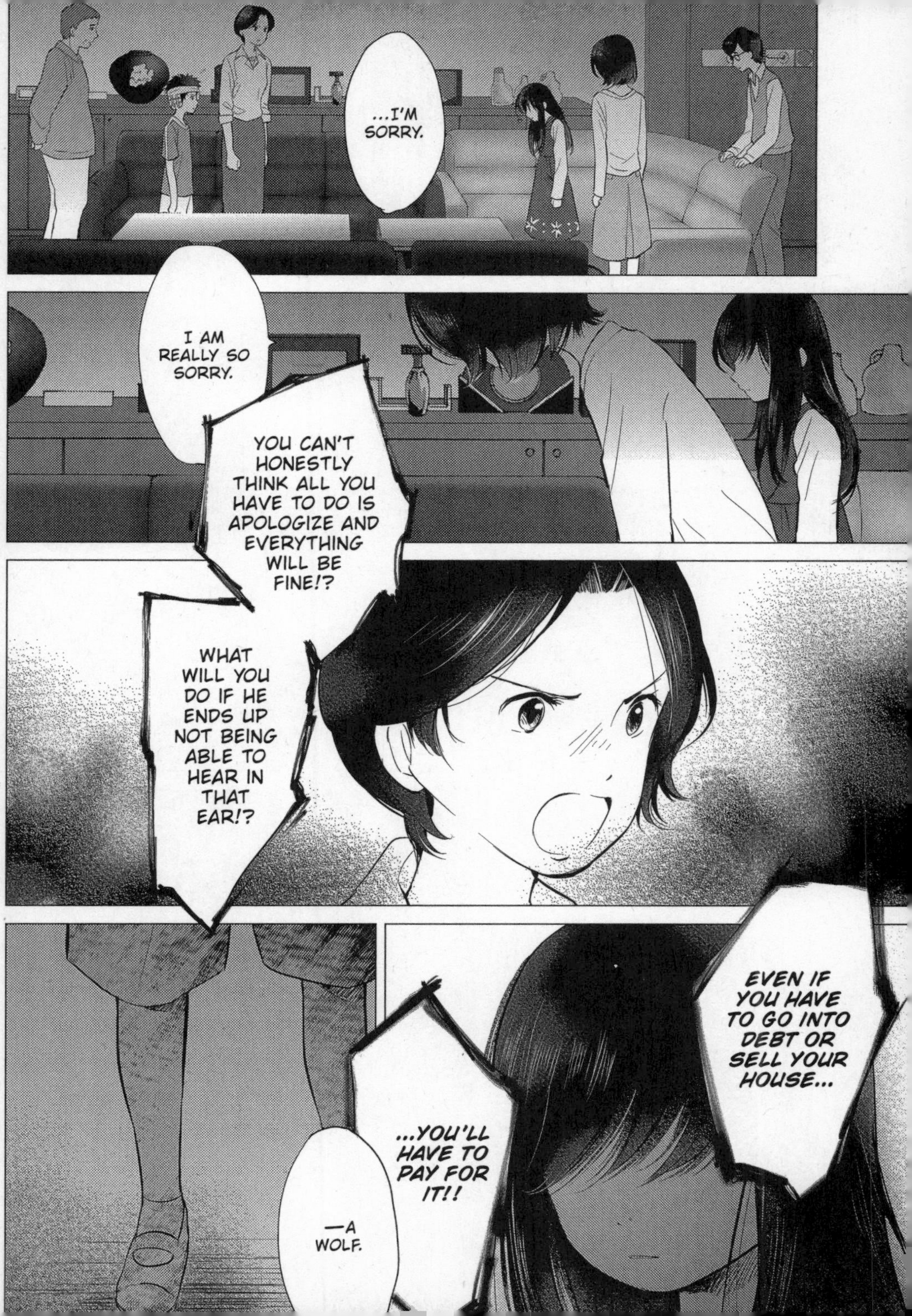
...I'M SORRY.
I AM REALLY SO SORRY.
YOU CAN'T HONESTLY THINK ALL YOU HAVE TO DO IS APOLOGIZE AND EVERYTHING WILL BE FINE!?
WHAT WILL YOU DO IF HE ENDS UP NOT BEING ABLE TO HEAR IN THAT EAR!?
EVEN IF YOU HAVE TO GO INTO DEBT OR SELL YOUR HOUSE...
...YOU'LL HAVE TO PAY FOR IT!!
—A WOLF.

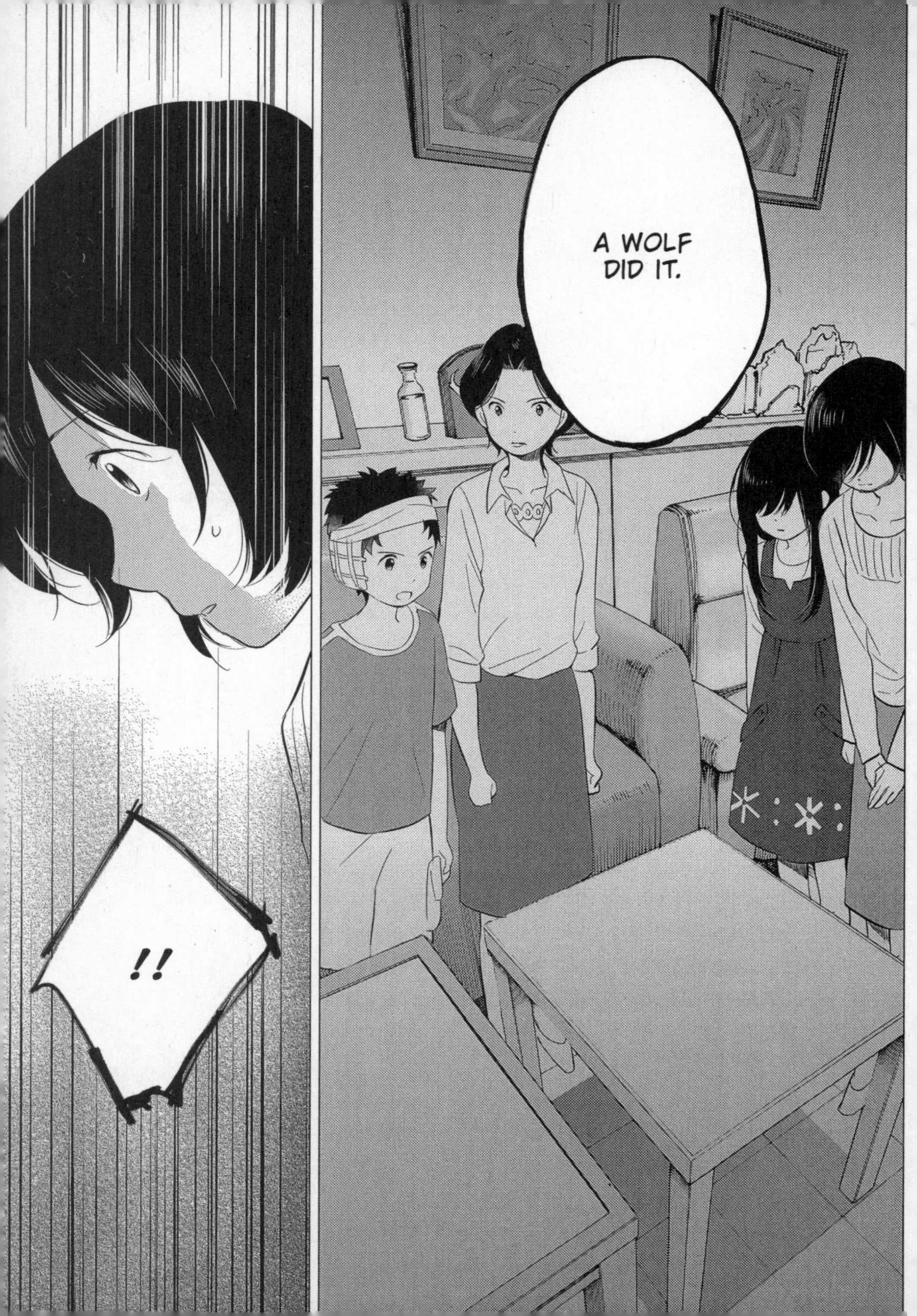
A WOLF DID IT.
!!

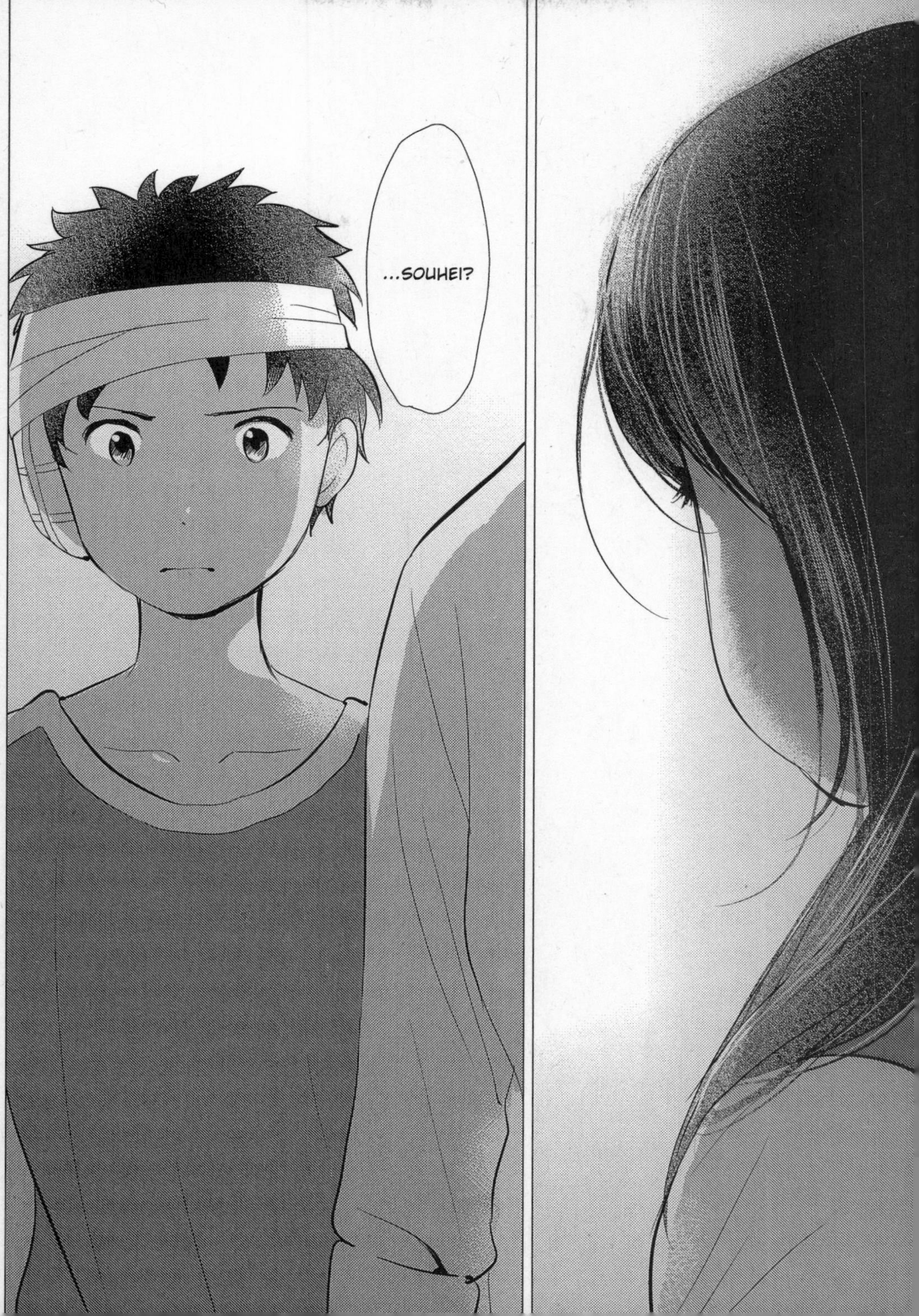
...SOUHEI?

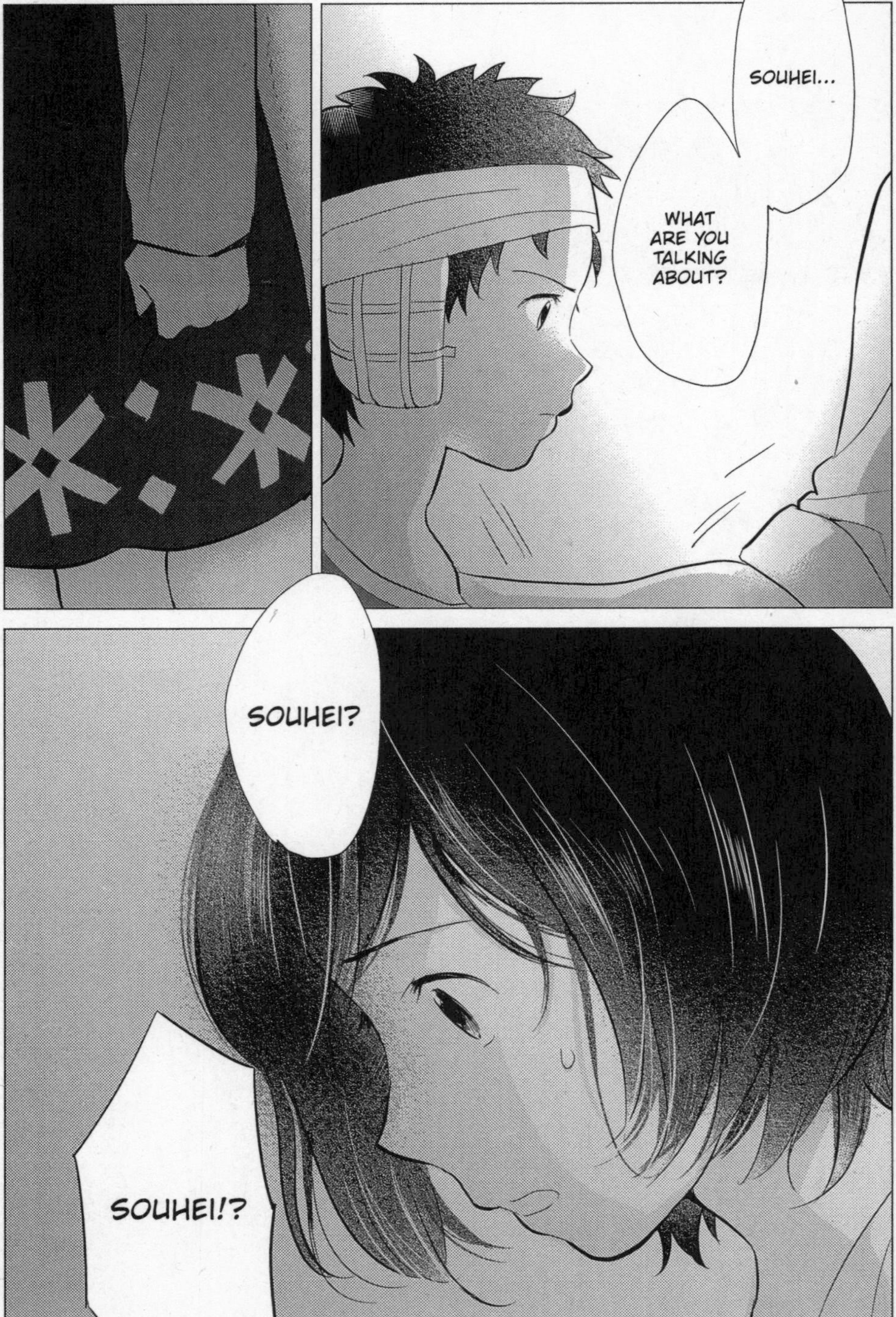
SOUHEI...
WHAT ARE YOU TALKING ABOUT?
SOUHEI?
SOUHEI!?

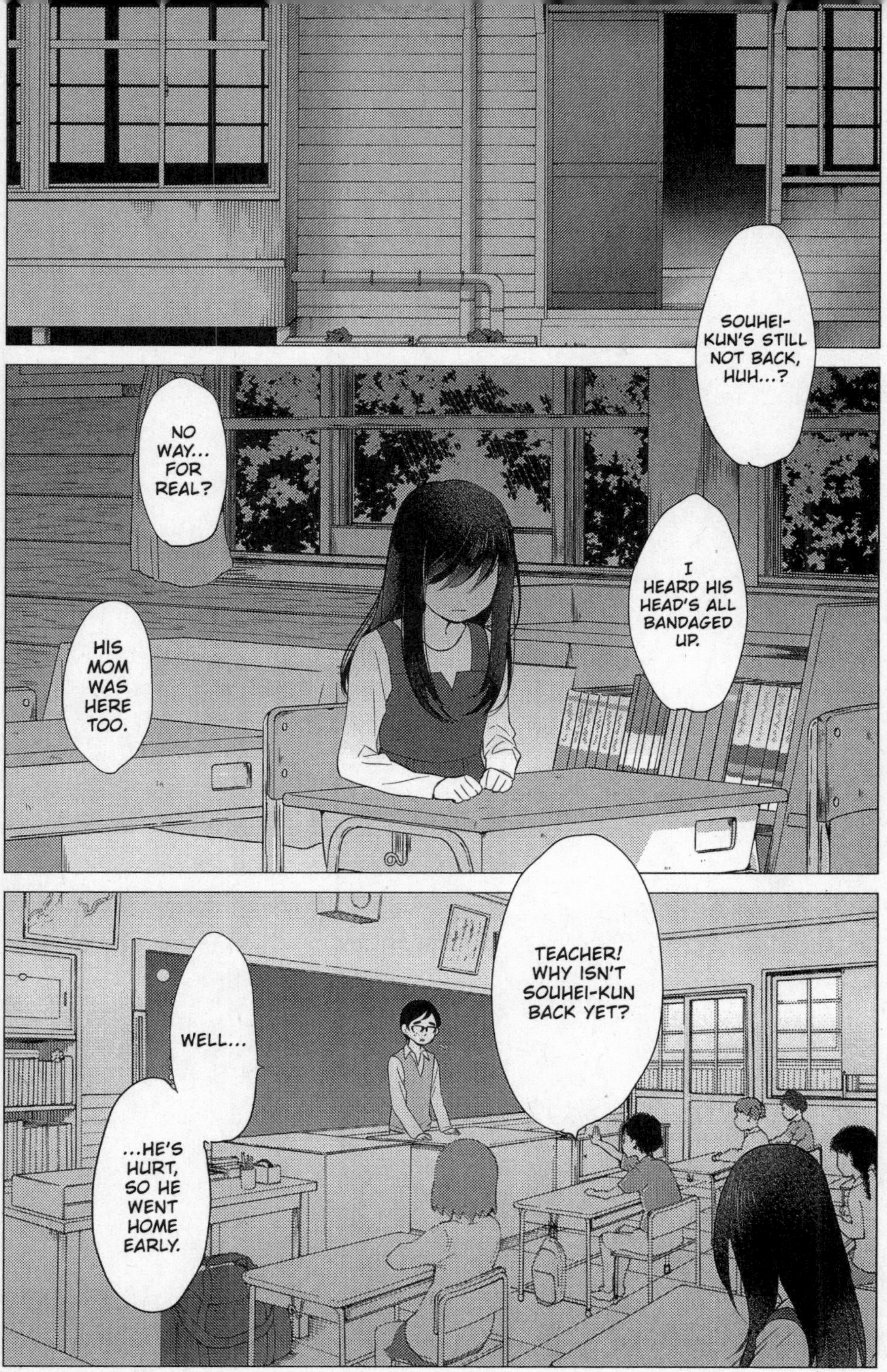
SOUHEI-KUN'S STILL NOT BACK, HUH...?
I HEARD HIS HEAD'S ALL BANDAGED UP.
NO WAY... FOR REAL?
HIS MOM WAS HERE TOO.
TEACHER! WHY ISN'T SOUHEI-KUN BACK YET?
WELL...
...HE'S HURT, SO HE WENT HOME EARLY.

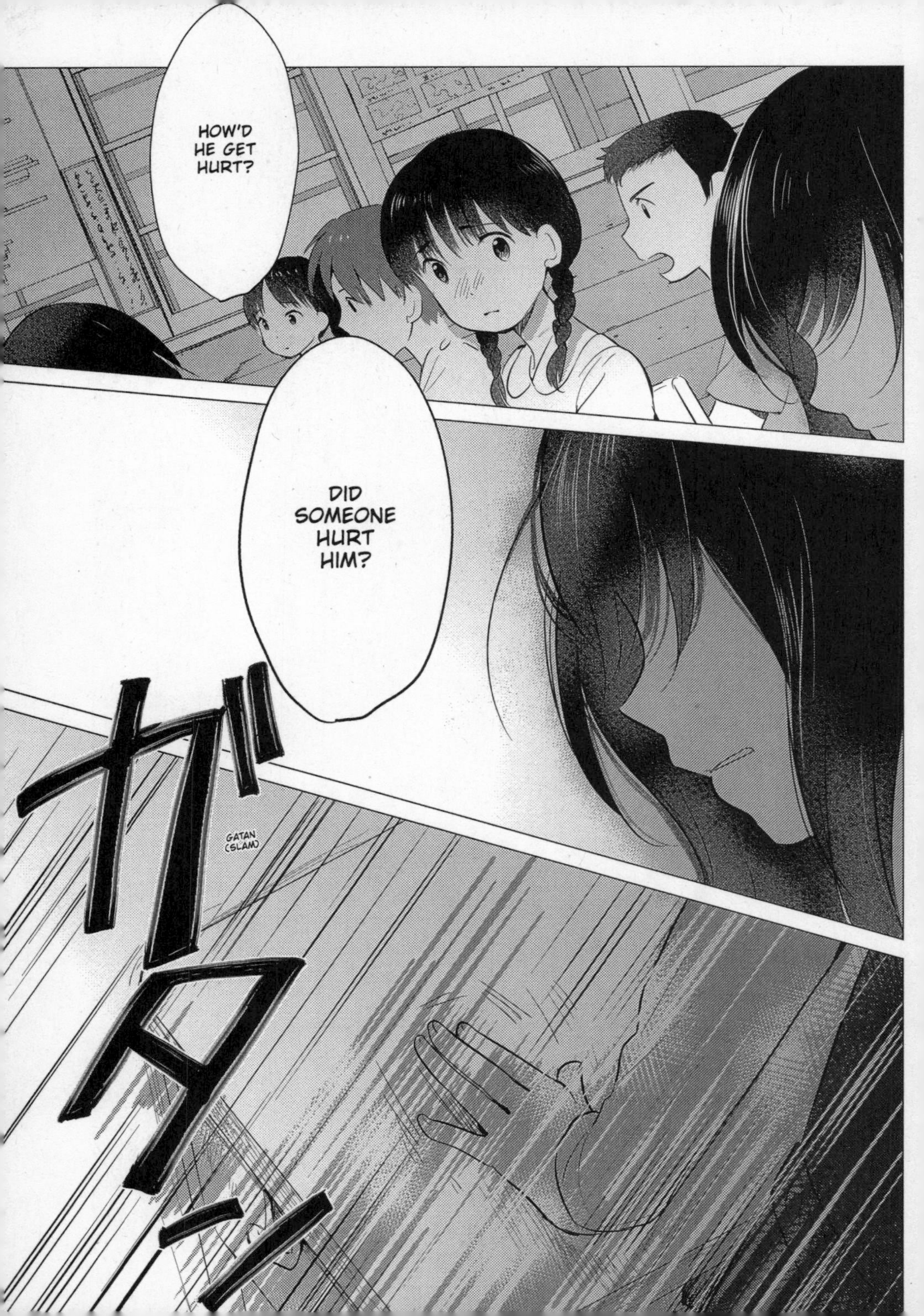
HOW'D HE GET HURT?
DID SOMEONE HURT HIM?
ガタン
GATAN (SLAM)

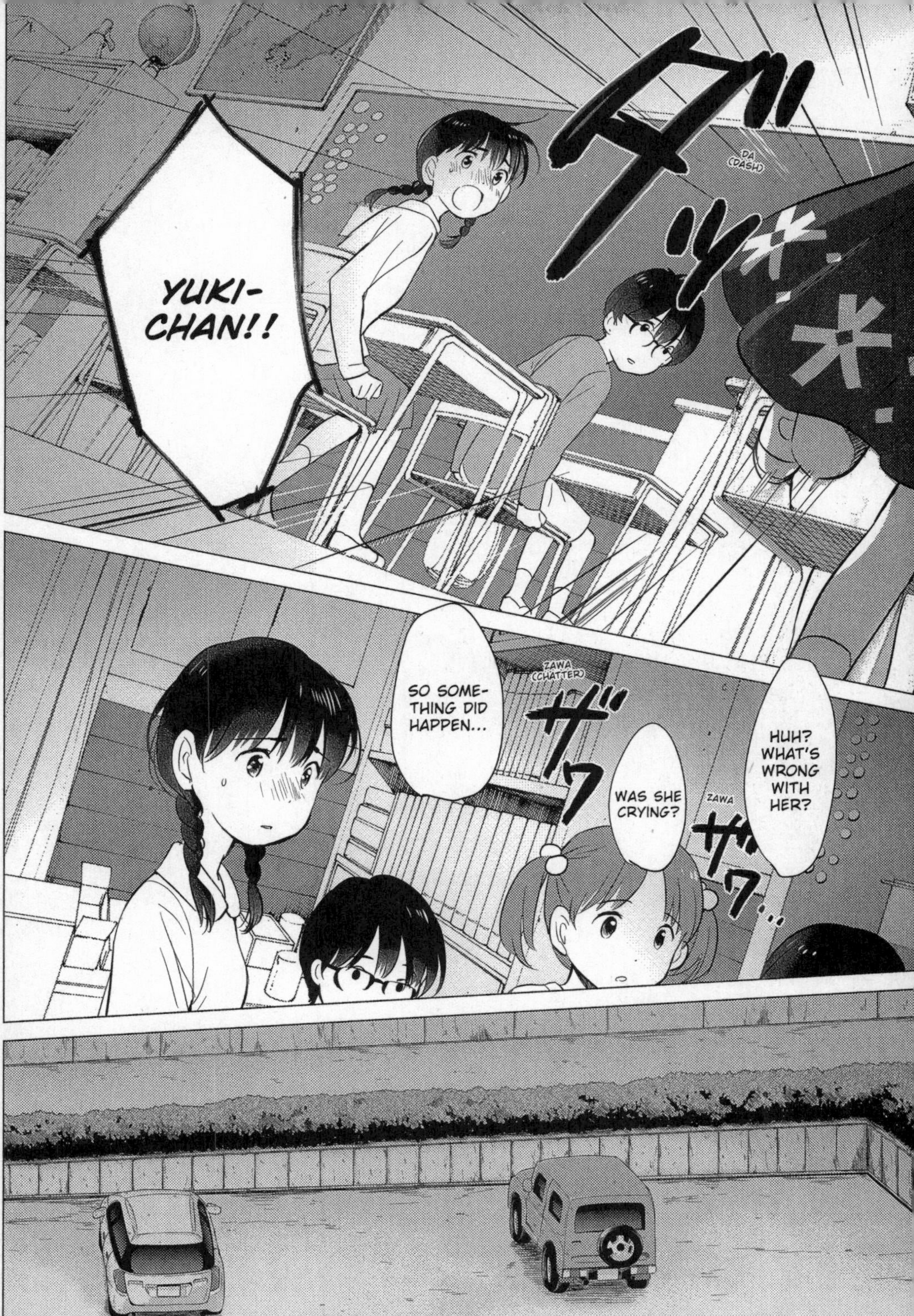
DA (DASH)
YUKI-CHAN!!
HUH? WHAT'S WRONG WITH HER?
ZAWA
WAS SHE CRYING?
ZAWA (CHATTER)
SO SOMETHING DID HAPPEN...

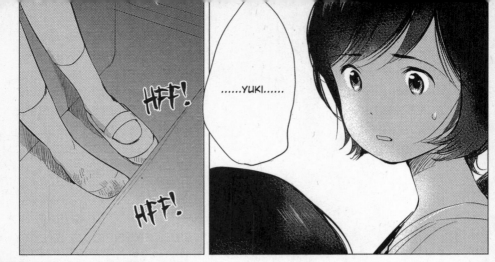

HFF!

HFF!

......YUKI......

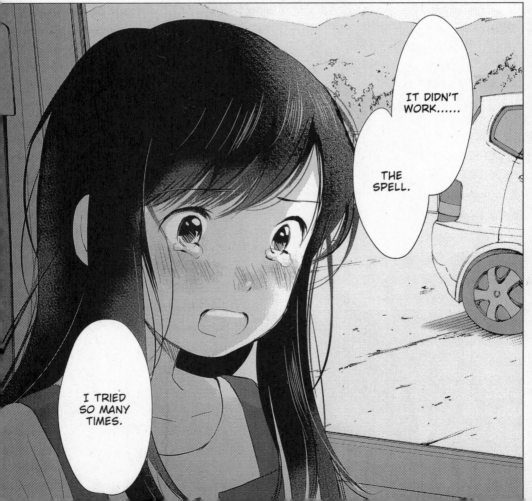

IT DIDN'T WORK......

THE SPELL.

I TRIED SO MANY TIMES.

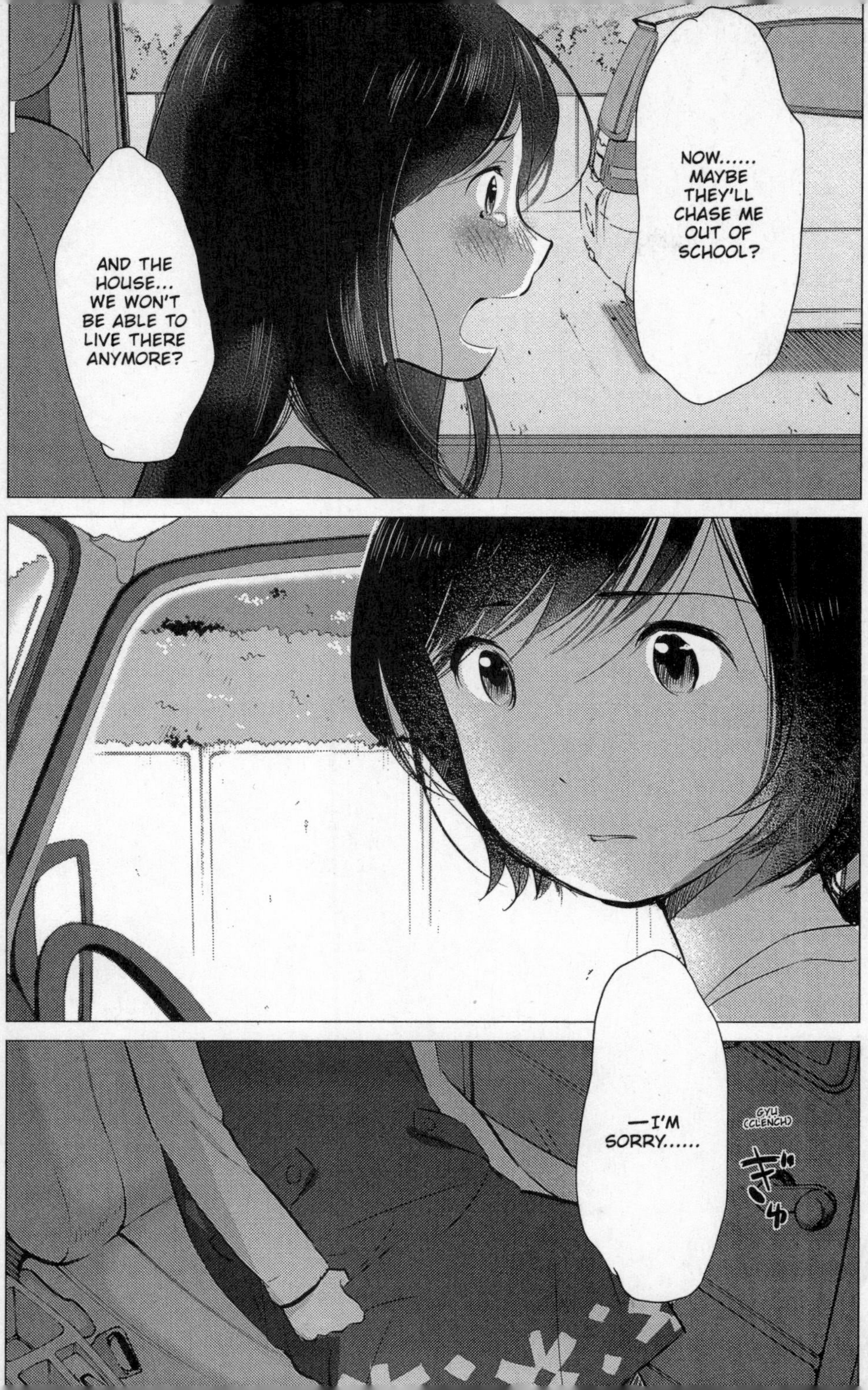
NOW...... MAYBE THEY'LL CHASE ME OUT OF SCHOOL?
AND THE HOUSE... WE WON'T BE ABLE TO LIVE THERE ANYMORE?
—I'M SORRY......
GYU (CLENCH)
ぎゅ

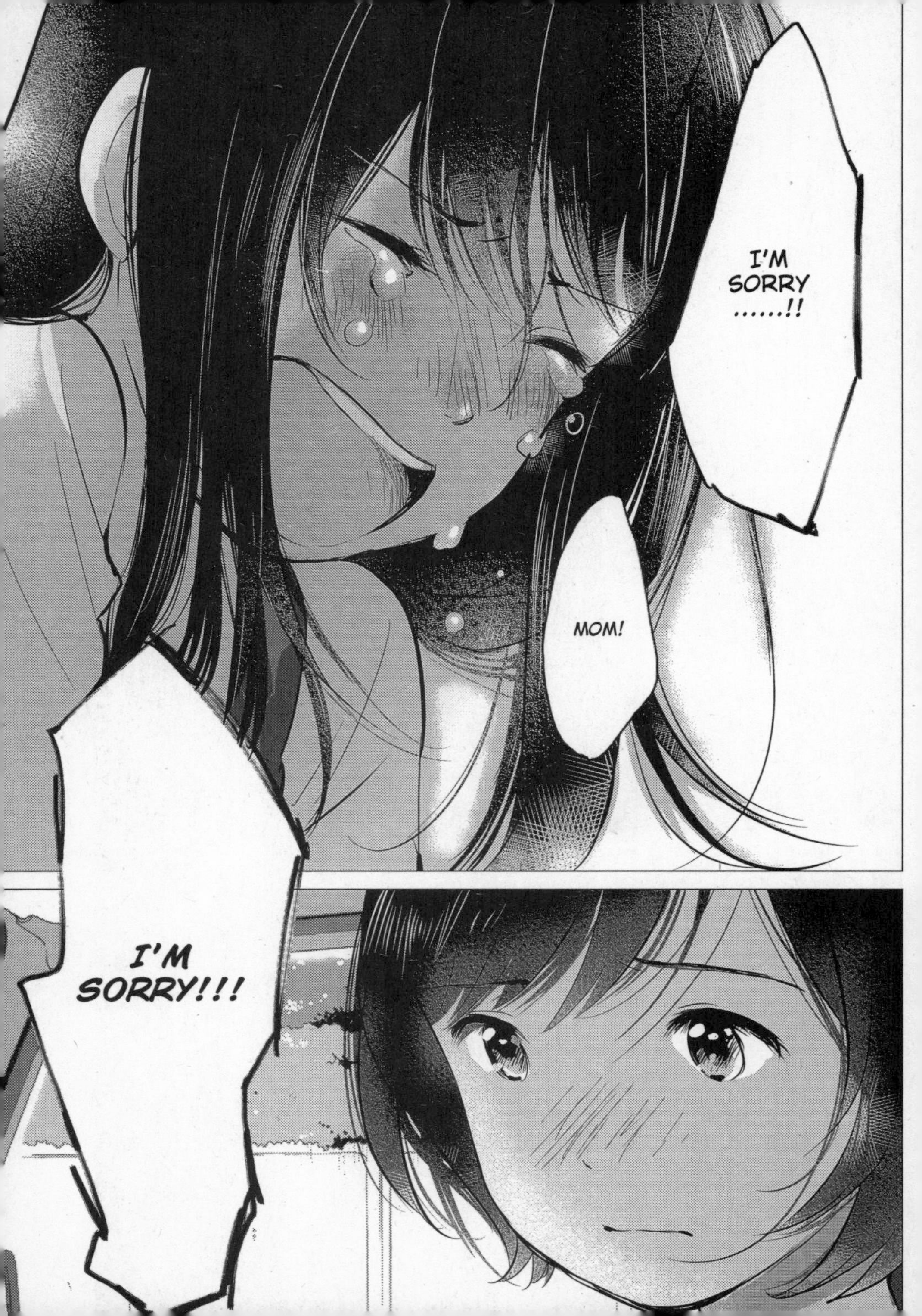
I'M SORRY ......!!
MOM!
I'M SORRY!!!

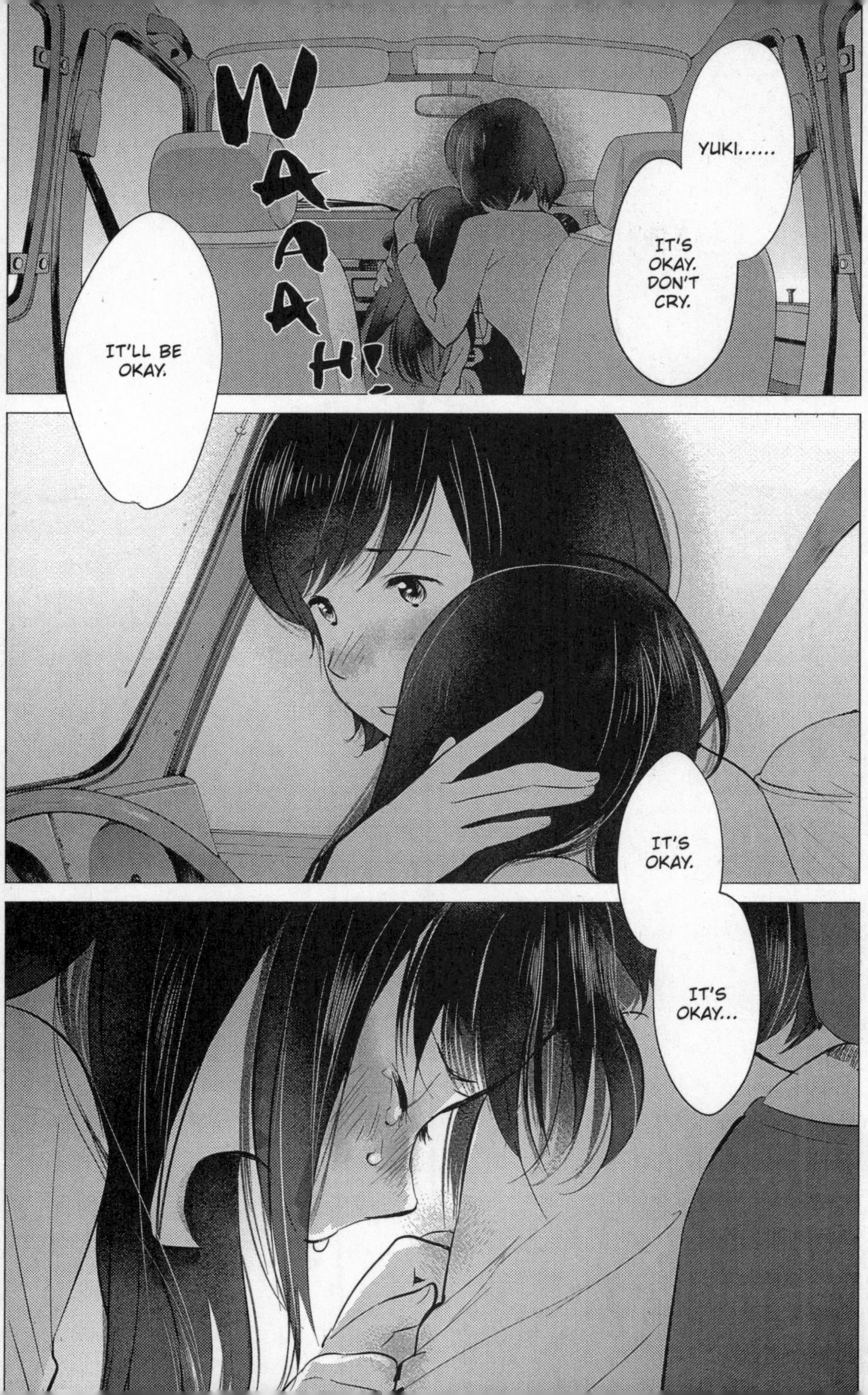
YUKI......
IT'S OKAY. DON'T CRY.
WAAAH!
IT'LL BE OKAY.
IT'S OKAY.
IT'S OKAY...

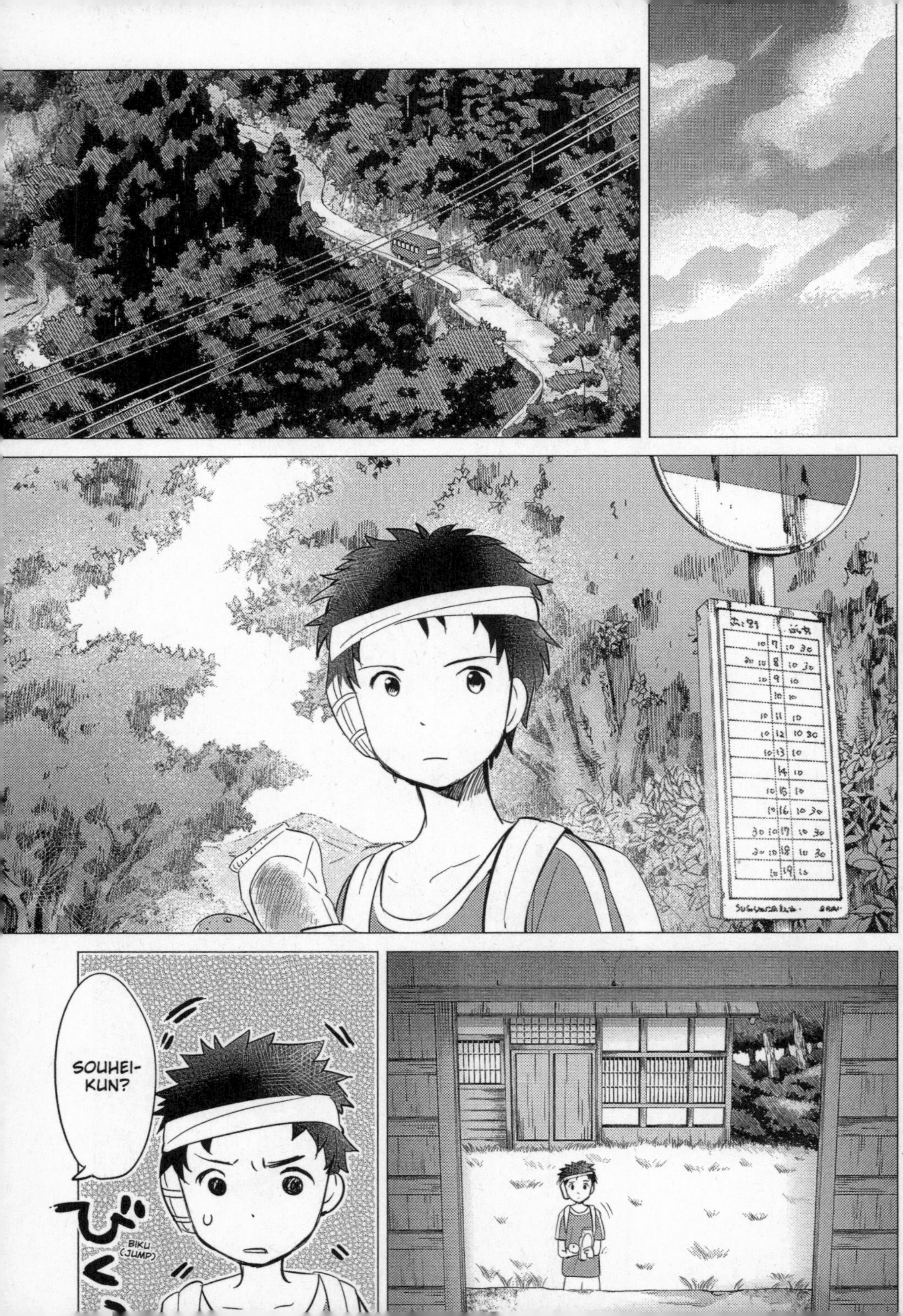
SOUHEI-KUN?
BIKU (JUMP)

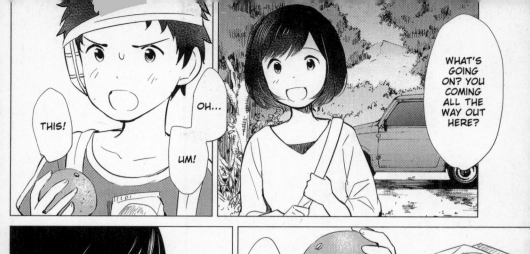

THIS!

OH...

UM!

WHAT'S GOING ON? YOU COMING ALL THE WAY OUT HERE?

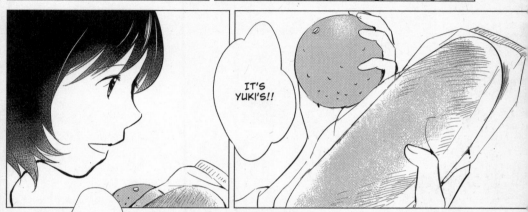

IT'S YUKI'S!!

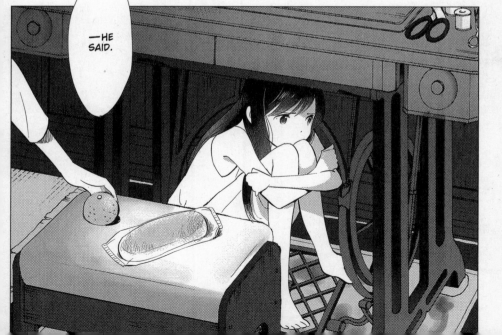

—HE SAID.

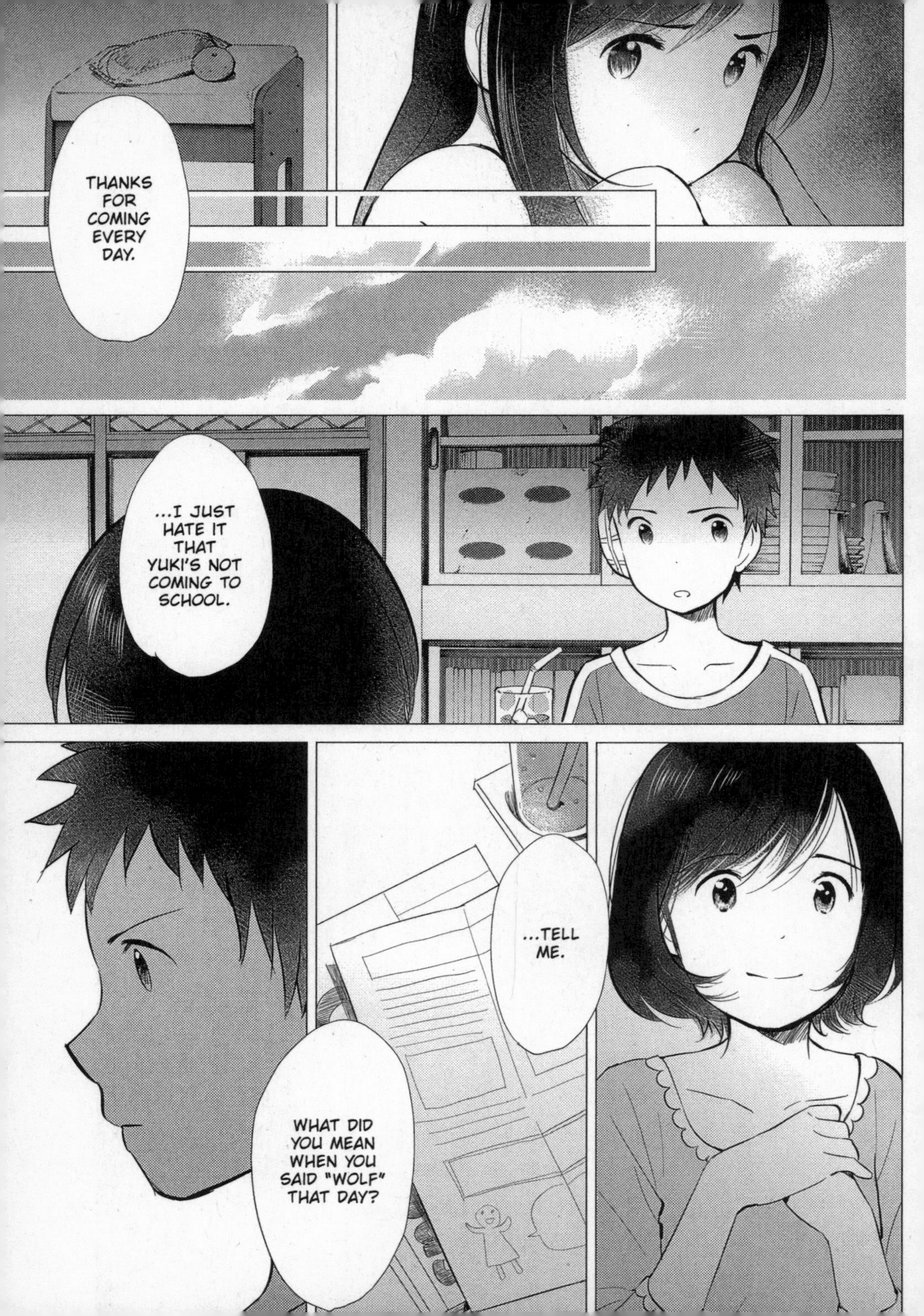
THANKS FOR COMING EVERY DAY.
...I JUST HATE IT THAT YUKI'S NOT COMING TO SCHOOL.
...TELL ME.
WHAT DID YOU MEAN WHEN YOU SAID "WOLF" THAT DAY?

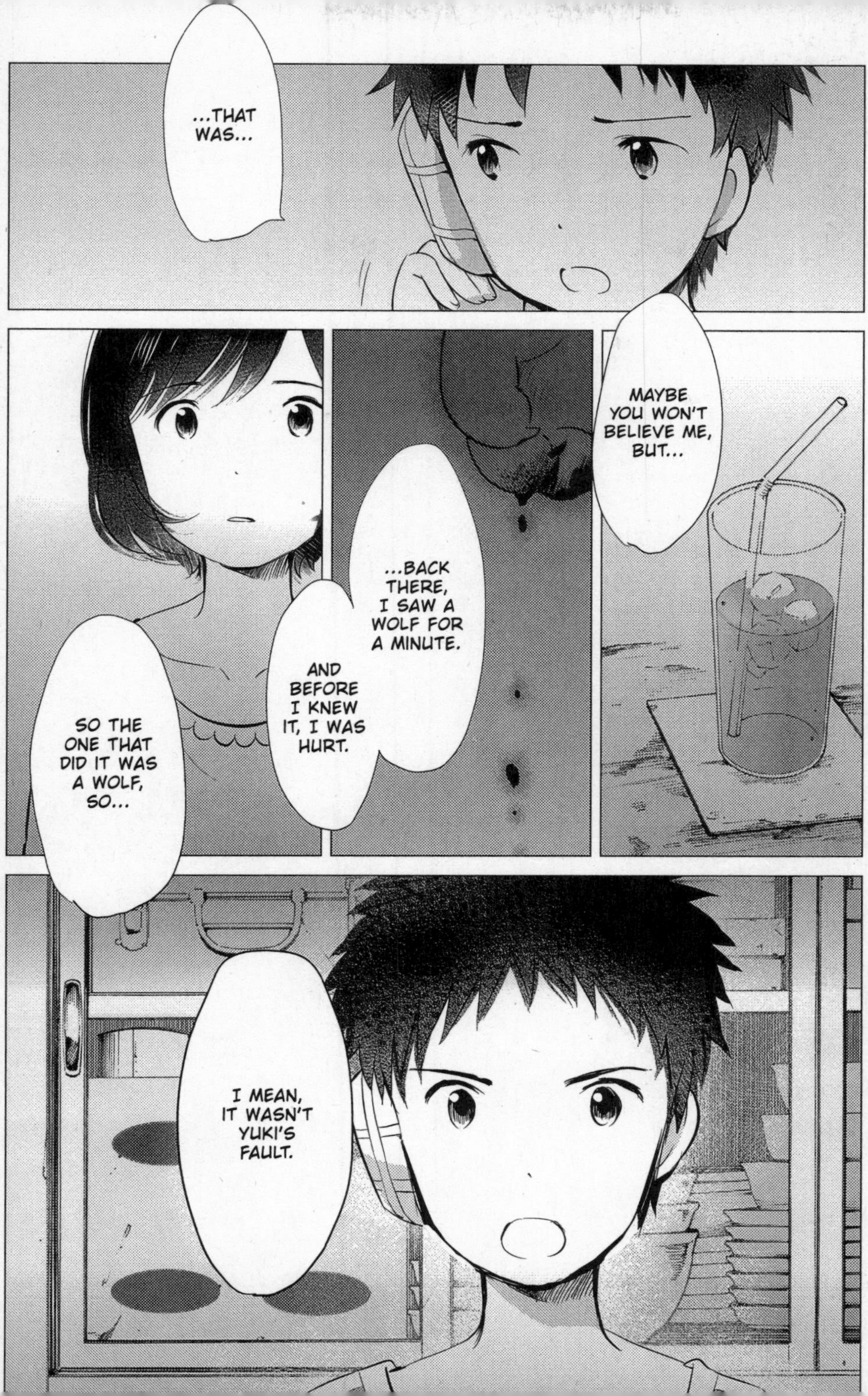
...THAT WAS...
MAYBE YOU WON'T BELIEVE ME, BUT...
...BACK THERE, I SAW A WOLF FOR A MINUTE.
AND BEFORE I KNEW IT, I WAS HURT.
SO THE ONE THAT DID IT WAS A WOLF, SO...
I MEAN, IT WASN'T YUKI'S FAULT.

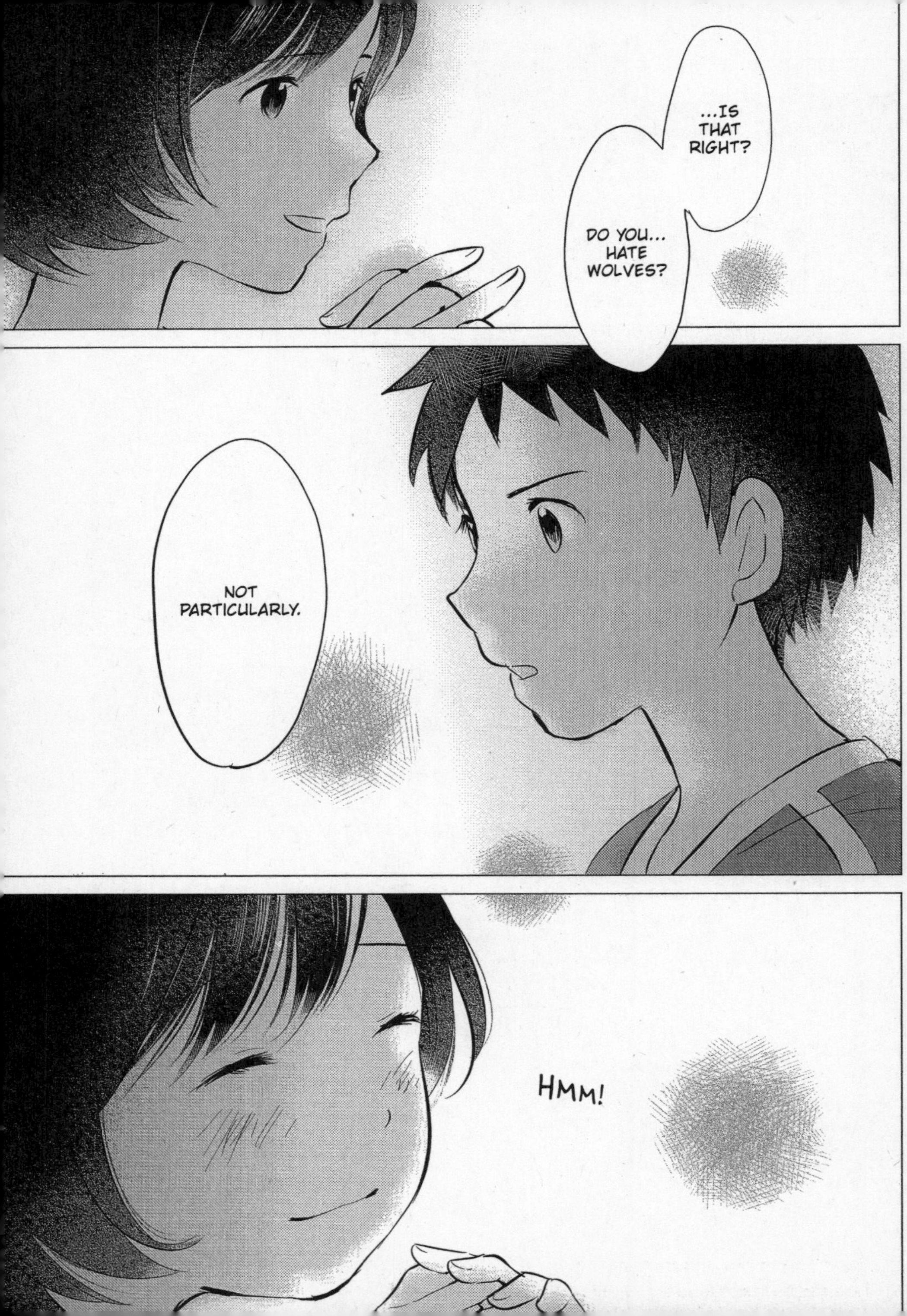
...IS THAT RIGHT?
DO YOU... HATE WOLVES?
NOT PARTICULARLY.
HMM!

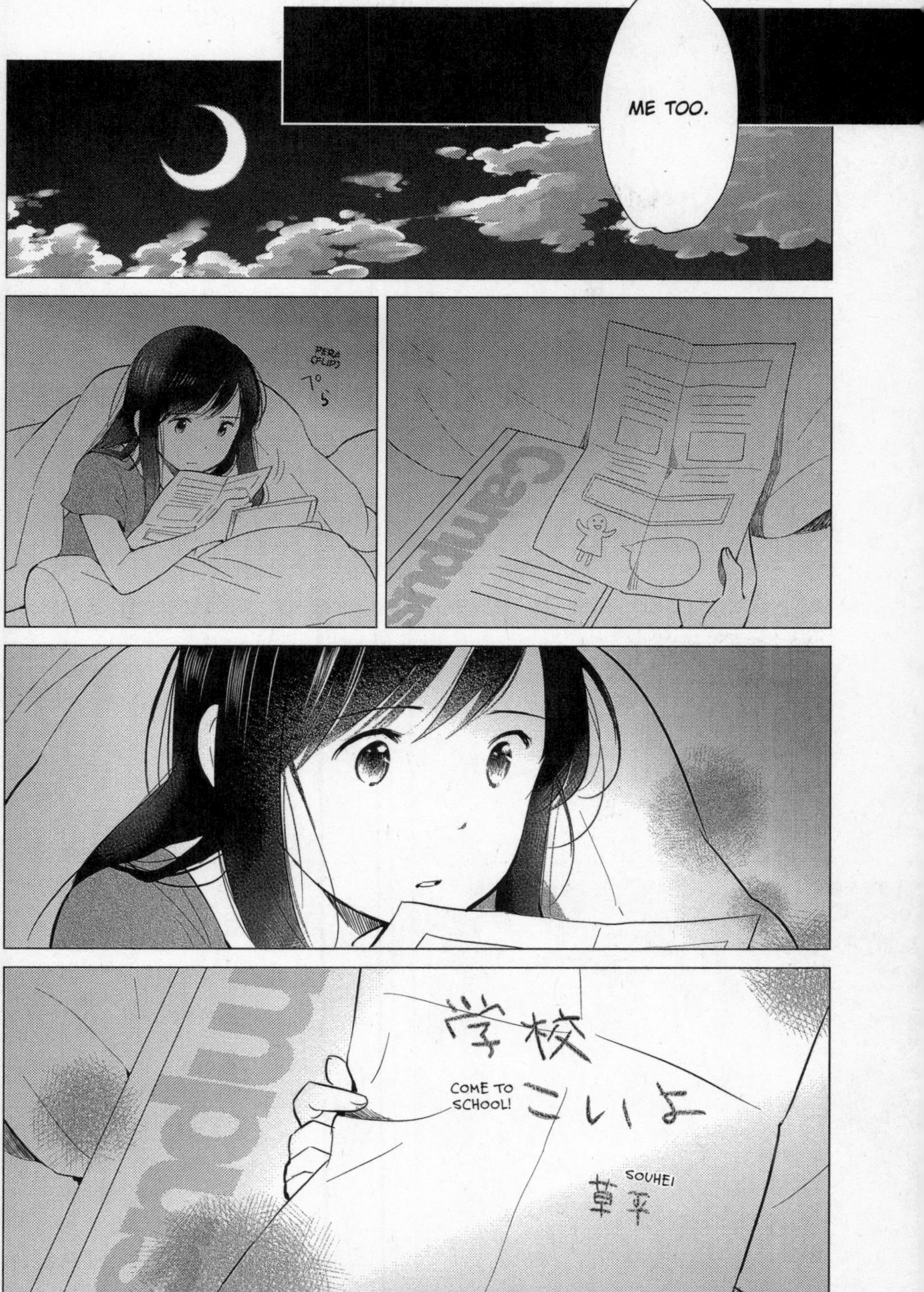
ME TOO.
PERA (FLIP)
ぺら
学校
こいよ
COME TO SCHOOL!
草平
SOUHEI

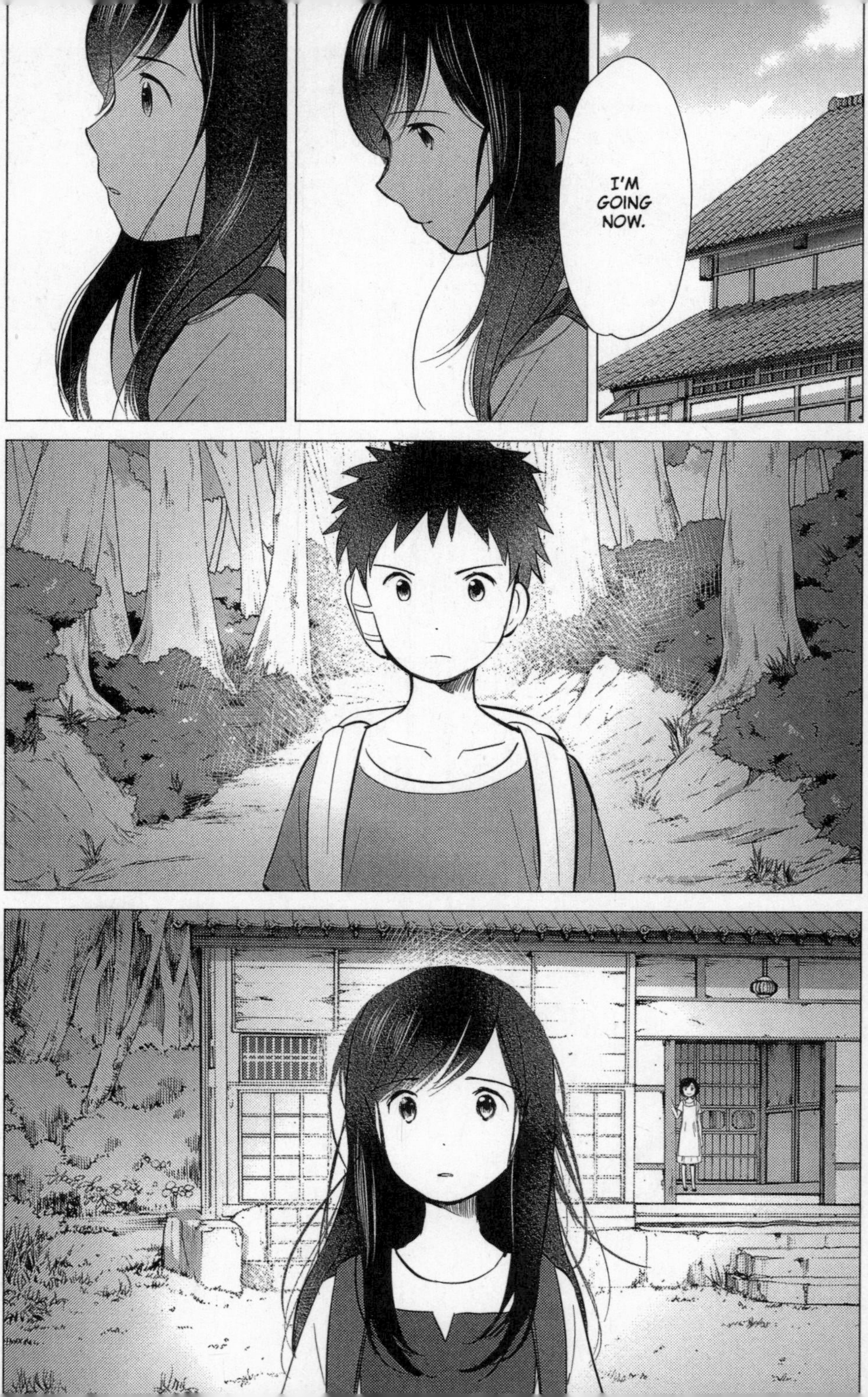
I'M GOING NOW.

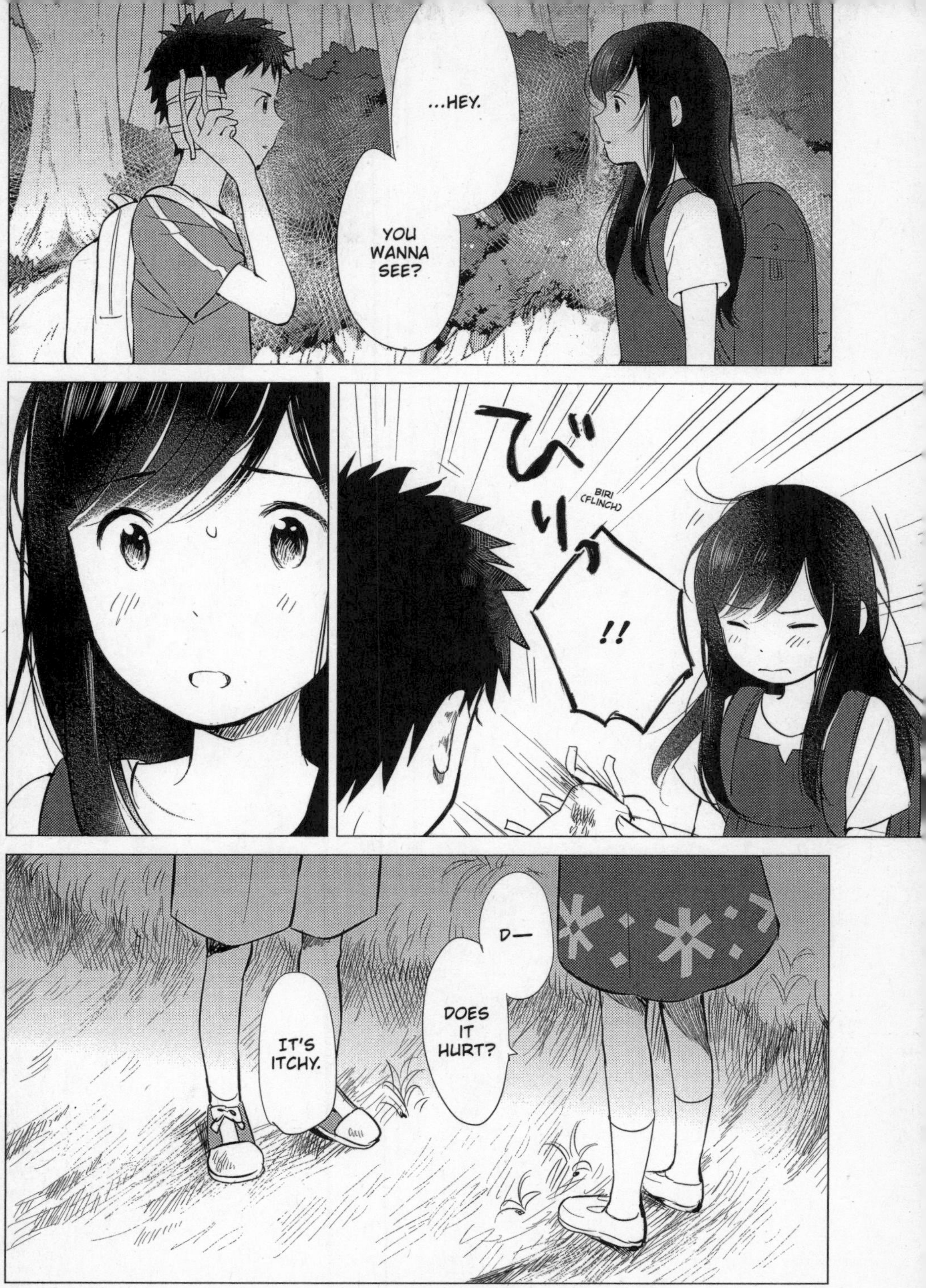
...HEY.
YOU WANNA SEE?
びりっ
BIRI (FLINCH)
!!
D—
DOES IT HURT?
IT'S ITCHY.

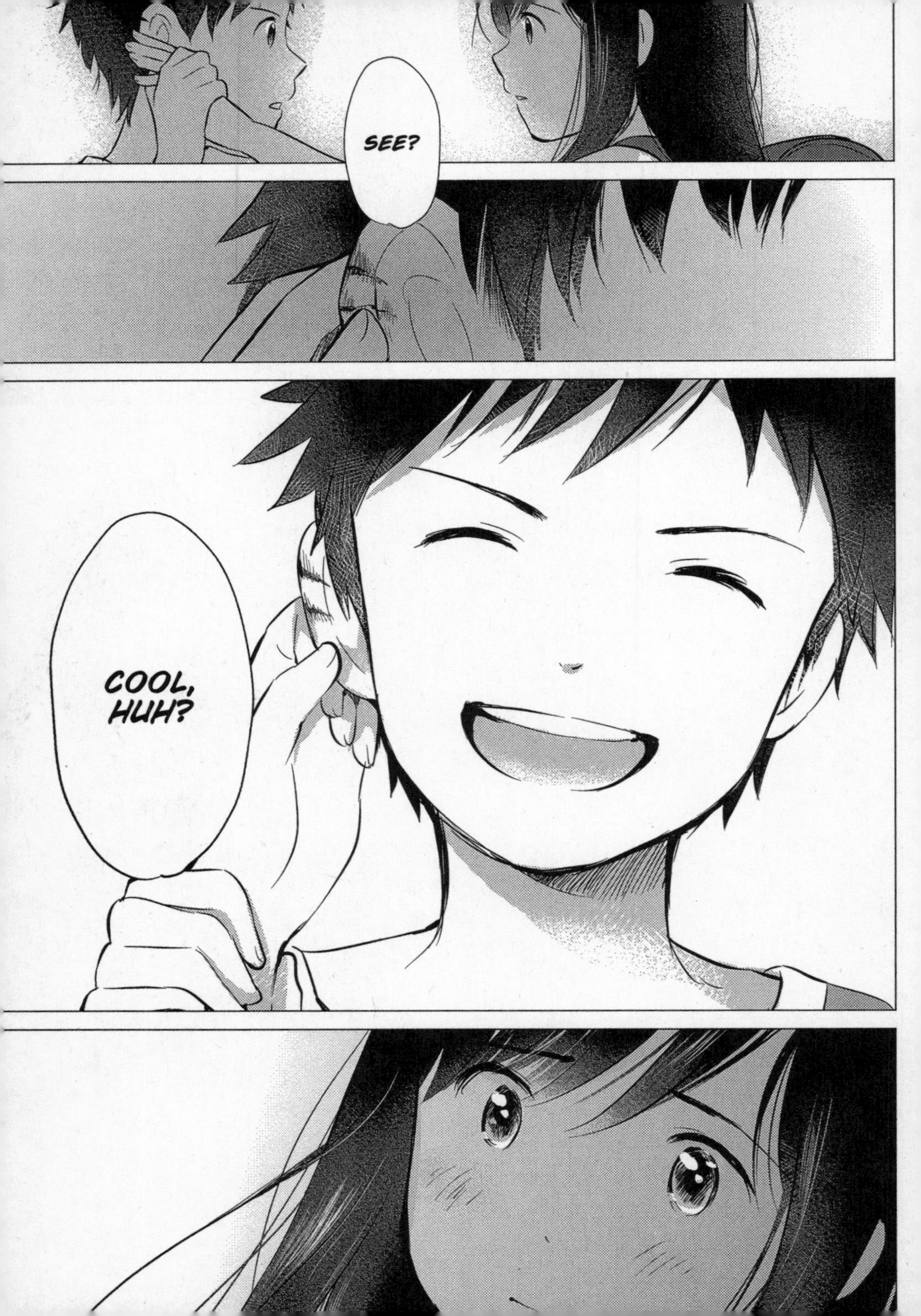
SEE?
COOL, HUH?

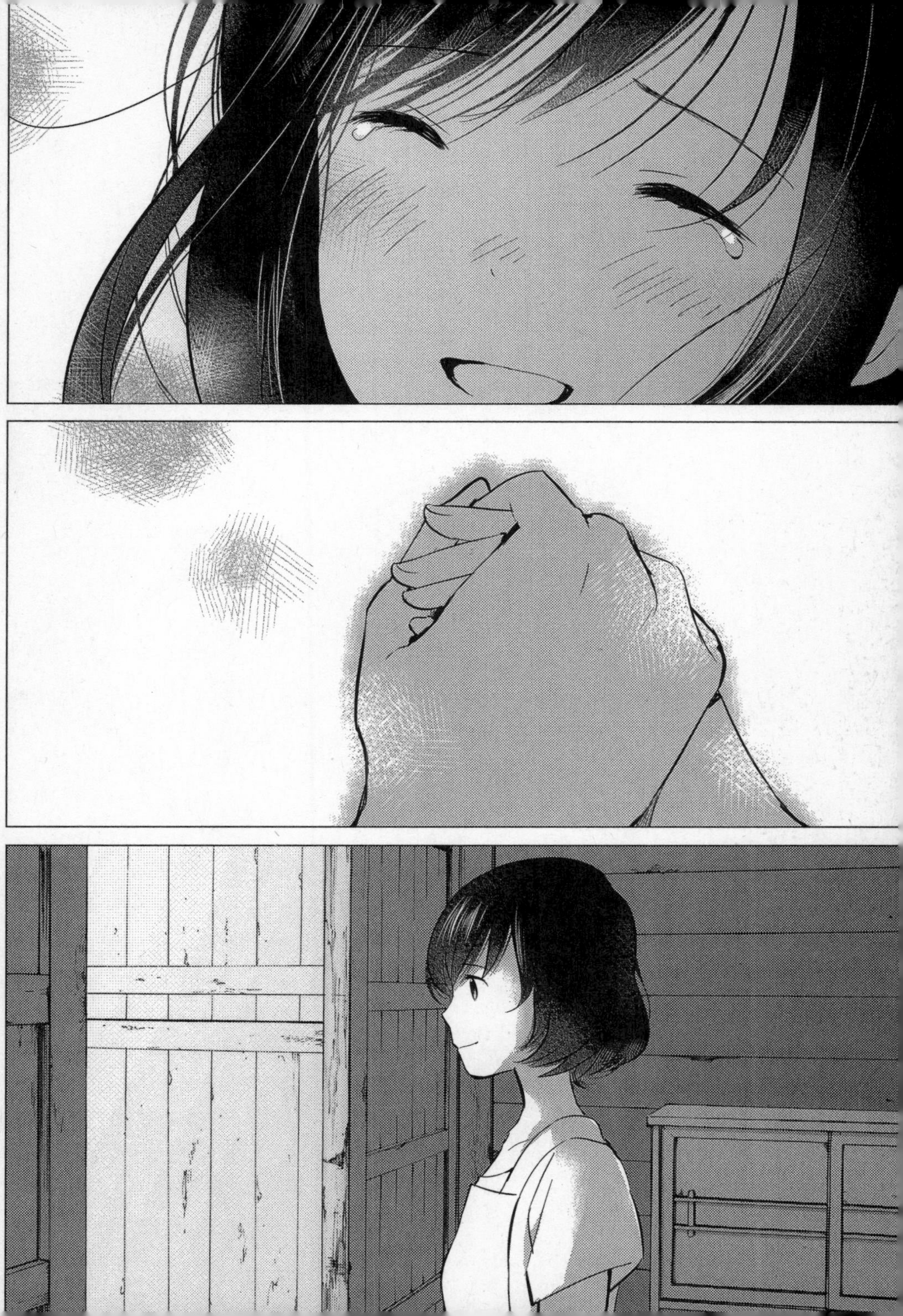

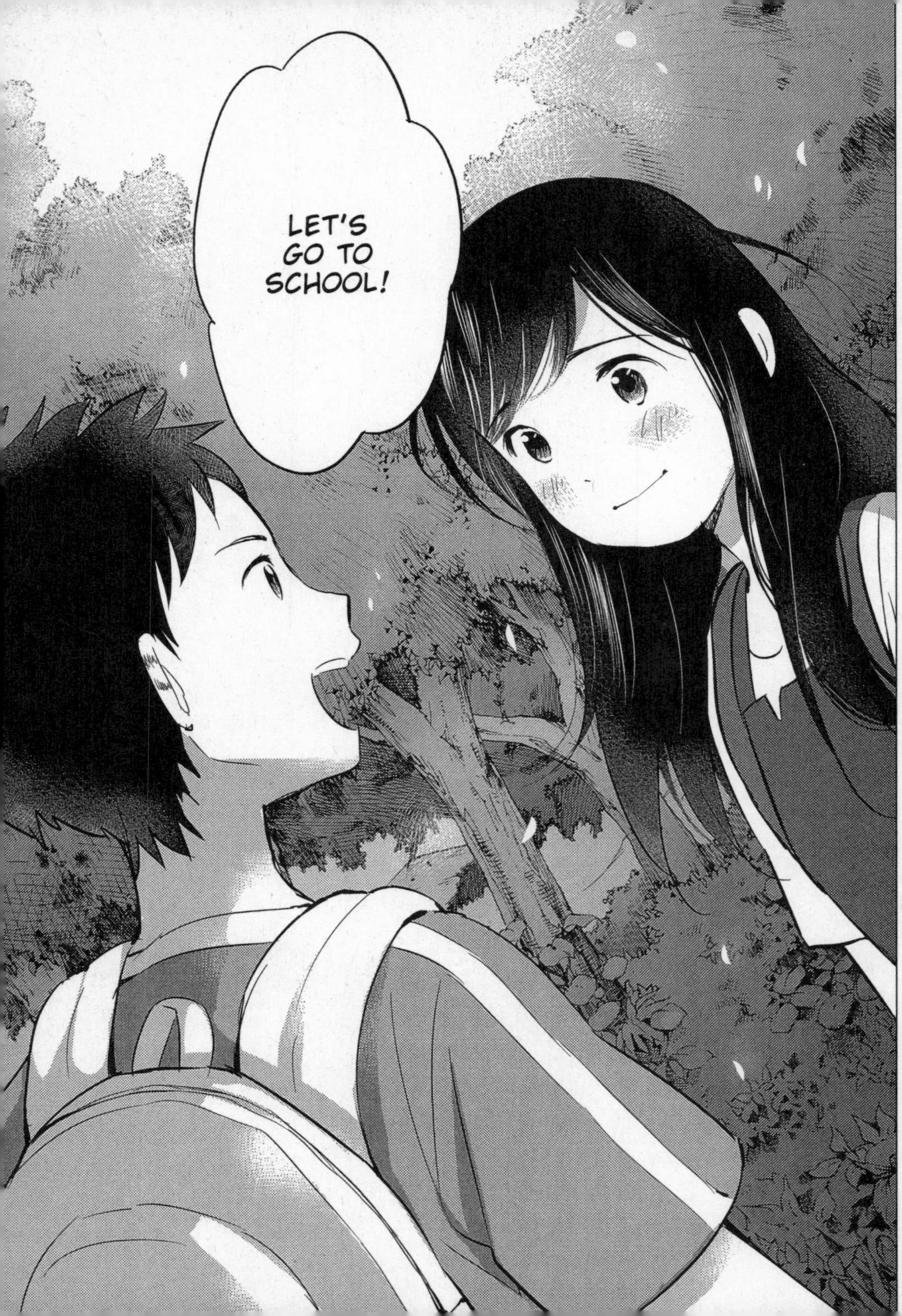
LET'S GO TO SCHOOL!

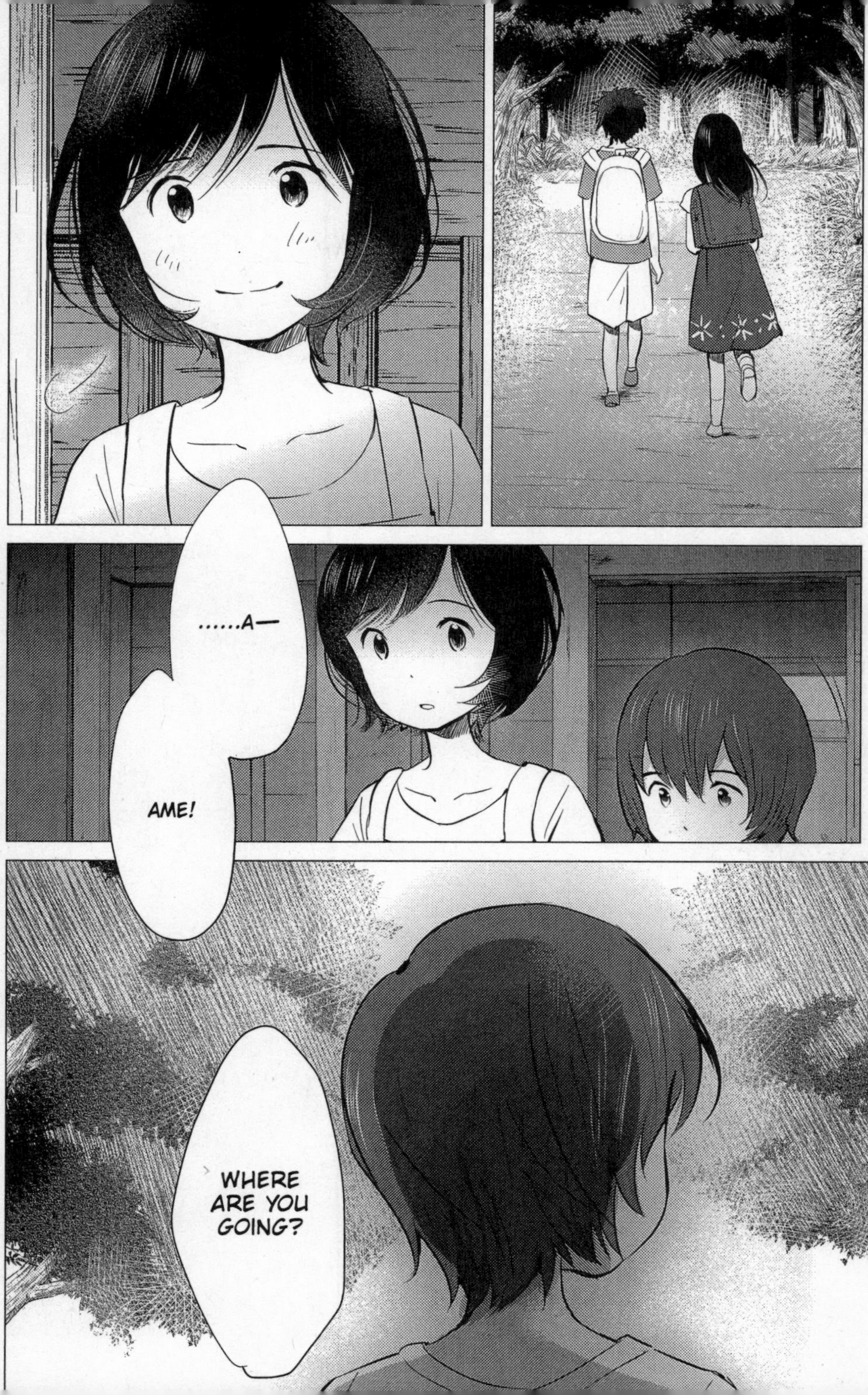
......A—
AME!
WHERE ARE YOU GOING?

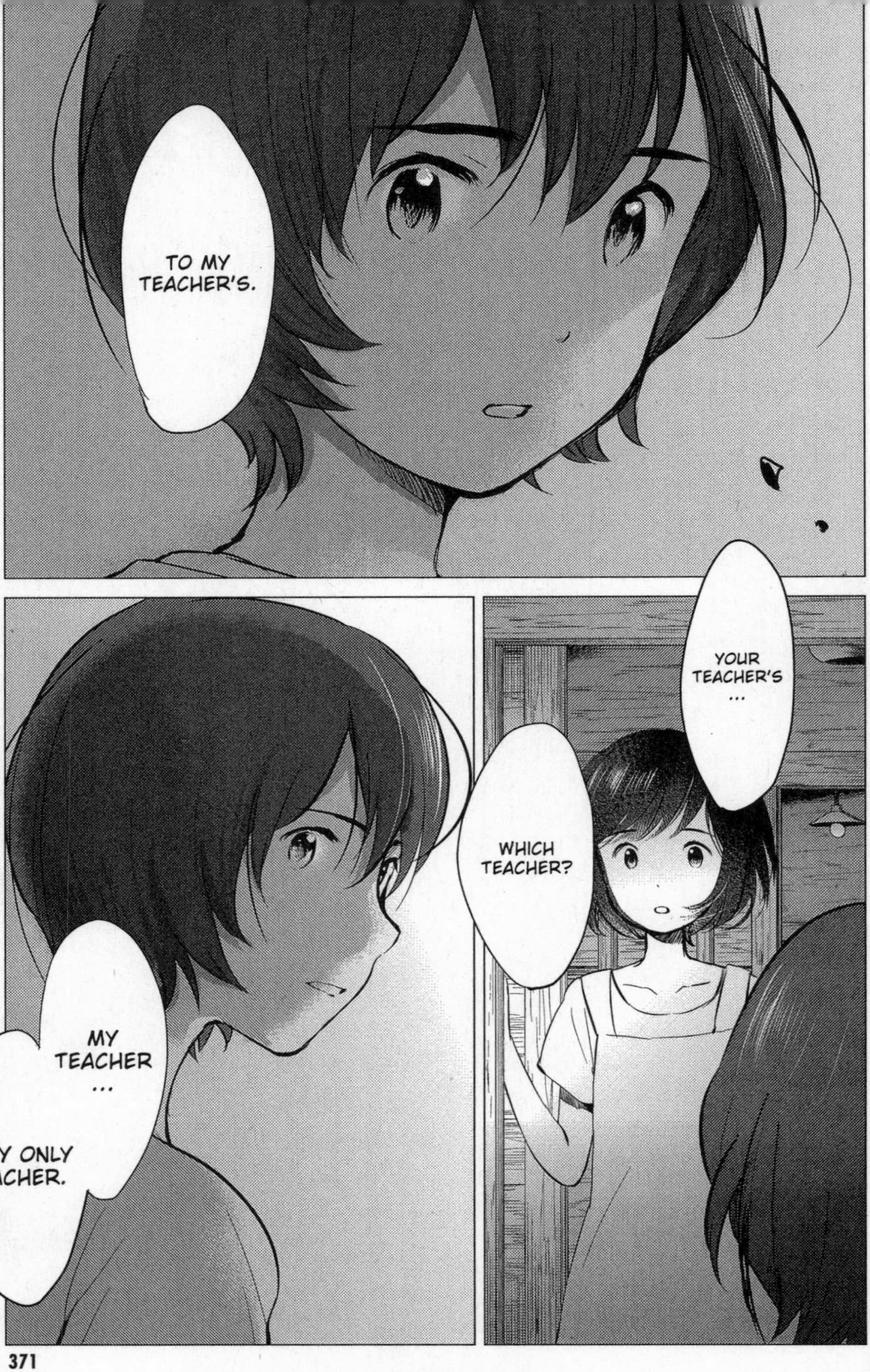
TO MY TEACHER'S.
YOUR TEACHER'S ...
WHICH TEACHER?
MY TEACHER ...
...MY ONLY TEACHER.

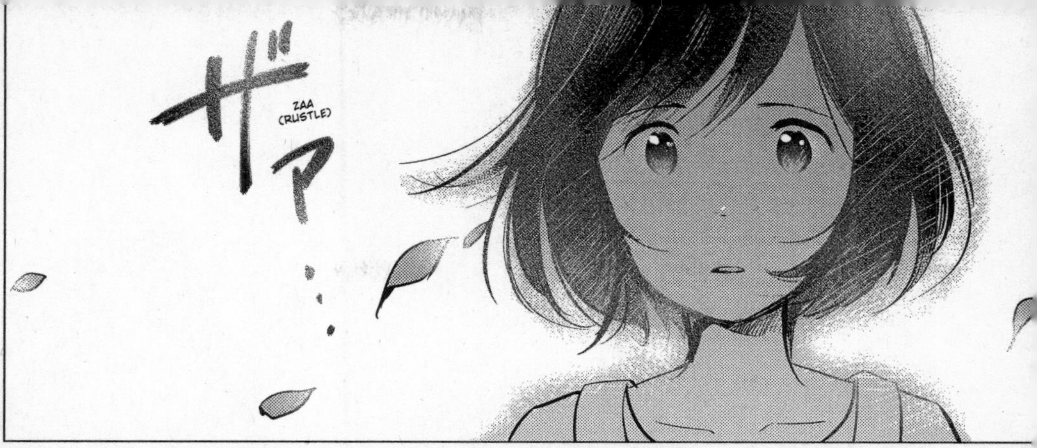
ザァ
ZAA
(RUSTLE)
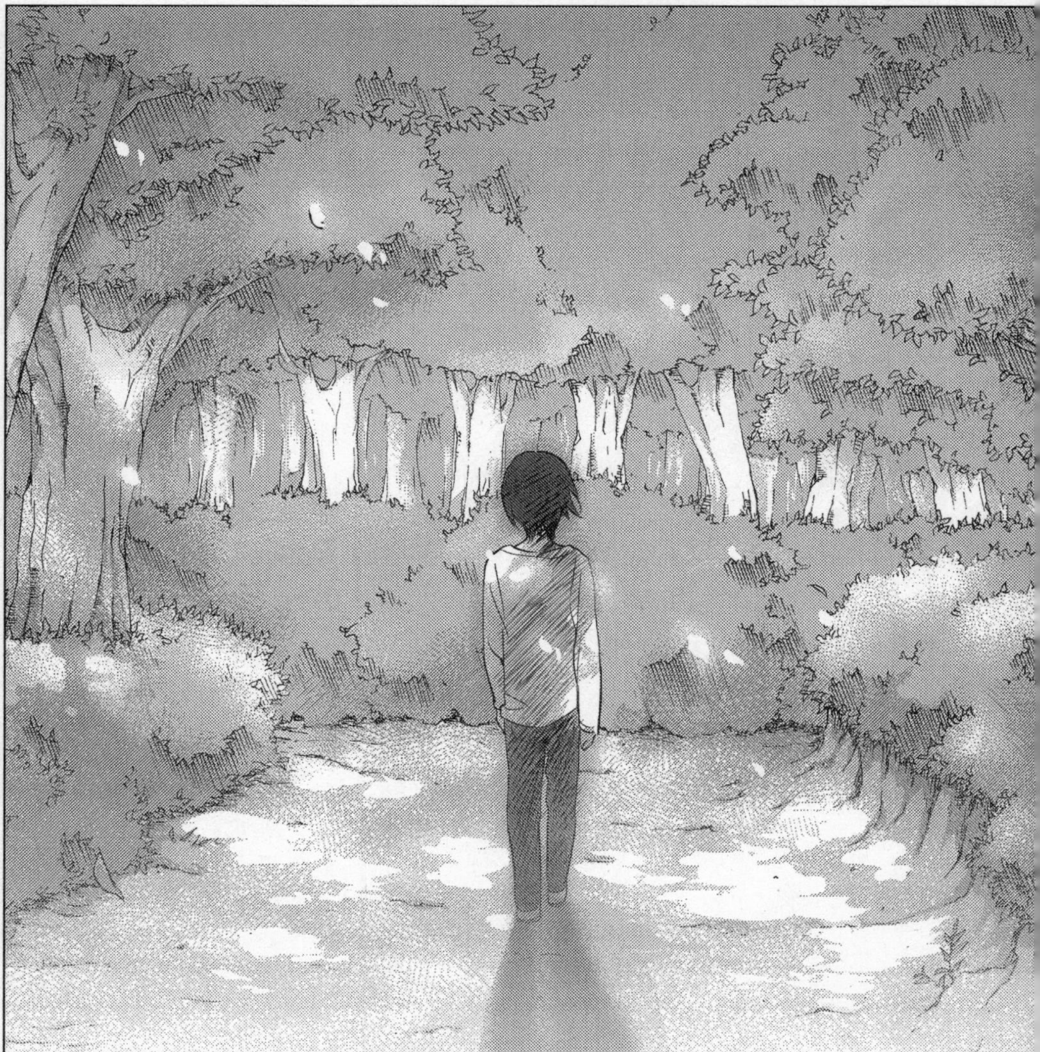

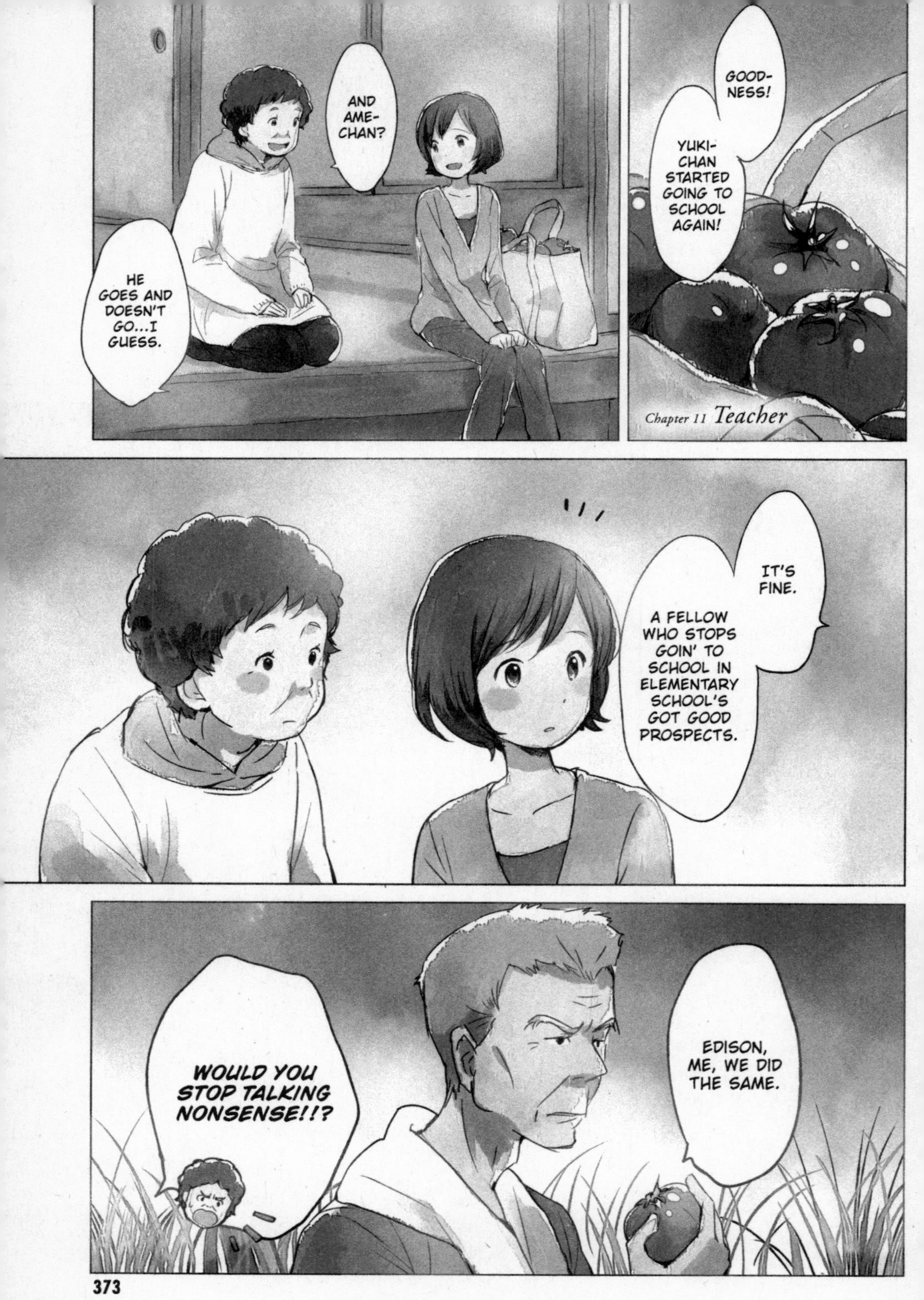
GOOD-NESS!
YUKI-CHAN STARTED GOING TO SCHOOL AGAIN!
Chapter 11 Teacher
AND AME-CHAN?
HE GOES AND DOESN'T GO...I GUESS.
IT'S FINE.
A FELLOW WHO STOPS GOIN' TO SCHOOL IN ELEMENTARY SCHOOL'S GOT GOOD PROSPECTS.
EDISON, ME, WE DID THE SAME.
WOULD YOU STOP TALKING NONSENSE!!?

Chapter 11 Teacher

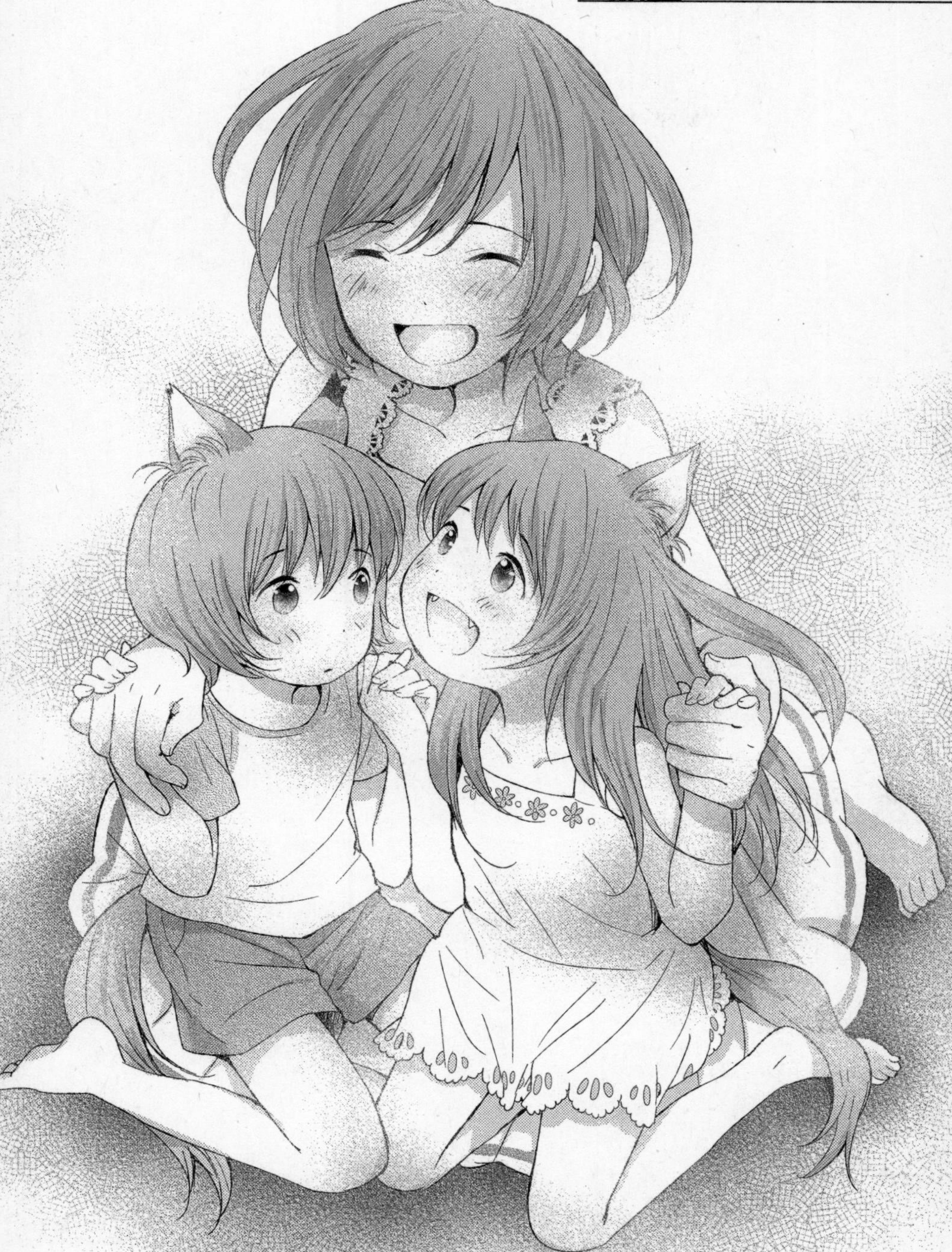

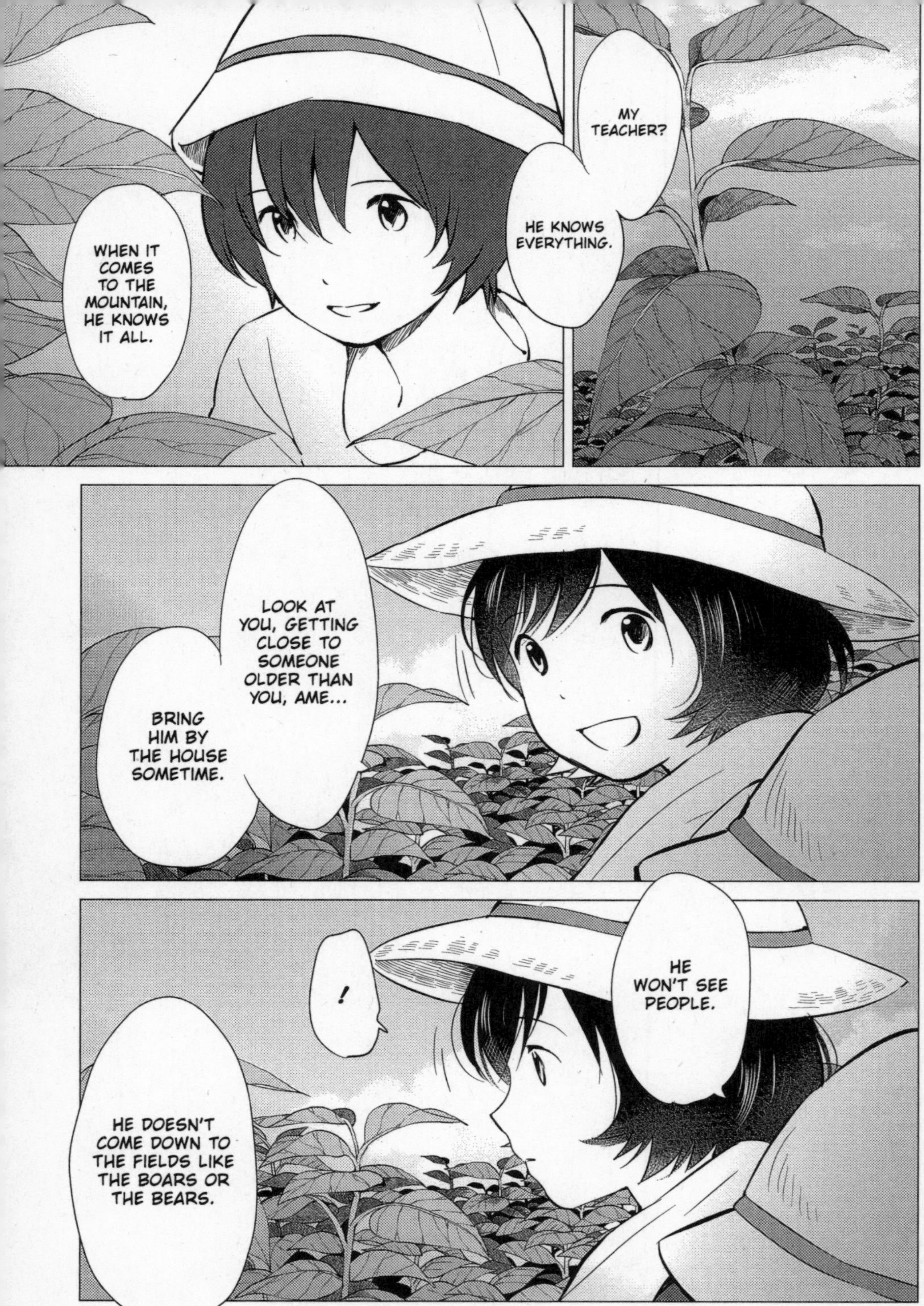
MY TEACHER?
HE KNOWS EVERYTHING.
WHEN IT COMES TO THE MOUNTAIN, HE KNOWS IT ALL.
LOOK AT YOU, GETTING CLOSE TO SOMEONE OLDER THAN YOU, AME...
BRING HIM BY THE HOUSE SOMETIME.
HE WON'T SEE PEOPLE.
!
HE DOESN'T COME DOWN TO THE FIELDS LIKE THE BOARS OR THE BEARS.

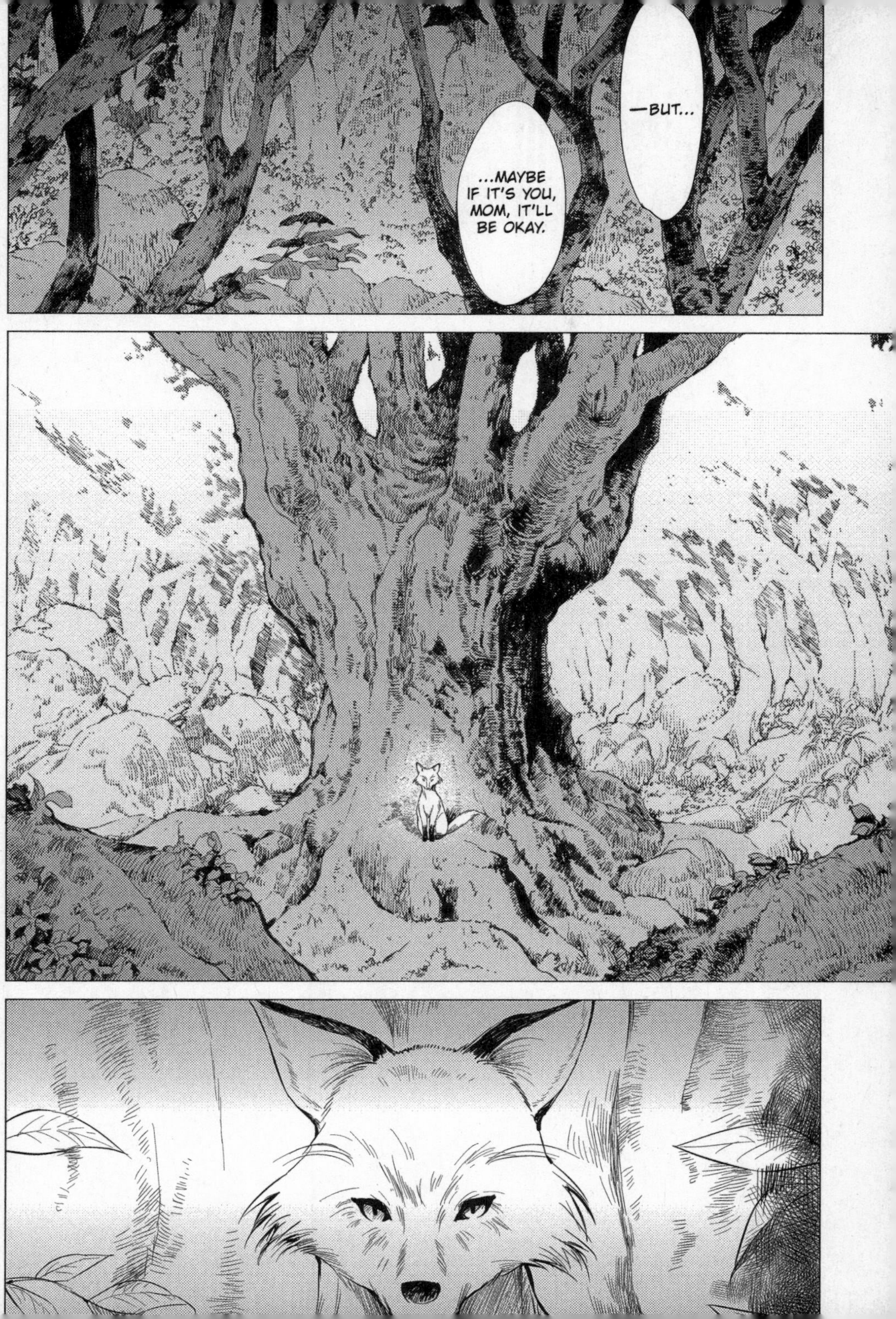
—BUT...
...MAYBE IF IT'S YOU, MOM, IT'LL BE OKAY.

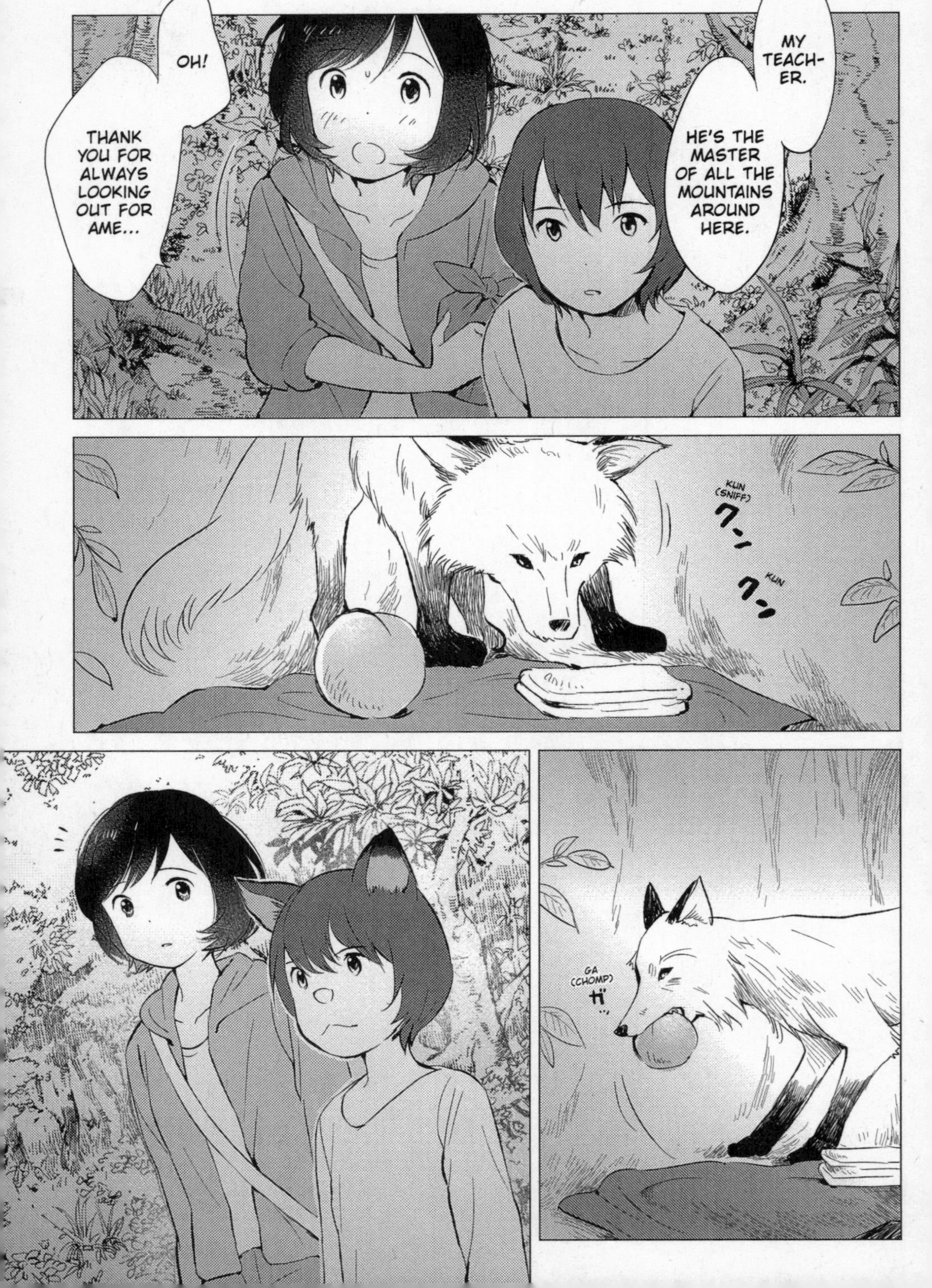
MY TEACHER.
HE'S THE MASTER OF ALL THE MOUNTAINS AROUND HERE.
OH!
THANK YOU FOR ALWAYS LOOKING OUT FOR AME...
KUN (SNIFF)
クン
KUN
クン
GA (CHOMP)
ガ

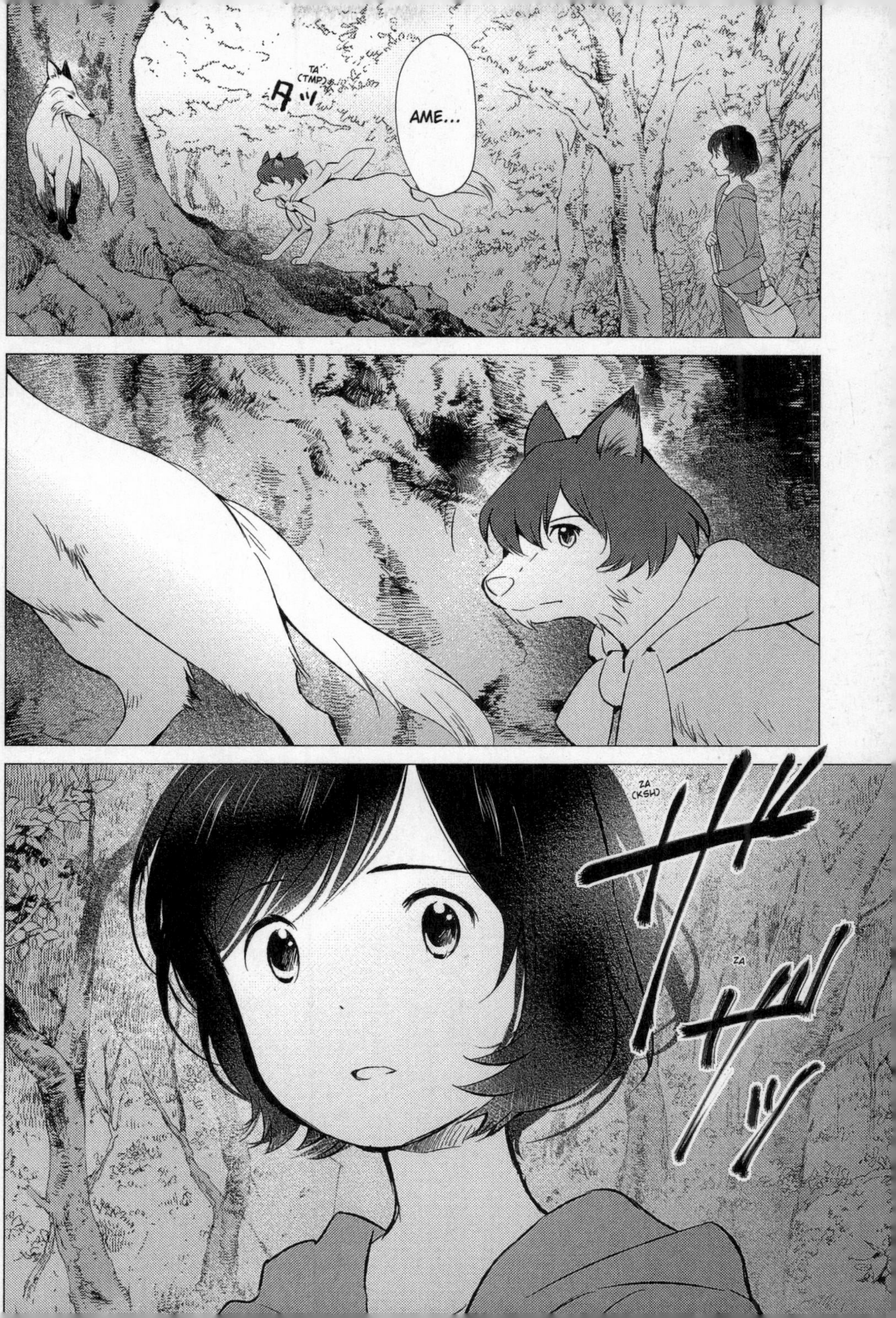
AME...
TA (TMP)
タッ
ZA (KSH)
ザッ
ZA
ザッ

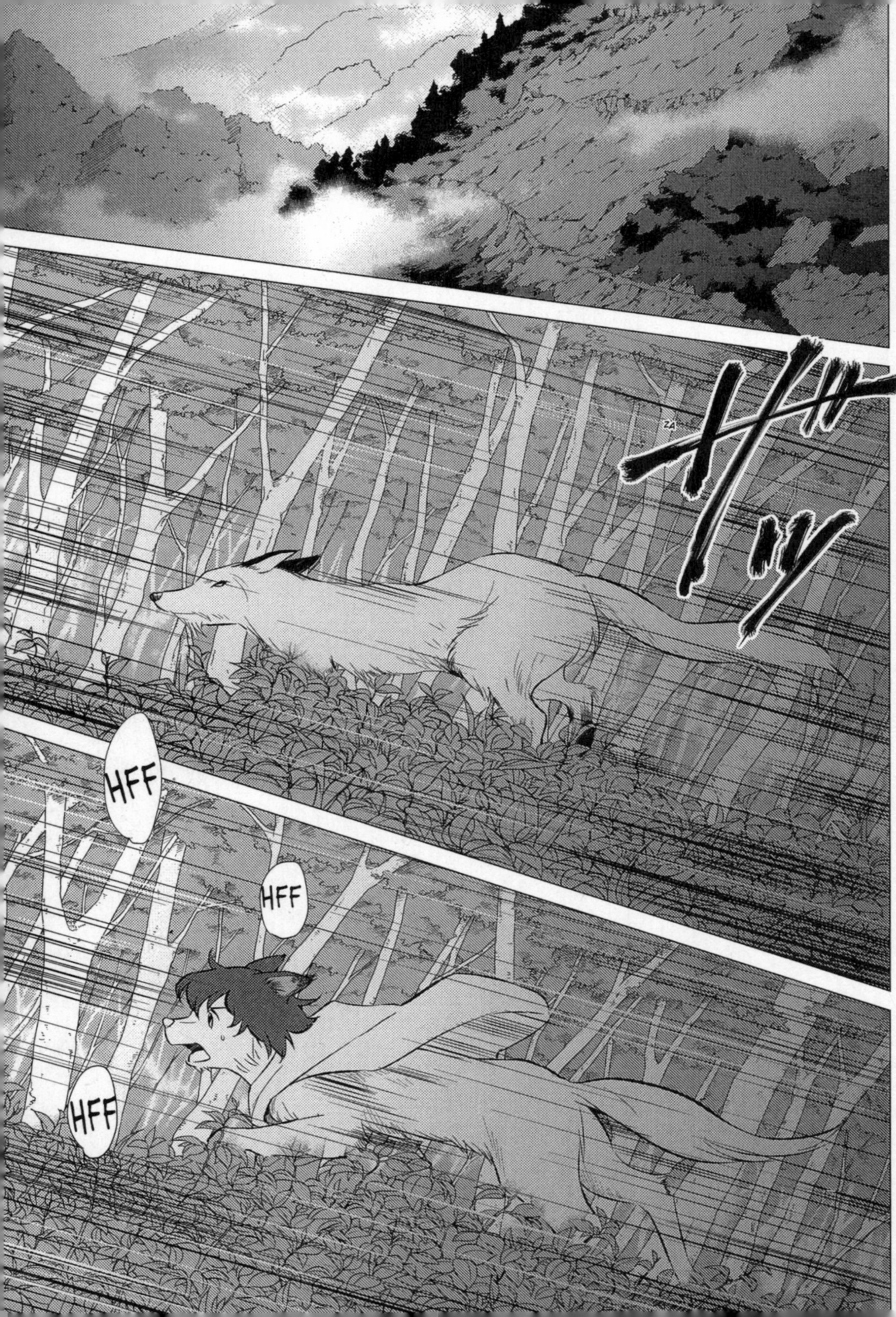
ザッ
ZA
HFF
HFF
HFF

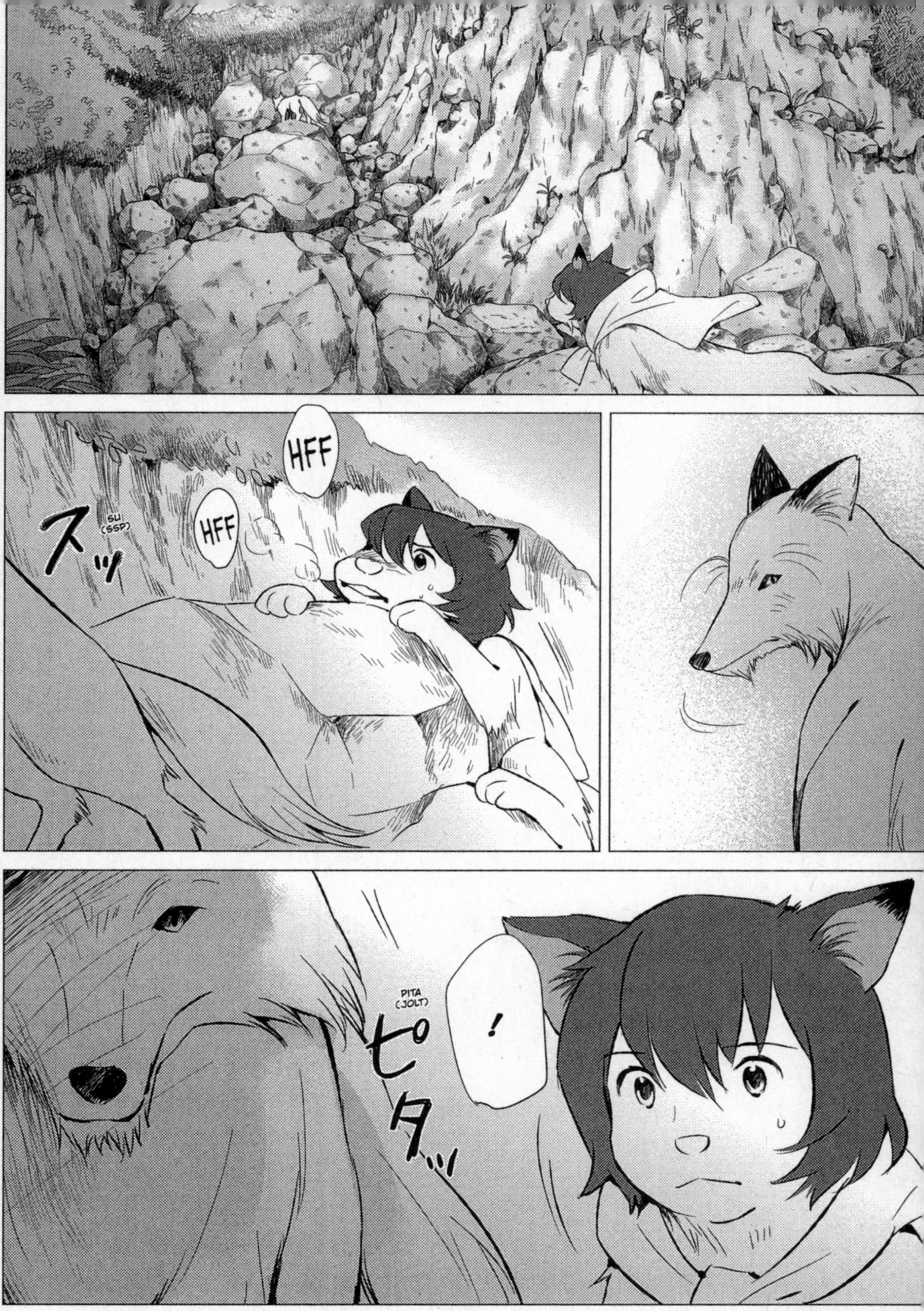
HFF
HFF
スッ
SU (SSP)
ピタッ
PITA (JOLT)
!

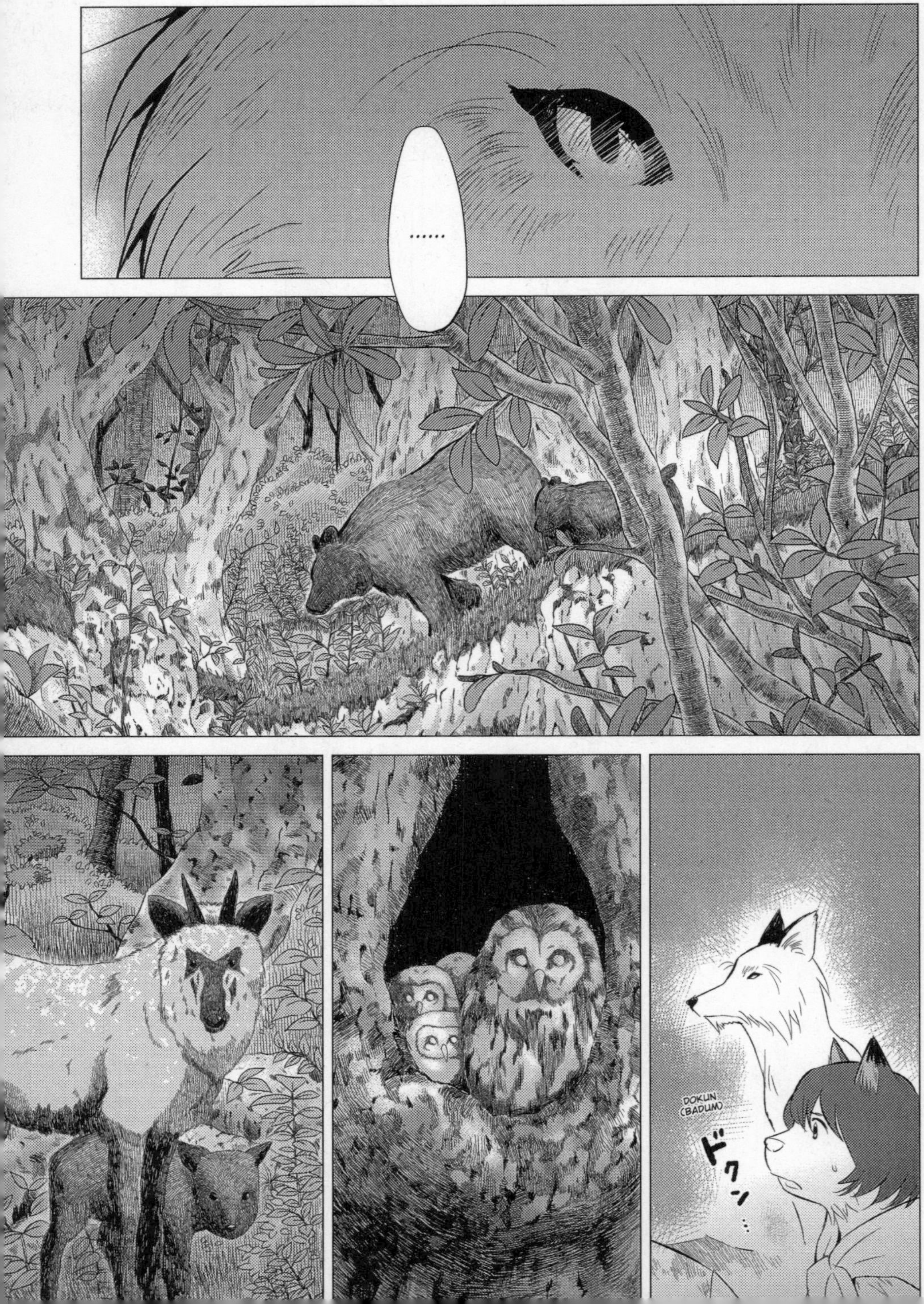
......
DOKUN (BADUM)
ドクン…

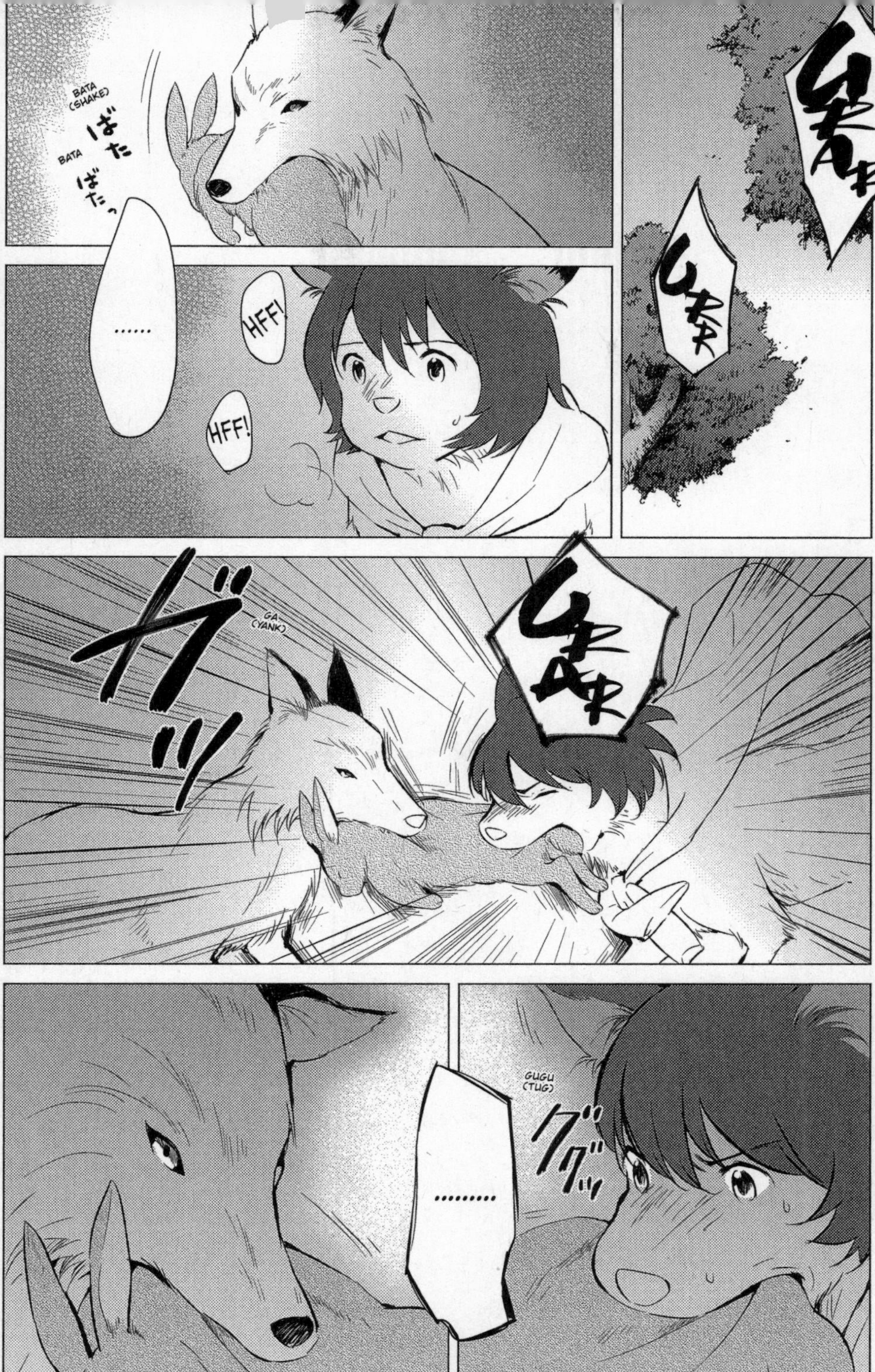
GRRR
URRR
BATA (SHAKE)
ばた
BATA
ばたっ
......
HFF!
HFF!
GA (YANK)
ガッ
URRR
GUGU (TUG)
ググッ
....

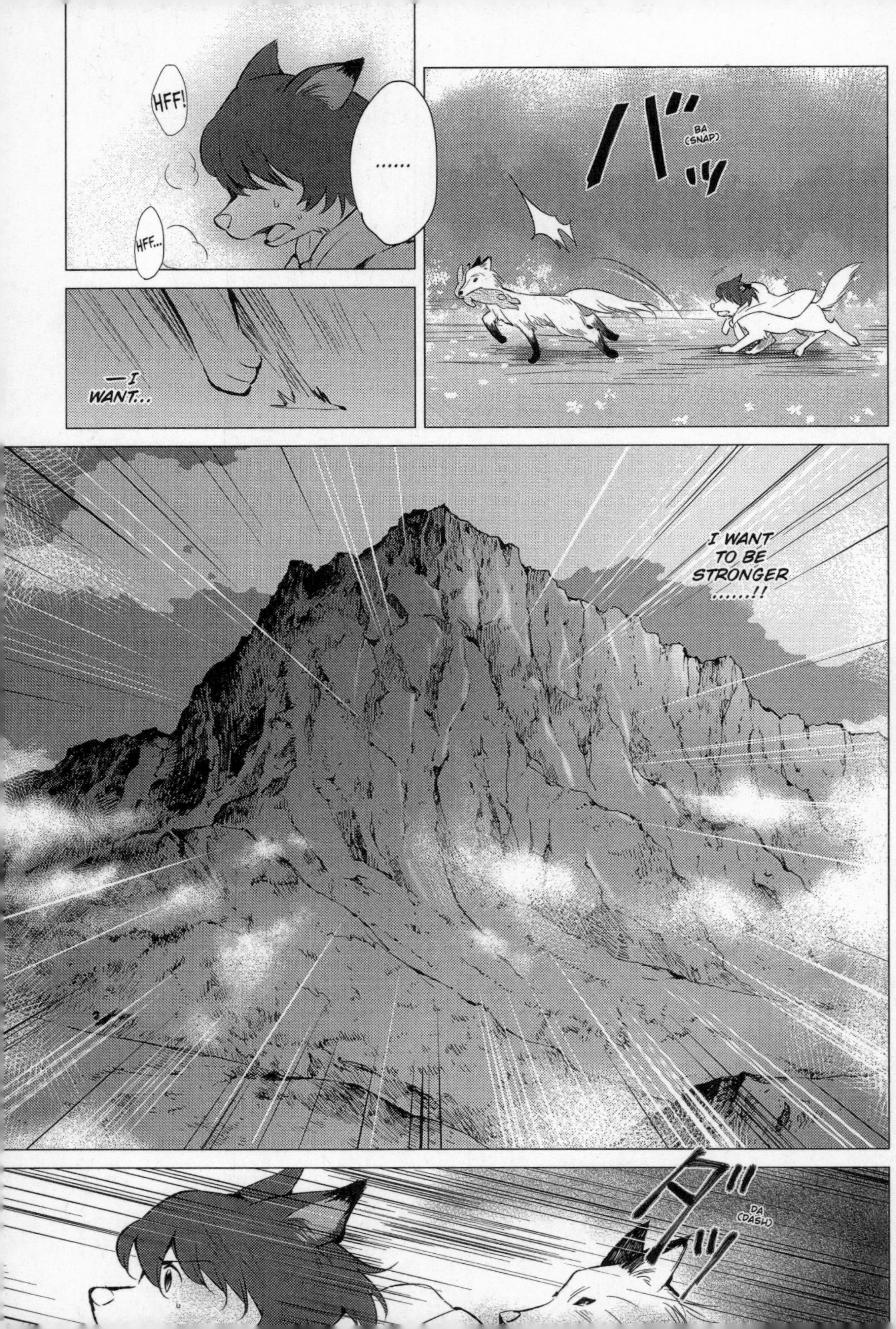

バッ
BA (SNAP)
......
HFF!
HFF...
—I WANT...
I WANT TO BE STRONGER ......!!
ダッ
DA (DASH)

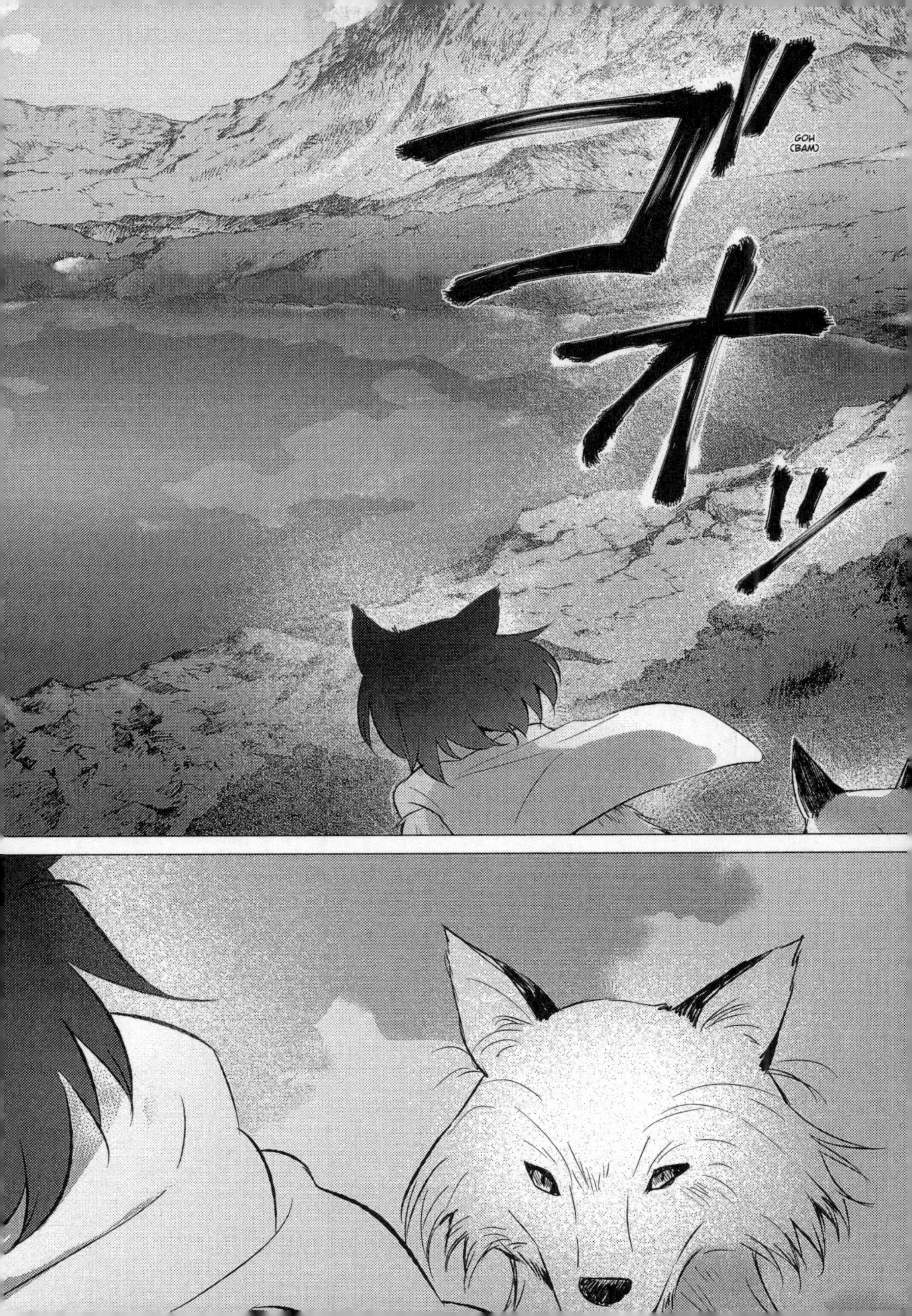
ゴオッ
GOH
(BAM)

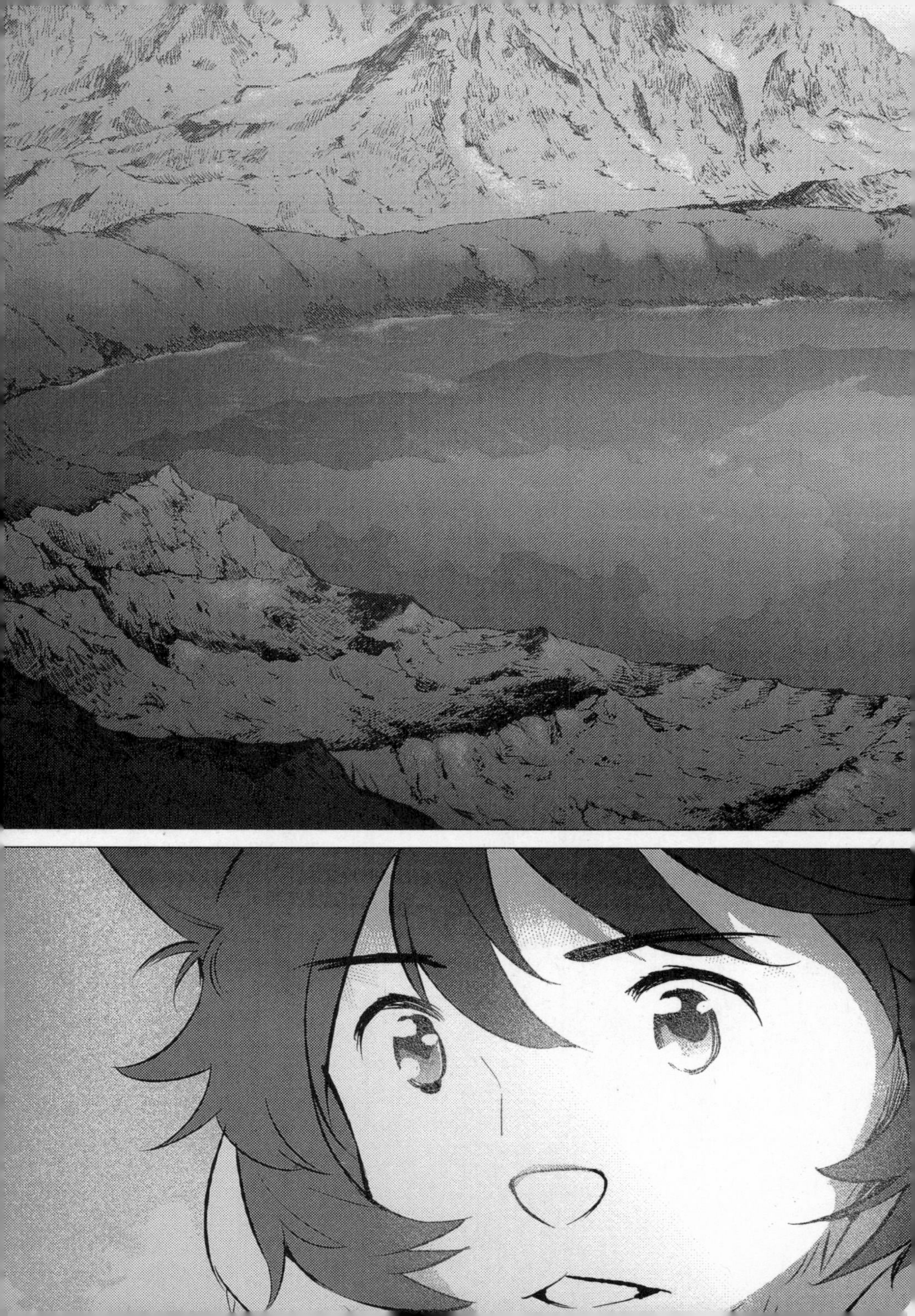

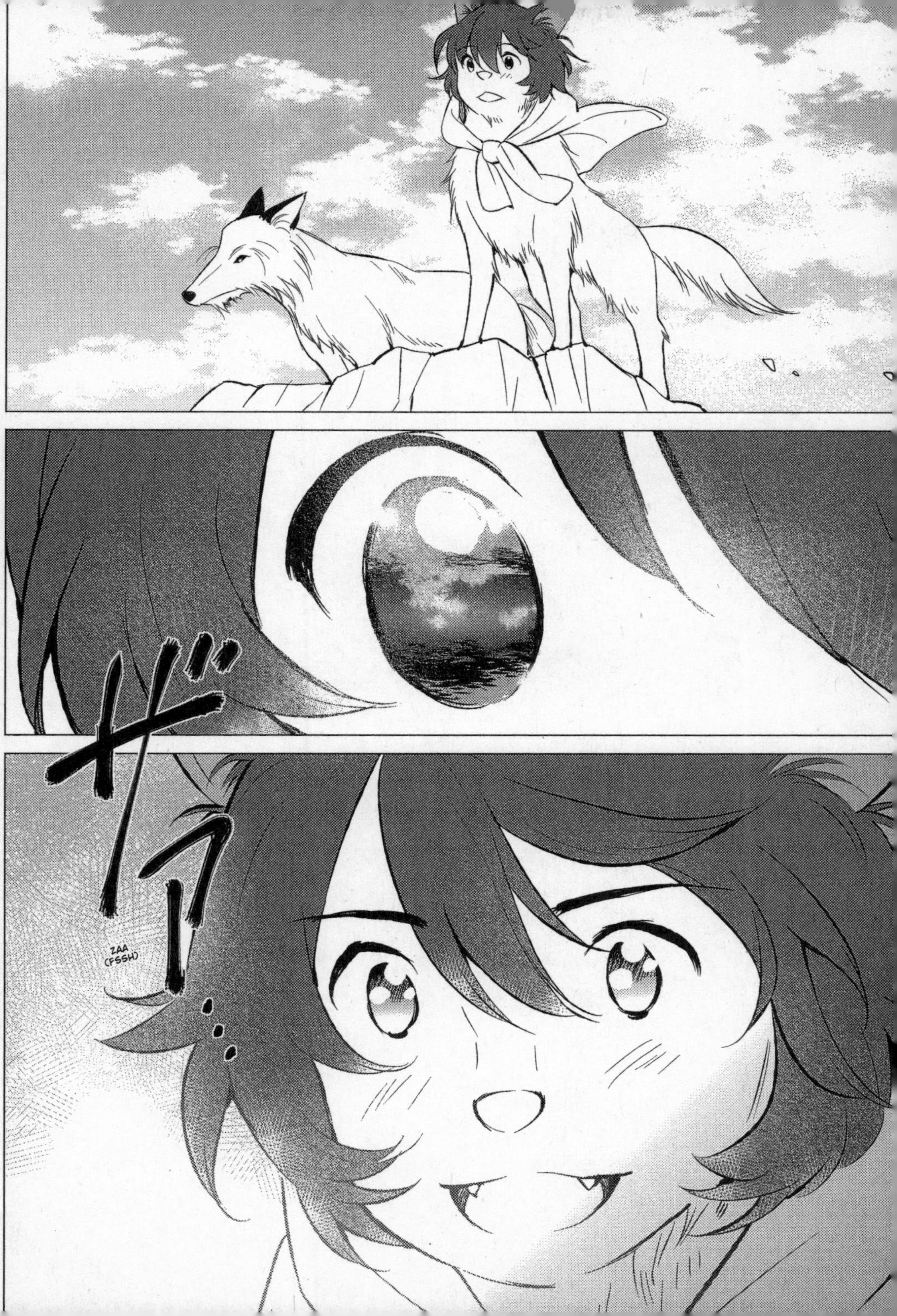
ザァ…
ZAA
(FSSH)

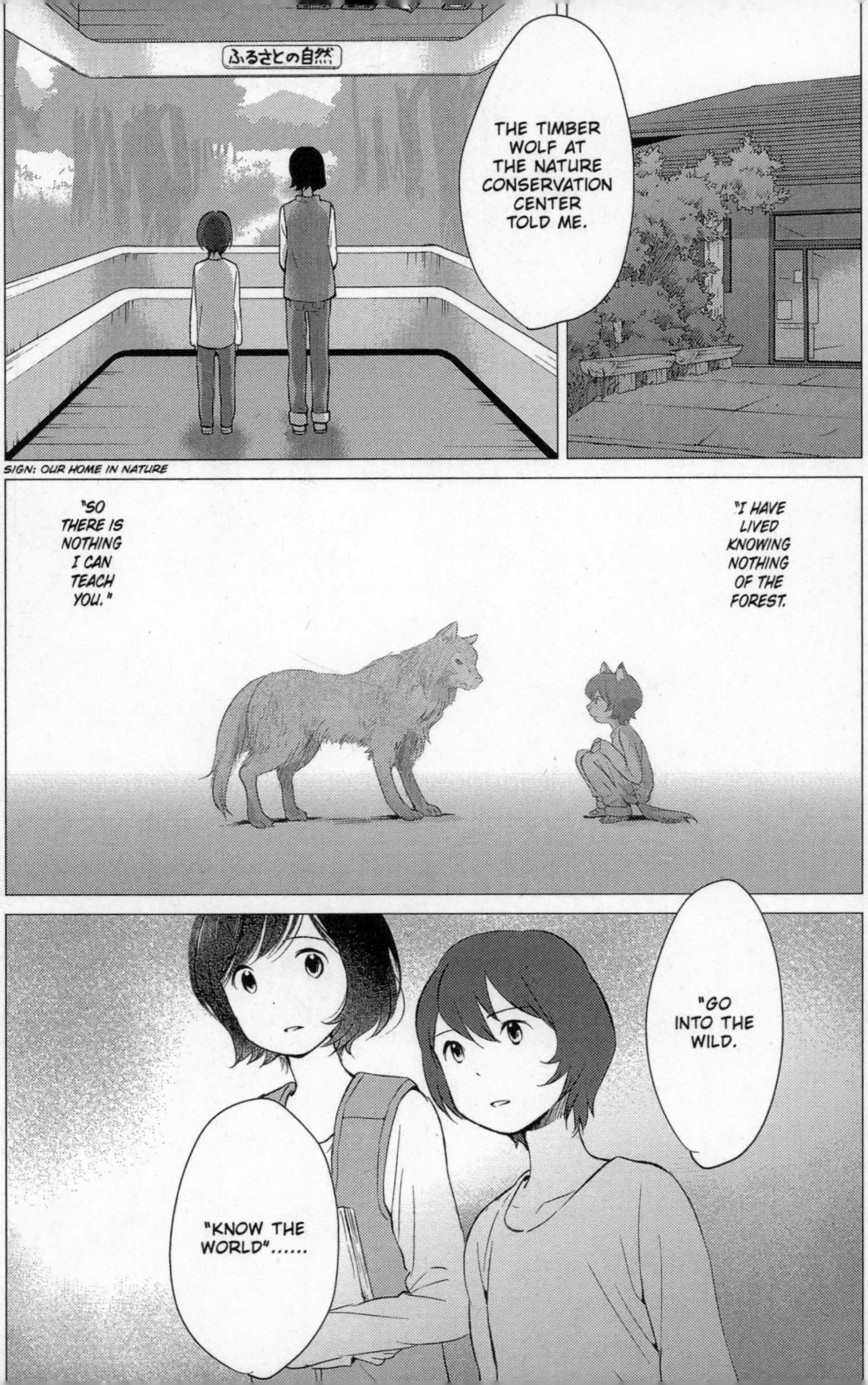
THE TIMBER WOLF AT THE NATURE CONSERVATION CENTER TOLD ME.
ふるさとの自然
SIGN: OUR HOME IN NATURE
"I HAVE LIVED KNOWING NOTHING OF THE FOREST.
"SO THERE IS NOTHING I CAN TEACH YOU."
"GO INTO THE WILD.
"KNOW THE WORLD"......

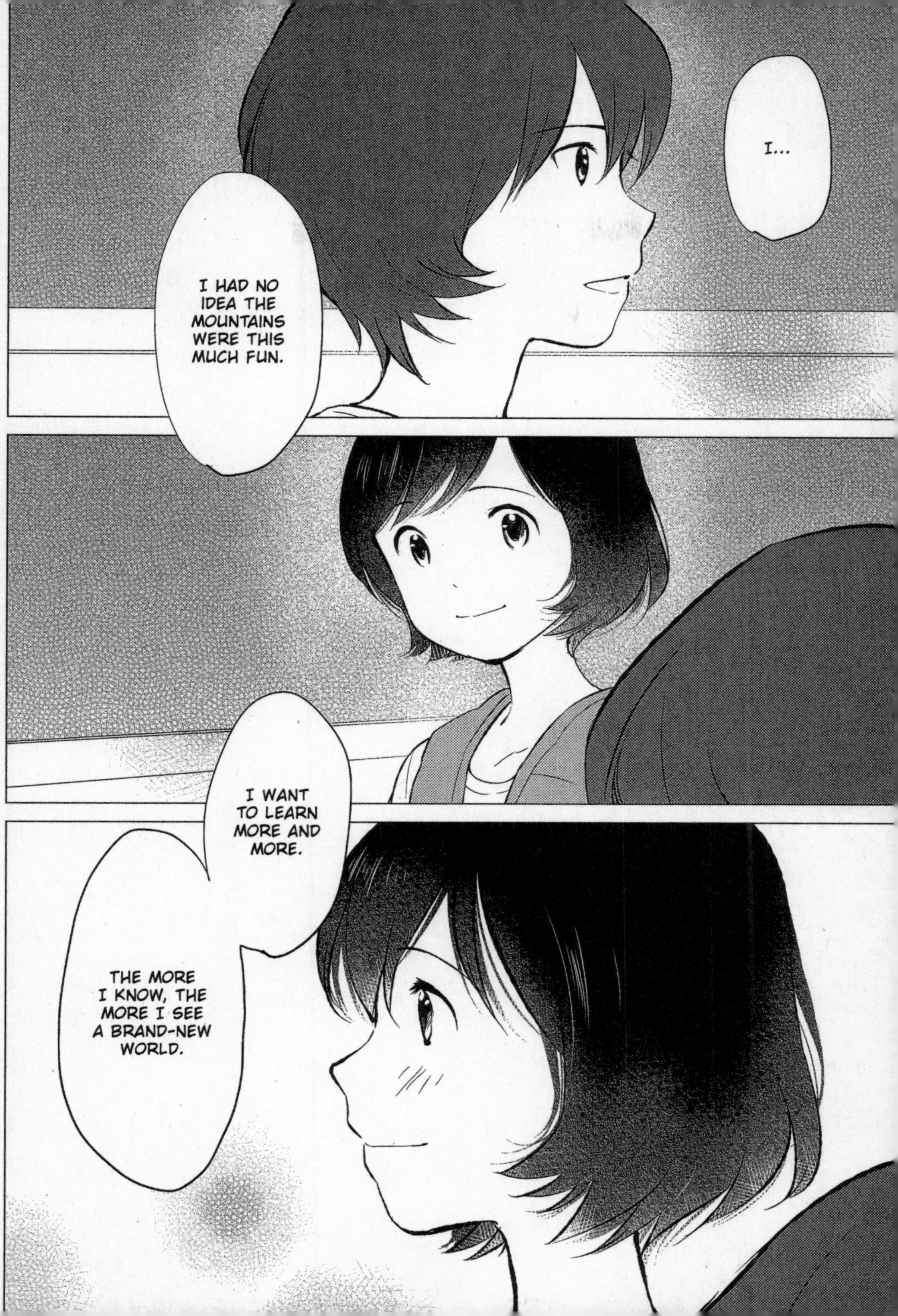
I...
I HAD NO IDEA THE MOUNTAINS WERE THIS MUCH FUN.
I WANT TO LEARN MORE AND MORE.
THE MORE I KNOW, THE MORE I SEE A BRAND-NEW WORLD.

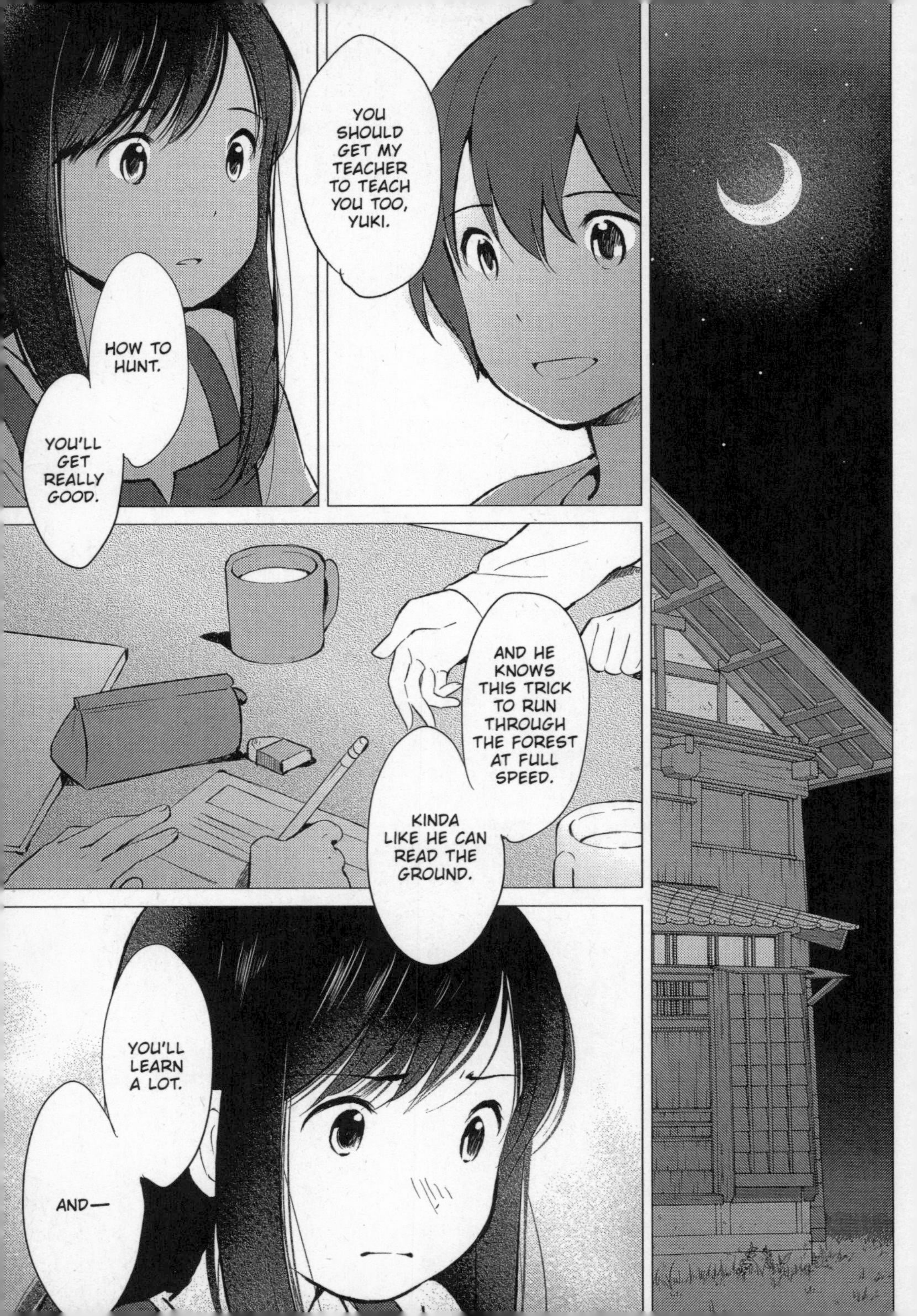
YOU SHOULD GET MY TEACHER TO TEACH YOU TOO, YUKI.
HOW TO HUNT.
YOU'LL GET REALLY GOOD.
AND HE KNOWS THIS TRICK TO RUN THROUGH THE FOREST AT FULL SPEED.
KINDA LIKE HE CAN READ THE GROUND.
YOU'LL LEARN A LOT.
AND—

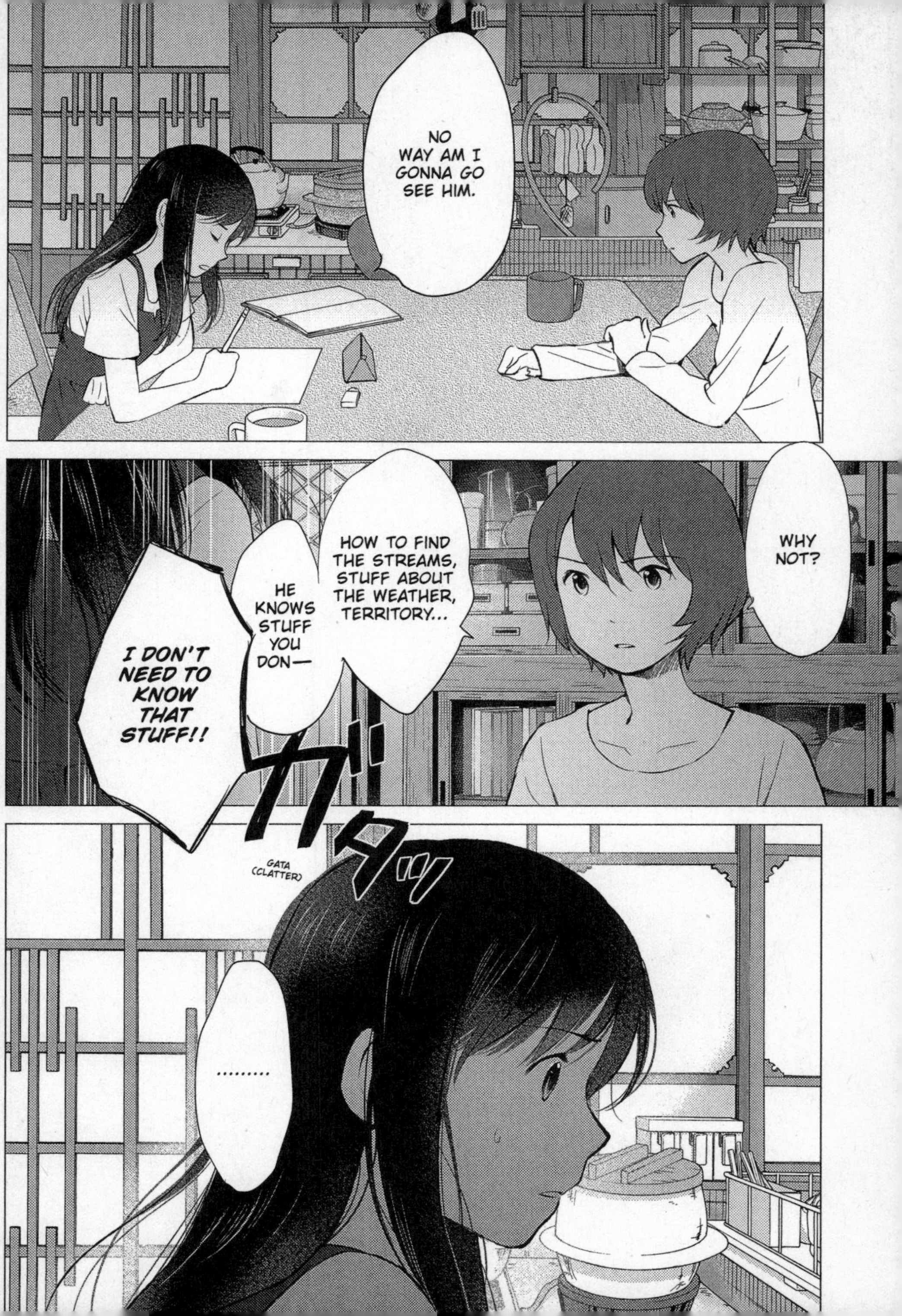
NO WAY AM I GONNA GO SEE HIM.
WHY NOT?
HOW TO FIND THE STREAMS, STUFF ABOUT THE WEATHER, TERRITORY...
HE KNOWS STUFF YOU DON—
I DON'T NEED TO KNOW THAT STUFF!!
GATA (CLATTER)
....

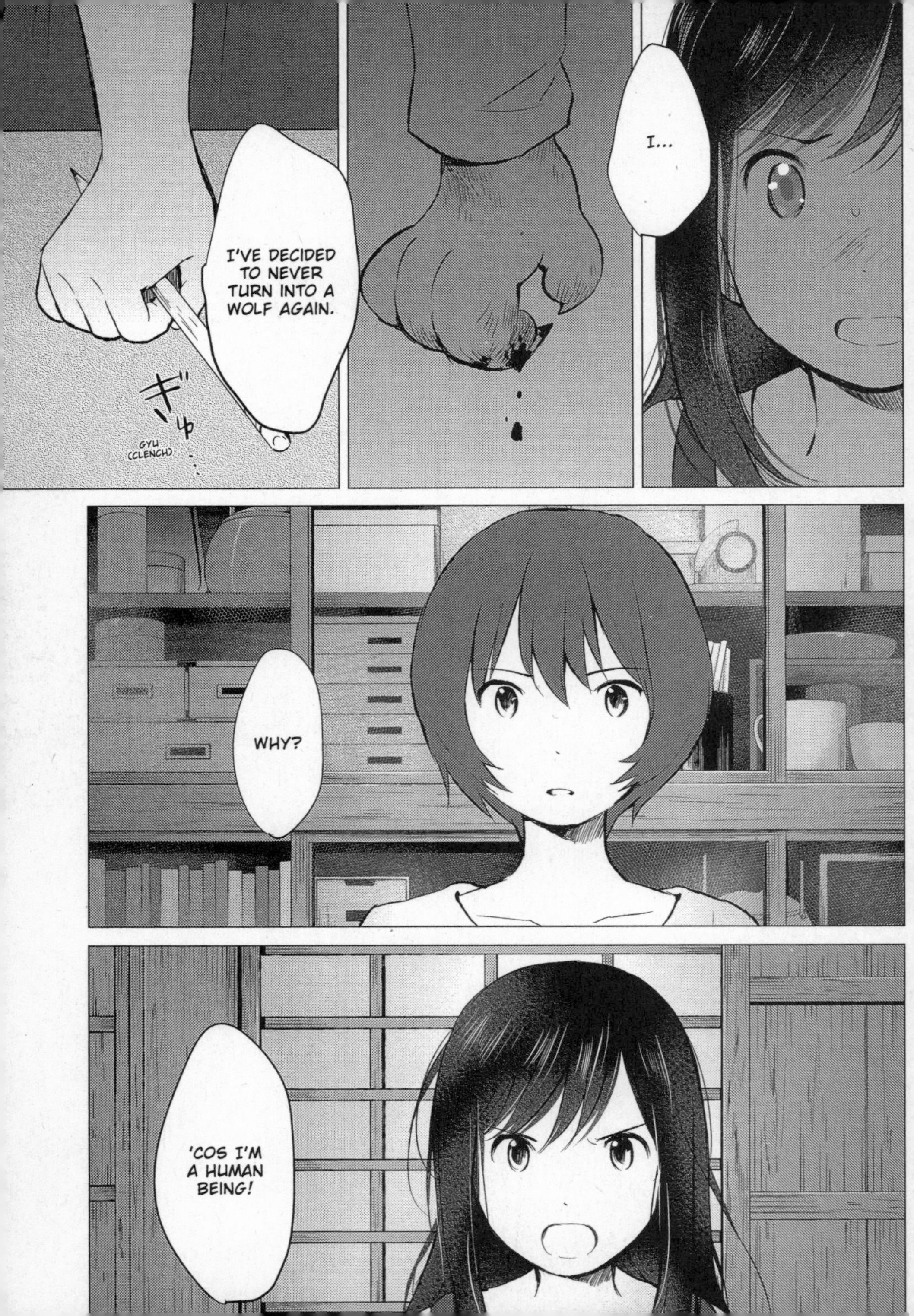
I...
I'VE DECIDED TO NEVER TURN INTO A WOLF AGAIN.
ぎゅ
GYU (CLENCH)
WHY?
'COS I'M A HUMAN BEING!

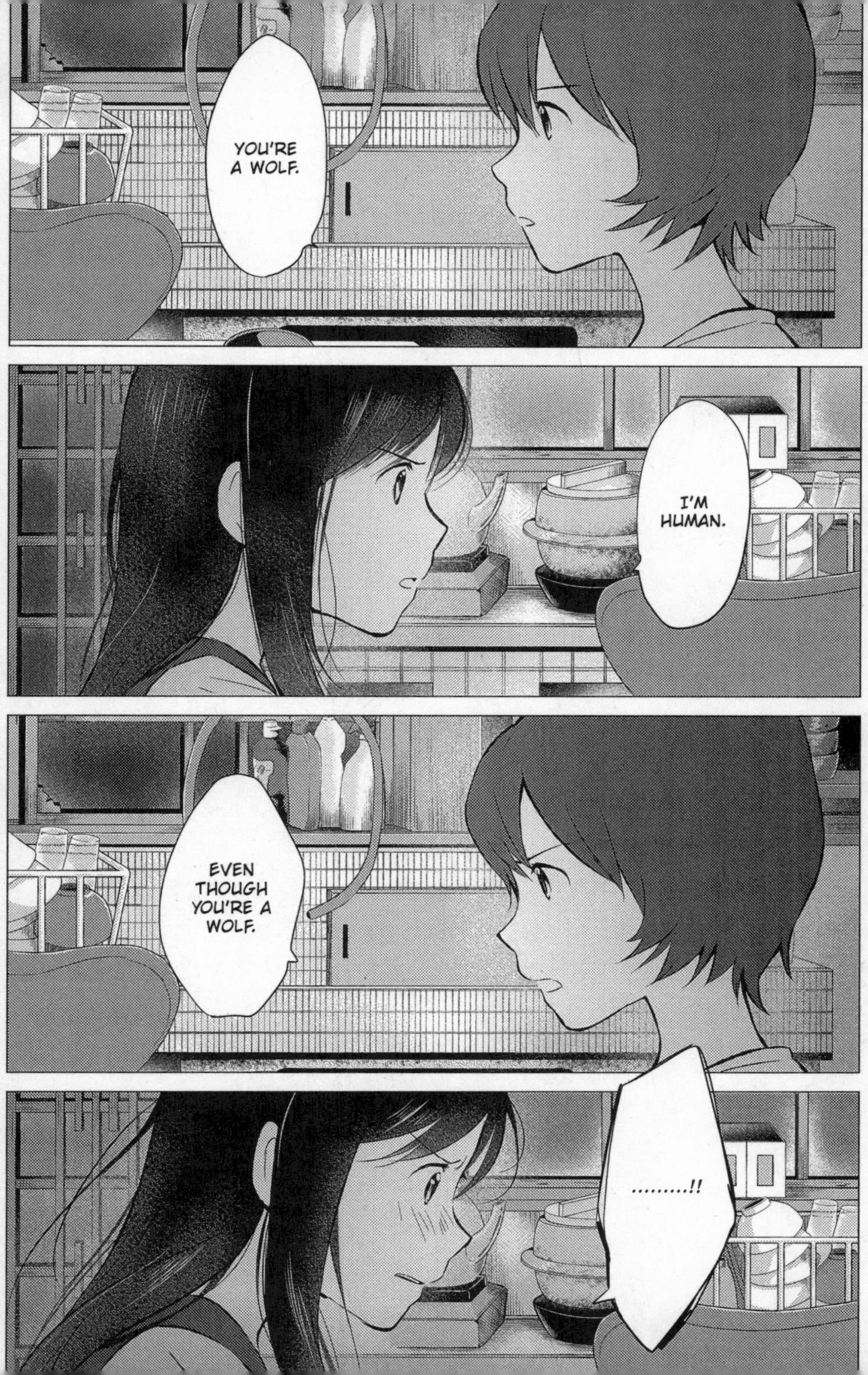
YOU'RE A WOLF.
I'M HUMAN.
EVEN THOUGH YOU'RE A WOLF.
..........!!

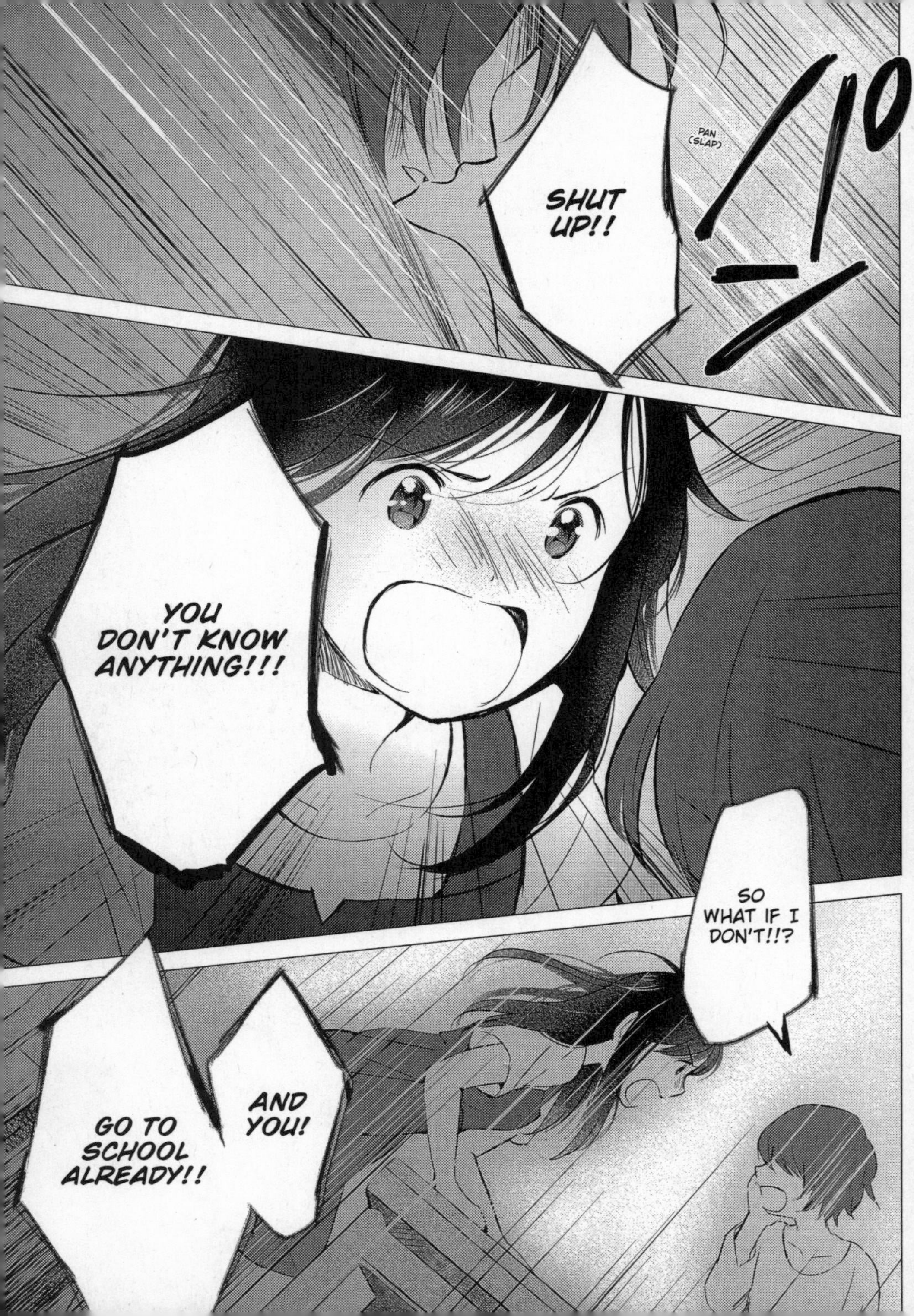
PAN (SLAP)
SHUT UP!!
YOU DON'T KNOW ANYTHING!!!
SO WHAT IF I DON'T!!?
AND YOU!
GO TO SCHOOL ALREADY!!

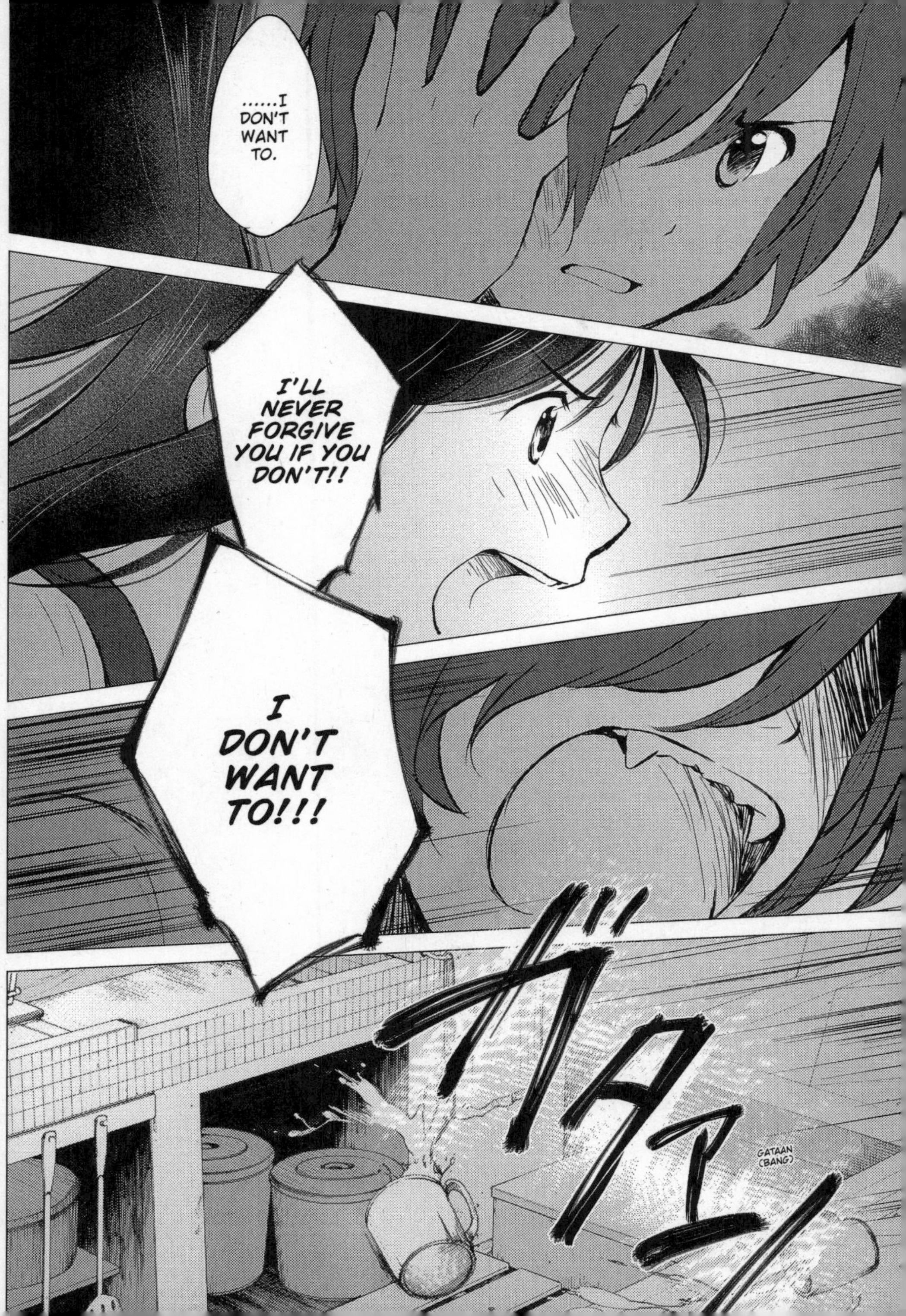
......I DON'T WANT TO.
I'LL NEVER FORGIVE YOU IF YOU DON'T!!
I DON'T WANT TO!!!
GATAAN (BANG)

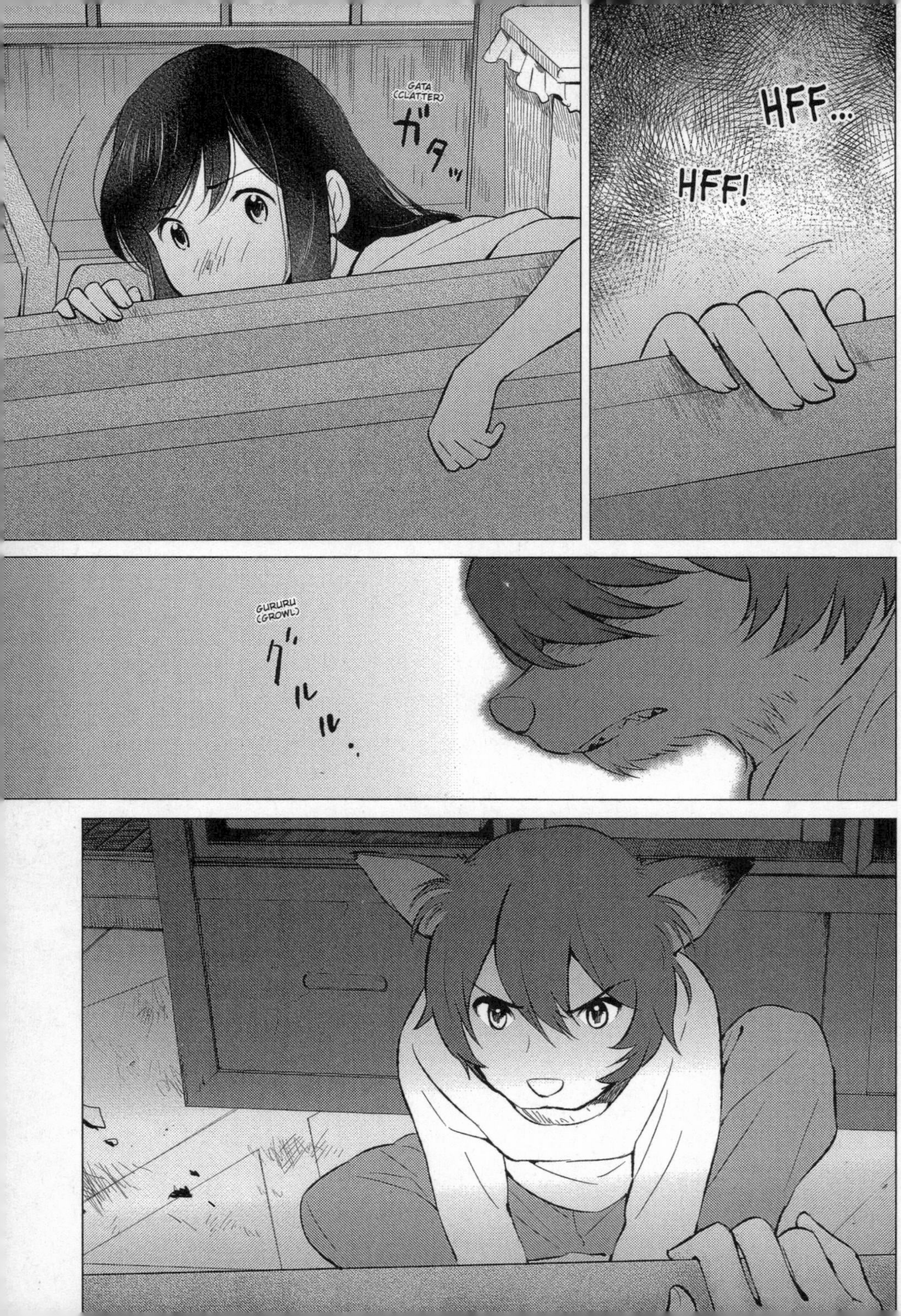
HFF...
HFF!
GATA (CLATTER)
ガタッ
GURURU (GROWL)
グルル..

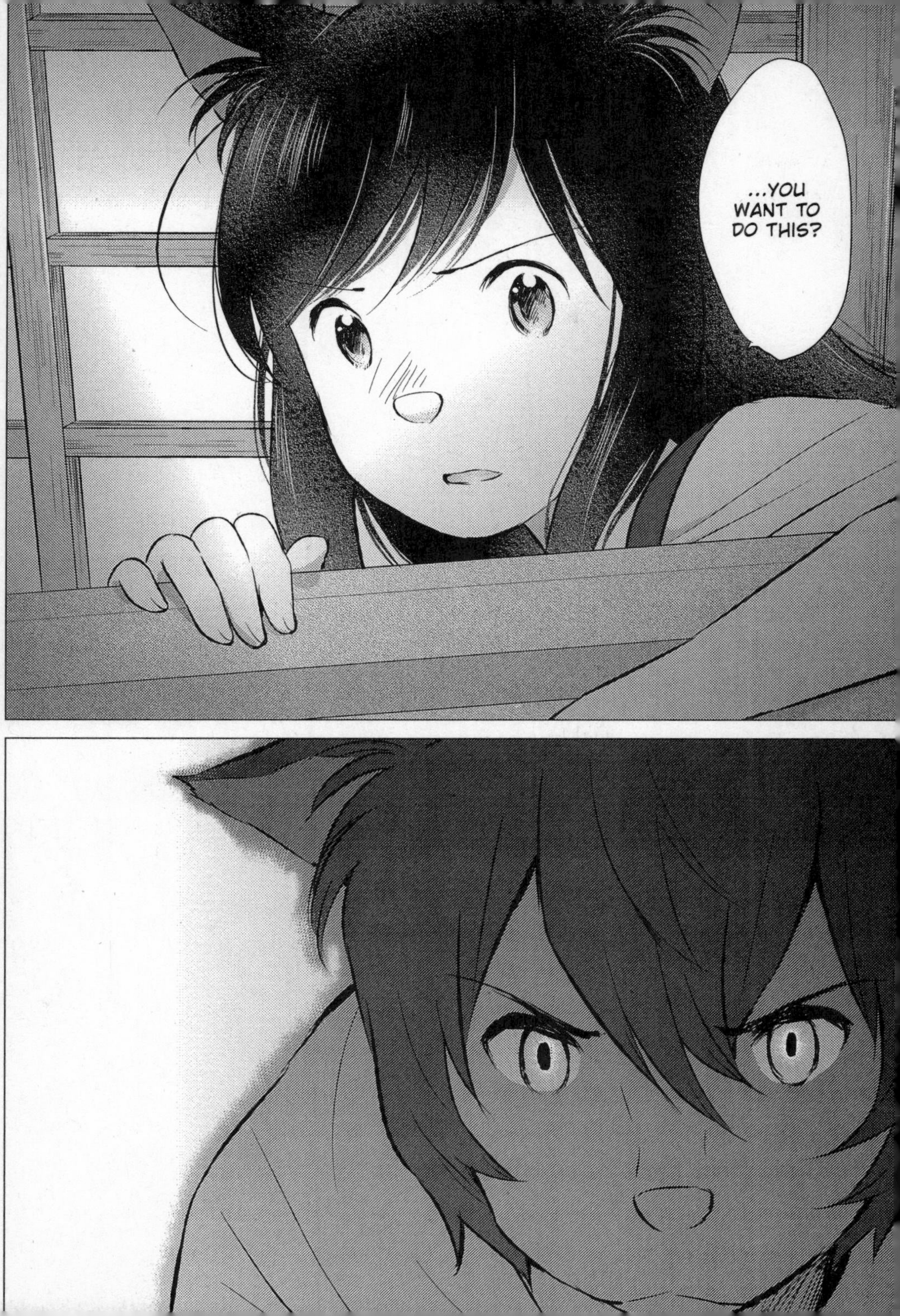
...YOU WANT TO DO THIS?

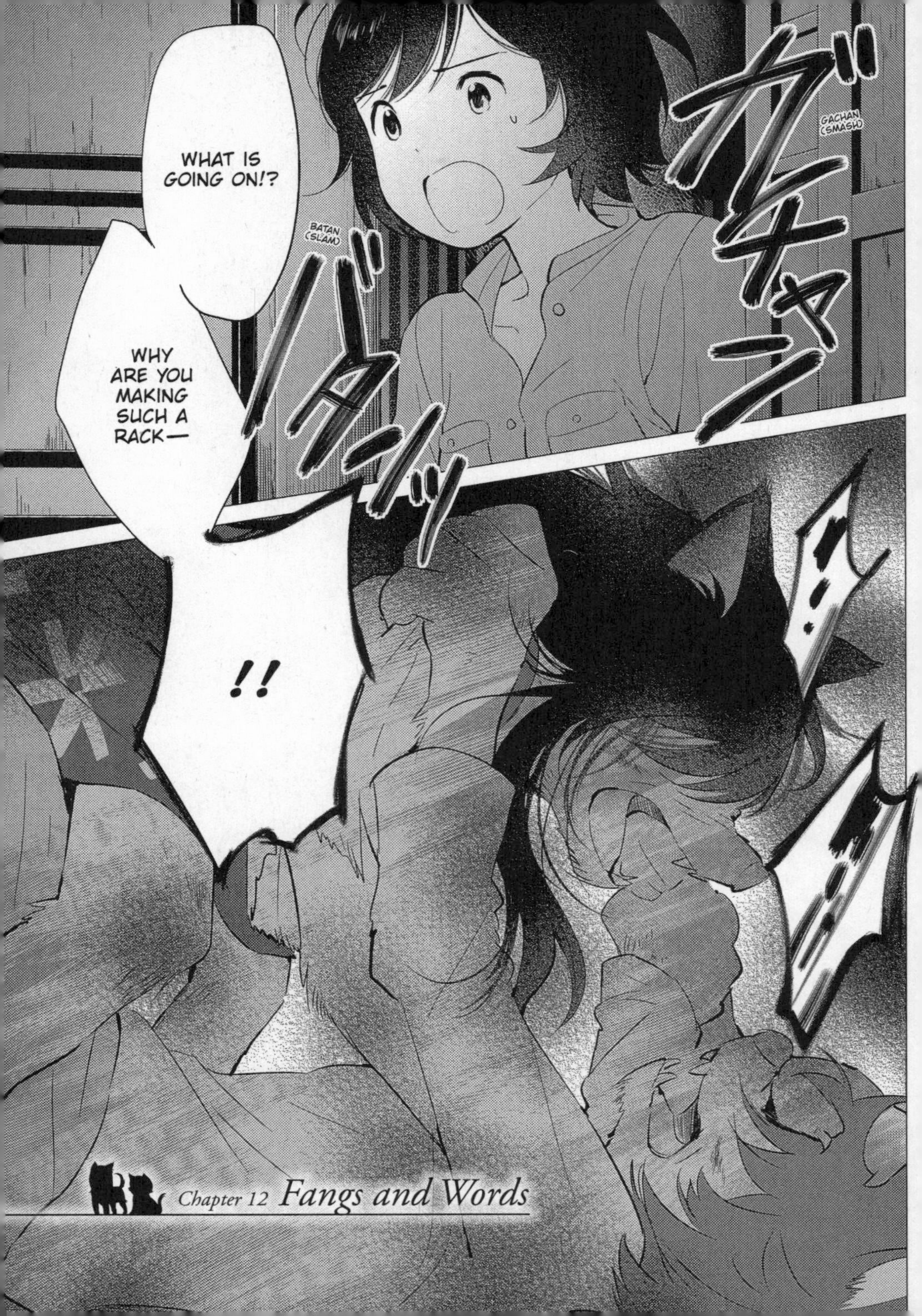
GACHAN (SMASH)
WHAT IS GOING ON!?
BATAN (SLAM)
WHY ARE YOU MAKING SUCH A RACK—
!!

Chapter 12 Fangs and Words

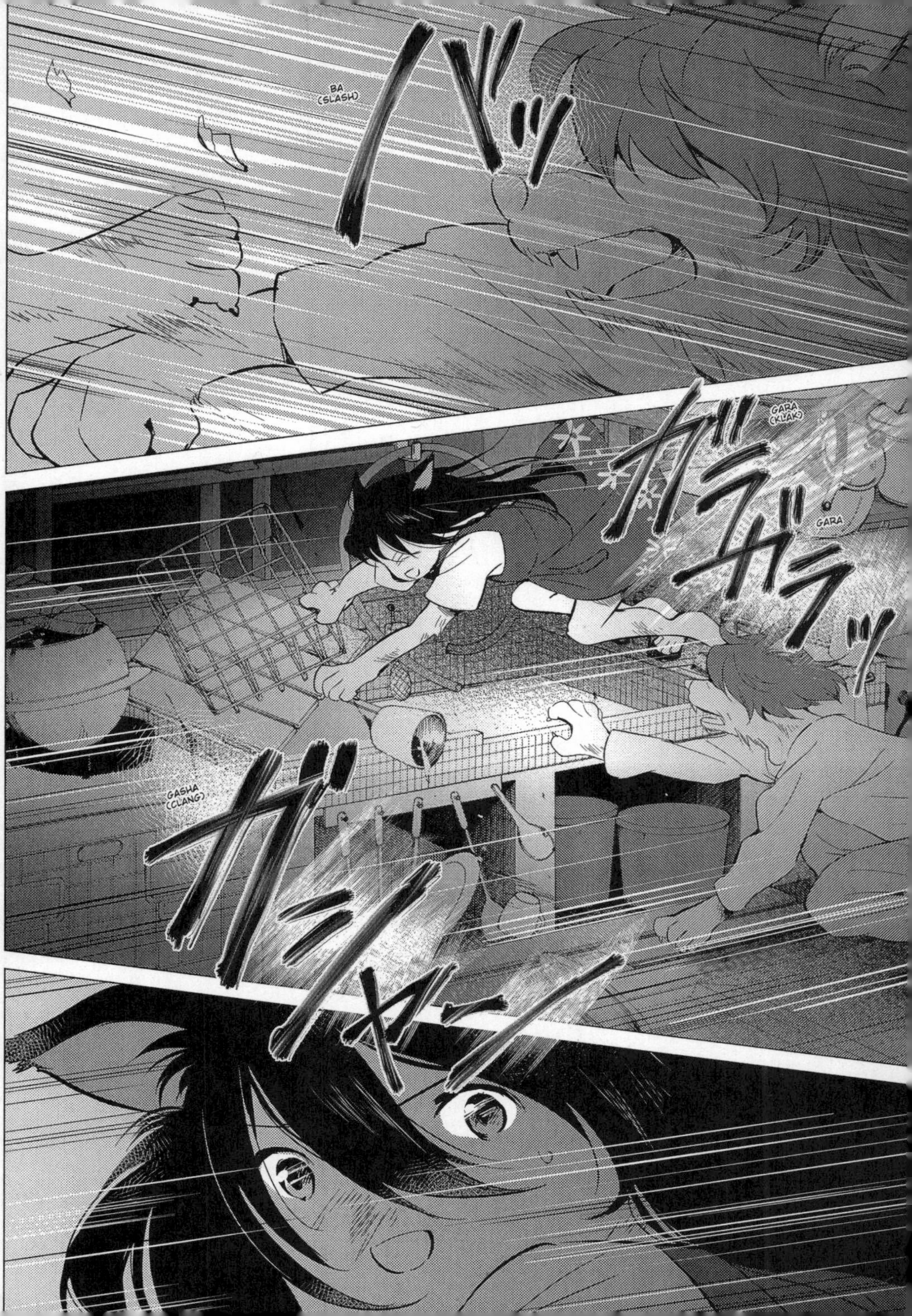
BA (SLASH)
GARA (KLAK)
GARA
GASHA (CLANG)

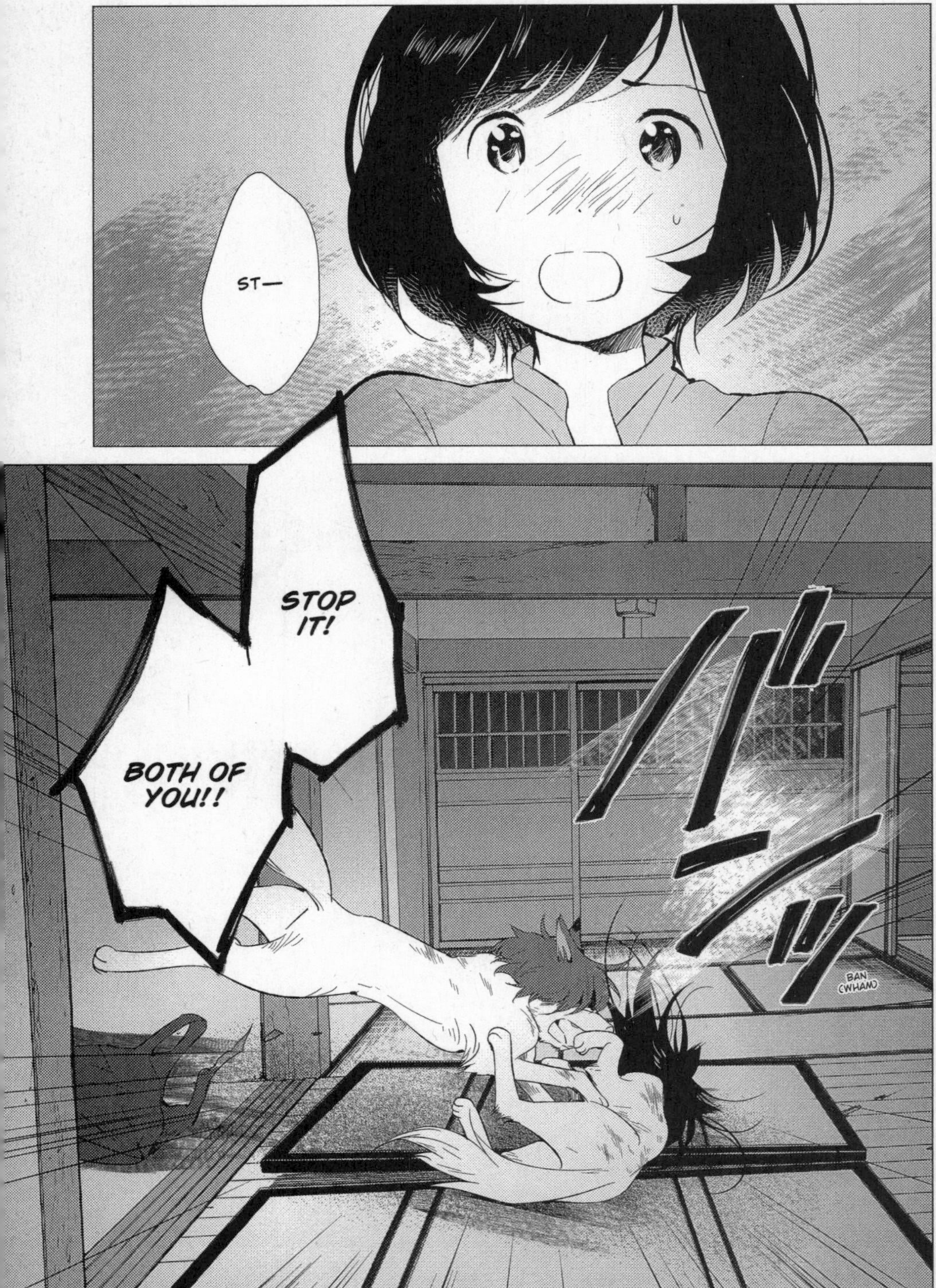
ST—
STOP IT!
BOTH OF YOU!!
BAN (WHAM)

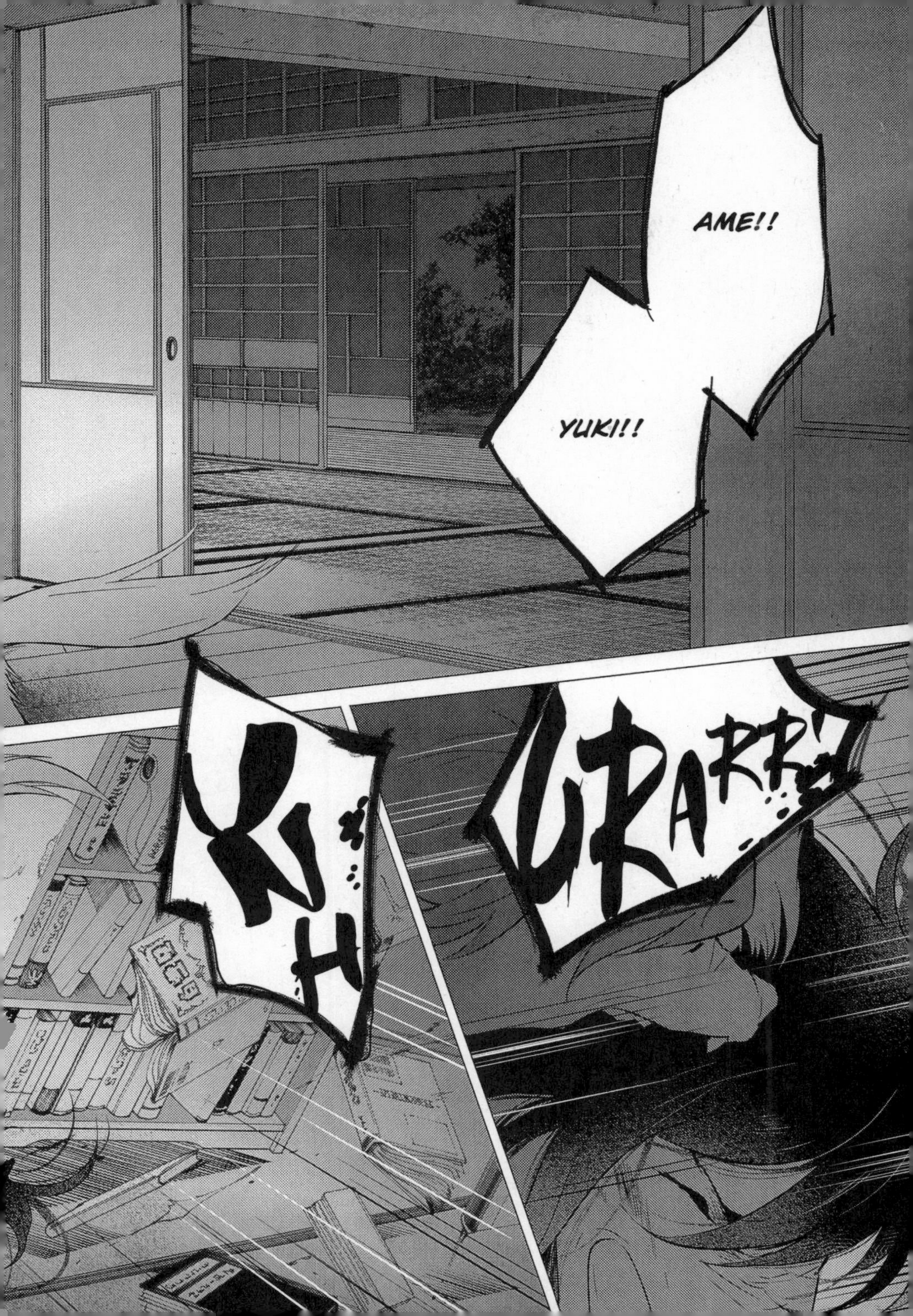
AME!!
YUKI!!
GRARR!
GUH

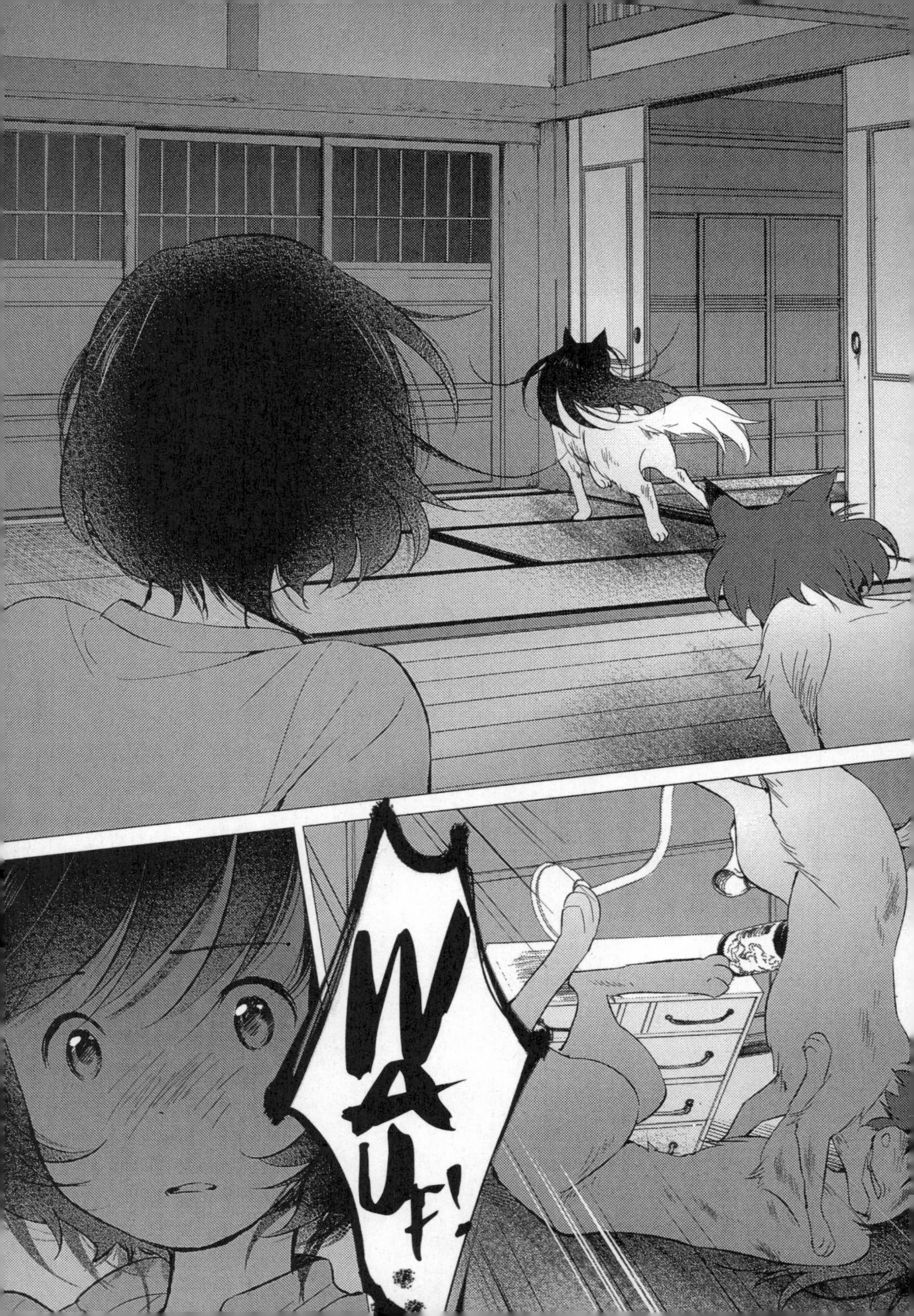
WAUF!

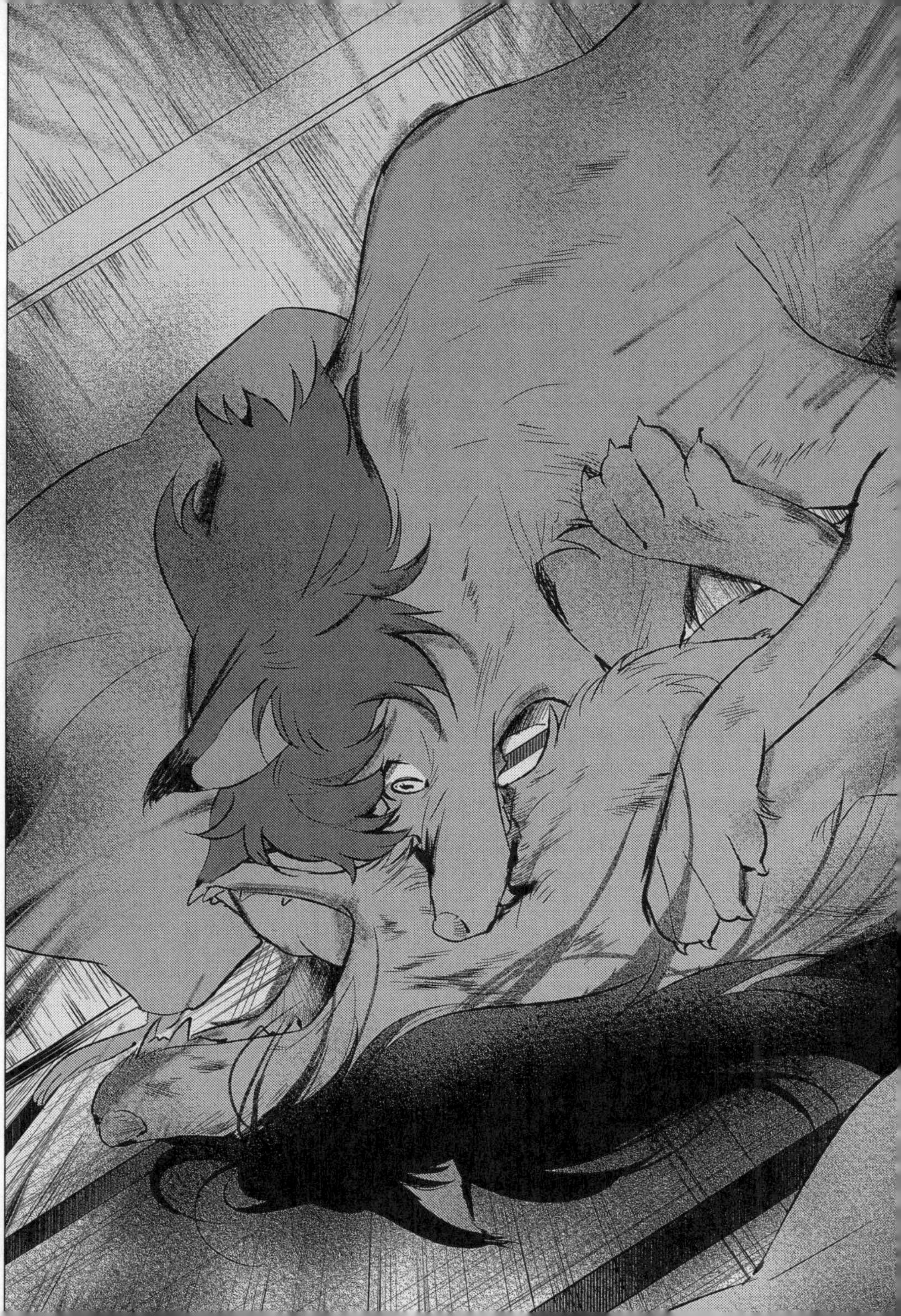

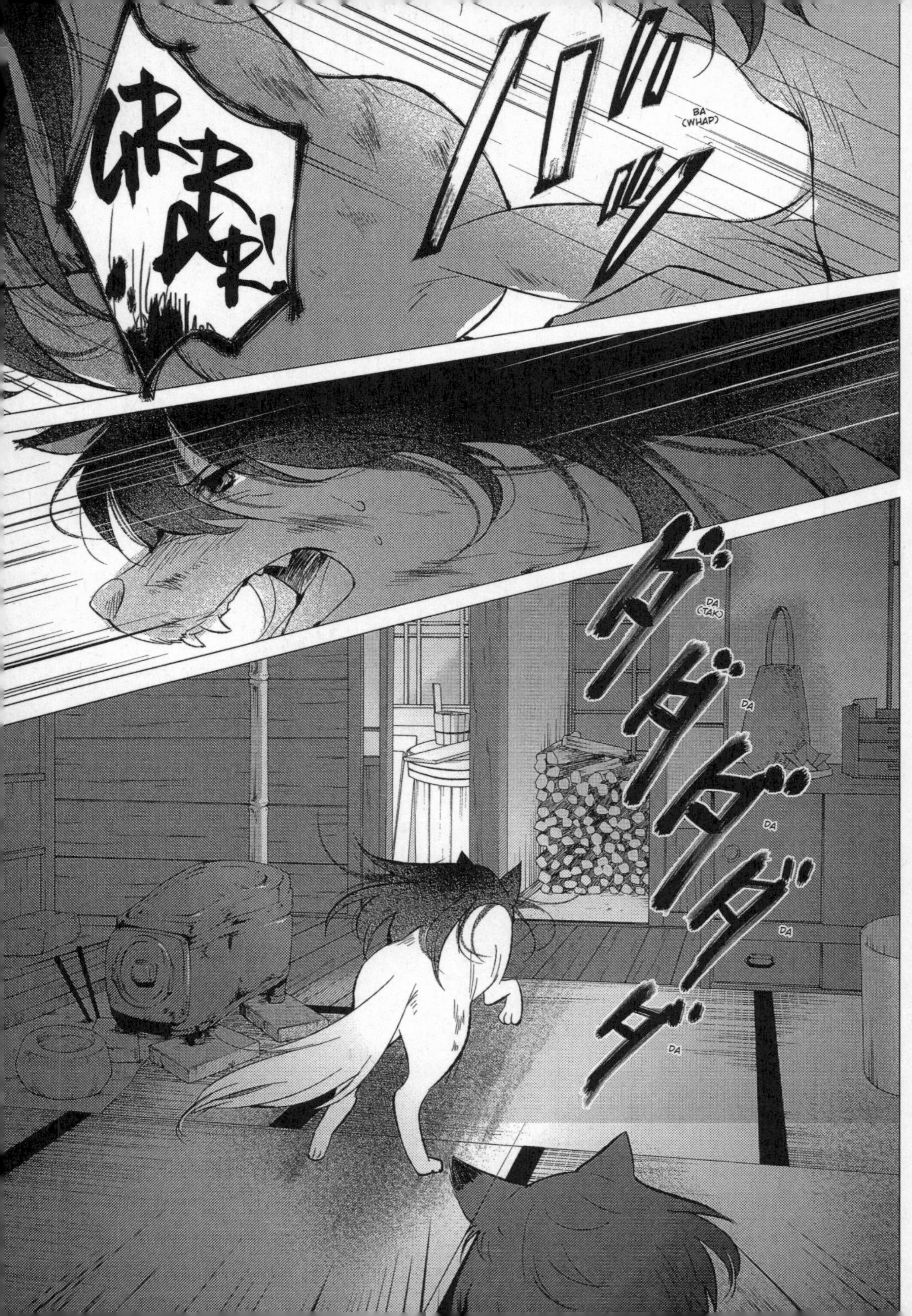
バッ
BA
(WHAP)
ダダダダダ
DA
(TAK)
DA
DA
DA
DA

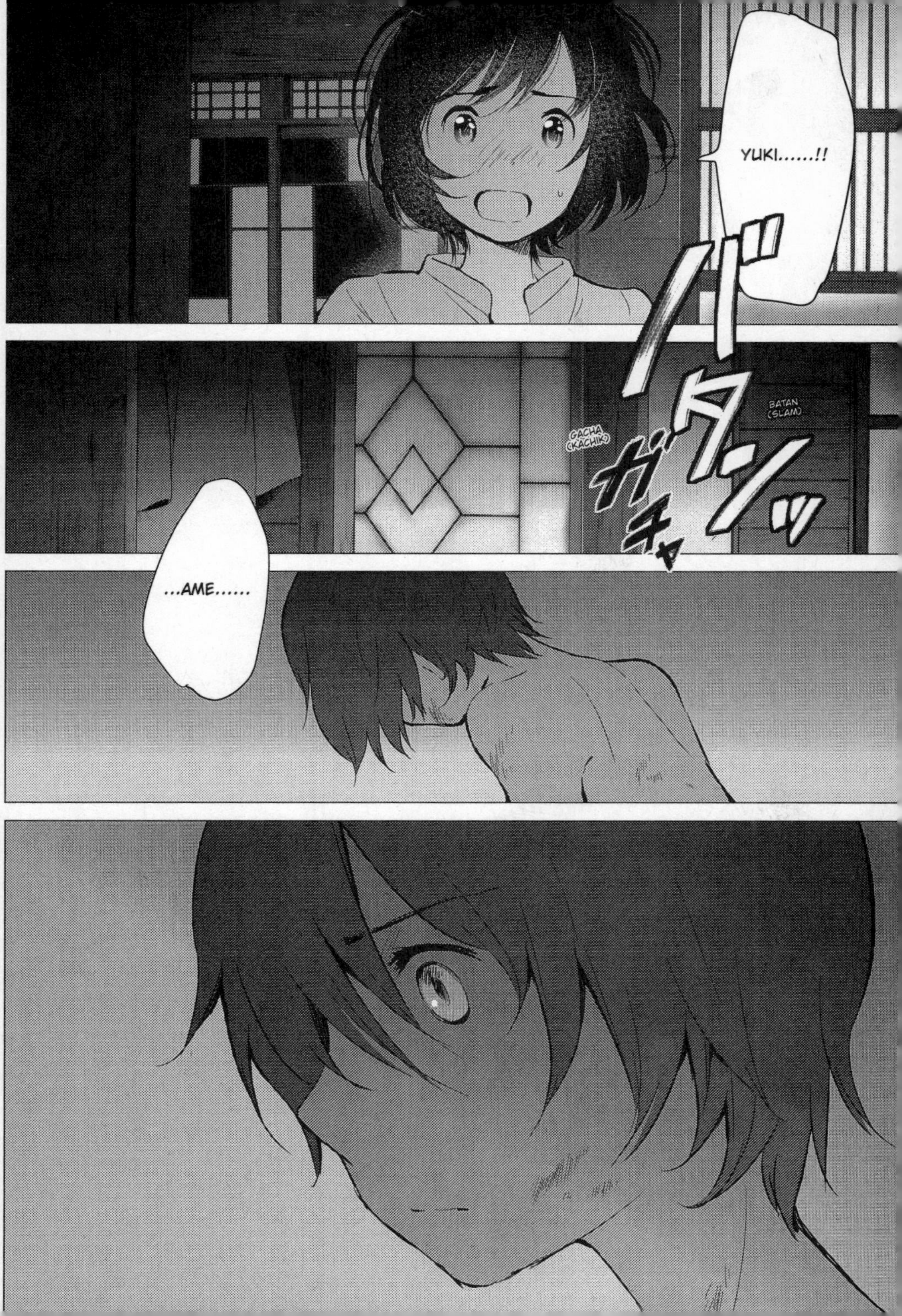
YUKI......!!
BATAN (SLAM)
GACHA (KACHIK)
...AME......

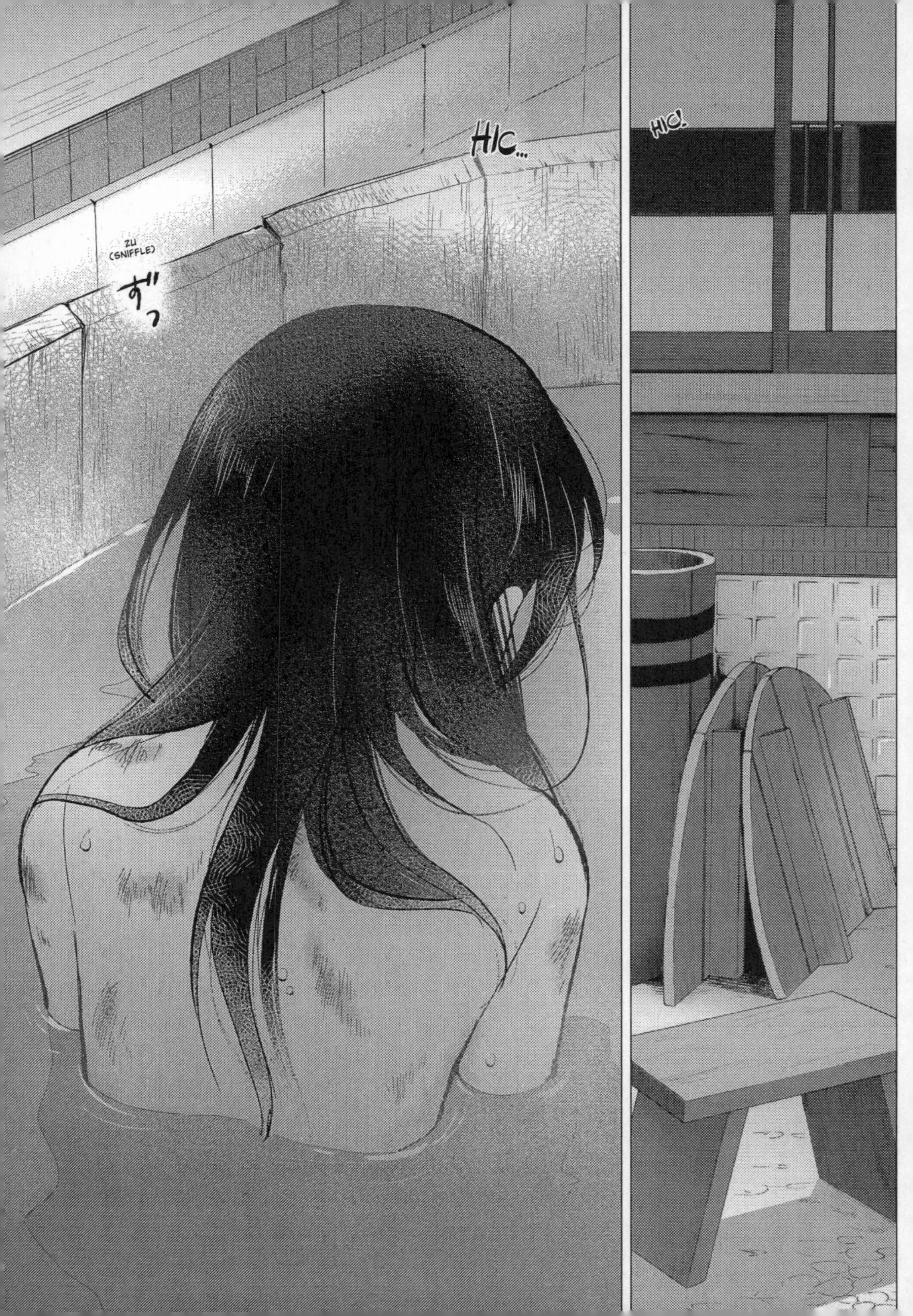
HIC!
HIC...
ZU (SNIFFLE)
ずっ

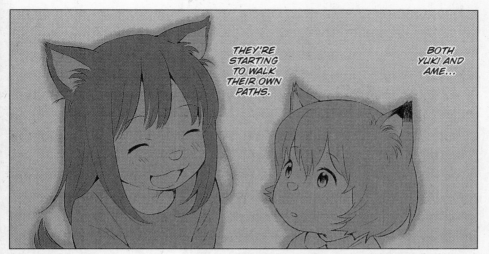

BOTH YUKI AND AME...

THEY'RE STARTING TO WALK THEIR OWN PATHS.

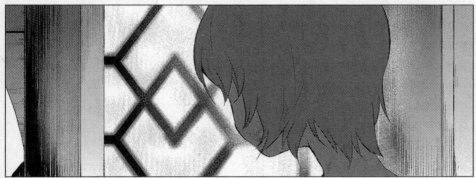

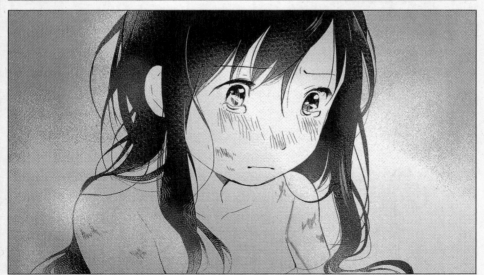

406

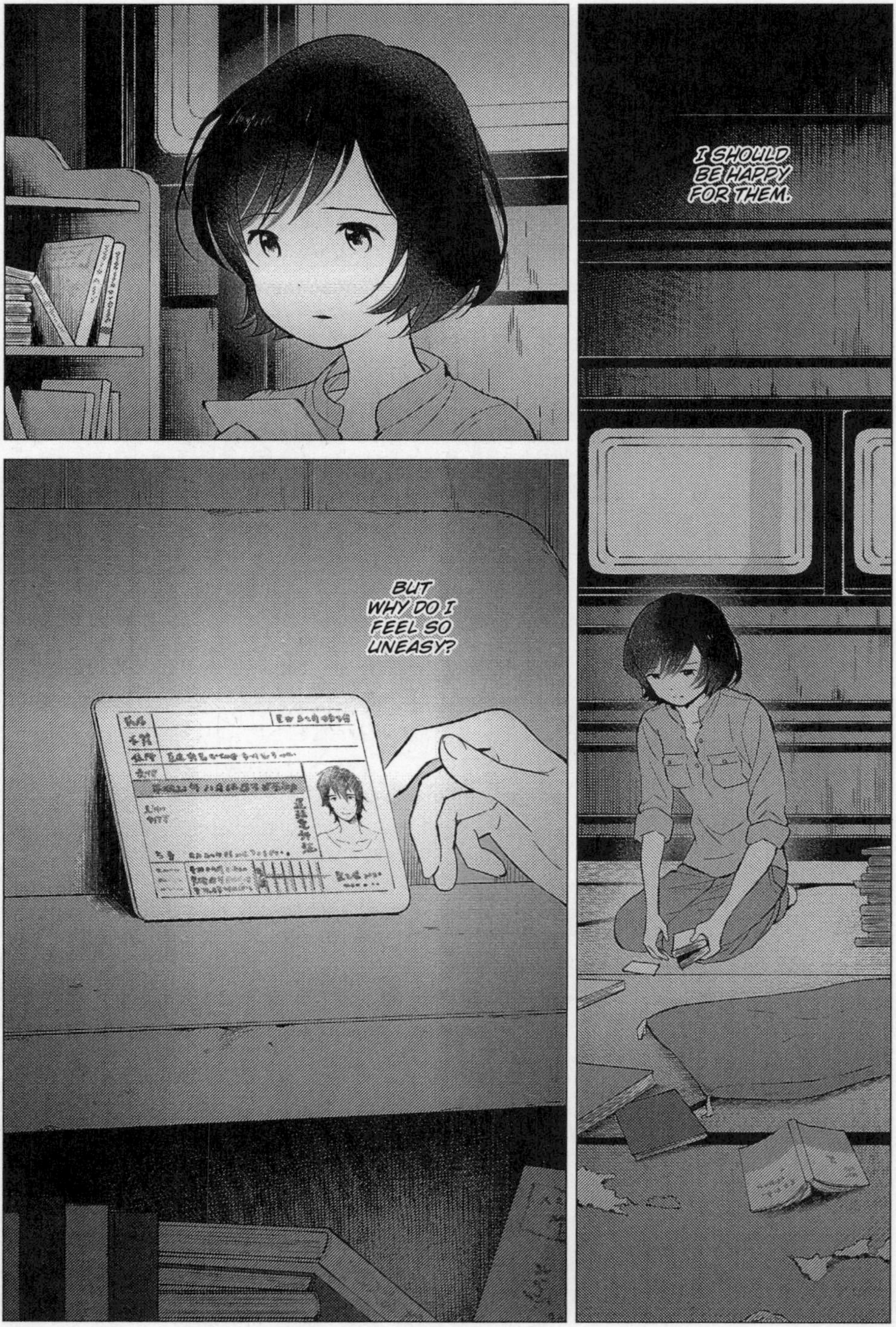
I SHOULD BE HAPPY FOR THEM.
BUT WHY DO I FEEL SO UNEASY?

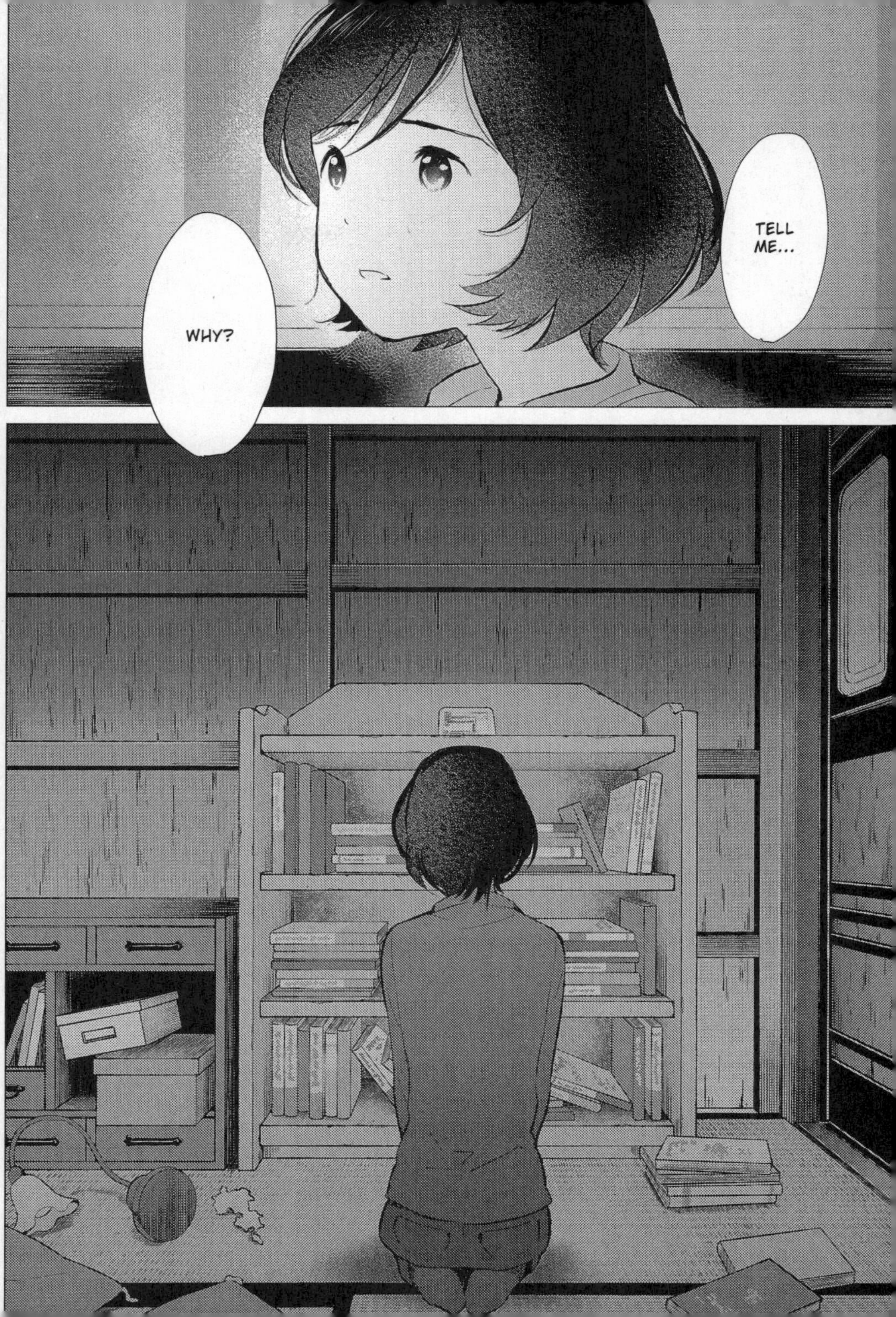
TELL ME...
WHY?

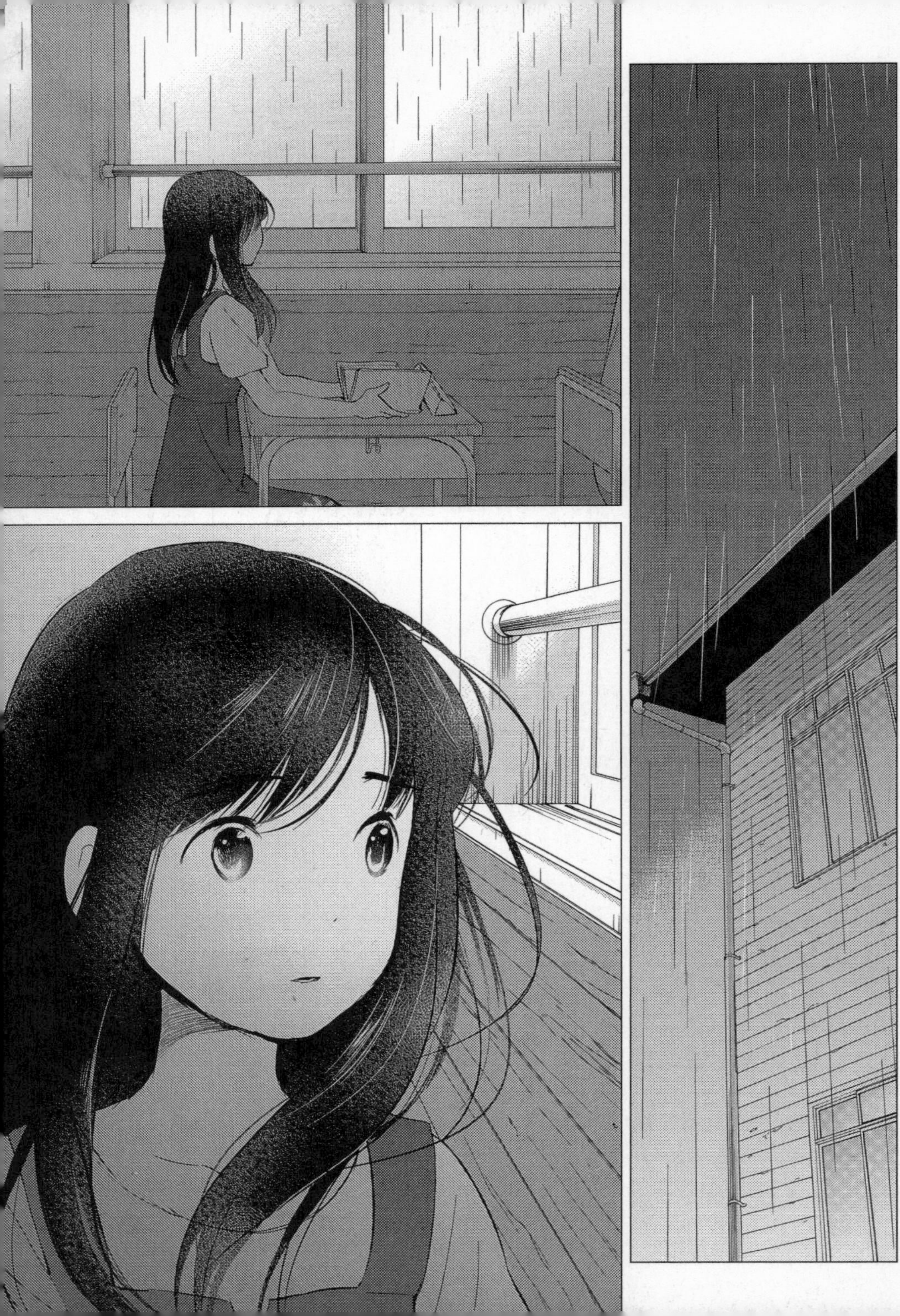

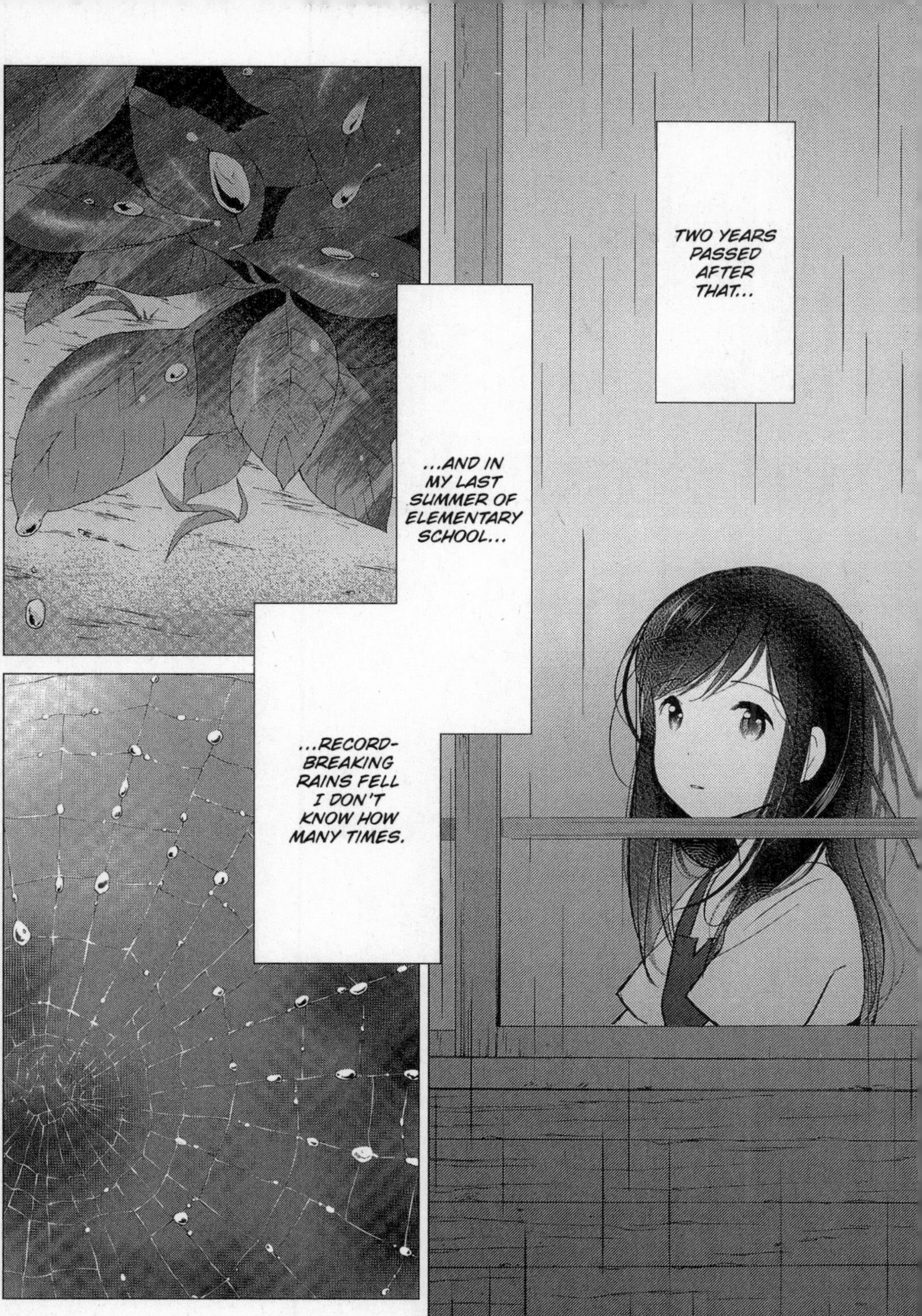
TWO YEARS PASSED AFTER THAT...
...AND IN MY LAST SUMMER OF ELEMENTARY SCHOOL...
...RECORD-BREAKING RAINS FELL I DON'T KNOW HOW MANY TIMES.

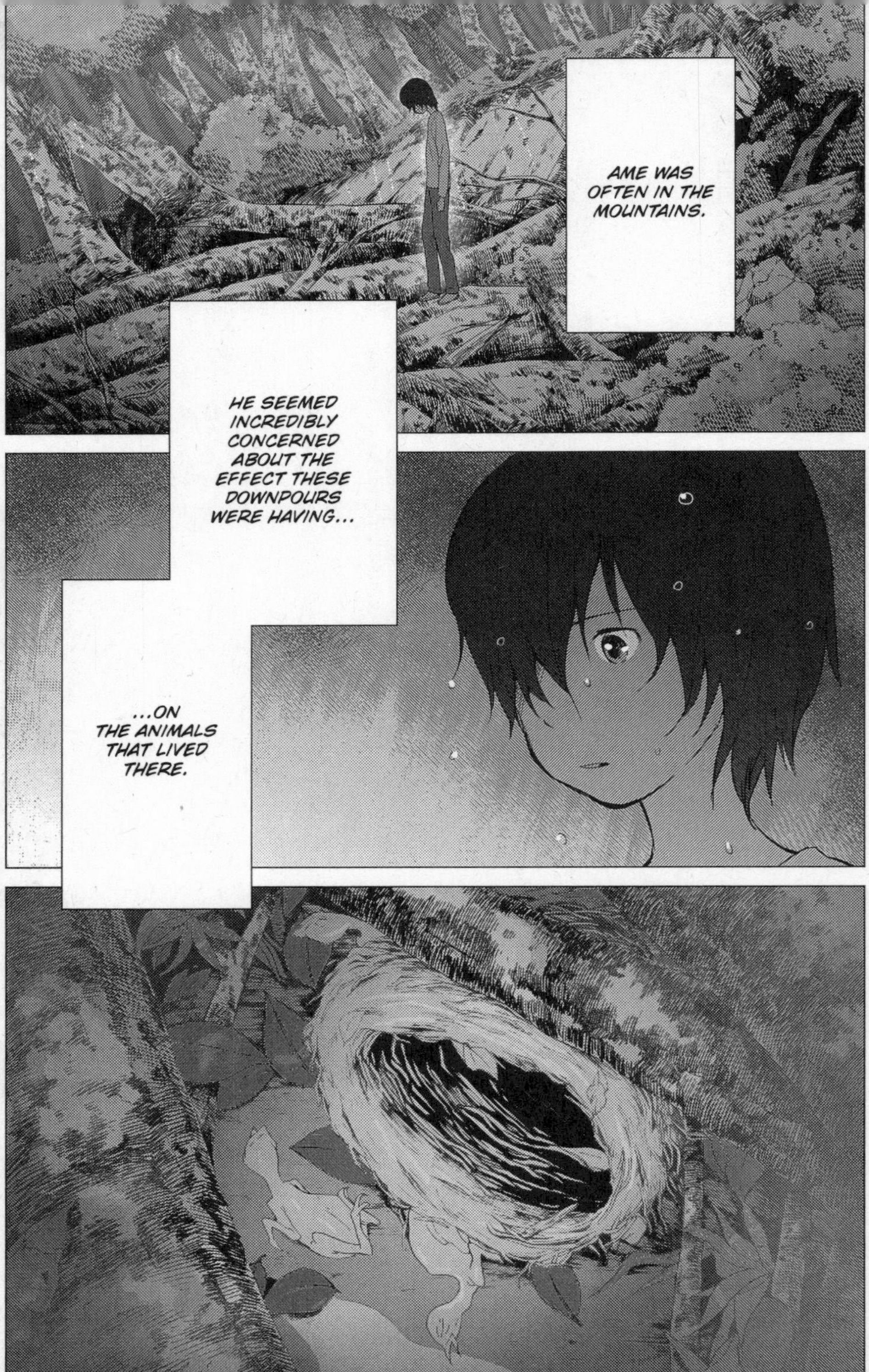
AME WAS OFTEN IN THE MOUNTAINS.
HE SEEMED INCREDIBLY CONCERNED ABOUT THE EFFECT THESE DOWNPOURS WERE HAVING...
...ON THE ANIMALS THAT LIVED THERE.

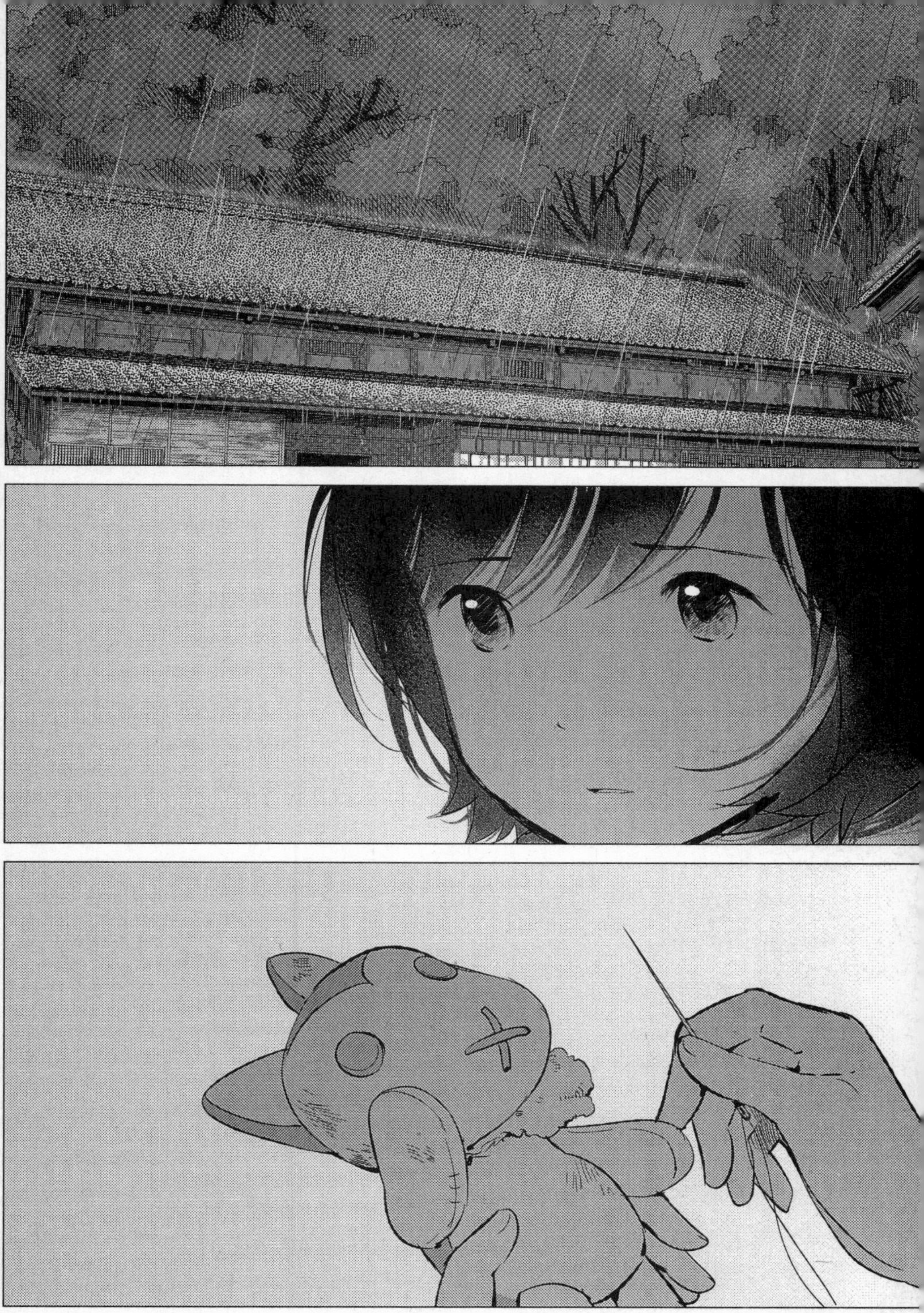

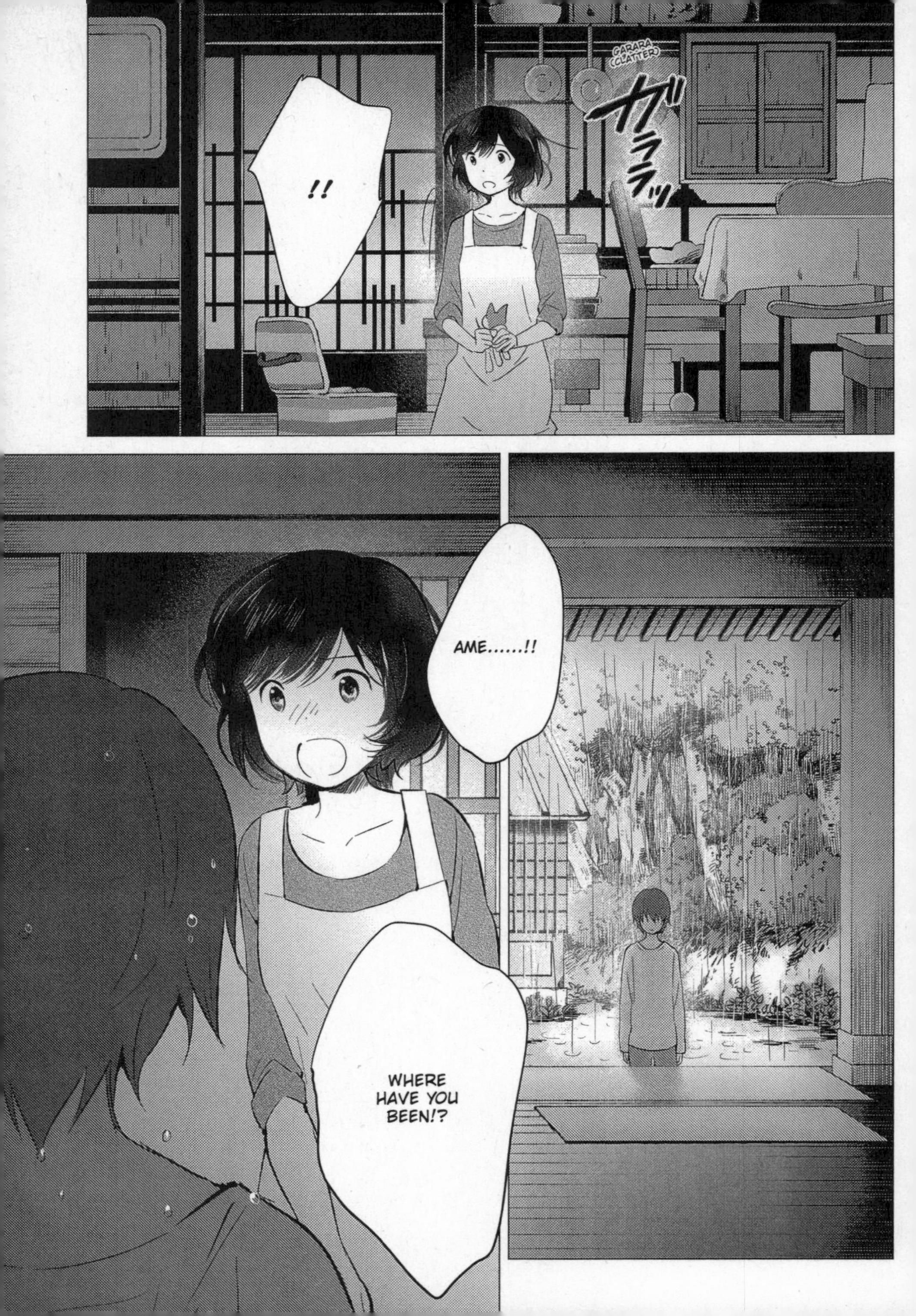
GARARA (CLATTER)
ガララッ
!!
AME......!!
WHERE HAVE YOU BEEN!?

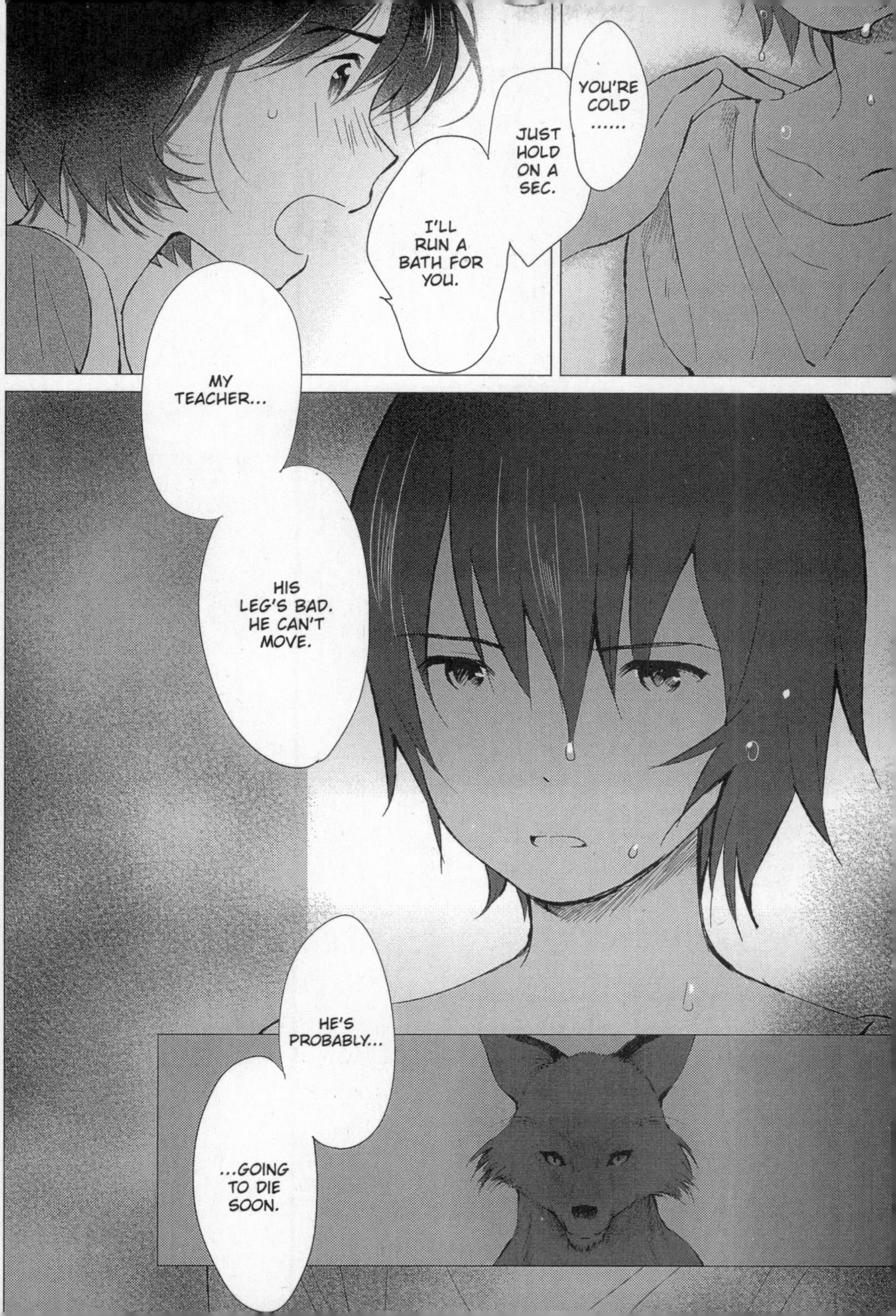
YOU'RE COLD ......
JUST HOLD ON A SEC.
I'LL RUN A BATH FOR YOU.
MY TEACHER...
HIS LEG'S BAD. HE CAN'T MOVE.
HE'S PROBABLY...
...GOING TO DIE SOON.

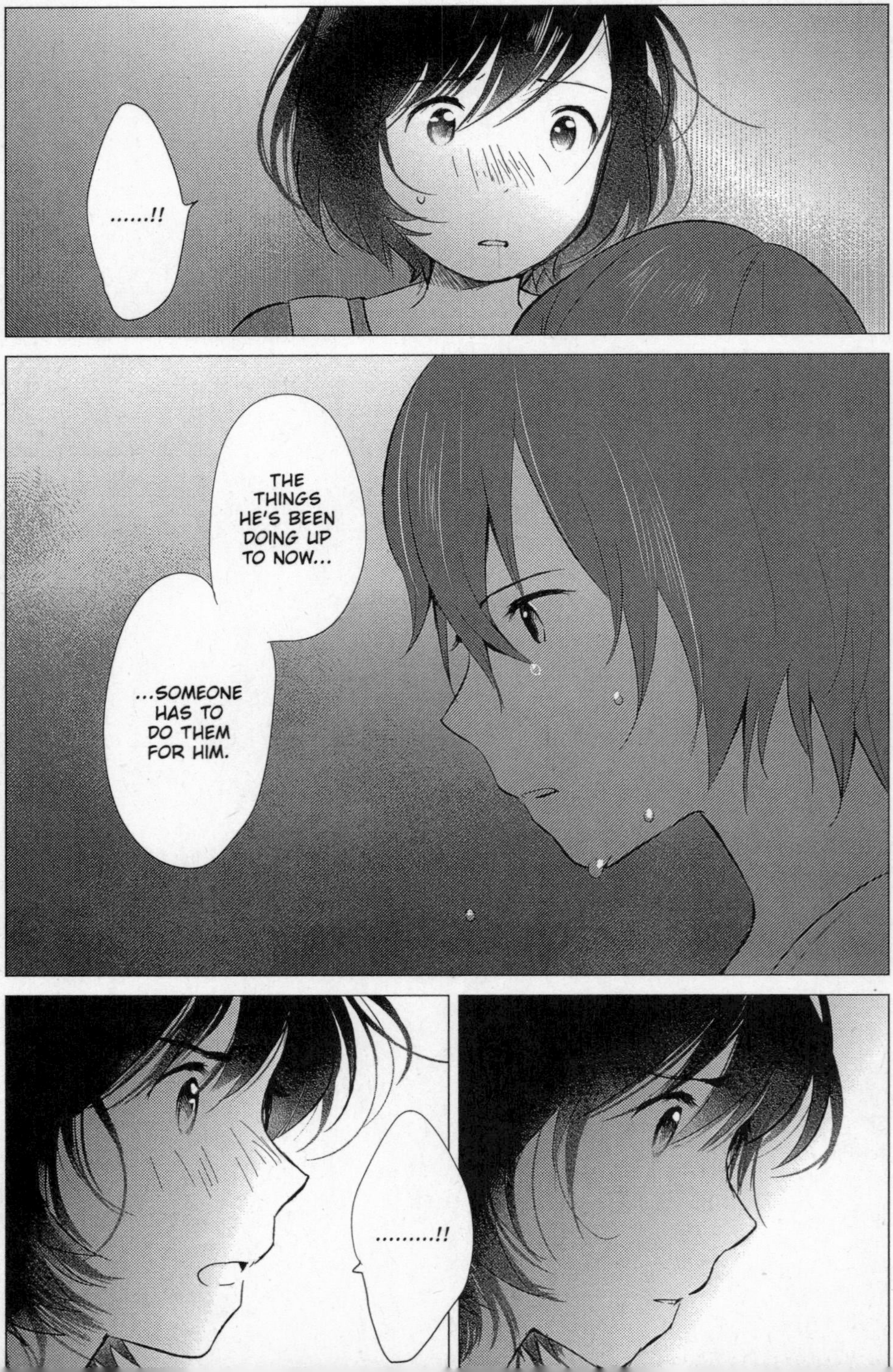
......!!
THE THINGS HE'S BEEN DOING UP TO NOW...
...SOMEONE HAS TO DO THEM FOR HIM.
.........!!

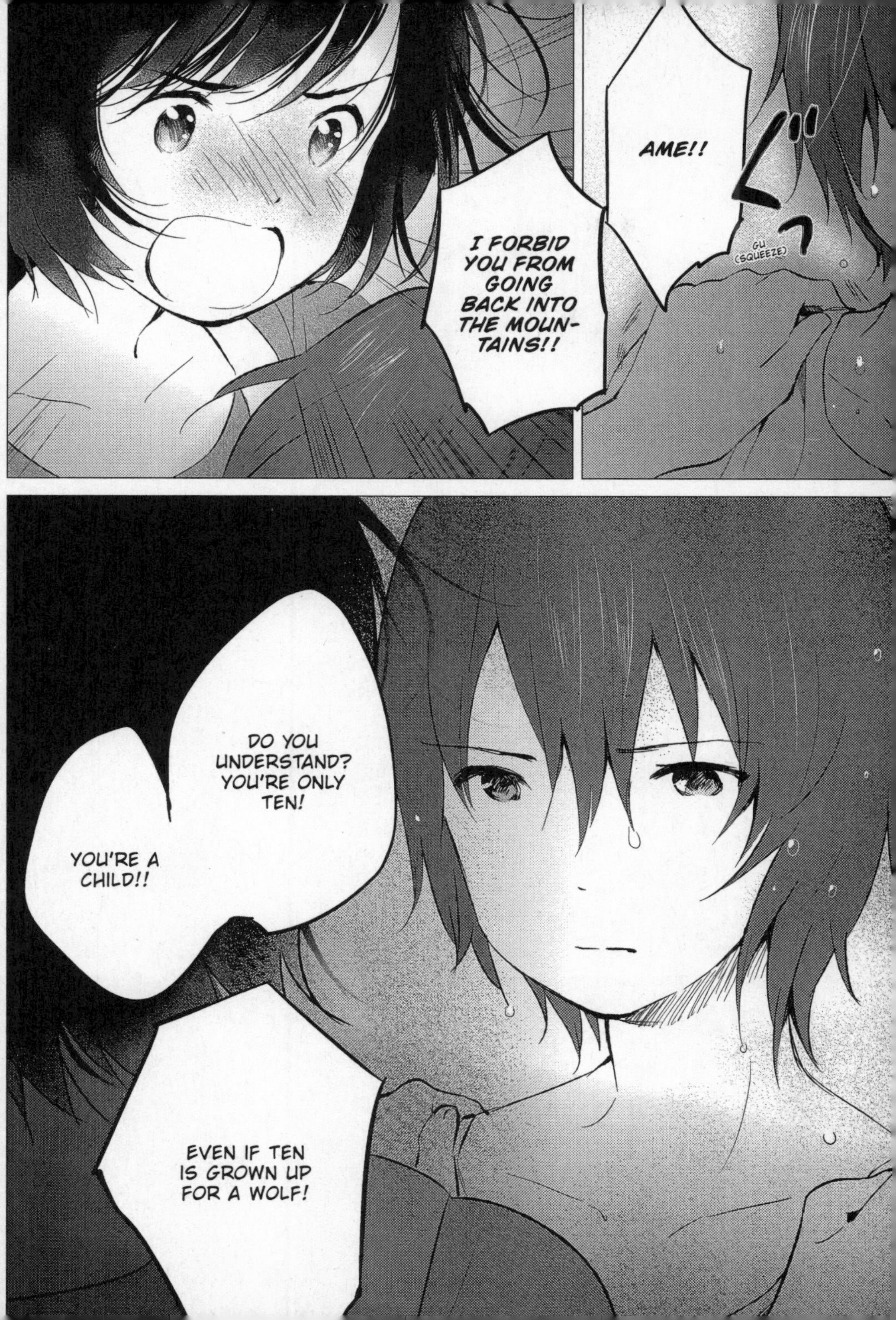

AME!!
GU (SQUEEZE)
I FORBID YOU FROM GOING BACK INTO THE MOUN-TAINS!!
DO YOU UNDERSTAND? YOU'RE ONLY TEN!
YOU'RE A CHILD!!
EVEN IF TEN IS GROWN UP FOR A WOLF!

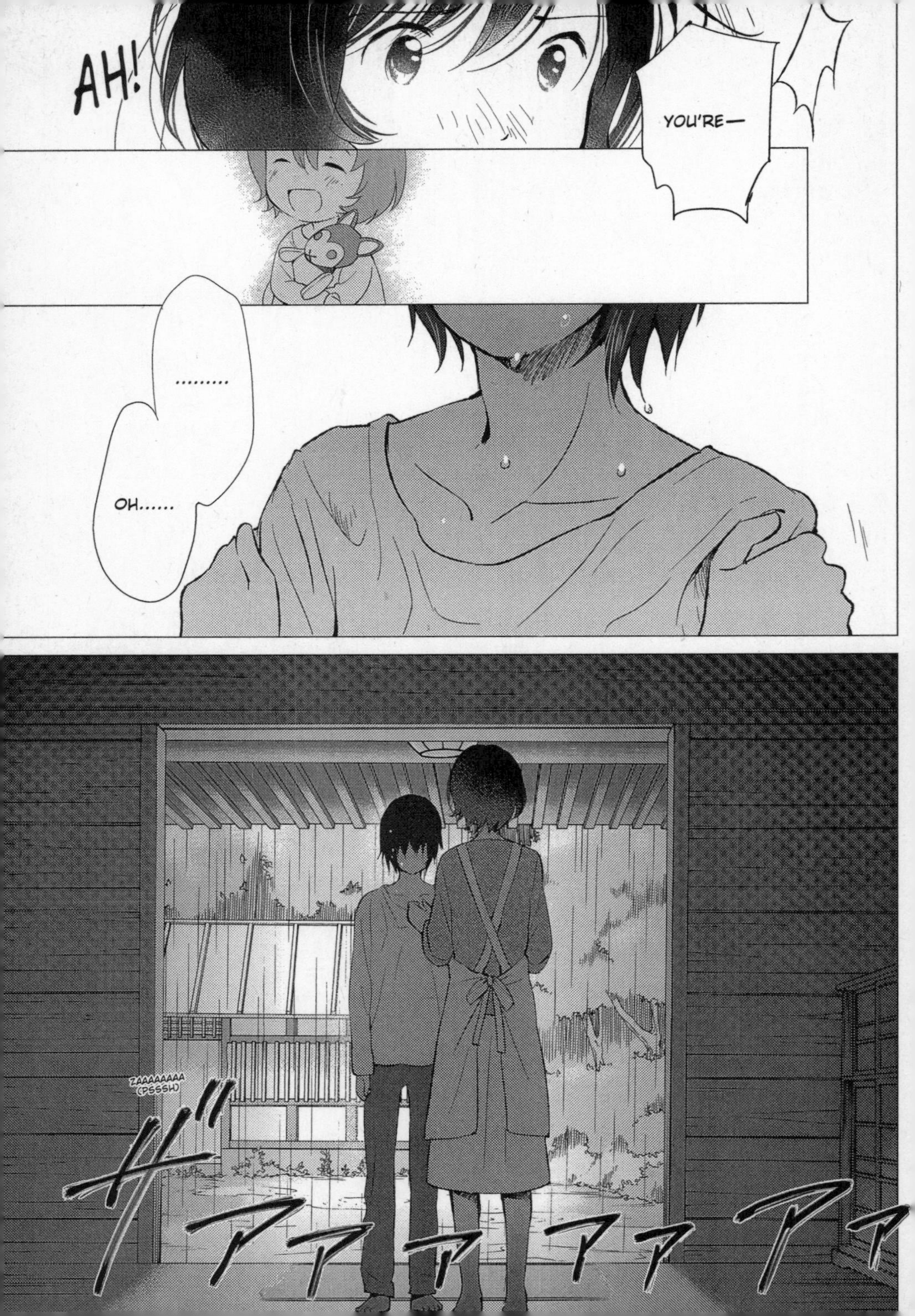
AH!
YOU'RE—
....
OH......
ZAAAAAAAA (PSSSH)
ザァァァァァ

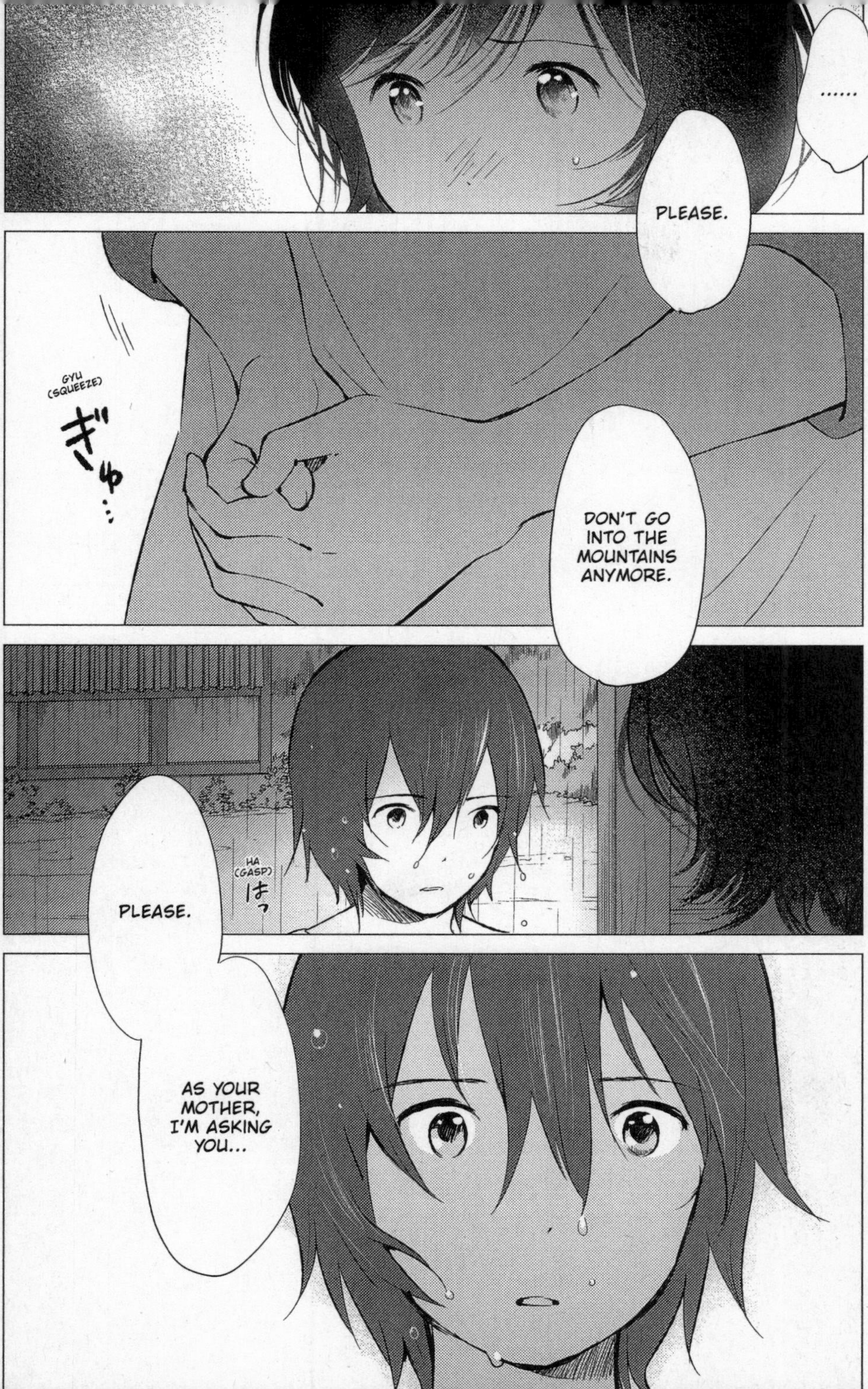
......
PLEASE.
DON'T GO INTO THE MOUNTAINS ANYMORE.
GYU (SQUEEZE)
ぎゅ…
HA (GASP)
はっ
PLEASE.
AS YOUR MOTHER, I'M ASKING YOU...

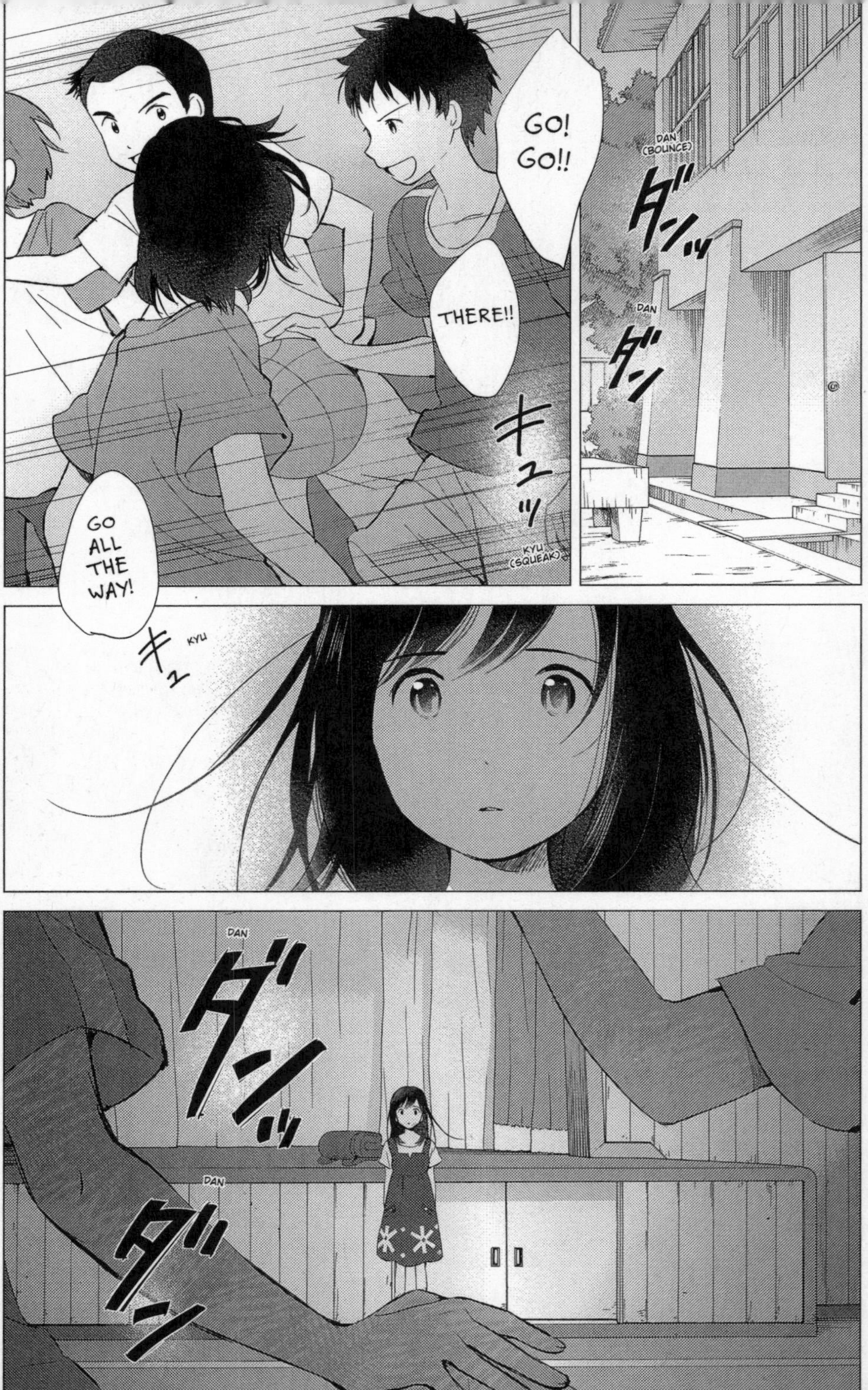

ダンッ
DAN (BOUNCE)
ダン
DAN
GO! GO!!
THERE!!
キュッ
KYU (SQUEAK)
GO ALL THE WAY!
キュ
KYU
ダンッ
DAN
ダン
DAN

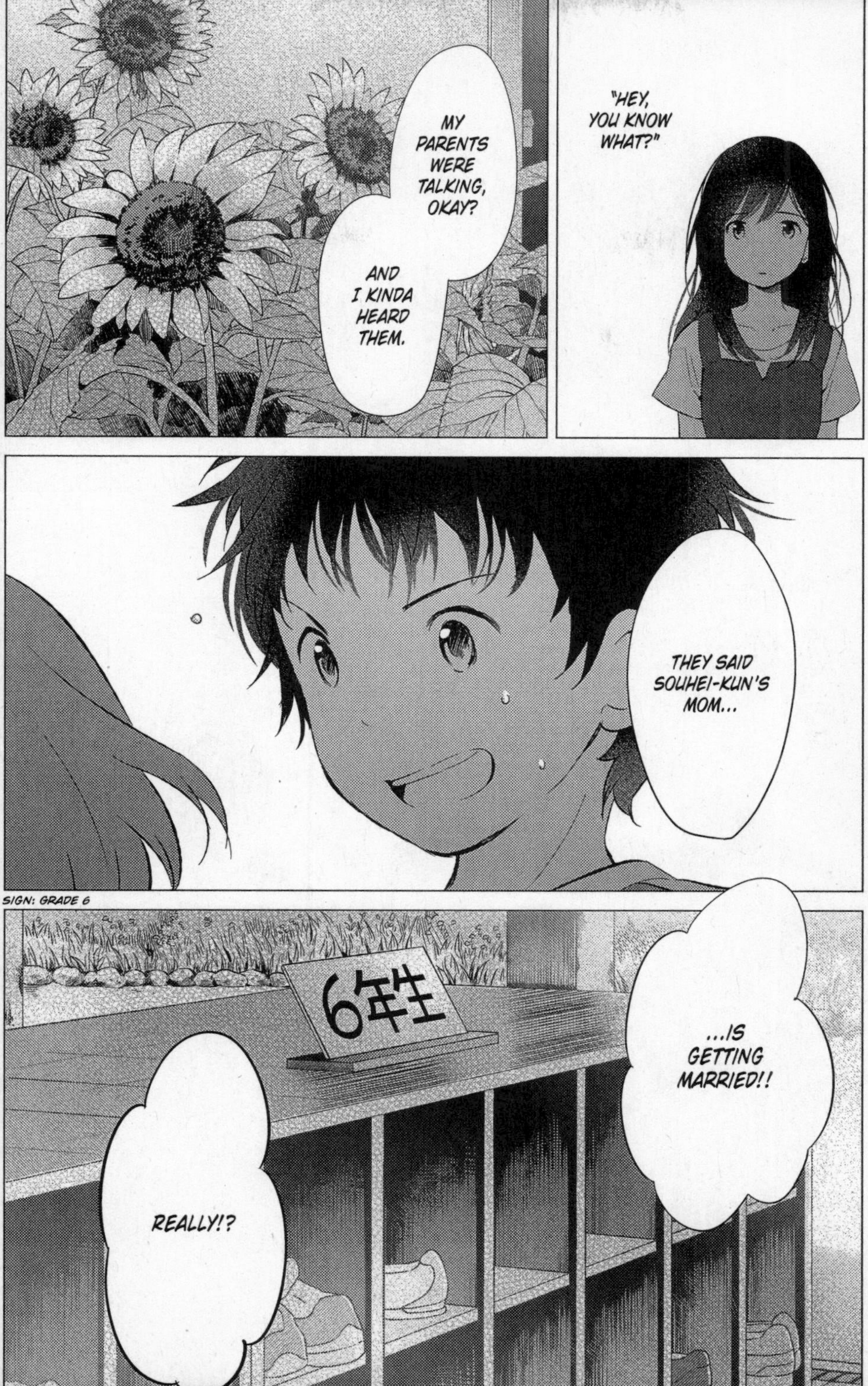
"HEY, YOU KNOW WHAT?"
MY PARENTS WERE TALKING, OKAY?
AND I KINDA HEARD THEM.
THEY SAID SOUHEI-KUN'S MOM...
SIGN: GRADE 6
6年生
...IS GETTING MARRIED!!
REALLY!?

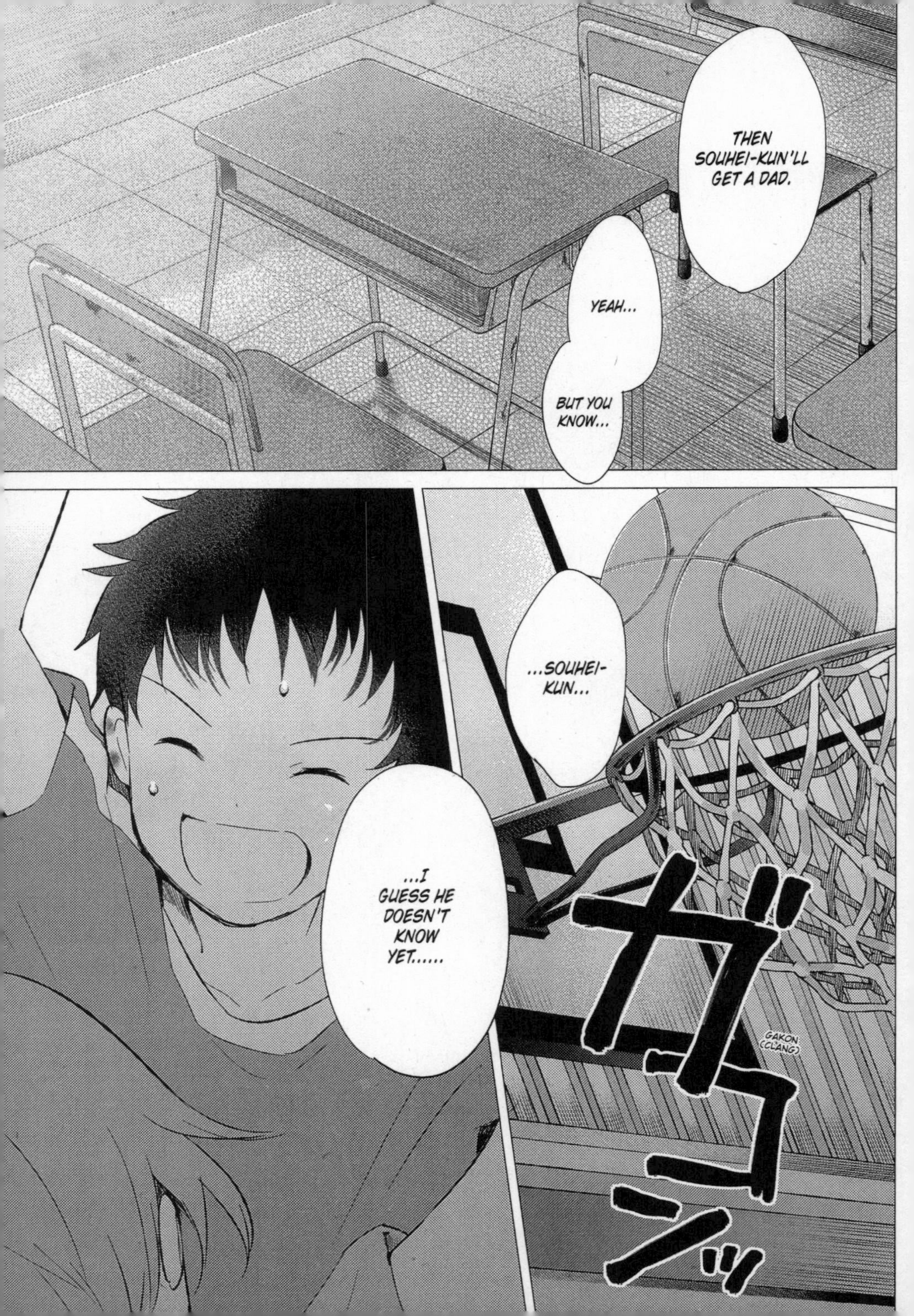
THEN SOUHEI-KUN'LL GET A DAD.
YEAH...
BUT YOU KNOW...
...SOUHEI-KUN...
ガゴンッ
GAKON (CLANG)
...I GUESS HE DOESN'T KNOW YET......

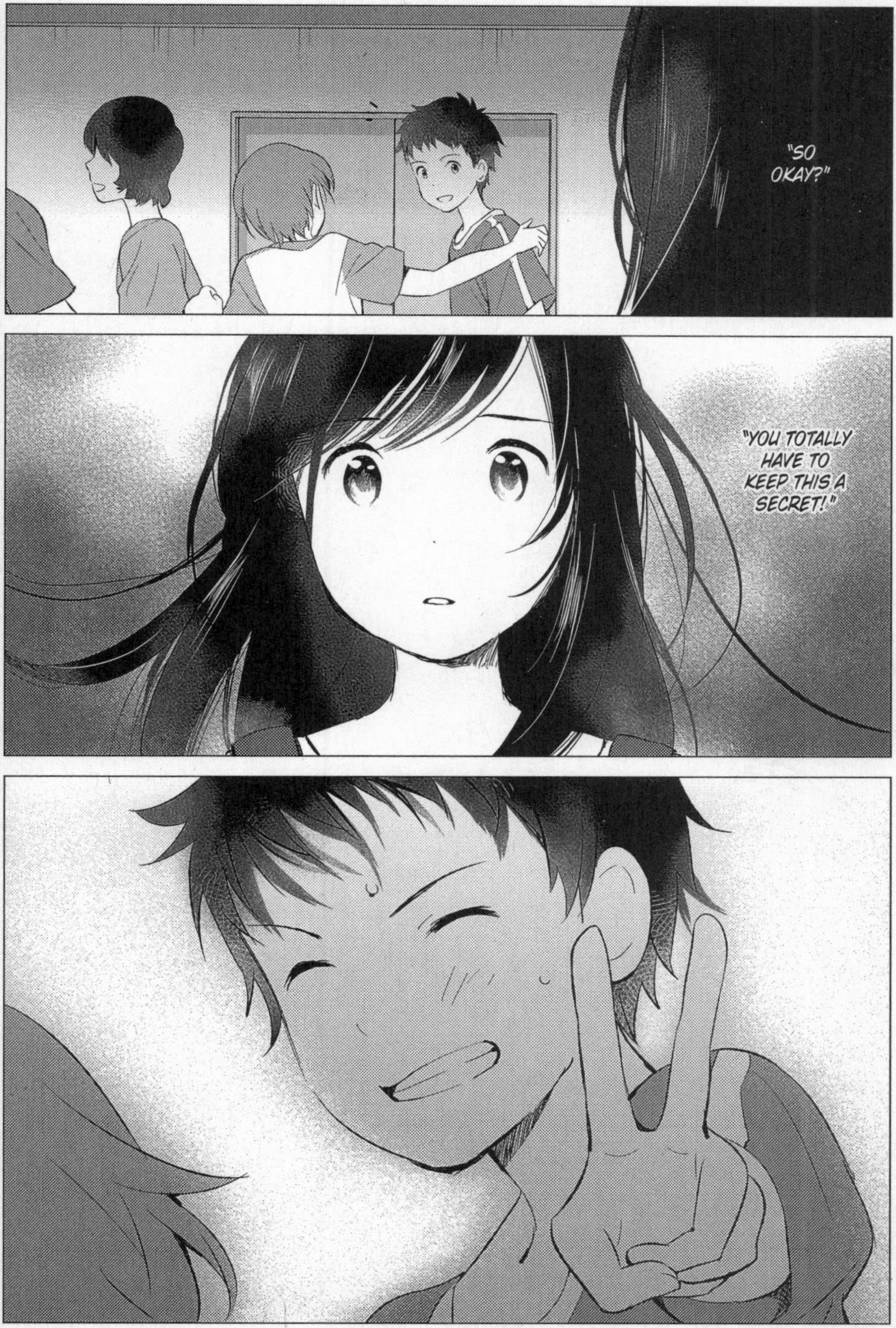
"SO OKAY?"
"YOU TOTALLY HAVE TO KEEP THIS A SECRET!"

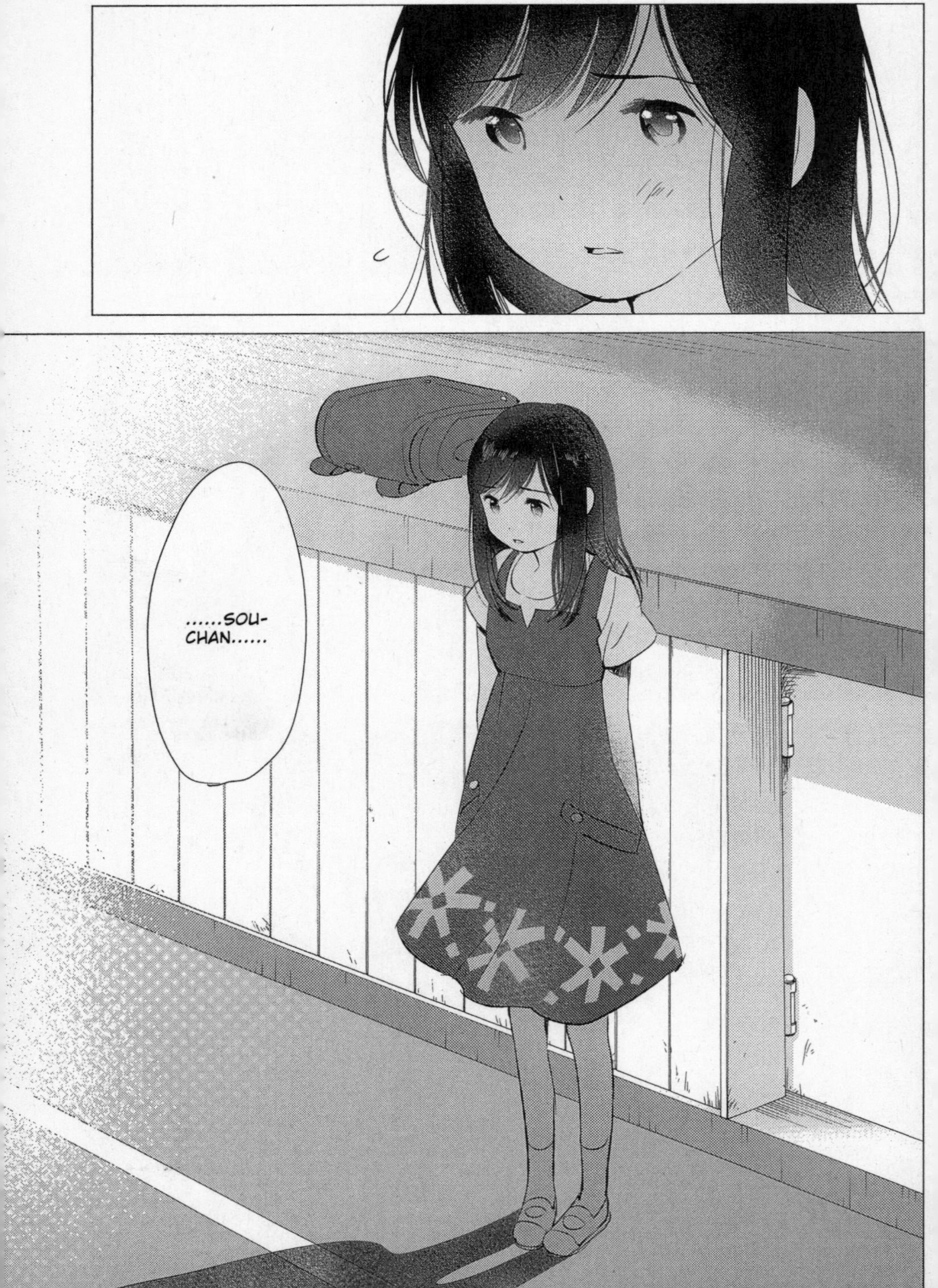

......SOU-CHAN......

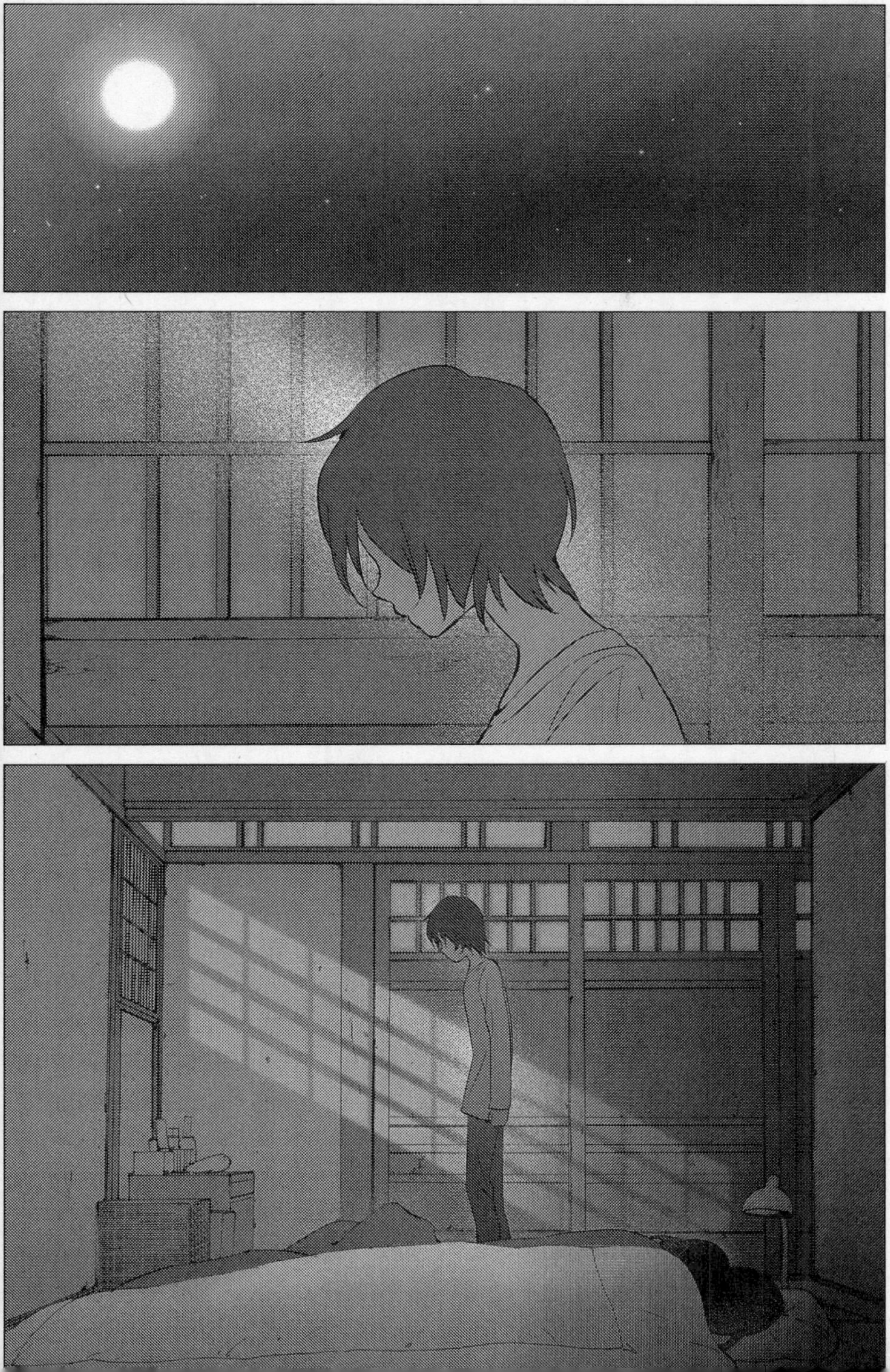

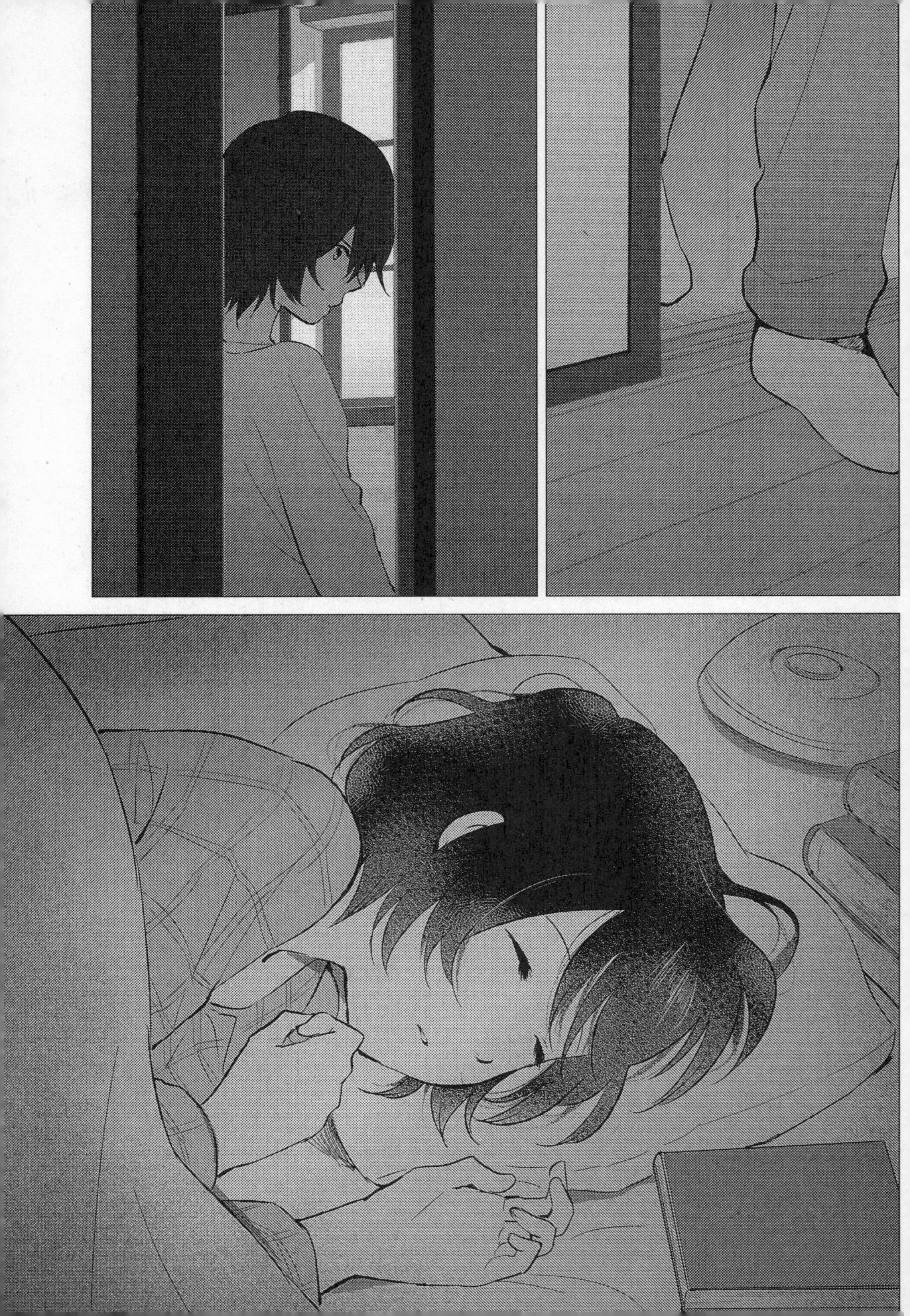

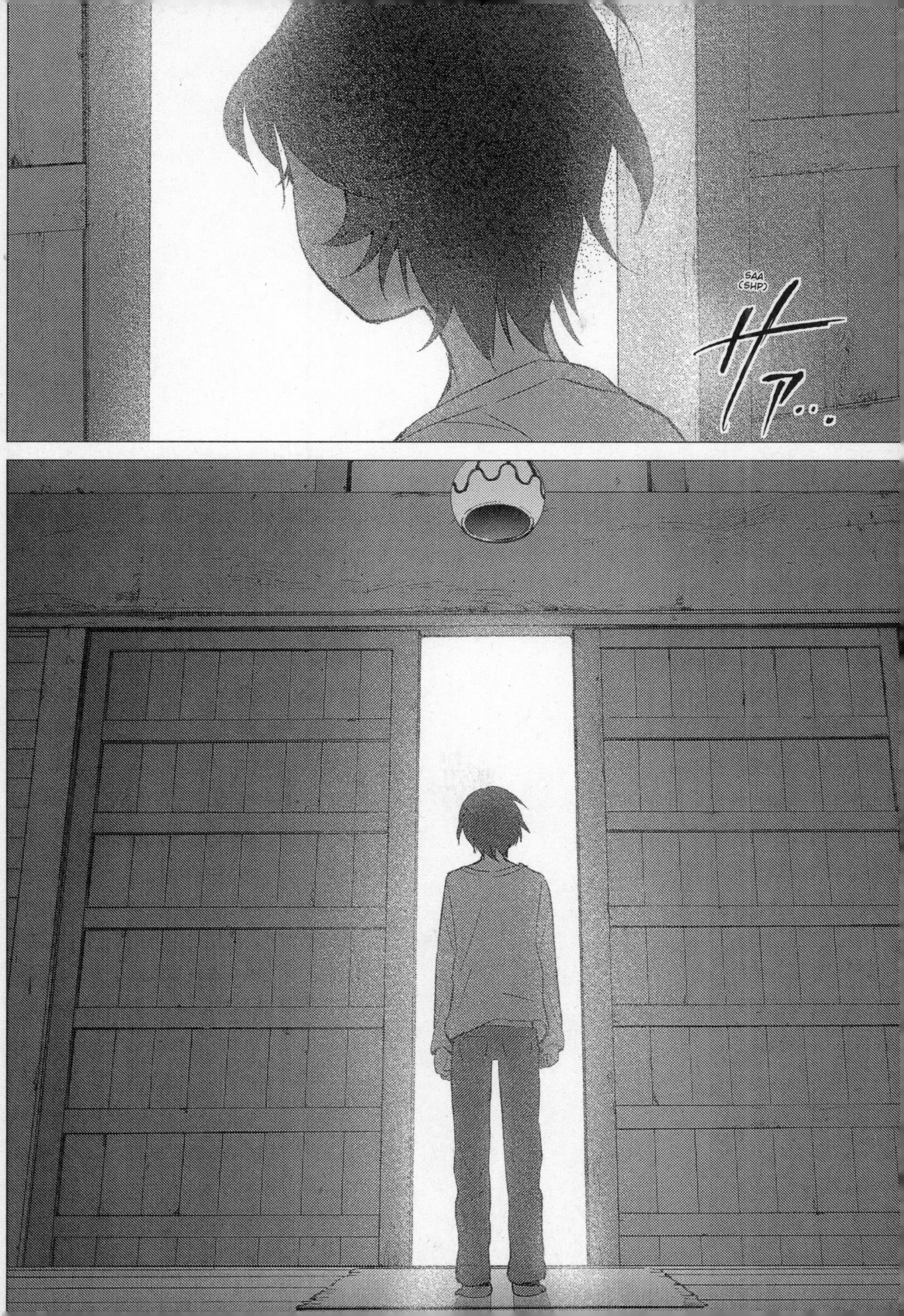
SAA (SHP)
サァ…

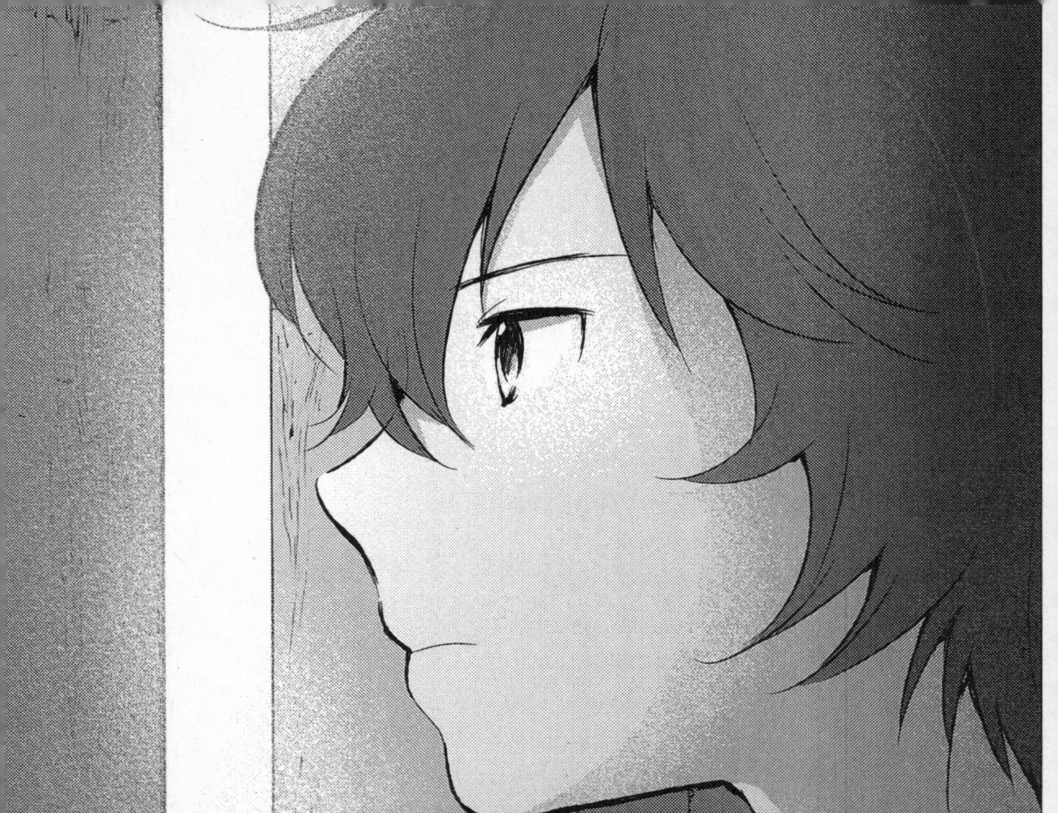

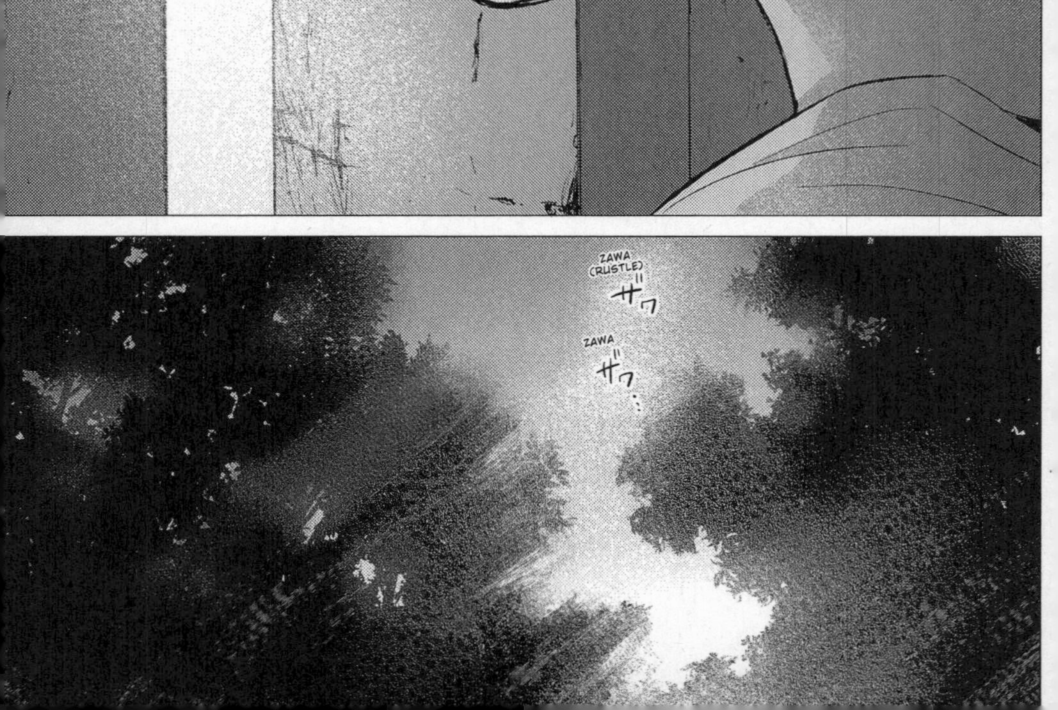
ZAWA (RUSTLE)
ザワ
ZAWA
ザワ…

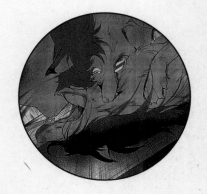

Chapter 13 After the Clouds

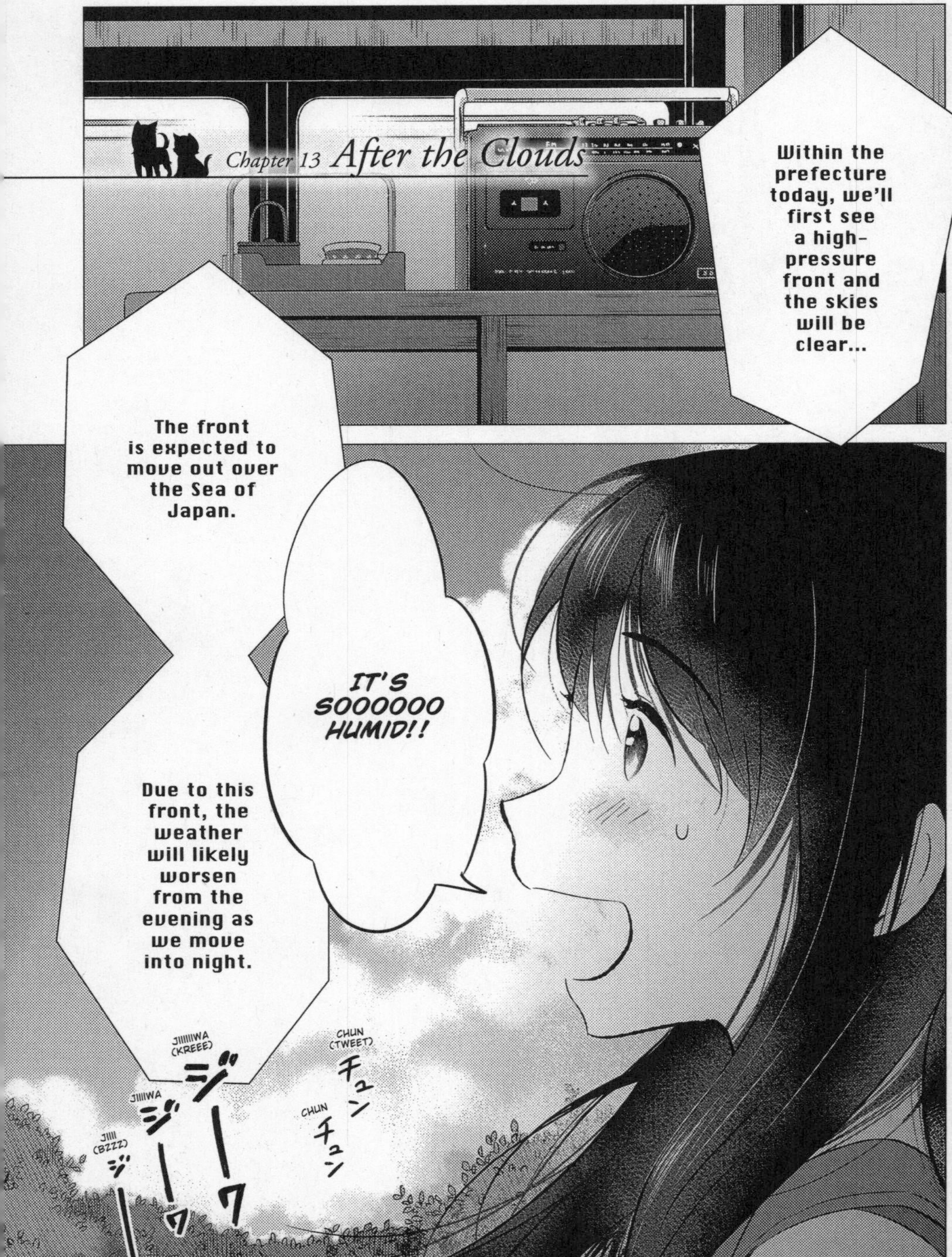
Within the prefecture today, we'll first see a high-pressure front and the skies will be clear...
The front is expected to move out over the Sea of Japan.
IT'S SOOOOOO HUMID!!
Due to this front, the weather will likely worsen from the evening as we move into night.
CHUN (TWEET) チュン
CHUN チュン
JIIIIIWA (KREEE) ジーワ
JIIIIWA ジーワ
JIIII (BZZZ) ジー

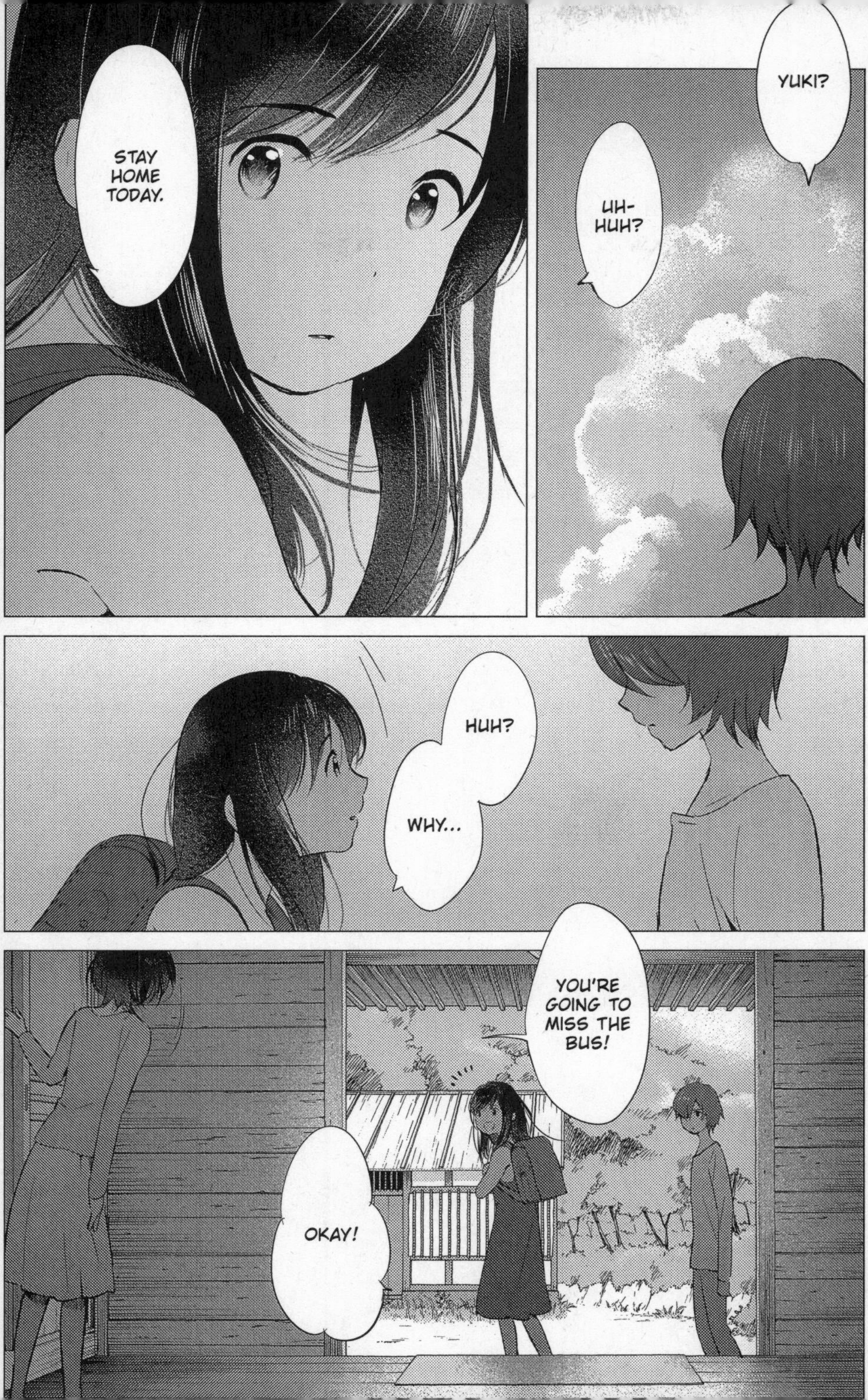
YUKI?
UH-HUH?
STAY HOME TODAY.
HUH?
WHY...
YOU'RE GOING TO MISS THE BUS!
OKAY!

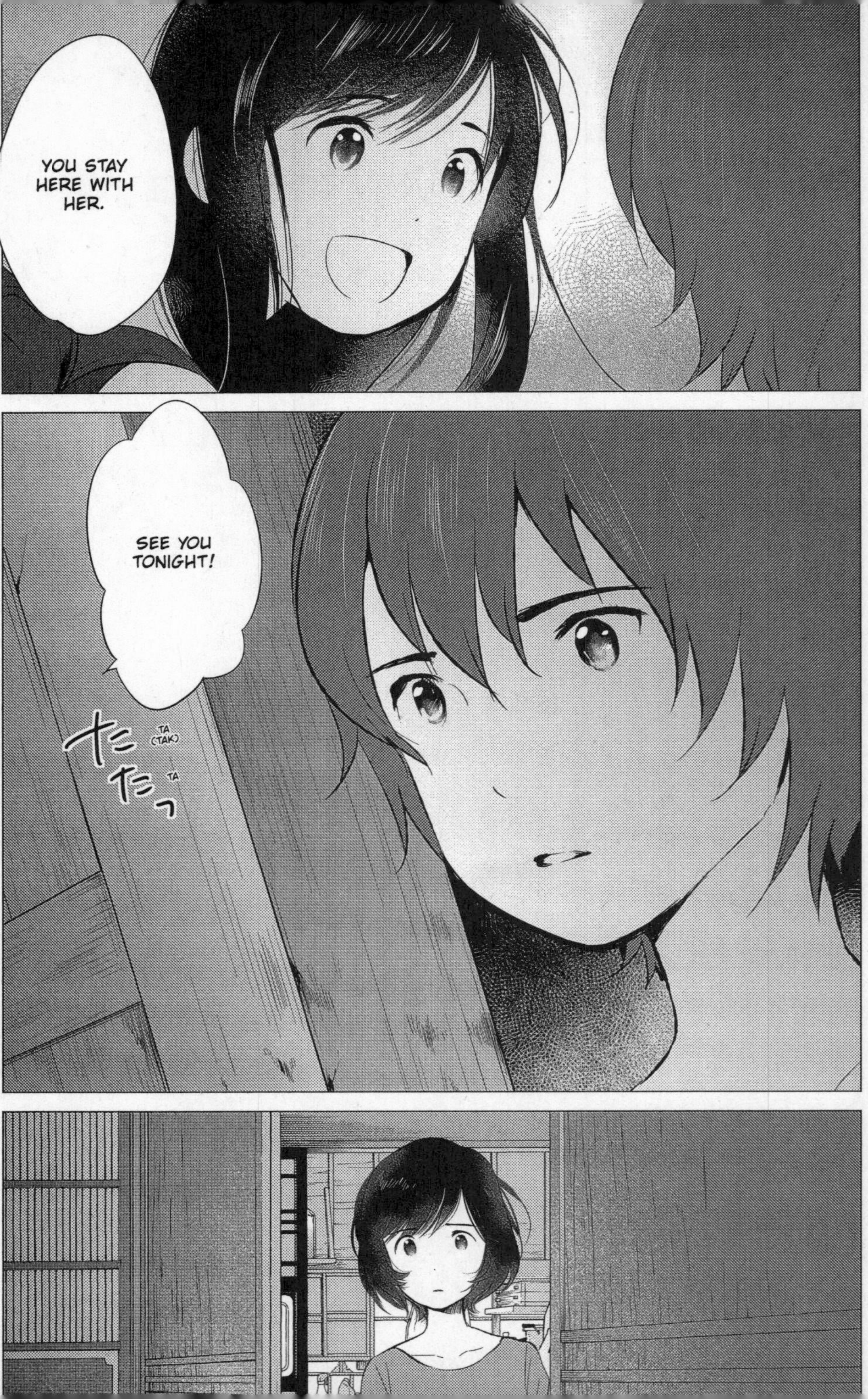
YOU STAY HERE WITH HER.
SEE YOU TONIGHT!
TA (TAK) TA

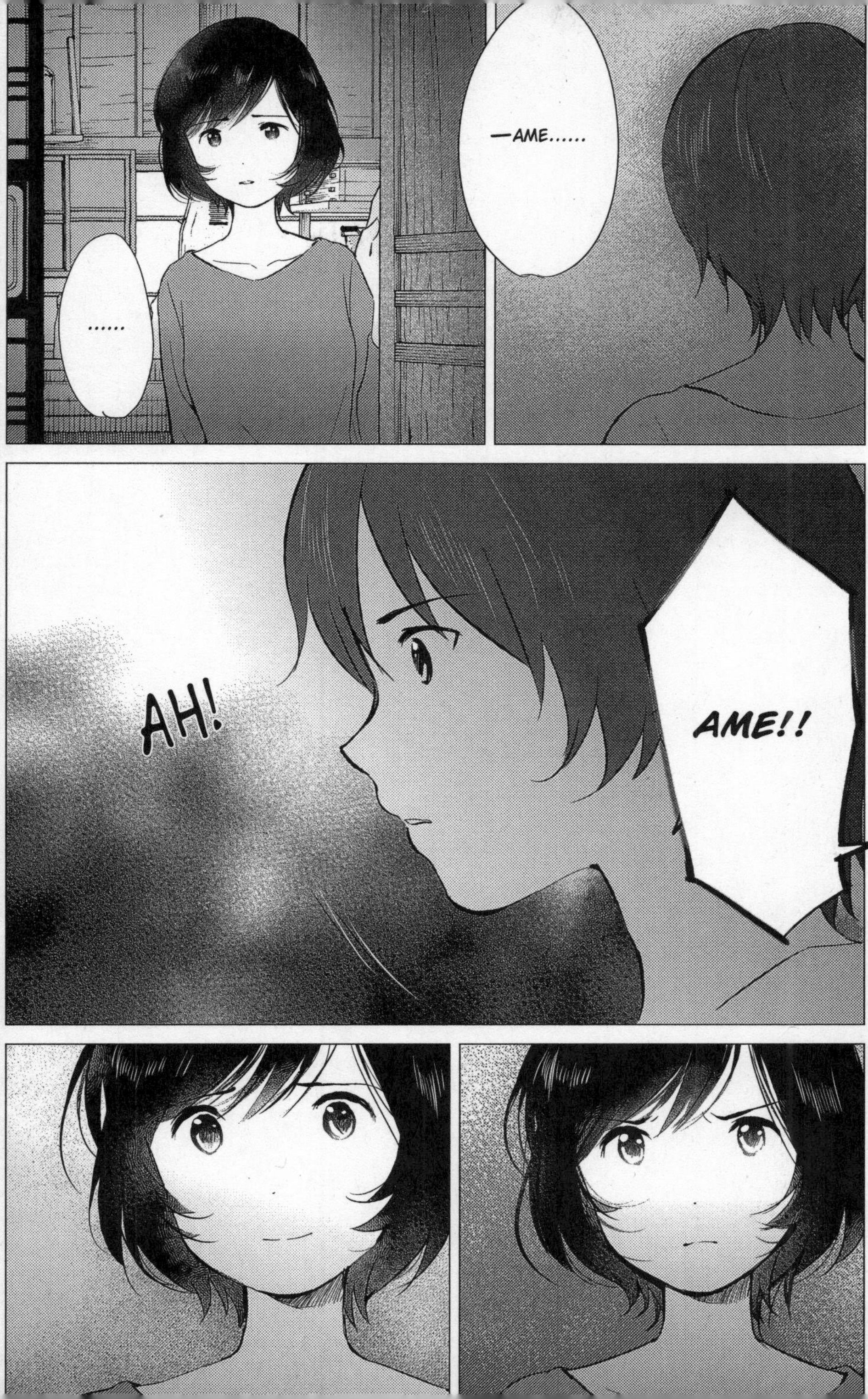
—AME......
......
AME!!
AH!

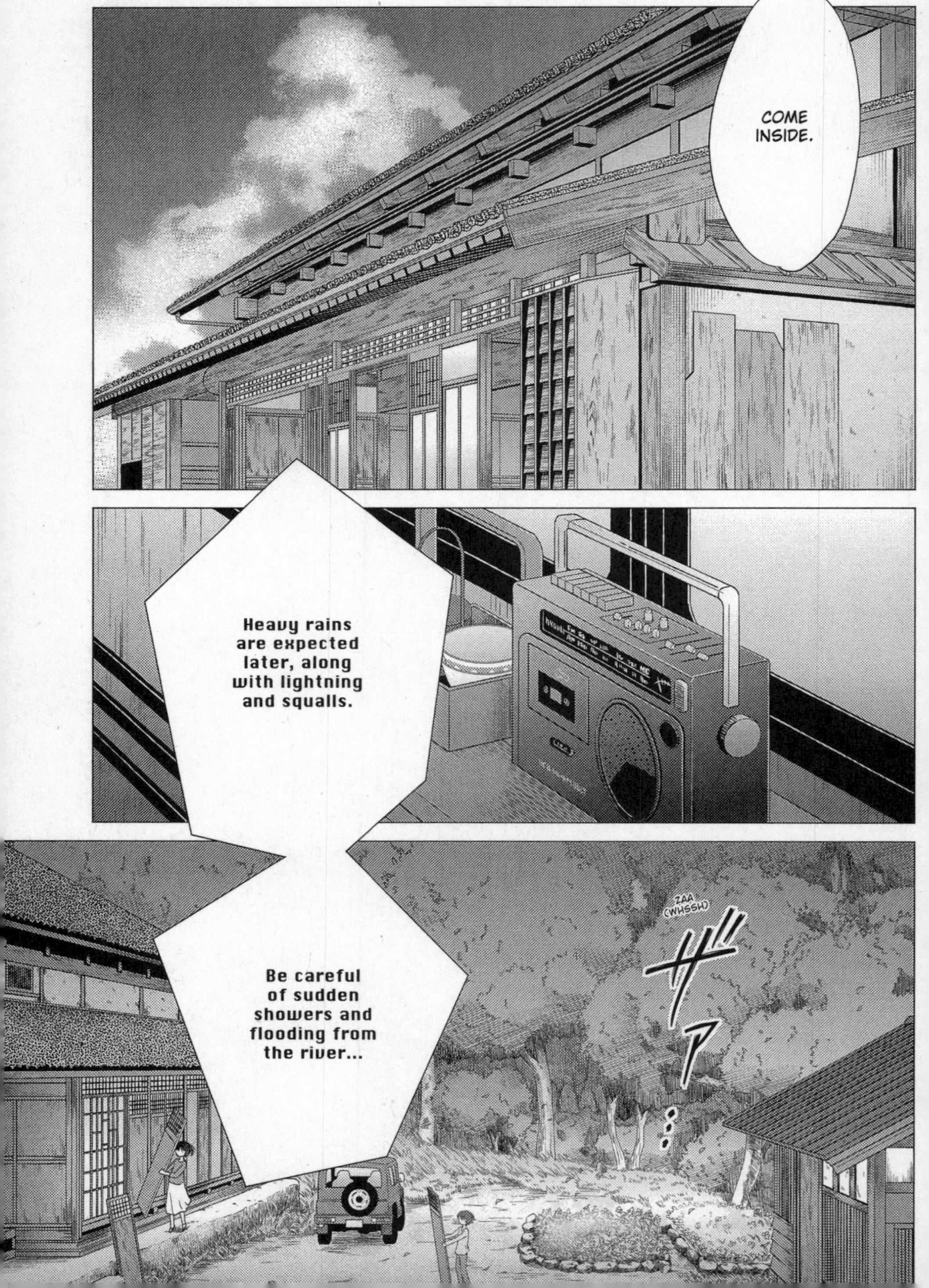
COME INSIDE.
Heavy rains are expected later, along with lightning and squalls.
Be careful of sudden showers and flooding from the river...
ZAA (WHSSH)

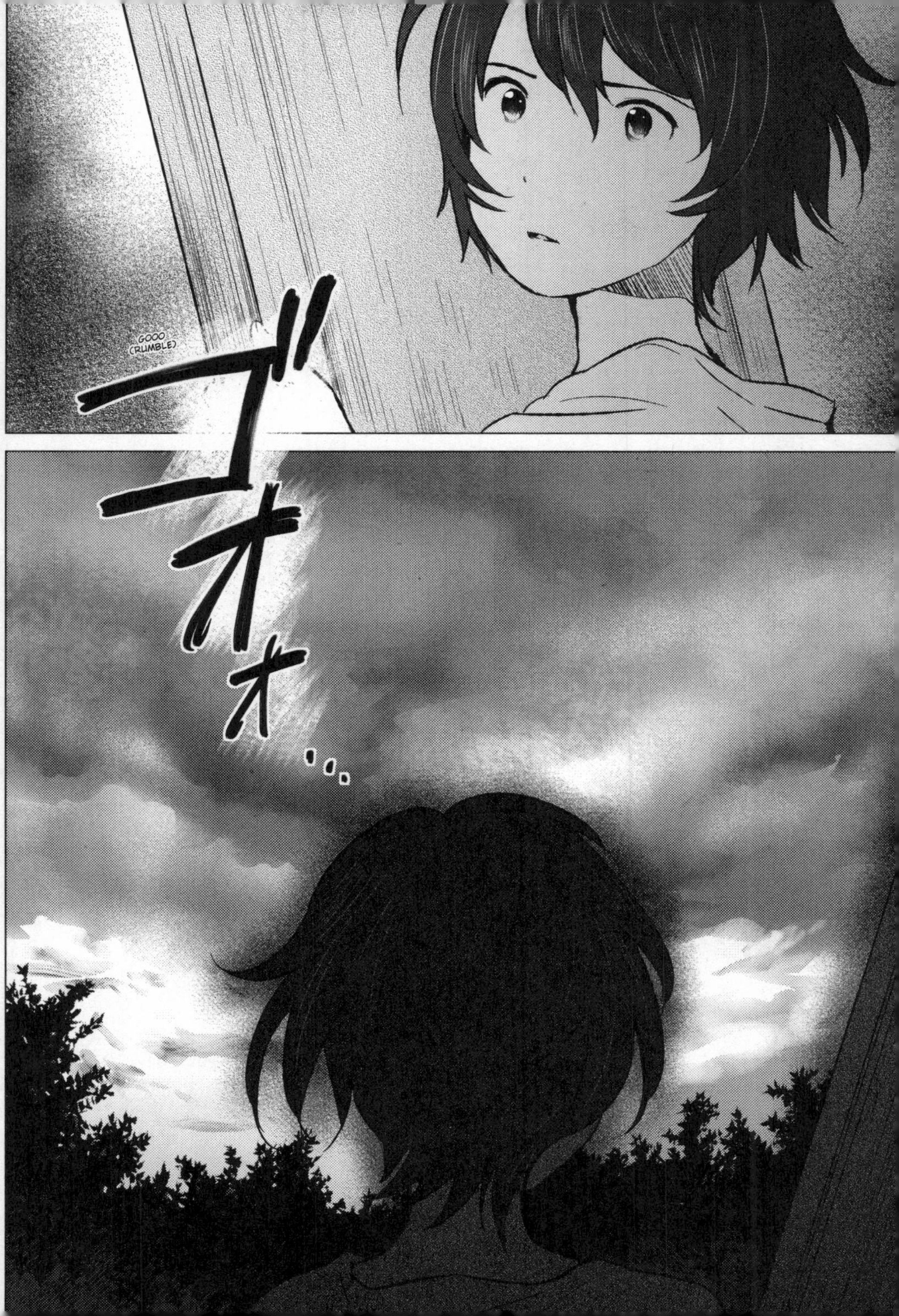

GOOO (RUMBLE)
ゴオォ…

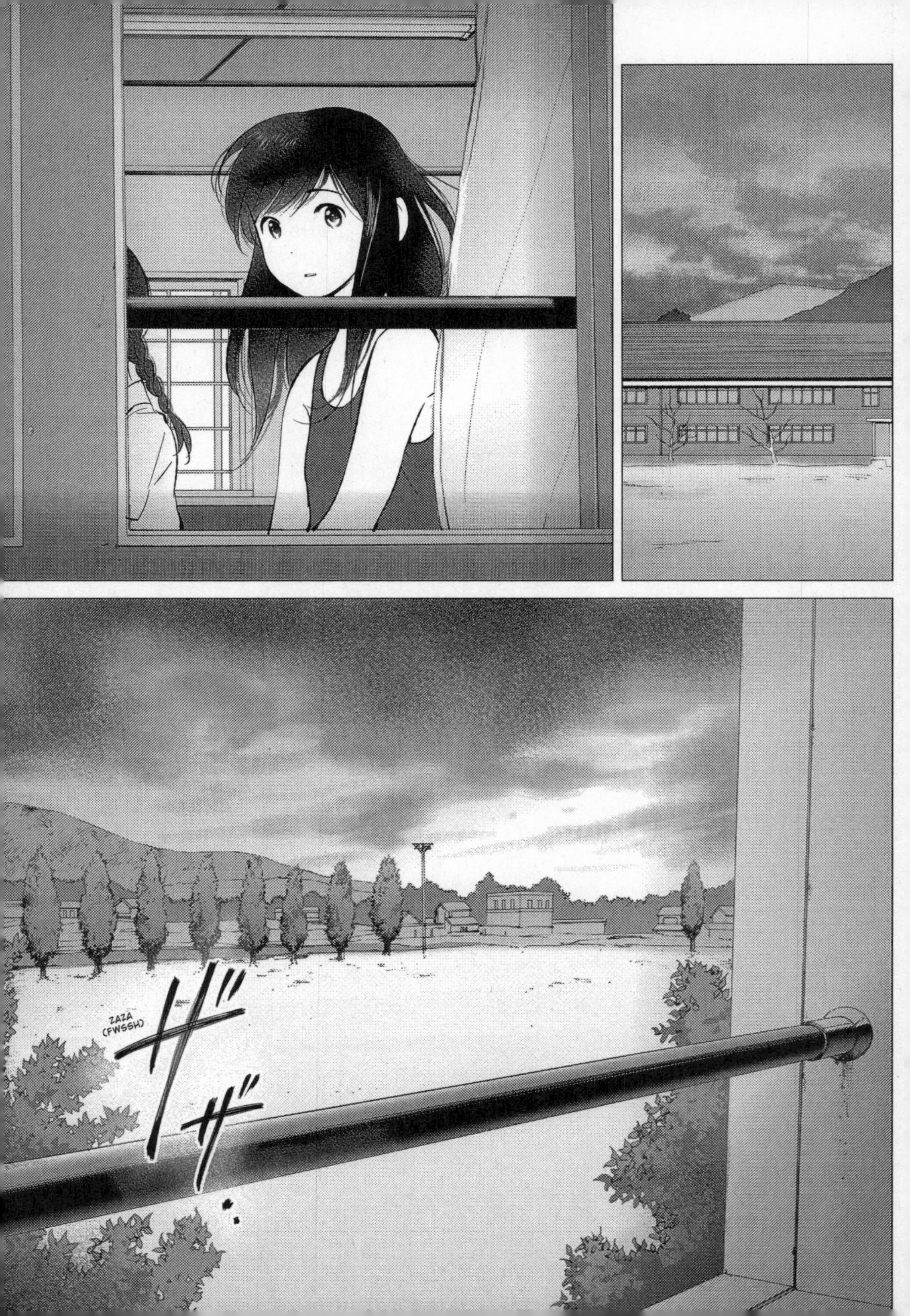
ザザ
ZAZA
(FWSSH)

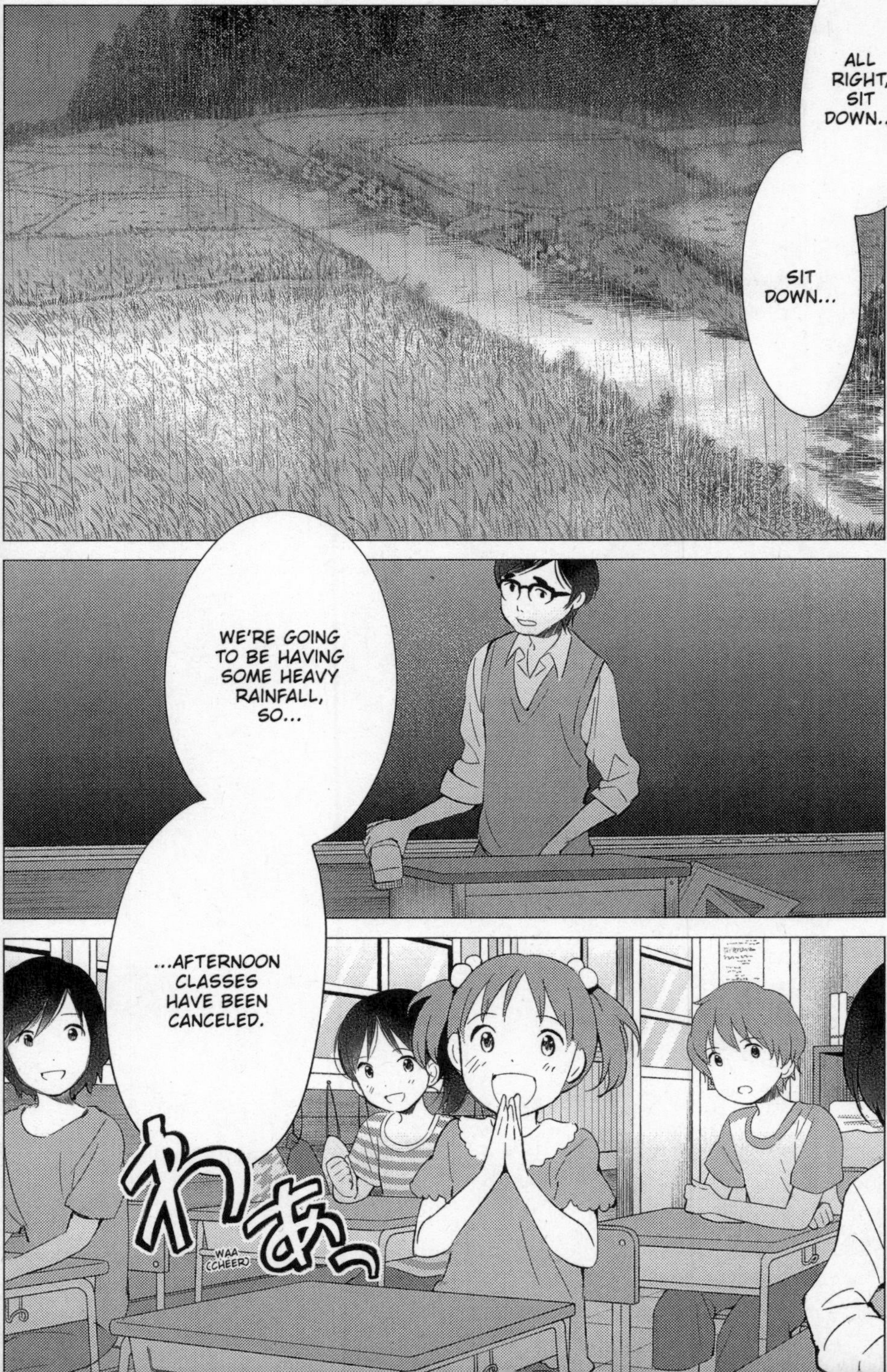
ALL RIGHT, SIT DOWN...
SIT DOWN...
WE'RE GOING TO BE HAVING SOME HEAVY RAINFALL, SO...
...AFTERNOON CLASSES HAVE BEEN CANCELED.
わぁっ
WAA (CHEER)

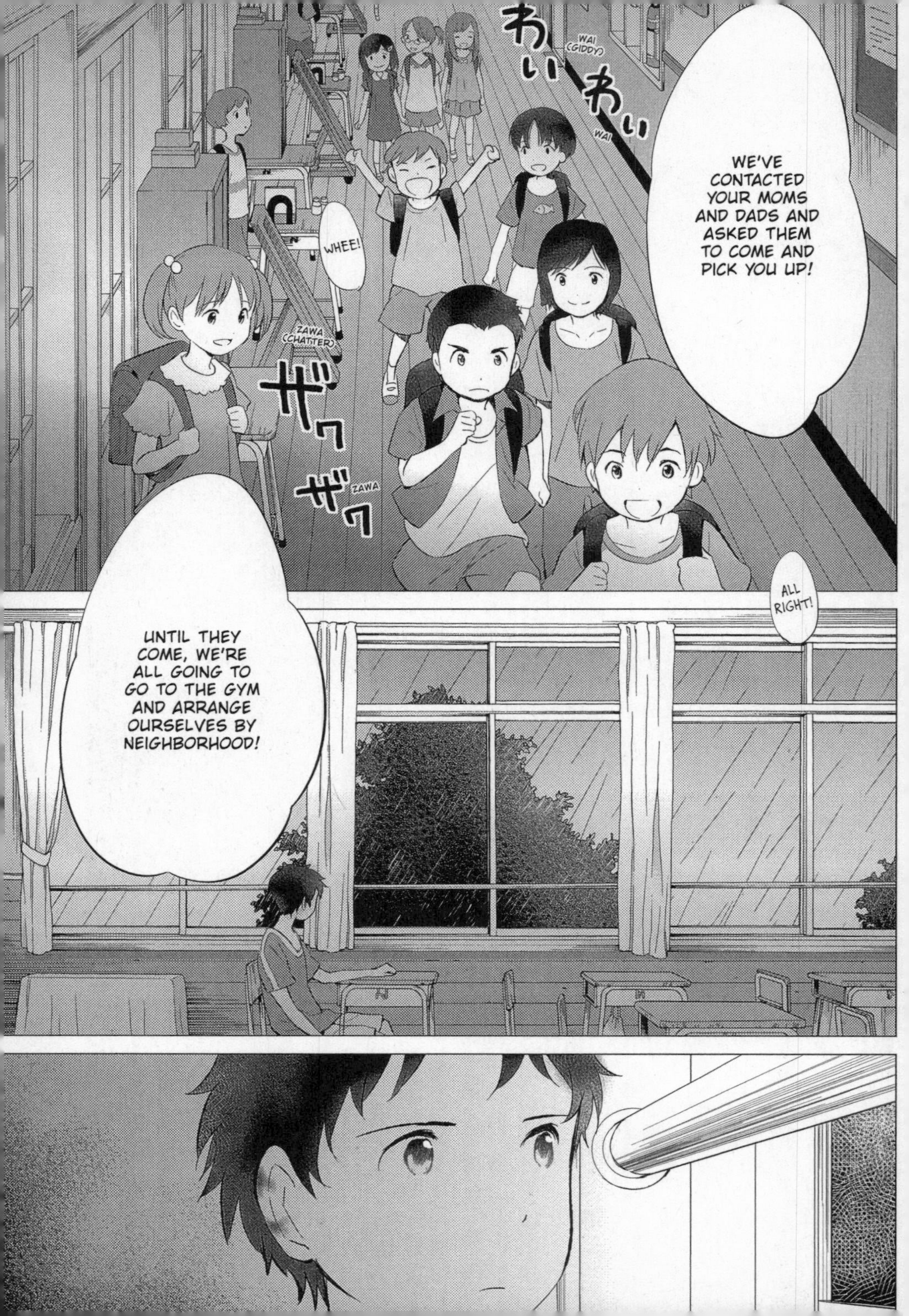
わい WAI (GIDDY)
わい WAI
WE'VE CONTACTED YOUR MOMS AND DADS AND ASKED THEM TO COME AND PICK YOU UP!
WHEE!
ザワ ZAWA (CHATTER)
ザワ ZAWA
UNTIL THEY COME, WE'RE ALL GOING TO GO TO THE GYM AND ARRANGE OURSELVES BY NEIGHBORHOOD!
ALL RIGHT!

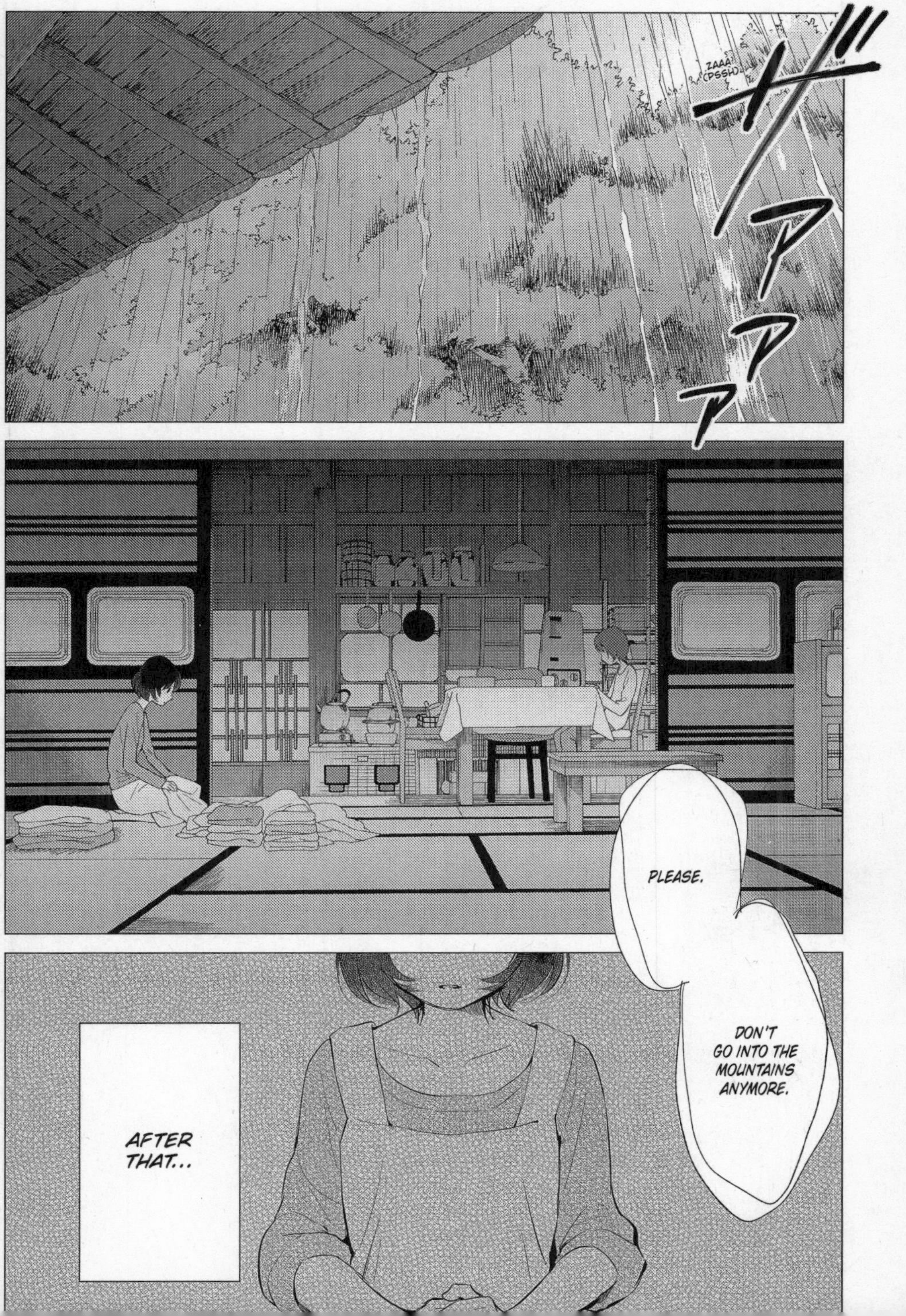
ザアアア
ZAAA (PSSH)
PLEASE.
DON'T GO INTO THE MOUNTAINS ANYMORE.
AFTER THAT...

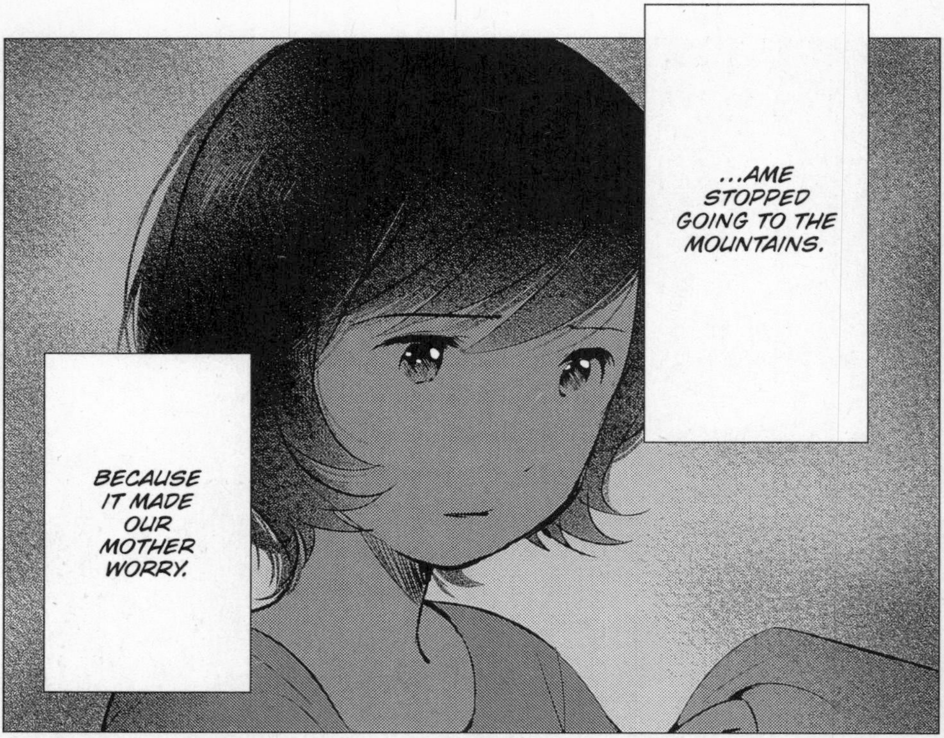
...AME STOPPED GOING TO THE MOUNTAINS.
BECAUSE IT MADE OUR MOTHER WORRY.

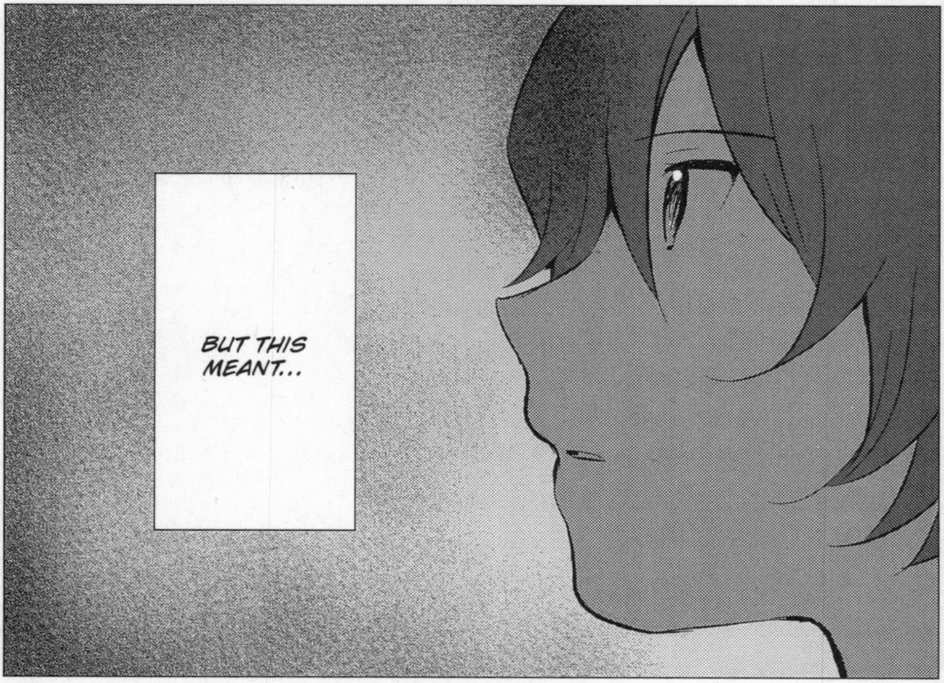
BUT THIS MEANT...

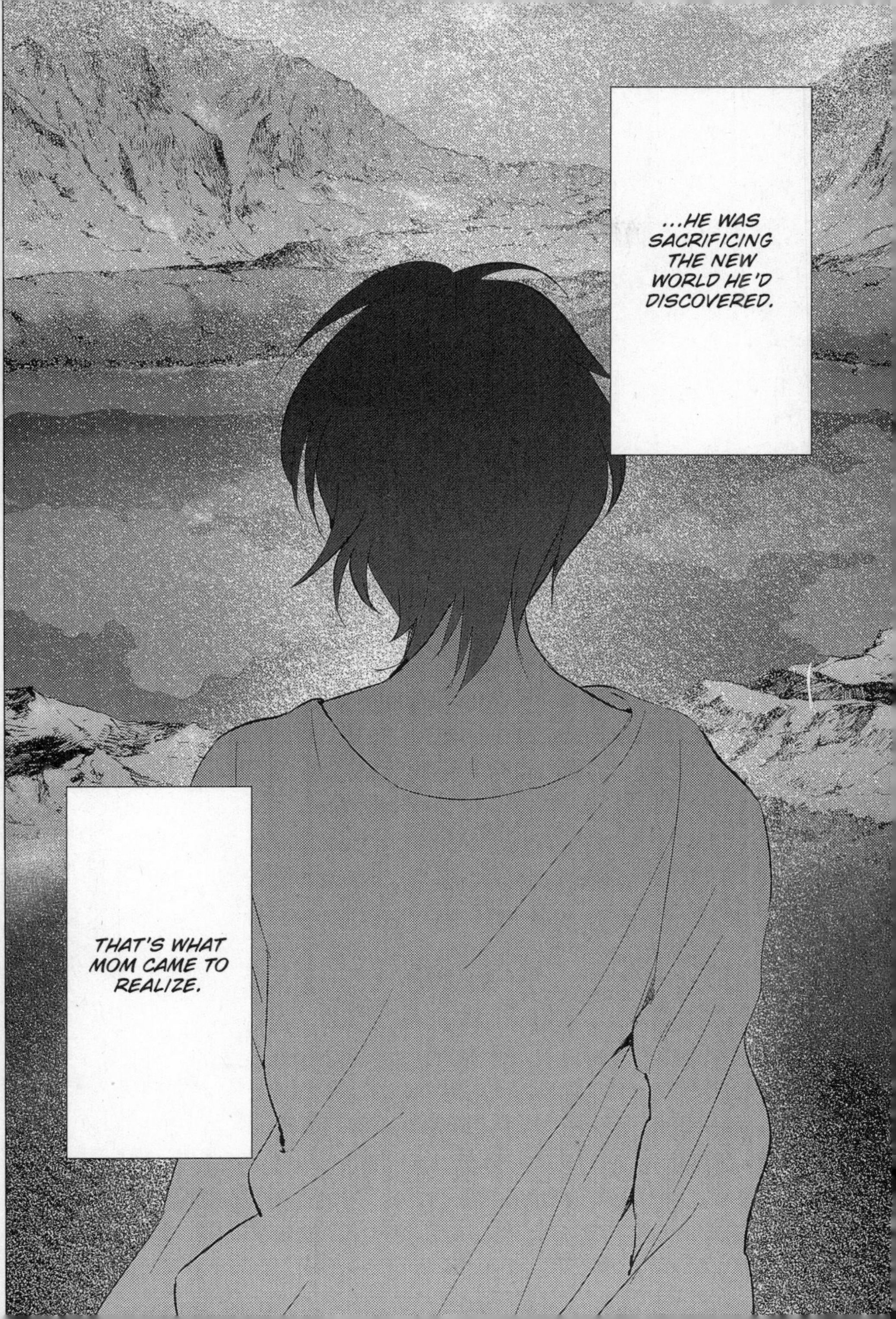
...HE WAS SACRIFICING THE NEW WORLD HE'D DISCOVERED.
THAT'S WHAT MOM CAME TO REALIZE.

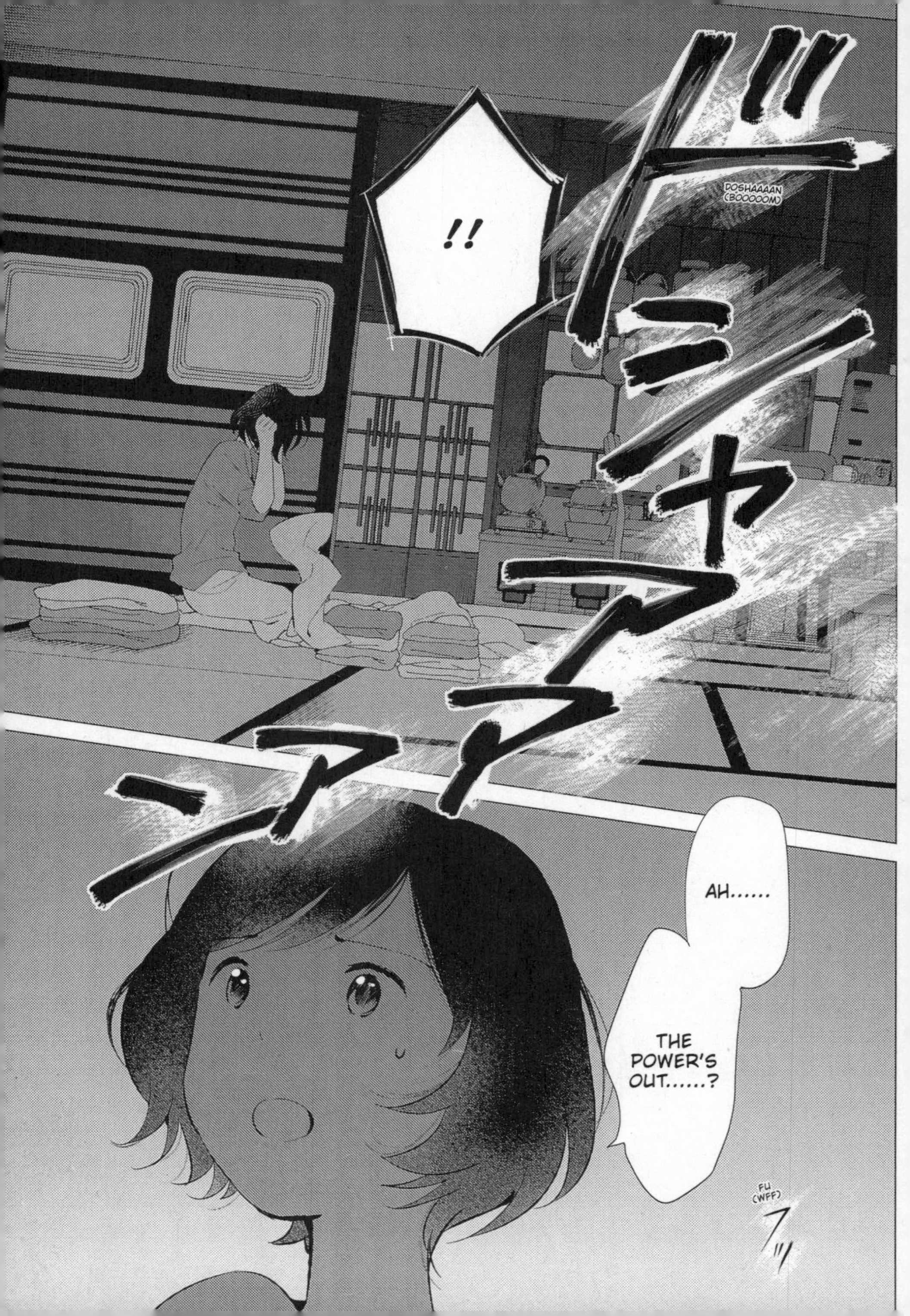
DOSHAAAAN
(BOOOOOM)
!!
AH......
THE POWER'S OUT......?
FU
(WFF)

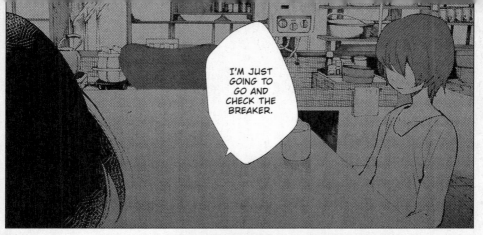

I'M JUST GOING TO GO AND CHECK THE BREAKER.

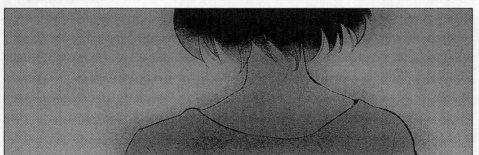

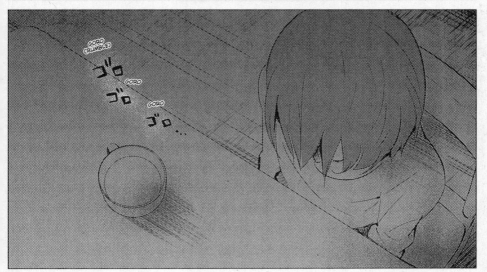

GORO (CRUMBLE)
GORO
GORO

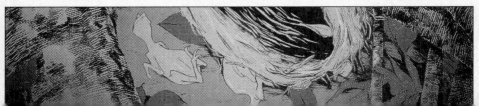

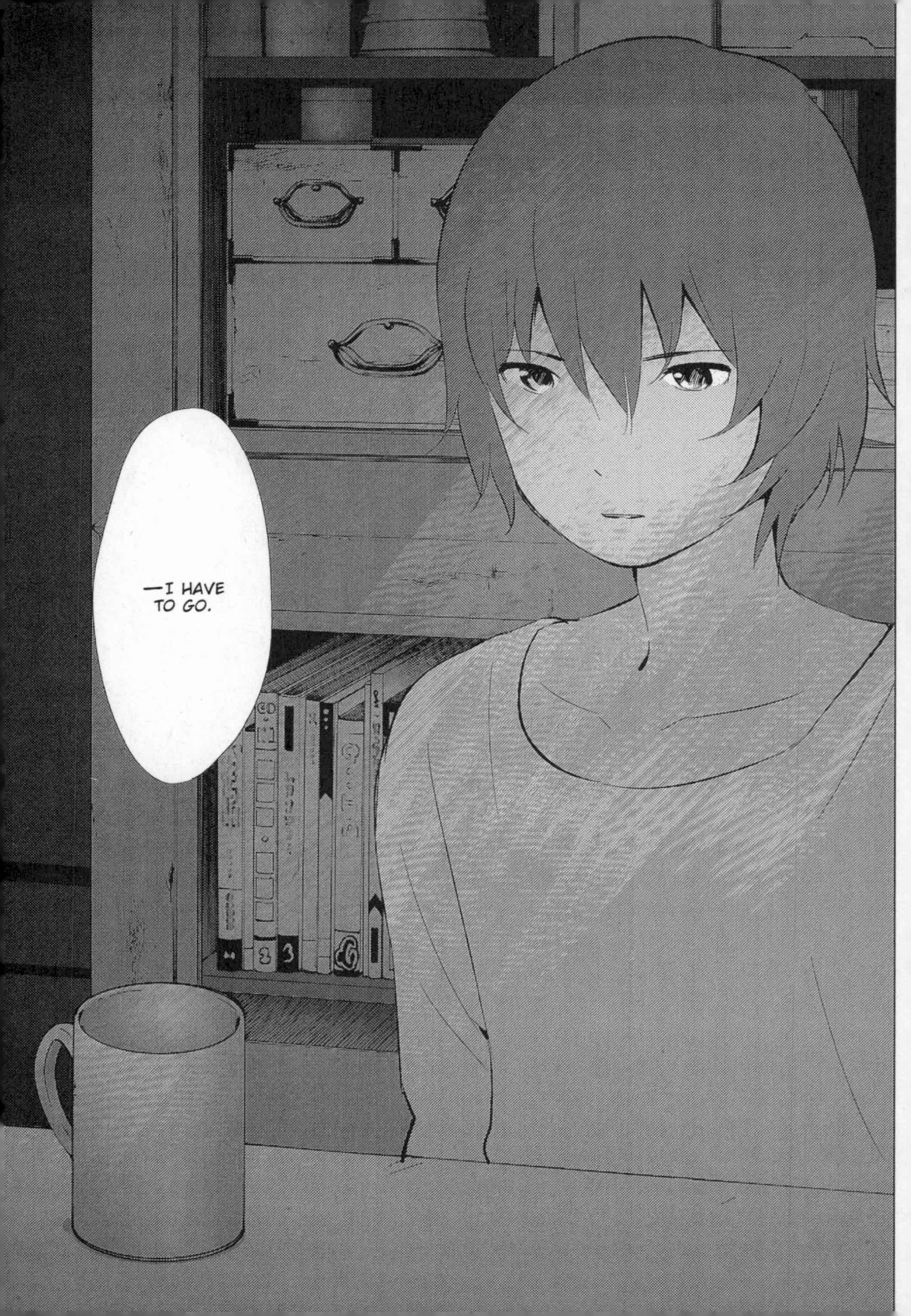
—I HAVE TO GO.

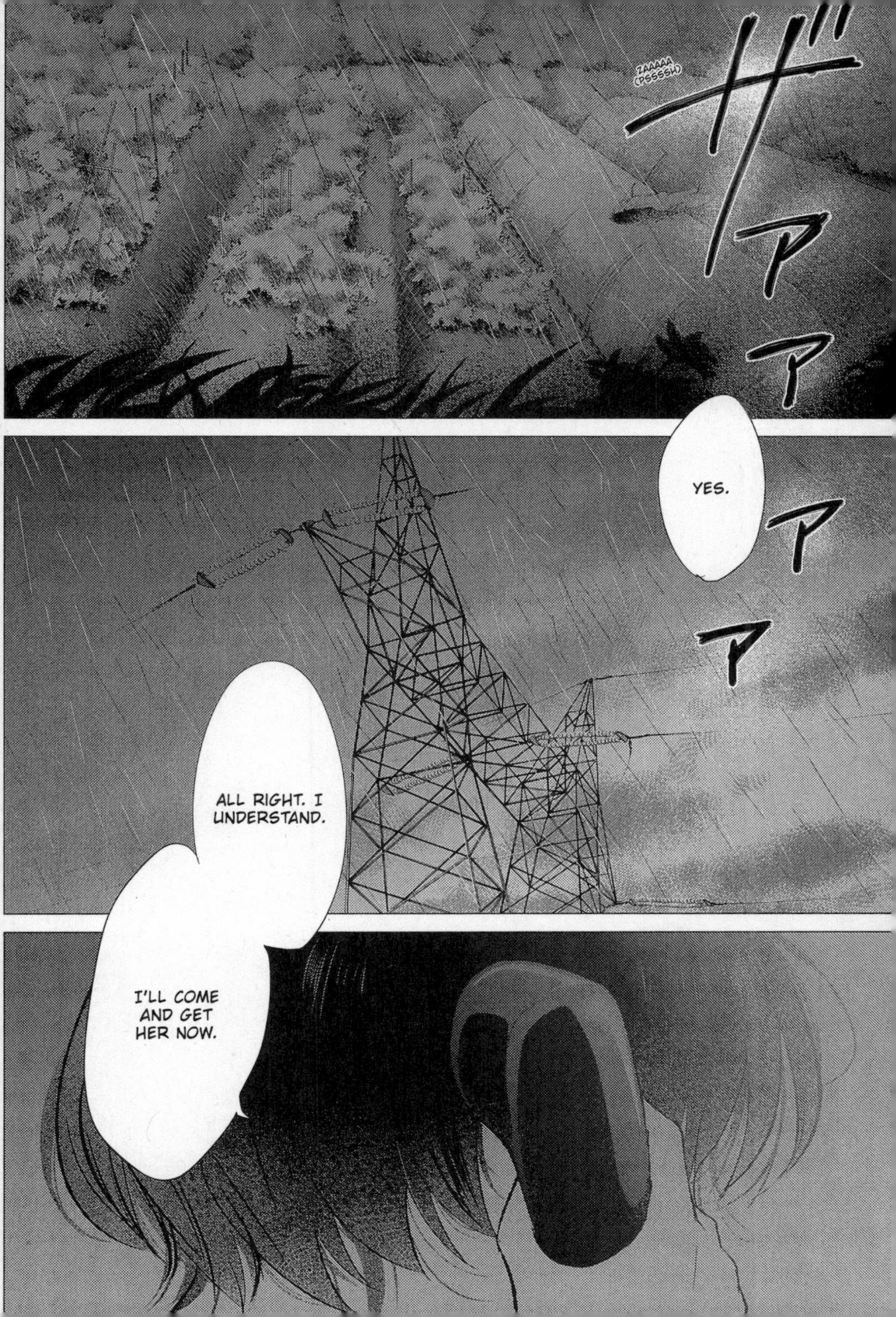
ザァァァァ
ZAAAAA (PSSSSH)
YES.
ALL RIGHT. I UNDERSTAND.
I'LL COME AND GET HER NOW.

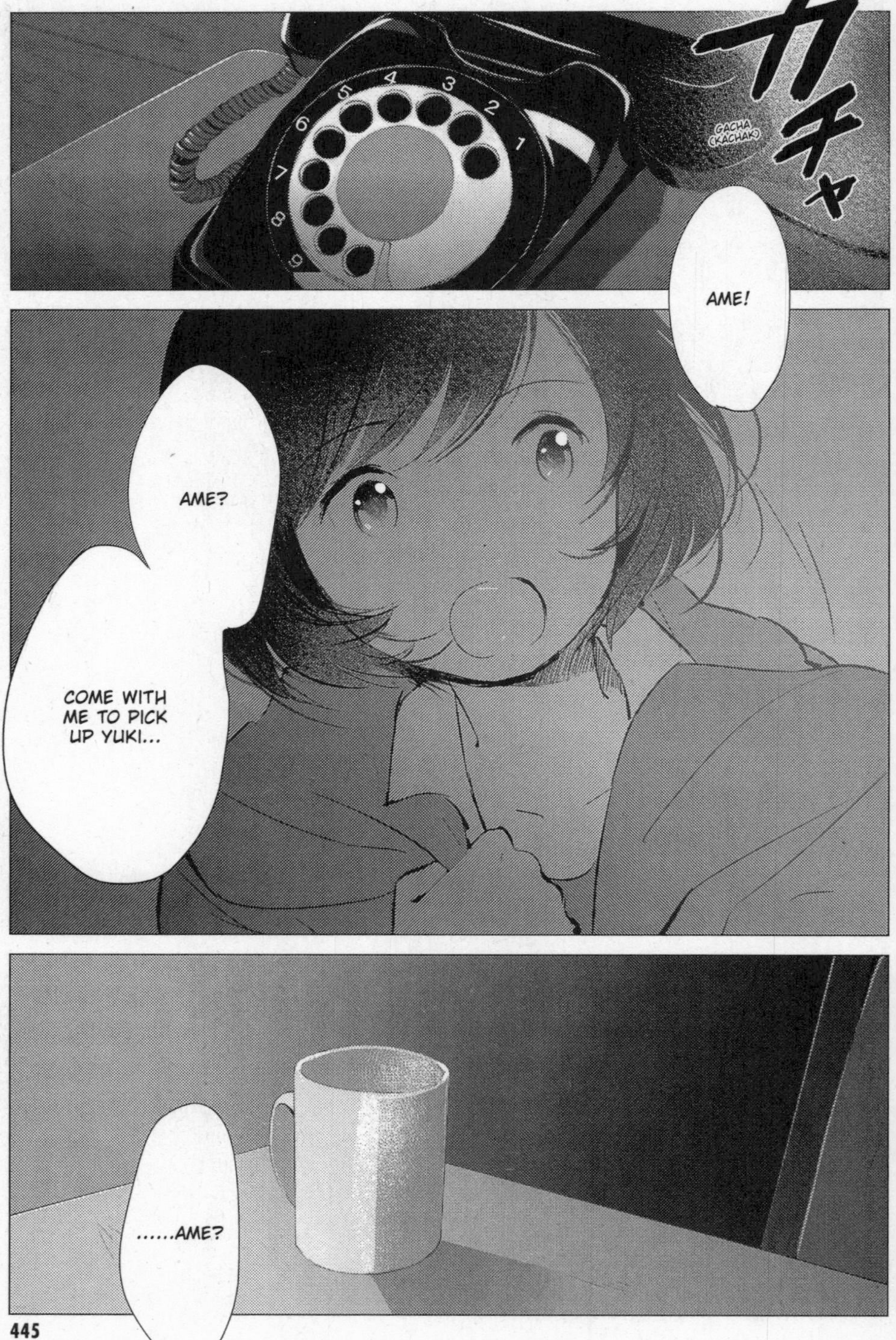
ガチャ
GACHA (KACHAK)
AME!
AME?
COME WITH ME TO PICK UP YUKI...
......AME?

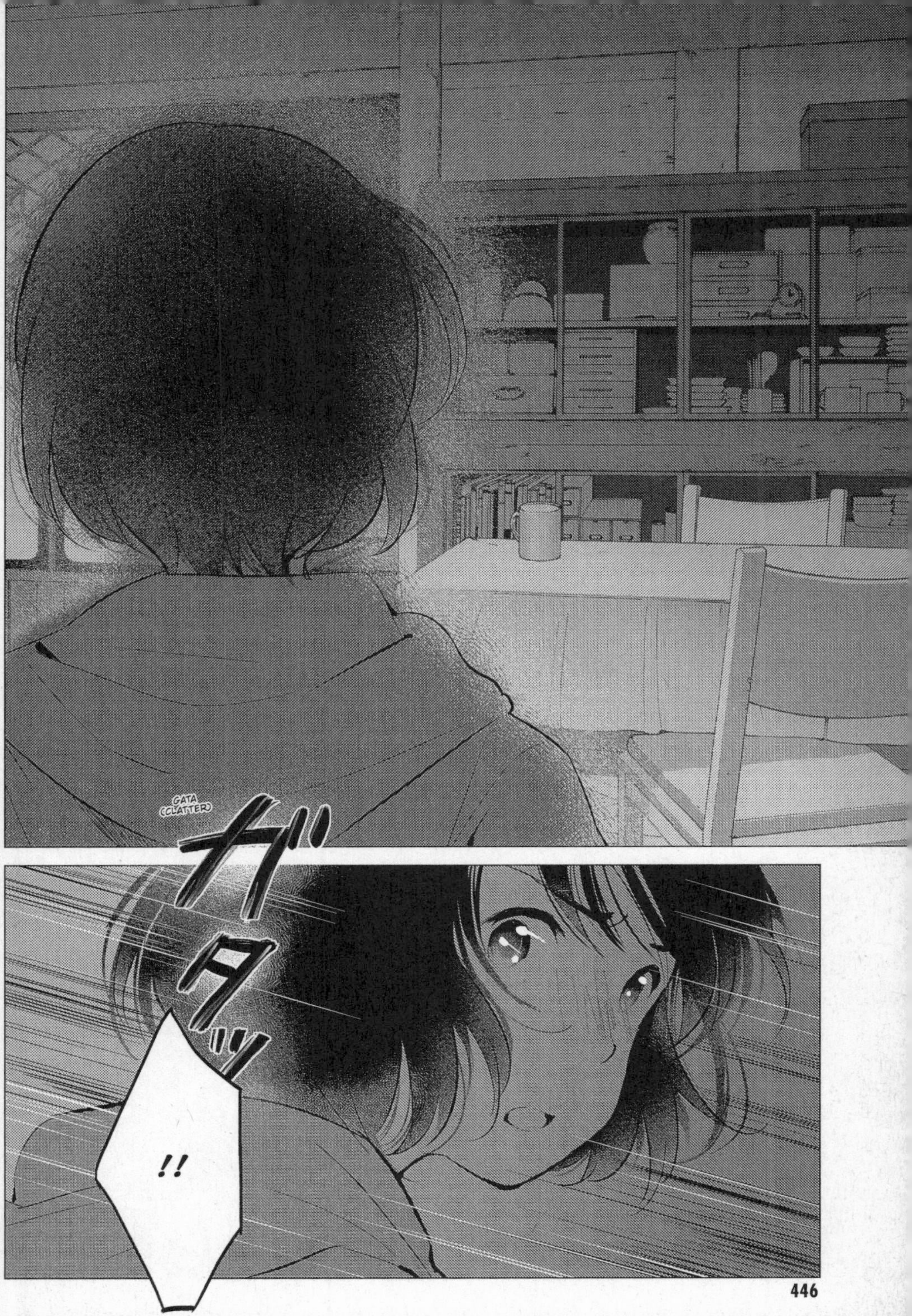
GATA (CLATTER)
ガタッ
!!

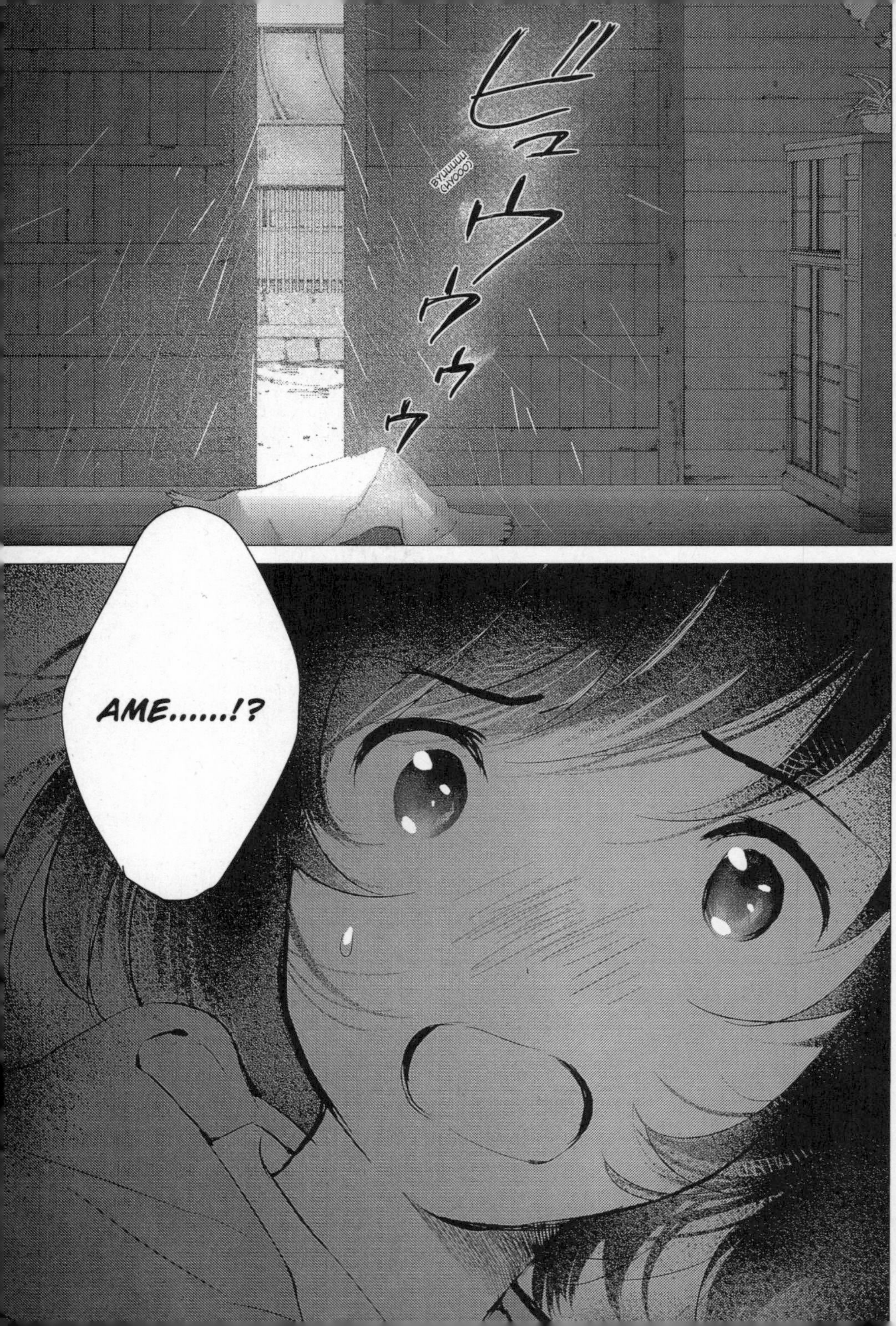
ビュウウゥゥゥ
BYuuuuu
(HYOOO)
AME......!?

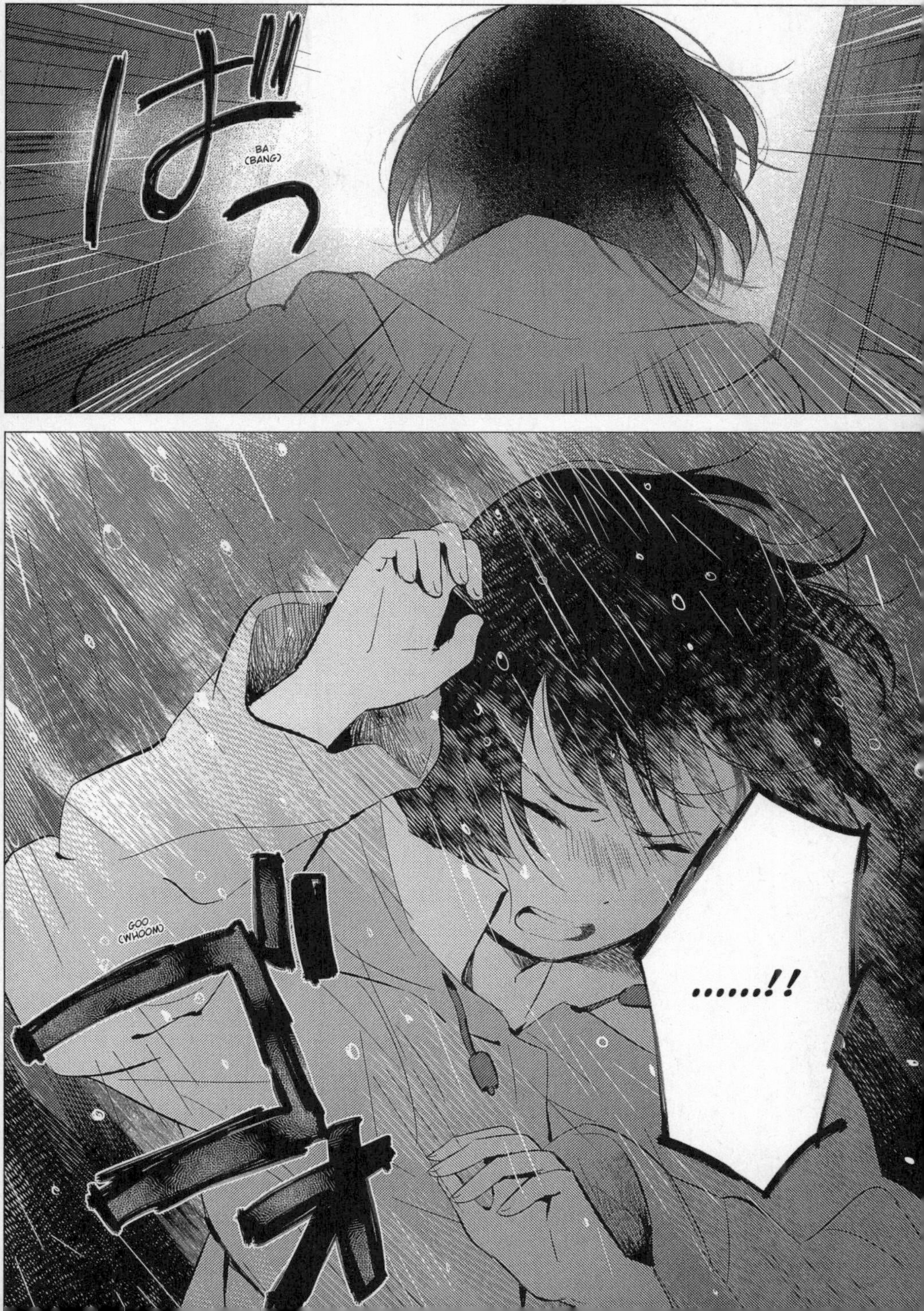
ばっ
BA (BANG)
......!!
ゴォ
GOO (WHOOM)

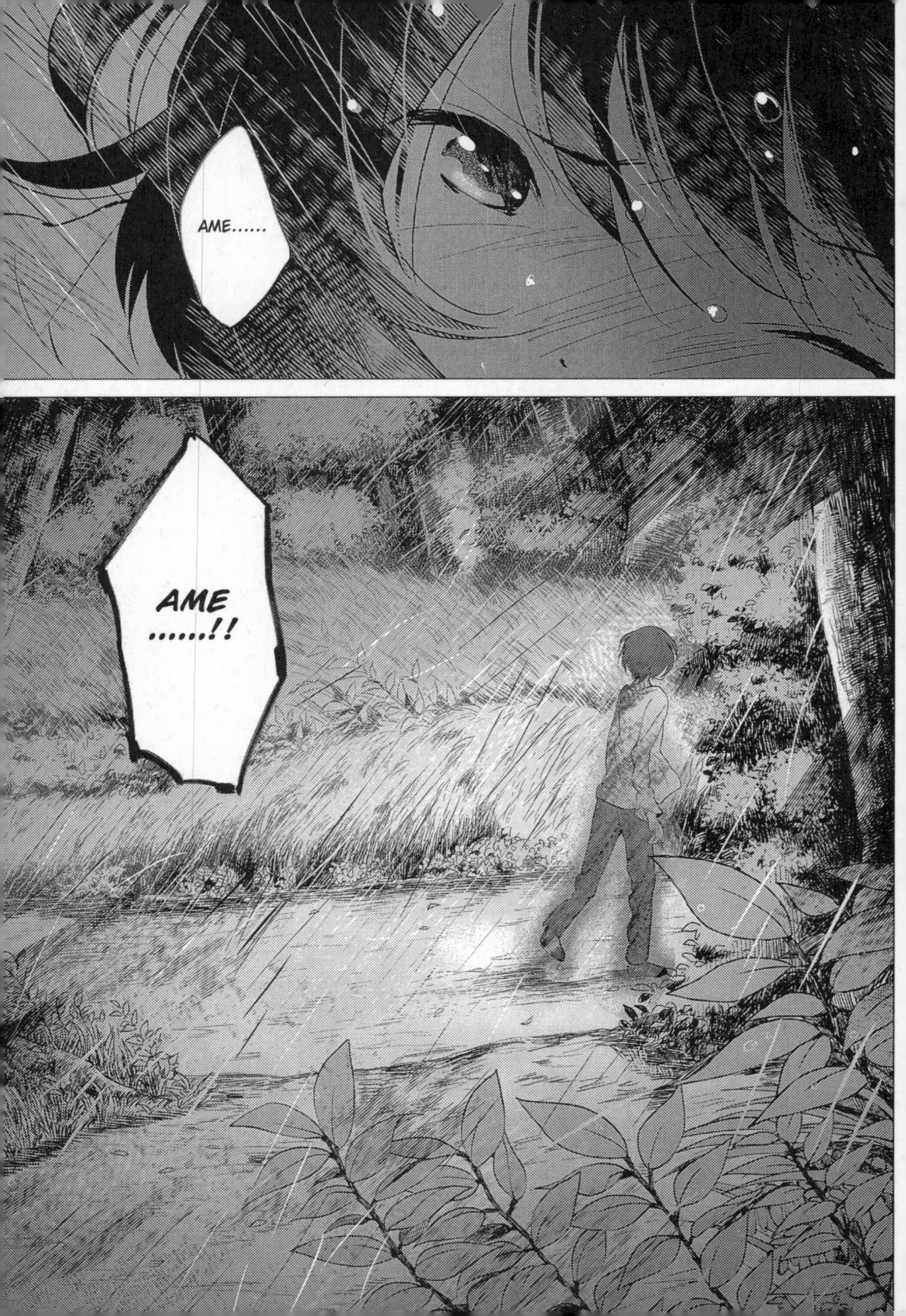
AME......
AME ......!!

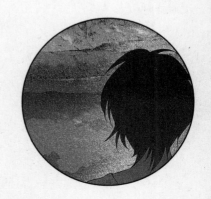

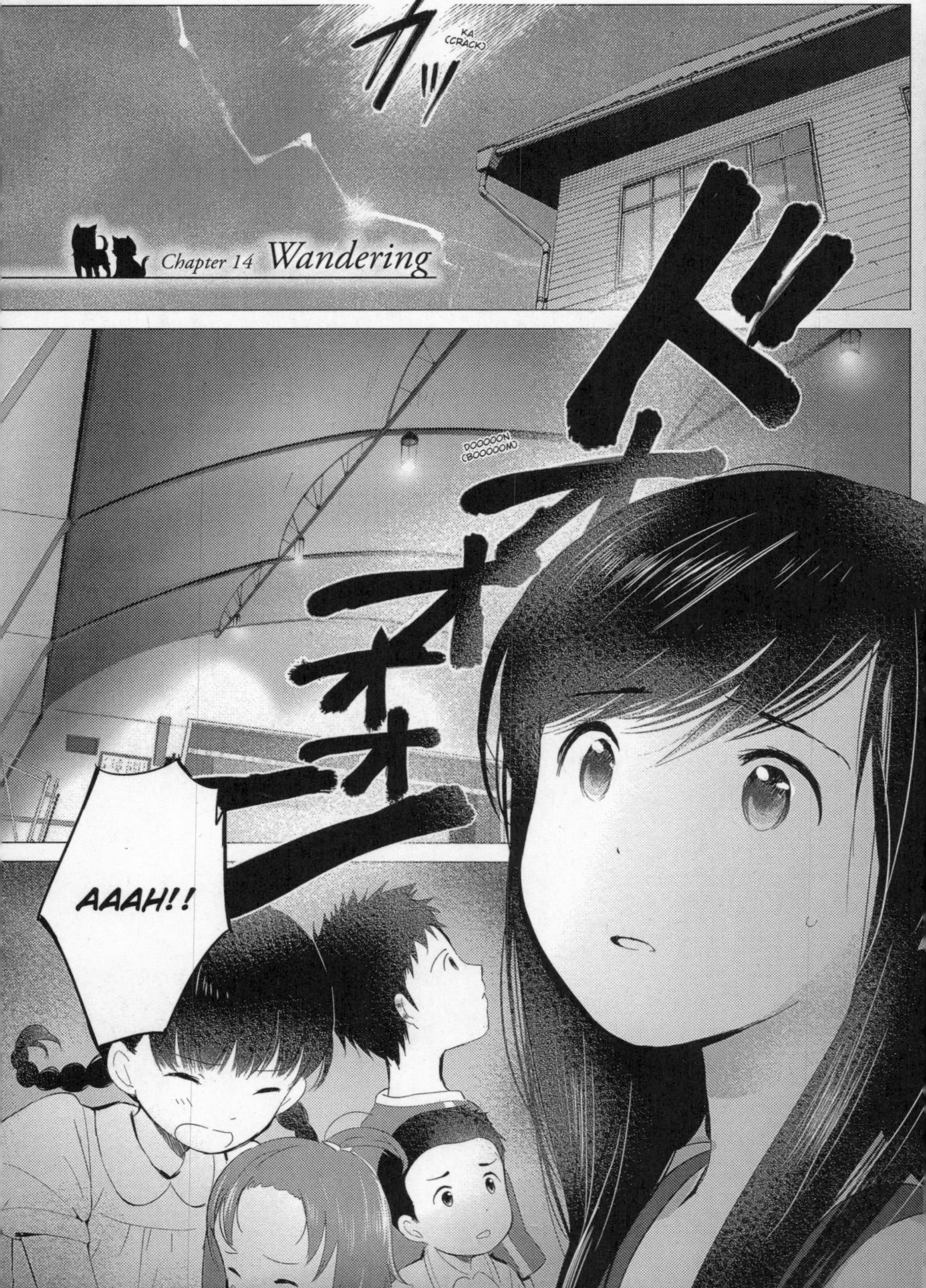
KA
(CRACK)
Chapter 14 Wandering
DOOOOON
(BOOOOOM)
AAAH!!

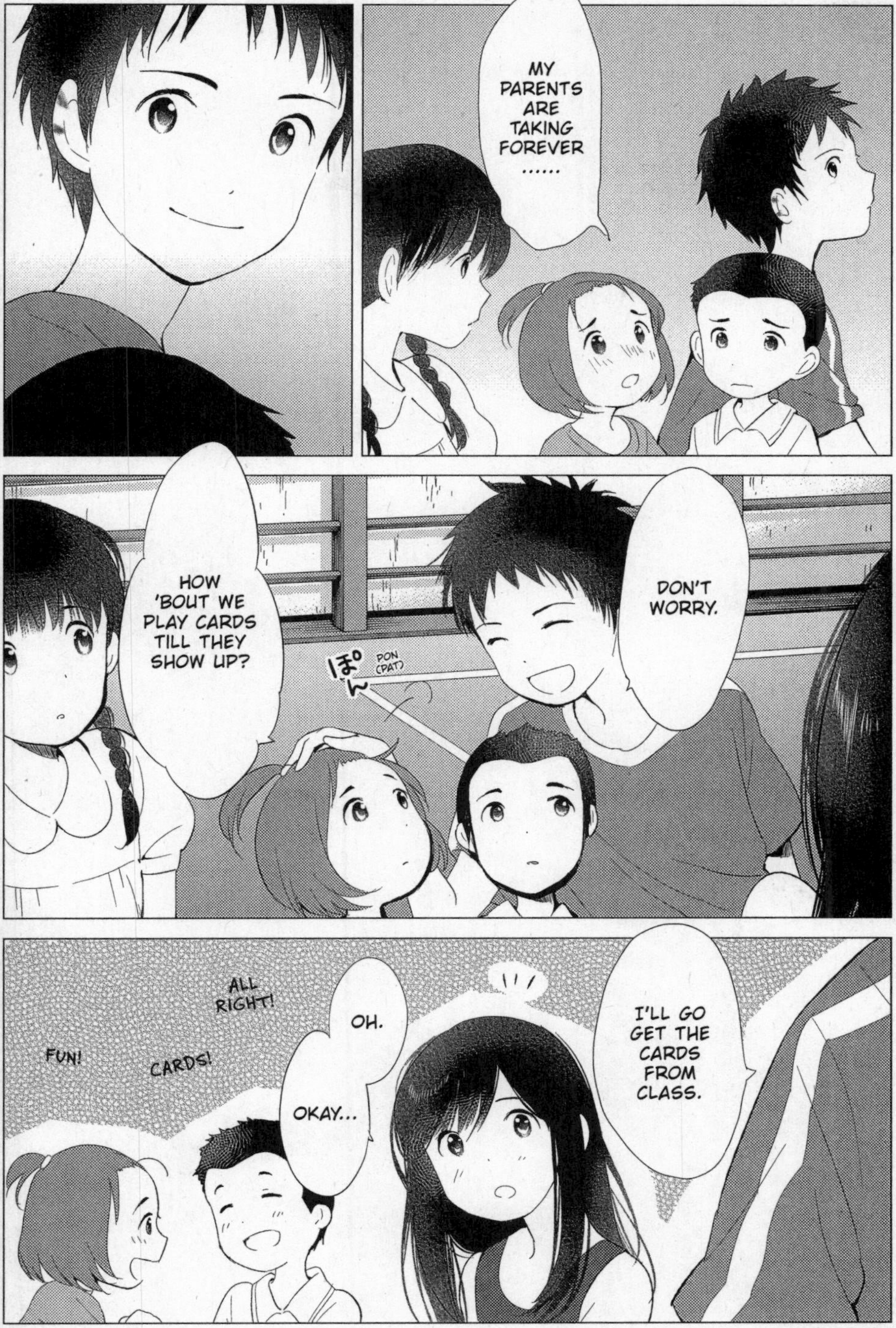
MY PARENTS ARE TAKING FOREVER ......
DON'T WORRY.
ぽん
PON (PAT)
HOW 'BOUT WE PLAY CARDS TILL THEY SHOW UP?
I'LL GO GET THE CARDS FROM CLASS.
OH.
OKAY...
ALL RIGHT!
CARDS!
FUN!

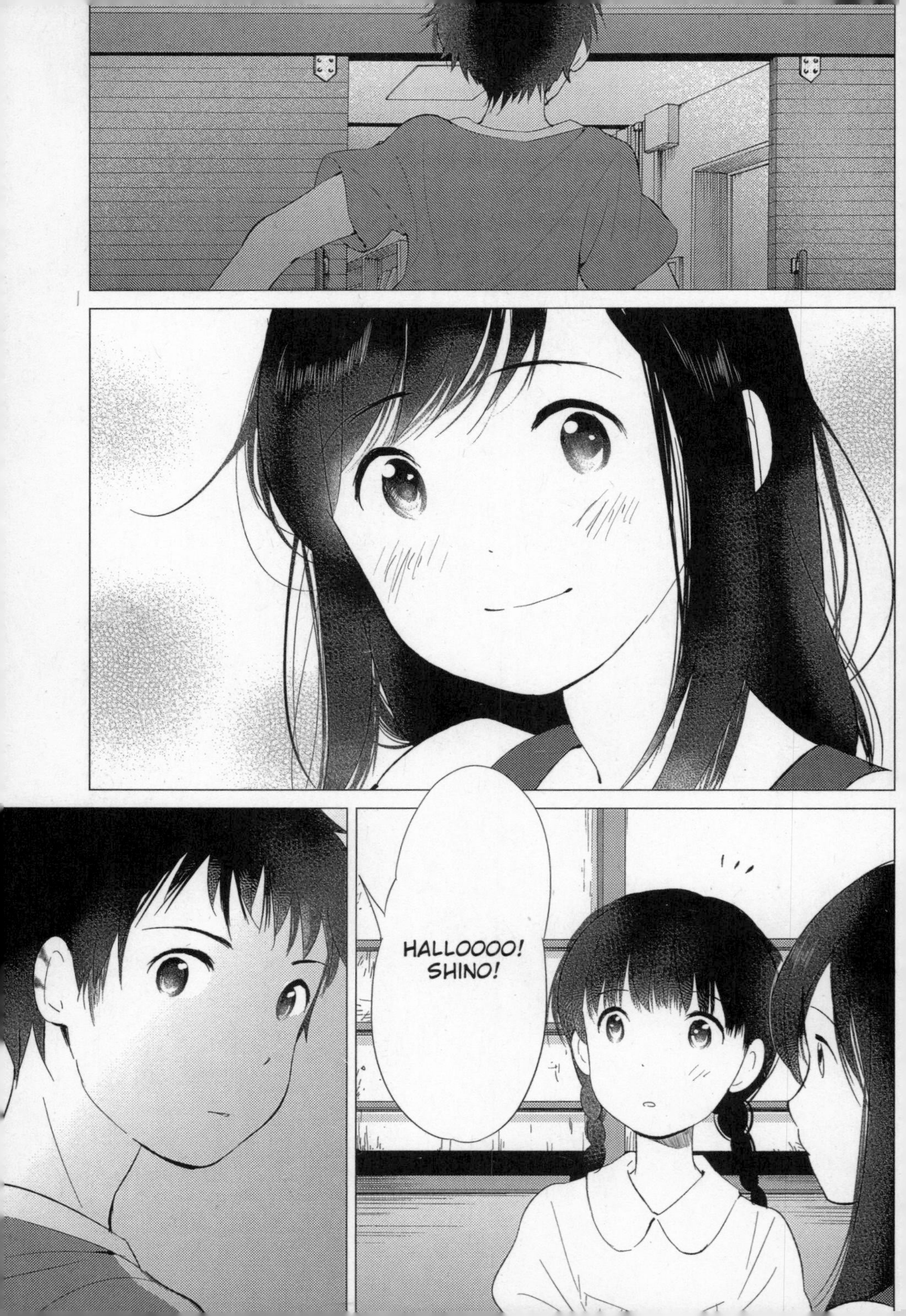
HALLOOOO!
SHINO!

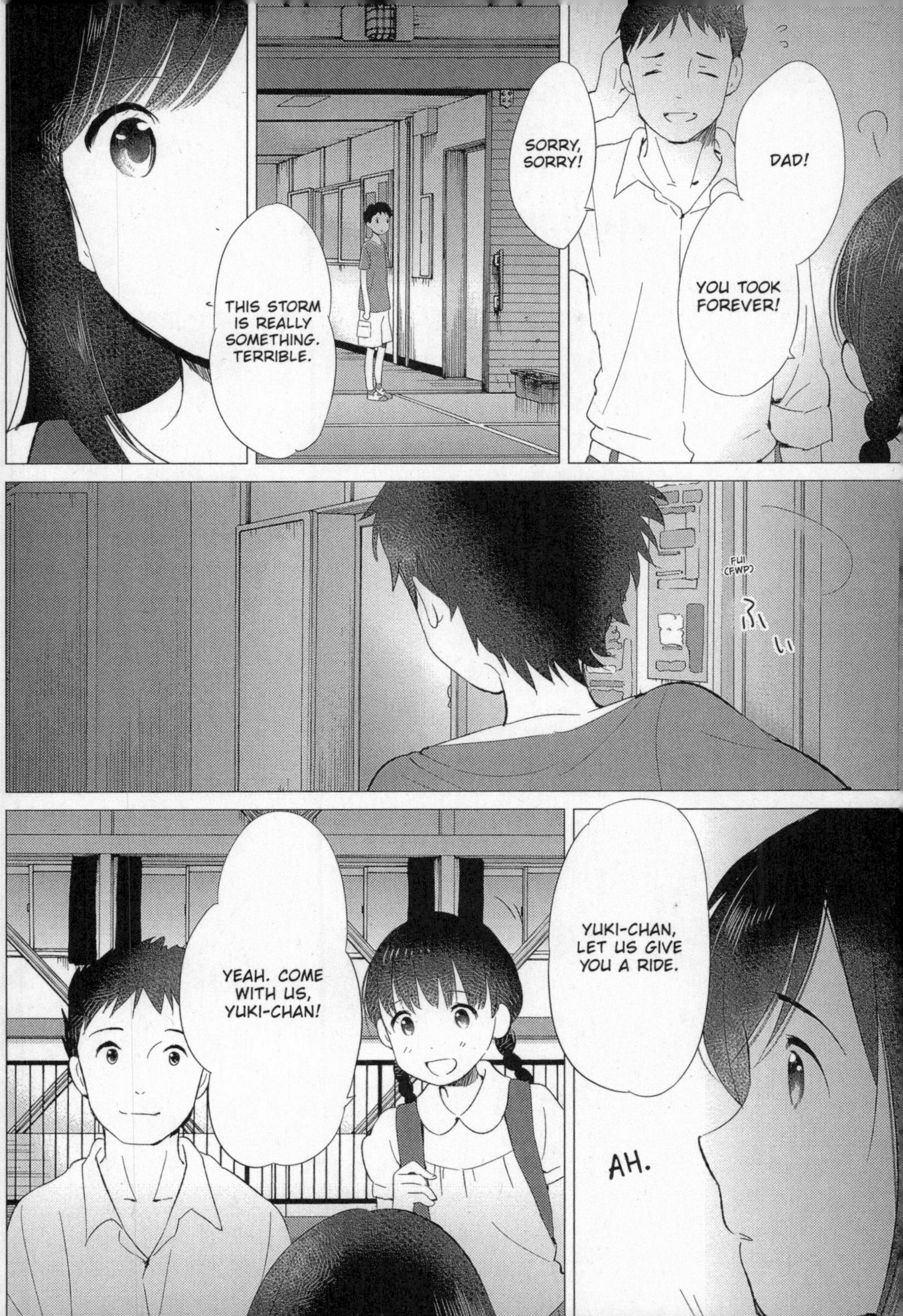
DAD!
YOU TOOK FOREVER!
SORRY, SORRY!
THIS STORM IS REALLY SOMETHING. TERRIBLE.
FUI (FWP)
ふい
YUKI-CHAN, LET US GIVE YOU A RIDE.
AH.
YEAH. COME WITH US, YUKI-CHAN!

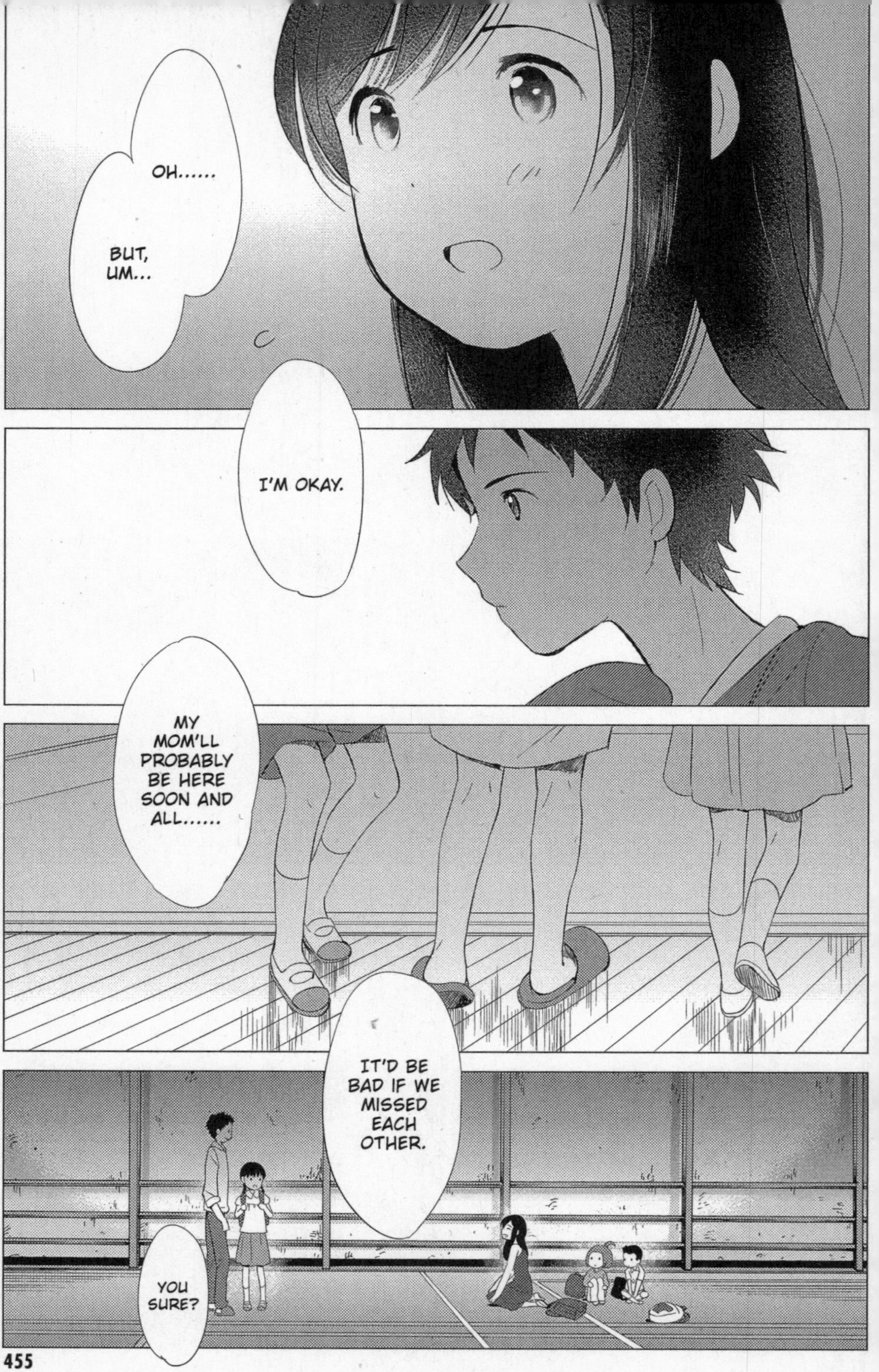
OH......
BUT, UM...
I'M OKAY.
MY MOM'LL PROBABLY BE HERE SOON AND ALL......
IT'D BE BAD IF WE MISSED EACH OTHER.
YOU SURE?

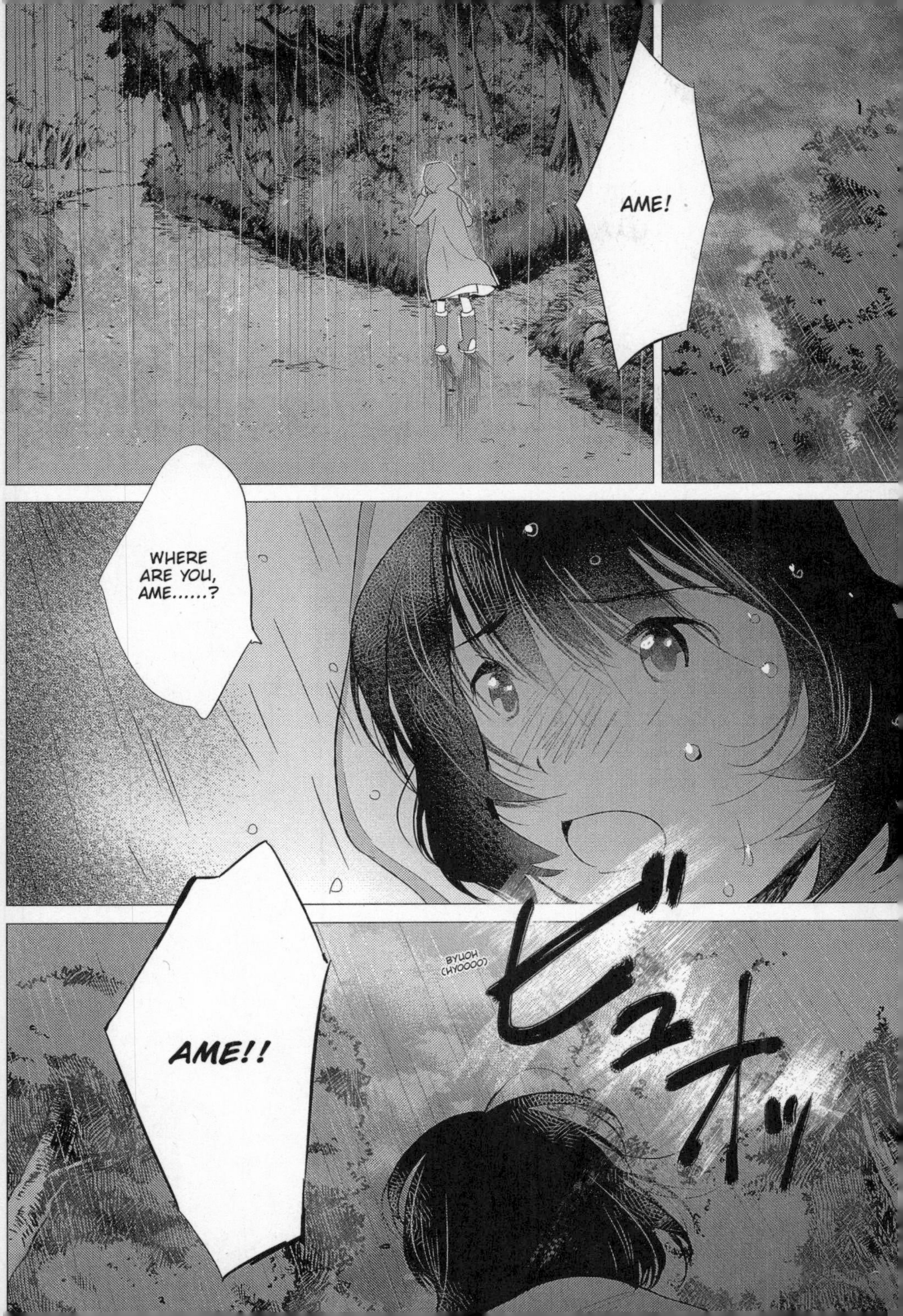
AME!
WHERE ARE YOU, AME......?
ビュオッ
BYUOH (HYOOOO)
AME!!

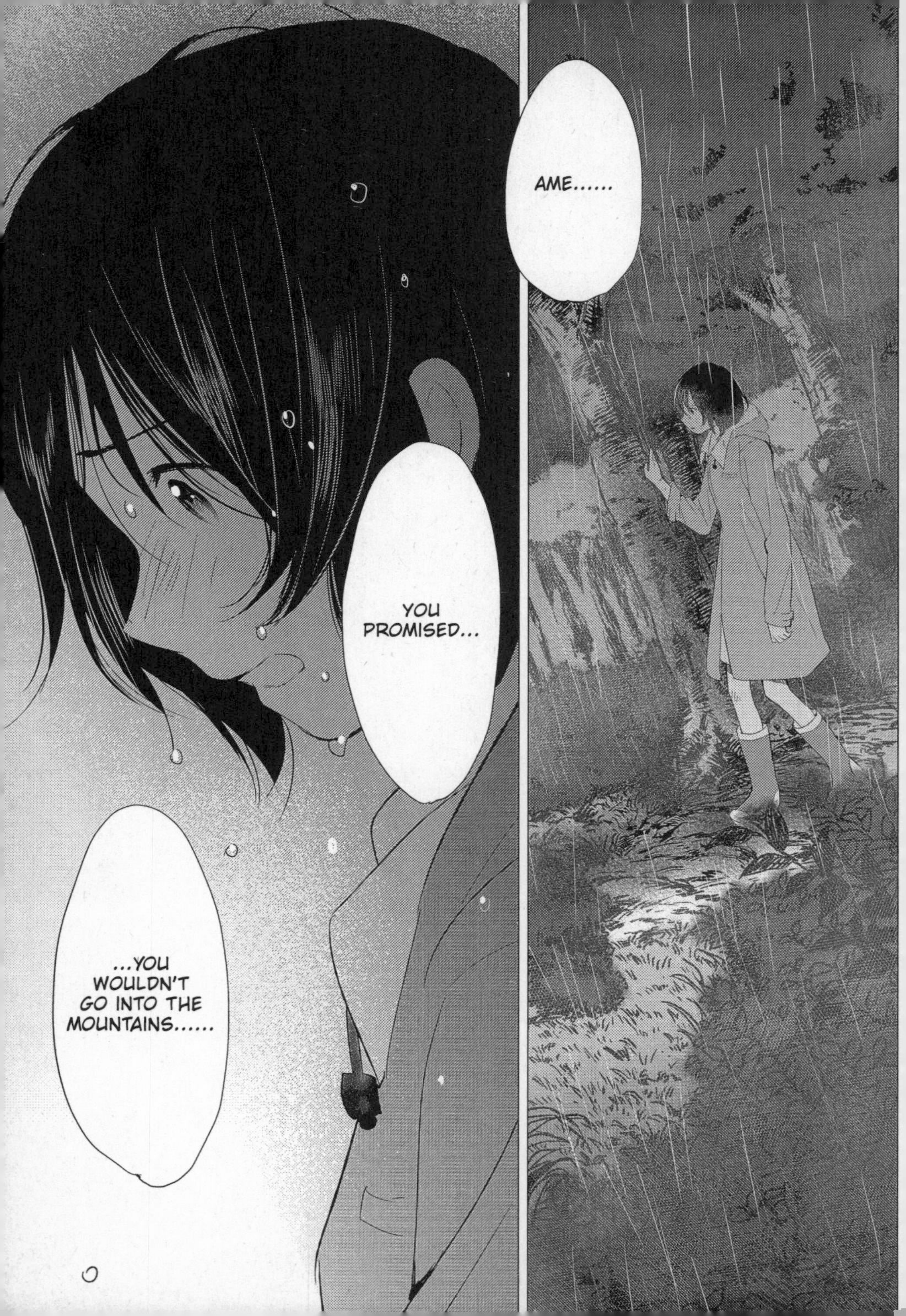
AME......
YOU PROMISED...
...YOU WOULDN'T GO INTO THE MOUNTAINS......

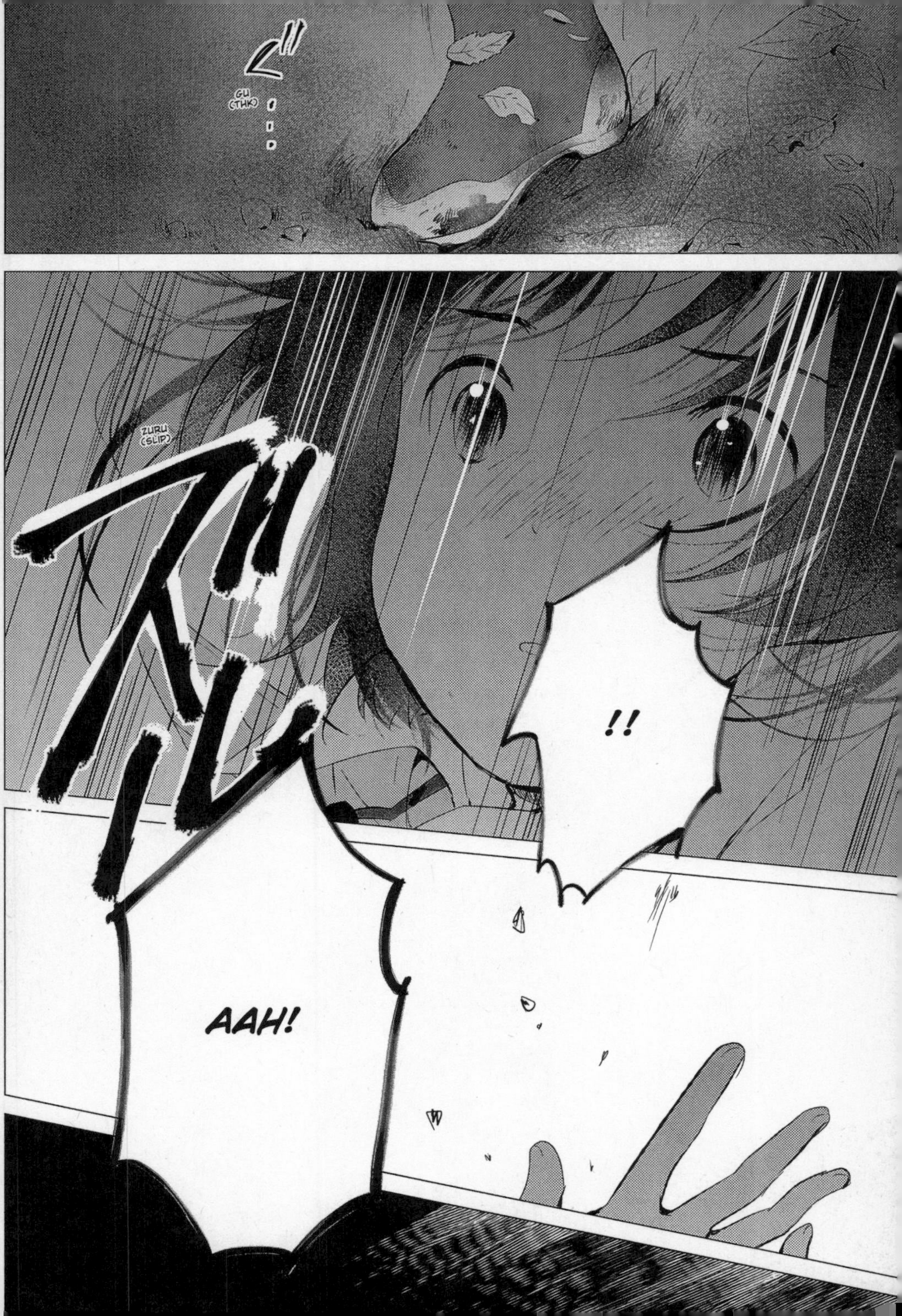
GU (THK)
ZURU (SLIP)
!!
AAH!

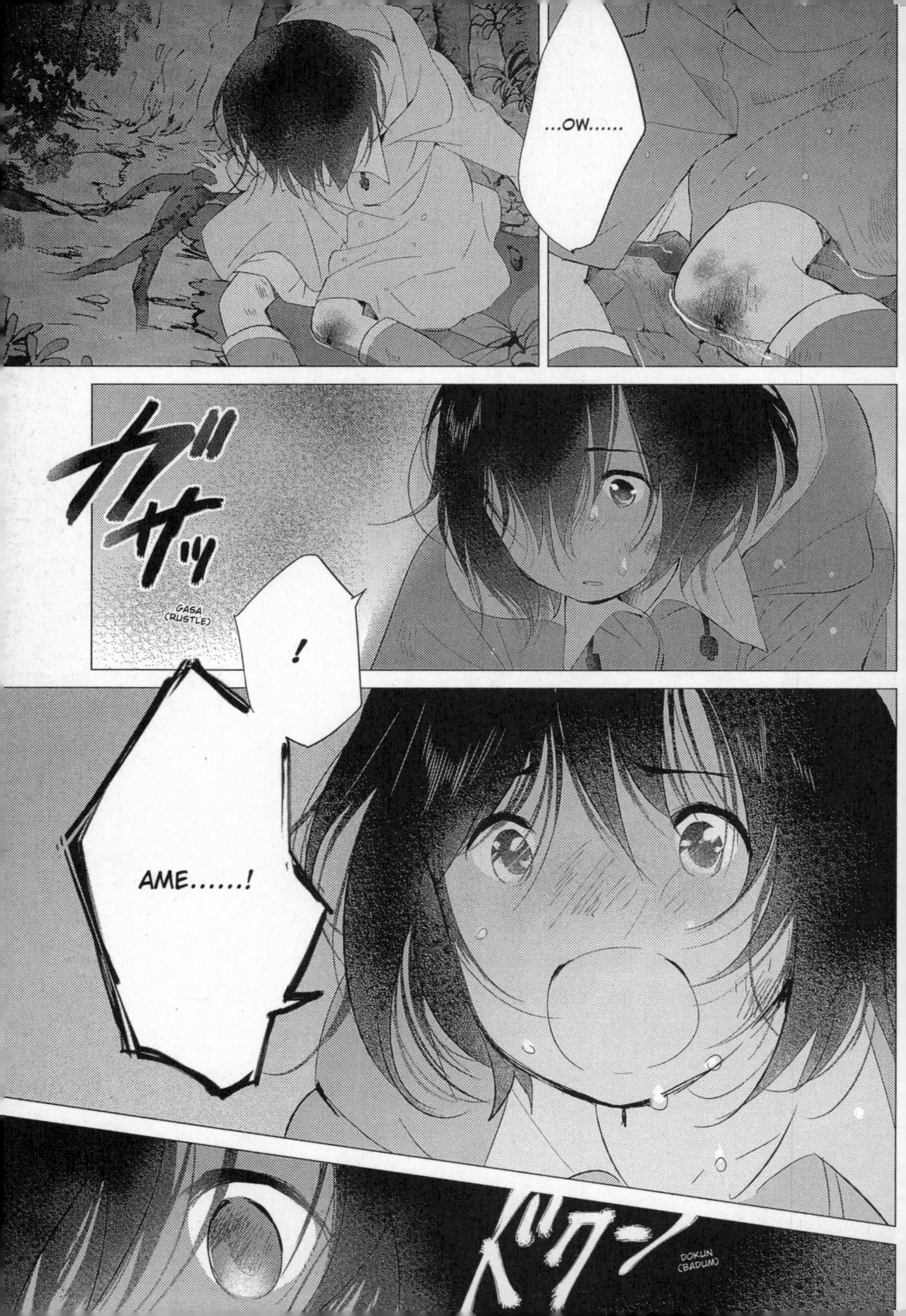
...OW......
GASA (RUSTLE)
!
AME......!
DOKUN (BADUM)

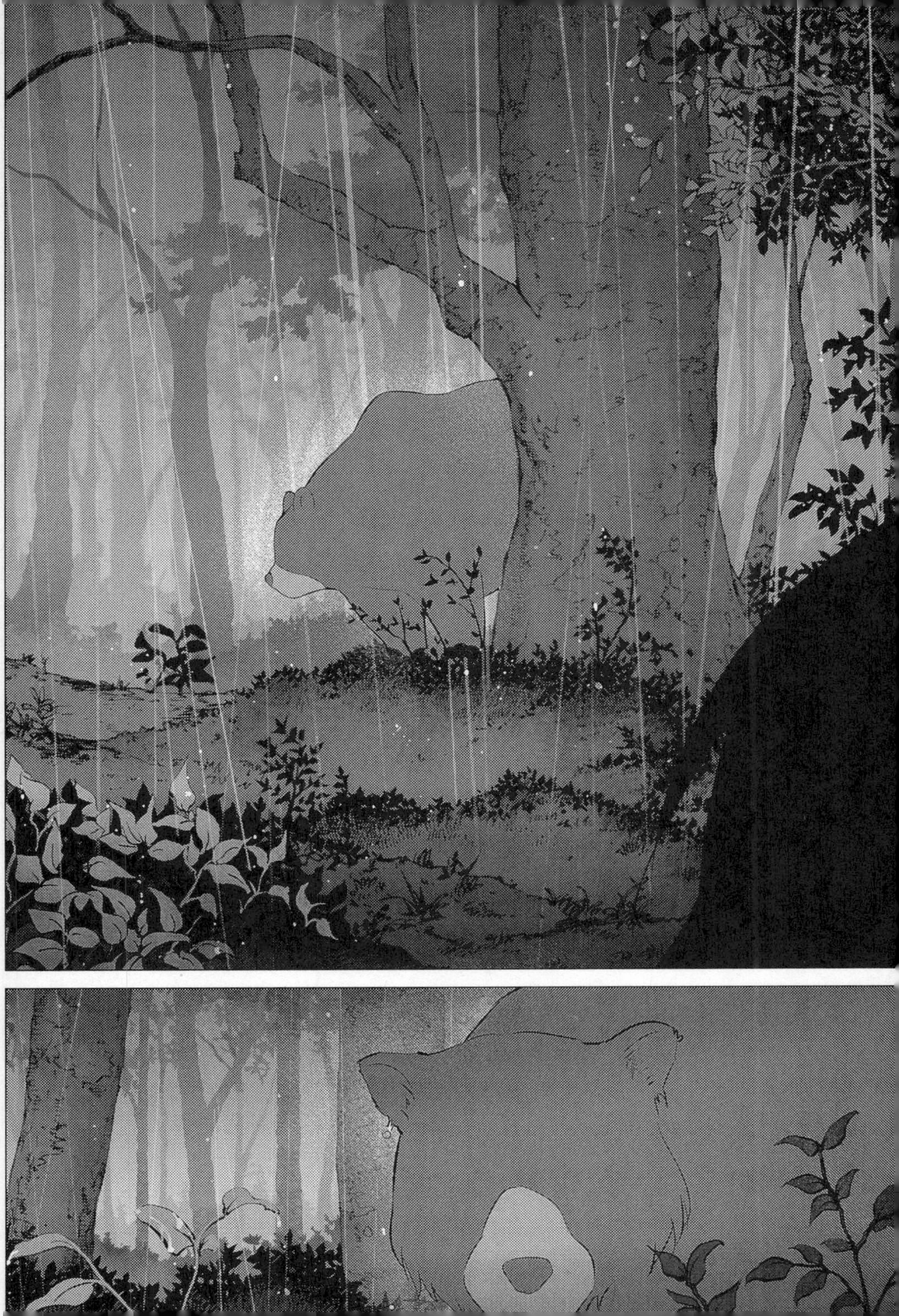

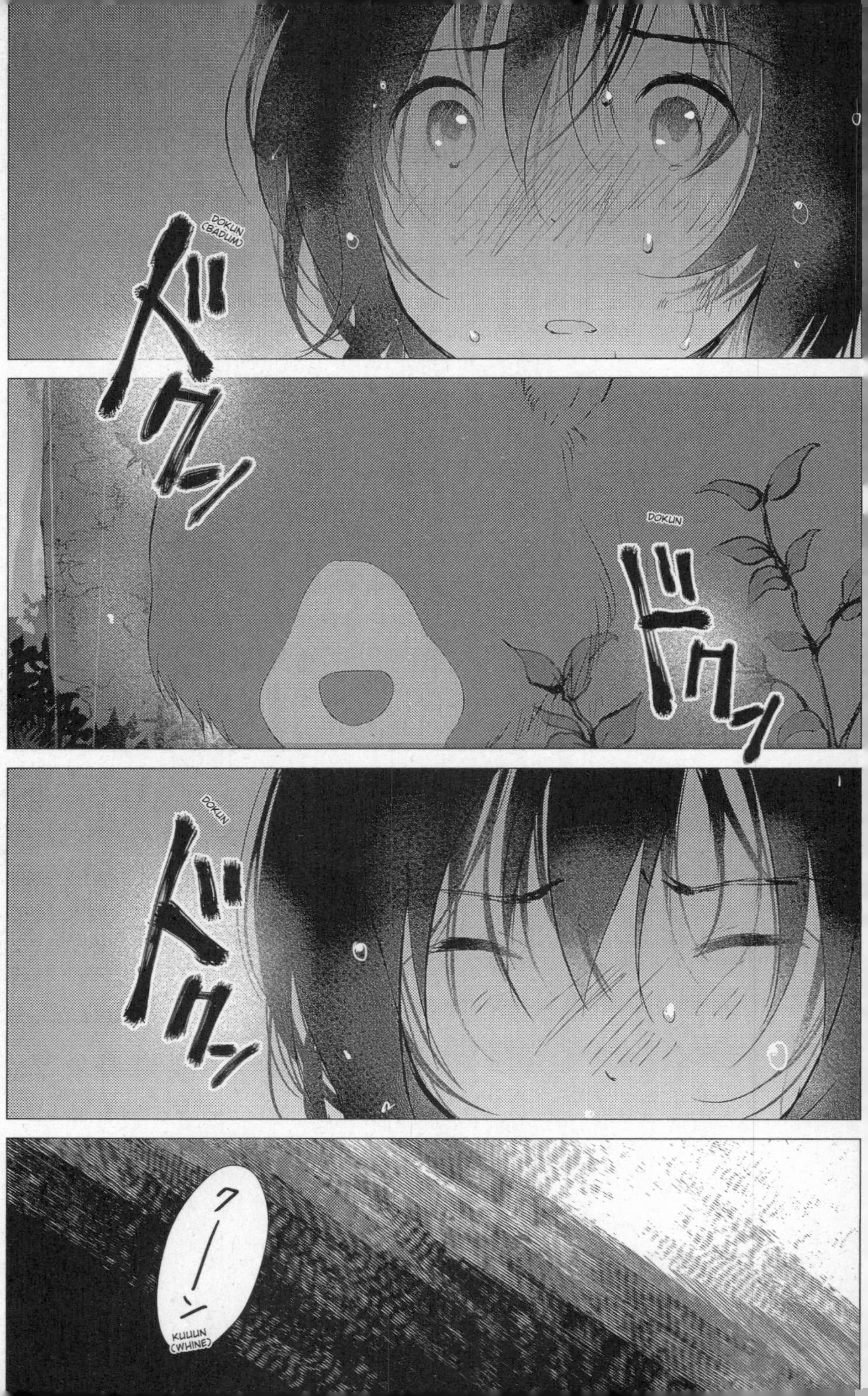

ドクン
DOKUN (BADUM)
ドクン
DOKUN
ドクン
DOKUN
クーン
KUUUN (WHINE)

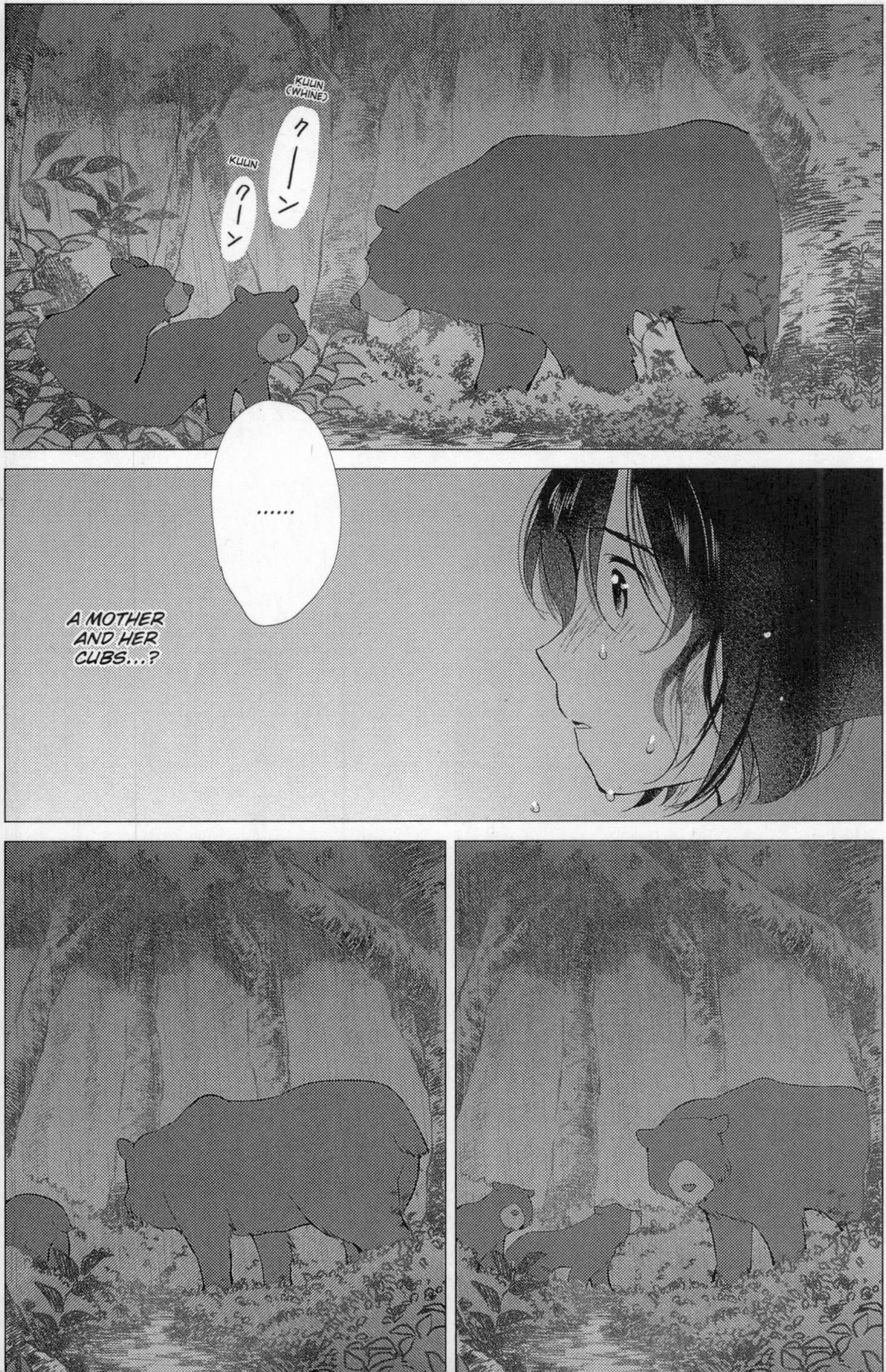
KUUN (WHINE)
クーン
KUUN
クーン
......
A MOTHER AND HER CUBS...?

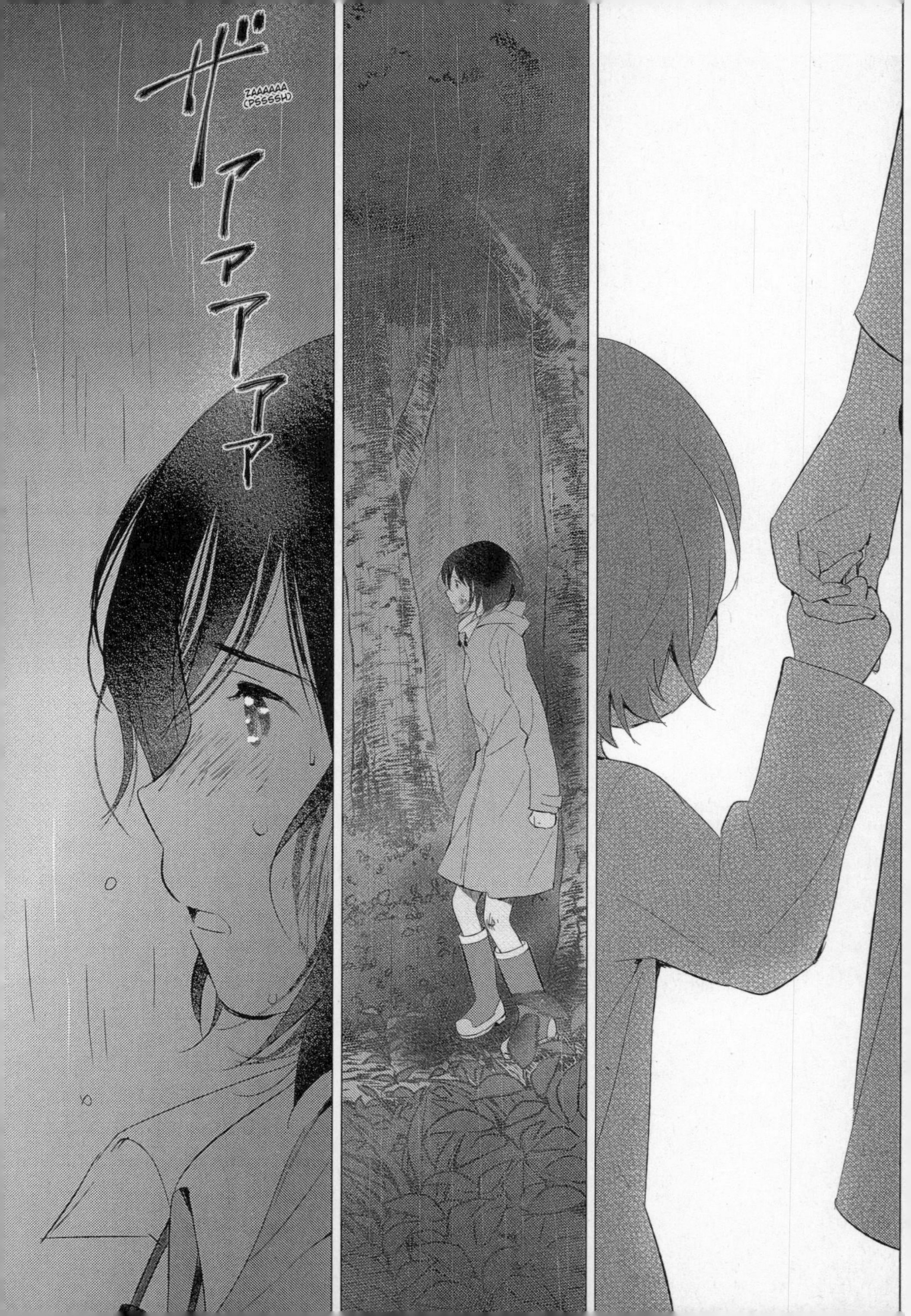
ザアアアアア
ZAAAAAA
(PSSSSH)

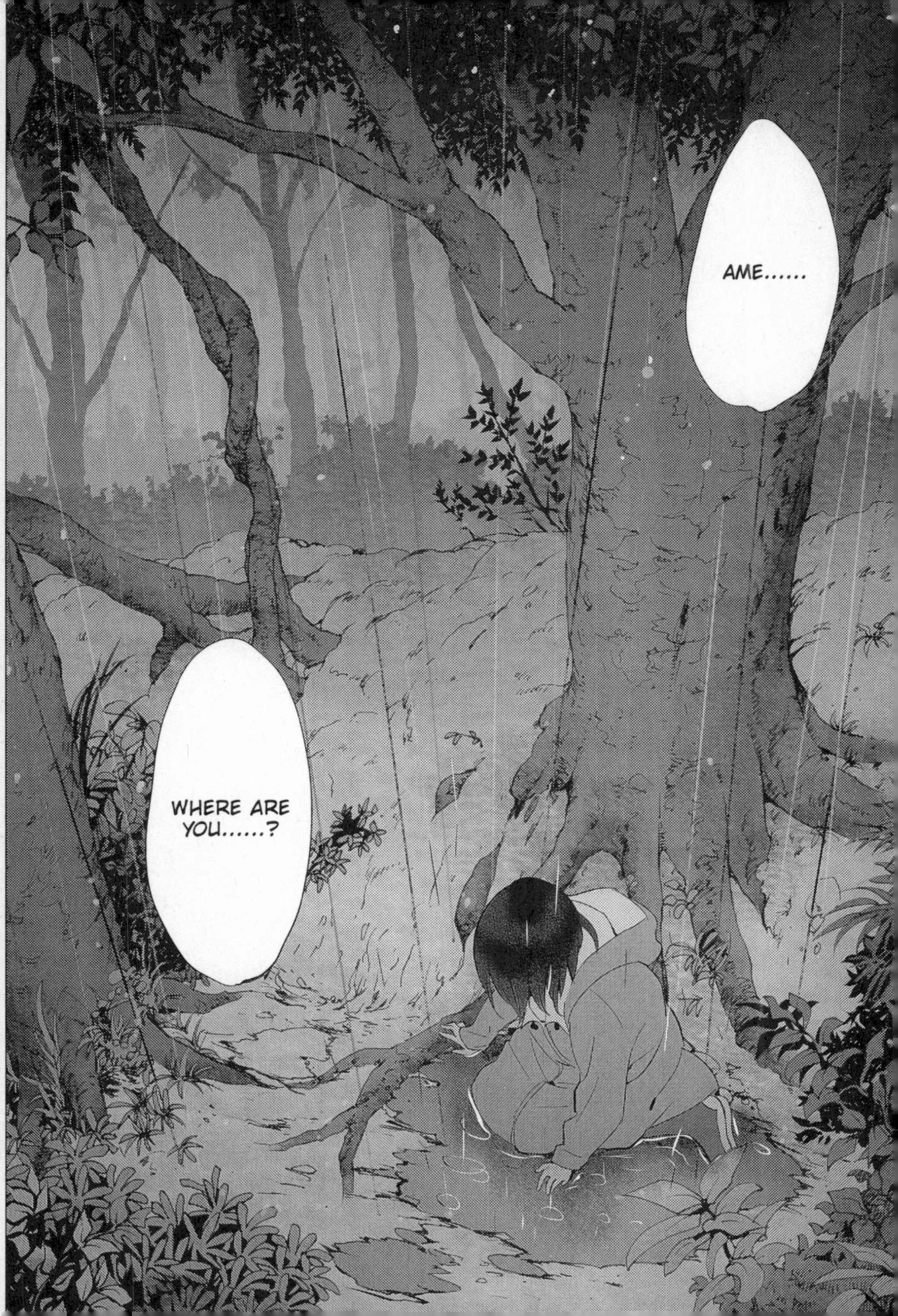
AME......
WHERE ARE YOU......?

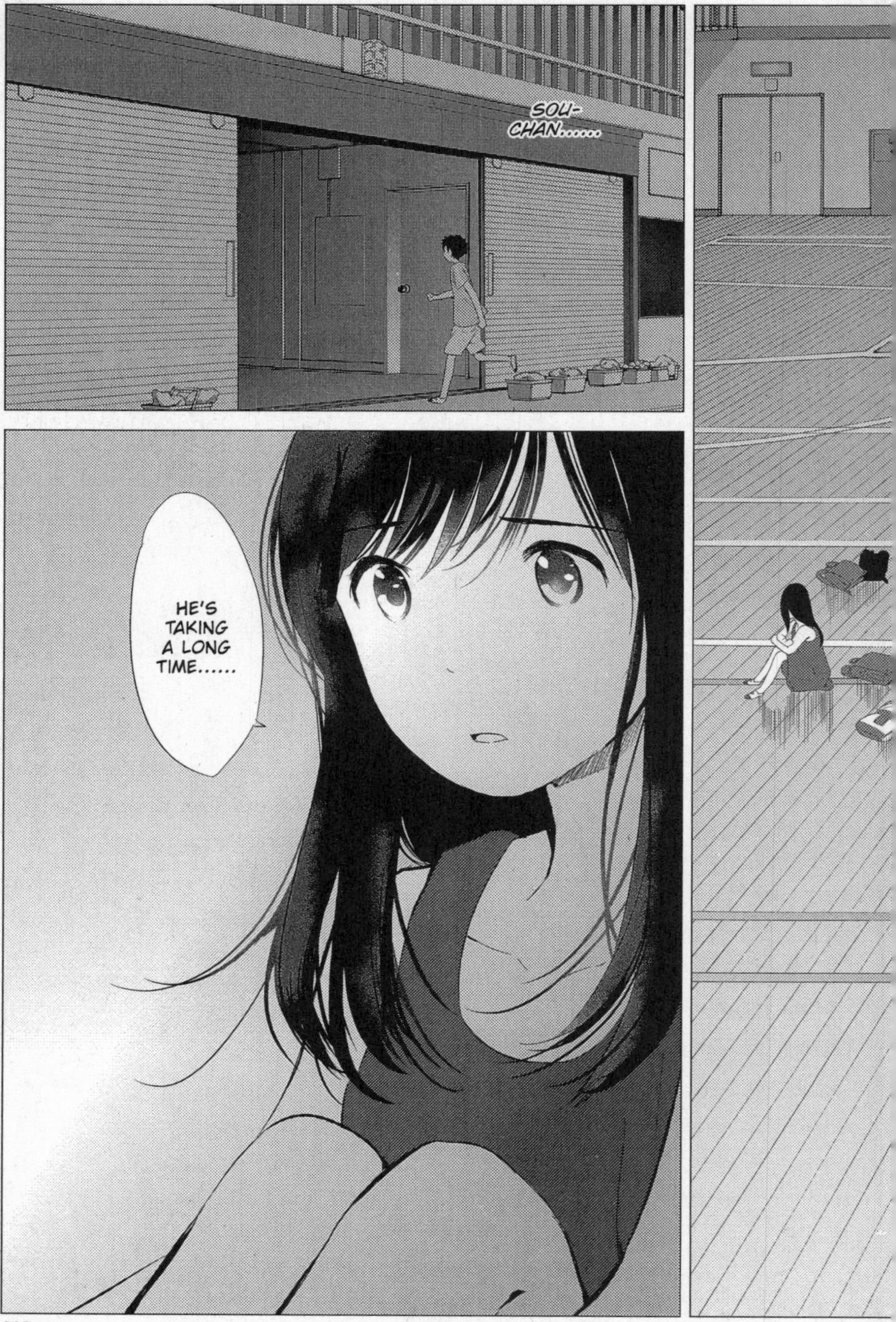
SOU-CHAN......
HE'S TAKING A LONG TIME......

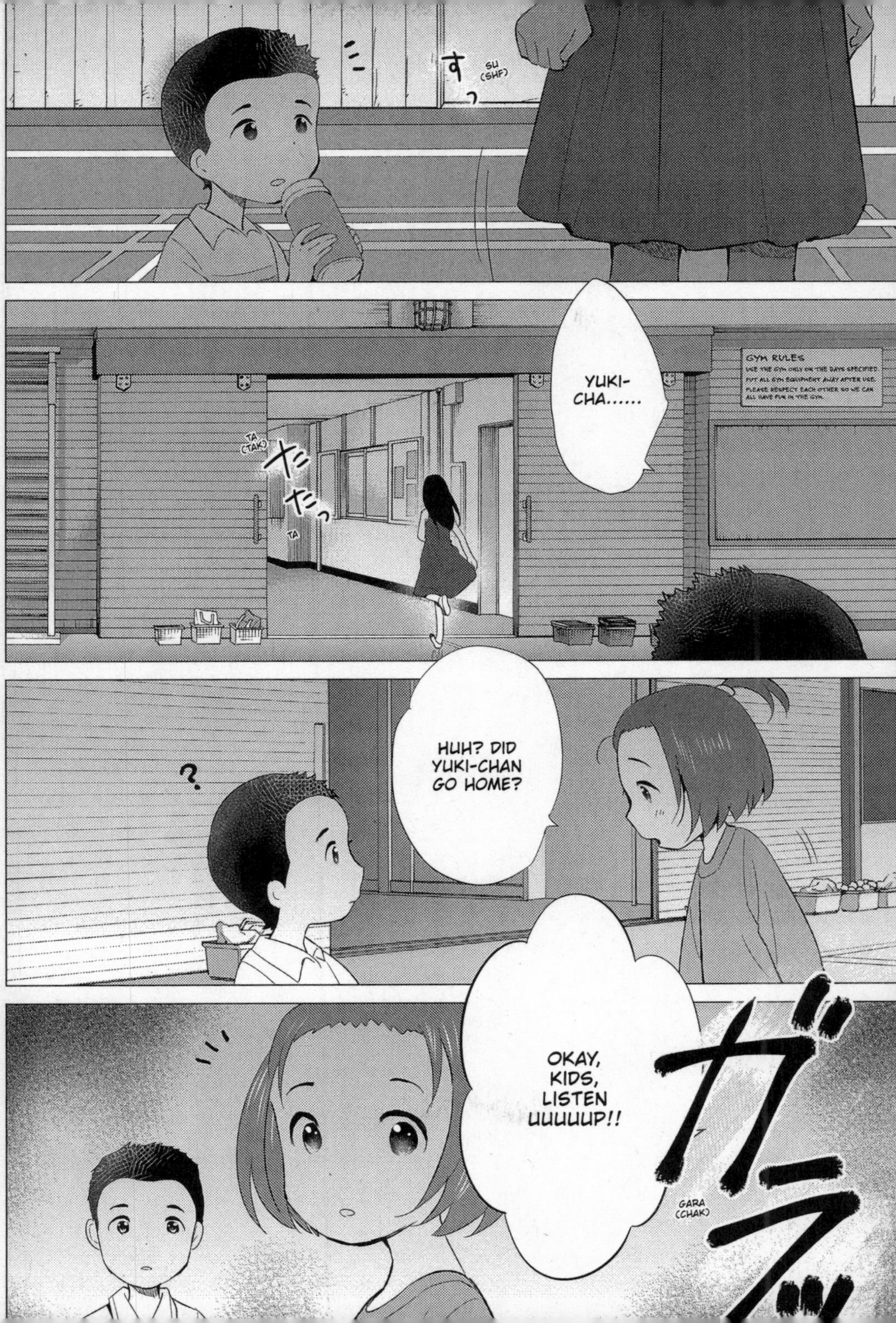
す
SU (SHF)
YUKI-CHA......
GYM RULES
USE THE GYM ONLY ON THE DAYS SPECIFIED.
PUT ALL GYM EQUIPMENT AWAY AFTER USE.
PLEASE RESPECT EACH OTHER SO WE CAN ALL HAVE FUN IN THE GYM.
たったっ
TA (TAK) TA
HUH? DID YUKI-CHAN GO HOME?
?
ガラッ
GARA (CHAK)
OKAY, KIDS, LISTEN UUUUUP!!

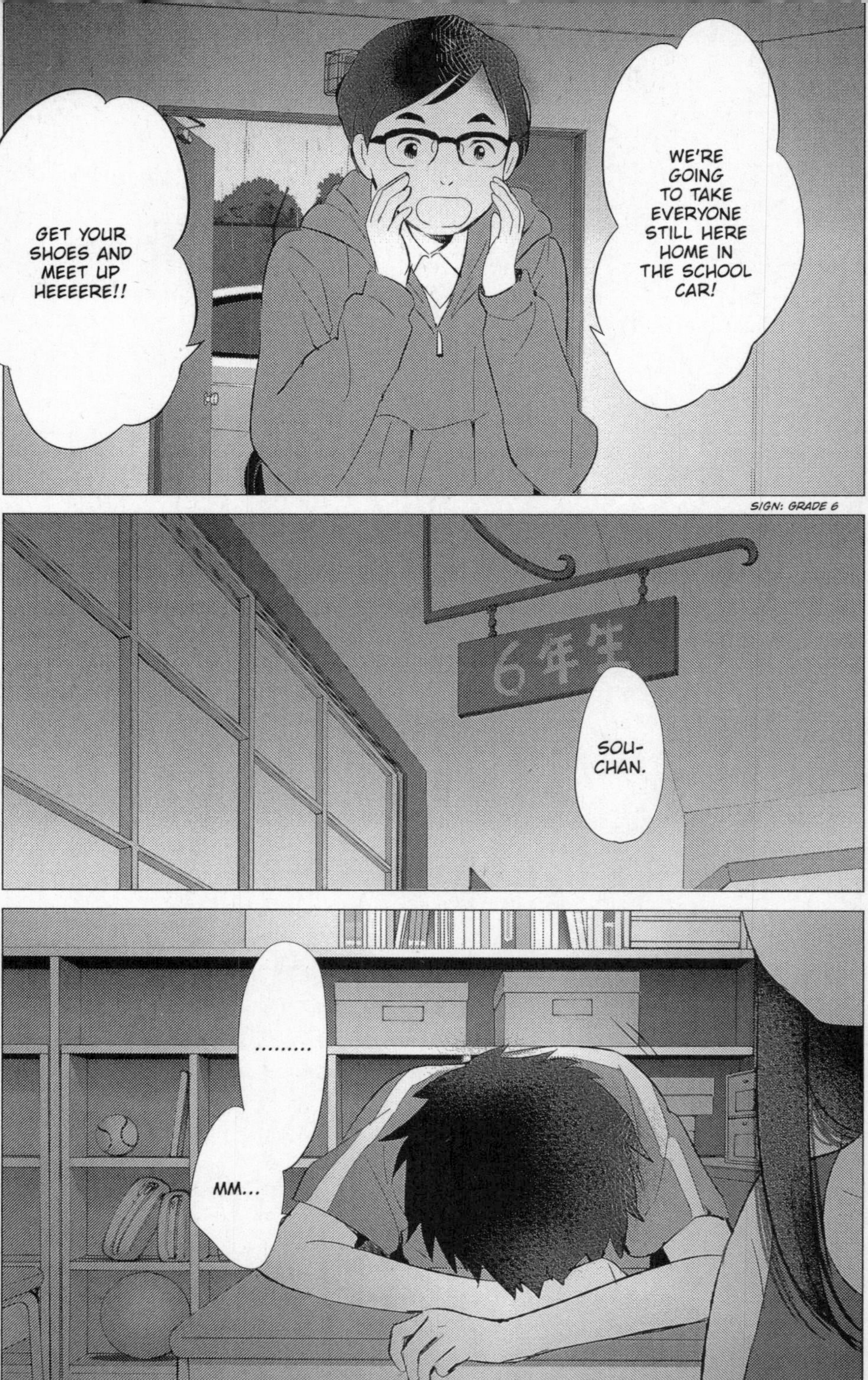

WE'RE GOING TO TAKE EVERYONE STILL HERE HOME IN THE SCHOOL CAR!
GET YOUR SHOES AND MEET UP HEEEERE!!
SIGN: GRADE 6
6年生
SOU-CHAN.
....
MM...

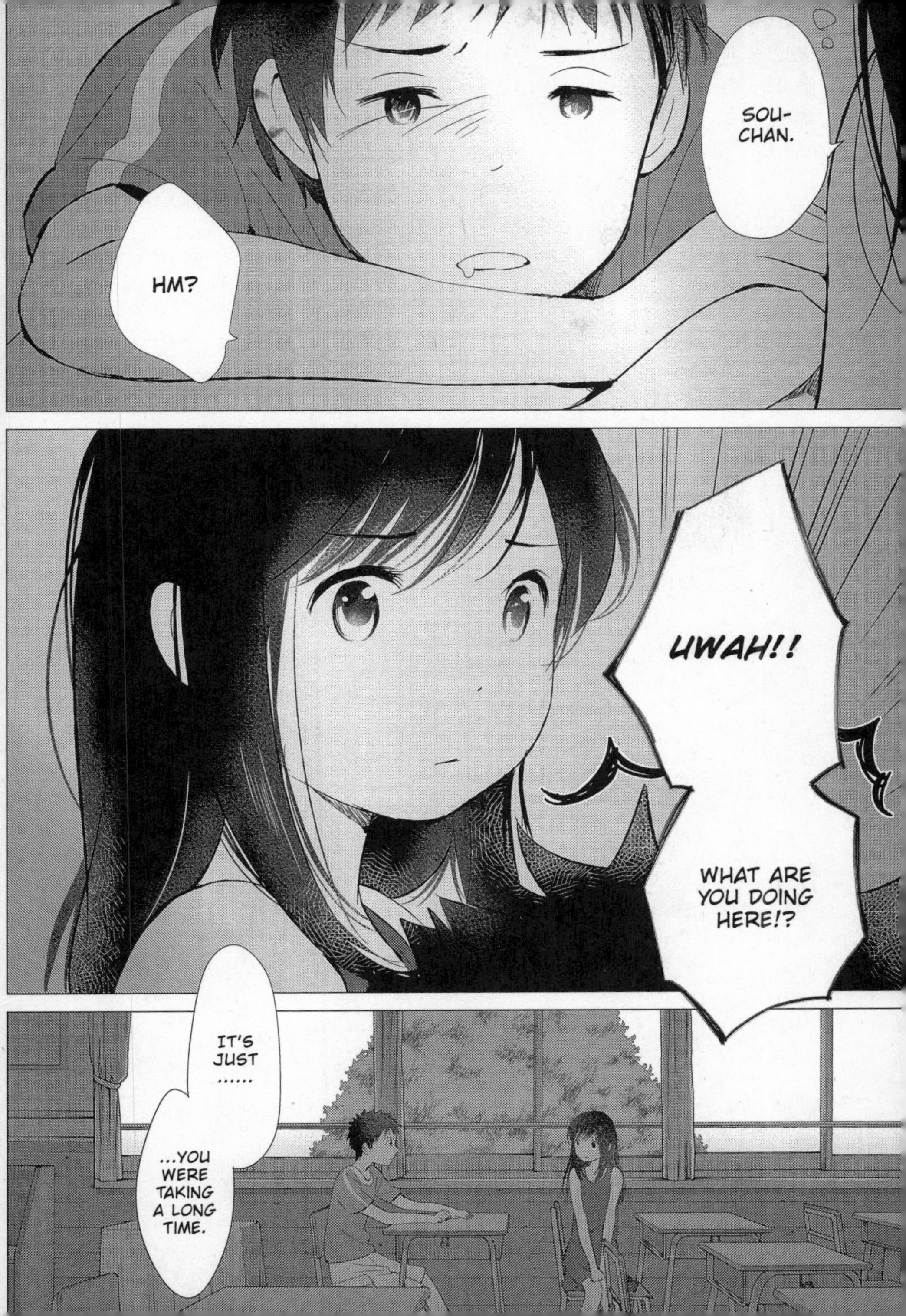
SOU-CHAN.
HM?
UWAH!!
WHAT ARE YOU DOING HERE!?
IT'S JUST ......
...YOU WERE TAKING A LONG TIME.

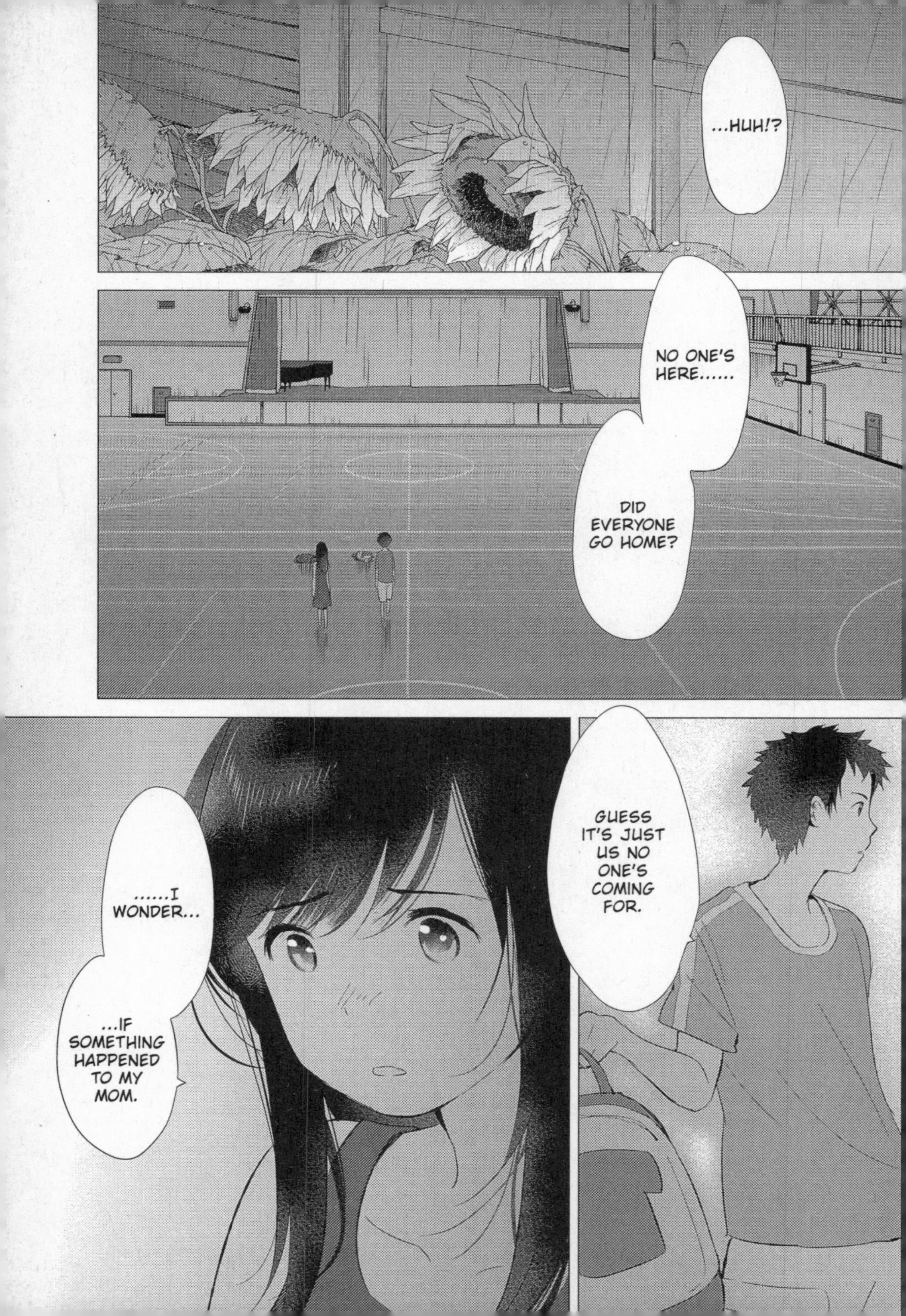
...HUH!?
NO ONE'S HERE......
DID EVERYONE GO HOME?
GUESS IT'S JUST US NO ONE'S COMING FOR.
......I WONDER...
...IF SOMETHING HAPPENED TO MY MOM.

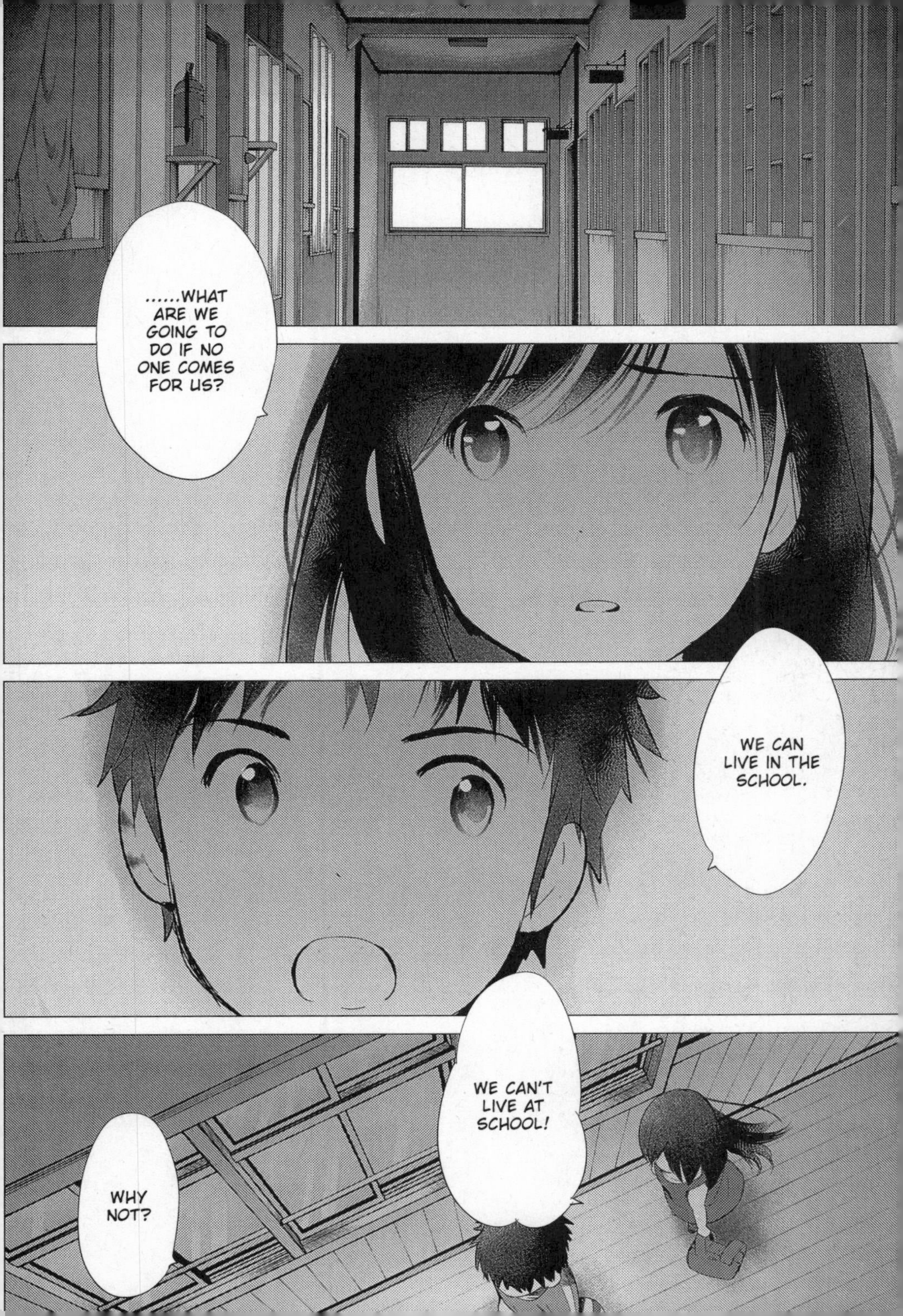
......WHAT ARE WE GOING TO DO IF NO ONE COMES FOR US?
WE CAN LIVE IN THE SCHOOL.
WE CAN'T LIVE AT SCHOOL!
WHY NOT?

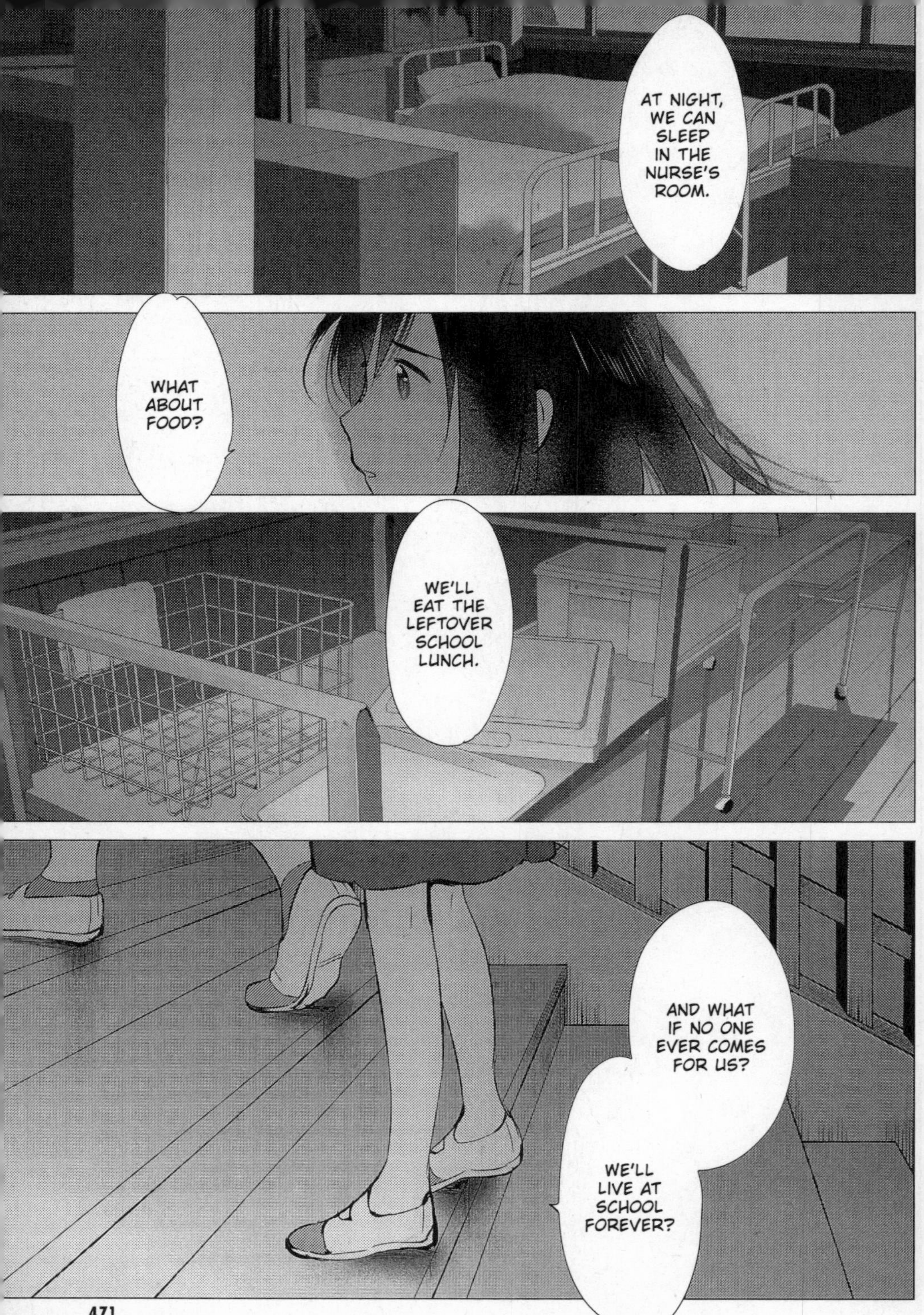
AT NIGHT, WE CAN SLEEP IN THE NURSE'S ROOM.
WHAT ABOUT FOOD?
WE'LL EAT THE LEFTOVER SCHOOL LUNCH.
AND WHAT IF NO ONE EVER COMES FOR US?
WE'LL LIVE AT SCHOOL FOREVER?

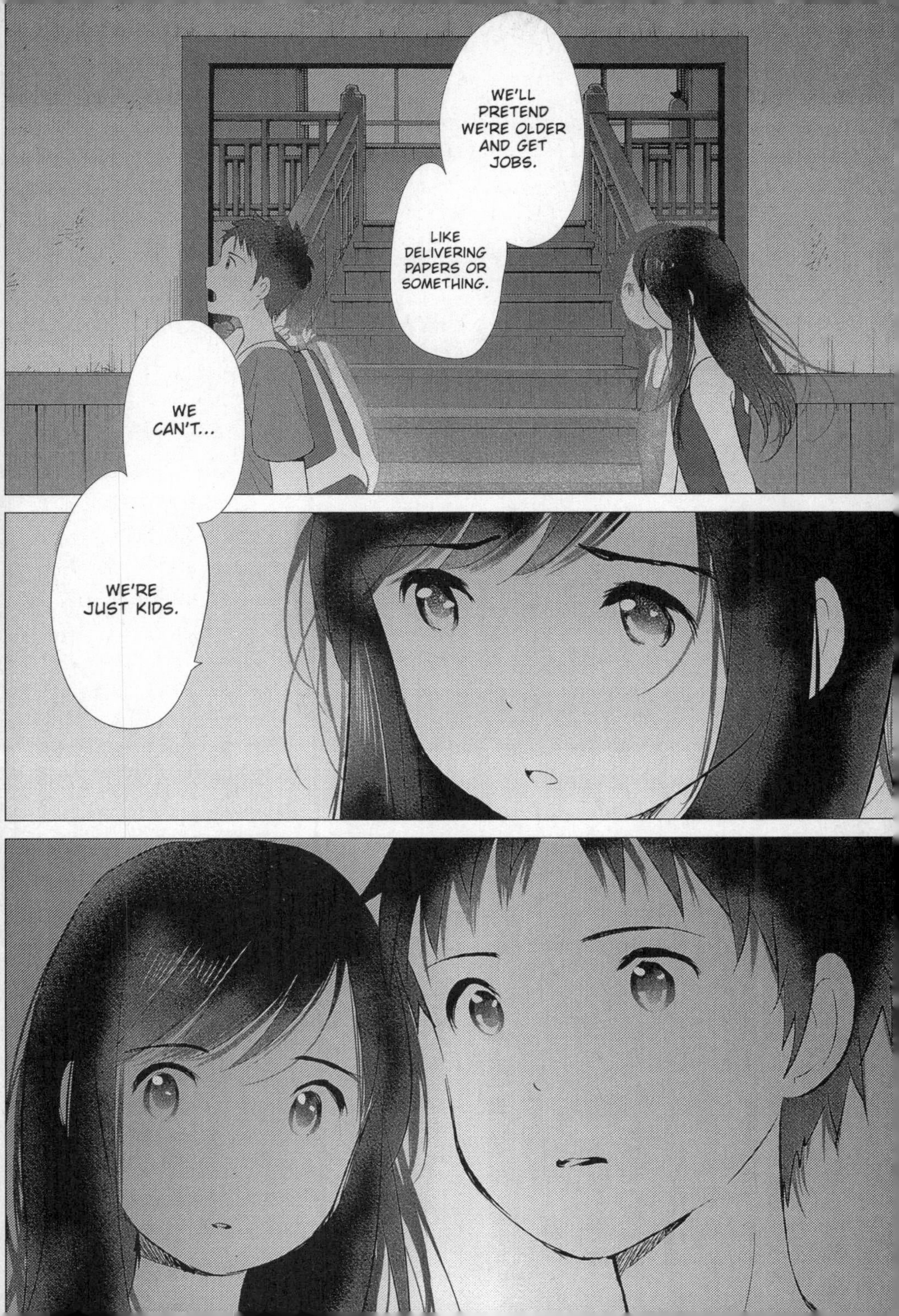
WE'LL PRETEND WE'RE OLDER AND GET JOBS.
LIKE DELIVERING PAPERS OR SOMETHING.
WE CAN'T...
WE'RE JUST KIDS.

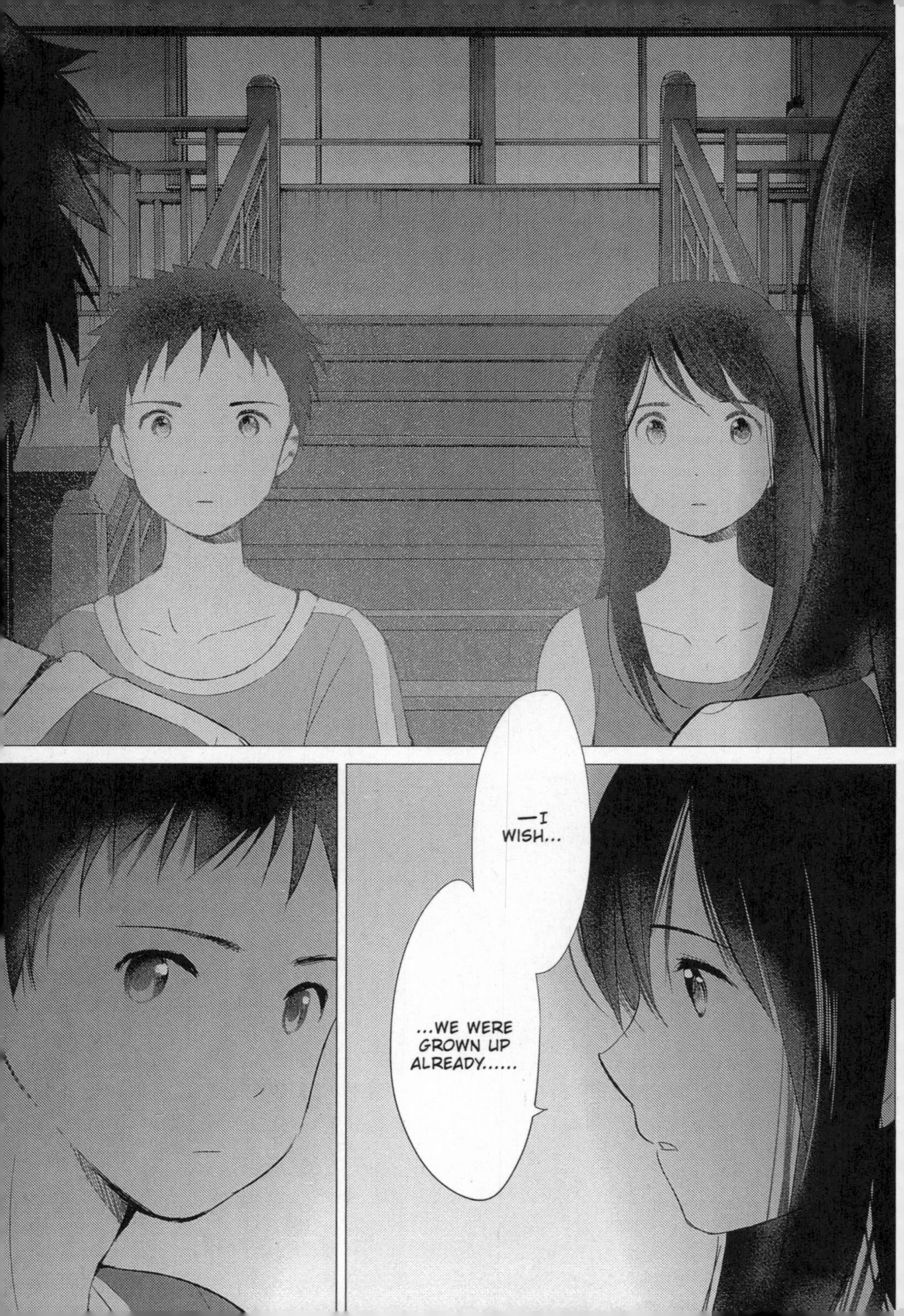
—I WISH...
...WE WERE GROWN UP ALREADY......

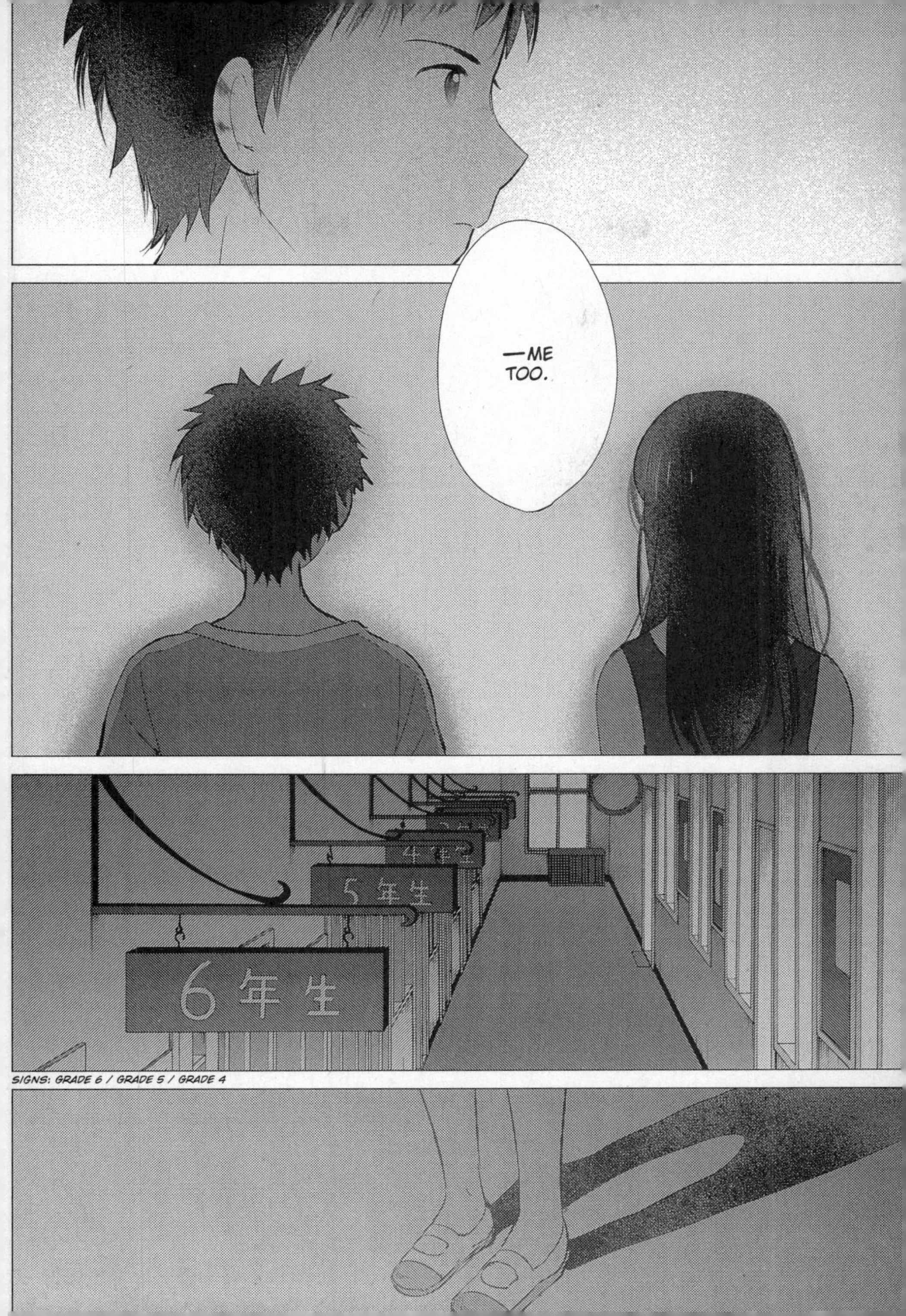
—ME TOO.
6年生
5年生
SIGNS: GRADE 6 / GRADE 5 / GRADE 4

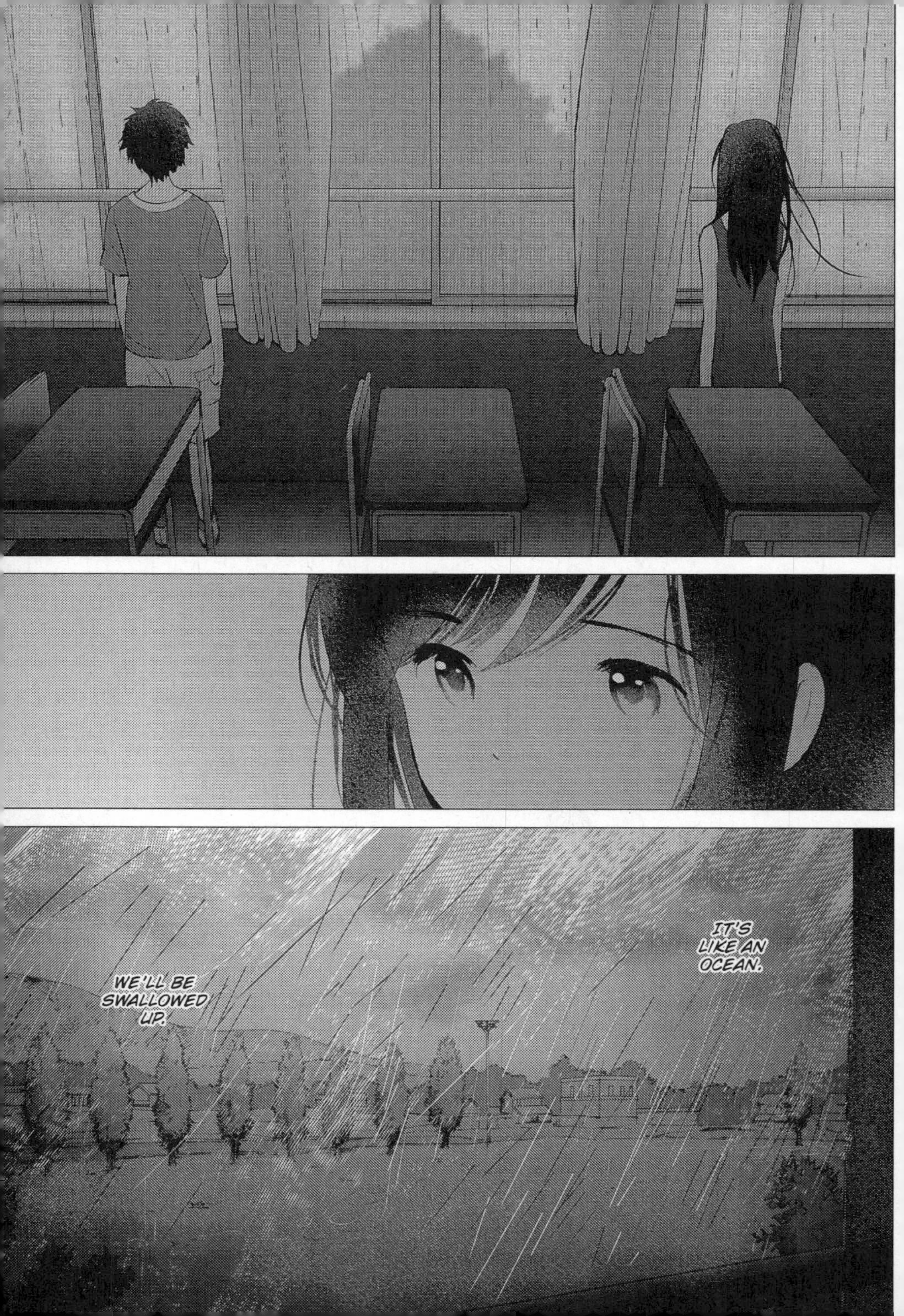
IT'S LIKE AN OCEAN.
WE'LL BE SWALLOWED UP.

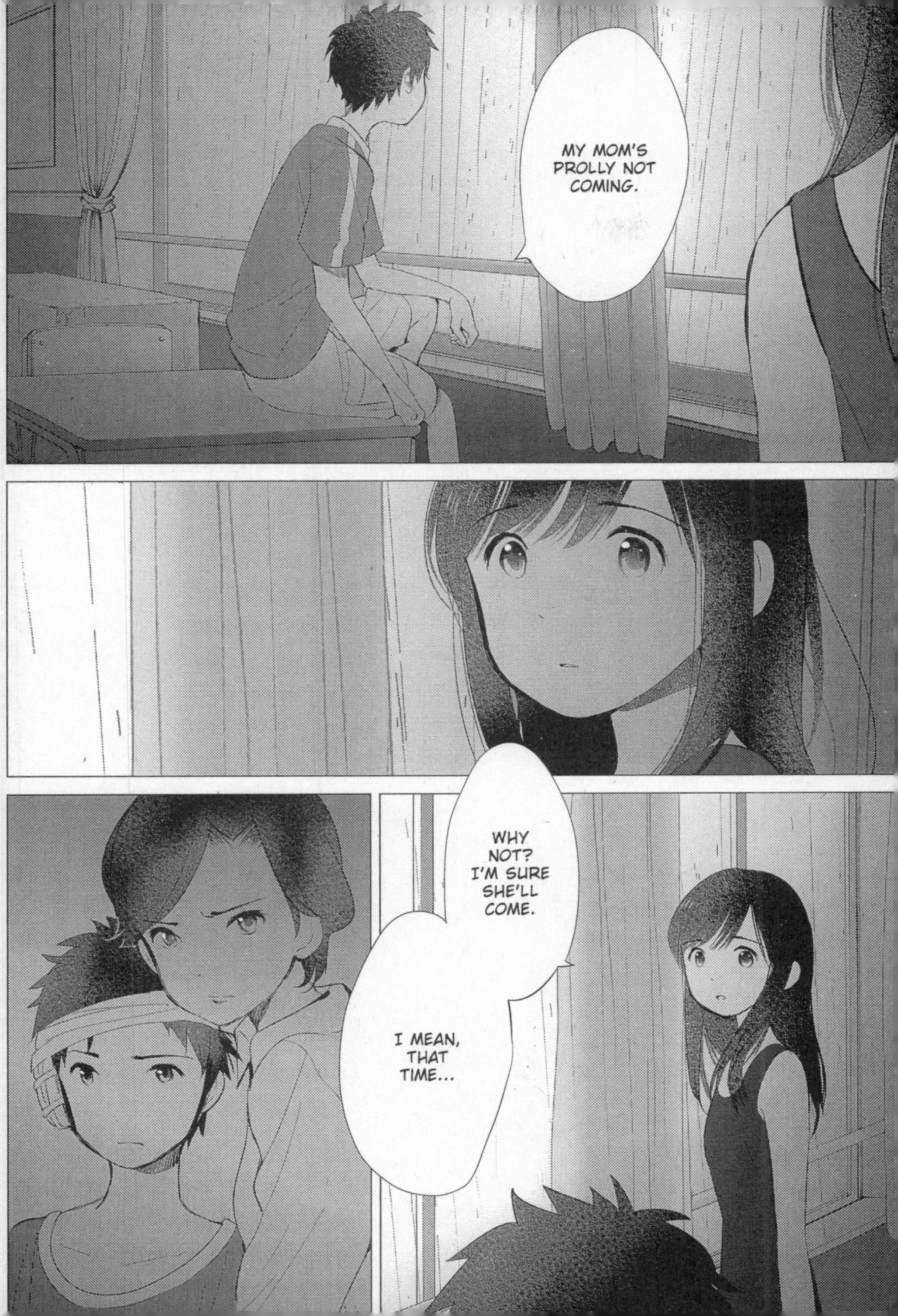
MY MOM'S PROLLY NOT COMING.
WHY NOT? I'M SURE SHE'LL COME.
I MEAN, THAT TIME...

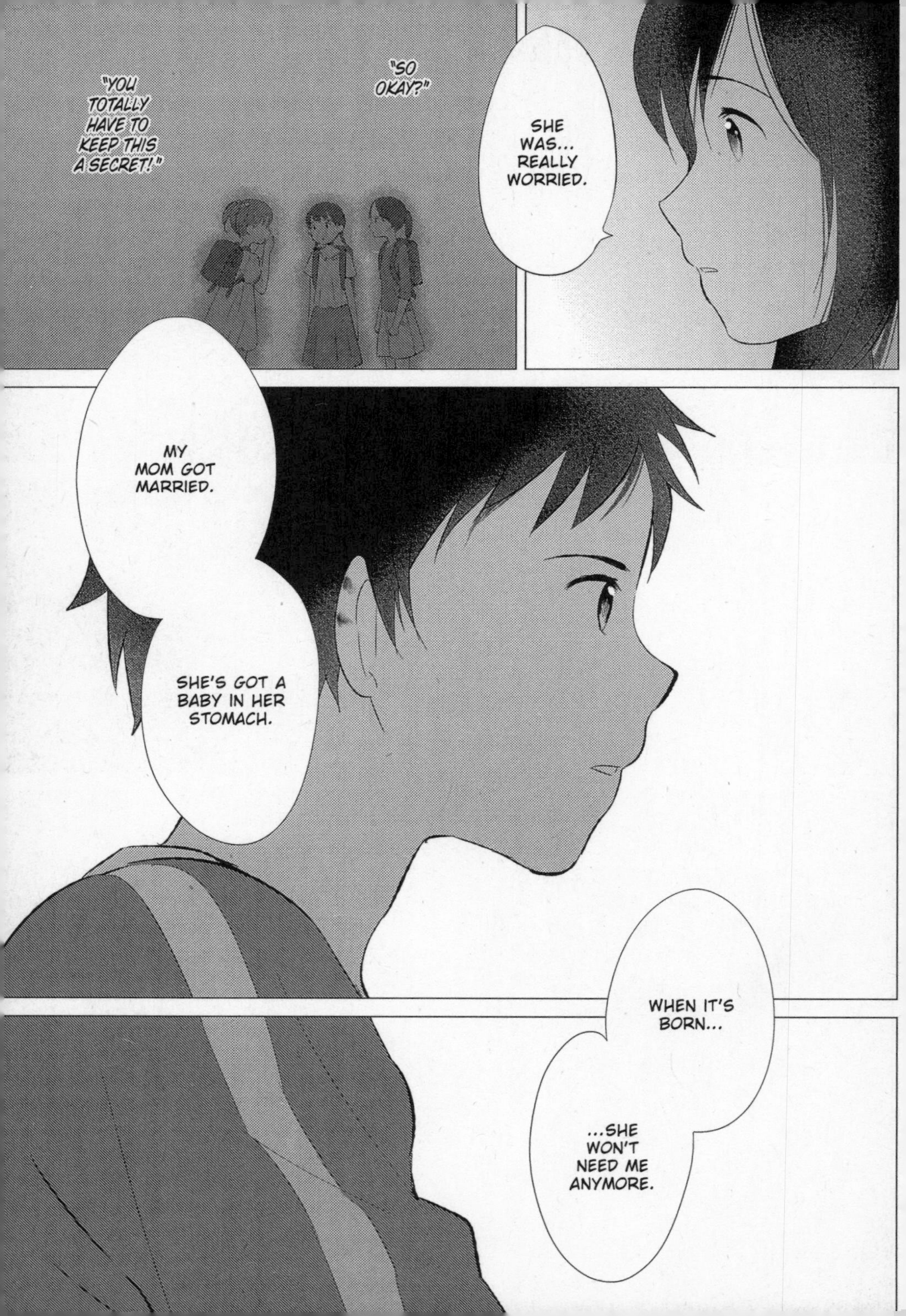
SHE WAS... REALLY WORRIED.
"SO OKAY?"
"YOU TOTALLY HAVE TO KEEP THIS A SECRET!"
MY MOM GOT MARRIED.
SHE'S GOT A BABY IN HER STOMACH.
WHEN IT'S BORN...
...SHE WON'T NEED ME ANYMORE.

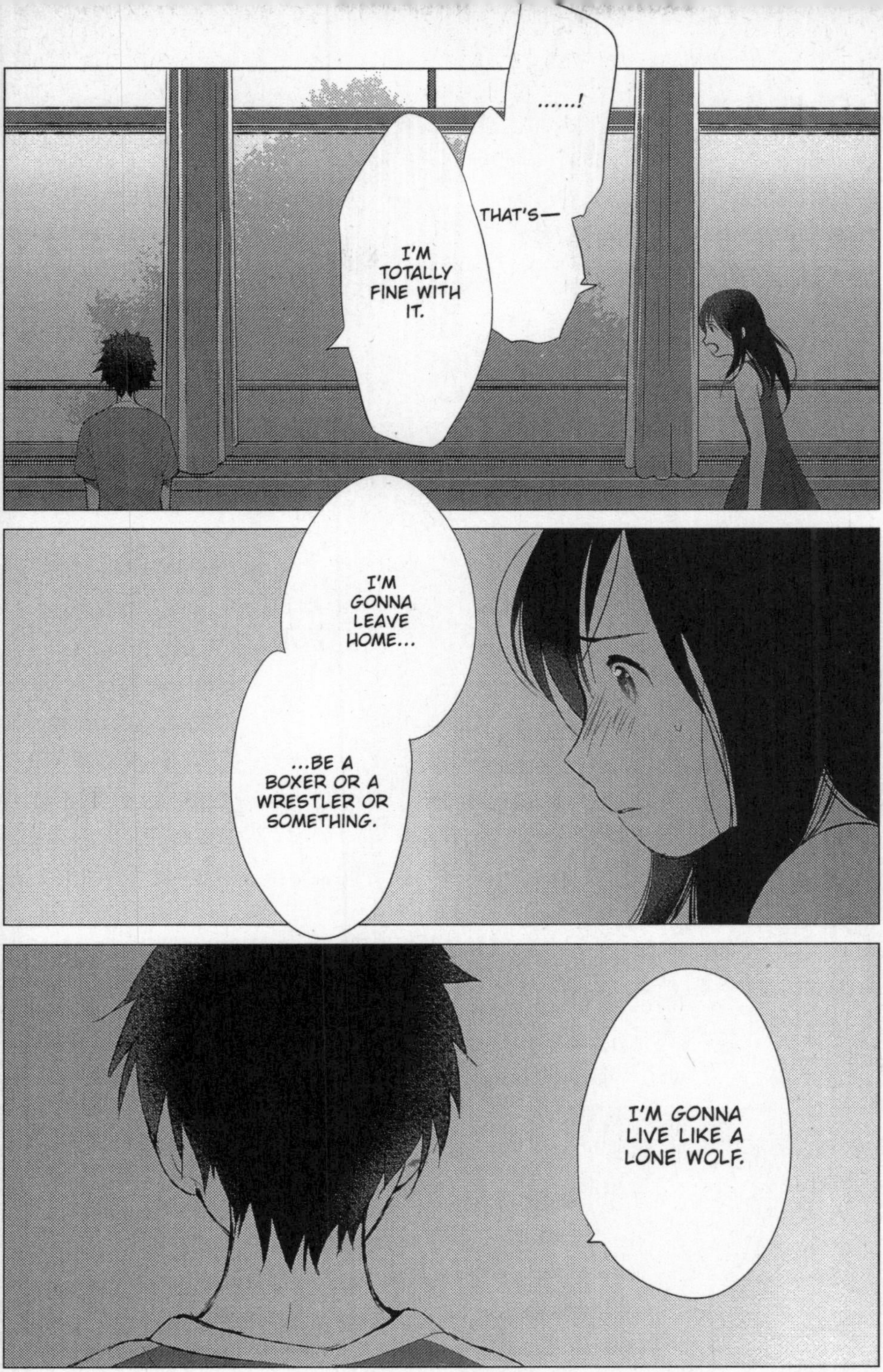
......!
THAT'S—
I'M TOTALLY FINE WITH IT.
I'M GONNA LEAVE HOME...
...BE A BOXER OR A WRESTLER OR SOMETHING.
I'M GONNA LIVE LIKE A LONE WOLF.

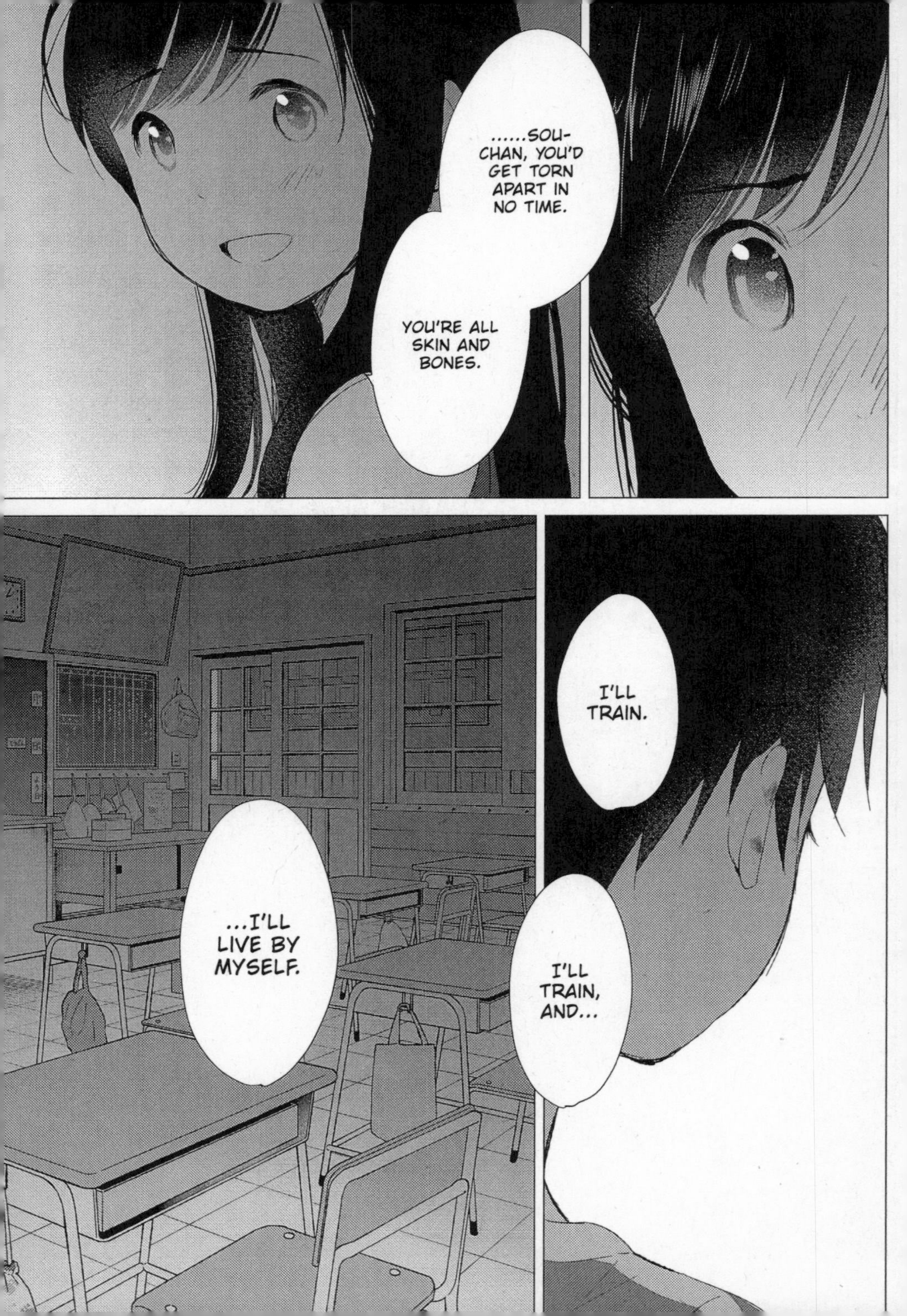

......SOU-CHAN, YOU'D GET TORN APART IN NO TIME.
YOU'RE ALL SKIN AND BONES.
I'LL TRAIN.
I'LL TRAIN, AND...
...I'LL LIVE BY MYSELF.

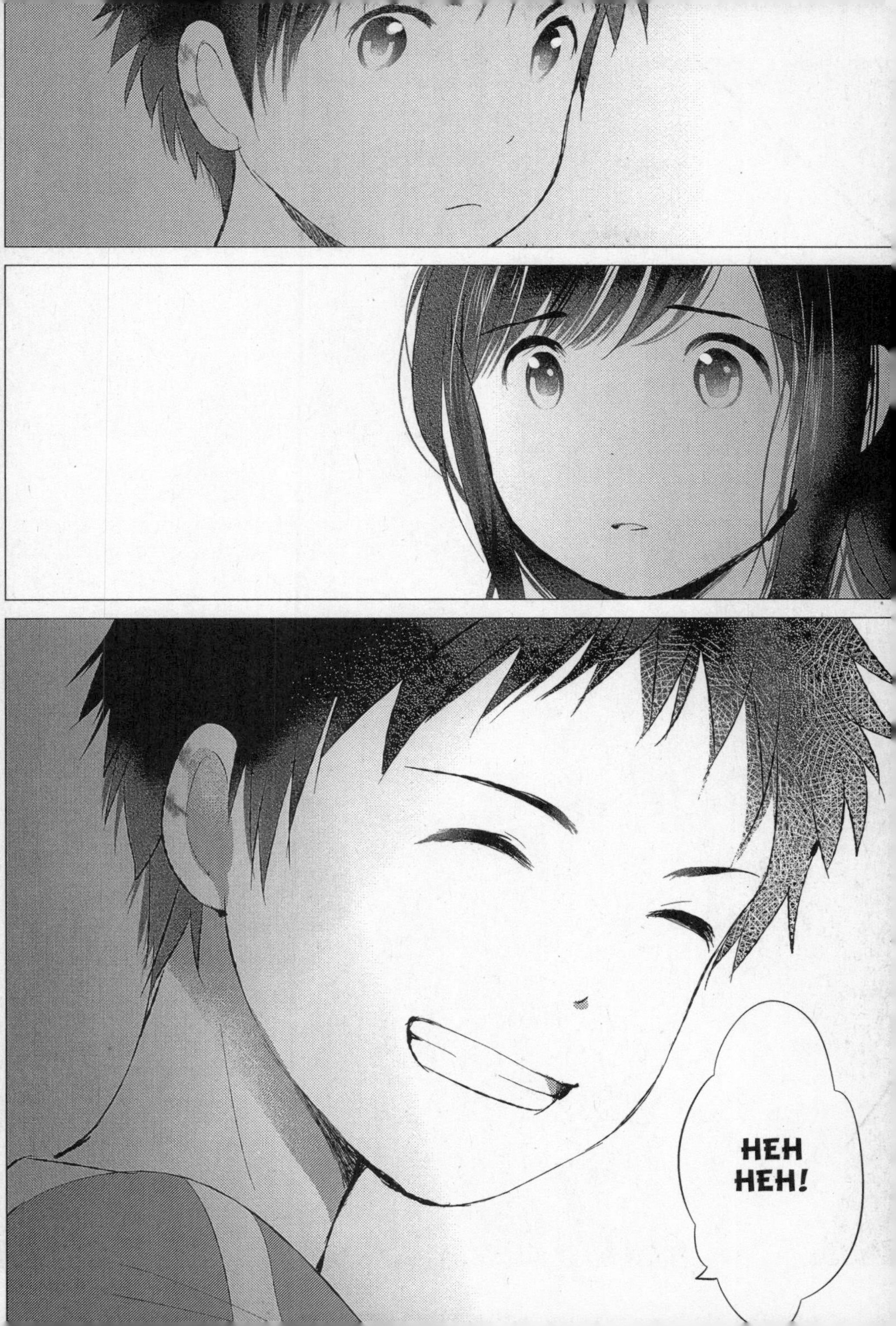
HEH HEH!

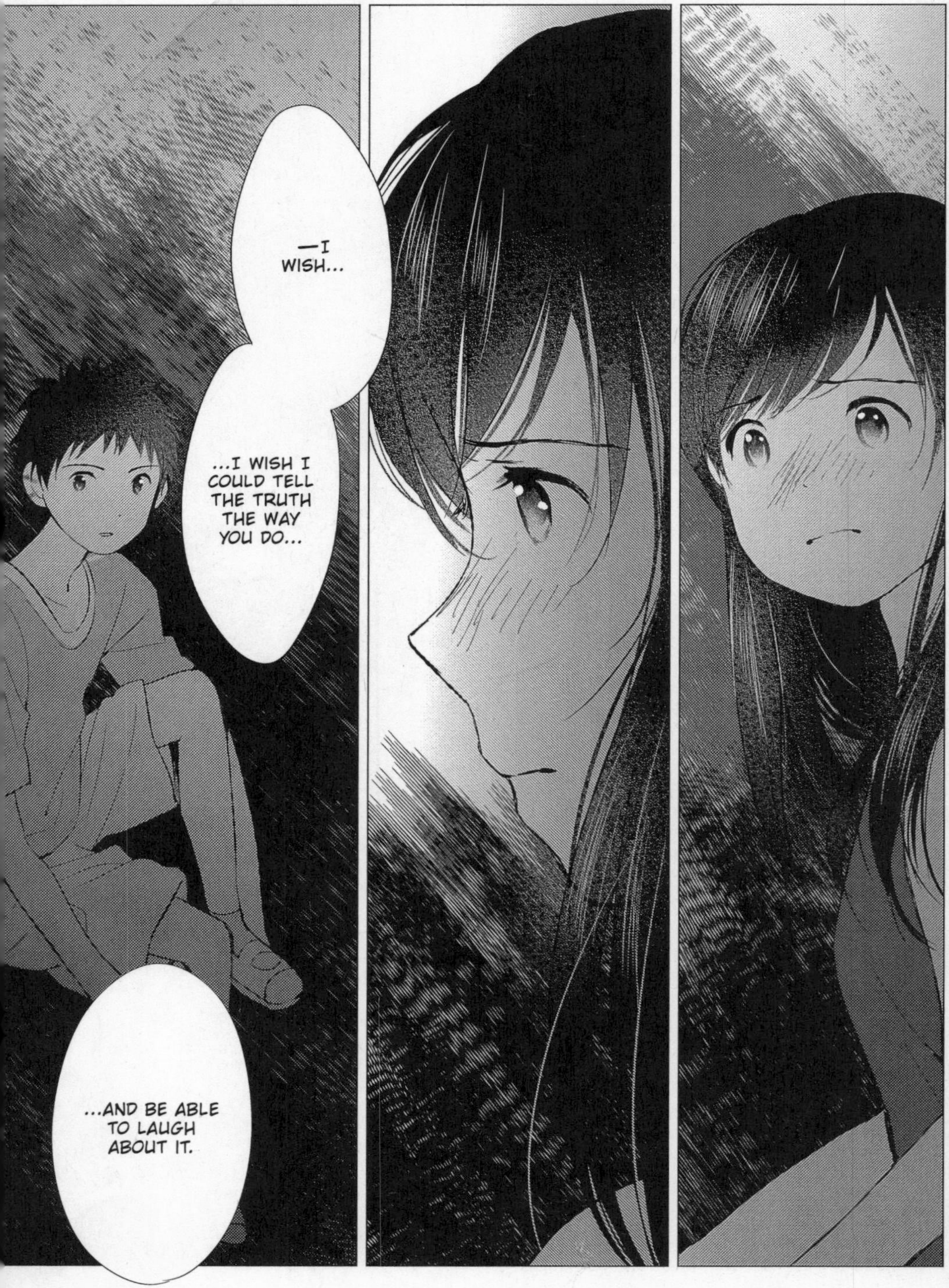
—I WISH...
...I WISH I COULD TELL THE TRUTH THE WAY YOU DO...
...AND BE ABLE TO LAUGH ABOUT IT.

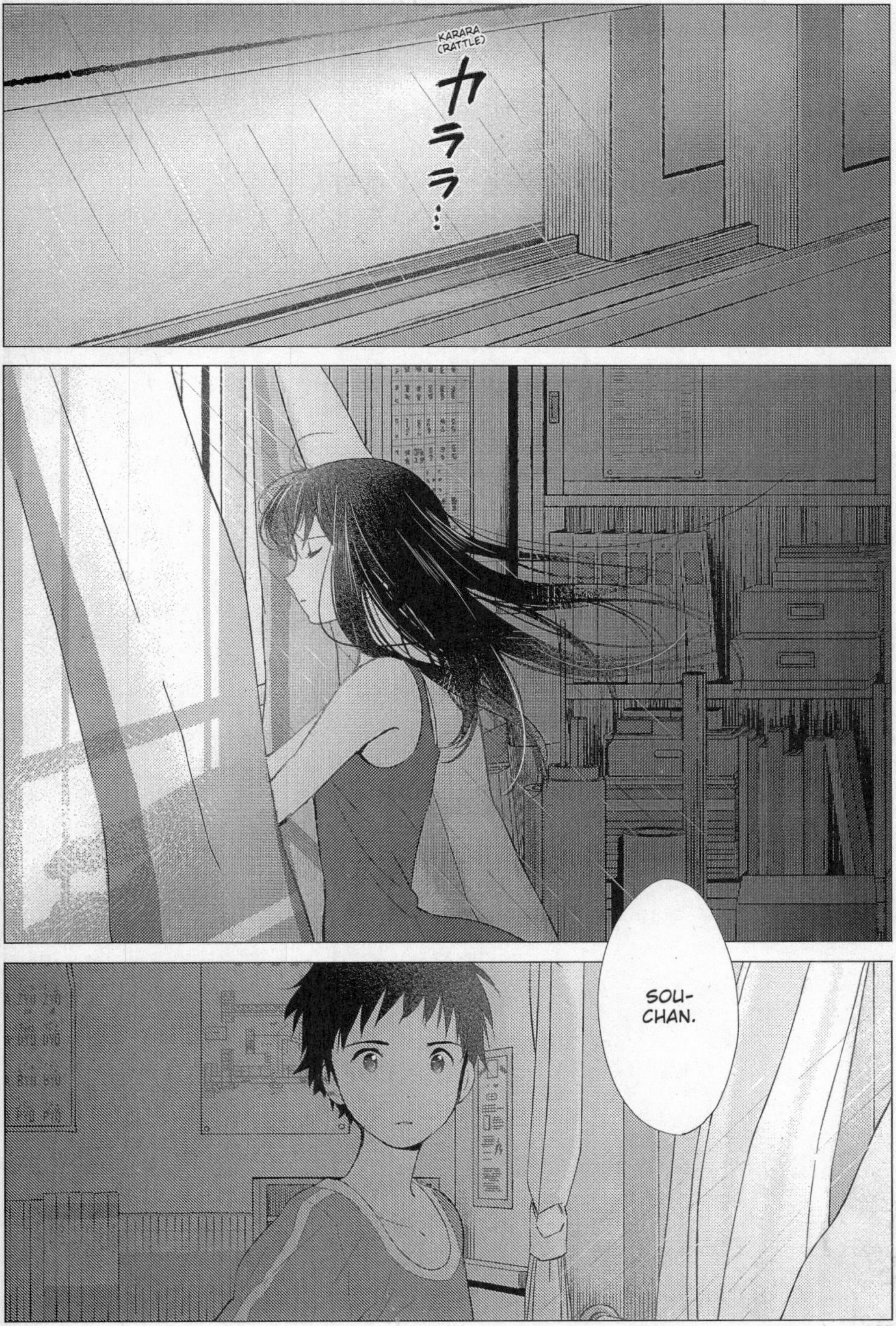
KARARA (RATTLE)
カララ…
SOU-CHAN.

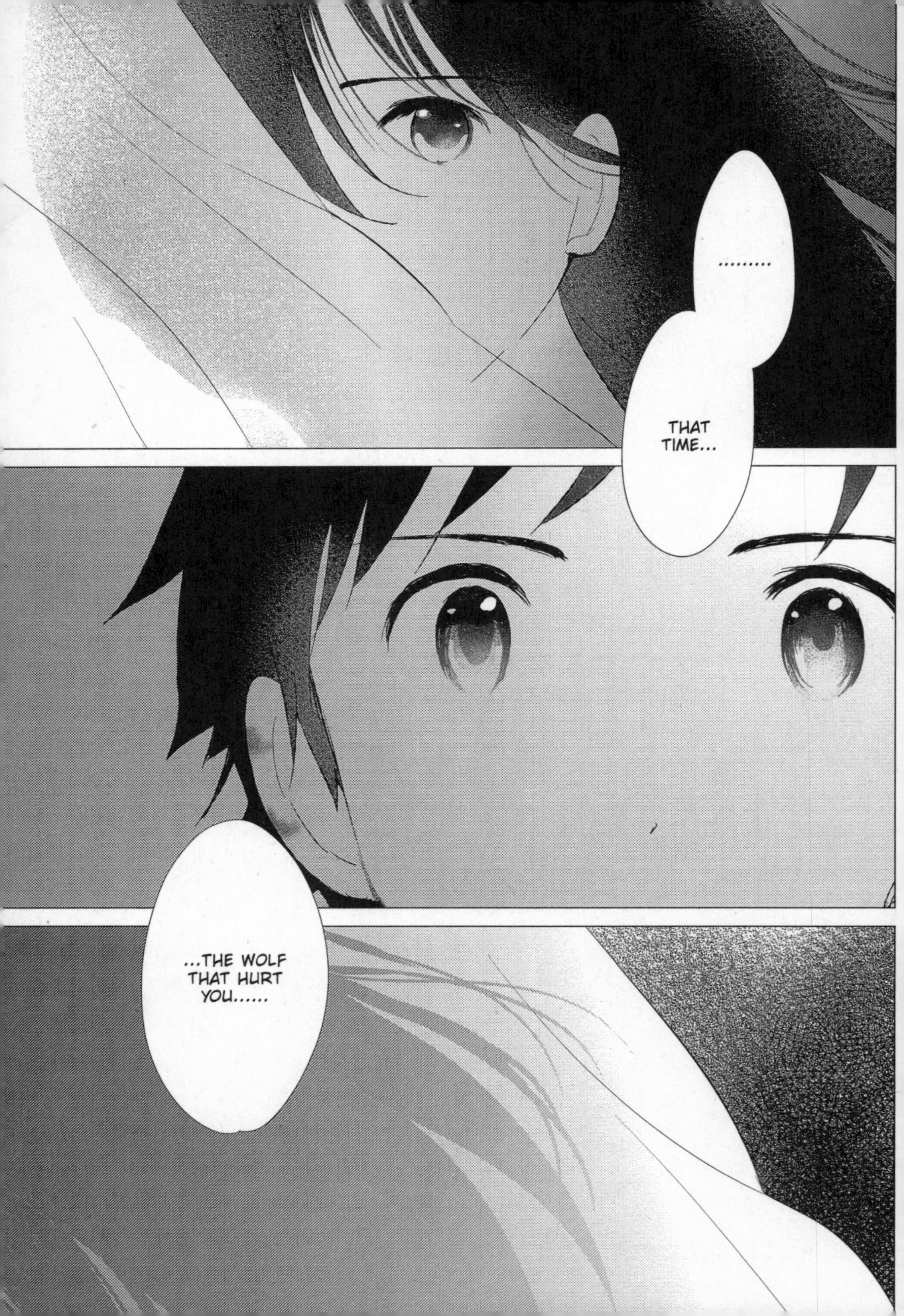
....
THAT TIME...
...THE WOLF THAT HURT YOU......

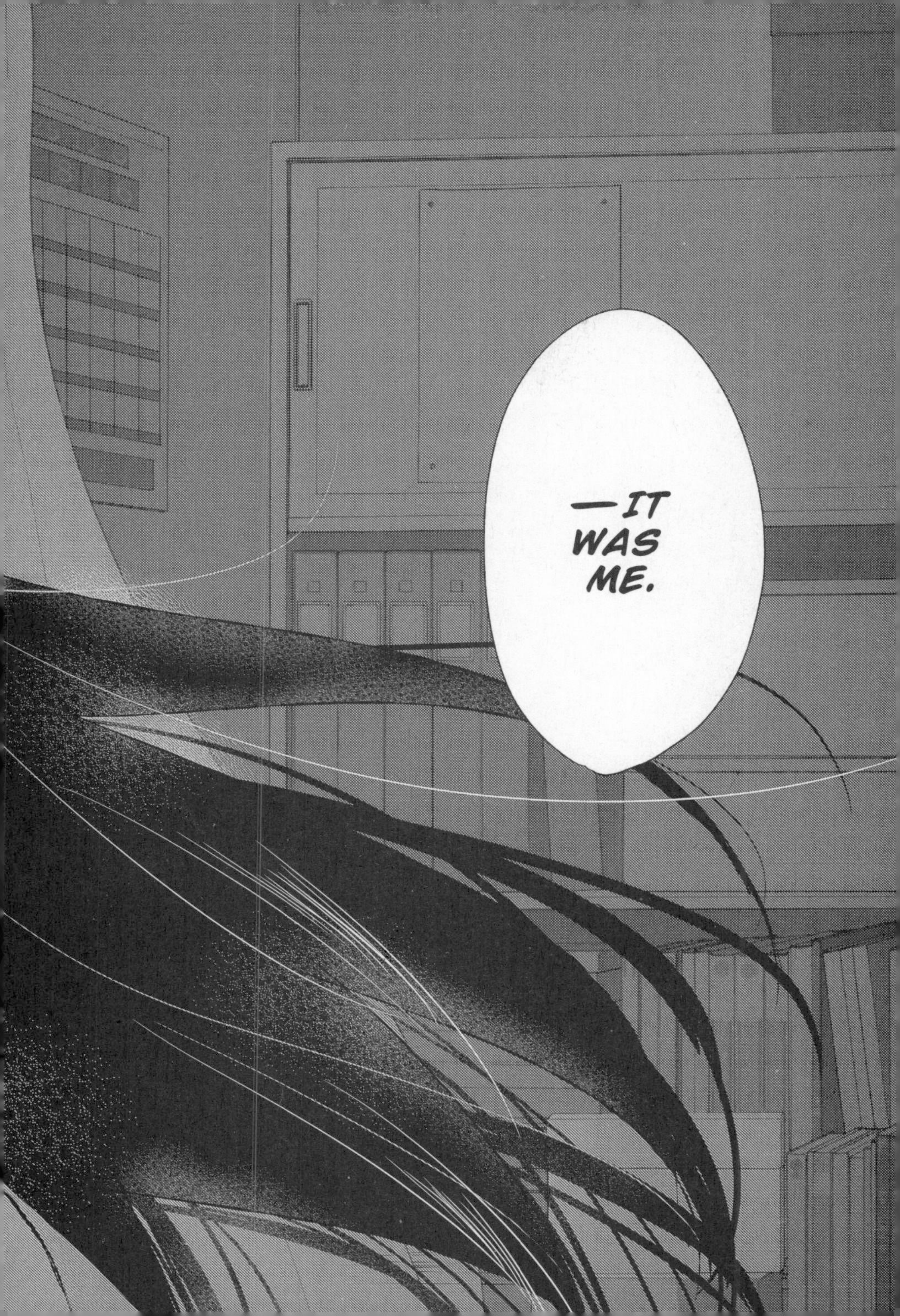
—IT WAS ME.

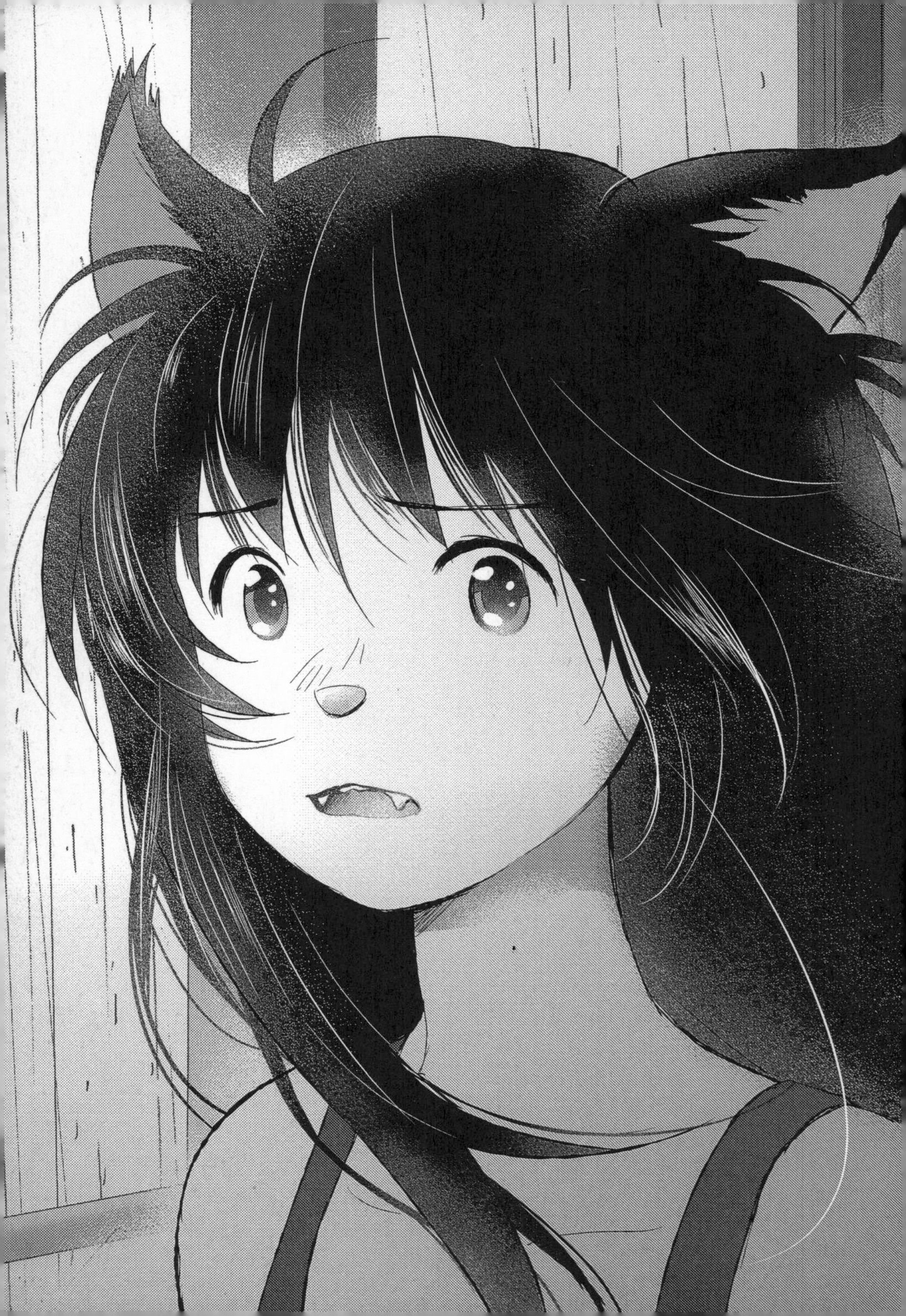

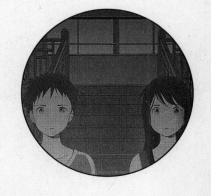

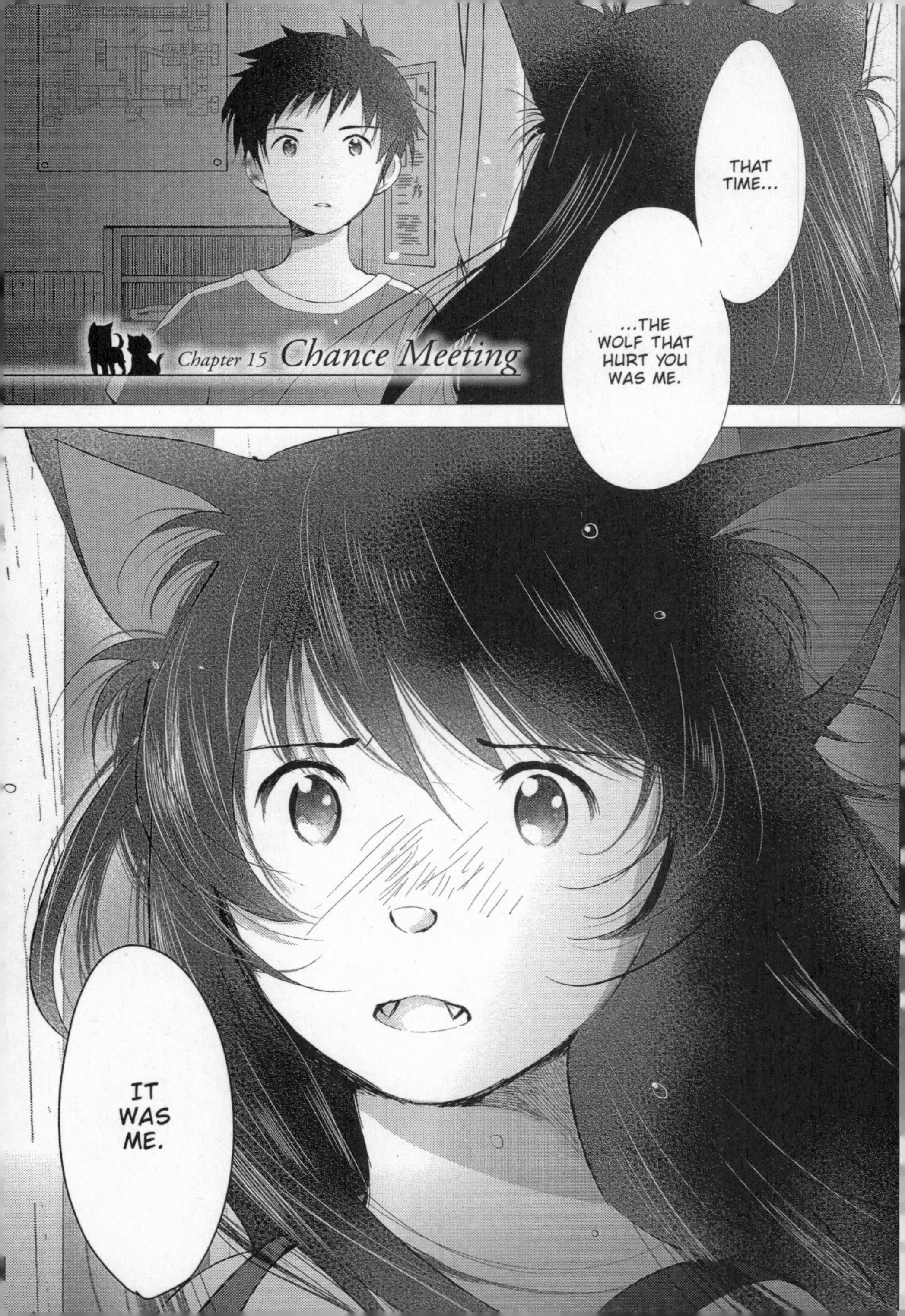
Chapter 15 Chance Meeting
THAT TIME...
...THE WOLF THAT HURT YOU WAS ME.
IT WAS ME.

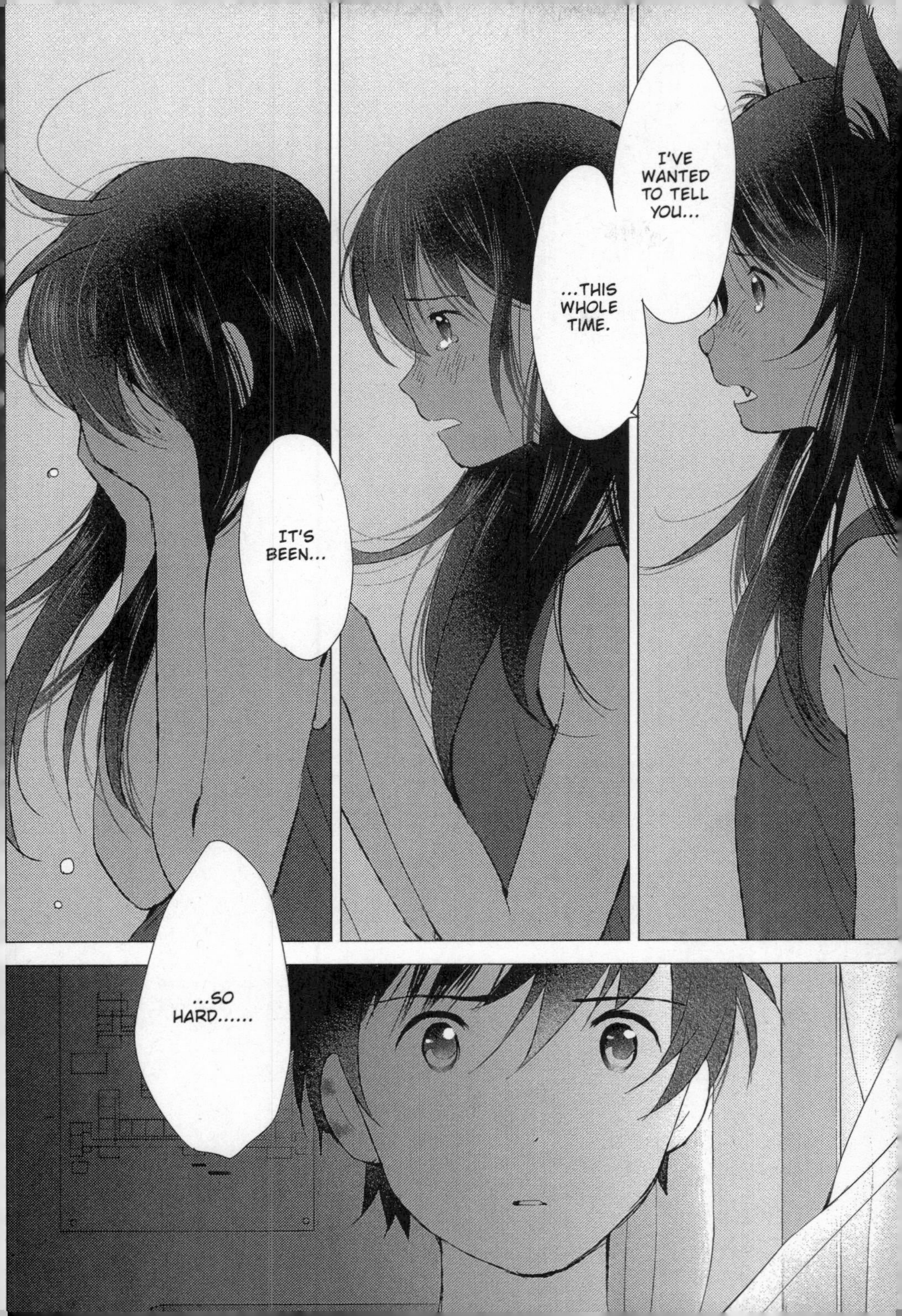
I'VE WANTED TO TELL YOU...
...THIS WHOLE TIME.
IT'S BEEN...
...SO HARD......

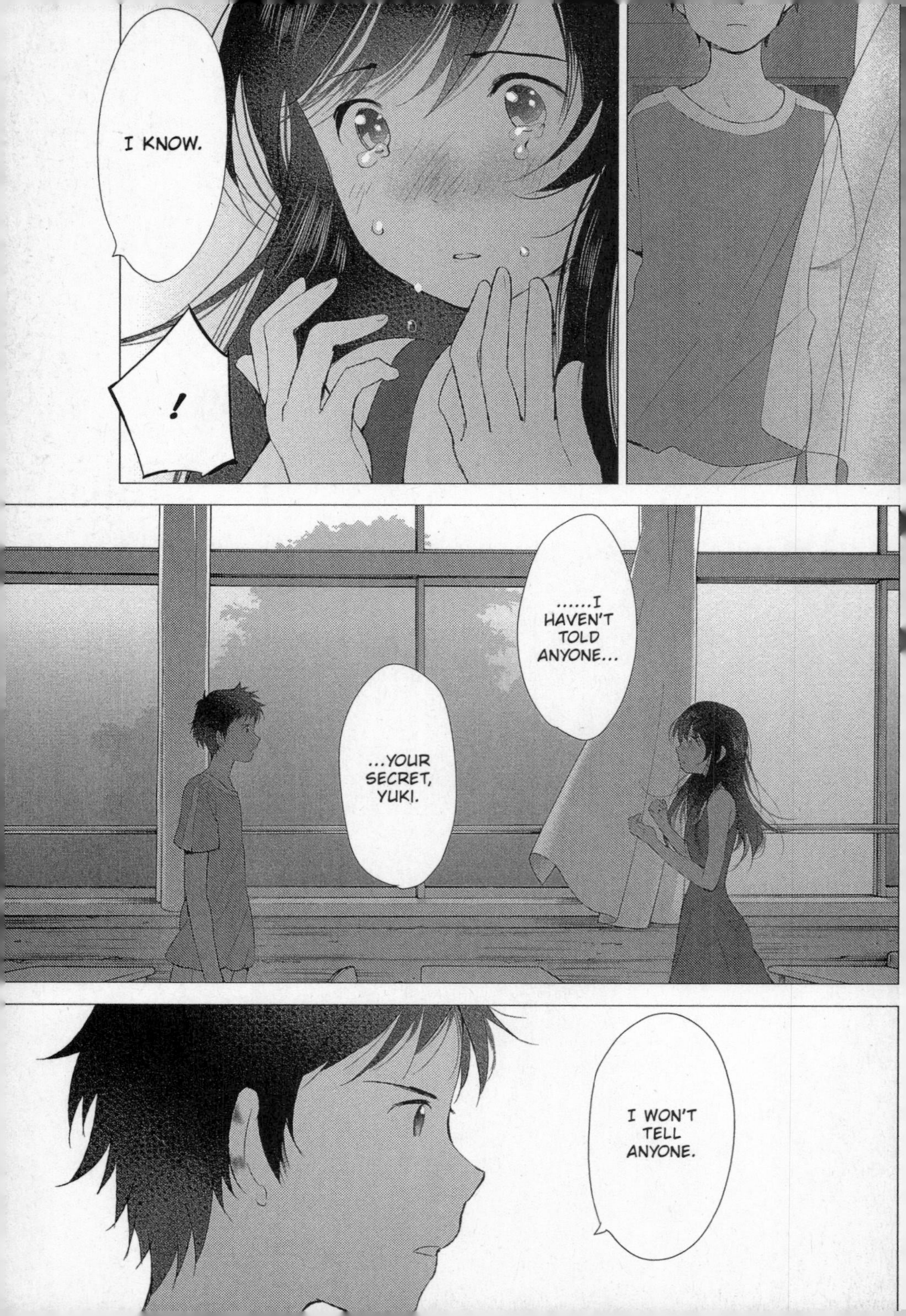
I KNOW.
!
......I HAVEN'T TOLD ANYONE...
...YOUR SECRET, YUKI.
I WON'T TELL ANYONE.

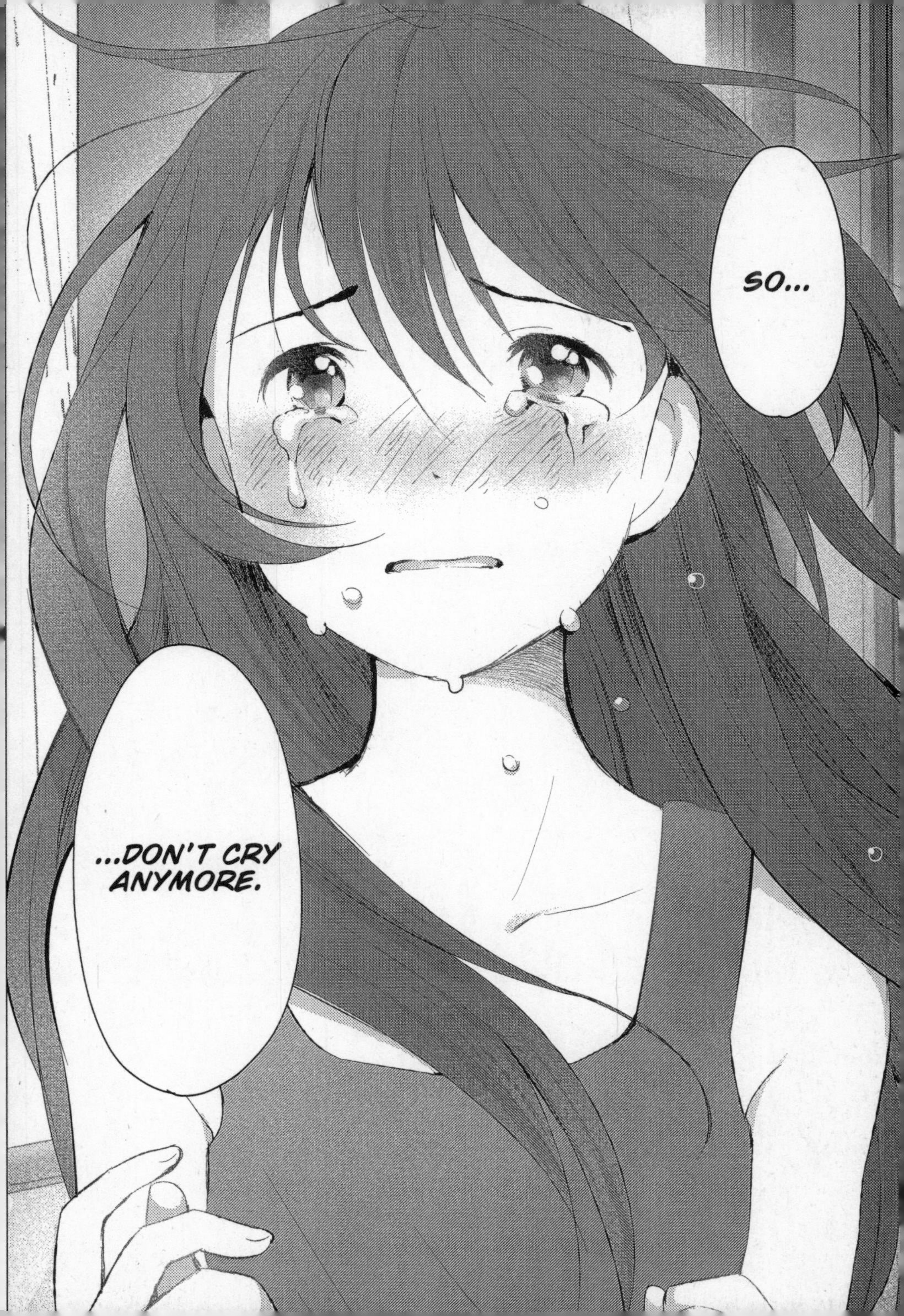
SO...
...DON'T CRY ANYMORE.

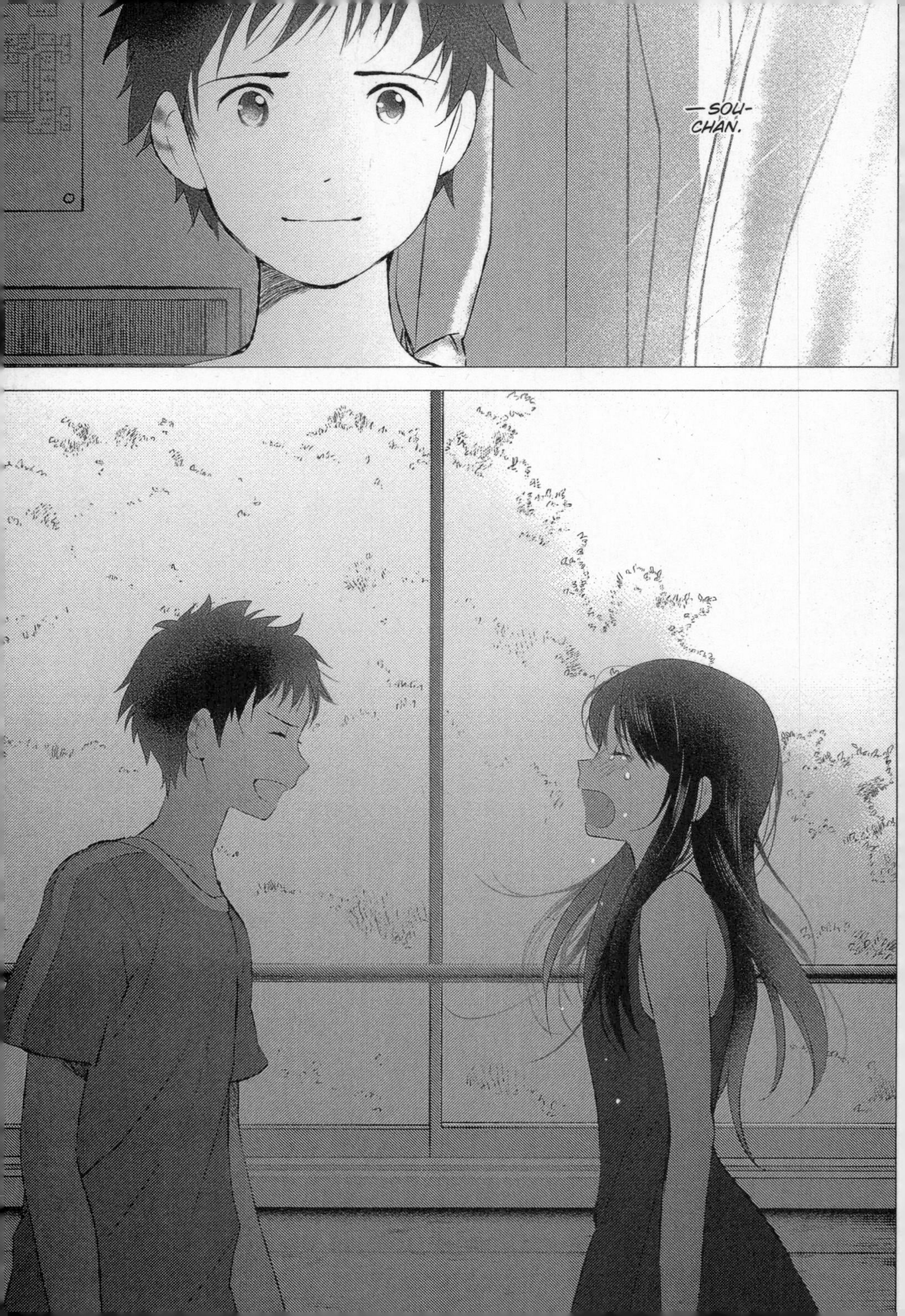
—SOU-CHAN.

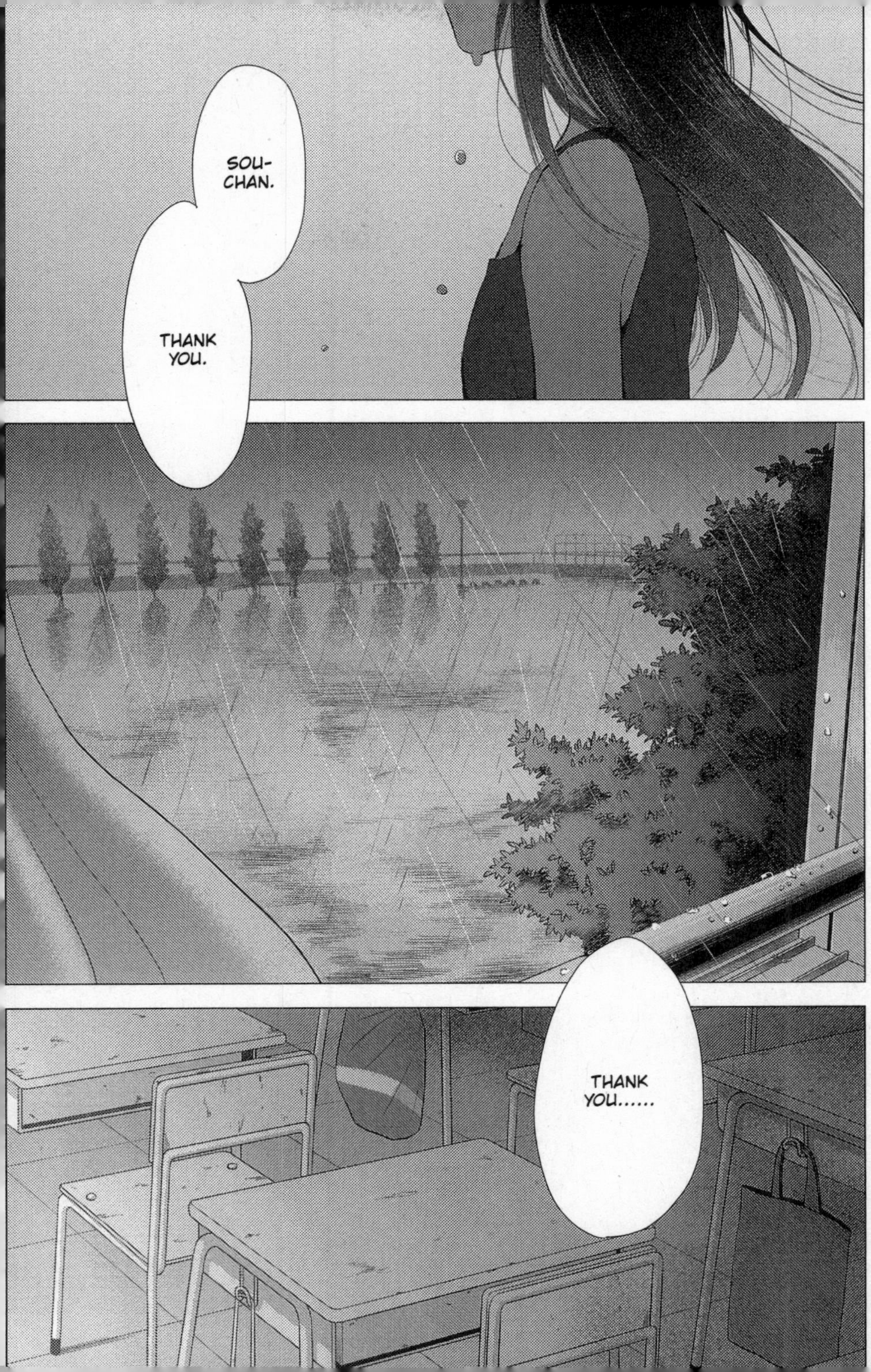
SOU-CHAN.
THANK YOU.
THANK YOU......

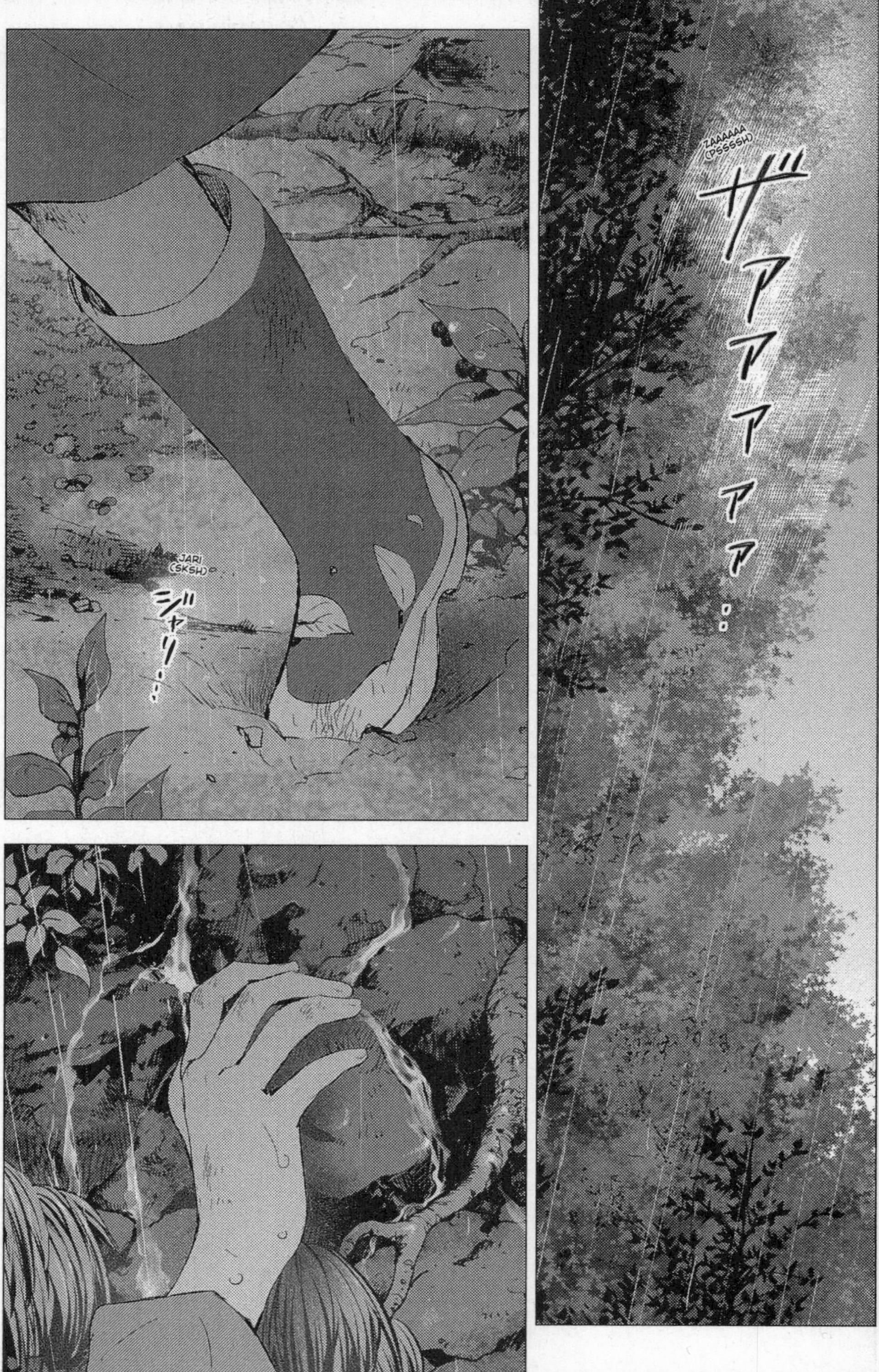
ZAAAAAA (PSSSSH)
ザアアアアア..
JARI (SKSH)
ジャリ...

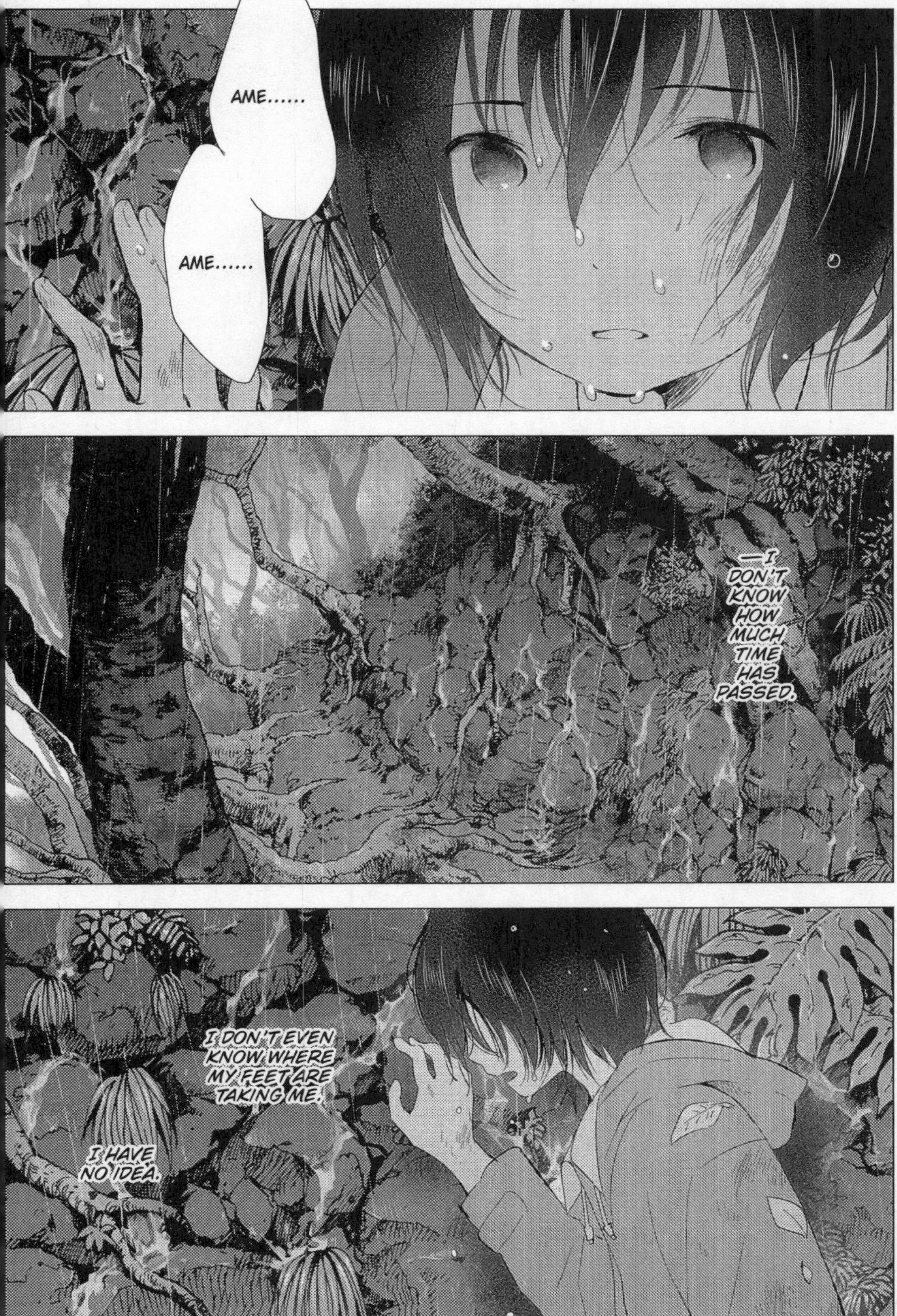
AME......
AME......
—I DON'T KNOW HOW MUCH TIME HAS PASSED.
I DON'T EVEN KNOW WHERE MY FEET ARE TAKING ME.
I HAVE NO IDEA.

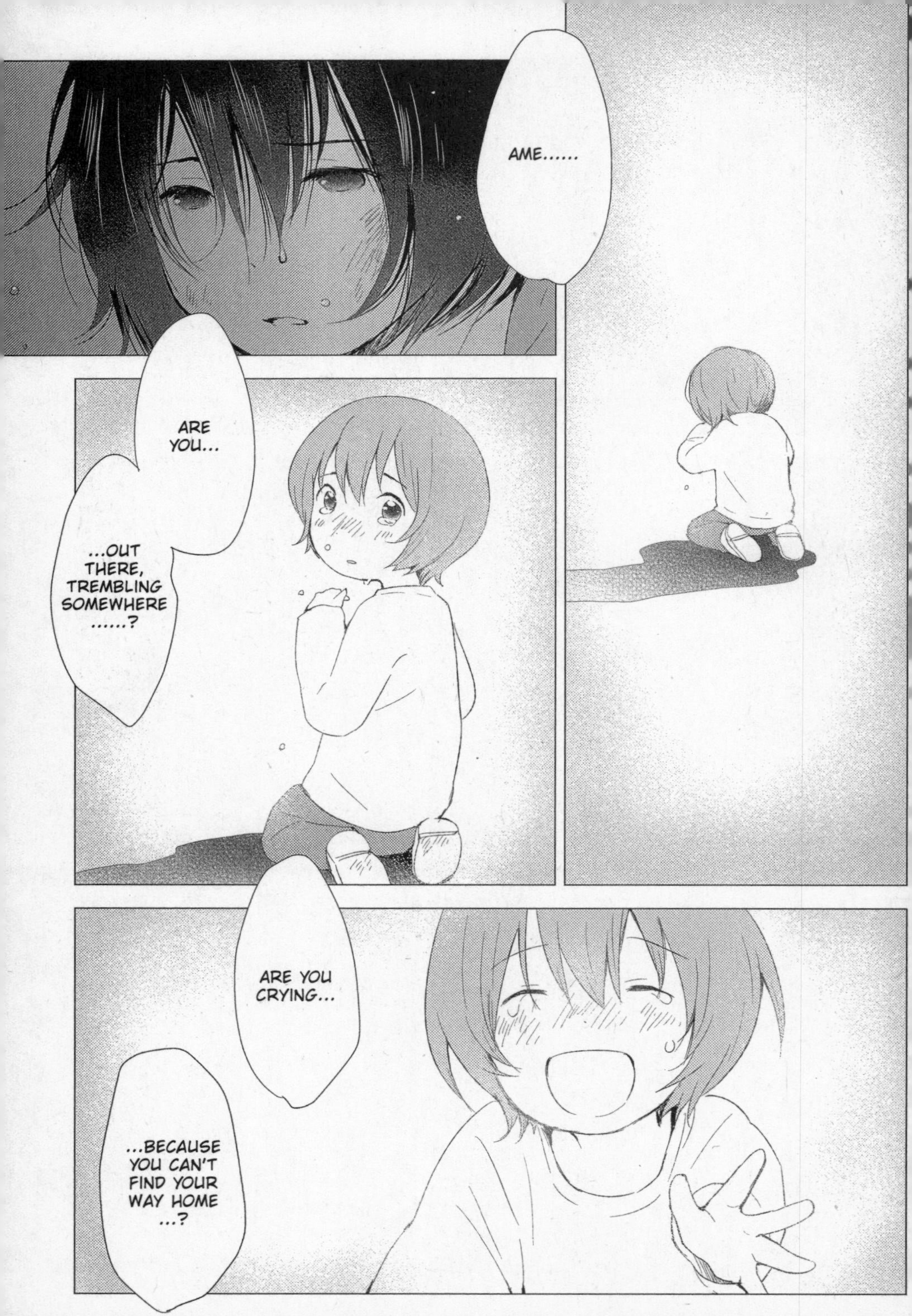
AME......
ARE YOU...
...OUT THERE, TREMBLING SOMEWHERE ......?
ARE YOU CRYING...
...BECAUSE YOU CAN'T FIND YOUR WAY HOME ...?

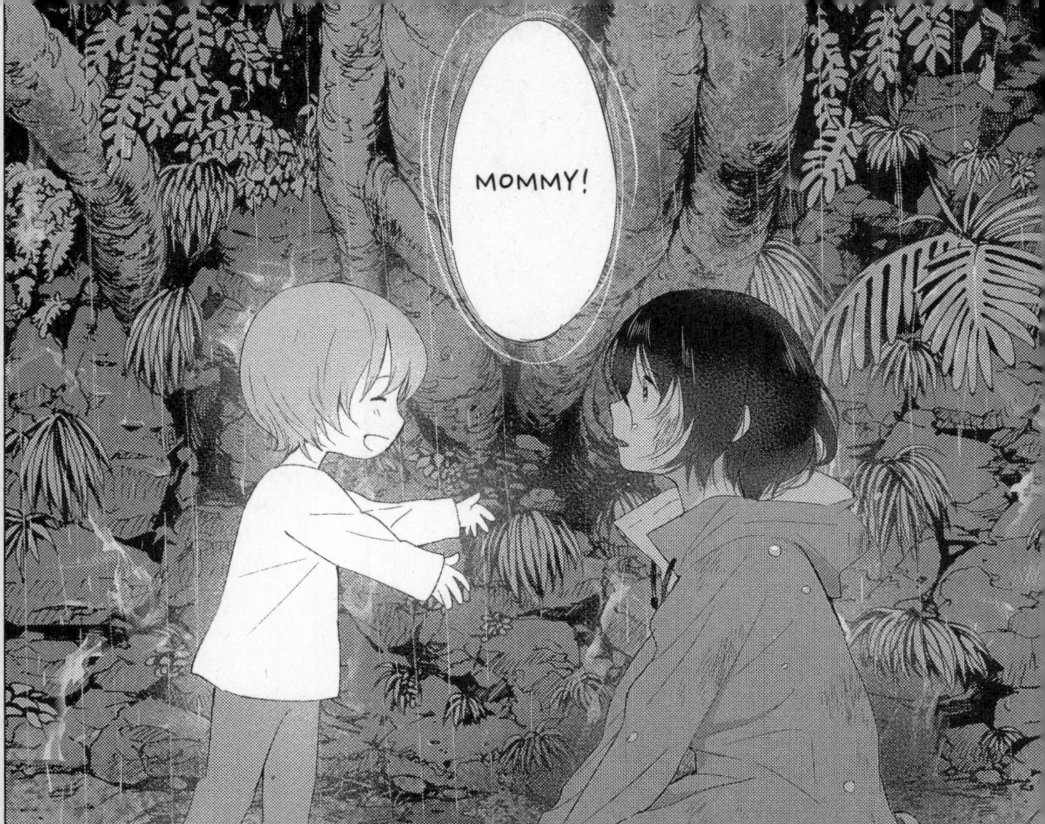
MOMMY!
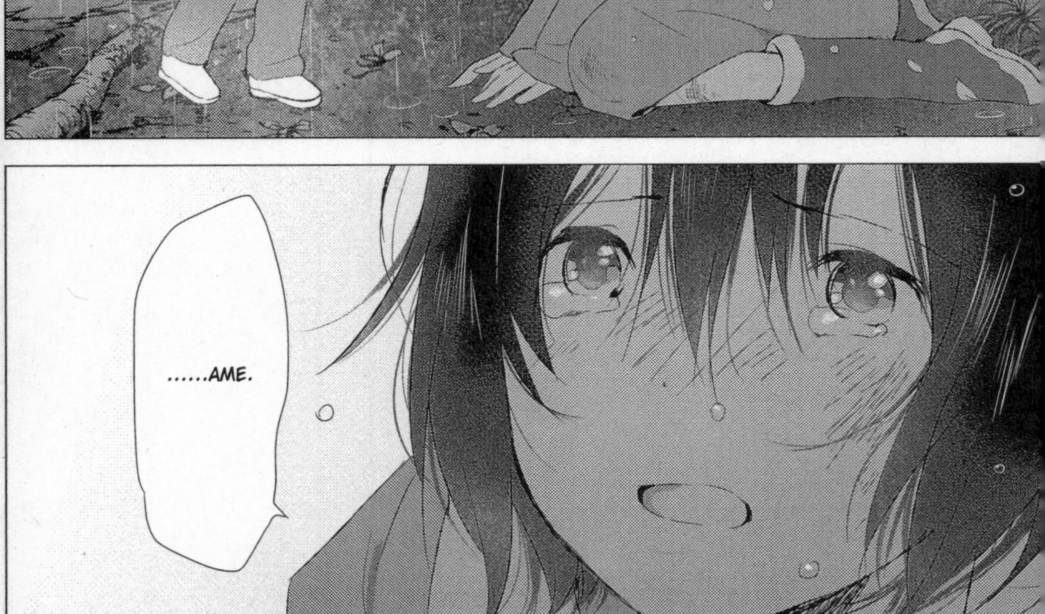
......AME.

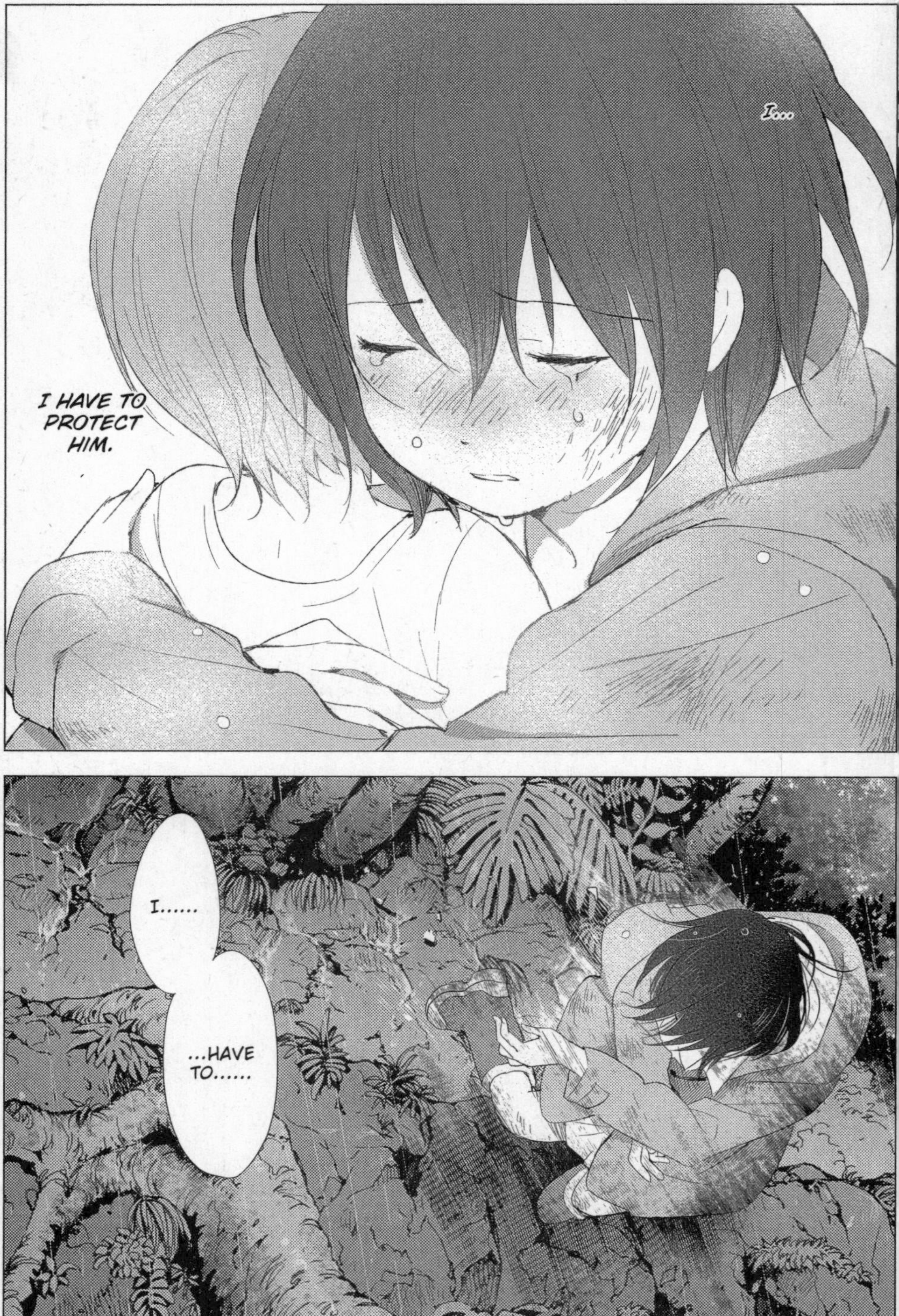
I...
I HAVE TO PROTECT HIM.
I......
...HAVE TO......

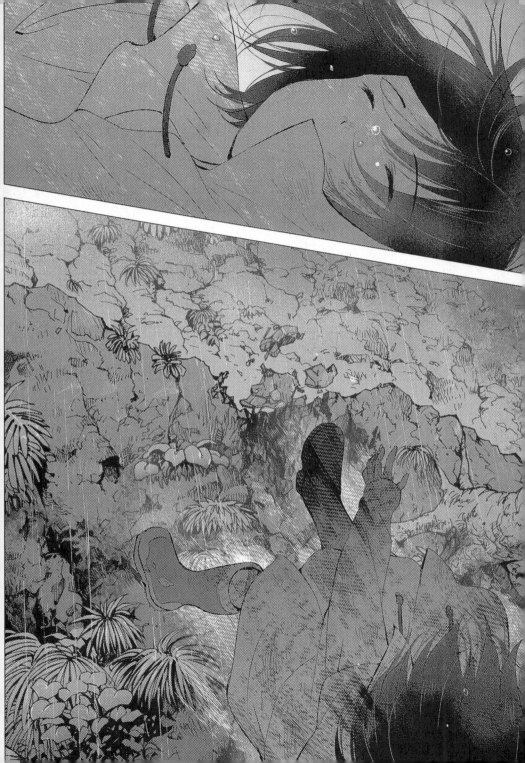

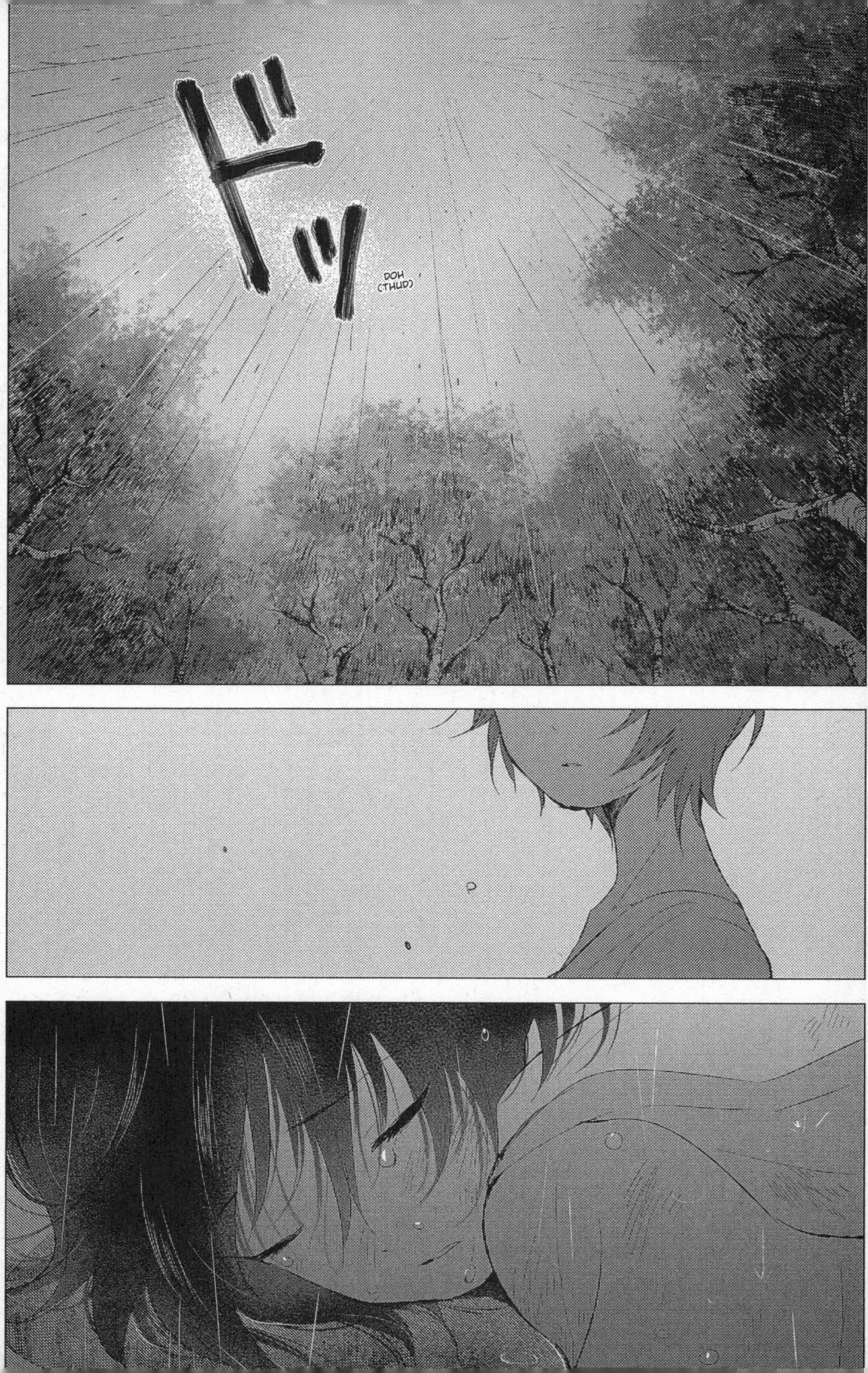
ドッ
DOH
(THUD)

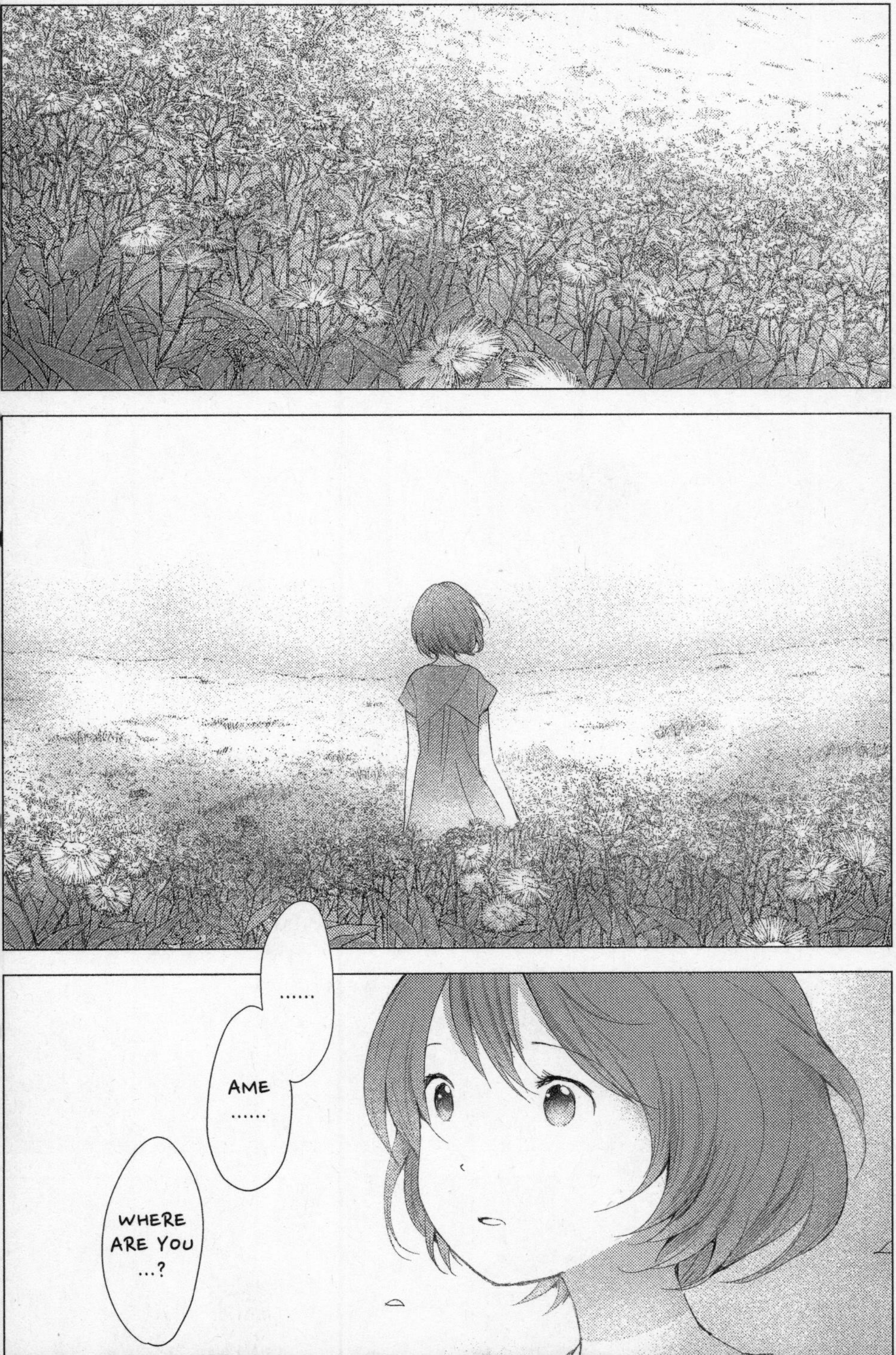
……
AME ……
WHERE ARE YOU …?

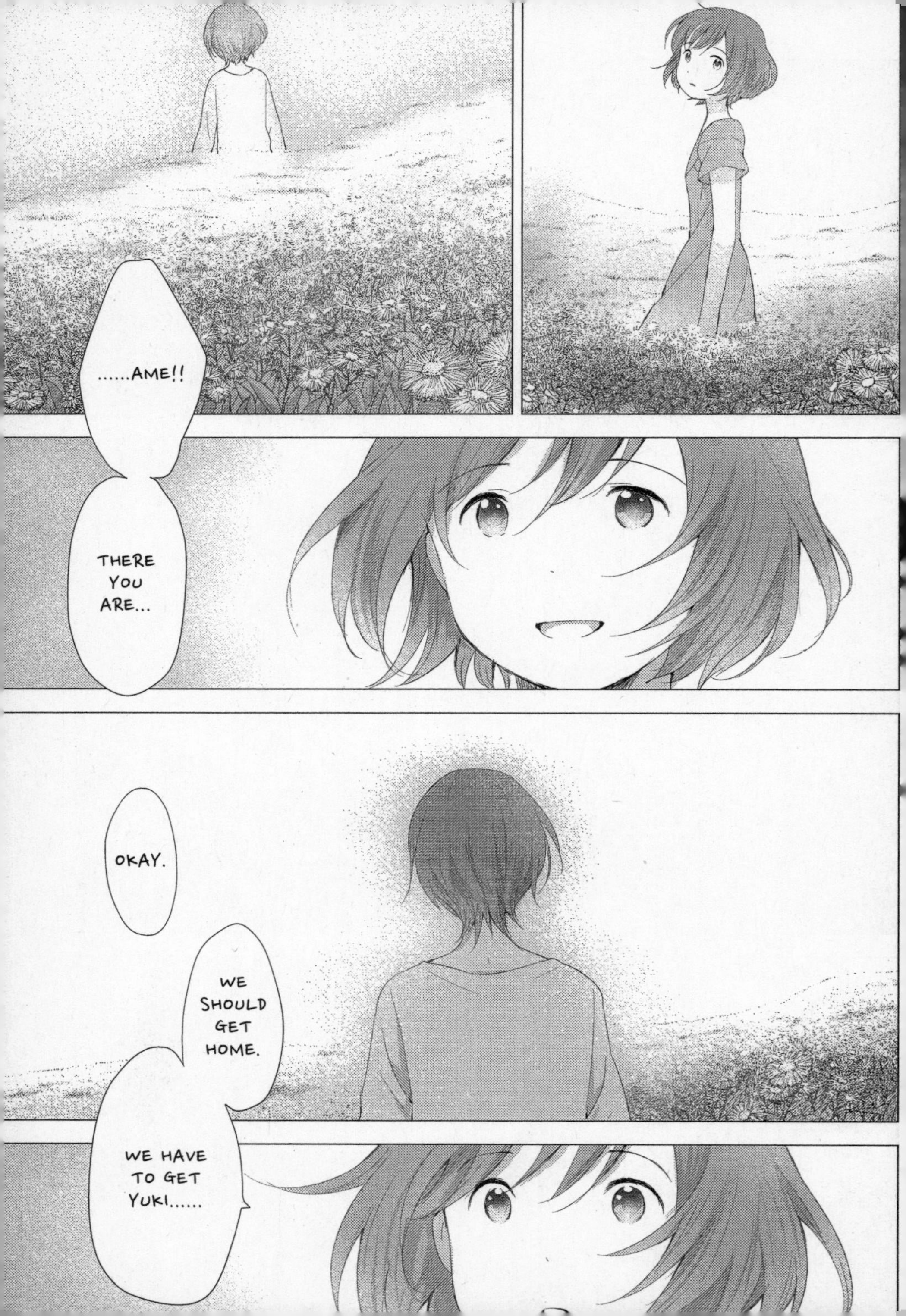
......AME!!
THERE YOU ARE...
OKAY.
WE SHOULD GET HOME.
WE HAVE TO GET YUKI......

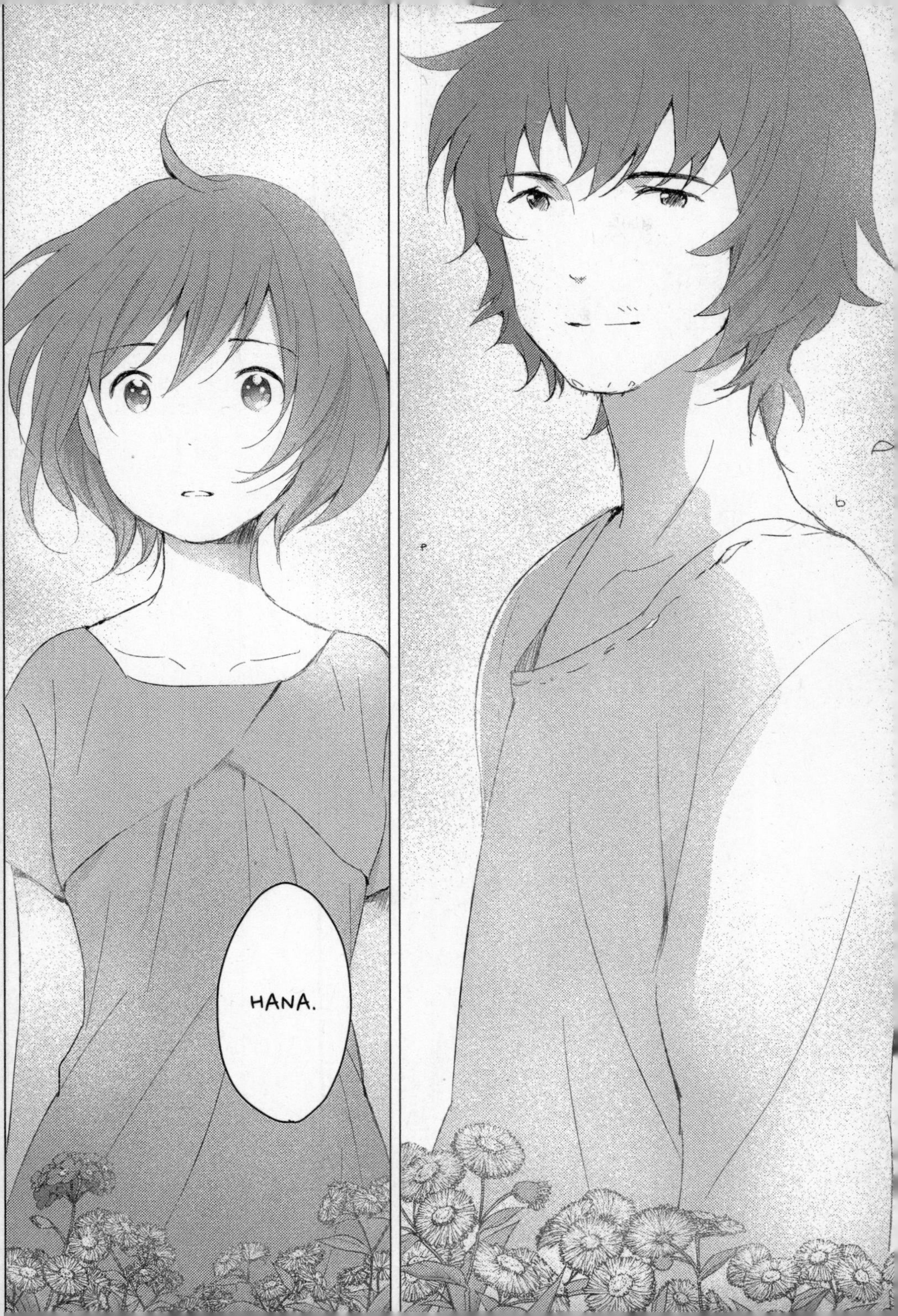
HANA.

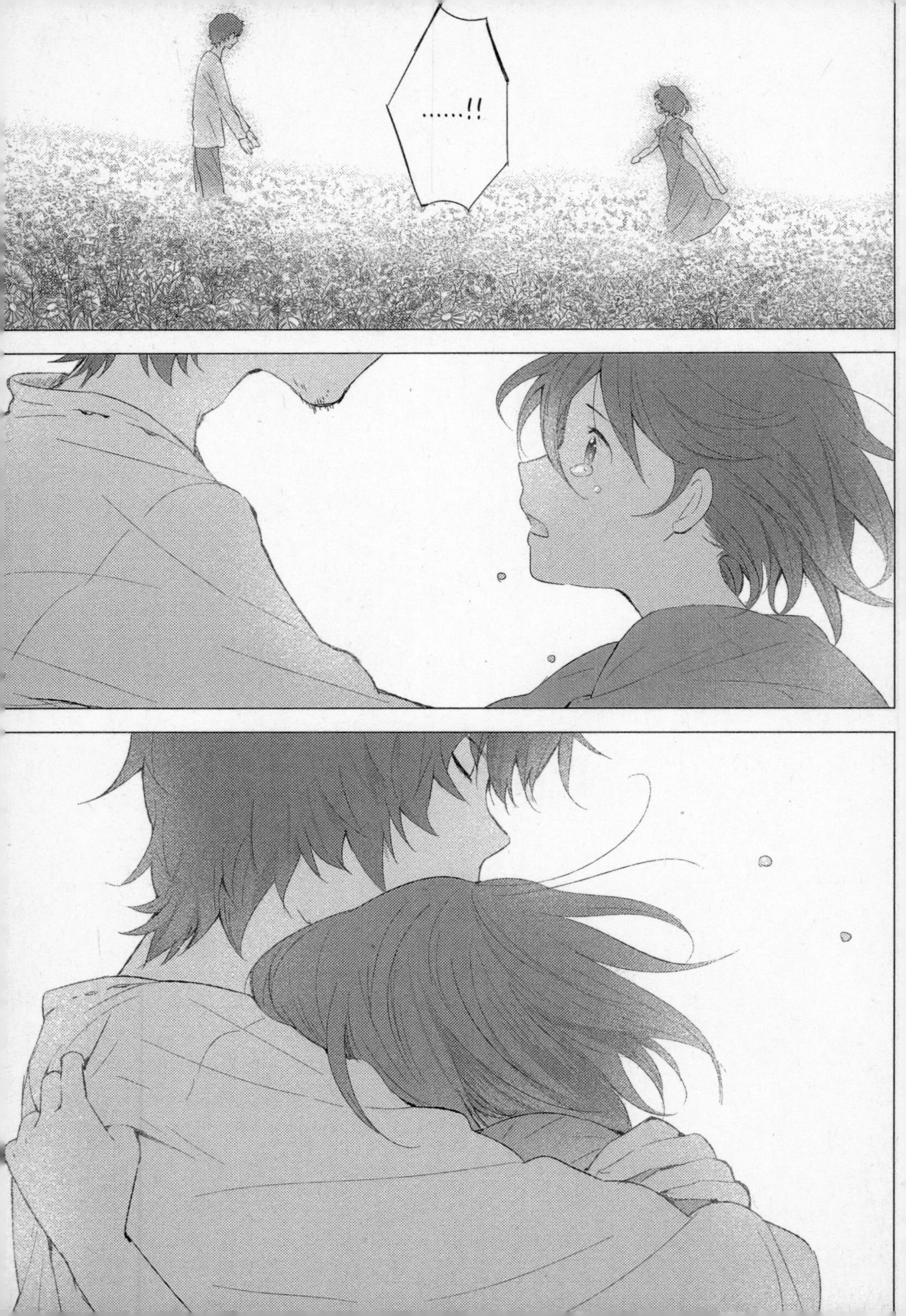
......!!

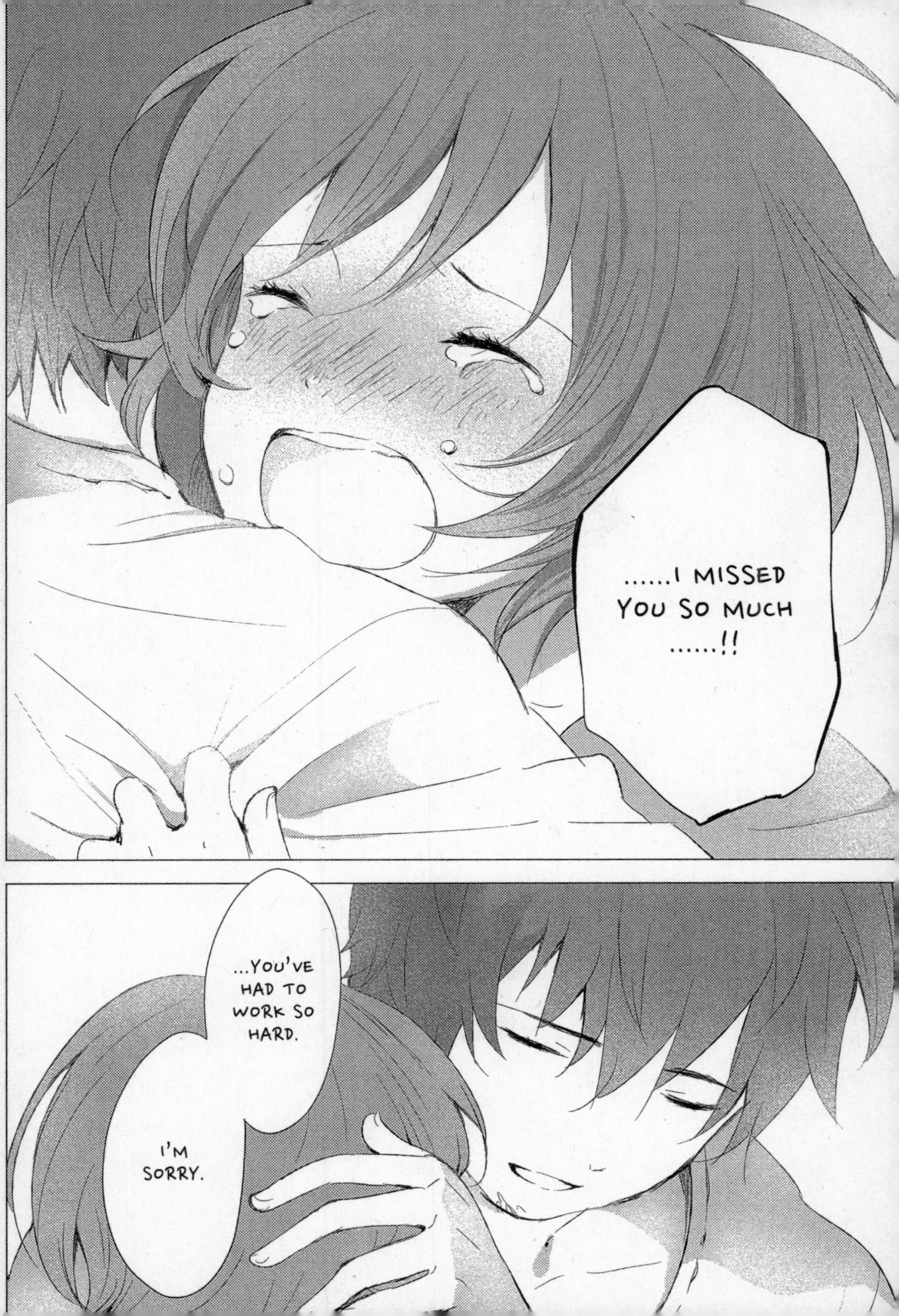
......I MISSED YOU SO MUCH ......!!
...YOU'VE HAD TO WORK SO HARD.
I'M SORRY.

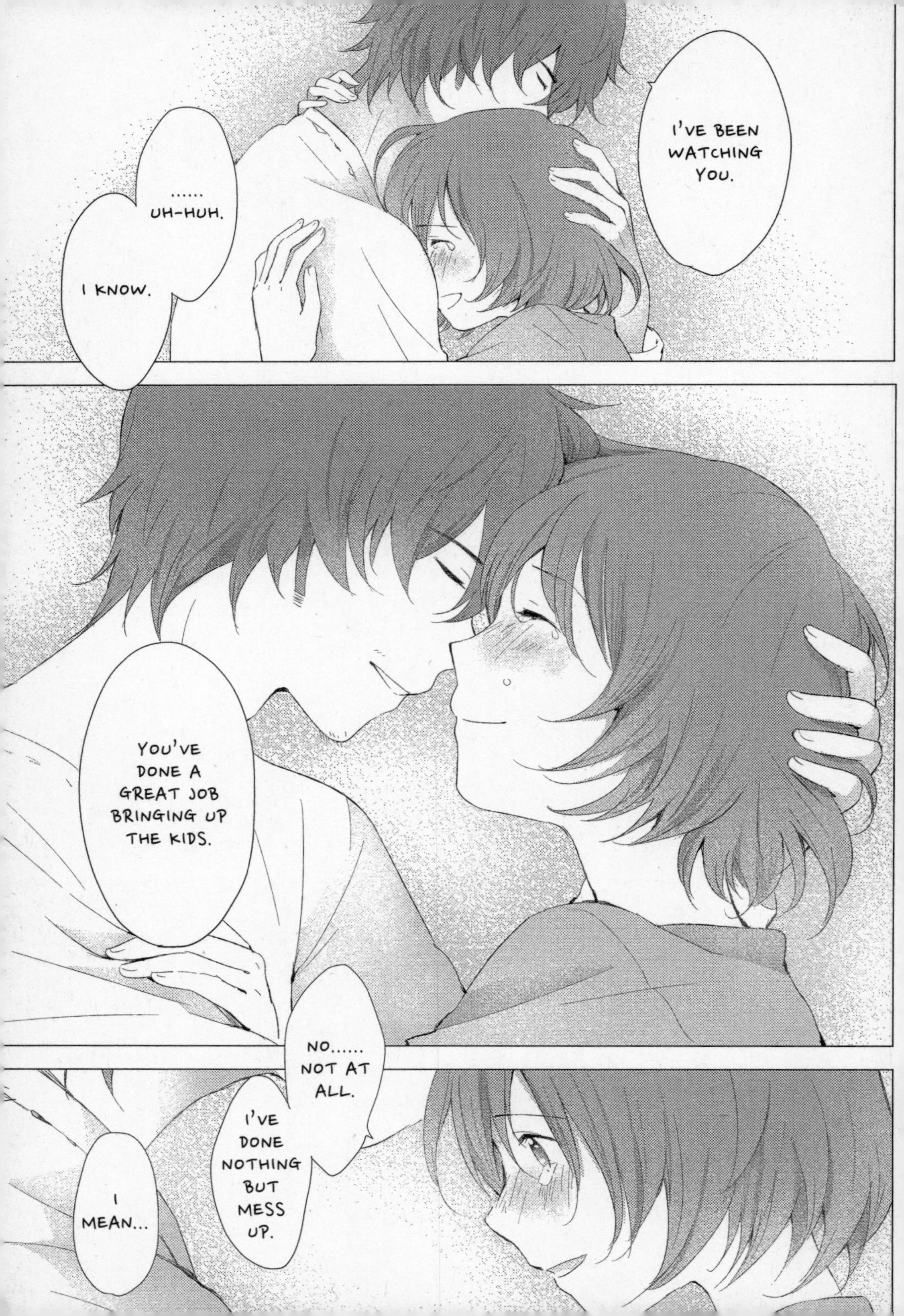
I'VE BEEN WATCHING YOU.
...... UH-HUH.
I KNOW.
YOU'VE DONE A GREAT JOB BRINGING UP THE KIDS.
NO...... NOT AT ALL.
I'VE DONE NOTHING BUT MESS UP.
I MEAN...

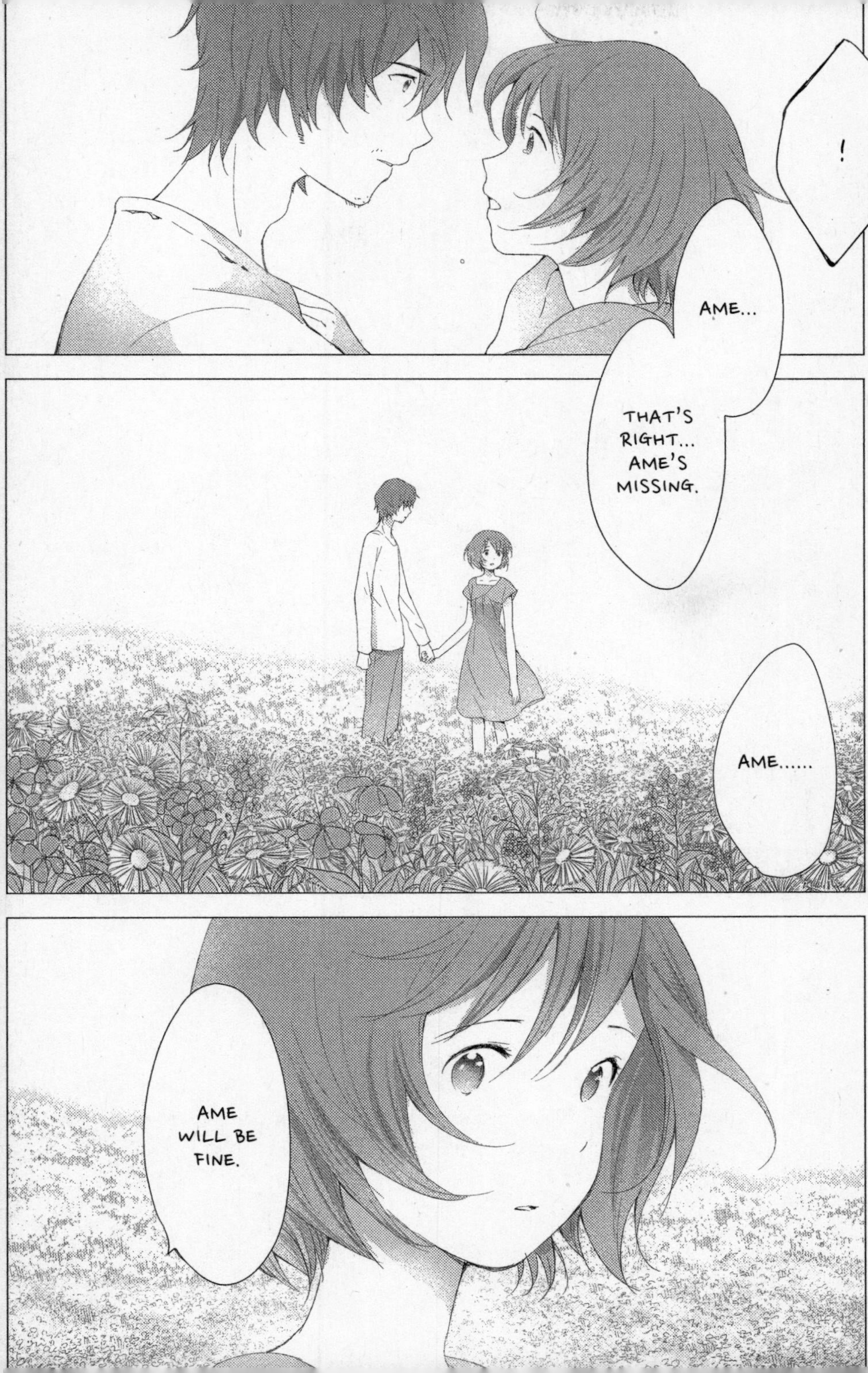
!
AME...
THAT'S RIGHT... AME'S MISSING.
AME......
AME WILL BE FINE.

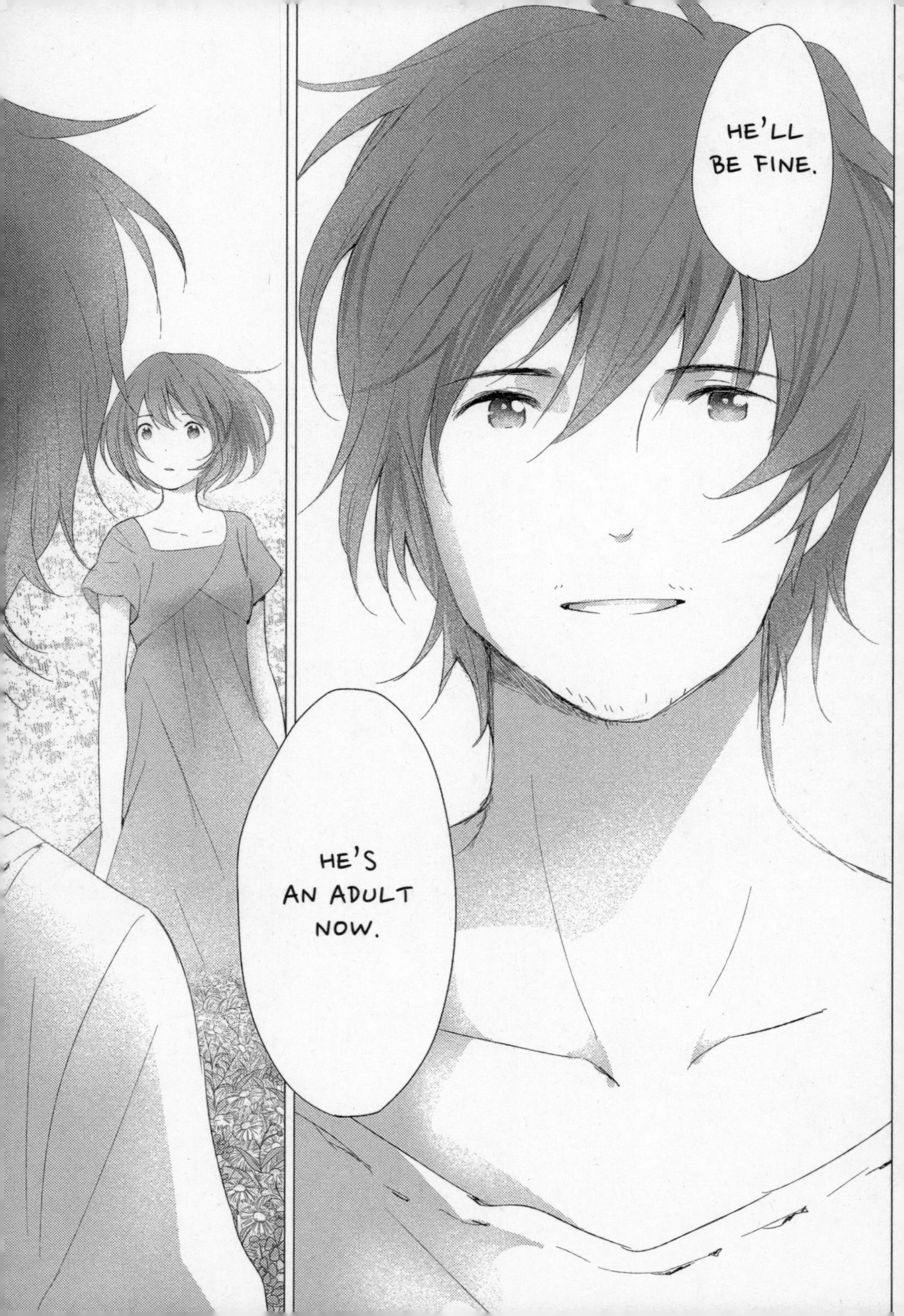
HE'LL BE FINE.
HE'S AN ADULT NOW.

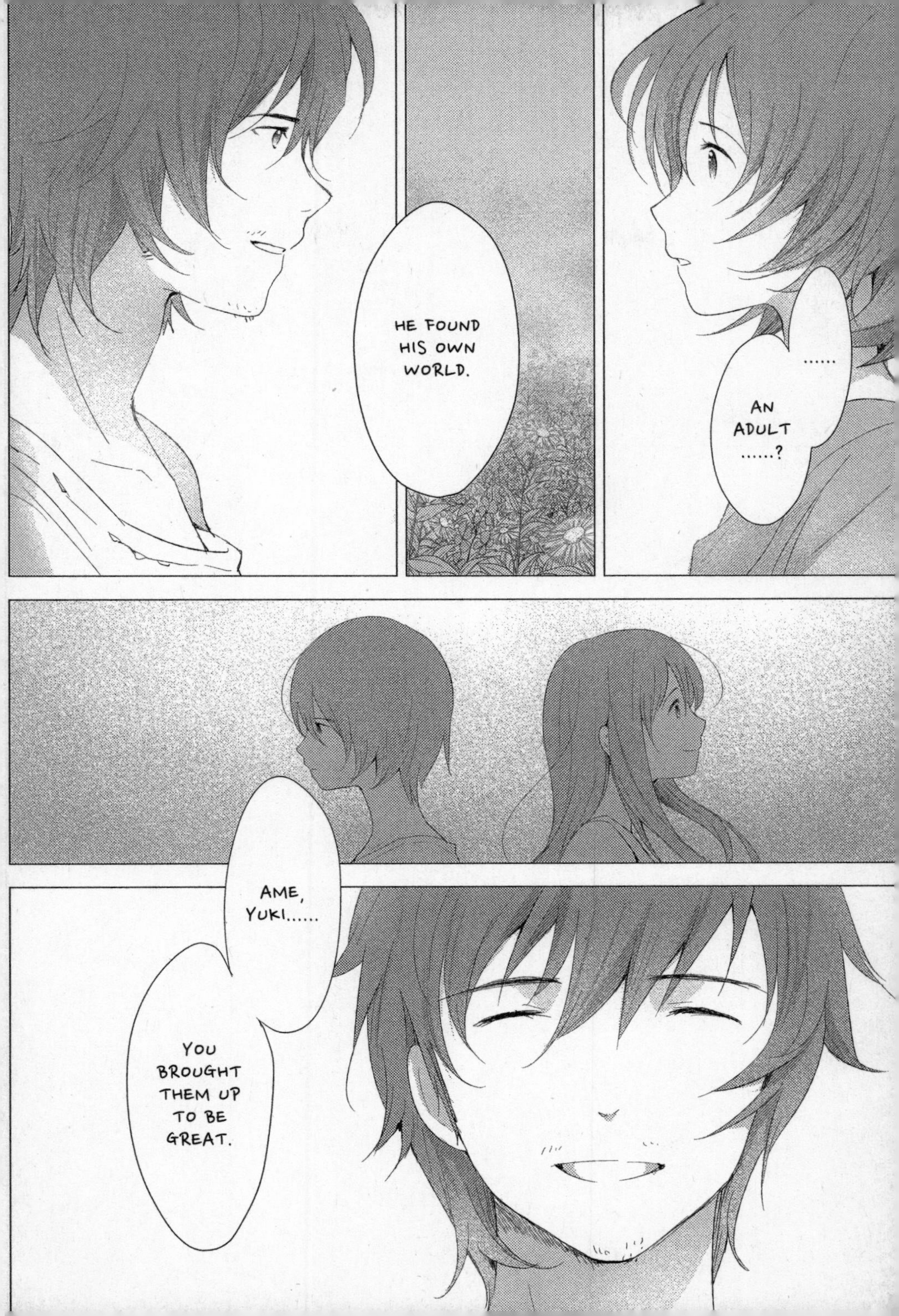
......
AN ADULT ......?
HE FOUND HIS OWN WORLD.
AME, YUKI......
YOU BROUGHT THEM UP TO BE GREAT.

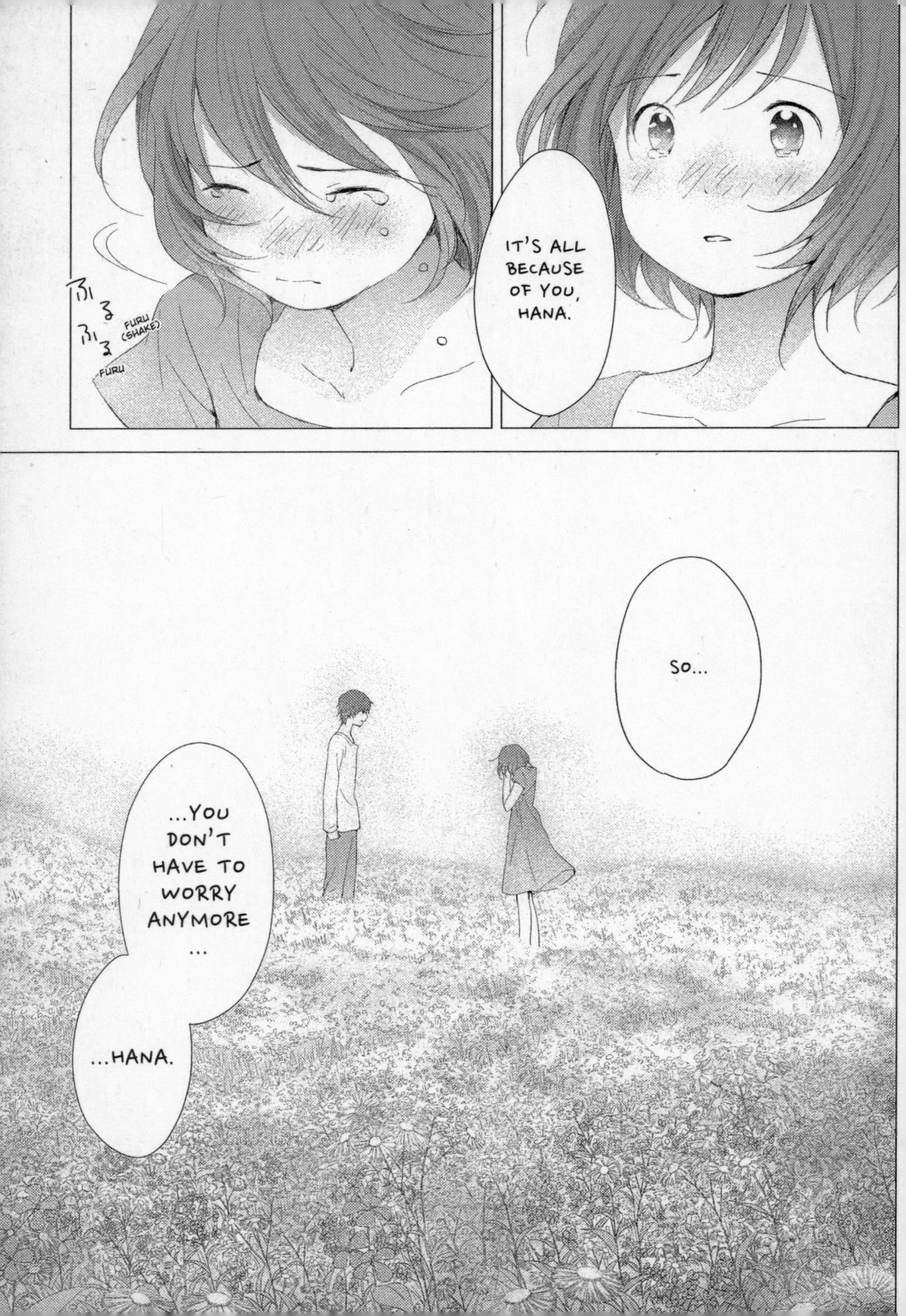
IT'S ALL BECAUSE OF YOU, HANA.
ふるふる
FURU (SHAKE)
FURU
SO...
...YOU DON'T HAVE TO WORRY ANYMORE ...
...HANA.

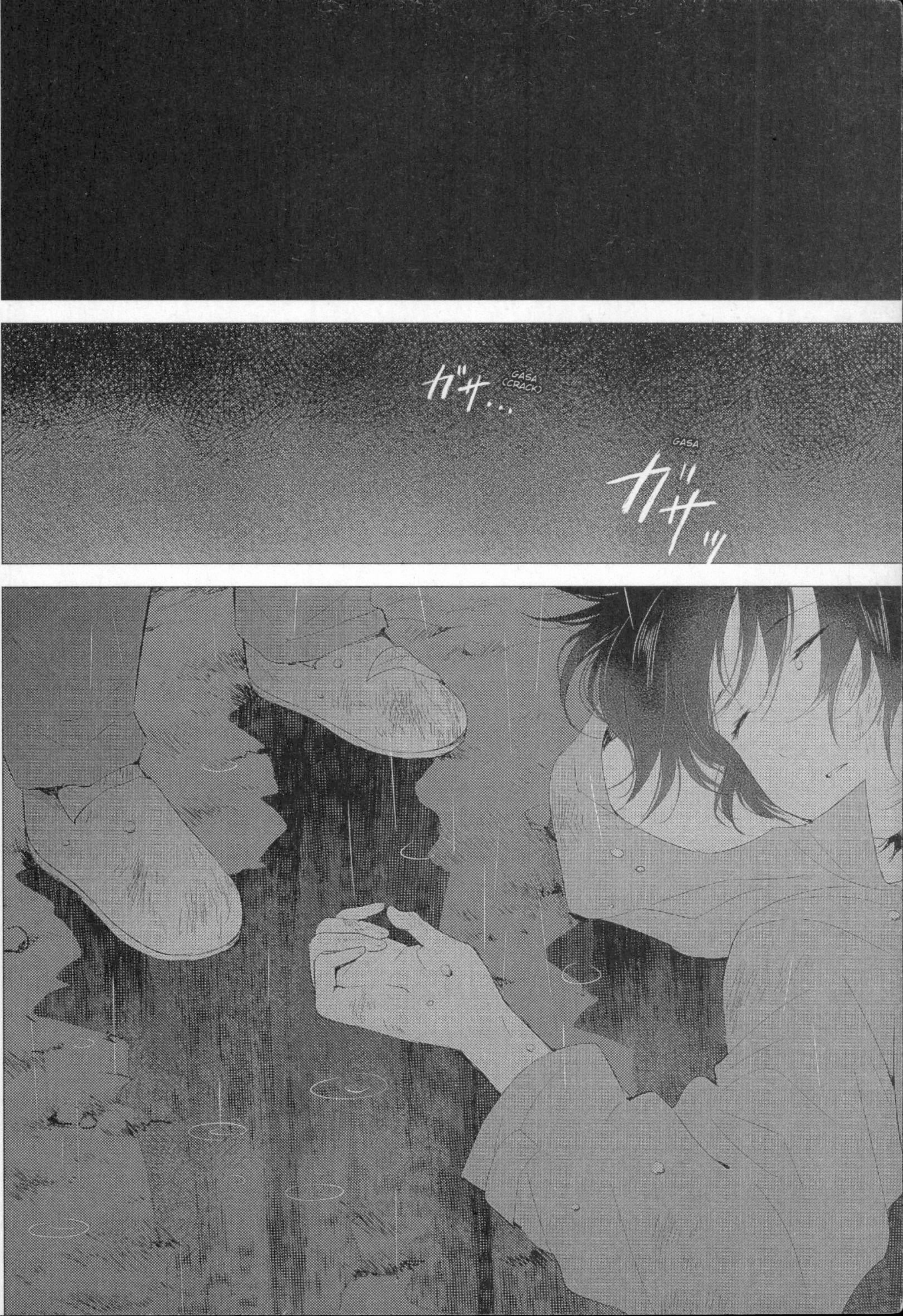
ガサ…
GASA (CRACK)
ガザッ
GASA

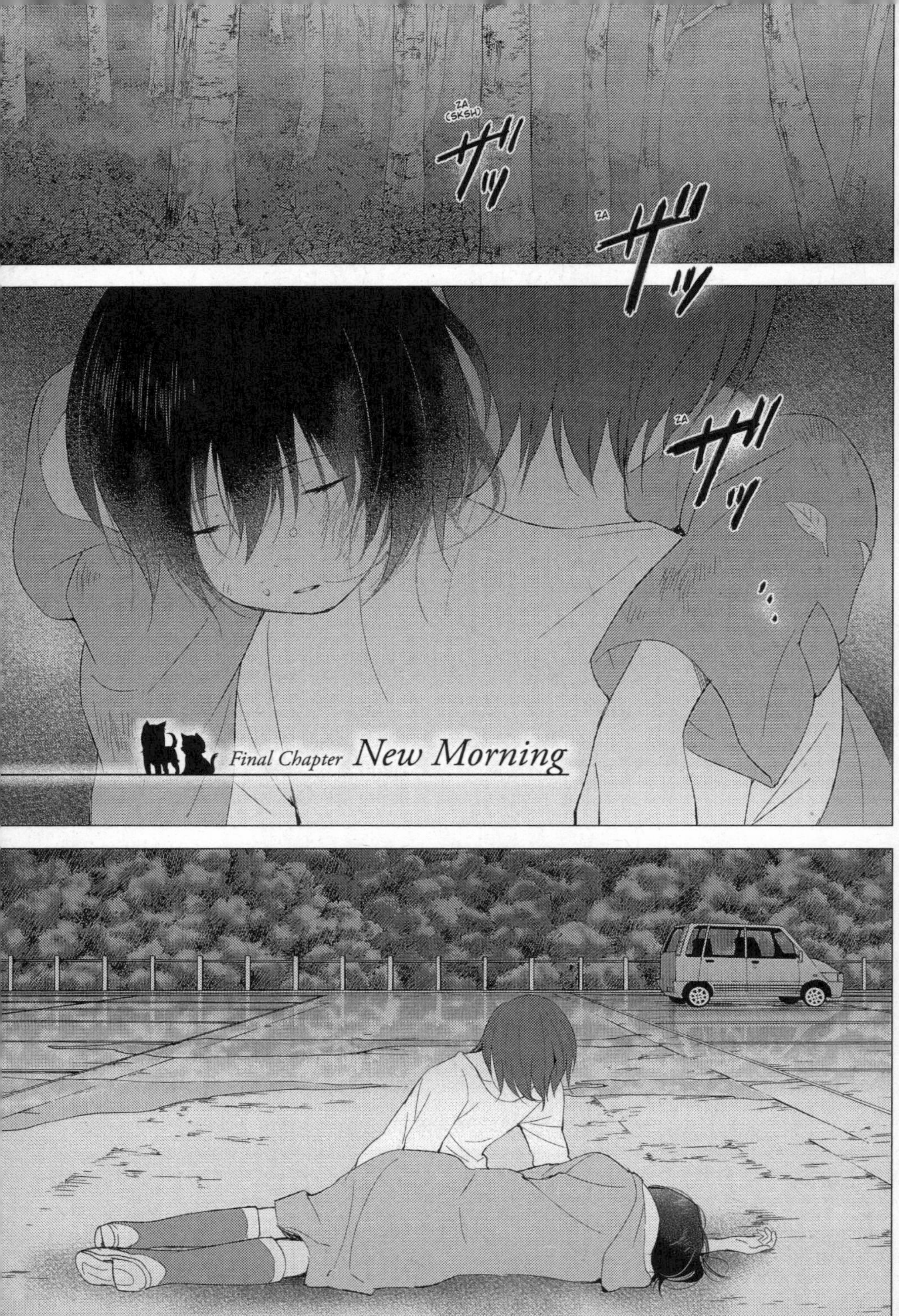
ZA (SKSH)
ザッ
ZA
ザッ
ZA
ザッ
...
Final Chapter New Morning

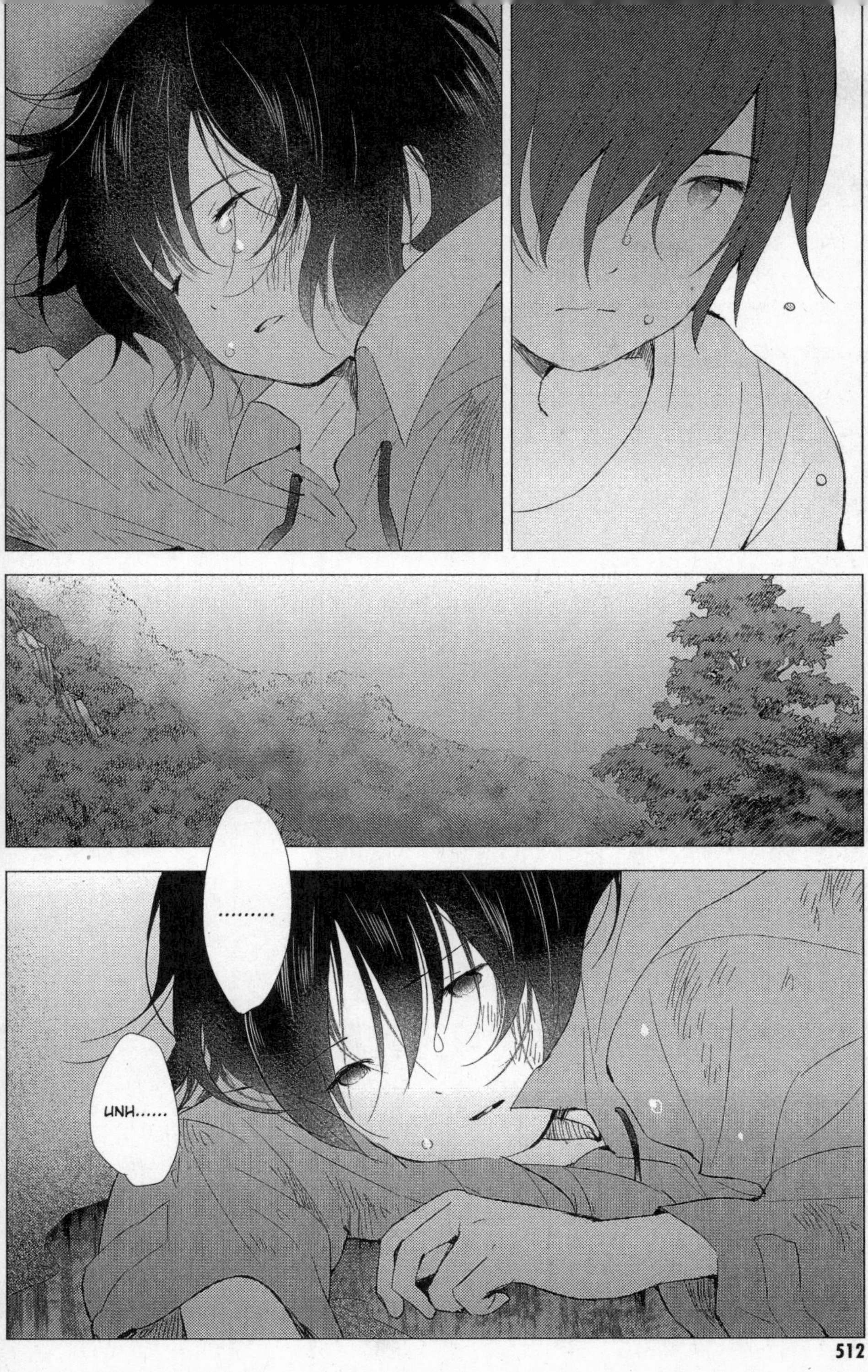
....
UNH......

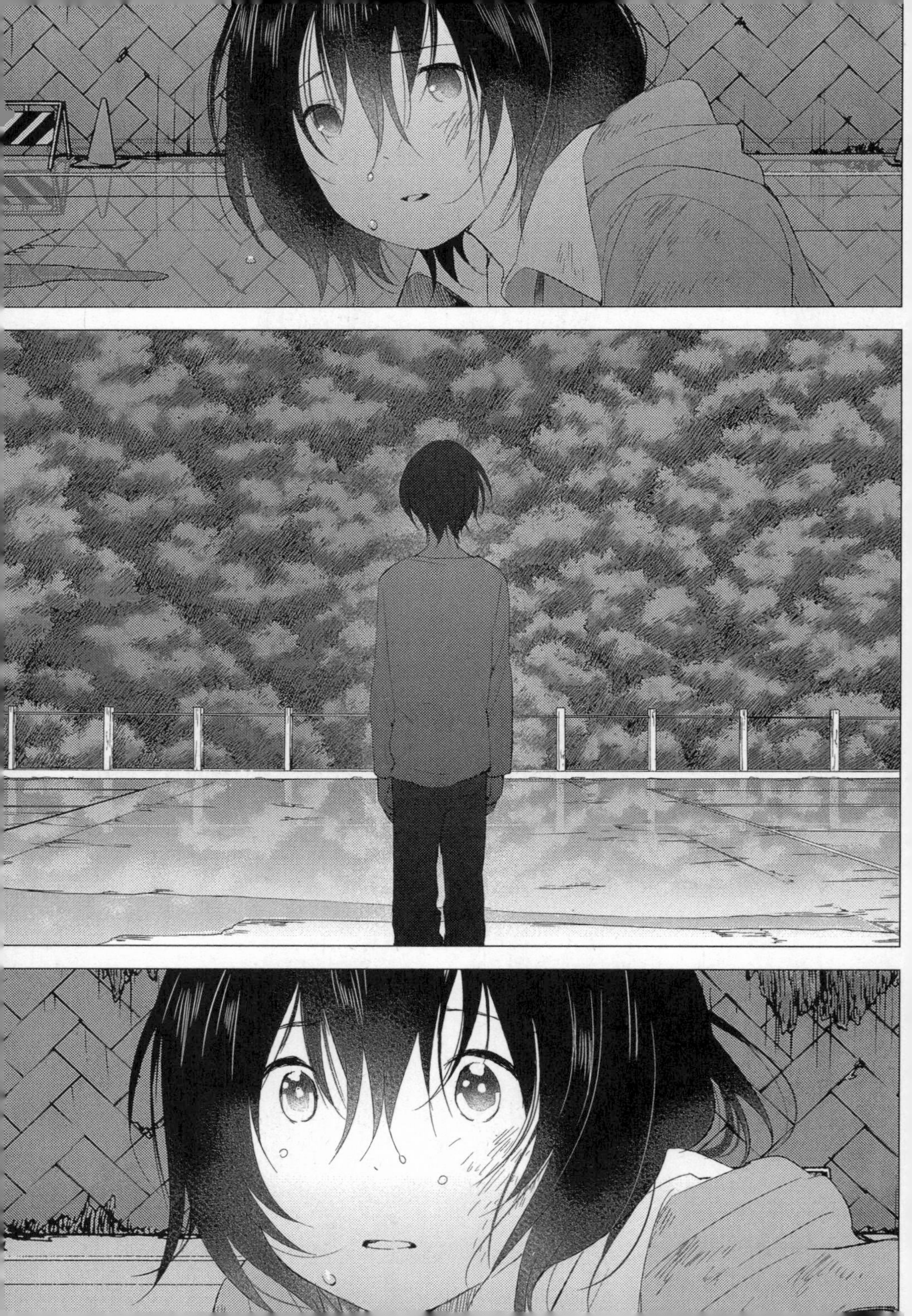

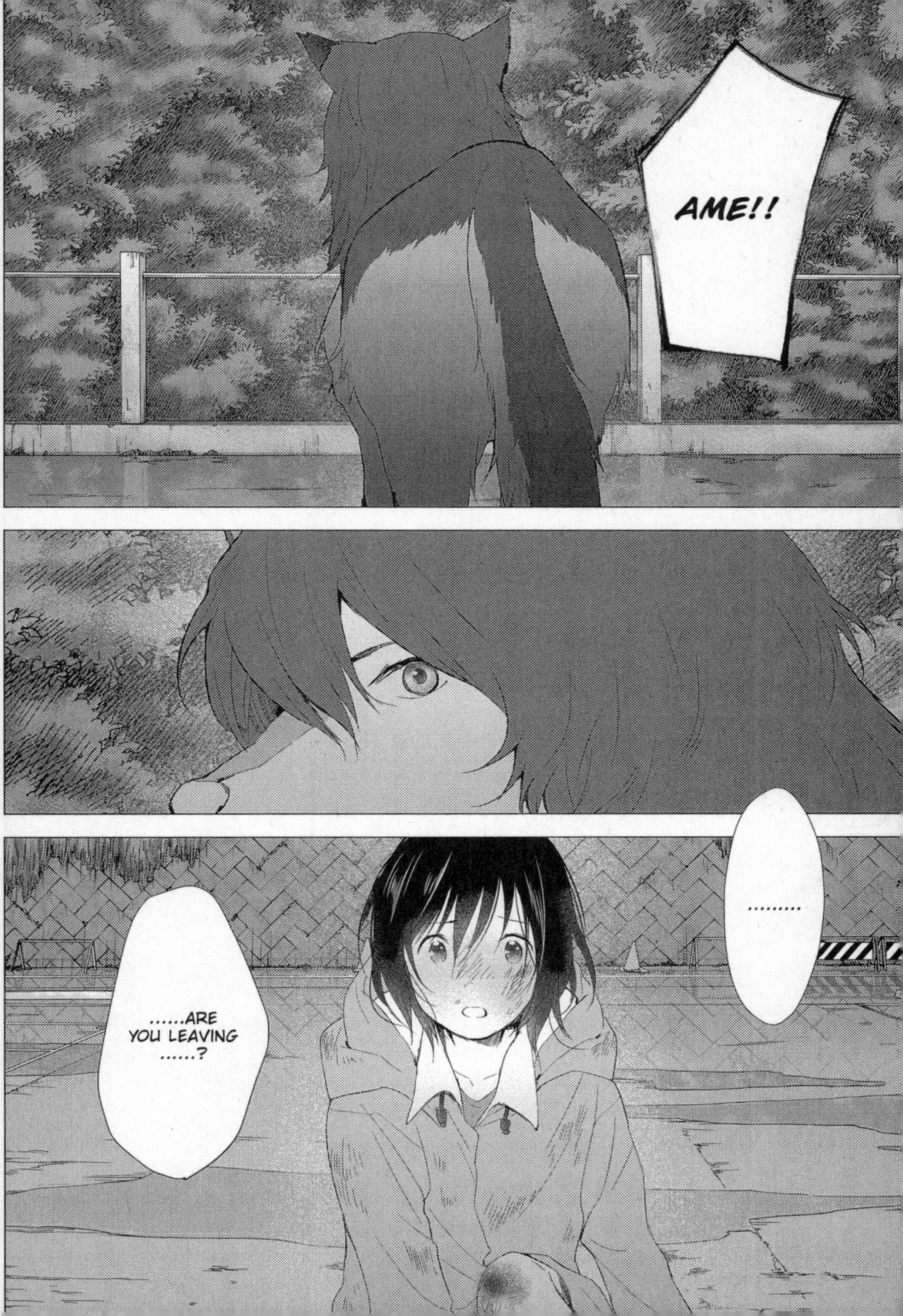
AME!!
....
......ARE YOU LEAVING ......?

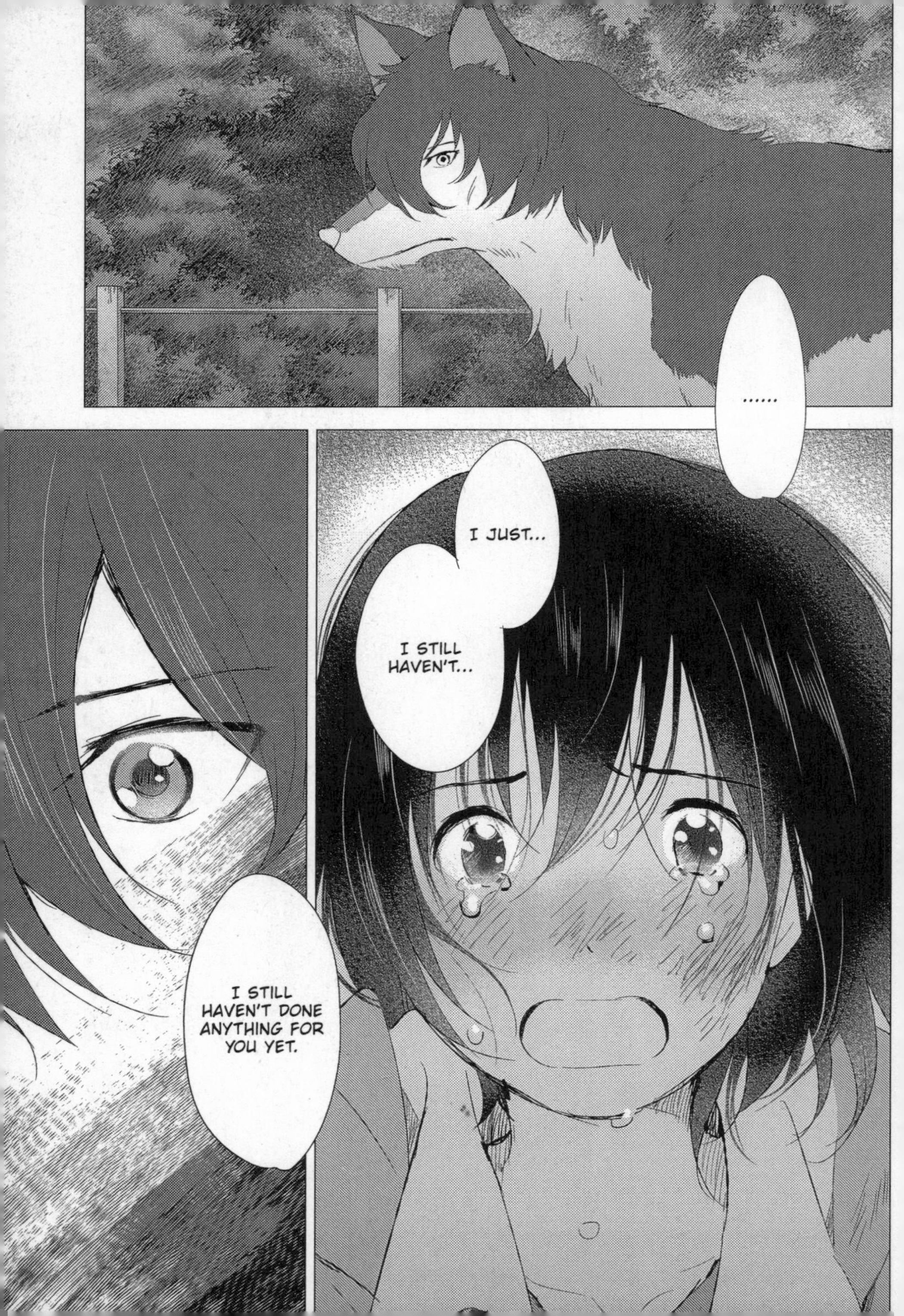
......
I JUST...
I STILL HAVEN'T...
I STILL HAVEN'T DONE ANYTHING FOR YOU YET.

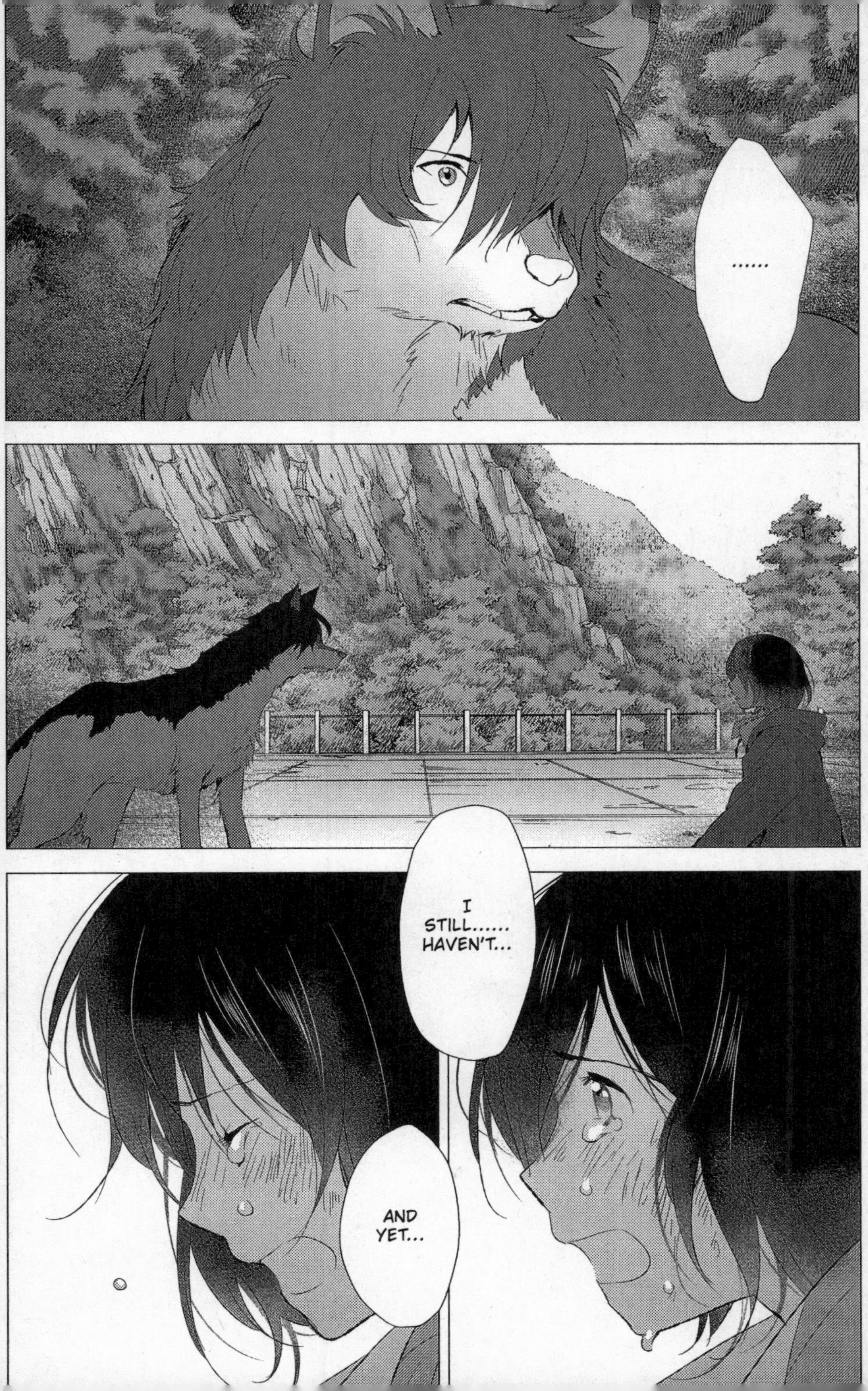
......
I STILL...... HAVEN'T...
AND YET...

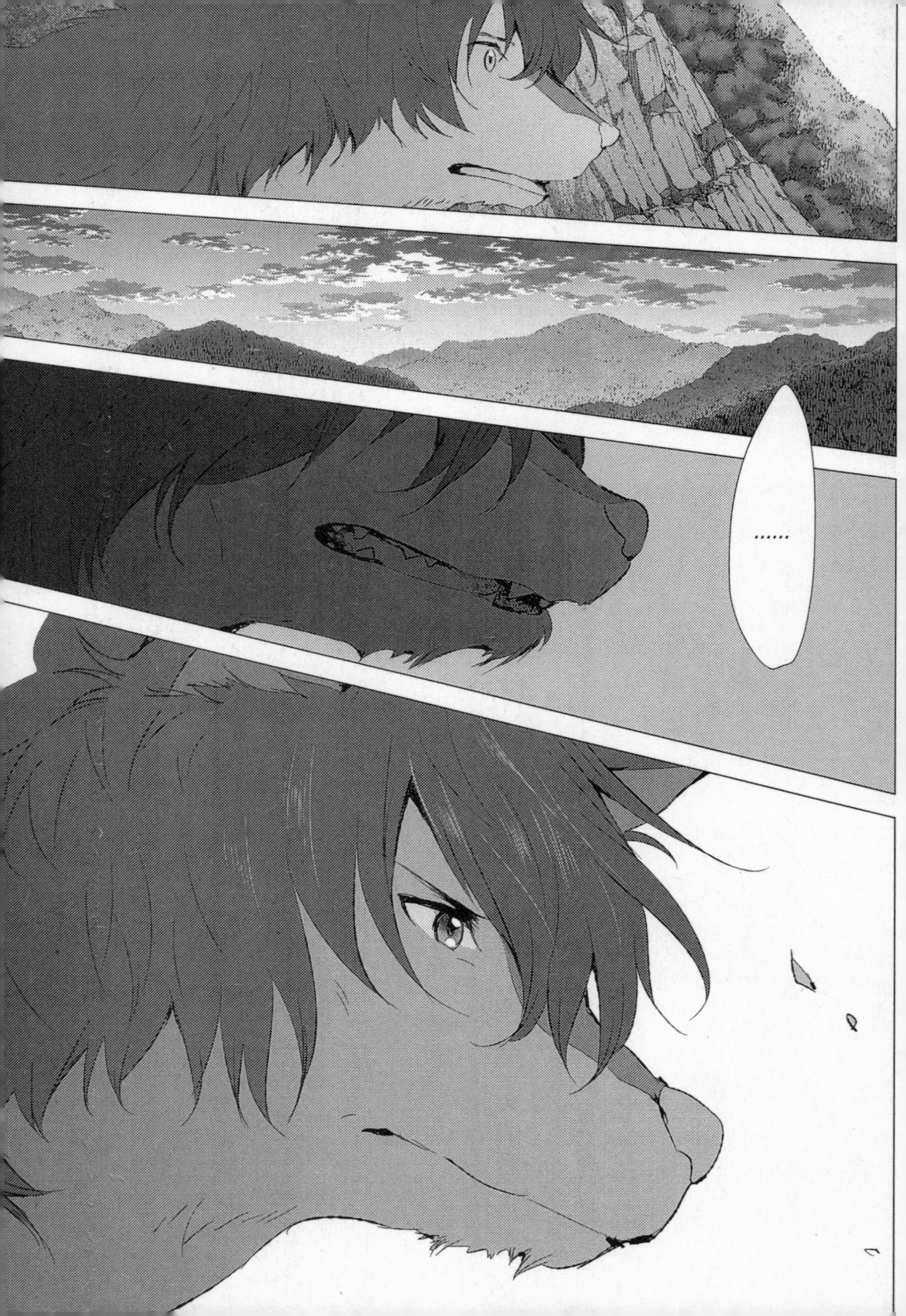
......

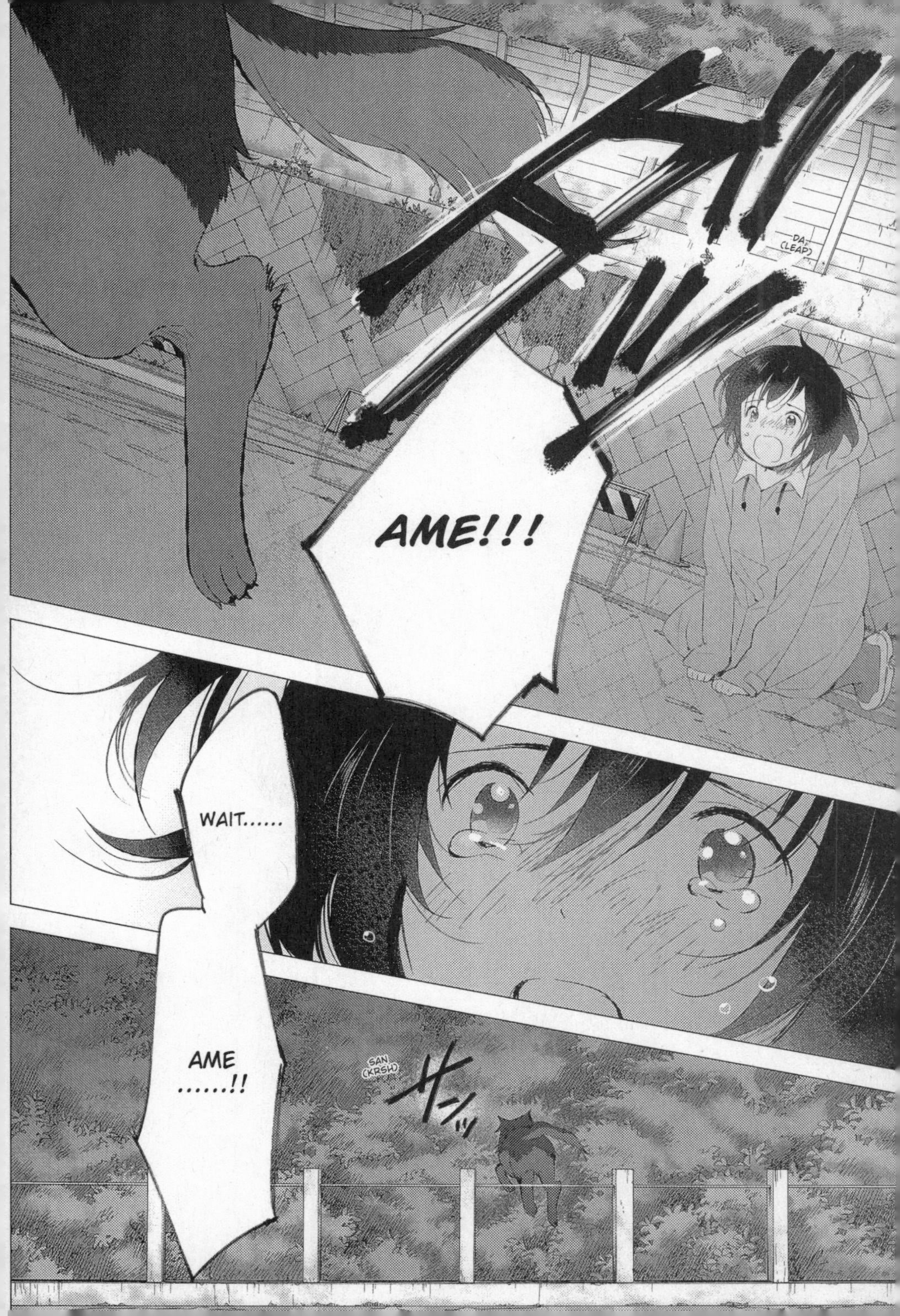
DA (LEAP)
AME!!!
WAIT......
AME
......!!
SAN (KRSH)

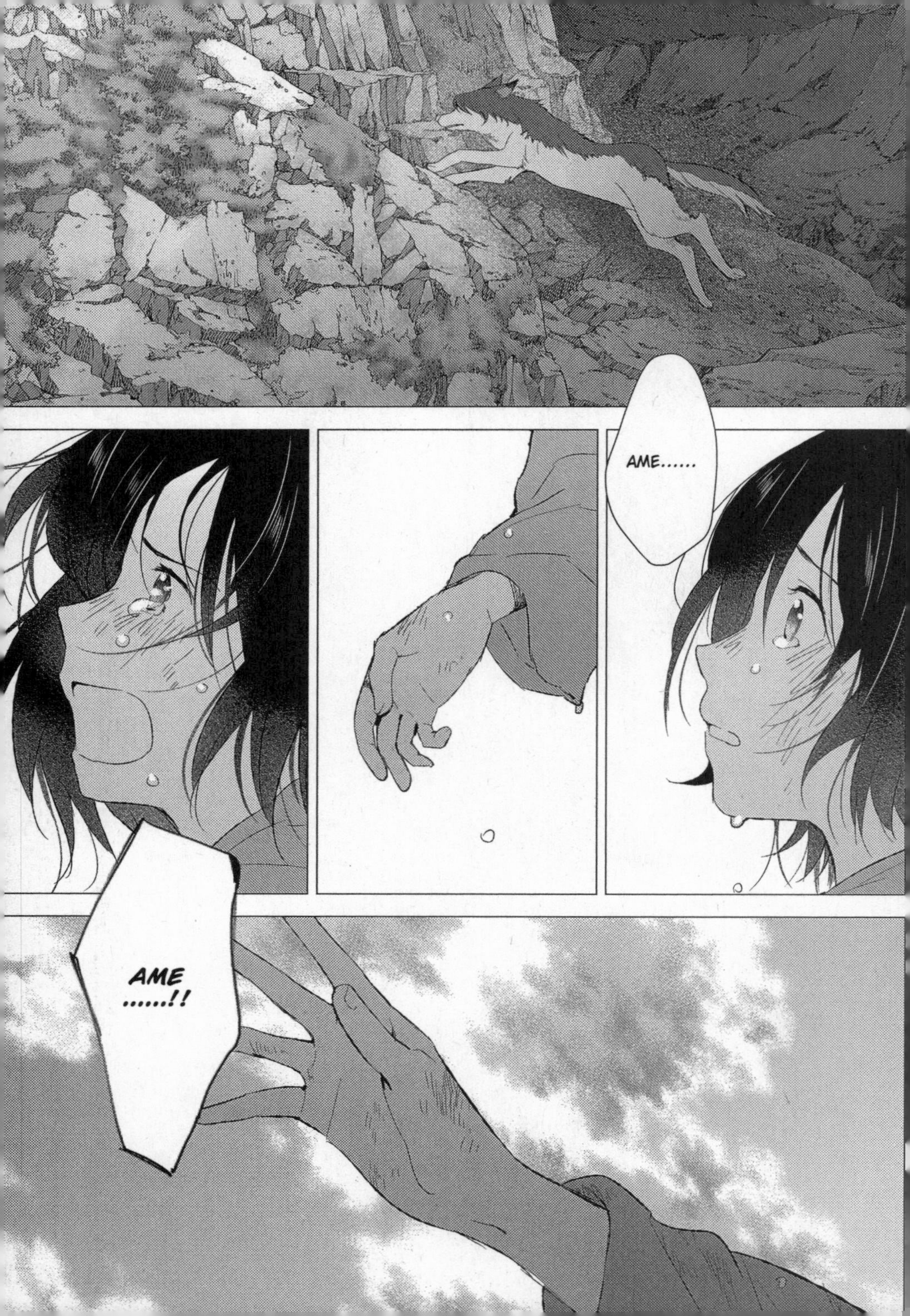
AME......
AME ......!!

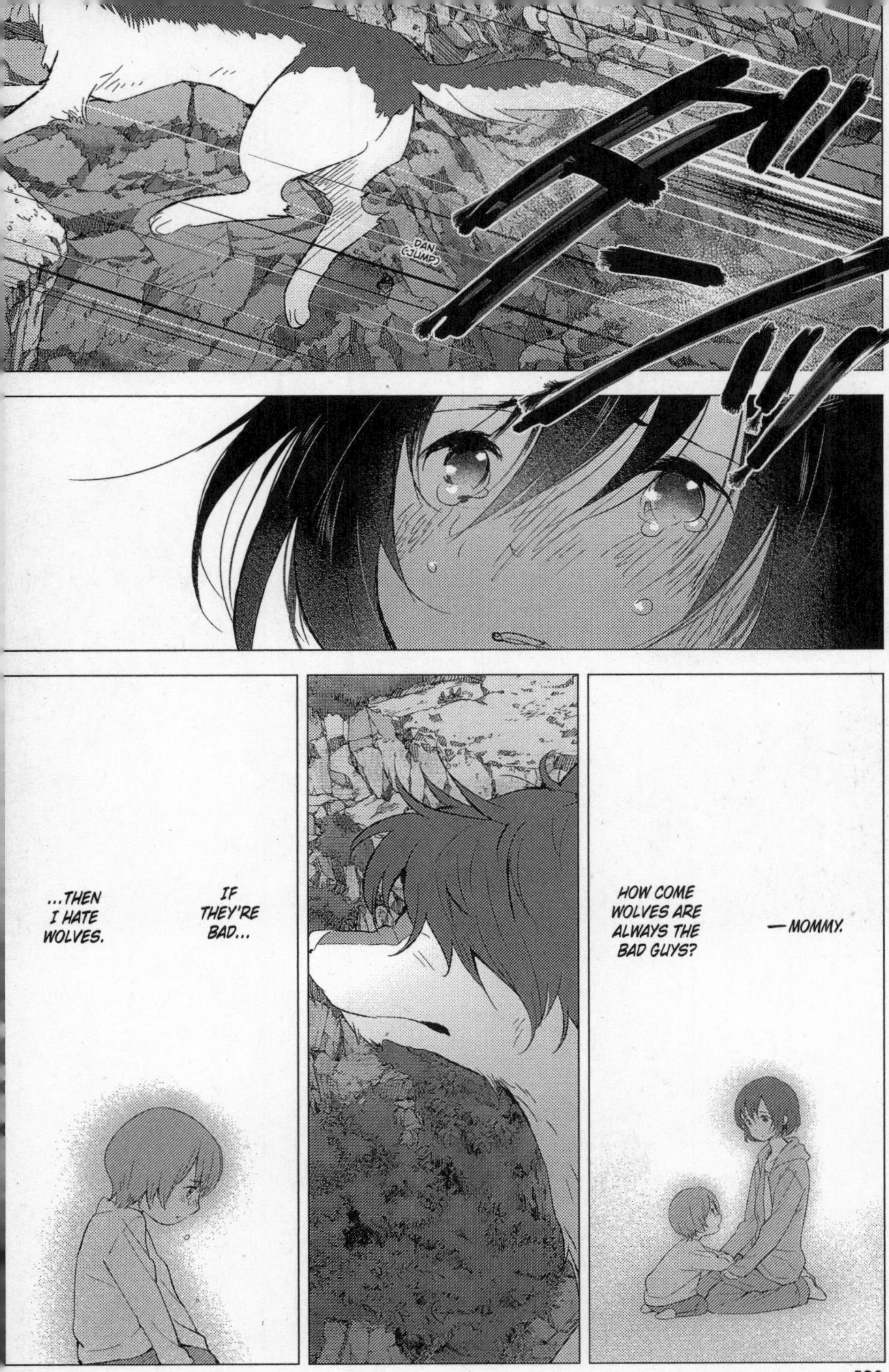
DAN (JUMP)
—MOMMY.
HOW COME WOLVES ARE ALWAYS THE BAD GUYS?
IF THEY'RE BAD...
...THEN I HATE WOLVES.

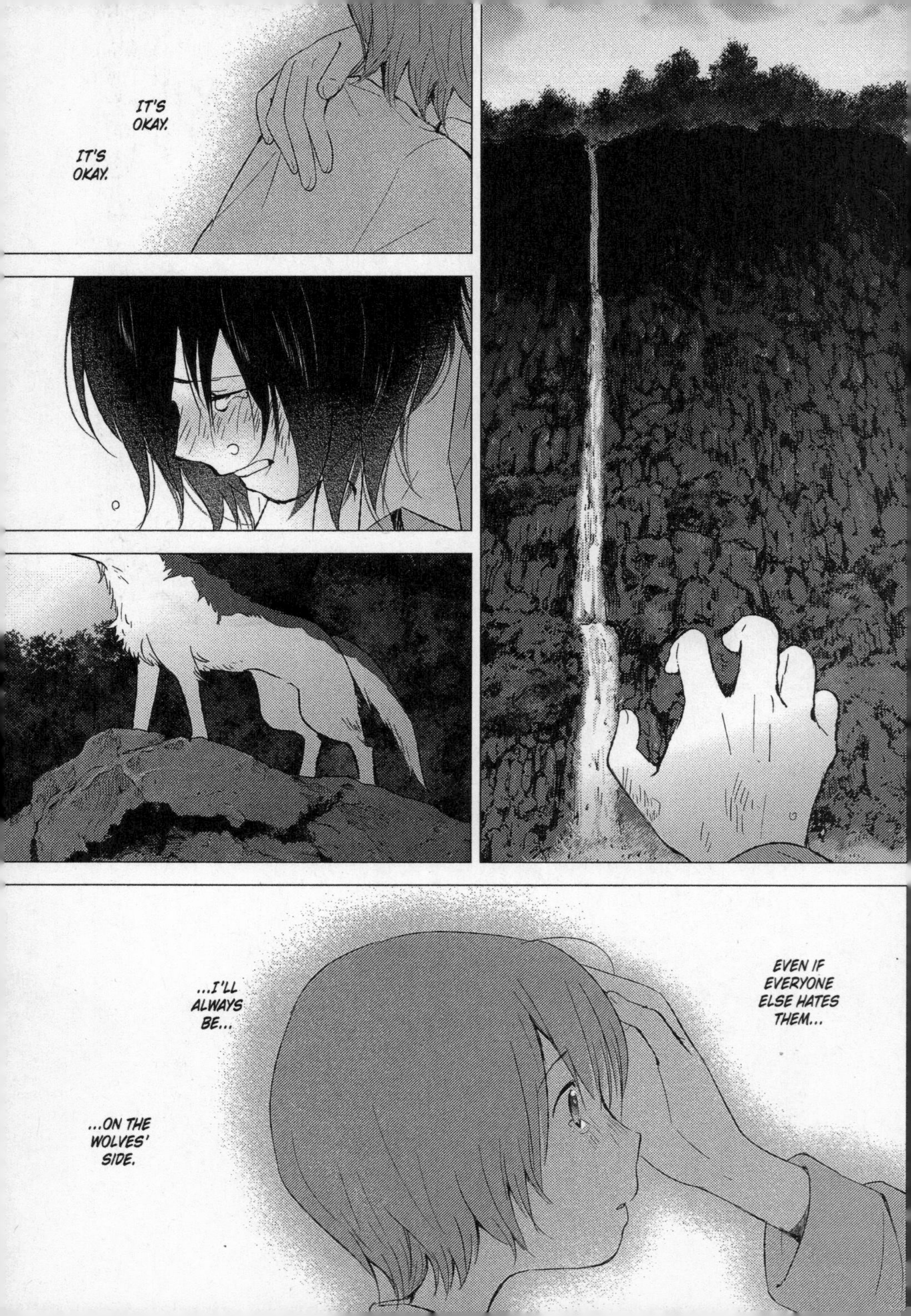
IT'S OKAY.
IT'S OKAY.
EVEN IF EVERYONE ELSE HATES THEM...
...I'LL ALWAYS BE...
...ON THE WOLVES' SIDE.

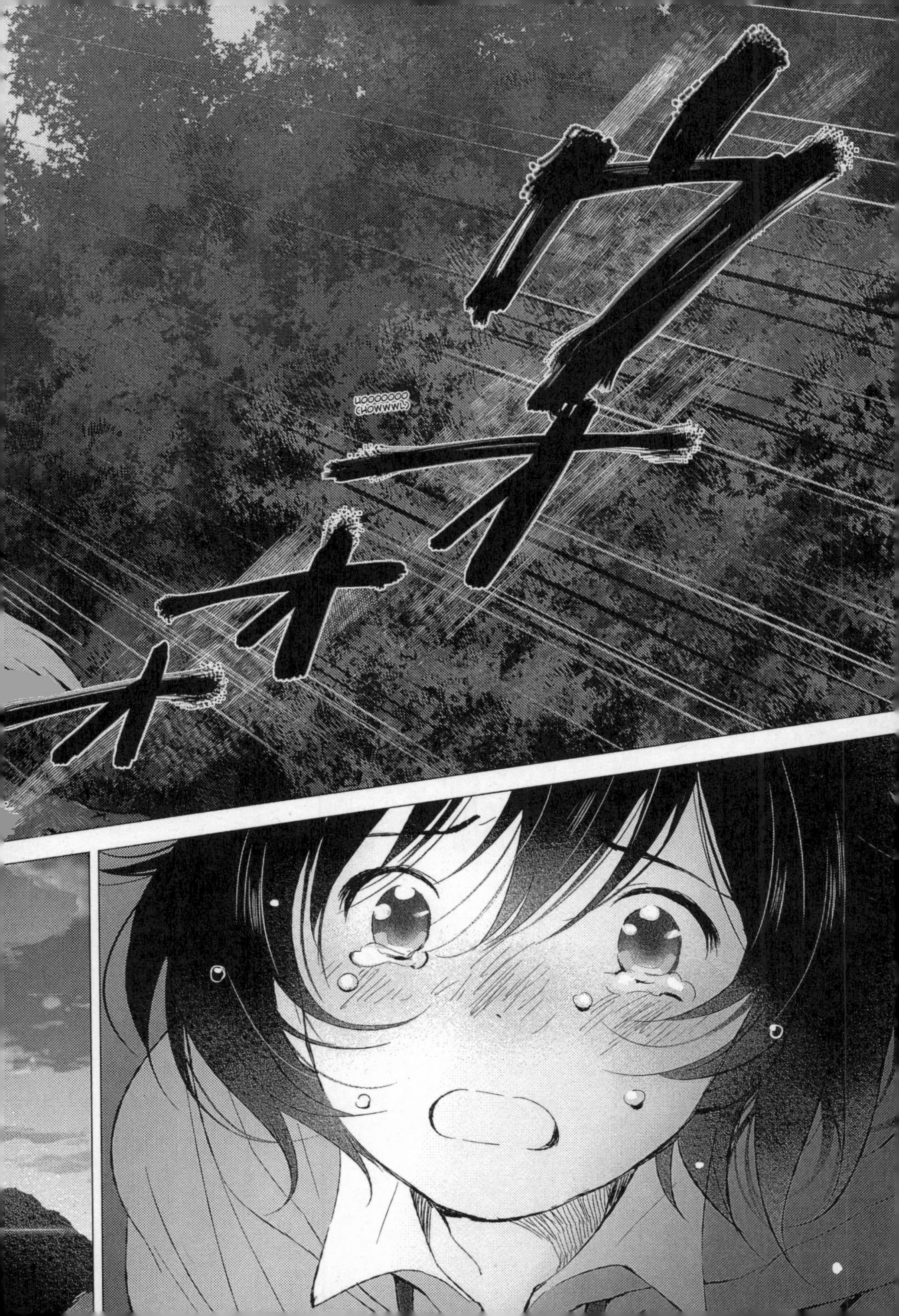
UOOOOOOO
(HOWWWL)

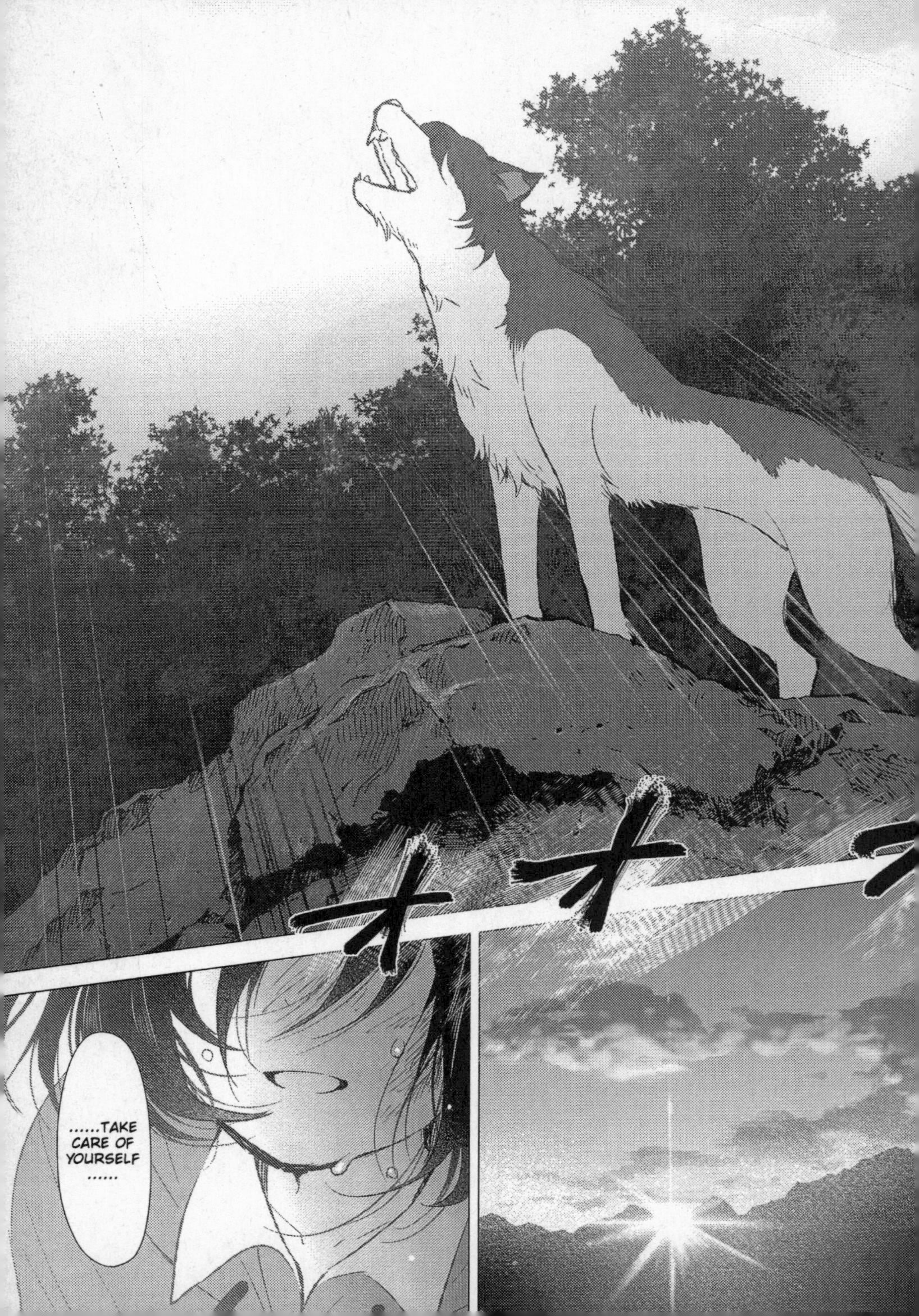
......TAKE CARE OF YOURSELF ......

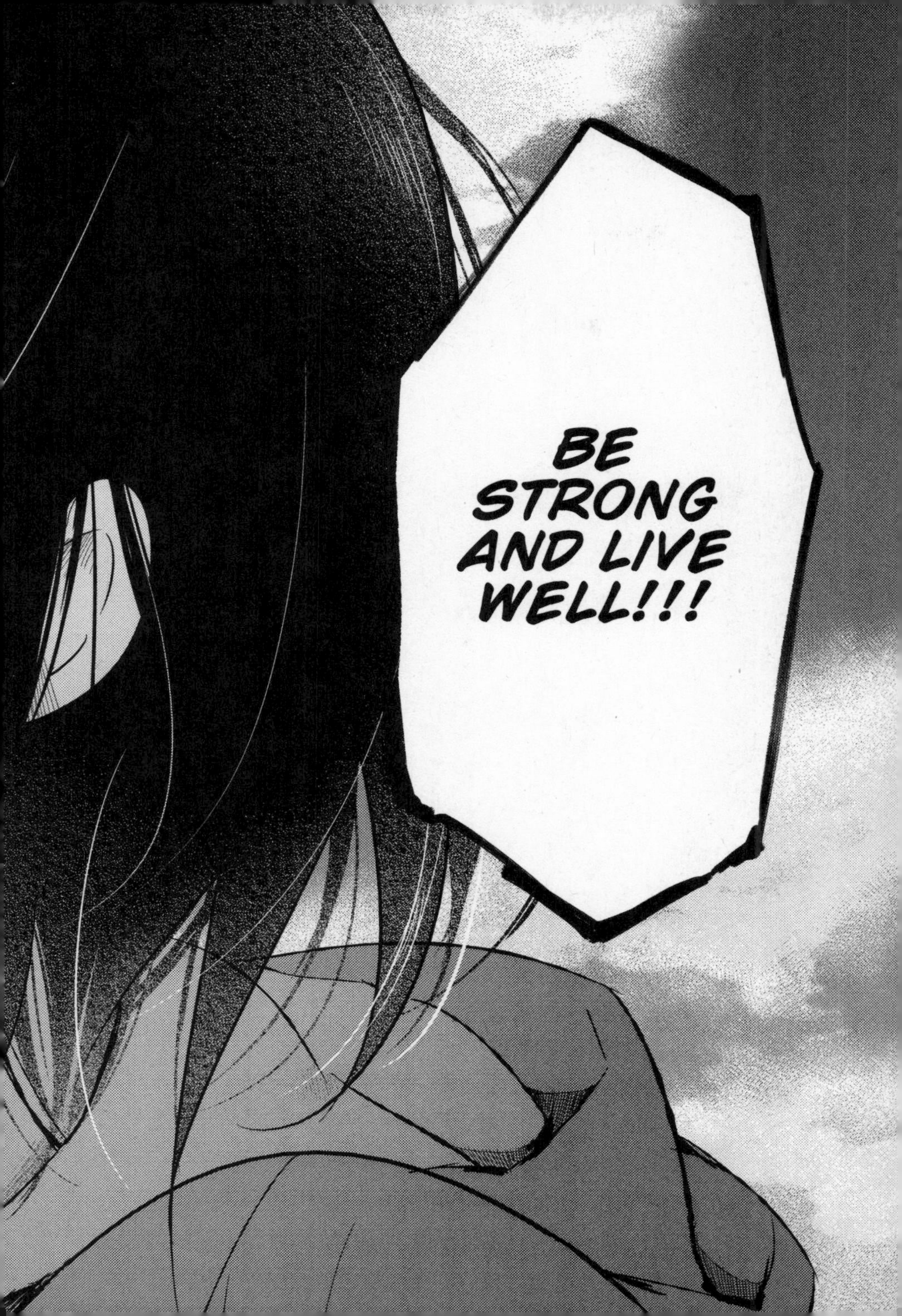
BE STRONG AND LIVE WELL!!!

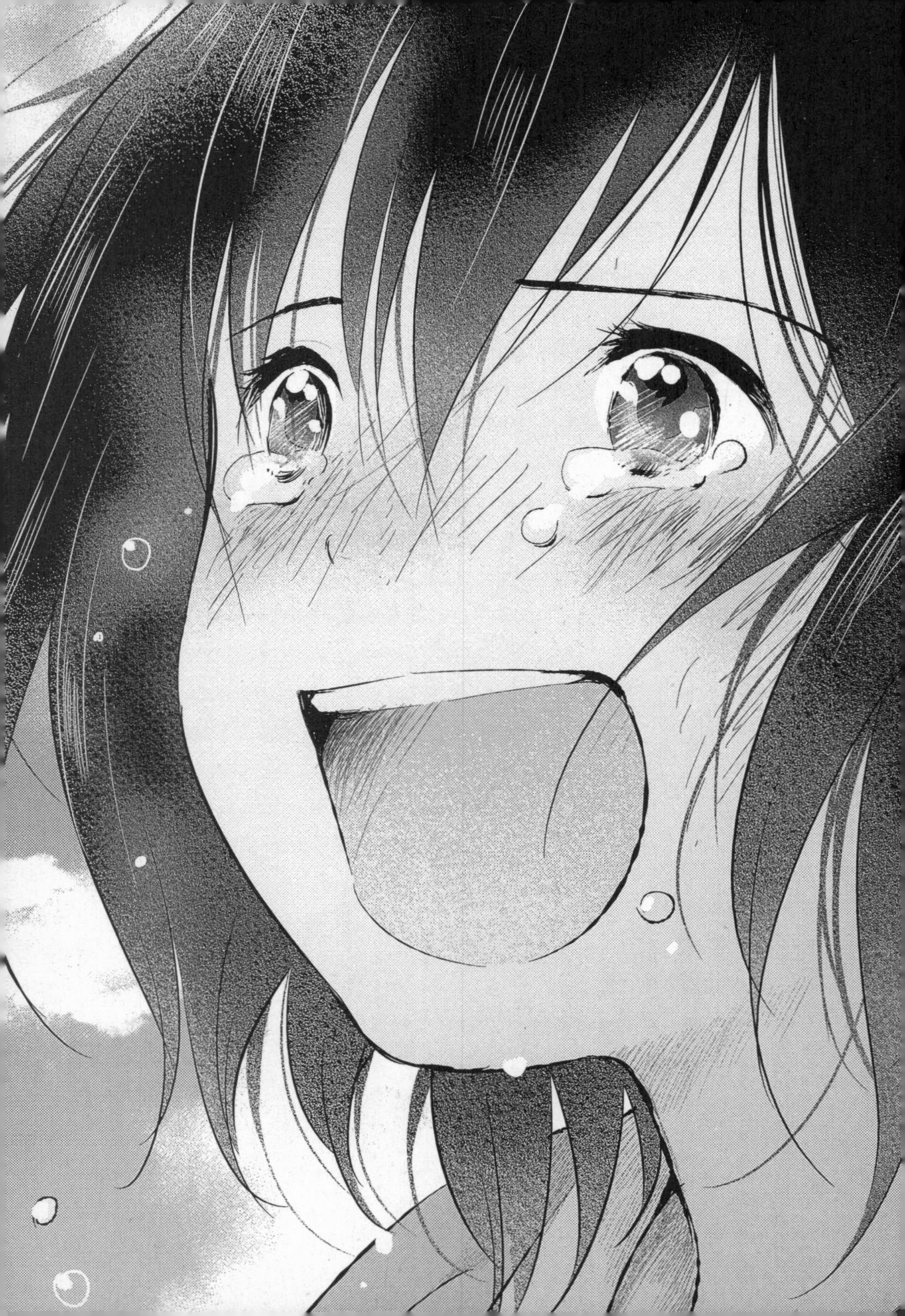

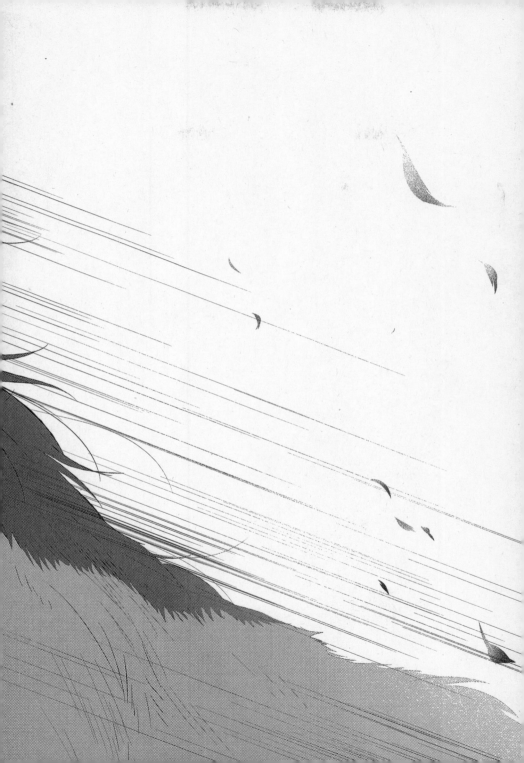

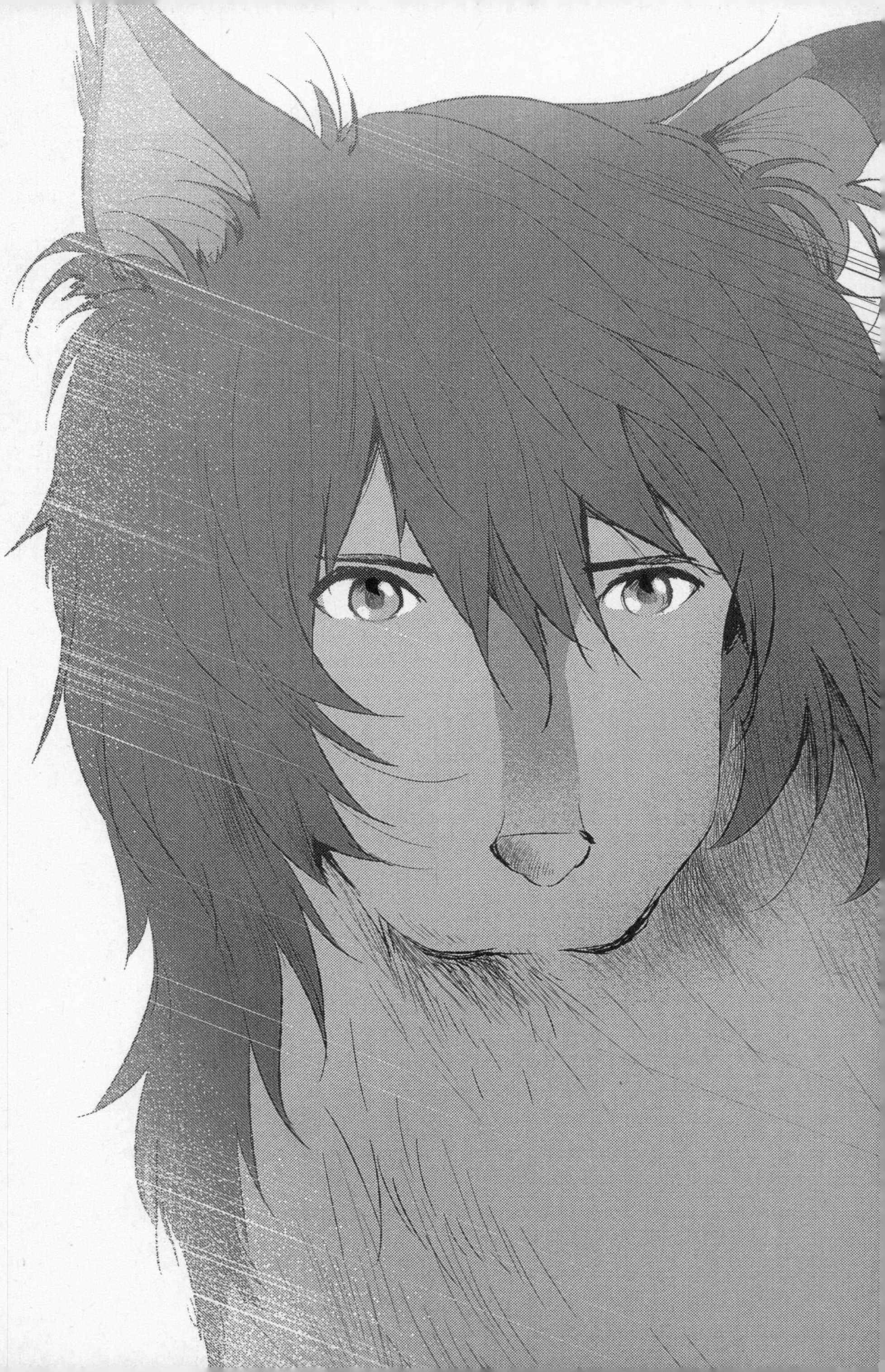

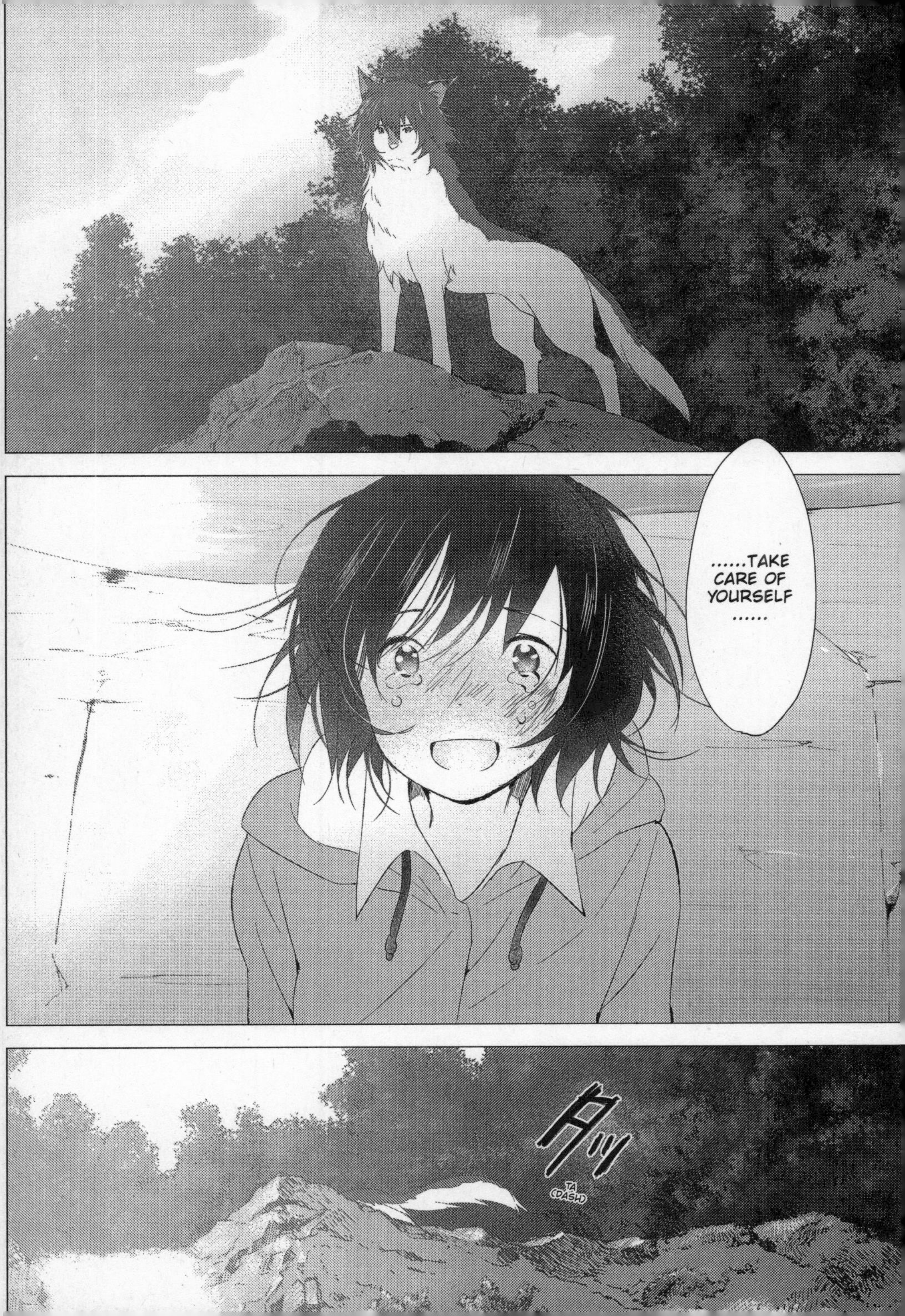
......TAKE CARE OF YOURSELF ......
TA (DASH)

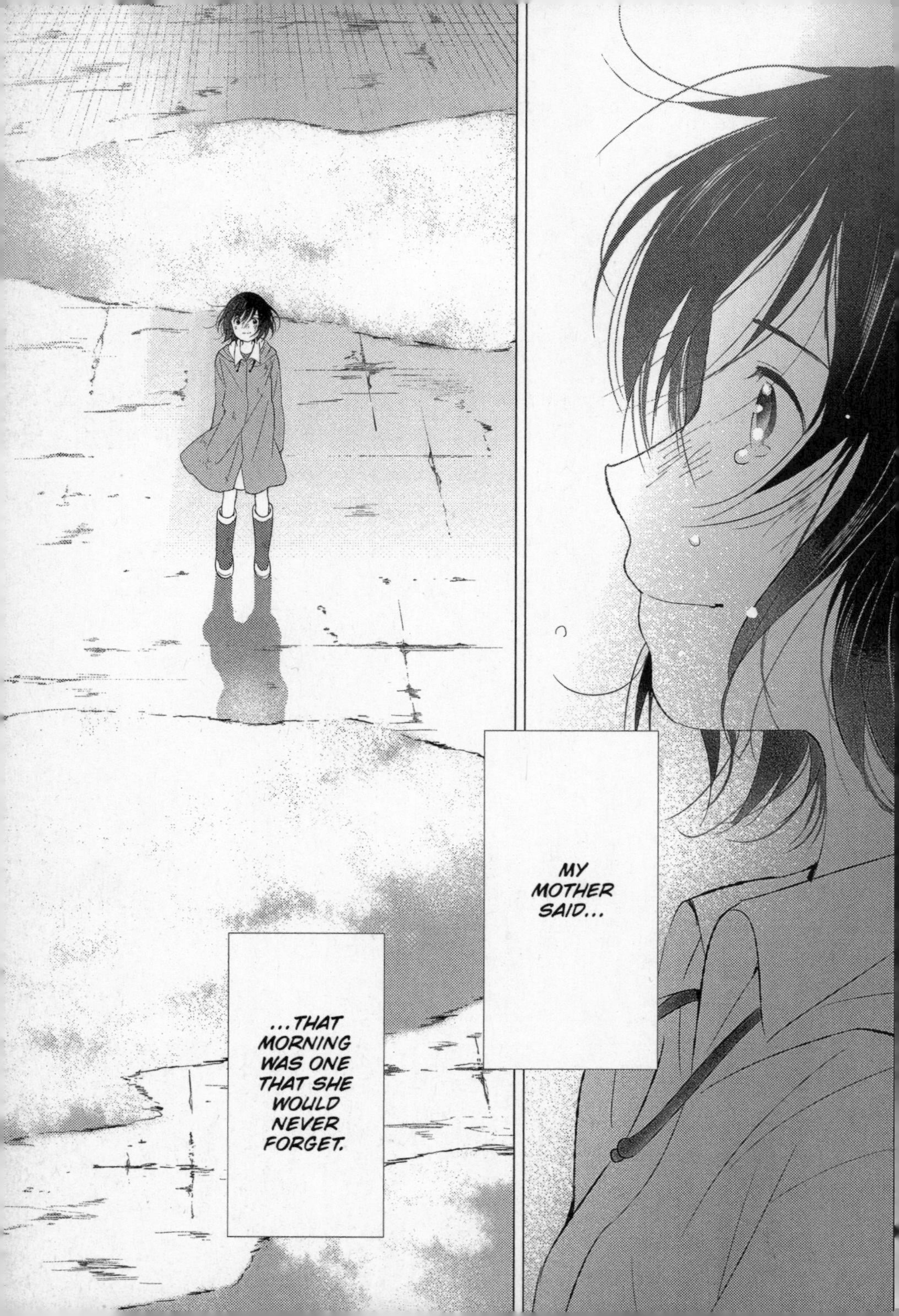
MY MOTHER SAID...
...THAT MORNING WAS ONE THAT SHE WOULD NEVER FORGET.

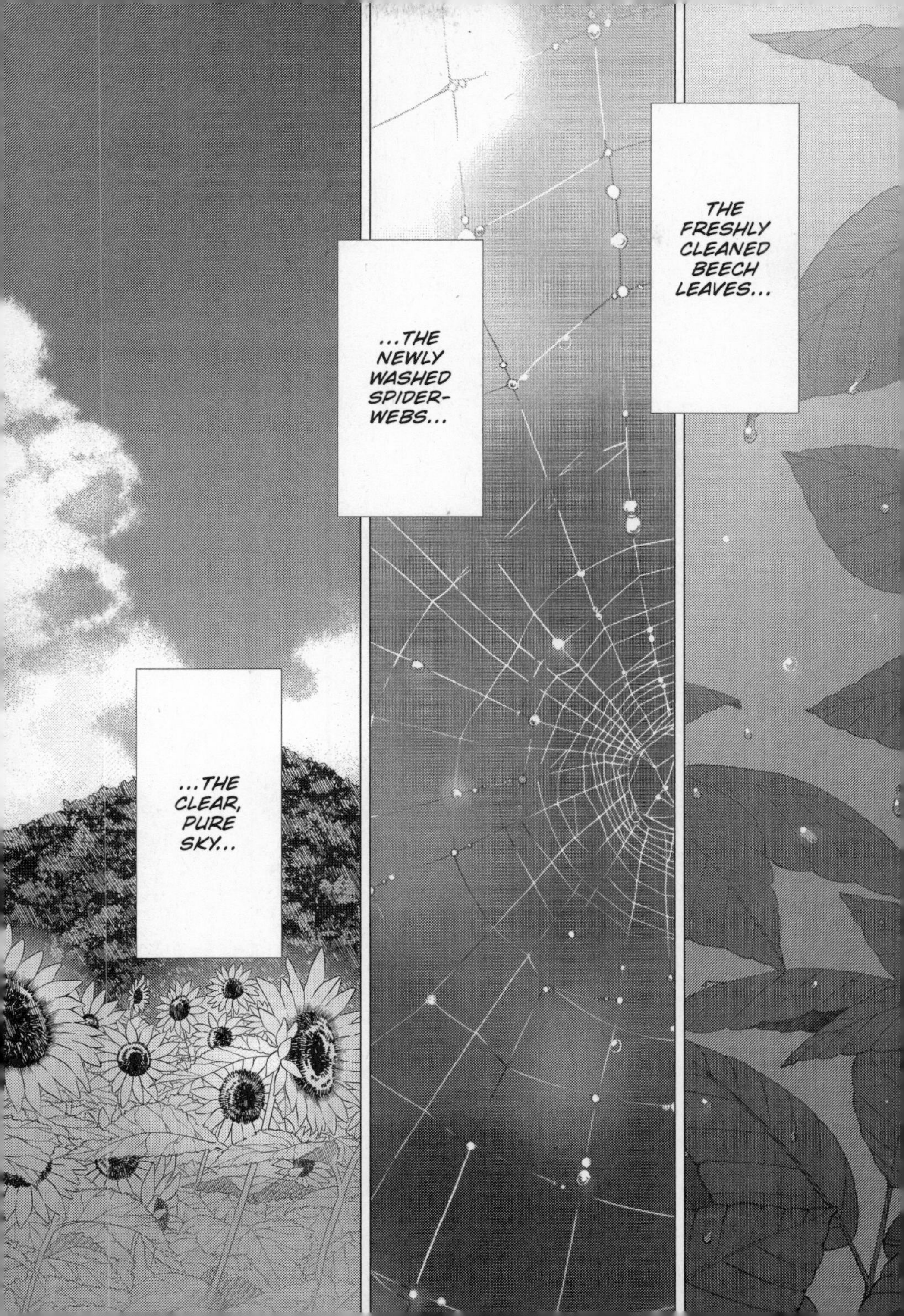
THE FRESHLY CLEANED BEECH LEAVES...
...THE NEWLY WASHED SPIDER-WEBS...
...THE CLEAR, PURE SKY...

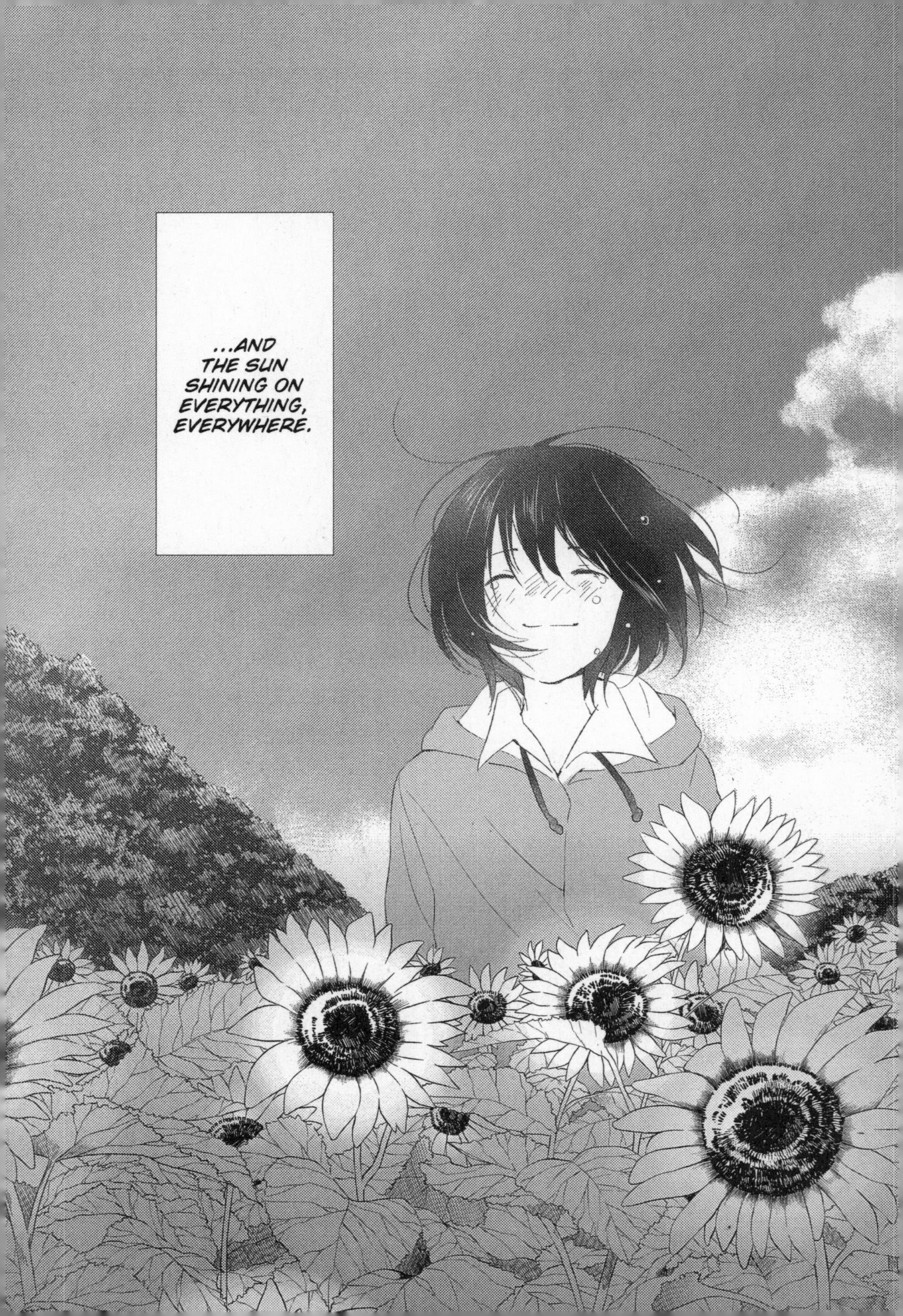
...AND THE SUN SHINING ON EVERYTHING, EVERYWHERE.

It was like the
whole world had
been reborn in a
single night...

...is what she
thought.

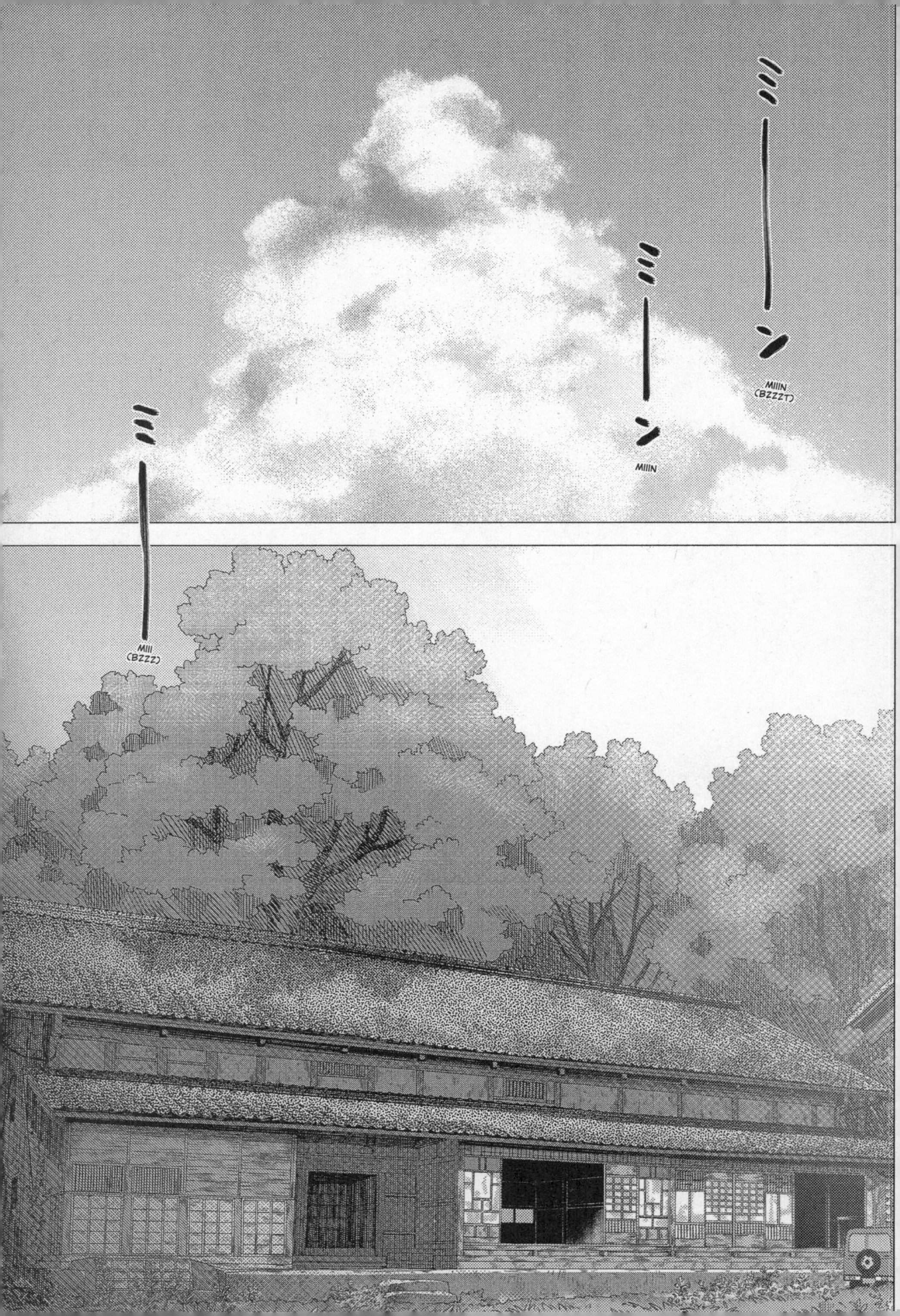
ミーーン
MIIIN (BZZZT)
ミーン
MIIIN
ミー
MIII (BZZZ)

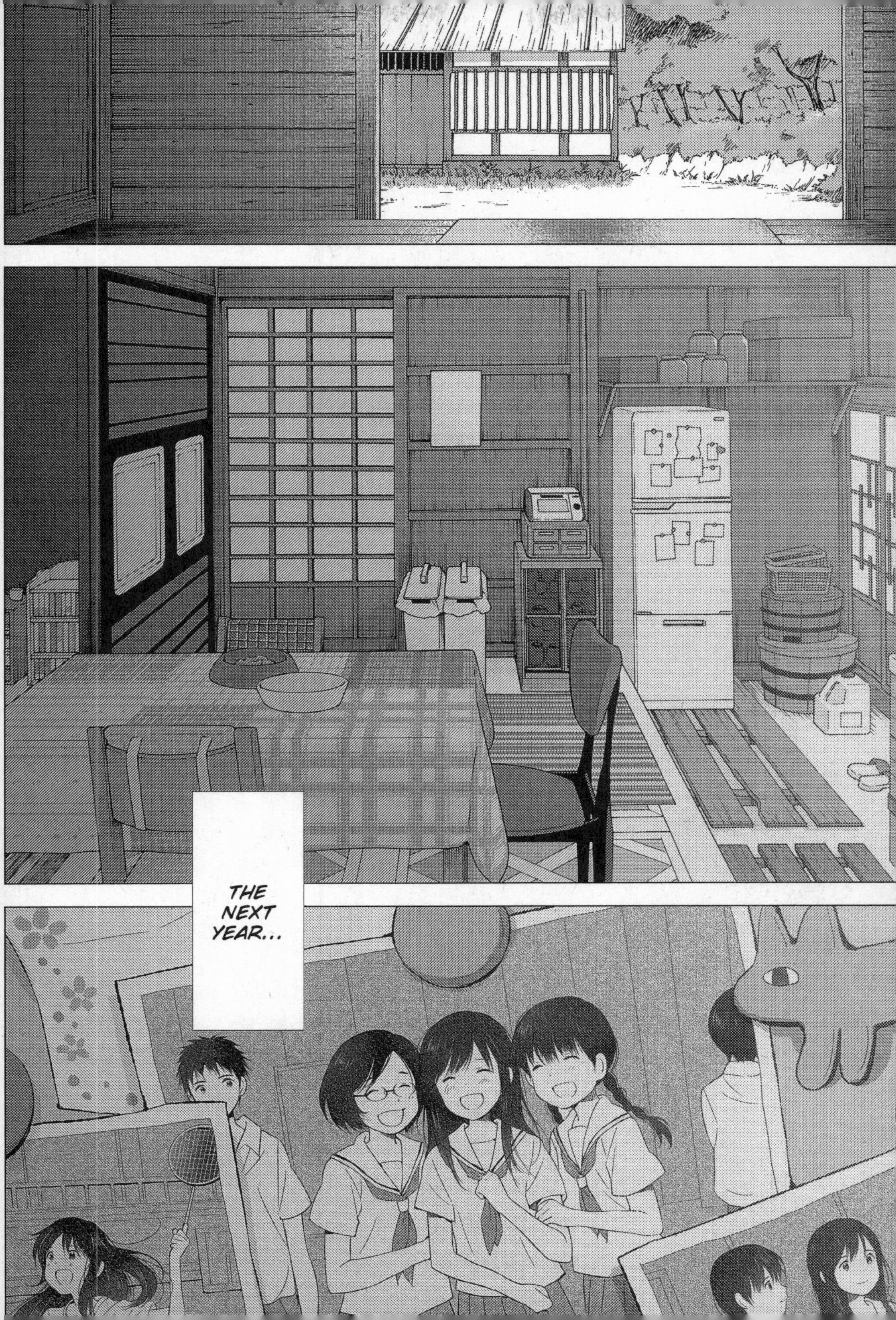
THE NEXT YEAR...

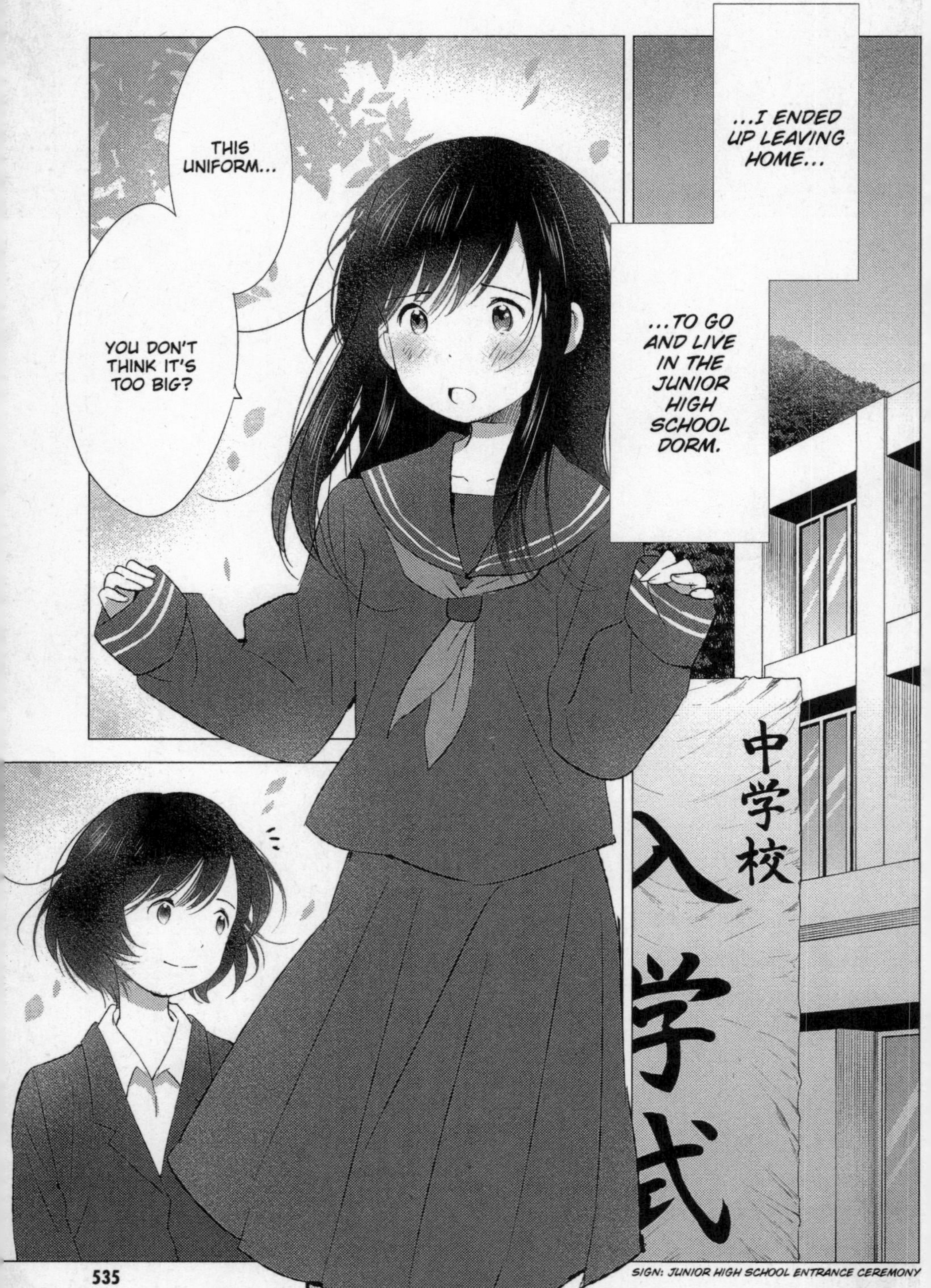
...I ENDED UP LEAVING HOME...
...TO GO AND LIVE IN THE JUNIOR HIGH SCHOOL DORM.
THIS UNIFORM...
YOU DON'T THINK IT'S TOO BIG?
中学校
入学式

SIGN: JUNIOR HIGH SCHOOL ENTRANCE CEREMONY

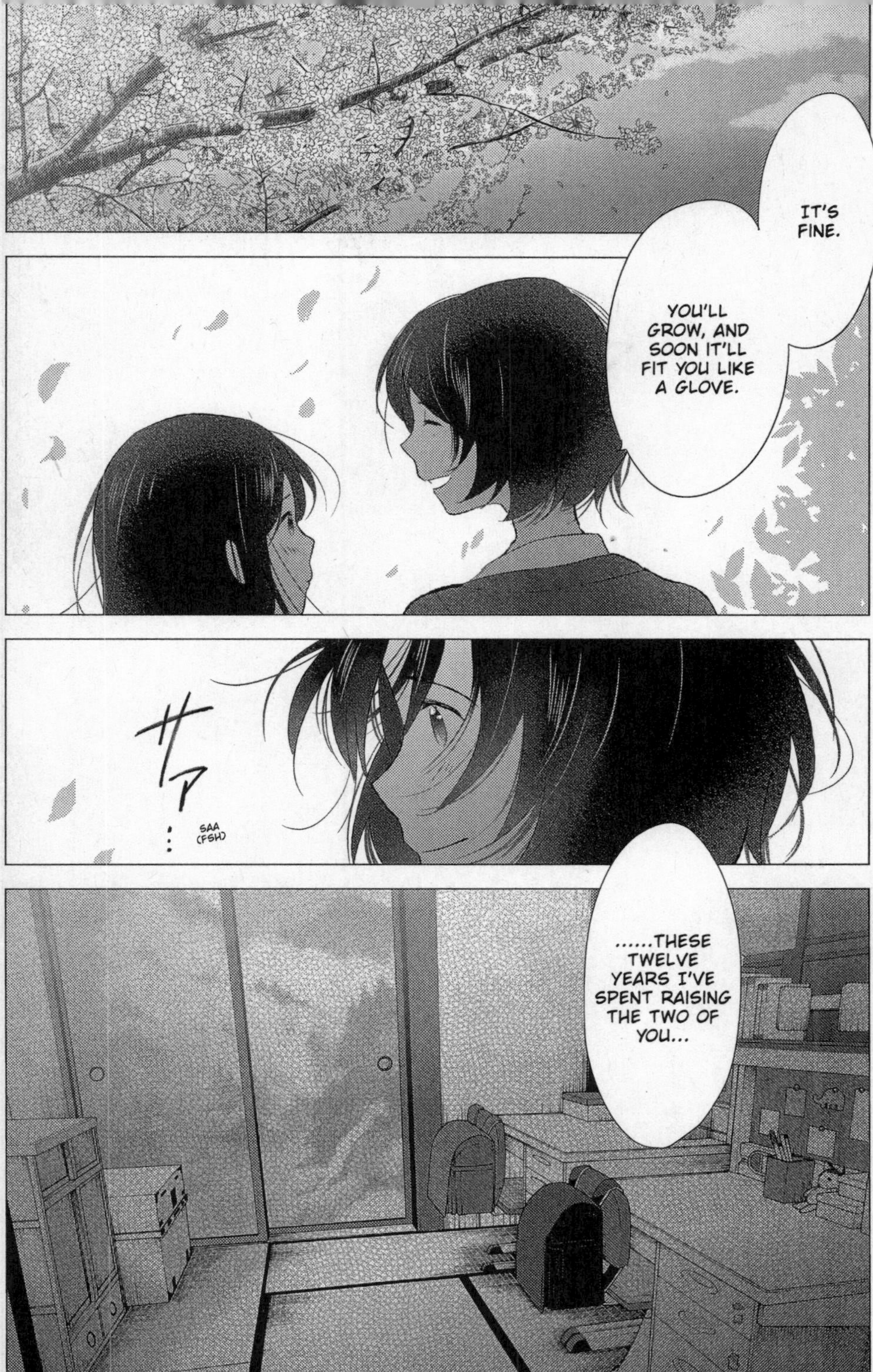
IT'S FINE.
YOU'LL GROW, AND SOON IT'LL FIT YOU LIKE A GLOVE.
サァ
SAA (FSH)
......THESE TWELVE YEARS I'VE SPENT RAISING THE TWO OF YOU...

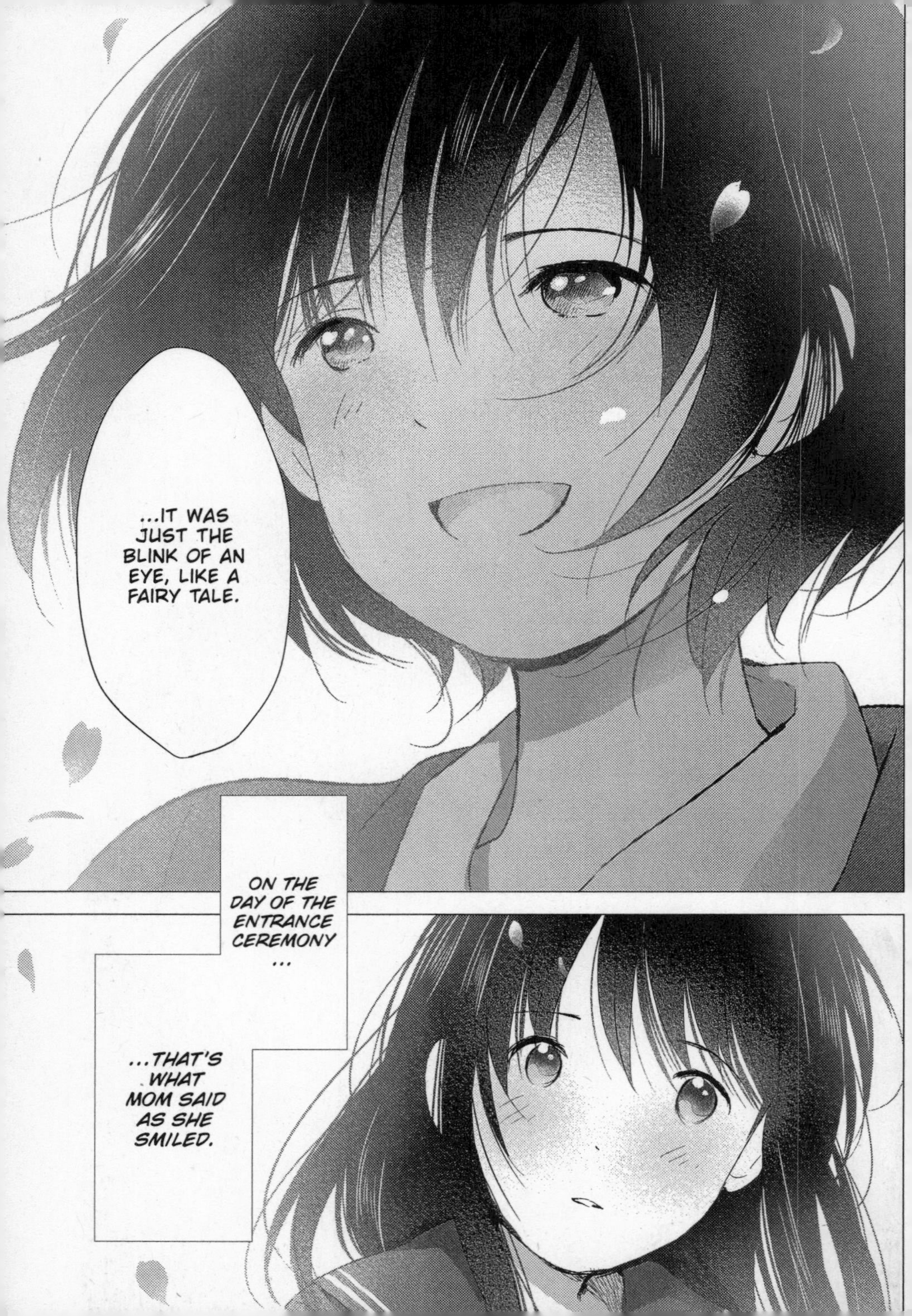
...IT WAS JUST THE BLINK OF AN EYE, LIKE A FAIRY TALE.
ON THE DAY OF THE ENTRANCE CEREMONY ...
...THAT'S WHAT MOM SAID AS SHE SMILED.

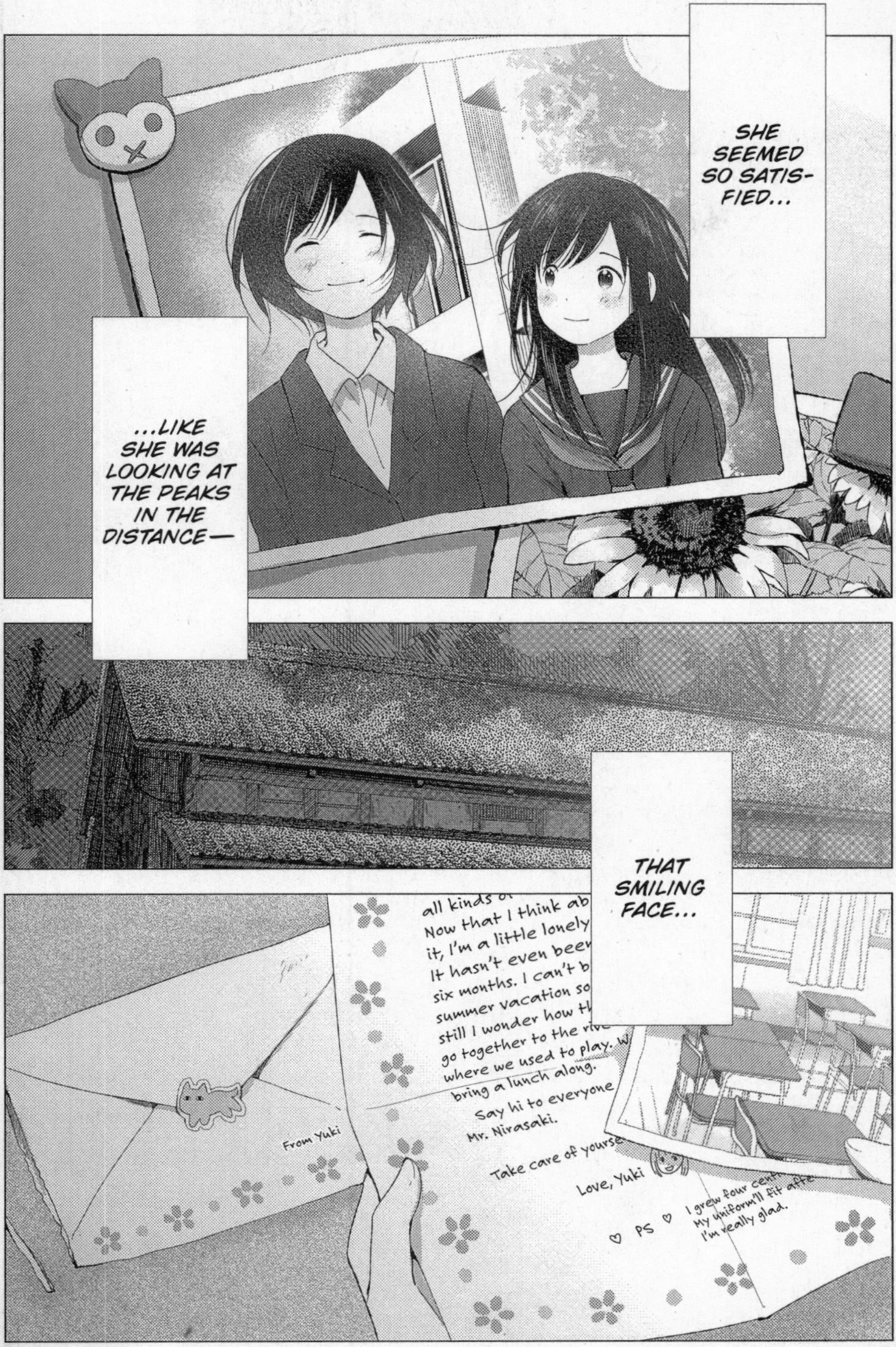
SHE SEEMED SO SATIS-FIED...
...LIKE SHE WAS LOOKING AT THE PEAKS IN THE DISTANCE—
THAT SMILING FACE...
Now that I think ab
it, I'm a little lonely
It hasn't even been
six months. I can't b
summer vacation so
still I wonder how th
go together to the rive
where we used to play.
bring a lunch along.
Say hi to everyone
Mr. Nirasaki.
Take care of yourse
Love, Yuki
PS
I grew four cent
My uniform'll fit afte
I'm really glad.
From Yuki

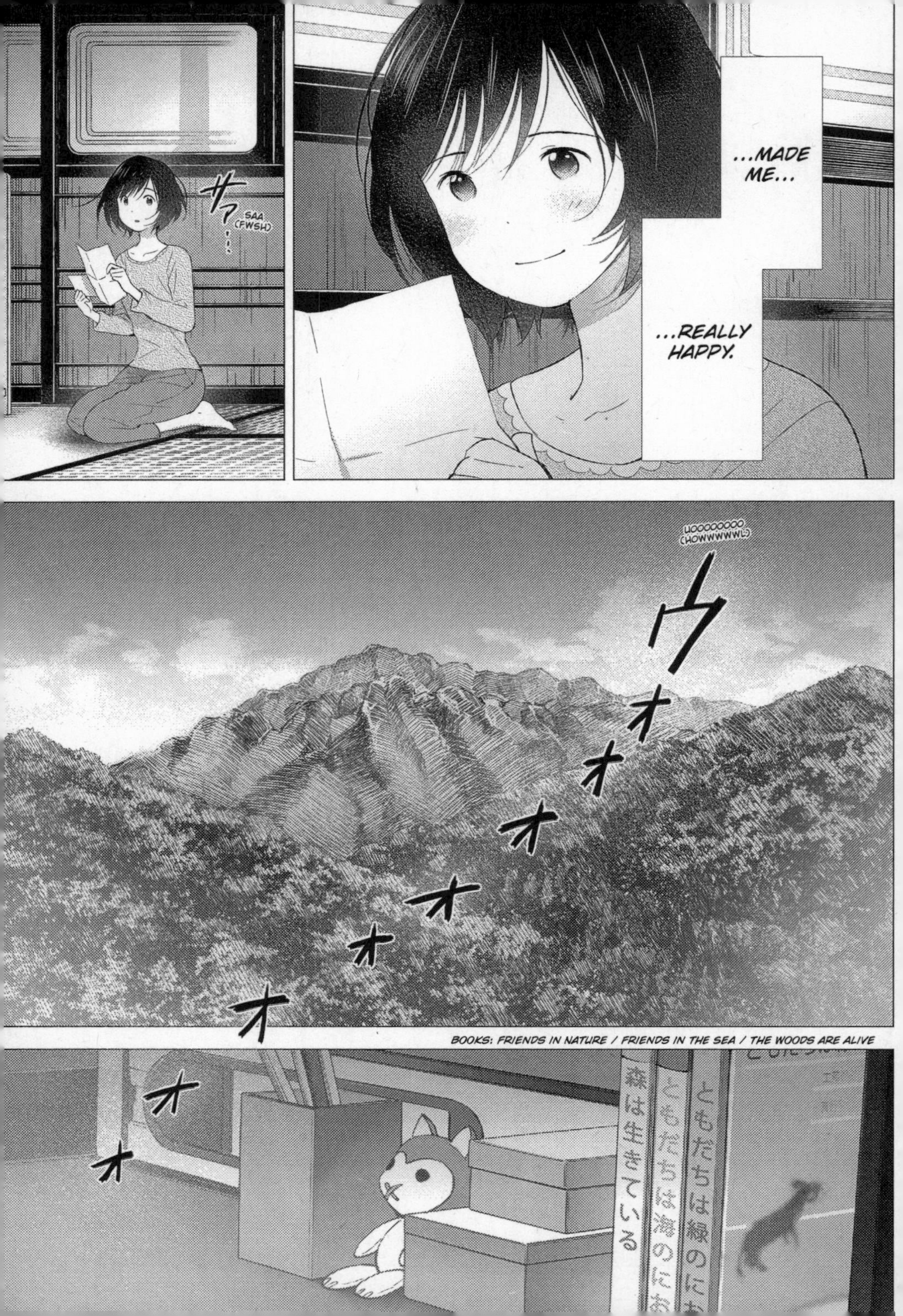
...MADE ME...
...REALLY HAPPY.
サァ・・・
SAA (FWSH)
UOOOOOOOO (HOWWWWWL)
ウオオオオオオオオ
BOOKS: FRIENDS IN NATURE / FRIENDS IN THE SEA / THE WOODS ARE ALIVE
森は生きている

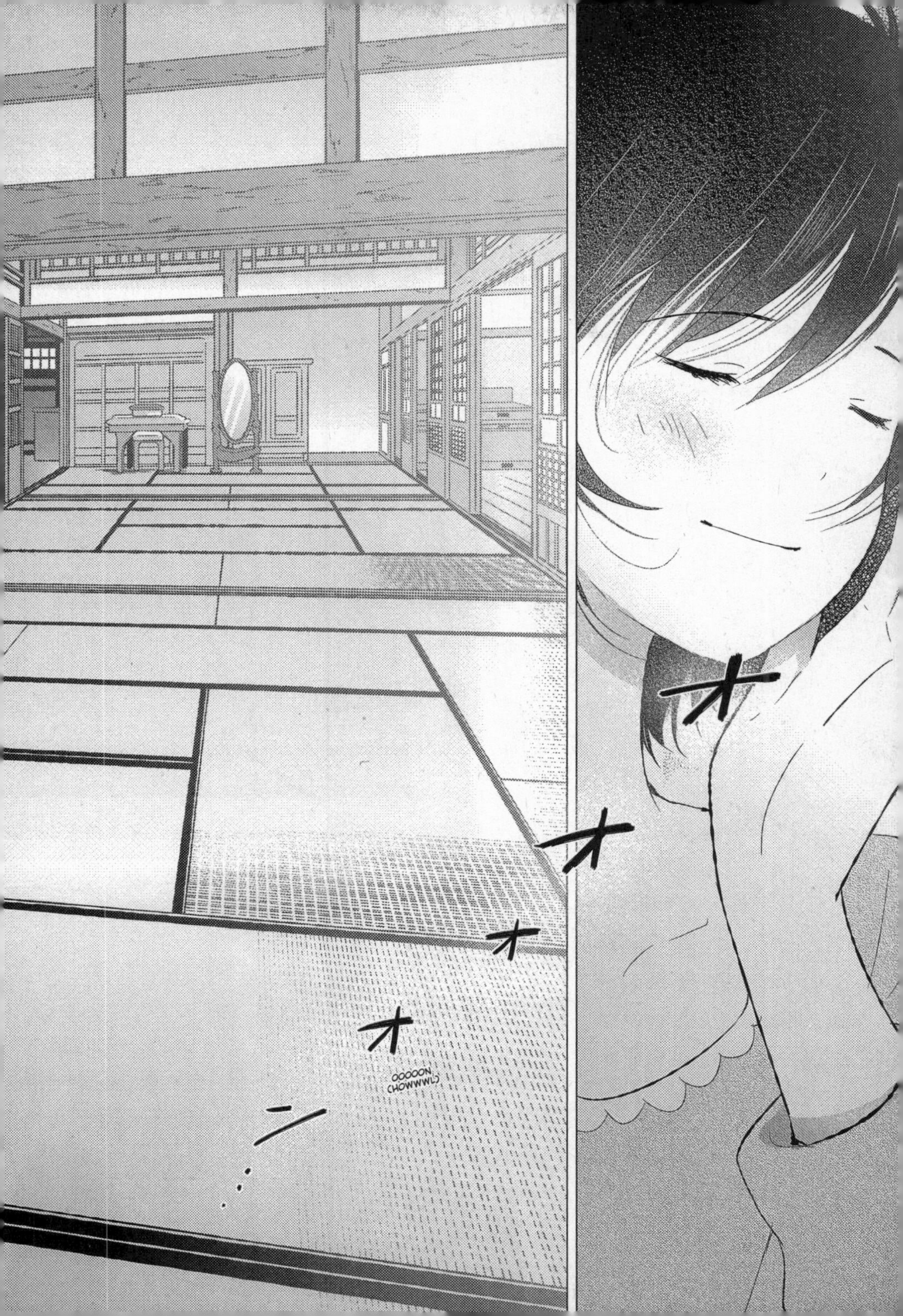
OOOOON
(HOWWWL)

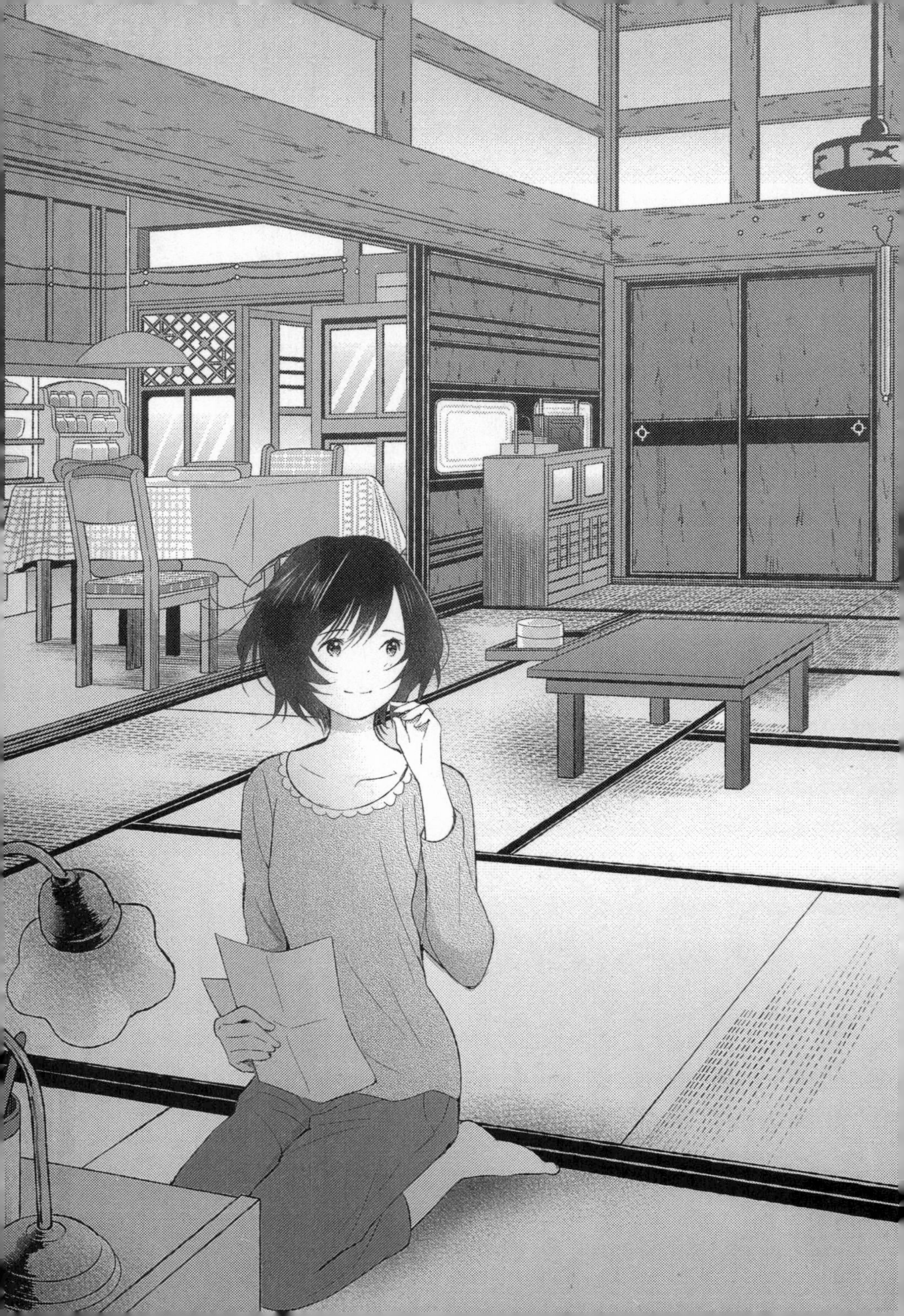

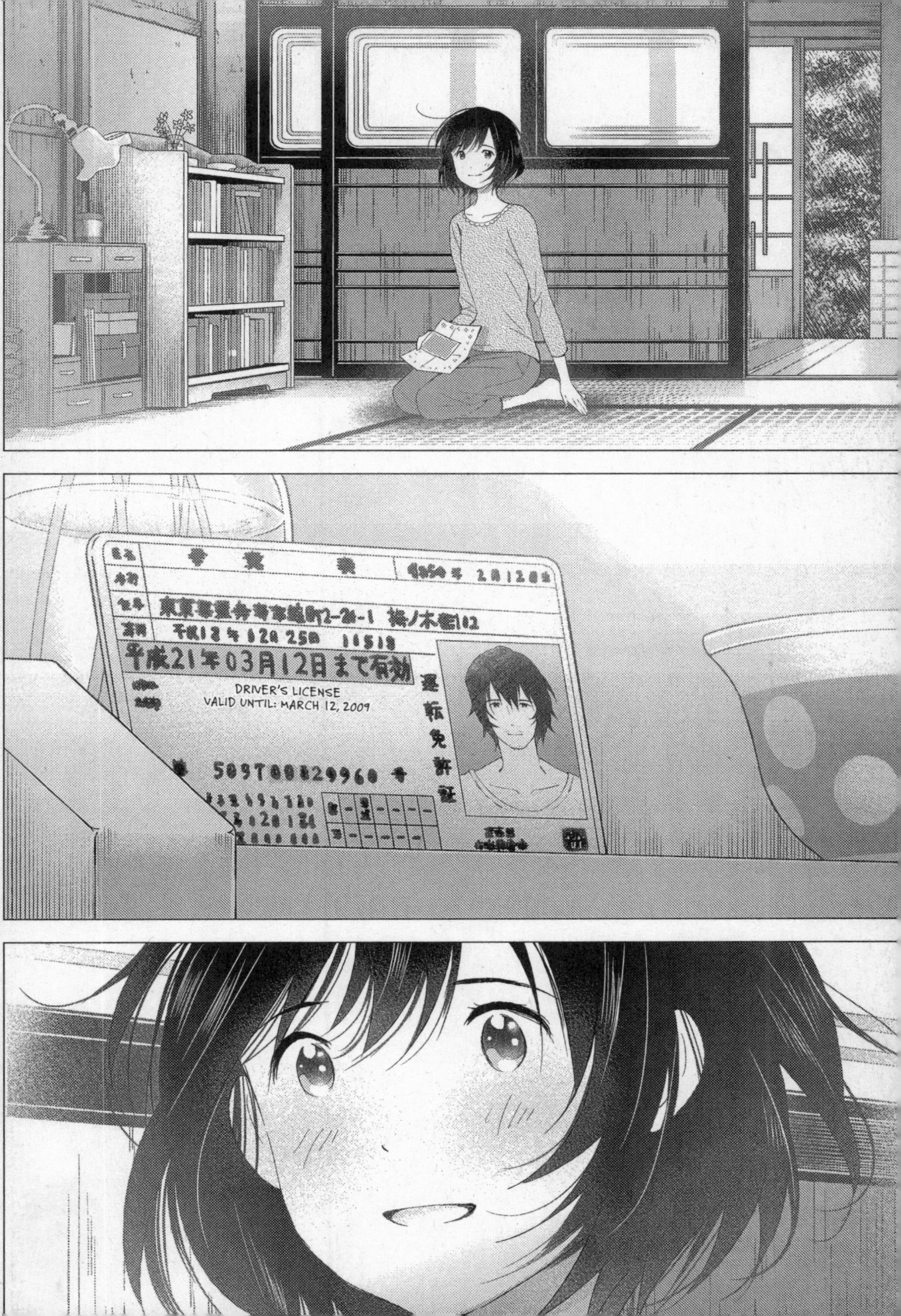
平成21年03月12日まで有効
DRIVER'S LICENSE
VALID UNTIL: MARCH 12, 2009
運転免許証

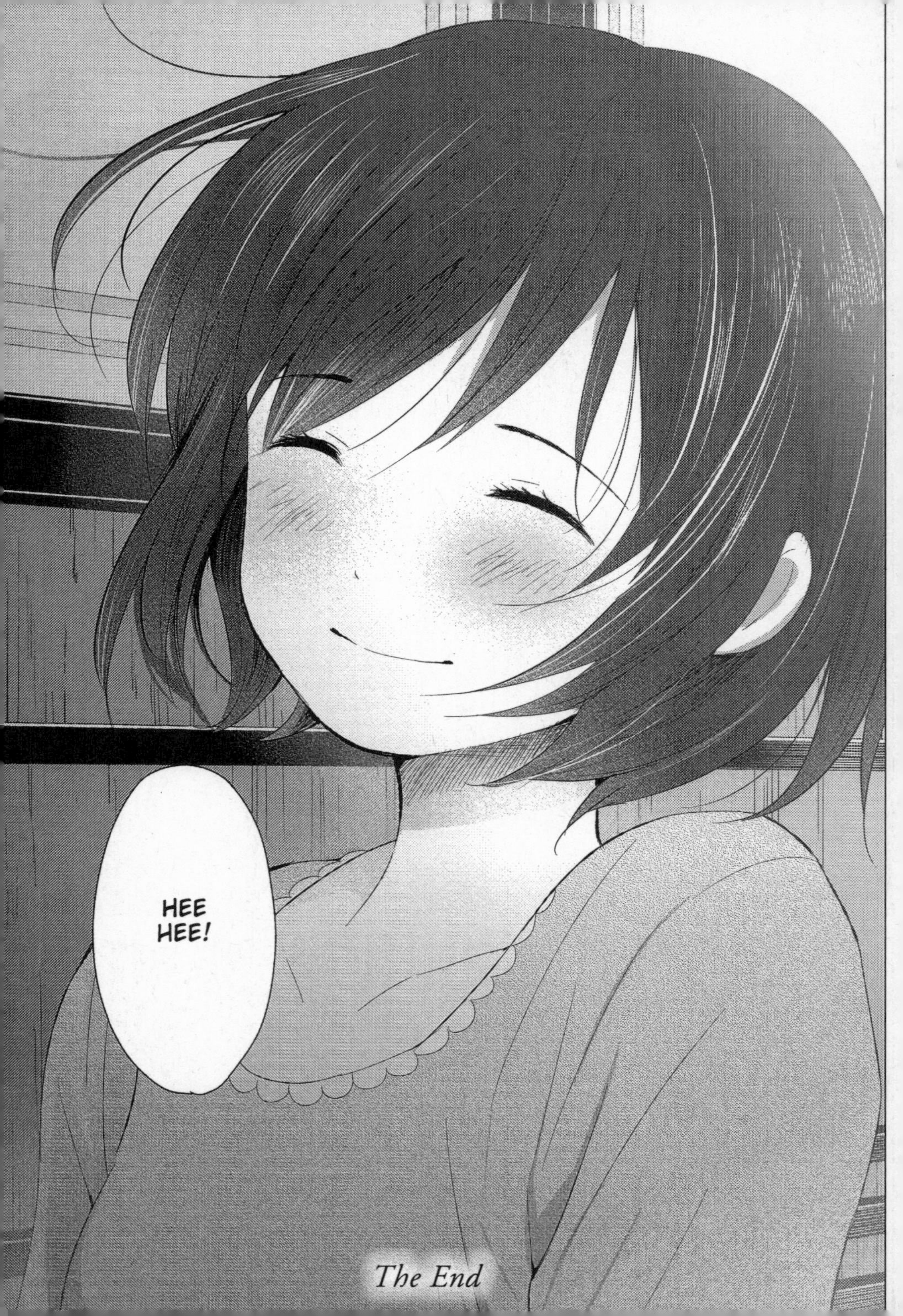
HEE HEE!
The End

WOLF CHILDREN
AME & YUKI

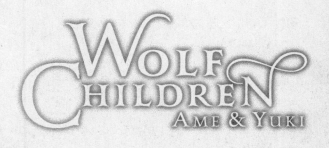

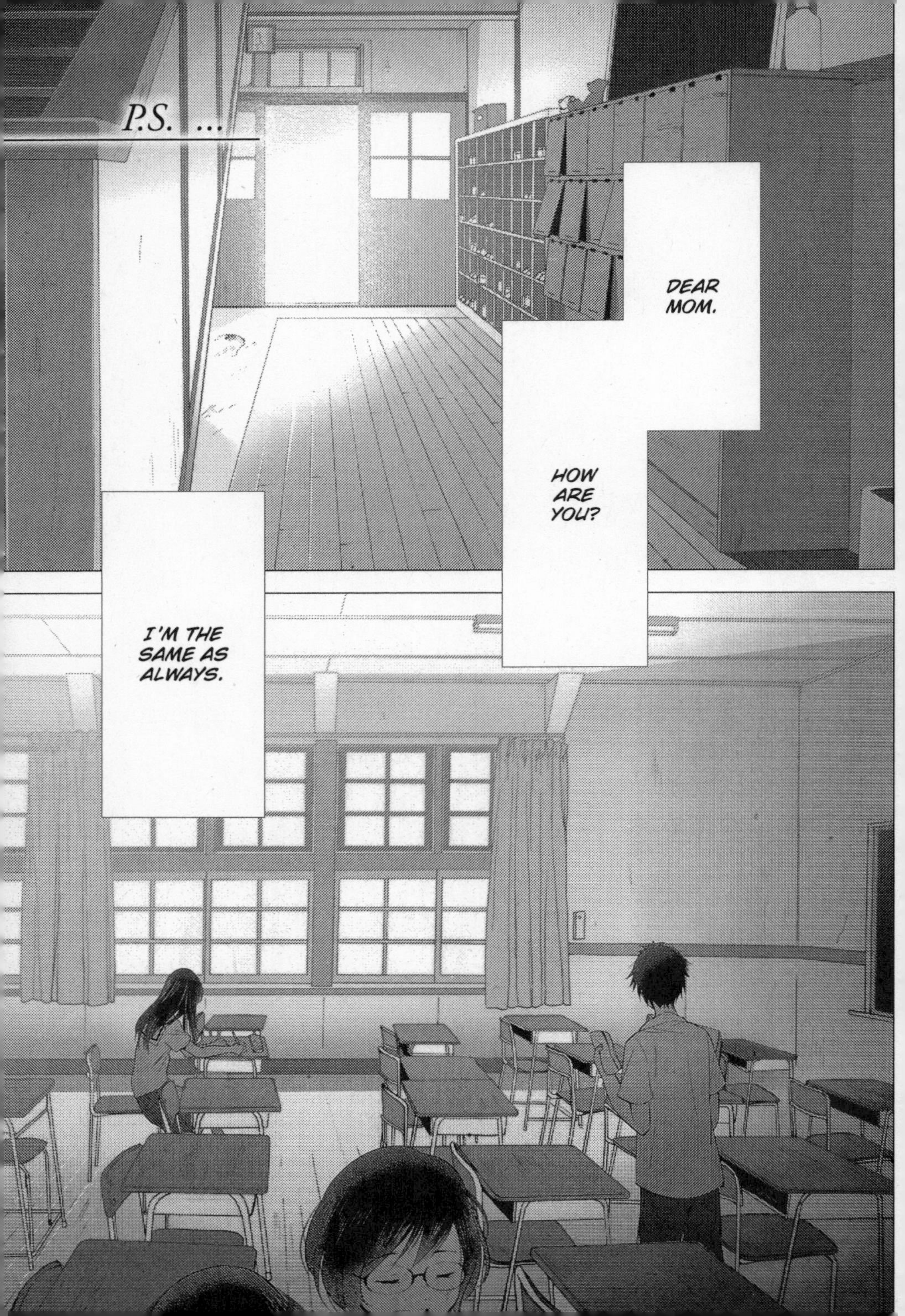
P.S. ...
DEAR MOM.
HOW ARE YOU?
I'M THE SAME AS ALWAYS.

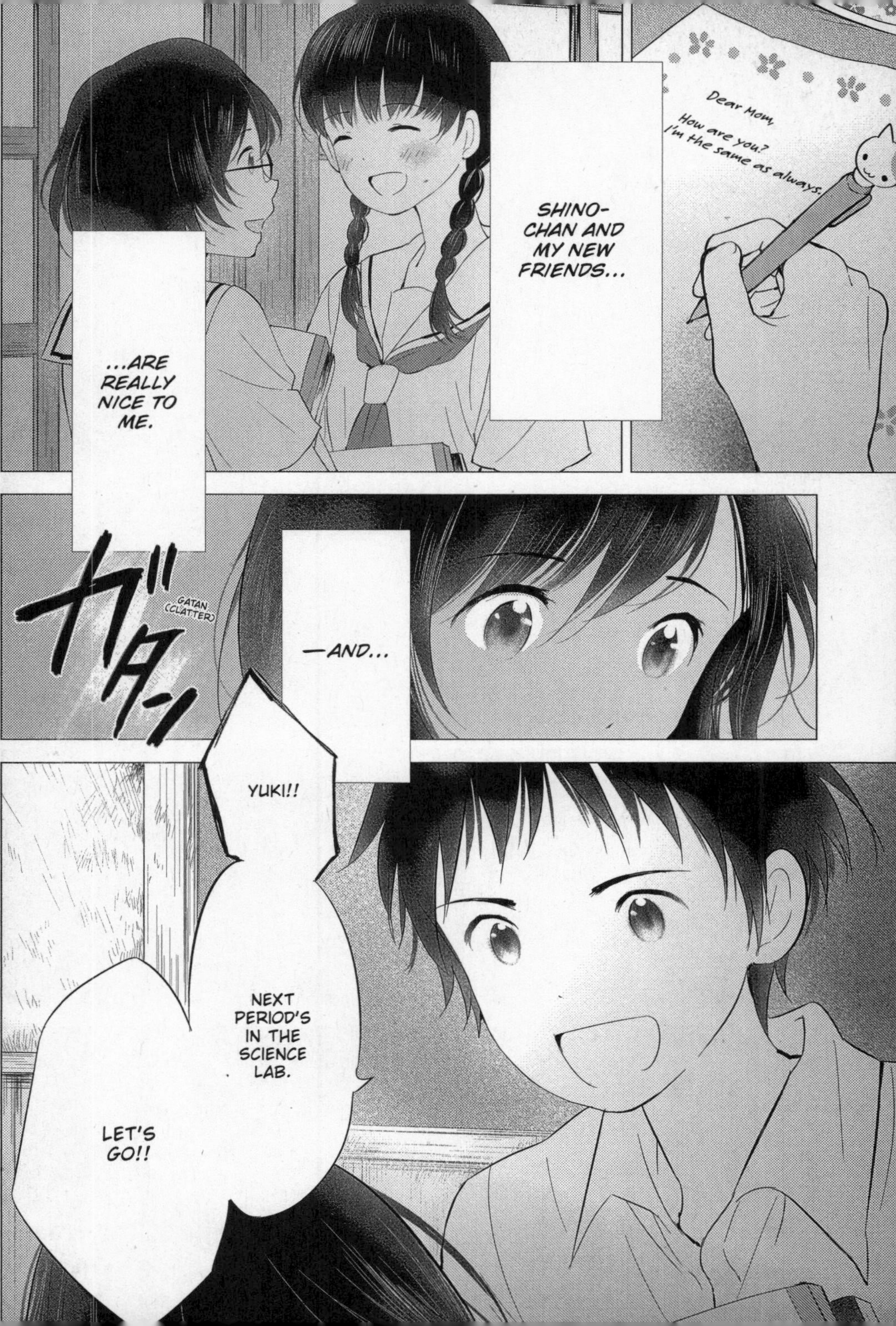
Dear Mom,
How are you?
I'm the same as always.
SHINO-CHAN AND MY NEW FRIENDS...
...ARE REALLY NICE TO ME.
GATAN (CLATTER)
—AND...
YUKI!!
NEXT PERIOD'S IN THE SCIENCE LAB.
LET'S GO!!

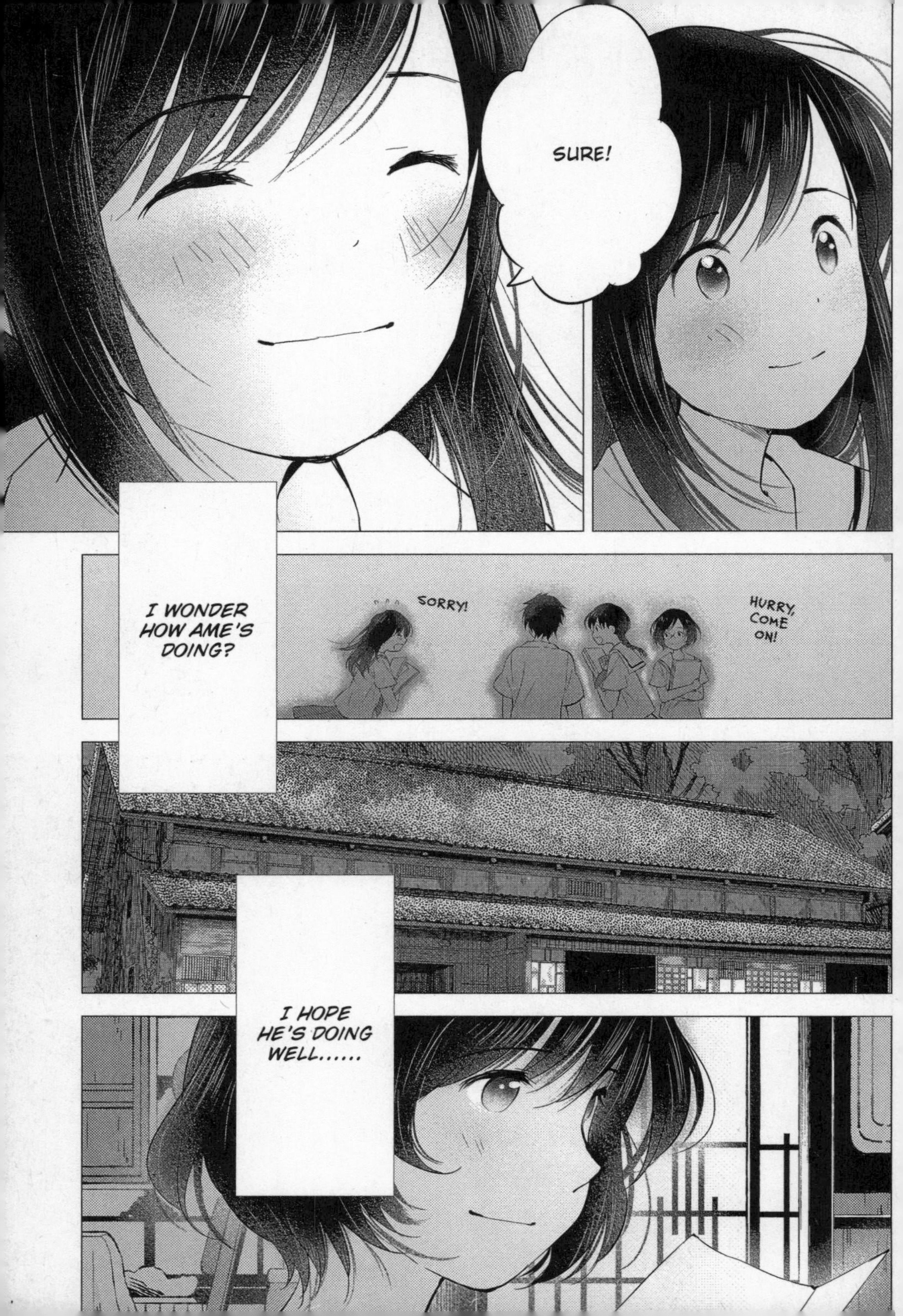
SURE!
I WONDER HOW AME'S DOING?
HURRY, COME ON!
SORRY!
I HOPE HE'S DOING WELL......

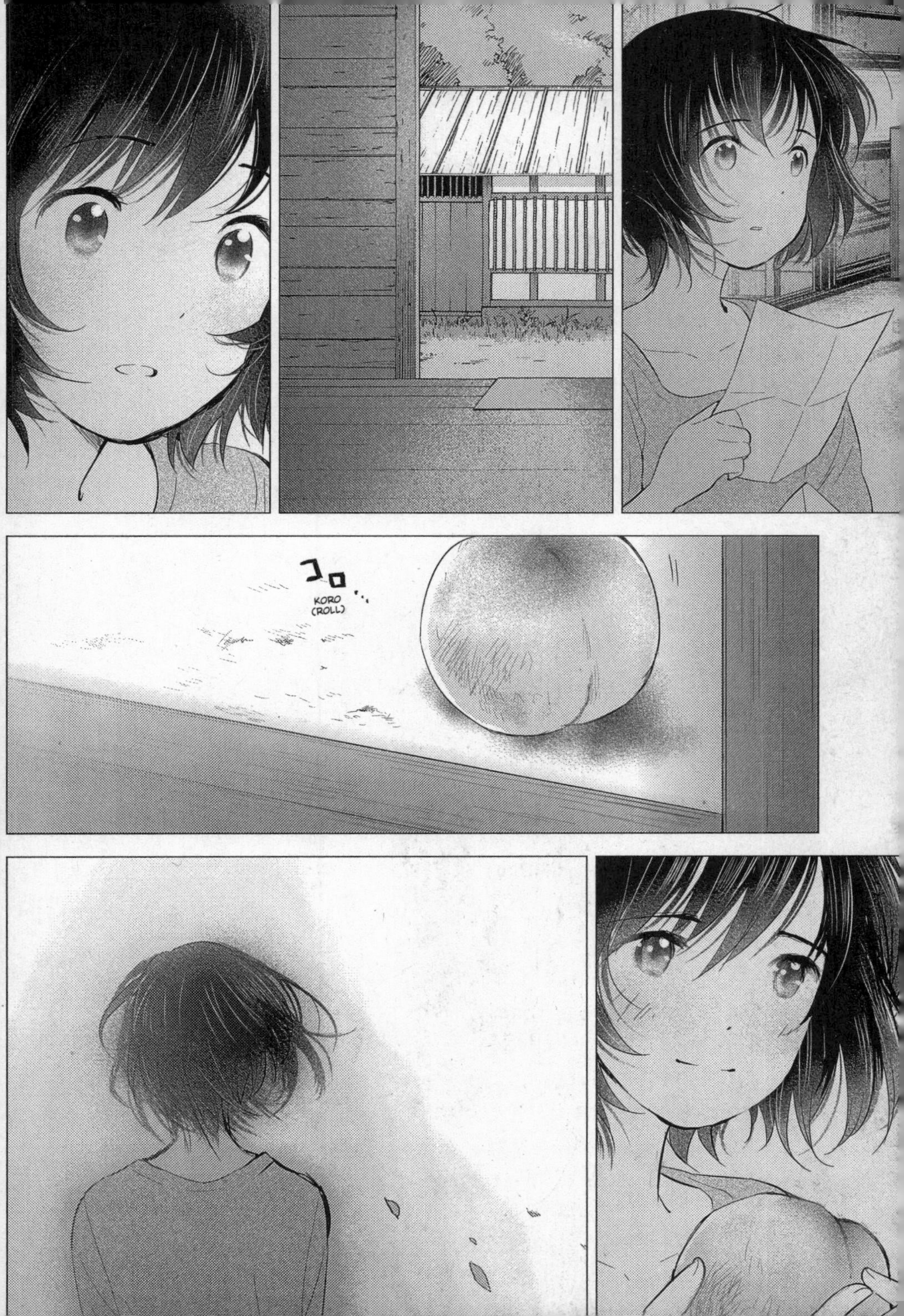
コロ…
KORO
(ROLL)

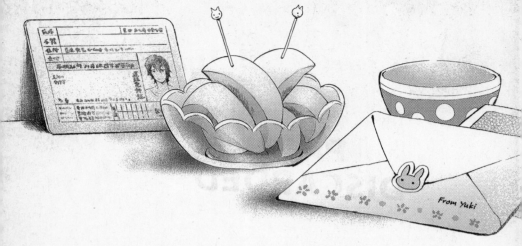

From Yuki

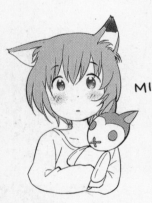 ✿ **SPECIAL THANKS** ✿

MIKI KAMIYA-SAN
YUKINA SUZUKI-SAN
JURO SHIMIZU-SAN
MIKI KAWARABAYASHI-SAN
AYUKO SUZUKI-SAN
EDITOR:
NAKAZAWA-SAN
AND YOU.

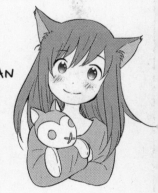

THIS IS THE FINAL VOLUME.
I WANT TO THANK FROM THE BOTTOM OF MY HEART
MAMORU HOSODA, EVERYONE INVOLVED WITH THE MAKING
OF THE FILM, ALL THE PEOPLE WHO SUPPORTED
ME IN MAKING THE COMIC, AND EVERYONE WHO READ
THE BOOKS. I AM REALLY, HONESTLY DELIGHTED TO
HAVE BEEN ABLE TO BE INVOLVED WITH *WOLF
CHILDREN AME & YUKI*. THANK YOU SO, SO MUCH.

優
YU

Wolf Children Ame & Yuki

Original Story **Mamoru Hosoda** · *Art* **Yu**
Character Design **Yoshiyuki Sadamoto**
A Studio Chizu Production

Translation: Jocelyne Allen · Lettering: Tania Biswas, Lys Blakeslee

OOKAMIKODOMO NO AME TO YUKI
© 2012 "WOLF CHILDREN" FILM PARTNERS © Yu 2012, 2013
Edited by KADOKAWA SHOTEN. First published in Japan in 2012, 2013 by KADOKAWA CORPORATION, Tokyo. English translation rights arranged with KADOKAWA CORPORATION, Tokyo, through TUTTLE-MORI AGENCY, INC., Tokyo.

Translation © 2014 by Hachette Book Group, Inc.

Yen Press
Hachette Book Group
237 Park Avenue, New York, NY 10017

www.HachetteBookGroup.com
www.YenPress.com

Yen Press is an imprint of Hachette Book Group, Inc.
The Yen Press name and logo are trademarks of Hachette Book Group, Inc.

First Yen Press Edition: March 2014

ISBN: 978-0-316-40165-4

10 9 8 7 6 5

BVG

Printed in the United States of America